ROBERT LUDLUM
Three Great Novels

Robert Ludlum

Three Great Novels

Trevayne
The Cry of the Halidon
The Rhinemann Exchange

ORION

This edition first published in Great Britain in 2005 by
Orion
An imprint of Orion Books Ltd
Orion House, 5 Upper St Martin's Lane,
London WC2H 9EA

1 3 5 7 9 10 8 6 4 2

ISBN 0 75287 274 5

Typeset by Deltatype Ltd, Birkenhead, Merseyside

Printed and bound in Great Britain by
Clays Ltd, St Ives plc

Contents

Trevayne

For Gail and Henry

To the Savoy! To Hampton!
To Pont Royal and Bernini!
And everything else
My thanks

Introduction

Every now and then throughout the human odyssey, forces seem almost accidentally to come together producing men and women of startling wisdom, talent and insight, and the results are wondrous indeed. The arts and the sciences speak for themselves, for they are all around us, embellishing our lives with beauty, longevity, knowledge and convenience. But there is another area of human endeavour that is both an art *and* a science, and it, too, is all around us – either enriching our lives or destroying them.

It is the guardianship of a given society under the common laws of governance. I'm not a scholar, but the courses in Government and Political Science that I was exposed to in college indelibly left their marks on me. I was hooked, fascinated, smitten, and were it not for stronger proclivities, I might have become the worst politician in the western world. My 'cool' levels off around 300 degrees Fahrenheit.

For me, one of the truly great achievements of man is open, representative democracy, and the greatest of all the attempts throughout history to create such a system was the magnificent American experiment as expressed in our Constitution. It's not perfect, but to paraphrase Churchill, it's the best damn thing on the block. But wait.

Someone's always trying to louse it up.

That's why I wrote *Trevayne* nearly two decades ago. It was the time of Watergate and my pencil flew across the pages in outrage. Younger – not youthful – intemperance made my head explode with such words and phrases as *Mendacity! Abuse of Power! Corruption! Police State!*

Here was the government, the highest of our elected and appointed officials entrusted with the guardianship of our system, not only lying to the people but collecting millions upon millions to perpetuate the lies and thus the controls they believed were theirs alone to exercise. One of the most frightening statements to come out of the Watergate hearings was the following, delivered, in essence, by the nation's chief law enforcement officer:

'There's nothing I would not do to keep the presidency . . .'

I don't have to complete the exact sentence, the meaning was clear. *Ours.* The presidency and the country was *theirs.* Not yours, or mine, or even the neighbours' across the street with whom we frequently disagreed on things

1

political. Only *theirs*. The rest of us somehow neither relevant nor competent. *They* knew better, therefore the lies had to continue and the coffers of ideological purity kept full so the impure were *blitzkrieg*ed by money and buried at the starting gates of political contests.

I also had to publish *Trevayne* under another name, hardly because of potential retribution, but because the 'conventional wisdom' of the time was that a novelist did not author more than a book a year. Why? Damned if I could figure it out – something to do with 'marketing psychology', whatever the hell that is. But wait. All that was nearly twenty years ago.

Plus ça change, plus c'est la même chose, say the French. The more things change, the more they stay the same. Or perhaps history repeats its follies *ad nauseam* because man is a creature of helter-skelter appetites and keeps returning to the troughs of poison that make him ill. Or perhaps the sins of the generational parent are borne by the offspring because the kids are too stupid to learn from our glaring mistakes. Who knows? All that's truly documented from time immemorial is that man continues to kill without needing the meat of his quarry; he lies in order to avoid accountability or, conversely, to seize the reins of accountability to the point where the social contract between the government and the governed is his alone to write; he seeks endlessly to enrich himself at the expense of the public weal, and while he's at it tries all too frequently to turn his personal morality or religion into everyone else's legality or religiosity, no quarter to the unbelievers of pariahdom. Good heavens, we could go on and on, couldn't we? But wait.

As I write, the United States of America has just witnessed two of the most disgraceful, debasing, inept, disingenuous and insulting presidential campaigns that living admirers of our system can recall. The candidates were 'packaged' by cynical manipulators of the public's basest fears; 'sound bite zingers' were preferable to intelligent statements of position; image took precedence over issues. The presidential debates were neither presidential nor debates but canned Pavlovian 'responses' more often than not having little or nothing to do with the questions. The ground rules for these robotic pavanes were drawn up by glib intellectual misfits who thought so ill of their clients that they refused to allow them to speak beyond *two minutes*! The orators of the cradle that was ancient Athens can be heard vomiting wherever they are. Perhaps one bright day ahead we'll return to legitimate, civilized campaigns where an open exchange of ideas can be heard, but not, I'm afraid, until those who persuade us to buy deodorants hie back to the armpits. They've worn out their welcome in the election process for they have committed the two cardinal sins of their profession – at the same time. They've made their 'products' simultaneously appear both offensive and boring. Of course, there's a solution. If I were either candidate, I'd refuse to pay them on the grounds of moral turpitude – hell, it's as good as any, and which of those image-makers would go into court expounding one way or the other on that one? Enough. The campaigns turned off the country.

And this numbing fiasco followed barely twenty-four months after we citizens of the Republic were exposed to a series of events so ludicrous they would have been a barrel of laughs but for their obscenity. Stripped of its asininity, unelected (?) officials fuelled the fires of terrorism by selling arms to a terrorist state while demanding that our allies do no such thing. Guilt became innocence; malfeasance brought honour-to-office; zealous, obsequious poseurs were heroes; to be present was to be absent; and to have creatures soiling the basement was a sign of efficient house management. By comparison, Alice's looking-glass world was a place of incontestable logic. But *wait* – all right, you're ahead of me.

Someone's always trying to louse it up. That great experiment, that wonderful system of ours based on open checks and balances. *Mendacity? Abuse of Power? Corruption? Police State?*

Well, certainly not with lasting effect as long as citizens can voice such speculations and shout their accusations, however extreme. We can be heard; that's our strength and it's indomitable.

So, in a modest way, I'll try to be heard again in that voice from another time, another era, always remembering that I'm fundamentally and merely a storyteller who hopes you enjoy the entertainment, but perhaps will permit me an idea or two.

Lastly, I have not attempted to 'update' the novel or adjust the licences I took with actual events or geography for they served the story I was writing. As anyone who has built or remodelled a home will tell you, once you start tinkering, you might as well throw away the schematics. It becomes another house.

Thanks for your time.

Robert Ludlum
a.k.a. (briefly) Jonathan Ryder
November 1988

3

Part One

1

The smoothly tarred surface of the road abruptly stopped and became dirt. At this point on the small peninsula the township's responsibility ended and the area of private property began. According to the United States Post Office, South Greenwich, Connecticut, the delivery route was listed on the map as Shore Road, Northwest, but to the carriers who drove out in the mail trucks it was known simply as High Barnegat, or just Barnegat.

And the carriers drove out frequently, three or four times a week, with special-delivery letters and certified-receipt-requested manila envelopes. They never minded the trip, because they received a dollar each time they made a delivery.

High Barnegat.

Eight acres of ocean property with nearly a half-mile bordering directly on the sound. Most of the acreage was wild, allowed to grow unhampered, untamed. What seemed contradictory in spirit was the compound – the house and grounds seventy yards up from the central beach. The long rambling house was contemporary in design, great expanses of glass encased in wood looking out over the water. The lawns were deep green and thick, manicured and broken up by flagstone paths and a large terrace directly above the boathouse.

It was late August, the best part of the summer at High Barnegat. The water was as warm as it would ever be; the winds came off the sound in gusts which made the sailing more exciting – or hazardous – depending on one's point of view; the foliage was at its fullest green. In late August a sense of calm replaced the hectic weeks of summer fun. The season was nearly over. Men thought once again of normal weekends and five full days of business; women began the agonizing process of selection and purchase that signalled the start of the new school year.

Minds and motives were slowly changing gears. Frivolity was ebbing; there were more serious things to consider.

And the steady flow of house guests diminished at High Barnegat.

It was four thirty in the afternoon, and Phyllis Trevayne reclined in a lounge chair on the terrace, letting the warm sun wash over her body. She thought, with a degree of satisfaction, that her daughter's bathing suit fitted her rather comfortably. Since she was forty-two and her daughter seventeen, satisfaction could have turned into minor triumph if she allowed herself to dwell on it. But she couldn't because her thoughts kept returning to the telephone, to the call from New York for Andrew. She had answered on the terrace phone, because the cook was still in town with the children and her husband was still a small white sail far out on the water. She'd nearly let the phone ring unanswered, but only very good friends and very important – her husband preferred the word 'necessary' – business associates had the High Barnegat number.

'Hello, Mrs Trevayne?' had asked the deep voice on the other end of the line.

'Yes?'

'Frank Baldwin here. How are you, Phyllis?'

'Fine, just fine, Mr Baldwin. And you?' Phyllis Trevayne had known Franklyn Baldwin for several years, but she still couldn't bring herself to call the old gentleman by his first name. Baldwin was the last of a dying breed, one of the original giants of New York banking.

'I'd be a lot better if I knew why your husband hasn't returned my calls. Is he all right? Not that I'm so important, God knows, but he's not ill, is he?'

'Oh, no. Not at all. He's been away from the office over a week now. He hasn't taken any messages. I'm really to blame; I wanted him to rest.'

'My wife used to cover for me that way, too, young lady. Instinctively. Jumped right into the breach, and always with the right words.'

Phyllis Trevayne laughed pleasantly, aware of the compliment. 'Really, it's true, Mr Baldwin. Right now the only reason I know he's not working is that I can see the sail of the catamaran a mile or so off-shore.'

'A cat! God! I forget how young you are! In my day no one your age ever got so damned rich. Not by themselves.'

'We're lucky. We never forget it.' Phyllis Trevayne's voice spoke the truth.

'That's a very nice thing to say, young lady.' Franklyn Baldwin also spoke the truth, and he wanted her to know that. 'Well, when Captain Ahab bounds ashore, do ask him to call me, will you, please? It's really most urgent.'

'I certainly shall.'

'Goodbye, my dear.'

'Goodbye, Mr Baldwin.'

But her husband *had* been in touch with his office daily. He'd returned dozens of calls to far less important people than Franklyn Baldwin. Besides which, Andrew liked Baldwin; he'd said so a number of times. He'd gone to Baldwin on many occasions for guidance in the tangled webs of international finance.

Her husband owed a great deal to the banker, and now the old gentleman needed him. Why hadn't Andrew returned the calls? It simply wasn't like him.

The restaurant was small, seating no more than forty people, and situated on Thirty-eighth Street between Park and Madison avenues. Its clientele was generally from the ranks of the approaching-middle age executives with suddenly more money than they'd ever made before and a desire, a need, perhaps, to hold on to their younger outlooks. The food was only fair, its prices high, and the drinks were expensive. However, the bar area was wide, and the rich panelling reflected the soft, indirect lighting. The effect was a throwback to all those collegiate spots from the fifties that these drinkers remembered with such comfort.

It was designed precisely with that in mind.

Considering this, and he always considered it, the manager was slightly surprised to see a short, well-dressed man in his early sixties walk hesitantly through the door. The man looked around, adjusting his eyes to the dim light. The manager approached him.

'A table, sir?'

'No ... Yes, I'm meeting someone ... Never mind, thank you. We have one.'

The well-dressed man spotted the person he was looking for at a table in the rear. He walked abruptly away from the manager and sidled awkwardly past the crowded chairs.

The manager recalled the man at the rear table. He'd insisted on that particular table.

The elderly man sat down. 'It might have been better to meet someplace other than a restaurant.'

'Don't worry, Mr Allen. No one you know comes here.'

'I certainly hope you're right.'

A waiter approached, and the order was given for drinks.

'I'm not so sure *you* should be concerned,' said the younger man. 'It strikes me that I'm the one taking the risk, not you.'

'You'll be taken care of; you know that. Let's not waste time. Where do things stand?'

'The commission has unanimously approved Andrew Trevayne.'

'He won't take it.'

'The feeling is that he will. Baldwin's to make the offer; he may have done so already.'

'If he has, then you're *late*.' The old man creased the flesh around his eyes and stared at the tablecloth. 'We heard the rumors; we assumed they were a smokescreen. We relied on you.' He looked up at Webster. 'It was our understanding that you would confirm the identity before any final action was taken.'

'I couldn't control it; no one at the White House could. That commission's off-limits. I was lucky to zero in on the name at all.'

'We'll come back to that. Why do they think Trevayne will accept? Why should he? His Danforth Foundation is damn near as big as Ford or Rockefeller. Why would he give it up?' Allen asked.

'He probably won't. Just take a leave of absence.'

'No foundation the size of Danforth would accept a leave for that length of time. Especially not for a job like this. They're *all* in trouble.'

'I don't follow you . . .'

'You think they're immune?' asked Allen, interrupting. 'They need friends in your town. Not enemies . . . What's the procedure? If Baldwin *has* made the offer. If Trevayne accepts?'

The waiter returned with the drinks and both men fell silent. He left, and Webster answered.

'The conditions are that whoever the commission selects receives the President's approval and is subject to a closed hearing with a bipartisan committee in the Senate.'

'All right, all right.' Allen raised his glass and swallowed a large portion of his drink. 'Let's work from there; we can do something there. We'll disqualify him at the hearing.'

The younger man looked puzzled. 'Why? What's the point? *Someone's* going to chair that subcommittee. I gather this Trevayne's at least a reasonable man.'

'You gather!' Allen finished his drink rapidly. 'Just what *have* you gathered? What do you know about Trevayne?'

'What I've read. I did my research. He and his brother-in-law – the brother's an electronics engineer – started a small company dealing in aerospace research and manufacturing in New Haven in the middle fifties. They hit the motherlode seven or eight years later; they were both millionaires by the time they were thirty-five. The brother-in-law designed, while Trevayne sold the hell out of the products. He cornered half the early NASA contracts and set up subsidiaries all over the Atlantic seaboard. Trevayne pulled out when he was thirty-seven and took on a job with the State Department. Incidentally, he did a whale of a job for State.' Webster raised his glass, looking over the rim at Allen. The young man expected to be complimented on his knowledge.

Instead, Allen dismissed his companion's words. 'Shit. *Time*-magazine material. What's important is that Trevayne's an original . . . He doesn't cooperate. We know; we tried reaching him years ago.'

'Oh?' Webster put his glass down. 'I didn't realize . . . Oh, Christ. Then he knows?'

'Not a great deal; perhaps enough. We're not sure. But you still miss the point, Mr *Webster*. It seems to me that you've missed the point from the beginning . . . We don't *want* him chairing that goddamned subcommittee. We don't want him or anyone *like* him! That kind of choice is unthinkable.'

'What can you do about that?'

'Force him out . . . if he's actually accepted. The back-up will be the Senate hearing. We'll make damn sure he's rejected.'

'Say you succeed, then what?'

'We'll nominate our own man. What should have been done in the first place.' Allen signalled the waiter, gesturing at both glasses.

'Mr Allen, why didn't you stop him? If you were in a position to do that, why didn't you? You said you heard the rumors about Trevayne; that was the time to step in.'

Allen avoided Webster's look. He drained the ice water in his glass, and when he spoke, his voice had the sound of a man trying very hard to maintain his authority; with lessening success. 'Frank Baldwin, that's why. Frank Baldwin and that senile son-of-a-bitch Hill.'

'The Ambassador?'

'The goddamned Ambassador-at-large with his goddamned embassy in the White House ... Big Billy Hill! Baldwin and Hill; they're the relics behind this bullshit. Hill has been circling like a hawk for the last two or three years. He talked Baldwin into the Defense Commission. Between them they picked Trevayne ... Baldwin put up his name; who the hell could argue? ... But *you* should have told us it was final. If we'd been certain, we could have prevented it.'

Webster watched Allen closely. When he replied, there was a hardness he hadn't displayed before. 'And I think you're lying. Somebody else blew it; you or one of the other so-called specialists. First, you thought this investigation would burn itself out in the forming, be killed in committee ... You were wrong. And then it was too late. Trevayne surfaced, and you couldn't stop it. You're not even sure you can stop him now. That's why you wanted to see me ... So let's dispense with this crap about my being late and missing the point, shall we?'

'You watch your tongue, young man. Just remember who I represent.' The statement was made without commensurate strength.

'And you remember that you're talking to a man personally appointed by the President of the United States. You may not like it, but that's why you came to me. Now, what is it? What do you want?'

Allen exhaled slowly, as if to rid himself of anger. 'Some of us are more alarmed than others ...'

'You're one of them,' interjected Webster quietly.

'Yes ... Trevayne's a complicated man. One-part boy genius of industry – which means he knows his way around the board rooms; one-part sceptic – he doesn't subscribe to certain realities.'

'Seems to me those assets go together.'

'Only when a man's dealing from strength.'

'Get to the point. What's Trevayne's strength?'

'Let's say he never needed assistance.'

'Let's say he refused it.'

'All right, all right. That's valid.'

'You said you tried reaching him.'

'Yes. When I was with ... Never mind. It was the early sixties; we were consolidating then and thought he might be a valuable addition to our ... community. We even offered to guarantee the NASA contracts.'

'Sweet Jesus! And he turned you down.' Webster made a pronouncement, not an inquiry.

'He strung us along for a while, then realized he could get the contracts without us. As soon as he knew that, he told us to go to hell. Actually, he went a lot further. He told me to tell my people to get out of the space programme, get out of the government money. He threatened to go to the Attorney General.'

Bobby Webster absently picked up his fork and slowly made indentations on the tablecloth. 'Suppose it had been the other way around? Suppose he *had* needed you? Would he have joined your "community"?'

'That's what we don't know. Some of the others think so. But they didn't talk to him; I did. I was the intermediary. I was the only one he really had ... I never used names, never said who my people were.'

'But you believe the fact that they *were* was enough? For him.'

'The unanswerable question. He threatened us after he got *his*; he was sure he didn't need anyone but himself, his brother-in-law, and his goddamned company in New Haven. We simply can't afford to take the chance now. We can't allow him to chair that subcommittee ... He's unpredictable.'

'What am I supposed to do?'

'Take every reasonable risk to get close to Trevayne. The optimum would be for you to be his White House connection. Is that possible?'

Bobby Webster paused, then answered firmly. 'Yes. The President brought me into the session on the subcommittee. It was a classified meeting; no notes, no transcripts. There was only one other aide; no competition. I'll work it out.'

'You understand, it may not be necessary. Certain preventive measures will be taken. If they're effective, Trevayne will be out of the picture.'

'I can help you there.'

'How?'

'Mario de Spadante.'

'No! Absolutely no! We've told you before, we don't want any part of him.'

'He's been helpful to you people. In more ways than you realize. Or want to acknowledge.'

'He's *out*.'

'It wouldn't hurt to establish a minor friendship. If you're offended, think of the Senate.'

Allen's wrinkled frown dissolved. He looked almost appreciatively at the presidential aide. 'I see what you mean.'

'Of course, it will raise my price considerably.'

'I thought you believed in what you're doing.'

'I believe in protecting my flanks. The best protection is to make you pay.'

'You're an obnoxious man.'

'I'm also very talented.'

2

Andrew Trevayne ran the twin hulls of the catamaran before the wind, catching the fast current into the shore. He stretched his long legs against a connecting spar and reached over the tiller to make an additional wake in the stern flow. No reason, just a movement, a meaningless gesture. The water was warm; his hand felt as though it was being propelled through a tepid, viscous film.

Just as he was being propelled – inexorably propelled – into an enigma that was not of his choosing. Yet the final decision would be his, and he knew what his choice would be.

That was the most irritating aspect; he understood the furies that propelled him, and he disliked himself for even contemplating submission to them. He had put them behind him.

Long ago.

The cat was within a hundred yards of the Connecticut shoreline when the wind abruptly shifted – as winds do when buffeted against solid ground from open water. Trevayne swung his legs over the starboard hull and pulled the mainsheet taut as the small craft swerved and lurched to the right toward the dock.

Trevayne was a large man. Not immense, just larger than most men, with the kind of supple coordination that bespoke a far more active youth than he ever bothered to reminisce about. He remembered reading an article in *Newsweek*, surprised at the descriptions of his former playing-field prowess. They'd been greatly exaggerated, as all such descriptions were in such articles. He'd been good, but not that good. He always had the feeling that he *looked* better than he was, or his efforts camouflaged his shortcomings.

But he knew he was a good sailor. Maybe more than good.

The rest was meaningless to him. It always had been, except for the instant of competition.

There would be intolerable competition facing him now. If he made the decision. The kind of competition that allowed no quarter, that involved strategies not listed in any rule-book. He was good at those strategies, too. But not from participation; that was important, immeasurably important to him.

Understand them, be capable of manoeuvre, even skirt the edges, but

13

never participate. Instead, use the knowledge to gain the advantage. Use it without mercy, without quarter.

Andrew kept a small pad fastened to a steel plate on the deck next to the tiller. Attached to the plate was a thin rustproof chain that housed a waterproof casing with a ballpoint pen. He said these were for recording times, markers, wind velocities – whatever. Actually, the pad and pen were for jotting down stray thoughts, ideas, memoranda for himself.

Sometimes things . . . just 'things' that seemed clearer to him while on the water.

Which was why he was upset when he looked down at the pad now. He had written one word. Written it unconsciously, without realizing it.

Boston.

He ripped off the page, crumpled it with far more intensity than the action called for, and threw it into the sound.

Goddamn! Goddamn it! he thought. No!

The catamaran pulled into the slip, and Trevayne reached over the side and held the edge of the dock with his right hand. With his left he pulled the release sheet, and the sail fluttered as it buckled. He secured the boat and stood up, pulling down the rest of the canvas, rolling it around the horizontal mast as he did so. In less than four minutes he had dismantled the tiller, stowed the jacket, lashed the sail, and tied off the boat at four corners.

He looked up beyond the stone wall of the terrace to the wood and glass structure that jutted from the edge of the hill. It never ceased to excite him. Not the material possession; that wasn't important any longer. But that it had all come out the way he and Phyl planned it.

They had done it together; that fact was very important. It might never make up for other things, perhaps. Sadder things. But it helped.

He walked to the stone path by the boathouse and started up the steep incline to the terrace. He could always tell what kind of shape he was in by the time he reached midpoint of the climb. If he was out of breath, or his legs ached, he would silently vow to eat less or exercise more. He was pleased to find that there was little discomfort now. Or perhaps his mind was too preoccupied to relate the stress.

No, he was feeling pretty good, he thought. The week away from the office, the continuous salt air, the pleasantly energetic end of the summer months; he was feeling fine.

And then he remembered the pad and the unconsciously – subconsciously – written word. *Boston.*

He didn't really feel fine at all.

He rounded the last steps to the flagstone terrace and saw that his wife was lying back in a deck chair, her eyes open, staring out at the water, seeing nothing he would see. He always felt a slight ache when he watched her like that. The ache of sad, painful memories.

Because of *Boston*, goddamn it.

He realized that his sneakers had covered the sound of his steps; he didn't want to startle her.

'Hi,' he said softly.

'Oh?' Phyllis blinked. 'Have a good sail, darling?'

'Fine. Good sleep?' Trevayne crossed over to her and kissed her lightly on her forehead.

'Great while it lasted. It was interrupted.'

'Oh? I thought the kids drove Lillian into town.'

'It wasn't the kids. Or Lillian.'

'You sound ominous.' Trevayne reached into a large rectangular cooler on the patio table and withdrew a can of beer.

'Not ominous. But I am curious.'

'What are you talking about?' He ripped off the flip-top on the can and drank.

'Franklyn Baldwin telephoned . . . Why haven't you returned his calls?'

Trevayne held the beer next to his lips and looked at his wife. 'Haven't I seen that bathing suit on someone else?'

'Yes, and I thank you for the compliment – intended or not – and I'd still like to know why you haven't called him.'

'I'm trying to avoid him.'

'I thought you liked him.'

'I do. Immensely. All the more reason to avoid him. He's going to ask me for something, and I'm going to refuse him. At least, I think he'll ask me, and I want to refuse him.'

'What?'

Trevayne walked absently to the stone wall bordering the terrace and rested the beer can on the edge. 'Baldwin wants to recruit me. That's the rumour; I think it's called a "trial balloon". He heads up that commission on defence spending. They're forming a subcommittee to make what they politely phrase an "in-depth study" of Pentagon relationships.'

'What does that mean?'

'Four or five companies – conglomerates, really – are responsible for seventy-odd per cent of the defence budget. In one way or another. There's no effective control any longer. This subcommittee's supposed to be an investigative arm of the Defense Commission. They're looking for a chairman.'

'And you're it?'

'I don't want to be it. I'm happy where I am. What I'm doing now is positive; chairing that committee would be the most negative thing I can think of. Whoever takes the job will be a national pariah . . . if he only half works at it.'

'Why?'

'Because the Pentagon's a mess. It's no secret; read the papers. Any day. It's not even subtle.'

'Then why would anyone be a pariah for trying to fix it? I understand making enemies, not a national pariah.'

Trevayne laughed gently as he carried the beer over to a chair next to his wife and sat down. 'I love you for your New England simplicity. Along with the bathing suit.'

'You're pacing too much. Your thinking-feet are working overtime, darling.'

'No, they're not; I'm not interested.'

'Then answer the question. Why a national pariah?'

'Because the mess is too ingrained. And widespread. To be at all effective, that subcommittee's going to have to call a lot of people a lot of names. Fundamentally act on a large premise of fear. When you start talking about monopolies, you're not just talking about influential men shuffling around stock issues. You're threatening thousands and thousands of jobs. Ultimately, that's any monopoly's hold, from top to bottom. You exchange one liability for another. It may be necessary, but you cause a lot of pain.'

'My God,' said Phyllis, sitting up. 'You've done a lot of thinking.'

'Thinking, yes. Not doing.' Andrew bounced out of the chair and walked to the table, extinguishing his cigarette in an ashtray. 'Frankly, I was surprised the whole idea got this far. These things – in-depth studies, investigations, call them what you want – are usually proposed loudly and disposed of quietly. In the Senate cloakroom or the House dining room. This time it's different. I wonder why.'

'Ask Frank Baldwin.'

'I'd rather not.'

'You should. You owe him that, Andy. Why do you think he chose you?'

Trevayne crossed back to the terrace wall and looked out over the Long Island Sound. 'I'm qualified; Frank knows that. I've dealt with those government-contract boys; I've been critical in print about the overruns, the open-end arguments. He knows that, too. I've even been angry, but that goes back a long time ago ... Mainly, I think, because he knows how much I despise the manipulators. They've ruined a lot of good men, one especially. Remember?' Trevayne turned and looked at his wife. 'They can't touch me now. I haven't a thing to lose but time.'

'I think you've just about convinced yourself.'

Trevayne lit a second cigarette and leaned against the ledge, his arms folded in front of him. He continued to stare at Phyllis. 'I know. That's why I'm avoiding Frank Baldwin.'

Trevayne pushed the omelette around the plate, not really interested in it. Franklyn Baldwin sat opposite him in the bank's executive dining room. The old gentleman was speaking intensely.

'The job's going to get done, Andrew; you know that. Nothing's going to prevent it. I just want the best man to do it. And I think you're the best man. I might add, the commission's voice was unanimous.'

'What makes you so sure the job'll get done? I'm not. The Senate's always yelling about economies; it's a hell of an issue, and always will be. That is, until a highway project or an aircraft plant is closed down in some district. Then suddenly the shouting stops.'

'Not this time. It's beyond cynicism now. I wouldn't have become involved if I thought otherwise.'

'You're expressing an opinion. There has to be something else, Frank.'

Baldwin removed his steel-rimmed glasses and laid them beside his plate. He blinked several times and gracefully massaged the bridge of his patrician nose. He smiled a half-smile, half-sadly. 'There is. You're very perceptive . . . Call it the legacy of two old men whose lives – and the lives of their families for a number of generations – have been made most pleasantly productive in this country of ours. I daresay we've contributed, but the rewards have been more than ample. That's the best way I can put it.'

'I'm afraid I don't understand.'

'Of course not. I'll clarify. William Hill and I have known each other since childhood.'

'Ambassador Hill?'

'Yes . . . I won't bore you with the eccentricities of our relationship – not today. Suffice it to say, we can't possibly stay around too many more years; not sure that I'd want to . . . This Defense Commission, the subcommittee – they're our ideas. We intend to see them become working realities. That much we can guarantee; in our different ways we're powerful enough to do that. And to use that dreadful term, sufficiently "respectable".'

'What do you think you'll gain?'

'The truth. The extent of the truth as we believe it to be. This country has the right to know that, no matter how much it may hurt. To cure any disease, a correct diagnosis has to be made. Not indiscriminate labels hung by self-righteous zealots, nor vindictive charges hurled by malcontents . . . The truth, Andrew. Merely the truth. That gift will be ours, Billy's and mine. Perhaps our last.'

Trevayne had the desire to move, to be physically in motion. The old gentleman opposite him was succeeding in doing exactly what he thought he'd do. The walls were closing in, the corridor defined.

'Why can this subcommittee do what you say? Others have tried; they failed.'

'Because, through you, it will be both apolitical and in no way self-seeking.' Baldwin replaced his glasses; the magnification of his old eyes hypnotized Trevayne. 'Those are the necessary factors. You're neither Republican nor Democrat, liberal nor conservative. Both parties have tried to recruit you, and you've refused both. You're a contradiction in this age of nomenclature. You have nothing to gain or lose. You'll be believed. That's the important thing . . . We've become a polarized people, slotted into intransigent, conflicting positions. We desperately need to believe once again in objective truth.'

'If I accept, the Pentagon and everyone connected with it will run to the hills – or their public relations' mimeographs. That's what they usually do. How are you going to prevent this?'

'The President. He has assured us; he's a good man, Andrew.'

'And I'm responsible to no one?'

'Not even me. Only yourself.'

'I hire my own staff; no outside personnel decisions?'

'Give me a list of those you want. I'll have it cleared.'

'I call it as I find it. I get the cooperation I deem necessary.' Trevayne didn't ask these last questions, he made statements which, nevertheless, anticipated answers.

'Total. That I'll guarantee. That I can promise you.'

'I don't want the job.'

'But you'll take it.' Another statement, this time from Franklyn Baldwin.

'I told Phyllis. You're persuasive, Frank. That's why I was avoiding you.'

'No man can avoid what he's meant to do. At the moment he's meant to do it. Do you know where I got that?'

'Sounds Hebraic.'

'No ... But close. Mediterranean. Marcus Aurelius. Have you met many bankers who've read Aurelius?'

'Hundreds. They think he's a mutual fund.'

3

Steven Trevayne looked at the expressionless mannequins clad in tweed jackets and varying shades of grey flannel slacks. The subdued lighting of the College Shoppe was appropriate for the quietly wealthy image sought after by the residents of Greenwich, Connecticut. Steven looked down at his own Levi's, soiled sneakers, and then noticed that one of the buttons on his old corduroy jacket was about to fall off.

He consulted his watch and was annoyed. It was nearly nine. He'd told his sister that he'd drive her and her friends back to Barnegat, but he'd stipulated that they were to meet him by eight thirty. He had to pick up his date over on Cos Cob by nine fifteen. He was going to be late.

He wished to hell his sister hadn't picked this particular night to have an all-girl gathering at home, or at least not to have promised rides for everyone. His sister wasn't allowed to drive at night – an edict Steven Trevayne thought was ridiculous; she was seventeen – so when these occasions arose, he was elected.

If he refused, his father might just find that all their cars were in use and he'd be without wheels.

He was almost nineteen. He'd be off to college in three weeks. Without a car. His father said no car while he was a freshman.

Young Trevayne laughed to himself. His father was right. There was no earthly reason why he should have a car. He didn't want to travel first class; not that way.

He was about to cross the street to the drugstore and telephone his date when a police car pulled up to the curb in front of him.

'You Steven Trevayne?' asked the patrolman at the near window.

'Yes, sir.' The young man was apprehensive; the policeman spoke curtly.

'Get in.'

'Why? What's the matter? I'm just standing here ...'

'You got a sister named Pamela?'

'Yes. Yes, I do. I'm waiting for her.'

'She won't make it down here. Take my word for it. Get in.'

'What's the matter?'

'Look, fella, we can't reach your folks; they're in New York. Your sister said you'd be down here, so we came after you. We're doing you both a favour. Now, get in!'

The young man pulled open the back door of the car and got in quickly. 'Was there an accident? Is she all right?'

'It's always an accident, isn't it?' said the policeman who was driving.

Steven Trevayne gripped the back of the front seat. He was frightened now. 'Please, tell me what happened!'

'Your sister and a couple of girl friends started out with a pot party,' answered the other patrolman. 'At the Swansons' guest house. The Swansons are in Maine ... naturally. We got a tip about an hour ago. When we got there, we found it was a little more complicated.'

'What do you mean?'

'That was the accident, young fellow,' interjected the driver. 'Hard stuff. The accident was that we found it.'

Steven Trevayne was stunned. His sister may have had a stick now and then – who hadn't? – but nothing hard. That was out.

'I don't believe you,' he said emphatically.

'You'll see for yourself.'

The patrol car turned left at the next corner. It was not the way to Police Headquarters.

'Aren't they at the station?'

'They're not booked. Not yet.'

'I don't understand.'

'We don't want any story out. If they're booked, we can't control it. They're still at the Swansons'.'

'Are the parents there?'

'We told you, we haven't been able to reach them,' answered the driver. 'The Swansons are in Maine; your folks are in town.'

'You said there were others. Girl friends.'

'Out-of-staters. Friends from boarding school. We want the local parents first on this one. We've got to be careful. For everyone's sake. You see, we found two packages of uncut heroin. An educated guess would put the price around a quarter of a million dollars.'

Andrew Trevayne took his wife's elbow as they walked up the short flight of concrete steps to the rear door of the Greenwich Police Station. It had been agreed that they would use this entrance.

The introductions were polite, abrupt, and the Trevaynes were ushered into a Detective Fowler's office. Their son was standing by a window and walked rapidly to his parents the moment they entered the door.

'Mom! Dad! ... This is a bunch of crap!'

'Just calm down, Steve,' said the father sternly.

'Is Pam all right?'

'Yes, Mother. She's fine. They're still at the Swansons'. She's just confused. They're all confused, and I don't blame them one goddamned bit!'

'I said cool it!'

'I'm perfectly calm, Dad. I'm just angry. Those kids don't know what uncut horse is, much less how or where to sell it!'

'Do you?' asked Detective Fowler impersonally.

'I'm not the issue, cop!'

'I'll tell you once more, Steve, get hold of yourself or shut up!'

'No, I won't! . . . I'm sorry, Dad, but I won't! These jokers got a phone tip to check out the Swansons'. No name, no reason. They . . .'

'Just a second, young man!' broke in the police officer. 'We're not "jokers" and I would advise you not to use that kind of language!'

'He's right,' added Trevayne. 'I'm sure Mr Fowler can explain what happened. What was this phone call, Mr Fowler? You didn't mention it when we spoke.'

'Dad! He won't *tell* you!'

'I don't *know*! . . . That's the truth, Mr Trevayne. At seven-ten this evening the desk got a phone call that there was some grass at the Swansons'; that we should look into it because there was a lot more involved. The caller was male, spoke with kind of a . . . well, high-toned speech. Your daughter was the only one mentioned by name. We followed it up . . . Four kids. They admitted sharing a single cigarette between them during the last hour or so. It was no party. Frankly, the patrolman suggested we forget it. But by the time they radioed in their report, we'd gotten another call. Same voice. Same person. This time we were told to look in the milk box on the Swansons' guest-house porch. We found the two packages of heroin. Uncut; we figure two hundred, two hundred and fifty thousand. That's a lot of involvement.'

'It's also the most transparent, trumped-up incrimination I've ever heard of. It's completely unbelievable.' Trevayne looked at his watch. 'My attorney should be here within a half-hour; I'm sure he'll tell you the same thing. Now, I'll stay and wait, but I know my wife would like to go out to the Swansons'. Is that all right with you?'

The detective sighed audibly. 'It's fine.'

'Do you need my son any longer? May he drive her?'

'Sure.'

'Can we take her home?' asked Phyllis Trevayne anxiously. 'Take all of them back to our house?'

'Well, there are certain formalities . . .'

'Never mind, Phyl. Go on out to the Swansons'. We'll call you as soon as Walter gets here. Don't worry. Please.'

'Dad, shouldn't I stay? I can tell Walter . . .'

'I want you to go with your mother. The keys are in the car. Now, go on.'

Trevayne and Detective Fowler watched the two of them leave. When the door was shut, Trevayne reached into his pocket for a pack of cigarettes. He offered one to the police officer, who refused.

'No, thanks. I eat pistachio nuts instead these days.'

'Good for you. Now, do you want to tell me what this is all about? You don't believe there's any connection between that heroin and those girls any more than I do.'

'Why don't I? It's a very expensive connection.'

'Because if you did, you'd have them down here and booked. Precisely because it *is* expensive. You're handling the entire situation in a very unorthodox manner.'

'Yes, I am.' Fowler walked around his desk and sat down. 'And you're right, I don't believe there's a connection. On the other hand, I can't dismiss it. Circumstantially, it's explosive; I don't have to tell you that.'

'What are you going to do?'

'This'll surprise you, but I may be guided by your attorney.'

'Which reinforces my statement.'

'Yes, it does. I don't think we're on opposite sides, but I've got problems. We've got the evidence; I certainly can't ignore it. On the other hand, the manner of our getting it raises questions. I can't legally hang it on the kids – not considering everything . . .'

'I'd have you in court on false arrest. *That* could be expensive.'

'Oh, come on, Mr Trevayne. Don't threaten. Legally, those girls, including your daughter, admitted using marijuana. That's against the law. But it's minor, and we wouldn't press it. The other is something else. Greenwich doesn't want that kind of publicity; and a quarter of a million dollars' worth of uncut heroin is a lot of publicity. We don't want a Darien here.'

Trevayne saw that Fowler was sincere. It *was* a problem. It was also insane. Why would anyone want to incriminate four young girls to the extent of throwing away such an enormous sum of money? It was an extraordinary gesture.

Phyllis Trevayne came down the stairs and walked into the living room. Her husband stood in front of the huge glass wall looking out over the sound. It was long after midnight, and the moon was an August moon, shining brightly on the water.

'The girls are in the adjoining guest rooms. They'll be talking till dawn; they're scared out of their wits. Can I get you a drink?'

'That'd be nice. We both could use one.'

Phyllis crossed to the small built-in bar to the left of the window. 'What's going to happen?'

'Fowler and Walter worked it out. Fowler will release the finding of the packages and the fact that they were uncovered as a result of telephone tips. He's forced to do that. But he won't mention any names or locations on the grounds that an investigation is under way. If he's pressed, he'll say that he has no right incriminating innocent people. The girls can't tell him anything.'

'Did you talk to the Swansons?'

'Yes. They panicked; Walter calmed them down. I told them Jean would stay with us and join them tomorrow or the day after. The others are heading home in the morning.'

Phyllis handed her husband a drink. 'Does it make any sense to you? At all?'

'No, it doesn't. We can't figure it out. The voice on the phone was moneyed, according to Fowler and the desk sergeant. That could mean any of thousands; narrowed somewhat because he knew the Swansons' guest house. That is, he didn't hesitate calling it "the guest house"; he didn't describe it as a separate building or anything like that.'

'But *why*?'

'I don't know. Maybe someone has it in for the Swansons; *really* in for them, a quarter of a million dollars' worth. Or . . .'

'But, Andy,' Phyllis interrupted, remembering and choosing her words carefully. 'The man who called used Pam's name. Not Jean Swanson's.'

'Sure. But the heroin was left on the Swansons' property.'

'I see.'

'Well, I don't,' said Trevayne, raising his glass to his lips. 'It's all guesswork. Walter's probably right. Whoever it was was probably caught in the middle of two transactions and panicked. The girls came along; on the surface, rich, spoiled, easy scapegoats for an alibi.'

'I can't think like that.'

'I can't either, really. I'm quoting Walter.'

The sound of an automobile could be heard in the circular driveway in front of the house.

'It must be Steve,' said Phyllis. 'I told him not to be too late.'

'Which he is,' added Trevayne, looking at the mantel clock. 'But no lectures, I promise. I liked the way he behaved himself tonight. His language left something to be desired, but he wasn't intimidated. He might have been.'

'I was proud of him. He was his father's son.'

'No, he was just calling it as he saw it. I think the word is "bummer".'

The front door opened, and Steven Trevayne walked in, closing it slowly, firmly behind him. He seemed disturbed.

Phyllis Trevayne started toward her son.

'Wait a minute, Mom. Before you come near me, I want to tell you something . . . I left the Swansons' around ten forty-five. The cop took me downtown for my car. I drove over to Ginny's, and we both went to the Cos Cob Tavern. We got there about eleven thirty. I had three bottles of beer, no grass, nothing else.'

'Why are you telling us this?' asked Phyllis.

The tall boy stammered, unsure of himself. 'We left the place about an hour ago and went out to the car. The front seat was a mess; someone had poured whisky or wine or something all over it; the seat covers were ripped, ashtrays emptied. We figured it was a lousy joke, a really lousy joke . . . I dropped off Ginny and started for home. When I got near the townline intersection, I was stopped by a police car. I wasn't speeding or anything; no one chased me. This patrol car just flagged me down at the side of the road. I thought maybe he was stuck, I didn't know . . . The cop came over and asked me for my licence and registration, and then he smelled the inside and told me to get out. I tried to explain, but he wasn't buying any of it.'

'Was he from the Greenwich police?'

'I don't know, Dad. I don't think so; I was still in Cos Cob.'

'Go on.'

'He searched me; his partner went over the car like it was the French Connection. I thought they were going to haul me in. I sort of hoped they would; I was sober and everything. But they didn't. They did something else. They took a Polaroid shot of me with my arms against the car – they made me stretch out so they could search my pockets – and then the first cop asked me where I'd come from. I told him, and he went to his patrol car and called someone. He came back and asked me if I'd hit an old man on the road about ten miles back. I said of course not. Then he tells me this old guy is in critical condition in the hospital. . . .'

'What hospital? What *name*?'

'He didn't say.'

'Didn't you *ask*?'

'No, Dad! I was scared to death. I didn't *hit* anyone. I never even saw anyone walking on the road. Just a couple of cars.'

'Oh, my God!' Phyllis Trevayne looked at her husband.

'What happened then?'

'The other policeman took more pictures of the car and a close-up shot of my face. I can still see the flash-bulb . . . Christ, I was scared . . . Then, just like that, they told me I could go.' The boy remained in the hallway, his shoulders slumped, the frightened bewilderment obvious in his eyes.

'You've told me everything?' asked Trevayne.

'Yes, sir,' replied the son, his fear clouding his nearly inaudible voice.

Andrew walked to the end table by the couch and picked up the telephone. He dialled the operator and asked for the number of the Cos Cob Police Department. Phyllis went to her son and led him into the living room.

'My name is Trevayne, Andrew Trevayne. I understand one of your patrol cars stopped my son on . . . where, Steve?'

'Junction Road, at the intersection. About a quarter of a mile from the railroad station.'

'. . . Junction Road, near the station at the intersection; no more than a half-hour ago. Would you mind telling me what the report says? Yes, I'll hold.'

Andrew looked at his son, sitting in a chair, Phyllis standing beside him. The boy shivered and took several deep breaths. He watched his father, afraid, not understanding.

'Yes,' said Trevayne impatiently into the telephone. 'Junction Road, Cos Cob side . . . Of course I'm sure. My son is right here! . . . Yes. Yes . . . No, I'm not positive . . . Just a minute.' Andrew looked at the boy. 'On the police car; did you see the Cos Cob name?'

'I . . . I didn't actually look. It was off on the side. No, I didn't see it.'

'No, he didn't, but it would have to be yours, wouldn't it? He was in Cos Cob . . . Oh? . . . I see. You couldn't check it out for me, could you? He was stopped in your township, after all . . . Oh? All right, I understand. I don't *like* it, but I see what you mean. Thanks.'

Trevayne replaced the telephone and took a pack of cigarettes out of his pocket.

'What is it, Dad? Wasn't it them?'

'No. They have two patrol cars, and neither one has been near Junction Road for the past two hours.'

'Why didn't you "like" but "understand"?' asked Phyllis.

'They can't check the cars of the other towns. Not without a formal request, which has to be recorded in the violations file. They don't like to do that; they have arrangements. In case police cars cross municipal lines going after someone, they just haul them back informally.'

'But you've got to find out! They took photographs, they said Steve *hit* someone!'

'I know. I will ... Steve, go on up and take a shower. You smell like an Eighth Avenue bar. And relax. You didn't do anything wrong.'

Trevayne moved the telephone to the coffee table and sat down.

Westport, Darien. Wilton. New Canaan. Southport.

Nothing.

'Dad, I didn't dream it up!' Steven Trevayne shouted; he was in his bathrobe.

'I'm sure you didn't. We'll keep trying; we'll call the New York stations.'

Port Chester. Rye. Harrison. White Plains. Mamaroneck.

The picture of his son stretched forward, hands clamped to the hood of an automobile soaked with alcohol, being questioned by untraceable police on a dark road about an unknown man struck down – photographs, accusations. It made no sense; there was an abstract quality of unbelievability. As unbelievable, as unreal as his daughter and her friends and two hundred and fifty thousand dollars' worth of uncut heroin found in a milk box on the Swansons' guest-house porch.

Insanity.

Yet it all had happened.

'The girls finally fell asleep,' said Phyllis, walking into the living room. It was nearly four o'clock. 'Anything?'

'No,' replied her husband. He turned to his son, who sat in a chair by the large wall window. The boy was staring outside, his fear intermittently replaced with angry bewilderment. 'Try to recall, Steve. Was the patrol car some other colour than black? Perhaps dark blue or green?'

'Dark. That's all. I suppose it could have been blue or green. It wasn't white.'

'Were there any stripes? Any kind of insignia, no matter how vague.'

'No ... Yes, I guess so. I just didn't look. I didn't think ...' The boy brought his hand to his forehead. 'I didn't *hit* anyone! I *swear* I didn't!'

'Of course you didn't!' Phyllis went to him and bent down, touching her cheek to his. 'It's a terrible mistake, we know that.'

'On top of a terrible joke,' added Trevayne, puzzled.

The telephone on the coffee table rang. Its effect was frightening, a jarring intrusion on private fears. Trevayne swiftly picked it up.

'Hello! ... Yes, yes. This is his residence; I'm his father.'

Steven Trevayne leaped out of the chair and walked rapidly to the back of the couch. Phyllis remained by the window, afraid of the immediate moment.

'My God! I've been phoning all over Connecticut and New York! The boy's a minor, the car's in my name! I should have been called immediately! I'd like an explanation, please.'

For the next several minutes Trevayne listened without comment. When finally he spoke, it was five words.

'Thank you. I'll expect them.'

He hung up the telephone and turned to his wife and son.

'Andy? Is everything all right?'

'Yes ... The Highport Police Station; it's a small village about fifteen miles north of Cos Cob. Their patrol car was following an automobile down Coast Road, a robbery suspect they were checking out over their radio before an arrest. They lost him and swung west on Briarcliff Avenue, when they saw a man ran down by a car that looked like yours, Steve. They radioed for an ambulance, informed the Cos Cob police, and after everything was taken care of, started back for Highport. They spotted you on Junction, swung onto a parallel street, and caught up with you a mile down the road by the intersection ... They could have let you go the minute they checked with Cos Cob; the hit-and-run had turned himself in. But they smelled the car and thought they'd give you a scare ... They're sending us the photographs.'

The terrible night was over.

Steven Trevayne lay on his bed looking up at the ceiling; the radio was tuned to one of those endless all-night talk shows where everyone shouted over everyone else. The boy thought the cacophony might help him sleep.

But sleep would not come.

He knew he should have said something; it was stupid *not* to say anything. But the words wouldn't come, any more than sleep came now. The relief had been so total, so complete, so needed; he hadn't dared resurrect a doubt.

His father had first mentioned the words, unknowingly.

Try to recall, Steve. Was the patrol car some other colour than black...

Maybe. Maybe a dark blue or green.

But it was a *dark* colour.

That's what he should have remembered when his father said 'Highport'.

Highport-on-the-Ocean was the name on the sign on Coast Road. Highport *was* a small village; tiny, actually. It had two or three great beaches – off by themselves, and privately owned. During hot summer nights he and a few friends – never more than a few – often parked a couple of hundred yards down Coast Road and crept through the private property to reach one of the beaches.

But they had to be careful; they always had to keep an eye out for the Yellowbird.

That's what they called it. *The Yellowbird.*
The village of Highport-on-the-Ocean's single patrol car.
It was bright yellow.

4

Andrew Trevayne boarded the 707 jet at John F. Kennedy Airport for the hour's flight to Washington.

He unlatched the seat belt once the aircraft completed its ascent and the warning lights were extinguished. It was three fifteen, and he'd be late for his meeting with Presidential Assistant Robert Webster. He'd had his office at Danforth call Webster at the White House; say he was detained and that if because of the delay Webster wished to change the meeting place, he should leave instructions for him at Dulles Airport. It didn't matter to Trevayne; he'd accepted the fact that he'd have to stay overnight.

He reached for the vodka martini from the pretty young stewardess and took a long sip. Placing the glass on the small tray in front of him, Trevayne latched the seat halfway back and spread a hastily purchased *New York* magazine on his lap.

Suddenly he was aware that the passenger next to him was staring at him. He returned the man's look and immediately realized he knew the face. The man was large, his head enormous, his complexion deeply tanned – more from birth than from the sun. He was, perhaps, in his early fifties, and wore thick horn-rimmed glasses. The man spoke first.

'Mr Trevayne, isn't it?' The voice was soft but deep, with a trace of a rasp. It was a gentle voice, however.

'That's right. I know we've met, but forgive me, I don't remember...'

'De Spadante. Mario de Spadante.'

'Of course,' said Trevayne, his memory instantly activated. Mario de Spadante went back to the New Haven days, the latter part, at any rate, about nine years ago. De Spadante had represented a construction firm involved with some buildings Trevayne and his brother-in-law were financing. Trevayne had rejected the bid – the builders had an insufficient history. But Mario de Spadante had gone a long way since those days a brief nine years ago. That is, if the newspapers were to be believed. He was reputed to be a power in the underworld now. 'Mario the Spade' was the name often used – referring to his swarthy complexion and the fact that he had buried a number of enemies. He was never convicted of the latter, however.

'Must be nine, ten years ago, I'd say,' said de Spadante, smiling pleasantly. 'You remember? You turned me down on a construction job. And you were absolutely correct, Mr Trevayne. Our company didn't have the experience for it. Yes, you were right.'

'At best, it's always an educated guess. Glad you don't resent it.'

'Of course not. Never did, to tell you the truth.' De Spadante winked at Trevayne and laughed quietly. 'It wasn't my company. Belonged to a cousin ... Him I resented, not you. He made me do his work. But everything always equals out. I learned the business, his business, better than he did. It's my company now ... Look, I interrupted your reading. Me, I got to go over some reports – a bunch of long-winded, eight-cylinder paragraphs with figures way beyond any math I ever took at New Haven High. If I get stuck on a word, I'm going to ask you to translate. That'll make up for your turning me down ten years ago. How about it?' De Spadante grinned.

Trevayne laughed, taking his martini off the miniature shelf. He raised the glass an inch or two toward de Spadante. 'It's the least I can do.'

And he did. About fifteen minutes before landing at Dulles, Mario de Spadante asked him to clarify a particularly complex paragraph. It was so complicated that Trevayne read it several times before advising de Spadante to have it simplified, put in cleaner form before accepting it.

'I really can't make much more sense out of this than to tell you they expect you to figure the large items first before tackling the smaller ones.'

'So what else is new? I use a square-foot unit plus profit, which includes the whole thing.'

'I think that's what this means. I gather you're a subcontractor.'

'That's right.'

'That general contractor wants it done in stages. At least, I think that's what it means.'

'So I build him half a door, or maybe just the frame, and he buys the rest from somebody else?'

'I'm probably wrong. You'd better get it clarified.'

'Maybe I won't. Cost him double with that kind of bidding. Nobody wants to do half of somebody else's job ... You just made up for ten years ago. I'll buy you a drink.'

De Spadante took the papers from Trevayne and signalled the stewardess. He placed the papers in a large manila envelope and ordered drinks for Trevayne and himself.

As Trevayne lit a cigarette, he felt the plane gradually descend. De Spadante was looking out the window, and Trevayne noticed the printing – upside down – on the large manila envelope on de Spadante's lap. It read:

Department of the Army
Corps of Engineers

Trevayne smiled to himself. No wonder the language was so obscure. The Pentagon engineers were the most exasperating men in Washington when it came to doing business.

He should know.

*

The message at the reservation desk consisted of Robert Webster's name and a Washington telephone number. When Trevayne called, he was surprised to learn that it was Webster's private line at the White House. It was only a little after four thirty; he could have telephoned the switchboard. In Trevayne's government days presidential aides never gave out their private numbers.

'I wasn't sure when you'd get in; the stack-ups can be terrible,' was Webster's explanation.

Trevayne was confused. It was a minor point, not worth mentioning, really, but Trevayne was bothered. The White House switchboard didn't have hours.

Webster suggested they meet after dinner in the cocktail lounge of Trevayne's hotel. 'It'll give us a chance to go over a few things before tomorrow. The President wants to chat briefly with you around ten or ten-thirty in the morning. I'll have his firm schedule in an hour or so.'

Trevayne left the telephone booth and walked toward the main exit of the airport terminal. He'd packed only a change of shirt, shorts, and socks; he would have to ascertain the swiftness of the hotel's cleaning and pressing facilities if he was going to have a White House audience. He wondered why the President wished to see him. It seemed a little premature, the formalities of his acceptance not having been completed. It was possible that the President simply wished to reaffirm personally Franklyn Baldwin's statement that the highest office in the country was behind the proposed subcommittee.

If so, it was generous and meaningful.

'Hey, Mr Trevayne!' It was Mario de Spadante standing by the curb. 'Can I give you a lift into town?'

'Oh, I don't want to inconvenience you. I'll grab a cab.'

'No inconvenience. My car just got here.' De Spadante gestured at a long, dark-blue Cadillac parked several yards to the right.

'Thanks, I appreciate it.'

De Spadante's chauffeur opened the back door, and the two men got in.

'Where are you staying?'

'The Hilton.'

'Fine. Just down the street. I'm at the Sheraton.'

Trevayne saw that the interior of the Cadillac was appointed with a telephone, miniature bar, television set, and a back-seat stereo cassette machine. Mario de Spadante had, indeed, come a long way since the New Haven days.

'Quite a car.'

'You press buttons and dancing girls come out of the dashboard. Frankly, it's too ostentatious for my taste. I called it my car, but it's not. It belongs to a cousin.'

'You have a lot of cousins.'

'Big family ... Don't misunderstand the term. I'm a construction boy from New Haven who made good.' De Spadante laughed his soft, infectious laugh. 'Family! What they *print* about me! Holy Christ! They should be writing movies. I don't say there's no mafiosi; I'm not that dumb, but I wouldn't know one if I fell over him.'

'They have to sell papers.' It was the only thing Trevayne could think of saying.

'Yeah, sure. You know, I got a younger brother, about your age. Even *him*. He comes up to me and says "What about it, Mario? Is it true?" . . . "What about what?" I ask. "You know me, Augie. You know me forty-two years. I got it so easy? I don't have to spend ten hours a day cutting costs, fighting the unions, trying to get paid on time?" . . . Hah! If I was what they say; I'd pick up a phone and scare the bejesus out of them. As it is, I go to the banks with my tail between my guinea ass and plead.'

'You look like you're surviving.'

Mario de Spadante laughed once more and winked his innocent, conspiratorial wink, as he had done on the plane. 'Right on, Mr Trevayne. I survive. It's not easy, but with the grace of God and a lot of hard work, I manage . . . Your foundation got business in Washington?'

'No. I'm here on another matter, just meeting some people.'

'That's Washington. Greatest little meeting place in the Western Hemisphere. And you know something? Whenever anyone says he's "just meeting people", that's the sign not to ask who he's meeting.'

Andrew Trevayne just smiled.

'You still live in Connecticut?' asked de Spadante.

'Yes. Outside of Greenwich.'

'Nice territory. I'm doing some residential work down there. Near the sound.'

'I'm on the sound. South shore.'

'Maybe we'll get together sometime. Maybe I can sell you a wing on your house.'

'You can try.'

Trevayne walked through the arch into the lounge and looked around at the various people seated in the soft easy chairs and low couches. A headwaiter, dressed in a tuxedo, approached.

'May I help you, sir?'

'Yes. I'm to meet a Mr Webster here. I don't know if he made a reservation.'

'Oh, yes. You're Mr Trevayne.'

'That's right.'

'Mr Webster telephoned that he'd be a few minutes late. I'll show you to a table.'

'Thank you.'

The tuxedoed waiter led Trevayne to a far corner of the lounge that was conspicuous by its lack of customers. It seemed as if this particular location was roped by an invisible cordon to isolate it. Webster had requested such a table, and his position guaranteed it. Trevayne ordered a drink and let his memory wander back to his days in the State Department.

They had been challenging, exciting, almost as stimulating as the early years with the companies. Primarily because few people believed he could accomplish the major assignment given him. It had been to coordinate trade agreements with several eastern satellite countries – guaranteeing the business sectors of each country the most favourable conditions possible – without upsetting political balances. It hadn't been difficult. He remembered that at the very first conference he had disarmed both sides by suggesting that the US State Department and its Communist counterpart hold an international press conference in one room categorically rejecting everything the other side stood for, while in the next room the businessmen negotiated their agreements.

The ploy had its effect; the laughter had been sincere, and the tone set for future meetings. Whenever the negotiations got heated, someone would playfully suggest that his adversary belonged in that 'other room' – with the propagandists.

He had enjoyed his Washington days. There had been the exhilaration of knowing he was close to corridors of real power, that his judgments were listened to by men of great commitments. And they *were* men of commitment, regardless of their individual political affiliations.

'Mr Trevayne?'

'Mr Webster?' Trevayne stood up and shook the hand of the presidential assistant. He saw that Webster was about his own age, perhaps a year or two younger, a pleasant-looking man.

'Sorry as hell to be late. There was a flap over tomorrow's schedule. The President told the four of us to lock ourselves in a room and not come out till we got it in order.'

'I gather that was accomplished.' Trevayne sat down as Webster did the same.

'Damned if I know.' Webster laughed, flagging a waiter. 'I got you cleared for eleven fifteen and let the rest of them figure out the afternoon.' He gave his order and collapsed back into the chair, sighing audibly. 'What's a nice Ohio farmboy like me doing in a job like this?'

'I'd say it was quite a leap.'

'It was. I think they got the names mixed up. My wife keeps telling me there's a guy named Webster wandering around the streets of Akron wondering why he spent all that money for campaign contributions.'

'It's possible,' replied Trevayne, knowing well that Webster's appointment was no mistake. He had been a bright young man who had risen rapidly in Ohio State House politics, credited with keeping the governorship in the President's column. Franklyn Baldwin had told Trevayne that Webster was a man to watch.

'Did you have a good flight?'

'Yes, thanks. Much smoother than your afternoon, I think.'

'I'm sure of that.' The waiter returned with Webster's drink; the two men remained silent until he left. 'Have you talked with anyone but Baldwin?'

'No, I haven't. Frank suggested that I don't.'

'The Danforth people have no idea?'

'There wasn't any point. Even if Frank hadn't cautioned me, nothing's definite yet.'

'It is as far as we're concerned. The President's delighted. He'll tell you that himself.'

'There's still the Senate hearing. They may have different ideas.'

'On what possible grounds? You're houndstooth material. The only thing they might spring on you is your favourable press in Soviet publications.'

'My what?'

'They like you over at Tass.'

'I wasn't aware of it.'

'It doesn't matter. They like Henry Ford, too. And you were doing a job for State.'

'I have no intention of defending myself against something like that.'

'I said it doesn't matter.'

'I would hope not . . . However, there *is* something else, from my point of view. I've got to have certain . . . well, I guess you'd call them understandings. They've got to be clear.'

'What do you mean?'

'Basically, two things. I mentioned them to Baldwin. Cooperation, and no interference. Both are equally important to me. I can't do the job without them. I'm not even sure I can do it *with* them; without them, impossible.'

'You won't have any trouble there. That's a condition anyone would make.'

'Easily made, difficult to get. Remember, I worked in this town once.'

'I don't follow you. How could anyone interfere?'

'Let's start with the word "classified". Then jump to "restricted". Along with which can be found "secret", "top-secret", even "priority".'

'Oh, hell, you're cleared for all that.'

'I want it spelled out up front. I insist on it.'

'Then ask for it. You'll get it . . . Unless you've managed to fool everyone, your dossier's a study in respectability; they'd let you carry around the little black box.'

'No, thanks. It can stay right where it is.'

'It will . . . Now, I wanted to brief you on tomorrow.'

Robert Webster spelled out the routine for a White House audience, and Trevayne realized how little had changed since his past appearances. The arrival time half an hour to forty-five minutes before admittance to the Oval Room; the specific entrance to be used; the pass supplied by Webster; the suggestion that Trevayne carry no metallic objects larger than a key ring; the realization that the meeting was restricted to just so many minutes and might well be cut short – if the Chief Executive had said what he wanted to say or heard what he wanted to hear. If time could be saved, it should be.

Trevayne nodded his understanding and approval.

Their business nearly finished, Webster ordered a second and final drink.

'I promised you on the phone a couple of explanations; I'm flattered you haven't pressed me for them.'

'They weren't important and I assumed that the President would answer the one uppermost in my mind.'

'That being ... why he wants to see you tomorrow?'

'Yes.'

'It's all related. It's why you have my private number and why you and I will make arrangements so that you'll be able to reach me anytime of day or night, no matter where I am, here or overseas.'

'Is that necessary?'

'I'm not sure. But it's the way the President wants it. I'm not going to argue.'

'Neither am I.'

'The President naturally wants to convey his support for the subcommittee, and his personal endorsement of you. That's primary. And there's another aspect – I'll put it in my words, not his; if I make a mistake, it's *my* mistake, not his.'

Trevayne watched Webster carefully. 'But you've discussed what you're about to tell me, so the variation would be minor.'

'Naturally. Don't look so concerned; it's for your benefit ... The President has been through the political wars, Trevayne. He's a savvy old duck. The State machine, the House, the Senate – he's been where the action is, and he knows what you're going to face. He's made a lot of friends and I'm sure that slate is balanced by an equal number of enemies. Of course, his office removes him from those battles now, but it also allows him certain latitudes, certain pressure points. He wants you to know they're at your disposal.'

'I appreciate it.'

'But there's a catch. You're never to try to reach him by yourself. I'm your sole contact, your only bridge to him.'

'It would never occur to me to try to reach him personally.'

'And I'm sure it never occurred to you that the official weight of the presidency was behind you in the most practical way. Namely, at the moment you may need it.'

'No, I guess I didn't. I'm a corporation man; I'm used to the structures. I see what you mean. I *do* appreciate it.'

'But he's never to be mentioned, you understand that.' Webster's statement was spoken firmly. He wanted no room for doubt.

'I understand.'

'Good. If he brings it up tomorrow, just tell him we've discussed everything. Even if he doesn't, you might volunteer that you're aware of his offer; you're grateful, or however you want to put it.'

Webster finished his drink and stood up. 'Wow! It's not even ten thirty yet. I'll be home before eleven; my wife won't believe it. See you tomorrow.' Webster reached down to shake Trevayne's hand.

'Fine. Good night.'

Trevayne watched the younger man dodge between the armchairs, making his way rapidly toward the arch. Webster was filled with that particular energy which was at once the fuel he needed and the sustenance he took from his work. The exhilaration syndrome, Trevayne reflected. This was the town for it; it was never really the same anywhere else. There were semblances of it in the arts, or in advertising, but the rates of failure were too pronounced in those fields – there was always an underlying sense of fear. Not in Washington. You were either in or out. If you were in, you were on top. If you were at the White House, you were standing on the summit.

The electorate got a lot of talent for the money it paid, Trevayne had long ago decided. All in exchange for the syndrome.

He looked at his watch; it was too early to try to sleep, and he didn't feel like reading. He'd go up to his room and call Phyllis and then look at the newspaper. Perhaps there was a movie on television.

He signed the check and started out, feeling his coat pocket to make sure the room key was there. He walked through the arch and turned left toward the bank of elevators. As he passed the newsstand he saw two men in neat, pressed suits watching him from the counter. They started toward him, and when he stopped in front of the first elevator, they approached.

The man on the right spoke, while taking a small black identification case from his pocket. The other man also removed his identification.

'Mr Trevayne?'

'Yes?'

'Secret Service. White House detail,' said the agent softly. 'May we speak with you over here, sir?' He indicated an area away from the elevators.

'Of course.'

The second man held his case forward. 'Would you mind confirming, Mr Trevayne? I'm going outside for a minute.'

Trevayne checked the photograph against the man's face. It was authentic, and he nodded. The agent turned and walked away.

'What is this?'

'I'd like to wait until my partner returns, sir. He'll make sure everything's clear. Would you care for a cigarette?'

'No, thank you. But I would like to know what this is all about.'

'The President would like to see you tonight.'

5

The brown Secret Service car was parked at the side entrance to the hotel. The two agents rushed Trevayne down the step while the driver held the rear door open. They sped off down the street, turning south on Nebraska Avenue.

'We're not going to the White House, Mr Trevayne. The President's in Georgetown. His schedule is such that it's more convenient this way.'

After several minutes the car bounced along the narrow cobblestone streets that marked the residential area. Trevayne saw that they were heading east toward the section with the large, five-story townhouses, rebuilt remnants of a gracious era. They drove up in front of a particularly wide brownstone structure with many windows and sculptured trees on the sidewalk. The Secret Service man on the curb side got out, signalling Trevayne to do the same. There were two other plainclothesmen at the front door, and the minute they recognized their fellow agent, they nodded to each other and removed their hands from their pockets.

The man who first had spoken to Trevayne in the hotel led him inside through the hallway to a tiny elevator at the end of the corridor. They entered; the agent pulled the brass grill shut and pushed the automatic button: four.

'Close quarters in here,' said Trevayne.

'The Ambassador says his grandchildren play in it for hours when they visit. I think it's really a kiddie elevator.'

'The Ambassador?'

'Ambassador Hill. William Hill. This is his house.'

Trevayne pictured the man. William Hill was in his seventies now. A wealthy eastern industrialist, friend-to-Presidents, roving diplomat, war hero. 'Big Billy Hill' was the irreverent nickname given by *Time* magazine to the articulate, soft-spoken gentleman.

The elevator stopped, and the two men got out. There was another hallway and another plainclothesman in front of another door. As Trevayne and the agent approached him, the man unobtrusively withdrew a small object from his pocket, slightly larger than a pack of cigarettes, and made several crisscross motions in Trevayne's direction.

'Like being given a benediction, isn't it?' said the agent. 'Consider yourself blessed.'

'What is it?'

'A scanner. Routine, don't be insulted. Come on.' The man with the tiny machine opened the door for them.

The room beyond the door was an immense library-study. The bookcases were floor-to-ceiling, the Oriental carpets thick, the furniture heavy wood and masculine. The lighting was indirect from a half-dozen lamps. There were several leather armchairs and a large mahogany table which served as the desk. Behind the table sat Ambassador William Hill. In an armchair to the right sat the President of the United States.

'Mr President. Mr Ambassador ... Mr Trevayne.' The Secret Service man turned and walked out, closing the door behind him.

Hill and the President rose as Trevayne approached the latter, gripping the hand extended to him. 'Mr President.'

'Mr Trevayne, good of you to come. I hope I didn't inconvenience you.'

'Not at all, sir.'

'You know Mr Hill?'

Trevayne and the Ambassador shook hands. 'A pleasure, sir.'

'I doubt it, at this hour,' William Hill laughed, coming around the table. 'Let me get you a drink, Trevayne. Nothing in the Constitution says you have to be abstemious during any meeting called after six o'clock.'

'I wasn't aware that there were any strictures before six, either,' said the President.

'Oh, I'm sure there are some eighteenth-century phrases which might apply. What'll you have, Trevayne?' asked the old gentleman.

Trevayne told him, realizing that the two men were trying to put him at ease. The President gestured for him to sit down and Hill brought him his glass.

'We met once before, but I don't suppose you recall, Mr Trevayne.'

'Of course, I do, Mr President. It was four years ago, I think.'

'That's right. I was in the Senate, and you had done a remarkable job for State. I heard about your opening remarks at the trade conference. Did you know that the then-Secretary of State was very annoyed with you?'

'I heard rumours. He never said anything to me, though.'

'How could he?' interjected Hill. 'You got the job done. He'd boxed himself into a corner.'

'That's what made it so amusing,' added the President.

'At the time, it seemed the only way to thaw the freeze,' said Trevayne.

'Excellent work. Excellent.' The President leaned forward in the armchair, looking at Trevayne. 'I meant what I said about inconveniencing you this evening. I know we'll meet again in the morning, but I felt tonight was important. I won't waste words; I'm sure you'd like to get back to your hotel.'

'No hurry, sir.'

'That's kind of you.' The Chief Executive smiled. 'I know you met with Bobby Webster. How did it go?'

'Very well, sir. I think I understand everything; I appreciate your offer of assistance.'

'You're going to need it. We weren't sure we were going to ask you to come out here tonight. It depended on Webster . . . The minute he left you he telephoned me here. On my instructions. Then we knew we had to get you over.'

'Oh? Why was that?'

'You told Webster that you'd spoken with no one but Frank Baldwin about the subcommittee. Is that correct?'

'Yes, sir. Frank indicated that I shouldn't. At any rate, there was no reason to talk to anyone about it; nothing was set.'

The President of the United States looked over at William Hill, who stared intently at Trevayne. Hill returned the Chief Executive's look, then pulled his attention back to Trevayne. Hill spoke softly, but with concern.

'Are you *absolutely sure*?'

'Of course.'

'Did you mention it to your wife? Could she have said anything?'

'I did, but she wouldn't. I'm positive about that. Why do you ask?'

The President spoke. 'You're aware that we sent out rumors that you were being approached for the job.'

'They reached me, Mr President.'

'They were meant to. Are you also aware that the Defense Commission is composed of nine members – leaders in their respective fields, some of the most honored men in the country?'

'Frank Baldwin said as much.'

'Did he tell you that they agreed to a man not to reveal any decisions, any progress, any concrete information?'

'No, he didn't, but I can understand it.'

'Good. Now, I must tell you this. A week ago we sent out another rumor. An authenticated rumor – agreed to by the commission – that you had categorically rejected the post. We left no room for doubt as to where you stood. The rumor was that you violently objected to the whole concept, considered it a dangerous encroachment. You even accused my administration of police-state tactics. It was the sort of suppressed information that experience tells us is most readily believed, because it's embarrassing.'

'And?' Trevayne did not try to conceal his annoyance. Not even the President of the United States had the right to attribute such judgments to him.

'Word came back to us that you had not rejected, but, instead, accepted the post. Civilian and military intelligence established the fact that in certain powerful sectors it was common knowledge. Our denial was ignored.'

The President and the Ambassador remained silent, as if to let the importance of their revelation have an effect on Trevayne. The younger man looked bewildered, unsure of his reaction.

'Then my "refusal" wasn't believed. That doesn't surprise me. Those who know me probably doubted it – the way it was phrased, at any rate.'

'Even when personally confirmed to selected visitors by the President?' asked William Hill.

'Not simply *me*, Mr Trevayne. The *office* of the President of the United States. Whoever that man is, he's a tall fellow to call a liar. Especially in an area like this.'

Trevayne looked over at both men. He was beginning to understand, but the picture was still out of focus. 'Is it ... was it necessary to create the confusion? Does it matter whether I take the job, or someone else?'

'Apparently it does, Mr Trevayne,' answered Hill. 'We know the proposed subcommittee is being watched; that's understandable. But we weren't sure of the intensity. We surfaced your name and then proceeded to deny – vehemently deny – your acceptance. It should have been enough to send the curious out speculating on other nominees. It wasn't. They were sufficiently concerned to dig further, dig until they learned the truth.'

'What the Ambassador means – forgive me, Bill – is that the possibility of your heading up the subcommittee was so alarming to so many people that they went to extraordinary lengths to ascertain your status. They had to make sure you were out. They discovered otherwise, and rapidly spread the word. Obviously in preparation.'

'Mr President, I assume this subcommittee, if it functions properly, will touch a great many people. Of course, it'll be watched. I expected that.'

William Hill leaned forward over his desk. 'Watched? ... What we've described goes far beyond the meaning of the word "watched" as I understand it. You may be assured that large sums of money have been exchanged, old debts called in, a number of dangerous embarrassments threatened. These things had to happen, or a different conclusion would have been arrived at.'

'Our purpose,' said the President, 'is to make you aware, to alert you. This is a frightened city, Mr Trevayne. It's frightened of you.'

Andrew slowly put down his glass on the small table next to the chair. 'Are you suggesting, Mr President, that I reconsider the appointment?'

'Not for a minute. And if Frank Baldwin knows what he's talking about, you're not the sort of man who'd be affected by this kind of thing. But you have to understand. This isn't an interim government appointment made to a respected member of the business community for the sake of mollifying a few outraged voices. We are committed – I am committed – to see it produce results. It must follow that there will be a considerable degree of ugliness.'

'I think I'm prepared for that.'

'Are you?' asked Hill, leaning back once again in his chair. 'That's very important, Mr Trevayne.'

'I believe so. I've thought it over, talked it out at length with my wife ... my very discreet wife. I have no illusions that it's a popular assignment.'

'Good. It's necessary you understand that ... as the President says.' Hill picked up a file folder from the large maroon blotter on his table-desk. It was inordinately thick, bulky, and held together by wide metal hasps. 'May we dwell for a minute on something else?'

'Of course.' Trevayne looked at Hill as he answered, but he could feel the President's stare. He turned, and the President instantly shifted his eyes to the Ambassador. It was an uncomfortable moment.

'This is your dossier, Mr Trevayne,' said Hill, holding the file horizontally, as if weighing it. 'Damned heavy, wouldn't you say?'

'Compared to the few I've seen. I can't imagine its being very interesting.'

'Why do you say that?' asked the President, smiling.

'Oh, I don't know . . . My life hasn't been filled with the sort of events that make for exciting fiction.'

'Any man who reaches the level of wealth you did before he's forty makes fascinating reading,' said Hill. 'One reason for the size of this file is that I kept requesting additional information. It's a remarkable document. May I touch on a few points I found salient, several not entirely clear?'

'Certainly.'

'You left Yale Law within six months of your degree. You never made any attempt to finish or pursue the bar. Yet your standing was high; the university officials tried to convince you to stay, but to no avail. That seems odd.'

'Not really. My brother-in-law and I had started our first company. In Meriden, Connecticut. There was no time for anything else.'

'Wasn't it also a strain on your family? Law school?'

'I'd been offered a full scholarship. I'm sure that's listed.'

'I mean, in the sense of contributing.'

'Oh . . . I see what you're driving at. I think you're giving it more significance than it deserves, Mr Ambassador . . . Yes. My father declared bankruptcy in nineteen fifty-two.'

'The circumstances were untidy, I gather. Would it bother you to describe them?' asked the President of the United States.

Trevayne looked alternately at both men. 'No, not at all. My father spent thirty years building up a medium-sized woollens factory – a mill, actually – in Hancock, Massachusetts; it's a town outside of Boston. He made a quality product, and a New York conglomerate wanted the label. They absorbed the mill with the understanding – my father's understanding – that he'd be retained for life as the Hancock management. Instead, they took the label, closed the factory, and moved south to cheaper labour markets. My father tried to reopen, illegally used his old label, and went under. Hancock became a New England mill-town statistic.'

'An unfortunate story.' The President's statement was made quietly. 'Your father had no recourse in the courts? Force the company to make restitution on the basis of default?'

'There was no default. His understanding was predicated on an ambiguous clause. And talk. Legally, he had no grounds.'

'I see,' said the President. 'It must have been a terrible blow to your family.'

'And to the town,' added Hill. 'The statistic.'

'It was an angry time. It passed.' Andrew recalled only too well the anger, the frustration. The furious, bewildered father who roared at the silent men who merely smiled and pointed to paragraphs and signatures.

'Did that anger cause you to leave law school?' asked William Hill. 'The events coincided; you had only six months to go for your degree; you were offered financial aid.'

Andy looked at the old Ambassador with grudging respect. The line of questioning was becoming clearer. 'I imagine it was part of it. There were other considerations. I was very young and felt there were more important priorities.'

'Wasn't there really just one priority, Mr Trevayne? One objective?' Hill spoke gently.

'Why don't you say what you want to say, Mr Ambassador? Aren't we both wasting the President's time?'

The President offered no comment; he continued to watch Trevayne, as a doctor might study a patient.

'All right, I will.' Hill closed the file and tapped lightly with his ancient fingers. 'I've had this dossier for nearly a month. I've read it and reread it perhaps twenty times over. And as I've told you, I repeatedly asked for additional data. At first it was merely to learn more about a successful young man named Trevayne, because Frank Baldwin was – and is – convinced that you're the only man to chair that subcommittee. Then it became something else. We had to find out why, whenever your name was mentioned as a possible nominee, the reactions were so hostile. Silently hostile, I might add.'

'"Dumbstruck" might be more appropriate, Bill,' interjected the President.

'Agreed,' said Hill. 'The answer had to be here, but I couldn't find it. Then, as the material was processed – and I placed it in chronological order – I found it. But I had to go back to March of nineteen fifty-two to understand. Your first compulsive, seemingly irrational action. I'd like to capsule . . .'

As Ambassador Hill droned on, summarizing his conclusions point by point, Andrew wondered if the old man really did understand. It was all so long ago; yet yesterday. There had been only one priority, one objective. To make a great deal of money, massive amounts that once and for all would eliminate the remotest possibility of ever having to experience what he witnessed his father living through in that Boston courtroom. It wasn't so much a sense of outrage – although the outrage was there – as it was a feeling of waste; the sheer waste of resources – financial, physical, mental: that was the fundamental crime, the essential evil.

He saw his father's productivity thwarted, warped, and finally stopped by the inconvenience of sudden poverty. Fantasy became the reality; vindication an obsession. At last the imagination lost all control, and a once proud man – moderately proud, moderately successful – was turned into a shell. Hollow, self-pitying, living through each day propelled by hatreds.

A familiar, loving human being had been transformed into a grotesque stranger because he hadn't the price of survival. In March of 1952 the final gavel was sounded in a Boston courtroom and Andrew Trevayne's father was informed that he was no longer permitted to function in the community of his peers.

The courts of the land had upheld the manipulators. The *best-efforts, endeavors, whereases,* and *therebys* buried forever the work of an adult lifetime.

The father was rendered impotent, a bewildered eunuch appealing in strained, falsely masculine roars to the unappealable.

And the son was no longer interested in the practice of law.

As with most histories of material success, the factor of coincidence, of timing, played the predominant role. But whenever Andrew Trevayne gave that simple explanation, few believed it. They preferred to look for deeper, more manipulative reasons.

Or in his case an emotional motive, based on revulsion, that lucked in. Nonsense.

The timing was supplied by the brother of the girl who became his wife. Phyllis Pace's older brother.

Douglas Pace was a brilliant, introverted electronics engineer who worked for Pratt and Whitney in Hartford: a painfully shy man happiest in the isolation of his laboratory, but also a man who knew when he was right and others were wrong. The others in his case were the Pratt and Whitney executives who firmly refused to allocate funds for the development of close-tolerance spheroid discs. Douglas Pace was convinced that the spheroid disc was the single most vital component of the new high-altitude propulsion techniques. He was ahead of his time – but only by about thirty-one months.

Their first 'factory' consisted of a small section of an unused warehouse in Meriden; their first machine a third-hand Bullard purchased from a tool-and-die company liquidating its assets; their first jobs odd-lot assignments of simple jet-engine discs for the Pentagon's general contractors, including Pratt and Whitney.

Because their overhead was minuscule and their work sophisticated, they took on a growing number of military subcontracts, until second and third Bullards were installed and the entire warehouse rented. Two years later the airlines made an industry decision: the way of the jet aircraft was the way of the commercial future. Schedules were projected calling for operational passenger carriers by the late fifties, and suddenly all the knowledge acquired in the development of the military jet had to be adapted to civilian needs.

And Douglas Pace's advanced work in spheroid discs was compatible with this new approach; compatible and far ahead of the large corporate manufacturers.

Their expansion was rapid and paid for up front, their backlog of orders so extensive they could have kept ten plants working three shifts for five years.

And Andrew discovered several things about himself. He had been told he was a major salesman, but it didn't take a high degree of salesmanship to corner markets in which the product was so sought after. Instead, other gifts came into play. The first, perhaps, was the soft-science of administration. He wasn't just good; he was superb, and he knew it. He could spot talent and place it under contract – at some other company's loss – in a matter of hours. Gifted men believed him, wanted to believe him, and he was quick to establish the weaknesses of their current situations; to hammer at them and offer viable alternatives. Creative and executive personnel found climates in which they could function, incentives which brought out their best work under his aegis. He could talk to union leadership, too. Talk in ways it readily understood. And no labour contract was ever signed without the precedent he'd fought for in the company's first expansion in New Haven – the productivity clause that locked in wages with the end result of assembly-line statistics. The wage scales were generous, outstripping competition, but never isolated from the end results. He was called 'progressive', but he realized that the term was simplistic, misleading. He negotiated on the theory of enlightened self-interest; and he was totally convincing. As the months and years went by, he had a track record to point to; it was irrefutable.

The most surprising asset Andrew found within himself was completely unexpected, even inexplicable. He had the ability to retain the most complex dealings without reference to contracts or notes. He had wondered briefly if he possessed a form of total recall, but Phyllis shot down that conceit by pointing out that he rarely remembered a birthday. Her explanation was, he felt, nearer the truth. She said he never entered any negotiation without absolute commitment, exhaustive analysis. She gently implied that this pattern might be traced to his observation of his father's experience.

It all would have been enough – the airlines, the expansion, the production network that began to extend throughout the Atlantic seaboard. On balance, it should have appeared that they had gone as far as they could hope for; but, suddenly again, the end was nowhere in sight.

For on the night of 4 October 1957, an announcement was made that startled mankind.

Moscow had launched Sputnik 1.

The excitement started all over again. National and industrial priorities were all about to be altered drastically. The United States of America was relegated to second status, and the pride of the earth's most inventive constituency was wounded, its people perplexed. Restoration to primacy was demanded, the cost inconsequential.

On the evening of the Sputnik news, Douglas Pace had driven out to Andy's home in East Haven, and Phyllis kept the coffee going until four o'clock in the morning. A decision was reached that ensured the Pace-Trevayne Company's emergence as the Space Administration's largest independent contractor of spheroid discs capable of sustaining rocket thrusts of ultimately six hundred thousand pounds. The decision was to concentrate on space. They would maintain a bread-and-butter margin with the airlines, but retool with space objectives, anticipating the problems to merge with the larger aircraft surely to be demanded in the late sixties.

The gamble was enormous, but the combined talents of Pace and Trevayne were ready.

'We reach a remarkable period in this . . . most remarkable document, Mr Trevayne. It leads directly into the area of our concerns – the President's and mine. It is, of course, related to March of nineteen-fifty-two.'

Oh, Christ, Phyllis. They've found it! The 'game', you called it. The game that you despised because you said it made me 'dirty'. It began with that filthy little bastard who dressed like a faggot tailor. It began with Allen . . .

'Your company made an audacious move,' continued Big Billy Hill. 'Without guarantees, you restructured seventy per cent of your factories – nearly all of your laboratories – to accommodate an uncertain market. Uncertain in the sense of its realistic demand.'

'We never doubted the market; we only underestimated the demand.'

'Obviously. And you proved correct. While everyone else was still on the drawing board, you were ready for production.'

'With respect, Mr Ambassador, it wasn't that simple. There was a two-year period when the national commitment was more rhetorical than financial. Another six months, and our resources would have been exhausted. We sweated.'

'You needed the NASA contracts,' said the President. 'Without them, you were on dangerous ground; you were in too far to reconvert.'

'That's true. We counted on our preparation schedules, our timing. No one could compete with us; we banked on that.'

'But the extent of your conversions was known within the industry, wasn't it?' asked Hill.

'Unavoidable.'

'And the risks?' Hill again.

'To a degree. We were a privately owned company; we didn't broadcast our financial statement.'

'But it could be assumed.' Hill was centring in.

'It could.'

Hill removed a single sheet of paper from the top of the file, turning its face toward Andrew. 'Do you recall this letter? It was written to the Secretary of Defense, with copies to the Senate Appropriations and House Armed Services committees. Dated April 14, 1959.'

'Yes. I was angry.'

'In it you stated categorically that Pace-Trevayne was wholly owned and in no way associated with any other company or companies.'

'That's right.'

'When questioned privately, you said you'd been approached by outside interests who implied that their assistance might be necessary to obtain the NASA contracts.'

'Yes. I was upset. We were qualified on our own.'

Ambassador Hill leaned back and smiled. 'This letter, then, was really a highly strategic device, wasn't it? You scared hell out of a lot of people. In essence, it assured you of the work.'

'That possibility occurred to me.'

'Yet in spite of your proclaimed independence, during the next several

years, when Pace-Trevayne became the acknowledged leader in its field, you
actively sought outside associations . . .'

Do you remember, Phyl? You and Doug were furious. You didn't understand.

'There were advantages to be gained.'

'I'm sure there were, if you had been serious in your intentions.'

'Are you implying that I wasn't?'

Oh, Lord, I was serious, Phyl! I was concerned. I was young and angry.

'I arrived at that conclusion, Mr Trevayne. I'm sure others did also . . . You
let the word out that you'd be interested in exploratory talks of merger. One
by one you held successive conferences with no less than seventeen major
defence contractors over a three-year period. A number of these were written
up in the newspapers.' Hill flipped through the file and removed a sheaf of
clippings. 'You certainly had an impressive assortment of suitors.'

'We had a great deal to offer.'

Only 'offer', Phyl. Nothing else; never anything else.

'You even went so far as to arrive at tentative agreements with several.
There were a number of startling fluctuations on the New York exchange.'

'My accountants will confirm that I was not in the market then.'

'With reason?' asked the President.

'With reason,' answered Trevayne.

'Yet none of the exploratory conferences, none of these tentative
agreements, was ever satisfactorily concluded.'

'The obstacles were insurmountable.'

The people were insurmountable. The manipulators.

'May I suggest, Mr Trevayne, that you never intended to reach any firm
agreements?'

'You may suggest that, Mr Ambassador.'

'And would it be inaccurate to suggest further that you gained a relatively
detailed working knowledge of the financial operations of seventeen major
corporations involved in defence spending?'

'Not inaccurate. I'd stress the past tense, however. It was over a decade
ago.'

'A short period of time when you're talking about corporate policy,' said
the President. 'I imagine that most of the executive personnel remain the
same.'

'Probably so.'

William Hill rose from his chair and took several steps to the edge of the
mahogany table. He looked down at Trevayne and spoke quietly, good-
naturedly. 'You were exorcising a few demons, weren't you?'

Andrew met the old gentleman's eyes and couldn't help himself; he smiled
slowly, with a marked degree of defeat.

'Yes, I was.'

'You were repaying the sort of people who destroyed your father . . .
March, nineteen fifty-two.'

'It was childish. A hollow kind of revenge; they weren't responsible.'

Remember, Phyl? You told me: 'Be yourself. This isn't you, Andy! Stop it!'

'Satisfying, however, I would think.' Hill walked around the desk and leaned against the front edge between Trevayne and the President. 'You forced a number of powerful men to make concessions, lose time, become defensive; all for a young man barely in his thirties who held a large carrot in front of their faces. I'd say that was very satisfying. What I can't understand is why you so abruptly stopped. If my information is correct, you were in a position of extreme strength. It's not inconceivable that you might have emerged as one of the world's richest men. Certainly possible that you could eventually have ruined a number of those you considered the enemy. Especially in the market.'

'I suppose I could say I got religion.'

'It's happened before, I'm told,' said the President.

'Then let's call it that . . . It occurred to me – with my wife's help – that I had involved myself in the same form of waste I found so appalling in . . . March of nineteen fifty-two. I was on the other side, but the waste was the same . . . And that, Mr President, Mr Ambassador, is all I care to say about it. I sincerely hope it's acceptable.'

Trevayne smiled as best he could, for he *was* sincere.

'Entirely.' The President reached for his highball as Hill nodded and returned to his chair. 'Our questions have been answered; as the Ambassador said, we were curious, we had to know. Among other things, your state of mind – which, frankly, we never doubted.'

'We assumed it would be healthy.' Hill laughed as he spoke. 'Anyone who leaves his own company to take on a thankless State Department job and then assumes the headaches of a philanthropic foundation is no ruthless Caesar of the financial world.'

'Thank you.'

The President leaned forward, locking his eyes with Andrew's. 'It's of paramount importance that this job be carried out, Mr Trevayne; go the distance. The spectre of financial and political collusion is always ugly; it becomes worse if it's suspected of being covered up. In other words, once you commit yourself, that's it. There's no turning back.'

Andrew realized that the President was giving him his last opportunity to reconsider. But the decision had really been made when he'd first heard the rumors. He knew he was the man to do it. He *wanted* to do it. For many reasons.

Among them, the memory of a Boston courtroom.

'I'd like the post, Mr President. I won't quit.'

'I believe you.'

6

Phyllis Trevayne wasn't often annoyed with her husband. He was careless, but she attributed that to his extraordinary concentration on whatever project he currently undertook, not to indifference. He had little patience with the niceties, but he was a nice person, time permitting. Abrupt, but gentle in his relationships. Abrupt even with her sometimes, but always considerate. And he had been there when she needed him most. The awful years.

She was annoyed with him this evening, however.

He had told her – asked her, really – to meet him in town. In the Palm Court at the Plaza Hotel. He specifically had said seven thirty; there was no reason why he should be late, he'd expressly pointed that out.

It was eight fifteen, and no message had arrived to explain his absence. She was hungry as hell, among other things. And besides, she had had her own plans for the evening. Both children were leaving for their respective schools within the week; Pamela back to Miss Porter's, Steve to Haverford. Husbands never understood the preparations; there were as many logistic decisions to be made prior to sending children away for three months as there were in most business dealings. Probably more. She had wanted to spend the evening making a few of those decisions, not driving into New York.

Besides, she had a lecture to prepare. Well, not really; that could wait.

She was going to talk to Andy about getting a chauffeur. She hated that goddamned Lincoln. She hated the idea of a chauffeur, too, but she hated the Lincoln more. And Andy wouldn't let her drive a smaller car into New York. When she objected, he produced statistics about the vulnerability of small cars on the highway.

Oh, *damn! damn! damn!* Where was he?

It was eight twenty now. Carelessness was rapidly becoming rudeness.

She'd ordered a second vermouth-cassis and nearly finished it. It was an innocuous drink, a feminine drink, and the best to sip while waiting, because she didn't really like it. And of course it was necessary that she didn't like it. She was flattered that several men had passed her table and given her second looks. Not at all bad for forty-two – about to be forty-three – and two grown children. She must remember to tell Andy about them. He'd laugh and say something like: What did you expect, you think I married a mongrel?

47

She had a good sex life, Phyllis reflected. Andy was a passionate man, an inquisitive man. They both enjoyed the bed. What had Tennessee Williams said? Was it Williams? Yes, it had to be . . . Some character in an early play, a play about Italians . . . Sicilians, had said it. *If the bed's okay, the marriage's okay!* . . . Something like that.

She liked Tennessee Williams. He was a poet as much as a playwright. Perhaps more of a poet.

Suddenly Phyllis Trevayne felt sick, terribly sick. Her eyes lost their focus, the entire Palm Court seemed to spin around and around. And then she heard voices above her.

'Madame, madame! Are you ill? Madame! Boy! Boy! Get smelling salts!'

Other voices, crescendos of volume, a blurring of words . . . nothing made sense, nothing was real. There was a hardness against her face, and she vaguely knew it was the marble floor of the room. Everything began to go dark, black. And then she heard the words.

'I'll take care of her! It's my wife! We've a suite upstairs! Here, give me a hand! It's all right!'

But the voice wasn't that of her husband.

Andrew Trevayne was furious. The taxi he'd taken from his office at Danforth had rammed into a Chevrolet sedan, and the policeman had insisted he remain on the scene until all the statements were taken. The wait was interminable. When he told the police officer he was in a hurry, the patrolman replied that if the passenger in the Chevrolet could wait, prone on his back, for an ambulance, the least Trevayne could do was wait for the statements to be taken.

Twice Trevayne had gone to a corner pay phone to call his wife at the Plaza and explain, but each time he reached the bell captain to have her paged, he was told she wasn't in the Palm Court. The traffic down from Connecticut was probably lousy, and she'd be doubly upset if she arrived late and found him not there.

Goddamn it! Goddamn it!

Finally, at eight twenty-five, he'd given his statement to the police and was allowed to leave the scene.

As he flagged down another cab, he vaguely thought about the fact that the second time he'd called the Plaza, the bell captain seemed to recognize his voice. Or, at least, the time span between his requesting the paging of his wife and the answer seemed much shorter than on the first call. But Trevayne knew his impatience was heightened when he was angry. Perhaps that was it.

And yet, if that were so, why didn't it seem longer?

Not shorter.

'Yes, sir! Yes, sir! The description is the same! She sat right there!'

'Then where *is* she?'

'Her husband, sir! Her husband took her upstairs to their rooms!'

'*I'm* her husband, you goddamned idiot! Now, *tell* me!' Trevayne had the waiter by the throat.

'Please, sir!' The waiter screamed, as most of the Palm Court turned in the direction of the loud voices, heard above the punctuated strains of the violin quartet. Two Plaza house detectives pulled Trevayne's hands away from the pleading waiter. 'He said they had rooms – a suite upstairs!'

Trevayne threw the arms off him and raced to the desk. When one of the detectives came up behind him, he did something he wouldn't have thought he was capable of doing. He slammed his fist into the man's neck. The detective fell backward as his fellow officer withdrew a pistol.

Simultaneously, the frightened clerk behind the desk spoke hysterically.

'Here, sir! Trevayne! Mrs A. Trevayne. Suite Five H and I! The reservation was made this afternoon!'

Trevayne didn't think about the man behind him. He ran to the door marked 'Stairs' and raced up the concrete steps. He knew the detective followed; the shouts came at him to stop, but he refused. It was only necessary to reach a suite at the Plaza Hotel marked 'Five H and I'.

He pushed his full weight into the corridor door and emerged on the thin rug that bespoke of better times. The doors in front of him read 'Five A', then 'B', then 'Five C and D'. He rounded the corner and the letters stared him in the face.

'H and I.'

The door was locked, and he threw himself against it. It gave only slightly under his weight. Trevayne moved back several feet and slammed the heel of his foot against the lock area.

It cracked, but did not open.

By now the winded, middle-aged house detective approached.

'You goddamn son-of-a-bitch! I could have shot you! Now, get away from there or I *will*!'

'You will *not*! My wife's in there!'

The strident urgency of Trevayne's command had its effect. The detective looked at the panicked husband and lent his own foot to Trevayne's next assault. The door came off the upper left hinge, crashing down obliquely into the short foyer. Trevayne and the detective rushed into the room.

The detective saw what he had to see and turned away. He'd seen it before. He'd wait in the doorframe, both eyes on the husband, to make sure there was no violence.

Phyllis Trevayne was naked in the white sheets of the bed; the covers were at the foot, lumped as if thrown off carelessly. On the night table, on the left side, was a bottle of Drambuie, two glasses half-full.

On Phyllis Trevayne's breasts were lipstick marks. Phalluses outlined toward the nipples.

The detective assumed that somebody had had a ball. He hoped to Christ the third party had left the premises.

Goddamn fool if he hadn't.

Phyllis Trevayne sat up in the bed drinking coffee, wrapped in towels. The doctor had finished his examination and motioned to Trevayne to come into the other room.

'I'd say a very powerful sedative, Mr Trevayne. A Mickey Finn, if you like. There won't be much after effect, perhaps a headache, upset stomach.'

'Was she ... was she assaulted?'

'Debatable, without a more thorough examination than I can perform here. If she was, it was a struggle; I don't believe there was penetration ... But I think an attempt was made, I won't disguise that.'

'She's not aware of the ... attempt, is she?'

'I'm sorry. Only she can answer that.'

'Thank you, doctor.'

Trevayne returned to the front room of the suite and took his wife's hand, kneeling down beside her.

'You're a rough old lady, you know that?'

'Andy?' Phyllis Trevayne looked at her husband calmly, but with a fear he rightfully had never seen before. 'Whoever it was tried to rape me. I remember that.'

'I'm glad you do. He didn't.'

'I don't think so ... Why, Andy, why?'

'I don't know, Phyl. But I'm going to find out.'

'Where *were* you?'

'In a traffic accident. At least, I thought it was an accident. I'm not sure now.'

'What are we going to do?'

'Not we, Phyl. Me. I have to reach a man in Washington. I don't want any part of them.'

'I don't understand you.'

'Neither do I, really. But I think there's a connection.'

'The President's in Camp David, Mr Trevayne. I'm sorry, it wouldn't be convenient to reach him now. What's the matter?'

Trevayne told Robert Webster what had happened to his wife. The presidential aide was speechless.

'Did you hear what I said?'

'Yes ... Yes, I did. It's horrible.'

'Is that all you can say? Do you know what the President and Hill *told* me last week?'

'I have a good idea. The chief and I discussed it; I explained that.'

'Is this connected? I want to know if this is part of it! I have a right to know!'

'I can't answer you. I don't think he could, either. You're at the Plaza? I'll call you back in a few minutes.'

Webster hung up, and Andrew Trevayne held the disconnected telephone in his grip. They could all go *screw*! The Senate hearing was scheduled for two thirty the next afternoon, and he'd tell them all to go to hell! Phyllis was no part of the bargain! It was one thing to go after him; he could handle that. Not his family. He'd level those bastards at two thirty tomorrow as they'd never been levelled! And he'd hold a press conference afterward. He'd let the whole goddamn country know what kind of pigs inhabited a town called Washington, DC! He didn't need it! He was *Andrew Trevayne*!

He replaced the telephone in its cradle and walked over to the hotel bed. Phyllis was asleep. He sat down on a chair and stroked her hair. She moved slightly, started to open her eyes, and then shut them again. She'd been through so much. And now this!

The telephone rang, its bell causing him to jerk his head up, frightened, furious.

He ran to it.

'Trevayne! It's the President. I've just heard. How's your wife?'

'Asleep, sir.' Trevayne was amazed at himself. In the midst of his anguish he still found the presence of mind to say 'Sir.'

'Christ, boy! I haven't any words! What can I say to you? What can I do?'

'Release me, Mr President. Because if you don't, I'm going to have a great deal to say tomorrow afternoon. Inside the hearing and out.'

'Of course, Andrew. It goes without saying.' The President of the United States paused before speaking further. 'She's all right? Your wife *is* all *right*?'

'Yes, sir . . . It was a . . . terror tactic, I guess. An obscene . . . *obscene* thing.' Trevayne had to hold his breath. He was afraid of the words that might come out of his mouth.

'Trevayne, listen to me. Andrew, listen! You may never forgive me for what I am about to say to you. If you feel strong enough, I'll accept the consequences and expect your roughest condemnation tomorrow. I won't rebut you . . . But you must think now. With your *head*. I've had to do it hundreds of times – granted, not like this – but, nevertheless, when it hurt badly . . . The country knows you've been chosen. The hearing is only a formality now. If you tell them to shove it up their ass, how are you going to do it without paining your wife further? . . . Don't you see? This is exactly what they want!'

Trevayne took a deep breath and replied evenly. 'I have no intention of paining my wife further or of allowing any part of you to touch us. I don't need you, Mr President. Do I make myself clear?'

'You certainly do. And I agree with you completely. But I have a problem. I need *you*. I said it would be ugly . . .'

Ugly! Ugly! That goddamn terrible word!

'Yes, ugly!' Trevayne roared viciously into the telephone.

The President continued as if Trevayne had not shouted. 'I think you should think about what's happened . . . If it can happen to you, and by all our estimates you're one of the better ones, think what can happen to others . . . Are we to stop? Is that what we should do?'

'Nobody elected me to anything! I'm not beholden, and you know damn well I'm not! I don't want it to concern me.'

'But you know it does. Don't answer me now. Think ... Please, talk to your wife. I can postpone the hearing for several days – on illness.'

'It won't do any good, Mr President. I want out.'

'Think about it. I ask you to give me a few hours. The *office* asks you that. Speaking as a man and not as your President, however, I must tell you that I'm pleading. The lines are drawn now. We can't turn back. But as a man, I'll understand your refusal ... My greatest sympathy and well-wishes to your wife ... Good night, Andrew.'

Trevayne heard the click of the disconnection and slowly replaced the telephone. He reached into his shirt pocket for his cigarettes, and extracting one, lit it with the all-maroon matches labelled 'The Plaza'. There wasn't much to think about. He wasn't about to change his mind for the tactics of a very persuasive President.

He was Andrew Trevayne. Every once in a while he had to remind himself of that. He didn't need anyone. Not even the President of the United States.

'Andy?'

Trevayne looked over at the bed. His wife's head was propped sideways against the pillow, and her eyes were open.

'Yes, darling?' He got out of the chair and walked rapidly to the bedside. His wife was only half-conscious.

'I heard. I heard what you said.'

'Just don't worry about a thing. The doctor'll be back in the morning; we'll head up to Barnegat first thing. You're fine. Sleep now.'

'Andy?'

'What, sweetheart?'

'He wants you to stay, doesn't he?'

'It doesn't make any difference what he wants.'

'He's right. Don't you see that? If you quit ... they've beaten you.'

Phyllis Trevayne shut her eyes deliberately. Andrew felt deeply for the pained expression on her exhausted face. Then he realized as he watched his wife that her pain was mixed with something else.

With loathing. With anger.

Walter Madison closed the door of his study and turned the brass knob, locking himself in. He'd gotten the call from Trevayne at the restaurant, and in spite of his panic, had followed Andy's instructions. He'd reached the Plaza security man and made sure no police report would be filed. Trevayne was adamant that Phyllis be spared – the family, the children, spared – any press coverage of the assault. Phyllis couldn't help with descriptions of either the man or the event; everything had been blurred for her, incoherent.

The Plaza security man had read something else into Madison's instructions – the explicit instructions of the powerful attorney for the more powerful Andrew Trevayne – and didn't bother disguising his interpretation. For several minutes Madison had considered offering the man money, but the lawyer in him prevented that; retired police officers adding to their pensions in stylish hotels had a proclivity for stretching out such understand-ings.

Better the man believe what he wanted to believe. There was nothing criminal involved, so long as the hotel property was paid for.

Madison sat down at his desk; he saw that both his hands shook. Thank God his wife was asleep. Asleep or passed out, what difference?

He tried to understand, tried to put everything into perspective, into some kind of order.

It had begun three weeks ago, with one of the most lucrative offers in his career. A silent retainer, conceived and executed in confidence. With him alone, unrelated to his partners or his firm. It wasn't an unusual practice, although he had entered into very few such agreements. Too often they weren't worth the strain – or the secrecy.

This agreement was. Seventy-five thousand dollars a year. Untaxable, untraceable. Paid out of Paris into a Zurich account. Length of contract: forty-eight months. Three hundred thousand dollars.

Nor was there any attempt to hide the reasons behind the offer.

Andrew Trevayne.

He, Walter Madison, was Trevayne's attorney; he had been for over a decade.

The conflict – so far – was minor. As Trevayne's lawyer he was to advise his new clients of any startling or extraordinary information related to Andrew and this proposed subcommittee – which wasn't even in existence as yet. And there was no guarantee that Andrew would advise *him*.

That was understood.

The risk was undertaken solely by the clients; they understood that.

It was entirely possible that no conflict would ever arise. Even if it did, whatever information he might transmit *could* be unearthed from a dozen sources. And in his bracket, it would take him a considerable length of time to bank three hundred thousand dollars.

But his agreement tolerated nothing in the area of what happened that evening at the Plaza.

Nothing!

To associate him with such an act was beyond imagination.

He unlocked the top drawer of his desk and withdrew a small leather notebook. He thumbed to the letter 'K' and wrote the number on a scratch pad.

He picked up his telephone and dialled.

'Senator? Walter Madison...'

A few minutes later the attorney's hands stopped trembling.

There was no connection between his new clients and the events of the evening at the Plaza Hotel.

The Senator had been horrified. And frightened.

7

The closed hearing comprised eight senators, as diversified as possible within the opposing camps, and the candidate for confirmation, Andrew Trevayne.

Trevayne took his seat, Walter Madison beside him, and looked up at the raised platform. On the platform was the usual long table with the necessary number of chairs, microphones in their places in front of each chair, and the flag of the United States centred against the wall. A small desk with a stenotype machine was below the platform on the main level.

Men were standing around in groups talking with one another, gesturing with quiet intensity. The clock reached two thirty, and the groups began to disperse. An elderly man Trevayne recognized as the senior Senator from Nebraska – or was it Wyoming – climbed the three steps of the platform and walked to one of the two centre chairs. His name was Gillette. He reached over for a gavel and lightly tapped it.

'May we clear the room, please?'

It was the sign for those not part of the hearing to leave quickly. Last-second instructions were given and received, and Trevayne was aware that he was the object of a great many looks. A youngish man dressed in a sober, dark suit approached the table and put an ashtray in front of Trevayne. He smiled awkwardly, as if he wished he could say something. It was a curious moment.

The panel of senators began assembling; cordialities were exchanged. Trevayne saw that the smiles were abrupt, artificial; a taut atmosphere prevailed. It was emphasized by an incident that would have gone unnoticed under more relaxed conditions. Senator Alan Knapp, mid-forties, straight black hair combed carefully back from his wide forehead, pressed the button on his microphone and blew through the meshed globe. The amplified rush of air caused a number of the panel to react sharply. They looked – apprehensively, perhaps – at their colleague. It might have been Knapp's reputation for uncompromising investigation, even rudeness, that made the reaction so totally serious. Another curious moment.

Old Senator Gillette – Wyoming? No, it was Nebraska, thought Trevayne – perceived the tension and rapidly, softly tapped the gavel. He cleared his throat and assumed the responsibility of the chair.

'Gentlemen. Distinguished colleagues, Mr Undersecretary. Senate hearing

54

number six-four-one commences session on this date at the hour of two-thirty; so let the record state.'

As the stenotypist, staring at nothing, effortlessly touched the muted keys, Trevayne realized that the 'Undersecretary' was himself. He had been 'Mr Undersecretary'; *an* undersecretary, one of many.

'Having been appointed generously by my colleagues as chairman of this hearing, I shall open with the usual statement outlining the purposes of our gathering. At the conclusion of this brief statement I welcome any additions or clarifications – I hope no contradictions, as our objective is fully bipartisan.'

There were perceptible nods of agreement, several unhumoured smiles, one or two deep breaths signifying the start of Senate hearing six-four-one. Gillette reached for a folder in front of him and opened it. His voice had the drone of a court-martial charge.

'The state of the defence economy is appalling; an opinion shared by every knowledgeable citizen. As elected representatives, it is our duty-by-oath to use the powers granted us by the Constitution to ascertain these deficiencies and correct them wherever possible. We can and should do no less. We have made provision for the forming of an investigative subcommittee, so requested by the Defense Allocation Commission – a subcommittee the purpose of which is to make a thorough study of the major contracts now existing and submitted for congressional approval between the Department of Defense and those corporations doing business with Defense. To limit the scope of the inquiry – and surely it must be limited, for reasons of time – an arbitrary contractual figure of one-point-five million has been suggested for the subcommittee's guidelines. All Defense agreements in excess of this amount are subject to the scrutiny of the subcommittee. It will, however, be at the discretion of the subcommittee to make all such investigatory decisions.

'Our purpose this afternoon is to examine and confirm or deny the appointment of Mr Andrew Trevayne, formerly Undersecretary of State, to the position of chairman of the above-mentioned subcommittee. This hearing is closed, and the record will remain classified for an indeterminate period, so I urge my colleagues to search their consciences, and where doubts exist, should they exist, express them. Again, further—'

'Mr Chairman.' Andrew Trevayne's soft-spoken, hesitant interruption so startled everyone in the room that even the stenotypist lost his appearance of uninterest and looked over at the man who had dared to interrupt the opening remarks of the chair. Walter Madison instinctively reached out and put his hand on Trevayne's arm.

'Mr Trevayne? . . . Mr Undersecretary?' asked the bewildered Gillette.

'I apologize . . . Perhaps this isn't the time; I'm sorry.'

'What is it, sir?'

'It was a matter of clarification; it can wait. My apologies again.'

'Mr Chairman!' It was the aquiline Senator Knapp. 'The Undersecretary's lack of courtesy to the chair is strange, indeed. If he has anything to say in the nature of clarification, it certainly *can* wait for the proper time.'

'I'm not that familiar with procedures, Senator. I didn't want it to slip my mind. You're right, of course.' Trevayne reached for a pencil, as if to write a note.

'It must have struck you as most pertinent, Mr Undersecretary.' It was the Senator from New Mexico who now spoke; a man in his fifties, a respected chicano. It was apparent that he disliked Alan Knapp's intimidating rebuke.

'It did, sir.' Trevayne lowered his eyes to the paper. There was a momentary silence in the room. The interruption was now complete.

'Very well, Mr Trevayne.' Senator Gillette seemed unsure of himself. 'It's quite possible that you are correct, though unorthodox. I've never held to the theory that the chair's remarks were sacrosanct. I've been tempted far too often to cut them short myself. Please. Your clarification, Mr Undersecretary.'

'Thank you, sir. You stated that it was the responsibility of this panel to search for and express doubts . . . I'm not sure how to say it, but I feel that a similar responsibility is shared by this table. Quite honestly, I've had doubts myself, Mr Chairman.'

'Doubts, Mr Trevayne?' asked Mitchell Armbruster, the small, compact Senator from California whose wit was as much a part of his reputation as his judgment. 'We're born with doubts; at least, we grow to recognize them. What doubts do you refer to? Pertinent to this hearing, I mean.'

'That this subcommittee will be given the degree of cooperation it needs in order to function. I sincerely hope the panel will consider the implications of this question.'

'That sounds suspiciously like an ultimatum, Mr Trevayne.' Knapp spoke.

'Not at all, Senator; that would be totally unwarranted.'

'It nevertheless strikes me that your "implications" are insulting. Is it your intention to put the Senate of the United States on trial here?' continued Knapp.

'I wasn't aware that this was a trial,' replied Trevayne pleasantly, without answering the question.

'Damn good point,' added Armbruster with a smile.

'Very well, Mr Undersecretary,' said Gillette. 'Your clarification has been placed into the record and duly noted by this panel. Is that satisfactory?'

'It is, and thank you again, Mr Chairman.'

'Then I shall conclude my opening remarks, and we may proceed.'

Gillette droned on for several minutes, outlining the questions which should be raised and answered. They fell into two categories. First, the qualifications of Andrew Trevayne for the position under consideration, and second the all-important factor of conceivable conflicts of interest.

At his conclusion, the chairman made the customary statement. 'Any additions or clarifications, beyond Mr Trevayne's previous inclusions?'

'Mr Chairman?'

'The Senator from Vermont is recognized.'

James Norton, early sixties, close-cropped gray hair, down-easter accent very pronounced, looked at Trevayne. 'Mr Undersecretary. The distinguished chairman has described the areas of this inquiry in his usual clear and forthright manner. And we certainly will raise the questions of competence and conflict. However, I submit there is a third territory that should be explored. That is your philosophy, Mr Undersecretary. You might say, where you *stand*. Would you grant the privilege to us?'

'No objections, Senator.' Trevayne smiled. 'I might even hope that we could exchange such views. My own and the panel's collective position, of course, relative to the subcommittee.'

'*We* are not standing for confirmation!' Alan Knapp's voice crackled harshly through the speakers.

'I respectfully refer the Senator to my previous remarks,' answered Trevayne softly.

'Mr Chairman?' Walter Madison placed his hand once more on Trevayne's arm and looked up at the platform. 'May I have a word with my client, if you please.'

'Certainly, Mr ... Madison.'

The Senate panel, in the courtesy of such hearings, talked among themselves and shuffled papers. Most, however, kept their eyes on Trevayne and Walter Madison.

'Andy, what are you doing? Are you trying to deliberately confuse the issues?'

'I made my point ...'

'Unforgettably. Why?'

'I want to make sure there's no misunderstanding. I want this record to specify – not indicate, but *specify* – that I'm putting everyone on notice. If they clear me, they do so knowing what I expect from them.'

'For God's sake, man, you're reversing the function of the hearing. You're confirming the *Senate!*'

'I guess I am.'

'What's your point? What are you trying to do?'

'Setting up the battleground. If they take me, it won't be because they want to; they'll have to. It'll be because I've challenged them.'

'Challenged them? What for? What about?'

'Because there's a profound difference between us.'

'What does *that* mean?'

'It means we're natural enemies.' Trevayne smiled.

'You're crazy!'

'If I am, I'll apologize. Let's get this over with.' Trevayne looked up at the panel. He took the time to rest his eyes on each place, each member. 'Mr Chairman, my attorney and I have concluded our discussion.'

'Yes. Yes, of course ... I believe the Senator from Vermont submitted an addition in the form of the Undersecretary's ... basic philosophy. The chair assumes that to mean *fundamental* political beliefs – not *partisan* – but of a more general application. None other are pertinent to this hearing.' Gillette looked over his glasses at Vermont's Norton, so to be sure he understood his meaning.

'Perfectly acceptable, Mr Chairman.'

'I was hoping it would be, Senator,' added California's Armbruster with a chuckle. Armbruster and Norton were not only from different sides of the aisle, but as separated in partisan politics as their states were in geography.

Knapp spoke without petitioning the chair. 'If I'm not mistaken, the Undersecretary countered our colleague's addition with one of his own. I think he said he reserved the right to raise similar questions with the members of this panel. A right I seriously doubt should be granted.'

'I don't believe I made such a request, Senator.' Trevayne spoke softly but with firmness into his microphone. 'If it was so construed, I apologize. I *have* no right – or reason – to question your individual persuasions. I'm concerned only that this panel, as one deliberative body, assure me, as I must assure it, of a sense of commitment. A *collective* commitment.'

'Mr Chairman?' The petitioner was the elderly Senator from West Virginia, a man named Talley. He was little known outside the club, but within it was well liked, as much for his easygoing temperament as for his intelligence.

'Senator Talley.'

'I'd like to ask Mr Trevayne why he even raises the issue. We want the same thing; none of us would be here otherwise. Frankly, I thought this would be one of the shortest hearings on record. Speaking personally, I have great confidence in you, sir. Isn't that confidence returned? If not personally, at least collectively – to use your term, sir?'

Trevayne looked over at the chairman, silently requesting permission to answer the question. Senator Gillette nodded.

'Of course, it is, Senator Talley. And immense respect. It's precisely because of my confidence *in* you, my respect *for* you, that I wish to be able to refer to this transcript and have it specify that we've understood each other. The subcommittee for the Defense Commission will be impotent unless it has the responsible backing of such impartial and influential men as yourselves.' Trevayne paused and ingenuously looked from one side of the panel table to the other. 'If you confirm me, gentlemen, and incidentally, I hope that you do, I'm going to need help.'

The West Virginian did not notice the discomfort of several colleagues. 'Let me then rephrase my supplication, Mr Undersecretary. I'm old enough, or naïve enough, or perhaps both, to believe that men of good will – albeit different opinions – can join together in a common cause. The confidence you seek in us I might hope would be documented by what we say to one another in this room. Should it not be to your satisfaction, you have every right to bring it up. Why not find out first?'

'I couldn't hope for sounder advice, Senator Talley. I'm afraid my initial nervousness clouded my perspective. I'll try not to raise the issue again.'

Gillette, peering once more over his glasses, looked at Trevayne, and when he spoke, it was clear that he was annoyed. 'You may raise whatever issues you wish, sir. As will this panel.' He looked down at the legal pad in front of him, at his own notations. 'Senator Norton. You brought up the aspect of Mr Trevayne's general philosophy. Would you amplify – briefly, if you please – so we may clear the question and get on. I presume you wish to be satisfied that our guest at least nominally endorses the fundamental laws of the land.'

'Mr Undersecretary.' Norton's heavy Vermont dialect seemed more pronounced than necessary as he eyed the candidate. Norton always knew when to use the Yankee approach. It had served him in many such Senate hearings – especially when television cameras were on the premises. It made him seem so bound-to-the-earth American. 'I shall be brief; for both our sakes ... I'd like to ask you if you *do* subscribe to the political system under which this country lives?'

'Of course, I do.' Trevayne was surprised by the naïvety of the question. But not for long.

'Mr Chairman ...' Alan Knapp spoke as if on cue. 'I, for one, am frankly disturbed by an aspect of the Undersecretary's political history. Mr Undersecretary, you're what is known as an ... independent, if I'm not mistaken.'

'*That's correct.*'

'That's interesting. Of course, I'm aware that in many sectors the term "political independent" is revered. It has a nice, rugged sound to it.'

'That's not my intention, Senator.'

'But there's another aspect of such a posture,' continued Knapp without acknowledging Trevayne's answer. 'And I don't find it particularly independent ... Mr Trevayne, it's true, is it not, that your companies profited considerably from government contracts – especially during the maximum space expenditures?'

'True. I think we justified whatever profits we made.'

'I would hope so ... I wonder, however, if your lack of partisanship wasn't perhaps shaped by other than ideological motivations. By being neither on one side nor the other, you certainly removed yourself from any political conflict, didn't you?'

'Again, not my intention.'

'I mean, it would be difficult for anyone to take issue with you on political grounds, since your opinions were ... are ... buried under the classification of "independent".'

'Just one minute, Senator!' The chairman, visibly upset, spoke sharply.

'I'd like to comment, if I may—'

'You *may*, Mr Trevayne, after my own observations. Senator Knapp, I thought I'd made it clear that this is a bipartisan hearing. I find your remarks irrelevant and, frankly, distasteful. Now, you may comment, Mr Undersecretary.'

'I'd like to inform the Senator that anyone, at any time, may ascertain my political opinions by simply asking for them. I'm not shy. On the other hand, I wasn't aware that government contracts were granted on the basis of political affiliations.'

'Exactly my point, Mr Trevayne.' Knapp turned toward the centre of the table. 'Mr Chairman, in my seven years in the Senate I have many times supported those whose politics differed from my own and, conversely, denied support to members of my own party. In such cases my approval or disapproval was based on the specific questions on the floor. As men of conscience, we all practise the same ethics. What bothers me about our candidate is that he elects to be called "non-partisan". That worries me. I fear such people in places of power. I wonder at their so-called *independence*. I wonder, if, instead, it's merely a convenience to be a companion of the strongest wind?'

There was a momentary silence in the room. Gillette removed his glasses and turned toward Knapp.

'Hypocrisy is a most serious insinuation, Senator.'

'Forgive me, Mr Chairman. You asked us to search our consciences . . . As was pointed out by Justice Brandeis, honesty by itself is not enough. The appearance of integrity must be concomitant. Caesar's wife, Mr Chairman.'

'Are you suggesting, Senator, that I join a political party?' asked Trevayne incredulously.

'I'm not suggesting anything. I'm raising doubts, which is the function of this panel.'

John Morris, Senator from Illinois, broke his silence. He was the young est man on the panel, in his mid-thirties, and a brilliant attorney. Whenever Morris was assigned to a committee, he was invariably called the 'house teenager'. It was a substitute for another phrase. For Morris was black, a Negro who had swiftly worked his way up within the system. 'You haven't . . . Oh, Mr Chairman?'

'Go ahead, Senator.'

'You haven't raised a doubt, Mr Knapp. You've made an accusation. You've accused a large segment of the voting public of potential deceit. You've relegated it to a position of . . . of a second-class franchise. I understand the subtleties you employ, even grant their validity in certain situations. I don't think they apply here.'

The Senator from New Mexico, the admired chicano, leaned forward and looked at Morris as he spoke. 'There are two of us here who understand only too well the meaning of a second-class franchise, Senator. In my opinion, the issue is valid – to be raised, that is. One always looks for checks and balances; that's the meaning of our system. However, I think, also, that once having been raised, the issue can be put to rest by a succinct answer from the man standing for confirmation . . . Mr Undersecretary? For the record, may we assume that you are not a . . . sworn companion of the wind? That your judgments are, indeed, as independent as your politics?'

'You may, sir.'

'That's what I thought. I have no further questions on this subject.'

'Senator?'

'Yes, Mr Trevayne?'

'Are *yours*?'

'I beg your pardon?'

'Are yours? Are your judgments – and the judgments of every member of this panel – independent of external pressures?'

Several senators started talking angrily at once into their microphones; Armbruster of California laughed, Senator Weeks of Maryland's Eastern Shore stifled a smile by withdrawing a handkerchief from his well-tailored blazer, and the chairman reached for the gavel.

As order was restored by the rapid clatter of Gillette's hammer, Vermont's Norton touched the sleeve of Senator Knapp. It was a sign. Their eyes met, and Norton shook his head – imperceptibly, but the message was clear.

Knapp lifted up the pad in front of him and unobtrusively removed a file folder. He reached down for his briefcase and opened it, slipping the folder inside.

On the top of the folder was a name: 'Mario de Spadante'.

8

The Recess was called at four fifteen, the hearing to be resumed at five o'clock. The forty-five minutes would give everyone a chance to call home, rearrange minor schedules, confer with aides, dismiss assistants outside.

Since the eruption of Andrew's polite but explosively unexpected question, Gillette had managed to steer the inquiry rapidly through the ensuing invective and reach less abstract ground in Trevayne's qualifications.

Andrew was prepared; his answers were quick, concise, and complete. He surprised even Walter Madison, who was rarely surprised by his extraordinary client. Trevayne had no need of the numerous pages and charts filled with past figures and long-ago estimates. He rattled off facts and explanations with such assurance that even those who tried to sustain their antagonism found it difficult.

His total command of his own past economic relationships frequently left the panel speechless – and led Senator Gillette to voice the opinion that, following a recess, they might conclude the hearing by seven that night – at the latest.

'You're hot on all burners, Andy,' said Madison, stretching as he rose from his chair.

'I haven't begun, counsellor. That's in act two.'

'Don't revert to Charlie Brown, *please*. You're doing fine. We'll be out of here by six o'clock. They think you're a computer, with a human thought process; don't louse it up.'

'Tell *them*, Walter. Tell them not to louse it up.'

'Jesus, Andy! What are you—'

'Very impressive performance, young man.' The elderly Talley, the former county judge from the state of West Virginia, walked up to the two of them, unaware that he was intruding.

'Thank you, sir. My attorney, Walter Madison.'

The men shook hands.

'You must feel somewhat unnecessary, I should think, Mr Madison. It's not often you high-powered New York lawyers get off so easy.'

'I'm used to it with him, Senator. It's the most undeserved retainer in legal history.'

'Which means it isn't, or you couldn't afford to say so. I was on the bench for damn near twenty years.'

Alan Knapp joined the group, and Trevayne felt himself grow tense. He didn't like Knapp, not only because of his unwarranted rudeness, but because Knapp had about him the unhealthy look of an inquisitor. What had Ambassador Hill said? What were Big Billy's words? '. . . we don't want an inquisitor . . .'

But the Knapp now standing in front of Trevayne did not seem to be the same man who sat so coldly on the dais. He was smiling affably, infectiously, as he shook Trevayne's hand.

'You're doing splendidly! You really are. You must have boned up for this like the chief does for a televised press conference . . . Senator? Mr Madison?'

Hands were again shaken, the camaraderie so opposed to the atmosphere of five minutes ago. Trevayne felt uncomfortable, artificial; and he didn't like the feeling.

'You're not making it any easier for me,' he said, smiling coldly at Knapp.

'Oh, Lord, don't personalize it, man. I do my job; you do yours. Right, Madison? Isn't that right, Senator?'

West Virginia's Talley did not agree as quickly as Madison. 'I suppose so, Alan. I'm not a scrapper, so I don't cotton to the unpleasantness. Must admit, though, it doesn't bother most of you.'

'Never think about it . . .'

'I'll substantiate that, gentlemen.' It was Armbruster of California, who spoke between puffs on his pipe. 'Nice work, Trevayne . . . Tell you all something. Knapp was in the process of crucifying his – the President's – H.E.W. man, I mean nailing him hands and feet, and yet when the hearing was over, the two of them couldn't wait to talk to each other. I thought, "Goddamn, they're young enough to start throwing punches!" Instead, they were hurrying out to get a taxi. Their wives were waiting for them at a restaurant. You're an original, Senator.'

Knapp laughed. 'Did you know he was an usher at my wedding fifteen years ago? The President's H.E.W. appointment?'

'Mr Undersecretary?' At first the title didn't register on Trevayne. Then a hand was placed on his shoulder. It was Norton of Vermont. 'May I see you a minute?'

Trevayne stepped away from the group as Madison and Knapp argued a fine point of law and Armbruster questioned Talley as to the upcoming autumn hunting in West Virginia.

'Yes, Senator?'

'I'm sure everyone's told you by now. You're tacking right through the rough waters, and a port's in sight. We'll be outta here by twelve bells . . .'

'I'm from Boston, Senator, and I like sailing, but I'm not a whaling man. What is it?'

'Very well. We'll eliminate the compliments – though you deserve them, let me tell you. I've conferred briefly with several of my colleagues; as a fact, we also spoke at length before the hearing. We want you to know that we feel as the President does. You're the very best man for the job.'

'You'll forgive me if I find the methods of endorsement a little strange.'

Norton smiled the thin-lipped smile of a Yankee tradesman – and he was trading now, no doubt about it. 'Not strange, Trevayne. Merely necessary. You see, young fella, you're in the hot spot. In case anything goes wrong – which nobody thinks will, by the way – this hearing's got to be one of the strongest on record. Try to understand that; it's nothing personal.'

'That's what Knapp said.'

'He's right . . . I don't suppose old Talley understands, though. Hell, down in West Virginia they don't even put up a man to run against him. Not seriously, that is.'

'Then Talley isn't one of the colleagues you met with.'

'Frankly, no.'

'And you still haven't said what you wanted to say, have you?'

'Goddamn, fella, just slow down! I'm trying to explain a point of procedure so you'll understand. The confirmation's yours . . . That is, it will be, unless you force us into opposition. None of us would like that.'

Trevayne looked hard at Norton; he'd seen many lean and wrinkled men like this bending over farm fences or squinting beyond the dunes out at the sea in Marblehead. One never knew how much perception was hidden in those weathered eyes. 'Look, Senator, all I want from this panel is the assurance that the subcommittee will act as a free agent. If I can't get your active assistance, I at least need your guarantee that you'll protect the subcommittee from interference. Is that so much to ask?'

Norton spoke laconically, the Yankee peddler fingering his merchandise. 'Free agent? Eheah . . . Well, let me tell you, son. Some people get a touch nervous when a man insists that he's got to be a . . . free agent; that he won't tolerate pressures. You can't help but wonder. There's good pressures and not-so-good pressures. Nobody likes the latter, but good pressures, that's something else again. It's comforting to know that a man is accountable to somebody other than God, isn't that so?'

'Certainly, I'd be accountable. I never expected otherwise.'

'But it's kind of a second thought, isn't it? . . . The intent of this subcommittee is not to satisfy the personal ego of any one man, Trevayne. It has a job to do that's bigger than any one person. You may not have the temperament for it. That's what I mean by "intent". We don't want a Savonarola.'

Norton held Trevayne's eyes with his own. The Yankee was trading abstractions as though they were horseflesh, and he was good at it. He never once hinted that he was anything but the philosophical salt of the good brown earth.

Trevayne stared back, trying to pry loose the hypocrisy he felt was behind Norton's words. It wasn't possible.

'You'll have to make that decision, Senator.'

'Do you mind if I have a word with your attorney? What's his name?'

'Madison. Walter Madison. No objection at all. However, I think he'll tell you that I'm a terrible client. He's convinced I never pay attention when I should.'

'No harm trying, young fella. You're obstinate. But I like you.' Norton turned and walked toward Madison and Knapp.

Trevayne looked at his watch. In twenty minutes the hearing would resume. He'd try the hotel and see if Phyllis was back from shopping. The President had urged him to bring her down. He wanted Phyllis to come to the White House with her husband after the hearing. Another photograph would be taken showing the President endorsing Trevayne personally – this time with Trevayne's wife by his side. Phyllis had understood.

James Norton extended his hand to Madison and if anyone in the room had been watching them it would have been assumed that the Senator was merely introducing himself.

It wasn't the case.

'Goddamn, Madison! What the hell *is* this!?' Norton spoke with quiet urgency. 'He smells something! You didn't tell us that!'

'I didn't *know* it! I just told Knapp, I don't know *what's* going on.'

'You'd better find out,' said Alan Knapp coldly.

The hearing resumed at seven minutes past five, the delay due to three senators unable to complete their outside business. The seven minutes, however, gave Walter Madison a chance to speak with his client alone at the table.

'That fellow Norton talked to me.'

'I know; he asked permission.' Trevayne smiled.

'Andy, there's a logic in what he says. They're not going to confirm you if they think you're going to play power broker. If you were in their shoes, you wouldn't either. You'd be rougher than they are, and I think you know that.'

'Agreed.'

'What's bothering you, then?'

Trevayne spoke, looking straight ahead. 'I'm not that sure I want the job, Walter. I certainly don't want it if I can't do it my way. I told you that; I said it to Baldwin and Robert Webster, too.' Trevayne now turned to his attorney. 'There's nothing in my record that gives credence to the Savonarola charge.'

'The what?'

'That's what Norton threw at me. Savonarola. You called it "power broker". That's not me, and they know it . . . If I'm confirmed, I've got to be able to walk into the office of every senator on this panel, and if I need assistance, get it without argument. I *must* be able to do that . . . This panel wasn't chosen indiscriminately, by straws. Each of these men's states is heavily committed to Pentagon contracts; a few less than the others, but they're a minority – window dressing. The Senate knew exactly what it was doing when it put this crowd together. The only way I can make sure that subcommittee isn't interfered with by the Senate is to force these watchdogs of their own constituencies on the defensive.'

'What?'

'Make them justify themselves to me . . . in the transcript. This panel will have to go on record as being a necessary adjunct to the subcommittee. A working partnership.'

'They won't do it! The purpose here is to confirm you, that's all. There's no other requirements.'

'There is if I make perfectly clear that the subcommittee can't function without the cooperation of the Senate, the active participation of this panel in particular. If I can't get a commitment from *them*, there's no point in continuing.'

Madison stared at his client. 'And what'll you gain by this?'

'They become a working part of the . . . inquisition. Each man an inquisitor himself, none sure of the extent of his "distinguished colleague's" involvement . . . Share the wealth, share the responsibility.'

'And share the risks?' asked Madison softly.

'You said it; I didn't.'

'What happens if they turn you down?'

Trevayne looked up at the gathering panel of senators. His eyes were remote, his voice flat and cold. 'I'll call a press conference tomorrow morning that will rip this goddamn city apart.'

Walter Madison knew there was nothing more to be said.

Trevayne knew it had to come out of the proceedings. Come as a slowly revealed necessity; logically, without stress. He wondered who would say the words first and force the question.

Not surprisingly, it was old Senator Talley, the gnarled county judge from West Virginia; a minority member, window dressing. Not one of Norton's 'colleagues'.

It happened at five fifty-seven. Talley leaned forward, looking at the chair; receiving the floor, he turned to the candidate and spoke.

'Mr Trevayne, if I understand you, and I think I do, your primary concern is the degree of practical cooperation you'll get from those of us who can offer it. I can understand that; it's a valid point . . . Well, you should know, sir, that the Senate of the United States is not merely a great deliberative body, but a coming together of dedicated gentlemen. I'm sure I speak for all when I tell you that *my* office is open to you, sir. There are a number of government installations in the state of West Virginia; I hope you'll use whatever information my office can provide.'

My God, thought Trevayne, he's utterly sincere. Government installations!

'Thank you, Senator Talley. Not only for your offer, but for clarifying a practical issue. Thank you again, sir. I would hope that you speak for all.'

California's Armbruster smiled and spoke slowly. 'Would you have any reason to think otherwise?'

'None whatsoever.'

'But you'd feel more confident,' continued the Californian, 'more desirous of our endorsement, if the proceedings this afternoon included a joint resolution to aid your subcommittee in every way we can.'

'I would, Senator.'

Armbruster turned to the centre of the table. 'I find nothing objectionable in that request, Mr Chairman.'

'So be it.' Gillette had been staring at Trevayne. He rapped his gavel harshly, just once. 'Let the record state . . .'

It happened. One by one the senators made their individual statements, each as sincere, each as genuine as the preceding declaration.

Trevayne sat back in his chair and listened to the well-chosen words, abstracting phrases he knew he would soon commit to memory. He had managed it; he had manoeuvred the panel into its voluntary resolution. It made little difference that few, if any, would honour the words. It would be nice but it didn't really matter. What mattered was the fact that he could point to them, quote them repeatedly.

Webster at the White House had promised him a copy of the transcript; it would be a simple thing to leak isolated sections to the press.

Gillette looked down from his perch of sanctum sanctorum at Trevayne. His voice was flat, his eyes – enlarged behind the bifocal lenses of his glasses – cold and hostile.

'Does the candidate wish to make a statement before he is excused?'

Andrew returned the chairman's stare. 'I do, sir.'

'I might hope it could be brief, Mr Undersecretary,' said Gillette. 'The panel must try to conclude its business – at the President's request – and the hour is late.'

'I'll be brief, Mr Chairman.' Trevayne separated a page from the papers in front of him and looked up at the senators. He did not smile; he did not convey any measure of emotion whatsoever. He spoke simply. 'Before you conclude the business of confirming or denying my appointment, gentlemen, I think you should be aware of the results of the preliminary studies I've made. They will serve as the basis for my approach – the subcommittee's approach – should confirmation be granted. And since this is a closed hearing, I'm confident that my remarks will go no farther . . . I have spent the past several weeks – courtesy of the Controller General's office – analysing the defence commitments with the following companies and corporations: Lockheed Aircraft, ITT Corporation, General Motors, Ling-Tempco, Litton and Genessee Industries. It is my judgment that one, two or possibly three have acted either individually or in concert to achieve extraordinary authority within the decision-making processes of the federal government; this is malfeasance in the extreme. From everything I've been able to fit together, I must tell you now that I firmly believe it is one company that has been primarily involved in this malfeasance. I recognize the severity of the charge; it will be my intention to justify it, and until I do, I will not name that company. That is my statement, Mr Chairman.'

The room was silent. Each member of the panel kept his eyes on Andrew Trevayne; none spoke, none moved.

Senator Gillette reached for the gavel, then stopped and withdrew his hand. He spoke quietly.

'You are excused, Mr Undersecretary ... And thank you.'

9

Trevayne paid the taxi and got out in front of the hotel. It was warm, the night breeze tepid. September in Washington. He looked at his watch; it was nearly nine thirty, and he was starved. Phyllis had said she would order dinner in their rooms. She claimed to be exhausted from shopping; a quiet dinner upstairs was just what she wanted. A quiet dinner with two round-the-clock guards – courtesy of the White House – in the hotel corridor. A goddamned hotel corridor.

Trevayne started for the revolving door on the right when a chauffeur who'd been standing by the main entrance came up to him.

'Mr Trevayne?'

'Yes?'

'Would you be so kind, sir?' The man gestured toward the curb, to a black Ford LTD, obviously a government-rented automobile. Trevayne approached the car and saw Senator Gillette, his glasses still on the bridge of his nose, his expression still half-scowling, seated in the back. The window electronically rolled down, and the old gentleman leaned forward.

'Could you spare me five minutes, Mr Undersecretary? Laurence here will just drive us around the block.'

'Of course.' Trevayne climbed into the back seat.

'Most everyone thinks spring in Washington is the best season,' said Gillette as the car started off down the street. 'I don't. I've always enjoyed autumn better. But then, I'm contrary.'

'Not necessarily. Or maybe I'm contrary, too. September and October are the best months for me. Especially in New England.'

'Hell, everybody says that. All your poets . . . The colours, I imagine.'

'Probably.' Trevayne looked at the politician, and his expression carried the message.

'But I didn't ask you to take a drive in order to discuss your New England autumn, did I?'

'I wouldn't think so.'

'No, no, of course, I didn't . . . Well, you have your confirmation. Are you pleased?'

'Naturally.'

'That's gratifying,' said the Senator with disinterest, looking out the window. 'You'd think the traffic would ease up by now, but it won't. Goddamn tourists; they should turn off the Mall lights. All the lights.' Gillette turned to Trevayne. 'In all my years in Washington, I've never seen such an insufferable display of tactical arrogance, Mr Undersecretary ... Perhaps you were subtler, with more honeybuckets, than Bloated Joe – I refer to the deceased and not too distinguished McCarthy, of course – but your objectives were every bit as censurable.'

'I don't agree with you.'

'Oh? ... If it *wasn't* tactical, it was instinctive. That's even more dangerous. If I believed that, I'd reconvene the hearing and do my damnedest to have you denied.'

'Then you should have made your feelings known this afternoon.'

'What? And hand you your issue wrapped in ribbons? Come, Mr Undersecretary, you're not talking to old Judge Talley. Oh, no! I went right along with you. I gave everyone of us a very vocal opportunity to join your *holy crusade*! Nothing else would *do*! No, *sir*! There was no alternative, and you know it.'

'Why would there be an alternative tomorrow? I mean, if you reconvened and withdrew confirmation.'

'Because I'd have eighteen hours to pull apart every week of your life, young man. Pull it apart, rearrange a number of ingredients, and put it all back together again. When I got finished, you'd be on the Attorney General's list.'

It was Trevayne's turn to look out the window. The President had said it; this was the town for it. It could happen so easily because accusations always appeared on page one, denials on page thirty, apologies on page forty-eight, sandwiched between cheap advertisements.

That was the town; that was the way things were.

But he didn't need the town. He didn't have to accept the way things were, and it was about time he let people know it.

'Then why don't you do just that, Mr Chairman.' It was not a question.

'Because I phoned Frank Baldwin ... And why don't you call a halt to that arrogance? It doesn't become you, sir.'

Trevayne was thrown by Baldwin's name. 'What did Baldwin say?'

'That you wouldn't have done what you did unless you'd been provoked. He said he's known you damn near ten years; he couldn't be mistaken.'

'I see.' Trevayne reached into his pocket for cigarettes and lit one. 'And you accepted that?'

'If Frank Baldwin told me every astronaut was a fairy, I'd consider it holy writ ... What I want to know from you is, what happened?'

'Nothing. Nothing ... happened.'

'You didn't force every senator on that panel to *counter* your insinuations of guilt with protestations of innocence for no reason! Because that's what you did! You ridiculed the process of confirmation ... And I didn't appreciate it, sir.'

'Do you people always add a "sir" when you're pontificating?'

'There are a number of ways to deliver the word "sir", Mr Undersecretary.'

'I'm sure you're a master, Mr Chairman.'

'Was Frank Baldwin right? Were you provoked ... mightily? And by whom?'

Trevayne tapped his cigarette carefully on the rim of the ashtray and looked at the older man. 'Assuming there was provocation, what would you do about it?'

'Ascertain first whether it was provocation and not an incident or incidents magnified out of proportion, easily resolved. Should provocation prove to be the case, I'd call those responsible into my office and run them out of Washington ... This subcommittee is not to be tampered with.'

'You sound as if you mean that.'

'I do, sir. The time is due and overdue for this work to begin. If there's been any interference, any attempt to seek influence, I want it stopped in the strongest measures possible.'

'I think I accomplished that this afternoon.'

'Are you telling me there were senators in that hearing who tried to reach you improperly?'

'I have no idea.'

'Then what *are* you saying?'

'There *was* provocation, I'll admit that; where it emanated from, I don't know. I just know that if it continues, I'm in the position of spreading it around. Or stopping it completely.'

'If there was impropriety, it is incumbent upon you to report it.'

'To whom?'

'To the proper authorities; there are any number!'

'Maybe I did.'

'Then you were obliged to inform the panel!'

'Mr *Chairman*, that hearing was loaded this afternoon. The majority off those men represent states whose economies are largely dependent on government installations and contracts.'

'You've judged us all guilty!'

'I've judged no one. I'm only taking measures that seem appropriate under the circumstances. Measures to make sure these men cannot hinder me.'

'You're wrong; you've misinterpreted.' Old Gillette saw that the car had rounded another corner and was approaching Trevayne's hotel. He leaned forward in the seat. 'Pull up, Laurence. We'll only be a few moments ... Trevayne, I find your judgment lacking. You make surface observations and proceed to draw erroneous conclusions. You deliver inflammatory insinuations and refuse to justify them. Most damaging, you withhold pertinent and, I gather, extraordinary information, setting yourself up as an arbitrary censor of what the Senate may be told. In my opinion, Frank Baldwin and his commission made a great mistake in recommending you; the President, too, is in error following their lead ... Tomorrow morning I shall insist upon a reconvening of the panel and use all the powers of my office to have your confirmation withdrawn. Your arrogance is not in keeping with the public interest; you'll have your chance to answer then. Good night, sir.'

Trevayne opened the door and stepped out on the curb. Before closing it he bent down and spoke to the old man. 'I assume you intend using the next eighteen hours to ... what was it? Oh, yes. To pull apart my life week by week.'

'I wouldn't waste my time, Mr Undersecretary. You're not worth it. You're a damned fool.' Gillette reached over to his left and touched a button. The car window rose as Trevayne pushed the door shut.

'Congratulations, darling!' Phyllis jumped up from the chair and dropped her magazine on the lamp table. 'I heard it on the seven o'clock news.'

Trevayne closed the door and walked into his wife's arms, kissing her lightly on the lips. 'Well, don't go out and rent a house yet. It's not settled.'

'What are you talking about? They interrupted some local story to read the bulletin. I was so proud; they said it was a bulletin. *You, a bulletin!*'

'I've got another flash for them. They may have a second bulletin tomorrow night. The confirmation may be withdrawn.'

'What?'

'I've just spent a startling few minutes riding around the block with the distinguished chairman of the hearing. I'm leaving messages for Walter all over New York. I've got to talk to him.'

'What in heaven's name are you saying?'

Trevayne had crossed to the telephone and picked it up. He gestured to his wife to hold her questions until he'd finished his calls. She was used to this; she went to the hotel window and looked out over the lighted city. Her husband spoke first to Madison's wife, and when the conversation ended, he pressed the button, holding the telephone in his hand. He hadn't been satisfied with Mrs Madison's words – Mrs Madison was not the most reliable woman after seven o'clock in the evening. He released the button and put through a call to La Guardia Airport, to the airline desk of the Washington shuttle.

'If he doesn't call back in an hour or so, I'll try his home again. His plane gets in at ten-something,' he said, hanging up.

'What happened?' Phyllis saw that her husband was not only angry, but confused. Andy wasn't often confused.

'He surprised me. For the wrong reasons. He said my arrogance wasn't in keeping with the public interest; I withheld facts. Also, I was a damned fool.'

'Who said it?'

'Gillette.' Trevayne took off his jacket and threw it on a chair. 'From his viewpoint, he's probably right. On the other hand, I know damned well *I'm* right. He may be the most honorable man in Congress; probably is, but that doesn't mean he can guarantee the rest of them. He may *want* to, but that doesn't mean it's so.'

Phyllis understood her husband's non sequiturs; he'd told her what he intended doing that afternoon. At least, the objectives. 'This was the man in the car?'

'Yes. The Senate's venerable Gillette. He says he's going to reconvene the panel and withdraw the confirmation.'

'Can he do that? I mean, after they gave it to you?'

'I guess so. He'll call it new disclosures, or something . . . Sure he can.'

'Then you got them to agree, to work with you.'

'Sort of. On the record, anyway. Webster was getting me the transcript tomorrow. But that's not it.'

'This Gillette saw through what you were doing?'

'They all did!' Trevayne laughed. 'Most of them looked like they'd swallowed mouthfuls of papier mâché . . . Oh, they'll be relieved as hell! Just the fact that I withheld information will be sufficient.'

'What are you going to do?'

'First, see if my desk at Danforth can be salvaged. It's probably too late, but it's worth trying; I *do* like the job. Walter'll know better . . . Then the important question: how far can I go tomorrow afternoon without being subject to a subpoena from the Justice Department?' He looked at his wife.

'Andy, I think you should tell them exactly what happened.'

'I won't do that.'

'You're far more sensitive about it than I am. How many times do I have to tell you. I am *not* embarrassed. I *will not* be a freak. Nothing *happened*!'

'It was ugly.'

'Yes, it was. And ugly things happen every day. You think you're protecting me, and I don't need that kind of protection.' She walked to the table where she'd put the magazine and spoke deliberately. 'Has it occurred to you that the best protection I might have would be to tell what happened in headlines?'

'It has, and I reject it. That approach simply implants ideas . . . Like kidnapping.'

Phyllis knew there was no point in pursuing the subject. He didn't want to talk about it. 'All right,' she said, turning to him. 'Tomorrow just tell them all to go to hell in a basket and you'll be happy to buy them the biggest basket made. Tax-deductible, of course.'

He saw the hurt in her face and knew in some illogical way she held herself responsible. He went to her and took her into his arms. 'We don't really like Washington, anyway. Last time, we couldn't wait for the weekends, remember? We found every excuse we could to get back to Barnegat.'

'You're a sweet man, Andrew. Remind me to buy you a new sailboat.' It was an old joke between them. Years ago when the company was struggling for existence, he once proclaimed that he'd feel successful only when he could go out and buy a small cat and not think about the price. It had come to mean all things.

He released her. 'I'm going to order some dinner.' He went to the coffee table, where there was a room-service menu.

'Why do you have to talk to Walter? What can he do?'

'I want him to describe the legal definitions between opinion and factual evaluation. The first gives me plenty of leeway to be angry; the second invites the Justice Department.'

'Is it so important that you be angry?'

Trevayne was reading the menu, but his thoughts were on his wife's questions. He looked over at her. 'Yes, I think it is. Not just for the satisfaction; I don't really need that. But because they all consider themselves so damned sacred. Whoever eventually chairs that subcommittee is going to need all the support he can get. If I shake them up a bit, maybe the next nominee will have it easier.'

'That's generous, Andy.'

He smiled, carrying the menu over to the telephone. 'Not entirely. I'm going to enjoy watching those pompous bastards squirm; especially several ... I extracted figures and percentages from the defence index. The most damaging thing I'll do tomorrow is simply read them off. All *eight states.*'

Phyllis laughed. 'That's terrible. Oh, Andy, that's devastating.'

'It's not bad. If I don't say anything else, it'd be enough ... Oh, hell, I'm tired and hungry, and I don't want to think anymore. I can't do anything until I reach Walter.'

'Relax. Have something to eat; take a nap. You look exhausted.'

'Talking about exhausted warriors home from battle ...'

'Which we weren't.'

'... you look awfully attractive.'

'Order your dinner ... You might include a nice bottle of red wine, if you've a mind to.'

'I've a mind to; you owe me a sailboat.'

Phyllis smiled warmly as Trevayne picked up the telephone and asked for room service. She went into the bedroom to change into a negligee. She knew her husband would have dinner and they'd both finish a bottle of Burgundy and then they'd make love.

She wanted that very much.

They lay in the hotel bed, Trevayne's arm around his wife, her head against his chest. Both still felt the warm effects of the lovemaking and the wine, and there was a splendid comfort between them. As there always was during such moments.

Trevayne removed his arm gently and reached for his cigarettes.

'I'm not asleep,' said Phyllis.

'You should be; that's the way it is in the movies. Smoke?'

'No, thanks ... It's eleven fifteen.' Phyllis raised herself against the headboard, pulling the sheet over her naked body, looking at the travel clock. 'Are you going to try Walter again?'

'In a few minutes. What with the stack-ups and the taxis, he's probably not home yet. I don't relish a conversation with Ellen Madison at this hour.'

'She's very sad; I'm sorry for her.'

'I still don't want to talk to her. And he obviously didn't get the message at the terminal.'

Phyllis touched her husband's shoulder, then rubbed his arm affectionately, slowly. It was an unconscious but meaningful touch of ownership. 'Andy, are you going to talk to the President?'

'No. I've kept my part of the bargain. I didn't quit. And I don't think he'd appreciate my running to him now. When it's over, I'll get the usual solicitous phone call. Probably breakfast, come to think of it, since I won't mention him tomorrow.'

'He's going to be grateful for that. He should be. My God, when you think about it. You may lose a job you like; you're insulted; the waste of time . . .'

'I don't qualify as a charity case,' interrupted her husband. 'I was warned. Wow, was I warned!'

The phone rang, and Trevayne reached for it. 'Hello?'

'Mr Trevayne?'

'Yes?'

'I realize there's a "do-not-disturb" on your room, but the messages are piling up, and—'

'A *what*? What do-not-disturb? I never gave those instructions! Phyllis?'

'Of course not,' said his wife, shaking her head.

'The *d-n-d* is clearly marked, sir.'

'It's a mistake!' Trevayne flung his legs over the side of the bed. 'What are the messages?'

'The *d-n-d* was given to the board at nine thirty-five, sir.'

'Now, listen! We never requested it! I asked you, what messages?'

The operator paused for a moment; she wasn't going to be abused by forgetful guests. 'As I started to say, sir, there's a Mr Madison on the line who insisted that I ring through. He said it was urgent.'

'Put him on, please . . . Hello, Walter? I'm sorry; I don't know where that goddamned switchboard—'

'Andy, it's terrible! I knew you'd want to talk; that's why I insisted.'

'What?'

'It's tragic. It's a tragedy!'

'How do *you* know? Where did you hear it?'

'Hear it? It's on every newscast. It's all over – radio, television.'

Trevayne held his breath for a split second before speaking. His voice was calm, precise. 'Walter, what are you talking about?'

'The Senator. Old Gillette. He was killed a couple of hours ago. Car went out of control over a Fairfax bridge . . . What're *you* talking about?'

10

The account of the accident was bizarre enough to be real. According to the hospitalized chauffeur, Laurence Miller, he drove Gillette from midtown – no mention of the hotel, none of Trevayne – back to the Senate Office building, where Miller was instructed to go to his employer's second-floor office and retrieve a forgotten briefcase. He returned to the car, drove across the Potomac River into Virginia, when the Senator insisted on taking a back route to his Fairfax home. The chauffeur had argued mildly – the back road was partially under construction, there were no street lamps – but the crusty old man was adamant; Laurence Miller didn't know why.

A mile or so from Gillette's property was one of those small offshoots of the Potomac which infiltrate the Virginia woods. A short, metal-ribbed bridge spanned the water and dipped sharply to the right before the Fairfax entrance. The Senator's car was at midpoint when another automobile came careening up from the other side approaching the bridge, its headlights at high beam, its speed enormous. Gillette's driver had no choice on the narrow bridge but to hug the right rail so as to avoid a direct collision. The opposing car skidded in its turn, and the chauffeur, again with no alternative but head-on impact, accelerated instantly, trying to race through the gap left by the onrushing car's skid. He managed the manoeuvre, and once over the planked entrance, hit the steep decline and slammed on his brakes. The LTD swerved to the left and descended sideways down the short, steep hill. Old Gillette was thrown bodily into the right window structure, crashing his head on the metal door frame with such force that the doctor said death was instantaneous.

The second automobile sped over the bridge and left the scene. The chauffeur could give no description of it; he'd been blinded by the lights, and his concentration was on survival.

The time of the accident was put at 9:55.

Andrew read the account in the Washington *Post* over breakfast in their suite. He read it several times, trying to find a false note, a variation not heard on the previous night's newscasts.

There was none. Except the drive to the Senate Office Building, the forgotten briefcase.

His eyes kept pivoting on the estimated time of the tragedy: 9:55.

Twenty minutes after someone – who? – had placed a 'do-not-disturb' on his hotel telephone.

And why had it been done? For what purpose?

It certainly was no guarantee that he wouldn't hear of the accident. He or Phyllis might have had the radio or the television set on; they usually did, at least the radio.

Why, then?

Why would anyone want him incommunicado from 9:35 to – when did Madison get through – 11:15. Nearly two hours.

Unless it was a mistake at the switchboard; that was entirely possible.

And he didn't believe it for a minute.

'I still can't get over it,' said Phyllis, coming out of the bedroom. 'It's scary! What are you going to do?'

'I don't know. I suppose I should call Webster and tell him about our conversation. How the old boy wanted me out.'

'No! Why should you?'

'Because it happened. Also, on another level, Gillette may have said something to the others, told them he was going to put me on the spit. I'd hate to find myself confirming a conversation like that without volunteering it first.'

'I think you ought to wait. On *both* levels, thank you ... You don't deserve being pilloried. I think that's what someone called it. You believe you're right; you said so last night.'

Trevayne drank his coffee, buying a few seconds of time before answering his wife. He wanted above all else to keep his suspicions from her. She accepted Gillette's death as 'scary' but nevertheless an accident; there was no reason to think otherwise. He wanted to keep it that way.

'Webster may agree with you; so might the President. But to keep it straight, I want them to know.'

The President of the United States did, indeed, agree with Phyllis Trevayne. He instructed Webster to tell Andrew to say nothing unless the matter came up from other quarters, and even then, to be vague about specific aspects of his talk with Gillette until subsequent contact with the White House.

Webster also informed Trevayne that Ambassador Hill's considered opinion was that the old Senator was merely testing him. Big Billy had known the cantankerous war horse for years; it was a personal tactic. Hill doubted that Gillette would have reconvened the hearing. He simply would have let the candidate 'stew', and if Trevayne stuck to his guns, let the confirmation stand.

It was a complicated rationalization.

And Trevayne didn't believe *it* for a minute, either.

Phyllis had promised herself a look at the NASA exhibition at the Smithsonian, and so, White House guard intact, she left Andrew at the hotel. The truth was that she realized he'd be on the telephone constantly; she knew he preferred being alone during such times.

Trevayne showered and dressed and had a fourth cup of coffee. It was nearly ten thirty, and he'd promised to call Walter Madison before noon. He wasn't sure what he was going to say to him. He would tell him about the ride around the block; Walter should know about it in the event the hearing *was* reopened. It had crossed his mind to mention it during their tense conversation eleven hours ago. But everything had been so confused, the attorney inexplicably so agitated, that he decided not to complicate the already complex state of things. He recognized Madison's semi-hysteria and thought he knew what brought it about; a terrible afternoon in the Senate chamber; the return home to an ill wife – ill in the sense that he wasn't there to help her stay sober; and finally the bizarre account of the tragedy on a back-country Fairfax bridge. Even brilliant, sophisticated Manhattan lawyers had their thresholds of pressure.

He'd wait until noon before calling; everyone's head would be clearer then.

There was a knock at the hotel door; Trevayne looked again at his watch. It was probably maid service.

He opened the door and was greeted by the polite, formal smile of an Army officer, a major in a creased uniform with gleaming brass and three rows of ribbons.

'Mr Trevayne?'

'Yes?'

'Major Paul Bonner, Department of Defense. I suppose you've been briefed; nice to meet you.' The Major held out his hand, and Trevayne, by reflex, shook it.

'No, Major, I haven't been briefed.'

'Oh ... That's a hell of a beginning. I'm your man Friday; at least until your office and staff are set up.'

'Really? Well, come on in. I wasn't aware I was in business yet.'

Bonner walked into the room with the assurance of a man used to command. He was, perhaps, in his late thirties or early forties, with close-cropped hair and the complexion of a man often outdoors.

'You're in business, all right. You want it; I get it ... Whatever. Those are my orders.' He threw his hat on a chair and faced Trevayne with an infectious grin. 'I understand you're happily married; maybe more to the point, your wife's here in Washington with you. So that rules out one area ... You're rich as Croesus, so there's nothing to be gained by offering you a boat ride on the Potomac; you probably own the river. Also, you've worked for State, so I can't intrigue you with DC gossip. You probably know more than I do ... So what's left? I drink; I assume you do, too. You sail; I try. I ski very well. You're at best on the intermediate slope; no sense in flying us to Gstaad ... So we find you a nice set of offices and start hiring.'

'Major, you overwhelm me,' said Trevayne, closing the door and approaching the officer.

'Good, I'm on target.'

'You sound as though you'd read a biography I haven't written.'

'You didn't; "Big Uncle" wrote it. And you bet your life I read it. You're high-priority material.'

'Also, you sound as if you didn't approve; am I correct about that, too?'

Bonner stopped smiling for the briefest of moments. 'You may be, Mr Trevayne. It wouldn't be fair for me to say it, though. I've heard only one side of the story.'

'I see.' Trevayne walked to the breakfast table and indicated the coffee. 'Thanks. It's too early for a drink.'

'I've got that too, if you like.'

'Coffee's fine.'

Trevayne poured a cup, and Bonner crossed to the table and took it. No sugar, no cream.

'Why the come-on-strong, Major?'

'Nothing personal. I resented the assignment, that's all.'

'Why? Not that I know what your assignment is; I still don't understand. Is there some combat situation somewhere that you're missing?'

'I'm not the late-late show, either.'

'Neither am I.'

'Sorry . . . again.'

'You're blowing it, that's for sure; whatever it is.'

'Sorry. For a third time.' Bonner took his coffee and sat down in an armchair. 'Mr Trevayne, two days ago I was given your file and told that I was assigned to you. I was also told that you were a VIP of the first water, and whatever I could do for you – *whatever* had no latitude or longitude, just *whatever* – I was to make sure you got it . . . Then yesterday the word came through. You're out to nail us, hands and feet, with big, fat spikes. I'm a lousy go-between in this kind of a situation.'

'I'm not out to nail anybody.'

'Then my job's easier. I admit you don't look like a nut. Or sound like one, either.'

'Thank you. I'm not entirely sure I can say the same.'

Bonner smiled again, more relaxed than before. 'Sorry. For a fourth time, or is it the fifth?'

'I lost count.'

'Actually, I rehearsed that little speech. I wanted to give you a chance to complain; I'd be taken off.'

'It's still possible. What's this "nailing people" supposed to mean?'

'In short words, you're one of the virulent antimilitary. You don't like the way the Pentagon operates; incidentally, neither does the Pentagon. You think Defense spends zillions more than it has to; so does Defense. And you're going to spell it all out with a subcommittee, and our heads will roll. Is that fairly accurate, Mr Trevayne?'

'Perhaps. Except, as with most such generalizations, you imply questionable accusations.' Trevayne stopped for a moment, remembering that the dead Gillette had said pretty much the same thing to him in the car last night. He finished the Senator's spoken judgment with a feeling of irony. 'I don't think they're justified.'

'If that's so, then I'm relieved. We'll—'

'Major,' interrupted Trevayne quietly, 'I don't give a damn whether you're relieved or not. If you're going to stay on, we'd better have that clear. Okay?'

Paul Bonner took an envelope from his tunic. He opened it and removed three typewritten pages, handing them to Trevayne. The first was a listing of available government offices; it read like a real-estate prospectus. The second was a Xerox copy of the names Andrew had given Frank Baldwin almost two weeks ago – before the terrible events at the Plaza. They were the names of those men and women Andy wanted on his staff; the major positions. There were eleven: four lawyers, three accountants, two engineers – one military, one civilian – and two secretaries. Of the eleven, five had enigmatic checks beside their names. The third page was again a list of names – all unfamiliar to Trevayne. To the right of each was a one-word description of his or her employment classification and the previous government position held. Trevayne looked over at Major Bonner.

'What the hell is this?'

'Which?'

Andrew held up the last page. 'This list here. I don't know any of these people.'

'They've all been cleared for high-intermediate-level security employment.'

'That's what I thought. And I assume these checks . . .' Trevayne held up the second page, his list. 'They mean these people haven't been cleared?'

'No. As a matter of fact, they have.'

'And six haven't?'

'That's right.'

Andrew removed the first two pages and placed them on the coffee table. He took the last page and carefully folded it, then proceeded to tear the fold in half. He held out the torn paper for Bonner. The Major reluctantly approached and took it. 'Your first job, Major, is to deliver this back to whoever gave it to you. I'll hire my own staff. Get those pretty little checks inked in for those other six people.'

Bonner started to speak and then hesitated as Trevayne picked up the pages from the coffee table and sat down on the couch. Finally Bonner took a long breath and addressed the civilian.

'Look, Mr Trevayne, nobody cares who you hire, but they've got to submit to security checks. This substitution list just makes it easier, quicker.'

'I'll bet it does,' mumbled Trevayne, marking off addresses on the office sheet. 'I'll try not to employ anyone in the pay of the Presidium . . . This suite at the Potomac Towers; isn't that an apartment building?'

'Yes. Government lease has fourteen months to run. It was rented last year for an engineering project, and then the funds were cut . . . It's out of the way, though. It might be inconvenient.'

'What would you suggest?'

'Someplace nearer Nebraska or New York Avenue. You'll probably be seeing a lot of people.'

'I'll pay for the taxis.'

'I hadn't thought of it that way. I just assumed they'd be calling on *you*.'

'Very good, Major.' Trevayne rose from the chair and looked at the officer. 'There's five places I've checked off. Look them over and tell me what you think.' He crossed to Bonner and handed him the page. 'I've some phone calls to make; I'll use the bedroom. Then we'll get going. Have some more coffee.'

Trevayne went into the bedroom and closed the door. There was no sense in waiting any longer to call Madison. He'd have no place to make the call other than a government office or a pay phone. It was quarter to eleven; Madison should be routined and calm by now.

'Andy, I'm still shook up,' said the attorney, sounding very much relaxed. 'It's simply terrible.'

'I think I should tell you the rest. That's pretty terrible, too.'

He did, and Walter Madison was, as Trevayne expected, stunned.

'Did Gillette give you any indication that he'd spoken to the others?'

'No. I gathered he hadn't. He said he was going to call a reopening in the morning.'

'He might have gotten too much resistance for that ... Andy, do you think that the accident was anything else?'

'I keep wondering, but I can't come up with a reason that makes sense. If it wasn't an accident and he was killed because he was going to reopen the hearing – that means *they*, whoever they are, *if* they are, *want* me to chair the subcommittee. I can understand someone wanting me out; I can't understand anyone wanting to make sure I'm in.'

'And I can't buy the theory that these extremes would be used. Money, persuasion, even outright influence; that's possible. Certainly not killing. As I gathered from the reports, that isn't feasible anyway. His car couldn't have gone into the water; the rail was too high. It couldn't have been forced into a roll; it simply slid sideways and threw the old man into the frame ... It was an accident, Andy. Simply terrible, but an accident.'

'I think it has to be.'

'Have you spoken to anyone about this?'

Trevayne was about to tell Madison the truth, that he'd been in touch with Webster at the White House. Instead, he hesitated. Not for any reason related to Walter's confidence, only because he felt an obligation to the President. To mention Webster would mean involving the President of the United States – the office, if not the man.

'No. No, I haven't. Just to Phyllis, that's all.'

'We may want to change that, but for the time being, telling me is sufficient. I'll phone around and let you know.'

'Who are you going to call?'

For several seconds Walter Madison said nothing, and both men recognized the awkwardness of the moment. 'I don't know yet. I haven't had time to think. Perhaps a couple of the men at the hearing, the ones I met. Easy enough to do; I'm solicitous, my client wants to know if he should make a statement. Anything . . . I'll get the drift.'

'Right. You'll call me back?'

'Of course.'

'Make it late in the day. I've got my own major from the Defense Department. He's going to help me set up shop.'

'Christ! They don't waste a minute. What's his name?'

'Bonner. First name, Paul, I think he said.'

Madison laughed. It was a laugh of recognition, and not entirely pleasant. 'Paul *Bonner*? They're not very subtle, are they?'

'I don't understand. What's so funny?'

'Bonner's one of the Pentagon's Young Turks. The original bad boy of Southeast Asia. Remember a few years ago? A half-dozen or so officers got thrown out of Indo-China for some highly questionable activities beyond the borders, behind the lines?'

'Yes, I do. The inquiry was squashed.'

'You *know* it. It was too damned hot. This Bonner was in command.'

11

By two o'clock Trevayne and Banner had scouted three of the five office suites. The Army liaison tried to maintain a neutral attitude, but he was too candid. Trevayne realized that in several ways Bonner was like himself; at close range, it was difficult for the officer to disguise his opinion.

It was obvious that Bonner felt all the locations they'd seen were satisfactory. He couldn't understand why Trevayne insisted on visiting the last two, both quite far from the central city. Why not pick one of the others?

Trevayne, on the other hand, had seen the first three out of courtesy, so it wouldn't appear that he was subject to snap decisions. Bonner had allowed that the offices at the Potomac Towers *did* look out on the river; Trevayne had suspected as much, and that fact, in itself, was enough to convince him.

His offices would be at the Potomac Towers.

But he would find other reasons than the river, the water. He wouldn't give Major Paul Bonner, the Young Turk of the Pentagon, the opportunity of saying that his VIP had a thing about water. He wouldn't lend himself to the ridicule that might so easily come from the blunt observations of a man whose actions had frightened the Department of the Army a few short years ago.

'There's nothing against our taking a lunch break, is there, Major?'

'Christ, no. I'll get my ass chewed if it doesn't appear on my chit sheet. As a matter of fact, I'll get reamed anyway for letting you make this tour. Frankly, I thought you'd have someone else do it for you.'

'Who, for instance?'

'Hell, I don't know. Don't you people always have other people do these things? Get offices and stuff like that?'

'Sometimes. But not if it's a concentrated job that's going to require a lot of time on the premises.'

'I forgot. You're a self-made millionaire, according to the reading material.'

'Only because it was easier, Major.'

They went to the Chesapeake House, and Trevayne was at first amused, then amazed, at Bonner's alcoholic capacity. The Major ordered double bourbons – three before lunch, two during, and one after. And they were generous singles to begin with.

83

Yet Bonner did not display the slightest indication of having had a drink.

Over coffee, Trevayne thought he'd try a more friendly approach than he'd shown throughout the morning.

'You know, Bonner, I haven't said it, but I do appreciate your taking on a thankless chore. I can see why you resent it.'

'I don't mind, really. Not now. Actually, I pictured you as some kind of computerized . . . prick, if you'll forgive the expression. You know, a mincing slide-rule type who made his bread and thinks everyone else is worthless.'

'Did the "reading material" indicate that?'

'Yeah. I think it did. Remind me to show it to you in a couple of months . . . If we're still speaking.' Bonner laughed and drank the remainder of his bourbon. 'It's crazy, but they didn't have any photographs of you. They never do with civilians, except in security cases. Isn't that nuts? In the field I'd never look at a file unless there were at least three or four photographs. Not just one; I'd never accept just one.'

Trevayne thought for a moment. The Major was right. One photograph was meaningless for a dozen reasons. Several were not.

'I read about your . . . field activity. You made a large impression.'

'That's off-limits, I'm afraid. I won't talk about that, which means I'm not supposed to admit I was ever west of San Diego.'

'Which strikes me as silly.'

'Me, too . . . So I've got a couple of programmed statements which don't mean a damned thing. Why bring them up?'

Trevayne looked at Bonner and saw that he was sincere. He didn't want to restate the programmed replies he'd been fed; yet there seemed to be something else he was perfectly willing to discuss. Andrew wasn't sure, but it was worth a try.

'I'd like a brandy. How about you?'

'Stick to bourbon.'

'A double?'

'That's right.'

The drinks came and were half-finished before Trevayne's observation proved out.

'What's this subcommittee all about, Mr Trevayne? Why is everyone so uptight?'

'You said it this morning, Major. Defense is spending "zillions" more than it should.'

'I understand that; nobody would argue. But why are we the heavies right off the top? There are thousands involved. Why are *we* singled out as the prime targets?'

'Because you issue contracts. Simple as that.'

'We issue contracts that congressional committees *approve.*'

'I don't want to generalize, but it seems to me that Congress usually approves one figure and then is forced to approve another – the second being a lot higher than the first.'

'We're not responsible for the economy.'

Trevayne lifted his half-empty brandy glass, and revolved it. 'Would you accept that kind of reasoning in the field, Major? I'm sure you'd accept the fact that your intelligence teams had a margin for error, but would you tolerate a hundred per cent inaccuracy?'

'It's not the same.'

'They're both information, aren't they?'

'I refuse to equate lives with money.'

'I find that argument specious; you had no such consideration when your "field activity" cost a great *many* lives.'

'Horseshit! That was a statistical-combat situation.'

'Double horseshit. There were an awful lot of people who thought the situation was totally uncalled for.'

'Then why the hell didn't they do something about it? Don't cry *now*.'

'As I recall, they tried,' said Trevayne, staring at his glass.

'And failed. Because they didn't read their problem correctly. Their strategy was very un-pro.'

'That's an interesting statement, Major . . . Provocative, too.'

'Look, I happen to think that particular war was necessary for all the reasons brighter men than me have stated time and again. I can also understand how a lot of those reasons could be rejected, traded off because of the price. That's what those people didn't concentrate on. They didn't emphasize it.'

'You fascinate me.' Trevayne finished his brandy. 'How could . . . those people have done that?'

'Visual-tactical manoeuvres. I could even break down the logistics of cost and geography.'

'Please do,' said Trevayne, returning the Major's smile.

'The visual: fifteen thousand coffins in three units of five thousand each. The real things – government issue, pine construction. Cost, two hundred dollars per item on bulk purchase. Geography: New York, Chicago, Los Angeles – Fifth Avenue, Michigan Avenue, Sunset Boulevard. Tactic: placing the coffins laterally at one-foot spacings, with every hundredth casket open and displaying a corpse. Mutilated, if possible. Personnel requirements: two men per coffin, with a side task force of one thousand per city employed to distract police or to prevent interference. Total troop requirements: thirty-three thousand . . . and a hundred and fifty corpses . . . Three cities completely immobilized. Two miles of corpses, real and symbolic, blocking major thoroughfares. Total impact. Revulsion.'

'That's incredible. And you think it would have worked?'

'Have you ever seen civilians standing around on a street corner watching a hearse go by? It's the ultimate identification . . . What I just described would have turned the stomachs of eight to ten million people on the scenes, and another hundred million through the media. A mass burial rite.'

'It couldn't have been done. It would have been prevented. There's the police, national guard . . .'

'Logistics, again, Mr Trevayne. Diversionary tactics; surprise, silence. The quiet grouping of personnel and equipment, say, on a Sunday morning or early Monday – minimum-police-activity hours. The execution of the manoeuvre so precisely timed that it could be accomplished in less than forty-five minutes in each city . . . Only thirty-odd thousand men – women, too, probably. You had damn near a half-million in the Washington march alone.'

'It's chilling.' Trevayne was not smiling; he also was aware that Bonner had used the word 'you' for the first time. Trevayne's position had been clear on IndoChina, and the soldier wanted him to know he knew it.

'That's the point.'

'Not only the manoeuvre, but that you could conceive of it.'

'I'm a professional soldier. It's my job to conceive strategies. And once having conceived them, also to create countermeasures.'

'You've created one for this?'

'Definitely. It's not very pleasant, but unavoidable. It's reduced to swift retaliation; immediate and complete suppression. Confrontation by force and superior weaponry so as to establish military supremacy. Suspension of all news media. Replace one idea with another. Fast.'

'And spill a considerable amount of blood.'

'Unavoidable.' Bonner looked up and grinned. 'It's only a game, Mr Trevayne.'

'I'd rather not play.'

Bonner looked at his watch. 'Gosh! It's almost four o'clock. We'd better check out those last two addresses, or they'll be locked up.'

Trevayne got out of his chair just a little bit numbed. Major Paul Bonner had spent the last few minutes telling him something. Spelling out the harsh reality that Washington was inhabited by many Paul Bonners. Men who were committed – rightfully, justifiably, by their lights – to the promulgation of their authority and influence. Professional soldiers who were capable of outthinking their opponents because they were equally capable of thinking *for* them. Generous, too; tolerant of the hazy, muddled thinking of their soft civilian counterparts. Secure in the knowledge that in this era of potential holocaust there was no room for the indecisive or undecided. The protection of the nation was directly related to the enormity and effectiveness of its strike force. For such men as Bonner it was inconceivable that any should stand in the way of this goal. That they could not tolerate.

And it seemed incongruous that Major Bonner could say so ingenuously: *Gosh! It's almost four o'clock.* And not a little frightening.

The Potomac Towers provided its own reason for being selected, unrelated to the view of the river. Bonner accepted it. The other suites all had the normal five offices and a waiting room; the Towers included an additional kitchenette and a study. The latter was designed for quiet reading or conferences, even overnight accommodations by way of a huge leather couch in the main office. The Potomac Towers had been leased for an engineering crash programme and outfitted to accommodate the pressurized schedule. It was ideal for Trevayne's purposes, and Bonner made the requisition, relieved that the tour was finished.

The two men returned to Trevayne's hotel.

'Would you care to come up for a drink?' asked Trevayne, getting out of the Army vehicle with the insignia on both doors that allowed for parking just about anywhere.

'Thanks, but I'd better report in. There are probably a dozen generals walking in and out of the men's room, watching my office, waiting for me.' Bonner's face lit up, his eyes smiling; he was pleased with the image he'd just created. Trevayne understood. The Young Turk enjoyed the position he was in – a position undoubtedly assigned for reasons Bonner didn't like, and now, perhaps, could be turned on his superiors.

Trevayne wondered what those reasons were.

'Well, have fun. Ten in the morning?'

'Right on. I'll alert security; that list of yours will be cleared. If there are any real problems, I'll call you myself. You'll want others, though. I'll set up interviews.' Bonner looked at Andrew and laughed. '*Your* interviews, massa.'

'Fine. And thanks.' Trevayne watched the Army car start up and enter the congested flow of Washington's five-thirty traffic.

The hotel desk informed Trevayne that Mrs Trevayne had picked up their messages at precisely five ten. The elevator operator tipped three fingers to his visor and said, 'Good evening,' addressing him by name. The first guard, seated in a chair by the row of elevators on the ninth floor, smiled; the second guard, standing in the corridor several yards from his door, nodded his head in recognition. Trevayne had the feeling that he'd just passed through a hall of mirrors, his image reflected a thousandfold, but not necessarily for him. For the benefit of others.

'Hello, Phyl?' Trevayne closed the door and heard his wife speaking on the telephone in the bedroom.

'Be with you in a sec,' she called out.

He took off his jacket, loosened his tie, and went to the bar, where he poured himself a glass of ice water. Phyllis came out of the bedroom, and Trevayne saw a trace of concern in her eyes, beyond the smile.

'Who was that?'

'Lillian.' She referred to their housekeeper, cook, aide-for-all-seasons at High Barnegat. 'She had some electrical trouble; it'll be all right. The repairmen said they'd be out soon.'

They kissed their customary kiss, but Trevayne was hardly aware of it. 'What do you mean, trouble?'

'Half the lights went out. The north side. She wouldn't have known except for the radio; it went off.'

'Didn't it go right back on again?'

'I guess not. It's all right, the men are coming.'

'Phyl, we have an auxiliary generator. It cuts in when a circuit breaker fails.'

'Darling, you don't expect us to know about *those* things. The men'll fix it ... How did everything go? Where *did* you go, incidentally?'

It was possible, Trevayne supposed, for there to be an electrical malfunction at Barnegat, but unlikely. Barnegat's entire electrical system was designed by Phyllis' brother; a labour of love and enormous sophistication. He'd call his brother-in-law later; ask him, jokingly perhaps, to check into it.

'Where did I go? ... all over town with a nice young fellow whose late-night reading is restricted to Clausewitz.'

'Who?'

'The science of ... military supremacy will do.'

'That must have been rewarding.'

'"Enlightening" would be more accurate ... We settled on the offices. Guess what? They're on the river.'

'How did you manage that?'

'I didn't. They were just available.'

'You haven't heard anything, then? About the hearing, the confirmation?'

'Nope. At least, not so far. The desk said you stopped for the messages. Did Walter call?'

'Oh, they're on the table. Sorry. I saw Lillian's and forgot.'

Trevayne went to the coffee table and picked up the notes. There were an even dozen, mostly friends, a few quite close, others vaguely remembered. There was no message from Madison. But there was one from a 'Mr de Spadante'.

'That's funny. A call here from de Spadante.'

'I saw the name; I didn't recognize it.'

'Met him on the plane. He goes back to early New Haven. He's in construction.'

'And probably wants to take you to lunch. After all, you're a bulletin.'

'I think, under the circumstances, I won't return the call ... Oh, the Jansens phoned. We haven't seen them in almost two years.'

'They're nice. Let's suggest dinner tomorrow or Saturday, if they're free.'

'Okay. I'm going to shower and change. If Walter calls and I'm in the john, get me, will you, please?'

'Sure.' Phyllis absently took the remainder of her husband's ice water from the bar and drank it. She walked to the couch and sat down, reaching for the messages. Several names were completely unfamiliar to her; business friends of Andy's, she presumed. The rest only peripherally recognizable, except for the Jansens and two others, the Fergusons and the Priors. Old Washington cronies from the State Department days.

She heard the shower running and considered the fact that she, too, would have to dress when Andy was finished. They'd accepted a dinner invitation over in Arlington – a duty call, as Andy termed it. The husband was an attaché at the French embassy, a man who years ago had helped him during the conferences in Czechoslovakia.

The Washington carousel had begun, she reflected. God, how she hated it!

The telephone rang, and for a second Phyllis hoped it was Walter Madison and that he had to meet with Andy, thus canceling the Arlington dinner.

No, she thought further; that would be worse. Quickly called meetings were always terrible in Washington.

'Hello?'

'Mr Andrew Trevayne, if you'd be so kind.' The voice was a touch raspy, but soft, polite.

'I'm sorry, he's in the shower. Who's calling, please?'

'Is this Mrs Trevayne?'

'Yes.'

'I haven't had the pleasure; my name is de Spadante. Mario de Spadante. I've known your husband, not well, of course, for a number of years. We met again yesterday, on the plane.'

Phyllis remembered that Andy had said he wouldn't return de Spadante's call. 'Then I'm doubly sorry. He's way behind schedule, Mr de Spadante. I'm not sure he'll be able to call you back right away.'

'Perhaps, I'll leave a number anyway, if it's not too much trouble. He may want to reach me. You see, Mrs Trevayne, I was to be at the Devereaux's over in Arlington, *too*. I've done some work for Air France. Your husband might prefer that I find an excuse and not be there.'

'Why in heaven's name would he do that?'

'I read in the papers about his subcommittee ... Tell him, please, that since I got into Dulles Airport I've been followed. Whoever it is knows he drove into town with me.'

'What does he mean, he was followed? Why does your driving into town with him have any bearing on anything?' Phyllis spoke to her husband as he came out of the bathroom.

'It shouldn't – my driving in with him; he offered me a lift. If he says he was followed, he's probably right. And used to it. He's supposed to be in the rackets.'

'At Air France?'

Trevayne laughed. 'No. He's a builder. He's probably involved with air-terminal construction. Where's the number?'

'I wrote it on the blotter. I'll get it.'

'Never mind.' Trevayne, in undershirt and shorts, walked into the living room to the white desk with the green hotel blotter. He picked up the telephone and slowly dialled as he deciphered his wife's hastily scribbled numbers. 'Is this a nine or a seven?' he asked her as she came through the door.

'A seven; there was no nine ... What are you going to say?'

'Straighten him out. I don't give a damn if he rents the rooms next door. Or takes pictures of me on May Day ... I don't play those games, and he's got a hell of a nerve thinking I do ... Mr de Spadante, please.'

Trevayne calmly but with obvious irritation informed de Spadante of his feelings and suffered through the Italian's obsequious apologies. The conversation lasted a little over two minutes, and when Trevayne hung up he had the distinct feeling that Mario de Spadante had enjoyed their dialogue.

Which was precisely the case.

Two miles away from Trevayne's hotel, in the northwest section of Washington, de Spadante's dark-blue Cadillac was parked in front of an old Victorian house. The house, as the street – the area itself – had seen better, more affluent times. Yet there was a grandeur; decaying, perhaps, but still being clung to in spite of the declining values. The inhabitants of this particular section fell into roughly three categories: the dying elders whose memories or lack of money prevented their moving away; the youngish couples – usually early-rung-on-the-government-ladder – who could lease a fair amount of space for comparatively little rent; and finally – in sociological conflict – a scattering of subculture youth enclaves, groups of young nomads wandering into sanctuaries. The wail of Far Eastern sitars, the hollow vibrations of Hindu woodwinds continued long into the morning; for there was no day or night, only grey darkness and the moans of very personal survival.

Hard drugs.

The suppliers and the supplied.

The old Victorian house beyond de Spadante's Cadillac was recently taken over by a cousin, another cousin whose influence was felt in Washington's Police Department. The house was a substation in the subculture, a minor command post for narcotics distribution. De Spadante had stopped off with some colleagues to inspect the real-estate investment.

He sat in a room with no windows, the indirect lighting illuminating the psychedelic posters on the walls, covering the cracks. Except for one other person, he was alone. He replaced the telephone in its cradle and leaned back in his chair behind a filthy table.

'He's edgy; he just told me off. That's good.'

'It would have been better if you goddamn fools had let things take their course! That hearing would have been reconvened and the confirmation withdrawn. Trevayne would have been out!'

'You don't think; that's your problem. You look for quick solutions; that's very dumb. It's especially dumb right now.'

'You're wrong, Mario!' said Robert Webster, spitting out the words, the muscles in his neck tense. 'You didn't solve anything, you only gave us a potentially dangerous complication. And a crude one!'

'Don't talk to me *crude*! I laid out two hundred thousand up in Greenwich; another five for the Plaza!'

'Also crude,' blistered Webster. 'Crude and unnecessary. Your out-of-date waterfront tactics damn near exploded in our faces! You watch your step.'

The Italian leaped out of the chair. 'Don't you tell me, Webster! One of these days you pricks will kiss my ass for what I got on him!'

'For God's sake, lower your voice. And don't use my name. The biggest mistake we ever made was getting mixed up with you! Allen's right about that. They all are!'

'I didn't ask for any engraved invitation, Bobby. And you didn't get my name out of no telephone book. You came to me, baby! You needed help, and I gave it to you . . . I've been helping you for a long time now. So don't talk to me like that.'

Webster's expression betrayed his reluctant acceptance of de Spadante's words. The mafioso had been helpful, helpful in ways few others dared to be. And he, Bobby Webster, had called upon him more than anyone else. The day had long since come and gone when Mario de Spadante could be so easily dismissed. It reduced itself to controlling him.

'Don't you understand? We wanted Trevayne out. A reconvened hearing would have accomplished that.'

'You think so? Well, you're wrong, Mr Lace Pants. I talked to Madison last night; I told him to call me from the airport before he boarded. I figured *someone* ought to know what Trevayne was doing.'

The unexpected information caused Webster to check his hostility, replace it with a concern he hadn't anticipated.

'What did Madison say?'

'That's different, huh? None of you smart asses thought of it, huh?'

'What did he say?'

De Spadante sat down again. 'The esteemed attorney was very uptight. He sounded like he was going to head home and climb into a bottle with that lush wife of his.'

'What did he *say*?'

'Trevayne figured that panel of senators for what it was – a big roomful of loaded dice; he made that clear. And Madison made no bones that he sweated out the confirmation – not Trevayne, he didn't sweat piss – *Madison* sweated. For a very goddamn good reason. Trevayne told him if those bastards turned him down he wasn't leaving town quietly. He was going to call in the newspapers, television; he had a lot of things he wanted to say. Madison didn't guess any of it was too good.'

'About what?'

'Madison doesn't know. He only knows it's very heavy. Trevayne said it would rip the city apart; those were the words. *Rip the city apart.*'

Robert Webster turned away from the mafioso; he breathed deeply to control his ire. The sour-sweet odor that permeated the old house was offensive. 'It makes absolutely no sense. I've talked with him every day this past week. It doesn't make sense.'

'Madison didn't lie, either.'

Webster turned back to de Spadante. 'I know. But what is it?'

'We'll find out,' answered the Italian with quiet confidence. 'Without having our asses in a sling over some press conference. And when you girls put it all together, you'll see I was right. If that hearing was reconvened and Trevayne thrown out, he would have shot off his cannon. I *know* Trevayne, from way back. He doesn't lie, either. None of us are ready for that; the old man had to die.'

Webster stared at the heavyset man sitting so arrogantly in the filthy chair. 'But we don't know what it was he was going to say. Has it crossed your Neanderthal mind that it might have been something as simple as the Plaza Hotel? We could have – and would have immediately – disassociated ourselves from anything like that.'

De Spadante didn't look up at the White House aide. Instead he reached into his pocket, and while Webster watched apprehensively, with a certain unbelieving fear, de Spadante removed a pair of thick tortoiseshell glasses. He put them on and began scanning some papers. 'You try too hard to get me pissed off, Bobby . . . "Might have", "could have"; what the hell is that? The fact is, we didn't know. And we weren't going to risk finding out on the seven-o'clock news. I think maybe you ought to go back to the lace parade, Bobby. They're probably sewing up a storm.'

Webster shook his head, dismissing de Spadante's invective as he walked to the shabby door. Hand on the broken glass doorknob, he turned to look once again at the Italian. 'Mario, for your own good, don't make any more unilateral decisions. Consult us. These are complicated times.'

'You're a bright boy, Bobby, but you're still very young, very green. You get older, things don't seem so complicated . . . Sheep don't survive in the desert; a cactus doesn't grow in a wet jungle. This Trevayne, he's in the wrong environment. It's as simple as that.'

12

The rambling white house, with the four Ionic pillars supporting an impractical balcony above the front porch, was situated in the middle of a landscaped three-acre plot. The driveway was as impractical as the balcony; it bordered the right side of a weedless, carpetlike front lawn and veered – inexplicably – again to the right, ending in a half-circle *away* from the house. The real-estate agent told Phyllis that the original owner had planned a garage apartment at the end of the semicircle, but before he could build it, he was transferred to Muscaton, South Dakota.

It was no High Barnegat, but it had a name – a name Phyllis wished she could obliterate. It was in raised lettering in the white stone beneath the impractical balcony.

Monticellino.

Since the year's lease did not entitle her to sandblast the letters, Phyllis decided the name would remain between God, the original owner, and Thomas Jefferson.

Tawning Spring, Maryland, was no Greenwich, although there were similarities. It was rich, ninety-eight per cent white, and catered to the upward-mobility syndrome; it was essentially imitative – of itself – and insular; it was inhabited by people who knew exactly what they were buying: the penultimate rewards of the corporate dream. The ultimate – when admitted – was southeast: McLean or Fairfax, in the Virginia hunt country.

What the people who were buying the penultimate rewards didn't know, thought Phyllis, was that they were also getting, without additional charge, all of the unbearable problems that went with their purchases.

Phyllis Trevayne had had them. *Those* problems. Five years' worth; nearer six, really. Six years in a half-hell. It was no one's fault. And everyone's. It was the way things were. Someone once decreed that a day should have twenty-four hours – not thirty-seven or forty-nine or sixteen – and that was that.

It was too short. Or too long.

Depending.

In the beginning, of course, there were no such philosophical thoughts about time. The first exhilaration of love, the excitement, the unbelievable energies the three of them – Andy, Douglas, herself – put into the shabby

93

warehouse they called a company; if there were any thoughts of time then, it was usually in the form of where-the-hell-did-it-go.

She did triple duty. She was the secretary so needed to keep Andy organized; she was the bookkeeper filling ledger after ledger with unpronounceable words and unbelievably complicated figures. And finally she was the wife.

Their marriage had been comfortably situated – as her brother phrased it – between a Pratt and Whitney contract and an upcoming presentation to Lockheed. Andy and Doug had agreed that a three-week honeymoon in the Northwest would be ideal. The couple could see the San Francisco lights, catch some late skiing in Washington or Vancouver, and Andrew could make a side trip to Genessee Industries in Palo Alto. Genessee was an enormous conglomerate – everything from trains to aircraft, prefabricated housing to electronics research.

She knew when they began – those awful years. At least, the day she saw the outlines of what was coming. It was the day after they got back from Vancouver.

She had walked into the office and met the middle-aged woman her brother had hired to fill in during her absence. A woman who somehow exuded a sense of purpose, who seemed so committed to accomplishing far more than eight hours would permit – before dashing home to husband and children. A delightful person without the slightest trace of competitiveness about her, only a profound gratitude at being permitted to work. She didn't actually need the money.

Phyllis would think of her often during the coming years. And understand.

Steven came; Andrew was ecstatic. Pamela arrived, and Andrew was the clichéd, bumbling father filled with love and awkwardness.

When he had the time.

For Andrew was also consumed with impatience; Pace-Trevayne was growing rapidly – too rapidly, she felt. There were suddenly awesome responsibilities accompanied by astronomical financing. She wasn't convinced her young husband could handle it all. And she was wrong. He was not only capable, but adaptable to the changing pressures, the widening pressure. When he was unsure or frightened – and he was often both – he simply stopped and made everyone else stop with him. He told her that his fear and uncertainty were the results of not understanding, not knowing. It was better to lose a contract – painful as it might be – than to regret the acceptance later.

Andrew never forgot the courtroom in Boston. That wouldn't happen to him.

Her husband was growing; his product filled a void that desperately needed filling, and he instinctively parried in point-counterpoint until he was assured of the advantage. A fair advantage; that was important to Andy. Not necessarily moral, just important, thought Phyllis.

But she wasn't growing; the children were. They talked, they walked, they filled uncountable pails of diapers and spewed out unmeasurable amounts of cereal and bananas and milk. She loved them with enormous joy and faced their beginning years with the happiness of the new experience.

And then it all began to slip away. Slowly at first, as with so many others. She understood that, too.

The schoolday was the initial shock. Pleasant to begin with – the abrupt cessation of the high-pitched, demanding voices. The silence, the peace; the wonderful first aloneness. Alone except for the maid, the laundry man, an occasional repairman. Essentially alone, however.

The few really close friends she'd known had moved away – with husbands or with dreams of their own having little to do with the New Haven-Hartford environs. The neighbours in their upper-middle-class suburb were pleasant enough for an hour or two, but no more. They had their own drives – company drives; East Haven was the territory for them. And there was something else about the East Haven wives. They resented Phyllis Trevayne's lack of need and appreciation for their corporate strivings. That resentment – as resentment so often does – led to a form of quiet, progressive isolation. She wasn't one of them. And she couldn't help them.

Phyllis realized that she'd been thrust into a strange, uncomfortable limbo. The thousands of hours, hundreds of weeks, scores of months that she'd devoted to Andrew, Doug, and the company had been replaced by the all-day, everyday needs of her children. Her husband was more often away than at home; it was necessary, she understood that, too. But the combination of all things left her without a functioning world of her own.

So there was the first, free-of-cares, purposeful venturing out on a regular, daily basis; unencumbered by infant concerns. No patient explanations to impatient maids, no elaborate preparations for noontime, snacktime, playtime, friendtime. The children were in private schools. They were picked up at eight thirty in the morning and returned conveniently at four thirty, just prior to the rush-hour traffic.

The 'eight-hour parole' was the term used by the other young, white, rich mothers of the white, rich youngsters attending the old, white, rich private schools.

She tried relating to their world and joined the proper clubs, including the Golf and Country; Andrew enthusiastically endorsed them but rarely set foot on the premises. They palled on her as rapidly as the members did, but she refused to admit the disenchantment. She began to believe the fault was hers, the inadequacy hers. Was there guilt? Then that was hers also.

What in God's name did she *want*? She asked that question of herself and found no answer.

She tried returning to the company – no longer a warehouse, now a sprawling complex of modern buildings, one of several branches. Pace-Trevayne was running at high speed on a very fast track in an extraordinarily complicated race. It wasn't comfortable for the wife of the energetic young president to be seated at a desk doing uncomplicated chores. She left, and she thought Andrew breathed easier.

Whatever it was she sought eluded her, but there was relief to be found, starting at lunch. In the beginning it was a delicate glass of Harvey's Bristol Cream. Then graduation to the single Manhattan, which swiftly became a double. In several years her degree was awarded by the switch to vodka – the no-telltale, very viable substitute.

Oh, God! She understood Ellen Madison! Poor, bewildered, rich, soft, pampered Ellen – hushed-up Ellen Madison. Never, never phone her after six p.m.!

She recalled with painful clarity the late rainy afternoon Andy found her. She'd been in an accident, not serious, but frightening; her car had skidded on the wet pavement into a tree about a hundred yards from the driveway. She'd been hurrying home from a very long lunch. She'd been incoherent.

In her panic she'd raced from the smashed car to the house, locked the front door, and run to her room, locking that also.

A hysterical neighbour ran over, and Phyllis' maid called the office.

Andrew convinced her to unlock their bedroom door, and with five words her life was changed, the awful years terminated.

'For God's sake, help me!'

'Mother!' Her daughter's voice intruded on the stillness of the new bedroom that opened on the impractical balcony. Phyllis Trevayne had nearly finished unpacking; it had been an early photograph of her children that had triggered her silent reminiscing. 'There's a special delivery letter from the University of Bridgeport for you. Are you lecturing this fall?'

Pam's transistor radio filled the downstairs. Phyllis and Andy had laughed when they met their daughter at Dulles Airport the night before; Pam's radio was turned on before she reached the passenger gate. 'Only biweekly seminars, dear. Bring it up, will you, please?'

The University of Bridgeport.

The coincidence of the letter and her thoughts was appropriate, she considered. For the letter from such a place as Bridgeport was a net result of her 'solution', as she called it.

Andy had realized that her drinking had become more than a social habit but had refused to accept it as a problem. He had more problems than he needed; he attributed her excess to the temporary condition of household pressures and too little outside activity. It wasn't uncommon; he'd heard other men speak of it. 'Cooped up' was the phrase usually accompanying their rationalizations. It would pass. Further, he'd proved it to himself. For whenever they took vacations or were travelling with each other, there was no problem at all.

But that rainy afternoon they both knew there was a problem and they had to face it together.

The solution had been Andy's, although he let her think it was hers. It was to immerse herself completely in some project with a specific objective in view. A project in which she found a great deal of pleasure; an objective ambitious enough to make the time and energy worthwhile.

It didn't take her long to find the project; the fascination had been there since she was first introduced to medieval and Renaissance history. It was the chronicles: Daniel, Holinshed, Froissart, Villani. An incredible, mystical, marvellous world of legend and reality, fact and fantasy.

Once she began – cautiously at first, auditing graduate courses at Yale – she found herself as impatient as Andrew was with the expanding concerns of Pace-Trevayne. She was appalled by the dry academic approach to these vivid, full-bodied histories. She was infuriated with the musty, cobwebbed, overly cautious literateness given these – her – poetic novelist-historians of the ages. She vowed to open the rust-caked doors and let the fresh air of new appreciation circulate among the ancient archives. She thought in terms of contemporary parallels – but with the splendour of past pageantry.

If Andrew had his fever, she caught one, too. And the more she immersed herself, the more she found everything else falling into organized place. The Trevayne household was a busy, energetic home again. In less than two years Phyllis had her master's degree. Two and a half years later, the once-described objective – now merely an accepted necessity – was reached. She was formally conferred a Doctor of English Literature. Andrew threw a huge party celebrating the event – and in the quiet love of the aftermath told her he was going to build High Barnegat.

They both deserved it.

'You're almost finished,' said Pamela Trevayne, coming through the bedroom door. She handed her mother the red-stamped envelope and looked around. 'You know, Mom, I don't resent the speed you get things straightened up in, but it doesn't have to be so organized, too.'

The more she immersed herself, the more she found everything falling into organized place.

'I've had lots of experience, Pam,' said Phyllis, her mind still on her previous thoughts. 'It wasn't always so ... tidy.'

'What.'

'Nothing. I said I've done a lot of unpacking.' Phyllis looked at her daughter as she rather absently thumbed open the back of the envelope. Pam was growing so tall; the light-brown hair fell loose, framing the sharp young features, the wide brown eyes that were so alive. So eager. Pam's face was a good face – a very feminine version of her brother's. Not quite beautiful, but much more, much deeper than pretty. Pam was emerging as a most attractive adult. And beneath the surface exuberance there was a fine intelligence, a questioning mind impatient with unsatisfactory answers.

Whatever the hang-ups of her immediate growth period – boys, transistor radios turned these days to mournful, back-country folk ballads, pop posters, poor marches and Boone's Apple Farm – Pam Trevayne was part of the vast 'now'. And that was fine for everybody, thought Phyllis as she watched her daughter part the curtains over the door of the impractical balcony.

'This is a crazy porch, Mother. With luck you could get a whole folding chair out there.'

Phyllis laughed as she read the letter from Bridgeport. 'I don't think we'll use it for dinner parties . . . Oh, Lord, they've got me scheduled for Fridays. I asked them not to.'

'The seminars?' asked Pam, turning from the curtains.

'Yes. I said any time from Monday through Thursday, so they assign me Fridays. I want Friday open for weekends.'

'That's not very dedicated, Madame Professor.'

'One dedicated member of the family is enough right now. Your dad's going to need the weekends – if he can take them off. I'll phone them later.'

'Today's Saturday, Mom.'

'You're right. Monday, then.'

'When's Steve getting here?'

'Your father asked him to take the train up to Greenwich and drive the station wagon down. He has a list of things to bring; Lillian said she'd pack the wagon.'

Pam uttered a short cry of disappointment. 'Why didn't you tell me? I could have taken the bus home and driven down with him.'

'Because I need you here. Dad's been living in a half-furnished house with no food and no help while I've been at Barnegat. We womenfolk have to put things to rights.' Phyllis shoved the letter back in the envelope and propped it against the bureau mirror.

'I'm against your approach. In principle.' Pam smiled. 'Womenfolk are emancipated.'

'Be against, be emancipated; and also go unpack the dishes. The movers put them in the kitchen – the oblong box.'

Pam walked to the edge of the bed and sat down, tracing an imaginary crease on her Levi's. 'Sure, in a minute . . . Mom, why didn't you bring down Lillian? I mean, it would be so much easier. Or hire someone?'

'Perhaps later. We're not sure what our schedule will be. We'll be in Connecticut a lot, especially weekends; we don't want to close the house . . . I didn't realize you were so maid-conscious.' Phyllis gave her daughter a raised eyebrow of mock disapproval.

'Oh, sure. I get uptight when I can't find my ladies-in-waiting.'

'Then why ask?' Phyllis rearranged some articles on the bureau and looked casually at her daughter in the mirror.

'I read the article in the Sunday *Times*. It said that Dad had taken on a job that would keep him busy for ten years – with no time off – and then it would only be half-done; that even *his* well-known abilities were up against the impossible.'

'Not impossible; they used the word "incredible". And the *Times* is prone to exaggerate.'

'They said *you* were a leading authority on the Middle Ages.'

'They don't always exaggerate.' Phyllis laughed again and lifted an empty suitcase off a chair. 'What is it, dear? You've got that I-want-to-say-something look.'

Pam leaned back against the headboard; Phyllis was relieved to see that her daughter did not have shoes on. The bedspread was silk. 'Not "say". "Ask."'

I've read the newspaper stories, the stuff in the magazines; I even saw that TV news thing of Eric Sevareid's – they called it a commentary. It was very big on campus; he's grooved these days . . . Why is Dad taking this on? Everyone says it's such a mess.'

'Precisely because it is a mess. Your father's a talented man. A lot of people think he can do something about it.' She carried the suitcase to the doorway.

'But he can't, Mom.'

Phyllis looked over at her daughter. She'd been only half-listening, parent-child listening, more concerned with the thousand and one things that needed to get done 'What?'

'He can't do anything.'

Phyllis walked slowly back to the foot of the bed. 'Would you mind explaining that?'

'He can't change things. No committee, no government hearing or investigation, can make things any different.'

'Why not?'

'Because the government's investigating itself. It's like an embezzler being made the bank examiner. No way, Mom.'

'That remark sounds suspiciously out of character, Pam.'

'I admit it isn't mine, but it says it. We talk a lot you know.'

'I'm sure you do, and that's good. But I think that kind of statement oversimplifies, to say the least. Since there's a general agreement that a mess exists, what's your solution? If you've arrived at a criticism you must have an alternative.'

Pam Trevayne sat forward, her elbows on her knees. 'That's what everyone always says, but we're not sure it's so. If you know someone's sick, but you're not a doctor, you shouldn't try to operate.'

'Out of character . . .'

'No, that's mine.'

'I apologize.'

'There *is* an alternative. But it'll probably have to wait; if we're not too far gone or dead by then . . . A whole big change. Top to bottom, a huge replacement. Maybe a *real* third party . . .'

'Revolution?'

'God, no! That's a freak-out; that's the violent-jocks. They're no better than what we've got; they're *dumb*. They split heads and think they're solving something.'

'I'm relieved – I'm not condescending, dear. I mean that,' said Phyllis, reacting to her daughter's sudden questioning look.

'You see, Mom, the people who make all the decisions have to be replaced with people who'll make other decisions. Who'll listen to the *real* problems and stop making up fake ones or exaggerating the little ones for their own benefit.'

'Maybe your father can point out . . . things like that. If he backs them up with facts, they'll have to listen.'

'Oh, sure. They'll listen. And nod; and say he's sure a great guy. Then there'll be other committees to look into *his* committee, and then a committee to look into *them*. That's the way it'll be; it's the way it always is. In the meantime, nothing changes. Don't you see, Mom? The *people* up there have to change *first*.'

Phyllis watched her daughter's excited expression. 'That's very cynical,' she said simply.

'I guess it is. But I've got an idea you and Dad don't feel so differently.'

'What?'

'Well, it seems to me everything's kind of ... impermanent. I mean, Lillian's not here, this house isn't exactly the kind of place Dad digs ...'

'There are good reasons for the house; there aren't many available. And Dad hates hotels, you know that.' Phyllis spoke rapidly, offhandedly. She didn't care to spell out the fact that the small guest cottage in the back was ideally situated for the two Secret Service men assigned to them. The '1600 Patrol' was the name she'd read on a memorandum from Robert Webster.

'You said the place was only half-furnished ...'

'We haven't had time.'

'... you're still lecturing up in Bridgeport.'

'I made the commitment; it was near home.'

'You even said you weren't sure of your schedule.'

'Darling, you're taking isolated, disconnected statements and making them support a preconceived judgment.'

'Come on, Mother, you're not building a case against somebody's footnotes.'

'I might as well be. I've seen an awful lot just as misleading. And extraneous ... What your father's doing is very important to him. He's made some agonizing decisions; they weren't easy, and they hurt. I don't like to hear you imply that he's not serious. Or part of a sham.'

'Oh, wow! I'm sending out the wrong vibes.' Pam rose from the edge of the bed and stammered, embarrassed that she'd so obviously upset her mother. 'I'm not saying that, Mom. I'd never say that about Dad. Or you. I mean, you *level*.'

'Then I misunderstood you.' Phyllis walked aimlessly back to the bureau. She was annoyed with herself; there was no reason to pick at Pam for saying what men – and women – far more knowledgeable than her daughter were saying all over Washington. Not the sham; the aspect of futility.

The waste. And Andrew hated waste.

Nothing would change. That's what they were saying.

'I just meant that Dad maybe wasn't sure, that's all ...'

'Of course,' said Phyllis turning, showing her daughter an understanding smile. 'And you may be right ... about the difficulty of changing things. But I think we ought to give him a crack at it, don't you?'

The daughter, relieved by her mother's smile, returned one of her own. 'Gosh, yes. I mean, he might switch the whole Navy around, make it a sailing fleet.'

'The ecologists would approve. Go on, now, get those dishes out. When Steve arrives, he'll be hungry.'

'He's always hungry.' Pam went to the door.

'Speaking of your father, where is the elusive man? He conveniently disappears when chores are in order.'

'He's out back. He was looking at that oversized doll house in the south forty. And that nutty driveway that looks like someone goofed with a cement mixer.'

'"Monticellino", dear.'

'Mom, what *does* that mean?'

'Monticello got pregnant, I guess.'

'Oh, wow!'

Trevayne closed the door on the small guest cottage, satisfied once again that the equipment for the 1600 Patrol had been properly installed and was functioning. There were two speakers that picked up any sound from the main-house hallway and living room as soon as a switch underneath the living-room rug was stepped on. He had done so, and he'd just heard the front door open and a brief conversation between his daughter and a postman, followed by Pam's shouting to Phyllis that a special delivery had arrived. Further, he'd placed a book on the ledge of an open window in the downstairs rec room – so that it horizontally broke the vertical space – and noted, again with satisfaction, that a high, piercing hum was emanating from a third speaker beneath a numbered panel when he'd entered the cottage. Every room in the main house had a number that corresponded with one on the panel. No object or person could cross a window space without activating the electronic scanner.

He'd asked the two Secret Service men to wait in their car up the street during the day while the children were down for the weekend. Andy suspected that they had additional materials in their automobiles that were somehow connected with the guest-cottage equipment, but he didn't inquire. He'd find a way to tell the kids about the 1600 Patrol, but he didn't want them alarmed; under no circumstances were they to learn of the reasons for the protection. The two agents had worked out their own schedules with alternate men, and were sympathetic.

His agreement with Robert Webster – with the President – was simple enough. His wife was to be given around-the-clock safety surveillance; he learned that 'safety surveillance' was the term, not 'protection'. For some reason the former gave 'wider latitude' and was more acceptable to the Justice Department. His two children were to receive 'spot-check surveillance' on a daily basis provided by local authorities through federal request. The schools were to be informed of the 'routine' exercise and asked to cooperate.

It was agreed that Trevayne himself would be allocated the minimum 'safety surveillance'. A personal assault against him was considered unlikely, and he refused any formal association with Justice on the basis of conceivable conflict. Bobby Webster told him the President had laughed when informed that he objected to the 'wider-latitude' phrase employed by the Justice Department.

A previous Attorney General named Mitchell had left his mark indelibly on such manipulative language.

Trevayne heard the sound of a horn and looked up. The station wagon, driven by his son, had gone partially beyond the entrance and was now in reverse, preparing to turn into the driveway. The back was filled practically to the roof, and Andy wondered how Steve could use the rear-view mirror.

The boy drove to the front path and accurately judged the parallel positioning of the tailgate so the unloading would be made easier. He climbed out of the front seat, and Andy realized – somewhat ruefully, but with amusement – that his son's long hair was now shaped almost biblically.

'Hi, Dad,' said Steve, smiling, his shirt overlapping his flared trousers, his shoulders equal in height to the roof of the station wagon. 'How's the nemesis of the incredible?'

'The who of the what?' asked Andy, shaking his son's hand.

'That's what the *Times* said.'

'They exaggerate.'

The house was 'organized' – far more than Andy thought possible by late afternoon. He and his son had unloaded the wagon and then stood around in their shirtsleeves, awaiting the next command from Phyllis, who had them shuffle furniture as though it were chess pieces. Steve announced that the hourly charges of the new moving company of Trevayne and Trevayne were going up rapidly, with double wages every time a heavy piece was moved back into a previous position. At one point he whistled loudly and stated with equal fervour that it was a union break for a can of beer.

His father, who had been relegated to vice president by a unanimous vote of one, thought his shop steward a cunning negotiator. The beer break came between one couch and two armchairs – all out of place. For them to get back in position, the can of beer was a small additional price.

By five thirty Phyllis was as satisfied as she'd be, the movers' cartons and sisal removed to the back of the house, the kitchen in order; and Pam came downstairs announcing that the beds were made – her brother's in a way she hoped he'd appreciate.

'If your IQ was one point lower, you'd be a plant,' was Steve's only comment.

The original owner of Monticellino – or, as he was referred to without much affection, *him* – had installed one desirable appliance in the kitchen: a char-broil grate. The collective decision was reached for Andrew to drive into Tawning Spring, find a butcher shop, and come back with the largest sirloin steak he could buy. Trevayne thought it was a fine idea; he'd stop and chat with the 1600 Patrol on the way.

He did so. And not to his surprise but to his liking, he saw beneath the dashboard of the government automobile, the largest, most complicated assortment of radio dials he could imagine in one vehicle outside of a spacecraft.

That was fine, too.

The original owner's char-broil grate had one disadvantage: it smoked up most of the downstairs. As this required multiple windows to be opened, Trevayne remembered the rug switch to the guest-house panel, stepped on it, and loudly – if inexplicably to the children – complained redundantly about *him* and *his* char-broil fiasco.

'You know, Mom,' said Steven Trevayne, watching his father open and close the front door, fanning the not currently overpowering smoke, 'I think you'd better get him back on a sailboat. Dry land does something to his lobotomy.'

'I think you'd better feed him, Mother,' added Pam. 'What did you say? He's been here for three weeks with no food.'

Trevayne saw his wife and children laughing and realized the apparent ridiculousness of his actions, vocal *and* physical. 'Be quiet or I'll cancel your subscriptions to *Child Life*.'

The outsized steak was good, but no more than that. Several other decisions were made concerning the butcher shop and *his* char-broil grate. Pam and Phyllis brought on the coffee as Steve and Andy carried off the remaining dishes.

'I wonder how Lillian's doing?' asked Pam. 'Up there all by herself.'

'That's the way she likes it,' said Steve, pouring a half-cup of heavy cream into his coffee. 'Anyway, she can tell off the gardening service. She says Mom's too easy with them.'

'I'm not easy or hard. I rarely see them.'

'Lillian thinks you should look. Remember?' Steve turned to his sister. 'She told us when we drove her into town last month that she didn't like the way they kept changing the crews. There was too much time wasted explaining, and the rock gardens were always loused up. She's a regular Louis the Fourteenth.'

Andrew suddenly but unobtrusively looked up at his son. It was a small thing, if *anything*, but it caught his attention. Why had the gardening service changed personnel? It was a family business, and as the family was Italian and large, there was never any dearth of employees. At one time or another they'd *all* worked the grounds of Barnegat. He'd look into the gardening service; he'd make some enquiries into the Aiello Landscapers. He would dismiss them.

'Lillian's protective,' he said, backing off the subject. 'We should be grateful.'

'We are. Continuously,' replied Phyllis.

'How's your committee coming, Dad?' Steve added some coffee to his heavy cream.

'Subcommittee, not committee; the difference is significant only in Washington. We've got most of the staff together now. The offices are in shape. Incidentally, very few beer breaks.'

'Unenlightened management, probably.'

'Positively.' Andy nodded.

'When do you start blasting?' asked the son.

'Blasting? Where did you pick up that word?'

'Saturday morning cartoons,' interjected Pam.

'Your father means relative to him,' said Phyllis, watching her husband's concerned look.

'Well, aren't you going to out-Nader the raiders?' Steve smiled without much humour.

'Our functions are different.'

'Oh? How so, Dad?'

'Ralph Nader's concerned with overall consumer problems. We're interested in specific contractual obligations pertaining to government agreements. There's a big difference.'

'Same people,' said the son.

'Not necessarily.'

'Mostly,' added the daughter.

'Not really.'

'You're qualifying.' Steve drank from his cup, his eyes on his father. 'That means you're not sure.'

'He probably hasn't had the time to find out, Steve,' said Phyllis. 'I don't think that's "qualifying" anything.'

'Of course it is, Phyl. A legitimate qualification. We're *not* sure. And whether they're the same people Nader's gone after or different people, that's not the issue. We're dealing in specific abuses.'

'It's all part of the larger picture,' said Steve. 'The vested interests.'

'Now hold it a minute.' Trevayne poured himself more coffee. 'I'm not sure of your definition of "vested interests", but I assume you mean "well financed". Okay?'

'Okay.'

'Heavy financing has brought about a lot of decent things. Medical research, I'd put first; then advanced technology in agriculture, construction, transportation. The results of these heavily financed projects help everyone. Health, food, shelter; vested interests can make enormous contributions. Isn't that valid?'

'Of course. When making contributions has something to do with it. And not just a by-product of making money.'

'Your argument's with the profit motive, then?'

'Partially, yes.'

'It's proved pretty viable. Especially when compared to other systems. The competition's built in; that makes more things available to more people.'

'Don't mistake me,' said the son. 'No one's against the profit motive as such, Dad. Just when it becomes the only motive.'

'I understand that,' Andrew said. He knew he felt it deeply himself.

'Are you sure you do, Dad?'

'You don't believe I can?'

'I want to believe you. It's nice to read what reporters and people like that say about you. It's a good feeling, you know?'

'Then what prevents you?' asked Phyllis.

'I don't know, exactly. I guess I'd feel better if Dad was angry. Or ang*rier*, maybe.'

Andrew and Phyllis exchanged glances. Phyllis spoke quickly.

'Anger's not a solution, darling. It's a state of mind.'

'It's not very constructive, Steve,' added Trevayne lamely.

'But, Jesus! It's a starting point, Dad. I mean, *you* can *do* something. That's heavy; that's a real opportunity. But you'll blow it if you're hung up on "specific abuses".'

'Why? *Those* are *actual* starting points.'

'No, they're not! They're the sort of things that clog up the drains. By the time you get finished arguing every little point, you're drowning in a sewer. You're up to your neck—'

'It's not necessary to complete the analogy,' interrupted Phyllis.

'. . . in a thousand extraneous facts that high-powered law firms delay in the courts.'

'I think, if I understand you,' said Andrew, 'you're advocating a spiked broom. That kind of cure could be worse than the disease. It's dangerous.'

'Okay. Maybe it's a little far out.' Steven Trevayne smiled earnestly without affection. 'But take it from the "guardians of tomorrow". We're getting impatient, Dad.'

Trevayne stood in his bathrobe in front of the miniature French door that opened on the impractical balcony. It was one o'clock in the morning; he and Phyllis had watched an old movie on the bedroom television set. It was a bad habit they'd gotten into. But it was fun; the old films were sedatives in their way.

'What's the matter?' asked Phyllis from the bed.

'Nothing. I just saw the car go by; Webster's men.'

'Aren't they going to use the cottage?'

'I told them it was all right. They hedged. They said they'd probably wait a day or so.'

'Probably don't want to upset the children. It's one thing telling them that routine precautions are taken for subcommittee chairmen; it's quite another to see strangers prowling around.'

'I guess so. Steve was pretty outspoken, wasn't he?'

'Well . . .' Phyllis fluffed her pillow and frowned before answering. 'I don't think you should put too much emphasis on what he said. He's young. He's like his friends: they generalize. They can't – or won't – accept the complications. They prefer "spiked brooms".'

'And in a few years they'll be able to use them.'

'They won't want to then.'

'Don't bank on it. Sometimes I think that's what this whole thing's all about . . . There goes the car again.'

Part Two

13

It was nearly six thirty; the rest of the staff had left over an hour ago. Trevayne stood behind his desk, his right foot carelessly on the seat of his chair, his elbow resting on his knee. Around the desk, looking at the large charts scattered over the top, were the subcommittee's key personnel, four men reluctantly 'cleared' by Paul Bonner's superiors at Defense.

Directly in front of Trevayne was a young lawyer named Sam Vicarson. Andrew had run across the energetic, outspoken attorney during a grant hearing at the Danforth Foundation. Vicarson had represented – vigorously – the cause of a discredited Harlem arts organization reapplying for aid. The funds, by all logic, should have been denied, but Vicarson's imaginative apologies for the organization's past errors were so convincing that Danforth resubsidized. So Trevayne had made inquiries about Sam Vicarson, learned that he was part of the new breed of socially conscious attorneys, combing 'straight', lucrative employment during the daytime with ghetto 'store-front' work at night. He was bright, quick, and incredibly resourceful.

On Vicarson's right, bending over the desk, was Alan Martin, until six weeks ago the comptroller of Pace-Trevayne's New Haven plants. Martin was a thoughtful middle-aged former stats analyst; a cautious man, excellent with details and firm in his convictions, once they were arrived at. He was Jewish and given to the quiet humour of ironies he'd heard since childhood.

On Vicarson's left, curling smoke out of a very large-bowled pipe, stood Michael Ryan, who, along with the man next to him, was an engineer. Both Ryan and John Larch were specialists in their fields – respectively aeronautical and construction engineering. Ryan was in his late thirties, florid convivial, and quick to laugh but deadly serious when faced with an aircraft blueprint. Larch was contemplative, sullen in appearance, thin-featured, and always seemingly tired. But there was nothing tired about Larch's mind. In truth, each of these four minds worked constantly, at very high speeds.

These men were the nucleus of the subcommittee; if any were equal to the Defense Commission's objectives they were.

'All right,' said Trevayne. 'We've checked and rechecked these.' He gestured wearily at the charts. 'You've each had your part in compiling them; all of you studied them individually, without the benefit of one another's comments. Now, let's spell it out.'

'The moment of truth, Andrew?' Alan Martin stood up. 'Death in the late afternoon?'

'Bullshit.' Michael Ryan took the pipe out of his mouth and smiled. 'All over the arena.'

'I think we ought to bind these and offer them to the highest bidder,' said Sam Vicarson. 'I could develop a penchant for the good life in Argentina.'

'You'd end up in the Tierra del Fuego, Sam.' John Larch moved slightly away from Ryan's pipe smoke.

'Who wants to begin?' asked Trevayne.

A quartet of statements was the reply. Each voice assertive, each expecting to dominate the others. Alan Martin, by holding up the palm of his hand, prevailed.

'From my point of view, there are holes in all the replies so far. But since the audits generally concern projects with subcontracting fluctuations, it's expected. Subsequent staff interviews are generally satisfactory. With one exception. In all cases of any real magnitude, bottom-line figures have been given. ITT was reluctant, but they came over. Again, one exception.'

'Okay, hold it there, Alan. Mike and John. You worked separately?'

'We cross-checked,' said Ryan. 'There was – and is – a lot of duplication; as with Alan, it's in the subcontracting areas. Ticking off: Lockheed and ITT have been cooperative down the line. ITT presses computer buttons, and out shoot the cards; Lockheed is centralized and still gets the shakes—'

'They should,' interrupted Sam Vicarson. 'They're using my money.'

'They told me to thank you,' said Alan Martin.

'GM and Ling-Tempco have problems,' continued Ryan. 'But to be fair about it, it's not so much evasion as it is just plain tracing who's responsible for what. One of our interviewers spent a whole day at General Motors – in the turbine engineering offices – talking to a guy who was trying to locate a unit design head. Turned out it was himself.'

'There are also the usual corporation tremors,' added John Larch. 'Especially at GM; conformity and inquiry aren't happy bedfellows.'

'Still, we generally get what we want. Litton is crazy. Smart-like-a-fox crazy. They finance; that puts them one to ten places removed from any practical application. I'm going to buy stock in those boys. Then we come to the big enigma.'

'We'll get to it.' Trevayne removed his foot from the chair and picked up his cigarette. 'How about you, Sam?'

Vicarson mocked a bow to Andrew. 'I'd like to take this opportunity to thank the gods for bringing me in contact with so many prestigious law firms. My modest head is swimming.'

'Translated,' said Alan Martin, 'he stole their books.'

'Or the silver,' said Ryan between puffs on his pipe.

'Neither. I have, however, juggled many offers of employment . . . There's no point in recapping what's come in on a relatively satisfactory basis. I disagree with Mike; I think there's been a hell of a lot of evasion. I agree with John; corporation tremors – or delirium tremens – are everywhere. But with enough perseverance, you get the answers; at least enough to satisfy. With all but one ... It's Alan's "exception" and Mike's "enigma". For me it's a legal jigsaw never covered in Blackstone.'

'And there we are,' said Trevayne, sitting down. 'Genessee Industries.'

'That's where it's at,' replied Sam. 'Genessee.'

'Leopards and spots and nothing changes.' Andrew crushed out his hardly smoked cigarette.

'What's that mean?' asked Larch.

'Years ago,' answered Trevayne, 'twenty, to be exact, Genessee waltzed Doug Pace and me around for months. One presentation after another. I'd just gotten married; Phyl and I travelled out to Palo Alto for them. We gave them everything they wanted. So well, they threw us out and used variations on our designs and went into production for themselves.'

'Nice people,' said Vicarson. 'Couldn't you get them for patent theft?'

'Nope. They're better than that and you can't patent Bernoulli's principle. They made the variation in the metal-lurgical tolerances.'

'Indigenous and unprovable.' Michael Ryan tapped his pipe into an ashtray. 'Genessee has laboratories in a dozen different states, proving grounds in twice as many. They could predate mockups with authenticated affidavits, and the courts wouldn't know what the hell was going on. They'd win.'

'Exactly,' agreed Andrew. 'But that's another story, another time. We've got enough to think about. Where are we? What do we do?'

'Let me try to put it together.' Alan Martin picked up the cardboard chart marked 'Genessee Industries'. Each chart was twenty-four inches by twenty-four; there were outlined boxes with headings above subdivisions. Underneath and to the right of every title was inserted – stapled – typewritten data pertaining to the areas of contractual commitment, engineering and construction, financial operations, and legal entanglements – usually concerning the financial operations. There were scores of index markings that referred the reader to this or that file. 'The advantage of the financial picture is that it pervades all areas ... During the past weeks we've sent out hundreds of questionnaires – routine, all the companies got them. As you all know, they were coded, just like advertising coupons in newspapers. The codes gave us mailing times and locations. We then followed up with staff interviews. We found that with Genessee there was an abnormal amount of shifting. Answers we assumed would be sent from logically designated departments and locations were transferred to others – not so logical. Executive personnel our staff went out to interview *routinely* were suddenly no longer in their positions. Genessee had sent them to other divisions, subsidiaries; hundreds, even thousands of miles away. Some to overseas branches ... We began setting up conferences with union leadership. Same story, only less subtle. The word went out across the country – from one coast to the other – no local discussions. The nationals were deciding what to do about government interference. In short words, Genessee Industries has been engaged in a very efficient and massive cover-up.'

'Not completely efficient, obviously,' said Trevayne quietly.

'Pretty damned good Andrew,' rejoined Martin. 'Remember, Genessee has over two hundred thousand employees, multimillion-dollar contracts every fifteen minutes – under one name or another – and real estate rivalling the Department of the Interior. As long as those questionnaires kept coming back, and with Genessee's diversification, the shuffling might easily go unnoticed.'

'Not with you, you financial raccoon.' Vicarson sat on the arm of an easy chair and reached over, taking the Genessee chart from Martin.

'I didn't say they were *that* good.'

'What struck me,' continued Sam, 'and it probably wasn't so great a shock to Mike and John or even Al here, was the sheer size of Genessee. Its subsidiary structure is goddamned unbelievable. Sure, we've all heard Genessee *this* and Genessee *that* for years, but it never really impressed me before. Like those one-page ads you see in magazines – institutional things; you figure, okay, it's a company. That's nice; it's a nice display. But this one! It's got more names than a telephone book.'

'And no antitrust action,' said Andrew.

'Gesco, Genucraft, SeeCon, Pal-Co, Cal-Gen, See Cal . . . So help me, it's double crostics!' Sam Vicarson tapped his finger on the Genessee chart's 'Subsidiary' heading. 'What bothers me is that I'm beginning to think there are dozens more we haven't traced.'

'Let them be,' said John Larch with a pained expression on his thin face. 'We've got enough to work with.'

14

Major Paul Bonner parked in an empty space on the river side of the Potomac Towers lot. He stared out the windscreen at the water, growing sluggish with the progressing fall season. It had been seven weeks to the day since he'd first driven into that parking area; seven weeks since he'd first met Andrew Trevayne. He had begun the liaison position with resentment – against both the man and the job. The resentment against the job remained, perhaps grew; he found it difficult to sustain any real dislike of the man.

Not that he approved of Trevayne's goddamn subcommittee; he didn't. It was all horseshit. Scattershot horseshit conceived by the pols on the Hill for the sole purpose of shifting – or at least diluting – the responsibility for that which was necessary. That's what made Major Paul Bonner so hostile; no one could dispute the necessity – no one! Yet everyone gave the appearance of shocked disbelief when dealing with acknowledged reality.

Time was the enemy. Not people. Couldn't they see that? Hadn't they learned that in the space programme? Certainly Apollo 14 cost twenty million when it was launched in February of seventy-one. If, instead, it had been scheduled for seventy-two, it would have cost ten; six months later, probably five to seven and a half. Time was the ultimate factor in the goddamn civilian economics and since they, the military, had to reckon with time, they also had to accept the economic – civilian – penalties.

Over the weeks he'd tried to impress Andy Trevayne with his theory. But Trevayne only acknowledged it to be *a* factor, not *the* factor. Trevayne insisted that Bonner's theory was simplistic, then roared with laughter when Bonner reacted explosively to the term. Even the Major had smiled – 'simplistic' was no less a code name for 'idiocy' than his use of 'civilian'.

Checkmate.

But Trevayne did allow that if one eliminated time, a degree of corruption could be dispensed with; if there was all the time in the world, one could sit back and wait for reasonable prices. He agreed to that.

But it was only one aspect, he insisted. Trevayne knew the marketplace. Corruption went much further than the purchase of time.

And Bonner knew he was right.

Checkmate.

The fundamental difference between the two men was the importance each gave to the time factor, however. For Bonner it was paramount; for Trevayne it wasn't. The civilian held to the judgment that there was a basic international intelligence that would prohibit global holocaust. The Major did not. He'd seen the enemy, fought him, witnessed the fanaticism that propelled him. It filtered down from austere halls in national capitals through field commanders to battalions; from battalions down into the ranks of the half-uniformed, sometimes half-starved troops. And it was powerful. Bonner was not so simplistic, he felt, as to reduce the enemy to a political label; he'd made that clear to Andy. The enemy wasn't a Communist, or a Marxist, or a Maoist or a Lumumbaist. Those were merely convenient titles.

The enemy was three-fifths of the earth emerging from ignorance and thrust forward by the *idea* of revolution; the *idea* of finally – after centuries – possessing its own identity. And once possessing it, forcing its imprimatur on the rest of the world.

No matter the reasons, even the justifications; no matter the rationalizations, filled with motivational theories and diplomatic convolutions. The enemy was people. A few in control of millions upon millions; and these few, with their newly found power and technology, were subject to human weakness and their own fanatical commitments.

The rest of the world had to be prepared to deal decisively, emphatically, overpoweringly with this enemy. Paul Bonner didn't give a damn what it was called.

That it was, was enough.

And that meant time. Time had to be bought, no matter the price or the petty manipulations of the suppliers.

He got out of the Army car and started to walk slowly across the tarred surface toward the entrance of the apartment-office complex. He was in no hurry, no hurry whatsoever. If it were possible, he'd prefer not being there at all. Not today.

For today was the start of his real assignment, what he'd been primed for, manoeuvred into. Today was when he was to begin bringing back concrete information to his superiors at Defense.

He'd known it all along, of course. He realized at the beginning that he hadn't been selected as Trevayne's liaison because of any outstanding qualifications. He had none for that type of work. He knew, further, that the constant but innocuous questioning he'd received to date was only a lead-in to what had to follow. His superiors weren't really interested in such mundane matters as: How are things going? Are the offices satisfactory? Is the staff up to snuff? Is Trevayne a nice fellow? ... No, the colonels and the brigadiers had other things on their minds.

Bonner stopped by the steps and looked up. Three Phantom 40s, their jetstreams sharply defined in white against the blue sky, streaked west at an enormous altitude. There was no sound, only the barely visible outlines of three tiny triangles gracefully, like miniature silver arrowheads, piercing the air corridors of the horizon.

Strike force – bomb and rocket tonnage capable of obliterating five battalions; flight manoeuvrability – complete mastery of dynamics from ground zero to seventy thousand feet; speed – Mach three.

That's what it was all about.

But he wished it didn't have to happen *this* way.

He thought back to the morning, a brief three hours ago. He'd been sitting in his office trying to make sense out of some Light-colonel's appraisal of new installations at Benning. It was nonsense, the summation more concerned with the officer's egotistical evaluation of his own observations than with the equipment. The request had been for eighty per cent replacement; said request a put-down of the previous officer in charge. It was an Army game played by second-raters.

As Bonner had scribbled his negative recommendation across the bottom of the page, his intercom rang. He was ordered to report immediately to the fifth floor – 'Brasswares', as all below the rank of colonel called it – to Brigadier General Cooper. Lester Cooper, a white-haired, tough, facile-tongued exponent of the Pentagon's requirements. An ex-commandant of West Point whose father had held the same position. A man of and for the Army.

The Brigadier had spelled it out. Not just what he was to do, but without using the specific words, why he was selected to do it. As most military strategies, it was simple – simplistic? – and to the point. Paul Bonner, for the sake of military necessity was to be an informer. In the event any impropriety was charged, he was expendable.

But the Army would take care of him. As it had taken care of him once before in Southeast Asia; protected him once before and showed him its gratitude.

It was all a question of priorities; the Brigadier had made that clear. Ordered it to be clear.

'You must understand, Major. We support this Trevayne's efforts. The Joint Chiefs have requested that we cooperate in every way and we have. But we can't allow him to cripple vital production. You of all people should see that ... Now, you're on a friendly basis with him. You've ...'

It was during the next five minutes that Brigadier General Cooper nearly lost his informer. He alluded to several get-togethers between Bonner and Trevayne that the Major had not listed in any report or spoken of in the office. There was no reason to; they were entirely social, in no way related to the Department of Defense. One had been a weekend he'd spent with the Trevaynes in Connecticut at High Barnegat. Another was a small dinner party Bonner's current mistress, a divorcée in McLean, had given for Andy and Phyllis. Still another, an afternoon of horseback riding and a fall barbecue in the Maryland hunt country. None was remotely connected with Trevayne's subcommittee or Bonner's liaison assignment; none was paid for with government funds. The Major was annoyed.

'General, why have I been under surveillance?'

'You haven't. Trevayne has.'

'Is he aware of it?'

'He may be. He's certainly aware of the rotating patrols from Treasury. White House orders. He takes damn good care of them.'

'Do they act as surveillance?'

'Frankly, no.'

'Why not . . . sir?'

'That question may be beyond your province, Bonner.'

'I don't wish to disagree with the General, but since I'm delegated to . . . act very closely with Trevayne, I think I should be informed of such matters. It was my understanding that the guards were assigned by "1600" for precautionary measures. Since they're in a maximum position by us – and we assign additional personnel, it strikes me that we're either duplicating or at cross-purposes.'

'Which means you object to my reading of information you haven't given this office.'

'Yes, sir. That information had nothing to do with this office. If there was surveillance, I should have been informed. I've been placed in an unreasonably prejudiced position.'

'You're a hardnose, Major.'

'I doubt I'd've been given this job if I wasn't.'

The Brigadier got out of his chair and went to a long briefing table against the wall. He turned and leaned against it, facing Bonner. 'All right, I'll accept "cross-purposes". I won't pretend that we have a solid working relationship with everyone in this administration. Nor will I deny that there are a number of people surrounding the President whose judgments we find lacking. No, Major, we're not about to let "1600" control our surveillance . . . or filter it.'

'I understand that, General. I still think I should have been told.'

'An oversight, Bonner. If it was anything else, my telling you now eliminates that, doesn't it?'

The two officers stared at each other briefly. The understanding was complete – Bonner was at that moment accepted into the highest echelons of Defense.

'Understood, General,' said Bonner quietly.

The erect, white-haired Cooper turned back to the long table and opened a thick, plastic-bound notebook with huge metal rings. 'Come here, Major. This is the book. And I mean *the* book, soldier.'

Bonner read the typed words on the front page: 'GENESSEE INDUSTRIES'.

Bonner entered the glass doors of the Potomac Towers and walked on the thick blue carpet toward the elevators. If he'd timed everything right, if his telephone calls had resulted in the correct information, he'd arrive at Trevayne's office at least a half-hour before Trevayne himself returned. That was the plan; over in the Senate Office Building, where Trevayne was in conference, others were also watching the clock.

He was such a familiar sight in Trevayne's suite of rooms that he was greeted now with complete informality. Bonner knew he was accepted by the small civilian staff because he seemed to be an anomaly. The professional soldier who possessed few of the unattractive military trappings; whose outlook, even his conversation, seemed easygoing, with a continuous undercurrent of humour. When civilians found a man in uniform – especially the sort of overdressed uniform required daily at the Pentagon – who seemed to contradict the accepted manifestations of his profession, they warmed quickly. It was standard procedure.

It would be no problem at all for him to wait in Trevayne's inner office. He would take off his tunic, and stand in the doorway, and joke with Trevayne's secretary. Then he might wander into one of the other rooms – his tie undone, his collar unbuttoned – and pass a few minutes with several of the staff. Men like Mike Ryan or John Larch. Perhaps the bright young attorney, Sam Vicarson. He'd tell them a couple of stories – stories which ridiculed a pompous, well-advertised general or two. Finally, he'd say he was going to stop bothering them and read the morning paper in Trevayne's office. They'd protest in good humor of course, but he'd smile and suggest a few drinks after work, perhaps.

It would all take six or seven minutes.

He would then return to Trevayne's office, passing the secretary once again – this time complimenting her on her dress or her hair or whatever – and walk to the armchair by the window.

But he would not read the paper nor sit in the chair.

Instead he would go to the file cabinet on the right wall and open it. He would select the drawer that held the Gs.

Genessee Industries, Palo Alto, California.

He would extract the folder, close the drawer, and return to the chair. He would have a safe maximum of fifteen minutes to make notes before replacing the information.

The entire operation would take less than twenty-five minutes, and there would be only one moment of risk. If Trevayne's secretary or a staff member walked in while the cabinet was open. In that event he would have to say he found it open and pass his actions off casually as 'curiosity'.

But of course the cabinet would never have been open; it was always locked. Always.

Major Paul Bonner would unlock it with a key given him by Brigadier General Lester Cooper.

It was all a question of priorities; and Bonner felt sick to his stomach.

15

Trevayne rushed up the steps of the Capitol Building, conscious of the fact that he had been followed. He knew it, because he had made two out-of-the-way stops from his office to the centre of town: at a bookstore on Rhode Island Avenue, where the traffic was slight, and a spur-of-the-moment detour to Georgetown, Ambassador Hill's residence. The Ambassador wasn't home.

On Rhode Island Avenue he'd noticed a grey Pontiac sedan manoeuvre into a parking space half a block behind him – heard the Pontiac's rear tyres scraping the curb.

Twenty minutes later, as he had walked to the front door of Hill's Georgetown house, he had heard the bells of a knife-sharpening truck, a small van driving slowly down the cobblestone street soliciting business from the uniformed maids. He had smiled, thinking the sight an anachronism, a throwback to his teenage Boston memories.

Then he saw it again; there was the grey Pontiac. It was behind the slow-moving van, its driver obviously annoyed; the street was narrow, and the small truck was not accommodating. The Pontiac was unable to pass.

As Trevayne reached the top of the Capitol's steps he made a mental note to check with Webster at the White House. Perhaps Webster had assigned separate guards for him, although such precautions were unnecessary. Not that he was brave; he was simply too well known a figure now, and he rarely travelled alone. This afternoon was an exception.

He turned on the last step and looked down at the street. The grey Pontiac wasn't in sight, but there were dozens of automobiles – some parked, with drivers inside, some moving slowly past. Any one of them might have been radioed from Georgetown.

He entered the building and went immediately to the information desk. It was almost four o'clock, and he was expected at the office of National District Statistics before the end of the day. He wasn't sure what the NDS information would prove, if, indeed, he could extract any information to begin with, but it was another alley, another possible connection between seemingly unrelated facts.

National District Statistics was a computerized laboratory that more logically should have been housed at Treasury. That it wasn't was merely another inconsistency in this town of contradictions, thought Trevayne. National District Statistics kept up-to-the-month records of regional employment directly affected by government projects. It duplicated the work of a dozen other offices but was somewhat different in the sense that its information was general; 'projects' included everything from partial payment of state highways to federal participation in school construction. From aircraft factories to the renovation of park areas. In other words, it was a catch-all for explaining the allocation of tax money, and as such was used incessantly, prodigiously, by politicians justifying their existences. The figures could, of course, be broken down into categories, if one preferred, but that was rarely the case. The totals were always more impressive than their collective parts.

As he neared the NDS door, Trevayne reconsidered the logic of its location; it was, after all, quite proper that NDS be close to the offices of those who needed it most.

In essence, why he was there.

Trevayne put the papers down on the table. It was a few minutes after five, and he'd been reading in the small cubicle for nearly an hour. He rubbed his eyes and saw that one of the minor custodians was looking through the glass-panelled door; it was past closing, and the clerk was anxious to shut the office and leave. Trevayne would give him a ten-dollar bill for the delay.

It was a ludicrous exchange. Information involving – at a rough estimate – two hundred and thirty million for the gratuity of ten dollars.

But there it was – two increases of 148 million and 82 million respectively. Each increase predominantly the result of defence contracts – coded as 'DF' in the schedules; both 'unexpected', if Trevayne's newspaper reading was accurate. Sudden windfalls for each constituency.

Yet both had been predicted with incredible accuracy by the two candidates running for re-election in their respective states.

California and Maryland.

Senators Armbruster and Weeks. The short, compact pipe-smoking Armbruster. And Alton Weeks, the polished aristocrat from Maryland's Eastern Shore.

Armbruster had faced a tough challenger for his incumbency. Northern California's unemployment was dangerously, if temporarily, high, and the polls indicated that his opponent's attacks on Armbruster's failure to garner government contracts were having an effect on the voters. Armbruster, in the last days of the campaign, suddenly injected a subtle note that probably turned the election in his favour. He insinuated that he was in the process of obtaining defence money in the neighbourhood of one hundred and fifty million. A figure which even the state economists admitted was sufficient to prime the pumps of the state's northern recovery.

Weeks: also an incumbent, but faced not so much by competition as by a campaign deficit. Money was tight in the Maryland coffers, and the prestigious Weeks family reluctant to underwrite the entirety. According to the Baltimore *Sun*, Alton Weeks met privately with a number of Maryland's leading business figures and told them Washington's purse strings were loosening. They could be assured of a minimum of eighty million directed into Maryland's industrial economy ... Weeks's campaign resources were suddenly substantial.

Yet the election of both senators had taken place six months prior to each allocation. And although it was possible that both men had been huddling with defence appropriations, it wasn't logical that they could have been so precise as to the amounts. Not unless arrangements were made; arrangements more concerned with politics than with national security.

And both senators dealt with the same Defense contractor.

Genessee Industries.

Armbruster funded developments in Genessee's new high-altitude Norad interceptors, a questionable project from the outset.

Weeks had managed to finance an equally suspect undertaking with a Maryland subsidiary of Genessee's. A coastal radar network improvement 'justified' by two isolated aircraft penetrating the coastal screen several years ago.

Trevayne gathered the papers together and stood up. He signaled the clerk through the glass panel and reached into his pocket.

Out on the street he considered going to a pay phone and calling William Hill. He had to see Hill about another 'project', one that dealt with naval intelligence and might surface in a matter of days, perhaps hours, because of Trevayne. It was why he'd driven out to Georgetown earlier; it was not the sort of conversation one had on the telephone.

The Navy Department had been authorized to equip four atomic submarines with the most sophisticated electronic intelligence instruments available, the equipment to be installed within twelve months of authorization. The due date had long since passed; two of the electronics firms contracted had declared bankruptcy; the four submarines were still in dry dock, essentially inoperable.

During his staff's preliminary work an angry lieutenant commander, one of the four submarine skippers, had openly criticized the operation. Word of the naval officer's complaints to an official audience had reached an aggressive Washington newsman named Roderick Bruce, who threatened to break the story in print. The Central Intelligence Agency and the Navy Department were in panic, genuine panic. Making public the undersea electronic installations was dangerous in itself; acknowledging the foul-ups compounded that danger, and admitting the current inoperability of the ships was an open invitation for Russian and Chinese sabre-rattling.

It was a sensitive situation, and Trevayne's subcommittee was being blamed for creating risks far greater than any good it might achieve.

Trevayne knew that sooner or later the spectre of 'dangerous intrusion' would be raised. He had prepared himself for it, made clear his fundamental opposition to burying incompetence – or worse – under the label of 'classified, top secret'.

For such labels were too easily come by; even if sincerely arrived at, they were only judgments, singular positions.

There were other judgments, opposing positions. And he would not back off unless those opinions were analysed as well. Once he did, once he retreated, his subcommittee would be emasculated. He could not allow that precedent.

And there was a side issue – unprovable, only rumour, but in line with everything they were learning.

Genessee Industries once again.

The back-room legal talk was that Genessee was preparing to submit bids to take over the electronics installation of the submarines. The gossip was that Genessee had brought about the bankruptcies; had created sufficient subcontracting problems for the remaining two, that their agreements with the Navy Department were as good as void.

Trevayne walked into a drugstore, to the telephone booth, and dialled Hill's number.

The Ambassador, of course, would see him immediately.

'To begin with, the CIA's assumption that the Russians and the Chinese are oblivious to the situation is ridiculous. Those submarines have been beached in New London for months; simple observation tells them their conditions.'

'Then I'm right to press it?'

'I'd say so,' answered Hill behind the mahogany table which served as his desk. 'I'd also suggest that you give the Agency and the Navy the courtesy of talking to this newsman, this Bruce fellow; see if you can't get him to ease up a bit. Their fears are real to them, if only for their own skins.'

'I've no objection to that. I just don't want to be put in the position of taking my staff off a project.'

'I don't think you should ... I don't think you will.'

'Thank you.'

William Hill leaned back in his chair. His advice dispensed with, he wanted to chat. 'Tell me, Trevayne. It's been two months. What do you think?'

'It's crazy. I know that's a frivolous word, but at this point it's the most descriptive. The economics of the biggest corporation in the world are run by lunatics ... Or, perhaps, that's the image that's meant to be projected.'

'I assume you refer to the aspect of ... "you'll-have-to-check-with-someone-else".'

'Exactly. Nobody makes a decision—'

'Responsibility's to be avoided at all costs,' interrupted Hill with a benign smile. 'Not much different from the outside. Each to his own level of incompetence.'

'I'll accept that in the private sector. It's a form of survival-waste, if there's such a term. But it's controllable, when control is wanted. But that's private, not public money ... Down here that theory shouldn't prove out. This is civil service. Given a period of time – say, enough so as to be in a decision-making position – a man's security is automatic. The games aren't necessary. Or they shouldn't be.'

'You're oversimplifying.'

'I know, but it's a starting point.' Trevayne recalled with amusement that he used his son's words.

'There are formidable pressures on people in this town. The results often lead to ostracism, which can be as important as security to all but the strongest. Scores of departments, including the Pentagon, demand commitments in the name of national interest; manufacturers demand the contracts and send highly paid lobbyists to get them; organized labour plays them all off against each other and threatens with strikes *and* votes. Finally, the senators and congressmen – their districts cry out for the economic benefits derived from the whole bundle ... Where do you find the independent, or incorruptible, man without such a system?'

Trevayne saw that Big Billy Hill was staring at the wall. Staring at nothing anyone else would see. The Ambassador had not asked the question of his guest, but of himself. William Hill was ultimately, after a long life, a profound cynic.

'The answer to that, Mr Ambassador, lies somewhere between our being a nation of laws, and the checks and balances of a relatively free society.'

Hill laughed. It was the tired laugh of an old man who still possessed his juices. 'Words, Trevayne, words. You throw in the Malthusian law of economics – which can be reduced to the human condition of wanting more, to somebody else's less – and the pot goes to the man who has raised the biggest bet ... or bank. That's what our friends in the Soviet Union have found out; why the primary theories of Marx and Engels won't wash. You can't change the human condition.'

'I don't agree; not about the Russians, the human condition. It changes constantly. We've seen that over and over again, especially in times of crisis.'

'Certainly, *crisis*. That's *fear*. Collective fear. The member subordinates his individual wants to tribal survival. Why do you think our socialist co-earthlings continually cry "emergency"? They've learned that much ... They've also learned that you can't project crises ad infinitum; that's against the human condition, too.'

'Then I'd go back to the checks and balances ... and a free society. You see, I really do believe it all works.'

Hill leaned forward in his chair, putting his elbows on the table. He looked at Trevayne, and there was humor in his eyes. 'Now I know why Frank Baldwin's on your side. You're like him in several ways.'

'I'm flattered, but I never thought there was any similarity...'

'Oh, but there is. You know, Frank Baldwin and I often talk as we're talking now. For hours. We sit in one of our clubs, or in our libraries ... surrounded by all this.' Hill gestured with his right hand, including – somewhat derisively – the entire room. 'There we are, two old men sitting around making pronouncements. Reaching for our very expensive brandies; servants checking out of the corners of their eyes to see if we're in need of anything. Comfort the prime consideration for our tired, breathing ... rich corpses. And there we sit, dividing up the planet; each trying to convince the other what this part of the world *will* do and that part *won't* do ... That's what it all comes down to, you know. Anticipate the opposing interests; motives are no problem any longer. Just modus vivendis. The *whats* and *hows*; not the *whys*.'

'Tribal survival.'

'Precisely ... And Frank Baldwin, the toughest of the money lenders, a man whose signature can bankrupt small nations, tells me as you tell me now that underneath the frantic deceits – this global mendacity – there's a workable solution. And I tell him there isn't; not in his sense of the word. Nothing that can be set on a permanent course.'

'There'll always be change, granted. But I side with him; there has to be a solution.'

'The solution, Trevayne, is in the ever-present search for one. Cycles of build-up and retreat. That's your solution. *Paratus*, paratus.'

'I thought you said that sort of thing was against the human condition; nations couldn't project crises ad infinitum.'

'Not inconsistent. Relief is constantly setting in. It's in the retreats. They're the breathing spells.'

'That's too dangerous; there has to be a better way.'

'Not in this world. We've gone beyond that.'

'I disagree again. We've just arrived at the point where it's mandatory.'

'All right. Let's take your present bailiwick. You've seen enough; how are you going to implement your checks and balances? Your problems aren't unlike the larger sphere of interacting nations; very similar in many ways. Where do you begin?'

'By finding a pattern. A pattern with designs common to all the rest; as near as possible, at any rate.'

'The Controller General's done that, and so we formed the Defense Allocations Commission. The United Nations did the same, and we got the Security Council. The crises still exist; nothing much has changed.'

'We have to keep looking—'

'The solution, then,' interrupted Hill with a small triumphant smile, 'is in the search. You see what I mean now? As long as the search goes on, we can breathe.'

Trevayne shifted his position in the soft leather armchair. It was the same chair, he reflected, in which he had sat during the hastily summoned conference ten weeks ago. 'I can't accept that, Mr Ambassador. It's too impermanent, too subject to miscalculation. There's better machinery than half-constructed scaffolds. We'll find it.'

'I repeat. Where do you begin?'

'I've begun ... I meant what I said about finding a pattern. A single enterprise, large enough to require enormous funding; complex enough to involve scores, hundreds of contractors and subcontractors. A project which reaches into a dozen states for its components . . . I've found it.'

William Hill brought the thin fingers of his right hand to his chin. He kept his eyes on Trevayne. 'Is your point to concentrate on one venture; to make an example?' The tone of Hill's voice was unmistakably that of disappointment.

'Yes. Assistants will continue with the other work; there'll be no loss of continuity. But my four top men and I are concentrating on one corporation.'

Hill spoke quietly. 'I've heard the rumours. Perhaps you'll find your enemy.'

Trevayne lit a cigarette, watching the butane flame of his lighter reduce itself to a tiny yellow ball through the loss of fuel. 'Mr Ambassador, we're going to need help.'

'Why?' Hill began doodling on a notepad. The scratches of the pencil were deliberate, controlled – and angry.

'Because a pattern is emerging that disturbs us very much. Let me put it this way: the clearer that pattern becomes, the more difficult it is to get specific information; we think we've nailed something, it eludes us. Explanations deteriorate to . . . what did you say a few minutes ago? "Words". "Check here", "check there", "check somewhere else". Specifics must be avoided at all costs, apparently.'

'You must be dealing with a very diversified, spreadout organization.' Hill spoke in a monotone.

'It has a subsidiary complex – to use one of my staff's phrases – that is "goddamned unbelievable". The major plants are centralized on the West Coast, but the Chicago offices run its administration. Its dictatorship is enormous and—'

'Read like a cross-section of the West Point-Annapolis honor rolls.' Hill interrupted rapidly, quietly, the humor fading from his eyes.

'I was going to include a number of highly placed – or once highly placed – residents of Washington. A few former senators and representatives, three or four cabinet appointments – going back over the years, of course.'

William Hill picked up the notepad on which he'd been scratching, and put down his pencil.

'It strikes me, Trevayne, that you're taking on the Pentagon, both houses of Congress, a hundred different industries, organized labour, and a few state governments thrown into the bargain.'

Hill turned the pad around toward Trevayne.

On it, hundreds of tiny lines converged to spell out two words. 'Genessee Industries'.

16

His name was Roderick Bruce, and its sound was as intelligently contrived as the man. An ear-catching, theatrical name; a fast tongue; and a hard stare were the extensions of his reporting personality.

He was syndicated in 891 papers across the country, had a standard lecture fee of three thousand dollars, which he invariably – publicly – donated to diverse charities, and, most surprising, was very much liked by his peers.

The reason for his popularity within the fourth estate was easily explained, however. Rod Bruce – of the 'Washington-New York media axis' – never forgot that he was born Roger Brewster of Erie, Pennsylvania, and among his journalist brothers, was generous and always humorous in a self-deprecating way about his public image.

In short, Rod was a nice guy.

Except when it came to his sources of information and the intensity of his curiosity.

He guarded the first zealously and was relentless in the second.

Andrew Trevayne had learned this much about Bruce and looked forward to meeting him. The columnist was perfectly willing to discuss the story of the four inoperable atomic submarines. But he'd made it clear that the sub-committee chairman would have to present an incredibly strong argument for the newsman to suppress the story. It was scheduled for release in three days.

And in what seemed an unusual courtesy, considering the situation, Bruce suggested that he come to Trevayne's suite at the Potomac Towers at ten in the morning.

When Trevayne saw the columnist enter his outer office, he was surprised by Bruce's appearance. Not the face; the face was familiar through years of newspaper photographs accompanying the man's columns – sharp features, deep-set eyes, longish hair before it was stylish. But his size. Roderick Bruce was a very short man, and this characteristic was accentuated by his clothes. Dark, conservative; seemingly overpressed. He looked like a little boy all dressed up for a Sunday-morning church service in a Norman Rockwell *Saturday Evening Post* cover. The longish hair being the one aspect of allowed independence, a little boy's independence, in a newspaperman well into his fifties.

Bruce followed the secretary through the door and extended his hand to Trevayne. Andrew was almost embarrassed to stand up and come around the desk. Bruce seemed actually shorter, smaller, at close proximity. But Roderick Bruce was no amateur at first meetings on a professional basis. He smiled as he gripped Trevayne's hand firmly.

'Don't let my size fool you; I'm wearing my elevator shoes ... Nice to meet you, Trevayne.'

In this brief salutation Bruce took care of two objectives. He humorously smoothed the awkward, obviously unmentionable aspect of his size, and by the use of Trevayne's single last name, let Andy know they were on equal footing.

'Thank you. Please, sit down.' Trevayne looked over at his secretary as she started out. 'Hold my calls, will you, Marge? And close the door, please.' He returned to his chair as Roderick Bruce sat down in front of the desk.

'These offices are certainly off the beaten track, aren't they?'

'I apologize; I hope the trip wasn't inconvenient. I'd have been happy to meet you in town; it's why I suggested lunch.'

'No trouble. I wanted to scout this place for myself; a lot of people are talking about it. Funny, I don't see any racks or whips or iron maidens.'

'We keep that equipment locked up in a back room. More centralized that way.'

'Good answer; I'll use it.' Bruce took out a small notebook – a *very* small notebook, as if scaled to his size – and jotted down several words as Trevayne laughed. 'You never can tell when a good direct quote will come in handy.'

'It wasn't particularly good.'

'All right, then, humanizing. A lot of Kennedy's quips were just as much humanizing as they were bright, you know.'

'Which one?'

'Jack's. Bobby's were laboured, thought out. Jack was instinctively human ... and humorous in a vulnerable way.'

'I'm in good company.'

'Not bad. But you're not running for anything, so it doesn't matter, does it?'

'You took out the notebook, I didn't.'

'And it's going to stay out, Mr Trevayne ... Shall we talk about four submarines, each costing roughly one hundred and eighty million apiece, currently boondoggled in dry dock? Seven hundred and twenty million dollars' worth of nothing ... You know it, I know it. Why shouldn't the people who paid for it know also?'

'Perhaps they should.'

Bruce hadn't expected Trevayne's reply. He shifted his position in the chair and crossed his short legs. Andy wondered for a second if the newsman's feet were touching the floor.

'That's very good, too. I won't bother to write it down, because I'll remember it.' Bruce folded the flap of his tiny notebook. 'Then I assume you have no objection to my story.'

'To be perfectly frank with you, I have no objections at all. Others have; I don't.'

'Then why did you want to see me?'

'To ... plead their case, I guess.'

'I've turned them down. Why wouldn't I turn you down?'

'Because I'm a disinterested party; I can objectify. I think you have sound reasons for making public a very expensive fiasco, and if I were you, I'd probably release it without hesitation. On the other hand, I don't have your experience. I wouldn't know where to draw the line between a necessary reporting of incompetence and invading the areas of national security. I might shed light on that part.'

'Oh, come on, Trevayne.' Roderick Bruce uncrossed his legs in annoyance. 'I've heard that argument, and it won't wash!'

'You're sure of that?'

'For reasons more valid than you'd ever suspect.'

'If that's the case, Mr Bruce,' said Trevayne, taking out a pack of cigarettes, 'you should have accepted my offer of lunch. We could have spent the rest of the meal in pleasant conversation. You don't know it, but I'm an avid reader of yours. Cigarette?'

Roderick Bruce stared at Trevayne, his lower lip fallen from his mouth. Since he did not reach for a cigarette, Trevayne shook one out for himself and leaned back in his chair while lighting it.

'Jesus! You mean it,' said Bruce quietly.

'I certainly do. I ... suspect ... the valid reasons you refer to cover the areas of security. If so, and I know damned well you didn't get where you are by lying in these matters, I can't offer any further argument.'

'But my breaking it isn't going to help you, is it?'

'No, it's not. It'll be one bitch of a hindrance, to tell you the truth. But that's my problem, not yours.'

Bruce leaned slightly forward, his miniature frame somewhat ludicrous in the large leather chair. 'You don't have to have a problem ... And I don't *care* if the room is bugged.'

'If it's what?' Trevayne sat up.

'I don't care if we're taped; I gather we're not. I'll trade you off, Trevayne ... No hindrance from me; no problems with the New London mess. Simple trade. I'll even give you a selection.'

'What the hell are you talking about?'

'We'll start with yesterday.' Bruce lifted the right flap of his coat jacket and slowly reinserted his notebook. He did so stylistically, as if the action were symbolic of confidence. He held his gold pencil in his hands and revolved both ends between his fingers. 'You spent an hour and twenty minutes at National District Statistics yesterday; from shortly after four to past closing. You requested the volumes for the states of California and Maryland for the periods covering the past eighteen months. Now, given time, my office could easily go through the books and probably find what you were researching, but let's face it, there are several thousand pages and a couple of hundred thousand insertions. What interests me is that you did the legwork yourself. Not a secretary, not even an aide. You were playing close poker. What did you get?'

Trevayne tried to absorb Bruce's words, the implications behind his words.

'You were the grey Pontiac. You followed me in a grey Pontiac.'

'Wrong, but interesting.'

'You were on Rhode Island Avenue, and then you were in Georgetown. Behind a knife-sharpening truck.'

'Sorry. Wrong again. If I want you followed, you'll never know it. What did you go after at NDS? That's selection one. If it's worth it, I'll kill the sub story.'

Trevayne's mind was still on the Pontiac. He'd call Webster at the White House as soon as he got rid of Bruce ... He'd nearly forgotten about the Pontiac.

'No deal, Bruce. It's not worth it, anyway. It was background.'

'All right, I'll put my staff on the NDS books. We'll find it ... Selection two. This is rougher. There's a rumor that six weeks ago, after your somewhat spectacular appearance at the Senate hearing, you met with the old boy from Nebraska a few hours before the Fairfax accident; that you had harsh words. Is it true, and what was the substance?'

'The only person who could have heard that conversation was a man named Miller ... Laurence Miller, as I recall. The chauffeur. Ask him. He's told you this much, why not the rest?'

'He's loyal to the old man. He was also taken care of with a bequest. He won't say; claims he never listened to back-seat talk. There was too much of it.'

'No deal again. It was an honourable disagreement. If Miller tells you anything else, I'd question it if I were you.'

'You're not me ... One more selection; your last, Trevayne. If you cop out, I'll be a big hindrance. I may even mention your attempt to "plead the case" for suppression. How about that?'

'You're a revolting little man. I don't think I'll read your column anymore.'

'Your words.'

'Followed by others; out of context.'

'Tell me about Bonner.'

'Paul Bonner?' Trevayne had an uncomfortable feeling that Roderick Bruce's last *selection* was the real reason he was there. Not that the first two choices were innocuous – they weren't, they were unacceptable – but the newsman's voice betrayed a degree of intensity absent from his other questions; his threat more direct.

'Major Paul Bonner, no-middle-initial, serial number 158–3288; Special Forces, Intelligence Section, currently attached to Department of Defense. Recalled from Indo-China, nineteen seventy after spending three months' isolation in a military stockade – officer's quarters, of course – awaiting court-martial. No interviews permitted; no information available. Except a happy little descriptive phrase coined by a general in Eye Corps: the "killer from Saigon". That's the Bonner I'm referring to, Mr Trevayne. And if you're the avid reader of my work you say you are, you know I've stated that the mad Major should be locked up in Leavenworth, not walking the streets.'

'I must have missed that day's paper.'

'*Those* days. What's Bonner's function? Why was he assigned to you? Did you know him before? Did you request him?'

'You talk awfully fast.'

'I'm awfully interested.'

'Taking your questions in order – if I can; Bonner's merely a liaison with Defense. If I need something he gets it. Those are his words, incidentally and he's been damned efficient. I have no idea why he was assigned to me; I'm also aware that he's not particularly happy with the job. I didn't know him, so obviously I couldn't have requested him.'

'Okay.' Bruce kept his eyes on Trevayne. He made small rapid vertical motions with his gold pencil against the air, against nothing. Again it was a gesture, an irritating one. 'That checks out; that's programmed. Now . . . do you believe it?'

'Believe what?'

'That the "killer from Saigon" is simply a messenger boy? You really believe that?'

'Of course I do. He's been very helpful. These offices, arranging transportation, reservations all over the country. Whatever his opinions, they have no bearing on what he does around here.'

'You mentioned your staff. Did he help you assemble it?'

'Of course not.' Trevayne found himself raising his voice. His anger, he realized was triggered because in the beginning Paul Bonner had tried to help him 'assemble' a staff. 'To anticipate you, Major Bonner holds convictions which differ considerably from my own. We both understand that; neither expects to convert the other. Regardless, I trust him. Not that there's any reason to use the term; he's not involved with our work.'

'I'd say he's very much involved. He's in a position to know what you're doing. Who you're talking to, which companies you're looking into—'

'That kind of information is hardly classified, Mr Bruce,' interrupted Trevayne. 'Frankly, I'm not sure what you're driving at.'

'It's obvious. If you're investigating a gang of thieves, you don't rely on one of the biggest crooks in town to help you out.'

Trevayne recalled Walter Madison's initial reaction to Bonner. The attorney had observed that Defense wasn't practising much subtlety. 'I think I can relieve your anxiety, Mr Bruce. Major Bonner is in no way responsible for any decisions here. We don't discuss our progress with him – except in the most general terms and if I'm not mistaken, usually with humour. He simply takes care of routine details; and as a matter of fact, far less so than at the beginning. My secretary has assumed most of those responsibilities and calls on Bonner only when she has problems. Defense is quite good at securing a difficult airlines reservation or locating a corporation man whose company has a Pentagon contract. I repeat he's been very helpful.'

'You'll grant his being here on these premises is unusual.'

'The military is not famous for its sensitivity, Mr Bruce. I think that's perhaps a good thing . . . Look, we're dealing with Defense economies; we need a liaison. Why the Army assigned Bonner, I can't presume to say. But it did, and he's been satisfactory. I won't say he's been inspired; I don't think he has much use for us. However, he's a good soldier. I believe he'd carry out whatever assignments given him, regardless of his personal feelings.'

'Nicely said.'

'There's no other way to say it.'

'You're telling me he doesn't try to represent the Pentagon viewpoint?'

'On the few occasions when I've asked his opinion, he very *much* represents the military point of view. I'd be alarmed if he didn't. Wouldn't you be? . . . If you're attempting to unearth some kind of conspiracy, you're not going to find it. Using your own logic Mr Bruce, we were aware of Bonner's reputation. Or became aware of it. Naturally, we were concerned. Those concerns proved unwarranted.'

'You're not giving me what I want, Trevayne.'

'It seems to me you want a headline for your column that says Bonner's impeding the subcommittee's progress. That he's been assigned here so he can transmit classified information to his superiors. I told you, I've read your byline, Bruce. It was a nice try, very logical. But it's not true. It's too goddamned obvious, and you know it.'

'What are some of his opinions? I might settle for that. What's he said that represents the "military point of view"?'

Trevayne watched the diminutive columnist. He was becoming edgy; he was nervous now, as if he sensed he was about to lose something he wanted desperately. Andy recalled Paul Bonner's harrowing counterstrategy against the hypothetical peace march – the troops, the swift repression – and knew this was the sort of thing Roderick Bruce wanted to print.

'You're paranoid. You're willing to settle for just about anything that colours Bonner dirty, aren't you?'

'You got it, Trevayne. Because he *is* dirty. He's a mad dog who should have been gassed three years ago.'

'That's a pretty strong indictment. If you feel that way, you've got the audience; tell them . . . if you can back it up.'

'They cover for that son-of-a-bitch. They *all* cover for him. Up and down the line he's sacred territory. Even with those who hate his guts – from the Mekong to Danang – no one'll say a word. That bothers me. I'd think it would bother you, too.'

'I don't have your information. I've got enough problems without creating more from half-truths or half-lies. Put plainly, I'm not that interested in Major Bonner.'

'Maybe you should be.'

'I'll think about it.'

'Think about something else, too. I'll give you a couple of days. You've had conversations with Bonner; he spent a weekend with you in Connecticut. Call me and tell me about them. What he's said to you may seem inconsequential. But coupled with what I've got could be important. You might be doing yourself and the country considerable service.'

Trevayne rose from the chair, looking down at the small reporter. 'Take your Gestapo tactics somewhere else, Mr Bruce. No sale here.'

Roderick Bruce knew through experience the disadvantages of standing up. He remained seated, fingering his gold pencil. 'Don't make an enemy of me, Trevayne. That's foolish. I can shape that submarine story in such a way as to make you untouchable. People'll run from you. Maybe worse; maybe they'll just be laughing.'

'Get out of here before I throw you out.'

'Intimidating the press, Mr Chairman? Threatening physical violence on a man of my size?'

'Describe it any way you like. Just get out,' said Trevayne calmly.

Roderick Bruce rose slowly, replacing the gold pencil in his breast pocket. 'A couple of days, Trevayne. I'll expect your call. You're upset now, but things will clear up for you. You'll see.'

Trevayne watched the little-boy/old-man walk firmly with his short strides toward the office door. Bruce didn't look back; he grasped the knob, pulled the door, and walked out. The heavy door banged against a chair in its backward path and vibrated slightly.

Brigadier General Lester Cooper slammed his fist on the long briefing table. His face was flushed, the veins in his neck pronounced.

'That little *bastard*. That goddamned pygmy *prick!* What the hell is he after?'

'We don't know yet. Could be just about anything,' answered Robert Webster from across the room. 'Our guess is Bonner; we calculated that possibility when we put him on.'

'*You* calculated it. We didn't want any part of it.'

'We know what we're doing.'

'I'd feel better if you could convince *me*. I don't like the possibility that everyone's expendable.'

'Don't be ridiculous. Tell Bonner his old friend Bruce may be stalking him again, to be careful.' Webster approached Cooper; there was a hint of a smile on his lips. 'But don't lay it on too thick. We wouldn't want him overly careful; just tell him. He's aware of Trevayne's surveillance; don't let somebody else tell him first.'

'I understand . . . However, I think you people should find a way to force Bruce out of this. He shouldn't be anywhere near it.'

'That'll come in time.'

'It should be *now*. The longer you wait, the greater the risk. Trevayne's going after Genessee.'

'That's exactly why we're not making any sudden moves. Especially not now. Trevayne won't get anywhere. Roger Brewster might.'

17

Andrew Trevayne looked out the window at the rolling Potomac. Brown leaves now, brackish water; Saturday-afternoon football games, pro contests on Sunday. Congress filled the newspapers with more talk than achievement; middle autumn in Washington.

The meeting had gone well, his nucleus had confidentially compiled enough data to justify personal confrontations with a number of Genessee Industries' top management.

Especially one man. James Goddard. The one man at Genessee Industries who had the answers. San Francisco.

That was the next stop.

It had been a singularly effective effort on everyone's part, made more difficult by the unorthodox methods Andy had called for. Very little of the work was done in the offices, almost all of it accomplished in the basement recreation room of his rented house in Tawning Spring. And those involved were limited to Alan Martin, Michael Ryan, John Larch, and the irrepressible Sam Vicarson.

He initially conceived of these methods, this secrecy, for very uncomplicated reasons. When the last responses came in from Genessee plants and contractors across the country, the volume was enormous. File cabinets were filled in a matter of several weeks. Then as these reports proved consistently unsatisfactory and additional requests were sent to the company's offices, Trevayne realized that Genessee was going to crowd out everything else they were working on. Simple collating between the voluminous replies became a major compilation, brought about by evasive responses.

Andrew found himself obsessed with the tactics of Genessee Industries. The only way to untangle the mess was to take each strand of the web and follow it through the myriad patterns to its source, adding up the misinformation and those responsible as one went along. It was a complex, gargantuan task, and it seemed logical to move this one area of the subcommittee's work to a single place, a comfortable environment conducive to late hours and long weekends.

From this unsophisticated reasoning, another, more concerning motive surfaced that further justified the move. Interference. Ryan and Larch were approached – indirectly, with extreme subtlety – and asked about the subcommittee's inquiries at Genessee. Veiled hints of payment were dropped; humorous allusions to Caribbean holidays made.

Only nobody was kidding. Ryan and Larch understood that.

Beyond these two half-explored contacts three other incidents occurred in which Genessee figured – again subtly, indirectly, in shadow conversation.

Sam Vicarson was invited to the country club at Chevy Chase by an apartment neighbour. What began as a small cocktail party for semi-acquaintances rapidly accelerated into a drinking bout of fairly hardcore dimensions. Acquaintances were suddenly close friends; a number of friends quickly developed enmities. The evening became alcoholically electric, and Sam Vicarson found himself on the golf course with the wife of a minor congressman from California.

As he related the story to Trevayne, and admittedly there were gaps brought on by the liquor, the young, ebullient lawyer and the girl commandeered a golf cart, drove several hundred yards, when the vehicle stopped, its charge diminished. The wife became frightened; it was a potentially bad scene, and she'd been the instigator, making it clear she was attracted to Sam. The two of them started back toward the clubhouse, when they were confronted by the Congressman and an unknown friend.

What followed was ugly, swift, and made indelible by the husband's final words. The Congressman was drunk to the edge of incoherence; he slapped his wife across the mouth and lurched at Vicarson. Sam stepped back, defending himself as best he could against the husband's onslaught, when the unknown man interceded, pinning the Congressman's arms and pushing him to the ground.

The stranger kept ordering the subdued man to be quiet, that he was making a fool of himself.

At which point the minor Congressman from California made a futile attempt to lunge upward, to free himself, then screamed at his subduer.

'Take your goddamn Palo Alto out of my life!'

The wife raced across the lawn toward the parking lot.

The unknown man lashed the back of his hand against the Congressman's mouth, pulled him to his feet, and shoved him after the girl.

Sam Vicarson had stood on the grass, aware through the liquor that in some strange, inexplicable way, a setup had just been aborted.

Palo Alto. Genessee Industries.

Trevayne agreed, knowing beyond a doubt that the young lawyer would be more circumspect in the future about invitations from neighbours.

The second incident was told to Trevayne by his own secretary. The girl was going through the last stages of a soured engagement. When, contrary to their agreed-upon separation, the ex-fiancé asked to move in again, she couldn't understand, the relationship was dead, amicably finished.

He said he needed to come back – just for a few days.

For appearances.

And if anyone ever inquired, she should remember he asked her a lot of questions.

Which he wouldn't ask. He didn't give a damn; he was getting out of Washington and just needed a few recommendations. Thanks to her, he got them.

On the day he left for Chicago and a new job, he phoned Trevayne's secretary.

'Tell your boss a lot of people on Nebraska Avenue are interested in GIC They're very uptight.'

And so she told him.

GIC Genessee Industries Corporation.

The third and last incident that he *knew* about reached Trevayne through Franklyn Baldwin, the New York banker who'd recruited him.

Baldwin came to Washington for a granddaughter's wedding. The girl was being married to an Englishman, an attaché at the British embassy with a viscount somewhere in his family background. As Baldwin phrased it, 'The dullest damned reception in nuptial history. Times don't change; tell an American mother her daughter's found a title, and she doesn't plan a wedding, she mounts a funereal coronation.'

This introduction from Baldwin was his way of telling Trevayne that he'd left the reception the minute he received a likely invitation to do so. It came from an old friend, a retired diplomat who suggested they plead geriatric exhaustion and head for one of Virginia's better watering spots.

They did so. To the home of a mutual friend, a rear admiral, also retired, who, to Baldwin's surprise, expected them.

At first, Baldwin said, he'd been delighted by the playful conspiracy of two old cronies; made him feel as though they were all youngsters again, ingenuously avoiding tiresome duties.

As the visit lengthened, however, Baldwin became upset. A supposedly pleasant get-together wasn't pleasant at all. The Admiral initiated the unpleasantness by referring to Roderick Bruce's article about the beached atomic submarines. From that point it was a short leap to Trevayne's understanding of military – especially Navy Department – problems; he obviously had none.

Finally, Baldwin continued, he found himself in a heated argument; after all, the Defense Commission was his responsibility. Trevayne's approval had been unanimous, not only within the commission itself, but with the President and the Senate as well. Those approvals stood; the military – including the Navy Department – had better damn well accept the fact.

However, the Admiral wouldn't. As Baldwin was leaving, the old Navy hand suggested that yesterday's approval might turn into today's revulsion. Especially if Trevayne continued to harass one of the great institutions – '*institutions,* mind you' – upon which the nation in large measure depended – '*depended,* goddamn it, that's what he said!'

That *institution* was Genessee Industries.

As Andrew continued to stare at the river, he reflected that these five fragments – the two guarded contacts with Ryan and Larch, Sam Vicarson in Chevy Chase, his secretary, and Franklyn Baldwin – these were what he *knew* about. How many others were there that he was not aware of? The subcommittee staff numbered twenty-one; had others been reached? Were there variations on the theme of interference that would remain silent?

He couldn't possibly hold a 'team meeting' and ask; not only was such a tactic abhorrent to him, but it wouldn't work. If anyone had been contacted and hadn't spoken of it, he wasn't going to do so now. The delay would appear incriminating.

And if, in the remote but possible chance there was an informer inside the subcommittee, the information he carried back would be worthless. For until this afternoon the vital papers concerning Genessee Industries had been kept in Tawning Spring.

The office files on Genessee – all the pertinent ones – were clearly marked in plastic tape: 'Status – Current. Complete. Satisfactory.' Several which were minor Genessee transactions had another tape: 'Status – Current. Pending.' These were unimportant.

The coding of 'Satisfactory' was not born of suspicion; instead, it was simply more convenient. Since only five people – the top four men and Trevayne – would have reason to use these files, each knew what the term meant. If anyone else, for any reason, came across them, there was no necessity for elaborate explanations.

'Satisfactory' was sufficient.

Andrew left the window and returned to his desk, where the three looseleaf notebooks were piled on top of one another. The Genessee notebooks, the partially unravelled threads of the web; a small clearing inside a labyrinth of very warped mirrors. He wondered where the hell they would lead?

He also wondered what a man like Roderick Bruce – Roger Brewster – would do if they were in his possession?

Roderick Bruce, diminutive slayer of dragons.

Yet he hadn't slain *him*. In spite of the columnist's threats, he'd been extraordinarily gentle about Andy's part of the submarine story.

No reasons given; none asked for.

There'd even been a kind of compliment:

The tough, unresponsive chairman of the subcommittee remains unreachable by panicked high personnel of the intelligence departments. He leaves media relations to others – which may not be smart, but that kind of brightness isn't required in his job. All they can do is dump him, and they probably will. Is that what he wants?

Trevayne wondered why Bruce had decided not to expose his 'plea for suppression'. Not that it mattered. He didn't give a goddamn about Roderick Bruce *or* his readership. He wouldn't have called Bruce back under any conditions. Whatever Paul Bonner stood for – and Christ knew it was ponderously antediluvian – the man was authentic. His beliefs were profoundly arrived-at concerns, not unthinking, blunt reactions to change.

The Bonners of this world had to be convinced, not sacrificed as goats in ideological skirmishes.

Above all, *convinced.*

Trevayne picked up the top notebook, the plastic tape on the right-hand corner imprinted with the Roman numeral I. It constituted his immediate itinerary; the first stop, San Francisco.

Routine. Nothing vital.

That's the way it was arranged. That's the way it was described. The subcommittee chairman was merely making a personal tour of West Coast companies – a number of them. If concerned executives took the trouble to check – and it was certain they would – they'd be relieved to learn that Andrew Trevayne was dropping in on a dozen or so firms. Nothing much of any depth could be accomplished with such a schedule.

It was even suggested off-handedly to several that the subcommittee chairman wasn't averse to a game of golf or a couple of sets of tennis – weather permitting.

The climate of his tour was, therefore, established. There were rumours of an early demise of the subcommittee; that Trevayne's cross-country trip was a kind of farewell appearance, a symbolic finish to an impossible production.

That was fine; that was the way he wanted it.

It wouldn't be possible if a Roderick Bruce had access to the Genessee notebooks.

God forbid that should ever be the case! What had to be avoided at all costs now were blanket accusations, inclusive condemnations. It was far too complicated for simple conclusions.

The telephone interrupted his meandering thoughts. It was after five; he'd let everyone go early – five o'clock was early at the Potomac Towers. He was alone.

'Hello?'

'Andy? Paul Bonner.'

'You're psychic. I was just thinking about you.'

'Nice thoughts, I hope.'

'Not particularly. How've you been? Haven't seen you in a couple of weeks.'

'I've been out of town. In Georgia. Every six months or so the brass sends me down to Benning to run around obstacle courses, stay in shape. Or that's what they think.'

'Probably nothing to do with it. They figure to beat out your hostilities, or give the Washington ladies a breather.'

'Better than cold baths. What are you doing tonight?'

'I'm meeting Phyl for dinner at L'Avion. Care to join us?'

'Sure. If I'm not intruding.'

'Not at all. Forty-five minutes?'

'Good. It'll give us a chance to go over this crazy tour of yours.'

'What?'

'I'm back as your major-domo, massa. Whatever you want, snap your fingers or whistle; I'll scurry around and get it for you.'

'I didn't know,' said Trevayne hesitantly.

'I just got the orders. I understand we'll be hitting the links and a few tennis courts. You've loosened up.'

'Sounds that way. See you at L'Avion.'

Trevayne replaced the phone and looked at the Genessee notebook in his left hand.

No request had been made of the Defense Department for a military aide. As a matter of fact, the Pentagon had not been apprised of the trip.

At least not by his office.

18

Mario de Spadante stepped off the second-floor escalator at the San Francisco Airport and headed for the observation lounge. His gait was fast, remarkably agile for a man of his girth. He dodged and overtook passengers and clerks; he was impatient with a black porter who blocked his path with an unwieldy luggage dolly. He pushed open the glass door of the lounge and rapidly walked past the hostess, acknowledging her unspoken question with a gesture of his hand. His party was already seated; they were expecting him, two men at a corner table.

'If you don't mind my saying so, Mr de Spadante, I think you're unnecessarily agitated.'

'I do mind your saying it, Mr Goddard. I mind very much, because I think you're a fucking idiot.' De Spadante's voice remained gentle, only the rasp slightly more pronounced than usual. He turned to the other man, an older man somewhere in his sixties, stylishly tailored. A man named Allen. 'Has Webster been in touch?'

'I haven't seen him or spoken with him since New York. Months ago, before Baldwin approached this Trevayne. We should have killed it then.'

'The big machers didn't listen, because your suggestion was not only dumb but also hopeless. I took other measures; everything was under control – including emergency procedures. That is, it was until now.' De Spadante reverted his look to Goddard. Goddard's cherubic face was still flushed with anger over the Italian's insult. Goddard was middle-aged, middle-fat, and middle-brow, the essence of the pressurized corporate executive, which he was – for Genessee Industries. De Spadante purposely did not speak. He just stared at Goddard. It was the executive's turn, and he knew it.

'Trevayne gets in tomorrow morning, around ten thirty. We've scheduled lunch.'

'I hope you eat well.'

'We have no reason to think the conference is anything more than what we've been told: a friendly meeting. One of many. He's scheduled conferences with half a dozen companies within a few hundred miles, all within several days.'

'You kill me, Mr Just-a-Minute. I mean, I'd be rolling on the floor laughing, except for the pain . . . "No reason to think"! You're beautiful! Like the kids say . . . very *heavy*, man.'

'You're offensive, Mr de Spadante.' Goddard withdrew a handkerchief and blotted his chin.

'Don't talk to me "offensive". There's nothing more offensive on this earth than stupidity. Except maybe conceited stupidity.' De Spadante spoke to Allen while his eyes remained on Goddard. 'Where did you high types come up with this *capo-zuccone*?'

'He's not stupid, Mario,' replied Allen softly. 'Goddard was the best cost accountant GIC ever had. He's shaped the company's economic policies for the past five years.'

'A bookkeeper! A lousy bookkeeper who sweats on his chin! I know the type.'

'I have no intention of taking your abuse any longer.' Goddard moved his chair back, prepared to stand. However, Mario de Spadante's hand shot out, and with the grip of a man who was no stranger to hard work and coarse methods, he held the arm. The chair rocked to a stop as Goddard's legs went tense.

'You sit. You stay. We have problems bigger than your intentions . . . Or mine, Mr Bookkeeper.'

'Why are you so sure?' asked Allen.

'I'll tell you. And maybe you'll understand some of my agitation. Also my anger . . . For weeks all we've heard is that everything's just fine. No real problems; a number of items had to get straightened out, but they were taken care of. Then we get word that even the major questions are marked "satisfactory". Complete, finished, kaput . . . clear sailing. I even bought it myself.' De Spadante released the chair but held the men with his eyes darting back and forth between them without shifting his head. 'Only except a couple of very curious fellows in New York decide to run a check. They're a little nervous, because they're paid to solve problems. When they don't see any problems, they look for them; they figure it's better than missing them because of an oversight . . . They take five – just five – very, very important inquiries which have been returned. All five have been accepted as satisfactory – we're told. They send supplementary information to Trevayne's office. Nothing that couldn't be explained but, by God, explanations were called for! . . . Do I have to tell you what happened?'

Goddard, who'd been holding his handkerchief in his hand, brought it once again to his chin. His look betrayed his fear. He spoke three words quietly, tensely. 'Reverse double entries.'

'If that fancy language means the office files were dummies, you're right on, Mr Bookkeeper.'

Allen leaned forward in his chair. '*Is* that what you mean, Goddard?'

'In essence, yes. Only I jumped a step. It would depend on whether the status of the office files was returned to "pending".'

'They weren't,' said Mario de Spadante.

'Then there's a second set of files.'

'Very good. Even us *tontos* figured that one out.'

'But where?' asked Allen, his composure losing some of its confidence.

'What difference does it make? You're not going to change what's in them.'

'It would be a great help to know, however,' added Goddard, no longer hostile; instead, very much afraid.

'You should have thought about such things these last couple of months, instead of sitting with your thumb up your ass figuring you're so smart. "Friendly meetings".'

'We had no cause . . .'

'Oh, shut up! Your chin's all wet . . . A lot of people may have to hang. But there are a lot of other people we won't let that happen to. We've still got certain emergency procedures. We did *our* work.' Suddenly, with great but silent intensity, Mario de Spadante clenched his fist and grimaced.

'What is it?' The man named Allen stared at the Italian apprehensively.

'That son-of-a-bitch Trevayne!' De Spadante whispered hoarsely. 'The Honourable – so fucking honourable – Undersecretary! Mr Clorox! . . . That bastard's as dirty as any pig in the cesspool. I hadn't figured on it.'

Major Paul Bonner watched Trevayne from across the aisle. Bonner had the window seat on the right side of the 707; Trevayne, flanked by Alan Martin and Sam Vicarson, sat directly opposite. The three of them were engrossed in a document.

Beavers, thought Bonner. Earnest, intense, chipping away at a thousand barks so the trees would fall and the streams would be dammed. Natural progression thwarted? Trevayne would call it something like ecological balance.

Horseshit.

It was far more important that the fields below be irrigated than a few earnest beavers survive. The beavers wanted to parch the land, to sacrifice the crops in the name of concerns only beavers cared about. There were other concerns, frightening ones that the smaller animals would never understand. Only the lions understood; they had to, because they were the leaders. The leaders stalked all areas of the forests and the jungles; they knew who the predators were. The beavers didn't.

Paul Bonner knew this jungle; had crawled on his bleeding stomach over the incredibly infested, ever-moving slime. He'd come face to face with the eyes, the commitment of pure hate. Had recognized the fact that he must kill the possessor of the hatred, put out the eyes. Or be killed.

His enemy.

Their enemy.

What the hell did the beavers know?

He saw that Trevayne and his two assistants began putting their papers back into their briefcases. They'd be in San Francisco soon; the 'fasten-your-seat-belts' light was on, the no-smoking sign as well. Another five minutes.

And then what?

His orders were less specific, vaguer than they had been before. Conversely, the atmosphere around Defense – that part of it dealing with Trevayne – was infinitely tauter. After his dinner with Andy and Phyllis, General Cooper had interrogated him as though he were a *Charleysan* guerilla with American dog tags around his neck. The Brigadier was damned near apoplectic. *Why hadn't Trevayne alerted Defense about this tour? What was the exact itinerary? Why so many stops, so many different conferences? Were they a smoke screen?*

Finally, Bonner had gotten angry. He didn't know the answers, hadn't sought them. If the General needed specific information, he should have briefed him on what it was. Bonner reminded Cooper that he had brought out over fifty separate reports from the Potomac Towers. Information *stolen* from Trevayne's private files, actions that laid him wide open to civilian prosecution.

He understood the reasons, accepted them as well as the risks, and relied on his superiors' judgment. But, goddamn it, he wasn't clairvoyant.

The Brigadier's reaction to his outburst stunned Bonner. Cooper had become hesitant, flustered; he started to stutter, and for Bonner it was inconceivable that such an old line man as Cooper would stutter. It was apparent that Brigadier General Cooper was dealing with totally new, unevaluated data.

And he was afraid.

Bonner had wondered what it was. What had produced the fear? The Major knew that he wasn't the only one bringing information out of the Towers. There were two others he knew about. One was a dark-haired stenographer, the nominal head of Trevayne's typing pool. He'd seen her photograph and résumé on Cooper's desk with several expense vouchers clipped underneath. Standard procedure.

The second was a blond man, late twenties, a Ph.D. from Cornell who, if he remembered correctly, Trevayne had hired as a favor to an old friend. Bonner had left late one night just as the blond man was going into the freight entrance. To the rear elevators invariably used by informers on scheduled runs. He'd looked up; Brigadier Cooper's fifth-floor office lights were still on.

Cooper had been too upset to be evasive or even subtle. So Bonner had been given his orders: Whatever Trevayne said, whatever either of the two aides traveling with him said – regardless of how inconsequential it might seem – commit it to memory and report by telephone direct on Cooper's private line. Try to find out the substance of any conference with anyone connected with Genessee Industries. Use whatever moneys might be needed, promise whatever immunities requested, but uncover facts.

Any facts.

Was he to look for specific . . .

Anything!

Bonner grudgingly admitted to himself that he'd caught a touch of the Brigadier's fever. He didn't like being fired up by someone else's anger – or panic – but he' had been. Trevayne had no right meddling in Genessee. At least, not to the extent that caused Cooper's extraordinary degree of concern. Genessee Industries was, in its own way, a necessary line of the nation's defence. Certainly more important than any extraterritorial ally. Surely more reliable.

The fighters – rocket jets – better than anything in their class in the air; fourteen different styles of helicopters – from the massive troop-, vehicle-, and weapons-carrying jet combinations to the fast, silent 'snakes' that hedged men like himself into tiny jungle locations; armour developed in dozens of Genessee laboratories that housed a hundred different types of protective cover saving thousands of square feet of human flesh from high-caliber shells and the refraction of napalm fire; even artillery – Genessee controlled scores of armaments plants, and thank God they did! – the finest, most destructive weaponry on earth.

Strike force! Power!

Goddamn it to goddamn hell! Couldn't 'they' understand?

It wasn't just the *possession*! It was the *protection*! Their protection!

What the hell did the beavers know?

What the hell did Trevayne know?

19

James Goddard walked out on his back lawn. The descending sun washed the Los Altos hills with misty hues of yellow and orange. As always, the view had a palliative effect on Goddard. It had been the primary reason he'd taken the gamble twelve years ago and bought the house in Los Altos. It had been far too expensive, but he'd reached that point at Genessee where either the future held such a home or there was no future at Genessee.

It really hadn't been much of a gamble. Twelve years ago he'd just begun his rapid ascendancy with *one* of the inner circles of Genessee Industries. The nature of his work ensured his survival, his eventual proprietorship of a corner office.

Finally, the penthouse. President, San Francisco Division.

But at times the pressure became too much.

Now was such a time.

The conference with Trevayne that afternoon had been nerve-wracking. Nerve-wracking because its objectives, at first, were totally unclear. A little of this, a little of that. A great deal of nodding-in-agreement, a fair amount of quizzical looks followed by further nods or just blank stares. Notes taken at seemingly inappropriate moments; innocuous questions asked by Trevayne's innocuous assistants. One Jewish; that was obvious. The other too young; that was insulting.

The whole meeting had been disjointed, without any discipline of agenda. As the immediate spokesman for Genessee, Goddard had tried to impose a sense of order, tried to elicit a schedule of inquiry. He'd been gently rebuffed by Trevayne; the subcommittee chairman unconvincingly played the role of a patriarchal uncle – everything would be covered sufficiently. The morning was only to establish general areas of responsibility.

General areas of responsibility.

The phrase had hit James Goddard's brain like a bolt of electricity.

But he had simply nodded as his three adversaries had nodded and smiled. A ritual dance of deceit, he'd decided.

When the meeting ended, around three thirty or so, he'd returned to his office from the conference room and immediately pleaded a splitting headache to his secretary. He had to get out, drive around, think over every aspect of what had been said during the past two and a half hours. For in spite of the nebulous approach, a great deal *had* been said. The problem was that it hadn't been said in figures. He understood figures. He could recite by rote P-and-L statements from scores of divisions going back years. He could take a handful of isolated numbers and prepare projections that, given a variance of four per cent, would prove out. He astonished so-called economists – academic theorists, usually Jewish – with the swiftness and accuracy of his market analyses and employment stats.

Even the Senator, California's Armbruster, had called upon him for advice last year.

He had refused any payment; after all, Armbruster was his political choice, and Genessee wasn't going to get hurt. However, he *had* accepted a token gift through a friend of the Senator. A ten-year company pass on Trans Pacific Airways.

His wife liked Hawaii, although he constantly had to reassure her that cat meat wasn't part of the cooking.

He'd left the office and driven damn near fifty miles. Along the ocean drive, over into Ravenswood, then across to Fair Oaks.

What had Trevayne been after?

Whenever Goddard had attempted to explain a specific overrun or underestimated cost – and weren't those explanations the essence of the subcommittee's function? – he'd been discouraged from elaborating on them. Instead, there was only a general discussion of the items; their validity, their functionability, their operational capacities, the engineering, the designs, the men who conceived the plans, those responsible for putting them into execution.

Abstractions and median-level personnel.

What in heaven's name could be the purpose of such a conference?

But as he approached the upward slope of the road leading to his isolated, view-calming house on his miniature mountain, James Goddard – cost-accountant-cum-division-president of Genessee Industries – saw with frightening clarity the purpose of Trevayne's conference.

Names.

Only names.

It explained the hastily written notes at seemingly inappropriate times, the innocuous questions from innocuous aides.

Names.

That was what they were after.

His own staff kept repeatedly going back into the papers. *This* engineering head, *that* design consultant; *this* labour negotiator, *that* stats analyst. Always buried under and sandwiched between unimportant judgments.

They weren't figures! They weren't numbers!

Only *people.*

Persons anonymous!

But that's what Trevayne was after.

And Mario de Spadante had said a lot of people might have to hang.

People.

Persons anonymous.

Was he one of them?

James Goddard watched a bird – a sparrow hawk – dip suddenly downward and just as swiftly come up from behind the trees and catch the wind, soaring to the sky, no quarry in his beak.

'Jimmy! ... Jimmeee!'

His wife's voice – full-throated yet somehow nasal – always had the same effect on him, whether it was shouting from a window or talking over the dinner table.

Irritation.

'Yes?'

'Really, Jim, if you're going to commune, for God's sake put the telephone outside. I'm busy on *my* line.'

'Who's calling?'

'Someone named de Spad ... de Spadetti, or something; I don't know! Some *wop*. He's on "hold".'

James Goddard took a last look at his precious view and started for the house.

At least one thing was clear. Mario de Spadante would be given the very best efforts a 'bookkeeper' could provide. He would tell him digit by digit the areas of inquiry Trevayne had asked for; no one could fault a 'bookkeeper' for that.

But Mario de Spadante would not be privy to the 'bookkeeper's' conclusions.

This 'bookkeeper' was not for hanging.

Paul Bonner walked through the door of the cellar café. It was like a hundred other San Francisco basements-with-licences. The amplified, ear-shattering sound from the tiny bandstand was an assault on his sensibilities – all of them – and the sight of the freaked-out, bare-breasted dancers no inducement.

The place was a mess.

He wondered what the effect might have been if he'd worn his uniform. As it was, he felt singularly out of place in a sport coat and denims. He quickly undid his paisley tie and stuffed it into his pocket.

The place was crazy with weed; more hash than 'grass' at that.

He went to the far end of the bar, took out a pack of cigarettes – French, Gauloise – and held them in his left hand. He ordered a bourbon – shouted his request, actually – and was surprised to find that the drink was an excellent sour mash.

He stood as best he could in one spot, jostled continually by the bearded drinkers and half-naked waitresses, a number of whom took second glances at his clean-shaven face and close-cropped hair.

Then he knew he saw him. Standing about eight feet away in tie-dyed Levi's and sandals, his shirt a variation of winter underwear. But there was something wrong with the hair, Bonner thought. It was shoulder-length and full, but there was something – a neatness, a sheen; that was it. The man's hair was a wig. A very good wig, but by the nature of its in-place effect, inconsistent with the rest of his appearance.

Bonner unobtrusively raised the pack of Gauloise and lifted his glass in greeting.

The man approached, and when he stood next to Paul he leaned over and spoke through the noise close to Bonner's ear.

'Nice place, isn't it?'

'It's . . . overwhelming. You look like you fit in, though. Are you sure you're the right guy? No intermediaries; I made that clear.'

'These are my civilian clothes, Major.'

'Very appropriate. Now, let's get out of here.'

'Oh, no, man! We stay. We talk here.'

'It's impossible! Why?'

'Because I know what these vibes do to a pickup.'

'No tapes; no pickups. Come on, be reasonable. There's no call for that sort of thing. Christ, I'd be frying myself.'

The unkempt mod with the neat hair looked closely at Bonner. 'You've got a point, man. I hadn't thought of it that way. You've *really* got a point! . . . The bread, please.'

Bonner replaced the Gauloises in his shirt pocket and then withdrew his wallet. He took out three one-hundred dollar bills and handed them to the man. 'Here.'

'Oh, come on, Major! Why don't you write me a cheque?'

'What?'

'Get the bartender to change them.'

'He won't do that.'

'Try.'

Bonner turned toward the bar and was surprised to see the bartender standing close by, watching the two of them. He smiled at the Major and held out his hand. Sixty seconds later Bonner was holding another assortment of bills – fives, tens, twenties. Three hundred dollars' worth. He gave them to the contact.

'Okay. Let's split, man. We'll walk the streets, just like cowboys. But we'll walk where *I* say, got it?'

'Understood.'

Out on O'Leary Lane the two men headed south, slowly weaving their way among what was left of the Haight-Ashbury tribes. The sidewalk stalls and curbside vendors noisily proclaimed the tribes' acceptance of a laissez-faire economy. A lot of profit was being made on O'Leary Lane.

'I suppose, in line with your obvious cautions, you haven't written anything down for me.'

'Of course not. Nothing to prevent *you* from taking notes, though. I remember everything.'

'That conference lasted damn near three hours.'

'I didn't get to be Genessee Jim's top accountant because of a bad memory,

Major.' The long-haired man gestured left, toward an alley. 'Let's head in here. Not so frenetic.'

They leaned against a brick wall covered with semi-pornographic posters, mostly torn, all marked with graffiti; the light from the street lamps on O'Leary Lane was just enough to illuminate their faces. Bonner manoeuvred his contact so the light was shining on him. Paul Bonner always watched a man's face during interrogations – whether in the field or in a San Francisco alley.

'Where do you want to begin, man?'

'Forget the tea and cookies. Start with the major items; we'll work back to the less important.'

'All right. In descending order ... The F-90's overrun – specifically, the design conversions of fan metals mandated by innovations called for in the Houston labs. They were first conceived of because of the flap at Rolls-Royce, if you recall.'

'What about them?'

'What do you mean, what about them? Those inno's had a price tag of one-zero-five mill; that's what about them.'

'That's no secret.'

'I didn't say it was. But Trevayne's crowd wanted to know dates. Maybe there was a time lag you people haven't thought about ... But that's not my bag. I'm no J. Edgar; I provide data, you evaluate. Isn't that what that honky used to say?'

'Go on.' Bonner had withdrawn a spiral notepad and began writing.

'Next. Down south, Pasadena ... The plants are eight months behind with the tool and dies for the big chopper armour plates. That's a bad one, man. They're so fucked up they'll never find ozone. Labour troubles, pollution complaints, blueprint alterations, base-metal compos; you name it, they fell over it. Armbruster's got to bail those plants out and still make it with the pure-breathers.'

'What did Trevayne want with this one?'

'Funny. He was sort of sympathetic. Honest mistakes, environment concerns; that kind of thing. He didn't dwell on the bread; he seemed more interested in the boys who had the problems ... Next. Right here in our beloved Northwest Pack. The lines up south of Seattle. As you know, there's a little diversification going on; Genessee took over the Bellstar Companies and has thrown a mighty tax chunk into making them work. So far, it's a large pair of snake-eyes.'

'Those are the rocket plants, aren't they?'

'Rockets, propulsion fuel, pads, launch tracks ... the Peenemünde of the Pacific, as we affectionately call that mess.'

'They're necessary. They've got to keep functioning ...' Bonner caught himself.

'Ah, so, Mr Moto! ... Don't burden me with evaluations, man. Remember?'

'I know; not your bag ... So what about them?'

'So they're a loss leader, and I *do* mean the leader of the losses, Charlie. And for a very good reason that Trevayne suspects. Genessee has no business buying from itself.'

'That was thrown out of court.'

'My turn to evaluate.' The long-haired, wigged accountant laughed. 'The court was thrown out of court. Because a few other people made evaluations ... Trevayne wants more information on Bellstar. Only, here again, like Pasadena and Houston, he's mining some personnel files. Frankly, I don't dig; they're not going to tell him anything. Wrong turn on his part. He doesn't pass "Go".'

Bonner wrote in his notebook. 'Did he get any more specific?'

'No, man. He couldn't. Your Mr Trevayne is either very dull or very cosy.'

A drunk careened off the wall at the far end of the short alley. He was a tourist, obviously; dressed in a jacket, slacks, tie, and an American Legion barracks cap. He leaned against the brick, unzipped his trousers, and proceeded to urinate. The accountant turned to Bonner.

'Come on, let's get out of here. The neighbourhood's going to hell. And if that's a tail, Major, I'll grant you're imaginative.'

'You may not believe this, *man*, but I hate those professional heroes.'

'I believe you, man. You look like you hate good ... I know a quiet mahogany a few blocks west. We'll finish up there.'

'Finish up! We haven't begun! I figure you've got about two hundred and ninety dollars to go ... *Man!*'

'We'll make it, soldier-boy.'

An hour and ten minutes later, Bonner had just about filled his small spiral pad with notes. He was getting his three hundred dollars' worth – at least in terms of the accountant's recollections. The man was amazing; he was capable – if he was to be believed – of recalling exact phrases, specific words.

What it all meant would be up to someone else, however. All Bonner could make of the information was that Trevayne and company covered a lot of ground but didn't do much digging. However, again, that could be an erroneous conclusion on his part.

Others would know better.

'That about does it, Major,' said the Genessee executive from under the long, false hair. 'Hope it gets you a pair of "birds"; that is, if you're really a soldier type and not some kind of crusading nut.'

'Suppose I was the latter?'

'Then I hope you nail GIC.'

'You can be flexible, I see.'

'Pure rubber. I've got the objectives of a scavenging mongrel. *I'm* my cause.'

'That must be nice to live with.'

'Very comfortable ... And I've got you boys to thank for that comfort.'

'What?'

'Oh, yes, man! A few years ago I *really* dressed like this. I mean, I meant it!

Protests, peace marches, walkathons for the dried-up Ganges, every man was my brother – black, white and yellow; I was going to change the world . . . Then you mothers sent me to 'Nam. Bad scene, man. I got half my stomach blown out. And for what? The pious, plastic men with their square-jawed bullshit?'

'I'd think that kind of experience might have renewed your energies; to change the world, I mean.'

'Maybe some, not me. I lost too much meat around the middle; I paid my dues. The saints are pimps, and Jesus Christ is not a superstar. It's *all* a bad scene. I want mine.'

Bonner rose from the small, dirty barroom table. 'I'll pass the word. Maybe they'll make you president of Genessee Industries.'

'It's not out of the question . . . And, soldier, I meant what I said. I want mine. If Trevayne's in the market, I'll let him bid; I want you to know that.'

'It could be dangerous for you. I might have to blow out the other half of your stomach. I wouldn't think twice about it.'

'I'm sure you wouldn't . . . But I'm fair about such things. I'll call you first and give you a chance to meet the price . . . If he's in the market, that is.'

Bonner looked at the accountant's enigmatic smile and the somewhat crazy expression on his face. The Major wondered whether the evening was one hell of a mistake. The Genessee man was toying with him in a very unhealthy way. Bonner leaned over, his hands gripping the sides of the table, and spoke firmly but calmly.

'If I were you, I'd be awfully careful about fishing on both sides of the river. The natives can get very unfriendly.'

'Relax, Major. I just wanted to see you spin; you spin like a top . . . No sweat. I like what's left of my stomach . . . Ciao.'

Paul pushed himself up. He hoped he'd never have to see this strange, unhealthy young man again. He was the worst type of informer – and usually the best at his job: a sewer rat who scurried around the tunnels of filth and had no fear of the sunlight, only a certain disdain. His only commitment being to himself.

But then, he'd admitted that.

'Ciao.'

20

The young attorney, Sam Vicarson, had never seen Fisherman's Wharf. It was a silly thing to want to do, he supposed, but he'd promised himself. And now he had two hours to himself, before the five-thirty session in Trevayne's room. The subcommittee chairman had called the two hours a bonus for extraordinarily good behaviour during the Genessee conference.

Sam Vicarson suggested they be given Academy Awards instead.

The taxi pulled up to a clam bar with baskets filled with seaweed and large hemp nets piled in front.

This is where the wharf begins, mister. Straight north, along the waterfront. Do you want to go someplace special? Di Maggio's maybe?'

'No, thanks; this'll be fine.'

Vicarson paid the driver and climbed out of the cab. He was immediately aware of the heavy odor of fish, and wondered – since the whole area had a contrived appearance – if it was piped in. He smiled to himself as he started down the street with the curio shops and the 'atmosphere' bars, the fishing boats bobbing up and down in their slips, nets everywhere. A half-mile travelogue prepared by a very knowledgeable Chamber of Commerce.

It was going to be fun. It was going to be a fun two hours.

He wandered into a number of shops, and for laughs sent postcards to several cynical friends – the most atrocious postcards he could find. He bought Trevayne and Alan Martin two grotesque little flashlights about three inches long and shaped like sharks; the mouths lit up by pressing the dorsal fins.

He strolled out to the far end of the pier, where the boats had an authentic look about them; or, more correctly, the men around them seemed intent on making their living from the water, not from the tourists. He started back, stopping every twenty yards or so to watch the various crews unload their catches, hose down the slicks. The fish were fascinating. Different shapes; odd speckling of colors amidst the predominant greys; the lidless eyes so wide, so blank, so dead yet knowing.

Vicarson looked at his watch. It was almost four fifteen. The Mark Hopkins was a twenty-minute taxi ride, and he wanted to allow himself time for a shower. That left him just about fifteen minutes for a drink at one of the waterfront bars.

That had to be on his wharf agenda.

As he looked up from his watch for a second time and increased his calculations, he saw two men standing perhaps fifty feet away. They were looking at him. They quickly turned and began talking to each other – too rapidly, too artificially. Then Vicarson realized what he'd just done. The San Francisco sun had caused a glare on his watch, so he'd turned to recheck the time in his own shadow; he'd made the movement at the last second. The men hadn't expected it.

Vicarson wondered. Or was Trevayne's constant reminder of caution causing his imagination to overwork?

A group of Girl Scouts accompanied by a large contingent of adult guides began filling up the base of the pier. They were preparing for an assault march to the far end amid squeals of laughter and parental reprimands. They started out; the tourists backed away to let Troop 36, Oakland Brownies, pass through.

Vicarson headed into the group, loudly apologizing as he worked his way through. He reached the last rows under the critical eyes of several adults and emerged within ten yards of the street. He dashed into the thoroughfare and turned right, entering the flow of human traffic on the waterfront side.

Two blocks south he saw a crowded café which advertised 'Drinks on the Bay' and rapidly walked through the door. The bar was in the shape of a horseshoe, the open end by the front entrance, the bar itself following the odd contours of the building, extending out over the water.

'Drinks on the Bay,' indeed.

Vicarson positioned himself halfway around the horseshoe so he could observe both the north side of the dock and the street. He ordered a Fisherman's Punch and waited, wondering if he'd see the two men again.

He did. Only when they came into view they'd been joined by a third man. A large, somewhat obese man in his fifties, or thereabouts.

Sam Vicarson nearly dropped his frosted glass of Fisherman's Punch.

He'd seen the third man before; he wasn't likely to forget, in spite of the circumstances of the meeting – perhaps because of them.

The last time – the only time – he'd seen the large man was on a golf course in the middle of the night three thousand miles away. At Chevy Chase in Maryland. This was the man who'd hammerlocked the drunken Congressman from California and slapped him to the ground.

Trevayne stood by the hotel window and listened to Vicarson's description but kept his own counsel. The young lawyer had described Mario de Spadante. And if he was correct, if de Spadante was in San Francisco, then there were side issues coming into play with Genessee Industries that he hadn't considered.

Mario de Spadante had to be scrutinized. The 'construction boy from New Haven who, with hard work and the grace of God, had made good, bore immediate looking into. Trevayne hadn't made any such connection before. There had been no reason to look for one.

'I'm not mistaken, Mr Trevayne. It was the same man. Who the hell is he?'

'I may be able to answer that after a few phone calls.'

'No kidding?'

'I wish I were ... We'll go into it later. Let's talk about this afternoon.' Trevayne crossed to an armchair; Alan Martin and Sam sat on the couch, papers on the coffee table in front of them. 'We've had time to mull it over, get a little perspective. What's your opinion, Alan? How do you think it went?'

The middle-aged accountant glanced at his papers. He pinched the bridge of his nose and spoke first with his eyes shut. 'Goddard was running scared but did his damnedest to conceal it.' Martin opened his eyes. 'He was also confused. He kept pressing his fingertips on the table; you could see the veins working. Here, I made some notes.' Martin picked up a clipboard from the coffee table. 'One of the first things that threw him was the Pasadena labour settlement. I don't think he expected it. He wasn't happy when Sam pushed his boys for the name of the AFL-CIO negotiator.'

'What was his name?' asked Trevayne.

'Manolo. Ernest Manolo,' answered Vicarson, looking down at his papers on the coffee table. 'The contract wasn't too rough from a local-conditions viewpoint, but if it's used as any sort of national guideline, consider it a giveaway.'

'Will it be?'

'That's up to Manolo and his crowd, I guess. Goose-and-gander reciprocity will be the issue,' replied Vicarson.

'You mean the AFL-CIO delegates that kind of authority to this ... Manolo?'

'Manolo was a medium-paced starter, but he's rising fast. Not much is delegated to him. He just takes. He's a firebrand – crusader type. Like Chavez; but with the benefit of an education. Economics, University of New Mexico.'

'Go ahead, Al.' Trevayne took an envelope out of his pocket.

'I think you fuzzed Goddard when you didn't pursue a number of Genessee's underestimates. He had the files on the Pittsburgh Cylinder Company; the Detroit armature run; the alloy steel – also Detroit; the Houston laboratories; the Green Agency, advertising, New York; and God knows what else. He was ready to throw volumes at us, justifications ... I did get the design-unit head, though. In Houston. His name never appeared in any of *our* files before. Ralph Jamison. Goddard couldn't figure that one out; a lousy lab man behind a one-hundred-and-five-million-dollar conversion ... Then he practically put his fingers through the table when we asked for the Bellstar projections. That's understandable; Genessee had antitrust problems with Bellstar.'

'Speaking as the most brilliant practising attorney here,' said Sam Vicarson with a grin, 'if the Bellstar decision had been rendered by anyone but old Judge Studebaker, it would have been challenged months ago.'

'Sam, why do you say that? I've heard it before.'

'Oh, Lord, Mr Trevayne, ask any trust lawyer who knows his books. The Genessee-Bellstar brief was filled with holes. But Joshua Studebaker was given the case. Old Josh is a little-known bench tradition, but a tradition nevertheless. He might have gone farther, but he prefers to sit in his chambers up in Seattle. He's a quiet, up-from-slavery legal diamond. He's black, Mr Trevayne. When you talk about little kids being whipped, and rickets, and scratching the ground for a potato that's divided, you're talking about old Josh. He's really been there. Even Justice would not challenge him.'

'I never realized that.' Alan Martin was fascinated by this newly acquired information. 'I never heard of him.'

'Neither did I,' said Trevayne.

'It's not surprising. Studebaker's assiduously devoted to being a private person. No interviews, no books; articles involving only the most complex legalistics in superacademic law journals. He's spent forty years or so complicating and uncomplicating legal decisions . . . Some say he's slipped in recent years – they're beginning to understand him.'

'You're saying he's untouchable?' Trevayne asked a question.

'For a number of reasons. He's a genius; he's black; he's eccentric-in-his-fashion; he's got a positively frightening grasp of legal abstractions; he's black. Do I draw a picture?'

'He's black and he made it,' said Alan Martin with resignation.

'To the very-most top of the mountain.'

'You're leaving out a pretty important piece of information . . . or judgment,' said Trevayne.

'Why did he render the decision?' Sam Vicarson leaned forward on the couch. 'I told you his rep is in legal complexities . . . abstractions. He used the phrase "mass human endeavor" in balancing, then overriding, obvious Genessee irregularities. He justified certain questionable economic relation-ships by ascertaining the necessity of "compatible motives" in large-scale financing. Lastly, he threw the hooker: in nothing words, the government hadn't proved the need for viable competition.'

'What does that mean?' asked Alan Martin, his eyes betraying a complete lack of understanding. 'Other than that you read the goddamn papers?'

'Nobody else had the loot.'

'Which has nothing to do with the legality of the situation,' said Trevayne.

'Conclusion?' Sam leaned back on the couch. 'Either old Josh wandered back through the legal gymnastics to the essential truth with all of its human imperfections, or he had an ulterior motive. Frankly, I can't subscribe to the latter. No . . . "compatible motive", to use the judge's own words. Lastly, he's a stand-up legal encyclopedia. Even though a lot of us are convinced there are holes, he might just be able to fill every one.'

'So much for Bellstar.' Trevayne wrote a note to himself on the back of the envelope in his hand. 'What else, Alan?'

'Goddard was angry – I mean he blinked and smiled and damn near tore his fingernails on the wood – when you skirted the question of Armbruster. The Senator's off-limits with him. I don't think he knew what you were driving at. Neither did I, to tell you the truth ... Armbruster's been a thorn to big corporations, especially monoliths like Genessee. He couldn't understand your question about Armbruster being consulted about employment statistics.'

'Because Armbruster wasn't consulted. *He* did the consulting.'

'I still don't understand.'

'The liberal Senator did some rather illiberal cogitations during the last election.'

'No kidding?' Vicarson's eyes were wide.

'I wish I were,' answered Trevayne.

'The last thing I put down – I left the legal stuff to Sam – was the downright evasions they all gave us, in unison, on the aircraft lobby. They were primed on this one. By their percentage figures they're accountable for a maximum of twenty-two per cent of the lobby's funding. Yet according to the lobby's own stats, Genessee's responsible for twenty-seven per cent that we know about, and probably another twelve that's buried. If I really ran a subsidiary check and pulled in the Green Agency in New York, I swear I'd find an additional twenty per cent. I know goddamned well Genessee plies a minimum of seven million into the lobby, but they refuse to admit it. I tell you, they've got more labels for public relations than Sears Roebuck has in a catalogue.'

Labels. A nation of labels, thought Andrew Trevayne.

'Who runs Green in New York?'

'Aaron Green,' answered Sam Vicarson. 'Philanthropist, patron of the arts, publisher of poetry at his own expense. Very high type.'

'A co-religionist of mine,' added Alan Martin. 'Only he came from Birmingham's "Our Crowd", not from New Britain, Connecticut, where us kids ate Kielbasa or got rapped by Polack knuckles ... That's all I wrote down.'

Labels, a nation of labels.

Andrew Trevayne unobtrusively made another notation on the back of the Mark Hopkins envelope. 'Grade A, pass, Rabbi Martin. Shall we bar-mitzvah young Sam?'

'After all my erudition? You're a hard man, Mr Chairman.'

'We grant you're erudite, don't we, Alan? We also grant your exquisite taste in gifts.' Trevayne picked up his shark lighter from the lamp table and pressed the dorsal fin. No light appeared in the mouth. 'You owe me a battery ... Now, what has the learned counsellor deemed to provide us?'

'Crap ... Funny, I don't even like the word, but I use it a lot. Now, it fits,' Vicarson rose from the couch and walked toward the hotel television set and fingered the top.

'What's the crap?' asked Trevayne.

'The term is *no-volotore*. At least it's *my* term.' Vicarson turned around and faced Martin and Trevayne. 'Goddard had a lawyer there this afternoon, but he didn't know what the hell was transpiring. *No-volotore*; he couldn't *offer* anything. He was there to make sure no one contradicted himself legally

– that's *all*. He wasn't allowed to know much of anything. It's one hell of a position.'

'Christ, I'm repeating myself,' said Martin, 'but I don't understand.'

'Dumb yiddle.' Vicarson lobbed an empty ashtray at Martin, who caught it effortlessly with his left hand. 'He was a front. A surface front who watched both sides like a biased referee. He kept picking us up on phrases, asking for classifications – *not* on substance, only on verbiage. You dig? . . . He made sure some future record was clean. And take my word for it, there was nothing said this afternoon that anyone could use in court.' Vicarson leaned against the back of a chair and feigned a push-up on it.

'All right, Mr Blackstone. Why does that disturb you so?' Trevayne shifted his position so he could give young Sam the benefit of his full attention.

'Simple, my leader. No one puts a lawyer, especially a *corporate* lawyer, in that kind of position unless he's frightened out of his tree. You *tell* him something! . . . That man didn't *know* anything. Believe me true, Mr Trevayne, he was in a much darker area than we were.'

'You're employing Judge Studebaker's tactics, Sam. Abstractions,' said Trevayne.

'Not really; that's for openers.' Vicarson suddenly stopped his juvenile gyrations and walked rapidly back to the couch. He sat down and picked up one of the pages on the coffee table. 'I made a couple of notes, too. Not so elaborate as Al's – I was dodging the evil people – but I figured out a few things . . . For a first raise, what would you say to collusion?'

Both listeners looked at each other, then at Vicarson.

'I thought nothing was said this afternoon that could be used in court.' Trevayne spoke while lighting a cigarette.

'Qualification – not by itself. In conjunction with other information, and a lot of digging, there's a good possibility.'

'What is it?' asked Martin.

'Goddard dropped the fact that he – "he" being Genesee Industries – hadn't been apprised of the steel quotas set by the President's Import Commission in March of last year before the official release date. The fact that Genessee had an armada of Tamishito ingot shipped from Japan just under the wire was ascribed to favorable market conditions and an astute purchasing board. Am I right?'

Trevayne nodded; Martin toyed with his grotesque little flashlight. 'So?' he asked.

'In August, Genessee floated a bond issue. Some one hundred million dollars . . . We lawyers keep an eye on such things; we always wish we were a member of the firm that gets the job. That's big-bonus time. I stray . . . The firm which took on the bond issue was a Chicago office, Brandon and Smith; very big, very aristocratic. But why Chicago? There are a dozen tried-and-trues just down the street in New York.'

'Come on, Sam,' said Trevayne. 'What's your point?'

'I have to tell it this way. I need the background . . . Two weeks ago,

Brandon and Smith took on a third principal partner. One Ian Hamilton, an irreproachable member of the bar and—'

It was as far as Vicarson got. Andrew sat forward, holding the envelope in his hand. 'Ian Hamilton was on the President's Import Commission.'

'The commission was formally adjourned after the report was given to the White House. In February; nine months ago. Although no one knew whether the President would accept the recommendations, the five members of the commission were expected – legally required – to keep silent about their findings.'

Trevayne sat back and wrote another note on his envelope. 'All right, Sam ... It's a traceable item. What else?'

'Minor stuff, mostly. You may pick up something though.'

The three men talked for an additional forty-five minutes. Trevayne wrote nothing further on the back of the Mark Hopkins envelope. During the conversation Andy made martinis from the ingredients ordered from room service.

The dissection of the Genessee conference was nearly complete.

'You've picked our – laughingly called – brains, Mr Trevayne,' said Vicarson. 'What did *you* think?'

Trevayne rose from his chair and held up the envelope. He approached the two aides on the couch and dropped it on the coffee table. 'I think we've got what we came for.'

Vicarson picked up the envelope and held it between himself and Martin. They read the carefully printed names:

ERNEST MANOLO – *Pasadena*
RALPH JAMISON – *Houston*
JOSHUA STUDEBAKER – *Seattle*
MITCHELL ARMBRUSTER – *DC*
AARON GREEN – *NYC*
IAN HAMILTON – *Chicago*

'Very well-rounded list, Andrew,' said Alan Martin.

'Very. Each is intrinsic to a Genessee operation involving unusual and expensive circumstances. It's across the board; that's what makes it interesting. Starting with Manolo, there's a labour settlement; Jamison: project design, production; Studebaker: a highly questionable legal decision – federal, too; Armbruster: right into the Senate – there are others in that area, but none have dealt directly with Genessee in California; Aaron Green is distributing a large part of a national lobby's finances – courtesy of GIC ... Ian Hamilton? Who knows? But I get nervous when a man with his presidential ties is that close to a hundred-million-dollar bond issue with a major Defense contractor.'

'What do you want to do?' Martin took the envelope from Sam. 'We can get background material on each, I would think.'

'Can we get it without arousing undue interest, though?'

'I think I can,' said Sam Vicarson.

'I had an idea you could,' replied Andy, smiling. 'I want each of these people researched thoroughly, quickly. Then I want Manolo, Jamison, and Studebaker interviewed, confronted with – in order – the ALF-CIO negotiation in Pasadena, the design conversions at the Houston laboratories, and the Bellstar court decision in Seattle. We may get nothing, each may be an isolated action, but I don't think so. I think we'll find some sort of outline or pattern of how Genessee operates. Even if they're not related, we'll get a very good idea of Genessee's methods.'

'What about the last three? The Senator, Green, and Hamilton?' asked Martin.

'We'll hold on them until we interview the others,' said Trevayne. 'What's important now is that we move quickly, without giving anyone a clue as to what we're doing. To use a Bonnerism, a surprise pincer attack; no one has the chance to create explanations ... We're on a junket right now; the word is out that the three of us are pulling routine drop-ins at various plants – from San Francisco to Denver. Okay, that's what the story remains. We continue. Only there'll be some absenteeism.'

'Absenteeism? What's that?' Sam Vicarson seemed entranced by Andrew's rapid manipulations.

'Alan, I want you to go down to Pasadena; reach Manolo. You've had experience in labour stats; you and I negotiated union stuff all over New England years ago. Find out how Manolo did it without any of the big labour boys. And how come he's so quiet about it; why the settlement hasn't developed as a union guideline. Manolo should have been crowned and moved into the Washington headquarters. He hasn't.'

'When do I go?'

'Tomorrow morning. If Sam here can come up with enough Manolo biography to give you something to work with.'

Vicarson wrote on his notes. 'It'll be a long night, but I think I can.'

'I'll get hold of Mike Ryan back east. He's an aeronautics engineer; that's close enough to this Jamison's work in Houston. I want him to get to the Genessee labs, find out how Jamison was able to get away with a conversion that cost one hundred and five million. What kind of man is given that kind of responsibility ... Sam, if we could find more hours for the night, could you dig up material on Jamison?'

Vicarson put down his pencil. 'Someone in his position at the Genessee labs has to have clearance, doesn't he?'

'Definitely,' answered Alan Martin.

'I know a disenchanted friend at the FBI. I went to school with him. He was never in the Hoover camp, but the Hoover contingent doesn't know it. He'll help us; no one will know.'

'Good. And now you, Sam. Get out all the information you can find on the Bellstar decision, Studebaker's decision. Read it until you can recite it backwards. As soon as Alan returns, I want you to go to Seattle. Studebaker's your assignment.'

'It's my pleasure,' said Vicarson. 'That man's a giant; maybe some of his stuff will rub off.'

'Let's hope it is the right stuff,' answered Trevayne.

'Andrew?' Alan Martin seemed concerned. 'You say you want this all to be done with no flak, no one knowing what we're doing. That's going to be difficult. How do you explain the absenteeism?'

'A few years ago, Henry Kissinger got the "touristas" in Taiwan; instead of being in his hotel room, he was in Peking.'

'Okay,' answered Martin. 'That part's okay. But he had rather special transportation. If anyone's watching us – and we know damned well they are – airline reservations are easily traced.'

'Good point,' answered Trevayne, addressing both men.

'And we'll have special transportation, too. I'll call my brother-in-law, Doug Pace, in New Haven. He can arrange private planes here and in DC. Ryan will be watched also.'

'You haven't lost your touch, Andrew,' said Martin. 'Doug may have apoplexy, but he'll do it.'

'He still hasn't forgiven me for kidnapping you, you know.'

'My wife brings him chicken soup at the office. She's afraid he won't take me back.' Martin smiled; Andrew laughed.

'Mr Trevayne?' Sam Vicarson was staring at his notes.

'Yes?'

'I see a problem.'

'Only one?' asked Martin. 'I'm relieved.'

'I think it's a big one. How do we know that the minute these guys – Manolo, Jamison, Studebaker – see us, they won't throw panic switches and call the Genessee management?'

'That *is* a problem. I think the only way to solve it is to use concrete threats. The approach to each should be that he is a small part of a much, much larger concern. The interviews are confidential; to break that confidence could be indictable. Since Defense is involved, maybe we could use the National Security Act.'

'Section three-five-eight!' Vicarson was impressed with himself. 'I picked that up from Bonner during an argument.'

'We'll try it . . . Now, you've both got a lot to do, and I have calls to make. Was Paul going to have dinner with us?'

'No,' answered Sam. 'He said he was going out catting. The son-of-a-bitch didn't even ask me to come along.'

'He'd be court-martialled for corrupting minors,' said Martin, chuckling.

'Thanks, Father Ben-Gurion.'

'We'll break, then.' Trevayne reached down for the envelope. 'The day after tomorrow we're in Boise, Idaho; that ITT subsidiary. Try to coordinate and meet us there, Alan. I'll call your room after I talk to Doug. From Boise, Sam, you head up to Seattle.'

'Join a subcommittee and see the world,' said Sam Vicarson, finishing his martini.

*

Trevayne leaned back on the pillow and put his feet up on the bed. The telephone calls had been made. Phyllis missed him; she'd gone back to Barnegat while he was away. Life was uneventful. Pam and Steve were surviving at their schools. Pam had won some kind of award this semester in chemistry; how did she *ever* come by *that* talent? Phyllis was having the Swansons over for dinner tomorrow. They were still upset over the heroin episode; Officer Fowler at Police Headquarters was no further along than before.

His brother-in-law would take care of the small-plane arrangements. Charter and flight plans would be in his, Pace's, name, and the first field would probably be the small private airport outside of Redwood City. Not San Francisco International. He'd call back. Further, his brother-in-law would discreetly, but thoroughly, check around the Hartford–New Haven area and uncover the whereabouts of Mario de Spadante. It wouldn't be difficult; de Spadante delegated very little authority in his company. Any number of problems could be raised – invented – that required his immediate attention.

Trevayne reached Mike Ryan, who was still in his office at Potomac Towers. Ryan made the evening brighter by telling Andrew he knew Ralph Jamison. Knew him quite well, as a matter of fact. They'd both been called in on the SST mock-up at Lockheed – consulting specialists.

'He's a *crazy* bastard, Andy. But they don't come any better in metallurgy. He's a goddamn genius. And *man*, does he *live*! I'll pump him dry.'

Ryan would be called directly by Doug Pace in New Haven; he understood the reasons for secrecy and felt certain he could handle Jamison in that area. Ryan would try to complete the job and meet them in Boise. If he wasn't able to make it by then, he'd get to Denver, the junket's next stop.

Andrew made a final telephone call to Washington. To Robert Webster on the White House aide's private line. He eventually reached him at home. He asked Webster to compile everything he could about Mario de Spadante.

Webster agreed to do so.

Trevayne looked down at the envelope in his hand. It was wrinkled, creased by his constant folding and unfolding. But the writing was still clear:

ERNEST MANOLO – *Pasadena*
RALPH JAMISON – *Houston*
JOSHUA STUDEBAKER – *Seattle*
MITCHELL ARMBRUSTER – *DC*
AARON GREEN – *NYC*
IAN HAMILTON – *Chicago*

This was the real itinerary. Six men who might help him understand the apparent majesty of Genessee Industries.

21

Sam Vicarson walked into the small passenger terminal at the Ada County Airport, ten miles from Boise. Douglas Pace's Lear jet had brought him back from Tacoma; while in Tacoma he'd rented a car and driven to Seattle.

To see Judge Joshua Studebaker.

It was a meeting he'd remember for the rest of his life.

It was also a meeting he could describe only to Andrew Trevayne alone. Not with Alan Martin, not with Mike Ryan. It was too private, too terrible, somehow, for any ears but Trevayne's.

Vicarson knew that Mike had gotten into Boise from Houston several hours ago; Alan had returned from the Manolo interview two days ago, when he turned the Lear jet over for the Seattle run.

They were to meet that night in Trevayne's hotel room. They were to put it all together then.

Sam had to find Trevayne before the meeting. Trevayne would know what to do.

Vicarson felt tired, exhausted, and depressed; he thought about stopping off at a bar for a few drinks. But he knew he wouldn't.

He'd get roaring drunk, and that wouldn't do anyone any good.

Especially not Joshua Studebaker.

Alan Martin stared out of the car window. He was alone; Andrew had left the meeting with ITT's subsidiary early, without explanation. Sam Vicarson had called from the airport; something was the matter.

The sign on the highway read: 'Boise, Idaho; State Capital; Population 73,000; Heart of the Columbia Basin.'

It was difficult for Alan Martin to think of Boise, think of the unnecessary conferences they were holding, for cover.

He couldn't get his mind off Pasadena. Pasadena and a fiery little man named Ernest Manolo. An incredibly *young* fiery man. Andrew didn't want to discuss Manolo until they all got together that night. There was logic in that; save the information, don't lose details in the retelling. Andrew was right; they could all trigger each other.

It wasn't so much Manolo; Andrew was right again. Manolo was only a cog, a single spike in a frightening wheel.

Ernest Manolo, AFL-CIO negotiator for the entire district of southern California, had his own considerable fiefdom.

How many others were there across the country?

Michael Ryan sat at a booth in the hotel's coffee shop. He was annoyed with himself. He should have known better than to be so obvious; he should have gotten a room and just stayed there until Trevayne called him.

Goddamn!

He just wasn't thinking!

The first person he'd run into in the goddamn coffee shop was Paul Bonner!

Bonner was surprised, of course. And when he, Ryan, couldn't come up with a decent explanation, Bonner's surprise turned into something else.

It was there, in the soldier's eyes. That something else.

Goddamn!

His carelessness, Ryan realized, was due to an old friend, Ralph Jamison. Stupid, insane, crazy-head Jamison! Falsifying decisions to get Genessee Industries a hundred and five million of Defense funds.

How could he have *done* it? How could he *do* it?

Sold, lock, stock, and barrel to Genessee Industries. Jamison, with his three ex-wives, his four kids from who-knew-which, his middle-aged peccadilloes that were right out of some goddamn fifth-rate porno movie.

Genessee took care of Ralph Jamison. Jamison told him it was standard operating procedure. 'Ma Gen' took care of its talent.

Bank accounts in Zurich!

Insane!

It had been three days since Trevayne and his subcommittee aides had left San Francisco, but James Goddard couldn't get them out of his mind. Something had gone wrong. The final two conferences were merely prolonged embarrassments.

Without the accountant. The accountant hadn't been there. And it didn't make sense for this Martin to be absent. Alan Martin was the cost man; just as he, Goddard, was a cost man. Without Martin, too many details were overlooked; Martin would have caught the details.

Trevayne had joked about his aide. The subcommittee chairman had laughed and said that Martin was holed up at the Mark Hopkins with a bad case of 'San Francisco water'.

After the last conference. Goddard decided to inquire. He could do so easily, even be solicitous. He called the hotel.

Alan Martin had checked out two days ago.

Why had Trevayne lied? Why had the other aide, Vicarson, lied? Where had Martin gone?

Had he suddenly gone to get follow-up data on information revealed during the conferences?

Revealed by him; revealed by James Goddard, president, San Francisco Division, Genessee Industries?

Which? What?

How could he find out what it was without others becoming alarmed?

That was important. Mario de Spadante said some might have to hang so those farther up could remain untouched. Goddard knew he was considered vital. Good *Lord;* he *was* vital! He was the figure man. He arranged the numbers, created the projections upon which the decisions were made. Even he wasn't sure who ultimately made those decisions, but without *him* they couldn't be made.

He was the keystone ... a keystone.

But he also knew that underneath the attention they gave him, the respect they surfacely rendered, there was a certain contempt. The contempt associated with a man who could only propose, never dispose.

A 'bookkeeper'.

But this bookkeeper wasn't for hanging.

Goddard signalled a cab, and as it pulled up to the curb he made his own decision. He'd return to his office and remove a number of highly confidential papers. He would carefully put them at the bottom of his briefcase and take them home.

Numbers. His numbers. Genessee's numbers. Not names.

He knew how to deal with numbers.

A man had to protect himself. Perhaps against names.

Andrew Trevayne jumped out of the cab and walked into the hotel lobby. He'd promised Sam Vicarson he'd meet him in Vicarson's room. But before he did, he knew it was time to talk to Bonner. Regardless of what was learned from Sam and Alan and Mike Ryan, he had to get on Pace's Lear jet tonight and go to Washington.

And depending on what was learned from his three aides about Manolo, Jamison, and Studebaker, he might well go from Washington to New York and on to Chicago.

Mitchell Armbruster. Aaron Green. Ian Hamilton.

Either way, it was time to use Paul Bonner.

Bonner was waiting for him in the cocktail lounge. The meeting would be brief.

Trevayne was of two minds. He knew he had to do what he was doing; by using Paul Bonner, Washington would be convinced of the 'legitimacy' of his temporarily abandoning his subcommittee, but there was another aspect.

He was actively, wilfully engaging in much the same type of manipulation he'd been recruited to expose – calculated deception. The difference, he rationalized, was the absence of financial profit, and for a while he accepted this rationalization as fundamentally justifiable. But there were other 'profits', equally important rewards. He didn't need money ... Was he somehow applying the intensity others used for making money to reach something else?

He couldn't dwell on it; the decision had been made.

He was going to relive – for the record – one of the most difficult periods of his life. It would give flexibility to time.

Six years ago Phyllis had entered the hospital for an exploratory. It was before mammography had been perfected, and she had developed lumps on her breasts. He had been beside himself, trying his best to be outwardly confident, knowing the children suspected something far more serious than what they'd been told – perceiving his anguish.

Now, six years later, Paul Bonner was to be given a current variation of the incident. An unspecific account, clouded with doubt and filled with apprehension. And a request: would Paul sit in on the upcoming subcommittee conferences with two subcontractors of General Motors and Lockheed? They were in Denver; the next few days. The conferences needed the 'weight' of his, Bonner's, inclusion. Sam Vicarson was simply too young, Alan Martin seemingly too lacking in authority. The aides would fill him in.

So that he, Andrew Trevayne, could get home to his wife.

Phyllis was entering a private hospital Friday afternoon. No one knew anything about the exploratory other than Sam and Alan. Even the two men from 1600 who stayed on the Barnegat property knew only that Phyllis was going for a check-up. One way or the other Trevayne would return to Denver on Monday.

When the drinks were finished, Andy found it difficult to look at Paul Bonner. The Major was genuinely concerned for him; he agreed to do anything, take whatever worries he could from Andy's mind.

Oh, God! thought Trevayne. *In this nation of labels this man is my enemy. Yet look at his eyes! They're frightened – for me.*

Paul Bonner walked slowly down the hotel corridor to his room. He unlocked the door, entered, and slammed it shut. He swung it with such force that two paintings – poor reproductions selected by a tasteless Boise management – vibrated on the wall. He crossed to his bureau, where there was the ever-present bottle of bourbon, and poured himself a large drink.

He poured himself another and drank it rapidly.

It was entirely possible, he reflected, that he might just stay in his room the remainder of the day, order another bottle, and get quietly, thoroughly drunk.

But then, that would preclude the charade. He'd be too hungover in the morning for his meeting with Alan Martin and Sam Vicarson, during which time they were to give him the background on the subcontractors in Denver.

Horseshit!

The beavers were so inept. And the head beaver was playing a dirty game – a very personally dirty game – of dam building. He hadn't thought Andrew Trevayne could roll in that kind of filth. Even the possessors of hatred – they might use their women to run guns and contraband, alert the jungles, smuggle narcotics, but they wouldn't use them *this* way. They wouldn't trade in painfully intimate confidences. There was no dignity in that, no essential strength.

Bonner carried his glass to his bed, sat down, and reached for the hotel telephone. He gave the operator the private Washington number of Brigadier General Lester Cooper.

It took Major Bonner less than a minute to get the basic information.

'. . . the cover is his wife. He says he's flying east to be with her. She's supposed to enter a quote – private hospital – unquote; cancer exploratory. It's a lie.'

'Are you sure?'

'Damned near positive,' answered Bonner, swallowing the remainder of the bourbon in his glass.

'Why? That's pretty hairy.'

'Because it follows!' Bonner realized he spoke too sharply to his superior; he couldn't help himself. His anger with Trevayne was too personal. 'Alan Martin disappeared for a day and a half; Vicarson was gone for two. No explanation given, just subcommittee business. Then this afternoon, who the hell do I run into? In Boise . . . Mike Ryan. Something's going on, General. It stinks.'

Brigadier General Cooper paused before speaking. His fear carried over the wire. 'We can't afford to be mistaken, Bonner.'

'For God's sake, General, I'm an experienced man; I've interrogated the best of them. Trevayne's learning, I'm sorry to say, but he's still a bad liar. It hurt him to look at me.'

'We've got to find out where the other three were . . . I'll put out tracers with the airlines. We've got to know.'

'Let me do that, General.' Bonner didn't want the Pentagon amateurs coming on the scene. 'There are only half a dozen lines coming in here. I'll find out where they flew in from.'

'Call me as soon as you learn something. This is priority, Major. In the meantime, I'll put surveillance on his wife. To be sure; in case he shows up.'

'You're wasting your time, sir. She's a cooperative girl. The "1600" team will vouch that she's going for a check-up. Trevayne's a rotten liar, but I'm sure he's methodical about this sort of thing. He's in new territory now; he'll be thorough.'

22

Sam Vicarson leaned against the writing desk as Trevayne settled into an armchair.

'All right, Counsellor,' said Andrew, looking up, 'why the private conference? What's the matter?'

'Joshua Studebaker made a mistake forty years ago. They're making him pay for it. He thinks thirty years of judicial decisions will go out of the window if he's called. As he put it, the source of his decisions would become suspect in every court in the land.'

Trevayne whistled softly. 'What did he do? Shoot Lincoln?'

'Worse. He was a Communist. Not the radical-chic variety, but a real card-carrying, cell-organized, Kremlin-instructed Marxist ... The country's first black judge west of the Rocky Mountains spent five years – again, as he put it – in dimly lit rooms preparing cases for his practising colleagues that tied up the courts with manipulative language. For the cause.'

'His practising colleagues?'

'He was disbarred in Missouri. He'd won one appeal in the State Supreme Court; he wasn't welcome after that. He went underground, landed in New York, and became part of the movement. He got the Red fever; for five years he really believed it was the answer.'

'What's that got to do with Genessee Industries? With the Bellstar decision?'

Vicarson pulled the chair out from under the writing desk and straddled it, his arms resting on the back. 'The Genessee attorneys got to him. Very subtly. Veiled but explicit threats of exposure.'

'And he sold out. He sold the bench.'

'It's not that simple, Mr Trevayne. That's why I wanted to see you alone, without the others ... I don't want to write up a report on Studebaker.'

Andrew's voice was clipped, cold. 'I think you'd better explain, Sam. That decision isn't yours to make.'

And Sam Vicarson tried to explain.

Joshua Studebaker was in his seventies. A large, magnificently gifted Negro, he was the son of an itinerant crop hand named Joshua, as *his* father before him was Joshua. In 1907, during one of Theodore Roosevelt's last-gasp reform programmes, young Joshua was selected to receive some minimum schooling.

Studebaker's government-sponsored education lasted an extraordinary seven years, six more than the counter-reformers anticipated. During those years the young boy crammed an equally extraordinary amount of knowledge into his previously illiterate head. But at sixteen he was told there was no more; he was to be grateful for what he'd been given. It was certainly no birthright, not in the year 1914 in the state of Missouri, USA.

However, the tools had been provided, and Joshua Studebaker took care of the rest. He sought, begged, stole, and fought for the remainder of an education. The years were migrant years, but instead of following the crops, he went to where the classrooms were open for him. He lived in squalor, when it was available; more often in railroad yards and dump shacks with corrugated metal roofs and fires kindled by refuse. At twenty-two Joshua Studebaker found a small experimental college that prepared him for the law. At twenty-five he was a lawyer. At twenty-seven he'd astounded the bar in Missouri by successfully appealing a case before the State Supreme Court.

He was not welcome in Missouri.

He was soon thereafter without a practice in Missouri, disbarred over technical preparations. He'd been put in his proper place.

There followed years of running, eking out whatever living he could – teaching when possible in back-country schools, more often doing manual labour. His prized lawyer's certificate was next to worthless. Negro attorneys were not sought after in the twenties; a disbarred Negro attorney not at all.

Studebaker drifted north to Chicago, where he made contact with the disciples of Eugene Debs, living out his last years writing and lecturing among the socialist intelligentsia. Joshua's talents were perceived by the extremists in Debs's circles, and he was sent to New York – to the soft, hot core of the Communist party.

For the next five years of his adult life he was a vital, unknown legal manipulator, hidden by anonymity, doing the work of headlining radicals. He was getting even with the Eden that had cast him so unfairly from its garden.

Then Franklin Roosevelt was elected President, and the Marxists went into panic. For Roosevelt went about saving the capitalistic system by boldly implementing social reforms the Leninists held as their own.

Joshua Studebaker was approached by the Marxists to enter into another phase of operation. He was ordered to form an elitist subcell, the end result of which was the training of insurgent teams used for the physical disruption of government reform programmes. Offices, job camps, food-distribution centres, were to be sabotaged; files stolen, welfare caseloads destroyed; any and all tactics employed that might cripple or make ineffective by delay the cures for the economic ills of the lingering Depression.

'It was appalling that they should have chosen me,' Joshua Studebaker had said to Sam Vicarson. 'They misunderstood my zeal ... As a thinker, a strategist, perhaps, I accepted the *principle* of violence. As an activist I could not accept participation. I specifically could not accept it when the first results were directed at those who were helpless.'

Joshua Studebaker, after reading in a newspaper the aftermath of a life-taking fire at a CCC camp in New York State, went to the Justice Department.

It was the time of welcoming back errants; it was also a time of rewarding those who could help the Roosevelt administration wash off the taint of the Red brush. Joshua fit into both categories. He was quietly hired by the government, and all his legal privileges were restored. For the first time in his life Joshua Studebaker could stop running, stop scratching, stop lashing out at the horrors – real and unreal – that had pursued him. Eden became a productive, serpentless garden.

And finally, as if the circle of experimentation were complete, Joshua Studebaker was awarded the first black judgeship west of the Rocky Mountains. It was a safe experiment – a small appointment with a constituency generously peopled by transient lumbermen and Tacomack Indians, but a judgeship, nevertheless.

Ironically, it was later, during the McCarthy madness, that Studebaker received his 'promotion', as it were, to Seattle. It was someone's sense of outrage that a once dangerous though anonymous radical was put forth. It balanced someone's scale.

'He's spent thirty years fighting vested advocacy, Mr Trevayne. I guarantee you that; look at the law books, at the supportive adjudications used by thousands of Legal Aid attorneys in the ghettos, in the barrios. I know, sir. I've been there. From land condemnation to restraints, from undue process to abridged rights. Studebaker's been a one-man barricade against the self-interest groups. If we expose what he was, all that could be in jeopardy.'

'*Why?*' Andrew was annoyed. 'For something that happened forty years ago, Sam? You're unreasonable.'

'No, I'm not, sir! He never recanted, there was no public confessional, no grovelling for forgiveness ... His court decisions have been interpreted as ideologically left of center. If his past is brought up, they'll be labelled something else.'

Labels. A nation of labels, thought Trevayne.

'Don't you see?' continued Vicarson. 'He doesn't care about himself. He cares deeply about his work. And whatever the reasons – even justifications – he *was* a subversive. In the real meaning of the word. The prospects of ulterior motive *could* be attributed to every major decision he's ever made. It's called "dishonorable source". It usually overrides everything else.'

'And that's why you don't want to write the report?'

'Yes, sir. You'd have to meet him to understand. He's an old man; I think a great man. He's not afraid for himself; I don't think the years he has left are important to him. What he's accomplished *is*.'

'Aren't you forgetting something, Sam?' asked Trevayne slowly.

'What?'

'The Bellstar decision. Didn't you say it was full of holes? Are we to let the Genessee lawyers get away with the most corrupt sort of practice?'

Vicarson smiled sadly. 'I have an idea they wasted their time. Studebaker might have reached the same decision without them. Of course, we'll never know, but he's pretty damned convincing.'

'How?'

'He quoted Hofstader: antitrust is "a faded passion of reform". And Galbraith: modern technology has brought about the "industrialized state". Competition, per se, is no longer a viable, built-in regulator. The huge economic resources demanded by our technology bring about a concentration of financing . . . Once this is accepted – and the law has to deal with practicalities – it's the government's responsibility, and the law's, to act as the regulator, the protector of the consumer. The civilizer, if you will . . . Put in blunt terms, the country needed the Bellstar products. The company was going under; there was no one else but Genessee Industries who had sufficient economic resources to assume the responsibility.'

'He said that?'

'Almost verbatim. It wasn't so clear in the decision; at least, not to me. He told me I wasn't the best student he'd ever met.'

'But if he believed that, why didn't he just say so? Why did he tell you all the rest of it?'

Sam Vicarson got out of the chair; there was a restless, uncomfortable expression on his face. 'I'm afraid I forced him. I said that if I didn't understand the Bellstar decision, if I thought it was suspect – and for the record, I'm considered a bright bastard – then he had an obligation to make a public clarification. He flatly refused. No way; he was adamant. I felt awful, but I told him he was copping out, and I wouldn't buy it. I was going to subpoena him.'

'I would have done the same thing.'

Vicarson was by the hotel window, staring out at the Boise skyline. 'He didn't expect that; I don't think he realized we had subpoena powers.'

'Honored in the breach, I hope,' said Trevayne. 'We haven't used them.'

Vicarson turned. 'It shook him, Mr Trevayne. It was a terrible sight. And it wasn't for *himself*; you've got to believe that.'

Trevayne got out of the chair and stood facing the young man. He spoke quietly but firmly.

'Write the report, Sam.'

'*Please* . . .'

'Don't file it. Give it to me. One copy.' Andrew walked to the door. 'See you at eight o'clock. My room.'

23

The coffee table served as a communal desk. The reports and memoranda were in file folders in front of each man. The conference in Trevayne's room had begun with Alan Martin's description of Ernest Manolo, president of the Lathe Operators Brotherhood of the District of Southern California and the all-powerful negotiator of the AFL-CIO. According to Martin, Ernest Manolo looked like a twelve-year-old bullfighter.

'He travels with his own picadors; two big fellows, they're always flanking him.'

'Are they guards?' asked Trevayne. 'And if so, why?'

'They are, and he needs them. Fast Ernie – that's what he's called, Fast Ernie – has a goodly share of resentful brothers in his brotherhood.'

'Good Lord, why?' Andrew was sitting next to Sam Vicarson on the couch. 'He got them a hell of a settlement.' Vicarson started to interrupt as Martin answered quickly.

'Sam knows. It was in his bio material. Incidentally, buddy,' said Martin to the young attorney, 'that was a good job.'

'Thanks,' answered a subdued Vicarson. 'It wasn't hard. When he was running for office he had a lot of promotion material circulated. Easy to zero in on.'

'That's why he travels with his two friends,' continued Martin. 'Fast Ernie's twenty-six years old. He had to jump over a lot of seasoned union stewards to get the job. Most of them don't like the way he did it.'

'Which was how?' asked Mike Ryan, sitting across from Martin.

'A lot of the hard-hat brothers think he used dirty money. They figure it had to be dirty, because he had so much of it. He brought into office with him a whole new breed of union management. Young, bright, college-educated. They don't shout arguments in union halls, they issue position papers with lots of charts and logistics. The old-timers don't like it. They're suspicious of three syllables.'

'Still,' said Andrew, 'he got them a decent contract. That's the name of the game, Alan.'

'It's also the name of Fast Ernie's problem. It's both his best weapon and his highly suspect manoeuvre ... It was the quickest settlement Genessee ever made. No big fights, no all-night bargaining sessions; when it was concluded, there weren't any celebrations; no dancing in the streets. No words of congratulation from the old war horses like Meany and his boys on the Labor Council. Most important, the settlement in the Southern California District will *not* be used as a guideline anywhere else. It's isolated, jurisdictional.'

Mike Ryan leaned forward in his chair. 'I'm an engineer, not a union-watcher. Is that unusual?'

'You can bet your blueprints on it,' answered Martin. 'Any major labour contract serves as the basis for upcoming negotiations. But not this one.'

'How do you know?' asked Trevayne.

'I backed Manolo into a corner. I told him I was surprised, even astounded, that he hadn't been given his proper due; that the DC Labor Council had brushed him off. I knew a few of those old buzzards, and I was going to raise the issue ... Manolo didn't want any part of my solicitous-ness. In fact, he was goddamned upset. He began retreating to his charts and employment stats relative to district conditions. He reiterated more times than I care to recall how the old-time labour clods couldn't understand the new jurisdictional economic theories. What was applicable to southern California wasn't to west Arkansas ... Do you begin to see?'

'He's Genessee's man. They put him in and bought him with the single contract,' interjected Vicarson.

'They're doing it all over the country – including west Arkansas,' said Martin. 'Genessee Industries is well on its way to controlling its own labour markets. I made a surface check this afternoon, based on Manolo's districting pattern. It's surface, mind you, but I found similarities in Genessee companies and subsidiaries in twenty-four states.'

'Jesus,' said Mike Ryan softly.

'Will Manolo run to Genessee? That could be a problem for us right now.' Andrew frowned as he asked the question.

'I don't think so. I can't guarantee it, but I think he's going to sit on the tightrope; at least for a while. I told him I was perfectly satisfied, and I think he bought it. I also implied that I'd be just as happy if our meeting was kept between the two of us. If others got involved – especially Genessee management – I'd have to spend a lot more time in Pasadena ... I think he'll keep quiet.'

'So much for Manolo. What about this Jamison in Houston, Mike?'

Ryan seemed to hesitate as he reached for the folder on the coffee table. He looked over at Trevayne and for several moments said nothing. The expression on his face was questioning. Finally he spoke. 'I'm trying to figure out a way to say this. I listen to Al's words here and find myself nodding my head, saying, "Yes, sure, that's the way it is." Because suddenly I realize he's describing Houston. And probably Palo Alto, Detroit, Oak Ridge, and twenty or so other Genessee design shops and laboratories in God knows how many places. Only you substitute "scientific community" for "labour markets", dirty up the players a bit more, and it's the same ballgame.'

Michael Ryan had flown into Houston International using a plane also chartered by Douglas Pace, flight plans filed under Pace's name. After checking the Genessee laboratories, he found Ralph Jamison, metallurgical specialist, at a yacht club on Galveston Bay. It was in Megans Point, a haven for oil-rich Texans, the Southwest's Riviera.

Ryan feigned an unexpected reunion, completely accepted by Ralph Jamison. The two men had become friends while they were at Lockheed; each an extrovert, each a lover of good times and a good deal of good liquor.

Each, too, a brilliant man.

Afternoon became evening and then, swiftly, the early-morning hours. Ryan found that Jamison continuously evaded questions about his projects at Genessee. It was frustrating, because it wasn't natural; shop talk among top aeronautical men – especially with both cleared for the highest classification – was the normal, anticipated, looked-forward-to indulgence.

'Then I got an inspiration, Andy,' said Mike Ryan, interrupting his narrative. 'I decided to offer Ralph a job.'

'Where?' asked Trevayne, smiling. 'Doing what?'

'Who the hell cared? We were both fried out of our skulls; him more than me, I'm happy to say . . . I made it sound like I was a lab raider. I was with a company that was in a bind; we needed him. I'd actually come looking for him. I offered him three, maybe four times what I figured he was pulling down at Genessee.'

'You were pretty damned generous,' said Alan Martin. 'What were you going to do if he accepted?'

Ryan stared down at the coffee table. His eyes had a sadness about them. 'By then I'd accurately predicted that he wouldn't.' Ryan looked up. 'Or couldn't.'

Ralph Jamison, faced with a firm, incredible offer made by a man who – drunk or sober – would not have made it without authorization, had to find explanations commensurate with his illogical refusal. The words, at first, came easily: loyalty, current projects that concerned him at Genessee, lab problems he couldn't leave, again loyalty, stretching back over the years.

Ryan countered each with growing irritation, until Jamison – by now nearly incoherent, and pressured by his total belief in Ryan's extraordinary offer – dropped the words.

'You can't understand. Genessee has taken care of us. All of us.'

'Taken care?' Trevayne repeated the words reported by Mike Ryan. 'All of them? . . . Who? What did he mean?'

'I had to piece it together. He never came out and made any blanket admissions . . . except one. But it's there, Andy. All the top talent – especially lab and design – are paid below the line.'

'Under the table, I presume, is another, more accurate description,' said Alan Martin.

'Yes,' answered Ryan. 'And not little driblets in expense vouchers. Fair-sized amounts, usually paid outside the country and wending their way to Zurich and Bern. Coded bank accounts.'

'Unreported income,' supplied Martin.

'Untraceable,' added Sam Vicarson. 'Because no one cries fraud. And no country's tax laws are recognized in Switzerland. Even when violated, it's not fraud as far as the Swiss are concerned.'

'It starts early, as I understand it,' said Ryan. 'Genessee spots a comer, a real potential, and the loving begins. Oh, they check out the person; they work slowly, gradually. They find weaknesses – that was Ralph's admission, incidentally, I'll get to it – and when they find them they cross-pollinate them with plain, outright, hidden bonuses. In ten or fifteen years a guy has a sweet nest egg of a hundred, a hundred and fifty thousand salted away. That's mighty inducive.'

'And he's inexorably bound to Genessee Industries,' said Trevayne. 'It's a collusion pact; he does what Genessee tells him to do. Because if he doesn't, that's conducive to something else. I assume payments are made by . . . let's say, expendable intermediaries.'

'Right.'

'A rough estimate, Mike: how many Ralph Jamisons are there?' asked Trevayne.

'Well, figure Genessee has a hundred installations – general and subsidiary – like the Houston labs. Not as big, certainly, but substantial. You can estimate between seven and ten top men at each site. Seven hundred to a thousand.'

'And these people control project decisions, production lines?' Trevayne wrote on notepaper.

'Ultimately, yes. They're responsible.'

'So for a few million a year, Genessee extracts obedience from a powerful sector of the scientific community,' said Andrew, scratching over the figures he'd written. 'Men who have control over, say, a hundred project installations, which in turn make the decisions for all of the Genessee plants and subsidiaries. Assembly lines and contracts involving billions.'

'Yes. I'd guess it's growing every year; they start young.' The dejected, questioning expression returned to Ryan's face. 'Ralph Jamison's a sad casualty, Andy. He's better than that. He's got a big problem.'

'He drinks with the Irish crazies,' said Alan Martin gently, seeing the pain in Ryan's eyes.

Ryan looked at Martin, smiled, and paused before replying softly. 'Hell no, Al, he's an amateur. He goes out New Year's Eve . . . Ralph's at the real genius level. He's made great contributions to metallurgical research; we'd never have made the moon without him. But he burns himself out in the shops. He's been known to work seventy-two hours straight. His whole life is committed to the laboratory.'

'Is that his problem?' asked Andy.

'Yes. Because he can't take the time for anything else. He runs from personal commitments; he's frightened to death of them. He's had three wives – quick selections. They gave him among them four children. The ladies have bled him in alimony and support. But he's nuts about the kids; he worries about them so because he knows himself and those girls. That was his admission to me. Every February he goes to Paris, where a Genessee small-timer gives him twenty thousand in cash, which he takes to Zurich. It's for his kids.'

'And he's one of the men who put us on the moon.' Sam Vicarson made the statement quietly and watched Trevayne. It was apparent to all in the room that Sam was referring to something – someone else.

And each knew that Sam had been to Seattle, Washington. To Joshua Studebaker.

Andrew accepted Vicarson's words and his unspoken appeal. He turned back to Ryan. 'But you're not suggesting that we disregard Jamison's report, are you, Mike?'

'Christ, no.' Ryan exhaled slowly. 'I don't like nailing him, but what I've learned about Genessee Industries scares the hell out of me; I mean *really scares* me. I know what those design shops and laboratories are turning out.'

'That's physical, not sociological,' said Vicarson quickly, firmly.

'Sooner or later those two get together if they're not already, fella,' answered Ryan.

'Thanks, Mike.' Trevayne's voice indicated that he wanted no tangential discussions at the moment.

Vicarson leaned forward on the couch and picked up his file folder. 'Okay. I guess it's my turn,' he said with a shrug that conveyed far more than resignation.

Andrew interrupted. 'May I, please?'

Sam looked at Trevayne, surprised. 'What?'

'Sam came to me earlier this evening. The Studebaker report isn't complete. There's no question that he was reached and threatened by Genessee, but we're not sure of the degree of influence that had on the antitrust decision regarding Bellstar. The judge claims that it didn't; he justifies the decision in legal and philosophical terms, using contemporary definitions. We *do* know the Justice Department had no real interest in pursuing the action.'

'But he *was reached*, Andrew?' Alan Martin was concerned. 'And threatened?'

'He was.'

'Threatened with what?' asked Ryan.

'I'm going to ask you to let me wait before answering that.'

'It's so filthy?' asked Martin.

'I'm not sure it's relevant,' said Trevayne. 'If it turns out to be, it'll be filed.'

Ryan and Martin looked at each other, then at Vicarson. Martin spoke, addressing Trevayne. 'I'd be a damn fool to start questioning your judgment after all these years, Andrew.'

'So, what else is new?' said Ryan casually.

'I'm leaving tonight. For Washington. Paul Bonner thinks I'm going to Connecticut; I'll explain . . . Genessee Industries is progressively eliminating all the checks and balances. It's time for Senator Armbruster.'

24

Brigadier General Lester Cooper walked up the flagstone path toward the front door of the suburban home. The coach lamp on the lawn was lighted; the metal plate beneath it, suspended by two small chains from a crossbar, read: 'The Knapps; 37 Maple Lane'.

Senator Alan Knapp.

There'd be at least one other senator inside, too, thought Cooper as he walked up the steps. He switched the attaché case to his left hand and pushed the button.

Knapp opened the door, his irritation obvious. 'For God's sake, Cooper, it's almost ten o'clock. We said nine!'

'I didn't *have* anything until twenty minutes ago.' The General spoke curtly. He didn't like Knapp; he simply had to tolerate him, not be polite. 'I didn't look upon this evening as a social call, Senator.'

Knapp feigned a smile; it was difficult for him. 'Okay, General, call off the artillery. Come on in ... Sorry, we're a little upset.'

'With damned good reason,' added Cooper as he stepped inside.

Knapp preceded the General into the living room. It was an expensive room, thought Cooper as he saw the French provincial furniture, the soft white rugs, and the ornate *objets d'art* scattered about. Knapp came from money; old money.

Vermont's Senator Norton looked out of place sitting in a delicate love seat. The craggy New Englander was not the sort of person for whom such pieces were designed. The other man, however – Cooper didn't know him – seemed very much at ease on the couch. His clothes looked English; dark, thin pinstripes and cut close.

The White House's Robert Webster was the fourth man.

'You know Norton and Webster, General. May I introduce Walter Madison ... Madison, General Cooper.'

The men shook hands. Knapp indicated a chair for Cooper and said, 'Mr Madison is Trevayne's attorney.'

'What?' The Brigadier looked questioningly at the Senator.

'It's all right, Cooper.' Norton shifted in the stiffly upholstered love seat as he spoke. He didn't feel the need to add anything further.

Webster, standing by the piano, highball in hand, was more understanding. 'Mr Madison is aware of our problems; he's cooperating with us.'

The Brigadier unlocked his attaché case, opened it, and extracted several typewritten pages. Madison elegantly uncrossed and crossed his legs. He asked calmly, 'How is Andrew? I haven't heard from him in weeks.'

Cooper looked up from his papers. It was obvious that he thought Madison's question was foolish. 'He's busy.'

'What have you learned?' Norton was impatient. He rose and walked to the couch – to the opposite end from Madison. Knapp kept his eyes on Cooper; he sat down in an armchair to the right of the General.

'Major Bonner spent the better part of the afternoon and evening trying to find the subcommittee's airline reservations. There were none. Thinking they might have used false names, he ran tracers on all male passengers coming into and out of the Boise airport during the past several days. They all proved out. He went to private aircraft; same answer.' Cooper paused briefly; he wanted the pols to recognize the thoroughness of Defense personnel. 'He then questioned several pilots and learned there was another airfield used exclusively for noncommercial aircraft; runway, medium-sized. Five thousand feet; sufficient for small jets. On the other side of Boise, eight to ten miles out of town. It's called Ada County Airport.'

'General?' It was Knapp who was impatient now. The military was usually circumlocutory about a problem it hadn't solved. 'I'm sure Major Bonner is an efficient officer, but I wish you'd get to the point.'

'I'll *do* that, Senator. But I'll get there by giving you this information, because you should have it. *We* should have it. It bears considerably on the subcommittee's actions.'

'I stand corrected. Go ahead, if you please.'

'Ada County has a lot of corporate traffic. The flight plans generally list only the pilot, the company, and, perhaps, the executive who ordered the aircraft. Rarely passengers. Bonner thought it might be a dead end. Trevayne knows a lot of people in companies that fly their own planes; his staff personnel could be unlisted passengers ... Then he found it. Two Lear jets chartered in the name of Douglas Pace.'

Walter Madison abruptly uncrossed his legs and sat forward.

'Who the hell is Douglas Pace?' asked Norton.

Walter Madison answered. 'He's Trevayne's brother-in-law.'

Robert Webster whistled softly by the piano. General Cooper turned to Knapp. 'Trevayne not only avoided all the commercial airlines, he also used an out-of-the-way field and flight plans under another name.'

Knapp wasn't convinced that Trevayne's caution required Cooper's elaborate explanation, but Knapp decided to let him enjoy the moment. 'Commendable job ... Where had they flown in from?'

Cooper looked down at the papers. 'According to Flight Service Stations, the first Lear was traced back to San Francisco, where Air Traffic Control confirmed its destination as San Bernardino. No amended flight plan filed with ATC.'

'What?' Senator Norton was constantly annoyed by the Army's use of short, staccato-sounding agencies and departments he'd never heard of or knew little about.

Webster, still by the piano, was once again understanding; this time on Norton's behalf. 'Flight plans can be amended within several minutes after a plane leaves the field, Senator. The information is filed with Traffic Control, not FSS. Flight Service rarely gets the information for hours, if at all. It's one way to confuse tracers.'

Norton looked over his shoulder at Webster with suspicious respect. He didn't know what Webster was talking about. Cooper continued.

'While the aircraft was in San Bernardino, Trevayne remained in San Francisco. Alan Martin did not.'

'He's the comptroller from Pace-Trevayne in New Haven, isn't he?' asked Knapp.

'Yes,' replied Cooper. 'And San Bernardino's twenty minutes from Pasadena. Genessee plants; there've been a lot of problems down there.'

Knapp looked at Norton. 'Go on, General.'

'The Lear left Thursday morning, destination Boise, Idaho. It remained at the Ada County field for only an hour and then took off for Tacoma, Washington. Bonner confirms that at that point Alan Martin returned, and the young lawyer, Sam Vicarson, was removed from the scene.'

'Tacoma!' shouted Norton angrily. 'What the hell is in Tacoma?'

Robert Webster drank his drink; he was getting drunk. He looked down at the dishevelled New Englander. 'Tacoma is in the state of Washington, Senator Norton. An hour's drive up the Puget is a city called Seattle. Just outside that city is a complex of buildings with ten-foot-high fences all around. By coincidence it has something to do with Genessee Industries. Its name is Bellstar.'

'Oh, Jesus!' Norton did not look at the White House aide this time. He was staring at Knapp, who addressed General Cooper.

'What about the second Lear? Do you have anything on it?'

'Everything,' answered Cooper. 'Tracing the FPs back from Boise, the plane was flown from Houston International. Its point of origin was Dulles Airport. Our informants at the Potomac Towers tell us that an aeronautical engineer named Michael Ryan was absent from the offices. Bonner confirms that Ryan showed up in Boise.'

Alan Knapp spoke quietly. 'Then Ryan was in Houston. We can presume he was at the Genessee laboratories. They have check-in ledgers. Let's find out who he went to see.' He rose from his chair and started for an antique desk with a French telephone on its sculptured top. 'I know who to call.'

'Don't bother, Senator. We called. Ryan never went to the labs.'

Knapp stopped and turned to Cooper. 'Are you sure? I mean, how can you be sure?'

'We also know who to call. *I* know who to call.' Both men stared at each other. It was checkmate, and then some. The permanent career officer had made it clear to this elected – impermanent – official that there were doors the military could unlock effortlessly that the politicians might not be able to find. Knapp understood.

There were such doors.

'All right, General. Ryan wasn't at the labs. Where was he? Why did he go to Houston?'

'Since I learned within the hour that he wasn't on Genessee property, I haven't had time to find out.'

'Can you?'

'Again, time.'

'We don't *have* time!' interjected Norton from the couch. 'Goddamn it! This is rough weather!'

'Oh, for God's sake, stow that crap!' yelled Knapp. Senator Alan Knapp had been a decorated naval officer, and Norton's excessive use of sea language maddened him.

'Now, just a minute!'

'All right, all right!' Knapp retreated. 'Sorry, Jim ... What are you figuring on, General?'

'I thought we'd discuss that ... Along with a prior consideration.'

Robert Webster moved from the piano and spoke. 'Trevayne sends a top financial analyst to Pasadena. To see who? Why? ... An aeronautical engineer – one of the best, by the way – to Houston. Ryan may not have been *in* the labs, but he sure as hell was in Houston to see someone connected with them ... And a lawyer to Bellstar; that's dangerous. I don't like it.' Webster sipped his replenished drink and stared straight ahead, at nothing. 'Trevayne's cutting near a jugular.'

'I *think*' – Walter Madison stretched his arms through his fashionable sleeves and leaned back on the couch – 'that you all should be reminded that Andrew could not, *can* not, come up with anything more than minor corruption. It's just as well that he finds it, if he does. It will satisfy his puritan streak.'

'That's a pretty goddamn blanket statement, Madison.' Knapp returned to his chair. He remembered how bewildered the lawyer had been at the hearing, months ago. He was astonished now at his calm.

'It's simply true. Legally, every overrun at Genessee has been substantially vindicated. And that's what he's looking into; that's what he's going after. I've spent weeks examining every congressional question. I've put my best staff on every problem. A little stealing, yes; and Andrew will nail it. Beyond that, nothing.'

'You're supposed to be a good man,' said Norton. 'I hope you're as good as the supposers say you are.'

'I can assure you I am, Senator. My fees might help to convince you.'

'I still want to know what Trevayne's been after. You'll find out, General?' asked Senator Knapp.

'Within forty-eight hours.'

25

Friday morning in Washington, and no one knew he was there. The Lear jet landed at Dulles at seven thirty, and at ten minutes past eight Trevayne walked into the rented house in Tawning Spring. He showered, changed clothes, and allowed himself an hour to sit and collect his thoughts, let the pressures of the fast trip from Boise wear off. He was good at pacing himself, he believed. He worked well under tension, because he tried never to permit tension and exhaustion to be simultaneous – mental exhaustion. And he was aware that now, during these next few days, he had to be very careful. It would be so easy for his mind, his imagination, to work itself into such a state of anxiety that thinking clearly might be impossible.

He phoned for a Tawning Spring taxi and was driven into Washington to the Senate Office Building.

It was ten twenty-five; Senator Mitchell Armbruster would be returning to his office within minutes. He had been on the floor for a quorum demanded by his party, but there was no other business of consequence. Armbruster was expected back by ten thirty at the latest. For a routine Friday-morning meeting with his staff.

Andy stood in the corridor outside Armbruster's door and waited. He leaned against the wall and halfheartedly leafed through the Washington *Post*. The editorial once again was a scathing appraisal of Congress' progress; the House criticized for its indecisiveness, the Senate for its obfuscation of pertinent business.

Late November in Washington; perfectly normal.

Trevayne was aware of the fact that Armbruster had seen him first. The small, compact Senator had literally stopped walking; he stood motionless, as if momentarily frozen in astonishment. Indeed, it was this sudden break in the moving human traffic that caused Trevayne to look up from the newspaper.

Armbruster resumed his casual, relaxed posture as he approached Trevayne. He smiled his warm, laconic smile and held out his hand. The moment of silent revelation had passed, but it was absolute, and both men recognized it.

'Well, Mr Trevayne, this is a delightful surprise. I thought you were out in my state, enjoying the scenic wonders of our Pacific.'

'I was, Senator. Then Idaho. But I found it necessary to make a brief, unscheduled return ... To see you.'

Armbruster, the handshake completed, looked questioningly at Trevayne as his smile diminished. 'That's certainly direct ... I'm afraid I have a full calendar today. Perhaps tomorrow morning; or if you like, we could have drinks around five thirty. Dinner's taken.'

'May I suggest that it is most urgent, Senator. I'm seeking the help and advice of your office. Shall we say, on labour statistics in northern California?'

There was a short halt to Mitchell Armbruster's breathing. He was silent for a few moments, his eyes wandering from Trevayne's face. 'I'd rather not speak with you here, in my office ... I'll meet you in an hour.'

'Where?'

'Rock Creek Park. Near the outdoor pavilion. Do you know it?'

'Yes, I do. In an hour ... And, Senator, one more suggestion. Hear what I have to say before you get in touch with anyone. You don't *know* what I'm going to say, sir. It would be best.'

'I said you were direct, Mr Trevayne ... I'll keep my own counsel; because I also think you're an honorable man. But then, I said that before, too. During the hearing.'

'Yes, you did. In an hour, sir.'

The two men walked along the wooded path in Rock Creek Park, the shorter one intermittently lighting his pipe with fresh matches. Trevayne realized that Armbruster's pipe acted as some kind of psychological crutch, an anchor, for the Senator. He remembered during the hearing how Armbruster had toyed with it – fondled it, really – packing and repacking the bowl, scraping the burned-out contents into an ashtray with methodical precision. Now, here in Rock Creek Park, walking casually along a path, he clutched it, held it between his teeth with such force that the muscles of his jaw stood out.

'So you've concluded that I've taken advantage of my office for personal gain,' said Armbruster calmly, his eyes staring straight ahead.

'I do, sir. I don't know any other way to put it. You determined the maximum funding Genessee Industries could handle; made sure it was sufficient for the unemployment recovery – at least, you had the economists back you up; and then guaranteed the amounts. You *had* to get both labour and management support. It won you the election.'

'And that was bad?'

'It was a political manipulation engineered at considerable expense. The country will be paying for it for a long time to come ... Yes, I'd say it was bad.'

'Oh, you rich Brahmins are too holy for words! What about the thousands of families I represent? In some areas unemployment had reached the levels of twelve, thirteen per cent! It was a constituency priority, and I'm damned proud I was able to help. Do I have to remind you that I'm the senior

Senator from the state of California, young man? . . . If you want to know the truth, Trevayne . . .' Armbruster paused and looked up at Andy, chuckling his pleasant, throaty laugh. 'You sound faintly ridiculous.'

Trevayne returned the good-humored laugh and saw that Armbruster's eyes weren't laughing at all. If anything, they were more probing than they had been in the corridor of the Senate Office Building.

'In other words, I'm ridiculous because I don't recognize that what you did was not only good politics – I mean "good" in all senses of the word – but also sound economics? And in line with defence objectives.'

'You're damned right. You're *goddamned* right, young man.'

'It was a question of priorities? A constituency . . . emergency?'

'You're almost poetic. 'Course, you don't scan.'

'It's done every day, that's what you're saying.'

'It's done several *hundred* times a day, and you know it as well as I do. In the House, the Senate, every agency in Washington. What in heaven's name do you think we're in this town for?'

'Even with such extraordinary sums of money?'

'That description is relative.'

'Contracts worth hundreds of millions are relative?'

'What in hell are you driving at? You sound like a ten-year-old.'

'Only one question, Senator. How often are these politically sound, economically feasible arrangements made with Genessee Industries? All over the country.'

Mitchell Armbruster stopped. They were on a small wooden bridge spanning one of Rock Creek Park's many streams. Armbruster stood by the grey-oak railing and looked down at the rushing water. He took his pipe from his mouth and tapped it against the wood.

'That's why you flew in on your . . . unscheduled detour.' He made the statement without any emotion whatsoever.

'Yes.'

'I knew it was . . . Why me, Trevayne?'

'Because I was able to make the practical, provable connection. I think coincidence. Frankly, I wish it were somebody else; but I don't have the time.'

'Is time that important?'

'If what I believe has happened, it is.'

'I'm minor. I fight for political survival so I can present a point of view that's progressively disappearing. It's important that I do that.'

'Tell me.'

Armbruster slowly removed a tobacco pouch from his jacket pocket and began refilling his pipe. He looked up at Trevayne several times, as if searching, wondering. Finally he lit the pipe and leaned his short elbows against the railing.

'What's there to tell? You join an organization, you understand the bylaws, the fundamental rules. As you go on, you find that in order to achieve certain objectives, those bylaws have to be, must be, circumvented. Otherwise you can't get the job done. If you're dedicated, I mean *passionately committed*, to your objectives, you become a very frustrated human being. You begin to doubt your own capabilities, your political virility. You think you're a eunuch ... Then, after a while – at first very subtly – you're told that there *are* ways, if you stop shouting off your big, fat *liberal* mouth. Stop trying to turn everything upside down with rhetoric. Be a little more accommodating ... It's easy to assimilate; they call it the process of maturing. *You* call it at-last-achieving-something. You see the good you're doing; you give just a little, but you get so much more in return ... Goddamn it, it's worth it! Bills are given your name, amendments are named after you. You see the good ... only the good ...'

Armbruster seemed to weary, to tire of his own logic, obviously circulated and recirculated throughout his ever-active brain. Trevayne knew he had to jar the man, make him respond.

'What about Genessee Industries?'

'It's the goddamned key!' Armbruster whipped his head around and stared at Andy. 'It's the funnel ... It's *accepted;* what more can I tell you? It's the watering hole we constantly replenish, it never runs dry ... It's got Mother, God, Country, Liberal, Conservative, Republican, Democrat, Bullmoose, and so help me Christ, the Communes, all wrapped into *one*! It's the answer to every political animal's hunger ... And the strangest thing of all is that it does a good job. That's what's remarkable.'

'I don't think you settle for that, Senator.'

'Of course I don't, young man! ... I've got two more years to go; I won't run again. I'll be sixty-nine years old, that's enough ... Then, perhaps, I'll sit back and wonder.'

'With a Genessee directorship?'

'Probably. Why not?'

Trevayne leaned his back against the railing and took out his cigarettes. Armbruster lit one for him. 'Thank you ... Let me try to put this into perspective, Senator.'

'Do more than that, Trevayne. Drop it from your schedule. Go after the profiteers; what you and your subcommittee *should* be doing. Genessee doesn't qualify. It may be too big, but it produces. It's borne scrutiny well.'

It was Trevayne's turn to laugh, and he did. Out loud and derisively. 'It's borne scrutiny because it's too damned big, too complicated to *scrutinize*! And you know it as well as *I* know what's happening in ... what did you say? – "every agency in Washington". That flag won't get up the pole, Senator. Genessee Industries, the "watering hole", is the fifty-first state. The difference being that the other fifty are beholden to it. Obligated, I think, in a very dangerous way.'

'That's overstating the case.'

'It's understating it. Genessee has no constitution, no two-party system, no checks and balances ... What I want to know from you, Senator, is who are the princes? Who rules this self-contained, self-sufficient, ever-expanding kingdom? And I don't refer to the corporate structure.'

'I don't know that anybody . . . rules. Other than its management.'

'Which management? I've met them; even the money man, Goddard. I don't believe it.'

'Its board of directors.'

'That's too easy. They're place cards at a dinner table.'

'Then I can't answer you. Not "won't", "can't".'

'Are you implying that it just grew – a Topsy?'

'That may be more accurate than you realize.'

'Who speaks for Genessee to the Senate?'

'Oh, Lord, scores of people. There are a dozen committees in which Genessee figures. It's the predominant factor in the aircraft lobby.'

'Aaron Green?'

'I've met Green, of course. Can't say I know him.'

'Isn't he the real account man?'

'He owns an advertising agency, if that's what you mean. Along with ten or twenty other companies.'

'It wasn't a pun, Senator. The accounts I refer to go beyond advertising, although they may be considered part of it.'

'I don't follow you.'

'We've established that Aaron Green administers between seven and twelve million a year – conceivably more – for the purposes of convincing the Washington bureaucracy of the patriotic validity of Genessee Industries and—'

'All registered—'

'Most buried. Anyone with that kind of fiscal responsibility generally has the authority that goes with it.'

'You're speculating.'

'I certainly am. Over unbelievable amounts of petty cash. Year after year . . . Does Green hold the reins?'

'Goddamn, son, you're looking for villains! "Account men", "rulers", "kingdoms", "holding reins" . . . "Fifty-first *state*"!' Armbruster tapped his pipe violently against the railing, clearing out the bowl. Several specks of burning tobacco fell on the back of the Senator's hand, which shook in anger, but Armbruster did not seem to feel the pain. 'Listen to me. For all my political life I've clashed with the big boys! I haven't shrunk. Read over some of those speeches I've made at conventions! I've *set* policy! If you recall, a whole goddamn contingent of right-wingers walked out on me – walked out – in the fifty convention! I didn't waver; I was right!'

'I remember. You were quite a hero.'

'I was right! That's the important thing . . . But I was also wrong. You didn't expect me to say that, did you? I'll tell you where I was wrong. I didn't try to understand; I didn't try hard enough to get to the roots of their thinking, their fears. I didn't try to use the powers of reason. I just condemned. I found my villains, raised my sword of wrath, and smote the hordes of Lucifer . . . Some awfully good men went out of the hall that day. They never came back.'

'Are you drawing a parallel?'

'Of course I am, young man. You think you've found *your* villain, your emissary from Lucifer. Your villain is a concept – bigness. And you're prepared to impale anyone who accepts any aspect of it with *your* sword of wrath ... And that could be a tragic error.'

'Why?'

'Because Genessee Industries has been responsible for a great deal of social good. Very progressive accomplishments. Did you know, for example, that there are drug clinics, day-care centres, mobile medical units in the hearts of some of California's worst ghetto areas, thanks to Genessee? A retraining centre for ex-convicts in Cape Mendocino that's considered a model rehabilitation operation? Genessee financing, Mr Trevayne. There's even the Armbruster Research Cancer Clinic in San Jose. Yes, my name, Trevayne; I convinced Genessee to donate the land and much of the equipment ... Lower your sword, young man.'

Trevayne turned away, just enough to avoid having to look at Mitchell Armbruster. To avoid watching a man who'd traded the voting strength of millions for tax-deductible marbles.

'Then there's no harm in bringing it all out in the open. Let the country know how it's twice blessed. It gets Genessee's superior products as well as its charity.'

'You do that, and they'll phase out the programmes.'

'Why? For being publicly thanked?'

'You know as well as I do that whenever the business community takes on these projects it reserves the right to release only the information it wishes. They'd be swamped.'

'They'd be suspect.'

'Whatever. The losers are in the ghettos, the barrios. Do you want to be responsible?'

'For God's *sake*, Senator, I want *someone* to be responsible!'

'Not everyone's as fortunate as you, Trevayne. We can't all sit in our lofty perches and look down with such impunity – and, I suspect, no little disdain – at the struggle beneath us. Most of us join in that struggle and do the best we can. For others as well as ourselves.'

'Senator, I'm not going to argue utilitarian philosophy with you. You're a debater, I'm not. Maybe we have no quarrel. I don't know. You said your term expires in two years; I've got about two months. Our report will be finished by then. For what it's worth, I think you've accommodated in good faith; you've contributed a great deal of good to a great many people. You may be on the side of the angels, while I'm the one making pacts with Lucifer. Maybe.'

'We all of us do what we can. The best way we can.'

'Again, maybe. Don't interfere with my two months, and I'll do my damnedest not to create any problems for your two years. A simple accommodation, Senator.'

Trevayne's Lear jet climbed rapidly to its cruising altitude of thirty-eight thousand feet. He'd be landing at Westchester airport in a little over an hour. He had decided to surprise Phyllis at the Darien Hospital. He needed the rest, needed the comfort of her gentle humor, her essential reasonableness. And, too, he wanted to allay her fears; she'd been afraid but was too unselfish to burden him.

Then tomorrow morning or afternoon or evening there was Aaron Green.

Four down, two to go.

Aaron Green, New York.

Ian Hamilton, Chicago.

26

Major Paul Bonner found himself actually issuing orders to Brigadier General Lester Cooper. Orders to use only the best CID undercover men and have them span out through Pasadena, Houston and Seattle. To reach Genessee or Bellstar personnel substantively related to any of the issues raised at the San Francisco conference. In Houston, since it was already established that Ryan hadn't gone to the labs, the agents should check with NASA high-level personnel. There had to be any number who knew Ryan; perhaps leads should be unearthed.

Bonner even suggested covers for the agents to use. The men should state that the subcommittee had received threatening communications – letters, telephone calls, et cetera.

It was the sort of cover that led easily into expansive conversations. Civilians were always eager to help the military when it was *protecting* someone. The mere confidence broke down reticence, especially when the inquiries had nothing to do with *them*.

Something was bound to turn up.

And if and when it did, Bonner asked the General to please alert him before taking action, before confronting anyone. He knew Andrew Trevayne better than Cooper did, better than anybody at Defense. He might have suggestions.

The Brigadier was delighted to share his responsibility with the Young Turk.

The last request Bonner made of his superior officer was to have a fighter jet sent down from the Air Force base at Billings, Montana.

If it became necessary, he was going to follow Andrew Trevayne.

It *would* become necessary if he could learn who Trevayne had gone to see. That he'd left for Washington, Bonner knew; the Lear flight plan had been filed with Ada County Traffic Control.

But who in Washington?

There was a chance of finding out, but it would have to wait until morning. He was having breakfast with Alan and Sam; he wondered if Mike Ryan would be there. After breakfast Martin and Vicarson had a final short meeting in Boise; they were all meeting at the airport for a noon plane to Denver.

During that hour or two, Major Paul Bonner would do some reconnoitring.

Paul watched Alan Martin and Sam Vicarson leave the hotel dining room, off to their final Boise conference.

He waited until they'd gone through the dining-room door, then rapidly left the table and followed them into the lobby. Martin stopped at the newsstand, while Vicarson went to the information desk. Bonner kept his back to them, pretending to look over the 'Nightly Entertainment' case. Thirty seconds later Vicarson joined Martin at the newsstand, and the two men walked toward the front entrance. Bonner went to the lobby window and watched them get into a cab.

He'd try Vicarson's room first. Sam seemed closer to Trevayne – or at least the one Andy delegated more authority to. If the front desk balked, he'd give a simple explanation that Sam forgot important papers. The clerk was the one on duty when they'd checked in together. If the clerk proved difficult, Bonner would produce several plastic identifications that would scare the hell out of him.

But when Bonner asked for the key, the laconic clerk handed it to him without question.

Inside Vicarson's room he started with the bureau drawers. There was nothing in them, and Bonner smiled; Sam *was* young. He lived out of a suitcase and a closet.

The suitcase was filled with unlaundered shirts, socks, and underwear. Vicarson was not only young but sloppy, thought Bonner.

He closed the suitcase, lifted it off the bed, and since the desk was nearest, he sat down at it and opened the single top drawer. Stationery had been used, not the envelopes. He picked up the wastebasket and removed two pages of crumpled paper.

One had figures with dollar signs, and Bonner recognized the information as pertinent to a Lockheed subcontractor he'd heard them all talking about.

The other had numbers also, but not dollars. Times. And several notations: '7:30–8:00 Dls.; 10:00–11:30 SA Qu.; Data – Grn. NY.'

Bonner looked at the paper. The '7:30–8:00' was Trevayne's arrival time; he'd learned that from Ada Traffic Control. The '10:00–11:30 SA Qu.' was indecipherable. So, too, was the last line 'Data – Grn. NY.' He took out his ball-point pen and copied the words onto a fresh page, folded it, and put it in his pocket.

He recrumpled the stationery, threw it in the wastebasket, and put the receptacle back on the floor.

In Vicarson's closet he separated the trousers from the jackets and began going through the pockets. He found it in the breast pocket of the second jacket. It was a precisely folded, precisely lettered note from a small appointments book, and it was between several baggage claim-checks. It was the sort of reminder a bright but often careless man might jot down because the information seemed so vital. It read: 'Armbruster. $178 Mill. Duplications. No Defense request. Six-month time lapse. Guarantees confirmed by J.G.'s top acct., L.R. Paid L.R. $300. L.R. offers add'l. data on Pasadena, Bellstar, etc. Price – 4 figures.'

Bonner stared at the note, his anger rising. Had Sam Vicarson met 'L.R.' in a crowded, dimly lit San Francisco cellar with a heavy odor of 'hash' and a bartender only too willing to exchange large bills for smaller ones? Had Sam been told he could make whatever notes he wished as long as he didn't ask 'L.R.' to write anything? Had 'L.R.' fed Vicarson that garbage about a blown-out stomach and a justifiable eagerness to steal from whoever was an accessible mark? Sam was not only young and sloppy, he was also naïve and an amateur. He paid for conjectures, for lies, and then forgot to destroy his notes. Bonner had burned his own notebook. It was so easy to forget – if one was an inept beaver.

The Major instantly made up his mind to carry out his threat; he'd find 'L.R.' and blow out the rest of his stomach.

Later.

Now he had to reach Trevayne. Andrew had to understand that the sewer rats, the double-a's, dealt in lies. Lies and half-lies were their merchandise. Find opponents and feed them – scraps, fragments, appetisers. Always with the promise of vital, explosive information to follow.

Better, *create* opponents.

Trevayne wasn't standing by a possibly diseased wife – such a cheap, undistinguished artifice; he was in Washington seeing the Senator from California. Armbruster was a good man, a friend to Genessee, a powerful friend. But he *was* a senator. Senators were easily frightened. They pretended not to be, but they always were.

Bonner put Vicarson's note in his pocket and left the room. Down in the lobby he returned the key to the front desk and went to a pay phone; he couldn't use the telephone in his room – hotels recorded numbers. He called the airport and asked for Operations.

The stand-by fighter jet from Air Force, Billings, Montana, was to be prepared immediately. Flight plan, straight through to Andrews Field, Virginia. Priority clearance, Defense Department.

As he started for the elevator to go to his room, pack, and check out, Paul Bonner had two reasons to reach Trevayne. One professional, the other personal.

Trevayne had involved himself and his goddamned subcommittee in a witch hunt that had to stop now. They were playing games they didn't understand. They didn't know the jungles. Beavers never did.

The other reason was the very personal lie.

That was sickening.

27

Phyllis Trevayne sat in the chair and listened to her husband as he paced the private hospital room. 'It sounds like an extraordinary monopoly, complete with state and federal protection.'

'Not just protection, Phyl. Participation. The active participation of the legislative and the judicial. That makes it more than a monopoly. It's some kind of giant cartel without definition.'

'I don't understand. That's semantics.'

'Not when the election of a senior senator from the country's most populous state is one result. Or when a decision rendered by an eminent jurist is a Justice Department compromise. That decision – even if eventually appealed and overturned – will cost millions ... billions, before it gets through the courts.'

'What will you learn from these last two? This Green and Ian Hamilton?'

'Probably more of the same. At different levels. Armbruster used the term "funnel", referring to the Genessee appropriations. I think it also applies to Aaron Green. Green's the funnel in which enormous sums of house money are poured, and he allocates it. Year after year ... Hamilton's the one that scares me. He's been a presidential adviser for years.'

Phyllis heard the fear in her husband's voice. He had walked to the window by the bed and leaned against the sill, his face next to the glass. Outside, the late-afternoon sky was overcast; there would be snow flurries by nightfall.

'It seems to me you should be careful before you make assumptions.'

Andy looked over at his wife and smiled with affection, with relief. 'If you knew how many times I've reminded myself of that; it's the toughest part.'

'I should think it would be.'

The telephone rang on the night table. Phyllis went to it. Andy remained by the window. The patrol from 1600 knew he was there, and the doctor. No one else.

'Certainly, Johnny,' said Phyllis as she handed the telephone to her husband. 'It's John Sprague.'

Trevayne pushed himself away from the window. John Sprague, M.D., F.A.C.S., was an across-the-street boyhood friend from Boston. He was now as close a friend as he had been then. And their family physician.

'Yes, Johnny?'

'I don't know how far you want to go with this Hasty Pudding stuff, but the switchboard says there's a call for you. If you're not here, the call's supposed to be given to Phyl's doctor. I can handle it, Andy.'

'Who is it?'

'Man named Vicarson.'

'God, isn't he *something*.'

'He may be. He's also got the price of a toll call.'

'I know. Denver. Can you have it switched here, or shall I go down to the board?'

'Please! With the contributions you make, my partners would fire me. Hang up. It'll ring in a couple of seconds.'

'It's nice to know big shots.'

'It's better to know money. Hang up, Croesus.'

Trevayne pressed down on the telephone button while holding the instrument in his hand. He turned to Phyllis. 'It's Sam Vicarson. I didn't tell him I was coming here. I was to call him later, after his meetings. He's in Denver now. I didn't think he'd be finished by now.' Andy spoke disjointedly, and his wife realized that he was troubled.

The telephone rang; the sound was short, merely a signal.

'Sam?'

'Mr Trevayne. I took a chance you might have driven over there; the airport said the Lear was going to Westchester.'

'Is anything the matter? How did the meetings go with the GM and Lockheed subs?'

'Short and to the point. They've got to come up with better cost sheets, or we threatened penalties. That's not why I'm calling. It's Bonner.'

'What happened?'

'He's gone.'

'What?'

'Just blew. Never showed up for the meetings, checked out of the hotel in Boise this morning, and never met us at the airport. No word, no messages, nothing. We thought you ought to know.'

Andy held the telephone firmly in his hand. He tried to think quickly; he realized that Vicarson expected instructions. 'When did you last see him?'

'This morning at breakfast. In Boise.'

'How did he seem?'

'Fine. A little quiet, but okay. I think he was tired, or hung. He was going to join us at the airport. He never showed.'

'Did I come up in the conversation?'

'Sure; normal. Our concern for your wife, how well you were taking it; that sort of thing.'

'That's all?'

'He did ask what flight you took out last night; figured you had to make rotten connections. Said he might have been able to get you a Defense jet, so it—'

'How did you answer that, Sam?' interrupted Trevayne sharply.

'No problem. We told him we didn't know. We kind of laughed and said with your connections and . . . your money, you probably bought an airline. He took it fine.'

Andy switched the telephone to his other hand and gestured Phyllis to light him a cigarette. He spoke quietly but with assurance to Vicarson.

'Listen to me, Sam. This is what I want you to do. Send a telegram, a very routine telegram, to Bonner's superior . . . No. Wait a minute; we're not sure who that is. Just to the senior personnel officer, Department of Defense. Say you assume Bonner was given a leave for some reason or other. Ask, in the event we *do* need any assistance, who we should reach in Washington. But make the whole thing sound like an afterthought, do you know what I mean?'

'Sure. We just happened to notice he was missing. Probably wouldn't have, except that he was to have dinner with us or something.'

'Exactly. They'll expect some reaction from us.'

'If they know he's not here.'

Mario de Spadante sat at the kitchen table in shirtsleeves. His obese wife was in the process of removing dishes; his daughter, equally obese, dutifully placed a bottle of Strega in front of her father. Mario's younger brother, in a J. Press suit and a wide regimental tie, sat opposite de Spadante, drinking coffee.

Mario waved his wife and daughter out of the room. Alone with his brother, he poured the yellow liquid into a brandy glass and looked up.

'Go on. Be clear, be accurate.'

'There's not much more to tell you. The questions seemed phony: Where was Mr de Spadante? . . . We can only speak with Mr de Spadante . . . It seemed like someone just wanted to know where you were. Then, when I heard they came from Torrington Metals – that's Gino's brother's place – we leaned. This guy Pace, Trevayne's partner, was the one who wanted the information.'

'And you told him I was in Miami.'

'Even gave him the hotel, the one that always says you just checked out.'

'Good. Now Trevayne's back east?'

'That's the word. They took his wife to a hospital in Darien. Cancer tests.'

'Better they should run a few on him. Trevayne's a sick man; he doesn't know how sick he is.'

'What do you want me to do, Mario?'

'Find out exactly where he is. In Darien. Or whether he's in Greenwich and drives back and forth. Or in a motel or some friend's house – Darien's crawling with his type . . . When you find him, let me know. Don't bother before you do. I stopped off in Vegas; I'm drained, Augie, all the way down.'

Augie de Spadante rose from the table. 'I'll go there myself. I'll call you . . . Suppose I find him this afternoon? Tonight?'

'Then you call; isn't that what I said?'

'But you're beat.'

'I'll revive quickly . . . There's been too goddamn much cock-kissing; too much *alternative* bullshit. It's time for Trevayne to get shook. I'm looking forward to that. It'll help make up for nine years ago . . . Arrogant prick! Velvet pig!'

Mario de Spadante spat on his own kitchen table.

28

The hospital dinner was not an ordinary hospital dinner, even by Darien standards. John Sprague had sent an ambulance – albeit no siren – to the best restaurant in the area; it had returned with trays of steak and lobster and two bottles of Châteauneuf du Pape. Dr Sprague also reminded his boyhood friend that the New Year's fund drive would be coming up soon. He looked forward to Andrew's communication.

Phyllis tried to get her husband to talk of other things than his all-consuming subcommittee, but it was impossible. The news of Paul Bonner's disappearance both confused and angered him.

'Couldn't he simply have decided to take a couple of days off? You said he doesn't do much; perhaps he just got fed up, bored. I can easily imagine Paul feeling that way.'

'Not after my heartbreaking story the other morning. He was ready to commandeer the entire Army Medical Corps, do whatever I wanted him to do. Those two conferences – to recall his words – were the least he could do.'

'Darling.' Phyllis put the wineglass on the table-cart and curled her feet under her in the chair. She was suddenly concerned by Andrew's words. 'I like Paul. Oh, I know his opinions are extreme, and you two argue a lot, but I know why I like him ... I've never heard him angry. He always seems so kind, so willing to laugh and have a good time. He's been very nice to us, when you think about it.'

'What's your point? I agree with you.'

'Yet there must be a great deal of anger in him. To do what he's done, be what he is.'

'I'll vouch for it. What else?'

'You didn't tell me before that you had given him such a ... heartbreaking story. You said you'd just told him I was going in for tests.'

'I didn't elaborate, because I'm not very proud of myself.'

'I'm not either ... Which brings me back to Paul. If you say he accepted your story about me and now he's disappeared without a word to anyone, I think he's learned the truth and is trying to find you.'

'That's one hell of a leap!'

'Not really. I think Paul trusts you – trusted you. He disagreed with you,

193

but he trusted you. If there's as much anger in him as we both believe, he won't settle for secondhand explanations. Or postponed ones, either.'

Trevayne understood his wife's logic. It went to the essence of a man like Paul Bonner. A man who looked at *people*, giving them classifications – labels – only when he believed those descriptions fit and were not simply popular. Such a man confronted those who mocked his judgment; he wouldn't wait for third parties to do it for him. Yet Phyllis' assumption was based on Paul's learning the truth – the truth about her. That was impossible. Only three people knew. Sam Vicarson, Alan Martin, and Mike Ryan. Impossible.

'It couldn't be,' said Andy. 'There's absolutely no way he could know.'

'You're an awful liar, Trevayne.' Phyllis smiled.

'I'm getting better. He believed me.'

They settled back in their chairs, and Andy turned on the television set for the seven-o'clock news.

'Maybe we'll find out he left Boise and started a little war somewhere. He'd call it a diversionary tactic,' said Trevayne.

'How are you going to get to Green tomorrow? How do you even know he's in the city?'

'I don't. Not yet ... But I'll reach him. I'll drive over to Barnegat in an hour or so; Vicarson expects my call at ten. He'll have everything he can get on Green, and between us we'll figure something out ... You know, Phyl, I've discovered a very interesting fact of life during the past week.'

'I can't wait.'

'No, it's true.' Andy lifted the glass of wine to his lips. His look was bemused. 'All this nonsense about so-called undercover work – intelligence gathering, whatever name you want to give it. It's really very simple; I mean, it's childish. It's like a game.' He drank the wine and put the glass back on the table-cart. He looked over at his wife – his so goddamned lovely, understanding wife – and added sadly, 'If only the people playing it were children.'

Mario de Spadante was in bed watching the seven-o'clock news. He'd called his wife into his bedroom twice. The first time to bring him an ice-cold Coca-Cola, the second to wheel the portable color set several feet to the left so the reflection of the gold crucifix above his pillow wouldn't interfere with the picture.

Then he told her he was going to sleep soon. She shrugged; she and Mario had had separate bedrooms for years. Separate worlds, really. They barely spoke except at weddings and funerals and when their infant grandchildren were over. But she had a big, beautiful house now. And a big garden and a big kitchen; even a big car and someone to drive her.

She would go back down to the big kitchen and cook something and watch her own television. Maybe call a friend on the fancy French telephone on the marble counter.

There was nothing of consequence within the first three minutes of the news programme, and Mario knew the rest would be twenty-five minutes of 'fill' interspersed with commercials. He reached out for the remote control and turned the set off. He was tired, but not for the reasons he gave his brother. He had stopped off in Las Vegas, but his whoring had been confined to one quick ball, and even then he had to tell the girl to leave immediately; there were too many phone calls coming in. He hadn't gone near the tables, because one of the phone calls had been from the White House contact, Webster. He had to leave Vegas Wednesday, midnight flight.

For Washington.

Even the cool Webster was beginning to lose his grip. Mario realized that everybody was sitting around making plans. Contingency this, contingency that.

Crap!

There was a time for talk and a time to carve flesh. He was finished bugging the electrical system at Barnegat.

Trevayne was for cutting. Now.

A quiet report from another wound-down subcommittee, quietly, respectfully received by those requesting it – buried and forgotten.

That's the way it was going to be.

The telephone rang, and de Spadante was annoyed. Then his annoyance left him; he saw that the lighted button was his private line, not the house phone. Everyone understood that his private line was used only for important business.

'Yes?'

'Mario? Augie.' It was his brother. 'He's here.'

'Where?'

'In the hospital.'

'You sure?'

'Positive. There's a rented car in the parking lot with a Westchester Airport sticker. We checked. It was taken out at three thirty this afternoon. In his own name, too.'

'Where are you calling from?'

De Spadante's brother told him. 'I've got Joey watching the lot.'

'Stay where you are. Tell Joey to follow him if he leaves; don't lose him! Give Joey the number there. I'll meet you as soon as I can.'

'Listen, Mario. There're two guys at the hospital. One's outside the front entrance, the other's inside somewhere. He comes out every now and then—'

'I know. I know who they are. They'll be out of there in a half-hour. Tell Joey to stay out of sight.'

De Spadante held his finger down on the telephone button, then released it. He dialled Robert Webster's private number at the White House. Webster was about to leave for home and was upset that de Spadante had used that number.

'I told you, Mario—'

'*I'm* doing the telling now. Unless you want a couple of unexplained sacks in your files!'

And with unsubtle, barely coded phrases, de Spadante gave his orders. He didn't care how Bobby Webster did it, but he wanted the 1600 Patrol removed immediately.

Mario replaced the telephone and got out of bed. He dressed quickly and after combing his sparse hair opened the top drawer of his bureau. He removed two items.

One was a .38-calibre magazine-clip pistol. The other, an ominous-looking object of black metal with four rings attached to one another above a flat base of ridged iron.

With a clenched fist it would break off a man's jaw from the neck joints. With an open hand it would rip a man's flesh to the bone.

The F-40 jet was given a priority clearance from its holding pattern and landed on runway five at Andrews Air Force Base. At the end of the strip the aircraft made its turn and stopped. The Major climbed out, waved to the pilot, and walked rapidly to a waiting jeep.

Paul Bonner ordered the driver to take him immediately to Operations. The driver pressed the accelerator without greeting or comment. The Major looked like a tight-ass; you didn't try to be friendly with that type.

Bonner walked rapidly into Operations and requested a private office for ten or fifteen minutes. The Operations duty officer, a lieutenant colonel who only minutes ago had called Defense to find out 'What kind of frigging priority this clown Bonner had,' offered the Major his own office. The Lieutenant Colonel had been told what kind of priority was due Major Bonner. By an aide to Brigadier General Lester Cooper.

Paul thanked the Lieutenant Colonel as the latter closed his office door, leaving Bonner alone. The Major instantly reached for the telephone and dialled Cooper's private number. He looked at his watch. It read two forty, which meant that it was twenty to six, eastern time. He cupped the telephone under his chin and began to set the correct time on his watch, but before he was able to do so, Cooper answered.

The General was furious; the Pentagon's Young Turk had no right making decisions that transported him three-quarters across the country without prior consultation, without *permission*, really.

'Major, I think we deserve an explanation,' said the General tersely, knowing Bonner would expect the reprimand.

'I'm not sure there's time, General—'

'*I'm sure there is!* We've covered your request from Billings to Andrews. Now, I think you'd better explain ... Has it occurred to you that even *I* might have to explain?'

'No, it hadn't,' lied Bonner. 'I don't want to argue, General: I'm trying to help, help all of us. I think I can, if I'm able to reach Trevayne.'

'Why? What happened?'

'He's being fed information by a psychopath.'

'*What?* Who?'

'One of Goddard's men. The same one who dealt with us.'

'Oh, Christ!'

'Which means whatever we've learned could be all fouled-up crap ...
He's a sick one, General. He's not after money; I should have spotted that
when he negotiated so low. If what he gave us was on target, he could have
asked three times the amount and we wouldn't have blinked.'

'What he gave *you*, Major. Not *us*.' What Cooper implied put Paul Bonner
on notice. The first of its kind he'd ever received.

'All right, General. What he gave *me* ... And whatever he gave me I
passed on to you, and you acted on it. I don't move in those circles.'

Lester Cooper controlled his anger. The Young Turk was actually
threatening him. There'd been too many threats; the General was wearying of
them. He wasn't capable of dealing with these constant assaults of subtlety.
'There's no cause for insubordination, Major. I'm merely defining lines of
intelligence. We're in this together.'

'In what, General?'

'You know perfectly well! The erosion of military influence; the accelerated
lessening of defence necessities. We're paid to uphold this country's state of
preparedness, not watch it disintegrate!'

'I read you, General.' And Bonner did. Except he suddenly had grave
doubts about his superior's ability to cope with the situation. Cooper was
spewing out Pentagon clichés as though they were biblical revelations. He
was not thoroughly in control of himself, and the circumstances called for
absolute stability. And at this moment of doubt, Bonner made a decision he
knew was not his to make. He would withhold the detailed specifics of why
he came to Washington from Cooper. At least for the time being, until he
spoke to Trevayne.

'... since you condescend to agree with me, Major, I'll expect you in my
office by nineteen hundred. That's an hour and fifteen minutes.' Cooper had
been talking, but Paul was barely aware of it. In some unconscious way he
had dismissed his superior officer.

'General, if that's an order, I'll obey, of course. But I submit sir, that every
minute I spend *not* trying to reach Trevayne could have serious consequences ... He'll *listen* to me.'

There was a pause on the other end of the line, and Bonner knew he'd
win. 'What will you tell him?'

'The truth – as I see it. He's been talking to the wrong person. A
maladjusted psychopath. Perhaps more than one; it's happened before. And
if this source is symptomatic of his other contacts – and it probably is, they
all know each other – he should be told that he's getting biased data.'

'Where is he now?' Bonner could sense the slight relief in the General's
voice.

'All I know is that he's in Washington. I think I can find him.'

Paul could hear Cooper inhale over the wire. The Brigadier was struggling
to make his decision seem wise and strong and well thought-out, when in
reality it was the only decision that could be made. 'I'll expect you to phone
me with a progress report by twenty-three hundred. I'll be at home.'

Bonner was tempted to dispute the order; he had no intention of calling the General at twenty-three hundred. Unless he was doing absolutely nothing.

After lighting one of his infrequent cigarettes, Bonner again picked up the phone and called a friend he knew was on a twelve-to-eight post at Army G-2. A minute later he had the telephone number of Senator Mitchell Armbruster's office and home.

He found him at home.

'Senator, I have to locate Andrew Trevayne.'

'Why call me?' The total lack of expression in Armbruster's voice betrayed him. And like the tumblers in a lock falling into place, Bonner suddenly understood the meaning of Sam Vicarson's notation: '10:00–11:30 SA Qu.'

Senator Armbruster had been in a quorum call on the Senate floor; the call was scheduled between those times, and Trevayne had to know it if he wanted to intercept the man.

'I don't have time for explanations, Senator. I assume you met with Trevayne around noon ...' Bonner paused to hear a denial or a confirmation. There was none, which was the same as the latter. 'It's imperative I find him. In quick words, he's been given highly misleading information; information that compromises a great many people who are completely above reproach – you among them, sir.'

'I have no idea what you're talking about, Major ... Bonner, was it?'

'Senator! There's a hundred and seventy-eight million dollars that Defense can substantiate as a long-standing priority request. Does that give you some idea?'

'I have nothing to say ...'

'You may have if I don't find Trevayne and tell him he's been dealing with enemies of this country! I can't put it any plainer.'

Silence.

'Senator Armbruster!'

'He instructed the cab to take him to Dulles Airport.'

'Thank you, *sir*.'

Bonner slammed down the phone. He leaned back in the Lieutenant Colonel's chair and brought his hand to his forehead. Oh Christ! he thought, the age of instant mobility! He reached for the telephone once again and called Traffic Control, Dulles.

The Lear jet under charter to Douglas Pace has left the airport at two-seventeen in the afternoon. Destination: Westchester, New York. Arrival time: three twenty-four.

So Trevayne had gone home – or near home. And if that was so, he would see his wife – especially under the strained circumstances. Of course, he'd go to his wife! It was inconceivable that he wouldn't. Andy had that rare thing, a wife he *liked* – beyond the love, thought Bonner. Trevayne would travel miles, take hours, to be in her company, even for short periods of time. Most married men he knew would travel miles and take hours to avoid theirs.

Paul walked to the door, opened it, and looked for the Lieutenant Colonel.

He was standing by a complex panel of instruments studying some pages on a clipboard.

'Colonel, I need a pilot. Would you have my plane refuelled and checked out as soon as possible?'

'Hey, wait a minute, Major. We don't run Andrews Field for your personal convenience!'

'I need a pilot, Colonel. Mine's been on call for over twenty-four hours.'

'That could just be *your* problem.'

'Colonel, do you want General Cooper's private telephone number and *you* tell *him* it's my problem? I'll be happy to give it to you.'

The Lieutenant Colonel lowered the clipboard and searched the face of the Major. 'You're with counter-intelligence, aren't you?'

Bonner waited a few seconds before making his reply.

'You know I can't answer that.'

'Which gives me my answer.'

'Do you want the General's private number?'

'You'll have your pilot ... When do you want to be airborne?'

Paul looked up at the numerous dials on the wall. It was just seven o'clock, eastern time.

'An hour ago, Colonel.'

29

Bonner had gotten the name of the private hospital from 1600 Security. He then processed a driving route from Andrews Transport, secured a vehicle to be at his disposal once he arrived at Westchester, and thanked the Lieutenant Colonel with as much sincerity as he could muster.

The vehicle turned out to be a motor-pool sedan which an Army corporal from some totally obscure post in Nyack, New York, had driven over to the Westchester airport.

Since the Corporal expected he would be the Major's driver, Bonner gave him twenty dollars to find his way back to his unmapped base in Nyack. The Major also informed the Corporal that there was no point in his returning before noon on the following day, and gave him a note so specifying. The Corporal was delighted.

Bonner drove up to the open iron gates of the hospital and entered the circular drive. The clock on the dashboard read nine thirty-five. There were no automobiles in the circle; two illuminated signs directed cars to a parking lot on the far side of the building. Bonner was not about to be so directed. Instead, he clung to the right of the driveway – so as to let other cars pass – and parked half on the grass. There were flurries of snow descending; wet, not sticking to the ground for long before melting. He got out of the car and automatically expected the 1600 Patrol to approach. It was, after all, an Army vehicle. He was prepared to deal with them. Explain, if necessary; which, of course, it would be.

No one came into view.

Bonner was confused. He'd read the rigid instructions the 1600 Patrol were to follow. With such buildings as the private hospital, housing a singular vehicular entrance and no more than three stories in height, one man was to remain outside, the other within, both in constant radio contact. The men from 1600 were the best in matters of security. They would not deviate except in an emergency.

To make certain it was not simply a case of observance without contact, Bonner walked slowly around the car and spoke clearly, projecting his voice slightly, not shouting.

'Bonner, Paul. Major, DOD "Sixteen hundred", please respond ... Repeat. "Sixteen hundred", please reply.'

Nothing. Only the silent tone of the night, the muted hum of the peaceful building.

Paul Bonner reached under his tunic to his belt. He withdrew his 'civilian' pistol – a custom-tooled, short-barreled, heavy .44. It would blow a human being into a jack-knifed, flying corpse.

He raced across the drive to the front entrance of the private hospital. He couldn't know what was happening inside. His uniform might be a deterrent or a provocation – it was certainly a target. He put the pistol in his tunic pocket and kept his hand on the stock, his finger curled in the trigger housing; with his thumb he released the safety and held the weapon in a horizontal position. He was prepared to fire through the cloth.

He turned the large brass knob quietly, and swiftly opened the white colonial door, startling an attractive, intelligent-looking nurse behind an admissions counter. She'd been reading at the desk; there was no panic within. He approached and spoke calmly.

'Miss, my name is Bonner. I understand Mrs Andrew Trevayne is a patient here.'

'Yes ... Colonel.'

'"Major" is fine.'

'I can never get those insignias straight,' said the girl pleasantly, getting out of the chair.

'I have trouble myself; the Navy stripes always confuse me.' Bonner looked around for the 1600 Patrol.

No one.

'Yes, Mrs Trevayne's a patient. Is she expecting you? It's somewhat after the usual visiting hours, Major.'

'Actually, I'm looking for *Mr* Trevayne. I was told I'd find him here.'

'I'm afraid you've missed him. He left about an hour ago.'

'Oh? Then I wonder ... perhaps I might speak with Mrs Trevayne's driver. I believe arrangements were made for a driver and a secretary; I think ...'

'It's all right, Major,' said the nurse, smiling. 'Our registration book is filled with "captains and kings", and people who keep them from being bothered by other people. I gather you're referring to the two gentlemen who arrived with Mrs Trevayne. Nice guys.'

'That's who I'm referring to. Where are they?'

'It's not your night, Major. *They* left before Mr Trevayne.'

'Did they say where they were going? It's really quite urgent that I talk to them.'

'No ... Mr Callahan, the one in the corridor, got a phone call around seven thirty. All he said was that he and his friend had the night off. I think he liked the idea.'

'Who took the call? I mean, do you know where it came from?' Bonner tried to conceal his anxiety, none too successfully.

'The switchboard.' The nurse understood the look in Paul's eyes. 'Shall I ask the operator if she can recall?'

'Please.'

The girl crossed rapidly to a white paneled door to the right, behind the counter, and opened it. Bonner could see a small switchboard and a middle-aged woman seated in front of it. He thought how different things were in a private hospital; even a switchboard was kept from public scrutiny. No large glass walls with impersonal robots plugging in wires; no starched, hard mannequins announcing institutional names over the hectic drone of mechanized activity. Everything secreted gracefully, everything personal, so nonpublic; elegant, somehow.

The nurse returned. 'The call was long-distance; a Washington, DC, operator. Person-to-person for Mr Callahan, Mrs Trevayne's party.'

'And then he left?' Paul's anxiety turned to concrete fear. On several levels; for a number of reasons. There had to be an explanation, and he had to know what it was.

'That's right,' answered the girl, 'Major? Would you like to use the telephone?'

Bonner felt relief at the nurse's perception. 'I would very much. Is there—'

'There's a phone in the waiting room. Right through there.' She pointed at an open door across the hall. 'On the table next to the window. Just tell the operator to bill it to room . . . two-twelve. You'll have privacy.'

'You're very kind.'

'You're very uptight.'

The 'waiting room' was a living room, gracefully secreted, warmly appointed, rugs on the floor. So different from the plastic couches and the confusing array of magazine racks usually found in hospitals.

Paul gave the Washington number to the operator, and before the first ring was completed, 1600 Security answered.

'It's Major Bonner again. Is this the same—'

'Right, Major. Four-to-twelve shift. Did you find the place?'

'Yes, I'm calling from there. What happened?'

'What happened where?'

'Here. Darien. Who relieved the men?'

'Relieved? What are you talking about?'

'The men were relieved. They were released at seven-thirty, or around then. Why?'

'No one released anybody, Bonner. What the hell are you talking about?'

'The men aren't *here*.'

'Look around, Major. They're there. They may not want you to know it, but—'

'I'm telling you, they *left*. Do you have a man named Callahan?'

'Hold it. I'll get the route sheet; it's right over here . . . Yes, Callahan and Ellis. They're on till two A.M.'

'They're *not* on, goddamn it! Callahan got a phone call from Washington. At seven thirty. He left; he told the nurse he and his partner had the night off.'

'That's crazy! No release went out. If it did, I'd know about it; it'd be listed on the route sheet. Damn it, Bonner, I'd be the one to make contact.'

'Are you telling me Callahan lied? He's not here; take my word for it. Neither of them is.'

'There'd be no reason for Callahan to lie. On the other hand, he couldn't have been released unless the call came from here. He *couldn't* have—'

'Why not?'

'Well, routine procedures ... you know. ID codes change every twenty-four hours. Those words are locked tight. He'd have to be given a code phrase before he accepted any instructions. *You* know ...'

'Then somebody's got your words, buddy, 'cause the boys have gone.'

'That's just *crazy*!'

'Look, I don't want to argue; get the next team over.'

'They're due at two—'

'Now!'

'They'll be pissed off; I may have trouble finding—'

'Then use locals! Get this post covered within fifteen minutes! I don't care if you have to use the Darien Boy Scouts! And find out who called Callahan.'

'Take it easy, Major. You're not running this office.'

'You may not be either if a foul-up like this can happen!'

'Hey, wait a minute! You know who could have released them?'

'Who?'

'Trevayne.'

'He was upstairs with his wife when the call came.'

'He could have told them *before*, you know. I mean Callahan's call could have been personal. Those guys *do* have wives and families, you know. People don't think of that. *I* have to.'

'You sound just dandy, buddy. Do as I tell you; I'll have DOD Security check up on you.' Bonner replaced the phone with irritation. And then he thought about 1600's suggestion. *If* Andy had spoken to the Patrol, it was conceivable that he wasn't giving them time off but, instead, sending them somewhere else. It was remote but possible. And if it was possible, it meant that Andy expected an emergency somewhere else. Otherwise he wouldn't leave Phyllis exposed for even a short period.

But if he hadn't released the patrol, it meant someone else had. Without authorization.

Andrew Trevayne was either setting a trap or the object of one.

Paul walked back through the door to the admissions desk. The nurse greeted him.

'Hi. Everything okay?'

'I think so. You've been a great help, and I'm going to have to burden you further ... We're security people, and we always make errors on the side of caution. Do you have a night watchman or a guard?'

'Yes. Two.'

Bonner calmly requested that the men be stationed, one outside Phyllis' door, the other in the lobby, which, he presumed, would cover the man's normal duties. He explained that a simple scheduling mistake had taken place, and it was necessary – formally, if for no other reason – that men be posted. Others would be sent shortly to relieve them.

'I understand, Major,' said the girl, with equal calm. And Bonner believed she did.

'You said room two-twelve. I assume that's the second floor? I'd like to see Mrs Trevayne. May I?'

'Of course. Up the stairs to the left. It's the room at the end of the corridor. Shall I ring through?'

'If you have to, by all means. I'd rather you didn't.'

'I don't.'

'Thank you . . . You're very kind. But I said that, didn't I?' As Paul Bonner looked at the assured, lovely face of the girl, he recognized a professional; as he was a professional. He felt that she knew it, too. It happened so seldom these days.

'I'd better go up,' he said.

Bonner raced up the stairs and into the second floor corridor. He ran to the end. Room two-twelve was closed; most of the others were open. He knocked rapidly, and the instant he heard Phyllis' voice, he opened it.

'Paul! My God!' She was sitting in the chair reading a book.

'Phyllis, where's Andy?'

'Just calm down, Paul!' Phyllis was obviously afraid for her husband. Paul Bonner had a wild look about him. She hadn't seen that look before. 'I *knew* it; but you don't understand. Now, close the door, and let me talk to you.'

'*You* don't understand, and *I* don't have time. Where did he go?' The Major saw that Phyllis was going to stall him, stall for her husband. He didn't want to tell her about the removal of the patrol, but he had to get his message across. He closed the door and approached the chair. 'Listen to me, Phyllis. I want to help Andy . . . Sure, I'm mad as hell about this whole hospital bull, but that can wait. Right now I've got to *find* him!'

'Something's happened.' Phyllis' fear took another turn. 'Is he in trouble?'

'I'm not sure, but he could be.'

'You didn't follow him all the way from Boise or Denver unless you *were* sure. What is it?'

'*Please*, Phyl! Just tell me where he is.'

'He drove back to Barnegat . . .'

'I don't know the area. Which road would he take?'

'Merritt Parkway. It's about a half-mile to your left as you leave the hospital. On Calibar Lane.'

'What exit on the parkway?'

'First Greenwich toll. You turn right out of the ramp and get on Shore Road. Stay on it for about six miles. There's a fork; the left is Shore Road, Northwest . . .'

'That's the one that becomes dirt?'

'It's our property line . . . Paul, what *is* it?'

'I . . . I just have to talk to him. Goodbye, Phyl.' Bonner opened the door and closed it rapidly behind him. He didn't want Phyllis to see him running down the corridor.

The exit ramp at the first Greenwich toll station had a speed limit of twenty-five miles an hour. Paul Bonner was going over forty, although making sure the tires gripped the wet pavement. On Shore Road he passed car after car, scrutinizing each one as best he could while the speedometer crept toward seventy.

He reached the fork, travelled about a mile and a half, and the road became dirt. He had entered the property of High Barnegat.

He slowed down; the snow was falling heavier now, the reflection of the headlights creating thousands of dancing white spots. He had driven the road perhaps three or four times during the weekend he'd spent with the Trevaynes, but he wasn't sure of the turns.

Suddenly he had to stop. A flashlight was waving in small circles about a hundred yards ahead. A man came running towards the car. Bonner's window was open.

'Mario. Mario ... It's Joey.' The voice was urgent but not loud.

Bonner waited in the seat, his hand gripping his pistol. The stranger stopped. The car was not the car he expected. The night, the wet snow, the glare of the headlights on the private back road, had caused the man to see what he anticipated, not what was there. An Army vehicle with its unmistakable dull-brown finish. He reached into his jacket – to a holster, for a weapon, thought Paul.

'Hold it! Stay where you are! You move, you're dead!' The Major opened his door and crouched.

Four shots, muffled by a silencer, was the stranger's reply. Three bullets embedded themselves in the metal of the door; one shattered the windshield above the steering wheel, leaving a tiny hole in the centre of the cracked glass. Bonner could hear the man begin to back away on the soft, snow-covered road. He raised his head; another puff of the silencer was heard, and a bullet whistled through the air above him.

Paul whipped to the rear of the car, protected by the open door, and flung himself on the ground. Underneath, between the two front tires, he could see the man running towards the woods, looking back, shielding his eyes against the glare of the lights. The man stopped at the edge of the trees, his body in shadows about forty yards down the road. It was obvious that the man wanted to come back to the Army car, to see if he'd hit Paul with his last shot. But he was afraid. Yet for some reason he couldn't leave the scene; couldn't run away. Then the man disappeared into the woods.

Bonner understood. The man with the gun had first come out with his flashlight to stop a car he was expecting. Now he had to get around the Army vehicle – with its alive or dead driver – and intercept the automobile he'd been waiting for.

That meant he'd make his way west through the dense forest of High Barnegat to a point behind Paul on Shore Road.

Major Paul Bonner felt a surge of confidence. He had learned his lessons in the Special Forces, in the scores of remote fire bases in Laos and Cambodia where his life and the lives of his team depended upon the swift, silent killing of enemy scouts. He knew the man with the gun who shielded his eyes from the headlights was no match.

Paul quickly estimated the man's distance – the distance to the point at which he'd entered the woods. No more than a hundred and twenty-five feet. Bonner knew he had the time. If he was fast – and quiet.

He dashed from the car to the woods and bent his elbows to fend the branches in front of him – never letting them slap back, never letting them break. He assumed a semi-crouch, his legs thrust forward, his feet nearly balletic as he tested the dark earth beneath him. Once or twice his foot touched a hard object – a rock or a fallen tree limb – and like a trained tentacle, it dodged or went above the object without interrupting the body's motion. In this manner Bonner silently, rapidly made his way thirty feet into the wet, dense foliage. He angled his incursion line on an oblique left course so that when he had penetrated as far as he wished, he was directly parallel to the beams of the headlights out on Shore Road. He found a wide tree trunk and stood up, positioning himself so that whoever crossed between the trunk of the tree and the lights on the road would be silhouetted; Paul would see the man without any chance of being seen.

As he pressed himself against the bark and waited, Bonner recalled how often he had employed this tactic – using the light of the sun at dawn or a low moon at night – to singularly ambush a scout or an infiltrator.

He was good. He knew the jungles.

What did the beavers know?

The man came into view. He was awkwardly sidestepping his way through the woods, shouldering the branches, his eyes on the road, his pistol raised, prepared to fire at any moving thing. He was about fifteen feet from Paul, concentrating on the obscure outline of the Army vehicle.

Paul picked the least obstructed path between himself and the man with the gun and prejudged the timing. He would have to divert the stranger for a second or two; do it in such a way as to cause him to stop at precisely that spot where their paths would meet. He reached down and felt the ground for a rock, a stone. He found one, rose to his feet, and silently counted the man's steps.

He threw the rock with all his strength just above the heavy ground cover toward the car on the road. The sound of the rock's impact on the automobile's hood caused the man to freeze, to fire his reloaded pistol repeatedly. There were five puffs from the silencer, and by the time the man crouched instinctively for protection, Bonner was on him.

He simultaneously grabbed the man's hair and right wrist, crashing his left knee into the gunman's rib cage with enormous force. Paul could hear the crack of the bone tissue as the man screamed in anguish. The pistol dropped, the neck wrenched back, blood matted the scalp where the hair was torn from the flesh.

It was over in less than ten seconds.

The man with the gun was immobilized, pain racking his entire body – but, as Bonner had planned, not unconscious.

He pulled the man out of the woods to the car and threw him into the front. He ran around, got in the driver's seat, and sped down the remaining dirt road to the Trevayne driveway.

The immobilized gunman wept and groaned and pleaded for aid.

Paul remembered that the drive in front of Trevayne's house had an offshoot that led to a large, four-car garage to the left of the main building. He drove into it and pulled the Army vehicle up to an open garage door. There was no automobile inside, so he entered, and as he did so, the man beside him began groaning again in pain. Bonner parked the car, grabbed the man's coat so that the head fell forward, and clenched his fist as tightly as he could. He then punched the anguished man just below the chin line so the blow would render him instantly unconscious, but with no danger of death.

In a way, the Major reflected, it was a humanitarian gesture; there was nothing quite so painful as broken ribs. He turned off the lights and got out of the car.

Running back toward the front entrance, he saw that the door was open. The maid, Lillian, was standing in the light.

'Oh, Major Bonner. I thought I heard a car. How are you, sir?'

'Fine, Lillian. Where's Mr Trevayne?'

'He's downstairs in his study. He's been on the phone since he arrived. I'll ring down and tell him you're here.'

Paul remembered Andy's soundproof study that overlooked the water. He wouldn't have heard the car. Or anything else, for that matter. 'Lillian, I don't want to alarm you, but we've got to turn off all the lights. We've got to do it quickly.'

'I beg your pardon.' Lillian was a modern servant but retained the old traditions. She accepted orders from her employers, not from guests.

'Where is the phone to Mr Trevayne's study?' asked Bonner as he stepped into the hallway. There was no time to convince Lillian.

'Right there, sir,' answered the maid, pointing to a telephone by the staircase. 'Third button, and press "Signal".'

'Paul! What are you doing *here*?'

'We can discuss that – argue it, if you like – later. Right now I want you to tell Lillian to do as I say. I want all the lights off . . . I'm *serious*, Andy.'

Trevayne didn't hesitate. 'Put her on.'

Lillian uttered four words. 'Right away, Mr Trevayne.'

If she hurried, thought Bonner as he looked through to the living room and recalled the few lights on upstairs, it shouldn't take her long. He couldn't take time to help her; he had to talk to Trevayne.

'Lillian, when you've finished, come downstairs to Mr Trevayne's study. There's nothing to worry about. I just want to make sure he doesn't have to meet with someone . . . he doesn't wish to see. It would be embarrassing for both of them.'

The explanation worked. Lillian sighed, half-humorously. She would be calm now; Paul had eliminated the essential fear. He started for the lower-level staircase, which was at the rear of the hallway, careful to keep his walk relaxed. Once on the stairs, he took them three at a time.

Trevayne was standing by his desk, its surface covered with torn-off pages of a yellow pad. 'For God's sake, what is it: What *are* you doing here?'

'You mean, neither Sam nor Alan called you?'

'Sam did. You left in a hurry. Is this ... current tactic so you can take me apart? The Army way. You could probably do it.'

'Oh, shut up! Not that you haven't given me reason.'

Bonner crossed to the single large window.

'You're right. I'm sorry. I thought it was necessary.'

'Don't you have curtains or a shade here?'

'They're electric. Buttons on either side. Here, I'll show—'

'Stay back there!' Bonner barked his order sharply as he found the button and two slatted, vertical blinds came out of each side of the window. 'Jesus! Electronic shades.'

'My brother-in-law; he's obsessed with gadgets.'

'One Douglas Pace. Two Lear jets. Chartered between such diverse locations as San Francisco, San Bernardino, Houston, Boise, Tacoma, and Dulles Airport.' The blind closed, and Bonner turned to face Trevayne. For several moments neither spoke.

'You've put your well-known resourcefulness to work, haven't you, Paul?'

'It wasn't difficult.'

'I don't imagine it was. I've been engaged in a little behind-the-lines work myself. It's overrated.'

'You're understaffed. You don't know what you've left back there ... Someone's after you, Andy. I judge no more than a couple of miles – if we're lucky.'

'What are you talking about?'

Bonner told him as rapidly as possible, before the maid came downstairs. Trevayne's reaction to the patrols was immediate, panicked concern for Phyllis. Paul reduced the issue by explaining the precautions he'd taken. He minimized the encounter in the Barnegat woods, saying only that the injured man was unconscious in Trevayne's garage.

'Do you know anyone named Mario?'

'De Spadante,' answered Andy without a pause.

'The Mafia boss?'

'Yes. He lives in New Haven. He was in San Francisco a couple of days ago. His people tried to cover for him, but we assume it was him.'

'He's on his way here.'

'Then we'll see him.'

'All right, but on our terms. Remember, he was able to remove the patrol. That connects him with someone – someone very important – in Washington. His man tried to kill me.'

'You didn't put it that way,' Andrew replied in a monotone, as if he didn't quite believe Paul.

'Details are time-consuming.' Bonner reached into his tunic and withdrew a gun, handing it to Andy. 'Here's a weapon; I reloaded it. There's a full magazine.' He crossed to Trevayne's desk and took out bullets from his trouser pocket. He put them on the blotter; there were eleven. 'Here are extra shells. Put the gun in your belt; it'll frighten what's-her-name, Lillian ... Is there a door down here, or back here, that can get me to the garage without going out front?'

'Over there.' Trevayne pointed to a heavy oak door that once had been a ship's hatch. 'It goes out to the terrace. There's a flagstone path to the left, past that window—'

'It leads to a side door at the garage,' interrupted Paul, remembering.

'That's right.'

The sound of the maid's footsteps could be heard on the stairs.

'Does Lillian scare easily?' asked Bonner.

'Obviously not. She stays here alone, often for weeks at a time. We've offered to get her a companion; she's always refused. Her husband – he's dead – was a New York cop. What about Phyllis? The hospital. You said you'd check.' Andrew watched Bonner closely.

'Will do.' Paul reached down on the desk for the telephone as Lillian opened the door. Before closing it, she snapped the wall switch in the lower-level hallway, and the lights went out. Trevayne took her aside and spoke softly while Bonner put through a call to 1600 Security.

The Major suffered through the whining discourse of 1600's problems but was satisfied that the relief men were on their way to the hospital, if they weren't there already. His memory temporarily wandered back to the nurse ... Phyllis was in good hands. Bonner hung up as Trevayne spoke from across the room.

'I've told Lillian the truth. As you've told it to me.'

Paul turned and looked at the maid. There was only the single light of the desk lamp, and it was difficult for him to see her eyes. Always the eyes. But he did see that the strong, middle-aged face was calm, the head firm.

'Good.' Bonner crossed to the hatch door. 'I'm going to bring in our friend from the garage. If I hear or see anything, I'll get back here fast, with or without him.'

'Don't you want me to help?' asked Trevayne.

'I don't want you to leave this room! Lock the door behind me.'

30

The man named Joey was slumped forward in the front seat of the Army vehicle, his forehead resting on the dashboard, the blood from his scalp partially congealed in splotches. Bonner pulled him out the door and lifted the gunman's midsection so he could slide his shoulder underneath and carry him fireman-style.

He returned to the side door of the garage and started back toward the terrace. Outside the door he walked along the side of the garage to where the driveway veered to the right, the flagstone path straight ahead toward the rear of the house.

He stopped. There was a dim reflection of light far off on the approach road. If he judged correctly, it was several hundred yards away, near where the man now slumped over his shoulder had tried to kill him. The light moved up and down, the motion emphasized by the falling snow. It was an automobile going over the bumps in the dirt road, the driver travelling slowly. Perhaps looking for a gunman.

Paul ran with his charge back to the study door and knocked. 'Hurry up!'

The door opened, and Bonner raced in, throwing the gunman down on the couch.

'Good Lord, he's a mess!' said Andy.

'Better him than me,' replied the Major. 'Now, listen. There's a car up the road . . . I'm going to let it be your decision, but I want to present my case before you choose an alternative.'

'You sound very military. Is this Fifth Avenue? Sunset Boulevard again? Are *you* bringing out coffins?'

'Cut it out, Andy!'

'Was *that* necessary?' Trevayne spoke angrily, pointing to the unconscious, brutalized man on the couch.

'*Yes!* Do you want to call the police?'

'I certainly do, and I will.' Trevayne started for the desk. Bonner overtook him and leaned across the top, between Andrew and the telephone.

'Will you *listen* to me?'

'This is no private mock battlefield, Major! I don't know what you people are trying to do, but you won't do it *here*. These tactics don't frighten me, soldier-boy.'

'Oh, *Jesus*, you're not reading me.'

'I'm just *beginning* to!'

'Hear me out, Andy. You think I'm part of something that's against you; in a way, maybe I am, but not *this*.'

'You have a remarkable ability for tracing itineraries. Doug Pace, two Lear jets . . .'

'Okay. But not this! Whoever's in that car was able to reach right up into "sixteen hundred". That's out of line!'

'We both know how, though, don't we Major? Genessee Industries!'

'No. Not *this* way. Not a Mario whatever-his-name-is.'

'What *are* you people—'

'Give me a chance to find out. Please! If you call in the police, we never will.'

'Why not?'

'Police matters mean courts and lawyers and horseshit! Give me ten, fifteen minutes.'

Trevayne searched Bonner's face. The Major wasn't lying; the Major was too angry, too bewildered to lie.

'Ten minutes.'

It was Laos again for Paul. He recognized the weakness of his exhilaration but rationalized it by telling himself that a man was cheated if he couldn't practise what he was trained for; and no one was trained better than he. He ran to the end of the terrace, and by instinct, looked down the slope at the stone steps leading to the dock and the boathouse. Always know your environs, commit them to memory; you might use them.

He crept up the lawn, staying close to the side of the house, until he reached the front. There were no headlights in the distance now, no sound but that of the falling snow. He had to assume that whoever was in the car up the road had stopped, shut off the engine, and was on foot.

Good. He knew the area. Not well, but probably better than the intruders.

He saw that the snow was holding to the ground a bit better than it had been, so he removed his tunic in the shadows. A light khaki shirt was less obvious than the dark cloth of a uniform. A little thing, but then, there were no little things – not when patrols were removed without authorization and murder attempted. He dashed across the open lawn to the outer perimeter of the drive and began making his way silently through the bordering woods, toward the dirt road.

Two minutes later he had reached the end of the straight approach to the driveway. He could see the outline of an automobile several hundred feet down the road. And then he saw the glare of a cigarette within.

Suddenly there was the beam of a flashlight pointed downward on the side of the road, his side. It had come from the woods. Then there were voices, agitated, rising and falling, but never loud. Quietly shrill.

Bonner instantly knew what provoked the excitement. The flashlight on the side had come out of the woods precisely where he had pulled the bleeding gunman to the Army car. The snow, still thin, still wet, had not yet covered the blood on the road. The footprints.

A second beam of light emerged from the opposite side. There were three men. The man inside the car got out and threw away his cigarette. Bonner crept forward, every nerve taut, every reflex ready to spring into motion.

He was within a hundred feet now, and began to discern the spoken words. The man who had come out of the automobile was issuing orders.

He instructed the one on his right to go down the road to the house and cut the telephone wires. The 'lieutenant' seemed to understand, which told Bonner something about the man. The second, addressed as 'Augie', was told to walk back behind the car and watch for anyone driving up the road. If he saw anything, he was to shout.

The man called Augie said 'Okay, Mario. I can't think what happened!' 'You can't *think*, fratello!'

So Mario de Spadante was protecting his flanks.

Good, thought Bonner. He'd remove the artillery, expose the flanks.

The first man was really quite simple. He never knew what happened. Paul followed the telephone cables as he was sure the 'lieutenant' would do, and waited in the darkness by a tree. As the man reached into his pocket for a knife, Bonner came forward and crashed a karate hand into the base of his neck. The man fell, urinating through his trousers. The Major removed the knife from the immobile hand.

Since he was a short distance from the study, Paul ran down the slope to the terrace and knocked quietly on the door. It was a time for instilling calm. In others. Andrew spoke through the thick wood.

'Paul?'

'Yes.' The door opened. 'Everything's going to be fine. This de Spadante's alone,' he lied. 'He's waiting in the car; probably for his friend. I'm going to talk to him.'

'Bring him here, Paul. I insist on that. Whatever he's got to say, I want to hear it.'

'My word. It may take a little more time. He backed his car up, and I want to approach him from the rear. So there won't be any trouble. I just wanted you to know. No sweat. I'll have him here in ten, fifteen minutes.' Bonner left quickly, before Trevayne could speak.

It took Bonner less than five minutes to pass de Spadante's car in the woods. As he came parallel, he could see the huge Italian standing by the hood, lighting a cigarette, cupping the flame. He seemed to be kneading something in his hand. He removed the cigarette with his left and then did a strange thing; he placed his right hand on the car and scraped the hood. It was a harsh, grating sound, and incomprehensible to Bonner. It was some kind of furious, destructive gesture with metal against metal.

The man called Augie was sitting on a large white-washed rock in a bend on the road. He held an unlit flashlight in his left hand, a pistol in his right. He was staring straight ahead, shoulders hunched against the cold wetness. He was also on the opposite side of the road from Paul.

Bonner swore to himself in irritation and backtracked swiftly, to cross the road unseen into the opposite woods. Once there, he edged his way west until he was within ten feet of his target. The man had not moved, and Paul realized he was faced with a problem. It would be so easy for the pistol to be fired in surprise, and even if it was silenced, as had been the weapon fired by his assailant, de Spadante would distinguish the sound. If there was no silencer, the report might be heard by Trevayne back in the study. Even soundproof rooms weren't guaranteed against gunfire. Trevayne would telephone the police.

The Major did not want the police. Not yet.

Bonner knew he would have to risk murder.

He withdrew the knife he'd taken from the man at the telephone wires and inched his way forward. The knife was a large utility knife that locked into position. Its point was sharp, its edge like a razor. He knew that if he inserted the blade in the lower-right midsection of a body, the reaction would be spastic: appendages, fingers, would fly out, open, rather than be clutched. The neck would arch back, again spastically, and there would be a brief instant before the windpipe had enough air to emit sound. During that instant he would have to yank the man's mouth nearly out of his head in order to keep him silent, and simultaneously crack the pistol out of his wrist.

The man's life was dependent upon three problems of the assault: the length of blade penetration – internal bleeding; shock, coupled with the temporary cutting off of air, which could cause a death paralysis; and the possibility that the knife would sever vital organs.

There was no alternative; a weapon had been fired at him. The intent was to kill. This man, this mafioso of Mario de Spadante, would not weep for him.

Bonner lunged at the sitting figure and executed the attack. There was no sound but the quick retch of air as the body went limp.

And Major Paul Bonner knew his execution had not been perfect, but, nevertheless, complete. The man called 'Augie' was dead.

He pulled the body off the road, into the woods, and began making his way back toward de Spadante's car. The snow was heavier, wetter now. The juxtaposition of ocean and land created a moisture inhospitable to clean, dry snow. The earth beneath him was getting soft, almost muddy.

He reached a position parallel to the automobile. Mario de Spadante wasn't there. He bent down and crept to the edge of the road.

No one.

And then he saw the outline of the footsteps in the snow. De Spadante had gone toward the house. As he looked closer, he realized that the first few imprints were separated only by inches, then immediately by over a foot or two. The track signs of a man who'd started to run. Something had caused de Spadante to race toward the house.

Bonner tried to imagine why. The 'lieutenant' by the telephone wires would remain unconscious for at least three or four hours; Paul had made sure of that. He'd moved the body out of sight and used the man's belt to tie his legs. It hadn't been pleasant. He'd had trouble with the belt, and the man's trousers had been drenched with urine; he'd rubbed his hands in the snow to try to cleanse them.

Why had de Spadante suddenly, in such a hurry, run to Trevayne's house?

There was no time to speculate. Trevayne's safety was uppermost, and if de Spadante was near the house, that safety was in jeopardy.

Time couldn't be wasted using the woods, either. Bonner started down the road, keeping the footsteps in view. They became clearer, newer, as he approached the drive. Once in sight of the house, his instincts told him to take cover, not expose himself on the open driveway, assess the area before entering it. But his concern for Trevayne overrode his alarms. The footsteps led to the telephone cables, and then sharply angled away onto the driveway, toward the front of the house.

De Spadante was searching, obviously for the man he'd sent to cut the wires. He had to know there'd been a fight, thought Paul. The ground around the telephone housing was disturbed, the snow parted by his dragging the body to the woods.

It was then that Bonner knew he'd been taken – or was about to be taken if he wasn't careful. Of course, de Spadante had seen the ground and the interrupted patterns in the newly fallen snow. Of course, he saw the path created by the immobile body pulled into the tall grass. And he'd done what any man used to the hunt would do; he'd faked out the hunter. He'd tracked away from the area and then doubled back somewhere, somehow, and was waiting; perhaps watching.

Paul rushed to the steps of the front entrance, where the footprints stopped. Where? How?

And then he saw what de Spadante had done, and a grudging respect surfaced for the mafioso. Along the base of the building, behind the shrubbery, the earth was simply damp, black with dirt and peat moss; the snow deflected from above. There was a straight, clear border nearly two feet wide heading straight to the end of the house, to the corner where the telephone wires descended. Bonner bent down and could see the fresh print of a man's shoe.

De Spadante had doubled back, hugging the side of the house. The next logical thing for him to do would be to wait in the shadows. Wait until he found the man who'd attacked his 'lieutenant'.

De Spadante had seen him on the road approaching the drive, had waited, perhaps yards away, for him to run toward the front steps from the telephone wires. Only seconds ago.

But where was he now?

Again the logic of the hunter – or the hunted: de Spadante would use the existing tracks in the wet snow and follow them into the woods.

The Major could not underestimate his opponent. They both were quarry, both hunters now.

He quickly slipped around the front steps to the other side of the raised entrance, dashed to the end of the house, and entered the offshoot drive toward the garage. Once near the garage, he turned right onto the flagstone path that led to the terrace and the stone steps above the dock and the boathouse. Instead of crossing onto the terrace, Bonner jumped over the brick wall and steadied himself on the rocky slope beneath. He made his way around to the stone steps and continued beyond, to a point directly above the boathouse. He crept to the top of the promontory and was at the edge of the ocean side of the Barnegat woods.

He remained on his hands and knees and crawled in the direction of the spot where he'd left the first man. He shut his eyes several times for periods of five seconds so as to make them more sensitive to the darkness. It was a theory doctors disputed, but sworn to by Special Forces infiltrators.

Thirty to forty feet inside the small section of the forest he saw him.

Mario de Spadante squatted by a large fallen tree limb. He was facing the house, a gun in his left hand, his right gripping a low branch to steady his hulking weight. The Italian had positioned himself quite far from his 'lieutenant'. Mario de Spadante wanted to be able to reach the driveway quickly if alerted by the man up the road – the man who lay dead, the result of an imperfect assault.

Bonner rose silently to his feet. He withdrew his forty-four and held it straight out. He stood beside a wide tree, knowing he could dodge behind it at the first sign of hostility.

'The back of your head is my target. I won't miss.'

De Spadante froze, then tried to turn around. Bonner shouted. 'Don't move. You do, and I'll blow your head off . . . Open your fingers in front of you. *Open* them! . . . Now, shake the gun off.'

The Italian complied. 'Who the hell are you?'

'Someone you missed taking out at the hospital, you fat bastard.'

'What hospital? I don't know any hospital.'

'Of course you don't. You're just here making a survey. You don't know anyone named *Joey*; no one named Joey followed Trevayne, set him up for your personal attention.'

De Spadante was furious and unable to conceal it. 'Who sent you?' he asked Bonner in his rasping voice. 'Where are you from?'

'Get up. Slowly!'

De Spadante did so with difficulty. 'Okay . . . Okay. What do you want from me? You know who I am?'

'I know you sent a man down here to cut the telephone wires. That you posted another up the road. Are you expecting someone?'

'Maybe . . . I asked you a question.'

'You asked me several. Start walking out to the drive. And be careful, de Spadante. It wouldn't bother me one bit to kill you.'

'You *know* me!' De Spadante turned.

'Keep walking.'

'You touch me, an army comes after you.'

'Really? I may have one of my own to hold them off.'

De Spadante, now only feet ahead of Bonner, turned while walking, his hands angled in front of him to ward off the branches. In the very dim light he squinted the large eyes in his huge head. 'Yeah ... Yeah, that shirt; that shiny buckle. I saw. You're a soldier.'

'Not one of yours. No family; just colonels and generals. Turn around. Keep moving.'

They reached the edge of the woods and walked onto the driveway.

'Listen, soldier. You're making a mistake. I do a lot of work for you people. You know me, you should know that.'

'You can tell us all about it. Go down the side of the house. Straight ahead. Down to that terrace.'

'Then he *is* here ... Where's that little prick, Joey?'

'You tell me why you left the car in such a hurry to get down here, I'll tell you about Joey.'

'I told that son-of-a-bitch to cut the wires and signal with his flashlight. Cutting a couple of wires don't take no ten minutes.'

'Check. Your friend Joey's inside. He's not well.'

They walked down the sloping lawn on the right side of the house. De Spadante stopped midway to the terrace.

'Move it!'

'Wait a minute. Talk ... What can a little talk do? Two minutes.'

'Let's say I've got a time problem.' Bonner had checked his watch. Actually, he had probably five minutes before Trevayne would telephone the police. And then he wondered. Perhaps de Spadante might tell him something he wouldn't say in front of Trevayne. 'Go ahead.'

'What are you? A captain, maybe? You talk too good for a sergeant-type.'

'I've got rank.'

'Good. Very good. Rank. Very military. Tell you what; this rank of yours. I'll up it one, maybe two. How about that?'

'You'll do *what?*'

'Like I say, maybe you're a captain. What's next? A major? Then a colonel, right? Okay, I guarantee the major. But I can probably get you the colonel.'

'That's horseshit.'

'Come on, soldier. You and me, we have no argument. Put down that gun. We got the same fight; we're on the same side.'

'I'm not on any side of yours.'

'What do you want? Proof? Take me to a phone; I'll give you proof.'

Bonner was stunned. De Spadante was lying, of course; but his arrogance was convincing. 'Who would you call?'

'That's my business. Two-oh-two's the area code. You recognize it, soldier?'

'Washington.'

'I'll go further. The first two numbers of the exchange are eight-eight.'

Christ! Eight-eight-six, thought Bonner. *Defense Department.* 'You're lying.'

'I repeat. Take me to a phone. Before we see Trevayne. You'll never regret it, soldier ... Never.'

De Spadante saw the astonishment on Bonner's face. He also saw the military man's disbelief turning into unwanted reality. Unacceptable reality. And that left him no choice.

De Spadante's foot slid on the snow-covered slope. Not much, just a few inches. Enough to establish the possibility of falling on the wet lawn. He steadied himself.

'Who at Defense would you call?'

'Oh, no. If he wants to talk to you, let *him* tell you. Are you going to take me to a phone?'

'Maybe.'

De Spadante knew the soldier was lying. His other foot slipped, and once more he steadied himself. 'Fucking hill's like ice . . . Come on, soldier. Don't be dumb.'

For a third time de Spadante seemed to lose his balance.

Suddenly, instead of regaining his posture, the Italian's left hand lashed out at Bonner's wrist. With his right he slapped the flat of his palm across Bonner's forearm. The flesh tore open, the sleeve of the shirt instantly saturated with blood. De Spadante whipped his hand up into Bonner's neck; again the flesh ripped open in serrated lacerations.

Paul recoiled, aware that blood was pouring out of him, seeing strips of his own flesh beneath his eyes. Still he held on to the gun, which de Spadante tried to pry loose. He brought his knee into the soft flesh of the Italian's groin, but it had no effect. De Spadante pummelled the other side of Bonner's head with slaps, drawing more blood with each contact. Paul realized that de Spadante's weapon was some kind of razor-sharp implement fitted into his right fist. He had to grab that fist and hold it, keep it away.

De Spadante was beneath him, then above him. They rolled, twisted; slipped on the white, wet earth. Two animals in a death struggle. Still de Spadante locked his immensely strong fingers over the chamber of the forty-four in Bonner's hand; still Bonner held the razor-sharp iron knuckles away from his bleeding wounds.

Bonner kept bringing his knee up with crushing assaults into the Italian's testicles. The repeated hammering began to have an effect. De Spadante's grip lessened. Minutely so, but nevertheless he was weakening. Bonner exploded with his last – he believed it was his last – surge of strength.

The sound of the forty-four was thunderous. It echoed throughout the quiet, white stillness, and within seconds Trevayne came out on the terrace, pistol raised, ready to fire.

Paul Bonner, covered with blood, weaved as he stood up. Mario de Spadante lay in the snow, curled up, his hands clutched over his huge stomach.

Paul's senses were numbed. The images in front of his eyes blurred; his hearing was sporadic – words audible and then indistinguishable. He felt hands over his body. Flesh, his flesh, was being touched. But gently.

And then he heard Trevayne speak. Or, to be more accurate, he was able to make out the words of a single sentence.

'We'll need a tourniquet.'

The blackness enveloped Bonner. He knew he was falling. He wondered what a man like Trevayne knew about tourniquets.

31

Paul Bonner felt the moisture on his neck before he opened his eyes. And then he heard a man's voice quietly making pronouncements. He wanted to stretch, but when he tried, there was a terrible pain in his right arm.

The people came into focus first, then the room. It was a hospital room.

There was a doctor – he had to be a doctor, he was in a white cloth jacket – at his side. Andy and Phyllis were at the foot of the bed.

'Welcome, Major,' said the doctor. 'You've had quite an evening.'

'I'm in Darien?'

'Yes,' answered Trevayne.

'How do you feel, Paul?' Phyllis' eyes couldn't hide the anxiety she felt at the sight of Bonner's dressed wounds.

'Stiff, I guess.'

'You're liable to have a few scars on your neck,' said the doctor. 'He missed your face, fortunately.'

'Is he dead? De Spadante?' Paul found it difficult to speak. Not painful, just exhausting.

'They're operating now. In Greenwich. They give him sixty-forty – against him,' replied the doctor.

'We brought you up here. This is John Sprague, Paul. Our doctor.' Trevayne gestured with his head in Sprague's direction.

'Thank you, doctor.'

'Oh, I didn't do a hell of a lot. A few stitches. Luckily our benefactor here had you squeezed up in a couple of places. And Lillian held your neck in iced compresses for damn near forty-five minutes.'

'You give her a raise, Andy.' Bonner smiled weakly.

'She's got it,' answered Phyllis.

'How long will I be wrapped up like this? When can I get out of here?'

'A few days, perhaps a week. It depends on you. Those stitches have got to set. The right forearm and both sides of your neck are cut up pretty badly.'

'Those are controllable areas, doctor.' Bonner looked up at Sprague. 'An air-flow brace and a simple gauze casing on my arm would work fine.'

'Are you telling me?' Sprague smiled.

'I'm consulting ... I really have to get out of here. No offence, please.'

'Now, just a minute.' Phyllis walked around the bed to Paul's right side.

'As far as I'm concerned, you saved Andy's life. That makes you special material, Major Bonner. I won't have you abused. By you or anyone else.'

'That's sweet, honey, but he also saved—'

'This is getting saccharine,' interrupted Trevayne. 'You need rest, Paul. We'll talk in the morning. I'll be over early.'

'No. Not in the morning. Now.' Bonner looked at Andy, his eyes imploring but stern. 'A few minutes, please.'

'What do you say, John?' Trevayne returned Bonner's look while asking the question.

Sprague watched the interplay between the two men. 'A few minutes means just that. More than two, less than five. I assume you want to be alone; I'll take Phyllis back to her room.' He looked at Trevayne's wife. 'Did your considerate husband think to bring you some Scotch, or should we stop off at my office?'

'I brought it,' Phyllis answered as she bent over Paul and kissed him on the cheek. 'Thank you more than I can ever say. You're a very brave man . . . and very dear. And we apologize.'

John Sprague held the door for Phyllis. As she walked into the hospital corridor, Sprague turned and spoke to Bonner. 'You happen to be right, *doctor*. The neck and the forearm are mobility control areas. The medical concern, however, is that the control be exercised by the patient.'

The door closed, and the two men were alone.

'I didn't think anything like this would happen,' said Bonner.

'If I'd thought it was ever remotely possible, I would have stopped you; I would have phoned the police. A man was killed, Paul.'

'I killed him. They had guns out for you.'

'Then why did you lie to me?'

'Would you have believed me?'

'I'm not sure. All the more reason to call the police. I never thought they'd go this far. It's unbelievable.'

'*"They"* means us, doesn't it?'

'Obviously not *you*. You might have lost your life; you nearly did . . . Genessee Industries.'

'You're wrong. That's what I wanted to prove. I wanted to bring that fat bastard to you so you'd know the truth.' Bonner was finding it difficult to sustain his speech. 'Make him tell you the truth. He's not Genessee; he's not with us.'

'You can't believe that, Paul. Not after tonight.'

'Yes, I can. Just like the information you paid for in San Francisco. You bought it from a certifiable psychopath. "L.R." I know. I paid him, too. Three hundred dollars . . . Funny, isn't it?'

Trevayne couldn't help but smile. 'Actually, it is . . . You *have* been busy. And resourceful. But for accuracy's sake, it wasn't information, per se. It was confirmation. We had the figures.'

'On Armbruster?'

'Yes.'

'He's a good man. He thinks like you do.'

'He's a very good man. And a sad one. There are a lot of sad men. That's the tragedy of this whole thing.'

'In Houston? Pasadena? Tacoma? Or should I say, Seattle?'

'Yes. And right down the line in Greenwich. On an operating table. Only I don't think of him as sad, just filthy. He tried to kill you, Paul. He *is* part of it.'

Bonner looked away from Trevayne. For the first time since the beginning of their numerous serious and semi-serious arguments, Andy saw doubt on Paul's face. 'You can't be sure of that.'

'Yes, I can. He was in San Francisco when we were. He roughed up a congressman from California several weeks ago in Maryland. The Congressman made the mistake of mentioning Genessee when he was drunk . . . He's part of it.'

Bonner was exhausted and began breathing through his mouth. He knew the few minutes were up. He couldn't sustain much more. He could only make one last attempt to convince Trevayne. 'Back off, Andy. You're going to raise a lot more problems than you'll solve. We'll get rid of the scum. You'll magnify things out of proportion.'

'I've heard that before: I won't buy it, Paul.'

'Principles . . . Those goddamn principles your bank account bought for you?'

'Something like that, I guess. I said it at the beginning; I've nothing to gain or lose. I've repeated it several times since . . . for anyone who wants to listen.'

'You're going to do a lot of damage.'

'And there are a lot of people I'll feel genuinely sorry for. I'll probably end up giving them a hand, if that'll make you feel better.'

'Horseshit! I don't give a goddamn about people. I care, care deeply, about this country . . . There isn't *time* for you. We can't slide back!' Bonner was breathing too hard now, and Andy recognized it.

'Okay, Paul. Okay. I'll see you tomorrow.'

Bonner closed his eyes. 'Will . . . you listen to me tomorrow? Will you consider letting us clean our own house? . . . Will you stop? . . . We can clean our own house.' He opened his eyes and stared at Andy.

Trevayne thought for a moment of the rodentlike Roderick Bruce who wanted to crucify Paul Bonner. How he had refused to be cowed by the newsman's threat. Bonner would never know that. 'I respect you, Paul. If the rest were like you, I'd consider the question. But they're not, and the answer is no.'

'Then go to hell . . . Don't come around tomorrow; I don't want to see you.'

'All right.'

Bonner was falling off to sleep. The sleep of a wounded, hurt man. 'I'm going to fight you, Trevayne . . .'

His eyes closed, and Andy let himself out quietly.

32

Trevayne awoke early, before seven o'clock. Outside the bedroom window the morning looked incredibly peaceful. The snow had reached perhaps three inches; enough to cover, but not so heavy as to warp the perfect designs of nature. Beyond the pines and the thousands of speckled foliage on the ocean slope, the water was calm, slowed down for the winter months; only the waves hitting the rocks were irascible, still fighting for identity. This was, after all, the sea.

Andrew decided to make his own breakfast. He didn't want to ring Lillian. She had been through so much.

He spread the yellow pages he'd gathered up from his study desk over the kitchen table. The writing was large, hastily scribbled. It consisted of half-sentences and brief notations, proper nouns and corporate titles. It was the information Vicarson had compiled on Aaron Green: much of it extracted from *Who's Who*; some from public Securities Exchange prospectus files; the remainder – the specifics on personal habits – from a creative director of the Green Agency in New York. The creative head was under the impression that Sam represented a television documentary firm contemplating a feature on Green.

So simple . . . Games. But not for children.

Green was not from Birmingham's *Our Crowd*, as Alan Martin had suggested. There were no Lehmans or Strauses in his family background, no old German-Jewish money giving him entree into the hallowed houses of Seligman or Manfried. Instead, Aaron Green was an immigrant refugee from Stuttgart who arrived in the United States in 1939 at the age of forty. Very little was listed about his life in Germany other than the fact that he'd been a sales representative for a large printing company, Schreibwaren, with branch offices in Berlin and Hamburg. Apparently he'd been married in the late twenties, but the marriage ended before he left Germany just ahead of the Nazi boot. In America, Aaron Green's success was quiet but meteoric. Together with several other older refugees he formed a small printing company in lower Manhattan. Using the advanced plate techniques developed at Schreibwaren – soon to become Hitler's (Goebbels') propaganda printing base – the small firm's ability to outproduce larger competitors soon became apparent to New York's diverse publishing needs.

In a matter of two years the firm had expanded its quarters fourfold; Green, as spokesman, had obtained temporary patents of the Schreibwaren process in his own name; the rest was publishing-printing history.

With America's formal entry into the war and the resultant restrictions on paper and print, only the most efficient survived. And in an industry notorious for trial-and-error waste, Green's operation had a decided advantage. The Schreibwaren process reduced the waste factor to an unheard-of degree, and consequently the production speed was accelerated beyond competitors' imaginations.

Aaron Green's company was awarded huge government printing contracts.

War contracts.

'My old associates speak for Nazi *Schlange*, I, for the lady with the torch. I ask you, who is on the side of the angels?'

At this juncture, Aaron Green made several decisions which ensured his future. He bought out his partners, moved his plant out of Manhattan into inexpensive acreage in southern New Jersey, scoured the immigration rolls for grateful employees, and literally repopulated a dying town with European transplants.

The price of the New Jersey land was negligible, but wouldn't always remain so; the expanding payrolls were peopled with men and women who looked upon their employer as a saviour – the concept of organized labour, unionism, was unthinkable; and once the initial shock of 'all those Jews' moving into the area was overcome and a temple built, Aaron Green's millions were secure. For as his profits accumulated, he purchased additional land for postwar growth and diversification.

A ride down New Jersey's Garden State Parkway to this day bore witness to Green's financial acumen, thought Trevayne as he turned over a yellow page.

After the war, Aaron Green found new interests. He foresaw the enormous profits intrinsic to the rapidly developing television industry, and chose to reach them through advertising. The creativity of the written, spoken, and visualized word.

It was as if the postwar era was waiting for his combined talents. Aaron Green formed the Green Agency and staffed it with the brightest minds he could find. His millions allowed him to raid the best men in existing agencies; his printing facilities afforded him the capability of luring away accounts from others with contracts competitors couldn't match; his contacts within government circles kept antitrust suits at bay, and by the time the television revenue schedules were set, Green's sudden supremacy in magazines, newspapers, and print promotions made the Green Agency the most sought-after advertising firm in New York.

The personal life of Aaron Green was clouded. He had remarried; had two sons and a daughter; lived on Long Island in a mansion that had twenty-odd rooms and gardens rivalling the Tuileries; gave with extraordinary generosity to many charities; published quality literature with no thoughts of profit; and was an espouser of liberal causes. He contributed to political campaigns without much concern for parties, but with a sharp eye for social reform. He had, however, a quirk which ultimately caused him to be brought into court by the American Civil Liberties Union, joined, reluctantly, by the US Employment Service. He refused to hire employees of German extraction. A non-Jewish German name was sufficient to disqualify an applicant.

Aaron Green paid the fines and quietly continued the practice.

Trevayne finished his breakfast and tried to form a picture of Green.

Why Genessee Industries? Why the covert support of the same type of militaristic purpose he'd escaped from and obviously still held in contempt. A man who succoured the dispossessed and championed liberal reforms was not a logical advocate of the Pentagon.

At the Westchester airport he returned the rented car, made arrangements for the jet to be flown to La Guardia later in the day, and hired a helicopter to fly him to Hampton Bays in central Long Island.

At Hampton Bays he rented another car and drove south to the town of Sail Harbor. To Aaron Green's home.

He arrived at the gates at eleven o'clock, and when a startled Green greeted him in the living room, the look in Green's eyes told him that the old gentleman had been alerted.

Aaron Green's handsome Semitic features were creased; there was both sorrow and anger in his countenance. His voice – deep, vibrant, still possessed of an accent after more than thirty years – emerged like the gentle roll of kettle drums.

'It is the Hebrew Sabbath, Mr Trevayne. I might have thought you'd consider that; at least to the extent of a telephone call. This house is Orthodox.'

'My apologies; I didn't know. My schedule is very tight, the decision to drive over here a last-minute one. I was visiting friends nearby . . . I can return at another time . . .'

'Do not compound your offence. East Hampton is not Boise, Idaho. Come out to the porch.' Green led Trevayne to a large glass-enclosed room that looked out over the side and back lawns. There were plants everywhere, the furniture white wrought iron with dozens of printed cushions. It was like a summer garden set down in the middle of a winter snowfall.

It was completely charming.

'Would you care for coffee? Perhaps some sweet buns?' asked Green as Andrew sat down.

'No, thank you.'

'Come, don't let my short temper deprive you of excellent cakes. I can't speak that well of the coffee, but our cook is a superb baker.' Aaron Green, lips tight, smiled warmly.

'I deserved the short temper. I don't deserve your hospitality.'

'Good! Then you'll have some . . . To tell you the truth, I'd like a little *nosh* myself. They won't let me indulge; company is the only way I get around them.' Green walked to a glass-topped iron table by the wall and pressed a button on a white intercom. He spoke in his deep, resonant voice. 'Shirley, darling. Our guest would like coffee and some of your cakes which I have positively advertised. Bring enough for two, and it would be pointless to tell Mrs Green. Thank you, darling.' He returned to the chair opposite Trevayne.

'You're too kind.'

'No. I have merely changed attitudes – from irritation to common sense. That makes me *appear* kind. Don't be fooled ... I was expecting you to call upon me. One day; I wasn't sure when, and certainly did not think it would be so soon.'

'I understand the Defense Department is ... upset. I assume they've contacted you.'

'Most definitely. A number of others as well. You are causing excited reactions in many quarters, Mr Trevayne. You breed fear in men who are paid to be unafraid. I have told several they would not draw an additional week's salary from me. Unfortunately – and I use the word well – they are not in my hire.'

'Then I don't have to beat around the bush, do I?'

'Beating bushes was always a questionable method of hunting, used by the poor because they couldn't afford bait. It had two adverse possibilities. One: the game always had the advantage due to its smell detectors and could choose its avenue of escape. And two: if aroused, it could turn on the hunter and attack without warning. Unseen, as it were ... You can do better, Mr Trevayne. You're neither poor nor unintelligent.'

'On the other hand, I find the idea of placing bait a little distasteful.'

'Excellent! You're very quick; I like you.'

'And I understand why you have such a loyal following.'

'Ahh! Fooled again, my friend. My following – if I *really* have one – has been purchased. We both have money, Mr Trevayne. Surely you've learned, even at your young age, that money begets followers. By itself, isolated, money is useless, merely a by-product. But it can be a bridge. Used correctly, it promulgates the idea. The *idea*, Mr Trevayne. The idea is a greater monument than a temple ... Certainly I have followers. What's more important is that they transport and convey my *ideas*.'

A uniformed servant came through the porch door carrying a silver tray. Green introduced Shirley, and Trevayne stood up – to Green's obvious approval – and helped place the tray on the exquisite wrought-iron coffee table.

Shirley departed quickly, hoping Mr Trevayne would enjoy the cakes.

'A gem! An absolute gem,' said Green. 'I found her at the Israeli Pavilion at the Montreal Exposition. She was American, you know. I had to endow a half a dozen orange groves in Haifa to convince her to come back and work for us ... The cakes, the cakes. Eat!'

The cakes *were* delicious.

'These are marvellous.'

'I told you. Falsehoods may pass in this room with our ensuing conversation, but not about the cakes ... Come, let us enjoy them.'

Both men warily, with some humor, bandied about trivialities until the cakes were finished. Each sized up the other, each found himself confident but apprehensive, as two extremely good tennis players approaching a play-off match.

Green put down his coffee and sighed audibly. 'The *nosh* is finished. We talk ... What are your concerns, Mr Subcommittee Chairman? What brings you to this house under such unusual circumstances?'

'Genessee Industries. You dispense, partially through your agency, an acknowledged seven million a year – we estimate closer to twelve, possibly more – for the purposes of convincing the country that Genessee is intrinsic to our survival. We know you've been doing this for at least ten years. That totals anywhere between seventy and a hundred and twenty million dollars. Again, possibly more.'

'And those figures frighten you?'

'I didn't say that. You were right the first time. They concern me.'

'Why? Even the disparity between the figures can be accounted for; and you *were* right. It is the higher amount.'

'Perhaps accounted for; can they be justified?'

'That would depend on who seeks justification ... Yes, they can be justified. *I* justify them.'

'How?'

Green pressed his back into the chair. The patriarch about to dispense wisdom, thought Trevayne. 'To begin with, a million dollars in today's purchase market is not what the average citizen thinks it is. General Motors alone bills twenty-two million annually in advertising. The new Post Office Utility, seventeen.'

'And they happen to be the two largest consumer corporations on earth. Try again.'

'They're infinitesimal compared to the government. And since the government is the predominant client – consumer – of Genessee Industries, certain scholastic logic might be applicable.'

'But it isn't. Unless the client is, in fact, his own company. Its own source. Even I don't believe that.'

'Every viewpoint has its own visual frame, Mr Trevayne. You look at a tree, you may see the sun reflected off its leaves. I look at it, I see the sunlight filtering through. Two different trees if we described them, wouldn't you say?'

'I fail to see the analogy.'

'Oh, you're capable of seeing it; you simply refuse to. You see only the reflection, not what's underneath.'

'Riddles are annoying, Mr Green, set-up riddles, insulting. For your edification, sir, I've gotten a glimpse of what's underneath, and that's why I'm here under these unusual circumstances.'

'I see.' Green nodded his head. The patriarch again, thought Trevayne; this time tolerantly accepting the inconsequential judgment of an inferior. 'I see. You're a tough fellow. A very hard man . . . You have chutzpah.'

'I'm not selling anything. I don't need chutzpah.'

Suddenly Aaron Green slapped the flat of his hand against the hard metal of his chair. The slap was loud, ugly. 'Of course, you're selling!' The old Jew shouted, his deep voice seemed to echo, his eyes glared at Trevayne. 'You're selling the most despicable merchandise a man can peddle. The narcotic of complacency. Weakness! You should know better.'

'Not guilty. If I'm selling anything, it's the proposition that the country has the right to know how its money is spent. Whether those expenditures are the result of necessity or because an industrial monster has been spawned and become insatiable. Controlled by a small group of men who arbitrarily decide where the millions will be allocated.'

'Schoolboy! You are a schoolboy. You soil your pants . . . What is this "arbitrary"? Who is arbitrary? You set yourself up as a judge of necessity? You imply that from-sea-to-shining-sea there is some great intelligence that is all-knowing? Tell me, Wise Rabbi, where was this mass intellect in nineteen seventeen? In nineteen forty-one? Yes, even in nineteen fifty and sixty-five? I'll tell you where. Standing in weakness, in complacency. And this weakness, this complacency, was paid for. With the blood of hundreds of thousands of beautiful young men.' Green suddenly lowered his voice. 'With the lives of millions of innocent children and their mothers and fathers, marching, straggling naked into the cement walls of death. Do not speak to me of "arbitrary"; you are a fool.'

Trevayne waited until Aaron Green calmed himself. 'I submit, Mr Green, and I say it with respect, that you're applying solutions to problems that belong in another time. We're faced with different problems now. Different priorities.'

'Fancy talk. The reasoning of cowards.'

'The thermonuclear age doesn't have very much room for heroes.'

'More garbage!' Green laughed derisively. He put his two hands together, his elbows at his side. The patriarch toying with an unenlightened adversary, thought Trevayne. 'Tell me, Mr Subcommittee Chairman, what is my crime? You haven't made that clear.'

'You know as well as I do. Using funds inappropriately—'

'Inappropriately or illegally?' Green interrupted, separating his hands, holding them out with their palms up, his deep voice trailing off.

Trevayne paused before answering. By doing so he made clear his distaste. 'The courts decide those questions, when they're capable of it . . . We find out what we can and make recommendations.'

'Just how are these funds used . . . inappropriately?'

'For purposes of persuasion. I suspect an enormous barrel of pork that's distributed to retain support or eliminate opposition to Genessee contracts. In a dozen areas. Labour, talent, Congress, to mention three.'

'You *suspect*? You make charges on what you *suspect*?'

'I've seen enough. I chose those three on the basis of what I've seen.'

'And what *have* you seen? Men growing wealthy beyond their abilities to earn? Worthless endeavours paid for by Genessee Industries? Come, Mr Subcommittee, where is this moral decay? Who, may I ask you, has been so hurt, so corrupted?'

Andrew watched the calm but nearly triumphant expression on Aaron Green's face. And understood the pure genius behind Genessee's use of the bribe. At least with regard to the enormous sums dispensed by Green, the most important commitments. Nothing was paid out that couldn't legally, logically, or at least emotionally be justified. There was Ernest Manolo, the infant labour baron of southern California. What could be more logical than to contain the spiralling national union demands with petty-cash vouchers and jurisdictional guarantees for certain geographical areas? And the brilliant scientist, Ralph Jamison, Ph.D. Should such a mind stop functioning, stop contributing, because it was troubled with real or imaginary problems? And Mitchell Armbruster. Perhaps the saddest of all. The fiery, liberal Senator pushed into line. But who could argue the benefits of the Armbruster Cancer Clinic? The mobile medical units travelling throughout the California ghettos? Who could term such contributions corrupt? What manner of cruel inquisitor would manufacture connectives that surely would cause the generosity to cease?

Inquisitor.

We don't want an inquisitor. Big Billy Hill.

There was Joshua Studebaker, too, plaintively searching for a way to make permanent his past emancipations. But that wasn't Aaron Green's domain. Studebaker belonged somewhere else. Yet if Sam Vicarson spoke the truth, Studebaker and Green were alike. In so many ways; both brilliant, complex; both hurt yet giantlike.

'So?' Green was leaning forward on the chair. 'You find it difficult to be specific about this mass depravity you've uncovered? Come, Mr Subcommittee. At least a for-instance.'

'You're incredible, aren't you?'

'So?' Green was perplexed by Andrew's abruptly inserted question. 'What's incredible?'

'You must have volumes. Each case a history, every expenditure balanced. If I picked an isolated "for-instance", you'd have a story.'

Green understood. He smiled and once again sat back in his chair. 'I have learned the lesson of Sholom Aleichem. I do not buy a billy goat with no testicles. Select, Mr Subcommittee. Give me an example of this degeneracy and I will make a telephone call. Within minutes you will learn the truth.'

'Your truth.'

'The tree, Mr Trevayne. Remember the tree. Which tree are we describing? Yours or mine?'

Andrew pictured in his mind some steel-encased vault with thousands of carefully annotated insertions, a massive directory of corruption. Corruption for him; justification for Aaron Green. It had to be something like that.

To even begin to unravel such an encyclopedia – if he could find it – would take years. And each case a complication in itself.

'Why, Mr Green? Why?' asked Trevayne softly.

'Are we talking, as they say, not on the record?'

'I can't promise that. On the other hand, I don't expect to spend the rest of my life on this subcommittee. If I brought you in, brought in this extraordinary source material of yours, I have an idea that we'd become a permanent fixture in Washington. I'm not prepared for that, and I think you know it.'

'Come with me.' Green got up from his chair; it was the effort of an old man, a tired man. He walked to a glass-louvred door that led to the back lawn. On the wall by the door were several ornate coat hooks, a woollen muffler hanging from one of them. He reached for it and wrapped it around his neck. 'I am an old woman; I need my shawl. You are young; the cold air will be invigorating. The snow beneath your feet won't hurt good leather. I know. When I was a child in the Stuttgart winters, my shoe leather was ersatz. My feet were always cold.'

He opened the door and led Trevayne out on the snow-covered grass. They walked to the far end of the lawn, past burlap-covered bushes and a marble table which stood in front of a white latticed arbour. Summer tea, thought Trevayne. They went just beyond the arbour to the edge of a tall Japanese maple and turned right. This section of the lawn was narrow, bordered by the maple and a row of evergreens on the other side. It was actually a wide path.

The flickering immediately caught Trevayne's eye.

At the end of the wooded corridor was a bronze Star of David raised perhaps a foot above the ground. It measured no larger than twenty or twenty-five inches, and on each side there was a small recessed casing in which a flame burned steadily. It was like a miniature altar protected by fire, the two jets of flame somehow strong and fierce. And very sad.

'No tears, Mr Trevayne. No wringing of hands or mournful wails. It's been nearly half a century now; there's some comfort in that. Or adjustment, as the Viennese doctors say . . . This is in memory of my wife. My first wife, Mr Trevayne; and my first child. A little daughter. We last saw each other through a fence. An ugly, rust-covered fence that tore the flesh off my hands as I tried to rip it apart . . .'

Aaron Green stopped and looked up at Trevayne. He was perfectly calm; if it pained him to remember, the hurt was recessed far inside him. But the memory of horror was in his voice. Its quiet, utter violence was unmistakable.

'Never, *ever* again, Mr Trevayne.'

33

Paul Bonner adjusted the brace so the metal collar was less irritating. The flight from Westchester airport, in the cramped quarters of the plane's bucket seat, had caused considerable chafing on his neck. He'd told his fellow officers in the adjacent Pentagon rooms that he'd jumped the skiing season in Idaho and regretted it.

It wasn't what he was going to tell Brigadier General Lester Cooper. He would tell Cooper the truth.

And demand answers.

He got out of the elevator on the fifth floor – Brasswares – and walked to his left. To the last office in the corridor.

The Brigadier General stared at Paul's bandaged arm and neck and tried his best to hold his reaction in check. Violence, physical violence, was the *last* thing he wanted. *They* wanted. The Young Turk – accustomed to violence, so prone to seek it out – had taken action without authorization.

What, in God's name had he done?

Who had he involved?

'What happened to you?' asked the Brigadier coldly. 'How seriously are you hurt?'

'I'm fine ... As to what happened, sir, I'll need your help.'

'You're insubordinate, Major.'

'Sorry. My neck hurts.'

'I don't even know where you've been. How could I help you?'

'By first telling me why Trevayne's Patrols were removed by untraceable orders so Trevayne could be led into a trap.'

Cooper shot up from the desk. His face was suddenly white with shock. At first he couldn't find the words; he began to stutter, and once again Bonner found the impediment astonishing. Finally: 'What are you saying?'

'My apologies, General. I wanted to know if you'd been informed ... You haven't been.'

'Answer me!'

'I told you. Both sixteen hundreds. White House security men. Someone who knew the ID codes ordered them out of the area. Trevayne was subsequently followed and set up for execution. At least, I think that was the objective.'

'How do you know this?'

'I was there, General.'

'Oh, my God.' Cooper sat down at his desk, his voice trailing off inaudibly. When he looked up at Paul, his expression was that of a bewildered noncom, not that of a brigadier who had acquitted himself superbly in three wars; a man Bonner had held – until three months ago – in his highest esteem. A *commander*, with all that the name implied.

This was not that man. This was a disintegrating, frail human being.

'It's true, General.'

'How did it happen? Tell me what you can.'

So Bonner told him.

Everything.

Cooper simply stared at a picture on the wall as Paul related the events of the previous night. The picture was an oil painting of a remodelled eighteenth-century farmhouse with mountains in the distance: the General's home in Rutland, Vermont. He'd soon be there . . . permanently, thought the Major.

'No doubt you saved Trevayne's life,' said Cooper when Paul had finished.

'I operated on that basis. The fact that I was fired upon convinced me. However, we can't be sure they were there to kill him. If de Spadante lives, maybe we'll find out . . . What I have to know, General, is why de Spadante was there in the first place. What has he got to do with Trevayne? . . . With us?'

'How would I know?' Cooper's attention was back on the oil painting.

'No Twenty Questions, General. My tour of duty's been too inclusive for that. I'm entitled to something more.'

'You watch your mouth, soldier.' Cooper pulled his eyes off the painting, back to Bonner. 'Nobody ordered you to follow that man to the state of Connecticut. You did that on your own.'

'You authorized the plane. You gave me your consent by not counter-manding my proposed intentions.'

'I also ordered you to phone in a progress report by twenty-three hundred hours. You failed to do that. In the absence of that report, any decisions you made were of your own doing. If a superior officer is not apprised of a subordinate's progress—'

'Horseshit!'

Brigadier General Lester Cooper once more stood up, this time not in shock but in anger. 'This is not the barracks, *soldier*, and I'm not your company sergeant. You will apologize forthwith. Consider yourself fortunate that I don't charge you with gross insubordination.'

'I'm glad you can still fight, General. I was beginning to worry . . . I apologize for my expletive, *sir*, I'm sorry if I offended the General, *sir*. But I'm afraid I will *not* withdraw the question . . . *sir!* What has Mario de Spadante got to do with Trevayne's investigation of us? And if you won't tell me, *sir*, I'll go higher up to find out!'

'*Stop it!*' Cooper was breathing hard; his forehead had small rivulets of perspiration at the hairline. He lowered his voice and lost much of his posture. His shoulders came forward, his stomach loose. For Bonner, it was a pathetic sight. 'Stop it, Major. You're beyond your depth. Beyond *my* depth.'

'I can't accept that, General. Don't ask me to. De Spadante is garbage. Yet he told me he could make just one phone call to this building and I'd be a colonel. How could he *say* that? Who was he calling? How? *Why*, General?'

'And who.' Cooper quietly interjected the statement as he sat down in his chair. 'Shall I tell you *who* he was calling?'

'Oh, Christ.' Bonner felt sick.

'Yes, Major. His call would have come to me.'

'I don't believe it.'

'You don't want to believe it, you mean ... Don't make hasty assumptions, soldier. I would have taken the call; it doesn't mean I would have complied.'

'The fact that he was able to reach you is bad enough.'

'Is it? Is it any worse than the hundreds of contacts you've made? From Vientiane to the Mekong Delta to ... the last, I believe, was San Francisco? Is de Spadante so much less reputable than the "garbage" you've dealt with?'

'Entirely different. Those were intelligence runs, usually in hostile territory. You know that.'

'Bought and paid for. Thus bringing us nearer whatever our objectives were at the given times. No different, Major. Mister de Spadante also serves a purpose. And we're in hostile territory, in case you hadn't noticed.'

'What purpose?'

'I can't give you a complete answer; I don't have all the facts; and even if I did, I'm not sure you'd be cleared. I *can* tell you that de Spadante's influence is considerable in a number of vital areas. Transportation is one of them.'

'I thought he was in construction.'

'I'm sure he is. He's also in trucking and waterfront operations. Shipping lines listen to him. Trucking firms give him priority. He gets cooperation when it's necessary.'

'You're implying we *need* him,' said Bonner incredulously.

'We need every*thing* and every*body* we can get, Major. I don't have to tell you that, do I? Go up on the Hill and look around. Every appropriation we ask for gets put through a wringer. We're the politicians' whipping boys; they can't live *with* us. The only supporters we have belong in fruitcake farms. Or in the movies, charging up some goddamn San Juan Hill with Teddy Roosevelt ... We've got *problems*, Major Bonner.'

'And we solve them by using criminals, gunmen? We enlist the support of the Mafia – or aren't we allowed to use the term anymore?'

'We solve them any way we can. I'm surprised at you, Bonner. You amaze me. Since when did someone's way of making a living stop you from using them in the field?'

'Probably never. Because I knew *I* was using *them*, not the other way around. And whatever I did was pretty far down the line. Dog territory. You live differently down there. I had the mistaken idea that you people up here were better than we were. That's right, General, *better*.'

'So you found out we're not, and you're shocked ... Where the hell did you people in "dog territory" think you got your hardware, soldier? From little old ladies in tennis shoes who shouted, "Support our boys" and presto, there were ships full of jet fuel and cargoes of ammunition? Come off it, Major! The weapons you used in the Plain of Jars may have been loaded out of the San Diego waterfront courtesy of Mario de Spadante. The copter that picked you up ten miles south of Haiphong might just be the "snake" we squeezed off a production line somewhere because de Spadante's friends called off a strike. Don't be so particular, Bonner. It doesn't become the "killer from Saigon".'

Deals were made on the waterfront, in the factories. Paul knew that. But that was different. That was as far down the line as 'dog territory' was for him. De Spadante and his gunmen weren't on the waterfront or at a factory last night. They were at Trevayne's *house*. Couldn't the brigadier *see*?

'General.' Bonner spoke slowly but with intensity. 'What I made contact with eighteen hours ago, on the property of the chairman of a subcommittee appointed by the President and the Senate, were two hired killers and a Mafia boss who wore iron spikes on his fist and took a lot of skin off my arm and my neck. For me that's different from stealing files and trying to louse up or outsmart some congressional committee that's determined to knock us out of the box.'

'Why? Because the fight's physical? Not on paper but in the flesh?'

'Maybe ... Maybe it's as simple as that. Or maybe I'm just worried that the next step will be for the de Spadantes to be appointed to the Chiefs of Staff. Or made part of the faculty at the War College ... If they're not on both already.'

'Is he dead?' asked Robert Webster into the telephone, holding his briefcase between his knees in the booth on Michigan Avenue.

'No. He's a tough old guinea. They think he'll pull through now,' said the doctor at the other end of the line in another public phone booth in Greenwich, Connecticut.

'That's not particularly good news.'

'They worked on him for three hours. Tied up a dozen veins, spliced twice as many and patched walls all over. He'll be on critical for a few days, but the odds are he'll make it.'

'We don't want that, doctor. That's unacceptable to us ... There's got to be a miscalculation somewhere.'

'Forget it, Bobby. This place is swarming with guns. Every entrance, the elevators, even the roof. The nurses aren't even ours, they're his. Four priests rotate the last rites watch inside his room; if they're priests, I'm Mother Cabrini.'

'I repeat, *some way* has *got* to be found.'

'Then you find it, but not here. If anything happened to him now, they'd burn the hospital to the ground with all of us in it. And *that's* unacceptable to me.'

'All right, all right. No medical accidents.'

'You bet your ass! ... Why the elimination?'

'He asked too many favors; he got them. He's become too much of a liability.'

The doctor paused. 'Not here, Bobby.'

'All right. We'll think of something else.'

'By the way, the discharge papers came through. I'm clean. Thanks a lot. You didn't have to add the citation, but it was a nice touch.'

'Better than dishonourable. You must have made a killing.'

'I did.' The doctor laughed. 'If you're strapped for a buck, let me know.'

'Be in touch.' Webster hung up and awkwardly manipulated his briefcase and the phone-booth door. He had to figure out what to do about de Spadante. The situation could become dangerous. Somehow he'd use the doctor in Greenwich. Why not? The doctor's debt wasn't nearly paid off. The doctor had run a series of abortion mills, in one Army hospital after another. He'd used government equipment and goddamned near advertised in base newspapers. The doctor had made a fortune two years after he'd finished internship.

Webster hailed a taxi and was about to give the driver the White House destination. Then he changed his mind.

'Twelve-twenty-two Louisiana.'

It was the address of the Gallabretto Construction Company. Mario de Spadante's Washington firm.

The nurse opened the door solemnly, silently. The priest removed his hand from his jacket, and the gold chain with the cross attached rattled slightly. He got out of the chair and whispered to the visitor.

'His eyes are closed, but he hears every fuckin' word.'

'Leave us,' said the weak, rasping voice from the bed. 'Come back when William's gone, Rocco.'

'Sure, boss.'

The priest put his finger between the clerical collar and his skin and stretched his neck. He picked up his small leather missal and opened the door, slightly embarrassed.

The visitor and Mario de Spadante were alone.

'I can't stay more than a few minutes, Mario. The doctors won't let me. You're going to be all right, you know that, don't you?'

'Hey, you look good, William. Big West Coast lawyer now, huh? You dress *good*. You make me proud, little cousin. Real proud.'

'Don't waste breath, Mario. We've got several things to go over, and I want you cognizant.'

'Listen to the word. "Cognizant".' De Spadante smiled lamely. It took strength to smile, and he was pitifully weak. 'They sent *you* in from the Coast. Imagine that.'

'Let me do the talking, Mario. . . . First of all, you went to Trevayne's place in hopes that he might be home. You didn't have his unlisted number; you were in Greenwich on business – you're doing some work down here – and you'd heard his wife was in a hospital. You knew him in New Haven, reacquainted yourselves on the plane to Washington. You were simply concerned. That's all. It was purely a social call. Perhaps a bit presumptuous on your part, but that's not contradictory to your . . . expansiveness.'

De Spadante nodded, his eyes half-closed. 'Little Willie Gallabretto,' he said with his faint smile. 'You talk good, William. I'm real proud.' De Spadante kept nodding his frail affirmation. 'You talk so good. So quick, William.'

'Thank you.' The lawyer looked at his gold Rolex watch and continued. 'This is most important, Mario. At Trevayne's house your car got stuck in the snow. The *mud* and the snow. We've got confirmation from the police. Incidentally, it cost a thousand with a man named Fowler, and the tracks have been erased. But remember, the mud and the snow. That's all you remember until you were attacked. Have you got that?'

'Yes, *consigliori*, I've got that.'

'Good . . . Now, I should go. My associates in Los Angeles send you their best. You'll be fine, Uncle Mario.'

'Fine . . . Fine.' De Spadante raised his hand an inch or two off the blanket. The lawyer halted. 'Now you finished?'

'Yes.'

'Fine. Now, stop talking the fancy talk and hear me. Hear me good . . . You put out a contract on this soldier boy. I want it *tormento lento*. You put it out tonight.'

'No, Mario. No contract. He's Army, federal. No contract.'

'You *dispute me*? You a *caporegime* dare to talk back to *capo di tutti capi*! I say a contract. Ten big ones a contract. Put it out.'

'Uncle Mario, the days of *The Godfather* are finished.' William Gallabretto spoke calmly, sympathetically, to his relative. 'We have better ways.'

'Better. What's better than *tormento lento*? A slow death for the pig that took my brother! *You* know. *I* know. A knife in the back. *Miole*. A contract. I say no more.' De Spadante inhaled deeply and rested his head back on the pillow.

'Listen to me, Uncle Mario. This soldier, this Major Bonner, will be arrested. He'll be indicted for murder – one. He has no defence. It was wanton killing without provocation. He's been in trouble before—'

'A contract.' De Spadante interrupted, his voice growing weaker.

'*No*. It's not necessary. There are a lot of people who want to see this Bonner not only finished, but *discredited*. Right up to the top . . . We even have a newspaperman, a famous columnist. A writer named Roderick Bruce. This Bonner is a psycho. He'll draw life. And *then* – somewhere in a penitentiary – he'll get the knife.'

'It's no good. You talk crap . . . You stay out of the courts. No lawyer shit. That's no good. You put out my contract.'

William Gallabretto retreated from the bedside. 'All right, Uncle Mario,' he lied. 'You rest now.'

34

Trevayne sat on the hotel bed, fighting to keep his eyes open, to keep his attention on the neatly typed pages in front of him. He knew he was losing the fight, and so he reached for the telephone and requested a call for seven in the morning.

He'd left Aaron Green shortly after one o'clock, much earlier than he'd expected. Green had offered him lunch, but Andy had declined, making a feeble excuse that he had to drive into New York – business undisclosed. The truth was that he couldn't stand being near Green. There was nothing he could say to him. The old Jew had destroyed any argument he might have presented. What words could be found to counter the sight in Green's back lawn or lessen the motive created nearly forty years ago alongside a fence in Auschwitz?

Aaron Green was no anomaly. He was totally consistent by his lights. He *did* believe in all the liberal reforms for which he was noted; he *was* a compassionate man, a generous man, who lavished huge personal sums on causes that strived to better the plights of the unfortunate. And he would spend the last dollar of his fortune, use the last energies of his financial genius to make sure his adopted country would maintain the climate that permitted his philosophy. Such a nation had to be the strongest on earth. Its borders could not be weakened by the necessarily soft, flexible interior; the shell had to be impenetrable.

Green was blind to the fact that the more absolute strength permitted the protectors – the shell – the greater the possibility that they would usurp the rights of the protected – the interior. It was the classic manifestation, the *a priori* conclusion, but Green rejected it. If it were possible to build a fortress from the finances of the marketplace, that power would be penultimate, he thought; the ultimate would remain where it was conceived – in the civilian economy. It was a ludicrous assumption, as ludicrous as the *Wehrmacht* animals counting off numbers to which the naked dead were to march. But the memory of that sight shattered Aaron Green's perception.

And there was absolutely nothing Trevayne could say to alter the old man's thinking.

When the Lear jet had landed at Chicago's O'Hare Airport, Trevayne immediately telephoned Sam Vicarson in Salt Lake City. Vicarson told him the Ian Hamilton dossier was typed and waiting for him at his hotel. It had been a simple one. The American Bar Association was immensely proud of Ian Hamilton, and its professional biography was extensive. Additional information was supplied by Hamilton's son. The choice of the son was another Vicarson touch, thought Andrew. The Hamilton boy – young man – was the 'now' generation; the break with the family's long establishment tradition. He was a folk singer with his own group, a graduate of the acid-rock scene who made the transition to the new-new music successfully. He had no hang-ups talking about his father. The son considered – or arrived at the conclusion – that the old man did 'his thing' with more intelligence than imagination, but did it well because he was dedicated to the proposition that the elite had to show the way for the unenlightened.

That summation turned out to be the most perceptive analysis of Ian Hamilton that Trevayne would find.

Hamilton came from very old, very secure upstate New York money and traced his ancestry back to the British Alexander and his antecedents in Ayrshire, Scotland, where the Hamiltons were lairds of Cambuskeith. He had attended the proper schools – Rectory, Groton, Harvard – and been graduated near the top of his class at Harvard Law. A postlaw year at Cambridge in England opened the door for him to spend the war years in London as a Navy legal officer attached to Eisenhower's General Staff. He'd married an English girl from the small social sea of acceptable British fish, and their only child, the son, was born in the Naval Hospital in Surrey.

After the war, Ian Hamilton's credentials – and brains – secured him a series of enviable positions, culminating in a partnership with one of New York's most prestigious firms. Speciality: corporate law with heavy diversification in municipal bonds. His wartime associations, beginning with the Eisenhower administration, brought him frequently to Washington: so often that his firm opened a Washington office. In succeeding administrations Ian Hamilton became more and more identified with the Washington scene. Though nominally a Republican, he was not doctrinaire. His working relationships with a Democratic House and Senate were solid. John Kennedy offered him the London embassy – which was a logical and politically shrewd decision – but Hamilton gracefully declined. Instead, he continued his progress up the Washington law ladder to the rung that allowed him the description of 'adviser to presidents'. He was experienced enough to warrant attention and yet young enough – in his middle fifties – to be flexible. His friendship was an asset.

And then, two years ago, Ian Hamilton did what no one expected him to do. He quietly resigned from his firm and stated – again quietly, to friends – that he was going to take a 'long, I hope deserved, sabbatical'. There were the obvious jokes that he'd make more money managing his folk-rock, guitar-playing son, and less pleasant speculation on his health. Hamilton heard them and accepted them, characteristically, in good grace.

Nevertheless, he left Washington and with his wife took a world cruise for twenty-two weeks.

Six months ago Ian Hamilton again did the unexpected and, again, without fanfare or excessive press coverage. Hamilton joined the old Chicago firm of Brandon and Smith. He cut his ties with Washington and New York and moved into a mansion in Evanston on the shores of Lake Michigan. Ian Hamilton had apparently decided on a less hectic life and was welcomed – quietly – into the social confines of the Evanston executive rich.

There was the matter of the bond issue raised by Genessee Industries and given to the firm of Brandon and Smith – the result of Hamilton's breaking silence while a member of the President's Steel Import Commission.

Genessee Industries now had the services of the most esteemed law firm in the Midwest – Brandon, Smith, and Hamilton. Genessee was covered in the highest financial echelons on both coasts: Green in New York; the company plants and Senator Armbruster in California. So it was logical that they establish a seat of influence in Middle America.

If what Trevayne perceived was the emerging pattern was correct.

And with Ian Hamilton that pattern spread into the area of the executive branch of the government. The President of the United States. For Hamilton, adviser to presidents, moved cautiously with quiet but enormous power.

In the morning, Trevayne would drive out to Evanston and surprise Ian Hamilton on the Christian Sabbath, as he'd surprised Aaron Green on the Hebrew Sabbath in Sail Harbor.

Robert Webster kissed his wife good night and swore again at the telephone. When they lived in Akron, Ohio, they never got calls at midnight that required his leaving the house. Of course, when they lived in Akron they could never have afforded such a home for him to leave. And how many Akron boys got calls from the White House? Though, God knew, this call wasn't from there.

Webster backed his car out of the garage and sped off down the street. According to the message, he had to be at the intersection of Nebraska and 21st in ten minutes – eight minutes now.

He spotted the car, a white Chevrolet, with a man's arm out of the window.

He pushed the rim of his horn with two short blasts.

The white Chevrolet responded with one long sound of its horn.

Webster continued down Nebraska Avenue as the Chevrolet whipped out of its parking space and followed.

The two cars reached the immense parking lot of the old Carter Baron Amphitheatre and came to a stop adjacent to each other.

Robert Webster got out and walked around to meet the man. 'Christ! I hope this is worth it! I need a night's sleep!'

'It's worth it,' said the dark man in the shadows. 'Move against the soldier. Everybody's covered.'

'Who says?'

'Willie Gallabretto; that's who says. It's straight. I'm to tell you to go for the mark. Put him away. *Loud.*'

'What about de Spadante?'

'He's a corpse as soon as he gets back to New Haven.'

Robert Webster sighed and smiled at the same time. 'It's worth it,' he said as he turned and walked back to his car.

The iron sign with the brass letters read one word: 'Lakeside'.

Trevayne turned the car into the snow-ploughed drive and started down the gentle slope toward the main house. It was a large white Georgian structure that seemed uprooted from some antebellum plantation in the Carolinas. There were tall trees everywhere. Beyond the house and the trees were the mostly frozen waters of Lake Michigan.

As he drove his car into a parking area in front of the three-car garage, Trevayne saw a man in a mackinaw coat and a fur cap walking with a large dog on a path. The sound of the automobile caused the man to turn, and the dog, a beautiful Chesapeake retriever, to start barking.

Andrew recognized Ian Hamilton immediately. Tall, slender, elegant even in his lumberjack clothes. There was a quality about him that reminded Trevayne of Walter Madison, another eastern-establishment corporate lawyer; but Madison – as good as he was – had a slight vulnerability about him. Hamilton had none whatsoever.

'Yes? May I help you?' said Ian Hamilton, holding the retriever by the collar as he approached the car.

Trevayne had rolled down his window. 'Mr Hamilton?'

'Good Lord. You're Trevayne. Andrew Trevayne. What are *you* doing here?' Hamilton looked as though he'd misplaced his senses but would quickly find them again.

Another one alerted, thought Trevayne. Another player had received his warning. It was unmistakable.

'I was visiting friends several miles from here ...'

Trevayne repeated a variation of the lie, and other than serving as a social buffer to lessen the awkwardness, it was no more believed than his previous lies had been. Hamilton, ever-gracious, pretended to accept it – without enthusiasm – and led Trevayne into the house. There was a roaring fire in the living-room fireplace, the Sunday papers strewn about the sofa and on the floor around a gold velvet-covered reclining chair. On a table in front of a bay window looking over the lakefront was a silver coffee service and the remnants of a single breakfast.

'My wife will be down shortly,' said Hamilton, indicating a chair for Trevayne, taking his overcoat. 'We've had a twenty-year understanding. Every Sunday she reads and breakfasts in bed while I take my dogs – or dog, as the case is now – for a run. We both find a gratifying hour or so of solitude this way ... I imagine it sounds rather old-fashioned.' Hamilton removed his mackinaw and fur cap and carried Trevayne's overcoat into the hallway.

'Not at all,' answered Andy. 'It sounds very civilized.'

Hamilton returned from hanging up the coats and looked at Trevayne.

Even in a sloppy cardigan sweater, the lawyer had a custom-tailored appearance, thought Andrew. 'Yes. It *is* civilized ... Actually, I'm the one who formalized the routine. It gave me an excuse not to accept telephone calls ... or interruptions.'

'I stand rebuked.'

'I'm sorry.' Hamilton walked to the table by the bay window. 'That was unnecessarily rude of me; I *do* apologize. My life these days is really far less strenuous than it's been in decades. I have no right to complain. Have some coffee?'

'Thank you, no.'

'Decades ...' Hamilton chuckled as he poured himself coffee. 'I sound like an old man. I'm not really. Fifty-eight next April. Most men my age are in the heavy-thick of it now ... Walter Madison, for instance. You're a client of Madison's, aren't you?'

'Yes.'

'Give Walter my regards. I've always liked him ... Very agile but completely ethical. You have a fine attorney, Mr Trevayne.' Hamilton walked to the sofa opposite Trevayne and sat down, putting his cup and saucer on the solid oak coffee table.

'Yes, I know. He's spoken of you often. He considers you a brilliant man.'

'Compared to what? ... That's a deceptive word, "brilliant". Overworked these days. A brief is brilliant, a dancer's brilliant; a book, a hairpiece, eggs benedict, plans, machinery ... I recall last summer a neighbour up the road called the horse manure for his garden "brilliant".'

'I'm sure Walter's more selective.'

'Of course he is. And unduly flattering ... Enough about me, I'm really semiretired these days, just a name on the stationery. My son is rather prominent, though, wouldn't you say?'

'Extremely. That was a good story in *Life* the other month.'

'It was highly fictionalized, to tell you the truth.' Hamilton laughed his elegant laugh as he sipped coffee. 'You know, that story was intended to be derogatory. Nasty girl writer, up to her eyeballs in women's liberation and convinced my son made sex objects of all females. He found out, I'm told, seduced the poor crusading bitch, and the article turned out fine.'

'He's a remarkable talent.'

'I like what he's doing now more than I did his previous work. More reflective, less frantic ... Certainly you didn't drop by to chat about the Hamilton family's endeavors, Mr Trevayne.'

Andrew was startled by the lawyer's abrupt transition. Then he understood. Hamilton had used the small talk to marshall his thoughts, his defences, perhaps. He sat back on the sofa with the expression of a very knowledgeable debater.

'The Hamilton endeavors.' Trevayne paused as though his words were a title. 'That's accurate, as a matter of fact. I dropped in because I find it necessary to discuss your endeavors, Mr Hamilton. Relative to Genessee Industries.'

'On what possible presumption do you find this necessity?'

'As chairman of the subcommittee for the Defense Allocations Commission.'

'An *ad hoc* committee, if I'm not mistaken, although I know very little about it.'

'We've been granted power of subpoena.'

'Which, if exercised, I'd challenge immediately.'

'So far, there's been no need for such challenges.'

Hamilton let the point pass. 'Genessee Industries is a client of our firm. A substantial and respected client. I wouldn't for one second violate the sanctioned relationship between lawyer and client. You may have dropped in to no avail, Mr Trevayne.'

'Mr Hamilton, my interest in your endeavours for Genessee Industries precedes the lawyer-client relationship. By nearly two years. The subcommittee is trying to piece together a ... financial narrative, I guess you'd call it. How did we get where we are? A harmless variation on the Pentagon Papers.'

'Two years ago I had nothing to do with Genessee Industries. There *were* no endeavours.'

'Perhaps not directly. But there's speculation—'

'Neither directly nor indirectly, Mr Trevayne,' interrupted Hamilton.

'You were a member of the President's Steel Import Commission.'

'I certainly was.'

'A month or two prior to the commission's public ruling on steel quotas, Genessee Industries imported excessive tonnage from Tamishito in Japan, Genessee floated a bond issue, with Brandon and Smith handling the legal work. Three months after that, you became a partner with Brandon and Smith ... The diagram would seem apparent.'

Ian Hamilton sat rigidly in the couch, his eyes blazing in anger, but icily controlled. 'That is the most scurrilous distortion of fact that I've heard in thirty-five years of practice. Out-of-context assumption. Misplaced concretion. And you *know* it, sir.'

'I don't know it. Neither do several members of the subcommittee.'

Hamilton remained frozen, but Trevayne saw the lawyer's mouth twitch – imperceptibly – at the mention of 'several members of the subcommittee'. The ploy was working. It was the public speculation that Hamilton feared.

'To enlighten you ... and your exceedingly misinformed associates, any damn fool involved with steel two years ago knew a ruling was forthcoming. Japanese, Czechoslovakian ... yes, even Chinese mills by way of Canada, were surfeited with American orders. They couldn't possibly meet the demands ... In the basic rule of production, a single buyer is preferable to many. It's cheaper, Mr Trevayne ... Genessee Industries obviously had the wherewithal – more so than its competitors – and therefore became the major purchaser from Tamishito ... They didn't need me to tell them. Or anyone else, for that matter.'

'I'm sure that's logical for those who deal in such economics; I'm not sure it would cut ice with the citizen-taxpayer. And he *does* foot the bill.'

'Sophistry, Mr Trevayne. And, again, you know it. A false argument. The American citizen is the most fortunate man on earth. He has the best minds, the most dedicated men watching out for him.'

'I agree,' said Trevayne, and he did. 'However, I prefer the term, "working for", him, not "watching out". After all, they're paid.'

'Irrelevant. The definition is interchangeable.'

'I hope so . . . You *did* join Brandon and Smith at a propitious time.'

'That will be about enough! If you're suggesting there was reciprocity, I trust you're prepared to substantiate the charge. My integrity is well established, Trevayne. I wouldn't attempt a gutter assault, if I were you.'

'I'm aware of your reputation. And the high regard people have for you . . . It's why I came to warn you, give you time to prepare your answers.'

'You came to *warn* me?' Hamilton involuntarily sat forward. He was stunned.

'Yes. The question of impropriety *has* been raised. It will call for a reply from you.'

'To whom?' The lawyer couldn't believe what he was hearing.

'To the subcommittee. In open session.'

'In *open* . . .' Hamilton's expression was one of complete astonishment. 'You can't mean what you're saying.'

'I'm afraid I do.'

'You have no right to parade whomever you choose in front of an *ad hoc* committee. In open session!'

'The witnesses will be voluntary, Mr Hamilton, not paraded. That's the way we'd prefer it.'

'You'd *prefer*? You've lost your senses. We have laws to protect fundamental rights, Trevayne. You'll not indiscriminately impugn the characters of men *you* see fit to harass.'

'No harassments. After all, it won't be a trial—'

'You know perfectly well what I mean.'

'Are you telling me you won't accept our invitation?'

Hamilton abruptly frowned and stared at Trevayne. He recognized the trap and wasn't about to be ensnared. 'I will privately give you the information you seek relative to my professional association with the firm of Brandon and Smith. It will answer the question you raised and remove any grounds for my appearance before your subcommittee.'

'How?'

Hamilton didn't like being pressed. He knew the dangers of letting an adversary know too much of one's defence. Nevertheless, he could hardly refuse to answer. 'I will make available to you documents which show that in no way do I participate in any profits accruing from the Genessee bond issue. It was legal work obtained before our partnership agreement; I'm not entitled to participation, nor have I sought it.'

'Some might say documents like that are easily written. Easily amended at later dates.'

'Company audits and moneys due from existing contracts are not. No partnership is entered into without full audit disclosures.'

'I see.' Trevayne smiled and spoke pleasantly. 'Then it should be a simple matter for you to submit the papers and refute the allegation; over in two minutes.'

'I said I would make the documents available to *you*. I did not say I would submit to questioning. I will not dignify such allegations; no one in my position would.'

'You flatter me, Mr Hamilton. You're assuming me to be some kind of grand jury.'

'I assume you establish the ground rules for your subcommittee's procedures. Unless you're misrepresenting yourself.'

'Not intentionally. Or should I put it this way? Those kinds of documents – accounts, audits, whatever you call them – don't impress me much. I'm afraid I must insist on your appearance.'

It took all of Hamilton's control not to lash out at Trevayne. 'Mr Trevayne, I've spent the better part of two decades in Washington. I left it by choice, hardly necessity; there was no lack of interest in my capabilities. I still retain very solid relationships there.'

'Are you threatening me?'

'Only with enlightenment. I have personal reasons for not wishing to become part of any subcommittee circus maximus. I fully understand that such a road may be the only one for you to follow; by reputation you're not a lean-and-hungry man. But I must insist on my privacy.'

'I'm not sure what you're saying.'

Hamilton sat back on the sofa. 'Should you not accept my personal vindication, should you insist on my appearing before your *ad hoc* committee, I shall use all of my influence – including the Department of Justice – to see you branded for what I think you are. An egomaniac intent on building your reputation by slandering others. If I'm not mistaken, you were warned once before about this unfortunate tendency. The old gentleman was subsequently killed in an automobile accident in Fairfax, Virginia ... A number of questions might be raised.'

It was Trevayne now who leaned forward in his chair. He thought it was incredible. Ian Hamilton's anger – fear, anger, panic – had caused the lawyer to reveal the connection he was looking for. It was almost laughable, because it was – contradictorily – so naïve on Hamilton's part. As he looked at Hamilton, Andrew reflected that none of them took him at his word. *None of them.* They simply didn't believe him when he repeated over and over again that he had nothing to lose. Or gain.

'Mr Hamilton, I think it's time we both stopped making threats. Mainly for your sake ... Tell me, does your influence also include Mitchell Armbruster, Genessee's senator from California? Joshua Studebaker, Genessee's circuit court judge in Seattle? A labour leader named Manolo – and probably dozens like him – handling jurisdictional contracts all over the country? And a scientist named Jamison – probably hundreds like him, maybe thousands – bought and paid for and blackmailed into unswerving loyalty to the Genessee laboratories? Or Aaron Green? What can anyone say about Green? You've all convinced him that "never again" means creating the very same climate of military influence that led his wife and child into showers at Auschwitz. What about it, counsellor? Do you want to threaten me with these things, these people? Because I'll tell you, frankly, I'm scared to death right *now*.'

Ian Hamilton looked as though he'd just witnessed a swift, brutal hanging, a cruel execution. For several moments he was speechless, and Trevayne would not break the silence. Finally the lawyer spoke, almost inaudibly.

'What have you done?'

Trevayne remembered Green's words. 'My homework, Mr Hamilton. I've attended to my books. But I have an idea I've only just begun. There's also an impeccable fellow, a senator from Maryland, who's done very well. Another senator, this one from Vermont, hasn't done badly, I suspect. And the less respectable boys – on the surface less respectable. Men like Mario de Spadante and his organization of good-fellows, who happen to be experts with knives and guns. They're doing nicely, thank you . . . Oh, Christ, I'm sure I've a long way to go. Because while the rest of them have spheres of influence, you go right to the seat of power, don't you?'

'You don't know what you're saying.' Hamilton's voice was flat, almost guttural.

'Yes, I do. And it's why I saved you for last. The last one on my list. Because we're somewhat alike, Mr Hamilton. Every one else has an *ax*, or a *need*. Something he needs or wants in the money area, or something he has to have rectified or avenged. We don't. At least, I can't think what it might be. If you've got some kind of Rasputin complex, you picked a hell of way to exercise it; as you said, "semiretired". Out of Washington . . . I want answers, and I'll get them from you, or I'll parade you in front of that subcommittee as though you were the biggest float in the Tournament of Roses.'

'Stop it!' Hamilton sprang up from the couch and stood rigidly in front of Andrew. 'Stop it . . . You'll do extraordinary damage, Mr Trevayne. You have no idea how dangerous your interfering could be for this country.'

The lawyer walked slowly toward the bay window. It was apparent to Trevayne that Hamilton had nearly reached the decision to speak plainly.

'How is that? I'm not unreasonable.'

Hamilton looked out of the window. 'I hope that's true. I've spent years watching dedicated men drive themselves to unendurable lengths trying to wrench vital decisions from the bureaucracy. I've seen executives in agencies throughout the government openly weep, scream at their subordinates, even destroy their marriages . . . because they were caught in the political labyrinth, their ability to act numbed by the counterthrust of indecision. Most tragic, I've stood helplessly by while this nation very nearly was plunged into catastrophe because men were too frightened to take positions, too concerned with their constituencies to accept the mantles of responsibility.' Hamilton turned from the window and looked at Andrew. 'Our government has reached the point of unmanageability, Mr Trevayne. It's across the board; it's not restricted to any one area. We've become a grotesque, awkward, fumbling giant. Instant communications have brought the decision-making processes into the living rooms of two hundred million uninformed households. And in this democratization we've necessarily lowered our standards abysmally. We have settled, *strived* for . . . mediocrity.'

'That's a pretty bleak picture, Mr Hamilton. I'm not sure it's an accurate one; not to the extent you describe.'

'Of course it is, and you know it.'

'I wish you'd stop saying that. I *don't* know it.'

'Then you've lost your powers of observation. Take the past two decades. Forgetting for a minute the extraterritorial problems such as Southeast Asia, Korea, the Middle East, the Bay of Pigs, the Berlin Wall, NATO – all of which could have been handled with infinitely greater wisdom by unencumbered leaders – let's look at the country itself. An inscrutable, totally unreliable economy; terrible recessions, inflation, mass unemployment. The urban crises which threaten revolution, and I mean *armed* revolution, Mr Trevayne. The abusive riots; the overreactions of police and National Guard; labour and corporate corruption; uncontrolled strikes; utility services lost for weeks; a dissolute military, rife with incompetency and inadequate command. Can you say these are the products of an orderly society, Trevayne?'

'They're the result of a country undergoing a very sceptical self-examination. We have different viewpoints. A lot of it's terrible . . . even tragic; there's a lot that's healthy, too.'

'Nonsense . . . Tell me, you started a business; you made a success of it. Would you have done so if the decisions were allowed to be made by your clerks?'

'We were the specialists. It was our job to make the decisions.'

'Then can't you see? The *clerks* are making national and international decisions!'

'The clerks elect the specialists. The voting booth—'

'The voting booth is the answer to mediocrity's prayer! . . . If only restricted to these times.'

Trevayne looked up at the elegant lawyer, willing to give Hamilton more rope. 'Whatever your motives, the subcommittee has to be convinced there's no gross illegality. We're not . . . inquisitors; we're reasonable.'

'There's *no* illegality, Mr Trevayne,' Hamilton went on, more gently. 'We are an apolitical group of men who are trying solely to contribute. With no thoughts of self-aggrandizement.'

'How does Genessee Industries fit in? I have to know that.'

'Merely an instrument. An imperfect one, to be sure; but you've learned that . . .'

What followed frightened Trevayne more than he thought possible. Emphasized by Hamilton's quiet benevolence. The lawyer would not deal in specifics, but what he described in generous abstractions was a government potentially more powerful than the nation in which it was housed.

Genessee Industries was far more than 'an instrument'. It was – or was intended to become – a council of the elite. Through its mammoth resources those privileged to execute Genessee's policies would be capable of rushing in where national problems were critical – before those problems disintegrated into chaos. This capability was, of course, years off; but in lesser examples Genessee had already proven itself, justified the considered projections of its architects. There were unemployment areas pulled out of the doldrums by Genessee; labour disputes settled reasonably in scores of strike-bound plants; companies saved from bankruptcy, resurrected by Genessee management. These were essentially economic problems; there were other kinds. In science, the Genessee laboratories were working on major socioscientific studies that would be invaluable in the areas of ecology, pollution. Inner-city disease crises had been averted with Genessee medical units, and medical research itself was of primary interest to the company. And the military. It must always be closely watched, controlled, a true servant; but Genessee had made possible certain necessary armaments which had resulted in saving thousands upon thousands of lives. The military was beholden to Genessee. It would remain so.

The key to these successes was in the ability to move quickly and commit vast sums. Sums not hampered by political considerations.

Sums allocated by the judgment of an elite corps of wise men, good men, men dedicated to the promise of America.

And America for all, not a few.

It was simply the method.

'This country was founded as a republic, Mr Trevayne,' said Hamilton, sitting down on the sofa opposite Andrew. 'Democracy is an abstraction . . . One definition of "republic" is a state governed by those *entitled* to vote, to shape its policies. Not blanketly franchised. Now, of course, no one would conceive of implementing this definition. But to borrow in principle – if only slightly, temporarily – has historical precedence . . . The times we live in call for it.'

'I see.' Trevayne had to ask the question, if only to hear how Hamilton dodged it. 'Don't you run the risk of those entitled to shape policy . . . wanting to make sure the trains-run-on-time? Of seeking final solutions?'

'Never.' Hamilton answered with quiet sincerity. 'Because there's no motive. No such dark ambitions . . . You said something earlier that impressed me, Trevayne. You said you came to me because – as yourself – I had neither financial need nor vengeance to carry out . . . Of course, we never know the other fellow's problems, but you happen to be right. My needs are satisfied, my vengeances minor. You and I, no political comets, proven in the marketplace, thinkers who can be decisive, concerned for the less fortunate. We are the aristocracy that must run the republic. The time will shortly be upon us when we either accept the responsibility, or there'll be no republic.'

'The rule of benevolent monarchy.'

'Oh, no, not monarchy. Aristocracy. And not attained through bloodlines.'

'Does the President know about this?'

Hamilton hesitated. 'No, he does not. He's not even aware of the hundreds of problems we've solved for him. They just disappear . . . We are always at his disposal. In the most positive sense, I should add.'

Trevayne rose from his chair. It was time to leave, time to think. 'You've been candid, and I appreciate it, Mr Hamilton.'

'I've also been most general. I trust you appreciate that, too. No names, no specifics, only generalizations with examples . . . of corporate responsibility.'

'Which means if I allude to this conversation you would . . .'

'What conversation, Mr Trevayne?'

'Yes, of course.'

'You *do* see the good? The extraordinary possibilities?'

'They're remarkable. But you never know the other fellow's problems. Isn't that what you said?'

Trevayne drove down the snow-banked roads out of Evanston. He drove slowly, letting the infrequent Sunday drivers pass him, not thinking of the speed or his destination. Thinking only of the unbelievable information he'd learned.

A council of the elite.

The United States of Genessee Industries.

Part Three

35

Robert Webster walked out the east White House portico toward the staff parking area. He'd excused himself from the press conference briefing, leaving his suggestions – mostly anticipated questions – with one of the other aides. He had no time for protective presidential routines; he had far more important problems to control. To orchestrate, really.

The leak to Roderick Bruce would result in damaging rumours circulated throughout every important office – Senate, House, Justice, Defense – and then exploding into headlines. The sort of headlines that would destroy the effectiveness of any subcommittee chairman and reduce a subcommittee itself to rubble.

Webster was pleased with himself. The solution for Mario de Spadante led directly to the elimination of Trevayne. With amazing clarity. The only extra bonus needed was throwing Paul Bonner to Roderick Bruce.

The rest was already established as much as was necessary. The close working relationship between de Spadante and Trevayne. De Spadante's meeting Trevayne late at night in Connecticut when the subcommittee chairman was supposed to be away on subcommittee business. Trevayne's first trip to Washington with Mario as travelling companion. The limousine ride from Dulles Airport to the Hilton. Trevayne and de Spadante together in Georgetown at the home of a less-than-welcomed attaché of the French government, a man known to be involved with the American underworld.

It was all that was needed.

Andrew Trevayne and Mario de Spadante.

Corruption.

When de Spadante was murdered in New Haven, his death would be attributed to a Mafia war. But it would be in print and on the news programmes that Trevayne had been at his hospital bedside a week before the murder.

Corruption.

It was all going to be all right, thought Webster, as he turned left up Pennsylvania Avenue. De Spadante would be eliminated, and Trevayne effectively removed from Washington.

Trevayne *and* de Spadante had become too unpredictable. Trevayne could no longer be trusted to go through him to the President. Trevayne had covered extraordinary ground – from Houston to Seattle – yet the only request he'd made was for information about de Spadante. Nothing else. That was too dangerous. Ultimately Trevayne could be killed, if need be, but that could backfire into a full-scale investigation. They weren't ready for that.

De Spadante, on the other hand, *had* to be killed. He'd gone too far, infiltrated too deeply. Webster had brought the mafioso into the Genessee picture originally – and solely – to solve waterfront problems easily controlled by Mafia commands. Then de Spadante had seen the enormous possibilities of aiding powerful men in high federal places. He didn't let go.

But de Spadante had to be eliminated by his own. Not by elements outside his world; that could prove disastrous. He had to be murdered by other de Spadantes.

Willie Gallabretto understood. The Gallabretto family – both blood and organizational – was getting fed up with the musical theatrics of its Connecticut relative. The Gallabrettos were the new breed; the slim, conservatively groomed college graduates who had no use for the Old World tactics of their forebears or the pampered, long-haired dropouts of the 'now' generation.

They fell beautifully in between, within the borders of respectability – almost Middle America respectability. If it were not for their names, they'd be farther up a hundred thousand corporate ladders.

Webster turned right on 27th Street and watched the numbers of the buildings. He was looking for 112.

Roderick Bruce's apartment house.

Paul Bonner stared alternately at the letter and at the Captain from the Provost Marshal's office who'd delivered it. The Captain leaned nonchalantly against the door of Bonner's office.

'What the hell is this, Captain? One lousy fucking joke?'

'No joke, Major. You're confined to BOQ, Arlington, until further notice. You're being tried for murder in the first degree.'

'I'm *what?*'

'The state of Connecticut has filed charges. The prosecution has accepted our responsibility for your detention. That's a break. Whatever the verdict, the Army then faces a five-million-dollar suit from the family of the deceased, one August de Spadante ... We'll settle; no one's worth five million bucks.'

'Settle? Murder? Those sons-of-bitches were gunning for Trevayne. What was I supposed to do? Let them *kill* him!'

'Major, have you got one shred of evidence that August de Spadante was there to do injury? Even in a hostile frame of mind? ... Because if you do, you'd better let us have it; we can't find it.'

'You're funny. He was armed, ready to fire.'

'Your word. It was dark out; no weapon was found.'

'Then it was stolen.'

'Prove it.'

'Two Secret Service men from "sixteen hundred" were deliberately removed – contrary to orders. In Darien. At the hospital. I was shot at, driving into the Barnegat property. I rendered the man unconscious and took his weapon.'

The Captain pushed himself away from the door and approached Bonner's desk. 'We read that in your report. The man you say fired at you claims he didn't own a gun. You jumped him.'

'*And* took his piece; I can prove *that*! I gave it to Trevayne.'

'You gave *a* gun to Trevayne. An unregistered handgun with no other fingerprints on it but his and yours.'

'Where the hell did I get it, then?'

'Good question. The injured party says it's not his. I understand you have quite a collection.'

'Horseshit!'

'And no Secret Service men were removed from Darien, because they weren't scheduled to be there.'

'Double horseshit! Check the rosters!'

'We have. The Trevayne detachment was recalled to the White House for further assignment. Its duties were assumed by local authorities through the office of the County Sheriff, Fairfield, Connecticut.'

'That's a lie! I called them in; through 1600.' Bonner rose from his chair.

'A mistake at Security Control, maybe. No lie. Take it up with Robert Webster at 1600. Presidential Assistant Webster, I should add. He said he was sure his office advised Trevayne of the switch. Although it wasn't required to.'

'Then where *were* the locals?'

'In a patrol car in the parking lot.'

'I didn't see them!'

'Did you look?'

Bonner thought for a moment. He remembered the sign in the hospital driveway directing automobiles to the rear parking area. 'No, I didn't . . . If they were there, they were out of position!'

'No question about it. Sloppy work. But then, those cops aren't 1600.'

'You're telling me I misinterpreted everything that happened. The patrol, the shots. That hood with a gun . . . Goddamn it, Captain, I don't make mistakes like that!'

'That's the opinion of the prosecution, too. You *don't* make mistakes like that. You tell lies.'

'I'd go easy if I were you, Captain. Don't let this brace fool you.'

'Get off it, Major! I'm defending you! And one of the tougher aspects of that defence is your reputation for unprovoked assault. A proclivity, in the field, for *un*justifiable homicide. You're not going to do yourself any good if you beat me up.'

Bonner took a deep breath. 'Trevayne will back me up; he'll straighten it out. He was right there.'

'Did he hear any threats? Did he see any gestures – even at a distance – that could be interpreted as hostility?'

Bonner paused. 'No.'

'What about the housekeeper?'

'No, again ... Except she held my neck together; Trevayne put a tourniquet around my arm.'

'That's no good. Mario de Spadante claims self-defence. You held a weapon on him. According to him, you pistol-whipped his head.'

'After he tore me apart with those iron-spiked knuckles.'

'He admits the knuckles. It's a fifty-dollar fine ... Did either of the other two, the deceased and the one you "chopped", did they initiate any assaults?' The Captain watched Bonner carefully.

'No.'

'You're sure we couldn't find anything?'

'No.'

'Thanks for that. A lie wouldn't hold up under diagrams. They've got us with the first man. His injuries were caused by an attack from the rear. A lie would finish you.'

'I'm not lying.'

'Okay, okay.'

'Have you talked to Cooper? General Cooper?'

'We've got his deposition. He claims he gave you authorization for a plane in from Boise, Idaho, but had no knowledge of your trip to Connecticut. The operations officer at Andrews said you told him you *had* Cooper's authorization. Conflict there. Cooper also says you failed to phone in a progress report.'

'For Christ's sake, I was being ripped apart.'

The Captain moved away from Bonner's desk. He spoke with his back to Paul. 'Major, I'm going to ask you a question, but before I do, I want you to know that I won't use the answer unless I think it'll do us some good. Even then, you could stop me. Fair enough?'

'Go ahead.'

The Captain turned and looked at Bonner. 'Did you have some kind of an agreement with Trevayne and de Spadante? Have you been taken? Squeezed out after delivering something you can't admit to?'

'You're way off, Captain.'

'Then what *was* de Spadante doing there?'

'I told you. A job on Trevayne. I'm not wrong about that.'

'Are you sure? ... Trevayne was supposed to be in Denver, in conferences. That's an established fact. No reason for anyone to think otherwise – unless he was *told*. What was he doing back in Connecticut, unless it was to meet de Spadante?'

'Seeing his wife at the hospital.'

'Now you're way off, Major. We ran confidential interrogations all day long. With every technician at that hospital. There were no tests run on Mrs Trevayne. It was a setup.'

'What's your point?'

'I think Trevayne came back to see de Spadante, and you bungled into the biggest mistake of your career.'

Roderick Bruce, watchdog of Washington – once little Roger Brewster of Erie, Pennsylvania – pulled the page out of his typewriter and got out his specially constructed chair. The messenger from the paper was waiting in the kitchen.

He placed the page at the bottom of several others and leaned back to read.

His quest was about over. Major Paul Bonner wouldn't survive the week. And that was justice.

Chalk one up for Alex. Dear, gentle Alex.

Bruce read each page slowly, savouring the knifelike words. It was the sort of story every newspaperman dreamed of: the reporting of terrible events he'd forecast; reporting them before anyone else did – substantiating them with irrefutable proof.

Sweet, lonely Alex. Bewildered Alex, who cared only for his precious remnants of antiquity. And him, of course. He cared about Rod Bruce.

Had cared.

He'd always called him Roger, not Rod, or Roderick. Alex always said it made him feel closer to call him by his right name. 'Roger', he said, was a beautiful name, soft and sensitive.

Bruce reached the last page of his copy:

... and whatever the speculations on August de Spadante's background – and they are *only* speculations – he was a good husband; a father of five innocent children who, today, weep without comprehension over his casket. August de Spadante served with distinction in the armed forces. He carried shrapnel wounds from Korea to his death.

The *tragedy* – there is no other word but 'tragedy' – is that too often the citizen soldier, men like August de Spadante, serve in blood-soaked battles *created* (*created*, mind you) by ambitious, rank-conscious, half-crazed military butchers who feed on war, demand war, plunge us into war for their own obsessions.

Such a man, such a butcher, plunged a knife, drove it deeply into the back (*back*, mind you) of August de Spadante, waiting in darkness, on an errand of mercy.

This killer, this Paul Bonner, is no stranger to wanton murder, as readers of this column have surmised. But he's been protected; perhaps he was protecting others.

Are we as citizens going to allow the United States Army to harbour hired killers, killers let loose to make their own decisions as to who will live and who will die?

Bruce smiled as he clipped the pages together. He got up and stretched his five-foot-three-inch body. He went to his desk, took a manila envelope from a drawer, and placed the pages within it. He sealed the envelope and stamped both sides with his usual rubber stamp: 'Roderick Bruce Copy – Special: City Desk'.

He had started for the kitchen door when his eyes caught sight of the Chinese box in his walled bookcase. He stopped and crossed to it, putting the envelope down and reaching into his pocket for his key chain. He removed the box, inserted a tiny key into its lock and opened the lid.

Alex's letters.

All addressed to Roger Brewster and sent to a special general-delivery number in the large overburdened downtown Washington Post Office.

He had to be careful. They both had to be careful, but he had to be more careful than Alex.

Alex, young enough to be his son – his daughter. Only neither son nor daughter, but lover. Passionate, understanding, teaching Roger Brewster to vent the pent-up physical emotions of a lifetime. His first love.

Alex was an ex-graduate student, a young genius whose expertise in Far East languages and cultures led to scholarship after scholarship, and a doctoral thesis from the University of Chicago. He had been sent to Washington on a grant to evaluate Oriental artefacts willed to the Smithsonian.

But his deferment was ended; Alex was taken into the Army, and Roderick Bruce dared not interfere – although the temptation nearly drove him insane. Instead, Alex was commissioned because Rod Bruce *did* point out to certain military personnel that Alex's background could be put to good use in the Pentagon-based Asian Affairs Bureau. It seemed as though their life would go on – quietly, lovingly. Then, suddenly, without planning, without prior knowledge, without *warning*, Alex was told he had four hours to gather his belongings – no more than sixty-five pounds – straighten out whatever personal affairs he had, and report to Andrews Air Force Base.

He was being flown across the world to Saigon.

No one would tell him why. And Roderick Bruce, frightened for himself and his lover, overcame his fears and tried to find out what had happened.

It was too classified even for him.

And then Alex's letters started to arrive. He was part of an intelligence team in training for some sort of trip into the northeastern areas. He had been told that they needed an American interpreter – they couldn't trust the local agents and feared ARVN leaks – preferably a man with some knowledge of the religious habits and superstitions of the people. The computers had come up with his name; that's the way the commander of the unit had put it. A major named Bonner, who was nothing short of a maniac. Alex knew this Bonner despised him. 'He's a repressed you-know-what.' The Major drove Alex incessantly, was unrelenting in his harassment, brutal in his insults.

Then the letters stopped. For weeks Roderick Bruce made the trips downtown to the post office, sometimes two and three times a day. Nothing.

And then he confirmed the horror, *his* horror.

The name was simply a name on the Pentagon casualty list. One of thirty-eight that week. Discreet inquiry, on the pretext of knowing the parents, uncovered the fact that Alex had been taken prisoner in Chung-Kal in northern Cambodia near the border of Thailand. It had been an intelligence operation under the command of Major Paul Bonner – one of the six men to survive the mission. Alex's body had been found by Cambodian farmers.

He'd been executed.

And several months later the name Paul Bonner came up for another sort of scrutiny, a more public one, and Roderick Bruce knew he'd found the means to avenge his lover. His beautiful, studious, gentle lover who had opened a world of physical ecstasy to him. His lover, led to death by an arrogant major who now was being accused by his own colleagues of being a law unto himself.

The hunt began when Roderick Bruce informed his editors he was going to do a series of columns from Southeast Asia. A general covering, with, perhaps, concentration on the men in the field – a contemporary Ernie Pyle approach; no one had done that very well in Vietnam.

The editors were delighted. Roderick Bruce, reporting from Danang, or Son Toy, or the Mekong Delta, had a sound to it reminiscent of the best of vintage war reporting. It was bound to sell more papers and enhance the already superior reputation of the columnist.

It took Rod Bruce less than a month to file his first story about the Major being held incommunicado, awaiting a military court's decision as to whether it had grounds for charges. Several other columns followed, each more damaging than its predecessor. Six weeks after he left Washington Roderick Bruce unearthed the phrase 'killer from Saigon'.

He used it unmercifully.

But the military court wasn't listening. It had orders from some other place, and Major Paul Bonner was quietly released and sent back to the States for obscure duty in the Pentagon.

The military would listen now. Three years and four months after the death of Alex, his Alex, they'd listen. And they'd comply with his demands.

36

Trevayne was annoyed that Walter Madison hesitated. He curled the telephone cord around his finger, his eyes on the folded newspaper in front of him. He kept looking at the three-column story in the lower-left corner of the front page. Its caption was simple, understated: 'Army Officer Held in Slaying'.

The subheading was less restrained: 'Ex-Special Forces Major Accused of Murders in Indo-China Three Years Ago Charged with Brutal Killing in Connecticut'.

Madison was now muttering legalistic platitudes about caution.

'Walter, he's being railroaded! Let's not argue the merits; you'll see I'm right. I just want you to say you'll defend him, be his civilian attorney.'

'That's a tall order, Andy. There are several preliminaries we might not overcome; have you thought of that?'

'What preliminaries?'

'To begin with, he might not want us to represent him. And, frankly, I'm not sure I'd care to. My partners would object strenuously.'

'What the hell are you talking about?' Andrew found himself angry; Madison was going to refuse him. For convenience. 'I haven't noticed any strenuous objecting when I've brought you people a few hundred contract situations which were a damn sight more offensive than defending an innocent man. A man, incidentally, who saved my life, thus allowing me to continue to provide you with retainers. Do I make myself clear?'

'In your usual forthright manner . . . Calm down, Andy. You were on the scene; you're too close to it. I'm thinking of you. If we jump into the defence, we're tying you to Bonner and – *not* incidentally – to de Spadante. I don't think that's wise. You *do* retain me to make such judgments. You may not always like them, but—'

'I don't care about that,' interrupted Trevayne. 'I know what you're saying, and I appreciate it; but it doesn't matter. I want him to have the best.'

'Have you read Roderick Bruce's stuff? It's very unpleasant. So far he's left you on the sidelines; that's not going to be possible much longer. Even so, I'd like to keep him neutral where you're concerned. We can't accomplish that if we're Bonner's attorney.'

'For Christ's sake, Walter. What words do I have to use? I don't give a

258

goddamn on that level. I really don't; I wish you'd believe that. Bruce is a nasty little bastard with a lot of venom and a nose for blood. Bonner's a perfect target. *Nobody* likes him.'

'Apparently with reason. He seems to have a capacity for implementing his own rather violent solutions. Andy, it's not a question of likes and dislikes. It's justified disapproval. The man's a psychopath.'

'That's not true. He's been ordered into terribly violent situations. He didn't create them . . . Look, Walter, I don't want to hire a military crusader. I want a solid firm who's anxious to handle the job because it publicly thinks it can win an acquittal.'

'That could very well disqualify us.'

'I said "publicly"; I don't give a damn what you think personally. You'll change your mind when you've got the facts; I'm sure of that.'

There was a pause. Madison exhaled audibly into the telephone. 'What facts, Andy? Are there really any supportable *facts* that disprove the charge that Bonner stabbed the man without so much as determining who he was or what he was doing there? I've read the newspaper accounts *and* Bruce's columns. Bonner admits to the accusations. The only mitigating circumstance is his claim that he was protecting you. But from what?'

'He was shot at! There's an Army car with bulletholes in the door and through the glass.'

'Then you haven't read Bruce's follow-ups. That car had one bullet mark in the windscreen and three in the door pane. They very well could have been put there with a revolver owned by Bonner. The man denies he had a gun.'

'That's a lie!'

'I'm not a fan of Bruce, but I'd be reluctant to call him a liar. His facts are too specific. You know, of course, he ridicules Bonner's statement that the guards were removed.'

'Also a lie . . . Wait a minute . . . Walter, is all that stuff – Paul's statements, the car, the patrols – is that public?'

'How do you mean?'

'Is it public information?'

'It's easily pieced together from charges and defence statements. Certainly no problem for an experienced reporter. Especially someone like Bruce.'

'But Paul's Army counsel hasn't held any press conferences.'

'He wouldn't have to. Bruce wouldn't need them.'

Trevayne forgot for a moment his argument with Walter Madison. He was suddenly concerned with Roderick Bruce. With an aspect of the diminutive columnist that he hadn't thoroughly considered before. Trevayne had thought Bruce was after Paul Bonner for some mythical conspiratorial theory associated with right-wing politics, Paul being the symbol of the military fascist. But Bruce hadn't pursued the line of attack. Instead, he'd isolated Bonner, concentrated on the specifics related to the Connecticut incident alone. There were allusions to Indo-China, to the murders in the field; but that was all, just allusions. No conspiracy, no Pentagon guilt, no philosophical implications. Just Major Paul Bonner, the 'killer from Saigon', let loose in Connecticut.

It wasn't logical, thought Trevayne as his mind raced, knowing Madison expected him to speak. Bruce had the ammunition to go after the Pentagon hard-liners, the men who ostensibly issued orders to someone like Paul Bonner. But he hadn't; he hadn't even speculated on Bonner's superiors.

Again, just Bonner.

It was a subtle omission. But it was there.

'Walter, I know your position, and I won't play dirty games. No threats –'

'I should hope not, Andy.' It was Madison's turn to interrupt, and he recognized it. 'We've been through too many productive years to see them buried by an Army officer who, I gather, hasn't much use for you.'

'You're right.' Trevayne momentarily lowered his eyes to the telephone. Madison's statement confused him, but he didn't have time to go into it. 'Think it over; talk to your partners. Let me know in a couple of hours. If the answer's negative, I *will* want to be apprised of your reasons; I think I deserve that. If it's yes, I'll expect a whopping bill.'

'I'll get back to you this afternoon or early evening. Will you be at your office?'

'If I'm not, Sam Vicarson will know where to reach me. I'll be home later, Tawning Spring number. I'll expect your call.'

Trevayne hung up and made a decision. Sam Vicarson had a new research project.

By early afternoon Sam had gathered together every column Roderick Bruce had written that had any mention of Paul Bonner, the 'killer from Saigon'.

The writings revealed only that Bruce had latched onto a volatile story made more explosive by the government's insistence on keeping it classified three years ago. It was difficult to tell whether the extraordinary invective used against Paul Bonner was directed at him or at those in command who were protecting the Special Forces Major. The columns were semibalanced in this respect. But sporadically this posture appeared as an excuse, a springboard, to remount an attack on one man – the symbol of monstrosity that was Paul Bonner.

The attacks were superbly written exercises in character assassination. Bonner was both the creator and product of a brutal system of armed exploitation. He was to be scorned and pitied; the pity very much an afterthought and only to be employed as one pities a barbarian who impales the bodies of children because he believes they stem from evil ancestors. Pity the primitive motive, but first destroy the Hun.

And then – as Trevayne had accurately assessed – the current writings shifted. No longer was there any attempt to lock in Bonner with a system. No product now, only a creator.

An isolated monster who betrayed his uniform.

There *was* a difference.

'Man, he's out for a firing squad!' Vicarson whistled before making the pronouncement.

'He certainly is, and I want to know why.'

'I think it's there. Underneath the Savile Row clothes and expensive restaurants, Rod Bruce is the freaked-out new left.'

'Then why isn't he asking for more than one execution? ... Find out where they've got Bonner. I want to see him.'

Paul removed the irritating neck brace and leaned his back against the wall while sitting on the regulation Army bed. Andrew remained standing; the first few minutes of their meeting had been awkward. The BOQ room was small; there was an Army guard stationed in the corridor, and Trevayne had been startled at Bonner's explanation that he was not permitted outside the room except for exercise periods.

'It's better than a cell, I suppose,' said Andy.

'Not a hell of a lot.'

Trevayne began the questioning cautiously. 'I know you can't, or won't, discuss these things, but I want to help. I hope I don't have to convince you of that.'

'No. I'll buy it. But I don't think I'm going to need any.'

'You sound confident.'

'Cooper's expected back in a few days. I've gone through this before, remember? There's a lot of yelling, a lot of formalities; then somehow it all rides out, and I'm quietly transferred somewhere else.'

'You *believe* that?'

Bonner looked reflective. 'Yes, I do ... For a lot of reasons. If I were in Cooper's place – or in the shoes of the other guys up there in Brasswares – I'd do just what they're doing. Let the flap settle ... I've thought about it.' Paul smiled and gave a short laugh. 'The Army moves in mysterious ways.'

'Have you seen the newspapers?'

'Sure. I saw them three years ago, too. Back when I rated ten minutes on the seven o'clock news. Now, it's barely a couple of seconds ... But I appreciate your concern. Especially since I told you to go to hell the last time we talked.'

'I gather you won't give me a return-trip ticket.'

'No, I won't, Andy. You're doing a lot of damage. I'm only a minor – and temporary – casualty.'

'I hope you haven't lulled youself into a false sense of security.'

'That's civilian talk. We have a different meaning for security. What is it that you want to discuss that I won't, or can't?'

'Why you're the all-time pariah for Roderick Bruce.'

'I've often wondered. An Army psychiatrist told me that I'm sort of everything Bruce wishes he was but can't be; that he takes *his* aggression out on a typewriter ... The simpler explanation is that I stand for large DOD appropriations, and that's grist for his mill.'

'I can't accept either. You never met him?'

'Nope.'

'You never quashed any stories he might have written from Indo-China? For security – your version of it.'

'How could I? I was never in that position. And I don't think he was there when I was operating in the field.'

'That's right . . .' Trevayne walked to the single chair in the small room and sat down. 'He went gunning for you after our embassy in Saigon demanded that charges be brought against you . . . Paul, please answer this; I can get the information, take my word for it. Bruce's articles said you were charged with killing three to five men; that the CIA denied having given you the licence by using the term "extreme dispatch" or "prejudice" or whatever the hell it's called. Bruce has friends in every section of the government. By implicating the CIA, could you have caused the Agency to dismiss anyone? Someone he might have known?'

Bonner stared at Trevayne without answering for several moments. He raised his hand to touch the tender skin around his neck and spoke slowly. 'Okay . . . I'll tell you what happened . . . If only to get you off the CIA's butt; they've got enough trouble. There were five slants, double agents. I killed all five. Three because they surrounded my bivouac and let loose with enough firepower to blow up an airstrip. I wasn't inside, thanks to the CIA boys who'd alerted me. I dropped the last two at the Thai border when I caught them with North Vietnamese pouches. They were using our contact sheets and buying off the tribe leaders I'd busted my ass cultivating . . . To tell you the truth, the Agency quietly got me out of the whole mess. Any implications were the result of hotheaded Army lawyers; we told them all to go to hell.'

'Then why were the charges brought in the first place?'

'You don't know Saigon politics. There was never – in history – any corruption like Saigon corruption. Two of those double agents had brothers in the Cabinet . . . At any rate, you can forget CIA.'

Trevayne had removed a thin notebook from his pocket and flipped through the pages. 'The charges against you were made public in February. By March twenty-first Bruce was on your back. He travelled from Danang to the Mekong Delta interviewing anyone who had business with you.'

'He talked to the wrong people. I operated in Laos, Thailand, and northern Cambodia mostly. Usually with teams of six to eight, and they were almost exclusively Asian nonmilitary.'

Trevayne looked up from his notebook. 'I thought Special Forces travelled in units; their own units.'

'Some do. Mostly I didn't. I have a working knowledge of the Thai and Laotian languages – enough tonal understanding to get by – not Cambodian, though. Whenever I went into Cambodia I recruited, when we felt the security was tight enough. It usually wasn't. Once or twice we had to scour our own people to come up with someone we could train in a hurry.'

'Train for what?'

'To stay alive. We weren't always successful. A case in point was Chung Kal...'

They talked for fifteen minutes longer, and Trevayne knew he had found what he was looking for.

Sam Vicarson could put the pieces together.

Sam Vicarson rang the door chimes at Trevayne's rented home in Tawning Spring. Phyllis answered and greeted Sam with a firm handshake.

'Glad you're out of hospital, Mrs Trevayne.'

'If that's meant to be funny, I won't get you a drink.' Phyllis laughed. 'Andy's downstairs, he's expecting you.'

'Thanks. I really am glad you're out.'

'I never should have gone in. Hurry up; your chairman's anxious.'

Downstairs in the recreation-room-turned-office, Trevayne was on the telephone, sitting in a chair, listening impatiently. At the sight of Vicarson, his impatience heightened. In words bordering on rudeness, he extricated himself from the conversation.

'That was Walter Madison. I wish I hadn't promised to play fair. His partners don't want the Bonner case, even if it means losing me as a client; which Walter told them, of course, it wouldn't.'

'There's such a thing as changing your mind.'

'I might do that. Their reasoning's fatuous. They respect the prosecution's case and have none for the defendant.'

'Why is that fatuous?'

'They haven't heard, nor do they wish to hear, the defendant's story. They don't want to get involved; clients to protect, including me.'

'That's fatuous ... However, I think we can turn the hysterical newshound into an enthusiastic character witness for the maligned Major; that is, if we want to. The least we can do is shut him up.'

'Bruce?'

'In lavender spades.'

Vicarson's research had been accomplished with comparative ease. The man's name was Alexander Coffey. The Asian Affairs Bureau at the Pentagon – that is, the officer in charge at AAB – recalled that Roderick Bruce *had* brought to his attention Coffey's background. And AAB had been happy to catch the Ph.D. Far East scholars were hard to come by. The officer was, of course, saddened about the Chung Kal operation, but apparently some good had come out of it. At least, that's what he'd been told. It was always dangerous to put a research analyst into a combat situation ... He gave Coffey's file to Sam.

Vicarson had then gone to the Smithsonian Far East Archives. The head archivist there remembered Coffey clearly. The young man was a brilliant scholar but an obvious homosexual. It had surprised the archivist that Coffey hadn't used his deviation to avoid being drafted, but since his future would be involved with foundations, and foundations were conservative organizations, by and large, the Smithsonian assumed Coffey didn't want the proof on record. Also, the archivist had the suspicion that Coffey knew someone who could steer him into a pleasant military assignment. The man had heard that Coffey was stationed in Washington, and so presumed his suspicions were correct. He obviously didn't know about Coffey's death at Chung Kal, and Vicarson didn't bother to tell him. The archivist showed him Coffey's identification card. On it was an address on 21st Street, Northwest, and the name of a roommate.

As Vicarson learned, a former roommate.

The roommate still blamed the 'rich-bitch' Coffey had moved in with for Alex's death. Alex never told him who it was, but 'he came round often enough – to get away from that awful glutton'. Alexander Coffey 'came around' in new clothes, a new car, and new jewellery. He also came with news that his benefactor had arranged the perfect 'situation' in the Army that wouldn't require even one day of barracks, one day out of Washington. A simple exchange of clothes for the daytime, and the uniform would be custom-made in soft flannel. It was, according to Alex, the 'perfect solution' for his career. Even an Army commission thrown in into the bargain. What foundation could refuse him? And then he was 'hijacked', probably 'betrayed' by the 'rich-bitch'.

Vicarson had heard enough. He drove out to Arlington and saw Paul Bonner.

Bonner remembered Coffey. He had respected him; liked him, actually. The young man had an extraordinary knowledge of the north Cambodian tribes and came up with ingenious suggestions as to how to implement religious symbols in initial contacts. A bold method of operation never considered before.

One aspect of Coffey's joining the unit stood out in Bonner's memory. The man was totally soft, completely alien to the demands that would be made upon him in the hills. Probably a faggot, too. As a result of this knowledge, Bonner drove him hard, relentlessly. Not that six weeks would make up for a lifetime, but perhaps enough could be instilled to help him in a pinch.

But it hadn't been enough, and Coffey was captured in a 'scramble'. Bonner blamed himself for not having been tougher with the scholar; but as a professional, he couldn't dwell on it. He could only learn from it. If the situation ever arose again, where such a man was assigned to him, he'd be unmerciful. Then, perhaps, the man might survive.

'There it is, Mr Trevayne. Lover-didn't-come-back-to-me.'

Trevayne winced. 'Really, Sam. It's very sad.'

'Sure as hell is. But it's also enough to throw Bruce out of the box. I happen to *like* Paul Bonner; I don't give a shit for that cocksucker. I use the word with legal expertise, sir.'

'I'm sure you do. Now, just hold it on a front burner and we'll consider our options.'

'Look, if you're reluctant to get into this gutter, Mr Trevayne, I'm *not*. I mean, it's not very nice for someone like you, but I'm just a wandering legal genius who has no roots. Just influential employers who, I trust, will not forget my contributions … Let me kick him in the balls, I'd love it.'

'You're impossible, Sam.'

'Your wife once told me I reminded her of you. Best compliment I ever had. You shouldn't do it. It's my job.'

'My wife is an incurable romantic when it comes to energetic young men. And it's not your job. It's nobody's at the moment.'

'Why not?'

'Because Roderick Bruce isn't acting alone. He's being fed. He's not flying solo, Sam. He's got confederates; right among the people Paul Bonner thinks are his enthusiastic supporters.'

Vicarson lifted his glass as Phyllis Trevayne walked down the stairs and entered the room. 'Wow, that's a wrinkle.'

'You keep that up, Sam, you won't be invited to a candlelight dinner when Andy's away.'

'Which is tomorrow,' added Trevayne. 'Webster implied that the President thinks I should hear what de Spadante has to say in the morning … on Bonner's behalf. Which means I listen to Mario de Spadante tomorrow morning "up in Greenwich".'

'You'll be back by the afternoon. There goes our candlelight dinner, Mrs Trevayne.'

'Not at all,' said Andy. 'I want you and Alan here by five thirty. Light the candles, Phyl. We may need them.'

37

Mario de Spadante was annoyed that the nurse insisted the shades be raised so as to let in the morning sunlight. But she was a good nurse – not one of his, the hospital's – and Mario was a polite man to those not in his employ. He let the shades stay up.

Andrew Trevayne had just arrived; he was downstairs being met at a side entrance. He had driven into the parking lot two minutes ago and soon would be coming through the door. Mario had arranged the room as he felt it should look. He was raised in the bed as high as possible, the chair beside him low. The young, well-dressed guard on duty across the room smiled as de Spadante instructed him to crank the bed handle and move the furniture.

The young man was one of William Gallabretto's assistants from California. He realized that de Spadante might soon order him out of the room, and that meant he had very little time to accomplish his task.

For attached to his lapel in the form of a jeweled American flag was a miniature camera with a shutter-release wire threaded down to his left jacket pocket.

The door opened, and Andrew Trevayne walked into the room. The corridor guard closed the door, making a last-instant check that the third man was inside.

'Sit, sit, Mr Trevayne.' De Spadante held out his hand, and Andy had no choice but to take it.

The young man by the wall had his hand in his pocket, and, unseen by both men, his thumb made rapid compressions against a small flat metal plunger.

Trevayne sat in the chair, releasing the Italian's grip as swiftly as possible. 'I won't pretend that I looked forward to this visit, Mr de Spadante. I'm not sure we have anything to say to each other.'

That's right, thought the young man by the wall. *Move in a bit and look thoughtful, perhaps a little wary, Trevayne. It'll come out as fear.*

'We got a lot to say, *amico.* I got nothing against you. This soldier, yes. Him I owe for the death of my little brother. Not you.'

'That soldier was attacked, and you know it. I'm sorry about your brother, but he was armed and prowling around on my property. If you were responsible for his being there, look to yourself.'

'What is *this*? I walked into my neighbour's field, and he takes my *life*? What kind of world have we come to?'

'The analogy doesn't fit. Walking in a field is hardly the same as stalking at night with pistols, knives and ... what was it? Oh, yes, iron spikes wrapped around your fingers.'

Perfect, Trevayne, though the man by the wall. *That slight gesture with your palm up. Just right. You, the 'capo regime', explaining to your 'capo di tutti capi'.*

'I grew up having to defend myself, *amico*. My fancy schools were the streets, my teachers the big niggers who liked to hammer wop heads. A bad habit, I confess, but an understandable one that I often carry my fist in my pocket. But no guns; never guns!'

'Apparently you have no need for one.' Trevayne looked over at the young man by the wall with his left hand ominously in his jacket pocket. 'He looks like a cartoon.'

'*You're very funny, too, Trevayne*,' thought the young man by the wall.

'You! Out! ... A friend of a cousin; they're young, what can I do? They have great affection ... Out! Leave us.'

'Sure, Mr de Spadante. Whatever you say.' The young man removed his hand from his jacket pocket. In it he held a box of jujubes. 'Care for a candy, Mr Trevayne?'

'No, thank you.'

'Get out! ... Christ, penny candy they got!'

The door closed, and de Spadante shifted his huge bulk in the pillows. 'Now, we do some talking, okay?'

'It's why I flew up. I'd like to make it as short as possible. I want to hear what you have to say; I want you to hear me.'

'You shouldn't be so arrogant. You know, a lot of people say you're arrogant, but I tell them that my good *amico*, Trevayne, he's not like that. He's just practical; he doesn't waste words.'

'I don't need you defending me—'

'You need something,' interrupted de Spadante. 'Christ, you need *help*.'

'I'm here for one reason only. To tell you to back off from Paul Bonner. You may control your own hoods, de Spadante; get them to swear to whatever you say. But you won't stand up to the cross-examination we throw at you personally ... You're right, I don't waste words. You were seen mauling and threatening a congressman one night on a golf course in Chevy Chase. You were seen by a man who reported the incident to me and Major Bonner. That was an act of physical violence; knowledge of it was all the motive Bonner needed to be on guard. Later you were observed thirty-five hundred miles away, following me to San Francisco. We have sworn testimony to that. Major Bonner had every reason to fear for my life ... Beyond these irrefutable facts and subsequent reasonable concerns, there are other speculations. How does a man like you get off physically abusing a United States congressman? Because he had the temerity to mention an aircraft company? Why did you follow me to California? Were you trying to corner an assistant of mine down at Fisherman's Wharf? Attack him too? Why? What have you got to do with Genessee Industries, de Spadante? The court's going to be concerned with these questions. I'll make sure of it, because I'll tie them to your assault on Paul Bonner last Saturday night . . . I know a little more than I did on that shuttle flight to Dulles. You're finished . . . because you're too obvious. You're just not desirable.'

Mario de Spadante, through heavy-lidded eyes, looked at Trevayne with hatred. His voice, however, remained calm, only the rasp slightly more pronounced. 'That's a favourite word of your kind, isn't it? "Desirable". We're . . . "just not desirable".'

'Don't make a sociological case out of it. You're not an appropriate spokesman.'

De Spadante shrugged. 'Even your insults don't bother me, my good *amico*. You know why? . . . Because you're a troubled man, and a man with troubles has a bad tongue . . . No, I'm still going to help you.'

'You may, but I doubt that it'll be voluntary . . .'

'But first this soldier,' continued the Italian, as if Trevayne had not spoken. 'This soldier, you forget. There's not going to be any trial. This soldier is a dead man; believe me when I tell you this information. He may be breathing now, but he's a dead man. You forget him . . . Now, for your good news . . . Like I said, you got troubles; but your friend Mario is going to make sure that nobody takes advantage of you because of them.'

'What are you talking about?'

'You work hard, Trevayne; you spend a lot of time away from home . . .'

Andrew sat bolt upright in his chair. 'You make one lousy, rotten threat against my family, you filthy son-of-a-bitch, and I'll see you put away for the rest of your life! You'd better not even *think* in those terms, you *animal*. That's one area where the President has given me all the assurances I need! I'll make one telephone call, and you're locked up so far out of sight—'

'*Basta!* You got no right! You shut up!' De Spadante roared as loud as was possible for him, simultaneously clutching his stomach. Then, just as quickly as he had matched Trevayne's intensity, his voice descended to its raspy, quiet norm. 'That kind of talk doesn't belong in this room. I got respect for a man's house . . . his children, his brothers. That soldier, *he's* the animal, not me; not de Spadante.'

'You were the one who brought it up. I just want to make sure you know where you stand. That's out of bounds, and the man on Pennsylvania Avenue has guaranteed it. He's out of your league, hoodlum.'

Mario swallowed, his fury hidden poorly under his rasp. 'He doesn't guarantee an Augie de Spadante, does he? Not Augie; he's not desirable.'

Trevayne looked at his wristwatch. 'You have something to say, say it.'

'Sure. Sure, I'll say it. And the only guarantee you got is me. Like I said, you spend a lot of time away from home, picking up your chips. Maybe you don't have enough time left to give proper guidance to your loved ones. You got a wild boy who drinks too much and draws blanks after a bad night.

Now, that's not too terrible, but he also hits pedestrians. For instance, I got an old man in Cos Cob who was hurt pretty bad by your kid.'

'That's a lie.'

'We got photographs. We got at least a dozen photographs of a half-crazy kid by his car at night. The car and the kid, a mess. So, this old man who was hit; we paid him to be nice and not hurt a wild kid who didn't mean any harm. I've got the canceled cheques – and, of course, a statement. But that's not such a bad thing; millionaires' kids have different values. People understand that . . . We had a little more trouble with your girl. Yes, *that* was a bad thing; it was very touch-and-go for a while. Your friend Mario spared no expense to protect her . . . and you.'

Trevayne sat back in his chair; there was no anger in his expression, only disgust coupled with faint amusement. 'The heroin. That was you,' he said simply.

'Me? You don't hear good . . . A little girl, maybe bored, maybe just for kicks, gets hold of a bag of the best Turkish—'

'You *conceivably* think you can prove that?'

'The *best* Turkish; over two hundred thousand worth. Maybe she's got a little network of her own. Those fancy girls' schools are a big part of the scene today. You know that, don't you? There was a diplomat's daughter caught a few months ago; you saw that in the papers, no? He didn't have a friend like your friend Mario.'

'I asked you a question. Do you really think you could prove anything?'

'You think I couldn't?' De Spadante suddenly turned on Trevayne and spat out the words. 'Don't be so dumb. You're dumb, Mr Arrogance! You think you know everyone your little girl has been seen with? You think I can't give Lieutenant Fowler of the Greenwich Police Department a list of names and places? Who checks? Seventeen isn't that young these days, *amico*. Maybe you read about those rich kids with the nigger organizations, blowing up buildings, making riots . . . Now, I don't say your kid is *one* of them; but people got to *think*. They see it every day. And two hundred thousand . . .'

Trevayne stood up, his patience at an end. 'You're wasting my time, de Spadante. You're cruder – and denser – than I thought. What you're telling me is that you've engineered potential blackmail situations; I'm sure they're well thought-out. But you've made a serious mistake. Two mistakes. You're out of date, and you don't know your subjects. You know, you're right. Seventeen and nineteen *aren't* that young these days. Think about it. You're part of what the kids can't stand anymore. Now, whether you'll excuse me or not—'

'What about forty-two?'

'What?'

'Forty-two isn't a kid. You got a pretty wife. A well-stacked lady in her forties with plenty of money and maybe a hunger or two she don't get satisfied inside her big ranch house . . . or maybe in her fancy castle on the ocean. A lady who had a big drinking problem a few years ago?'

'You're on dangerous ground, de Spadante.'

'You listen, and you listen good! . . . Some of these classy ladies come into town and hang around the East Side saloons, the ones with French or Spanish names. Others head for the artsy-fartsy places in the Village where the rich fags go, too. Lots of studs down there who'll swing both ways for a buck . . . And then a few of the real genuine articles go to hotels like the Plaza—'

'I warn you!'

'Before they get to the Plaza – where naturally they got reservations – they make a telephone call to a certain number, these ladies do; these genuine articles. No fuss; no bother, no worries at all. Everything very discreet; satisfaction guaranteed . . . And the games they play! I tell you, *amico*, you wouldn't believe it!'

Trevayne abruptly swung around and started for the door. De Spadante's voice – louder but not loud – stopped him. 'I got a sworn affidavit from a very respected hotel security man. He's been around for a long time; he's seen them all. He can spot the genuine articles; he spotted yours. It's a very ugly statement. And it's true. What he saw.'

'You're filth, de Spadante.' It was all he could think to say.

'I like that better than "not desirable", *amico*. It's stronger, more positive, you know what I mean?'

'Have you finished?'

'Just about. I want you to know that the private troubles you got are going to stay very confidential. Your burdens are safe with me. No newspapers, no television or radio broadcasts; everything quiet. You want to know why?'

'I might be able to guess.'

'Yeah, sure you can . . . Because you're going to go back to Washington and wrap up your little subcommittee. Write a nice report that slaps a few wrists and makes a couple of people get fired – we'll tell you who – and call it a day. You got that?'

'And if I refuse?'

'Oh, Christ, *amico*. You want to put your loved ones through all this *rifiuti*. I mean, what the hell, a little old man in Cos Cob and all those pictures of the drunken kid. They'd look terrible in the newspapers. And a matter of two hundred thousand dollars' worth of uncut Turkish – the cops *found* it, you know what I mean? They couldn't say they didn't. Last, your pretty lady at the Plaza; that hotel security – he's a very respected retired police officer – he wrote up exactly what he saw. You don't even want to see it privately. It'd bring back all kinds of things; like the lady's big drinking problem. That was very real; we got a doctor to help her a few years back. You know how people think. They never really trust an ex-drunk. There's always that possibility that she's not so ex. Or maybe she's just substituted another hang-up. You know how people think.'

'Everything you say would be exposed for what it is. Lies.'

'Of course, you deny! . . . But enough of those items are solid, Trevayne. Real *solid*, you know what I mean? . . . And I read in a book once: accusations – especially with a little foundation, some background, a few photographs, they hit page one. Denials, they come later – on page fifty – between salami ads ... Take your choice, Mr Trevayne. But think it over good.'

Trevayne watched the slow smile emerge on the fat Sicilian lips; the satisfied hatred in the tiny eyes, surrounded by rolls of flesh.

'I get the idea you've waited a long time for this, de Spadante.'

'All my life, you snot-nosed, velvet pig. Now get out of here and do what I tell you. You're just like all the rest.'

38

Robert Webster received the telephone call in his White House office and knew it had to be an emergency. The caller said he had a message from Aaron Green and was instructed to deliver it personally. It couldn't wait; Webster was to meet him within the hour. By three o'clock.

The two men agreed on the Villa d'Este restaurant in Georgetown; second floor, cocktail lounge. The Villa d'Este was an insane conglomeration of Victorian pastiche and Italian renaissance, had six floors, and catered to a tourist luncheon crowd. No one of consequence in Washington arrived at the Villa d'Este until the late-evening hours, when a tourist couldn't get a reservation unless he had a personal introduction from his senator.

Webster arrived first, in itself a bad omen. Bobby Webster made it a point never to be the one waiting. The advantage of immediate control was too often lost while listening to low-keyed but impressive explanations of tardiness.

And so it was when Aaron Green's man finally showed up, fifteen minutes late. He spoke in rapid, short sentences, making his points apologetically but with an unmistakable air of condescension. He'd had a number of other calls to finish; Aaron Green expected him to accomplish one hell of a lot for a single day in Washington.

And now he could allocate the proper time to their immediate concerns.

Webster watched the man, listened to the understated but confident words, and suddenly realized why he felt uncomfortable, anxious. The man from Green was an operator, as he was an operator. He was comparatively young, as he was young. He was on his way up in the labyrinth world of conglomerate economics, as he was on his way up in the contradictory world of power politics. They both spoke well, carried themselves with assurance, had bearings that were at once strong and yet obedient to those to whom obedience was due.

But there was one profound difference between them, and both men knew it; it needed no elaboration. Green's man was dealing from the position of strength; Robert Webster was not and could not.

Something had happened. Something that directly affected Webster's value, his position of influence. A decision had been made somewhere, in some conference or over some very private dinner, that would alter the course of his immediate existence.

The emissary from Green was his first warning and the cause of Bobby Webster's profound sense of anxiety. For he recognized the preliminary stay of his own symbolic execution.

Webster knew he was on the way out. He'd failed to control the necessities; the best he might hope for was to retreat and salvage what he could.

'Mr Green is very concerned, Bobby. He understands that solutions have been agreed to without his having been consulted. It's not that he expects to be called every time a decision is made, but Trevayne is a sensitive area.'

'We're simply discrediting him. Linking him to de Spadante, that's all. Deballing his subcommittee. It's no big deal.'

'Perhaps not. But Mr Green thinks Trevayne might react differently than the way you've anticipated. He might make it a . . . big deal.'

'Then Mr Green hasn't been given an accurate picture. It doesn't make any difference how Trevayne reacts, because there won't be any charges leveled. Only speculations. And none of us will be involved . . . As we see it, he'll be compromised to the point of ineffectiveness.'

'By associating him with de Spadante?'

'More than verbal association. We have photographs – they came out beautifully. They place him unquestionably at the hospital in Greenwich. They're candids, and more damaging the longer they're looked at . . . Roderick Bruce will release the first of them in two days.'

'After de Spadante is taken to New Haven?' Green's man was staring hard at Webster, his voice skirting the edge of insult.

'That's right.'

'De Spadante will be very much in the news then, won't he? Mr Green understands he's to be removed from the chessboard.'

'That decision emanated from his own associates; they consider it imperative. It has nothing to do with us, except that it happens to be advantageous to our objectives.'

'Mr Green isn't convinced of that.'

'It's an underworld action. We couldn't stop it if we wanted to. And with those photographs, properly documented by a couple of Greenwich doctors, Trevayne becomes implicated in the entire mess. He's finished.'

'Mr Green thinks that's oversimplified.'

'It's not, because no one's going to claim anything. Can't you *see* that?' Webster now utilized the tone of impatient explanation. It was useless.

The conversation was no more than a ritual dance. The best Webster could expect was that Green's man – for his own protection – might carry back the total strategy to Green; that the old Jew would see the benefits and change his mind.

'I'm only an assistant, Bobby. A messenger.'

'But you *do* see the advantages.' It wasn't a question, but a statement.

'I'm not sure. This Trevayne is a determined man. He might not accept . . .
implications and quietly go away.'

'Have you ever seen anyone *turned off* in Washington? It's a hell of a sight.
He can yell all he cares to, but somehow no one wants to listen. No one
wants to get touched by the leper . . . even the President.'

'What about him? The President.'

'The simplest part of the exercise. I'll hold a group session with the aides,
and together we'll present a strong case for the President to extricate himself
from Trevayne. He'll listen to us; he's got too goddamned many other
problems. We'll give him the options of doing it gracefully or with acid. He'll
choose the former, of course. There's an election in eighteen months. He'll
see the logic. No one'll have to draw pictures.'

Green's man looked sympathetically at Webster as he spoke. 'Bobby, I'm
here to instruct you to call it all off. That was the exact way Mr Green put it.
"Instruct him to call everything off." He doesn't care about de Spadante; you
say you can't control that anyway. But Trevayne isn't to be touched . . .
That's the word. It's final.'

'It's *wrong*. I've thought this out to the last detail. I've spent weeks making
sure every goddamn piece falls into place. It's *perfect*.'

'*It's out*. There's a whole new set of circumstances now. Mr Green is
meeting with three or four others to clarify everything . . . I'm sure you'll be
apprised.'

Webster understood the throw-away quality of the man's last sentence. He
wouldn't be apprised of a damn thing unless they wanted something. Nor
could he force his way into the newly formed circle. Alliances were being
altered, or, conversely, made more interdependent, consolidated. Whichever,
he was excluded.

Webster probed for survival clues. 'If there are to be any substantial
changes of policy, I think I'd better be informed immediately. I don't like to
use the bromide, but the White House *is*, after all, where it's *at*.'

'Yes . . . Yes, of course.' Green's man looked at his watch.

'A number of questions will be directed at me. From a wide spectrum of
influential people. I should have answers.'

'I'll tell Mr Green.'

'He should *know* it.' Webster watched himself; he didn't want to appear
desperate.

'I'll remind him.'

He *was* being excluded, and in a manner that was far too cavalier, thought
Webster. The White House was being excluded. It was a moment for
audacity.

'Do more than "remind" him. Make it clear that there are a few of us
down here who wield pretty big sticks. There are some areas of Genessee
Industries that we're more knowledgeable about than anyone else. We like to
think of them as our insurance policies.'

The man from Green abruptly looked up from the table and locked his
eyes with Webster's. 'I'm not sure that's an apt term, Bobby. "Insurance

Policies", I mean. Unless you're thinking about double indemnity; that's expensive.'

The moment sustained itself. Green's man was telling Robert Webster of the White House that he, too, could be removed from the chessboard. Webster knew it was time to initiate the beginning of his retreat. 'Let's clarify; since there seems to be a lot of that going around. I'm not so concerned for myself; my credentials couldn't be much better. I can go back to Akron and pick and choose. My wife would like that best. And I wouldn't mind one bit . . . But there are others; they might not be *able* to pick and choose. None of them *has* the White House on his résumé. They could be troublesome.'

'I'm sure everything will work out. For all of you. You're experienced people.'

'Well, there aren't that many—'

'We know,' interrupted the emissary from Aaron Green. The statement implied far more than the understated way it was phrased. 'It's time for me to go. I've still got a lot to do today.'

'Sure. I'll pay for the drinks.'

'Thanks very much.' Green's man got up from the table. 'You'll get those photographs back from Rod Bruce? Kill any story?'

'He won't like it, but I will.'

'Good. We'll be in touch . . . And, Bobby. About Akron. Why don't you start preparing that résumé.'

39

The servants had turned on the table lamps in Aaron Green's glass-enclosed porch with the potted plants everywhere. Outside, toward the rear, two yellowish floodlights lit up the snow-covered lawn – the burlapped shrubbery and the far-off, ghostlike white arbour in the distance. A silver coffee service was on the glass-topped round table between the white wrought-iron furniture, cups and saucers in their places. Several yards away on still another glass-topped table – this one a rectangle, longer, higher, and against the wall – was a selection of liqueurs with crystal brandy glasses off to the side.

The servants had been excused. Mrs Green had retired to her sewing room upstairs; the lights in the rest of the house, except for the front hall and entrance, were extinguished.

Aaron Green was about to hold a meeting. A meeting with three men, but only one had been a guest for dinner. A Mr Ian Hamilton.

The other two were driving out to Sail Harbor together. Walter Madison would stop by Kennedy Airport and pick up Senator Alan Knapp, who was flying in from Washington; together they would drive to Sail Harbor. They would arrive around ten o'clock.

They did. Precisely at ten o'clock.

At six minutes past ten the four men entered the glass-enclosed porch.

'I shall pour coffee, gentlemen. The drinks – the brandies – are over there. I do not trust these old hands to tip a bottle into those tiny glasses. I also find it difficult to read the labels; consequently, I do not indulge . . . Perhaps it's fortunate I can find my chair.'

'Absolutely nothing wrong with you but sheer laziness, Aaron.' Ian Hamilton laughed, going to the brandy table. 'I'll pour.'

Walter Madison accepted his brandy and sat at Green's left. Hamilton brought Knapp's drink to the round table and placed it at Green's right; the Senator sat down promptly. Hamilton then pulled back the chair opposite Aaron Green and did the same, not too promptly.

'We could be sitting down for a hand of bridge,' said Madison.

'Or a rough game of poker,' added Senator Knapp.

'Perhaps baccarat unlimited might be more appropriate.' Ian Hamilton raised his glass to Green. 'Your health, Aaron . . . All our healths.'

'Also appropriate, my friend,' replied Green in his low voice. 'These are times that require the best of health. Health of body and mind. Especially the mind.'

They drank, and Knapp was the first to replace his glass on the table. He was impatient but knew that patience was a valued commodity at this table. Still, he was a respected senator, a man this table needed. There was no point in feigning a composure he did not feel. He was not famous for his tact; tact was irrelevant to him.

'I'll put my first card face-up on the table, Mr Hamilton, Mr Green. I'm not leaving you out, Walter, but I think your position here is somewhat the same as mine. All we've heard is that Andrew Trevayne is not to be ... "taken advantage of" is the best way to put it. Walter and I discussed it in the car. There's no point obscuring that fact. To be frank, I'll be damned if I can understand. Bobby Webster's strategy seemed to me a beautiful piece of work.'

Ian Hamilton looked over at Green, and after several seconds he nodded his head. It was a very slight motion; he was giving the old Jew permission to speak.

'Mr Webster's strategy *was* a beautiful piece of work, Senator,' said Green. 'As the General's brilliant manoeuvre might win a battle – to the great rejoicing of his command post – while in another section of the terrain the enemy mounts a blitzkrieg that will win the war.'

'You think,' asked Walter Madison, 'that rendering Andrew completely ineffective ... isn't sufficient? Who else is fighting us?'

Ian Hamilton spoke. 'Trevayne is in a unique position, Walter. He fully understands what we've done and why we've done it. What he may lack in hard evidence he's more than compensated for by his perception of our larger goals.'

'I don't understand that,' interrupted Knapp quietly.

'I'll answer,' said Green, smiling at Hamilton. 'We two are not lawyers, Knapp. If we were – I were – I think I'd say that our Mr Trevayne has only bits and pieces of directly damaging testimony, but volumes of circumstantial evidence. Is that correctly put, Counsellor Hamilton?'

'You may go to the head of the class, Aaron ... What Trevayne has done is something no one expected he would do. He threw away the book, the legal book. I suspect he threw it away very early in his research ... While we were concerned with a thousand legalities, ten thousand items of cost and processing and allocations, Trevayne was going after something else. Individuals. Men in key positions he correctly assumed were representative. Remember, he's a superb administrator; even those who despise him grant him that. He knew there had to be a pattern, a control process. A company as large and diverse as Genessee couldn't function on the executive-board level if one didn't exist. Especially under the circumstances. Strangely enough, Mario de Spadante's people first perceived it. They purposely sent in contradictory information and waited to be called up on it. They weren't. Of course, they didn't know what to do with what they'd discovered. De

Spadante crudely began making threats, upsetting everyone he came in contact with ... So much for de Spadante.'

'I'm sorry, Mr Hamilton.' Knapp leaned forward on the white wrought-iron chair with its floral-print cushions. 'Everything you say leads me right back to Bobby Webster's solution ... You imply that Trevayne has pieced together information that endangers everything we've worked for; what better moment to discredit him? Discredit him, we discredit his evidence. At least, sufficiently so for our purposes.'

'Why not *kill* him?' Aaron Green's deep voice thundered across the table. It was an angry question and stunned Madison and Knapp. Hamilton had no visible reaction. 'That shakes you, eh? Why? It is the unspoken thought, perhaps ... I've seen death closer than anyone at this table, so it does not shock *me*. But I will tell you why it is not plausible, just as this peddler Webster's solution is not plausible ... Such men as Trevayne are more dangerous in death and forced retirement than they are in active life.'

'Why?' asked Walter Madison.

'Because they leave *legacies*,' answered Green. 'They become rallying points for crusaders. They are the martyrs, the symbols. They cause the breeding of discontented rats that multiply and nibble away at your foundations! We have no time to spend stamping out their nests.'

Aaron Green's anger so upset him that his old hands shook. Ian Hamilton's voice was calm but nevertheless commanding. 'Don't excite yourself, Aaron. Nothing will be accomplished by it ... He's right, you know. We haven't the time for such endeavors. Not only are they distracting, they can't succeed. Men like Trevayne keep extensive records ... Instead, one must face a fundamental issue. We can neither obscure it nor sidestep it. We must understand and accept our own motives ... In light of the record, I primarily address myself to the Senator and Aaron. You arrived late on the scene, Walter; your participation, though immensely valuable, has not been one of long standing.'

'I know that,' said Madison softly.

'There are many who could call us power brokers, and they would be right. We dispense authority within the body politic. And though there are ego compensations in what we do, we are not driven by our egos to do it. We, of course, believe in ourselves; but only as instruments to gain our objectives. I explained this – abstractly, to be sure – to Trevayne, and I believe he can be convinced of our sincerity.'

Knapp had been staring down at the glass tabletop, listening. Suddenly he whipped his head up and looked at Hamilton in disbelief. 'You what?'

'Yes, Senator, that's what it came down to between us. Are you shocked?'

'I think you've lost your mind!'

'Why?' asked Aaron Green sharply. 'Have you ultimately done something for which you are ashamed, Senator? Are you more concerned for yourself than for our aims? Are you one of us, or are you something else?' Green leaned forward, his hand trembling on the handle of the coffee cup.

'It's not a question of being ashamed. It's simply one of being misjudged,

Mr Green. You act as a private individual; I am an elected representative. Before I'm held accountable, I want the results to be apparent. We haven't reached that point yet.'

'We're nearer than you think,' said Hamilton quietly, in counterpoint to both Green and Knapp.

'I fail to see any evidence of that,' replied the Senator.

'Then you haven't looked around you.' Hamilton raised his brandy glass and drank sparingly. 'Everything we've touched, every area we've managed, has been the better for our attentions. There can be no denying it. What we've done, in essence, is to build a financial base of such dimensions that it influences whole sections of the country. And wherever that influence has been felt, we've improved the status quo. Minorities – and majorities – are heeded; employment risen; welfare declined; production continued without interruption. As a result, segments of national interest have benefited. Our military posture has been strengthened unquestionably; geographical areas of the economy remain at high-gross-product levels; social reforms in housing, education, and medicine have been promoted painlessly wherever Genessee's imprimatur is found . . . What we've proved is that we can bring about social stability . . . Would you deny this summation, Senator? It's what we've worked for.'

Knapp was startled. Hamilton's rapid enumeration of points astonished him; gave him a sense of confidence – identification, perhaps – he had not felt before. 'I've been too close to the Washington machinery; obviously you have a better view.'

'Granted. I'd still like you to answer the question. Would you deny the facts . . . from what you *have* discovered?'

'No, I imagine I wouldn't . . .'

'You *couldn't*.'

'All right, "couldn't".'

'Then don't you see the corollary? . . . Don't you realize what we've done?'

'You've outlined the accomplishments; I accept them.'

'Not just accomplishments, Senator. I've outlined the leadership functions of the executive branch of the government . . . With *our* help. Which is why, after painstaking consideration and swift but exhaustive analysis, we are going to offer Andrew Trevayne the presidency of the United States.'

No one spoke for several minutes. Ian Hamilton and Aaron Green sat back in their chairs and let the newcomers absorb the information. Finally, Knapp spoke in a voice laced with incredulity.

'That's the most preposterous statement I've ever heard. You've got to be joking.'

'And you, Walter?' Hamilton turned to Madison, who sat staring at his glass. 'What's your reaction?'

'I don't know,' answered the attorney slowly. 'I'm still trying to digest it . . . I've been close to Andrew for many years. I think he's an extraordinarily talented man . . . But this? I just don't know.'

'But you are *thinking*,' said Aaron Green, looking not at Madison but at Knapp. 'You are using your imagination. Our "elected representative" reacts only to "preposterous".'

'For good and sufficient reasons!' snapped Alan Knapp. 'He has no political experience; he's not even a registered member of either party!'

'Eisenhower had no experience,' replied Green. 'And both parties tried to recruit him.'

'He has no stature.'

'Who had less at the beginning than Harry Truman?' rejoined the Jew.

'Eisenhower had worldwide exposure, popularity. Truman grew in the job he inherited. Irrelevant examples.'

'Exposure's no problem today, Senator,' interjected Hamilton with his prepossessing calm. 'There are thirteen months before the national conventions, eighteen before the election. Within that period of time, I daresay, Andrew Trevayne could be merchandised with extraordinary effect. He has all the qualifications for maximum results ... The key is not political experience or affiliation – actually, their absence could be an advantage; nor is it his current stature – which, incidentally, may be more than you think, Senator. Neither is it that abstraction, popularity ... It's voting blocs. Before and after whatever convention we decide to enter. And Genessee Industries will deliver those blocs.'

Knapp started to speak several times but stopped, as though rethinking his thoughts, trying to find the words to convey his bewilderment. At last he spread his hands down on the glass-topped table; it was a gesture of superimposing control on himself. 'Why? Why in God's name would you do it, even consider it?'

'Now you are *thinking*, "elected representative".' Aaron Green patted the back of Knapp's left hand. The Senator drew it off the table quickly.

'Put simply, Senator, it's our judgment that Trevayne would make an extremely competent President. Perhaps even a brilliant one. He would, after all, have the time to pursue those aspects of the office few presidents in this century have been afforded. Time to reflect, concentrate on the nation's foreign relationships, its negotiations and long-range policies ... Has it ever occurred to you why we are constantly being outflanked by our global adversaries? It's quite simple, you know. We expect *far* too much of the single man sitting in the Oval Office. He's torn in a thousand directions. He has no time to think. The Frenchman Pierre Larousse, I believe, said it best in the nineteenth century ... Our form of government is superb, with one significant imperfection. Every four years we must elect God as our President.'

Walter Madison watched Hamilton closely. As a good attorney he had spotted the quantum jump, and it wasn't in his training to let it slide by. 'Ian, do you think for one minute Trevayne would accept the condition that the majority of domestic problems be handled outside the decision sphere of the presidency?'

'Certainly not.' Hamilton smiled. He accepted the forensic challenge.

'Because the majority wouldn't be problems. Put another way, major problems wouldn't be allowed to develop, to the degree heretofore experienced. Questions of domestic irritation are something else again. Every President delegates them and makes the proper palliative statements. They're not time-consuming, and they allow for leadership exposure.'

'You know you haven't really answered my question, Mr Hamilton.' Knapp got up from his chair and went to the brandy. 'It's one thing to say a man will make a President. Good, bad, or brilliant, it's the making that counts first ... It's something else again to select this or that specific individual as your chosen candidate. That choice has to reflect something other than idealistic appraisal. Under the circumstances, given someone who's displayed such determination to be his own man, I still want to know why it's Trevayne ... Yes, Mr Green, I think it's preposterous!'

'Because when all the fancy talk is finished, Mr Elected Representative, we have no choice.' Green turned in his chair and looked up at Knapp. 'You'd like better so preposterous an idea that you're run out of office for a thief.'

'My record is spotless.'

'Your associations aren't so clean. Take my word.' Green turned back to the table and with his trembling hand reached for his cold coffee.

'Such talk is pointless,' said Hamilton, for the first time showing anger. 'Trevayne would not have been chosen – and you know this, Aaron – if we felt he wasn't qualified. It's been established that he's an extraordinary executive; that's exactly what the presidency requires.'

Knapp returned to the table as Aaron Green looked at Hamilton and spoke softly; with immense feeling. 'You know what I require. Nothing else concerns me, or will ever concern me. I want no peddlers to interfere with that. *Strength*. That's all.'

Walter Madison watched the old man and thought he understood. He'd heard rumors that Green had quietly financed training camps for the Jewish Defense League. He knew now they weren't just rumors. But Madison was disturbed. He turned to Hamilton, cutting off Knapp, who was about to speak.

'Obviously Andrew hasn't been approached. What makes you think he'll accept? Personally, I don't think he will.'

'No man of talent and vanity turns his back on the presidency. Trevayne has both. And he should have. If the talent's authentic, the vanity must follow.' Hamilton answered Madison but included Knapp. 'At first, his reaction will be no different from the Senator's. Preposterous. We'll expect that. But within a matter of days he will be shown graphically, *professionally*, that it is a feasible concept, that it's really within his grasp ... Spokesmen for labour, the business community, the sciences, will be brought to him. Leading political figures from all sections of the country will telephone him, letting him know that they are most interested – not committed, but interested – in the possibility of his candidacy. From these exploratory confrontations will emerge a practical campaign strategy. Aaron's agency will assume responsibility.'

'*Have* assumed it,' said Green. 'Already three of my most trusted people are working behind tight-shut doors. All are the very best, and each knows if there's a leak, he'll never work again except maybe in a ditch.'

Knapp's astonishment grew in proportion to the extraordinary information. 'You've actually begun all this?'

'It is our function to stay well ahead of tomorrow, Senator,' answered Hamilton.

'You can't possibly guarantee that labour, business, political leaders ... will agree.'

'We can, and those we've reached *have*. They've been contacted in utter sincerity; they've been sworn to confidence until told otherwise. They are part of a grass-roots groundswell. In many instances, they're most enthusiastic.'

'It's ... it's ...'

'We know, preposterous.' Green completed Knapp's exclamation. 'You think Genessee Industries is managed by Washington bureaucrats? By idiots? We're talking about two or three hundred people, maybe a few mayors, governors; our payrolls are several thousand times that.'

'What about the House, the Senate? Those are—'

'That House is under control,' interrupted Hamilton. 'The Senate? ... That's why you're here tonight.'

'*Me?*' Knapp's hands were once more back on the glass-topped table in front of him.

'Yes, Senator.' Hamilton spoke with calm conviction. 'You're a dedicated member of the Club. You've also got the reputation of a sceptic. I've seen in print where you've been called the "unpredictable sceptic of the Senate". You're going to be our key man in the cloakroom.'

'Otherwise,' added Aaron Green with a gesture, 'poof!'

Senator Knapp did not pursue the subject.

Walter Madison couldn't help but smile at the old Jew, but his smile faded quickly as he spoke. 'Let's grant, hypothetically, that everything you say is possible. Even probable. How do you propose to handle the current President? It's my impression that he intends to run for a second term.'

'By no means conclusive. His wife and family are very much against it. And remember, Genessee Industries has removed scores of major problems from his concerns. We can easily re-create them. Finally, if it comes to it, we have medical reports that could finish him a month before the election.'

'Are they true?'

Hamilton lowered his eyes. 'Partially. But I'm afraid that's irrelevant. We have them; that's relevant.'

'Second question. If Andrew is elected, how do you control him? How can you stop him from throwing all of you out?'

'Any man who sits in the president's chair learns one supreme lesson instantly,' replied Hamilton. 'That it's the most pragmatic of all jobs. He needs every bit of help he can get. Instead of throwing us out, he'll come running for assistance, try to convince us to come out of retirement.'

'Retirement?' Knapp's confusion was paramount, but Walter Madison's expression conveyed his understanding.

'Yes. Retirement, Senator. Walter knows. You must try to grasp the subtlety. Trevayne would never accept the proposition if he thought it was engineered by Genessee. Our position will be made clear. We'll be reluctant, but ultimately he has our backing, our endorsement; he's one of us. He's a product of the marketplace. Once he's elected, we have every intention of leaving the scene, living out the remainder of our lives in the comforts we've earned. We'll convince him of this ... If he needs us, we're there, but we'd rather not be called ... Of course, we have no intention of leaving at all.'

'And when he learns this,' summed up Walter Madison, attorney-at-law, 'it's too late. It's too late. It's the ultimate compromise.'

'Exactly,' agreed Ian Hamilton.

'My people behind the tight-shut doors have created a very effective campaign phrase ... "Andrew Trevayne, the Mark of Excellence".'

'I think they stole it, Aaron,' said Hamilton.

40

Trevayne read the newspaper story as a wave of relief swept over him. He never imagined that he could be so filled with joy – there was no other word but 'joy' – over a man's death, a man's brutal murder. But there it was, and he was consumed with a sense of deliverance.

'Underworld Chief Slain in Ambush Outside New Haven Home.'

The story went on to say how Mario de Spadante, while being transferred from an ambulance into his home on Hamden Terrace, was dropped to the ground and fired upon by six men who had been waiting on both sides of de Spadante's house. None of those carrying the stretcher or the others at the scene, presumably the gangster's personal guards, were injured. Thus the police authorities speculated that the killing was a multiple 'contract' issued by 'bosses' unhappy over de Spadante's expanding associations outside the Connecticut area. It was no secret that de Spadante, whose brother allegedly was killed by an Army officer – a Major Paul Bonner – had displeased Mafia chieftains with his involvement in government construction projects. There seemed to be a general agreement among underworld powers that de Spadante was exceeding his authority and courting widespread danger for organized crime with his Washington endeavours.

As a side issue, the daylight slaying lent considerable credence to Major Paul Bonner's claim that he was assaulted prior to having killed August de Spadante, the brother of the above. Reached in Arlington, Bonner's military defence attorney stated that the New Haven murder was further evidence that his client was caught in the crossfire of a gangland war; that Major Bonner performed outstandingly to protect Andrew Trevayne from attack. Mr Trevayne, the article pointed out, was chairman of a subcommittee investigating corporate relationships with the Defense Department; the de Spadantes were known to have profited from several Pentagon contracts.

There followed four photographs showing Mario de Spadante in various stages of his career. Two were police identification shots separated by fifteen years; another on a nightclub floor in the early fifties; and one with his brother, August, in which both were standing in front of a construction crane, grinning the grins of Caesars.

It was so tidy, thought Trevayne. The snuffing out of one life removed so much evil. He had not slept – or if he had, it didn't seem so – since leaving de Spadante's hospital bed. He had asked himself over and over again if it was all worth it. And the answer progressively became a louder and louder negative.

He finally had to admit to himself that de Spadante *had* reached him; *had* compromised him. The Italian succeeded because he had forced him to weigh the values, consider the terrible price. The *rifiuti*, as de Spadante had called it. The garbage that would have buried his wife and children, the stench of its conjecture lingering for years.

It wasn't worth it to him. He would not pay that price for a subcommittee he hadn't sought, for the benefit of a President he owed no debt to, for a Congress that allowed such men as de Spadante to buy and sell its influence. Why should he?

Let someone else pay the price.

And now that part of it was finished. De Spadante was finished. He could put his mind back to the subcommittee report he had attacked with such energy after he'd left Chicago. After he'd left Ian Hamilton.

Three days ago nothing else had seemed so necessary, so vital. He had been distracted by Paul Bonner's murder charge, but every minute away from that concern found him back at the report. He'd had the feeling then – three days ago – that time was the most important thing on earth; the report had to be completed and its summary made known to the highest levels of the government as soon as was humanly possible.

Yet now, as he stared down at the Genessee notebooks piled beside the folded newspaper, he found himself strangely reluctant to plunge back into the work he'd set aside three days ago. He'd travelled to and from his River Styx. Like Charon, he'd carried the souls of the dead across the turbulent waters, and now he needed rest, peace. He had to get out from the lower world for a while.

And Genessee Industries was the lower world.

Or was it? Or was it, instead, only the maximum efforts of misguided men seeking reasonable solutions in unreasonable times?

It was only nine fifteen in the morning, but Trevayne decided to take the rest of the day off. Perhaps one carefree day – one *free* of *care* – with Phyllis was what he needed.

To get the battery charged again.

Roderick Bruce threw the newspaper across the room and swore at the blue velour walls. That hard-on son-of-a-bitch had betrayed him! That Corn Belt butcher had waltzed him, and when the music stopped, kicked him in the balls and run back to the White House!

... the slaying lent considerable credence to Major Paul Bonner's claim ... assaulted prior to allegedly killing ... caught in the crossfire of a gangland war ... performed outstandingly ...

Bruce swept his tiny arm across the breakfast tray, sending the dishes crashing to the floor. He kicked the blankets off the bed – his and Alex's bed – and leaped onto the lime flotkati rug. He could hear the sound of the maid's footsteps; she was running down the outside corridor towards his room, and he shouted at the top of his lungs.

'Stay *out* of here, you black cunt!'

He ripped his Angkor Wat night shirt – the silk sleeping gown given him by Alex – as he pulled it over his head. Naked on the soft rug, his foot touched the upturned coffee cup; he reached down, picked it up, and slammed it against the onyx bedside table.

He sat down at his desk and purposely straightened his bare back so that it was flat, hard against the chair. He kept his muscles taut, his posture rigid. It was an exercise he used often to discipline himself. To gain control of excessive feelings.

He'd shown Alex one night; a rare evening when they'd fought. Over some silly thing that was inconsequential . . . the roommate, that was it. The dirty roommate from Alex's old apartment on 21st Street. The dirty, filthy roommate who wanted Alex to drive him up to Baltimore because he had too much luggage for the train.

They'd fought that night. But Alex finally understood how the dirty, filthy roommate was taking advantage of him, and so he called him up and told him absolutely *no*. After the telephone call, Alex was still upset, so Rod – Roger – showed him his bedroom desk exercise, and Alex began to laugh. It was a happy laugh; Alex was actually giddy. He told Roger that his exercise in discipline was almost pure Hindu Kantamani, an ancient religious punishment for young boys the priests found masturbating.

Bruce pressed his naked back harder into the chair. He could feel the buttons of the blue-velvet upholstery cutting into his flesh. But it was working; he was thinking clearly now.

Bobby Webster had given him two photographs of Trevayne and de Spadante together in de Spandante's hospital room in Greenwich. The first photograph depicted Trevayne seemingly explaining something to the bedridden gangster. The second showed Trevayne looking angry – 'disgruntled' was perhaps more accurate – at something de Spadante had just said. Webster had told him to hold them for seventy-two hours. That was important. Three days. Bruce would understand.

Then the following afternoon Webster had called him all over town, trying to find him. The White House aide was in a panic – as much of a panic as he allowed himself. He demanded the photographs back, and before he even heard the agreeable reply, began threatening White House retaliation.

And Webster had sworn to impose executive isolation if *one word* about Trevayne's visit to de Spadante was even *hinted* at in print.

Roderick Bruce relaxed his posture, let his back fall away from the chair. He recalled Webster's exact words when he asked the White House aide if Trevayne or de Spadante or the photographs would have any bearing on Paul Bonner's murder charge.

'None whatsoever. There's no connection; that stands as is. We're controlling that on all sides.'

But he hadn't controlled it. He hadn't even been able to manage the Army lawyer defending Bonner. A Pentagon lawyer!

Bobby Webster hadn't lied; he'd lost his clout. He was helpless. He used strong threats, but he hadn't the muscle to carry them out.

And if there was one thing Roger Brewster of Erie, Pennsylvania, had learned in the cosmopolitan world of the Washington orbit, it was to take advantage of a helpless man, especially one who'd recently lost his muscle. Specifically, one who was helpless and had lost his muscle and was close to power and closer still to panic.

Behind such a man was usually a hell of a story. And Bruce knew how to get it. He'd made copies of the photographs.

Brigadier General Lester Cooper watched the man with the attaché case walk down the path to his car. The Vermont snow was deep and the path not shovelled well. But the driveway was fine. The snow plough had done a fine job all the way out to the road. And the man's car was a heavy automobile with huge snow tyres. He'd be all right.

Such men were always all right. Men who worked in skyscrapers for other men like Aaron Green. They moved in cloud-high offices with soft carpeting and softer lights. They spoke quietly into telephones and referred to complex figures – most often with decimal points and percentages within those decimals.

They dealt in the subtleties Brigadier General Lester Cooper abhorred.

He watched the large automobile turn around in the small parking area and start off down the drive. The man waved, but there was no smile, no sense of friendliness. No thanks for having been treated hospitably in spite of the fact that he had arrived without warning, without announcement.

The subtleties.

And the news he brought to the Rutland farmhouse was a subtlety Lester Cooper felt he would never understand. But then, they didn't ask him to understand, just be aware of, follow instructions. For the good of everyone. The Pentagon would benefit more than any other area of the government; he was assured of that.

Andrew Trevayne, President of the United States.

It was incredible.

It was preposterous.

But if the man from Aaron Green said it was a realistic consideration, Andrew Trevayne was halfway to his inauguration.

Lester Cooper turned away from the path and started back toward the house. As he approached the thick Dutch door he changed his mind and veered off to the left. The powdered snow was lying loose above a hard base, and his feet sank in up to his ankles. He had no boots or galoshes on, but the cold wetness didn't bother him. There was the winter of forty-four, when he hopped off tanks into the snow-cold mud, and it hadn't bothered him then either. Patton, George Patton, kept yelling at him: '. . . Cooper, you stupid son-of-a-bitch! Get the goddamn regulation boots on! We're barrel-assing into a Kraut winter, and you act like it was springtime in Georgia! Take that shit-eating grin off your face!'

He'd yelled right back at George; always smiling, of course. Boots inhibited his tank driving. Shoes were fine.

Patton.

This would have been beyond him, too.

Cooper reached the end of the backyard lawn, fully covered with virgin snow. The sky was dull; one could hardly see the mountains in the distance. But they were there, and not treacherous, and he would look at them every day for the rest of his life – in a very short time.

As soon as he organized the logistics of Aaron Green's strategy – his part of it, the military end. It wouldn't be difficult; the combined services were all aware of the enormous contributions of Genessee Industries. They were also aware that the future held the greatest military promise in history if Genessee became – as they wanted it to become – the true civilian spokesman for all of them. And if Andrew Trevayne was Genessee's candidate, that was all that mattered.

The word would be passed throughout every post, airfield, training centre, and naval station in the world. No identification yet, only the alert. The advance cue that a name would be forthcoming, and that name was the man Genessee Industries and the Pentagon wanted as President. Schedules with proper allocations of space and time should be prepared, allowing for indoctrination courses for all officers and enlisted men and women. Under the heading of 'Current Affairs', of course. Separate facilities for regular and reserve personnel, as approaches would vary considerably.

It could be done. None of the uniformed services wanted to slide back to the days before Genessee Industries was such a large part of its line of supply.

And when the order came to release the name, Xeroxes and printing presses and mimeograph machines in all parts of the earth where the American serviceman was stationed or at sea would be activated around the clock. From Fort Dix, New Jersey, to Bangkok, Thailand; from Newport News to Gibraltar.

The military could deliver over four million votes.

Lester Cooper wondered if it would come to that. Would it really be Andrew Trevayne?

And why?

It would have been comforting to call Robert Webster and find out what he knew; that wasn't possible now. The man from Aaron Green had made it clear.

Webster was frozen out.

Of course, no one was to be told anything yet. But Bobby Webster wasn't even to be *talked* to. About *anything*. Cooper wasn't to initiate or accept any communications whatsoever from Webster.

He wondered what Webster had done.

It didn't matter. He wasn't even curious any longer, if the truth were known. He just wanted his part over with so he could come back to Rutland and spend the days at peace.

No more subtleties.

He just didn't care; he'd do the job for Green – he owed him that. Owed it to Genessee Industries and all his memories, his ambitions.

He even owed it to Paul Bonner, the poor son-of-a-bitch. Bonner was a sacrifice, a necessary casualty, as he understood it.

His only hope was, of all things, executive clemency.

From President Trevayne.

Wasn't that ironic?

The goddamn subtleties . . .

41

'Mr Trevayne?'

'Yes.'

'Bob Webster here. How are you?'

'Fine. And you?'

'A little shook up, I'm afraid. I think I led you into a rotten situation, a very bad scene.'

'What's the matter?'

'Before we go into it, I've got to make one thing clear; I mean, I have to *emphasize* it ... *I'm* the one responsible. Nobody else. Do you understand?'

'I do ... I think I do.'

'Good. That's damned important.'

'Now I'm sure I do. What is it?'

'Your visit to Greenwich. To de Spadante the other day. You were seen.'

'Oh? ... Is that a problem?'

'There's more, but that's primarily it.'

'Why's it so serious? We didn't advertise, that's true; on the other hand, we didn't try to hide it.'

'You didn't mention it to the papers, though.'

'I didn't think it was necessary. The office put out a short statement that violence wasn't the answer to anything. That's what they carried. Sam Vicarson issued it; I approved it. There's still nothing to hide.'

'Perhaps I'm not making myself clear. It looks as though you and de Spadante held a secret meeting ... There were photographs taken.'

'What? Where? I don't remember any photographer. Of course, there were a lot of people in the parking lot ...'

'Not in the parking lot. Inside the room.'

'Inside the room? What the hell ... Oh? Oh, good God! Jujubes.'

'What was that?'

'Nothing ... What about the photographs?'

'They're damaging. I saw a copy. Two copies, actually. You and de Spadante looked like you were engrossed in heavy conversation.'

'We were. Where did you see them?'

'Rod Bruce. He's the one who's got them.'

'Who from?'

'We don't know. He won't reveal his sources; we've tried before. He's planning to release everything tomorrow. He's threatened to make sure you're linked to de Spadante. And that's bad for Bonner, incidentally.'

'Well . . . what do you want me to do? Obviously you've got something in mind.'

'As we see it, the only way to deflate the story is for you to speak first. Issue a statement that de Spadante wanted to see you; you saw him two days before he was killed. You wanted the information public for Major Bonner's sake . . . Make up whatever you like about what was said. We've checked the room; there weren't any bugs.'

'I'm not sure I understand. What's Bruce's point? How does Paul fit in?'

'I *told* you . . . Sorry, it's been a rotten morning over here . . . Bruce thinks it's another hook into Paul Bonner. If you and de Spadante were still talking to each other . . . it's not very likely he was out to kill you a week ago as Bonner claims.'

'I see . . . All right, I'll issue a statement. And I'll take care of Bruce.'

Trevayne held down the button for several seconds, released it, and dialed a number. 'Sam Vicarson, please. Mr Trevayne calling . . . Sam, it's time for Bruce. No, not you. Me . . . Find out where he is and call me back. I'm home . . . No, I won't reconsider. Call me as soon as you can. I want to see him this afternoon.'

Trevayne replaced the phone on the bedside table and looked over at his wife, who was in her slip by the dresser, putting the final touches on her make-up. She watched him in the mirror.

'I got the gist of that. Something tells me our day off, antique-wandering, just got postponed.'

'Nope. Fifteen or twenty minutes, that's all. You can wait in the car.'

Phyllis walked over to the bed and laughed as she pointed her finger at the rumpled blankets and sheets. 'I've heard that before. You're a beast, Mr Trevayne. You dash home from the office, ravish an unsullied maiden, of indeterminate years, plying her with promises; then, the minute your lusts are satisfied and you have a nap, you start telephoning . . .'

Andrew pulled her down on his lap, feigning a melodramatic grab for her breasts. He touched them, caressed them alternately as she kissed his ear. Their laughter subsided as he gently rolled her off his legs back onto the bed.

'Oh, Andy, we can't.'

'We certainly can. It'll take Sam the better part of an hour.' He stood and unbuckled his trousers as Phyllis pulled up the sheet, flipping over a side, waiting for him.

'You're incorrigible. And I love it . . . Who are you going to see?'

'A nasty little man named Roderick Bruce,' he answered as he removed his shirt and shorts and got into the bed.

'The newspaperman?'

'He wouldn't approve of us.'

Bobby Webster folded his arms in front of him on the desk. He lowered his head and closed his eyes and knew he was very close to tears. He'd locked his office door; no one could barge in on him. Half-consciously he wondered why the tears did not come. The semiconscious answer was so appalling he rejected it. He'd lost the ability to cry ... to cry out.

Reductio ad manipulatem.

Was there such a phrase? There should be. The years of contrivance; the untold, unremembered, unaccounted for – hundreds, thousands? – plots and counterplots.

Will it work?

That was all that mattered.

The human factor was only an *X* or a *Y*, to be considered or discarded as the case may be. Certainly not taken for more than that, more than part of a formula.

Even himself.

Bobby Webster felt the welling of tears in his eyes. He was going to cry. Uncontrollably.

It was time to go home.

Trevayne walked down the thickly carpeted hallway to the short flight of steps underneath the small sign printed in Old English: 'The Penthouse; Roderick Bruce.'

He climbed the five steps, approached the door, and pushed the button, causing inordinately loud chimes to be heard beyond the black-enamelled entrance with the shiny brass hardware. He could hear muffled voices inside; one was agitated. Roderick Bruce.

The door was opened, and a large black maid in a starched white uniform stood imposingly, forbiddingly in the small foyer. She blocked any view beyond her.

'Yes?' she asked in a lilting dialect formed somewhere in the Caribbean.

'Mr Bruce, please.'

'Is he expecting you?'

'He'll want to see me.'

'I'm sorry. Please leave your name; he'll be in touch with you.'

'My name is Andrew Trevayne, and I'm not leaving until I see Mr Bruce.'

The maid started to close the door; Trevayne was about to shout when suddenly Roderick Bruce darted into view like a tiny ferret from a hidden nest. He'd been listening from a doorway several yards away.

'It's all right, Julia!' The huge maid gave Trevayne the benefit of a last, unpleasant look, turned, and walked rapidly down the hall out of sight. 'She's Haitian, you know. Her six brothers are all Ton Ton Macoute. It's a cruel streak that runs in the family ... What do you want, Trevayne?'

'To see you.'

'How did you get up here? The doorman didn't ring through.'

'He thinks I'm seeing another tenant. Don't bother to trace it down; my office arranged it. The other party doesn't know anything.'

'The last time we talked, you threatened me, if I remember correctly. In your office. Now, you come to my office, to me; and you don't look so menacing. Am I to assume you're here to make a trade? Because I'm not sure I'm interested.'

'I don't feel menacing; I feel sad. But you're right. I'm here to make a trade ... Your kind of trade, Bruce.'

'You don't have anything I want; why should I listen?'

Trevayne watched the little man with the small, deep-set eyes and the confident, tiny mouth pursed in satisfaction. Andy felt sick to his stomach as he said the name quietly.

'Alexander Coffey.'

Roderick Bruce stood there motionless. His tight jaw slackened, his lips parted, and his face lost all poise of arrogance.

Part Four

42

It seemed preposterous.

It *was* preposterous.

And the most preposterous aspect of it was that no one wanted anything – except his commitment. That had been made totally clear; no one expected him to change one word of the subcommittee report. It was anticipated that he would complete it, present copies to the President, the Congress, and the Defense Allocation Commission and be thanked by a grateful government. Nothing altered, nothing compromised.

Chapter closed.

Another chapter about to begin.

It didn't seem to matter that the report was viciously uncompromising; he hadn't concealed the fact. It had even been suggested that the more severe the judgments, the greater stature it lent his proposed candidacy.

Candidacy.

A candidate for the nomination of President of the United States.

Preposterous.

But it wasn't preposterous at all, they'd insisted. It was the logical decision of an extraordinary man who'd spent five months, when the report was finished, making an independent study of the country's most massively complicated problem. It was time for an extraordinary man unwedded to political harems; the nation cried out for an individual dramatically separated from the intransient positions of doctrinaire politics. It needed a healer; but more than just a healer. It demanded a man who was capable of facing a giant challenge, of assembling the facts and weeding the truth from myriad deceits.

That was his track record, they'd told him.

At first, he thought Mitchell Armbruster was mad, desperately trying to flatter with such excess that his words nullified his intent. But Armbruster had been firm. The senior Senator from California readily admitted that the idea seemed grotesque to him too when first proposed by a nucleus of the National Committee, but the longer he had thought of it, the more plausible it had become – for men of his political inclinations. The President, whom he supported more than he opposed, was not of his party; Armbruster's party had no viable prospects, only pretenders. They were tired men, familiar men,

men like himself who'd had their chance at the brass ring and failed to grasp it. Or younger ones who were too brash, too irreverent to appeal to the classic middle. The middle American really didn't want to 'rap' or be 'right on'.

Andrew Trevayne could cross the lines, fill the vacuum. There was nothing preposterous about that; it was eminently practical. It was political – within the craft of the possible that was politics. This was the National Committee's argument. It was sound.

But what of the report? The findings and judgments of the subcommittee weren't compiled in such a way as to win partisan support. And there would be no alterations made for any reasons; he was adamant about that.

So he should be, had been Armbruster's unexpected reply. The report of the Defense Allocations subcommittee was just that. A report. It was to be filed with the proper committees in the Senate and the House and, of course, the President. Its recommendations would be weighed by both the legislative and the executive; the prosecutable data handed directly to the Justice Department, and where indictments were called for, they would follow.

And Genessee Industries?

The major conclusion of the subcommittee report branded the company as a government unto itself, with powers political and economic that were unacceptable in a democracy. What of this judgment? What of the men responsible? What of men like Ian Hamilton who controlled, and men like Mitchell Armbruster who benefited?

The Senator from California had smiled sadly and restated the assurance of indictments where they were called for. He did not believe he had committed illegal acts. We were still a nation of laws, not insupportable speculations. He would stand on his record.

As for Genessee Industries, neither the Senate, the House, nor the President would settle for less than complete reforms. Obviously, they were mandatory. Genessee Industries was in large measure dependent on government purchases. If the company had abused the resultant privileges to the degree Trevayne believed, it would be severely curtailed until those reforms were instituted.

Andrew should sleep on the idea; say nothing, do nothing. It might all dissolve. Often the conjectures were mere flurries, political desperations. But the Senator, speaking for himself, had come to believe it made great sense.

There would be other conversations. Other meetings.

And there were.

The first took place at the Villa d'Este in Georgetown. In a private room on the sixth floor. Seven men had gathered together – all of the same party, with the exception of Senator Alan Knapp. Senator Alton Weeks of the Eastern Shore of Maryland – still wearing the blazer Trevayne remembered from the closed Senate hearing – took command.

'This is merely exploratory, gentlemen; I, for one, will need considerable enlightenment . . . Senator Knapp, who is with us out of a bipartisan spirit, has asked that he be allowed to speak and then leave. His remarks will be confidential, of course.'

Knapp leaned forward on the huge banquetlike table, his palms pressed down on the damask cloth. 'Thank you, Senator ... Gentlemen, my good friend and colleague from across the aisle, Mitchell Armbruster' – Knapp smiled a short noncommittal smile at Ambruster, who was at his side – 'told me of this meeting in response to a query of mine. As I'm sure you realize, the cloakroom has been alive with quiet rumours that a very dramatic announcement might be forthcoming. When I learned further the nature of this announcement, I felt that you should be aware of a little drama going on over in our section. Because, gentlemen, there's been an unexpected turn of events that might have bearing on your discussion this evening. I tell you not only in a bipartisan spirit, but because I share with you the concern with the direction this country takes, especially in these times ... The President very likely will not seek a second term.'

There was silence around the table. Slowly, without emphasis, but with consciousness, each man looked at Andrew Trevayne.

Shortly thereafter Knapp left the private room, and the process of dissecting Andrew began.

It lasted nearly five hours.

The second meeting was shorter. Barely an hour and a half, but infinitely more extraordinary to Trevayne. In attendance was the junior Senator from Connecticut, an old-middle-aged man from West Hartford whose record was lacklustre but whose appetites were reputed to be varied. He'd come to the meeting to announce his retirement; he was going back into private life. His reasons were bluntly financial. He'd been offered the presidency of a large insurance firm, and it wasn't fair to his family to refuse.

The Governor of Connecticut was prepared to offer Trevayne the appointment – provided, of course, that Andrew immediately enroll in the party. 'Immediately' meant within the month. Before the fifteenth of January.

By fulfilling the unexpired Senate term Trevayne would be propelled into the national spotlight. His political springboard was assured.

It had happened before; to lesser men, usually. The extraordinary man could capitalize on it brilliantly. The forum was ready-made. Positions could be established swiftly, with strength. Papers would be issued, making irrevocably clear the beliefs of Andrew Trevayne.

For the first time, Andrew faced the concrete reality.

It *was* possible.

Yet what were his beliefs? Did he believe in the checks and balances and independent judgments he so readily espoused? Did he believe – really believe – that the Washington talent was superior talent, needing only to be freed from contemptible influences such as Genessee Industries? And was he capable of leading that superior talent? Was he strong enough? Could he impose the strength of his own convictions on an immensely powerful adversary?

Much had been made at the Villa d'Este meeting of his work for the State

Department. The conferences in Czechoslovakia, where he'd brought seemingly implacable opponents together.

But Andy knew that Czechoslovakia was not the test at all.

The test was Genessee Industries.

Could he himself – alone – bring the company to heel? That was the test he wanted, needed.

43

Paul Bonner stood at attention as Brigadier General Cooper came through the door of his small room in Arlington. Cooper waved his hand, half in salute, half in a gesture of weariness, indicating that Bonner should relax, sit down again.

'I can't stay long, Major. I'm due at OMB shortly; there's always a budget crisis, isn't there?'

'As far back as I can remember, sir.'

'Yes ... Yes. Sit down. If I don't, it's only because I've been sitting all day. And most of this past weekend. I've been up to our place in Rutland. Sometimes it's even more lovely with the snow. You should visit us there sometime.'

'I'd like that.'

'Yes ... Yes. Mrs Cooper and I would like it, too.'

Paul sat down in the chair by his bare steel desk, leaving the single armchair for the General. But the Brigadier would not sit down. Cooper was nervous, agitated, unsure of himself.

'I gather you haven't brought very good news, General.'

'I'm sorry, Major.' Cooper looked down at Paul, his mouth drawn, his brow wrinkled. 'You're a good soldier, and everything will be done for you that can be done. We expect you'll be acquitted of the murder charge ...'

'That's nothing to be sorry about.' Bonner grinned.

'The newspapers, especially that little prick Bruce, have stopped demanding your neck.'

'I'm grateful. What happened?'

'We don't know, and nobody wants to ask. Unfortunately, it will have no bearing.'

'On what?'

Cooper walked to the small double window overlooking the BOQ courtyard. 'Your acquittal – if it's that – will be in a civil criminal court with military as well as civilian attorneys ... You are still subject to an Army court-martial. The decision has been made to proceed with dispatch immediately following your trial.'

'*What?*' Bonner got out of his chair slowly. The gauze around his throat was stretched as his neck muscles expanded in anger. 'On what basis? You can't try me twice. If I'm acquitted ... I'm acquitted!'

'Of murder. Not of gross neglect of duty. Not of disregarding orders, thus placing yourself at the scene of the trouble.' Cooper continued to look out the window. 'You had no right being where you were, Major. You might have jeopardized the safety of Trevayne and his housekeeper. And you involved the United States Army in areas beyond its province, thus impugning our motives.'

'That's goddamn double-talk!'

'That's the goddamn truth, soldier!' Cooper whipped around from the window. 'Pure and simple. *You* may have been shot at, legally constituting self-defence. I hope to Christ we can prove that. No one else was!'

'They've got the Army car. We *can* prove it.'

'The Army car. That's the point! Not Trevayne's car, not Trevayne ... Goddamn, Bonner, can't you see? There are too many other considerations. The Army can't afford you any longer.'

Paul lowered his voice as he stared at the Brigadier. 'Who's going to do the shithouse detail, General? You? ... I don't think you're up to it, *sir*.'

'I won't say that's not called for, Major. From your point of view, I suppose it is ... However, it may have struck you that I was under no obligation to come here this afternoon.'

Bonner realized the truth of Cooper's statement. It would have been much simpler for everyone except him had the General said nothing. 'Why did you, then?'

'Because you've been through enough; you deserve better than you're getting. I want you to know I know that. Whatever the outcome, I'll make sure you'll ... still be able to come and visit a retired superior officer in Rutland, Vermont.'

So the General *was* getting out, thought Paul. The commander wasn't commanding anymore, just making his last deals. 'Which means you'll keep me out of the stockade.'

'I promise you that. I've been given assurance.'

'But I lose the uniform?'

'Yes ... I'm sorry. We're approaching a very sensitive situation ... We have to go by the book. No deviations. We can't afford the Army's motives to be subject to question. We can't be accused of covering up.'

'There's that double-talk again, General. You're not very good at it, if you don't mind my saying so.'

'I don't mind, Major. I've tried, you know. I've tried to get better at it during the past seven or eight years. I don't seem to take to it; I just get worse. I like to think it's one of the better traits of us old-line men.'

'What you're telling me is the Army wants me conveniently tucked away somewhere. Out of sight.'

Brigadier Cooper slumped into the armchair, his legs extended, the repose position of a combat officer in his tent. The way most of them slept after a rotten day at a fire base. 'Out of sight, out of mind, out of the picture,

Major . . . If possible, out of the country; which I will propitiously suggest to you, once the court-martial is commuted.'

'Jesus! It's all been programmed, hasn't it?'

'There's one possibility, Bonner. It struck me as amusing the other day, around noontime in my backyard . . . with all the snow. Not funny, just ironic.'

'What is it?'

'You might get a presidential reprieve. An executive reversal, I think it's called nowadays. Isn't that ironic?'

'How would that be possible?'

Brigadier General Cooper got out of the armchair and walked slowly back to the window overlooking the courtyard.

'Andrew Trevayne,' he said quietly.

Robert Webster didn't say goodbye to anyone for the simple reason that no one other than the President and the head of the White House staff knew he was leaving.

The sooner the better.

The press release would read that Robert Webster of Akron, Ohio, for nearly three years a special assistant to the President, was relinquishing his post for reasons of health. The White House reluctantly accepted his resignation, wishing him well.

His audience with the President took exactly eight minutes, and as he was leaving the Lincoln Room he could feel the intense stare of the Man's eyes on his back.

The Man hadn't believed a word, thought Webster. Why should he have? Even the truth had sounded hollow. The words had tumbled forth, expressing, if nothing else, an exhaustion that was real; but the reality was obscured by his trying to explain it. That was hollow, false.

'Maybe you're temporarily burnt out, Bobby,' the President had suggested. 'Why not take a leave of absence, see how you feel in a few weeks? The pressure gets rough; I know that.'

'No, thank you, sir,' he'd replied. 'I've made my decision. With your permission, I'd like to make the break final. My wife isn't happy here. I'm not either, really. We want to start raising a family. But not in Washington . . . I think I strayed too far from the barn, sir.'

'I see . . . So you really want to go back to the hinterlands, raise kids, and be able to walk the streets at night. Is that it?'

'I know it sounds corny, but I guess it is.'

'Not corny. The American dream, Bobby. Your talents have helped make it possible for millions of others. No reason why you shouldn't have your share of the dream.'

'That's very generous of you, sir.'

'No, you've sacrificed. You must be damned near forty now . . .'

'Forty-one.'

'Forty-one and still no children . . .'

'There just wasn't the time.'

'No, of course, there wasn't. You've been very dedicated. And your lovely wife.'

Webster knew then that the Man was toying with him; he didn't know why. The President didn't like his wife.

'She's been very helpful.' Webster felt he owed his wife that, selfish bitch or no.

'Good luck, Bobby. I don't think you'll need luck, though. You're very resourceful.'

'Working here has opened a lot of doors, Mr President. I have you to thank for that.'

'That pleases me ... And reminds me, there's a revolving door in the lobby, isn't there?'

'What, sir?'

'Nothing. Nothing at all. It's unimportant ... Goodbye, Bobby.'

Robert Webster carried the last of his checked-out effects to his car in the west parking lot. The President's cryptic remark bothered him, but there was relief in knowing that it wasn't necessary to dwell on it. He didn't have to; he didn't care. No longer would he have to analyse and reanalyse a hundred cryptic remarks every time he or the office faced a problem. It was more than relief; he felt a sense of exhilaration. He was out of it.

Oh, Christ, what a magnificent feeling!

He pulled his car up to the sentry box by the gate and waved at the guard. It would be the last time. Tomorrow morning the gate would get the word. Robert Webster was no longer a fixture at the White House, his plastic pass with the sharp photograph and the brief description of his identifying marks no longer valid. Even the guards would ask questions. He was always polite and cheerful with the White House detachment. He never knew when it might be necessary to stretch a time-out check at either end. Cop a little extra time for himself; no big deal, just a few minutes – ten or fifteen, perhaps – so he could 'belt down an extra martini' or 'avoid some son-of-a-bitch'. The gate was always cooperative. They couldn't understand why someone like Bobby Webster ever worried about checkouts, but they accepted his bitchy comments about ducking this or that meeting. What the hell, they had their lousy inspections; Webster had his lousy meetings. Besides, he got them autographs.

How many slightly altered checkouts had there been? How many times had he managed those invaluable extra minutes in which startling information would come over the Teletype – information he'd use but be perfectly capable of proving he could not have received.

The Operator.

Everything slightly altered. For Genessee Industries.

No more. The Operator was out of business.

He sped off down Pennsylvania Avenue, oblivious to the car, a grey Pontiac, that took up the position behind him.

Inside the grey Pontiac, the driver turned to his companion.

'He's going too fast. He's liable to get a ticket.'

'Don't lose him.'

'Why not? It doesn't make any difference.'

'Because Gallabretto *said* so! That makes the difference. Every minute we know where he is, who he meets.'

'It's all a lot of shit. There's no contract till he gets to Ohio. To Akron, Ohio. Pick him up easy there.'

'If Willie Gallabretto says we stay on, we stay on. I used to work for Gallabretto's uncle. Look what happened to him.'

Ambassador William Hill paused in front of a framed, autographed cartoon on the wall of his study. It depicted a spindly-legged 'Big Billy' as a puppeteer holding strings tied to small recognizable models of past presidents and secretaries of state. The puppeteer was smiling, pleased that the puppets were dancing to the tune of his choice, the written notes of which were ballooned above his head.

'Did you know, Mr President, that it was a full year after this abomination appeared that I learned the music was "Ring-Around-the-Rosy"?'

The President laughed from across the room, seated in the heavy leather armchair that was his usual spot when visiting the Ambassador. 'Your artist friend wasn't very kind to the rest of us. He added injury to insult. If I remember correctly, the last line of that ditty is "all fall down".'

'It was years ago. You weren't even in the Senate then. He wouldn't have dared to include you anyway.' Hill walked over to the chair opposite the President and sat down. 'If *I* remember correctly, this is where Trevayne was seated when last here. Perhaps I'll have some psychic flashes.'

'Are you sure it wasn't in this chair? I wasn't with you then.'

'No, I recall. As most people who've been here with the two of us, he avoided that chair. Afraid of being presumptuous, I think'.

'He may be overcoming his shyness . . .' The telephone rang on Hill's table-desk, cutting the President's words short.

'Very well, Mr Smythe. I'll tell him. Thank you.'

'Jack Smythe?' asked the President.

'Yes. Robert Webster and his wife left on the Cleveland flight. Everything's fine. That was the message.'

'Good.'

'May I ask what it means?'

'Certainly. Surveillance showed that Bobby's been followed since leaving the White House gate two nights ago. I was worried about him. And curious, of course.'

'So was somebody else.'

'Probably for the same reason. Intelligence identified one of the men as a small-time leg-man, a "shadow", I think we called it in comic-book jargon . . . He didn't have any more to report than our people did. Webster didn't meet with anyone, see anyone, but the movers.'

'Telephone?'

'Airline reservations and a brother in Cleveland who'll drive Bobby and his wife down to Akron . . . Oh, and a Chinese restaurant. Not a very good one.'

'Probably filled with Chinamen.' Hill laughed softly as he returned to the chair. 'He knows nothing about the Trevayne situation?'

'I don't know. All I know is, he's running. Maybe he told the truth. He said he strayed too far from the barnyard, that it all became too much.'

'I don't believe it.' Hill leaned his gaunt frame forward on the chair. 'What about Trevayne? Would you like me to bring him in for a chat?'

'Oh, Billy! You and your goddamn puppet strings. I come over for a quiet chat, a restful drink, and you keep bringing up business.'

'I think *this* business is extremely important, Mr President. Even vital. Shall I call him in?'

'No. Not yet. I want to see how far he'll go, how bad the fever's got him.'

44

'When did they approach you?' asked Phyllis Trevayne, absently poking one of the huge logs in the High Barnegat fireplace.

'A little over three weeks ago,' replied Andy, sitting on the couch. He could see the wince of hurt around her eyes. 'I should have told you, but I didn't want you concerned. Armbruster said it might only be a ... political desperation.'

'You took them seriously?'

'Not at first; of course not. I practically threw Armbruster out of my office, accused him of all kinds of things. He said he was speaking for a caucus in the National Committee; that he was initially opposed to the idea and still not convinced ... but coming around.'

Phyllis hung the poker on the fireplace brick and turned to Trevayne. 'I think it's crazy. It's a blatant device having something to do with the subcommittee, and I'm surprised you went this far.'

'The only reason I went this far is that no one yet has hinted that I alter the report ... That's what intrigued me. I suppose I couldn't believe it. I've been waiting for someone, anyone, to bring up the slightest suggestion ... and I was going to burn them. But no one has.'

'Did *you* bring it up?'

'Continuously. I told Senator Weeks that he was liable to be embarrassed. He looked down his patrician nose and said he was perfectly capable' – here Andy mimicked the Eastern Shore politician – 'of answering any questions the subcommitttee might raise, but that was another matter. No part of the issue at hand.'

'Brave fellow ... But even so, why you? Why you at this particular time?'

'It's not very flattering, but there doesn't seem to be anyone else. At least that's what their polls tell them. "No viable contenders on the political horizon" was the way they put it. The heavyweights are worn out, and the young ones are lightweights. Or they wear their pants too tight or they're Jewish or Latin or black or some goddamn thing that makes them unacceptable to our democratized election process ... As Paul Bonner would say, "Horseshit!"'

Phyllis walked-wandered back to the couch, stopping along the way to take a cigarette from a box on the coffee table. Andy lit it for her.

'That's unfortunately perceptive.' She sat down next to her husband. 'What?'

'They're right. I was trying to think who they had.'

'I didn't know you were an authority.'

'Don't kid yourself, Mr ... What did that dreadful man call you? ... Mr Arrogance ... I haven't missed an election in years.'

Trevayne laughed. 'The seer of High Barnegat. We'll rent you to Nick the Greek.'

'No, really. I have a system. It works. Take the name of a candidate and put the word "President" in front. It either sounds real, you know, *all right*, or it doesn't. The only time I had trouble was in sixty-eight. It didn't sound right with either one.'

'A general consensus ...'

'Of course, it's a little more difficult when there's an incumbent; then you have to split hairs. Which brings to mind, the man in there now sounds pretty okay ... I thought you liked him.'

'He's not going to run again.'

Phyllis' controlled expression changed. She looked at Andy and spoke quietly, urgently. 'You didn't tell me that.'

'There are several things I haven't—'

'You should have told me that first.'

Trevayne understood. The game was no longer a game. 'I'm sorry. I was taking things in order of sequence.'

'Try in order of importance.'

'All right.'

'You're not a politician; you're a businessman.'

'I'm neither, really. My business interests are secure but peripheral. For the past five years I've worked for the State Department and one of the largest foundations in the world. If you want to categorize me, I'd go under the label of ... "public service", I suppose.'

'No! You're rationalizing.'

'Hey, Phyl ... We're talking, not fighting.'

'Talking? No. Andy, *you've* been talking. For weeks; with other people, not with me.'

'I told you. It was too loose, too speculative to raise hopes. Or doubts.'

'And now it isn't?'

'I'm not sure. I just know it's time we talked about it ... I gather I've lost your vote.'

'You certainly have.'

'Make a hell of a story. Probably the first time in history.'

'Andy, be serious. You're not ... not ...' Phyllis stammered, unsure of the words but certain of her feelings.

'Not presidential timber,' added Trevayne gently.

'I didn't say that; I don't mean that. You're not a ... political animal.'

'I'm told that's a plus for our side. I'm still not sure what it means.'

'You're not that kind of extrovert. You're not the sort of man who goes through crowds shaking hands, or makes a dozen speeches a day, or calls governors and congressmen by their first names when you don't know them. You're not comfortable doing those things, and that's what candidates do!'

'I've thought about . . . those things, and you're right, I don't like them. But maybe they're necessary; perhaps by doing them you prove something quite apart from position papers and executive decisions. It's a form of stamina. Truman said that.'

'My God,' said Phyllis softly, making no attempt to hide her fear. 'You *are* serious.'

'That's what I'm trying to tell you . . . I'll know more on Monday. On Monday I'm meeting with Green and Hamilton. On Monday it could all blow up.'

'You need their support? Do you want it?' The questions were asked with distaste.

'They wouldn't support me in a race with Mao Tse-tung . . . No, Phyl, I'm going to find out how good I really am.'

'I'll pass that . . . Let's stick to why Andy Trevayne suddenly thinks he's in the race for such a position.'

'Can't you say the word, Phyl? It's called the presidency.'

'No, I won't say it. It scares me.'

'You don't want me to go any further then.'

'I don't understand. Why would you want to? . . . You don't have those kind of demons, Andy; that kind of vanity. You have money, and money attracts flattery, but you're too realistic, too aware. I just can't believe it.'

'Neither could I when I first realized I was paying attention.' Trevayne laughed, more to himself than for his wife's benefit, and put his feet on the coffee table. 'I listened to Armbruster, went to the meetings, because I thought all the conversation was leading up to one thing – the report. And I was angry, angry as hell. Then I understood that wasn't the case. These were professionals, not frightened men caught with their fingers in the till. They're the talent hunters; I can't object to that. When the companies were growing, I spent months scouting corporations here and abroad luring away the best brain power I could buy. I still keep it in mind. Whenever I meet someone I think might be an asset, I make a mental note to call your brother . . . These men are doing the same thing I was . . . am still doing. Only on a larger scale, with far greater complications. And if in the first few weeks or months I fall on my face, they'll pull the rug out so fast I'll have mat burns. But I'm beginning to think it's important to give those first few months a try.'

'You haven't explained why.'

Trevayne withdrew his feet from the small table and stood up. He thrust his hands in his trouser pockets and walked on the patterns of the living-room rug, absently placing his feet at specific intervals as a small boy on a sidewalk playing step-on-a-crack. 'You really want the nitty-gritty, don't you?'

'Shouldn't I? I love you. I love the life we have, the lives our children have; I think everything is being threatened, and I'm scared to death.'

Andy looked down at his wife, his expression kind but his eyes remote, seeing her, yet not focusing sharply. 'I am, too, I think ... Why? ... All right, the "why". Because the truth might be that I can. I'm not kidding myself; I'm no genius. At least, I don't feel like one – whatever way a genius is supposed to feel. But I don't think the presidency requires genius. I think it does require the ability to absorb quickly, act decisively – not always impartially – and accept extraordinary pressure. Perhaps, above all, to listen. To distinguish between the legitimate cries for help and the hypocrisy. I think I can handle almost everything but the pressure – I don't know about that; not to the degree that's required ... But if I can prove to myself that I can jump that hurdle – and one other – I think I want to get into the fight. Because any country that allows a Genessee Industries needs all the help it can get. Frank Baldwin quoted something I made a joke of when he first approached me. He said no man can avoid what he's supposed to do when the time comes for him to do it. I think that's pretentious as hell, and not necessarily accurate. But if through a series of accidents the political cupboard is damned near empty and a good man is going to make it bare by leaving – and the kingmakers think, for their own reasons, that I can cut it – I'm not sure I've got a choice. I'm not sure *we've* got a choice, Phyl.'

Phyllis Trevayne watched her husband carefully; coldly, perhaps. 'Why have you chosen ... no, that's not right; why have you let this party choose you, and not the other? If the president isn't going to run for a second term—'

'For practical reasons,' interrupted Andy. 'I don't think it makes a whit of difference which banner a man runs under anymore. Both parties are splintered. It's the man that counts, not the bromides of Republican or Democratic philosophy – they're meaningless now ... The President will wait until the last possible minute before announcing his withdrawal; he's got too many bills in Congress. I'll need that time. If only to find out I'm not wanted.'

Phyllis remained staring at her husband, without discernible reaction. 'You're willing to expose yourself – and us – to that kind of agony, knowing that it might be a complete waste?'

Trevayne was by the side brick wall of the outsized fireplace. He leaned his back against it and returned his wife's look. 'I'd like your permission to ... For the first time in my life, I'm aware of a threat to everything I think I believe in. It's got nothing to do with parades and flags and enemies – no easy heroes and villains. It's a gradual but certain erosion of choice. Bonner uses the word a lot, "programmed". Though I don't think he really knows what it means, what its implications are ... But it's happening, Phyl. The men behind Genessee Industries want to run the country because they're convinced they know better than the voter on Main Street, and they have the power to convey their ideas into the system. And there are hundreds like them in corporate board rooms everywhere. Sooner or later they'll get together, and instead of being a legitimate part of the system, they'll *be* the system ... I don't agree with that. I'm not sure yet what I *do* agree with, but

I don't agree with that. We're ten steps away from our own particular police state, and I want people to know it.'

Trevayne pushed himself off the brick wall and walked back to the couch. He smiled at Phyllis, a little embarrassed, and slumped down beside her.

'That's quite a speech,' she said softly.

'Sorry ... I didn't mean it to be.'

She reached over and took his hand. 'An awful thing just happened.'

'What?'

'I just put that frightening title before your name, and it didn't sound at all unreal.'

'If I were you, I wouldn't start redecorating the East Room ... I may freeze in my first *Senate* speech, and it's back to the coupons.'

Phyllis released his hand, astonished. 'Good God, you've been busy! Do tell. In case I should order new Christmas cards or something. What Senate?'

45

James Goddard backed his car out of the sloping driveway and started off down the road. It was a clear Sunday morning, the air cold, the winds swirling out of the Palo Alto hills, chilling everything in front of them. It was a day meant for decisions; Goddard had made his.

He would finalize it, organize its implementation within an hour or two.

Actually, the decision had been made for him. They were going to let him hang, and James Goddard had promised himself that he wasn't for hanging. No matter the promises, regardless of the guarantees that he knew would be offered. He wasn't going to allow it. He wasn't going to let them solve their problems by having the accusing arrow settle in his direction; accepting the responsibility in exchange for the transfer of money into a coded Swiss bank account. That would be too easy.

He had nearly made that mistake himself – without any settlement. His preoccupation with past history – Gennessee history – had blinded him to the fact that he was using his own figures, his own intricate manipulations. There was another way, a better way.

Someone else's figures. Financial projections that couldn't possibly be his.

It was December 15. In forty-six days it would be January 31, the end of the fiscal year. All plants, divisions, departments, and assembly control offices of Genessee Industries had to have their year-end reports in by that date. Submitted in final form to his office.

They were simple P-and-L statements with lengthy addenda of required purchases and payroll adjustments. The thousands upon thousands of figures were fed into computer banks where necessary alterations and imbalances were spotted and taped out for correction.

They were balanced against the master tape of the previous year's budgets.

Simple arithmetic that leaped into the economic stratosphere of billions.

The master tape.

The master plan.

Every year the master tape was sent to the comptroller's office in San Francisco and kept in the Genessee vaults. It arrived sometime during the second week in December, on a private plane from Chicago. Always accompanied by a president of one division or another, and armed guards.

Every complex industry had to include budgeting projections for all

312

contractual obligations. But Genessee's master tape differed from the control data tapes of other corporations in a profound way.

For the commitments of others were generally public knowledge, while Genessee's Industries' master tape included thousands of unannounced commitments. And each December brought new surprises seen by less than a dozen pairs of eyes. They spelled out a major portion of the military armaments programme of the United States for the next five years. Pentagon commitments that neither the Congress nor the President knew existed. But they existed as surely as the steel and the politicians could be tempered.

Since the master tape was processed on the basis of five-year data – each December brought a fresh fifth year and constantly swelling information for the years preceding. Nothing was ever deleted, only added.

It was Goddard's function as the financial keystone of Genessee Industries to absorb and coordinate the massive influx of listed and unlisted – old and new – material with respect to changing market conditions; to allocate financing to the divisions as necessary; and to distribute contractual workloads among the plants – always operating on the assumption that 120 per cent of capacity was the median. Sufficient for optimum local employment statistics, yet not excessive to the point of affording unions undue strength. Seventy per cent of that capacity was convertible without profit concern; to be given or taken away as the children behaved.

And James Goddard knew that it was his ability, not the computers', that reduced the incredible mass into workable figures. He separated, isolated, appropriated; his eyes scanned the sheets and with the surefootedness of a large but supple cat he made his swift notations and shifted millions as though he were testing branches, prepared for the unexpected fall but always ready for that last step, that final inch that meant he could leap for the profit-kill.

There was no one like him. He was an artist with figures. Numbers were his friends; they didn't betray him, and he could make them do his bidding.

People betrayed him.

MEMORANDUM: Mr James Goddard, Pres., San Francisco Division

There is a problem that I believe imperatively warrants your attention.

L.R.

L.R. Louis Riggs. The Vietnam veteran Genessee had hired a year ago. A bright young man, unusually quick and decisive. He was quiet, but not without emotions, not without loyalty; that had been proved to Goddard.

Riggs had been wounded in the service. He was a hero and a fine young American; not an obscure ass or an indolent, drug-taking hippie the way most of the youth were today.

Lou Riggs had told him that something was going on he should be aware of. Riggs had been approached by one of Trevayne's assistants and offered a bribe to confirm information damaging to Genessee – especially to him as president of the San Francisco Division. Naturally, Riggs refused. Then, several days later, a man who identified himself as an Army officer attached to the Department of Defense threatened him – actually *threatened* him – to disclose private company records that bore specifically on Mr Goddard's reputation. He also refused, and if Mr Goddard recalled, Lou Riggs had sent a previous memo requesting a meeting – Mr Goddard didn't recall; there were so damned many memos. However, when Lou Riggs read in the newspaper that this same Army officer was the one involved with that killing in Connecticut, on Andrew Trevayne's property, he knew he had to see Mr Goddard immediately.

Goddard wasn't sure what was going on, but the outlines of a conspiracy were there. A conspiracy against him. Possibly being made between Trevayne and the Pentagon. Why else would DOD send an interrogation officer to back up one of Trevayne's assistants? And why had that same officer killed de Spadante's brother?

Why had Mario de Spadante been killed?

It seemed logical that de Spadante was trying to get off his own hook. *Some might be hanged so that others – higher up – would not have to hang.* De Spadante had said that. But perhaps de Spadante wasn't as 'high up' as he thought he was. Perhaps the Pentagon considered him too much a liability – God knew he was an undesirable fellow.

Whatever. James Goddard, the 'bookkeeper', had made up his mind. It was the moment to act, not reflect any longer. He needed only the most damaging of all information.

There would be approximately eleven thousand cards measuring three by seven inches. Cards with strange square perforations; cards that weren't to be folded, spindled, or mutilated. He had measured several thousand identically shaped cards, and found that eleven thousand would require four briefcases. He had them in the trunk of his car.

The computer itself was another matter. It was huge and required two men to operate. For security purposes the men had to be across the room from each other and punch simultaneously separate codes on the keys for it to function. The codes of each man were changed daily, and the two codes were kept in separate offices. The division president's and the comptroller's.

It hadn't been difficult for Goddard to get the second code for the twenty-four-hour period beginning Sunday morning. He'd simply walked into the comptroller's office and said innocently that he thought they'd been given identical code schedules by mistake. Equally innocently the comptroller withdrew his from the safe, and they matched figures. Instantly it was obvious that Goddard had been wrong; the codes were different. But within that instant James Goddard's eyes riveted on the Sunday figures. He committed them to memory.

Numbers were his only friends.

Still there was the physical aspect of the machine itself. He needed one other person who would be willing to spend nearly six hours in the basement computer room; someone whom he could trust, who realized that his actions were for the benefit of Genessee Industries, perhaps for the nation itself.

He'd been astonished when the man he'd selected had made a financial demand, but then, as he pointed out, it could be considered a promotion, an overdue promotion. Before he realized it, Goddard had hired a special assistant at an increase of ten thousand dollars a year.

It didn't matter. What mattered was this day's business, this day's decision.

He approached the gate and slowed down his car. The guard, recognizing first the automobile and then the driver, snapped a firm two fingers to his cap.

'Good morning. Mr Goddard. No Sunday off for the front office, eh, sir?'

Goddard didn't like the man's informality. It was out of place. However, there was no time for reprimands.

'No, I have work to do. And, guard, I've asked Mr Riggs to come in this morning. There's no need to check him out with security. Tell him to report directly to my office.'

'Mr Riggs, sir?'

'You *should* know him. He was wounded fighting for our country, protecting us, mister.'

'Yes, sir, Riggs, sir.' the guard wrote the name on his clipboard rapidly.

'He drives a small sports car,' added Goddard as an afterthought. 'Just wave him through. His initals are on the door panel. L.R.'

46

Sam Vicarson sank into the down-filled cushion of the velvet sofa and found his knees disconcertingly parallel with his shoulders. Andrew Trevayne sat at the room-service table and sipped coffee from a Limoges cup imprinted with the words 'Waldorf Towers, New York'. He was reading from a very thick red leather notebook.

'Jesus!' said Vicarson.

'What?'

'No wonder so many uptight conferences take place in these rooms. Once you sit down, you can't get up; you might as well talk.'

Trevayne smiled and went back to his reading. Sam stretched his legs, only to find the position less comfortable. With considerable effort he got up and wandered about the room looking at the various prints on the velour-covered walls and finally out the windows, thirty-five storys above Park Avenue and Fiftieth Street. Trevayne made a notation on a piece of paper, closed the red leather notebook, and looked at his watch.

'They're five minutes late. I wonder if that's a good sign in politics,' said Andrew.

'I'd be just as happy if they never showed up,' replied Sam, without answering the question. 'I feel outclassed. Christ. Ian *Hamilton*. He wrote the book.'

'Not any book I'd run out to buy.'

'You don't have to; you don't sell legal services, Mr Trevayne. This guy does. He walks with kings, and he threw away the common touch a long time ago. I don't think he had much use for it anyway.'

'Very accurate. You read the report.'

'I didn't have to. What did his kid say? That his old man does his thing because he figures no one else can do it as well. Anywhere's near as well.'

The chimes could be heard in the hotel suite's foyer. Vicarson involuntarily patted down his perpetually rumpled hair and buttoned his jacket. 'I'll get the door. Maybe they'll think I'm the butler; that'd be fine.'

The first ten minutes were like an eighteenth-century pavane, thought Trevayne. Slow, graceful, assured; essentially chartered, fundamentally ancient. Sam Vicarson was doing very well, Andy considered, watching the youthful attorney parry Aaron Green's thrusts of solicitousness, which barely concealed his annoyance. Green was angry that Vicarson was present; Hamilton barely acknowledged Sam's presence. For Hamilton, thought Trevayne, it was a time for giants; a subordinate was relegated to his properly unimportant status.

'I think you should realize, Trevayne, when your friends on the National Committee made their choice known to us, we were bitterly disappointed,' said Ian Hamilton.

'"Shocked" is more accurate,' added Green in his deep, resonant voice.

'Yes,' said Andy flatly. 'I'd like to discuss your reaction. It's one of the things I'm interested in. Except they're not my friends . . . I was wondering if they were yours, frankly.'

Hamilton smiled. The anglicized attorney crossed his legs and folded his arms, sinking into the soft cushions of the velvet sofa – the picture of elegance. Aaron Green had a hard-backed armchair next to Trevayne. Sam Vicarson sat slightly outside the triangle, at Andy's right but not in line with Trevayne's view of Hamilton. Even the seating arrangements seemed orchestrated to Andy. And then he realized that Sam had accomplished it; Sam Vicarson had indicated the places for each of them to sit. Sam was better than he thought he was, mused Trevayne.

'If you're considering the possibility that you are our choice,' said Hamilton, still smiling benignly, 'I think I can disabuse you.'

'How?'

'Quite simply, we favour the President. A perusal of our . . . combined contributions, both financial and otherwise, will substantiate that fact.'

'Then I wouldn't have your support under any conditions.'

'I should think not, speaking candidly,' replied Hamilton.

Suddenly Andrew got out of his chair and returned Hamilton's noningratiating smile. 'Then, gentlemen, I've made a mistake, and I apologize. I'm wasting your time.'

The abruptness of Trevayne's move startled the others, including Sam Vicarson. Hamilton was the first to recover.

'Come, Mr Trevayne, let's not play those games, which, if I remember correctly, you detest so . . . Circumstances dictate that we meet with you. Please sit down.'

Andrew did so. 'What are those circumstances?'

Aaron Green spoke. 'The President does not intend to seek a second term.'

'He might change his mind,' said Trevayne.

'He can't,' said Hamilton. 'He wouldn't live it out. I tell you this in the strictest confidence.'

Andrew was stunned. 'I didn't know that. I thought it was a personal choice.'

'What's more personal?' asked Green.

'You know what I mean . . . That's terrible.'

'So . . . we meet.' Green ended the topic of the President's health. 'Circumstances dictate.'

Trevayne was still thinking of the ill man in the White House while Hamilton continued.

'As I say, we were disappointed. Not that the idea of your candidacy is without merit; it's not. But, frankly, all things considered, we favour the President's party.'

'That's a non sequitur. Why should my candidacy concern you at all, then? The opposition has good men.'

'It has the *President's* men,' interrupted Green.

'I don't understand.'

'The President' – Hamilton paused, choosing his words carefully – 'as any man who has completed half a job that will be judged by history, is vitally concerned that his programmes be continued. He will dictate the choice of his successor. He'll pick one of two men because they *will* consent to his dictates. The Vice President or the Governor of New York. In conscience, we cannot support either. Neither has the strength of his own convictions; only the President's. They can't win, and they shouldn't.'

'A lesson. A lesson was learned,' said Green, sitting forward, his hands poised pontifically. 'In sixty-eight, Hubert didn't lose to Nixon because he was the lesser man, or because of money, or the issues. He lost the election with four words whined into the television after his nomination. "Thank you, Mr President." He never washed away those four words.'

Trevayne reached into his pocket for a cigarette, lighting it while no one spoke. 'So you've concluded that the President will ensure the defeat of his own party.'

'Precisely,' replied Hamilton. 'That is our dilemma. One man's vanity. The opposition has only to mount an attractive candidate, accentuate his strength of character – his independence, if you will – and the nationwide gossip will take care of the rest. The electorate has a visceral instinct about puppets.'

'Then you think I have a legitimate chance?'

'Reluctantly,' answered Green. 'You haven't much competition. Who else is there? In the Senate, the party has old men who tremble as I do, or loud-mouthed brats who soil their bell-bottom trousers. Only Knapp has possibilities, but he's so obnoxious he'd be buried. The House is filled with nonentities. A few big governors might give you a run, but they carry the urban messes on their backs ... Yes, Mr Andrew Trevayne; Mr Undersecretary in State Department, Mr Millionaire, Mr Foundation President, Mr Subcommittee Chairman. You've got a lot of marbles ... You could fall down on the issue of elective office, but you would get picked right up again on comparisons. The National Committee boys knew what they were doing when they pulled your name out. They don't like losers.'

'And neither do we,' concluded Ian Hamilton. 'So whether we like it or not, you're a political reality.'

Trevayne once again got up, breaking the triangle. He walked to the room-service table, picked up the thick red leather notebook, and returned, standing several feet behind his chair. 'I'm not sure your assessment is accurate, gentlemen, but it's as good a springboard as any I can think of for

what I have to say . . . This is the subcommittee report. It will be delivered to
the Defense Commission, the President, and the designated congressional
committees in five days. The report itself has been boiled down to six
hundred and fifty pages, with four volumes of subsequent documentations.
Of the report, over three hundred pages are devoted to Genessee Industries.
And two volumes of documentation . . . Now, I understand your "bitter
disappointment" at the prospect of my candidacy. I don't like you; I don't
approve of what you've done, and I intend to see you put out of business.
Simple? *Capisce?* As one of your departed colleagues might have said.'

'He was no part of us!' interrupted Aaron Green angrily.

'You *allowed* him; it's the same thing.'

'What's your point? I believe I smell a compromise,' said Hamilton.

'You do. But not your kind of compromise; you don't come out with
anything. Except, perhaps, the comfort of knowing you can spend the rest of
your lives outside the courts – *and* outside the country.'

'What?' Hamilton's complacency was replaced with his first hint of anger.

'You are a ridiculous man, Mr Subcommittee!' added Green.

'Not really. But the word "ridiculous" is well chosen, if not correctly
applied.' Trevayne walked back to the linen-covered table and threw the
notebook carelessly on top.

Hamilton spoke firmly. 'Let's talk sense, Trevayne. Your report is
damaging; we won't bother to deny it. However, it is – or certainly must be –
riddled with speculations, inconclusive conjectures. Do you think for one
minute we're not prepared for that?'

'No. I'm sure you are.'

'You realize, of course, that the worst you portend for us are accusations,
vehemently denied. Months, years, perhaps a decade in the courts?'

'That's entirely possible.'

'Then why should we even consider you a threat? Are you prepared for our
counterattack? Are you willing to spend years of your life defending yourself
in the libel courts?'

'No, I'm not.'

'Then we are at an impasse. We might as well accommodate each other.
After all, our objectives are identical. The good of the United States.'

'Our definitions differ.'

'That's impossible,' said Green.

'That's why we differ. You conceive of no other absolutes but your own.'

Hamilton shrugged elegantly and raised both his hands in a gesture of
compromise. 'We are prepared to discuss these definitions—'

'I'm not,' replied Andrew standing. 'I'm weary of your definitions, your
ersatz elitist logic; those tiring conclusions that give you the right to
implement only your own objectives. You don't have that right; you're
stealing it. And I'm crying "thieves!" – loud and repeatedly.'

'Who will listen?' shouted Green. 'Who will listen to a man propelled by a
vengeance twenty years old?'

'What did you say?'

'Twenty years ago Genessee Industries turned you down!' Green shook his finger at Andrew. 'For twenty years you're whining! We have proof—'

'You *disgust* me!' roared Trevayne. 'You're no better than the man you claim is no part of you. But you're kidding yourselves; you and the de Spadantes of this world are cut from the same cloth. "We have proof!" Good God, do you extort protection money from blind newsdealers, too?'

'The analogy is unfair, Trevayne,' said Hamilton, taking a disapproving eye off Green. 'Aaron is prone to get upset easily.'

'It's not unfair,' answered Trevayne quietly, his hands gripping the back of his chair. 'You're scheming, out-of-date old men playing an insane game of Monopoly. Buying up this, buying up that – using a hundred different subsidiaries – promising, bribing, blackmailing. Compiling thousands of individual dossiers and poring over them like demented gnomes. One stating that *his* ideas are greater monuments – what was it? – temples, cathedrals! My God, what pomposity ... The other. Oh, yes. There shouldn't be any blanket franchises. Only those entitled to vote should have a voice. That's not only out of date, it's out of sight!'

'I deny! I deny I ever said that!' Hamilton leaped to his feet, suddenly, profoundly frightened.

'Deny all you like. But you'd better know this. On Saturday, I was in Hartford; I signed the papers, Hamilton. I had reasons – out of focus but clear enough – to use another attorney. Mr Vicarson here has assured me everything is in order. On January fifteenth an irrevocable announcement is made by the Governor of Connecticut. I am right now, for all intents and purposes, A United States senator.'

'What?' Aaron Green looked as though he'd been slapped harshly.

'That's right, Mr Green. And I intend to use the immunity of that seat and the stature of that office to hammer away at you. I'm going to let the country know – over and over again. Every day, every quorum, every session; I won't stop. If need be – and I've considered it deeply – I'll have my own personal marathon, my own filibuster. I'll start at the beginning and read that entire report. Every word. All six hundred pages. You won't survive that. Genesee Industries won't survive.'

Aaron Green was breathing heavily, his eyes levelled at Trevayne, his voice deep with personal hatred. 'From Auschwitz to Babi-Yar. Pigs like you make trouble when there is trouble enough.'

'And the solutions are not your solutions. Your solutions lead right back to the camps. To the executions. Can't you *see* that?'

'I see only *strength*! Strength is the deterrent!'

'For God's sake, Green, make it a collective strength. A responsible strength. One that's shared, open. Not furtively manipulated by a select few. That doesn't belong here.'

'You are a schoolboy again! What is this "shared", this "open"? They're words, sterile words. They lead to chaos, to weakness. Look at the record.'

'I've looked at it. Hard and long. It's flawed, imperfect, frustrating. But, goddamn it, it's a better alternative than the one you're suggesting. Look at that track record! ... And if we're walking into a time when the system doesn't work, we'd better know that, too. Then we'll change it. But openly. By choice. Not by edict; and certainly not by your edict.'

'Very well, Mr Trevayne,' said Ian Hamilton, suddenly walking away from the others, his back to them. 'You've built a strong case. What are you suggesting we do?'

'Cut bait. Get out. I don't care where; Switzerland, the Mediterranean, the Scottish Highlands, or the English Lowlands. It doesn't make any difference. Just get out of this country. And stay out.'

'We have financial responsibilities,' protested Hamilton quietly.

'Delegate them. But severe all connections with Genessee Industries.'

'Impossible! Preposterous!' Aaron Green looked at Hamilton now.

'Easy, old friend ... If we do as you suggest, what is our guarantee?'

Trevayne crossed to the room-service table and pointed at the red leather notebook. 'This is the report as it stands—'

'You've made us aware of that,' interrupted Hamilton.

'We have also prepared an alternate report. One that considerably reduces the attention now given to Genessee Industries—'

'*So?*' Aaron Green's sudden interruption was stated emphatically, distastefully. 'The schoolboy's not so pure. He wasn't going to change a word. A single word.'

Trevayne paused before replying. 'I still mightn't. If I do, you have an Army major named Bonner to thank for it. And your own willingness to comply, of course ... Major Bonner made an observation once that stuck with me. Perhaps it dovetailed with other opinions, but, nevertheless, he gave the idea focus. He said I was destructive; that I was tearing down, not offering any alternatives. Just a total wipeout, the good and the bad down the drain together ... All right, let's try to salvage some of the good.'

'We want specifics,' said Hamilton.

'All right ... You get out and you stay out, and I turn over the alternate report, and the quiet process of cleaning up Genessee Industries begins. No cries of conspiracy – which it is; no demands for your necks – which should be demanded; no total wipeout. I'm sure a task force can be mounted to go after the existing financial fiefdoms. We won't bother with the root causes, because they'll be eliminated. You'll be eliminated.'

'That's excessively harsh.'

'You came here to make a deal, Hamilton. There it is, You're a political realist; I'm a political reality – your judgment, I believe. Take it. You won't get a better offer.'

'You're no match for us, *schoolboy*,' said Aaron Green, his emotion denying the confidence of his statement.

'Not by myself; of course not. I'm only an instrument. But through me two hundred million people will learn what you are. As opposed to you, I honestly believe they're capable of making decisions.'

The pavane was over. The music finished. The stately ancients took their leave of the newly established court with as much dignity as was possible.

'Would it have worked?' asked Sam Vicarson.

'I don't know,' answered Trevayne. 'But they couldn't take the chance.'

'Do you think they'll really get out?'

'We'll see.'

47

'I'm sorry. I think my letter makes clear the Army's position in the matter. I'm sure Major Bonner appreciates your retaining attorneys for him. From what I gather, there's every reason to anticipate a civilian acquittal.'

'But you're still going ahead with your own charges, General Cooper; you want him out of the Army.'

'We have no choice, Mr Trevayne. Bonner's stepped out of line once too often. He knows it. There's no defence against dereliction, disregarding the chain of command. Without that chain we have no military organization, sir.'

'I'll insist on seeing him defended in the court-martial proceedings, of course. Again, with my attorneys present.'

'You're wasting your money. The adjutant charge isn't murder or assault or even criminal intent. It's simply one of lying to an AF officer; misrepresenting his orders so as to gain access to government property. In this case, a jet aircraft. Furthermore, he refused to inform his superiors of his intentions. We simply can't tolerate that kind of behaviour. And Bonner is inclined to repeat this type of offence. There's no sound military justification.'

'Thank you, General. We'll see'.

Andrew hung up the phone and got out of his chair. He walked over to his office door, which he'd shut prior to his call to General Cooper. He opened it and spoke to his secretary.

'I saw the light on two; anything I should take care of, Marge?'

'The Government Printing Office, Mr Trevayne. I didn't know what to say. They wanted to know when you'd be sending over the subcommittee report. They're getting back-logged with congressional stuff and didn't want to disappoint you. I started to tell them it was completed and sent out late this morning, but I thought perhaps there was some kind of protocol we didn't know about.'

Trevayne laughed. 'I'll bet they didn't want to disappoint us! Lord! The eyes are everywhere, aren't they? . . . Call them back and tell them we weren't aware they expected our business. We saved the taxpayers' money and did it ourselves. All five copies. But first get me a cab. I'm going over to Arlington. To Bonner.'

During the ride from the Potomac Towers to the Army BOQ, Arlington, Andy tried to understand Brigadier General Lester Cooper and his legion of righteous indignants. Cooper's letter – the reply to his inquiry about Bonner – had been couched in Army jargon. *Section* this, *Article* that; Army regulations pertinent to the disposition of authority under the conditions of limited responsibility.

'Horseshit,' as Paul Bonner said – far too often for his own good.

The threat of the court-martial charge wasn't the Army's abhorrence of Bonner's behaviour; it was its abhorrence of Bonner himself. If it was explicitly the behaviour in *principle*, far more serious charges would have been filed against him, charges that could be argued back and forth. As it was, the Army chose the lesser indictment. Dereliction. Misprision, or concealment of intentions. Charges from which there would be no hard-won vindication. Not a slap-on-the-wrist; more a strap-on-the-back. It left the defendant no choice but to resign; there was no career left for him in the military.

He simply couldn't win the fight, because there was no fight. Just a pronouncement.

But *why*, for God's sake? If ever there was a man made for the Army, it was Paul Bonner. If ever there was an army that needed such a man, it was the demoralized Army of the United States. Instead of prosecuting him, Cooper and the rest of his 'Brasswares' should be out beating the bushes for Bonner's support.

Beating the bushes. What had Aaron Green said about 'beating bushes?' Beating was an undesirable tactic, because the quarry could turn on the hunter without warning.

Was that what the Army was afraid of?

That by supporting Paul Bonner, acknowledging his participation, his commitment to the military, the Army was exposing its own vulnerability?

Were Lester Cooper and his uniformed tribunals afraid of a surprise attack?

From whom? A curious public? That was understandable. Paul Bonner was a knowledgeable accessory.

Or were they afraid of the accessory? Afraid of Paul Bonner? And by discrediting him, they conveniently pushed him out of the picture, out of any frame of reference.

A nonperson.

Banished.

The taxi came to a stop at the gates of the BOQ. Trevayne paid the driver and started walking toward the huge entrance with the gold eagle over the double doors and the inscription: 'Through These Portals Pass the Best Damned Men in the Field'.

Andrew noticed that to the right, underneath the inscription was the date of the building's construction: 'April, 1944.'

History. Another era. A lifetime ago. A time when such inscriptions were perfectly natural, properly heroic.

The days of the disdainful cavaliers.

They were no more. They seemed a little silly now.

That, too, was unfair, thought Trevayne.

The guard outside Paul Bonner's room acknowledged Trevayne's presence, his standing access to the officer under barracks arrest, and opened the door. Bonner was seated at the small steel desk writing on a sheet of Army stationery. He turned in the chair and glanced up at Trevayne. He did not stand or offer his hand.

'I'll just finish this paragraph and be right with you.' He returned to the paper. 'I think I'm considered a spit-and-polish moron. Those two lawyers you hired are making me put everything I can remember down in writing. Said one thought leads to another if you see it in front of you, or something like that.'

'It makes sense. The sequence of thoughts, I mean. Go ahead; no hurry.' Trevayne sat down in the single armchair and kept silent until Bonner put down his pencil and shifted his position, throwing his shoulder over the back of the chair as he looked at the 'civilian'.

And he was looking at a 'civilian'; there was no mistaking the insult.

'I'll pay you back for the legal fees. I insist on that.'

'Not necessary. It's the least I can do.'

'I don't want you to do it. I asked them to bill me directly, but they said that wasn't possible. So, I'll pay you ... Frankly, I'm perfectly satisfied with my Army counsel. But I suppose you have your reasons.'

'Just added insurance.'

'For whom?' Bonner stared at Trevayne.

'For you, Paul.'

'Of course. I shouldn't have asked ... What do you want?'

'Maybe I'd better go out and come in again,' said Andrew with a questioning harshness. 'What's the matter with you? We're on the same side, remember?'

'Are we, Mr President?'

The sound of the words was like the crack of a lash across Trevayne's face. He returned Bonner's stare, and for several moments neither man spoke.

'I think you'd better explain that.'

So Major Paul Bonner did.

And Trevayne listened in astonished silence as the Army officer recounted his brief but extraordinary conversation with the soon-to-retire Brigadier General Lester Cooper.

'So nobody has to tell any elaborate stories anymore. All those complicated explanations aren't necessary.'

Trevayne got out of the chair and walked to the small window without speaking. There was a contingent – a platoon, perhaps – of young second lieutenants being lectured to by a wrinkle-faced full colonel in the courtyard. Some of the young men moved their feet, several cupped their hands to their lips, warding off the December chill in Arlington. The Colonel, open-shirted, laconic, seemed oblivious to the climate.

'What about the truth? Would you be interested in that, Major?'

'Give me some credit, *politician*. It's pretty goddamned obvious.'

'What's your version?' Trevayne turned from the window.

'Cooper said the Army couldn't afford me. The truth is that *you* can't ... I'm the lodestone around your presidential neck.'

'That's ridiculous.'

'Come off it! You ensure the trial, I'm acquitted – which I should be – and you're clean. Nobody can say you ran out on the soldier boy who was shot at. But that trial is controlled. No extraneous issues; just the pertinent facts, ma'am. Even the Army lawyer made that clear. Just Saturday night in Connecticut. No San Francisco, no Houston, no Seattle. No Genessee Industries! ... Then I'm quietly drummed out by kangaroos, the world goes on, and no one has to be embarrassed any longer. What pisses me off is that none of you can come out and say it!'

'I can't, because it's not true.'

'The hell it isn't! It's all wrapped up in a neat package. Man, when you sell out, you sell out *high*. I'll give you credit, you don't take second best.'

'You're way off, Paul.'

'Horseshit! Are you telling me you're not in the sweepstakes? I even hear you're going to get a seat in the Senate! Goddamn convenient, isn't it?'

'I swear to you I don't know where Cooper got that information.'

'Is it true?'

Trevayne turned his back on Bonner, looking once again out the window at the platoon of second lieutenants. 'It's ... all under consideration.'

'Oh, that's beautiful. "Under consideration." What do you do next? Run it up a flagpole and see if it gets off at Westport? Look, Andy, I'll tell you the same thing I told Cooper. I don't like this big new wrinkle – this sudden first-team switch – any more than I like a lot of the things I've found out during the past several months. Let's say I'm square enough to disapprove of the *MOs*. The methods of operation. I think they smell ... On the other hand, I'd be a first-class hypocrite if I started getting moralistic at this late date. I've spent my career believing that military goals were their own justifications. Let the elected civilians worry about the morals; that's always been a distant area to me ... Well, this is the *big game plan*, isn't it? I don't play in that ball park. Good luck!'

The platoon of second lieutenants was dispersing in the courtyard below; the open-shirted Colonel was lighting a cigarette. The lecture was over.

And Trevayne felt suddenly exhausted, weary. Nothing was as it seemed. He turned to face Bonner, who still remained insultingly casual in the desk chair.

'What do you mean, "game plan"?'

'You're getting funnier by the minute. You're going to make me blow any chance I may have for executive intervention.'

'Cut the clowning! Spell it out, Major.'

'You bet your ass, Mr President! They've got you, they don't need anyone else! The independent, incorruptible, Mr Clean. They couldn't have done any better if they called down John the Baptist, backed up with young Tom Paine. The Pentagon's worries are over.'

'Had it occurred to you that they may have just begun?'

Bonner lifted his shoulder off the back of the chair and laughed quietly – with maddening sincerity. 'You're the funniest nigger on the plantation, massa. But you don't have to tell those jokes; I won't interfere. I don't belong up there.'

'I asked you a question. I expect an answer. You're implying that I've been bought. Why do you think so?'

'Because I know those boys in "Brasswares". They're going to ensure your investiture. They wouldn't do that unless they had ironbound guarantees.'

48

Trevayne ordered the taxi to let him out nearly a mile from the Potomac Towers. It was a time to walk, to think, to analyse. To try to find logic within the illogical.

His thoughts were interrupted by the sound of automobile horns, blowing angrily at a brown sedan that seemed lost, unsure of its direction. The irritating cacophony fit his own sense of frustration.

Had he really been so naïve, so much the innocent, to have been used so completely? Had his confrontation with Ian Hamilton and Aaron Green been no more than an indulgence on their part? A sham?

No, that wasn't so. It couldn't be.

Hamilton and Green were frightened men. Hamilton and Green called the shots for Genessee Industries and Genessee ran the Pentagon.

A equals *B* equals *C*.

A equals *C*.

If he, as President, could control Ian Hamilton and Aaron Green – make them bend to his demands – then it was only logical that he could control the Pentagon. The means of that control would be in the dismembering of Genessee Industries, cutting the monolith down to size.

He had stated that clearly as his prime objective.

Yet, if Paul Bonner was to be believed – and why not? He couldn't have invented the scenario – Lester Cooper and his colleagues were throwing the full weight of the Pentagon behind his proposed candidacy.

And since their military opinion was formed in the conglomerate thought process of Genessee Industries, their support had to be directed – at least endorsed – by Ian Hamilton and Aaron Green.

A equals *B*.

Why, then? Why would Brigadier General Lester Cooper and his legion of brass willingly oversee the burial of their own strength? Why would they be *ordered* to?

A equals *C*.

It was one thing for Hamilton and Green to fade out – they had no choice – it was something else altogether for them to turn and instruct the Pentagon to support the candidate who was admittedly destroying them.

Yet apparently they had done just that.

Unless that support was ordered *before* the Waldorf confrontation.

Ordered and put into action before his threats ended the stately pavane high up in the Waldorf Towers.

In which case, Andrew realized that he was not what he thought he was. He wasn't the strong alternative, the man good political men had turned to; he wasn't the considered choice of seasoned professionals who looked into their smoke-filled crystal balls and determined him fit.

He was the candidate of Genessee Industries, personally selected by Ian Hamilton and Aaron Green. And all their talk of bitter disappointment was just that, talk.

Christ, the irony of it! The subtlety!

And the conclusion to be drawn; that was the most frightening part of the whole charade.

It mattered not one whit who held the office of the presidency. It mattered only that no one made waves through which the good ship Genessee could not navigate.

He had provided just that.

He had *delivered* just that.

Four hours ago he had delivered an extraordinary report, made more extraordinary by the fact that vital, incriminating evidence had been withheld.

Oh, Christ! What the hell had he done?

He saw the outlines of the twin steel-and-brick structure of the Potomac Towers in the distance. Perhaps a half-mile away. He began walking faster, then faster still. He looked up and down the avenue for a taxi, but there were none. He wanted to get to his office quickly now. He wanted to find out the truth; he *had* to find out.

There was only one way to do it.

Brigadier General Lester Cooper.

Sam Vicarson was pacing up and down outside the subcommittee's offices when Andrew emerged from the elevator into the corridor.

'Good God, am I glad to see you! I called Arlington and left messages at half a dozen places.'

'What's the matter?'

'We better go inside so you can sit down.'

'Oh, Jesus! Phyllis—'

'No, sir, I'm sorry ... I mean, I'm sorry if I made you ... it's not Mrs Trevayne.'

'Let's go inside.'

Vicarson closed the door of Trevayne's office and waited until Andy took off his overcoat and threw it on the couch. He began slowly, as if trying to recall the exact words he should repeat.

'The chief of the White House staff telephoned about forty-five minutes ago. Something happened this morning – it hasn't been released to the press yet, at least it hadn't been a half-hour ago – that caused the President to make a decision you should be aware of ... He temporarily exercised executive privilege and had the copies of the subcommittee's report impounded.'

'*What?*'

'He had them intercepted at all four destinations – the Defense Commission, the Attorney General's office, and the offices of the chairmen of the Senate and House committees; that's Appropriations and Armed Services ... He's talked to the four principals personally, and they've accepted his explanation.'

'What is it?'

'Robert Webster – you remember, the White House—'

'I remember.'

'He was killed this morning. I mean, he was murdered. Shot in his Akron hotel room ... A maid who was in the hallway gave the police a description of two men she saw running out of the room, and someone at the hotel had the presence of mind to call the White House. I mean, Webster was a hometown boy who made good and all that ... The White House went to work. Got the papers and the wire services to keep it quiet for a few hours ...'

'Why?'

'The description of the killers. It fit two men the White House had under surveillance ... That's not right. They had Webster under surveillance, and spotted them following Webster.'

'I don't understand you, Sam.'

'The two men were from Mario de Spadante's organization ... As I said, White House security went to work. Did you know that every conversation on every 1600 telephone, including the kitchen, is automatically put on a microtape and housed in the communications room; checked out, discarded, or kept every six months?'

'It doesn't surprise me.'

'I think it would have surprised Webster. 1600 said it isn't common knowledge. But they had to tell us.'

'What's your point? Why was the report impounded?'

'Bobby Webster was up to his ass with de Spadante. He was a paid informer. He's the one who removed the men in Darien. According to one conversation, you asked Webster for material on de Spadante.'

'Yes. When we were in San Francisco; Webster never delivered.'

'Regardless, the President thinks Webster was killed because de Spadante's men believe he was working with you. That he chickened and gave you the information that got de Spadante killed ... The assumption is that they cornered Bobby in the hotel room, forced him to tell them what was in the report, and when he couldn't, or didn't, they shot him.'

'And if the report involves de Spadante, his loyalists will go after me next?'

'Yes, sir. The President was concerned that if any details of the report were leaked, you might become a target. No one wanted to alarm you, but a security detail picked you up in Arlington. Or they were supposed to.'

Trevayne thought of the automobile behind his taxi; the brown sedan that had held up traffic. His brow creased in doubt; he looked at Sam. 'Just how long is this solicitous concern for me supposed to last?'

'Apparently until they catch the men who killed Webster. De Spadante's loyalists.'

Trevayne sat down behind his desk and reached into his pocket for a cigarette. He had the feeling that he was careering around a steep downhill curve, struggling to hold a wheel nearly out of control.

Was it possible? Was it possible, when he let the sunlight come into the dark corridors of his mind, that he was right, after all?

'As Paul Bonner would say,' said Trevayne softly, '"horseshit".'

'Why? The concerns seem legitimate to me, sir.'

'I hope you're right. I *pray* you're right. Because if you're wrong, Sam, a dying man is trying to protect his place in history.'

Vicarson understood; and the look on his face showed that his understanding was the most serious comprehension he'd ever experienced. 'Do you think the President is . . . Genessee Industries?'

'Get General Cooper on the phone.'

49

Brigadier General Lester Cooper sat in front of Andrew Trevayne's desk. He was exhausted – with the fatigue of a man who'd reached the limits of his ability to cope.

'Everything I've done, I consider it a privilege to have been in my province to accomplish, Mr Chairman.'

'There's no necessity for that title, General. The name's "Andy", or "Andrew", or "Mr Trevayne", if you insist. I respect you enormously; I'd consider it a privilege if you'd be less formal.'

'That's kind of you; *I'd* prefer the formality. You've manifestly accused me of dereliction, conspiracy, and disregard of my oath . . .'

'Goddamn it, *no*, General. I did not use those words. I *wouldn't* use them . . . I think you've operated in an impossible position. You have a hostile electorate that begrudges you every dollar of your budget. You have an Army that demands attention. You have to reconcile those two extremes in an area I know very well. Supply! . . . I'm only asking you if you made the very same compromises I would have made! That's neither dereliction nor conspiracy, General. That's goddamn common sense! If you didn't make them, that would be a violation of your oath.'

It was working, thought Trevayne with sad feelings of misgiving. The General was being primed. He stared at Trevayne, his look one of supplication.

'Yes . . . There's really nowhere to turn, you know. You know, of course. I mean, after all, you of all people . . .'

'Why me?'

'Well, if you are what they say you are . . .'

'What is that?'

'You *understand* . . . You wouldn't be where you are if you didn't. We're all aware of that . . . I mean, you'll have our complete, enthusiastic endorsement. It's far-reaching, but, of course, you know that . . .'

'Endorsement for what?'

'Please, Mr Trevayne . . . Are you testing me? Why is that necessary?'

'Perhaps it is. Maybe you're not good enough!'

'That's not right! You shouldn't say that! I've done *everything—*'

'For whom? For *me*?'

'I've done everything I was told to do. The logistics have gone out.'

'Where?'

'Everywhere! In every port, on every base. Every airfield. We've covered every spot on earth! ... Only the *name*. Only the name has to be supplied.'

'And what is that name?'

'*Yours* ... yours, for God's sake! What do you *want* from me?'

'Who gave you those orders?'

'What do you mean—'

'Who gave you the orders to put out my name?' Trevayne slapped the flat of his hand on his desk, flesh against hard wood, the sound sharp and distracting.

'I'm ... I'm ...'

'I asked you *who*?'

'The man from ... the man from ...'

'*Who?*'

'Green.'

'Who's Green?'

'You *know*! ... Genessee. Genessee Industries.' Brigadier General Cooper slumped in his seat; breathing hard.

But Trevayne hadn't finished. He leaned across the desk. '*How long ago*? Were you in *time*, General? Were you on *schedule*? How long ago?'

'Oh, my God! ... What *are* you?'

'*How long ago*?'

'A week, ten days ... What *are* you?'

'Your best friend! The man that gets you what you want! Would you like to believe that?'

'I don't know what to believe ... You people ... you people drain me.'

'None of that, General ... I asked you if you were on schedule.'

'Oh, Jesus!'

'What were the *other* schedules, General? Were you on schedule with everyone else?'

'Stop it! *Stop it!*'

'Answer me.'

'How do I know? *Ask them!*'

'Who?'

'I don't know!'

'Green?'

'Yes. Ask him!'

'Hamilton?'

'Yes, of course.'

'What can they guarantee?'

'Everything! You *know* that!'

'Spell it out, you *latrine private!*'

'You can't *say* that. You have no *right!*'

'*Spell it out.*'

'It will be what you need. The unions. Management ... All the psychological profiles in every section of the country ... we've got them in Army computers ... We'll act in *concert*.'

'Oh, my God ... Does the President know?'

'Certainly not from us.'

'And nobody's countermanded those orders within the last five days?'

'Of course not!'

Trevayne suddenly lowered his voice as he sat back in his chair. 'Are you sure, General?'

'Yes!'

Trevayne brought both his hands to his face and breathed into his palms. He had the feeling that he'd spun wildly off that long, steep downhill curve and was plunging uncontrollably into the turbulent waters below.

Why should there always be the sea?

'Thank you, General Cooper,' said Trevayne gently. 'I think we've finished.'

'I beg your pardon?'

'I meant what I said. I respect you. I don't know that I would have if it hadn't been for Paul Bonner ... You've heard of Major Bonner, General? I believe we've discussed him ... Now, I'm going to offer you some unsolicited advice. Get out, Cooper. Get out quick.'

Brigadier General Lester Cooper, his eyes bloodshot, looked at the civilian who covered his face with his hands.

'I don't understand.'

'It's come to my attention that you anticipate retiring soon ... May I respectfully suggest that you formally write that letter of resignation first thing tomorrow morning?'

Cooper started to speak and then stopped. Andrew Trevayne took his hands away from his face and looked into the General's tired eyes. The officer made a last West Point grasp at control, but it couldn't work.

'You're not ... you haven't ... Am I free?'

'Yes ... Christ knows you deserve it.'

'I hope so. Thank you, Mr Chairman.'

Sam Vicarson watched the General walk out of Trevayne's office. It was nearly six thirty. Andrew had timed the meeting with Cooper to begin after five; no one but the three of them would be in the subcommittee's office, and Sam could bar any late visitors or staff members who might unexpectedly show up.

The Brigadier General looked at Vicarson, but there was no recognition in his eyes, no sense of contact. Cooper stood motionless for several moments, his vacant, absently hostile expression concentrated on the young attorney. And then he did a strange – for Sam, a strangely terrible – thing. He stood erect and brought his right hand up to his visor and held it in a salute. He held his right hand in place until Sam Vicarson acknowledged by nodding his head silently. Only then did the General lower his hand, turn, and go out the door.

Sam walked quickly into Trevayne's office. The chairman of the subcommittee for the Defense Allocations Commission looked as exhausted as the decorated legend he had just confronted. Andrew was slumped back in his swivel chair, his chin resting in the palm of his right hand, his elbow on the arm of the chair. His eyes were closed.

'That must have been something,' said Sam quietly. 'I thought for a few minutes I should call for an ambulance. You should have seen Cooper outside. He looked as though he'd run head-on into a tank.'

'Don't sound so satisfied,' replied Trevayne, his eyes still shut. 'There's nothing to gloat over . . . I think we owe a lot to Cooper, to all the Coopers. We ask them to accomplish the impossible; give them no training – training, hell, we don't even warn them – on how to handle the political messiahs we force them to deal with. Finally we hold them up to ridicule when they try to cope.' Trevayne opened his eyes and looked up at Sam. 'Doesn't that strike you as unfair?'

'I'm afraid it doesn't, sir,' answered Vicarson, only slightly mitigating his refusal to agree. 'Men like Cooper – men who get that high – can find plenty of soap boxes, a lot of free time on television and radio on which to complain. At least, they can try that before going with Genessee Industries.'

'Sam, Sam . . .' said Trevayne wearily. 'You wouldn't "yes" me if my sanity depended on it. I suppose that's an asset.'

'Sure, I would. I may need a job someday.'

'I doubt it.' Trevayne got out of his chair, walked in front of his desk, and leaned back on the edge. 'Do you realize what they've done, Sam? They've structured my so-called candidacy in such a way that to win means I win as *their* candidate. Cooper was the proof of that.'

'So what? You didn't ask for it.'

'But I would have accepted it. Knowingly, consciously, I tacitly became an intrinsic part of the corruption I've claimed to be against . . . To smite Lucifer is to smite myself.'

'What?'

'Nothing. A little excess employed by Armbruster . . . Do you see, now? Caesar's wife, Sam. The Calpurnia complex. If elected – or even halfway into the campaign – I couldn't turn on Genessee Industries because I'm as guilty as it is. If I try before the election, I guarantee my loss; if after, I erode the public's confidence in me. They have the ammunition to cripple me: the amended report; they waded me out. It was extraordinary strategy . . . Thanks to Paul Bonner and a confused, overextended brigadier general, I found out before it was too late.'

'Why did they do it? Why did they pick you?'

'For the simplest of all reasons, Sam. The twentieth-century motif. They had no choice. No alternative . . . I was out to destroy Genessee Industries. And I could do it.'

Vicarson stared down at the floor. 'Oh, Jesus,' he said softly. 'I didn't understand . . . What are you going to do?'

Trevayne pushed himself off the edge of the desk. 'What I should have kept my mind on in the first place. Rip out Genessee . . . Root by goddamn root!'

'That blows your candidacy.'

'It certainly does.'

'I'm sorry about that.'

Andy stopped on his way back to the chair. He turned and looked in Sam's direction, but not at Sam. He looked beyond him to the windows, to the descending darkness that soon would be night in Washington, DC. 'Isn't it remarkable? I'm sorry, too. Genuinely sorry. How easily we convince ourselves . . . How much easier still are we mistaken.'

He continued back to the chair and sat down. He tore off the top page of a memorandum pad and picked up his Mark Cross pencil.

The telephone rang.

'I'll get it,' said Sam, getting up from the couch and crossing to the desk. 'Mr Trevayne's office . . . Yes, sir? Oh? Yes. I understand. Just one minute, please.' Vicarson pushed the 'hold' button and looked at Trevayne. 'It's James Goddard . . . He's in Washington.'

50

James Goddard, president, San Francisco Division, Genessee Industries, sat across the room while Trevayne and Vicarson studied the voluminous papers and computer cards spread out over the long conference table. The room was large, an executive suite at the Shoreham Hotel.

Goddard had been brief nearly four hours ago when Trevayne and his aide first walked through the door. There was no reason, he felt, for extraneous conversation. The figures, the reports, the printed results of the Genessee master tape were all that was necessary.

Let the numbers do the talking.

He had watched the two men; they'd approached the carefully sorted-out display apprehensively. At first they were guarded, suspicious. Then gradually the magnitude of the indictment shook their sense of reality. As their disbelief turned into reluctant acceptance, Trevayne started hammering questions at him; questions he answered – when he wanted to answer them – in the simplest of terms.

Let the numbers do the talking.

The subcommittee chairman then ordered Vicarson to return to their offices and bring back a small multipurpose desk computer. The sort of machine that added, subtracted, divided, multiplied, and held figures in six-column accruals until needed. Without it, Trevayne had said, they'd be there a week trying to reach their own conclusions. With it, and with luck, they might accomplish the job by morning.

James Goddard could have completed the job in two hours, three at the outside.

It was four hours now, and still they hadn't finished.

Amateurs.

Occasionally, then with growing rapidity, Trevayne turned to him and asked a question, expecting an immediate reply. Goddard laughed to himself as he 'thoughtfully' found that the answer was not within his grasp. Trevayne was reaching the end; he wanted the specific names now, the master planners of the master type. Goddard could easily supply them – Hamilton and Hamilton's faceless legion of 'vice presidents' in Chicago: men who stayed in deep cover, out of sight, manipulating the huge national and international commitments.

They never let him reach that level. They never gave him a chance to show he had the qualifications to set entire courses, to create – with even more accuracy – the fiscal projections spanning the five-year interregnums. How often had he found it necessary to make major alterations within his own sphere because the master tape had carried errors that would have led to financial crises within isolated sectors of Genessee's production? How many times had he sent irrefutable proof back to Chicago that he was not only the public figurehead of Genessee's finances but, in fact, the one man capable of overseeing the work of the master tape?

The replies from Chicago – never written, always a faceless voice over a telephone – were invariably the same. They thanked him, acknowledged his contribution, and restated the premise that his value as president of the all-important San Francisco Division was without parallel. All to say he'd reached the end of his line.

In the final analysis, he was expendable. The public figurehead ready at the crack of a whip for a public hanging. And once that hanging was set, what could he possibly do about it?

Nothing. Absolutely nothing. For his 'contributions' were there for all to see. And without the master tape, his 'contributions' stopped at his office door.

But there was a way out, his only way.

To move swiftly to the top – his top – of the one conglomerate larger than Genessee Industries.

The United States government.

The kind of deal that was made every day under a dozen guises: 'Consultant', 'Expert', 'Administrative Adviser'.

It meant giving up the house in Palo Alto; and the beautiful hills that calmed him so with their majesty. On the other hand, it meant also giving up his wife – she'd never, never consent – and that was a plus.

But the biggest gain of all was his own sense of well-being. For from now on his 'contributions' would not only be extraordinary – and acknowledged as such – but also indispensable. The history of Genessee Industries' ascent to its present position covered nearly twenty years. To untangle that extraordinary financial interweaving would take, perhaps, a decade.

And he, James Goddard, 'Expert', was the economic legend who could do it. It would have to be done, for it was, after all, an intrinsic part of the history of twentieth-century America. He would record for the millennia that history. Scholars for a thousand years would research his words, study his figures, hold his knowledge in reverence.

The government itself, right up to the highest reaches of decision making, would consider him the indispensable man.

No one could do what he would do now.

To have that acknowledged was all that he wanted. Couldn't Ian Hamilton and the faceless voices in Chicago understand? It wasn't money: it wasn't power.

It was respect. A respect that took him out of the realm of being primed for hanging.

It was nearly five hours now. Trevayne and his voluble, obnoxious assistant had gone through two pots of coffee. The chain-smoking chairman had stopped asking questions; the aide kept shoving cards and papers in front of Trevayne – they'd finally understood the pattern of financial sequence as he'd arranged it. They hadn't acknowledged it, of course, but they fell into a rhythm on the desk computer that silently betrayed the fact.

Soon it would come. The question.

Then the deal.

It would all be spelled out. Nothing left to speculation. It was really quite simple when one analysed it. He was merely changing sides, altering his allegiances.

He watched Andrew Trevayne get up from the table and rip the wide paper tape from the machine. The subcommittee chairman looked at it, placed it in front of his assistant, and began rubbing his eyes.

'Finished?'

'Finished?' answered Trevayne with the same question. 'I think you know better than that. It's just begun, I'm sorry to say.'

'Yes. Yes, of course. Precisely ... It *has* just begun. There are years, volumes to be completed. I'm well aware of it ... We must talk now.'

'Talk? Us? ... No, Mr Goddard. It may not be finished, but I am. You talk to others ... If you can find them.'

'What does that mean?'

'I won't pretend to understand your motives, Goddard. You're either the bravest man I've ever met ... or so consumed with guilt you've lost all sense of perspective. Either way, I'll try to help. You deserve that ... But I don't think anyone's going to want to touch you. Not the people who should ... They won't know where your leprosy ends. Or whether they've got a latent case, and standing next to you might make their skin fall off.'

51

The President of the United States rose from behind his desk in the Oval Office as Andrew Trevayne entered. The first thing that struck Trevayne was the presence of William Hill. Hill was standing across the room in front of the French doors, reading some papers in the harsh light of the early sun off the terrace. The President, seeing Andy's obvious reaction to a third party, spoke rapidly.

'Good morning, Mr Trevayne. The Ambassador is here at my request; my insistence, if you like.'

Trevayne approached the desk and shook the hand extended to him. 'Good morning, Mr President.' He turned and took several steps toward Hill, who met him halfway between the desk and the French doors. 'Mr Ambassador.'

'Mr Chairman.'

Trevayne felt the ice in Hill's voice, the title spoken in an emphasized monotone that skirted the edge of insult. The Ambassador was an angry man. That was fine, thought Andrew. Strange, but fine. He was angry himself. He returned his attention to the President, who indicated a chair – one of four forming a semicircle in front of the desk.

'Thank you.' Trevayne sat down.

'What is that quote?' asked the President with slim humour. '"We three do meet again . . ." Is that it?'

'I believe,' said Hill slowly, still standing, 'that the correct words are "*When shall we three meet again?*" The three in question had forecast the fall of a government; they weren't sure even they could survive.'

The President watched Hill; his eyes bore deeply into the old man's, his look a cross between compassion and irritation. 'I think that's highly interpretive, Bill. A bias I'm not sure would hold up academically.'

'Fortunately, Mr President, the academicians do not concern me.'

'They should, Mr Ambassador,' said the President curtly, turning to Trevayne. 'I can only assume, Mr Trevayne, that you requested this meeting as a result of my exercising executive privilege. I intercepted the subcommittee report on grounds you find suspect, and you'd like an explanation. You're entirely justified; the grounds I employed were fallacious.'

Andrew was surprised. He hadn't questioned the grounds at all. They were for his protection. 'I wasn't aware of that, Mr President. I accepted your explanation up front.'

'Really? I'm amazed. The device seemed so transparent to me. At least, I thought you'd think so ... Robert Webster's death was a private war, in no way connected with you. You don't know those people, you couldn't identify them. Webster did and could, and therefore had to be silenced. You're the last person on earth they'd want to touch.'

Trevayne flushed, partly in anger, more so because of his own ineptness. Of course, he was the 'last person on earth they'd want to touch'. Killing him would create a furore, bring about a relentless investigation, an intense pursuit for his killers: Bobby Webster was an embarrassment to everyone. Including the man who sat behind the desk at the Oval Office.

'I see. Thanks for the lesson in practicality.'

'That's what this job's all about.'

'Then I would like an explanation, sir.'

'You shall have it, Mr Chairman,' said William Hill as he crossed to the chair farthest away from Trevayne and sat down.

The President spoke quickly, attempting to vitiate Hill's invective. 'Of course, you will; you must. But, if you'll forgive me, I'd like to exercise another privilege. Let's not call it executive; let's just say the prerogative of an older man. Then we can get on ... I'm curious. Why did you consider this meeting so vital? If I've been accurately informed, you damn near told the appointments desk that you'd camp in the hallways until I saw you ... A tight morning schedule was rearranged ... The report's complete. The formalities of leave-taking aren't exactly priority functions.'

'I wasn't sure when you'd release the report.'

'And that concerns you?'

'Yes, Mr President.'

'*Why?*' interrupted William Hill harshly. 'Do you think the President intends suppressing it?'

'No ... It's not complete.'

There was silence for several seconds as the President and the Ambassador exchanged looks. The President leaned back in his chair. 'I stayed up most of the night reading it, Mr Trevayne. It seemed complete to me.'

'It's not.'

'What's missing?' asked Hill. 'Or should I ask, what's been removed?'

'Both are accurate, Mr Hill. Omitted and removed ... For what I believed at the time were reasoned judgments, I eliminated detailed – and indictable – information about the Genessee Industries Corporation.'

The President sat up and stared at Trevayne. 'Why did you do that?'

'Because I thought I was capable of controlling the situation in a less inflammatory manner. I was mistaken. It must be exposed. Completely.'

The President looked away from Andrew, his elbow on the arm of the chair, his fingers tapping a slow rhythm on his chin. 'Often first – reasoned – judgments are quite valid. Especially when they emanate from such reasonable men as yourself.'

'In the case of Genessee Industries, my judgment was in error. I was persuaded by an argument that proved groundless.'

'Would you please clarify?' asked Hill.

'Of course. I was led to believe – no, that's not right, I convinced myself – that I could bring about a solution by forcing the removal of those responsible. By eliminating them, the root motives could be altered. The corporation – or companies, hundreds of them – could then be subject to restructuring. Reshaped administratively and brought into line with compatible business practices.'

'I see,' said the President. 'Root out the corrupters, the corruption will follow, and chaos is averted. Is that it?'

'Yes, sir.'

'But the corrupters, in the final analysis, would not be rooted,' added Hill, avoiding Trevayne's eyes.

'That's my conclusion.'

'You're aware that your ... solution is infinitely preferable to the chaos that would result from ripping Genessee Industries apart. Genessee is the major producer for the country's defence programme. To lose confidence in such an institution would have extraordinary effects throughout the nation.' The President once more leaned back in his chair.

'That was my initial thinking.'

'I think it's sound.'

'It's no longer feasible, Mr President. As Mr Hill just said ... the corrupters can't be rooted.'

'But can they be used?' The President's tone was steady, not questioning.

'Ultimately, no. The longer they're entrenched, the more secure their control. They're building a base that will be passed on as they see fit; to whom they consider fit. And they deal in their own absolutes. A council of elite that will be inherited by their own kind – protected by unimaginable economic resources. Exposure's the only solution. Immediate exposure.'

'Aren't you now dealing in your own absolutes, Mr *Chairman*?'

Trevayne was annoyed once again by Hill's use of the title. 'I'm telling you the truth.'

'Whose truth?' asked the Ambassador.

'*The* truth, Mr Hill.'

'It wasn't the truth when you submitted your report. The truth changed. The judgment was altered.'

'Yes. Because the facts weren't known.'

William Hill lowered his voice and spoke with no apparent feeling. 'What facts? Or was it a *single* fact? The fact that you'd compromised your subcommittee for what you discovered was a hollow offer. The presidency of the United States.'

The muscles of Andrew Trevayne's stomach tensed. He looked at the President.

'You knew.'

'Did you really think I wouldn't?'

'Strangely enough, I hadn't given it much thought. I suppose that's asinine.'

'Why? It's not a betrayal of me. I asked you to do a job; I didn't demand political fidelity; or adherence.'

'But you did demand integrity, Mr President,' said Hill with conviction.

'Whose description of integrity, Mr Ambassador?' shot back the chief executive. 'Must I remind you of your own admonitions regarding truths and absolutes? ... Oh, no, Mr Trevayne, I'm not being kind. Or solicitous. I'm only convinced that you conducted yourself in good conscience – *as you understood it* ... Which makes my job easier. For the reason I intercepted the subcommittee report – my sole purpose in exercising privilege – was to stop you from tearing this country apart ... From using Genessee Industries as the means to destroy a large section of the economy unnecessarily. Depriving livelihoods, ruining reputations indiscriminately. You can imagine my astonishment when I read what you'd written.'

Andrew Trevayne returned the President's stare. 'I find that an extraordinary statement.'

'No more extraordinary than I found your report. And the fact that you refused to announce – at least to any of the proposed recipients – the exact date when you'd deliver the report. You made no arrangements with the Government Printing Office; you did not, as is customary, avail yourself of Justice Department attorneys prior to the final assembling—'

'I was not aware of those customs; and if I had been, I doubt I'd have complied.'

'Courtesy, expediency, and simple protection might have made you aware of them,' interjected Hill. 'As I gather, your mind was on other, more vital matters.'

'Mr Ambassador, you've been pressing me against the wall since I walked in. I don't like it! Now, with all due respect, I ask you to stop it.'

'With very little respect returned, Mr Trevayne, I shall be guided by my chosen vocabulary until the President asks otherwise.'

'Then I do ask it, Bill ... Mr Hill has worked closely with this office, with a number of my predecessors, Trevayne. He looks upon your action more severely than I do.' The President smiled gently. 'The Ambassador is not, nor will he ever be, a politician. He believes, quite simply, that you're trying to rob me of my second term. I wish you luck; I don't think you can. Or "could have", I assume, is more proper.'

Trevayne took a silent breath before speaking. 'If I had believed for one minute that you were going to run for re-election, none of this would have happened. I'm sorry. Sorrier than I can ever express to you.'

The President's smile diminished and was no more. Hill began to speak but was stopped by the President's hand, held up firmly, commanding silence. 'I think you'd better explain that, Mr Trevayne.'

'I was told you would not seek a second term ... the decision was irrevocable.'

'And you accepted that.'

'It was the basis of my discussions. Finally the only basis.'

'Were you told why?'

'Yes ... I'm sorry.'

The President searched Trevayne's face, and Andrew felt sick. He didn't want to look at this good, fine man, but he knew he could not waver.

'My health?' asked the President simply.

'Yes.'

'Cancer?'

'I inferred that ... I'm sorry.'

'Don't be. It's a lie.'

'Very well, sir.'

'You're not reading me, Mr Trevayne. It *is* a lie. The simplest, crudest lie that can be used in the political arena.'

Trevayne's jaw fell slack as he looked at the maturely lined, strong features of the man behind the desk. The President's eyes were steady, conveying the truth of his statement.

'Then I'm a damn fool.'

'I'd rather that than face the diminishing returns of cobalt ... I have every intention of assuming the standard of my party, campaigning, and being returned to office. Is that clear?'

'Yes.'

'Mr Trevayne.' William Hill spoke softly. 'Please accept my apologies. You're not the only damn fool in this room.' The old man attempted a tight-lipped smile. 'We're neck-and-neck on a slow track for last place ... We're both a little ludicrous.'

'Who specifically read you my premature obituary?'

'It was read twice. The first time was at the Villa d'Este in Georgetown. I went there a sceptic – to see who would try to buy off the subcommittee report. To my astonishment, no one did; quite the opposite, as a matter of fact. I emerged a three-quarters candidate.'

'You still haven't—'

'Sorry. Senator Alan Knapp. In what I think was called "true bipartisan spirit", he made the announcement that you were leaving at the end of your present term. And the good of the country came first.'

The President, turning his head only slightly in Hill's direction, spoke. 'You'll follow this up, Bill?'

'The energetic Senator will retire before the end of the month. Consider it a Christmas present, Mr President.'

'Go on, please.'

'The second instance was in New York. At the Waldorf. I held what I believed was a showdown with Aaron Green and Ian Hamilton ... I thought I'd won; therefore, the report as you read it. Hamilton said you wouldn't live out a second term; you were putting up either the Vice President or the Governor of New York. They couldn't accept either one.'

'Scylla and Charybdis strike again, eh, Bill?'

'They've gone too far!'

'They always do. Don't touch them.'

'I understand.'

Trevayne watched the short interplay between the two older men. 'Mr President, *I* don't understand. How can you *say* that? Those men should—'

'We'll get to that, Mr Trevayne,' interrupted the President. 'One last question. When did you learn that you'd been manipulated? Manipulated brilliantly, I might add, now that I see the pattern.'

'Paul Bonner.'

'Who?'

'Major Paul Bonner—'

'From the Pentagon,' said the President as a statement of fact. 'The one who killed that man up at your house in Connecticut?'

'Yes, sir. He saved my life; he'll be acquitted of the murder charge. He then faces court-martial; he's being drummed out.'

'You don't think that's justified?'

'I do not. I don't agree very often with the Major, but—'

'I'll review it,' cut in the chief executive as he hastily scribbled a note on his desk. 'What did this Bonner tell you?'

Andrew paused briefly; he wanted to be precise, completely accurate. He owed that to Bonner. 'That a brigadier general named Cooper, in a state of depression, anxiety, told him I was the Pentagon's candidate; that the irony of the Major's situation was that in the final analysis . . .' Trevayne paused again, embarrassed by his own words. 'Bonner's court-martial might be rescinded by executive intervention . . . My intervention.'

'Good Lord,' uttered Hill almost inaudibly.

'And?'

'It didn't make sense. I looked upon my meeting with Hamilton and Green as a success, a capitulation on their part. I was sure of two things. The first was that I was not their candidate; the second, that they accepted my terms. They were getting out . . . Bonner's information contradicted everything I believed.'

'So you called in Cooper,' said the President.

'I did. And I learned not only that I was the Pentagon's – Genessee Industries' – candidate, but I had been from the beginning. Every resource of the military – Army intelligence data banks, industrial collusion, even interservice voting indoctrinations – they'd all be used to ensure my election. Management, labour, the service ballot; voting blocs guaranteed by Genessee. There was no capitulation in New York; they weren't getting out. They were *wading me* out. If I got the nomination – God forbid the office – I'd be hanged. To be independent, to expose them at that point, would be to expose myself.'

'At which juncture – junctures – you'd destroy your candidacy or – God forbid – the national and international confidence of your administration,' completed the President.

'They took considerable risks,' said William Hill. 'It's not like them.'

'What alternative did they have, Bill? He couldn't be bought. Or persuaded. If our young friend hadn't gone to them, they would have come to him. Same solution, on the surface. Orderly retreat as opposed to economic chaos. I would have subscribed; so would you.'

'You talk as if you know all about . . . *them.*'

'A great deal, yes. Hardly "all". I'm sure there are areas you've covered that we're not aware of. We'd appreciate a full briefing. Classified, of course.'

'Classified? This material can't be classified, Mr President. It's got to be made public.'

'You didn't think so twenty-four hours ago.'

'The conditions weren't the same.'

'I've read the report; it's entirely satisfactory.'

'It's *not* satisfactory. I spent five hours last night with a man named Goddard—'

'Genessee. President, San Francisco Division,' said William Hill quietly, in response to the glance from the man behind the desk.

'He walked out of San Francisco with four briefcases filled with Genessee commitments – extending for years. A good percentage of which have never been *heard* of before.'

'I'm sure you'll cover that in your briefing. The report stands as submitted.'

'No. It can't! I won't accept that!'

'You *will* accept it!' The President's voice suddenly matched Trevayne's. 'You'll accept it because it is the decision of this office.'

'You can't enforce that decision! You have no control over me!'

'Don't be so sure of that. You submitted – *officially* submitted – your report to this office. The document is over your signature. Incidentally, we have in our possession four copies with the seals unbroken. To speculate that this single report is not authentic; that it must be recalled because it's been tampered with, shaped by the political ambitions of the subcommittee's chairman, would raise the gravest issues. To allow you to recall it – for whatever the stated reasons – would also make my administration suspect. Our adversaries would claim we demanded changes. I can't permit that. This office deals daily with both domestic and foreign complexities; you will not compromise our effectiveness in these areas because *your* ambitions have been thwarted. In this instance, we must remain above suspicion.'

Trevayne's voice conveyed his astonishment. He could hardly be heard. 'That's what they would have said.'

'I have no compunctions stealing someone's strategy if it has merit.'

'And if I stand up and say it's not authentic, not complete?'

'Outside of the personal anguish – and ridicule – to which you subject yourself and your family,' said William Hill quietly, staring at Trevayne, 'who would believe you? . . . You sold your credibility when you sent out that report yesterday morning. Now you wish to substitute a second? Perhaps there'll be a third – if a group of politicians recommend you for the governorship. Even a fourth – there are other offices, other appointments. Where does the flexible chairman stop? Just how many reports are there?'

'I don't care about other people's opinions. I've said it from the beginning – over and over again. I've nothing to gain or lose.'

'Except your effectiveness as a functioning, contributive individual,' said the President. 'You couldn't live without that, Mr Trevayne. No one with your abilities could. And it would be taken from you; you'd be isolated from the community of your peers. You'd never be trusted again. I don't think you could live that existence. We all need something; none of us is totally self-sufficient.'

Andrew, his eyes locked with the President's, understood the essential truth of the man's words. 'You'd do that? You'd have it come out that way?'

'I most certainly would.'

'*Why?*'

'Because I must deal in priorities. Quite simply, I need Genessee Industries.'

'No! . . . No. You can't mean that. You know what it *is!*'

'I know it serves a function; I know it can be controlled. That's all I have to know.'

'Today. Perhaps tomorrow. Not in a few years. It's out to destroy.'

'It won't succeed.'

'You can't guarantee that.'

The President suddenly slapped his hand on the arm of his chair and stood up. 'No one can guarantee anything. There are risks every time I walk into this room; dangers every time I walk out . . . You listen to me, Trevayne. I believe deeply in the capacity of this country to serve the decent instincts of her own people – and of mankind. But I'm practical enough to realize that in the service of this decency there must often be indecent manipulations . . . Does that surprise you? It shouldn't. For surely you know not all weapons will be turned into ploughshares; Cain will murder Abel; the locusts will plague the land; and the oppressed will get goddamn sick and tired of looking forward to inheriting the creature comforts of an afterlife! They want something down here! And whether *you* like it or not – whether *I* like it or not – Genessee Industries is doing something about these things! . . . It's my considered judgment that it is not a threat. It can and will be contained. *Used*, Mr Trevayne. *Used.*'

'With every turn,' said Hill with compassion, seeing the look of shock on Trevayne's face, 'there's the constant seeking of solutions. Do you remember my telling you that? That *search* is the solution. It is continuously applied to such entities as Genessee Industries. The President is right.'

'He's not right,' replied Andrew quietly, painfully, looking at the man who stood behind the desk. 'It's no solution; it's a surrender.'

'An employable strategy.' The President sat down. 'Eminently suited to our system.'

'Then the system's wrong.'

'Perhaps,' said the President, reaching for some papers. 'I haven't the time to indulge in such speculations.'

'Don't you think you should?'

'No,' answered the man, looking up from a page, dismissing Trevayne's plea. 'I have to run the country.'

'Oh, my God . . .'

'Take your moral outrage somewhere else, Mr Trevayne. Time. Time is what I must deal with. Your report stands.'

As if it were an afterthought, the President shifted the paper and extended his right hand over the desk as Andrew stood up.

Trevayne looked at the hand, held steady, as the man's eyes were steady. He did not accept it.

52

Paul Bonner looked around the courtroom for Trevayne. It was difficult to find him, for the crowds were milling, the voices pitched high, reporters demanding statements, and the incessant silent pops of flashbulbs were coming from all directions. Andrew had been there for the morning summations, and Paul thought it strange that he didn't remain – at least for a while – to see if the jury would return an early verdict.

It did.

In one hour and five minutes.

Acquittal.

Bonner hadn't worried. As the trial progressed he'd been confident that his own Army counsel could have handled the job without Trevayne's elegant, hard-as-nails attorneys from New York. But there was no denying the value of their collective image. They were the essence of respectability; whenever they referred to the de Spadantes or their associates, there was implied revulsion. So successful were they that several members of the jury nodded affirmatively when the comparison was made between the professional soldier who, for years, had risked his life in the murderous jungles defending the nation's institutions, and the brother-brokers who sought to bleed these same institutions of money and honour.

Trevayne was nowhere to be found.

Paul Bonner made his way through the crowd toward the courtroom door. He tried to maintain a grateful smile as he was jostled and yelled at. He promised to have a 'statement later', and mouthed the appropriate clichés about his abiding faith in the judicial system.

The empty, hollow phrases that contradicted the terrible knowledge inside him. In less than a month he'd know the wrath of military intransigence. He wouldn't win that fight. The battle had been decided.

On the courthouse steps he looked for his uniformed escort, for the brown sedan that would take him back to Arlington, to his barracks arrest. It wasn't in sight; it wasn't parked where he'd been told it would be.

Instead, a master sergeant, tunic and trousers creased into steel, shoes gleaming, approached Bonner.

'If you'll follow me, please, Major.'

The automobile at the curb was a tan-metallic limousine, two flags mounted in the front, one on each side of the hood above the wide grille. They rustled hesitantly in the December breeze. Enough to reveal four gold stars on each laterally across a red background.

The sergeant opened the right-rear door for Bonner as newsmen and photographers crowded around him firing questions and snapping pictures. Paul didn't need to speculate on the identity of the General in the back seat. The reporters had established it in loud, excited voices.

The Chairman of the Joint Chiefs of Staff of the United States.

The General offered no greeting as Bonner entered and sat beside him. He stared straight ahead at the glass partition separating the driver from his Very Important Passengers.

Outside, the sergeant shouldered his way around the vehicle and got behind the wheel. The car drove off; at first slowly, the driver coldly impatient with the crowd, pressing the horn continuously in an effort to clear his path.

'That little scene was ordered, Major. I hope you appreciate it.' The General spoke curtly, without looking at Bonner.

'You sound as though you didn't approve, sir.'

The senior officer looked abruptly at Bonner, and then, just as rapidly, turned away. He reached over to the left door panel, to the elasticized pocket, and withdrew a manila envelope. 'The second order I received was to deliver this to you personally. It is equally distasteful to me.'

He handed the envelope to Bonner, who, bewildered, responded with an inaudible thank you. The printing on the upper-left-hand corner told him that the contents were from the Department of the Army, not the Joint Chiefs of Staff. He ripped the flap open and extracted a single page. It was a copy of a letter from the White House, addressed to the Secretary of the Army and signed by the President of the United States.

The language was terse, to the point, and left no room for interpretation – other than the degree of anger, perhaps hostility, felt by the author.

The President directed the Secretary of the Army to terminate forthwith all contemplated charges against Major Paul Bonner. Said Major Bonner was to be elevated immediately to the permanent rank of full colonel and entered within the month to the War College for highest-level strategic training. Upon completion of the War College curriculum – an estimated six months – Colonel Bonner was to be assigned as a liaison officer to the Joint Chiefs of Staff.

Paul Bonner put the letter carefully back into the envelope and sat silently beside the General. He closed his eyes and thought about the irony of it all.

But he'd been right all along. That was the important thing.

It was back to work.

What did the beavers know?

Yet he was strangely troubled; he wasn't sure why. Perhaps it was the escalation in rank. Not one jump, but two. It was disconcertingly parallel to a promise made on an icy Connecticut slope, words that ended with ripped flesh and finally death.

But he wouldn't dwell on it. He was a professional.

It was a time for professionals.

Ian Hamilton patted the wet fur of his Chesapeake retriever. The large dog kept running ahead on the snow-covered path to pick up a stray branch or a loose rock, bringing it back to its master for approval.

It was a particularly gratifying Sunday morning, thought Hamilton. Ten days ago he wasn't sure he'd be taking any more Sunday walks; at least not on the shores of Lake Michigan.

All that was changed now. The fear was gone, and his normal sense of elation, the quiet elation that came with great accomplishment, returned. And the irony of it! The one man he had feared, the only one who had the real capacity to destroy them, had removed himself from the chessboard.

Or had been removed.

Either way, it proved that the course of action he'd insisted upon was the correct action. Aaron Green had nearly fallen apart; Armbruster spoke in panic of early retirement; Cooper – poor, beleaguered, unimaginative Cooper – had run to the Vermont hills, his uniform stained with the sweat of hysteria.

But he, Ian Hamilton, who could trace his family back to the origins of the infant colossus, whose forebears were the lairds of Cambuskeith, he'd held firm.

Practically speaking – *pragmatically* speaking – he'd felt secure. Far more so than the others. For he knew all they had to do was wait until Andrew Trevayne's 'abridged' version was released from the Potomac Towers. Once that happened, who would make, *could* make, the decision to allow him to submit the report in its original form? The rope would be on fire at both ends; Trevayne trapped by his own compromise, and the government's need for equilibrium.

William Hill as much as admitted it.

Big Billy. Hamilton wondered if Hill would ever realize how great a part – unknowingly, of course – he'd played in the development of Genessee Industries. He'd no doubt take his own life if he did. But it was true; Ambassador William Hill had been largely responsible. For over the Washington years Hamilton had watched Big Billy closely. They both were 'friends to', advisers to presidents; Hill much older, of course. He'd seen Big Bill's words stricken from the record more than once. He'd sympathized as Hill's advice to Eisenhower over the U-2 crisis in Paris had gone unheeded – the summit meeting aborted; he'd felt for the old man when McNamara persuaded Kennedy that Hill's judgment on Berlin was in error – the Wall was the result; he'd winced openly when those maniacs at the Pentagon convinced a perplexed, malleable Nixon that the 'incursion' into Cambodia was necessary – over the loud, intensely felt objections of William Hill.

Kent State, Jackson. An all but destroyed Joint Chiefs of Staff.

And Ian Hamilton realized that he'd been observing a man whose shoes he might jump into; a version of himself in a few years to come.

Unacceptable.

The alternative was the power and influence of Genessee Industries.

He'd concentrated on that. For everyone's good.

The Chesapeake retriever was now trying to separate a twig from a fallen limb. The twig held firm; Hamilton bent down and twisted it off.

It took considerable strength, he considered, but he wasn't even breathing hard.

Big Billy.

Big Billy had flown out to Chicago – an emissary from the President of the United States. They'd met in private in a suite at the Palmer House.

There were areas of mutual concern to be discussed. Mutual concern. The President wanted to see him, meet with him in Washington.

Accommodation would be reached.

The Chesapeake retriever had found another stick. But this one was different from the others; there were several sharp points where the bark had been stripped from the white wood. The dog whimpered, and Ian Hamilton could see that there was blood trickling down the mouth over the wet fur.

Sam Vicarson sat on top of the packed, sealed carton and looked around at the empty room. Empty except for the couch which had been there when the subcommittee had taken over the office. The movers were about finished. The chairs, the desks, the file cabinets had all disappeared, taken back to wherever chairs and desks and file cabinets went when there was no more use for them.

The cartons were his only concern. Trevayne had told him to oversee their crating and removal into the truck. The truck that would take them to Trevayne's house in Connecticut.

Why in God's name would he want them?

Who *would* want them?

Blackmailers, perhaps.

But these weren't the important files. The Genessee files.

Those had long since been removed from the Tawning Spring basement; sealed in wooden crates, with locks and guards and – as he understood it – driven directly to the underground vaults in the White House.

Cop-out.

Trevayne had copped out; they'd all copped out.

Trevayne tried to tell him that he hadn't; that the decisions made were for – what were the fatuous words? – the 'greater good'. Trevayne had forgotten that he, himself, had termed such words 'the twentieth-century syndrome'.

Cop-out.

He wouldn't have believed it a month ago. He wouldn't have considered it possible.

And, goddamn it, a man – a young man – had to look out for himself.

He had the options; Christ, did he have options! Trevayne had secured him offers from half a dozen top corporate firms in New York – including Walter Madison's. And Aaron Green – pretending to have been impressed with him at the Waldorf – had said he could go to work next week as the head of his agency's legal department.

But the best of all was right here in Washington. A man named Smythe, chief of the White House staff.

There was an opening.

What could look better on a résumé than the White House?

James Goddard sat on the thin, hard bed in the dingy rented room. He could hear the breathy wail of a woodwind – a primitive recorder, perhaps – and the intermittent, discordant twang of a Far East string instrument – a sitar, he thought. The players were on drugs, he knew that much.

Goddard wasn't a drinker, but he'd gotten drunk. Very drunk. In a filthy bar that opened early in the morning for the filthy, glassy-eyed drunks who had to have that drink before they went to their filthy jobs – if they had jobs.

He'd stayed in a back booth with his four briefcases – his precious briefcases – and had one drink after another.

He was so much better than anyone else in the bar – everyone could see that. And because he was better, the filthy bartender made it a point to be solicitous – which, God knew, he should have been. Then several of the filthy bar's filthy clientele had wandered over and been respectful – solicitous – also. He'd bought a number of drinks for the filthy people. Actually, he'd had no choice; the bartender said he couldn't change a hundred-dollar bill, so the natural solution was to purchase merchandise.

He'd mentioned to the filthy bartender that he wouldn't be averse to having a woman. No, not a woman, a young girl. A young girl with large breasts and firm thin legs. Not a woman with sagging breasts and fat legs, who spoke with a nasal twang and complained. It was important that the young girl with the large breasts and firm thin legs speak pleasantly – if she spoke at all.

The filthy bartender in the filthy apron found him several young girls. He'd brought them back to the booth for Goddard to make his selection. He chose the one who unbuttoned her blouse and showed him her large, pointed breasts. She actually unbuttoned her blouse and pushed her breasts above her brassiere and smiled at him!

And when she spoke, her voice was soft, almost melodious.

She needed money in a hurry; he didn't ask why. She said if she had money she'd calm down and give him a work-out he'd never forget.

If he gave her money, she'd take him to a wonderful old house in a quiet, old section of Washington where he could stay as long as he liked and no one would find him. And there were other girls there; young girls with large breasts ... and other wonderful things.

She'd sat down beside him in the booth and reached between his legs and held his organ.

His wife had never, never done that. And the girl's voice was soft; there wasn't the harsh hostility he'd put up with for nearly twenty-five years; there was no inherent complaint, only supplication.

He agreed, and showed her the money. He didn't give it to her, he only showed it.

He wasn't Genessee Industries 'keystone' for nothing.

But he had one last purchase to make from the filthy bartender before he left with the young, large-breasted girl.

The filthy bartender at first hesitated, but his hesitation disappeared when James Goddard produced another hundred-dollar bill.

The old Victorian house was everything the girl said it would be. He was given a room; he carried the briefcases himself; he wouldn't let anyone touch them.

And she did calm down; and she did come to his room. And when he'd finished, when he'd exploded in an explosion he hadn't experienced in twenty-five years, she quietly left, and he rested.

He was finished resting now. He sat on the bed – a bed of such memory – and looked at the four briefcases piled on a filthy table. He got up, naked except for his knee-length socks, and walked to the table. He remembered precisely which briefcase held the final purchase he'd made from the filthy bartender.

It was the second from the top.

He lifted the first briefcase off the stack and placed it on the floor. He opened the next.

Lying on top of the cards and the papers was a gun.

53

It had begun.

This doomed land, this Armageddon of the planet, this island of the power-damned where the greeds had fed upon themselves until the greatest good became the greatest evil. For the land belonged to the power-damned.

And the insanity was abruptly, shockingly made clear with a single act of horror.

Andrew Trevayne sat at the dining-room table in front of the large picture window overlooking the water, and his whole body trembled. The morning sun, careening shafts of blinding light off the surface of the ocean, did not herald the glory of morning, but offered, instead, a terrible foreboding. As if flashes of lightning kept crashing across the horizon through the bright sunlight.

An unending daytime of hell.

Trevayne forced his eyes back to the newspaper. The headlines stretched across The New York *Times*, roaring the impersonality of objective terror:

PRESIDENT ASSASSINATED:

SLAIN IN WHITE HOUSE DRIVEWAY

BY BUSINESS EXECUTIVE

Pronounced Dead at 5:31 p.m.

Assassin Takes Own Life; James Goddard, Pres., San Francisco Div. of Genessee Industries, Identified as Killer.
Vice President Sworn in Office at 7:00 p.m. Calls Cabinet Meeting. Congress Reconvened.

The act was ludicrously simple. The President of the United States was showing newsmen the progress of the Christmas decorations on the White House lawn when in a holiday spirit he greeted the last contingent of tourists leaving the grounds. James Goddard had been among them; as recalled by the guides, Goddard had made numerous tours of the White House during the past several days.

Merry Christmas, Mr President.

The inside pages were filled with biographical material about Goddard and

355

speculative conjectures about the atrocity. Interviews hastily written, hysteri-cally responded to, were given unthought-out importance.

And in the lower-right-hand corner of the front page was a report, the obscenity of which caused Trevayne to stare in disbelief.

REACTION AT GENESSEE

San Francisco, Dec. 18 – Private aircraft flew in from all over the country throughout the night bringing top Genessee management to the city. The executive personnel have been closeted in meetings, attempting to unravel the mystery behind the tragic events of yesterday in Washington. One significant result of these conferences is the emergence of Louis Riggs as the apparent spokesman for Genessee Industries' San Francisco Division, considered the company's headquarters. Riggs, a combat veteran of Vietnam, is the young economist who was Goddard's chief aide and top accountant. Insiders say that Riggs had for weeks been concerned over his superior's erratic behaviour; that the young aide had privately sent a number of confidential memoranda to other top-level management personnel stating his concerns. It was also revealed that Riggs will fly to Washington for a meeting with the newly sworn-in President.

It had begun.
And Andrew Trevayne knew he could not let it continue. He could not bear witness to the cataclysm without raising an anguished voice, without letting the country know.

But the country was in panic; the world was in panic. He could not compound that hysteria with his anguish.

That much he knew.

He knew also that he could not react as his wife had reacted, as his children had.

His daughter. His son.

The lost, bewildered guardians of tomorrow.

The girl had been the first to bring the news. Both children were home for the holidays, and both had been out separately: Pam involved with Christmas shopping, Steve with other young men of his age, regreeting one another, exaggerating their first semesters. Andy and Phyllis had been in the downstairs study quietly making plans for getting away in January.

Phyllis insisted on the Caribbean; a hot country where Andy could spend hours on his beloved ocean, sailing around the islands, letting the warm winds ease the hurt and the anger. They'd take a house in St Martin; they'd use some of their well-advertised money to help heal the wounds.

The door of the study was open, the only sound the hum of the wall vacuum being used by Lillian somewhere upstairs.

They'd both heard the crash of the front door, the hysterical sobs through the cries for help.

Cries for a mother and a father. For somebody.

They'd raced out of the study, up the stairs, and seen their daughter standing in the hallway, tears streaming down her face, her eyes afraid.

'Pam! For heaven's sake, what's the matter?'

'Oh, God! *God!* You don't *know*?'

'Know?'

'Turn on the radio. Call somebody. He was killed!'

'Who?'

'The President was killed! He was killed!'

'Oh, my God.' Phyllis spoke inaudibly as she turned to her husband and searched his face; Andrew instinctively reached for her. The unspoken statements – questions – were too clear, too intimate, too filled with agony and personal fear to surface the words.

'*Why? Why?*' Pamela Trevayne was screaming.

Andrew released his wife and silently, gently commanded her to go to their daughter. He walked rapidly into the living room, to the telephone.

There was nothing anyone could tell him but the terrible facts, the unbelievable narrative. Nearly every private line he knew in Washington was busy. The few that weren't had no time for him; the government of the United States had to function, had to secure continuity at all costs.

The television and radio stations suspended all broadcasts and commercial breaks as harried announcers began their fugues of repetition. Several news analysts wept openly, others betrayed angers that came close to outright condemnation of their vast, silent audiences. A number of the self-hustlers – second-rate politicians, third-rate journalists, a few pompous, pontificating articulators of academia – were by chance 'in the studios' or 'on the other end of the line', ready to make their bids for immediate recognition, spreading their tasteless perceptions and admonitions on a numbed public only too willing to be taught in its moment of confusion.

Trevayne left a single network station – the least irresponsible, he thought – on several sets throughout the house. He went to Pam's room, thinking Phyllis would be there. She wasn't. Pam was talking quietly with Lillian; the maid had been weeping, and the girl was comforting the older woman, conversely regaining her own control as she did so.

Andrew closed his daughter's bedroom door and walked down the hall to his and Phyllis' room. His wife sat by the window, the light of early night filtering through the woods, reflected up from the water.

Darkness was coming.

He went to her and knelt beside the chair. She stared at him, and he knew then that she knew what he was going to do before he did.

And she was terrified.

Steven Trevayne stood by the fireplace, his hands black with ash, the poker beside him, resting on the brick below the mantel. No one had thought to light a fire, and the fact seemed to annoy him. He had mixed new kindling with nearly burnt logs and held the Cape Cod lighter underneath the grate, oblivious to the heat and the dirt of the fireplace.

He was alone and looked over at the television set, its volume low, on only to impart whatever new information there might be.

The Vice President of the United States had just taken his hand off a Bible; he was now the world's most powerful man. He was President.

An old man.

They were all old men. No matter the years, their dates of birth. Old men, tired men, deceitful men.

'That's a good idea. The fire,' said Andrew quietly, walking into the living room.

'Yeah,' answered the boy without looking up, turning his head back toward the expanding flames. Then, just as abruptly, he stepped away from the fireplace and started for the hallway.

'Where are you going?'

'Out. Do you mind?'

'Of course not. It's a time to do nothing. Except, perhaps, think.'

'Please cut the bromides, Dad.'

'I will if you'll stop being childish. And sullen. I didn't pull the trigger, even symbolically.'

The boy stopped and looked at his father. 'I know you didn't. Maybe it would have been better if you had . . .'

'I find that a contemptible statement.'

'. . . "even symbolically" . . . For Christ's sake, then you would have done *something*!'

'That's off-base. You don't know what you're saying.'

'"Off-base?" What's *on*-base? You were there! You've been there for months. What did you *do*, Dad? Were you on-base? On target? . . . Goddamn it. *Some*body thought. Somebody did a terrible, lousy, rotten, fucking thing, and everybody's going to pay for it!'

'Are you endorsing the act?' Trevayne shouted, confused; he was as close to striking his son as he could ever recall.

'Jesus, no! Do *you*?'

Trevayne gripped his hands in front of him, the muscles in his arms and shoulders taut. He wanted the boy to leave. To run. Quickly.

'If that hurts, it's because that killing took place in your ball park.'

'He was insane, a maniac. It's isolated. You're being unfair.'

'Nobody thought so until yesterday. Nobody had any big files on *him; he* wasn't on anybody's list. No one detained him anywhere; they just gave him millions and millions to keep on building that goddamn *machine*.'

'That's asinine. You're trying to create a label out of one warped clump of insanity. Use your head, Steve. You're better than that.'

The boy paused; his silence was the stillness of grief and bewilderment. 'Maybe labels are the only things that make sense right now . . . And you lose, Dad. I'm sorry.'

'Why? Why do I lose?'

'Because I can't help thinking that you – or someone like you – could have stopped it.'

'That's not so.'

'Then maybe there's nothing left. If you're right.' Steven Trevayne looked down at his ash-black hands and rubbed them on his dungarees. 'I've got to wash my hands ... I'm sorry, Dad; I mean, I'm really sorry. I'm scared.'

The boy ran into the hallway; Trevayne could hear him descend the stairs toward the study and the terrace.

... *maybe there's nothing left.*

No.

No, he couldn't react like that. He couldn't allow himself the indulgence others gave vent to. Even among his family; within his family.

Not now.

Now he had to make himself felt, where it counted. Before the continuity was irrevocably established.

He had to jolt them, all of them. Make them realize he was serious. They could not be allowed to forget he held – held firmly – the weapons to depose them all.

And he would use those weapons, for they did not deserve to run the country. The nation demanded more.

'... maybe there's nothing left.'

Even if it meant using Genessee Industries. Using Genessee properly.

Properly.

Use it or destroy it once and for all.

He picked up the phone. He would stay on it until he reached Senator Mitchell Armbruster.

Part Five

54

The smoothly tarred surface of the road abruptly stopped and became dirt. At this point on the small peninsula the township's responsibility ended and the private property began. Only now it was under the jurisdiction of the federal government as well; watched, guarded, isolated, as it had been for eighteen months now.

High Barnegat.

The Connecticut White House.

The row of five automobiles sped through the gates of the Greenwich toll station without stopping. The guards on duty saluted as the motorcade went by; a patrolman inside the first booth received a signal from a man standing outside and picked up a telephone. The normal flow of traffic could continue now. The President's column had turned off onto the Shore Road exit, where the local police had cleared the area into the peninsula. The patrolman gave the release order to the Westchester station, waved to the man outside, who waved back, then climbed into a waiting automobile.

The 1600 Security men had dispersed throughout the property in teams of two. The Secret Service agent named Callahan had checked the beach area with his partner, and both men were walking up the steps to the terrace, their eyes professionally scanning the sloping woods as they did so.

Callahan had protected four presidents. Nearly twenty years of service; he was forty-six now. Still one of the best men 1600 had, and he knew it. No one could hold him responsible for the Darien business three years ago – that phone call from 1600 pulling him off duty at the hospital. Jesus! That'd been such a top-level fuck-up, he never did learn how it happened. How someone else had gotten the codes. He didn't ask, either; not after he'd been taken off the hook. And he was nowhere near the White House when the assassination took place. Everyone on that detail was relieved. Strange: he'd been reassigned to Trevayne and wrote in his surveillance report that his subject had met with James Goddard a week before the killing of the President. No one paid much attention, and he never brought it up afterward. Weird that nobody else did, though.

People – acquaintances, the small circle of friends he and his wife had –

kept asking him what he thought of whoever was President at the time. He always gave the same reply: sober approval bordering on reserved enthusiasm. Totally apolitical. It was the best way.

The only way; you never could tell.

But if the truth were told, Callahan didn't like any of them very much. He had devised a kind of scale for himself in judging a president. It was the balance between the public man and the private man as he saw him. There would always be differences, he understood that, but Jesus, some of them had gone too far.

To the point where *everything* was an act; the scales really tipped out. Meaningless smiles at public nothings, followed by torrents of private anger; furious attempts to be something that wasn't a person at all. An image.

Not trusting.

Worst of all, making a joke about it.

Perhaps that's why Andrew Trevayne got the best marks; he kept the scale nearer in balance. Not that he didn't have moments when his temper exploded over some goddamn thing or other that seemed inconsequential, but by and large the private man didn't deny the public man as often as the other presidents had. He seemed ... maybe more sure of himself; more sure he was right, and so he didn't have to yell about it or keep convincing people.

Callahan liked the man better for that, but he still didn't *like* him. Nobody who'd worked in the White House environment for any length of time could like a man who mounted such an assault for the Oval Office. A campaign that literally began within weeks of the assassination, within days after Trevayne had assumed the abandoned Senate seat from Connecticut. The sudden position papers, the cross-country tours that resulted in scores of dramatic press conferences and one television appearance after another. The man had a hunger, a driving, cold ambition that he mixed with a shyly ingratiating intelligence. A man with the answers, because he was a man of today. His supporters even coined a phrase, and it was used over and over again: 'The Mark of Excellence'. A minion at 1600 couldn't *like* a man like that. It was too obvious he wanted to move in.

Trevayne's preconvention manoeuvres had stunned the White House staff, still under the awesome weight of adjusting to the most terrible of power transfers, the unexpected, unwanted, unwarranted. No one was prepared, no one seemed to know how to stop the headstrong, authoritative, even charismatic Senator from Connecticut.

And at one point it occurred to Agent Callahan of 1600 Security, no one basically wanted to.

The motorcade streamed into the wide drive in front of the house; the doors of the first and third vehicles whipped open before the cars stopped, and men stood effortlessly half out of the automobiles, their arms gripping the interior frames, their feet ready to touch the pavement at the first reasonable instant.

Sam Vicarson leaned against the railing on the front steps. Sam wanted to be in evidence when Trevayne stepped out of the limousine. The President had come to expect that; expected him to be among the first of those who waited for him at any given destination. He told Sam that it gave him a sense of relief to know that there would be one person meeting him who'd give him the information he needed, not necessarily wanted.

Vicarson understood. It was one of the aspects of working in the White House that he found deplorable. No one wanted to displease the Man. If that meant burying unpleasant facts, or disguising them to fit a presidential judgment, that's what generally happened. It wasn't necessarily fear that provoked aides to behave this way. Often it was simply the knowledge that the Man had so damn many pressures on him that if a few could be lessened, why not?

But most of the time it was fear.

Even Sam had fallen into the trap. Both traps: the sympathy and the fear. He had shaped the précis of a trade report in such a way that upheld the President's thinking when actually there was room for disagreement.

'If you ever do that again, Sam, you're out!'

Vicarson often wondered if it would have been the same with Trevayne's predecessor.

Goddamn, he was a good president! A really *fine* president, thought Vicarson as he watched Andrew get out of the car and hold the door for Phyllis, simultaneously talking with the Secret Service men at his side. People had confidence in him; people everywhere. If comparisons were to be made with those in the recent past, a columnist for the New York *Times* had said it best: '. . . the calming nature of Eisenhower, the grace and fire of Kennedy, the drive of Johnson.'

Sam felt sorry for the opposition party, parties. After only eighteen months in office, Trevayne had set a tone, an outlook. He'd established an *attitude*. For the first time in years the country had a collective pride in its leadership. The Man before Trevayne had almost reached that level, but the sharpshooting snipers on the right and left had prevented him. Trevayne, because of either a general desire for tranquillity or the force of his own personality – and his ability to listen – had defused the extremists. It was probably a combination of both, thought Vicarson.

Trevayne was the right man for the right time. Another man might not be capable of sustaining the calm, sometimes more difficult than weathering a storm. Not that there was any lack of excitement. The Trevayne administration had made bold innovations in dozens of areas, but they were dramatic more in concept than in execution. And their announcements were subdued; they were called desirable shifts of priorities, not hailed as landmarks, which a number were. Housing, medicine, education, employment; long-range national strategies were implemented.

Sam Vicarson was enormously, realistically proud of President Andrew Trevayne.

So was the country, he felt.

Sam was surprised to see an old man getting out of the other side of the presidential limousine. It was Franklyn Baldwin, Trevayne's ancient banker friend from New York. Baldwin looked like hell, thought Vicarson. It was understandable; Baldwin had just buried William Hill, the friend he'd known since childhood. Big Billy Hill was gone; Baldwin had to be aware that his own time wasn't far off.

It was a mark of the President's sense of obligation that he had attended Hill's funeral; a mark of his swift grace that he'd insisted on saying a few words before the formal eulogy. A mark of his kindness that he'd brought old Frank Baldwin back with him to High Barnegat.

A 'Mark of Excellence'. That had been the very appropriate phrase used during the campaign.

Phyllis watched her husband helping Frank Baldwin up the short steps to the front door. Sam Vicarson offered assistance, but Andrew shook his head imperceptibly; enough so the young lawyer understood. The President alone would attend to Mr Baldwin.

Phyllis felt a surge of quiet pride when Andy did such things, gave meaning to gestures. *The prince doth render concern and the court doth follow, bettered by its better.* A description Froissart gave to the court of Chatillon in his First Chronicle ... Prince, young king – and not so young, thought Phyllis. There was much of Froissart, or what the Arthurian chronicler always wanted to find, in Andrew's White House. She knew her husband would laugh at such a suggestion. He'd tell her not to romanticize courtesy, not to find symbols where none were intended. That, too, was part of the aura that Andy exuded; the office magnified his quiet goodness, his confident modesty. Even his humor was laced with self-effacing irony.

She'd always loved her husband: he was a man to be loved. Now she found herself almost revering him, and she wasn't sure that was good or even healthy, but she couldn't help it. She realized that the awesomeness of the office lent itself to reverence, but Andy refused the mantle of heavy-lies-the-head. He gave out no stern reminders that the ultimate loneliness was his, no plaintive cries that decisions were never easy. No hollow dramatics of justification were to be found in his explanations.

But he had explained.

'A nation that is capable of reaching the planets can tend to its own land. A people who have taken so much from the earth can render a just portion back into it. A citizenry that has supported – fairly and unfairly – the expenditures of millions beyond its borders, can certainly build within . . .'

And he had proceeded to expedite these deceptively simple inaugural beliefs.

Phyllis followed her husband and Frank Baldwin into the house, where a military aide took their coats. They walked into the large living room, where some considerate soul – probably Sam, thought Phyllis – had lighted a fire. She'd been worried about old Baldwin. The funeral service for William Hill had been one of those long High Anglican chores, and the church draughty, the stone floor cold.

'Here, Frank,' said Trevayne, holding the back of an armchair, turning it slightly toward the fireplace. 'Relax. Let me get you a drink. All of us; we could use it.'

'Thank you, Mr President,' answered Baldwin, sitting down. Phyllis crossed to the long couch and saw that Sam Vicarson had moved a second armchair opposite Baldwin. Sam was so good at that sort of thing.

'Scotch, isn't that right, Frank? Rocks?'

'You always remember what a man drinks. I think that's how you became President.' Baldwin laughed, winking his old eye at Phyllis.

'Much easier, believe me. Sam, would you do the honors for me? Scotch on the rocks for Mr Baldwin; Phyl and I will have the usual.'

'Certainly, sir,' replied Vicarson, turning toward the hall.

Trevayne sat down in the chair facing Baldwin, Phyllis next to him at the end of the couch. He reached over and held her hand briefly, releasing it when the old man smiled at the sight.

'Don't stop. It's nice to know a man can be President and still hold his wife's hand without a camera around.'

'Good Lord, Frank, I've been known to kiss her.'

'Now you *may* stop,' added Baldwin with a soft laugh. 'I keep forgetting how young you are ... It was most kind of you to invite me here, Mr President. It's much appreciated.'

'Nonsense. I wanted your company; I was afraid I was imposing.'

'That's a gracious thing to say; but then, I read so often in the newspapers that you possess such qualities. I always knew you did.'

'Thank you.'

'It's all been remarkable, hasn't it? Do you remember, my dear?' asked Baldwin of Phyllis. 'I remember, because I'd never been up here. I always picture in my mind an office, or a home, a club – whatever – when I telephone someone. Especially if I don't know the surroundings. In your case it was a window looking out on the water. I recall distinctly your saying that Andrew ... the President, was out in a sailboat. A cat.'

'I remember.' Phyllis smiled gently. 'I was on the terrace.'

'So do I,' said Trevayne. 'The first thing she asked me when I got in was why I hadn't returned your calls. I was honest; I told her I was trying to avoid you.'

'Yes, I remember your saying that at the bank. At lunch ... I beg you to forgive me for interrupting your life so completely.' The old man's tired eyes showed that he was, indeed, asking forgiveness.

'Aurelius, Frank.'

'Who?'

'Marcus Aurelius. You quoted him. "No man can avoid ..."'

'Oh, yes. "What he's meant to do. At the moment ..." You called him a mutual fund.'

'A what?' asked Phyllis.

'An inept joke, Phyl. As I came to learn.'

Sam Vicarson returned with a silver tray on which there were three glasses. He offered the tray first to Phyllis, and as she nodded, he caught Trevayne's glance. Although it was customary to serve the President after the First Lady, he would approach Baldwin next.

'Thank you, young man.'

'You're a regular maître d', Sam,' said Phyllis.

'It's all those parties on Embassy Row.' Trevayne laughed, taking a glass. 'Will you join us, Sam?'

'Thank you, sir, but I'd better stay with communications.'

'He's got a girl in the kitchen,' mocked Phyllis in a stage whisper.

'From the French embassy,' added Andrew.

The three of them laughed while Baldwin looked on with amusement. Sam bowed slightly to the old man.

'Nice to see you again, Mr Baldwin.' He left as Baldwin inclined his head.

'I see what they mean. Or I think I do,' said the banker.

'What's that?' asked Phyllis.

'About the atmosphere around the White House these days. The easy relationships; even when things aren't easy. The pundits give you a lot of credit for that, Mr President.'

'Oh, Sam? He became my right arm, and sometimes my left as well, three years ago. He came with the subcommittee.'

Phyllis couldn't help herself. She wouldn't let Andy continuously sidestep the compliments he deserved. 'I agree with you and the pundits, Mr Baldwin. Andrew's made considerable progress in deformalizing the privy chambers. If the word's still in use.'

'My wife, the doctor,' interrupted Trevayne with a chuckle. 'Which word?'

'"Deformalizing." It's rarely used, but it should be. I haven't heard it recently.'

'I thought you meant "privy chamber". Whenever I come across the term in history books, I think of a bathroom.'

'That's historically sacrilegious, isn't it, Mr Baldwin?'

'I'm not sure, my dear . . .'

'Just don't tell the pundits I'm turning the White House rest rooms into playgrounds.'

The small laughter that followed warmed Phyllis. Old Baldwin was being amused, taking his mind off the sadness of the day. His sadness.

And then she realized the humorous byplay was only a momentary deflection. Baldwin's memories wouldn't be lightened. He spoke.

'Billy Hill and I honestly believed that the subcommittee was our well-conceived gift to the country. We never dreamed that our gift, in reality, would be the next President of the United States. When we finally understood that, it frightened us.'

'I would have given anything in the world to have had it otherwise.'

'Of course you would. A man has to possess extraordinary drives to want to be president, in the ordinary process. He has to be out of his mind to want the office under the conditions . . .' Baldwin stopped, aware of his indiscretion.

'Go on, Frank. It's all right.'

'I apologize, Mr President. That was unwarranted and not meant . . .'

'You don't have to explain. I think I was as surprised as you. And the Ambassador. Certainly as frightened.'

'Then may I presume to ask you why?'

Phyllis watched her husband closely. For in spite of the fact that the question had been raised a thousand times publicly, ten times that privately, the answer – answers – had never really satisfied her. She wasn't sure there *was* an answer beyond the best instincts of a brilliant, anguished man who measured his own abilities against that which he had seen, observed closely, and was horrified by. If such a man could hold the seat of power and deliver – as Andy had said to her in very private moments – even his second best, it had to be better than what he'd witnessed. If there were any answers beyond this simple truth, her husband wasn't capable of verbalizing them.

Not to her satisfaction.

'In all honesty, what I provided was unlimited funds for both campaigns. The preconvention and the election; beyond whatever the party could raise. Under a dozen different labels, of course. I'm not proud of it, but that's what I did.'

'That's the "how", Mr President. Not the "why". As I understand you.'

Phyllis now watched the old banker. Baldwin wanted his answer; his eyes pleaded.

And Baldwin was right, of course. The how was relatively inconsequential. But God, it has been insane, thought Phyllis. Limousines arriving at all hours of the day and night, extra phones installed, endless conferences – Barnegat, Boston, Washington, San Francisco, Houston; Andrew had plunged into the eye of a hurricane. Eating, sleeping, resting; they were forgotten.

She forgotten. The children forgotten.

'You've read all that, Frank.' Her husband was smiling his shy smile, which Phyllis had come to suspect. 'I meant what I said in all those speeches. I felt I was qualified to weld together a great many conflicting voices; that's not a good metaphor. I guess one doesn't weld voices. Perhaps "orchestrate" is better; reduce the dissonance. If the level of shouting was lowered, we could get at the root causes. Get to work.'

'I can't fault that, Mr President. You've succeeded. You're a popular man. Undoubtedly the most popular man the White House has had in years.'

'I'm grateful for that, but more important, I think it's all working.'

'Why were you and Ambassador Hill frightened?' Phyllis found herself asking the question without thinking. Andy looked at her, and she knew he would have preferred her not to pursue the subject.

'I'm not sure, my dear. I find that the older I get, the less sure I am about anything. Billy and I agreed on that less than a week ago. And you must remember, we've always been so positive . . . Oh, why were we frightened.' A statement. 'I imagine it was the responsibility. We proposed a subcommittee chairman and found we'd unearthed a viable candidate for president. Quite a jump.'

'But viable,' said Phyllis, now concerned by the sound of old Baldwin's voice.

'Yes.' The banker looked at Andrew. 'What frightened us was the sudden, inexplicable determination you displayed . . . Mr President. If you think back, perhaps you'll understand.'

'It wasn't my question, Frank. It was Phyl's.'

'Oh, yes, of course. It's been a difficult day; Billy and I won't have our lengthy debates anymore. No one ever won, you understand. He often told me, Andrew, that you thought as I did.' Baldwin's glass, at his lips, was nearly empty, and he looked at the rim; he had used the President's first name and obviously was sorry that he had.

'That's a superb compliment, Frank.'

'Only history will confirm that, Mr President. If it's true.'

'Regardless, I'm flattered.'

'But you *do* understand?'

'What?'

'Our concerns. According to Billy's reports, Bobby Kennedy's machine was a Boy Scout troop compared to yours. His words, incidentally.'

'I can bear them,' said Andrew with a half-smile on his lips. 'You were offended?'

'We couldn't understand.'

'There was a political vacuum.'

'You weren't a politician . . .'

'I'd seen enough politicians. The vacuum had to be filled quickly. I understood that. Either I was going to fill it, or someone else was. I looked around and decided I was better equipped. If anyone else had come along to alter that judgment, I would have bowed out.'

'Was anyone else given the chance, Mr President?'

'They – he – never appeared.'

'I think,' said Phyllis Trevayne somewhat defensively, 'my husband would've been very happy to have gone scot-free. As you say, he's not basically a politician.'

'You're wrong, my dear. He's the *new* politics, in all its pristine glory. The remarkable thing is that it works! Utterly and completely. It is a far greater reformation than any revolutionist could conceive of – right, left, or up the middle. But he knew he could do it. What Billy and I could never understand was *why* he knew he could.'

There was silence, and Phyllis realized, once again, that only her husband could reply. She looked at him and saw that he would not respond. His thoughts were not for display, even for his old friend, this wonderful old man who had given him so much. Perhaps not even for her.

'Mr President.' Sam Vicarson walked rapidly into the room, his expression denying any emergency, and by so doing, giving the message that an emergency existed.

'Yes, Sam?'

'The confirmation on the media exchange came through. From Chicago. I thought you'd want to know.'

'Can you locate the principals?' Trevayne's words shot out quietly, sharply; on the edge of abrasiveness.

'In the process, sir.'

'Get them.'

'Three lines are working on it. The call will be put through downstairs.'

'You'll pardon me, Frank. I haven't taught Sam the corporate procedure of procrastination.' Trevayne rose from the chair and started out of the room.

'May I fix you another, Mr Baldwin?'

'Thank you, young man. Only if Mrs Trevayne . . .'

'Thank you, Sam,' said Phyllis, holding out her glass. She was tempted to ask the presidential aide to disregard the 'usual' and pour her some whisky, but she didn't. It was still afternoon; even after all the years, she knew she couldn't drink whisky in the afternoon. She'd watched her husband as he listened to Sam Vicarson. His jaw had tightened, his eyes momentarily had squinted, his whole body stiffened, if only for an instant.

People never understood that it was these moments, handled with such ease and apparent confidence, that sapped the energies of the man. Moments of fear, incessant, unending.

As with everything he ever engaged in, her husband drove himself beyond the endurance of ordinary men. And he had finally found the job in which there was no surcease. There were times when Phyllis thought it was slowly killing him.

'I mourn an old friend whose time had come, my dear,' said Baldwin, observing Phyllis closely. 'Yet the look on your face makes me somewhat ashamed.'

'I'm sorry.' Phyllis had been absently staring at the hallway. She turned to the banker. 'I'm not sure I know what you mean.'

'I've lost my friend. To the perfect natural finality of his long life. In some ways, you've lost your husband. To a concept. And your lives are so far from being over . . . I think your sacrifice is greater than mine.'

'I think I agree with you.' Phyllis tried to smile, tried to make the pronouncement lighter, but she could not.

'He's a great man, you know.'

'I'd like to believe that.'

'He's done what no one else could do; what some of us thought was beyond doing. He's put the pieces back together again, let us see ourselves more as we *can* be, not as we were. There's still a long way to go, but he's provided the essentials. The desire to be better than we are; and to face the truth.'

'That's a lovely thing to say, Mr Baldwin.'

Andrew looked at Sam Vicarson, who'd just shut the study door. They were alone. 'How far has it gone?'

'Apparently all the way, sir. Our information is that the papers were signed several hours ago.'

'What does Justice say?'

'No change. They're still researching, but there's not much hope. They restate their original thesis. The purchase – or absorption – simply can't be traced to Genessee Industries.'

'We traced it, Sam. We know we're right.'

'You traced it, Mr President.'

Trevayne walked to the study window and looked out. To the terrace and the water below. 'Because it was one thing they didn't have. One thing we kept from them.'

'May I say something, sir?'

'Two years ago, I doubt you would have asked. What is it?'

'Isn't it possible that you're overreacting? Genessee has acted responsibly; you've controlled ... them. They support you.'

'They don't *support* me, Sam,' said Trevayne softly, harshly, without looking at Vicarson, his eyes still on the water. 'We have a nonaggression pact. I signed a nonaggression pact with the twentieth-century syndrome. The no-alternative holy ghost.'

'It's worked, Mr President.'

'You may have to keep that judgment in the past tense.' Andrew turned and stared at the lawyer. 'The pact is broken, Sam. It's no longer tenable. It's smashed.'

'What are you going to do?'

'I'm not sure. I won't allow Genessee to control a large segment of the American press. And a chain of newspapers is exactly that. It can't be tolerated.' Trevayne walked to his desk. 'Newspapers ... then will come magazines, radio, television. The networks. That they will not have.'

'Justice doesn't know how to stop them, Mr President.'

'We'll find a way; we have to.'

The telephone hummed; it did not ring. Vicarson swiftly crossed to the desk beside Andrew and picked it up.

'President Trevayne's office.' Sam listened for several seconds. 'Tell him to stay where he is. The Man's in conference, but we'll get back to him. Tell him it's priority.' Vicarson hung up. 'Let him stew until you're ready, sir.'

Sam walked away as Andrew nodded his appreciation. Vicarson knew instinctively by now when the President wanted to be alone. This was one of those moments. He spoke as Trevayne sat down at his desk.

'I'll head back to communications.'

'No, Sam. If you don't mind, go up and keep Phyl and old Baldwin company. I don't imagine it's easy for either of them.'

'Yes, sir.' For two or three seconds the young aide just watched the President of the United States. Then he abruptly left the room, closing the door behind him.

Andrew picked up a pencil and wrote out a sentence in clear, precise letters. 'The only solution is in the constant search for one.'

Big Billy Hill.

And then he wrote one word: 'Horseshit.'

Paul Bonner.

And then he added: '?'

He picked up the telephone and spoke firmly.

'Chicago, please.'

Fifteen hundred miles away, Ian Hamilton answered.

'Mr President?'

'I want you out of that merger.'

'Perhaps it's academic, but you have no viable proof that we're involved. The little men from your Justice Department have been nuisances.'

'You know. I know. Get out.'

'I think you're beginning to show the strain, Mr President.'

'I'm not interested in what you think. Just make sure you understand me.'

There was a pause. 'Does it matter?'

'Don't press me, Hamilton.'

'Nor you us.'

Trevayne stared out of the window, at the ever-moving waters of the sound. 'There'll come a day when you're expendable. You should realize that. All of you.'

'Quite possibly, Mr President. However, not in our time.'

The Cry of
the Halidon

For all those who in strictest confidence helped me research this novel so many years ago – you know who you are, and I'm still forever grateful.

Introduction

A number of years ago – a quarter of a century to be precise – an author barely in his forties was so exuberant over the fact that he had actually *published* two novels that, like an addict, he relentlessly pursued the source of his addiction. Fortunately, it was the narcotic of writing, chemically not dangerous, mentally an obsession. That obsessed author, me, is now far older and only slightly wiser, and I *was* exhilarated until I was given a gentle lecture by a cadre of well-meaning publishing executives. I was stunned – walleyed and speechless.

Apparently, it was the conventional wisdom of the time that no author who sold more than a dozen or so books to his immediate family and very close friends should write more than one novel a year! If he did, he would automatically be considered a 'hack' by 'readers and critics alike.' (I loved this last dual-persona, as expressed.) Such writing giants of the past came to mind, like Dickens, Trollope, and Thackeray, fellows who thought nothing of filling up reams of copy for monthly and weekly magazines, much of said copy excerpts from their novels in progress. Perhaps, I thought silently, 'hack' had a different meaning then, like in 'he can't hack it,' which implies that to 'hack' is good, as opposed to 'he's a hack,' obviously pejorative. It was all too confusing, and, as I mentioned, I was speechless anyway. So I said nothing.

Nevertheless, I was the new kid on the block, more precisely on Publishers' Row. I listened to my more experienced betters and submitted *The Cry of the Halidon* as written by someone called 'Jonathan Ryder,' actually the first name of one of our sons and a contraction of my wife's stage name when she was a popular actress in New York and its environs.

I'd be foolish to deny the influence this novel had on subsequent books, for it was the first time I actively forced myself to research obscure history along with the roots of myth as opposed to well-documented, if difficult to unearth, historical records. For me, it was terrific. My wife, Mary, and I flew to Jamaica, where most of the novel was to take place. I was like a kid in a giant toy store. There was so much to absorb, to study! I even stole real names before I learned you weren't supposed to do that without permission. For example, 'Timothy Durell,' the first character we meet in the book, actually was the youngest and brightest manager of a large international resort that I'd ever met; 'Robert Hanley' is a pilot in the novel and was, as well, in everyday life. Among other detours, Bob ferried Howard Hughes around the Caribbean, and was on Errol Flynn's payroll as his private pilot when the motion-picture star lived in Jamaica. (Other liberties I really should not reveal – on advice of counsel.)

Of course, research is the dessert before an entrée, or conversely, the succulent shrimp cocktail before the hearty prime rib, the appetizer leading to serious dining. It is also both a trap and a springboard. A trap for it ensnares one in a world of geometric probabilities that an author resists leaving, and a springboard for it fires one's imagination to get on with the infinite possibilities a writer finds irresistible.

The first inkling I had regarding the crosscurrents of deeply felt Jamaican religiosity and myth came when my wife and I took our daughter, along with the regal lady who ran the kitchen at our rented house, to a native village market in Port Antonio. Our young daughter was a very blond child and very beautiful (still is). She became the instant center of attention, for this was, indeed, a remote thoroughfare and the inhabitants were not used to the sight of a very blond white child. The natives were delightful, as most Jamaicans are; they're gentle, filled with laughter and kindness and intelligent concern for the guests on their island. One man, however, was none of these. He was large, abusive, and kept making remarks that any parent would find revolting. The people around him admonished him; many shouted, but he simply became more abusive, bordering on the physical. I'd had enough.

Having been trained as a marine – and far younger than I am now – I approached this offensive individual, spun him around, hammerlocked his right arm, and marched him across the dirt road to the edge of a ravine. I sat him down on a rock, and vented my parental spleen.

Suddenly, he became docile, trancelike, then started to chant in a singsong manner words to the effect of: 'The Hollydawn, the Hollydawn, all is for the Hollydawn!' I asked him what he was talking about. 'You can never know, mon! It is not for you to know. It is the holy church of the Hollydawn! *Obeah, Obeah*. Give me money for the magic of the Hollydawn!'

I realized he was high on something – grass, alcohol, who knows? I gave him a few dollars and sent him on his way. An elderly Jamaican subsequently came up to me, his dark eyes sad, knowing. 'I'm sorry, young man,' he said. 'We watched closely and would have rushed to your assistance should you have been in danger.'

'You mean he might have had a gun, a weapon?'

'No, never a gun, no one allows those people to have guns, but a weapon, yes. He frequently carries a machete in his trousers.'

I swallowed several times, and no doubt turned considerably paler than I had been. But the episode did ignite the fuses of my imagination. From there, and courtesy of Bob Hanley and his plane, I crisscrossed the infamous Cock Pit jungles, flying low and seeing things no one in a commercial airliner could ever see. I traveled to Kingston, to waterfronts Bob thought I was nuts to visit. (Remember, I was much, much younger.) I explored the coves, the bays, and the harbours of the north coast, questioning, always questioning, frequently met by laughter and dancing eyes, but never once hostility. I even went so far as to initiate negotiations to purchase Errol Flynn's old estate, when, as I recall, Hanley hammerlocked *me* and dragged me back to the plane under sentence of bodily harm. (Much younger!)

I was having so much fun that one evening, while sipping cocktails in the glorious glow of a Jamaican sunset, Mary turned to me and, in her delightfully understated way, said, 'You were actually going to *buy* the Flynn estate?'

'Well, there is a series of natural waterfalls leading to a pool, and—'

'Bob Hanley has my permission to severely wound you. Your right hand excepted.' (I write in longhand.) 'Do you think you'll ever start the novel?'

'What novel?'

'I rest my case. I think it's time we go home.'

'What home . . . ?'

'The other children, our sons.'

'*I* know *them*! Big fellas!'

Do you get the picture? Call it island fever, a mad dog in the noonday sun, or a mentally impaired author obsessed with *research*. But my bride was right. It was time to go home and begin the hearty prime rib.

While rereading this novel for editorial considerations, I was struck by how much I'd forgotten, and the memories came flooding back over me. Not regarding the quality of the book – that's for others to comment on one way or another – but the things I experienced that gave rise to whole scenes, composite characters, back-country roads dotted with the great houses and their skeletons of bygone eras, the *cocoruru* peddlers on the white sandy beaches with their machetes decapitating the fruit into which was poured the rum . . . above all the countless hundreds of large dark eyes that held the secrets of centuries.

It was a beautiful time, and I thank all those who made it possible. I hope you enjoy the novel for I truly enjoyed working on it.

Robert Ludlum
Naples, Florida
January 1996

Part One

Port Antonio/London

1

Port Antonio, Jamaica

The white sheet of ocean spray burst up from the coral rock and appeared suspended, the pitch-blue waters of the Caribbean serving as a backdrop. The spray cascaded forward and downward and asserted itself over thousands of tiny, sharp, ragged crevices that were the coral overlay. It became ocean again, at one with its source.

Timothy Durell walked out on the far edge of the huge free-form pool deck, imposed over the surrounding coral, and watched the increasing combat between water and rock. This isolated section of the Jamaican north coast was a compromise between man and natural phenomenon. Trident Villas were built on top of a coral sheet, surrounded by it on three sides, with a single drive that led to the roads in front. The villas were miniature replicas of their names; guest houses that fronted the sea and the fields of coral. Each an entity in itself; each isolated from the others, as the entire resort complex was isolated from the adjoining territory of Port Antonio.

Durell was the young English manager of Trident Villas, a graduate of London's College of Hotel Management, with a series of letters after his name indicating more knowledge and experience than his youthful appearance would seem to support. But Durell was good; he knew it, the Trident's owners knew it. He never stopped looking for the unexpected – that, along with routine smoothness, was the essence of superior management.

He had found the unexpected now. And it troubled him.

It was a mathematical impossibility. Or, if not impossible, certainly improbable in the extreme.

It simply did not make sense.

'Mr Durell?'

He turned. His Jamaican secretary, her brown skin and features bespeaking the age-old coalition of Africa and Empire, had walked out on the deck with a message.

'Yes?'

'Lufthansa flight sixteen from Munich will be late getting into Montego.'

'That's the Keppler reservation, isn't it?'

'Yes. They'll miss the in-island connection.'

'They should have come into Kingston.'

'They didn't,' said the girl, her voice carrying the same disapproval as Durell's statement, but not so sternly. 'They obviously don't wish to spend the night in Montego; they had Lufthansa radio ahead. You're to get them a charter—'

'On three hours' notice? Let the Germans do it! It's their equipment that's late.'

'They tried. None available in Mo'Bay.'

'Of course, there isn't ... I'll ask Hanley. He'll be back from Kingston with the Warfields by five o'clock.'

'He may not wish to ...'

'He will. We're in a spot. I trust it's not indicative of the week.'

'Why do you say that? What bothers you?'

Durell turned back to the railing overlooking the fields and cliffs of coral. He lighted a cigarette, cupping the flame against the bursts of warm breeze. 'Several things. I'm not sure I can put my finger on them all. One I *do* know.' He looked at the girl, but his eyes were remembering. 'A little over twelve months ago, the reservations for this particular week began coming in. Eleven months ago they were complete. All the villas were booked ... for this particular week.'

'Trident's popular. What is so unusual?'

'You don't understand. Since eleven months ago, every one of those reservations has stood firm. Not a single cancellation, or even a minor change of date. Not even a day.'

'Less bother for you. I'd think you'd be pleased.'

'Don't you see? It's a mathematical imp – well, inconsistency, to say the least. Twenty villas. Assuming couples, that is forty families, really – mothers, fathers, aunts, uncles, cousins ... For eleven months nothing has happened to change anyone's plans. None of the principals died – and at our rates we don't cater exclusively to the young. No misfortunes of consequence, no simple business interferences, or measles or mumps or weddings or funerals or lingering illness. Yet we're not the Queen's coronation; we're just a week-in-Jamaica.'

The girl laughed. 'You're playing with numbers, Mr Durell. You're put out because your well-organized waiting list hasn't been used.'

'And by the way, they're all arriving,' continued the young manager, his words coming faster. 'This Keppler, he's the only one with a problem, and how does he solve it? Having an aircraft radio ahead from somewhere over the Atlantic. Now, you'll grant *that's* a bit much. The others? No one asks for a car to meet them, no in-island confirmations required, no concerns about luggage or distances. Or anything. They'll just be here.'

'Not the Warfields. Captain Hanley flew his plane to Kingston for the Warfields.'

'But *we* didn't know that. Hanley assumed that we did, but we didn't. The arrangements were made privately from London. He thought we'd given them his name; we hadn't. I hadn't.'

'No one else would ...' The girl stopped. 'But everyone's ... from all over.'

'Yes. Almost evenly divided. The States, England, France, Germany, and ... Haiti.'

'What's your point?' asked the girl, seeing the concern on Durell's face.

'I have a strange feeling that all our guests for the week are acquainted. But they don't want us to know it.'

London, England

The tall, light-haired American in the unbuttoned Burberry trench coat walked out the Strand entrance of the Savoy Hotel. He stopped for an instant and looked up at the English sky between the buildings in the court. It was a perfectly normal thing to do – to observe the sky, to check the elements after emerging from shelter – but this man did not give the normally cursory glance and form a judgment based primarily on the chill factor.

He looked.

Any geologist who made his living developing geophysical surveys for governments, companies, and foundations knew that the weather was income; it connoted progress or delay.

Habit.

His clear gray eyes were deeply set beneath wide eyebrows, darker than the light brown hair that fell with irritating regularity over his forehead. His face was the color of a man's exposed to the weather, the tone permanently stained by the sun, but not burned. The lines beside and below his eyes seemed stamped more from his work than from age, again a face in constant conflict with the elements. The cheekbones were high, the mouth full, the jaw casually slack, for there was a softness also about the man ... in abstract contrast to the hard, professional look.

This softness, too, was in his eyes. Not weak, but inquisitive; the eyes of a man who probed – perhaps because he had not probed sufficiently in the past.

Things ... things ... had happened to this man.

The instant of observation over, he greeted the uniformed doorman with a smile and a brief shake of his head, indicating a negative.

'No taxi, Mr McAuliff?'

'Thanks, no, Jack. I'll walk.'

'A bit nippy, sir.'

'It's refreshing – only going a few blocks.'

The doorman tipped his cap and turned his attention to an incoming Jaguar sedan. Alexander McAuliff continued down the Savoy Court, past the theater and the American Express office to the Strand. He crossed the pavement and entered the flow of human traffic heading north toward Waterloo Bridge. He buttoned his raincoat, pulling the lapels up to ward off London's February chill.

It was nearly one o'clock; he was to be at the Waterloo intersection by one. He would make it with only minutes to spare.

He had agreed to meet the Dunstone company man this way, but he hoped his tone of voice had conveyed his annoyance. He had been perfectly willing to take a taxi, or rent a car, or hire a chauffeur, if any or all were necessary, but if Dunstone was sending an automobile for him, why not send it to the Savoy? It wasn't that he minded the walk; he just hated to meet people in automobiles in the middle of congested streets. It was a goddamn nuisance.

The Dunstone man had had a short, succinct explanation that was, for the Dunstone man, the only reason necessary – for all things: 'Mr Julian Warfield prefers it this way.'

He spotted the automobile immediately. It had to be Dunstone's – and/or Warfield's. A St James Rolls-Royce, its glistening black, hand-tooled body breaking space majestically, anachronistically, among the petrol-conscious Austins, MGs, and European imports. He waited on the curb, ten feet from the crosswalk onto the bridge. He would not gesture or acknowledge the slowly approaching Rolls. He waited until the car stopped directly in front of him, a chauffeur driving, the rear window open.

'Mr McAuliff?' said the eager, young-old face in the frame.

'Mr Warfield?' asked McAuliff, knowing that this fiftyish, precise-looking executive was not.

'Good heavens, no. The name's Preston. Do hop in; I think we're holding up the line.'

'Yes, you are.' Alex got into the back seat as Preston moved over. The Englishman extended his hand.

'It's a pleasure. I'm the one you've been talking to on the telephone.'

'Yes ... Mr Preston.'

'I'm really very sorry for the inconvenience, meeting like this. Old Julian has his quirks, I'll grant you that.'

McAuliff decided he might have misjudged the Dunstone man. 'It was a little confusing, that's all. If the object was precautionary – for what reason I can't imagine – he picked a hell of a car to send.'

Preston laughed. 'True. But then, I've learned over the years that Warfield, like God, moves in mysterious ways that basically are quite logical. He's really all right. You're having lunch with him, you know.'

'Fine. Where?'

'Belgravia.'

'Aren't we going the wrong way?'

'Julian and God – basically logical, chap.'

The St James Rolls crossed Waterloo, proceeded south to the Cut, turned left until Blackfriars Road, then left again, over Blackfriars Bridge and north into Holborn. It was a confusing route.

Ten minutes later the car pulled up to the entrance canopy of a white stone building with a brass plate to the right of the glass double doors that read SHAFTESBURY ARMS. The doorman pulled at the handle and spoke jovially.

'Good afternoon, Mr Preston.'

'Good afternoon, Ralph.'

McAuliff followed Preston into the building, to a bank of three elevators in the well-appointed hallway. 'Is this Warfield's place?' he asked, more to pass the moment than to inquire.

'No, actually. It's mine. Although I won't be joining you for lunch. However, I trust cook implicitly; you'll be well taken care of.'

'I won't try to follow that. "Julian and God."'

Preston smiled noncommittally as the elevator door opened.

Julian Warfield was talking on the telephone when Preston ushered McAuliff into the tastefully – elegantly – decorated living room. The old man was standing by an antique table in front of a tall window overlooking Belgrave Square. The size of the window, flanked by long white drapes, emphasized Warfield's shortness. He is really quite a small man, thought Alex as he acknowledged Warfield's wave with a nod and a smile.

'You'll send the accrual statistics on to Macintosh, then,' said Warfield deliberately into the telephone; he was not asking a question. 'I'm sure he'll disagree, and you can both hammer it out. Goodbye.' The diminutive old man replaced the receiver and looked over at Alex. 'Mr McAuliff, is it?' Then he chuckled. 'That was a prime lesson in business. Employ experts who disagree on just about everything and take the best arguments from both for a compromise.'

'Good advice generally, I'd say,' replied McAuliff. 'As long as the experts disagree on the subject matter and not just chemically.'

'You're quick. I like that ... Good to see you.' Warfield crossed to Preston. His walk was like his speech: deliberate, paced slowly. Mentally confident, physically unsure. 'Thank you for the use of your flat, Clive. And Virginia, of course. From experience, I know the lunch will be splendid.'

'Not at all, Julian. I'll be off.'

McAuliff turned his head sharply, without subtlety, and looked at Preston. The man's first-name familiarity with old Warfield was the last thing he expected. Clive Preston smiled and walked rapidly out of the room as Alex watched him, bewildered.

'To answer your unspoken questions,' said Warfield, 'although you have been speaking with Preston on the telephone, he is not with Dunstone Limited, Mr McAuliff.'

Alexander turned back to the diminutive businessman. 'Whenever I phoned the Dunstone offices for you, I had to give a number for someone to return the call—'

'Always within a few minutes,' interrupted Warfield. 'We never kept you waiting; that would have been rude. Whenever you telephoned – four times, I believe – my secretary informed Mr Preston. At his offices.'

'And the Rolls at Waterloo was Preston's,' said Alex.

'Yes.'

'So if anyone was following me, my business is with Preston. Has been since I've been in London.'

'That was the object.'

'Why?'

'Self-evident, I should think. We'd rather not have anyone know we're discussing a contract with you. Our initial call to you in New York stressed that point, I believe.'

'You said it was confidential. Everyone says that. If you meant it to this degree, why did you even use the name of Dunstone?'

'Would you have flown over otherwise?'

McAuliff thought for a moment. A week of skiing in Aspen notwithstanding, there had been several other projects. But Dunstone was Dunstone, one of the largest corporations in the international market. 'No, I probably wouldn't have.'

'We were convinced of that. We knew you were about to negotiate with ITT about a little matter in southern Germany.'

Alex stared at the old man. He couldn't help but smile. 'That, Mr Warfield, was supposed to be as confidential as anything you might be considering.'

Warfield returned the good humor. 'Then we know who deals best in confidence, don't we? ITT is patently obvious ... Come, we'll have a drink, then lunch. I know your preference: Scotch with ice. Somewhat more ice than I think is good for the system.'

The old man laughed softly and led McAuliff to a mahogany bar across the room. He made drinks rapidly, his ancient hands moving deftly, in counterpoint to his walk. 'I've learned quite a bit about you, Mr McAuliff. Rather fascinating.'

'I heard someone was asking around.'

They were across from one another, in armchairs. At McAuliff's statement, Warfield took his eyes off his glass and looked sharply, almost angrily, at Alex. 'I find that hard to believe.'

'Names weren't used, but the information reached me. Eight sources. Five American, two Canadian, one French.'

'*Not* traceable to Dunstone.' Warfield's short body seemed to stiffen; McAuliff understood that he had touched an exposed nerve.

'I said names weren't mentioned.'

'Did you use the Dunstone name in any ensuing conversations? Tell me the truth, Mr McAuliff.'

'There'd be no reason not to tell you the truth,' answered Alex, a touch disagreeably. 'No, I did not.'

'I believe you.'

'You should.'

'If I didn't, I'd pay you handsomely for your time and suggest you return to America and take up with ITT.'

'I may do that anyway, mightn't I? I *do* have that option.'

'You like money.'

'Very much.'

Julian Warfield placed his glass down and brought his thin, small hands together. 'Alexander T. McAuliff. The "T" is for Tarquin, rarely, if ever, used. It's not even on your stationery; rumor is you don't care for it ...'

'True. I'm not violent about it.'

'Alexander Tarquin McAuliff, forty-four years old. B.S., M.S., Ph.D., but the title of Doctor is used as rarely as his middle name. The geology departments of several leading American universities, including California Tech and Columbia, lost an excellent research fellow when Dr McAuliff decided to put his expertise to more commercial pursuits.' The man smiled, his expression one of how-am-I-doing; but, again, not a question.

'Faculty and laboratory pressures are no less aggravating than those outside. Why not get paid for them?'

'Yes. We agreed you like money.'

'Don't you?'

Warfield laughed, and his laugh was genuine and loud. His thin, short body fairly shook with pleasure as he brought Alex a refill. 'Excellent reply. Really quite fine.'

'It wasn't that good.'

'But you're interrupting me,' said Warfield as he returned to his chair. 'It's my intention to impress you.'

'Not about myself, I hope.'

'No. Our thoroughness ... You are from a close-knit family, secure academic surroundings—'

'Is this necessary?' asked McAuliff, fingering his glass, interrupting the old man.

'Yes, it is,' replied Warfield simply, continuing as though his line of thought was unbroken. 'Your father was – and is, in retirement – a highly regarded agro-scientist; your mother, unfortunately deceased, a delightfully romantic soul adored by all. It was she who gave you the "Tarquin," and until she died you never denied the initial or the name. You had an older brother, a pilot, shot down in the last days of the Korean War; you yourself made a splendid record in Vietnam. Upon receipt of your doctorate, it was assumed that you would continue the family's academic tradition. Until personal tragedy propelled you out of the laboratory. A young woman – your fiancée – was killed on the streets of New York. At night. You blamed yourself ... and others. You were to have met her. Instead, a hastily called, quite unnecessary research meeting prohibited it ... Alexander Tarquin McAuliff fled the university. Am I drawing an accurate picture?'

'You're invading my privacy. You're repeating information that may be personal but hardly classified. Easy to piece together. You're also extremely obnoxious. I don't think I have to have lunch with you.'

'A few more minutes. Then it is your decision.'

'It's my decision right now.'

'Of course. Just a bit more ... Dr McAuliff embarked on a new career with extraordinary precision. He hired out to several established geological-survey firms, where his work was outstanding; then left the companies and underbid them on upcoming contracts. Industrial construction knows no national boundaries: Fiat builds in Moscow; Moscow in Cairo; General Motors in Berlin; British Petroleum in Buenos Aires; Volkswagen in New Jersey, USA; Renault in Madrid – I could go on for hours. And everything begins with a single file folder profuse with complicated technical paragraphs describing what is and is not possible in terms of construction upon the land. Such a simple, taken-for-granted exercise. But without that file, nothing else is possible.'

'Your few minutes are about up, Warfield. And, speaking for the community of surveyors, we thank you for acknowledging our necessity. As you say, we're so often taken for granted.' McAuliff put his glass down on the table next to his armchair and started to get up.

Warfield spoke quietly, precisely. 'You have twenty-three bank accounts, including four in Switzerland; I can supply the code numbers if you like. Others in Prague, Tel Aviv, Montreal, Brisbane, São Paulo, Kingston, Los Angeles, and, of course, New York, among others.'

Alexander remained immobile at the edge of his chair and stared at the little old man. 'You've been busy.'

'Thorough. Nothing patently illegal; none of the accounts is enormous. Altogether they total two million four hundred-odd US dollars, as of several days ago when you flew from New York. Unfortunately, the figure is meaningless. Due to international agreements regarding financial transfers, the money cannot be centralized.'

'Now I know I don't want to have lunch with you.'

'Perhaps not. But how would you like another two million dollars? Free and clear, all American taxes paid. Deposited in the bank of your choice.'

McAuliff continued to stare at Warfield. It was several moments before he spoke.

'You're serious, aren't you?'

'Utterly.'

'For a *survey*?'

'Yes.'

'There are five good houses right here in London. For that kind of money, why call on me? Why not use them?'

'We don't want a firm. We want an individual. A man we have investigated thoroughly; a man we believe will honor the most important aspect of the contract. Secrecy.'

'That sounds ominous.'

'Not at all. A financial necessity. If word got out, the speculators would move in. Land prices would sky-rocket, the project would become untenable. It would be abandoned.'

'What is it? Before I give you my answer, I have to know that.'

'We're planning to build a city. In Jamaica.'

2

McAuliff politely rejected Warfield's offer to have Preston's car brought back to Belgravia for him. Alex wanted to walk, to think in the cold winter air. It helped him to sort out his thoughts while in motion; the brisk, chilling winds somehow forced his concentration inward.

Not that there was so much to think about as to absorb. In a sense, the hunt was over. The end of the intricate maze was in sight, after eleven years of complicated wandering. Not for the money per se. But for money as the conveyor belt to independence.

Complete. Total. Never having to do what he did not wish to do.

Ann's death – murder – had been the springboard. Certainly the rationalization, he understood that. But the rationalization had solid roots, beyond the emotional explosion. The research meeting – accurately described by Warfield as 'quite unnecessary' – was symptomatic of the academic system.

All laboratory activities were geared to justifying whatever grants were in the offing. God! How much useless activity! How many pointless meetings! How often useful work went unfinished because a research grant did not materialize or a department administrator shifted priorities to achieve more obvious *progress* for *progress*-oriented foundations.

He could not fight the academic system; he was too angry to join its politics. So he left it.

He could not stand the companies, either. Jesus! A different set of priorities, leading to only one objective: profit. Only profit. Projects that didn't produce the most favorable 'profit picture' were abandoned without a backward glance.

Stick to business. Don't waste time.

So he left the companies and went out on his own. Where a man could decide for himself the price of immediate values. And whether they were worth it.

All things considered, everything ... everything Warfield proposed was not only correct and acceptable, it was glorious. An unencumbered, legitimate two million dollars for a survey Alex knew he could handle.

He knew vaguely the area in Jamaica to be surveyed: east and south of Falmouth, on the coast as far as Duncan's Bay; in the interior into the Cock

Pit. It was actually the Cock Pit territory that Dunstone seemed most interested in: vast sections of uninhabited – in some cases, unmapped – mountains and jungles. Undeveloped miles, ten minutes by air to the sophistication of Montego Bay, fifteen to the expanding, exploding New Kingston.

Dunstone would deliver him the specific degree marks within the next three weeks, during which time he was to assemble his team.

He was back on the Strand now, the Savoy Court several blocks away. He hadn't resolved anything, really; there was nothing to resolve, except perhaps the decision to start looking for people at the university. He was sure there would be no lack of interested applicants; he only hoped he could find the level of qualification he needed.

Everything was fine. Really fine.

He walked down the alley into the court, smiled at the doorman, and passed the thick glass doors of the Savoy. He crossed the reservations desk on the right and asked for any messages.

There were none.

But there was something else. The tuxedoed clerk behind the counter asked him a question.

'Will you be going upstairs, Mr McAuliff?'

'Yes ... yes, I'll be going upstairs,' answered Alex, bewildered at the inquiry. 'Why?'

'I beg your pardon?'

'Why do you ask?' McAuliff smiled.

'Floor service, sir,' replied the man, with intelligence in his eyes, assurance in his soft British voice. 'In the event of any cleaning or pressing. These are frightfully busy hours.'

'Of course. Thank you.' Alex smiled again, nodded his appreciation, and started for the small brass-grilled elevator. He had tried to pry something else from the Savoy man's eyes, but he could not. Yet he knew something else was there. In the six years he had been staying at the hotel, no one had ever asked him if he was 'going upstairs'. Considering English – Savoy – propriety, it was an unlikely question.

Or were his cautions, his Dunstone cautions, asserting themselves too quickly, too strongly?

Inside his room, McAuliff stripped to shorts, put on a bathrobe, and ordered ice from the floor steward. He still had most of a bottle of Scotch on the bureau. He sat in an armchair and opened a newspaper, considerately left by room service.

With the swiftness for which the Savoy stewards were known, there was a knock on his corridor door. McAuliff got out of the chair and then stopped.

The Savoy stewards did not knock on hallway doors – they let themselves into the foyers. Room privacy was obtained by locking the bedroom doors, which opened onto the foyers.

Alex walked rapidly to the door and opened it. There was no steward.

Instead, there was a tall, pleasant-looking middle-aged man in a tweed overcoat.

'Mr McAuliff?'

'Yes?'

'My name is Hammond. May I speak with you, sir?'

'Oh? Sure . . . certainly.' Alex looked down the hallway as he gestured the man to pass him. 'I rang for ice; I thought you were the steward.'

'Then may I step into your . . . excuse me, your lavatory, sir? I'd rather not be seen.'

'What? Are you from Warfield?'

'No, Mr McAuliff. British Intelligence.'

3

'That was a sorry introduction, Mr McAuliff. Do you mind if I begin again?' Hammond walked into the bed-sitting room. Alex dropped ice cubes into a glass.

'No need to. I've never had anyone knock on my hotel door, say he's with British Intelligence, and ask to use the bathroom. Has kind of a quaint ring to it . . . Drink?'

'Thank you. Short, if you please; a touch of soda will be fine.'

McAuliff poured as requested and handed Hammond his glass. 'Take off your coat. Sit down.'

'You're most hospitable. Thank you.' The Britisher removed his tweed overcoat and placed it carefully on the back of a chair.

'I'm most curious, that's what I am, Mr Hammond.' McAuliff sat by the window, the Englishman across from him. 'The clerk at the desk; he asked if I was going upstairs. That was for you, wasn't it?'

'Yes, it was. He knows nothing, however. He thinks the managers wished to see you unobtrusively. It's often done that way. Over financial matters, usually.'

'Thanks very much.'

'We'll set it right, if it disturbs you.'

'It doesn't.'

'I was in the cellars. When word reached me, I came up the service elevator.'

'Rather elaborate—'

'Rather necessary,' interrupted the Englishman. 'For the past few days, you've been under continuous surveillance. I don't mean to alarm you.'

McAuliff paused, his glass halfway to his lips. 'You just have. I gather the surveillance wasn't yours.'

'Well, you could say we observed – from a distance – both the followers and their subject.' Hammond sipped his whisky and smiled.

'I'm not sure I like this game,' said McAuliff quietly.

'Neither do we. May I introduce myself more completely?'

'Please do.'

Hammond removed a black leather identification case from his jacket pocket, rose from the chair, and crossed to McAuliff. He held out the flat

394

case and flipped it open. 'There is a telephone number below the seal. I'd appreciate it if you would place a call for verification, Mr McAuliff.'

'It's not necessary, Mr Hammond. You haven't asked me for anything.'

'I may.'

'If you do, I'll call.'

'Yes, I see ... Very well.' Hammond returned to his chair. 'As my credentials state, I'm with Military Intelligence. What they do not say is that I have been assigned to the Foreign Office and Inland Revenue. I'm a financial analyst.'

'In the Intelligence service?' Alex got out of his chair and went to the ice bucket and the whisky. He gestured at them. Hammond shook his head. 'That's unusual, isn't it? I can understand a bank or a brokerage office, not the cloak-and-dagger business.'

'The vast majority of intelligence gathering is allied with finance, Mr McAuliff. In greater or lesser degrees of subtlety, of course.'

'I stand corrected.' Alex replenished his drink and realized that the ensuing silence was Hammond's waiting for him to return to his chair. 'When I think about it, I see what you mean,' he said, sitting down.

'A few minutes ago, you asked if I were with Dunstone Limited.'

'I don't think I said that.'

'Very well. Julian Warfield – same thing.'

'It was a mistake on my part. I'm afraid I don't remember asking you anything.'

'Yes, of course. That's an essential part of your agreement. There can be no reference whatsoever to Mr Warfield or Dunstone or any*one* or -*thing* related. We understand. Quite frankly, at this juncture we approve wholeheartedly. Among other reasons, should you violate the demands of secrecy, we think you'd be killed instantly.'

McAuliff lowered his glass and stared at the Englishman, who spoke so calmly, precisely. 'That's preposterous,' he said simply.

'That's Dunstone Limited,' replied Hammond softly.

'Then I think you'd better explain.'

'I shall do my best. To begin with, the geophysical survey that you've contracted for is the second such team to be sent out—'

'I wasn't told that,' interrupted Alex.

'With good reason. They're dead. I should say, "disappeared and dead". No one's been able to trace the Jamaican members; the whites are dead, of that we are sure.'

'How so? I mean, how can you be sure?'

'The best of all reasons, Mr McAuliff. One of the men was a British agent.'

McAuliff found himself mesmerized by the soft-spoken Intelligence man's narrative. Hammond might have been an Oxford don going over the blurred complexities of a dark Elizabethan drama, patiently clarifying each twist of an essentially inexplicable plot. He supplied conjectures where knowledge failed, making sure that McAuliff understood that they were conjectures.

Dunstone Limited, was not simply an industrial-development company;

that was to say, its objectives went far beyond those of a conglomerate. And it was not solely British, as its listed board of directors implied. In actuality, Dunstone Limited, London, was the 'corporate' headquarters of an organization of international financiers dedicated to building global cartels beyond the interferences and controls of the European Common Market and its trade alliances. *That* was to say – by conjecture – eliminating the economic intervention of governments: Washington, London, Berlin, Paris, The Hague, and all other points of the financial compass. Ultimately, these were to be reduced to the status of clients, not origins of resource or negotiation.

'You're saying, in essence, that Dunstone is in the process of setting up its own government.'

'Precisely. A government based solely on economic trade factors. A concentration of financial resources unheard of since the pharaohs. Along with this economic catastrophe, and no less important, is the absorption of the government of Jamaica by Dunstone Limited. Jamaica is Dunstone's projected base of operations. They can succeed, Mr McAuliff.'

Alex put his glass on the wide windowsill. He began slowly trying to find words, looking out at the slate rooftops converging into the Savoy Court. 'Let me try to understand, from what you've told me and from what I know. Dunstone anticipates investing heavily in Jamaican development. All right, we agree on that, and the figures are astronomical. Now, in exchange for this investment, they expect to be awarded a lot of clout from a grateful Kingston government. At least, that's what I'd expect if I were Dunstone. The normal tax credits, importing concessions, employment breaks, real estate . . . general incentives. Nothing new.' McAuliff turned his head and looked at Hammond. 'I'm not sure I see any financial catastrophe . . . except, maybe, an English financial catastrophe.'

'You stand corrected; I stand rebuked,' said Hammond. 'But only in a minor way. You're quite perceptive; it's true that our concerns were – at *first* – UK oriented. English perversity, if you will. Dunstone is an important factor in Britain's balance of trade. We'd hate to lose it.'

'So you build a conspiracy—'

'Now, just a minute, Mr McAuliff,' the agent broke in, without raising his voice. 'The highest echelons of the British government do not *invent* conspiracies. If Dunstone were what it is purported to be, those responsible in Downing Street would fight openly for our interests. I'm afraid that is not the case. Dunstone reaches into extremely sensitive areas in London, Berlin, Paris, Rome . . . and, most assuredly, in Washington. But I shall return to that. I'd like to concentrate on Jamaica for the moment. You used the terms "concessions", "tax breaks", . . . "clout" and "incentives". I say "absorption".'

'Words.'

'*Laws*, Mr McAuliff. Sovereign; sanctioned by prime ministers and cabinets and parliaments. Think for a minute, Mr McAuliff. An existing, viable government in a strategically located independent nation controlled by a huge industrial monopoly with world markets. It's not outlandish. It's around the corner.'

Alex did think about it. For more than a minute. Prodded by Hammond's gently spoken, authoritatively phrased 'clarifications'.

Without disclosing MI5's methods of discovery, the Britisher explained Dunstone's modus operandi. Enormous sums of capital had been transferred from Swiss banks to Kingston's King Street, that short stretch of the block that housed major international banking institutions. But the massive cash flow was not deposited in British, American, or Canadian banks. Those went begging, while the less secure Jamaican banks were stunned by an influx of hard money unheard of in their histories.

Few knew that the vast new Jamaican riches were solely Dunstone's. But for these few, proof was supplied by the revolving transfers of a thousand accounts within an eight-hour business day.

Heads spun in astonishment. A few heads. Selected men in extraordinarily high places were shown incontrovertibly that a new force had invaded Kingston, a force so powerful that Wall Street and Whitehall would tremble at its presence.

'If you know this much, why don't you move in? Stop them.'

'Not possible,' answered Hammond. 'All transactions are covered; there's no one to accuse. It's too complex a web of financing. Dunstone is masterminded by Warfield. He operates on the premise that a closed society is efficient only when its various arms have little or no knowledge of each other.'

'In other words, you can't prove your case and—'

'We cannot expose what we cannot prove,' interrupted Hammond. 'That is correct.'

'You could threaten. I mean, on the basis of what you know damn well is true, you could raise one hell of a cry . . . But you can't chance it. It goes back to these "sensitive" areas in Berlin, Washington, Paris, et cetera. Am I correct about that, too?'

'You are.'

'They must be goddamn sensitive.'

'We believe they compromise an international cross-section of extraordinarily powerful men.'

'In governments?'

'Allied with major industries.'

'For instance?'

Hammond held Alex's eyes with his own. His message was clear. 'You understand that what I say is merely conjecture.'

'All right. And my memory is short.'

'Very well.' The Britisher got out of the chair and walked around it. His voice remained quiet, but there was no lack of precision. 'Your own country: conceivably the Vice President of the United States or someone in his office and, certainly, unknown members of the Senate and the President's cabinet. England: prominent figures in the House of Commons and undoubtedly various department directors at the Inland Revenue. Germany: ranking *vorsitzen* in the Bundestag. France: elitist holdovers from the pre-Algerian Gaullists. Such men as I have described must exist relative to Warfield. The progress made by Dunstone would have been impossible without influence in such places. Of that we are certain.'

'But you don't know who, specifically.'

'No.'

'And you think, somehow, I can help you?'

'We do, Mr McAuliff.'

'With all the resources you have, you come to me? I've been contracted for a Dunstone field survey, nothing else.'

'The *second* Dunstone survey, Mr McAuliff.'

Alexander stared at the Englishman.

'And you say that team is dead.'

Hammond returned to his chair and sat down once more. 'Yes, Mr McAuliff. Which means Dunstone has an adversary. One that's as deadly and powerful as Warfield's forces. And we haven't the slightest idea what it is, who they are. Only that it exists, *they* exist. We wish to make contact with those who want the same thing we do. We can guarantee the safety of your expedition. You are the key. Without you, we're stymied. Without us, you and your people might well be in extreme jeopardy.'

McAuliff shot out of the chair and stood above the British agent. He took several short, deep breaths and walked purposefully away from Hammond; then he aimlessly paced the Savoy room. The Englishman seemed to understand Alex's action. He let the moment subside; he said nothing.

'*Jesus!* You're something, Hammond!' McAuliff returned to his chair, but he did not sit down. He reached for his drink on the windowsill, not so much for the whisky as to hold the glass. 'You come in here, build a case against Warfield by way of an economics lecture, and then calmly tell me that I've signed what amounts to my last contract if I don't cooperate with you.'

'That's rather black and white, chap.'

'That's rather exactly what you just said! Suppose you're mistaken?'

'We're not.'

'You know goddamn well I can't prove that either. If I go back to Warfield and tell him about this little informal chat, I'll lose the contract the second I open my mouth. And the largest fee any surveyor was ever offered.'

'May I ask the amount? Just academic interest.'

McAuliff looked at Hammond. 'What would you say to two million dollars?'

'I'd say I'm surprised he didn't offer three. Or four. Why not? You wouldn't live to spend it.'

Alex held the Englishman's eyes. 'Translated, that means if Dunstone's enemies don't kill me, Dunstone will?'

'It's what we believe. There's no other logical conclusion. Once your work is finished.'

'I see . . .' McAuliff walked slowly to the whisky and poured deliberately, as if measuring. He did not offer anything to Hammond. 'If I confront Warfield with what you've told me, you're really saying that he'd ...'

'Kill you? Are those the words that stick, Mr McAuliff?'

'I don't have much cause to employ those kind of words, Mr Hammond.'

'Naturally. No one ever gets used to them ... Yes, we think he would kill you. Have you killed, of course. After picking your brains.'

McAuliff leaned against the wall, staring at the whisky in his glass, but not drinking. 'You're not giving me an alternative, are you?'

'Of course we are. I can leave these rooms; we never met.'

'Suppose someone sees you? That surveillance you spoke of.'

'They won't see me; you will have to take my word for that.' Hammond leaned back in the chair. He brought his fingers together pensively. 'Of course, under the circumstances, we'd be in no position to offer protection. From either faction—'

'Protection from the unprovable,' interjected Alex softly.

'Yes.'

'No alternative ...' McAuliff pushed himself away from the wall and took several swallows of whisky. 'Except one, Hammond. Suppose I cooperate, on the basis that there may be substance to your charges ... or theories, or whatever you call them. But I'm not accountable to you.'

'I'm not sure I understand.'

'I don't accept orders blindly. No puppet strings. I want that condition – on the record. If that's the phrase.'

'It must be. I've used it frequently.'

McAuliff crossed in front of the Englishman to the arm of his chair. 'Now put it in simple words. What am I supposed to do?'

Hammond's voice was calm and precise. 'There are two objectives. The first, and most vital, is Dunstone's opposition. Those knowledgeable enough and fanatical enough to have killed the first survey team. If uncovered, it is conceivable that they will lead you to the second and equally important objective: the names of Dunstone's unknown hierarchy. The faceless men in London, Paris, Berlin, Washington ... even one or two. We'd be grateful for anything specific.'

'How do I begin?'

'With very little, I'm afraid. But we do have something. It's only a word, a name, perhaps. We don't know. But we have every reason to think it's terribly important.'

'A word?'

'Yes. "Halidon."'

4

It was like working in two distinct spheres of reality, neither completely real. During the days, McAuliff conferred with the men and women in the University of London's geophysics laboratories, gathering personnel data for his survey team. The university was Dunstone's cover – along with the Royal Historical Society – and neither was aware that Dunstone's finances were behind the expedition.

During the nights, into the early morning hours, he met with R. C. Hammond, British Intelligence, in small, guarded houses on dimly lit streets in Kensington and Chelsea. These locations were reached by two changes of vehicles – taxis driven by MI5. And for each meeting Alex was provided with a cover story regarding his whereabouts: a dinner party, a girl, a crowded restaurant he was familiar with; nothing out of the ordinary, everything easily explained and verifiable.

The sessions with Hammond were divided into areas of instruction: the political and financial climate of Jamaica, MI5 contacts throughout the island, and basic skills – with instruments – in communication and countersurveillance.

At several sessions, Hammond brought in West Indian 'specialists' – black agents who were capable of answering just about any question McAuliff might raise. He had few questions; he had surveyed for the Kaiser bauxite interests near Oracabessa a little over a year ago, a fact he suspected had led Julian Warfield to him.

When they were alone, R. C. Hammond droned on about the attitudes and reactions Alex should foster.

Always build on part of the truth ... keeping it simple ... the basics easily confirmed ...

You'll find it quite acceptable to operate on different levels ... naturally, instinctively. Your concentration will separate independently ...

Very rapidly your personal antennae will be activated ... second nature. You'll fall into a rhythm ... the connecting link between your divided objectives ...

The British agent was never emphatic, simply redundant. Over and over again, he repeated the phrases, with minor variations in the words.

Alex understood. Hammond was providing him with fundamentals: tools and confidence.

'Your contact in Kingston will be given to you in a few days; we're still refining. Kingston's a mess; trust isn't easily come by there.'

'Whose trust?' asked McAuliff.

'Good point,' replied the agent. 'Don't dwell on it. That's our job. Memorize everyone else.'

Alex looked at the typewritten names on the paper that was not to be removed from the house in Kensington. 'You've got a lot of people on your payroll.'

'A few too many. Those that are crossed out were on double rosters. Ours and the CIA's. Your Central Intelligence Agency has become too political in recent years.'

'Are you concerned about leaks?'

'Yes. Dunstone Limited, is alive in Washington. Elusive, but very much alive.'

The mornings found him entering Dunstone's sphere of reality, the University of London. He discovered that it was easier than he'd thought to shut out the previous night's concerns. Hammond's theory of divided objectives was borne out; he did fall into a rhythm. His concentration was now limited to professional concern – the building of his survey team.

It was agreed that the number should not exceed eight, preferably fewer. The areas of expertise would be the normal ones: shale, limestone, and bedrock stratification; water and gas-pocket analyses; vegetation – soil and botanical research; and finally, because the survey extended into the interior regions of the Cock Pit country, someone familiar with the various dialects and outback customs. Warfield had thought this last was superfluous; Alex knew better. Resentments ran high in Jamaica.

McAuliff had made up his mind about one member of the team, a soil analyst from California named Sam Tucker. Sam was an immense, burly man in his fifties, given to whatever excesses could be found in any immediate vicinity, but a top professional in his field. He was also the most reliable man Alex had ever known, a strong friend who had worked surveys with him from Alaska to last year's Kaiser job in Oracabessa. McAuliff implied that if Julian Warfield withheld approval from Sam, he might have to find himself another surveyor.

It was a hollow threat, all things considered, but it was worth the risk of having to back down. Alex wanted Sam with him in Jamaica. The others would be new, unproven; Tucker had worn well over the years. He could be trusted.

Warfield ran a Dunstone check on Sam Tucker and agreed there was nothing prejudicial beyond certain minor idiosyncrasies. But Sam was to be no different from any other member; none was to be informed of Dunstone's interests. Obviously.

None would be. Alex meant it. More than Warfield realized. If there was *any* truth to R. C. Hammond's astonishing pronouncements. Everyone on the survey would be told the same story. Given a set of facts engineered by Dunstone Limited. Even the organizations involved accepted the facts as truth; there was no reason not to. Financial grants were not questioned; they were academic holy writ. Coveted, revered, never debated.

The geological survey had been made possible through a grant from the Royal Historical Society, encouraged by the Commonwealth Activities Committee, House of Lords. The expedition was to be a joint endeavor of the University of London and the Jamaican Ministry of Education. All salaries, expenses, disbursements of any kind were to be made through the bursar's office at the university. The Royal Society would establish lines of bank credit, and the university was to draw on those funds.

The reason for the survey was compatible with endeavors of the Commonwealth Committee at Lords, whose members peopled and paid for most royal societies. It was another not-to-be-forgotten link with Britannia. A study which would be acknowledged in textbooks for years to come. For, according to Jamaican ministry, there were no records of this particular territory having been subjected to a geophysical survey of any dimensions.

Obviously.

And if there was, certainly no one was going to bring them up.

Academic holy writ.

The university rip-off. One did not question.

The selection of Alexander McAuliff for the post of survey director was acknowledged to be an embarrassment to both the society and the university. But the American was the Jamaican ministry's choice. One suffered such insults from the former colonies.

One took the money; one did not debate.

Holy writ.

Everything was just complicated enough to be academically viable, thought McAuliff. Julian Warfield understood the environs through which he manoeuvred.

As did R. C. Hammond of British Intelligence.

And Alex began to realize that he would have to catch up. Both Dunstone Limited, and MI5 were committed to specific objectives. He could get lost in those commitments. In some ways, he had lost already. But choosing the team was his immediate concern.

McAuliff's personnel approach was one he had used often enough to know it worked. He would not interview anyone whose work he had not read thoroughly; anyone he did interview had already proven himself on paper. Beyond the specific areas of expertise, he cared about adaptability to the physical and climatic requirements, and to the give and take of close-quarters association.

He had done his work. He was ready.

'My secretary said you wanted to see me, Dr McAuliff.' The speaker at the door was the chairman of the Geophysics Department, a bespectacled, gaunt academician who tried not to betray his resentment of Alex. It was obvious that the man felt cheated by both the Royal Society and Kingston for not having been chosen for McAuliff's job. He had recently completed an excellent survey in Anguilla; there were too many similarities between that assignment and the Jamaican grant for comfort.

'Good Lord,' said Alex. 'I expected to come to your office.' He crossed to his desk and smiled awkwardly. He had been standing by the single window, looking out over a miniature quadrangle, watching students carrying books, thankful that he was no longer part of that world. 'I think I'll be ready to start the interviews this afternoon.'

'So soon?'

'Thanks mainly to you, Professor Ralston. Your recommendations were excellent.' McAuliff wasn't being polite; the academician's candidates were good – on paper. Of the ten final prospects, exactly half were from Ralston; the remaining five were freelancers highly thought of by two London survey firms. 'I'm inclined just to take your people without seeing any others,' continued Alex, now being polite. 'But the Kingston ministry is adamant that I interview these.' McAuliff handed Ralston a sheet of paper with the five nonuniversity names.

'Oh, yes. I recognize several,' said Ralston, his voice now pleasantly acknowledging Alex's compliment. 'A couple here are ... a couple, you know.'

'What?'

'Man-and-wife team. The Jensens.'

'There's one Jensen. Who's the woman?'

'R. L. Wells. That's Ruth Wells, Jensen's wife.'

'I didn't realize ... I can't say that fact is in their favor.'

'Why not?'

'I'm not sure,' answered Alex sincerely. 'I've never had a married couple on a survey. Silly reaction, isn't it? Do you know anybody else there?'

'One fellow. I'd rather not comment.'

'Then I wish you would.'

'Ferguson. James Ferguson. He was a student of mine. Very outspoken chap. Quite opinionated, if you know what I mean.'

'But he's a botanist, plant specialist, not a geology man.'

'Survey training; geophysics was his curriculum secondary. Of course, it was a number of years ago.'

McAuliff sorted out some papers on the desk. 'It couldn't have been too many. He's only been on three tours, all in the past four years.'

'It wasn't, actually. And you should see him. He's considered quite good, I'm told.'

'Here are your people,' said Alex, offering a second page to Ralston. 'I chose five out of the eight you submitted. Any more surprises there? Incidentally, I hope you approve.'

Ralston read the list, adjusting his spectacles and pursing his lips as he did so. 'Yes, I thought you'd select these. You realize, of course, that this Whitehall chap is not one of us. He was recommended by the West Indies

Studies. Brilliant fellow, according to the chairs. Never met him myself. Makes quite a lot of money on the lecture circuits.'

'He's black, isn't he?'

'Oh, certainly. He knows every tongue, every dialect, every cultural normality and aberration in the Antilles. His doctoral thesis traced no fewer than twenty-seven African tribes to the islands. From the Bushwadie to the Coromantees. His research of Indian-African integration is the standard reference. He's quite a dandy, too, I believe.'

'Anyone else you want to talk about?'

'No, not actually. You'll have a difficult time deciding between your shale-bedrock experts. You've two very decent ones here. Unless your ... immediate reactions take precedence. One way or the other.'

'I don't understand.'

Ralston smiled. 'It would be presumptuous of me to comment further.' And then the professor added quickly, 'Shall I have someone set up the appointments?'

'Thanks, I'd appreciate it. If schedules can be organized with all ten, I'd like an hour apiece over the next few days; whatever order is convenient for everyone.'

'An hour ...'

'I'll call back those I want to talk with further. No sense in wasting everyone's time.'

'Yes, of course.'

One applicant disqualified himself the moment he walked into McAuliff's cubicle. The fact that he was more drunk than sober at one o'clock in the afternoon might have been explained, but instead was used as the excuse to eliminate him for a larger problem: he was crippled in his right leg and unlikely to withstand the rigors of the expedition. Three men were crossed off for identical conditions: each was obviously hostile to West Indians – a spreading English virus, Britain's parallel to *Americus Redneckus*.

The Jensens – Peter Jensen and Ruth Wells – were delightful surprises, singly and together. They were in their early fifties, bright, confident, and good-natured. A childless couple, they were financially secure and genuinely interested both in each other and in their work. His expertise was ore minerals; hers, the sister science of paleontology – fossils. His had direct application, hers was removed but academically justifiable.

'Might I ask you some questions, Dr McAuliff?' Peter packed his pipe, his voice pleasant.

'By all means.'

'Can't say that I know much about Jamaica, but this seems like a damned curious trip. I'm not sure I understand. What's the point?'

Alex was grateful for the opportunity to recite the explanation created by Dunstone Limited. He watched the ore man closely as he spoke, relieved to see the light of recognition in the geologist's eyes. When he finished, he paused and added, 'I don't know if that clears up anything.'

'Oh my word, it certainly does, chap. *Burke's Peerage* strikes again!' Peter Jensen chuckled, glancing at his wife. 'The royal *H* has been hard pressed to find something to do. Its members at Lords simply provided it. Good show. I trust the university will make a pound or two.'

'I'm afraid the budget's not that loose.'

'Really?' Peter Jensen held his pipe as he looked at McAuliff. 'Then perhaps I *don't* understand. You'll forgive me, but you're not known in the field as a particularly inexpensive director ... quite rightfully, let me add. Your reputation precedes you.'

'From the Balkans to Australia,' added Ruth Wells Jensen, her expression showing minor irritation with her husband. 'And if you have a separate arrangement, it's none of Peter's bloody business.'

Alex laughed softly. 'You're kind, both of you. But there's nothing special. I got caught, it's as simple as that. I've worked for companies on the island; I hope to again. Often. All geophysical certificates are issued by Kingston, and Kingston asked for me. Let's call it an investment.'

Again McAuliff watched Peter Jensen closely; he had rehearsed the answer. The Britisher looked once more at his wife. Briefly. Then he chuckled, as he had done seconds before.

'I'd do the same, chap. But God help the survey *I* was director on.'

'It's one I'd avoid like a May Day in Trafalgar,' said Ruth, matching her husband's quiet laugh. 'Who have you set, if it's proper to ask? Anyone we might know?'

'Nobody yet. I've really just started—'

'Well,' interrupted Peter Jensen, his eyes alive with humor, 'since you suffer from inadequate freight charges, I should tell you we'd rather not be separated. Somewhat used to each other by now. If you're interested in one of us, the other would take half till to straggle along.'

Whatever doubts remained for Alex were dispelled by Ruth Wells Jensen's words. She mimicked her husband's professorial tones with good-natured accuracy. 'Half till, old chap, can be negotiated. Our flat's damned cold this time of year.'

The Jensens would be hired.

The third nonuniversity name, James Ferguson, had been accurately described by Ralston as outspoken and opinionated. These traits, however, were the results of energy and impatience, it seemed to McAuliff. Ferguson was young – twenty-six – and was not the sort to survive, much less thrive, in an academic environment. Alex recognized in Ferguson much of his younger self: consummate interest in his subject, intolerance of the research world in which it was studied. A contradiction, if not a conflict of objectives. Ferguson freelanced for agro-industry companies, and his best recommendation was that he rarely was out of work in a market not famous for excessive employment. James Ferguson was one of the best vegetation specialists around.

'I'd love to get back to Jamaica,' said the young man within seconds after the preliminary interview began. 'I was in Port Maria for the Craft

Foundation two years ago. It's my judgment the whole bloody island is a gold mine if the fruit and synthetic industries would allow development.'

'What's the gold?' asked McAuliff.

'The baracoa fibers. In the second growth stages. A banana strain could be developed that would send the nylon and the tricot boys into panic, to say nothing of the fruit shippers.'

'Can you prove it?'

'Damn near did, *I* think. That's why I was thrown out by the Foundation.'

'You were thrown out?'

'Quite unceremoniously. No sense hiding the fact; don't care to, really. They told me to stick to business. Can you imagine? You'll probably run across a few negatives about me, if you're interested.'

'I'm interested, Mr Ferguson.'

The interview with Charles Whitehall disturbed McAuliff. That was to say, the man disturbed him, not the quality of information received. Whitehall was a black cynic, a now-Londoner whose roots and expertise were in the West Indies but whose outlook was aggressively self-perpetuating. His appearance startled McAuliff. For a man who had written three volumes of Caribbean history, whose work was, in Ralston's words, 'the standard reference', Charles Whitehall looked barely as old as James Ferguson.

'Don't let my appearance fool you, Mr McAuliff,' said Whitehall, upon entering the cubicle and extending his hand to Alex. 'My tropic hue covers the years better than paler skin. I'm forty-two years old.'

'You read my thoughts.'

'Not necessarily. I'm used to the reaction,' replied Whitehall, sitting down, smoothing his expensive blazer, and crossing his legs, which were encased in pinstriped trousers.

'Since you don't waste words, Dr Whitehall, neither will I. Why are you interested in this survey? As I gather, you can make a great deal more money on the lecture circuit. A geophysical survey isn't the most lucrative employment.'

'Let's say the financial aspects are secondary; one of the few times in my life that they will be, perhaps.' Whitehall spoke while removing a silver cigarette case from his pocket. 'To tell you the truth, Mr McAuliff, there's a certain ego fulfillment in returning to one's country as an expert under the aegis of the Royal Historical Society. It's really as simple as that.'

Alex believed the man. For, as he read him, Whitehall was a scholar far more honored abroad than at home. It seemed that Charles Whitehall wanted to achieve an acceptance commensurate with his scholarship that had been denied him in the intellectual – or was it social? – houses of Kingston.

'Are you familiar with the Cock Pit country?'

'As much as anyone who isn't a runner. Historically and culturally, much more so, of course.'

'What's a runner?'

'Runners are hill people. From the mountain communities. They hire out as guides, when you can find one. They're primitives, really. Who have you hired for the survey?'

'What?' Alex's thoughts were on runners.

'I asked who was going with you. On the survey team. I'd be interested.'

'Well . . . not all the posts have been filled. There's a couple named Jensen – ores and paleo; a young botanist, Ferguson. An American friend of mine, a soil analyst, name of Sam Tucker.'

'I've heard of Jensen, I believe. I'm not sure, but I think so. I don't know the others.'

'Did you expect to?'

'Frankly, yes. Royal Society projects generally attract very high-caliber people.' Whitehall delicately tapped his cigarette on the rim of an ashtray.

'Such as yourself?' asked McAuliff, smiling.

'I'm not modest,' replied the black scholar, returning Alex's smile with an open grin. 'And I'm very much interested. I think I could be of service to you.'

So did McAuliff.

The second shale-bedrock analyst was listed as A. Gerrard Booth. Booth was a university applicant personally recommended by Ralston in the following manner:

'I promised Booth I'd bring these papers and articles to your attention. I do believe Booth would be a fine asset to the survey.'

Professor Ralston had given McAuliff a folder filled with A. Gerrard Booth's studies of sheet strata in such diverse locations as Turkey, Corsica, Zaire, and Australia. Alex recalling having read several of the articles in *National Geologist*, and remembered them as lucid and professional. Booth was good; Booth was better than good.

Booth was also a woman. A. Gerrard Booth was known to her colleagues as Alison; no one bothered with the middle name.

She had one of the most genuine smiles McAuliff had ever seen. It was more a half laugh – one might even say masculine, but the word was contradicted by her complete femininity. Her eyes were blue and alive and level, the eyes of a professional. Her handshake was firm, again professional. Her light brown hair was long and soft and slightly waved – brushed repeatedly, thought Alex, for the interview. Her age was anywhere from late twenties to middle thirties; there was no way to tell by observation, except that there were laugh lines at the corners of her eyes.

Alison Booth was not only good and a woman; she was also, at least on first meeting, a very attractive, outgoing person. The term 'professional' kept recurring to McAuliff as they spoke.

'I made Rolly – Dr Ralston – promise to omit the fact that I was a woman. Don't hold him responsible.'

'Were you so convinced I was antifeminist?'

She raised her hand and brushed her long, soft hair away from the side of her lovely face. 'No preformed hostility, Dr McAuliff. I just understand the practical obstacles. It's part of my job to convince you I'm qualified.' And then, as if she were aware of the possible double entendre, Alison Booth stopped smiling and smoothed her skirt ... professionally.

'In fieldwork and the laboratory, I'm sure you *are* qualified.'

'Any other considerations would be extraneous, I should think,' said the woman, with a slight trace of English aloofness.

'Not necessarily. There are environmental problems, degrees of physical discomfort, if not hardship.'

'I can't conceive of Jamaica being in that league with Zaire or the Aussie Outback. I've surveyed in those places.'

'I know—'

'Rolly told me,' interrupted Alison Booth, 'that you would not accept tour references until you had interviewed us.'

'Group isolation tends to create fallible judgments. Insupportable relationships. I've lost good men in the past because other good men reacted negatively to them for the wrong reasons.'

'What about women?'

'I used the term inclusively, not exclusively.'

'I have very good references, Dr McAuliff. For the right reasons.'

'I'll request them.'

'I have them with me.' Alison unbuckled the large leather purse on her lap, extracted two business envelopes, and placed them on the edge of McAuliff's desk. 'My references, Dr McAuliff.'

Alex laughed as he reached for the envelopes. He looked over at the woman; her eyes locked with his. There was both a good-humored challenge and a degree of supplication in her expression. 'Why is this survey so important to you, Miss Booth?'

'Because I'm good and I can do the job,' she answered simply.

'You're employed by the university, aren't you?'

'On a part-time basis, lecture and laboratory. I'm not permanent ... by choice, incidentally.'

'Then it's not money.' McAuliff made a statement.

'I could use it; I'm not desperate, however.'

'I can't imagine your being desperate anywhere,' he said, with a partial smile. And then Alex saw – or thought he saw – a trace of a cloud across her eyes, an instant of concern that left as rapidly as it had come. He instinctively pressed further. 'But why *this* tour? With your qualifications, I'm sure there are others. Probably more interesting, certainly more money.'

'The timing is propitious,' she replied softly, with precise hesitation. 'For personal reasons that have absolutely nothing to do with my qualifications.'

'Are there reasons why you want to spend a prolonged period in Jamaica?'

'Jamaica has nothing to do with it. You could be surveying Outer Mongolia for all that it matters.'

'I see.' Alex replaced the two envelopes on the desk. He intentionally conveyed a trace of indifference. She reacted.

'Very well, Dr McAuliff. It's no secret among my friends.' The woman held her purse on her lap. She did not grip it; there was no intensity about her whatsoever. When she spoke, her voice was steady, as were her eyes. She was the total professional again. 'You called me Miss Booth; that's incorrect. Booth is my married name. I regret to say the marriage was not successful; it was terminated recently. The solicitousness of well-meaning people during such times can be boring. I'd prefer to be out of touch.'

McAuliff returned her steady gaze, trying to evoke something beyond her words. There *was* something, but she would not allow his prying further; her expression told him that . . . professionally.

'It's not relevant. I apologize. But I appreciate your telling me.'

'Is your . . . responsibility satisfied?'

'Well, my curiosity, at any rate.' Alex leaned forward, elbows on the desk, his hands folded under his chin. 'Beyond that, and I hope that it's not improper, you've made it possible for me to ask you to have dinner with me.'

'I think that would depend on the degree of relevance you ascribed to my acceptance.' Alison's voice was polite, but not cold. And there was that lovely humor in her eyes.

'In all honesty, I do make it a point to have dinner or a long lunch, even a fair amount of drinks, with those I'm thinking about hiring. But right now, I'm reluctant to admit it.'

'That's a very disarming reply, Dr McAuliff,' she said, her lips parted, laughing her half laugh. 'I'd be delighted to have dinner with you.'

'I'll do my damnedest not to be solicitous. I don't think it's necessary at all.'

'And I'm sure you're never boring.'

'Not relevantly.'

5

McAuliff stood on the corner of High Holborn and Chancery Lane and looked at his watch. The numbers glowed in the mist-laden London darkness; it was 11:40. Preston's Rolls-Royce was ten minutes late. Or perhaps it would not appear at all. His instructions were that if the car did not arrive by midnight, he was to return to the Savoy. Another meeting would be scheduled.

There were times when he had to remind himself whose furtive commands he was following, wondering whether he in turn was being followed. It was a degrading way to live, he reflected: the constant awareness that locked a man into a pocket of fear. All the fiction about the shadowy world of conspiracy omitted the fundamental indignity intrinsic to that world. There was no essential independence; it was strangling.

This particular evening's rendezvous with Warfield had necessitated a near-panic call to Hammond, for the British agent had scheduled a meeting himself, for one in the morning. That is, McAuliff had requested it, and Hammond had set the time and the place. And at ten twenty that night the call had come from Dunstone: Be at the corner of High Holborn and Chancery Lane at eleven thirty, an hour and ten minutes from then.

Hammond could not, at first, be found. His highly secret, private telephone at MI5 simply did not answer. Alex had been given no other number, and Hammond had told him repeatedly never to call the office and leave his name. Nor was he ever to place a call to the agent from his rooms at the Savoy. Hammond did not trust the switchboards at either establishment. Nor the open frequencies of cellular phones.

So Alex had to go out onto the Strand, into succeeding pubs and chemists' shops to public telephones until Hammond's line answered. He was sure he was being observed – by someone – and thus he had to pretend annoyance each time he hung up after an unanswered call. He found that he had built the fabric of a lie, should Warfield question him. His lie was that he was trying to reach Alison Booth and cancel a lunch date they had for the following day. They did have a lunch date, which he had no intention of canceling, but the story possessed sufficient truth to be valid.

Build on part of the truth. Attitude and reaction. MI5.

Finally, Hammond's telephone was answered, by a man who stated casually that he had gone out for a late supper.

A late supper! Good God! ... Global cartels, international collusion in the highest places, financial conspiracies, and a late supper.

In reasoned tones, as opposed to McAuliff's anxiety, the man told him that Hammond would be alerted. Alex was not satisfied; he insisted that Hammond be at his telephone – if he had to wait all night – until he, Alex, made contact after the Warfield appointment.

It was eleven forty-five. Still no St James Rolls-Royce. He looked around at the few pedestrians on High Holborn, walking through the heavy mist. He wondered which, if any, was concerned with him.

The pocket of fear.

He wondered, too, about Alison. They had had dinner for the third night in succession; she had claimed she had a lecture to prepare, and so the evening was cut short. Considering the complications that followed, it was a good thing.

Alison was a strange girl. The professional who covered her vulnerability well; who never strayed far from that circle of quiet humor that protected her. The half laugh, the warm blue eyes, the slow, graceful movement of her hands ... these were her shields, somehow.

There was no problem in selecting her as his first choice ... professionally. She was far and away the best applicant for the team. Alex considered himself one of the finest rock-strata specialists on both continents, yet he wasn't sure he wanted to pit his expertise against hers. Alison Gerrard Booth was really good.

And lovely.

And he wanted her in Jamaica.

He had prepared an argument for Warfield, should Dunstone's goddamn security computers reject her. The final clearance of his selections was the object of the night's conference.

Where *was* the goddamned black ship of an automobile? It was ten minutes to midnight.

'Excuse me, sir,' said a deep, almost guttural voice behind McAuliff.

He turned, and saw a man about his own age, in a brown mackinaw; he looked like a longshoreman or a construction worker.

'Yes?'

'It's m' first time in London, sir, and I thinks I'm lost.'

The man then pointed up at the street sign, barely visible in the spill of the lamp through the mist. 'This says Chancery Lane, which is *supposed* to be near a place called Hatton, which is where I'm supposed to meet m' friends. I can't *find* it, sir.'

Alex gestured to his left. 'It's up there two or three blocks.'

The man pointed again, as a simpleton might point, in the direction of McAuliff's gesture. 'Up there, sir?'

'That's right.'

The man shook his arm several times, as if emphasizing. 'You're sure, sir?'

And then the man lowered his voice and spoke rapidly. 'Please don't react, Mr McAuliff. Continue as though you are explaining. Mr Hammond will meet you in Soho; there's an all-night club called The Owl of Saint George. He'll be waiting. Stay at the bar, he'll reach you. Don't worry about the time. He doesn't want you to make any more telephone calls. You're being watched.'

McAuliff swallowed, blanched, and waved his hand – a little too obviously, he felt – in the direction of Hatton Garden. He, too, spoke quietly, rapidly, '*Jesus!* If *I'm* being watched, so are *you*!'

'We calculate these things—'

'I don't like your addition! What am I supposed to tell Warfield? To let me off in *Soho*?'

'Why not? Say you feel like a night out. You've nothing scheduled in the morning. Americans like Soho; it's perfectly natural. You're not a heavy gambler, but you place a bet now and then.'

'Christ! Would you care to describe my sex life?'

'I could, but I won't.' The guttural, loud North Country voice returned. 'Thank you, sir. You're very kind, sir. I'm sure I'll find m' friends.'

The man walked swiftly away into the night mist toward Hatton Garden. McAuliff felt his whole body shiver; his hands trembled. To still them, he reached into his pocket for cigarettes. He was grateful for the opportunity to grip the metal of his lighter.

It was five minutes to twelve. He would wait until several minutes past and then leave. His instructions were to 'return to the Savoy'; another meeting would be set. Did that mean it was to be scheduled later that night? In the morning hours? Or did 'return to the Savoy' simply mean that he was no longer required to remain at the corner of High Holborn and Chancery Lane? He was free for the evening?

The words were clear, but the alternative interpretation was entirely feasible. If he chose, he could – with a number of stops – make his way into Soho, to Hammond. The network of surveillance would establish the fact that Warfield had not appeared for the appointment. The option was open.

My God! thought Alex. *What's happening to me? Words and meanings . . . options and alternates. Interpretations of . . . orders!*

Who the hell gave *him* orders!

He was *not* a man to be commanded!

But when his hand shook as he raised his cigarette to his lips, he knew that he was – for an indeterminate period of time. Time in a hell he could not stand; he was not free.

The dual hands on his wristwatch converged. It was midnight. To goddamn hell with all of them! He *would* leave! He would call Alison and tell her he wanted to come over for a drink . . . ask her if she would let him. Hammond could wait all night in Soho. Where was it? The Owl of Saint George. Silly fucking name!

To hell with him!

The Rolls-Royce sped out of the fog from the direction of Newgate, its deep-throated engine racing, a powerful intrusion in the otherwise still street. It swung alongside the curb in front of McAuliff and stopped abruptly. The chauffeur got out of his seat, raced around the long hood of the car, and opened the rear door for Alex.

It all happened so quickly that McAuliff threw away his cigarette and climbed in, bewildered; he had not adjusted to the swift change of plans. Julian Warfield sat in the far right corner of the huge rear seat, his tiny frame dwarfed by the vehicle's expansive interior.

'I'm sorry to have kept you waiting until the last minute, Mr McAuliff. I was detained.'

'Do you always do business with one eye on secrecy, the other on shock effect?' asked Alex, settling back in the seat, relieved to feel he could speak with confidence.

Warfield replied by laughing his hard, old-man's laugh. 'Compared to Ross Perot, I'm a used-car salesman.'

'You're still damned unsettling.'

'Would you care for a drink? Preston has a bar built in right there.' Warfield pointed to the felt back of the front seat. 'Just pull on that strap.'

'No, thank you. I may do a little drinking later, not now.' *Easy. Easy, McAuliff,* he thought to himself. *For Christ's sake, don't be obvious. Hammond can wait all night. Two minutes ago, you were going to let him do just that!*

The old man took an envelope from his jacket pocket. 'I'll give you the good news straight off. There's no one we objected to strenuously, subject to minor questions. On the contrary, we think you finalized your selections rather ingeniously...'

According to Warfield, the initial reaction at Dunstone to his list of first choices was negative. Not because of security – subject to those minor questions – nor quality. McAuliff had done his homework. But from a conceptual viewpoint. The idea of female members of a geological survey expedition was rejected out of hand, the central issue being that of less strength, not necessarily weakness. Any project entailing travel had, by tradition, a masculine identification; the intrusion of the female was a disquieting component. It could only lead to complications – any number of them.

'So we crossed off two of your first choices, realizing that by eliminating the Wells woman, you would also lose her husband, Jensen ... Three out of the first five rejected; knew you'd be unhappy, but then, you *did* understand ... Later, it came to me. By George, you'd outthought the lot of us!'

'I wasn't concerned with any strategies, Warfield. I was putting together the best team I could.' McAuliff felt he had to interject the statement.

'Perhaps not consciously, and qualitatively you have a splendid group. But the inclusion of the two ladies, one a wife and both superior in their fields, was a profound improvement.'

'Why?'

'It provides – they provide – a unique ingredient of innocence. A patina of scholarship, actually; an aspect we had overlooked. A dedicated team of men and women – on a grant from the Royal Society – so different somehow from an all-male survey expedition. Really, most remarkable.'

'That wasn't my intention. I hate to disabuse you.'

'No disabusement whatsoever. The result is the same. Needlessly said, I pointed out this consideration to the others, and they agreed instantly.'

'I have an idea that whatever you might "point out" would be instantly agreed to. What are the minor questions?'

'"Incidental information you might wish to consider" is a better description.' The old man reached up and snapped on a reading lamp. He then removed several pages from his overcoat, unfolded them, and placed them in front of the envelope. He adjusted his glasses and scanned the top paper. 'The husband and wife, this Jensen and Wells. They're quite active in leftish political circles. Peace marches, ban-the-bombing, that sort of thing.'

'That doesn't have any bearing on their work. I doubt they'll be organizing the natives.' McAuliff spoke wearily, on purpose. If Warfield intended to raise such 'questions,' he wanted the financier to know he thought them irrelevant.

'There is a great deal of political instability in Jamaica; unrest, to be precise. It would not be in our interests for any of your people to be outspoken on such matters.'

McAuliff shifted in his seat and looked at the little old man – tiny lips pursed, the papers held in his thin, bony fingers under the pin spot of yellow light, giving his ancient flesh a sallow color. 'Should the occasion arise – and I can't conceive of it – when the Jensens make political noises, I'll quiet them. On the other hand, the inclusion of such people might be an asset to you. They'd hardly, knowingly, work for Dunstone.'

'Yes,' said Warfield quietly. 'That, too, occurred to us. This chap Ferguson. He ran into trouble with the Craft Foundation.'

'He ran into a potentially vital discovery concerning baracoa fibers, that's what he ran into. It scared the hell out of Craft and Craft's funding resources.'

'We have no fight with Craft. We don't want one. The fact that he's with you could raise eyebrows. Craft's well thought of in Jamaica.'

'There's no one as good as Ferguson, certainly not the alternate, and he was the best of those remaining. I'll keep Ferguson away from Craft.'

'That is essential. We cannot permit him otherwise.'

Charles Whitehall, the black scholar-dandy, was a psychological mess, according to Dunstone's data banks. Politically he was a conservative, a black conservative who might have led the Kingston reactionaries had he remained on the island. But his future was not in Jamaica, and he had recognized it early. He was bitter over the fact. Warfield hastened to add, however, that his negative information was balanced – and more – by Whitehall's academic standing. His interest in the survey was ultimately a positive factor; his inclusion tended to remove any commercial stain from the project. To compound the complications of this very complex man, Whitehall was a

Class Triple A Black Belt practitioner of jukato, a more intricate and deadly development of judo.

'Our contacts in Kingston are quite impressed with his being with you. I suspect they'll offer him a chair at the West Indies University. I think he'll probably accept, if they pay him enough. Now, we come to the last submission.' Warfield removed his glasses, placed them on his lap with the papers, and rubbed the bridge of his thin bony nose. 'Mrs Booth . . . Mrs Alison Gerrard Booth.'

Alex felt the stirring of resentment. Warfield had already told him that Alison was acceptable; he did not want to hear intimate, private information dredged up by Dunstone's faceless men or whirring machines.

'What about her?' asked McAuliff, his voice careful. 'Her record speaks for itself.'

'Unquestionably. She's extremely qualified . . . and extremely anxious to leave England.'

'She's explained that. I buy it. She's just been divorced, and the circumstances, I gather, are not too pleasant . . . socially.'

'Is that what she told you?'

'Yes. I believe her.'

Warfield replaced his glasses and flipped the page in front of him. 'I'm afraid there's a bit more to it than that, Mr McAuliff. Did she tell you who her husband was? What he did for a living?'

'No. And I didn't ask her.'

'Yes . . . well, I think you should know. David Booth is from a socially prominent family – viscount status, actually – that hasn't had the cash flow of a pound sterling for a generation. He is a partner in an export–import firm whose books indicate a barely passable subsistence. Yet Mr Booth lives extremely well. Several homes – here and on the Continent – drives expensive cars, belongs to the better clubs. Contradictory, isn't it?'

'I'd say so. How does he do it?'

'Narcotics,' said Julian Warfield, as if he had just given the time of day. 'David Booth is a courier for Franco-American interests operating out of Corsica and Marseilles.'

For the next few moments both men were silent. McAuliff understood the implication, and finally spoke. 'Mrs Booth was on surveys in Corsica, Zaire, and Turkey. You're suggesting that she's involved.'

'Possibly; not likely. If so, unwittingly. After all, she did divorce the chap. What we are saying is that she undoubtedly learned of her husband's involvement; she's afraid to remain in England. We don't think she plans to return.'

Again, there was silence, until McAuliff broke it.

'When you say "afraid", I presume you mean she's been threatened.'

'Quite possibly. Whatever she knows could be damaging. Booth didn't take the divorce action very well. Not from the point of view of affection – he's quite a womanizer – but, we suspect, for reasons related to his travels.' Warfield refolded the pages and put them back into his overcoat pocket.

'Well,' said Alex, 'that's quite a ... minor explosion. I'm not sure I'm ready for it.'

'I gave you this information on Mrs Booth because we thought you'd find out for yourself. We wanted to prepare you, not to dissuade you.'

McAuliff turned sharply and looked at Warfield. 'You want her along because she might ... might possibly be valuable to you. And not for geological reasons.' *Easy, McAuliff. Easy!*

'Anything is conceivable in these complicated times.'

'I don't like it!'

'You haven't thought about it. It is our opinion that she's infinitely safer in Jamaica than in London. You are concerned, aren't you? You've seen her frequently during the past week.'

'I don't like being followed, either.' It was all Alex could think to say.

'Whatever was done was minimal and for your protection,' replied Warfield quickly.

'Against what? For Christ's sake, protection from whom?' McAuliff stared at the little old man, realizing how much he disliked him. He wondered if Warfield would be any more explicit than Hammond on the subject of protection. Or would he admit the existence of a prior Jamaican survey? 'I think I have a right to be told,' he added angrily.

'You shall be. First, however, I should like to show you these papers. I trust everything will be to your satisfaction.' Warfield lifted the flap of the unsealed envelope and withdrew several thin pages stapled together on top of a single page of stationery. They were onionskin carbons of his lengthy letter of agreement signed in Belgrave Square over a week ago. He reached above, snapped on his own reading lamp, took the papers from Warfield, and flipped over the carbons to the thicker page of stationery. Only it wasn't stationery; it was a Xerox copy of a letter deposit transfer from the Chase Manhattan Bank in New York. The figures were clear: On the left was the amount paid into his account by a Swiss concern; on the right, the maximum taxes on that amount, designated as income, to the Swiss authorities and the United States Internal Revenue Service.

The net figure was $1,270,000.

He looked over at Warfield. 'My first payment was to have been twenty-five per cent of the total contract upon principal work of the survey. We agreed that would be the team's arrival in Kingston. Prior to that date, you're responsible only for my expenses and, if we terminate, five hundred a day for my time. Why the change?'

'We're very pleased with your preliminary labours. We wanted to indicate our good faith.'

'I don't believe you—'

'Besides,' continued Warfield, raising his voice over Alex's objections, 'there's been no contractual change.'

'I know what I signed.'

'Not too well, apparently. Go on, read the agreement. It states clearly that you will be paid a *minimum* of twenty-five per cent; *no later* than the end of the business day we determined to be the start of the survey. It says nothing about an excess of twenty-five per cent; no prohibitions as to an earlier date. We thought you'd be pleased.' The old man folded his small hands like some kind of Gandhi the Nonviolent in Savile Row clothes.

McAuliff reread the transfer letter from Chase Manhattan. 'This bank transfer describes the money as payment for services rendered as of today's date. That's past tense, free and clear. You'd have a hard time recouping if I didn't go to Jamaica. And considering your paranoia over secrecy, I doubt you'd try too hard. No, Mr Warfield, this is out of character.'

'Faith, Mr McAuliff. Your generation overlooks it.' The financier smiled benignly.

'I don't wish to be rude, but I don't think you ever had it. Not that way. You're a manipulator, not an ideologue. I repeat: out of character.'

'Very well.' Warfield unfolded his delicate hands, still retaining the Gandhi pose under the yellow light. 'It leads to the protection of which I spoke and which, rightly, you question. You are one of us, Alexander Tarquin McAuliff. A very important and essential part of Dunstone's plans. In recognition of your contributions, we have recommended to our directors that you be elevated – in confidence – to their status. Ergo, the payments made to you are the initial monies due one of our own. As you say, it would be out of character for such excessive payments to be made otherwise.'

'What the hell are you driving at?'

'In rather abrupt words, don't every try to deny us. You are a consenting participant in our work. Should you at any time, for whatever motive, decide you do not approve of Dunstone, don't try to separate yourself. You'd never be believed.'

McAuliff stared at the now smiling old man. 'Why would I do that?' he asked softly.

'Because we have reason to believe there are . . . elements most anxious to stop our progress. They may try to reach you; perhaps they have already. Your future is with us. No one else. Financially, perhaps ideologically . . . certainly legally.'

Alex looked away from Warfield. The Rolls had proceeded west into New Oxford, south on Charing Cross, and west again on Shaftesbury. They were approaching the outer lights of Piccadilly Circus, the gaudy colors diffused by the heavy mist.

'Who were you trying to call so frantically this evening?' The old man was not smiling now.

McAuliff turned from the window. 'Not that it's any of your damned business, but I was calling – not frantically – Mrs Booth. We're having lunch tomorrow. Any irritation was due to your hastily scheduled meeting and the fact that I didn't want to disturb her after midnight. Who do you think?'

'You shouldn't be so hostile—'

'I forgot,' interrupted Alex. 'You're only trying to protect me. From . . . elements.'

'I can be somewhat more precise.' Julian Warfield's eyes bore into Alex's, with an intensity he had not seen before. 'There would be no point in your lying to me, so I expect the truth. What does the word "Halidon" mean to you, Mr McAuliff?'

6

The screaming, hysterical cacophony of the acid-rock music caused a sensation of actual pain in the ears.

The eyes were attacked next, by tear-provoking layers of heavy smoke, thick and translucent – the nostrils reacting immediately to the pungent sweetness of tobacco laced with grass and hashish.

McAuliff made his way through the tangled network of soft flesh, separating thrusting arms and protruding shoulders gently but firmly, finally reaching the rear of the bar area.

The Owl of Saint George was at its undulating peak. The psychedelic lights exploded against the walls and ceiling in rhythmic crescendos; bodies were concave and convex, none seemingly upright, all swaying, writhing violently.

Hammond was seated in a circular booth with five others: two men and three women. Alex paused, concealed by drinkers and dancers, and looked at Hammond's gathering. It was funny; not sardonically funny, humorously funny. Hammond and his middle-aged counterpart across the table were dressed in the 'straight' fashion, as were two of the three women, both of them past forty. The remaining couple was young, hip, and profuse with black leather and zippers. The picture was instantly recognizable: parents indulging the generation gap, uncomfortable but game.

McAuliff remembered the man's words on High Holborn. *Stay at the bar, he'll reach you.* He manoeuvred his way to within arm's length of the mahogany and managed to shout his order to the black Soho bartender with hair so short he looked bald. McAuliff wondered when Hammond would make his move; he did not want to wait long. He had a great deal to say to the British agent.

'Pardon, but you are a chap named McAuliff, aren't you?' The shouted question caused Alex to spill part of his drink. The shouter was the young man from Hammond's table. Hammond was not wasting time.

'Yes. Why?'

'My girl's parents recognized you. Asked me to invite you over.'

The following moments, McAuliff felt, were like a play within a play. A brief, staged exercise with acutely familiar dialogue, acted out in front of a bored audience of other, more energetic actors. But with a surprise that made Alex consider Hammond's skill in a very favorable light.

He *did* know the middle-aged man across from Hammond. And his wife. Not well, of course, but they were acquaintances. He'd met them two or three times before, on previous London trips. They weren't the sort of memorable people one recognized on the street – or in The Owl of Saint George – unless the circumstances were recalled.

Hammond was introduced by his correct name and McAuliff was seated next to him.

'How the hell did you arrange this?' asked Alex after five excruciating minutes remembering the unmemorable with the acquaintances. 'Do they know who you are?'

'Laugh occasionally,' answered Hammond with a calm, precise smile. 'They believe I'm somewhere in that great government pyramid, juggling figures in poorly lit rooms ... The arrangements were necessary. Warfield has doubled his teams on you. We're not happy about it; he may have spotted us, but, of course, it's unlikely.'

'He's spotted something, I guarantee it.' Alex bared his teeth, but the smile was false. 'I've got a lot to talk to you about. Where can we meet?'

'Here. Now,' was the Britisher's reply. 'Speak occasionally to the others, but it's perfectly acceptable that we strike up a conversation. We might use it as a basis for lunch or drinks in a day or two.'

'No way. I leave for Kingston the day after tomorrow in the morning.'

Hammond paused, his glass halfway to his lips. 'So soon? We didn't expect that.'

'It's insignificant compared to something else ... Warfield knows about Halidon. That is, he asked me what *I* knew about it.'

'*What?*'

'Mr McAuliff?' came the shouted inquiry from across the table. 'Surely you know the Bensons, from Kent ...'

The timing was right, thought Alex. Hammond's reaction was one of astonishment. Shock that changed swiftly to angered acceptance. The ensuing conversation about the unremembered Bensons would give Hammond time to think. And Alex wanted him to think.

'What *exactly* did he say?' asked Hammond. The revolving psychedelic lights now projected their sharp patterns on the table, giving the agent a grotesque appearance.

'The exact words.'

'"What does the word 'Halidon' mean to you?" That's what he said.'

'Your answer?'

'What answer? I didn't have one. I told him it was a town in New Jersey.'

'I beg your pardon?'

'Halidon, New Jersey. It's a town.'

'Different spelling, I believe. And pronunciation. Did he accept your ignorance?'

'Why wouldn't he? I'm ignorant.'

'Did you conceal the fact that you'd heard the word? It's terribly important!'

'Yes ... yes, I think I did. As a matter of fact, I was thinking about something else. Several other things—'

'Did he bring it up later?' broke in the agent.

'No, he didn't. He stared hard, but he didn't mention it again. What do you think it means?'

Suddenly a gyrating, spaced-out dancer careened against the table, his eyes half focused, his lips parted without control. 'Well, if it ain't old Mums and Dadsies!' he said, slurring his words with rough Yorkshire. 'Enjoying the kiddie's show-and-tell, Mums?'

'Damn!' Hammond had spilled part of his drink.

'Ring for the butler, Pops! Charge it to old Edinburgh. He's a personal friend, good old Edinburgh.'

The solo, freaked-out dancer bolted away as quickly as he had intruded. The other middle-aged straights were appropriately solicitous of Hammond, simultaneously scathing of The Owl's patrons; the youngsters did their best to mollify.

'It's all right, nothing to be concerned with,' said the agent good-naturedly. 'Just a bit of damp, nothing to it.'

Hammond removed his handkerchief and began blotting his front. The table returned to its prior and individual conversations. The Britisher turned to McAuliff, his resigned smile belying his words. 'I have less than a minute; you'll be contacted tomorrow if necessary.'

'You mean that ... collision was a signal?'

'Yes. Now, listen and commit. I haven't time to repeat myself. When you reach Kingston, you'll be on your own for a while. Quite frankly, we weren't prepared for you so soon—'

'Just a minute!' interrupted McAuliff, his voice low, angry. 'Goddamn you! *You* listen ... and commit! You guaranteed complete safety, contacts twenty-four hours a day. It was on that basis I agreed—'

'Nothing has changed.' Hammond cut in swiftly, smiling paternalistically – in contradiction to the quiet hostility between them. 'You have contacts; you've memorized eighteen, twenty names—'

'In the north country, not Kingston! You're supposed to deliver the Kingston names!'

'We'll do our best for tomorrow.'

'That's not good enough!'

'It will have to be, Mr McAuliff,' said Hammond coldly. 'In Kingston, east of Victoria Park on Duke Street, there is a fish store called Tallon's. In the last extremity – and only then – should you wish to transmit information, see the owner. He's quite arthritic in his right hand. But, mind you, all he can do is transmit. He's of no other use to you. Now, I really must go.'

'I've got a few other things to say.' Alex put his hand on Hammond's arm.

'They'll have to wait—'

'One thing. Alison Booth. You knew, didn't you?'

'About her husband?'

'Yes.'

421

'We did. Frankly, at first, we thought she was a Dunstone plant. We haven't ruled it out.... Oh, you asked about Warfield's mention of Halidon; what he meant. In my judgment, he knows no more than we do. And he's trying just as hard to find out.'

With the swiftness associated with a much younger man, Hammond lifted himself up from the booth, slid past McAuliff, and excused himself from the group. McAuliff found himself seated next to the middle-aged woman he presumed had come with Hammond. He had not listened to her name during the introductions, but as he looked at her now, he did not have to be told. The concern – the fear – was in her eyes; she tried to conceal it, but she could not. Her smile was hesitant, taut.

'So you're the young man ...' Mrs Hammond stopped and brought the glass to her lips.

'Young and not so young,' said McAuliff, noting that the woman's hand shook, as his had shaken an hour ago with Warfield. 'It's difficult to talk in here with all the blaring. And those godawful lights.'

Mrs Hammond seemed not to hear or be concerned with his words. The psychedelic oranges and yellows and sickening greens played a visual tattoo on her frightened features. It was strange, thought Alex, but he had not considered Hammond as a private man with personal possessions or a wife or even a private, personal life.

And as he thought about these unconsidered realities, the woman suddenly gripped his forearm and leaned against him. Under the maddening sounds and through the wild, blinding lights, she whispered in McAuliff's ear: 'For God's sake, go after him!'

The undulating bodies formed a violently writhing wall. He lunged through, pushing, pulling, shoving, finally shouldering a path for himself amid the shouted obscenities. He tried looking around for the spaced-out intruder who had signaled Hammond by crashing into the table. He was nowhere to be found.

Then, at the rear of the crowded, flashing dance floor, he could see the interrupted movements of several men pushing a single figure back into a narrow corridor. It was Hammond!

He crashed through the writhing wall again, toward the back of the room. A tall black man objected to Alex's assault.

'Hey, mon! Stop it! You own The Owl, I think not!'

'Get out of my way! Goddammit, take your hands off me!'

'With pleasure, mon!' The black man removed his hands from McAuliff's coat, pulled back a tight fist, and hammered it into Alex's stomach. The force of the blow, along with the shock of its utter surprise, caused McAuliff to double up.

He rose as fast as he could, the pain sharp, and lurched for the man. As he did so, the black man twisted his wrist somehow, and McAuliff fell into the surrounding, nearly oblivious, dancers. When he got to his feet, the attacker was gone.

It was a curious and very painful moment.

The smoke and its accompanying odors made him dizzy; then he understood. He was breathing deep breaths; he was out of breath. With less strength but no less intensity, he continued through the dancers to the narrow corridor.

It was a passageway to the rest rooms, 'Chicks' to the right, 'Roosters' to the left. At the end of the narrow hallway was a door with a very large lock, an outsized padlock, that was meant, apparently, to remind patrons that the door was no egress; The Owl of Saint George expected tabs to be paid before departure.

The lock had been pried open. Pried open and then reset in the round hasps, its curving steel arm a half-inch from insertion.

McAuliff ripped it off and opened the door.

He walked out into a dark, very dark, alleyway filled with garbage cans and refuse. There was literally no light but the night sky, dulled by fog, and a minimum spill from the windows in the surrounding ghettolike apartment buildings. In front of him was a high brick wall; to the right the alley continued past other rear doorways, ending in a cul-de-sac formed by the sharply angled wall. To his left, there was a break between The Owl's building and the brick; it was a passageway to the street. It was also lined with garbage cans, and the stench that had to accompany their presence.

McAuliff started down the cement corridor, the light from the streetlamps illuminating the narrow confines. He was within twenty feet of the pavement when he saw it. Them: small pools of deep red fluid.

He raced out into the street. The crowds were thinning out; Soho was approaching its own witching hour. Its business was inside now: the private clubs, the illegal all-night gambling houses, the profitable beds where sex was found in varying ways and prices. He looked up and down the sidewalk, trying to find a break in the patterns of human traffic: a resistance, an eruption.

There was none.

He stared down at the pavement; the rivulets of blood had been streaked and blotted by passing feet, the red drops stopping abruptly at the curb. Hammond had been taken away in an automobile.

Without warning, McAuliff felt the impact of lunging hands against his back. He had turned sideways at the last instant, his eyes drawn by the flickering of a neon light, and that small motion kept him from being hurled into the street. Instead, his attacker – a huge black man – plunged over the curb, into the path of an onrushing Bentley, traveling at extraordinary speed. McAuliff felt a stinging pain on his face. Then man and vehicle collided; the anguished scream was the scream at the moment of death; the screeching wheels signified the incredible to McAuliff. The Bentley raced forward, crushing its victim, and sped off. It reached the corner and whipped violently to the left, its tires spinning above the curb, whirring as they touched stone again, propelling the car out of sight. Pedestrians screamed, men ran, whores disappeared into the doorways, pimps gripped their pockets, and McAuliff stood above the bloody, mangled corpse in the street and knew it was meant to be him.

He ran down the Soho street; he did not know where, just away. Away from the gathering crowds on the pavement behind. There would be questions, witnesses ... people placing him at the scene – *involved*, not placed, he reflected. He had no answers, and instinctively he knew he could not allow himself to be identified – not until he had some answers.

The dead black man was the one who had confronted him in The Owl of Saint George, of that he was certain: the man who had stunned him with a savage blow to the stomach on the dance floor and twisted his wrist, throwing him into the surrounding gyrating bodies. The man who had stopped him from reaching Hammond in the narrow corridor that led past the 'Chicks' and the 'Roosters' into the dark alleyway beyond.

Why had the black man stopped him? Why for Christ Almighty's sake had he tried to kill him?

Where was Hammond?

He had to get to a telephone. He had to call Hammond's number and speak to someone, anyone who could give him some answers.

Suddenly, Alex was aware that people in the street were staring at him. Why? Of course. He was running – well, walking too rapidly. A man walking rapidly at this hour on a misty Soho street was conspicuous. He couldn't be conspicuous; he slowed his walk, his aimless walk, and aimlessly crossed unfamiliar streets.

Still they stared. He tried not to panic. What *was* it?

And then he knew. He could feel the warm blood trickling down his cheek. He remembered now: the sting on his face as the huge black hands went crashing past him over the curb. A ring perhaps. A fingernail ... what difference? He had been cut, and he was bleeding. He reached into his coat pocket for a handkerchief. The whole side of his jacket had been ripped.

He had been too stunned to notice or feel the jacket ripping, or the blood.

Christ! What a sight! A man in a torn jacket with blood on his face, running away from a dead black man in Soho.

Dead? Deceased? Life spent?

No. Murdered.

But the method meant for him: a violent thrust into the street, timed to meet the heavy steel of an onrushing, racing Bentley.

In the middle of the next block – what block? – there was a telephone booth. An English telephone booth, wider and darker than its American cousin. He quickened his pace as he withdrew coins from his pocket. He went inside; it was dark, too dark. Why was it so dark? He took out his metal cigarette lighter, gripping it as though it were a handle that, if released, would send him plunging into an abyss. He pressed the lever, breathed deeply, and dialed by the light of the flame.

'We know what's happened, Mr McAuliff,' said the clipped, cool British voice. 'Where precisely are you calling from?'

'I don't know. I ran ... I crossed a number of streets.'

'It's urgent we know where you are. When you left The Owl, which way did you walk?'

'I *ran*, goddammit! I *ran*. Someone tried to *kill* me!'

'Which *way* did you run, Mr McAuliff?'

'To the right ... four or five blocks. Then right again; then left, I think two blocks later.'

'All right. Relax, now. You're phoning from a call booth?'

'Yes. No, damn it, I'm *calling* from a *phone* booth! ... Yes. For Christ's sake, tell me what's happening! There aren't any street signs; I'm in the middle of the block.'

'Calm down, please.' The Englishman was maddening: imperviously condescending. 'What are the structures outside the booth? Describe anything you like, anything that catches your eye.'

McAuliff complained about the fog and described as best he could the darkened shops and building. 'Christ, that's the best I can do. I'm going to get out of here. I'll grab a taxi somehow; and then I want to see one of you! Where do I go?'

'You will *not* go *anywhere*, Mr McAuliff!' The cold British tones were suddenly loud and harsh. 'Stay right where you are. If there is a light in the booth, smash it. We know your position. We'll pick you up in minutes.'

Alex hung up the receiver. There was no light bulb in the booth, of course. The tribes of Soho had removed it. He tried to think. He hadn't gotten any answers. Only orders. More commands.

It was insane. The last half-hour was madness. What was he *doing*? Why was he in a darkened telephone booth with a bloody face and a torn jacket, trembling and afraid to light a cigarette?

Madness!

There was a man outside the booth, jingling coins in his hand and pointedly shifting his weight from foot to foot in irritation. The command over the telephone had instructed Alex to wait inside, but to do so under the circumstances might cause the man on the pavement to object vocally, drawing attention. He could call someone else, he thought. But who? Alison? No ... He had to think about Alison now, not talk with her.

He was behaving like a terrified child! With terrifying justification, perhaps. He was actually afraid to move, to walk outside a telephone booth and let an impatient man jingling coins go in. No, he couldn't behave like that. He could not freeze. He had learned that lesson years ago – centuries ago – in Vietnam. To freeze was to become a target. One had to be flexible within the perimeters of common sense. One had to, above all, use his natural antennae and stay intensely alert. Staying alert, retaining the ability and capacity to move swiftly, these were the important things.

Jesus! He was correlating the murderous fury of Vietnam with a back street in Soho. He was actually drawing a parallel and forcing himself to adjust to it. Too goddamn much!

He opened the door, blotted his cheek, and mumbled his apologies to the man jingling coins. He walked to a recessed doorway opposite the booth and waited.

The man on Hammond's telephone was true to his word. The wait wasn't long, and the automobile recognizable as one of those Alex and the agent had used several times. It came down the street at a steady pace and stopped by the booth, its motor running.

McAuliff left the darkness of the recessed doorway and walked rapidly to the car. The rear door was flung open for him, and he climbed in.

And he froze again.

The man in the back seat was black. The man in the back seat was supposed to be dead, a mangled corpse in the street in front of The Owl of Saint George!

'Yes, Mr McAuliff. It is I,' said the black man who was supposed to be dead. 'I apologize for having struck you, but then, you were intruding. Are you all right?'

'Oh my God!' Alex was rigid on the edge of the seat as the automobile lurched forward and sped off down the street. 'I thought . . . I mean, I saw . . .'

'We're on our way to Hammond. You'll understand better then. Sit back. You've had a very strenuous past hour. Quite unexpectedly, incidentally.'

'*I saw you killed!*' McAuliff blurted out the words involuntarily.

'You saw a black man killed, a large black man like myself. We do weary of the bromide that we all look alike. It's both unflattering and untrue. By the way, my name is Tallon.'

McAuliff stared at the man. 'No, it's not. Tallon is the name of a fish store near Victoria Park. In Kingston.'

The black laughed softly. 'Very good, Mr McAuliff. I was testing you. Smoke?'

Alex took the offered cigarette gratefully. 'Tallon' held a match for him, and McAuliff inhaled deeply, trying to find a brief moment of sanity.

He looked at his hands. He was both astonished and disturbed.

He was cupping the glow of the cigarette as he had once done centuries ago as an infantry officer in the jungles of Vietnam.

They drove for nearly twenty minutes, traveling swiftly through the London streets to the outskirts. McAuliff did not try to follow their route by looking out the window; he did not really care. He was consumed with the decision he had to make. In a profound way it was related to the sight of his hands – no longer trembling – cupping the cigarette. From the nonexistent wind? From betraying his position? From enemy snipers?

No. He was not a soldier, had never been one really. He had performed because it was the only way to survive. He had no motive other than survival; no war was his or ever would be his. Certainly not Hammond's.

'Here we are, Mr McAuliff,' said the black man who called himself Tallon. 'Rather deserted place, isn't it?'

The car had entered a road by a field – a field, but not grass covered. It was a leveled expanse of ground, perhaps five acres, that looked as though it was being primed for construction. Beyond the field was a riverbank; Alex presumed it was the Thames, it had to be. In the distance were large square structures that looked like warehouses. Warehouses along a riverbank. He had no idea where they were.

The driver made a sharp left turn, and the automobile bounced as it rolled over a primitive car path on the rough ground. Through the windshield, McAuliff saw in the glare of the headlamps two vehicles about a hundred yards away, both sedans. The one on the right had its inside lights on. Within seconds, the driver had pulled up parallel with the second car.

McAuliff got out and followed 'Tallon' to the lighted automobile. What he saw bewildered him, angered him, perhaps, and unquestionably reaffirmed his decision to remove himself from Hammond's war.

The British agent was sitting stiffly in the rear seat, his shirt and overcoat draped over his shoulders, an open expanse of flesh at his midsection revealing wide, white bandages. His eyes were squinting slightly, betraying the fact that the pain was not negligible. Alex knew the reason; he had seen the sight before – centuries ago – usually after a bayonet encounter.

Hammond had been stabbed.

'I had you brought here for two reasons, McAuliff. And I warrant you, it was a gamble,' said the agent as Alex stood by the open door. 'Leave us alone, please,' he added to the black man.

'Shouldn't you be in a hospital?'

'No, it's not a severe penetration.'

'You got cut, Hammond,' interrupted McAuliff. 'That's severe enough.'

'You're melodramatic; it's unimportant. You'll notice, I trust, that I am very much alive.'

'You're lucky.'

'Luck, sir, had nothing whatsoever to do with it! That's part of what I want you to understand.'

'All right. You're Captain Marvel, indestructible nemesis of the evil people.'

'I am a fifty-year-old veteran of Her Majesty's Service who was never very good at football ... soccer, to you.' Hammond winced and leaned forward. 'And it's quite possible I would not be in these extremely tight bandages had you followed my instructions and not made a scene on the dance floor.'

'What?'

'But you provoke me into straying. First things first. The instant it was apparent that I was in danger, that danger was removed. At no time, at no moment, was my life in jeopardy.'

'Because you say so? With a ten-inch bandage straddling your stomach? Don't try to sell water in the Sahara.'

'This wound was delivered in panic caused by you! I was in the process of making the most vital contact on our schedule, the contact we sought you out to make.'

'Halidon?'

'It's what we believed. Unfortunately, there's no way to verify. Come with me.' Hammond gripped the side strap, and with his right hand supporting himself on the front seat as he climbed painfully out of the car. Alex made a minor gesture of assistance, knowing that it would be refused. The agent led McAuliff to the forward automobile, awkwardly removing a flashlight from his draped overcoat as they approached. There were several men in shadows; they stepped away, obviously under orders.

Inside the car were two lifeless figures: one sprawled over the wheel, the other slumped across the rear seat. Hammond shot the beam of light successively on both corpses. Each was male, black, in his mid-thirties, perhaps, and dressed in conservative, though not expensive, business suits. McAuliff was confused: there were no signs of violence, no shattered glass, no blood. The interior of the car was neat, clean, even peaceful. The two dead men might have been a pair of young executives taking a brief rest off the highway in the middle of a long business trip. Alex's bewilderment ended with Hammond's next word.

'Cyanide.'

'Why?'

'Fanatics, obviously. It was preferable to revealing information ... unwillingly, of course. They misread us. It began when you made such an obvious attempt to follow me out of The Owl of Saint George. That was their first panic; when they inflicted ... this.' Hammond waved his hand just once at his midsection.

McAuliff did not bother to conceal his anger. 'I've about had it with your goddamn caustic deductions!'

'I told you it was a gamble bringing you here—'

'Stop *telling* me things!'

'Please bear in mind that without us you had a life expectancy of four months – at the outside.'

'Your version.' But the agent's version had more substance than McAuliff cared to think about at the moment. Alex turned away from the unpleasant sight. For no particular reason, he ripped the torn lining from the base of his jacket and leaned against the hood of the car. 'Since you hold me responsible for so much tonight, what happened?'

The Britisher told him. Several days ago, MI5's surveillance had picked up a second 'force' involved with Dunstone's movements. Three, possibly four, unidentifiable subjects who kept reappearing. The subjects were black. Photographs were taken, fingerprints obtained by way of restaurants, discarded objects – cigarette packs, newspapers, and the like – and all the data fed into the computers at New Scotland Yard and Emigration. There were no records; the subjects were 'negative' insofar as Dunstone was concerned. Obvious ... then proven without doubt earlier in the evening, when one of the subjects killed a Dunstone man who spotted him.

'We knew then,' said Hammond, 'that we had centered in; the target was accurate. It remained to make positive contact, sympathetic contact. I even toyed with the idea of bringing these men and you together in short order, perhaps this morning. So much resolved so damned quickly . . .'

A cautious preliminary contact was made with the subjects: 'so harmless and promising, we damn near offered what was left of the Empire. They were concerned, of course, with a trap.'

A rendezvous was arranged at The Owl of Saint George, a racially integrated club that offered a comfortable environment. It was scheduled for two thirty in the morning, after Hammond's meeting with McAuliff.

When Alex made his panicked – and threatening – call to Hammond's number, insisting that they meet regardless of time, the agent left his options open. And then made his decision. Why not The Owl of Saint George? Bring the American into Soho, to the club, and if it proved the wrong decision, McAuliff could be stopped once inside. If the decision was the right one, the circumstances would be optimal – all his parties present.

'What about Warfield's men?' asked Alex. 'You said he doubled his teams on me.'

'I lied. I wanted you to remain where you were. Warfield had a single man on you. We diverted him. The Dunstone people had their own anxieties: One of their men had been killed. You couldn't be held responsible for that.'

The night progressed as Hammond had anticipated: without incident. The agent made arrangements for the table – 'we know just about everyone you've met in London, chap' – and awaited the compatible merging of elements.

And then, in rapid succession, each component fell apart. First was Alex's statement that the survey team was leaving in two days – MI5 and its counterpart overseas, MI6, were not ready for them in Kingston. Then the information that Warfield had spoken the name of 'Halidon'; it was to be expected, of course. Dunstone would be working furiously to find the killers of the first survey team. But, again, MI5 had not expected Dunstone to have made such progress. The next breakdown was the spaced-out agent who crashed into the table and used the word 'Edinburgh' – used it twice.

'Each twenty-four-period we circulate an unusual word that has but one connotation: "abort, extreme prejudice." If it's repeated, that simply compounds the meaning: Our cover is blown. Or misread. Weapons should be ready.'

At that moment, Hammond saw clearly the massive error that had been made. His agents had diverted Warfield's men away from Alex, but not one of the black men. McAuliff had been observed in Warfield's company at midnight for a considerable length of time. Within minutes after he had walked into The Owl, his black surveillance had followed, panicked that his colleagues had been led into a trap.

The confrontation had begun within the gyrating, psychedelic madness that was The Owl of Saint George.

Hammond tried to stop the final collapse.

He broke the rules. It was not yet two thirty, but since Alexander McAuliff had been seen with him, he dared not wait. He tried to establish a bridge, to explain, to calm the raging outburst.

He had nearly succeeded when one of the black men – now dead behind the wheel – saw McAuliff leap from his seat in the booth and plunge into the crowds, whipping people out of his way, looking frantically – obviously – for Hammond.

This sight triggered the panic. Hammond was cut, used as a shield, and propelled out the rear door into the alley by two of the subjects while the third fled through the crowds in front to alert the car for escape.

'What happened during the next few minutes was as distressing as it was comforting,' said Hammond. 'My people would not allow my physical danger, so the instant my captors and I emerged on the pavement, they were taken. We put them in this car and drove off, still hoping to re-establish goodwill. But we purposely allowed the third man to disappear – an article of faith on our part.'

The MI5 had driven out to the deserted field. A doctor was summoned to patch up Hammond. And the two subjects – relieved of weapons, car key removed unobtrusively – were left alone to talk by themselves, hopefully to resolve their doubts, while Hammond was being bandaged.

'They made a last attempt to get away but, of course, there were no keys in the vehicle. So they took their deadly little vials or tablets and, with them, their lives. Ultimately, they could not trust us.'

McAuliff said nothing for several moments. Hammond did not interrupt the silence.

'And your "article of faith" tried to kill me.'

'Apparently. Leaving one man in England we must try to find: the driver. You understand that we cannot be held accountable; you completely disregarded our instructions—'

'We'll get to that,' broke in McAuliff. 'You said you brought me out here for two reasons. I get the first: Your people are quick, safety guaranteed . . . if instructions aren't "disregarded."' Alex mimicked Hammond's reading of the word. 'What's the second reason?'

The agent walked directly in front of McAuliff and, through the night light, Alex could see the intensity in his eyes. 'To tell you that you have no choice but to continue now. Too much has happened. You're too involved.'

'That's what Warfield said.'

'He's right.'

'Suppose I refuse? Suppose I just pack up and leave?'

'You'd be suspect, and expendable. You'd be hunted down. Take my word for that, I've been here before.'

'That's quite a statement from a – what was it, a financial analyst?'

'Labels, Mr McAuliff. Titles. Quite meaningless.'

'Not to your wife.'

'I beg your—' Hammond inhaled deeply, audible. When he continued, he did not ask a question. He made a quiet, painful statement. 'She sent you after me.'

'Yes.'

It was Hammond's turn to remain silent. And Alex's option not to break that silence. Instead, McAuliff watched the fifty-year-old agent struggle to regain his composure.

'The fact remains, you disregarded my instructions.'

'You must be a lovely man to live with.'

'Get used to it,' replied Hammond with cold precision. 'For the next several months, our association will be very close. And you'll do exactly as I say. Or you'll be dead.'

Part Two

Kingston

7

The red-orange sun burned a hole in the streaked blue tapestry that was the evening sky. Arcs of yellow rimmed the lower clouds; a purplish-black void was above. The soft Caribbean night would soon envelop this section of the world. It would be dark when the plane landed at Port Royal.

McAuliff stared out at the horizon through the tinted glass of the aircraft's window. Alison Booth was in the seat beside him, asleep.

The Jensens were across the 747's aisle, and for a couple whose political persuasions were left of center, they adapted to British Air's first-class accommodations with a remarkable lack of guilt, thought Alex. They ordered the best wine, the foie gras, duck à l'orange, and Charlotte Malakof as if they had been used to them for years. And Alex wondered if Warfield was wrong. All the left-oriented he knew, outside the former Soviet bloc, were humorless; the Jensens were not.

Young James Ferguson was alone in a forward seat. Initially, Charles Whitehall had sat with him, but Whitehall had gone up to the lounge early in the flight, found an acquaintance from Savanna-la-Mar, and stayed. Ferguson used the unoccupied seat for a leather bag containing photographic equipment. He was currently changing lens filters, snapping shots of the sky outside.

McAuliff and Alison had joined Charles Whitehall and his friend for several drinks in the lounge. The friend was white, rich and a heavy drinker. He was also a vacuous inheritor of old southwest Jamaican money, and Alex found it contradictory that Whitehall would care to spend much time with him. It was a little disturbing to watch Whitehall respond with such alacrity to his friend's alcoholic, unbright, unfunny observations.

Alison had touched McAuliff's arm after the second drink. It had been a signal to return to their seats; she had had enough. So had he.

Alison?

During the last two days in London there had been so much to do that he had not spent the time with her he had wanted to, intended to. He was involved with all-day problems of logistics: equipment purchases and rentals, clearing passports, ascertaining whether inoculations were required (none was), establishing bank accounts in Montego, Kingston, and Ocho Rios, and scores of additional items necessary for a long geological survey. Dunstone

435

stayed out of the picture but was of enormous help behind the scenes. The Dunstone people told him precisely whom to contact where; the tangled webs of bureaucracy – governmental and commercial – were untangled.

He had spent one evening bringing everyone together – everyone but Sam Tucker, who would join them in Kingston. Dinner at Simpsons. It was sufficiently agreeable; all were professionals. Each sized up the others and made flattering comments where work was known. Whitehall received the most recognition – as was appropriate. He was an authentic celebrity of sorts. Ruth Jensen and Alison seemed genuinely to like each other, which McAuliff had thought would happen. Ruth's husband, Peter, assumed a paternalistic attitude toward Ferguson, laughing gently, continuously at the young man's incessant banter. And Charles Whitehall had the best manners, slightly aloof and very proper, with just the right traces of scholarly wit and unfelt humility.

But Alison.

He had kept their luncheon date after the madness at The Owl of Saint George and the insanity that followed in the deserted field on London's outskirts. He had approached her with ambivalent feelings. He was annoyed that she had not brought up the questionable activities of her recent husband. But he did not accept Hammond's vague concern that Alison was a Warfield plant. It was senseless. She was nothing if not independent – as was he. To be a silent emissary from Warfield meant losing independence – as he knew. Alison could not do that, not without showing it.

Still, he tried to provoke her into talking about her husband. She responded with humorously 'civilized' clichés, such as 'let's let sleeping dogs lie', which he had. Often. She would not, at this point, discuss David Booth with him.

It was not relevant.

'Ladies and gentlemen,' said the very masculine in-charge tones over the aircraft's speaker. 'This is Captain Thomas. We are nearing the northeast coast of Jamaica; in several minutes we shall be over Port Antonio, descending for our approach to Palisados Airport, Port Royal. May we suggest that all passengers return to their seats. There may be minor turbulence over the Blue Mountain range. Time of arrival is now anticipated at eight twenty, Jamaican. The temperature in Kingston is seventy-eight degrees, weather and visibility clear . . .'

As the calm, strong voice finished the announcement, McAuliff thought of Hammond. If the British agent spoke over a loudspeaker, he would sound very much like Captain Thomas, Alex considered.

Hammond.

McAuliff had not ended their temporary disassociation – as Hammond phrased it – too pleasantly. He had countered the agent's caustic pronouncement that Alex do as Hammond instructed with a volatile provision of his own: He had a million dollars coming to him from Dunstone Limited, and he expected to collect it. From Dunstone or some other source.

Hammond had exploded. What good were two million dollars to a dead geologist? Alex should be paying for the warnings and the protection afforded him. But, in the final analysis, Hammond recognized the necessity for something to motivate Alexander's cooperation. Survival was too abstract; lack of survival could not be experienced.

In the early morning hours, a letter of agreement was brought to McAuliff by a temporary Savoy floor steward; Alex recognized him as the man in the brown mackinaw on High Holborn. The letter covered the condition of reimbursement in the event of 'loss of fees' with a *very* clear ceiling of one million dollars.

If he remained in one piece – and he had every expectation of so doing – he would collect. He mailed the agreement to New York.

Hammond.

He wondered what the explanation was; what could explain a wife whose whispered voice could hold such fear? He wondered about the private, personal Hammond, yet knew instinctively that whatever private questions he had would never be answered.

Hammond was like that. Perhaps all the people who did what Hammond did were like that. Men in shadows; their women in unending tunnels of fear. Pockets of fear.

And then there was . . .

Halidon.

What did it mean? What was it?

Was it a black organization?

Possibly. Probably not, however, Hammond had said. At least, not exclusively. It had too many informational resources, too much apparent influence in powerful sectors. Too much money.

The word had surfaced under strange and horrible circumstances. The British agent attached to the previous Dunstone survey had been one of two men killed in a bush fire that began inside a bamboo camp on the banks of the Martha Brae River, deep within the Cock Pit country. Evidence indicated that the two dead members of the survey had tried to salvage equipment within the fire, collapsed from the smoke, and burned in the bamboo inferno.

But there was something more; something so appalling that even Hammond found it difficult to recite it.

The two men had been bound by bamboo shoots to separate trees, each next to valuable survey equipment. They had been consumed in the conflagration, for the simple reason that neither could run from it. But the agent had left a message, a single word scratched on the metal casing of a geoscope.

Halidon.

Inspection under a microscope gave the remainder of the horror story: particles of human tooth enamel. The agent had scratched the letters with broken teeth.

Halidon . . . hollydawn.

No known definition. A word? A name? A man? A three-beat sound?

What did it mean?

'It's beautiful isn't it,' said Alison, looking beyond him through the window.

'You're awake.'

'Someone turned on a radio and a man spoke ... endlessly.' She smiled and stretched her long legs. She then inhaled in a deep yawn, which caused her breasts to swell against the soft white silk of her blouse. McAuliff watched. And she saw him watching, and smiled again – in humor, not provocation. 'Relevancy, Dr McAuliff. Remember?'

'That word's going to get you into trouble, Ms Booth.'

'I'll stop saying it instantly. Come to think, I don't believe I used it much until I met you.'

'I like the connection; don't stop.'

She laughed and reached for her pocketbook, on the deck between them. There was a sudden series of rise-and-fall motions as the plane entered air turbulence. It was over quickly, but during it Alison's open purse landed on its side – on Alex's lap. Lipstick, compact, matches, and a short thick tube fell out, wedging themselves between McAuliff's legs. It was one of those brief, indecisive moments. Pocketbooks were unfair vantage points, somehow unguarded extensions of the private self. And Alison was not the type to reach swiftly between a man's legs to retrieve property.

'Nothing fell on the floor,' said Alex awkwardly, handing Alison the purse. 'Here.'

He picked up the lipstick and the compact with his left hand, his right on the thick tube, which, at first, seemed to have a very personal connotation. As his eyes were drawn to the casing, however, the connotation became something else. The tube was a weapon, a compressor. On the cylinder's side were printed words:

312 GAS CONTENTS

FOR MILITARY AND/OR POLICE USE ONLY

AUTHORISATION NUMBER 4316

RECORDED: 1–6

The authorization number and the date had been handwritten in indelible ink. The gas compressor had been issued by British authorities a month ago.

Alison took the tube from his hand. 'Thank you,' was all she said.

'You planning to hijack the plane? That's quite a lethal-looking object.'

'London has its problems for girls ... women these days. There were incidents in my building. May I have a cigarette? I seem to be out.'

'Sure.' McAuliff reached into his shirt pocket and withdrew the cigarettes, shaking one up for her. He lighted it, then spoke softly, very gently. 'Why are you lying to me, Alison?'

'I'm not. I think it's presumptuous of you to think so.'

'Oh, come on.' He smiled, reducing the earnestness of his inquiry. 'The police, especially the London police, do not issue compressors of gas because of "incidents". And you don't look like a colonel in the Women's Auxiliary Army.' As he said the words, Alex suddenly had the feeling that perhaps he was wrong. Was Alison Booth an emissary from Hammond? Not Warfield, but British Intelligence?

'Exceptions are made. They really are, Alex.' She locked her eyes with his; she was not lying.

'May I venture a suggestion? A reason?'

'If you like.'

'David Booth?'

She looked away, inhaling deeply on her cigarette. 'You know about him. That's why you kept asking questions the other night.'

'Yes. Did you think I wouldn't find out?'

'I didn't care . . . no, that's not right; I think I wanted you to find out if it helped me get the job. But I couldn't tell you.'

'Why not?'

'Oh, Lord, Alex! Your own words; you wanted the best professionals, not personal problems! For all I knew, you'd have scratched me instantly.' Her smile was gone now. There was only anxiety.

'This Booth must be quite a fellow.'

'He's a very sick, very vicious man. But I can handle David. I was always able to handle him. He's an extraordinary coward.'

'Most vicious people are.'

'I'm not sure I subscribe to that. But it wasn't David. It was someone else. The man he worked for.'

'Who?'

'A Frenchman. A marquis. Chatellerault is his name.'

The team took separate taxis into Kingston. Alison remained behind with McAuliff while he commandeered the equipment with the help of the Jamaican government people attached to the Ministry of Education. Alex could feel the same vague resentment from the Jamaicans that he had felt with the academicians in London; only added now was the aspect of pigmentation. Were there no black geologists? they seemed to be thinking.

The point was emphasized by the Customs men, their khaki uniforms creased into steel. They insisted on examining each box, each carton, as though each contained the most dangerous contraband imaginable. They decided to be officially thorough as McAuliff stood helplessly by long after the aircraft had taxied into a Palisados berth. Alison remained ten yards away, sitting on a luggage dolly.

An hour and a half later, the equipment had been processed and marked for in-island transport to Boscobel Airfield, in Ocho Rios. McAuliff's temper was stretched to the point of gritted teeth and a great deal of swallowing. He grabbed Alison's arm and marched them both toward the terminal.

'For heaven's sake, Alex, you're bruising my elbow!' said Alison under her breath, trying to hold back her laughter.

'Sorry . . . I'm *sorry*. Those goddamned messiahs think they inherited the earth! The *bastards*!'

'This *is* their island—'

'I'm in no mood for anticolonial lectures,' he interrupted. 'I'm in the mood for a drink. Let's stop at the lounge.'

'What about our bags?'

'Oh. Christ! I forgot. It's this way, if I remember,' said Alex, pointing to a gate entrance on the right.

'Yes,' replied Alison. '"Incoming Flights" usually means that.'

'Be quiet. My first order to you as a subordinate is not to say another word until we get our bags and I have a drink in my hand.'

But McAuliff's command, by necessity, was rescinded. Their luggage was nowhere in sight. And apparently no one knew where it might be; all passenger baggage stored on Flight 640 from London had been picked up. An hour ago.

'*We* were on that flight. We did not pick up our bags. So, you see, you're mistaken,' Alex said curtly to the luggage manager.

'Then you look-see, mon,' answered the Jamaican, irritated by the American's implication that he was less than efficient. 'Every suitcase taken – nothing left. Flight Six Forty all *here*, mon! No place other.'

'Let me talk to the British Air representative. Where is he?'

'Who?'

'Your boss, goddammit!'

'I top mon!' replied the black man angrily.

Alex held himself in check. 'Look, there's been a mix-up. The airline's responsible, that's all I'm trying to say.'

'I think not, mon,' interjected the luggage manager defensively as he turned to a telephone on the counter. 'I will call British Air.'

'All heart.' McAuliff spoke softly to Alison. 'Our bags are probably on the way to Buenos Aires.' They waited while the man spoke briefly on the phone.

'Here, mon.' The manager held the phone for Alex. 'You talk, please.'

'Hello?'

'Dr McAuliff?' said the British voice.

'Yes. McAuliff.'

'We merely followed the instruction in your note, sir.'

'What note?'

'To First-Class Accommodations. The driver brought it to us. The taxi. Mrs Booth's and your luggage was taken to Courtleigh Manor. That is what you wished, is it not, sir?' The voice was laced with a trace of overclarification, as if the speaker were addressing someone who had had an extra drink he could not handle.

'I see. Yes, that's fine,' said Alex quietly. He hung up the telephone and turned to Alison. 'Our bags were taken to the hotel.'

'Really? Wasn't that nice.' A statement.

'No, I don't think it was,' answered McAuliff. 'Come on, let's find that bar.'

*

They sat at a corner table in the Palisados observation lounge. The red-jacketed waiter brought their drinks while humming a Jamaican folk tune softly. Alex wondered if the island's tourist bureau instructed all those who served visitors to hum tunes and move rhythmically. He reached for his glass and drank a large portion of his double Scotch. He noticed that Alison, who was not much of a drinker, seemed as anxious as he was to put some alcohol into her system.

All things considered – all things – it was conceivable that his luggage might be stolen. Not hers. But the note had specified his and Mrs Booth's.

'You didn't have any more artillery, did you?' asked Alex quickly. 'Like that compressor?'

'No. It would have set off bells in the airline X-ray. I'd declared this prior to boarding.' Alison pointed to her purse.

'Yes, of course,' he mumbled.

'I must say, you're remarkably calm. I should think you'd be telephoning the hotel, see if the bags got there . . . oh, not for me. I don't travel with the Crown jewels.'

'Oh, Lord, I'm sorry, Alison.' He pushed his chair back. 'I'll call right away.'

'No, please.' She reached out and put her hand over his. 'I think you're doing what you're doing for a reason. You don't want to appear upset. I think you're right. If they're gone, there's nothing I can't replace in the morning.'

'You're very understanding. Thanks.'

She withdrew her hand and drank again. He pulled his chair back and shifted his position slightly, toward the interior of the lounge. Unobtrusively, he began scanning the other tables.

The observation lounge was half filled, no more than that. From his position – their position – in the far west corner of the room, Alex could see nearly every table. And he slowly riveted his attention on every table, wondering, as he had wondered two nights ago on High Holborn, who might be concerned with *him*.

There was movement in the dimly lighted entrance. McAuliff's eyes were drawn to it: the figure of a stocky man in a white shirt and no jacket standing in the wide frame. He spoke to the lounge's hostess, shaking his head slowly, negatively, as he looked inside. Suddenly, Alex blinked and focused on the man.

He knew him.

A man he had last seen in Australia, in the fields of Kimberly Plateau. He had been told the man had retired to Jamaica.

Robert Hanley, a pilot.

Hanley was standing in the entranceway of the lounge, looking for someone inside. And Alex knew instinctively that Hanley was looking for him.

'Excuse me,' he said to Alison. 'There's a fellow I know. Unless I'm mistaken, he's trying to find me.'

McAuliff thought, as he threaded his way around the tables and through the subdued shadows of the room, that it was somehow right that Robert Hanley, of all the men in the Caribbean, would be involved. Hanley, the open man who dealt with a covert world because he was, above all, a man to be trusted. A laughing man, a tough man, a professional with expertise far beyond that required by those employing him. Someone who had miraculously survived six decades when all the odds indicated nearer to four. But then, Robert Hanley did not look much over forty-five. Even his close-cropped, reddish-blond hair was devoid of gray.

'Robert!'

'Alexander!'

The two men clasped hands and held each other's shoulders.

'I said to the lady sitting with me that I thought you were looking for me. I'll be honest, I hope I'm wrong.'

'I wish you were, lad.'

'That's what I was afraid of. What is it? Come on in.'

'In a minute. Let me tell you the news first. I wouldn't want the lady to uncork your temper.' Hanley led Alex away from the door; they stood alone by the wall. 'It's Sam Tucker.'

'*Sam?* Where is he?'

'That's the point, lad. I don't know. Sam flew into Mo'Bay three days ago and called me at Port Antone; the boys in Los Angeles told him I was here. I hopped over naturally, and it was a grand reunion. I won't go into the details. The next morning, Sam went down to the lobby to get a paper, I think. He never came back.'

8

Robert Hanley was flying back to Port Antonio in an hour. He and McAuliff agreed not to mention Sam Tucker to Alison. Hanley also agreed to keep looking for Sam; he and Alex would stay in touch.

The three of them took a taxi from Port Royal into Kingston, to Courtleigh Manor. Hanley remained in the cab and took it on to the small Tinson Pen Airfield, where he kept his plane.

At the hotel desk, Alex inquired nonchalantly, feeling no casualness whatsoever, 'I assume our luggage arrived?'

'Indeed, yes, Mr McAuliff,' replied the clerk, stamping both registration forms and signaling to a bellhop. 'Only minutes ago. We had them brought to your rooms. They're adjoining.'

'How thoughtful,' said Alex softly, wondering if Alison had heard the man behind the desk. The clerk did not speak loudly, and Alison was at the end of the counter, looking at tourist brochures. She glanced over at McAuliff; she had heard. The expression on her face was noncommittal. He wondered.

Five minutes later, she opened the door between their two rooms, and Alex knew there was no point speculating further.

'I did as you ordered, Mr Bossman,' said Alison, walking in. 'I didn't touch the—'

McAuliff held up his hand quickly signaling her to be quiet. 'The bed, bless your heart! You're all heart, luv!'

The expression now on Alison's face was definitely committal. Not pleasantly. It was an awkward moment, which he was not prepared for; he had not expected her to walk deliberately into his room. Still, there was no point standing immobile, looking foolish.

He reached into his jacket pocket and withdrew a small, square-shaped metal instrument the size of a cigarette pack. It was one of several items given him by Hammond. (Hammond had cleared his boarding pass with British Airways in London, eliminating the necessity of his declaring whatever metallic objects were on his person.)

The small metal box was an electronic scanner with a miniaturized high-voltage battery. Its function was simple, its mechanism complex, and Hammond claimed it was in very common use these days. It detected the presence of electronic listening devices within a nine- by nine-foot area. Alex had intended to use it the minute he entered the room. Instead, he absentmindedly had opened the doors to his small balcony and gazed for a brief time at the dark, majestic rise of the Blue Mountains beyond in the clear Kingston night.

Alison Booth stared at the scanner and then at McAuliff. Both anger and fear were in her eyes, but she had the presence of mind to say nothing.

As he had been taught, Alex switched on the instrument and made half circles laterally and vertically, starting from the far corner of the room. This pattern was to be followed in the other three corners. He felt embarrassed, almost ludicrous, as he waved his arm slowly, as though administering some occult benediction. He did not care to look at Alison as he went through the motions.

Then, suddenly, he was not embarrassed at all. Instead, he felt a pain in the center of his upper stomach, a sharp sting as his breath stopped and his eyes riveted on the inch-long, narrow bar in the dial of the scanner. He had seen that bar move often during the practice sessions with Hammond; he had been curious, even fascinated at its wavering, stuttering movements. He was not fascinated now. He was afraid.

This was not a training session in an out-of-the-way, safe practice room with Hammond patiently, thoroughly, explaining the importance of overlapping areas. It was actually happening; he had not really thought that it *would* happen. It all had been . . . well, basically *insincere*, somehow so improbable.

Yet now, in front of him, the thin, inch-long bar was vibrating, oscillating with a miniature violence of its own. The tiny sensors were responding to an intruder.

Somewhere within the immediate area of his position was a foreign object whose function was to transmit everything being said in this room.

He motioned to Alison; she approached him warily. He gestured and realized that his gestures were those of an unimaginative charade contestant. He pointed to the scanner and then to his lips. When she spoke he felt like a goddamned idiot.

'You promised me a drink in that lovely garden downstairs. Other considerations will have to wait . . . *luv*.' She said the words quietly, simply. She was very believable.

'You're right,' he answered, deciding instantly that he was no actor. 'Just let me wash up.'

He walked swiftly into the bathroom and turned the faucets on in the basin. He pulled the door to within several inches of closing; the sound of the rushing water was discernible, not obvious. He returned to where he had been standing and continued to operate the scanner, reducing the semicircles as the narrow bar reacted, entering in on the location of the object as he had been taught to do by Hammond.

The only nonstunning surprise was the fact that the scanner's tiny red light went on directly above his suitcase, against the wall on a baggage rack.

The red light indicated that the object was within twelve inches of the instrument.

444

He handed Alison the scanner and opened the case cautiously. He separated his clothes, removing shirts, socks, and underwear, and placing them – throwing them – on the bed. When the suitcase was more empty than full, he stretched the elasticized liner and ran his fingers against the leather wall.

McAuliff knew what to feel for; Hammond had showed him dozens of bugs of varying sizes and shapes.

He found it.

It was attached to the outer lining: a small bulge the size of a leather-covered button. He let it stay and, as Hammond had instructed, continued to examine the remainder of the suitcase for a second, back-up device.

It was there, too. On the opposite side.

He took the scanner from Alison, walked away from the area, and rapidly 'half circled' the rest of the room. As Hammond had told him to expect, there was no further movement on the scanner's dial. For if a transmitter was planted on a movable host, it usually indicated that it was the only source available.

The rest of the room was clean. 'Sterile' was the word Hammond had used.

McAuliff went into the bathroom; it, too, was safe. He turned off the faucets and called out to Alison.

'Are you unpacked?' *Now why the hell did he say that? Of all the stupid . . .*

'I'm an old hand at geo trips,' came the relaxed reply. 'All my garments are synthetic; they can wait. I really want to see that lovely garden. Do hurry.'

He pulled the door open and saw that she was closing the balcony door, drawing the curtains across the floor-to-ceiling glass. Alison Booth was doing the right thing, he reflected. Hammond had often repeated the command: *When you find a transmitter, check outside sight lines; assume visual surveillance.*

He came out of the bathroom; she looked across at him . . . No, he thought, she did not look at him, she stared at him.

'Good,' she said. 'You're ready. I think you missed most of your beard, but you're presentable. Let's go . . . *luv*.'

Outside the room, in the hotel corridor, Alison took his arm, and they walked to the elevator. Several times he began to speak, but each time he did so, she interrupted him.

'Wait till we're downstairs,' she kept repeating softly.

In the patio garden, it was Alison who, after they had been seated, requested another table. One on the opposite side of the open area; a table, Alex realized, that had no palms or plants in its vicinity. There were no more than a dozen other couples, no single men or unescorted women. McAuliff had the feeling that Alison had observed each couple closely.

Their drinks arrived; the waiter departed, and Alison Booth spoke.

'I think it's time we talked to each other . . . about things we haven't talked about.'

Alex offered her a cigarette. She declined, and so he lighted one for himself. He was buying a few seconds of time before answering, and both of them knew it.

'I'm sorry you saw what you did upstairs. I don't want you to give it undue importance.'

'That would be funny, darling, except that *you* were halfway to hysterics.'

'That's nice.'

'What?'

'You said "darling".'

'Please. May we stay professional?'

'Good Lord! Are you? Professional, I mean?'

'I'm a geologist. What are you?'

McAuliff ignored her. 'You said I was ... excited upstairs. You were right. But it struck me that you weren't. You did all the correct things while I was fumbling.'

'I agree. You were fumbling ... Alex, were you told to hire me?'

'No. I was told to think twice or three times before accepting you.'

'That could have been a ploy. I wanted the job badly; I would have gone to bed with you to get it. Thank you for not expecting that.'

'There was no pressure one way or the other about you. Only a warning. And that was because of your recent husband's sideline occupation, which, incidentally, apparently accounts for most of his money. I say money because it's not considered income, I gather.'

'It accounts for *all* of his money, and is not reported as income. And I don't for a minute believe the Geophysics Department of the University of London would have access to such information. Much less the Royal Society.'

'Then you'd be wrong. A lot of the money for this survey is a grant from the government funneled through the society and the university. When governments spend money, they're concerned about personnel and payrolls.' McAuliff was pleasantly surprised at himself. He was responding as Hammond said he would: creating instant, logical replies. *Build on part of the truth, keep it simple* ... Those had been Hammond's words.

'We'll let that dubious, American-oriented assessment pass,' said Alison, now reaching for his cigarettes. 'Surely you'll explain what happened upstairs.'

The moment had come, thought Alex, wondering if he could carry it off the way Hammond said: *Reduce any explanation to very few words, rooted in common sense and simplicity, and do not vary.* He lighted her cigarette and spoke as casually as possible.

'There's a lot of political jockeying in Kingston. Most of it's petty, but some of it gets rough. This survey has controversial overtones. Resentment of origin, jealousies, that sort of thing. You saw it at Customs. There are people who would kill to discredit us. I was given that goddamned scanner to use in case I thought something very unusual happened. I thought it had, and I was right.' Alex drank the remainder of his drink and watched the girl's reaction. He did his best to convey only sincerity.

'Our bags, you mean,' said Alison.

'Yes. That note didn't make sense, and the clerk at the desk said they got here just before we did. But they were picked up at Palisados over two hours ago.'

'I see. And a geological survey would drive people to those extremes? That's hard to swallow, Alex.'

'Not if you think about it. Why are surveys made? What's generally the purpose? Isn't it usually because someone – some people – expect to build something?'

'Not one like ours, no. It's too spread out over too great an area. I'd say it's patently, *obviously* academic. Anything else would—' Alison stopped as her eyes met McAuliff's. 'Good Lord! If it *was* anything else, it's unbelievable!'

'Perhaps there are those who do believe it. If they did, what do you think they'd do?' Alex signaled the waiter by holding up two fingers for refills. Alison Booth's lips were parted in astonishment.

'Millions and millions and *millions*,' she said quietly. 'My God, they'd buy up everything in sight!'

'Only if they were convinced they were right.'

Alison forced him to look at her. When, at first, he refused, and glanced over at the waiter, who was dawdling, she put her hand on top of his and made him pay attention. 'They *are* right, aren't they, Alex?'

'I wouldn't have any proof of it. My contract's with the University of London, with countersigned approvals from the Society and the Jamaican ministry. What they do with the results is their business.' It was pointless to issue a flat denial. He was a professional surveyor, not a clairvoyant.

'I don't believe you. You've been primed.'

'Not primed. Told to be on guard, that's all.'

'Those ... deadly little instruments aren't given to people who've only been told to be on guard.'

'That's what I thought. But you know something? You and I are wrong, Alison. Scanners are in common use these days. Nothing out of the ordinary. Especially if you're working outside home territory. Not a very nice comment on the state of trust, is it?'

The waiter brought their drinks. He was humming and moving rhythmically to the beat of his own tune. Alison continued to stare at McAuliff. He wasn't sure, but he began to think she believed him. When the waiter left, she leaned forward, anxious to speak.

'And what are you supposed to do now? You found those awful things. What are you going to do about them?'

'Nothing. Report them to the Ministry in the morning, that's all.'

'You mean you're not going to take them out and step on them or something? You're just going to leave them there?'

It was not a pleasant prospect, thought Alex, but Hammond had been clear: If a bug was found, let it remain intact and use it. It could be invaluable. Before eliminating any such device, he was to report it and await instructions. A fish store named Tallon's, near Victoria Park.

'They're paying me ... paying us. I suppose they'll want to quietly investigate. What difference does it make? I don't have any secrets.'

'And you *won't* have,' Alison said softly but pointedly, removing her hand from his.

McAuliff suddenly realized the preposterousness of his position. It was at once ridiculous and sublime, funny and not funny at all.

'May I change my mind and call someone now?' he asked.

Alison slowly – very slowly – began to smile her lovely smile. 'No. I was being unfair ... And I *do* believe you. You're the most maddeningly unconcerned man I've ever known. You are either supremely innocent or superbly ulterior. I can't accept the latter; you were far too nervous upstairs.' She put her hand back on top of his free one. With his other, he finished the second drink.

'May I ask why you weren't? Nervous.'

'Yes. It's time I told you. I owe you that ... I shan't be returning to England, Alex. Not for many years, if ever. I can't. I spent several months cooperating with Interpol. I've had experience with those horrid little buggers. That's what we called them. Buggers.'

McAuliff felt the stinging pain in his stomach again. It was fear, and more than fear. Hammond had said British Intelligence doubted she would return to England. Julian Warfield suggested that she might be of value for abstract reasons having nothing to do with her contributions to the survey.

He was not sure how – or why – but Alison was being used.

Just as he was being used.

'How did *that* happen?' he asked with appropriate astonishment.

Alison touched on the highlights of her involvement. The marriage was sour before the first anniversary. Succinctly put, Alison Booth came to the conclusion very early that her husband had pursued and married her for reasons having more to do with her professional travels than for anything else.

'... it was as though he had been ordered to take me, use me, absorb me ...'

The strain came soon after they were married: Booth was inordinately interested in her prospects. And, from seemingly nowhere, survey offers came out of the blue, from little-known but well-paying firms, for operations remarkably exotic.

'... among them, of course, Zaire, Turkey, Corsica. He joined me each time. For days, weeks at a time ...'

The first confrontation with David Booth came about in Corsica. The survey was a coastal-offshore expedition in the Capo Senetose area. David arrived during the middle stages for his usual two- to three-week stay, and during this period a series of strange telephone calls and unexplained conferences took place, which seemed to disturb him beyond his limited abilities to cope. Men flew into Ajaccia in small, fast planes; others came by sea in trawlers and small oceangoing craft. David would disappear for hours, then for days at a time. Alison's fieldwork was such that she returned nightly to the team's seacoast hotel; her husband could not conceal his behavior, nor the fact that his presence in Corsica was not an act of devotion to her.

She forced the issue, enumerating the undeniable, and brutally labeling David's explanations for what they were: amateurish lies. He had broken down, wept, pleaded, and told his wife the truth.

In order to maintain a lifestyle David Booth was incapable of earning in the marketplace, he had moved into international narcotics. He was primarily a courier. His partnership in a small importing–exporting business was ideal for the work. The firm had no real identity; indeed, it was rather nondescript, catering – as befitted the owners – to a social rather than a commercial clientele, dealing in art objects on the decorating level. He was able to travel extensively without raising official eyebrows. His introduction to the work of the *contrabandists* was banal: gambling debts compounded by an excess of alcohol and embarrassing female alliances. On the one hand, he had no choice; on the other, he was well paid and had no moral compunctions.

But Alison did. The ideological surveys were legitimate, testimonials to David's employers' abilities to ferret out unsuspecting collaborators. David was given the names of survey teams in selected Mediterranean sites and told to contact them, offering the services of his very respected wife, adding further that he would confidentially contribute to her salary if she was hired. A rich, devoted husband only interested in keeping an active wife happy. The offers were invariably accepted. And, by finding her 'situations', his travels were given a twofold legitimacy. His courier activities had grown beyond the dilettante horizons of his business.

Alison threatened to leave the Corsican job.

David was hysterical. He insisted he would be killed, and Alison as well. He painted a picture of such widespread, powerful corruption-without-conscience that Alison, fearing for both their lives, relented. She agreed to finish the work in Corsica, but made it clear their marriage was finished. Nothing would alter *that* decision.

So she believed at the time.

But one late afternoon in the field – on the water, actually – Alison was taking bore samples from the ocean floor several hundred yards offshore. In the small cabin cruiser were two men. They were agents of Interpol. They had been following her husband for a number of months. Interpol was gathering massive documentation of criminal evidence. It was closing in.

'Needless to say, they were prepared for his arrival. My room was as private as yours was intended to be this evening...'

The case they presented was strong and clear. Where her husband had described a powerful network of corruption, the Interpol men told of another world of pain and suffering and needless, horrible death.

'Oh, they were experts,' said Alison, her eyes remembering, her smile compassionately sad. 'They brought photographs, dozens of them. Children in agony, young men, girls destroyed. I shall never forget those pictures. As they intended I would not...'

Their appeal was the classic recruiting approach: Mrs David Booth was in a unique position; there was no one like her. She could do so much, provide *so* much. And if she walked away in the manner she had described to her husband – abruptly, without explanation – there was the very real question of whether she would be allowed to do so.

My God, thought McAuliff as he listened, *the more things change . . . The Interpol men might have been Hammond speaking in a room at the Savoy Hotel.*

The arrangements were made, schedules created, a reasonable period of time specified for the 'deterioration' of the marriage. She told a relieved Booth that she would try to save their relationship, on the condition that he never again speak to her of his outside activities.

For half a year Alison Gerrard Booth reported the activities of her husband, identified photographs, planted dozens of tiny listening devices in hotel rooms, automobiles, their own apartment. She did so with the understanding that David Booth – whatever the eventual charges against him – would be protected from physical harm. To the best of Interpol's ability.

Nothing was guaranteed.

'When did it all come to an end?' asked Alex.

Alison looked away, briefly, at the dark, ominous panorama of the Blue Mountains, rising in blackness several miles to the north. 'When I listened to a very painful recording. Painful to hear; more painful because I had made the recording possible.'

One morning after a lecture at the university, an Interpol man arrived at her office in the Geology Department. In his briefcase he had a cassette machine and a cartridge that was a duplicate of a conversation recorded between her husband and a liaison from the Marquis de Chatellerault, the man identified as the overlord of the narcotics operation. Alison sat and listened to the voice of a broken man drunkenly describing the collapse of his marriage to a woman he loved very much. She heard him rage and weep, blaming himself for the inadequate man that he was. He spoke of his refused entreaties for the bed, her total rejection of him. And at the last, he made it clear beyond doubt that he loathed using her; that if she ever found out, he would kill himself. What he had done, almost too perfectly, was to exonerate her from any knowledge whatsoever of Chatellerault's operation. He had done it superbly.

'Interpol reached a conclusion that was as painful as the recording. David had somehow learned what I was doing. He was sending a message. It was time to get out.'

A forty-eight-hour divorce in far-off Haiti was arranged. Alison Booth was free.

And, of course, not free at all.

'Within a year, it will all close in on Chatellerault, on David . . . on all of them. And somewhere, someone will put it together: Booth's wife . . .'

Alison reached for her drink and drank and tried to smile.

*

'That's it?' said Alex, not sure it was all.

'That's it, Dr McAuliff. Now, tell me honestly, would you have hired me had you known?'

'No, I would not. I wonder why I didn't know.'

'It's not the sort of information the university, or Emigration, or just about anyone else would have.'

'Alison?' McAuliff tried to conceal the sudden fear he felt. 'You *did* hear about this job from the university people, didn't you?'

The girl laughed and raised her lovely eyebrows in mock protest. 'Oh, Lord, it's tell-all time! . . . No, I admit to having a jump; it gave me time to compile that very impressive portfolio for you.'

'How did you learn of it?'

'Interpol. They'd been looking for months. They called me about ten or twelve days before the interview.'

McAuliff did not have to indulge in any rapid calculations. Ten or twelve days before the interview would place the date within reasonable approximation of the afternoon he had met with Julian Warfield in Belgrave Square.

And later with a man named Hammond from British Intelligence.

The stinging pain returned to McAuliff's stomach. Only it was sharper now, more defined. But he couldn't dwell on it. Across the dark-shadowed patio, a man was approaching. He was walking to their table unsteadily. He was drunk, thought Alex.

'Well, for God's sake, *there* you are! We wondered where the hell you were! We're all in the bar inside. Whitehall's an absolute riot on the piano! A bloody black Noel Coward! Oh, by the way, I trust your luggage got here. I saw you were having problems, so I scribbled a note for the bastards to send it along. If they could read my whisky slant.'

Young James Ferguson dropped into an empty chair and smiled alcoholically at Alison. He then turned and looked at McAuliff, his smile fading as he was met by Alex's stare.

'That was very kind of you,' said McAuliff quietly.

And then Alexander saw it in Ferguson's eyes. The focused consciousness behind the supposedly glazed eyes.

James Ferguson was nowhere near as drunk as he pretended to be.

9

They expected to stay up most of the night. It was their silent, hostile answer to the 'horrid little buggers'.

They joined the others in the bar and, as a good captain should, McAuliff was seen talking to the maître d'; all knew the evening was being paid for by their director.

Charles Whitehall lived up to Ferguson's judgment. His talent was professional; his island patter songs – filled with Caribbean idiom and Jamaican wit – were funny, brittle, cold, and episodically hot. His voice had the clear, high-pitched thrust of a Kingston balladeer; only his eyes remained remote. He was entertaining and amusing, but he was neither entertained nor amused himself, thought Alex.

He was performing.

And finally, after nearly two hours, he wearied of the chore, accepted the cheers of the half-drunken room, and wandered to the table. After receiving individual shakes, claps, and hugs from Ferguson, the Jensens, Alison Booth, and Alex, he opted for a chair next to McAuliff. Ferguson had been sitting there – encouraged by Alex – but the young botanist was only too happy to move. Unsteadily.

'That was remarkable!' said Alison, leaning across McAuliff, reaching for Whitehall's hand. Alex watched as the Jamaican responded; the dark Caribbean hand – fingernails manicured, gold ring glistening – curled delicately over Alison's as another woman's might. And then, in contradiction, Whitehall raised her wrist and kissed her fingers.

A waiter brought over a bottle of white wine for Whitehall's inspection. He read the label in the nightclub light, looked up at the smiling attendant, and nodded. He turned back to McAuliff; Alison was now chatting with Ruth Jensen across the table. 'I should like to speak with you privately,' said the Jamaican casually. 'Meet me in my room, say, twenty minutes after I leave.'

'Alone?'

'Alone.'

'Can't it wait until morning?'

Whitehall leveled his dark eyes at McAuliff and spoke softly but sharply. 'No, it cannot.'

James Ferguson suddenly lurched up from his chair at the end of the table and raised his glass to Whitehall. He waved and gripped the edge with his free hand; he was the picture of a very drunk young man. 'Here's to Charles the First of Kingston! The bloody black Sir Noel! You're simply fan*testic*, Charles!'

There was an embarrassing instant of silence as the word 'black' was absorbed. The waiter hurriedly poured Whitehall's wine; it was no moment for sampling.

'Thank you,' said Whitehall politely. 'I take that as a high compliment, indeed ... Jimbo-mon.'

'*Jimbo-mon!*' shouted Ferguson with delight. 'I love it! You shall call me *Jimbo-mon*! And now, I should like—' Ferguson's words were cut short, replaced by an agonizing grimace on his pale young face. It was suddenly abundantly clear that his alcoholic capacity had been reached. He set his glass down with wavering precision, staggered backward and, in slow motion of his own, collapsed to the floor.

The table rose en masse; surrounding couples turned. The waiter put the bottle down quickly and started toward Ferguson; he was joined by Peter Jensen, who was the nearest. 'Oh, Lord,' said Jensen, kneeling down. 'I think the poor fellow's going to be sick. Ruth, come help ... You there, waiter. Give me a hand, chap!'

The Jensens, aided by two waiters now, gently lifted the young botanist into a sitting position, unloosened his tie, and generally tried to reinstate some form of consciousness. Charles Whitehall, standing beside McAuliff, picked up two napkins and lobbed them across the table onto the floor near those administering aid. Alex watched the Jamaican's actions; it was not pleasant. Ferguson's head was nodding back and forth; moans of impending illness came from his lips.

'I think this is as good a time as any for me to leave,' said Whitehall. 'Twenty minutes?'

McAuliff nodded. 'Or thereabouts.'

The Jamaican turned to Alison, delicately took her hand, kissed it, and smiled. 'Good night, my dear.'

With minor annoyance, Alex sidestepped the two of them and walked over to the Jensens, who, with the waiters' help, were getting Ferguson to his feet.

'We'll bring him to his room,' said Ruth. 'I warned him about the rum; it doesn't go with whisky. I don't think he listened.' She smiled and shook her head.

McAuliff kept his eyes on Ferguson's face. He wondered if he would see what he saw before. What he had been watching for over an hour.

And then he did. Or thought he did.

As Ferguson's arms went limp around the shoulders of a waiter and Peter Jensen, he opened his eyes. Eyes that seemingly swam in their sockets. But for the briefest of moments, they were steady, focused, devoid of glaze. Ferguson was doing a perfectly natural thing any person would do in a dimly lit room. He was checking his path to avoid obstacles.

And he was – for that instant – quite sober.

Why was James Ferguson putting on such a splendidly embarrassing performance? McAuliff would have a talk with the young man in the morning. About several things, including a 'whisky-slanted' note that resulted in a suitcase that triggered the dial of an electric scanner.

'Poor lamb. He'll feel miserable in the morning.' Alison had come alongside Alex. Together they watched the Jensens take Ferguson out the door.

'I hope he's just a poor lamb who went astray for the night and doesn't make a habit of it.'

'Oh, come on, Alex, don't be old-auntie. He's a perfectly nice young man who's had a pint too many.' Alison turned and looked at the deserted table. 'Well, it seems the party's over, doesn't it?'

'I thought we agreed to keep it going.'

'I'm fading fast, darling; my resolve is weakening. We also agreed to check my luggage with your little magic box. Shall we?'

'Sure.' McAuliff signaled the waiter.

They walked down the hotel corridor; McAuliff took Alison's key as they approached her door. 'I have to see Whitehall in a few minutes.'

'Oh? How come? It's awfully late.'

'He said he wanted to speak to me. Privately. I have no idea why. I'll make it quick.' He inserted the key, opened the door, and found himself instinctively barring Alison in the frame until he had switched on the lights and looked inside.

The single room was empty, the connecting door to his still open, as it had been when they left hours ago.

'I'm impressed,' whispered Alison, resting her chin playfully on the outstretched, forbidding arm that formed a bar across the entrance.

'What?' He removed his arm and walked toward the connecting door. The lights in his room were on – as he had left them. He closed the door quietly, withdrew the scanner from his jacket, and crossed to the bed, where Alison's two suitcases lay alongside each other, he held the instrument above them; there was no movement on the dial. He walked rapidly about the room, laterally and vertically blessing it from all corners. The room was clean. 'What did you say?' he asked softly.

'You're protective. That's nice.'

'Why were the lights off in this room and not in mine?' He had not heard her words.

'Because I turned them off. I came in here, got my purse, used some lipstick, and went back into your room. There's a switch by the door. I used it.'

'I don't remember.'

'You were upset at the time. I gather my room isn't the center of attention yours is.' Alison walked in and closed the corridor door.

'No, it's not, but keep your voice low. Can those goddamn things listen through doors and walls?'

'No, I don't think so.' She watched him take her suitcases from the bed and carry them across the room. He stood by the closet, looking for a luggage rack. There was none. 'Aren't you being a little obvious?'

'What?'

'What are you doing with my bags? I haven't unpacked.'

'Oh.' McAuliff could feel the flush on his face. He felt like a goddamn idiot. 'I'm sorry. I suppose you could say I'm compulsively neat.'

'Or just compulsive.'

He carried the bags back to the bed and turned to look at her, the suitcases still in his hands. He was so terribly tired. 'It's been a rotten day . . . a very confusing day,' he said. 'The fact that it's not over yet is discouraging as hell; there's still Whitehall to go . . . And in the next room, if I snore or talk in my sleep or go to the bathroom with the door open, everything is recorded somewhere on a tape. I can say it doesn't bother me, but it doesn't make me feel any better, either. I'll tell you something else, too, while I'm rambling. You are a lovely, lovely girl, and you're right, I'm compulsive . . . for example, at this moment I have the strongest compulsion to hold you and kiss you and feel your arms around me, and . . . you are so goddamn desirable . . . and you have such a beautiful smile and laugh . . . and all I want to do is hold you and forget everything else . . . Now I'm finished rambling, and you can tell me to go to hell because I'm not relevant.'

Alison Booth stood silently, looking at McAuliff for what seemed to him far too long. Then she walked slowly, deliberately, to him.

'Do you know how silly you look holding those suitcases?' she whispered as she leaned forward and kissed him on the lips.

He dropped the bags; the noise of their contact with the floor made them both smile. He pulled her to him and the comfort was splendid, the warm, growing excitement a special thing. And as he kissed her, their mouths moistly exploring, pressing, widening, he realized Alison was trembling, gripping him with a strength that was more than a desire to be taken. Yet it was not fear; there was no hesitancy, no holding back, only anxiety.

He lowered her gently to the bed; as he did so, she unbuttoned the silk blouse and guided his hands to her breasts. She closed her eyes as he caressed her and whispered.

'It's been a terribly long time, Alex. Do you think Whitehall could wait a while longer? You see, I don't think I can.'

They lay beside each other, naked, under the soft covers. She rose on her elbow, her hair falling over her face, and looking at him. She traced his lips with her fingers and bent down, kissing him, outlining his lips now with her tongue.

'I'm absolutely shameless,' she said, laughing softly. 'I want to make love to you all night long. And most of the day . . . I'm parched and I've been to the well and I want to stay here.'

He reached up and let her hair fall through his fingers. He followed the strands downward to the swell of her body and cupped her left breast. 'We'll take the minimum time out for food and sleep.'

There was the faint ring of a telephone. It came from the direction of the connecting door. From his room.

'You're late for Charles Whitehall,' said Alison. 'You'd better go answer it.'

'Our goddamn Sir Noel.' He climbed out of the bed, walked rapidly to the door, opened it, and went into the room. As he picked up the telephone, he looked at the drawn curtains of his balcony doors; he was grateful for Alison's experience. Except for his socks – why his socks? – he was naked.

'I said twenty minutes, Mr McAuliff. It's nearly an hour.' Whitehall's voice was quietly furious.

'I'm sorry. I told you "thereabouts". For me, an hour is "thereabouts". Especially when someone gives me orders at this time of night and he's not bleeding.'

'Let's not argue. Will you be here soon?'

'Yes.'

'When?'

'Twenty minutes.' Alex hung up the telephone a bit harder than was necessary and looked over at his suitcase. Whoever was on the other end of that line knew he was going out of the room to meet someone who had tried to issue him orders at three o'clock in the morning. He would think about it later.

'Do you know how positively handsome you are? All over,' said Alison as he came back into the room.

'You're right, you're shameless.'

'Why do you have your knee socks on? It looks peculiar.' She sat up, pulling the sheet over her breasts, and reached for the cigarettes on the night table.

'Light me one, will you please? I've got to get dressed.' McAuliff looked around the bed for the clothing he had removed in such haste a half-hour ago.

'Was he upset?' She handed him a cigarette as he pulled on his trousers and picked up his shirt from the floor.

'He was upset. He's also an arrogant son of a bitch.'

'I think Charles Whitehall wants to strike back at someone or something,' said Alison, watching him absently. 'He's angry.'

'Maybe it's recognition. Not granted to the extent he thinks it should be.' McAuliff buttoned his shirt.

'Perhaps. That would account for his dismissing the compliments.'

'The what?' he asked.

'His little entertainment downstairs tonight was frighteningly thought out. It wasn't prepared for a nightclub. It was created for Covent Garden. Or the grand hall of the United Nations.'

He tapped gently on Whitehall's door, and when it opened, McAuliff found the Jamaican dressed in an embroidered Japanese *hopi* coat. Beneath the flowery garment, Whitehall wore his pinstriped trousers and velvet slippers.

'Come in, please. This time you're early. It's not yet fifteen minutes.'

'You're obsessed with time. It's after three in the morning; I'd rather not look at my watch.' Alex closed the door behind him. 'I hope you have something important to tell me. Because if you don't, I'm going to be damned angry.'

Whitehall had crossed to the bureau; he picked up a folded piece of paper from the top and indicated a chair for McAuliff. 'Sit down, please. I, too, am quite exhausted, but we must talk.'

Alex walked to the armchair and sat down. 'Go ahead.'

'I think it's time we had an understanding. It will in no way affect my contributions to the survey.'

'I'm relieved to hear that. I didn't hire you to entertain the troops downstairs.'

'A dividend,' said Whitehall coldly. 'Don't knock it; I'm very good.'

'I know you are. What else is new?'

The scholar tapped the paper in his hands. 'There'll be periods when it will be necessary for me to be absent. Never more than a day or two at a time. Naturally, I'll give you advance notice, and if there are problems – where *possible* – I shall rearrange my schedule.'

'You'll *what*?' McAuliff sat forward in the chair. 'Where ... *possible* ... you'll fit your time to *mine*? That's goddamn nice of you. I hope the survey won't be a burden.'

Whitehall laughed, impersonally. 'Not at all. It was just what I was looking for. And you'll see, you'll be quite pleased ... although I'm not sure why I should be terribly concerned. You see, I cannot accept the stated reasons for this survey. And I suspect there are one or two others, if they spoke their thoughts, who share my doubts.'

'Are you suggesting that I hired you under false pretenses?'

'Oh, come now,' replied the black scholar, his eyes narrowing in irritation. 'Alexander McAuliff, a highly confidential, one-man survey company whose work takes him throughout the world ... for very large fees, abruptly decides to become academically *charitable*? To take from four to six months away from a lucrative practice to head up a *university survey*?' Whitehall laughed like a nervous jackal, walked rapidly to the curtains of the room's balcony doors, and flipped one side partially open. He twisted the latch and pulled the glass panel several inches inward; the curtain billowed in the night breeze.

'You don't know the specifics of my contract,' said Alex noncommittally.

'I know what universities and royal societies *and* ministries of education pay. It's not your league, McAuliff.' The Jamaican returned to the bed and sat down on the edge. He brought the folded paper to his chin and stared at Alex.

McAuliff hesitated, then spoke slowly. 'In a way, aren't you describing your own situation? There were several people in London who didn't think you'd take the job. It was quite a drop in income for you.'

'Precisely. Our positions are similar; I'm sure for very different reasons ... Part of *my* reasoning takes me to Savanna-la-Mar in the morning.'

'Your friend on the plane?'

'A bore. Merely a messenger.' Whitehall held up the folded piece of paper. 'He brought me an invitation. Would you care to read it?'

'You wouldn't offer unless it was pertinent.'

'I have no idea whether it is or not. Perhaps *you* can tell *me*.'

Alex took the paper extended to him and unfolded it. It was hotel stationery. The Georges V, Paris. The handwriting was slanted, the strokes rapid, words joined in speed.

My dear Whitehall —

Forgive this hastily written note but I have just learned that we are both en route to Jamaica. I for a welcome rest and you, I understand, for more worthwhile pursuits.

I should deem it an honor and a pleasure to meet with you. Our mutual friend will give you the details. I shall be staying in Savanna-la-Mar, albeit incognito. He will explain.

I do believe our coming together at the earliest would be mutually beneficial. I have long admired your past (?) island activities. I ask only that our meeting and my presence in Jamaica remain confidential. Since I so admire your endeavors, I know you will understand.

Chatellerault

Chatellerault . . . ?

The Marquis de Chatellerault.

David Booth's 'employer'. The man behind a narcotics network that spread throughout most of Europe and the Mediterranean. The man Alison feared so terribly that she carried a lethal-looking cylinder of gas with her at all times!

McAuliff knew that Whitehall was observing him. He forced himself to remain immobile, betraying only numbness on his face and in his eyes.

'Who is he?' asked McAuliff blandly. 'Who's this Chatel . . . Chatellerault?'

'You don't know?'

'Oh, for Christ's *sake*, Whitehall,' said Alex in weary exasperation. 'Stop playing games. I've never heard of him.'

'I thought you might have.' The scholar was once again staring at McAuliff. 'I thought the connection was rather evident.'

'What connection?'

'To whatever *your* reasons are for being in Jamaica. Chatellerault is, among other things, a financier with considerable resources. The coincidence is startling, wouldn't you agree?'

'I don't know what you're talking about.' McAuliff glanced down at Chatellerault's note. 'What does he mean by your past, "question mark", island activities?'

Whitehall paused before replying. When he did, he spoke quietly, thus lending emphasis to his words. 'Fifteen years ago I left my homeland because the political faction for which I worked . . . devotedly, and in secret . . . was forced underground. Further underground, I should say. For a decade we have remained dormant – on the surface. But only on the surface. I have returned now. Kingston knows nothing. It therefore demands confidentiality. I have, with considerable risk, broken this confidence as an article of faith. For you ... please. Why are you here, McAuliff? Perhaps it will tell me why such a man as Chatellerault wishes a conference.'

Alex got out of the chair and walked aimlessly toward the balcony doors. He moved because it helped him concentrate. His mind was racing, some abstract thoughts signaling a warning that Alison was in danger ... others balking, not convinced.

He crossed to the back of the chair facing Whitehall's bed and gripped the cloth firmly. 'All right, I'll make a deal with you. I'll tell you why I'm here, if you'll spell out this ... activity of yours.'

'I will tell you what I can,' replied Charles, his eyes devoid of deceit. 'It will be sufficient, you will see. I cannot tell you everything. It would not be good for you.'

'That's a condition I'm not sure I like.'

'*Please.* Trust me.'

The man was not lying, that much was clear to Alex. 'Okay ... I know the north coast; I worked for Kaiser's bauxite. I'm considered very pro – that is, I've put together some good teams and I've got a decent reputation—'

'Yes, yes. To the point, please.'

'By heading up this job, the Jamaican government has guaranteed me first refusal on twenty per cent of any industrial development for the next six years. That could mean millions of dollars. It's as simple as that.'

Whitehall sat motionless, his hands still folded beneath his chin, an elegant little boy in a concerned man's body. 'Yes, that is plausible,' he said finally. 'In much of Kingston, everything's for sale. It could be a motive for Chatellerault.'

Alex remained behind the chair. 'All right. Now, that's why I'm here. Why are you?'

'It is good you told me of your arrangement. I shall do my best to see that it is lived up to. You deserve that.'

'What the hell does that mean?'

'It means I am here in a political capacity. A solely Jamaican concern. You must respect that condition ... and my confidence. I'd deny it anyway, and you would soil your foreigner's hands in things Jamaican. Ultimately, however, we will control Kingston.'

'Oh, Christ! Comes the goddamn revolution!'

'Of a different sort, Mr McAuliff. Put plainly, I'm a fascist. Fascism is the only hope for my island.'

10

McAuliff opened his eyes, raised his wrist from beneath the covers, and saw that it was ten twenty-five. He had intended to get up by 8:30–9:00 at the latest.

He had a man to see. A man with arthritis at a fish store called Tallon's.

He looked over at Alison. She was curled up away from him, her hair sprayed over the sheets, her face buried in the pillow. She had been magnificent, he thought. No, he thought, *they* had been magnificent together. She had been ... what was the word she used? Parched. She had said: 'I'm parched and I've been to the well ...' And she had been.

Magnificent. And warm, meaningful.

Yet still the thoughts came back.

A name that meant nothing to him twenty-four hours ago was suddenly an unknown force to be reckoned with, separately put forward by two people who were strangers a week ago.

Chatellerault. The Marquis de Chatellerault.

Currently in Savanna-la-Mar, on the southwest coast of Jamaica.

Charles Whitehall would be seeing him shortly, if they had not met by now. The black fascist and the French financier. It sounded like a vaudeville act.

But Alison Booth carried a deadly cylinder in her handbag, in the event she ever had occasion to meet him. Or meet with those who worked for him.

What was the connection? Certainly there had to be one.

He stretched, taking care not to wake her. Although he wanted to wake her and hold her and run his hands over her body and make love to her in the morning.

He couldn't. There was too much to do. Too much to think about.

He wondered what his instructions would be. And how long it would take to receive them. And what the man with arthritis at a fish store named Tallon's would be like. And, no less important, where in God's name was Sam Tucker? He was to be in Kingston by tomorrow. It wasn't like Sam to just take his leave without a word; he was too kind a man. And yet, there had been times ...

When would they get the word to fly north and begin the actual work on the survey?

He was not going to get the answers staring up at the ceiling from Alison

Booth's bed. And he was not going to make any telephone calls from his room.

He smiled as he thought about the 'horrid little buggers' in his suitcase. Were there horrid little men crouched over dials in dark rooms waiting for sounds that never came? There was a certain comfort in that.

'I can hear you thinking.' Alison's voice was muffled in the pillow. 'Isn't that remarkable?'

'It's frightening.'

She rolled over, her eyes shut, and smiled and reached under the blankets for him. 'You also stretch quite sensually.' She caressed the flatness of his stomach, and then his thighs, and then McAuliff knew the answers would have to wait. He pulled her to him; she opened her eyes and raised the covers so there was nothing between them.

The taxi let him off at Victoria's South Parade. The thoroughfare was aptly named, in the nineteenth-century sense. The throngs of people flowing in and out of the park's entrance were like crowds of brightly colored peacocks, strutting, half acknowledging, quickening steps only to stop and gape.

McAuliff walked into the park, doing his best to look like a strolling tourist. Intermittently he could feel the hostile, questioning glances as he made his way up the gravel path to the center of the park. It occurred to him that he had not seen a single other white person; he had not expected that. He had the distinct feeling that he was an object, to be tolerated but watched. Not essentially to be trusted.

He was a strange-toned outsider who had invaded the heart of this Man's playground. He nearly laughed when a young Jamaican mother guided a smiling child to the opposite side of the path as he approached. The child obviously had been fascinated by the tall, pinkish figure; the mother, quietly, efficiently, knew better. With dignity.

He saw the rectangular white sign with the brown lettering: QUEEN STREET, EAST. The arrow pointed to the right, at another, narrower gravel path. He started down it.

He recalled Hammond's words: *Don't be in a hurry. Ever, if possible. And never when you are making a contact. There's nothing so obvious as a man in a rush in a crowd that's not; except a woman. Or that same man stopping every five feet to light the same cigarette over and over again, so he can peer around at everyone. Do the natural things, depending on the day, the weather, the surroundings.*

It was a warm morning . . . noon. The Jamaican sun was hot, but there were breezes from the harbour, less than a mile away. It would be perfectly natural for a tourist to sit down and take the sun and the breeze; to unbutton his collar, remove his jacket, perhaps. To look about with pleasant tourist curiosity.

There was a bench on the left; a couple had just gotten up. It was empty. He took off his jacket, pulled at his tie, and sat down. He stretched his legs and behaved as he thought was appropriate.

But it was not appropriate. For the most self-conscious of reasons: He was too free, too relaxed in this Man's playground. He felt it instantly, unmistakably. The discomfort was heightened by an old man with a cane who walked by and hesitated in front of him. He was a touch drunk, thought Alex; the head swayed slightly, the legs a bit unsteady. But the eyes were not unsteady. They conveyed mild surprise mixed with disapproval.

McAuliff rose from the bench and swung his jacket under his arm. He smiled blankly at the old man and was about to proceed down the path when he saw another man, difficult to miss. He was white – the only other white man in Victoria Park. At least, the only one he could see. He was quite far away, diagonally across the lawns, on the north–south path, about a hundred and fifty yards in the distance.

A young man with a slouch and a shock of untrained dark hair. And he had turned away. He had been watching him, Alex was sure of that. Following him.

It was James Ferguson. The young man who had put on the second-best performance of the night at Courtleigh Manor last evening. The drunk who had the presence of mind to keep sharp eyes open for obstacles in a dimly lit room.

McAuliff took advantage of the moment and walked rapidly down the path, then cut across the grass to the trunk of a large palm. He was nearly two hundred yards from Ferguson now. He peered around the tree, keeping his body out of sight. He was aware that a number of Jamaicans sitting about on the lawn were looking at him; he was sure, disapprovingly.

Ferguson, as he expected, was alarmed that he had lost the subject of his surveillance. (It was funny, thought Alex. He could think the word 'surveillance' now. He doubted he had used the word a dozen times in his life before three weeks ago.) The young botanist began walking rapidly past the brown-skinned strollers. Hammond was right, thought McAuliff. A man in a hurry in a crowd that wasn't was obvious.

Ferguson reached the intersection of the Queen Street path and stopped. He was less than forty yards from Alex now; he hesitated, as if not sure whether to retreat back to the South Parade or go on.

McAuliff pressed himself against the palm trunk. Ferguson thrust forward, as rapidly as possible. He had decided to keep going, if only to get out of the park. The bustling crowds on Queen Street East signified sanctuary. The park had become unsafe.

If these conclusions were right – and the nervous expression on Ferguson's face seemed to confirm them – McAuliff realized that he had learned something else about this strange young man: He was doing what he was doing under duress and with very little experience. *Look for small things*, Hammond had said. *They'll be there; you'll learn to spot them. Signs that tell you there is valid strength or real weakness.*

Ferguson reached the East Parade gate, obviously relieved. He stopped and looked carefully in all directions. The unsafe field was behind him. The young man checked his watch while waiting for the uniformed policeman to halt the traffic for pedestrians. The whistle blew, automobiles stopped with varying levels of screeches, and Ferguson continued down Queen Street. Concealing himself as best he could in the crowd, Alex followed. The young man seemed more relaxed now. He wasn't as aggressive in this walk, in his darting glances. It was as thought, having lost the enemy, he was more concerned with explanations than with re-establishing contact.

But McAuliff wanted that contact re-established. It was as good a time as any to ask young Ferguson those questions he needed answered.

Alex started across the street, dodging the traffic, and jumped over the curb out of the way of a Kingston taxi. He made his way through the stream of shoppers to the far side of the walk.

There was a side street between Mark Lane and Duke Street. Ferguson hesitated, looked around, and apparently decided it was worth trying. He abruptly turned and entered.

McAuliff realized that he knew that street. It was a freeport strip interspersed with bars. He and Sam Tucker had been there late one afternoon a year ago, following a Kaiser conference at the Sheraton. He remembered, too, that there was a diagonally connecting alley that intersected the strip from Duke Street. He remembered because Sam had thought there might be native saloons in the moist, dark brick corridor, only to discover it was used for deliveries. Sam had been upset; he was fond of back-street native saloons.

Alex broke into a run. Hammond's warning about drawing attention would have to be disregarded. Tallon's could wait; the man with arthritis could wait. This was the moment to reach James Ferguson.

He crossed Queen Street again, now paying no attention to the disturbance he caused, or the angry whistle from the harassed Kingston policeman. He raced down the block; there was the diagonally connecting alley. It seemed even narrower than he remembered. He entered and pushed his way past half a dozen Jamaicans, muttering apologies, trying to avoid the hard stares of those walking in the opposite direction toward him – silent challenges, grown-up children playing king-of-the-road. He reached the end of the passageway and stopped. He pressed his back against the brick and peered around the edge, up the side street. His timing was right.

James Ferguson, his expression ferretlike, was only ten yards away. Then five. And then McAuliff walked out of the alley and confronted him.

The young man's face paled to a deathly white. Alex gestured him against the stucco wall; the strollers passed in both directions, several complaining.

Ferguson's smile was false, his voice strained. 'Well, hello, Alex ... Dr McAuliff. Doing a bit of shopping? This is the place for it.'

'*Have* I been shopping, Jimbo-mon? You'd know if I had, wouldn't you?'

'I don't know what you ... I wouldn't—'

'Maybe you're still drunk,' interrupted Alex. 'You had a lot to drink last night.'

'Made a bloody fool of myself, I expect. Please accept my apologies.'

'No apologies necessary. You stayed just within the lines. You were very convincing.'

'Really, Alex, you're a bit much.' Ferguson moved back. A Jamaican woman, basket balanced on her head, hurried past. 'I said I was sorry. I'm sure you've had the occasion to overindulge.'

'Very often. As a matter of fact, I was a hell of a lot drunker than you last night.'

'I don't know what you're implying, chap, and frankly, my head's too painful to play anagrams. Now, for the last time, I apologize.'

'For the wrong sins, Jimbo-mon. Let's go back and find some real ones. Because I have some questions.'

Ferguson awkwardly straightened his perennial slouch and whisked away the shock of hair on his forehead. 'You're really quite abusive. I have shopping to do.'

The young man started to walk around McAuliff. Alex grabbed his arm and slammed him back into the stucco wall. 'Save your money. Do it in London.'

'*No!*' Ferguson's body stiffened; the taut flesh around his eyes stretched further. 'No, *please,*' he whispered.

'Then let's start with the suitcases.' McAuliff released the arm, holding Ferguson against the wall with his stare.

'I *told* you,' the young man whined. 'You were having trouble. I tried to help.'

'You bet your ass I had trouble! And not only with Customs. Where did my luggage go? Our luggage? Who took it?'

'I don't know. I *swear* I don't!'

'Who told you to write that note?'

'*No* one told me! For God's sake, you're *crazy!*'

'Why did you put on that act last night?'

'What act?'

'You weren't drunk – you were sober.'

'Oh, Christ Almighty, I wish you had my hangover. Really—'

'Not good enough, Jimbo-mon. Let's try again. Who told you to write that note?'

'You won't *listen* to me—'

'I'm listening. Why are you following me? Who told you to follow me this morning?'

'By God, you're insane!'

'By God, *you're fired!*'

'No! ... You can't. Please.' Ferguson's voice was frightened again, a whisper.

'What did you say?' McAuliff placed his right hand against the wall, over Ferguson's frail shoulder. He leaned into the strange young man. 'I'd like to hear you say that again. What can't I do?'

'Please ... don't send me back. I beg you.' Ferguson was breathing through his mouth; spots of saliva had formed on his thin lips. 'Not now.'

'Send you back? I don't give a goddamn where you go! I'm not your keeper, little boy.' Alex removed his hand from the wall and yanked his jacket from under his left arm. 'You're entitled to return-trip airfare. I'll draw it for you this afternoon, and pay for one more night at the Courtleigh. After that, you're on your own. Go wherever the hell you please. But not with me; not with the survey.'

McAuliff turned and abruptly walked away. He entered the narrow alleyway and took up his position in the line of laconic strollers. He knew the stunned Ferguson would follow. It wasn't long before he heard him. The whining voice had the quality of controlled hysteria. Alex did not stop or look back.

'McAuliff! Mr McAuliff! *Please!*' The English tones echoed in the narrow brick confines, creating a dissonant counterpoint to the lilting hum of a dozen Jamaican conversations. 'Please, *wait* . . . Excuse me, excuse me, please. I'm sorry, let me pass, please . . .'

'What you do, mon?! Don't push me.'

The verbal objections did not deter Ferguson; the bodily obstructions were somewhat more successful. Alex kept moving, hearing and sensing the young man closing the gap slowly. It was eerily comic: a white man chasing another white man in a dark, crowded passageway that was exclusively – by civilized cautions – a native thoroughfare. McAuliff was within feet of the exit to Duke Street when he felt Ferguson's hand gripping his arm.

'*Please.* We have to talk . . . not here.'

'Where?'

They emerged on the sidewalk. A long, horse-drawn wagon filled with fruits and country vegetables was in front of them at the curb. The sombreroed owner was arguing with customers by a set of ancient scales; several ragged children stole bananas from the rear of the vehicle. Ferguson still held McAuliff's arm.

'Go to the Devon House. It's a tourist—'

'I know.'

'There's an outside restaurant.'

'When?'

'Fifteen minutes.'

The taxi drove into the long entrance of Devon House, a Georgian monument to an era of English supremacy and white, European money. Circular floral gardens fronted the spotless columns; rinsed graveled paths wove patterns around an immense fountain. The small outdoor restaurant was off to the side, the tables behind tall hedges, the diners obscured from the front. There were only six tables, McAuliff realized. A very small restaurant; a difficult place in which to follow someone without being observed. Perhaps Ferguson was not as inexperienced as he appeared to be.

'Well, hello, chap!'

Alex turned. James Ferguson had yelled from the central path to the fountain; he now carried his camera and the cases and straps and meters that went with it. 'Hi,' said McAuliff, wondering what role the young man intended to play now.

'I've got some wonderful shots. This place has quite a history, you know.' Ferguson approached him, taking a second to snap Alex's picture.

'This is ridiculous,' replied McAuliff quietly. 'Who the hell are you trying to fool?'

'I know exactly what I'm doing. Please cooperate.' And then Ferguson returned to his play-acting, raising his voice and his camera simultaneously. 'Did you know that this old brick was the original courtyard? It leads to the rear of the house, where the soldiers were housed in rows of brick cubicles.'

'I'm fascinated.'

'It's well past elevenses, old man,' continued an enthusiastic, loud Ferguson. 'What say to a pint? Or a rum punch? Perhaps a spot of lunch.'

There were only two other separate couples within the small courtyard restaurant. The men's straw hats and bulging walking shorts complemented the women's rhinestone sunglasses; they were tourists, obviously unimpressed with Kingston's Devon House. They would soon be talking with each other, thought McAuliff, making happier plans to return to the bar of the cruise ship or, at least, to a free-port strip. They were not interested in Ferguson or himself, and that was all that mattered.

The Jamaican rum punches were delivered by a bored waiter in a dirty white jacket. He did not hum or move with any rhythmic punctuation, observed Alex. The Devon House restaurant was a place of inactivity. Kingston was not Montego Bay.

'I'll tell you exactly what happened,' said Ferguson suddenly, very nervously; his voice once more a panicked whisper. 'And it's everything I know. I worked for the Craft Foundation, you knew all about that. Right?'

'Obviously,' answered McAuliff. 'I made it a condition of your employment that you stay away from Craft. You agreed.'

'I didn't have a choice. When we got off the plane, you and Alison stayed behind; Whitehall and the Jensens went on ahead to the luggage pickup. I was taking some infrared photographs of the airport ... I was in between, you might say. I walked through the arrival gate, and the first person I saw was Craft himself; the son, of course, not the old fellow. The son runs the Foundation now. I tried to avoid him. I had every reason to; after all, he sacked me. But I couldn't. And I was amazed – he was positively effusive. Filled with apologies; what outstanding work I had done, how he personally had come to the airport to meet me when he heard I was with the survey.' Ferguson swallowed a portion of his punch, darting his eyes around the brick courtyard. He seemed to have reached a block, as if uncertain how to continue.

'Go on,' said Alex. 'All you've described is an unexpected welcome wagon.'

'You've *got to understand*. It was all so strange – as you say, unexpected. And as he was talking, this chap in uniform comes through the gate and asks me if I'm Ferguson. I say yes and he tells me you'll be delayed, you're tied up; that *you* want me to have your bags sent on to the hotel. I should write a note to that effect so British Air will release them. Craft offered to help, of course. It all seemed so minor, quite plausible, really, and everything happened so fast. I wrote the note and this chap said he'd take care of it. Craft tipped him. Generously, I believe.'

'What kind of uniform was it?'

'I don't know. I didn't think. Uniforms all look alike when you're out of your own country.'

'Go on.'

'Craft asked me for a drink. I said I really couldn't. But he was adamant, and I didn't care to cause a scene, and you were delayed. You *do* see why I agreed, don't you?'

'Go on.'

'We went to the lounge upstairs . . . the one that looks out over the field. It's got a name . . .'

'Observation.'

'What?'

'It's called the Observation Lounge. Please go on.'

'Yes. Well, I was concerned. I mean, I told him there were my own suitcases and Whitehall, the Jensens. And you, of course. I didn't want you wondering where I was . . . especially under the circumstances.' Ferguson drank again; McAuliff held his temper and spoke simply.

'I think you'd better get to the point, Jimbo-mon.'

'I hope that name doesn't stick. It was a bad evening.'

'It will be a worse afternoon if you don't go on.'

'Yes . . . Craft told me you'd be in Customs for another hour and the chap in uniform would tell the others I was taking pictures; I was to go on to the Courtleigh. I mean, it was strange. Then he changed the subject – completely. He talked about the Foundation. He said they were close to a major breakthrough in the baracoa fibers; that much of the progress was due to my work. And, for reasons ranging from the legal to the moral, they wanted me to come back to Craft. I was actually to be given a percentage of the market development. Do you realize what that could mean?'

'If this is what you had to tell me, you can join them today.'

'Millions!' continued Ferguson, oblivious to Alex's interruption. 'Actually *millions* . . . over the years, of course. I've never had any money. Stony, most of the time. Had to borrow the cash for my camera equipment, did you know that?'

'It wasn't something I dwelled on. But that's all over with. You're with Craft now.'

'*No.* Not yet. That's the point. After the survey. I *must* stay with the survey – stay with *you.*' Ferguson finished his rum punch and looked around for the waiter.

'Merely stay with the survey? With me? I think you've left out something.'

'Yes. Actually.' The young man hunched his shoulders over the table; he avoided McAuliff's eyes. 'Craft said it was harmless, completely harmless. They only want to know the people you deal with in the government . . .

which is just about everyone you deal with, because most everyone's *in* the government. I am to keep a log. That's all; simply a diary.' Ferguson looked up at Alex, his eyes pleading. 'You *do* see, don't you? It *is* harmless.'

McAuliff returned the young man's stare. 'That's why you followed me this morning?'

'Yes. But I didn't mean to do it this way. Craft suggested that I could accomplish a great deal by just ... tagging along with you. Asking if I could join you when you went about survey business. He said I was embarrassingly curious and talked a lot anyway; it would be normal.'

'Two points for Craft.'

'What?'

'An obsolete American expression. Nevertheless, you followed me.'

'I didn't mean to. I rang your room. Several times. There was no answer. Then I called Alison ... I'm sorry. I think she was upset.'

'What did she say?'

'That she thought she heard you leave your room only minutes ago. I ran down to the lobby. And outside. You were driving away in a taxi. *Then* I followed you, in another cab.'

McAuliff put his glass aside. 'Why didn't you come up to me in Victoria Park? I saw you and you turned away.'

'I was confused ... and frightened. I mean, instead of asking to tag along, there I was, really following you.'

'Why did you pretend you were so drunk last night?'

Ferguson took a long nervous intake of breath. 'Because when I got to the hotel, I asked if your luggage had arrived. It hadn't. I panicked, I'm afraid ... You see, before Craft left, he told me about your suitcases—'

'The bugs?' interrupted Alex angrily.

'The what?' Instantly, James understood. 'No. *No!* I swear to you, nothing like that. Oh, God how *awful.*' Ferguson paused, his expression suddenly pensive. 'Yet, of course, it makes sense ...'

No one could have rehearsed such a reversal of reactions, thought Alex. It was pointless to explode. 'What about the suitcases?'

'What ... oh, yes, Craft. At the very end of the conversation, he said they were checking your luggage – *checking*, that's all he said. He suggested, if anyone asked, that I say I'd taken it upon myself to write the note; that I say you were having trouble. But I wasn't to worry, your bags would get to the hotel. But they weren't *there*, you see.'

McAuliff did not see. He sighed wearily. 'So you pretended to be smashed?'

'Naturally. I realized you'd have to know about the note; you'd ask me about it, of course, and be terribly angry if the luggage was lost; blame me for it ... Well, it's a bit unsporting to be hard on a fellow who's squiffed and tried to do you a good turn. I mean, it is, really.'

'You've got a very active imagination, Jimbo-mon. I'd go so far as to say convoluted.'

'Perhaps. But you didn't get angry, did you? And here we are and nothing has changed. That's the irony: Nothing has changed.'

'Nothing changed? What do you mean?'

Ferguson nervously smiled. 'Well ... I'm tagging along.'

'I think something very basic has changed. You've told me about Craft.'

'Yes. I would have anyway; that was my purpose this morning. Craft need never know; no way he could find out. I'll just tag along with you. I'll give you a portion of the money that's coming to me. I promise you that. I'll write it out, if you like. I've never had any money. It simply a marvelous opportunity. You do see that, don't you?'

11

He left Ferguson at the Devon House and took a cab into Old Kingston. If he was being followed, he didn't give a damn. It was a time for sorting out thoughts again, not worrying about surveillance. He wasn't going anywhere.

He had conditionally agreed to cooperate with Ferguson. The condition was that theirs was a two-way street; the botanist could keep his log – freely supplied with controlled names – and McAuliff would be kept informed of this Craft's inquiries.

He looked up at the street signs; he was at the corner of Tower and Matthew, two blocks from the harbour. There was a coin telephone on a stanchion halfway down the sidewalk. He hoped it was operable. It was.

'Has a Mr Sam Tucker checked in?' he asked the clerk on the other end of the line.

'No, Mr McAuliff. As a matter of fact, we were going over the reservations list a few minutes go. Check-in time is three o'clock.'

'Hold the room. It's paid for.'

'I'm afraid it isn't, sir. Our instructions are only that you're responsible; we're trying to be of service.'

'You're very kind. Hold it, nevertheless. Are there any messages for me?'

'Just one minute, sir. I believe there are.'

The silence that ensued gave Alex the time to wonder about Sam. Where the hell was he? McAuliff had not been as alarmed as Robert Hanley over Tucker's disappearance. Sam's eccentricities included sudden wanderings, impulsive treks through native areas. There had been a time in Australia when Tucker stayed four weeks with an outback aborigine community, traveling daily in a Land Rover to the Kimberleys survey site twenty-six miles away. Old Tuck was always looking for the unusual – generally associated with the customs and lifestyles of whatever country he was in. But his deadline was drawing near in Kingston.

'Sorry for the delay,' said the Jamaican, his lilt denying the sincerity of the statement. 'There are several messages. I was putting them in the order of their sequence.'

'Thank you. What are—'

'They're all marked urgent, sir,' interrupted the clerk. 'Eleven fifteen is the first; from the Ministry of Education. Contact Mr Latham as soon as possible. The next at eleven twenty is from a Mr Piersall at the Sheraton. Room fifty-one. Then a Mr Hanley called from Montego Bay at twelve-oh-six; he stressed the importance of your reaching him. His number is—'

'Wait a minute,' said Alex, removing a pencil and a notebook from his pocket. He wrote down the names 'Latham', 'Piersall', 'Hanley'. 'Go ahead.'

'Montego exchange, eighty-two-two-seven. Until five o'clock. Mr Hanley said to call in Port Antonio after six thirty.'

'Did he leave that number?'

'No, sir. Mrs Booth left word at one thirty-five that she would be back in her room at two thirty. She asked that you ring through if you telephoned from outside. That's everything, Mr McAuliff.'

'All right. Thank you. Let me go back, please.' Alex repeated the names, the gists of the messages, and asked for the Sheraton's telephone number. He had no idea who Mr Piersall was. He mentally scanned the twelve contact names provided by Hammond; there was no Piersall.

'Will that be all, sir?'

'Yes. Put me through to Mrs Booth, if you please.'

Alison's phone rang several times before she answered. 'I was taking a shower,' she said, out of breath. 'Rather hoping you were here.'

'Is there a towel around you?'

'Yes. I left it on the knob with the door open, if you must know. So I could hear the telephone.'

'If I was there, I'd remove it. The towel, not the phone.'

'I should think it appropriate to remove both.' Alison laughed, and McAuliff could see the lovely half smile in the haze of the afternoon sun on Tower Street.

'You're right, you're parched. But your note said it was urgent. Is anything the matter?' There was a click within the interior of the telephone box; his time was nearly up. Alison heard it, too.

'Where are you? I'll call you right back,' she said quickly.

The number had been deliberately, maliciously scratched off the dial's center. 'No way to tell. How urgent? I've got another call to make.'

'It can wait. Just don't speak to a man named Piersall until we talk. 'Bye now, darling.'

McAuliff was tempted to call Alison right back; who was Piersall? But it was more important to reach Hanley in Montego. It would be necessary to call collect; he didn't have enough change.

It took the better part of five minutes before Hanley's phone rang and another three while Hanley convinced a switchboard operator at a less-than-chic hotel that he would pay for the call.

'I'm sorry, Robert,' said Alex. 'I'm at a coin box in Kingston.'

'It's all right, lad. Have you heard from Tucker?' There was an urgency in Hanley's rapidly asked question.

'No. He hasn't checked in. I thought you might have something.'

'I have, indeed, and I don't like it at all. I flew back to Mo'Bay a couple of hours ago, and these damn fools here tell me that two black men picked up Sam's belongings, paid the bill, and walked out without a word.'

'Can they do that?'

'This isn't the Hilton, lad. They had the money and they did it.'

'Then where are *you*?'

'Goddammit, I took the same room for the afternoon. In case Sam tries to get in touch, he'll start here, I figured. In the meantime, I've got some friends asking around town. You still don't want the police?'

McAuliff hesitated. He had agreed to Hammond's command not to go to the Jamaican police for anything until he had checked with a contact first and received clearance. 'Not yet, Bob.'

'We're talking about an old friend!'

'He's still not overdue, Robert. I can't legitimately report him missing. And, knowing our old friend, I wouldn't want him embarrassed.'

'I'd sure as hell raise a stink over two strangers picking up his belongings!' Hanley was angry, and McAuliff could not fault him for it.

'We're not sure they're strangers. You know Tuck; he hires attendants like he's the court of Eric the Red. Especially if he's got some money and he can spread it around the outback. Remember Kimberleys, Bob.' A statement. 'Sam blew two months' wages setting up an agricultural commune, for Christ's sake.'

Hanley chuckled. 'Aye, lad, I do. He was going to put the hairy bastards in the wine business. He's a one-man Peace Corps with a vibrating crotch ... All right, Alex. We'll wait until tomorrow. I have to get back to Port Antone. I'll phone you in the morning.'

'If he's not here by then, I'll call the police and you can activate your subterranean network – which I'm sure you've developed by now.'

'Goddamn right. We old travelers have to protect ourselves. And stick together.'

The blinding sun on the hot, dirty Caribbean street and the stench of the telephone mouthpiece was enough to convince McAuliff to return to Courtleigh Manor.

Later, perhaps early this evening, he would find the fish store called Tallon's and his arthritic contact.

He walked north on Matthew Lane and found a taxi on Barry Street; a half-demolished touring car of indeterminate make, and certainly not of this decade, or the last. As he stepped in, the odor of vanilla assaulted his nostrils. Vanilla and bay rum, the scents of Jamaica: delightful in the evening, oppressive during the day under the fiery equatorial sun.

As the cab headed out of Old Kingston – harbour-front Kingston – where man-made decay and cascading tropical flora struggled to coexist, Alex found himself staring with uncomfortable wonder at the suddenly emerging new buildings of New Kingston. There was something obscene about the proximity of such bland, clean structures of stone and tinted glass to the rows of filthy, tin, corrugated shacks – the houses of gaunt children who played slowly, without energy, with bony dogs, and of pregnant young-old women hanging rags on ropes salvaged from the waterfront, their eyes filled with the bleak, hated prospect of getting through another day. And the new, bland, scrubbed obscenities were less than two hundred yards from even more terrible places of human habitation: rotted rat-infested barges, housing those who had reached the last cellars of dignity. Two hundred yards.

McAuliff suddenly realized what these buildings were: banks. Three, four, five ... six banks. Next to, and across from one another, all within an easy throw of a safe-deposit box.

Banks.

Clean, bland, tinted glass.

Two hundred yards.

Eight minutes later, the odd, ancient touring car entered the palm-lined drive of Courtleigh Manor. Ten yards in from the gates, the driver stopped, briefly, with a jerk. Alex, who was sitting forward, taking out his wallet, braced himself against the front seat as the driver quickly apologized. Then McAuliff saw what the Jamaican was doing. He was removing a lethal, thirty-inch machete from the worn felt next to him, and putting it under the seat. The driver grinned.

'I take a fare into old town, mon. Shack town. I keep long knife by me alla time there.'

'Is it necessary?'

'Oh, mon! True, mon. Bad people; dirty people. Not Kingston, mon. Better to shoot alla dirty people. No good, mon. Put 'em in boats back to Africa. Sink boats; yes, mon!'

'That's quite a solution.' The car pulled up to the curb, and McAuliff got out. The driver smiled obsequiously as he stated an inflated charge. Alex handed him the precise amount. 'I'm sure you included the tip,' he said as he dropped the bills through the window.

At the front desk, McAuliff took the messages handed to him; there was an addition. Mr Latham of the Ministry of Education had telephoned again.

Alison was on the small balcony, taking the afternoon sun in her bathing suit. McAuliff entered the room from his connecting door.

She reached out and he took her hand. 'Have you any idea what a lovely lady you are, lovely lady?'

'Thank you, lovely man.'

He gently released her hand. 'Tell me about Piersall,' he said.

'He's at the Sheraton.'

'I know. Room fifty-one.'

'You spoke to him.' Alison was obviously concerned.

'No. That was his message. Phone him in room fifty-one. Very urgent.'

'He may be there now; he wasn't when you called.'

'Oh? I got the message just before I talked to you.'

'Then he must have left it downstairs. Or used a pay phone in the lobby. Within minutes.'

'Why?'

473

'Because he was here. I talked with him.'

'Do tell.'

She did.

Alison had finished sorting out research notes she had prepared for the north coast, and was about to take her shower, when she heard a rapid knocking from Alex's room. Thinking it was one of their party, Alison opened her own door and looked out in the corridor. A tall, thin man in a white Palm Beach suit seemed startled at her appearance. It was an awkward moment for both. Alison volunteered that she had heard the knocking and knew McAuliff was out; would the gentleman care to leave a message?

'He seemed very nervous. He stuttered slightly, and said he'd been trying to reach you since eleven o'clock. He asked if he could trust me. Would I speak only to you? He was really quite upset. I invited him into my room, but he said no, he was in a hurry. Then he blurted it out. He had news of a man named Sam Tucker. Isn't he the American who's to join us here?'

Alex did not bother to conceal his alarm. He bolted from his reclining position and stood up. 'What about Tucker?'

'He didn't go into it. Just that he had word *from* him or *about* him. He wasn't really clear.'

'Why didn't you tell me on the phone?'

'He asked me not to. He said I was to tell you when I saw you, *not* over the telephone. He implied that you'd be angry, but you should get in touch with him before you went to anyone else. Then he left. Alex, what the hell was he talking about?'

McAuliff did not answer; he was on his way to her telephone. He picked up the receiver, glanced at the connecting door, and quickly replaced the phone. He walked rapidly to the open door, closed it, and returned to the telephone. He gave the Sheraton's number and waited.

'Mr Piersall, room fifty-one, please.'

The interim of silence was infuriating to McAuliff. It was broken by the soothing tones of a subdued English voice, asking first the identity of the caller and then whether the caller was a friend or, perhaps, a relative of Dr Piersall's. Upon hearing Alex's replies, the unctuous voice continued, and as it did so, McAuliff remembered a cold night on a Soho street outside The Owl of Saint George. And the flickering of a neon light that saved his life and condemned his would-be-killer to death.

Dr Walter Piersall had been involved in a terrible, tragic accident.

He had been run down by a speeding automobile in a Kingston street.

He was dead.

12

Walter Piersall, American, Ph.D., anthropologist, student of the Caribbean, author of a definitive study on Jamaica's first known inhabitants, the Arawak Indians, and the owner of a house called High Hill near Carrick Foyle in the parish of Trelawny.

That was the essence of the information supplied by the Ministry's Mr Latham.

'A tragedy, Mr McAuliff. He was an honored man, a titled man. Jamaica will miss him greatly.'

'*Miss* him! Who killed him, Mr Latham?'

'As I understand it, there is very little to go on: the vehicle sped away, the description is contradictory.'

'It was broad daylight, Mr Latham.'

There was a pause on Latham's part. 'I know, Mr McAuliff. What can I say? You are an American; he was an American. I am Jamaican, and the terrible thing took place on a Kingston street. I grieve deeply for several reasons. And I did not know the man.'

Latham's sincerity carried over the wire. Alex lowered his voice. 'You say "the terrible thing". Do you mean more than an accident?'

'No. There was no robbery, no mugging. It was an accident. No doubt brought on by rum and inactivity. There is a great deal of both in Kingston, Mr McAuliff. The men ... or children who committed the crime are undoubtedly well into the hills now. When the rum wears off, the fear will take its place; they will hide. The Kingston police are not gentle.'

'I see.' McAuliff was tempted to bring up the name of Sam Tucker, but he held himself in check. He had told Latham only that Piersall had left a message for him. He would say no more for the time being. 'Well, if there's anything I can do ...'

'Piersall was a widower, he lived alone in Carrick Foyle. The police said they were getting in touch with a brother in Cambridge, Massachusetts ... Do you know why he was calling you?'

'No idea.'

'A great deal of your survey will take place in Trelawny Parish. Perhaps he had heard and was offering you hospitality.'

'Perhaps ... Mr Latham, is it logical that he would know about the survey?' Alex listened intently to Latham's reply. Again, Hammond: *Learn to spot the small things.*

'Logical? What is logical in Jamaica, Mr McAuliff? It is a poorly kept secret that the Ministry – with the gracious help of our former mother country – is undertaking an overdue scientific evaluation. A secret poorly kept is not really much of a secret. Perhaps it is not logical that Dr Piersall knew; it is certainly possible, however.'

No hesitations, no overly quick responses, no rehearsed words.

'Then I guess that's what he was calling about. I'm sorry.'

'I grieve.' Again Latham paused; it was not for effect. 'Although it may seem improper, Mr McAuliff, I should like to discuss the business between us.'

'Of course. Go ahead.'

'All of the survey permits came in late this morning . . . less than twenty-four hours. It generally takes the best part of a week.'

The processing was unusual, but Alex had come to expect the unusual with Dunstone Limited. The normal barriers fell with abnormal ease. Unseen expediters were everywhere, doing the bidding of Julian Warfield.

Latham said that the Ministry had anticipated more, rather than less, difficulty, as the survey team would be entering the territory of the Cock Pit, miles of uninhabited country – jungle, really. Escorts were required, guides trained in the treacherous environs. And arrangements had to be made with the recognized descendants of the Maroon people, who, by a treaty of 1739, controlled much of the territory. An arrogant, warlike people, brought to the islands as slaves, the Maroons knew the jungles far better than their white captors. The British sovereign, George the First, had offered the Maroons their independence, with a treaty that guaranteed the Cock Pit territories in perpetuity. It was a wiser course than continuing bloodshed. Besides, the territory was considered unfit for colonial habitation.

For over 235 years that treaty was often scoffed at but never violated, said Latham. Formal permission was still sought by Kingston from the 'Colonel of the Maroons' for all those who wished to enter their lands. The Ministry was no exception.

Yet the Ministry, thought McAuliff, was in reality Dunstone Limited. So permissions were granted, permits obtained with alacrity.

'Your equipment was air-freighted to Boscobel,' said Latham. 'Trucks will transport it to the initial point of the survey.'

'Then I'll leave tomorrow afternoon or, at the latest, early the next day. I'll be hiring out of Ocho Rios; the others can follow when I'm finished. It shouldn't take more than a couple of days.'

'Your escort-guides, we call them "runners", will be available in two weeks. You will not have any need for them until then, will you? I assume you will be working the coast to begin with.'

'Two weeks'll be fine . . . I'd like a choice of runners, please.'

'There are not that many to choose from, Mr McAuliff. It is not a career that appeals to many young people; the ranks are thinning. But I shall do what I can.'

'Thank you. May I have the approved maps in the morning?'

'They will be sent to your hotel by ten o'clock. Goodbye, Mr McAuliff. And again, my deeply felt regrets over Dr Piersall.'

'I didn't know him either, Mr Latham,' said Alex. 'Goodbye.'

He did not know Piersall, thought McAuliff, but he had heard the name Carrick Foyle, Piersall's village. He could not remember where he had heard it, only that it was familiar.

Alex replaced the telephone and looked over at Alison, on the small balcony. She had been watching him, listening, and she could not conceal her fear. A thin, nervous man in a white Palm Beach suit had told her – less than two hours ago – that he had confidential information, and now he was dead.

The late afternoon sun was a Caribbean orange, the shadows shafts of black across the miniature balcony. Behind her was the deep green of the high palms, behind them the awesome rise of the mountain range. Alison Booth seemed to be framed within a tableau of chiaroscuro tropic colors. As though she were a target.

'He said it was an accident.' Alex walked slowly to the balcony doors. 'Everyone's upset. Piersall was liked on the island. Apparently, there's a lot of drunken hit-and-runs in Kingston.'

'And you don't believe him for an instant.'

'I didn't say that.' He lighted a cigarette; he did not want to look at her.

'You don't have to. You didn't say one word about your friend Tucker, either. Why not?'

'Common sense. I want to talk to the police, not an associate director of the Ministry. All he can do is babble and create confusion.'

'Then let's go to the police.' Alison rose from the deck chair. 'I'll go get dressed.'

'No!' McAuliff realized as he said the word that he was too emphatic. 'I mean, I'll go. I don't want you involved.'

'I spoke to the man. You didn't.'

'I'll relay the information.'

'They won't accept it from you. Why should they hear it secondhand?'

'Because I say so.' Alex turned away, ostensibly to find an ashtray. He was not convincing, and he knew it. 'Listen to me, Alison.' He turned back. 'Our permits came in. Tomorrow I'm going to Ocho Rios to hire drivers and carriers; you people will follow in a couple of days. While I'm gone I don't want you – or any member of the team – involved with the police or anybody else. Our job here is the survey. That's my responsibility; you're my responsibility. I don't want delays.'

She walked down the single step, out of the frame of color, and stood in front of him. 'You're a dreadful liar, Alex. Dreadful in the sense that you're quite poor at it.'

'I'm going to the police now. Afterwards, if it's not too late, I may drop over to the Ministry and see Latham. I was a little rough with him.'

'I thought you ended on a very polite note.'

It was Alison who spotted Hammond's small things, thought McAuliff. She was better than he was. 'You only heard me. You didn't hear him . . . If I'm not back by seven, why not call the Jensens and have dinner with them? I'll join you as soon as I can.'

'The Jensens aren't here.'

'What?'

'Relax. I called them for lunch. They left word at the desk that since it was a day off, they were touring. Port Royal, Spanish Town, Old Harbour. The manager set up their tour.'

'I hope they enjoy themselves.'

He told the driver that he wanted a half-hour's tour of the city. He had thirty minutes to kill before cocktails in Duke Street – he'd spot the restaurant; he didn't know the specific address – so the driver could do his imaginative best within the time span.

The driver protested: thirty minutes was barely sufficient to reach Duke Street from the Courtleigh in the afternoon traffic. McAuliff shrugged and replied that the time was not absolute.

It was precisely what the driver wanted to hear. He drove out Trafalgar, south on Lady Musgrave, into Old Hope Road. He extolled the commercial virtues of New Kingston, likening the progress to Olympian feats of master planning. The words droned on, filled with idiomatic exaggerations of the 'alla time big American millions' that were turning the tropical and human overgrowth that was Kingston into a Caribbean financial mecca. It was understood that the millions would be German or English or French, depending on the accent of the passenger.

It didn't matter. Within minutes, McAuliff knew that the driver knew he was not listening. He was staring out the rear window, watching the traffic behind them.

It was there.

A green Chevrolet sedan, several years old. It stayed two to three cars behind, but whenever the taxi turned or sped ahead of other vehicles, the green Chevrolet did the same.

The driver saw it too.

'You got trouble, mon?'

There was no point in lying. 'I don't know.'

'I know, mon. Lousy green car be'n d'ere all time. It stay in big parking lot at Courtleigh Manor. Two block sons of a bitch drivin'.'

McAuliff looked at the driver. The Jamaican's last statement triggered his memory of Robert Hanley's words from Montego Bay. *Two black men picked up Sam's things.* Alex knew the connection was far-fetched, coincidental at best in a black country, but it was all he had to go on. 'You can earn twenty dollars, friend,' he said quickly to the driver, 'if you can do two things.'

'You tell me, mon!'

'First, let the green car get close enough so I can read the licence plate, and when I've got it, lose them. Can you do that?'

'You watch, mon!' The Jamaican swung the wheel to the right; the taxi veered briefly into the right lane, narrowly missing an oncoming bus, then lurched back into the left, behind a Volkswagen. McAuliff crouched against the seat, his head pressed to the right of the rear window. The green Chevrolet duplicated the taxi's movements, taking up a position two cars behind.

Suddenly the cabdriver accelerated again, passing the Volks and speeding ahead to a traffic light that flashed the yellow caution signal. He swung the car into the left intersection; Alex read the street sign and the wording on the large shield-shaped sign beneath:

TORRINGTON ROAD

ENTRANCE

GEORGE VI MEMORIAL PARK

'We head into a racecourse, mon!' shouted the driver. 'Green son of a bitch have to stop at Snipe Street light. He come out'a d'ere fast. You watch good now!'

The cab sped down Torrington, swerving twice out of the left lane to pass three vehicles, and through the wide-gated entrance into the park. Once inside, the driver slammed on the brakes, backed the taxi into what looked like a bridle path, spun the wheel, and lurched forward into the exit side of the street.

'You catch 'em good now, mon!' yelled the Jamaican as he slowed the car down and entered the flow of traffic leaving the George VI Memorial Park.

Within seconds the green Chevrolet came into view, hemmed between automobiles entering the park. And then McAuliff realized precisely what the driver had done. It was early track time; George VI Memorial Park housed the sport of kings. Gambling Kingston was on the way to the races.

Alex wrote down the licence number, keeping himself out of sight but seeing clearly enough to know that the two black men in the Chevrolet did not realize that they had passed within feet of the car they were following.

'Them sons of bitches got to drive all way 'round, mon! Them dumb block sons of bitches! ... Where you want to go, mon? Plenty of time, now. They don't catch us.'

McAuliff smiled. He wondered if the Jamaican's talents were listed in Hammond's manual somewhere. 'You just earned yourself an extra five dollars. Take me to the corner of Queen and Hanover Streets, please. No sense wasting time, now.'

'Hey, mon! You hire my taxi alla time in Kingston. I do what you say. I don' ask questions, mon.'

Alex looked at the identification behind the dirty plastic frame above the dashboard. 'This isn't a private cab ... Rodney.'

'You make a deal with me, mon; I make a deal with the taxi boss.' The driver grinned in the rear-view mirror.

'I'll think about it. Do you have a telephone number?'

The Jamaican quickly produced an outsized business card and handed it back to McAuliff. It was the taxi company's card, the type that was left on hotel counters. Rodney's name was printed childishly in ink across the bottom. 'You telephone company, say you gotta have Rodney. Only Rodney, mon. I get the message real quick. Alla time they know where Rodney is. I work hotels and Palisados. Them get me quick.'

'Suppose I don't care to leave my name—'

'No name, mon!' broke in the Jamaican, grinning in the mirror. 'I got lousy sen-of-a-bitch memory. Don't want no name! You tell taxi phone . . . you the fella at the racecourse. Give place; I get to you, mon.'

Rodney accelerated south to North Street, left to Duke, and south again past the Gordon House, the huge new complex of the Kingston legislature.

Out on the sidewalk, McAuliff straightened his jacket and his tie and tried to assume the image of an average white businessman not entirely sure of which government entrance he should use. Tallon's was not listed in any telephone or shopping directory; Hammond had indicated that it was below the row of government houses, which meant below Queen, but he was not specific.

As he looked for the fish store, he checked the people around him, across the street, and in the automobiles that seemed to go slower than the traffic allowed.

For a few minutes he felt himself in the pocket of fear again; afraid that the unseen had their eyes on him.

He reached Queen Street and hurried across with the last contingent making the light. On the curb he turned swiftly to watch those behind on the other side.

The orange sun was low on the horizon, throwing a corridor of blinding light from the area of Victoria Park several hundred yards to the west. The rest of the street was in dark, sharply defined shadows cast from the structures of stone and wood all around. Automobiles passed east and west, blocking a clear vision of those on the north corner. Corners.

He could tell nothing. He turned and proceeded down the block.

He saw the sign first. It was filthy, streaked with runny print that had not been refinished in months, perhaps years:

TALLON'S

FINE FISH AND NATIVE DELICACIES

311½ QUEEN'S ALLEY

1 BLOCK – DUKE ST. WEST

He walked the block. The entrance to Queen's Alley was barely ten feet high, cut off by grillwork covered with tropical flowers. The cobblestone passage did not go through to the next street as is common in Paris and

Rome and Greenwich Village. Although it was in the middle of a commercial market area, there was a personal quality about his appearance, as though an unwritten sign proclaimed this section private: residents only, keys required, not for public usage. All that was needed, thought McAuliff, was a gate.

In Paris and Rome and Greenwich Village, such wide alleys held some of the best restaurants in the world, known only to those who cared.

In Shenzen and Macao and Hong Kong, they were the recesses where anything could be had for a price.

In Kingston, this one housed a man with arthritis who worked for British Intelligence.

Queen's Alley was no more than fifty feet long. On the right was a bookstore with subdued lighting in the windows, illuminating a variety of wares from heavy academic leather to nonglossy pornography. On the left was Tallon's.

He had pictured casements of crushed ice supporting rows of wide-eyed dead fish, and men in soiled, cheap white aprons running around scales, arguing with customers.

The crushed ice was in the window; so were several rows of glassy-eyed fish. But what impressed him was the other forms of ocean merchandise placed artistically: squid, octopus, shark, and exotic shellfish.

Tallon's was no Fulton Market.

As if to add confirmation to his thoughts, a uniformed chauffeur emerged from Tallon's entrance carrying a plastic shopping bag, insulated, Alex was sure, with crushed ice.

The double doors were thick, difficult to open. Inside, the counters were spotless; the sawdust on the floor was white. The two attendants were just that: attendants, not countermen. Their full-length aprons were striped blue and white and made of expensive linen. The scales behind the chromeframed glass cases had shiny brass trimmings. Around the shop, stacked shelves lighted by tiny spotlights in the ceiling, were hundreds of tins of imported delicacies from all parts of the world.

It was not quite real.

There were three other customers: a couple and a single woman. The couple was at the far end of the store, studying labels on the shelves; the woman was ordering from a list, being overly precise, arrogant.

McAuliff approached the counter and spoke the words he had been instructed to speak.

'A friend in Santo Domingo told me you had north-coast trout.'

The light-skinned black man behind the white wall barely looked at Alex, but within that instant there was recognition. He bent down, separating shellfish inside the case, and answered casually. Correctly. 'We have some freshwater trout from Martha Brae, sir.'

'I prefer saltwater trout. Are you sure you can't help me?'

'I'll see, sir.' The man shut the case, turned, and walked down a corridor in the wall behind the counter, a passageway Alex assumed led to large refrigerated rooms.

When a man emerged from a side door within the corridor, McAuliff caught his breath, trying to suppress his astonishment. The man was black and slight and old; he walked with a cane, his right forearm still, and his head trembled slightly with age.

It was the man in Victoria Park: the old man who had stared at him disapprovingly in front of the bench on the Queen Street path.

He walked to the counter and spoke, his voice apparently stronger than his body. 'A fellow saltwater trout lover,' he said, in an accent more British than Jamaican, but not devoid of the Caribbean. 'What are we to do with those freshwater aficionados who cost me so much money? Come, it is nearly closing. You shall have your choice from my own selection.'

A hinged panel of the butcher-block counter was lifted by the light-skinned attendant in the striped apron. Alex followed the arthritic old man down the short corridor and through a narrow door into a small office that was a miniature extension of the expensive outer design. The walls were paneled in fruitwood; the furniture was a single mahogany desk with a functional antique swivel chair, a soft leather couch against the wall, and an armchair in front of the desk. The lighting was indirect, from a lone china lamp on the desk. With the door closed, Alex saw oak file cabinets lined against the inner wall. Although the room was confining in size, it was eminently comfortable – the isolated quarters of a contemplative man.

'Sit, Mr McAuliff,' said the proprietor of Tallon's, indicating the armchair as he hobbled around the desk and sat down, placing his cane against the wall. 'I've been expecting you.'

'You were in Victoria Park this morning.'

'I did not expect you then. To be quite frank, you startled me. I'd been looking at your photograph minutes before I took my stroll. From nowhere the face of this photograph was in front of my eyes in Victoria.' The old man smiled and gestured with his palms up, signifying unexpected coincidence. 'Incidentally, my name is Tallon. Westmore Tallon. We're a fine old Jamaican family, as I'm sure you've been told.'

'I hadn't, but one look at your ... fish store would seem to confirm it.'

'Oh, yes. We're frightfully expensive, very exclusive. Private telephone number. We cater only to the wealthiest on the island. From Savanna to Montego to Antonio and Kingston. We have our own delivery service – by private plane, of course ... It's most convenient.'

'I should think so. Considering your extracurricular activities.'

'Which, of course, we must never consider to the point of discussion, Mr McAuliff,' replied Tallon quickly.

'I've got several things to tell you. I expect you'll transmit the information and let Hammond do what he wants.'

'You sound angry.'

'On one issue, I am. Goddamned angry ... Mrs Booth. Alison Booth. She was manipulated here through Interpol. I think that smells. She made one painful – and dangerous – contribution. I should think you people would let her alone.'

Tallon pushed his foot against the floor, turning the silent antique swivel to his right. He aimlessly reached over for his cane and fingered it. 'I am merely a . . . liaison, Mr McAuliff, but from what I understand, no pressure was exerted on you to employ Mrs Booth. You did so freely. Where was the manipulation?'

Alex watched the small, arthritic man toy with the handle of the cane. He was struck by the thought that in some strange way Westmore Tallon was like an artist's composite of Julian Warfield and Charles Whitehall. The communion of elements was disturbing. 'You people are very professional,' he said quietly, a touch bitterly. 'You're ingenious when it comes to presenting alternatives.'

'She can't go home, Mr McAuliff. Take my word for that.'

'From a certain point of view, she might as well . . . The Marquis de Chatellerault is in Jamaica.'

Tallon spun in the antique chair to face McAuliff. For an instant he seemed frozen. He stared at Alex, and when he blinked it was as though he silently rejected McAuliff's statement. 'This is impossible,' he said simply.

'It's not only possible, I don't even think it's a secret. Or if it is, it's poorly kept; and as somebody said about an hour ago, that's not much of a secret.'

'Who gave you this information?' Tallon held onto his cane, his grasp visibly firmer.

'Charles Whitehall. At three o'clock this morning. He was invited to Savanna-la-Mar to meet Chatellerault.'

'What were the circumstances?'

'The circumstances aren't important. The important fact is that Chatellerault is in Savanna-la-Mar. He is the house guest of a family named Wakefield. They're white and rich.'

'We know them,' said Tallon, writing a note awkwardly with his arthritic hand. 'They're customers. What else do you have?'

'A couple of items. One is extremely important to me, and I warn you, I won't leave here until something's done about it.'

Tallon looked up from his notepaper. 'You make pronouncements without regard for realistic appraisal. I have no idea whether I can do anything about anything. Your camping here would not change that. Please continue.'

Alex described James Ferguson's unexpected meeting with Craft at the Palisados Airport and the manipulation that resulted in the electronic devices in his luggage. He detailed Craft's offer of money in exchange for information about the survey.

'It's not surprising. The Craft people are notoriously curious,' said Tallon, writing painfully on his notepaper. 'Shall we get to the item you say is so vital?'

'I want to summarize first.'

'Summarize what?' Tallon put down his pencil.

'What I've told you.'

Tallon smiled. 'It's not necessary, Mr McAuliff. I take notes slowly, but my mind is quite alert.'

'I'd like us to understand each other ... British Intelligence wants the Halidon. That was the purpose – the only purpose – of my recruitment. Once the Halidon could be reached, I was finished. Complete protection still guaranteed to the survey team.'

'And so?'

'I think you've got the Halidon. It's Chatellerault and Craft.'

Tallon continued to stare at McAuliff. His expression was totally neutral. 'You have arrived at this conclusion?'

'Hammond said this Halidon would interfere. Eventually try to stop the survey. Diagrams aren't necessary. The marquis and Craft fit the prints. Go get them.'

'I see ...' Tallon reached once more for his cane. His personal scepter, his sword Excalibur. 'So, in one extraordinary simplification, the American geologist has solved the riddle of the Halidon.'

Neither man spoke for several moments. McAuliff broke the silence with equally quiet anger. 'I could get to dislike you, Mr Tallon. You're a very arrogant man.'

'My concerns do not include your approval, Mr McAuliff. Jamaica is my passion – yes, my *passion*, sir. What you think is not important to me ... except when you make absurd pronouncements that could affect my work ... Arthur Craft, *père et fils*, have been raping this island for half a century. They subscribe to the belief that theirs is a mandate from God. They can accomplish too much in the name of Craft; they would not hide behind a symbol. And Halidon *is* a symbol, Mr McAuliff ... The Marquis de Chatellerault? You were quite correct. Mrs Booth *was* manipulated – brilliantly, I think – into your survey. It was cross-pollination, if you like; the circumstances were optimum. Two kling-klings in a hibiscus, one inexorably forcing the other to reveal himself. She was bait, pure and simple, Mr McAuliff. Chatellerault has long been suspected of being an associate of Julian Warfield. The marquis is with Dunstone Limited.' Tallon lifted his cane up laterally, placed it across his desk, and continued to gaze blankly at Alex.

McAuliff said finally, 'You withheld information; you didn't tell me things I should have been told. Yet you expect me to function as one of you. That smells, Tallon.'

'You exaggerate. There is no point in complicating further an already complicated picture.'

'I should have been told about Chatellerault, instead of hearing his name from Mrs Booth.'

Tallon shrugged. 'An oversight. Shall we proceed?'

'All right. There's a man named Tucker. Sam Tucker.'

'Your friend from California? The soil analyst?'

'Yes.'

McAuliff told Hanley's story without using Hanley's name. He emphasized the coincidence of the two black men who had removed Tucker's belongings and the two Jamaicans who had followed his taxi in the green Chevrolet sedan. He described briefly the taxi owner's feats of driving skills in the racetrack park, and gave Tallon the licence plate number of the Chevrolet.

Tallon reached for his telephone and dialed without speaking to Alex. 'This is Tallon,' he said quietly into the phone. 'I want M.V. information. It is urgent. The licence is KYB four-four-eight. Call me back on this line.' He hung up and shifted his eyes to McAuliff. 'It should take no longer than five minutes.'

'Was that the police?'

'Not in any way the police would know ... I understand the Ministry received your permits today. Dunstone does facilitate things, doesn't it?'

'I told Latham I was leaving for Ocho Rios tomorrow afternoon. I won't if Tucker doesn't show up. That's what I want you to know.'

Once again, Westmore Tallon reached for his cane, but not with the aggressiveness he had displayed previously. He was suddenly a rather thoughtful, even gentle man. 'If your friend was taken against his will, it would be kidnapping. A very serious crime, and insofar as he's American, the sort of headline attraction that would be an anathema. It doesn't make sense, Mr McAuliff ... You say he's due today, which could be extended to this evening, I presume?'

'Yes.'

'Then I suggest we wait. I cannot believe the parties involved could – or would – commit such a gargantuan mistake. If Mr Tucker is not heard from by, say, ten o'clock, call me.' Tallon wrote a number on a piece of paper and handed it to Alex. 'Commit this to memory, please; leave the paper here.'

'What are you going to do if Tucker doesn't show?'

'I will use perfectly legitimate connections and have the matter directed to the most authoritative officials in the Jamaican police. I will alert highly placed people in the government; the governor-general, if necessary. St Croix has had its murders; tourism is only now coming back. Jamaica could not tolerate an American kidnapping. Does that satisfy you?'

'I'm satisfied.' Alex crushed out his cigarette in the ashtray, and as he did so, he remembered Tallon's reaction to Chatellerault's appearance in Savanna-la-Mar. 'You were surprised that Chatellerault was on the island. Why?'

'As of two days ago, he was registered at the Georges Cinque in Paris. There's been no word of his leaving, which means he flew here clandestinely, probably by way of Mexico. It is disturbing. You must keep a close watch on Mrs Booth. You have a weapon, I assume?'

'Two rifles in the equipment. An .030 Remington telescopic and a long-power .22 automatic. Nothing else.'

Tallon seemed to debate with himself, then make his decision. He took a key ring from his pocket, selected a key, and opened a lower drawer of his desk. He removed a bulky manila envelope, opened the flap, and shook a pistol onto his blotter. A number of cartridges fell out with the gun. 'This is a

.38 Smith & Wesson, short barrel. All markings have been destroyed. It's untraceable. Take it, please; it's wiped clean. The only fingerprints will be yours. Be careful.'

McAuliff looked at the weapon for several seconds before reaching out and slowly picking it up. He did not want it; there was a finality of commitment somehow attached to his having it. But again, there was the question of alternatives: Not having it might possibly be foolish, though he did not expect to use it for anything more than a show of force.

'Your dossier includes your military service and experience in small-arms fire. But that was a long time ago. Would you care to refresh yourself at a pistol range? We have several, within minutes by plane.'

'No, thank you,' replied Alex. 'Not too long ago, in Australia, it was the only diversion we had.'

The telephone rang with a muted bell. Tallon picked it up and acknowledged with a simple 'Yes?'

He listened without speaking to the party on the other end of the line. When he terminated the call, he looked at McAuliff.

'The green Chevrolet sedan is registered to a dead man. The vehicle's licence is in the name of Walter Piersall. Residence: High Hill, Carrick Foyle, parish of Trelawny.'

13

McAuliff spent another hour with Westmore Tallon, as the old Jamaican aristocrat activated his information network. He had sources all over the island. Before the hour was up, one important fact had been uncovered: the deceased, Walter Piersall of Carrick Foyle, parish of Trelawny, had in his employ two black assistants with whom he invariably traveled. The coincidence of the two men who had removed Sam Tucker's belongings from the hotel in Montego Bay and the two men who followed Alex in the green Chevrolet was no longer far-fetched. And since Piersall had brought up Sam's name with Alison Booth, the conclusion was now to be assumed.

Tallon ordered his own people to pick up Piersall's men. He would telephone McAuliff when they had done so.

Alex returned to Courtleigh Manor. He stopped at the desk for messages. Alison was at dinner; she hoped he would join her. There was nothing else.

No word from Sam Tucker.

'If there are any calls for me, I'll be in the dining room,' he said to the clerk.

Alison sat alone in the middle of the crowded room, which was profuse with tropical plants and open-grilled windows. In the center of each table was a candle within a lantern; these were the only sources of light. Shadows flickered against the dark red and green and yellow foliage; the hum was the hum of contentment, rising but still quiet crescendos of laughter; perfectly groomed, perfectly dressed manikins in slow motion, all seemingly waiting for the nocturnal games to begin.

This was the manikins' good hour. When manners and studied grace and minor subtleties were important. Later it would be different; other things would become important ... and too often ugly. Which is why James Ferguson knew his drunken pretense had been plausible last night.

And why Charles Whitehall arrogantly, quietly, had thrown the napkin across the table onto the floor. To clean up the foreigner's mess.

'You look pensive. Or disagreeable,' said Alison as Alex pulled out the chair to sit down.

'Not really.'

'What happened? What did the police say? I half expected a call from them.'

487

McAuliff had rehearsed his reply, but before delivering it he gestured at the cup of coffee and the brandy glass in front of Alison. 'You've had dinner, I guess.'

'Yes. I was famished. Haven't you?'

'No. Keep me company?'

'Of course. I'll dismiss the eunuchs.'

He ordered a drink. 'You have a lovely smile. It's sort of a laugh.'

'No sidetracking. What happened?'

McAuliff lied quite well, he thought. Certainly better – at least more persuasively – than before. He told Alison he had spent nearly two hours with the police. Westmore Tallon had furnished him with the address and even described the interior of the main headquarters; it had been Tallon's idea for him to know the general details. One could never tell when they were important.

'They backed up Latham's theory. They say it's hit-and-run. They also hinted that Piersall had a diversion or two that was closeted. He was run down in a very rough section.'

'That sounds suspiciously pat to me. They're covering themselves.' Alison's eyebrows furrowed, her expression one of disbelief.

'They may be,' answered Alex casually, sincerely. 'But they can't tie him to Sam Tucker, and that's my only concern.'

'He *is* tied. He told me.'

'And *I* told *them*. They've sent men to Carrick Foyle, that's where Piersall lived. In Trelawny. Others are going over his things at the Sheraton. If they find anything, they'll call me.' McAuliff felt that he was carrying off the lie. He was, after all, only bending the truth. The arthritic Westmore Tallon was doing these things.

'And you're satisfied with that? You're just going to take their word for it? You were awfully troubled with Mr Tucker a few hours ago.'

'I still am,' said Alex, putting down his glass and looking at her. He had no need to lie now. 'If I don't hear from Sam by late tonight . . . or tomorrow morning, I'm going to go to the American Embassy and yell like hell.'

'Oh . . . all right. Did you mention the little buggers this morning? You never told me.'

'The what?'

'Those bugs in your luggage. You said you were supposed to report them.'

Again McAuliff felt a wave of inadequacy; it irked him that he wasn't keeping track of things. Of course, he hadn't seen Tallon earlier, had not received his instructions, but that was no explanation. 'I should have listened to you last night. I can just get rid of them; step on them, I guess.'

'There's a better way.'

'What's that?'

'Put them someplace else.'

'For instance?'

'Oh, somewhere harmless but with lots of traffic. It keeps the tapes rolling and people occupied.'

McAuliff laughed; it was not a false laugh. 'That's very funny. And very practical. Where would they be, listening, I mean?'

Alison brought her hands to her chin; a mischievous little girl thinking mischievously. 'It should be within a hundred yards or so – that's usually the range tolerance between bugs and the receivers And where there's a great deal of activity ... Let's see. I complimented the headwaiter on the red snapper. I'll bet he'd bring me to the chef for the recipe.'

'They love that sort of thing,' added Alex. 'It's perfect. Don't go away. I'll be right back.'

Alison Booth, former liaison to Interpol, reported that two electronic devices were securely attached to the permanent laundry hamper under the salad table in the Courtleigh Manor kitchen. She had slipped them inside – and pushed them down – along with a soiled napkin, as an enthusiastic chef described the ingredients of his Jamaican red snapper sauce.

'The hamper was long, not deep,' she explained as McAuliff finished the last of his dinner. 'I pressed rather hard; the adhesive will hold quite well, I think.'

'You're incredible,' said Alex, meaning it.

'No, just experienced,' she replied, without much humor. 'You were only taught one side of the game, my darling.'

'It doesn't sound much like tennis.'

'Oh, there are compensations. For example, do you have any idea how limitless the possibilities are? In that kitchen for the next three hours or so, until it's tracked?'

'I'm not sure I know what you mean.'

'Depending upon who's on the tapes, there'll be a mad scramble writing down words and phrases. Kitchen talk has its own contractions, its own language, really. It will be assumed you've taken your suitcase to a scheduled destination, for reasons of departure, naturally. There'll be quite a bit of confusion.' Alison smiled, her eyes again mischievous, as they had been before he had gone upstairs to pry loose the bugs.

'You mean, "sauce Béarnaise" is really a code for submachine gun? "B.L.T." stands for "hit the beaches"?'

'Something like that. It's quite possible, you know.'

'I thought that sort of thing only happened in World War Two movies. With Nazis screaming at each other, sending Panzer divisions in the wrong directions.' McAuliff looked at his watch. It was nine fifteen. 'I have a phone call to make, and I want to go over a list of supplies with Ferguson. He's going to—'

He stopped. Alison had reached over, her hand suddenly on his arm. 'Don't turn your head,' she commanded softly, 'but I think your little buggers provoked a reaction. A man just came through the dining room entrance very rapidly, obviously looking for someone.'

'For us?'

'For you, to be precise, I'd say.'

'The kitchen codes didn't fool them very long.'

'Perhaps not. On the other hand, it's quite possible they've been keeping loose tabs on you and were double-checking. It's too small a hotel for round-the-clock—'

'Describe him,' interrupted McAuliff. 'As completely as you can. Is he still facing this way?'

'He saw you and stopped. He's apologizing to the man on the reservations book, I think. He's white; he's dressed in light trousers, a dark jacket, and a white – no, a yellow shirt. He's shorter than you by a bit, fairly chunky—'

'What?'

'You know, bulky. And middle-young, thirties, I'd say. His hair is long, not extreme, but long. It's dark blond or light brown; it's hard to tell in this candlelight.'

'You've done fine. Now I've got to get to a telephone.'

'Wait till he leaves; he's looking over again,' said Alison, feigning interested, intimate laughter. 'Why don't you leer a little and signal for the check. Very casually, my darling.'

'I feel like I'm in some kind of nursery school. With the prettiest teacher in town.' Alex held up his hand, spotted the waiter, and made the customary scribble in the air. 'I'll take you to your room, then come back downstairs and call.'

'Why? Use the phone in the room. The buggers aren't there.'

Damn! Goddamn! It had happened again; he wasn't prepared. The little things, always the little things. They were the traps. Hammond said it over and over again ... Hammond. The Savoy. Don't make calls on the Savoy phone.

'I was told to use a pay telephone. They must have their reasons.'

'Who?'

'The Ministry. Latham ... the police, of course.'

'Of course. The police.' Alison withdrew her hand from his arm as the waiter presented the bill for Alex to sign. She didn't believe him; she made no pretense of believing him. Why should she? He was a rotten actor; he was caught ... But it was preferable to an ill-phrased statement or an awkward response to Westmore Tallon over the phone while Alison watched him. And listened. He had to feel free in his conversation with the arthritic liaison; he could not have one eye, one ear on Alison as he talked. He could not take the chance that the name Chatellerault, or even a hint of the man, was heard. Alison was too quick.

'Has he left yet?'

'As you signed the check. He saw we were leaving.' Her reply was neither angry nor warm, merely neutral.

They walked out of the candlelit dining room, past the cascading arcs of green foliage into the lobby, toward the bank of elevators. Neither spoke. The ride up to their floor continued in silence, made bearable by other guests in the small enclosure.

He opened the door and repeated the precautions he had taken the previous evening – minus the scanner. He was in a hurry now; if he remembered, he would bless the room with electronic benediction later. He checked his own room and locked the connecting door from her side. He looked out on the balcony and in the bathroom. Alison stood in the corridor doorway, watching him.

He approached her. 'Will you stay here until I get back?'

'Yes,' she answered simply.

He kissed her on the lips, staying close to her, he knew, longer than she expected him to; it was his message to her. 'You are a lovely lady.'

'Alex?' She placed her hands carefully on his arms and looked up at him. 'I know the symptoms. Believe me, I do. They're not easy to forget ... There are things you're not telling me and I won't ask. I'll wait.'

'You're overdramatizing, Alison.'

'That's funny.'

'What is?'

'What you just said. I used those words with David. In Malaga. He was nervous, frightened. He was so unsure of himself. And of me. And I said to him: David, you're being overly dramatic ... I know now that it was at that moment he knew.'

McAuliff held her eyes with his own. 'You're not David and I'm not you. That's as straight as I can put it. Now, I have to get to a telephone. I'll see you later. Use the latch.'

He kissed her again, went out the door, and closed it behind him. He waited until he heard the metallic sounds of the inserted bolt, then turned toward the elevators.

The doors closed; the elevator descended. The soft music was piped over the heads of assorted businessmen and tourists; the cubicle was full. McAuliff's thoughts were on his imminent telephone call to Westmore Tallon, his concerns about Sam Tucker.

The elevator stopped at an intermediate floor. Alex looked up at the lighted digits absently, vaguely wondering how another person could fit in the cramped enclosure. There was no need to think about the problem; the two men who waited by the parting doors saw the situation, smiled, and gestured that they would wait for the next elevator.

And then McAuliff saw him. Beyond the slowly closing panels, far down in the corridor. A stocky man in a dark jacket and light trousers. He had unlocked a door and was about to enter a room; as he did so, he pulled back his jacket to replace the key in his pocket. The shirt was yellow.

The door closed.

'Excuse me! Excuse me, please!' said McAuliff rapidly as he reached across a tuxedoed man near the panel of buttons and pushed the one marked 2, the next number in descent. 'I forgot my floor. I'm terribly sorry.'

The elevator, its thrust suddenly, electronically interrupted, jerked slightly as it mindlessly prepared for the unexpected stop. The panels opened and Alex sidled past the irritated but accommodating passengers.

He stood in the corridor in front of the bank of elevators and immediately pushed the Up button. Then he reconsidered. Where were the stairs?

The EXIT – STAIRCASE sign was blue with white letters. That seemed peculiar to him; exit signs were always red. It was at the far end of the hallway. He walked rapidly down the heavily carpeted corridor, nervously smiling at a couple who emerged from a doorway at midpoint. The man was in his fifties and drunk; the girl was barely in her twenties sober and mulatto. Her clothes were the costume of a high-priced whore. She smiled at Alex; another sort of message. He acknowledged, his eyes telling her he wasn't interested but good luck, take the company drunk for all she could.

He pushed the crossbar on the exit door. Its sound was too loud; he closed it carefully, quietly, relieved to see there was a knob on the inside of the door.

He ran up the concrete stairs on the balls of his feet, minimizing the sound of his footsteps. The steel panel had the Roman numeral III stenciled in black over the beige paint. He twisted the knob slowly and opened the door onto the third-floor corridor.

It was empty. The nocturnal games had begun below; the players would remain in the competitive arenas until the prizes had been won or lost or forgotten in alcoholic oblivion. He had only to be alert for stragglers, or the overanxious, like the pigeon on the second floor who was being manoeuvred with such precision by the child-woman mulatto. He tried to recall at which door the man in the yellow shirt had stood. He had been quite far down the hallway, but not at the end. Not by the staircase; two-thirds of the way, perhaps. On the right; he had pulled back his jacket with his right hand, revealing the yellow shirt. That meant he was not inside a door on Alex's left. Reversing the viewpoint, he focused on three ... no, four doors on his left that were possible. Beginning with the second door from the suitcase, one-third the distance to the elevators.

Which one?

McAuliff began walking noiselessly on the thick carpet down the corridor, hugging the left wall. He paused before each door as he passed, his head constantly turning, his eyes alert, his ears listening for the sound of voices, the tinkling of glasses. For anything.

Nothing.

Silence. Everywhere.

He looked at the brass numbers – 218, 216, 214, 212. Even 210. Any farther would be incompatible with what he remembered.

He stopped at the halfway point and turned. Perhaps he knew enough. Enough to tell Westmore Tallon. Alison had said that the tolerance range for the electronic bugs was one hundred yards from first positioning to the receiving equipment. This floor, this section of the hotel, was well within that limit. Behind one of those doors was a tape recorder activated by a man in front of a speaker or with earphones clamped over his head.

Perhaps it was enough to report those numbers. Why should he look further?

Yet he knew he would. Someone had seen fit to intrude on his life in a way that filled him with revulsion. Few things caused him to react violently, but one of them was the actual, intended invasion of his privacy. And greed. Greed, too, infuriated him. Individual, academic, corporate.

Someone named Craft – because of his greed – had instructed his minions to invade Alex's personal moments.

Alexander Tarquin McAuliff was a very angry man.

He started back toward the staircase, retracing his steps, close to the wall, closer to each door, where he stopped and stood immobile. Listening.

212, 214, 216, 218 . . .

And back once again. It was a question of patience. Behind one of those doors was a man in a yellow shirt. He wanted to find that man.

He heard it.

Room 214.

It was a radio. Or a television set. Someone had turned up the volume of a television set. He could not distinguish the words, but he could hear the excitement behind the rapid bursts of dialogue from a clouded speaker, too loud to avoid distortion.

Suddenly, there was the sound of a harsh, metallic crack of a door latch. Inches away from McAuliff someone had pulled back the bolt and was about to open the door.

Alex raced to the staircase. He could not avoid noise, he could only reduce it as much as possible as he lurched into the dimly lit concrete foyer. He whipped around, pushing the heavy steel door closed as fast and as quietly as he could; he pressed the fingers of his left hand around the edge, preventing the door from shutting completely, stopping the sound of metal against metal at the last half-second.

He peered through the crack. The man in the yellow shirt came out of the room, his attention still within it. He was no more than fifty feet away in the silent corridor – silent except for the sound on the television set. He seemed angry, and before he closed the door he looked inside and spoke harshly in a Southern drawl.

'Turn that fuckin' thing down, you goddamn ape!'

The man in the yellow shirt then slammed the door and walked rapidly toward the elevators. He remained at the end of the corridor, nervously checking his watch, straightening his tie, rubbing his shoes over the back of his trousers until a red light, accompanied by a soft, echoing bell, signaled the approach of an elevator. McAuliff watched from the stairwell two hundred feet away.

The elevator doors closed, and Alex walked out into the corridor. He crossed to Room 214 and stood motionless for a few moments. It was a decision he could abandon, he knew that. He could walk away, call Tallon, tell him the room number, and that would be that.

But it would not be very satisfying. It would not be satisfying at all. He had a better idea: he would take whoever was in that room to Tallon himself. If Tallon didn't like it, he could go to hell. The same for Hammond. Since it was established that the electronic devices were planted by a man named Craft, who was in no way connected with the elusive Halidon, Arthur Craft could be taught a lesson. Alex's arrangements with Hammond did not include abuses from third and fourth parties.

It seemed perfectly logical to get Craft out of the chess game. Craft clouded the issues, confused the pursuit.

McAuliff had learned two physical facts about Arthur Craft: He was the son of Craft the Elder and he was American. He was also an unpleasant man. It would have to do.

He knocked on the door beneath the numerals 214.

'Yes, mon? Who is it, mon?' came the muffled reply from within.

Alex waited and knocked again. The voice inside came nearer the door. 'Who is it, please, mon?'

'Arthur Craft, you idiot!'

'Oh!' Yes sir, Mr Craft, mon!' The voice was clearly frightened. The knob turned; the bolt had not been inserted.

The door had opened no more than three inches when McAuliff slammed his shoulder against it with the full impact of his near two hundred pounds. The door crashed against the medium-sized Jamaican inside, sending him reeling into the center of the room. Alex gripped the edge of the vibrating door and swung it back into place, the slam of the heavy wood echoing throughout the corridor.

The Jamaican steadied himself, in his eyes a combination of fury and fear. He whipped around to the room's writing desk; there were boxed speakers on each side. Between them was a pistol.

McAuliff lurched forward, his left hand aiming for the gun, his right grabbing any part of the man it could reach. Their hands met above the warm steel of the pistol; Alex gripped the black man's throat and dug his fingers into the man's flesh.

The man shook loose; the gun went careening off the surface of the desk onto the floor. McAuliff lashed out with the back of his fist at the Jamaican man's face, instantaneously opening his hand and yanking forward, pulling the man's head down by the hair. As the head went down, Alex brought his left knee crashing up into the man's chest, then into his face.

Voices from a millennium ago came back to him: *Use your knees! Your feet! Grab! Hold! Slash at the eyes! The blind can't fight! Rupture!*

It was over. The voices subsided. The man collapsed at his feet.

McAuliff stepped back. He was frightened; something had happened to him. For a few terrifying seconds, he had been back in the Vietnam jungle. He looked down at the motionless Jamaican beneath him. The head was turned flat against the carpet; blood was oozing from the pink lips.

Thank God the man was breathing.

It was the gun. The goddamned *gun*! He had not expected a gun. A fight, yes. His anger justified that. But he had thought of it as a scuffle – intense, over quickly. He would confront, embarrass, forcibly make whoever was monitoring the tapes go with him. To embarrass; to teach an avaricious employer a lesson.

But not this.

This was deadly. This was the violence of survival.

The tapes. The voices. The excited voices kept coming out of the speakers on the desk.

It was not a television set he had heard. The sounds were the sounds of the Courtleigh Manor kitchen. Men shouting, other men responding angrily; the commands of superiors, the whining complaints of subordinates. All frantic, agitated ... mostly unintelligible. They must have driven those listening into a fury.

Then Alex saw the revolving reels of the tape deck. For some reason it was on the floor, to the right of the desk. A small, compact Wollensak recorder, spinning as if nothing had happened.

McAuliff grabbed the two speakers and crashed them repeatedly against each other until the wood splintered and the cases cracked open. He tore out the black shells and the wires and threw them across the room. He crossed to the right of the desk and crushed his heel into the Wollensak, grinding the numerous flat switches until a puff of smoke emerged from the interior and the reels stopped their movement. He reached down and ripped off the tape; he could burn it, but there was nothing of consequence recorded. He rolled the two reels across the floor, the thin strand of tape forming a narrow 'V' on the carpet.

The Jamaican groaned; his eyes blinked as he swallowed and coughed.

Alex picked up the pistol on the floor, and squeezed it into his belt. He went into the bathroom, turned on the cold water, and threw a towel into the basin.

He pulled the drenched towel from the sink and walked back to the coughing, injured Jamaican. He knelt down, helped the man into a sitting position, and blotted his face. The water flowed down on the man's shirt and trousers ... water mingled with blood.

'I'm sorry,' said Alex. 'I didn't mean to hurt you. I wouldn't have if you hadn't reached for that goddamned pistol.'

'*Mon!*' The Jamaican coughed his interruption. 'You *crazy-mon!*' The Jamaican held his chest and winced painfully as he struggled to his feet. 'You break up ... everyt'ing, mon!' said the injured man, looking at the smashed equipment.

'I certainly did! Maybe your Mr Craft will get the message. If he wants to play industrial espionage, let him play in somebody else's backyard. I resent the intrusion. Come on, let's go.' Alex took the man by the arm and began leading him to the door.

'No, mon!' shouted the man, resisting.

'*Yes*, mon,' said McAuliff quietly. 'You're coming with me.'

'Where, mon?'

'To see a little old man who runs a fish store, that's all.' Alex shoved him; the Jamaican gripped his side. His ribs were broken, thought McAuliff.

'Please, mon! No *police*, mon! I lost everyt'ing!' The Jamaican's dark eyes were pleading as he held his ribs.

'You went for a gun, mon! That's a very serious thing to do.'

'Them not my gun. Them gun got no bullets, mon.'

'*What?*'

'Look-see, mon! Please! I got good job ... I don't hurt nobody...'

Alex wasn't listening. He reached into his belt for the pistol.

It was no weapon at all.

It was a starter's gun; the kind held up by referees at track meets.

'Oh, for Christ's sake ...' Arthur Craft Junior played games – little boys' games with little boys' toys.

'Okay, mon. You just tell your employer what I said. The next time, I'll haul him into court.'

It was a silly thing to say, thought Alex, as he walked out into the corridor, slamming the door behind him. There'd be no courts; Julian Warfield or his adversary, R. C. Hammond, was far preferable. Alongside Dunstone Limited, and British Intelligence, Arthur Craft was a cipher. An unimportant intrusion that in all likelihood was no more.

He walked out of the elevator and tried to recall the location of the telephone booths. They were to the left of the entrance, past the front desk, he remembered.

He nodded to the clerks while thinking of Westmore Tallon's private number.

'Mr McAuliff, sir?' The speaker was a tall Jamaican with very broad shoulders, emphasized by a tight nylon jacket.

'Yes?'

'Would you come with me, please?'

Alex looked at the man. He was neat, the trousers pressed, a white shirt and a tie in evidence beneath the jacket. 'No ... why should I?'

'Please, we have very little time. A man is waiting for you outside. A Mr Tucker.'

'What? How did—'

'*Please*, Mr McAuliff. I cannot stay here.'

Alex followed the Jamaican out the glass doors of the entrance. As they reached the driveway, he saw the man in the yellow shirt – Craft's man – walking on the path from the parking lot; the man stopped and stared at him, as if unsure what to do.

'Hurry, please,' said the Jamaican, several steps in front of McAuliff, breaking into a run. 'Down past the gates. The car is waiting!'

They ran down the drive, past the stone gateposts.

The green Chevrolet was on the side of the road, its motor running. The Jamaican opened the back door for Alex.

'Get in!'

McAuliff did so.

Sam Tucker, his massive frame taking up most of the back seat, his shock of red hair reflecting the outside lights, extended his hand.

'Good to see you, boy!'

'Sam!'

The car lurched forward, throwing Alex into the felt. McAuliff saw that there were three men in the front seat. The driver wore a baseball cap; the third man – nearly as large as Sam Tucker – was squeezed between the driver and the Jamaican who had met him inside the Courtleigh lobby. Alex turned back to Tucker.

'What *is* all this, Sam? Where the hell have you been?'

The answer, however, did not come from Sam Tucker. Instead, the black man by the window, the man who had led Alex down the driveway, turned and spoke quietly.

'Mr Tucker has been with us, Mr McAuliff. If events can be controlled, we are your link to the Halidon.'

14

They drove for nearly an hour. Always climbing, higher and higher, it seemed to McAuliff. The winding roads snaked upward, the turns sudden, the curves hidden by sweeping waterfalls of tropic greenery. There were stretches of unpaved road. The automobile took them poorly; the whining of the low gear was proof of the strain.

McAuliff and Sam Tucker spoke quietly, knowing their conversation was overheard by those in front. That knowledge did not seem to bother Tucker.

Sam's story was totally logical, considering his habits and lifestyle. Sam Tucker had friends, or acquaintances, no one knew about, in many parts of the world. Not that he intentionally concealed their identities, only that they were part of his personal, not professional, life.

One of these people had been Walter Piersall.

'I mentioned him to you last year, Alexander,' said Tucker in the darkness of the back seat. 'In Ocho Rios.'

'I don't remember.'

'I told you I'd met an academic fellow in Carrick Foyle. I was going to spend a couple of weekends with him.'

That was it, thought McAuliff. The name Carrick Foyle; he had heard it before. 'I remember now. Something about a lecture series at the Kingston Institute.'

'That's right. Walter was a very classy type – an anthro man who didn't bore you to death. I cabled him I was coming back.'

'You also got in touch with Hanley. He's the one who set off the alarms.'

'I called Bob after I got into Montego. For a little sporting life. There was no way I could reach him later. We traveled fast, and when we got where we were going, there was no telephone. I figured he'd be mad as hell.'

'He was worried, not mad. It was quite a disappearing act.'

'He should know better. I have friends on this island, not enemies. At least, none either of us knows about.'

'What happened? Where did you go?'

Tucker told him.

When Sam arrived in Montego Bay, there was a message from Piersall at the Arrivals desk. He was to call the anthropologist in Carrick Foyle after he was settled. He did, but was told by a servant in Carrick Foyle that Piersall might not return until late that night.

Tucker then phoned his old friend Hanley, and the two men got drunk, as was their established custom at reunions.

In the morning, while Hanley was still sleeping, Sam left the hotel to pick up cigars.

'It's not the sort of place that's large on room service, boy.'

'I gathered that,' said Alex.

'Out on the street, our friends here' – Tucker gestured toward the front seat – 'were waiting in a station wagon—'

'Mr Tucker was being followed,' interrupted the Jamaican by the window. 'Word of this reached Dr Piersall. He sent us to Mo'Bay to look after his friend. Mr Tucker gets up early.'

Sam grinned. 'You know me. Even with the juice, I can't sleep long.'

'I know,' said Alex, remembering too many hotel rooms and survey campsites in which Tucker had wandered about at the first light of dawn.

'There was a little misunderstanding,' continued Sam. 'The boys here said Piersall was waiting for me. I figured, what the hell, the lads thought enough of me to stick out the night, I'd go with 'em straight off. Old Hanley wouldn't be up for an hour or so . . . I'd call him from Piersall's house. But, goddammit, we didn't go to Carrick Foyle. We headed for a bamboo camp down the Martha Brae. It took us damn near two hours to get there, a godforsaken place, Alexander.'

When they arrived at the bamboo camp, Walter Piersall greeted Sam warmly. But within minutes Tucker realized that something had happened to the man. He was not the same person that Sam had known a year ago. There was a zealousness, an intensity not in evidence twelve months before.

Walter Piersall was caught up in things Jamaican. The quiet anthropologist had become a fierce partisan in the battles being waged between social and political factions within Jamaica. He was suddenly a jealous guardian of the islanders' rights, an enemy of the outside exploiters.

'I've seen it happen dozens of times, Alexander,' said Sam. 'From the Tasman to the Caribbean; it's a kind of island fever. Possession . . . oneness, I think. Men migrate for taxes or climate or whatever the hell and they turn into self-proclaimed protectors of their sanctuaries . . . the Catholic convert telling the pope he's not with it . . .'

In his cross-island proselytizing, Piersall began to hear whispers of an enormous land conspiracy. In his own backyard in the parish of Trelawny. At first he dismissed them; they involved men with whom one might disagree, but whose integrity was not debated. Men of extraordinary stature.

The conspiratorial syndrome was an ever-present nuisance in any growing government; Piersall understood that. In Jamaica it was given credence by the influx of foreign capital looking for tax havens, by a parliament ordering more reform programs than it could possibly control, and by a small, wealthy island aristocracy trying to protect itself – the bribe was an all-too-prevalent way of life.

Piersall had decided, once and for all, to put the whispered rumors to rest. Four months ago he'd gone to the Ministry of Territories and filed a resolution of intent to purchase by way of syndication twenty square miles of land on the north border of the Cock Pit. It was a harmless gesture, really. Such a purchase would take years in the courts and involve the satisfactory settling of historic island treaties; his point was merely to prove Kingston's willingness to accept the filing. That the land was not controlled by outsiders.

'Since that day, Alexander, Piersall's life was made a hell.' Sam Tucker lit a thin native cigar; the aromatic smoke whipped out the open window into the onrushing darkness. 'He was harassed by the police, pulled into the parish courts dozens of times for nonsense; his lectures were canceled at the university and the Institute; his telephone tapped – conversations repeated by government attorneys . . . Finally, the whispers he tried to silence killed him.'

McAuliff said nothing for several moments. 'Why was Piersall so anxious to contact you?' he asked Tucker.

'In my cable I told him I was doing a big survey in Trelawny. A project out of London by way of Kingston. I didn't want him to think I was traveling six thousand miles to be his guest; he was a busy man, Alexander.'

'But you were in Kingston tonight. Not in a bamboo camp on the Martha Brae. Two of these men' – McAuliff gestured front – 'followed me this afternoon. In this car.'

'Let me answer you, Mr McAuliff,' said the Jamaican by the window, turning and placing his arm over the seat. 'Kingston intercepted Mr Tuck's cable; they made kling-kling addition, mon. They thought Mr Tuck was mixed up with Dr Piersall in bad ways. Bad ways for them, mon. They sent dangerous men to Mo'Bay. To find out what Tuck was doing—'

'How do you know this?' broke in Alex.

For the briefest instant, the man by the window glanced at the driver. It was difficult to tell in the dim light and rushing shadows, but McAuliff thought the driver nodded imperceptibly.

'We took the men who came to Mo'bay after Mr Tuck. That is all you need to know, mon. What was learned caused Dr Piersall much concern. So much, mon, that we flew to Kingston. To reach you, mon . . . Dr Piersall was killed for that.'

'Who killed him?'

'If we knew that there would be dead men hanging in Victoria Park.'

'What did you learn . . . from the men in Montego?'

Again, the man who spoke seemed to glance at the driver. In seconds he replied, 'That people in Kingston believed Dr Piersall would interfere further. When he went to find you, mon, it was their proof. By killing him they took a big sea urchin out of their foot.'

'And you don't know who did it—'

'Hired niggers, mon,' interrupted the black man.

'It's insane!' McAuliff spoke to himself as much as to Sam Tucker. 'People killing people . . . men following other men. It's goddamn crazy!'

'Why is it crazy to a man who visits Tallon's fish market?' asked the Jamaican suddenly.

'How did—' McAuliff stopped. He was confused; he had been so careful. 'How did you know that? I lost you at the racetrack!'

The Jamaican smiled, his bright teeth catching the light from the careening reflections through the windshield. 'Ocean trout is not really preferable to the freshwater variety, *mon*.'

The counterman! The nonchalant counterman in the striped linen apron. 'The man behind the counter is one of you. That's pretty good,' said McAuliff quietly.

'We're very good. Westmore Tallon is a British agent. So like the English: enlist the clandestine help of the vested interests. And so fundamentally stupid. Tallon's senile Etonian classmates might trust him; his countrymen do not.'

The Jamaican removed his arm from the seat and turned front. The answer was over.

Sam Tucker spoke pensively, openly. 'Alexander . . . now tell me what the hell is going on. What have you done, boy?'

McAuliff turned to Sam. The huge, vital, capable old friend was staring at him through the darkness, the rapid flashes of light bouncing across his face. Tucker's eyes held confusion and hurt. And anger.

What in hell *had* he done, thought Alex.

'Here we are, mon,' said the driver in the baseball cap, who had not spoken throughout the trip.

McAuliff looked out the windows. The ground was flat now, but high in the hills and surrounded by them. Everything was sporadically illuminated by a Jamaican moon filtering through the low-flying clouds of the Blue Mountains. They were on a dirt road; in the distance, perhaps a quarter of a mile away, was a structure, a small cabinlike building. A dim light could be seen through a single window. On the right were two other . . . structures. Not buildings, not houses or cabins, nothing really definable; just free-form, sagging silhouettes . . . translucent? Yes . . . wires, cloth. Or netting . . . They were large tentlike covers, supported by numerous poles. And then Alex understood: beyond the tents the ground was matted flat, and along the border, spaced every thirty or forty feet apart, were unlit cradle torches. The tents were camouflaged hangars; the ground was a landing strip.

They were at an unmarked airfield in the mountains.

The Chevrolet slowed down as it approached what turned out to be a small farmhouse. There was an ancient tractor beyond the edge of the building; field tools – plows, shoulder yokes, pitchforks – were scattered about carelessly. In the moonlight the equipment looked like stationary relics. Unused, dead remembrances only.

Camouflage.

As the hangars were camouflaged.

An airfield no map would indicate.

'Mr McAuliff? Mr Tucker? If you would come with me, please.' The black spokesman by the window opened the door and stepped out. Sam and Alex did the same. The driver and the third Jamaican remained inside, and when the disembarked passengers stepped away from the car, the driver accelerated and sped off down the dirt road.

'Where are they going?' asked McAuliff anxiously.

'To conceal the automobile,' answered the black man. 'Kingston sends out ganja air patrols at night, hoping to find such fields as these. With luck to spot light aircraft on narcotics runs.'

'This ganja country? I thought it was north,' said Tucker.

The Jamaican laughed. 'Ganja, weed, poppy ... north, west, east. It is a healthy export industry, mon. But not ours. Come, let us go inside.'

The door of the miniature farmhouse opened as the three of them approached. In the frame stood the light-skinned man whom Alex had first seen in a striped apron behind the counter at Tallon's.

The interior of the small house was primitive: wooden chairs, a thick round table in the center of the single room, an army cot against the wall. The jarring contradiction was a complicated radio set on a table to the right of the door. The light in the window was far from the shaded lamp in front of the machinery; a generator could be heard providing what electricity was necessary.

All this McAuliff observed within seconds of entering. Then he saw a second man, standing in shadows across the room, his back toward the others. The body – the cut of the coat, the shoulders, the tapered waist, the tailored trousers – was familiar.

The man turned around; the light from the table illuminated his features.

Charles Whitehall stared at McAuliff and then nodded once, slowly.

The door opened, and the driver of the Chevrolet entered with the third Jamaican. He walked to the round table in the center of the room and sat down. He removed his baseball cap, revealing a large shaved head.

'My name is Moore. Barak Moore, Mr McAuliff. To ease your concerns, the woman, Alison Booth, has been called. She was told that you went down to the Ministry for a conference.'

'She won't believe that,' replied Alex.

'If she cares to check further, she will be informed that you are with Latham at a warehouse. There is nothing to worry about, mon.'

Sam Tucker stood by the door; he was relaxed but curious. And strong; his thick arms were folded across his chest, his lined features – tanned by the California sun – showed his age and accentuated his leather strength. Charles Whitehall stood by the window in the left wall, his elegant, arrogant face exuding contempt.

The light-skinned black attendant from Tallon's fish market and the two Jamaican 'guerillas' had pulled their chairs back against the far right wall, away from the center of attention. They were telegraphing the fact that Barak Moore was their superior.

'Please, sit down.' Barak Moore indicated the chairs around the table.

There were three. Tucker and McAuliff looked at each other; there was no point in refusing. They walked to the table and sat down. Charles Whitehall remained standing by the window. Moore glanced up at him. 'Will you join us?'

'If I feel like sitting,' answered Whitehall.

Moore smiled and spoke while looking at Whitehall. 'Charley-mon finds it difficult to be in the same room with me, much less at the same table.'

'Then why is he here?' asked Sam Tucker.

'He had no idea he was going to be until a few minutes before landing. We switched pilots in Savanna-la-Mar.'

'His name is Charles Whitehall,' said Alex, speaking to Sam. 'He's part of the survey. I didn't know he was going to be here either.'

'What's your field, boy?' Tucker leaned back in his chair and spoke to Whitehall.

'Jamaica ... *boy.*'

'I meant no offense, son.'

'You are offensive,' was Whitehall's simple reply.

'Charley and me,' continued Barak Moore, 'we are at the opposite poles of the politic. In your country, you have the term "white trash"; he considers me "black garbage". For roughly the same reason. He thinks I'm too crude, too loud, too unwashed. I am an uncouth revolutionary in Charley-mon's eyes ... he is a graceful rebel, you see.' Moore swept his hand in front of him, balletically, insultingly. 'But our rebellions are different, *very* different, mon. I want Jamaica for *all* the people. He wants it for only a few.'

Whitehall stood motionless as he replied. 'You are as blind now as you were a decade ago. The only thing that has changed is your name, Bramwell Moore.' Whitehall sneered vocally as he continued. '*Barak* ... as childish and meaningless as the social philosophy you espouse; the sound of a jungle toad.'

Moore swallowed before he answered. 'I'd as soon kill you, I think you know that. But it would be as counterproductive as the solutions you seek to impose on our homeland. We have a common enemy, you and I. Make the best of it, *fascisti-mon.*'

'The vocabulary of your mentors. Did you learn it by rote, or did they make you read?'

'*Look!*' McAuliff interrupted angrily. 'You can fight or call names, or kill each other for all I give a damn, but I want to get back to the hotel!' He turned to Barak Moore. 'Whatever you have to say, get it over with.'

'He has a point, Charley-mon,' said Moore. 'We come later. I will, as they say, summarize. It is a brief summary, mon. That there are development plans for a large area of the island – plans that exclude the people – is now established. Dr Piersall's death confirms it. That your geological survey is tied to those plans, we logically assume. Therefore, the Ministry of Education and the Royal Society are – knowingly or unknowingly – concealing the identity of those financial interests. Furthermore, Mr McAuliff here is not unaware of these facts, because he deals with British Intelligence through the despicable

Westmore Tallon . . . That is the summary. Where do we go?' Moore stared at Alex, his eyes small black craters in a huge mountain of dark skin. 'We have the right to go somewhere, Mr McAuliff.'

'Before you shove him against the wall, boy,' interjected Sam Tucker, to Alex's surprise, 'remember, I'm no part of you. I don't say I won't be, but I'm not now.'

'I should think you'd be as interested as we are, Tucker.' The absence of the 'Mr', McAuliff thought, was Moore's hostile response to Sam's use of the word 'boy'. Moore did not realize that Tucker used the term for everyone.

'Don't mistake me,' added Sam. 'I'm interested. Just don't go running off too fast at the mouth. I think you should say what you know, Alex.'

McAuliff looked at Tucker, then Moore, then over at Whitehall. Nothing in Hammond's instructions included such a confrontation. Except the admonition to keep it simple; build on part of the truth.

'The people in British Intelligence – and everything they represent – want to stop this development as much as you do. But they need information. They think the Halidon has it. They want to make contact with the Halidon. I'm supposed to try and make that contact.'

Alex wasn't sure what to expect from his statement, but certainly not what happened. Barak Moore's blunt features, grotesque under the immense shaven head, slowly changed from immobility to amusement, from amusement to the pinched flesh of outright mirth; it was a humor based in cruelty, however. His large mouth opened, and a coughing, malevolent laugh emerged.

From the window there was another sound, another laugh: higher and jackallike. Charles Whitehall's elegant neck was stretched back, his head tilted toward the ceiling, his arms folded across his tailored jacket. He looked like some thin, black Oriental priest finding amusement in a novice's ignorance.

The three Jamaicans in the row of chairs, their white teeth gleaming in the shadows, were smiling, their bodies shaking slightly in silent laughter.

'What's so goddamn funny?' asked McAuliff, annoyed by the undefined humiliation.

'Funny, mon? Many times more than *funny*. The mongoose chases the deadly snake, so the snake wants to make friends?' Moore laughed his hideous laugh once again. 'It is not in any law of nature, mon!'

'What Moore is telling you, Mr McAuliff,' broke in Whitehall, approaching the table, 'is that it's preposterous to think the Halidon would cooperate with the English. It is inconceivable. It is the Halidons of this island who drove the British from Jamaica. Put simply, MI6 is not to be trusted.'

'What *is* the Halidon?' Alex watched the black scholar, who stood motionless, his eyes on Barak Moore.

'It is a force,' said Whitehall quietly.

McAuliff looked at Moore; he was returning Whitehall's stare. 'That doesn't say very much, does it?'

'There is no one in this room who can tell you more, mon.' Barak Moore shifted his gaze to Alex.

Charles Whitehall spoke. 'There are no identities, McAuliff. The Halidon is an unseen curia, a court that has no chambers. No one is lying to you. Not about this. This small contingent here, these three men; Moore's elite corps, as it were—'

'Your words, Charley-mon! We don't use them! *Elite!*' Barak spat out the word.

'Immaterial,' continued Whitehall. 'I venture to say there are no more than five hundred people in all Jamaica who have heard of the Halidon. Less then fifty who know for certain any of its members. Those who do would rather face the pains of Obeah than reveal identities.'

'*Obeah!*' Sam Tucker's comment was in his voice. He had no use for the jingoistic diabolism that filled thousands upon thousands of native minds with terror – Jamaica's counterpart of the Haitian voodoo. 'Obeah's horseshit, boy! The sooner your hill and village people learn that, the better off they'll be!'

'If you think it's restricted to the hills and the villages, you are sadly mistaken,' said Whitehall. 'We in Jamaica do not offer Obeah as a tourist attraction. We have too much respect for it.'

Alex looked up at Whitehall. 'Do *you* have respect for it? Are *you* a believer?'

Whitehall leveled his gaze at McAuliff, his eyes knowing – with a trace of humor. 'Yes, Mr McAuliff, I have respect for Obeah. I have traced its strains to its origins in Mother Africa. I have seen what it's done to the veldt, in the jungles. Respect; I do not say commitment or belief.'

'Then the Halidon is an organization.' McAuliff took out his cigarettes. Barak Moore reached over to accept one; Sam leaned forward in his chair. Alex continued. 'A secret society that has a lot of clout. Why? ... Obeah?'

'Partly, mon,' answered Moore, lighting his cigarette like a man who does not smoke often. 'It is also very rich. It is whispered that it possesses wealth beyond anyone's thinking, mon.'

Suddenly, McAuliff realized the obvious. He looked back and forth between Charles Whitehall and Barak Moore.

'Christ Almighty! You're as anxious to reach the Halidon as I am! As British Intelligence is!'

'That is so, mon.' Moore crushed out his barely smoked cigarette on the surface of the table.

'Why?' asked Alex.

Charles Whitehall replied. 'We are dealing with two giants, Mr McAuliff. One black, one white. The Halidon must win.'

15

The meeting in the isolated farmhouse high in the hills of the Blue Mountains lasted until two o'clock in the morning.

The common objective was agreed to: contact with the Halidon.

And since Barak Moore's and Charles Whitehall's judgment that the Halidon would not deal directly with British Intelligence was convincing, McAuliff further agreed to cooperate with the two black antagonists. Barak and his 'elite' guerillas would provide additional safety for the survey team. Two of the three men sitting against the wall of the farmhouse would fly to Ocho Rios and be hired as carriers.

If the Jamaicans suspected he knew more than he was telling them, they did not press him, thought Alex. They accepted his story – now told twice to Whitehall – that initially he had taken the survey as an investment for future work. From Kingston. MI6 was a complication thrust upon him.

It was as if they understood he had his own concerns, unrelated to theirs. And only when he was sure those concerns were not in conflict would he be completely open. Insane circumstances had forced him into a war he wanted no part of, but one thing was clear above all other considerations: the safety of those he had brought to the island.

Two things. Two million dollars.

From either enemy, Dunstone Limited, or British Intelligence.

'MI5 in London did not tell you, then, who is behind this land rape,' said Barak Moore – not asking a question – continuing immediately. 'It goes beyond their Kingston flunkies, mon.'

'If the British reach the Halidon, they'll tell them what they know,' said McAuliff. 'I'm sure of that. They want to pool their information, that much they've told me.'

'Which means the English assume the Halidon know a great deal,' added Whitehall pensively. 'I wonder if that is so.'

'They have their reasons,' said Alex cautiously. 'There was a previous survey team.'

The Jamaicans knew of it. Its disappearance was either proof of the Halidon's opposition or an isolated act of theft and murder by a roving band of primitive hill people in the Cock Pit. There was no way to tell.

Circles within circles.

What of the Marquis de Chatellerault? Why had he insisted upon meeting with Whitehall in Savanna-la-Mar?

'The marquis is a nervous man,' said Whitehall. 'He claims to have widespread interests on the island. He smells bad fish with this survey.'

'Has it occurred to you that Chatellerault is himself involved?' McAuliff spoke directly to the black scholar. 'MI5 and 6 think so. Tallon told me that this afternoon.'

'If so, the marquis does not trust his colleagues.'

'Did Chatellerault mention anyone else on the team?' asked Alex, afraid of the answer.

Whitehall looked at McAuliff and replied simply. 'He made several allusions, and I told him that I wasn't interested in side issues. They were not pertinent; I made that clear.'

'Thank you.'

'You're welcome.'

Sam Tucker raised his scraggy eyebrows, his expression dubious. 'What the hell *was* pertinent? What did he want?'

'To be kept informed of the survey's progress. Report all developments.'

'Why did he think you'd do that?' Sam leaned forward in the chair.

'I would be paid handsomely, to begin with. And there could be other areas of interest, which, frankly, there are not.'

'*Ha*, mon!' interjected Moore. 'You see, they believe Charley-mon can be bought! They know better with Barak Moore!'

Whitehall looked at the revolutionary, dismissing him. 'There is little to pay you for.' He opened his silver cigarette case; Moore grinned at the sight of it. Whitehall closed it slowly, placed it at his right, and lighted his cigarette with a match. 'Let's go on. I'd rather not be here all night.'

'Okay, mon.' Barak glanced at each man quickly. 'We want the same as the English. To reach the Halidon.' Moore pronounced the word in the Jamaican dialect: hollydawn. 'But the Halidon must come to us. There must be a strong reason. We cannot cry out for them. They will not come into the open.'

'I don't understand a damn thing about any of this,' said Tucker, lighting a thin cigar, 'but if you wait for them, you could be sitting on your asses a long goddamn time.'

'We think there is a way. We think Dr Piersall provided it.' Moore hunched his shoulders, conveying a sense of uncertainty, as if he was not sure how to choose his words. 'For months Dr Piersall tried to ... define the Halidon. To seek it out, to understand. He went back into Caribe history, to the Arawak, to Africa. To find meaning.' Moore paused and looked at Whitehall. 'He read your books, Charley-mon. I told him you were a bad liar, a diseased goat. He said you did not lie in your books ... From many small things, Dr Piersall put together pieces of the puzzle, he called it. His papers are in Carrick Foyle.'

'Just a minute.' Sam Tucker was irritated. 'Walter talked a goddamned streak for two days. On the Martha Brae, in the plane, at the Sheraton. He never mentioned any of this. Why didn't he?' Tucker looked over at the Jamaicans against the wall, at the two who had been with him since Montego Bay.

The black man who had spoken in the Chevrolet replied. 'He would have, mon. It was agreed to wait until McAuliff was with you. It is not a story one repeats often.'

'What did the puzzle tell him?' asked Alex.

'Only part, mon,' said Barak Moore. 'Only part of the puzzle was complete. But Dr Piersall arrived at several theories. To begin with, Halidon is an offshoot from the Coromanteen tribe. They isolated themselves after the Maroon wars, for they would not agree to the treaties that called upon the Maroon nation – the Coromantees – to run down and capture runaway slaves for the English. The Halidon would not become bounty hunters of brother Africans. For decades they were nomadic. Then, perhaps two hundred, two hundred and fifty years ago, they settled in one location. Unknown, inaccessible to the outside world. But they did not divorce themselves from the outside world. Selected males were sent out to accomplish what the elders believed should be accomplished. To this day it is so. Women are brought in to bear children so that the pains of inbreeding are avoided ... And two final points: The Halidon community is high in the mountains where the winds are strong, of that Piersall was certain. And last, the Halidon has great riches. These are the pieces of the puzzle; there are many missing.'

No one spoke for a while. Then Tucker broke the silence.

'It's a hell of a story,' said Sam, 'but I'm not sure where it gets us. Our knowing it won't bring them out. And you said we can't go after them. Goddamn! If this ... tribe has been in the mountains for two hundred years and nobody's found them, we're not likely to, boy! Where is "the way" Walter provided?'

Charles Whitehall answered. 'If Dr Piersall's conclusions are true, the *way* is in the knowledge of them, Mr Tucker.'

'Would you explain that?' asked Alex.

In an unexpected show of deference, the erudite scholar turned to the rough-hewn guerilla. 'I think ... Barak Moore should amplify. I believe the key is in what he said a few minutes ago. That the Halidon must have a strong reason to contact us.'

'You are not mistaken, mon. Dr Piersall was certain that if word got to the Halidon that their existence – and their great wealth – had been confirmed by a small band of responsible men, they would send an emissary. They guard their wealth above all things, Piersall believed. But they have to be convinced beyond doubt ... That is the way.'

'Who do you convince?' asked Alex.

'Someone must travel to Maroon Town, on the border of the Cock Pit. This person should ask for an audience with the Colonel of the Maroon people, offer to pay much, much money. It was Dr Piersall's belief that this man, whose title is passed from one generation to the next within the same tribal family, is the only link to the Halidon.'

'The story is told to him, then?'

'No, McAuliff, mon! Not even the Colonel of the Maroons is to be so trusted. At any rate, it would be meaningless to him. Dr Piersall's studies hinted that the Halidon kept open one perpetual line to the African brothers. It was called *nagarro*—'

'The Akwamu tongue,' broke in Whitehall. 'The language is extinct, but derivations exist in the Ashanti and Mossai-Grusso dialects. *Nagarro* is an abstraction, best translated to mean "a spirit materialized".'

'A spirit ...' Alex began to repeat the phrase, then stopped. 'Proof ... proof of something real.'

'Yes,' replied Whitehall.

'Where is it?' asked McAuliff.

'The proof is in the meaning of another word,' said Barak Moore. 'The meaning of the word "Halidon".'

'What is it?'

'I do not know—'

'*Goddamn!*' Sam Tucker exploded. Barak Moore held up his hand, silencing him.

'Piersall found it. It is to be delivered to the Colonel of the Maroon people. For him to take up into the mountains.'

McAuliff's jaws were tense; he controlled himself as best he could. 'We can't deliver what we don't have.'

'You will have it, mon.' Barak settled his gaze on Alexander. 'A month ago Dr Piersall brought me to his home in Carrick Foyle. He gave me my instructions. Should anything happen to him, I was to go to a place in the forests of his property. I have committed this place to memory, mon. There, deep under the ground, is an oilcloth packet. Inside the packet is a paper; on it is written the meaning of "Halidon".'

The driver on the ride back to Kingston was the Jamaican who was obviously Barak Moore's second-in-command, the man who had done the talking on the trip out to the airfield. His name was Floyd. Charles Whitehall sat in the front seat with him; Alex and Sam Tucker sat in back.

'If you need stories to say where you were,' said Floyd to all of them, 'there was a long equipment meeting at a Ministry warehouse. On Crawford Street, near the docks. It can be verified.'

'Who were we meeting with?' asked Sam.

'A man named Latham. He is in charge—'

'*Latham?*' broke in Alex, recalling all too vividly his telephone conversation with the Ministry man that afternoon. 'He's the one—'

'We know,' interrupted Floyd, grinning in the rearview mirror at McAuliff. 'He's one of us, mon.'

He let himself into the room as quietly as possible. It was nearly three thirty; Courtleigh Manor was quiet, the nocturnal games concluded. He closed the door silently and started across the soft carpet. A light was on in Alison's room, the door open perhaps a foot. His own room was dark. Alison had turned off all the lamps; they had been on when he left her five hours ago.

Why had she done that?

He approached the slightly open door, removing his jacket as he did so.

There was a click behind him. He turned. A second later, the bedside lamp was snapped on, flooding the room with its dim light, harsh only at the source.

Alison was sitting up in his bed. He could see that her right hand gripped the small deadly weapon 'issued by the London police'; she was placing it at her side, obscuring it with the covers.

'Hello, Alex.'

'Hello.' It was an awkward moment.

'I stayed here because I thought your friend Tucker might call. I wouldn't have heard the telephone.'

'I could think of better reasons.' He smiled and approached the bed. She picked up the cylinder and twisted it. There was the same click he had heard seconds ago. She placed the strange weapon on the night table.

'Also, I wanted to talk.'

'You sound ominous.' He sat down. 'I wasn't able to call you ... everything happened so fast, Sam showed up; he just walked through the goddamn lobby doors and wondered why I was so upset ... then, as he was registering, the call came from Latham. He was really in a hurry. I think I threw him with Ocho Rios tomorrow. There was a lot of equipment that hadn't been shipped to Boscobel—'

'Your phone didn't ring,' interrupted Alison quietly.

'What?'

'Mr Latham didn't ring through to your room.'

McAuliff was prepared; he had remembered a little thing. 'Because I'd left word we were having dinner. They were sending a page to the dining room.'

'That's very good, Alex.'

'What's the matter with you? I told the clerk to call you and explain. We were in a hurry; Latham said we had to get to the warehouse ... down on Crawford Street, by the docks ... before they closed the check-in books for the night.'

'That's not very good. You can do better.'

McAuliff saw that Alison was deadly serious. And angry. 'Why do you say that?'

'The front desk did not call me; there was no explaining *clerk*.' Alison pronounced the word 'clerk' in the American fashion, exaggerating the difference from English speech. It was insulting. 'An "assistant" of Mr Latham's telephoned. He wasn't very good, either. He didn't know what to say when I asked to speak to Latham; he didn't expect that. Did you know that Gerald Latham lives in the Barbican district of Kingston? He's listed right in the telephone book.'

Alison stopped; the silence was strained. Alex spoke softly as he made the statement. 'He was home.'

'He was home,' replied Alison. 'Don't worry. He didn't know who called him. I spoke to a woman first, and when he got on the phone I hung up.'

McAuliff inhaled a deep breath and reached into his shirt pocket for his pack of cigarettes. He wasn't sure there was anything to say. 'I'm sorry.'

'So am I,' she said quietly. 'I'll write you out a proper letter of resignation in the morning. You'll have to accept a promissory note for the airfare and whatever other expenses I'm liable for. I'll need what money I have for a while. I'm sure I'll find a situation.'

'You can't do that.' McAuliff found himself saying the words with strength, in utter conviction. And he knew why. Alison was perfectly willing to leave the survey; she was going to leave it. If her motive – or motives – for coming to Jamaica were not what she had said they were, she would not do that. 'For Christ's sake, you can't resign because I lied about a few hours! Damn it, Alison, I'm not accountable to you!'

'Oh, stop behaving like a pompous, wounded ass! You don't do that very well, either. I will *not* go through the labyrinth again; I'm sick to death of it. No more, do you hear!' Suddenly her voice fell and she caught her breath – and the fear was in her eyes. 'I can't stand it any longer.'

He stared at her. 'What do you mean?'

'You elaborately described a long interview with the Jamaican police this afternoon. The station, the district, the officers ... very detailed, Alex. I called them after I hung up on Latham. They'd never heard of you.'

16

He knew he had to go back to the beginning – to the very beginning of the insanity. He had to tell her the truth. There was relief in sharing it.

All of it. So it made sense, what sense there was to make.

He did.

And as he told the story, he found himself trying to understand all over again. He spoke slowly, in a monotone actually; it was the drone of a man speaking through the mists of confusion.

Of the strange message from Dunstone Limited, that brought him to London from New York, and a man named Julian Warfield. Of a 'financial analyst' at the Savoy Hotel whose plastic card identified him as 'R. C. Hammond, British Intelligence.' The pressurized days of living in two worlds that denied their own realities – the covert training, the secret meetings, the vehicle transfers, the hiring of survey personnel under basically false pretenses. Of a panicked, weak James Ferguson, hired to spy on the survey by a man named 'Arthur Craft the Younger,' who was not satisfied being one of the richest men in Jamaica. Of an arrogant Charles Whitehall, whose brilliance and scholarship could not lift him above a fanatic devotion to an outworn, outdated, dishonored concept. Of an arthritic little islander, whose French and African blood had strained its way into the Jamaican aristocracy and MI6 by way of Eton and Oxford.

Of Sam Tucker's odd tale of the transformation of Walter Piersall, anthropologist, converted by 'island fever' into a self-professed guardian of his tropic sanctuary.

And finally of a shaven-headed guerilla revolutionary, named Barak Moore. And everyone's search for an 'unseen curia' called the Halidon.

Insanity. But all very, very real.

The sun sprayed its shafts of early light into the billowing gray clouds above the Blue Mountains. McAuliff sat in the frame of the balcony door; the wet scents of the Jamaican dawn came up from the moist grounds and down from the tall palms, cooling his nostrils and so his skin.

He was nearly finished now. They had talked – he had talked – for an hour and forty-five minutes. There remained only the Marquis de Chatellerault.

Alison was still in the bed, sitting up against the pillows. Her eyes were tired, but she did not take them off him.

He wondered what she would say – or do – when he mentioned Chatellerault. He was afraid.

'You're tired; so am I. Why don't I finish in the morning?'

'It is morning.'

'Later, then.'

'I don't think so. I'd rather hear it all at once.'

'There isn't much more.'

'Then I'd say you saved the best for last. Am I right?' She could not conceal the silent alarm she felt. She looked away from him, at the light coming through the balcony doors. It was brighter now, that strange admixture of pastel yellow and hot orange that is peculiar to the Jamaican dawn.

'You know it concerns you . . .'

'Of course I know it. I knew it last night.' She returned her eyes to him. 'I didn't want to admit it to myself . . . but I knew it. It was all too tidy.'

'Chatellerault,' he said softly. 'He's here.'

'Oh, *God*,' she whispered.

'He can't touch you. Believe me.'

'He followed me. Oh my God . . .'

McAuliff got up and crossed to the bed. He sat on the edge and gently stroked her hair. 'If I thought he could harm you, I would never have told you. I'd simply have him . . . removed.' *Oh, Christ*, thought Alex. How easily the new words came. Would he soon be using *killed*, or *eliminated*?

'Right from the very start, it was all programmed. I was programmed.' She stared at the balcony, allowing his hand to caress the side of her face, as if oblivious to it. 'I should have realized; they don't let you go that easily.'

'Who?'

'All of them, my darling,' she answered, taking his hand, holding it to her lips. 'Whatever names you want to give them, it's not important. The letters, the numbers, the official-sounding nonsense . . . I was warned, I can't say I wasn't.'

'How?' He pulled her hand down, forcing her to look at him. 'How were you warned? Who warned you?'

'In Paris one night. Barely three months ago. I'd finished the last of my interviews at the . . . underground carnival, we called it.'

'Interpol?'

'Yes. I met a chap and his wife. In a waiting room, actually. It's not supposed to happen; isolation is terribly important, but someone got their rooms mixed up. They were English. We agreed to have a late supper together. He was a Porsche automobile dealer from Macclesfield. He and his wife were at the end of their tethers. He'd been recruited because his dealership – the cars, you see – were being used to transport stolen stock certificates from European exchanges. Every time he thought he was finished, they found reasons for him to continue – more often than not, without telling him. It was almost three years; he was about out of his mind. They were going to leave England. Go to Buenos Aires.'

'He could always say no. They couldn't force him.'

'Don't be naïve, darling. Every name you learn is another hook, each new method of operation you report is an additional notch in your expertise.' Alison laughed sadly. 'You've traveled to the land of the informer. You've got a stigma all your own.'

'I'll tell you again: Chatellerault can't touch you.'

She paused before acknowledging his words, his anxiety. 'This may sound strange to you, Alex. I mean, I'm not a brave person – no brimfuls of courage for me – but I have no great fear of him. The appalling thing, the fear, is *them*. They wouldn't let me go. No matter the promises, the agreements, the guarantees. They couldn't resist. A file somewhere, or a computer, was activated and came up with his name; automatically mine appeared in a data bank. That was it: factor X plus factor Y, subtotal – your life is not your own. It never stops. You live with the fear all over again.'

Alex took her by the shoulders. 'There's no law, Alison. We can pack; we can leave.'

'My darling, my darling ... You *can't*. Don't you see? Not that way. It's what's behind you: the agreements, the countless files filled with words, your words ... you can't deny them. You cross borders, you need papers; you work, you need references. You drive a car or take a plane or put money in a bank ... They have all the weapons. You can't hide. Not from them.'

McAuliff let go of her and stood up. He picked up the smooth, shiny cylinder of gas from the bedside table and looked at the printing and the inked date of issue. He walked aimlessly to the balcony doors and instinctively breathed deeply; there was the faint, very faint, aroma of vanilla with the slightest trace of a spice.

Bay rum and vanilla.

Jamaica.

'You're wrong, Alison. We don't have to hide. For a lot of reasons, we have to finish what we've started; you're right about that. But you're wrong about the conclusion. It does stop. It will stop.' He turned back to her. 'Take my word for it.'

'I'd like to. I really would. I don't see how.'

'An old infantry game. Do unto others before they can do unto you. The Hammonds and the Interpols of this world use us because we're afraid. We know what they can do to what we think are our well-ordered lives. That's legitimate; they're bastards. And they'll admit it. But have you ever thought about the magnitude of disaster we can cause *them*? That's also legitimate, because we can be bastards, too. We'll play this out – with armed guards on all our flanks. And when we're finished, we'll *be* finished. With them.'

Charles Whitehall sat in the chair, the tiny glass of Pernod on the table beside him. It was six o'clock in the morning; he had not been to bed. There was no point in trying to sleep; sleep would not come.

Two days on the island and the sores of a decade ago were disturbed. He had not expected it; he had expected to control everything. Not *be* controlled.

His enemy now was not the enemy – enemies – he had waited ten years to fight: the rulers in Kingston; worse, perhaps, the radicals like Barak Moore. It was a new enemy, every bit as despicable, and infinitely more powerful, because it had the means to control his beloved Jamaica.

Control by corruption; ultimately own . . . by possession.

He had lied to Alexander McAuliff. In Savanna-la-Mar, Chatellerault openly admitted that he was part of the Trelawny Parish conspiracy. British Intelligence was right. The marquis's wealth was intrinsic to the development of the raw acreage on the north coast and in the Cock Pit, and he intended to see that his investment was protected. Charles Whitehall was his first line of protection, and if Charles Whitehall failed, he would be destroyed. It was as simple as that. Chatellerault was not the least obscure about it. He had sat opposite him and smiled his thin Gallic smile and recited the facts – and names of the covert network Whitehall had developed on the island over the past decade.

He had capped his narrative with the most damaging information of all: the timetable and the methods Charles and his political party expected to follow on their road to power in Kingston.

The establishment of a military dictatorship with one, nonmilitary leader to whom all were subservient – the Praetorian of Jamaica was the title, Charles Whitehall the man.

If Kingston knew these things . . . well, Kingston would react.

But Chatellerault made it clear that their individual objectives were not necessarily in conflict. There were areas – philosophical, political, financial – in which their interests might easily be merged. But first came the activity on the north coast. That was immediate; it was the springboard to everything else.

The marquis did not name his partners – Whitehall got the distinct impression that Chatellerault was not entirely sure who they all were – but it was manifestly clear that he did not trust them. On one level he seemed to question motives, on another it was a matter of abilities. He spoke briefly about previous interference and/or bungling, but did not dwell on the facts.

The facts obviously concerned the first survey.

What had happened?

Was the Halidon responsible?

Was the Halidon *capable* of interference?

Did the Halidon really exist?

The Halidon.

He would have to analyse the anthropologist Piersall's papers; separate a foreigner's exotic fantasies from island reality. There was a time, many years ago, when the Rastafarians were symbols of African terror, before they were revealed to be children stoned on grass with mud-caked hair and a collective desire to avoid work. And there were the Pocomanians, with their bearded high priests inserting the sexual orgy into the abstract generosities of the Christian ethic: a socioreligious excuse for promiscuity. Or the Anansi sects –

inheritors of the long-forgotten Ashanti belief in the cunning of the spider, on which all progress in life was patterned.

There were so many. So often metaphysically paranoid; so fragmented, so obscure.

Was the Halidon – Hollydawn – any different?

At this juncture, for Charles Whitehall it didn't really matter. What mattered was his own survival and the survival of his plans. His aims would be accomplished by keeping Chatellerault at bay and infiltrating the structure of Chatellerault's financial hierarchy.

And working with his first enemy, Barak Moore.

Working with both enemies.

Jamaica's enemies.

James Ferguson fumbled for the light switch on the bedside lamp. His thrusts caused an ashtray and a glass to collide, sending both crashing to the floor. Light was coming through the drawn curtains; he was conscious of it in spite of the terrible pain in his eyes and through his head, from temple to temple. Pain that caused flashes of darkness to envelop his inner eye. He looked at his watch as he shaded his face from the dim spill of the lamp. It was six fifteen.

Oh, Christ! His head hurt so, tears welled in the far corners of his eyes. Shafts of pain – sharp, immobilizing – shot down into his neck and seemed to constrict his shoulders, even his arms. His stomach was in a state of tense, muscular suspension; if he thought about it, he knew he would be sick and vomit.

There was no pretense regarding the amount of alcohol he had consumed last night. McAuliff could not accuse him of play-acting now. He had gotten drunk. Very drunk. And with damn good reason.

He had been elated.

Arthur Craft had telephoned him in panic. In *panic*!

Craft the Younger had been caught. McAuliff had found the room where the taping was being done and beaten someone up, *physically beaten* him *up*! Craft had yelled over the telephone, demanding where McAuliff had gotten his name.

Not from him! Certainly not from Jimbo-mon. He had said nothing.

Craft had roared, swearing at the 'goddamned nigger on the tape machine', convinced the 'black fucker' had confessed to McAuliff, adding that the bastard would never get near a courtroom. 'If it came to that.'

If it came to that.

'You never *saw* me,' Craft the Younger had screamed. 'We never talked! We didn't meet! You get that absolutely clear, you shaky son of a bitch!'

'Of course . . . of course, Mr Craft,' he had replied. 'But then, sir . . . we *did* talk, didn't we? This doesn't have to change anything.'

He had been petrified, but he had said the words. Quietly, with no great emphasis. But his message had been clear.

Arthur Craft Junior was in an awkward position. Craft the Younger should not be yelling; he should be polite. Perhaps even solicitous.

After all, they *had* talked . . .

Craft understood. The understanding was first indicated by his silence, then confirmed by his next statement.

'We'll be in touch.'

It had been so simple. And if Craft the Younger wanted it different, wanted things as they were not, Craft controlled an enormously wealthy foundation. Certainly he could find something for a very, *very* talented botanist.

When he hung up the telephone last night, James had felt a wave of calm come over him. The sort of quiet confidence in a laboratory, where his eye and mind were very sure indeed.

He would have to be cautious, but he could do it.

He had gotten drunk when he realized that.

And now his head and stomach were in pain. But he could stand them; they were bearable now. Things were going to be different.

He looked at his watch. His goddamn Timex. It was six twenty five. A cheap watch but accurate.

Instead of a Timex there might be a Breitling chronometer in his future. And new, very expensive camera equipment. And a real bank balance.

And a new life.

If he was cautious.

The telephone rang on Peter Jensen's side of the bed, but his wife heard it first.

'Peter . . . Peter! For heaven's sake, the *phone*.'

'What? What, old girl?' Peter Jensen blinked his eyes; the room was dark, but there was daylight beyond the drawn curtains.

The telephone rang again. Short bursts of bell; the kind of rapid blasts hotel switchboards practise. Nimble fingers, irritated guests.

Peter Jensen reached over and switched on the light. The traveling clock read ten minutes to eight. Again the shrill bell, now steady.

'Damn!' sputtered Peter as he realized the instrument was beyond the lamp, requiring him to reach farther. 'Yes, *yes*? Hello?'

'Mr Peter Jensen, please?' said the unfamiliar male voice.

'Yes. What is it? This is Jensen.'

'Cable International, Mr Jensen. A wire arrived for you several minutes ago. From London. Shall I read it? It's marked urgent, sir.'

'No!' replied Peter quickly, firmly. 'No, don't do that. I've been expecting it; it's rather long, I should think.'

'Yes, sir, it is.'

'Just send it over right away, if you please. Can you do that? Courtleigh Manor. Room four-oh-one. It won't be necessary to stop at the desk.'

'I understand, Mr Jensen. Right away. There'll be a charge for an unscheduled—'

'Of course, of course,' interrupted Peter. 'Just send it over, please.'

'Yes, sir.'

Twenty-five minutes later, the messenger from Cable International arrived. Moments before, room service had wheeled in a breakfast of melon, tea, and scones. Peter Jensen opened the two-page cablegram and spread it over the linen cloth on his side of the table. There was a pencil in his hand.

Across from him, Ruth held up a page of paper, scanning it over the rim of her cup. She, too, had a pencil, at the side of the saucer.

'The company name is Parkhurst,' said Peter.

'Check,' said Ruth, putting down her tea. She placed the paper alongside, picked up the pencil, and made a mark on the page.

'The address is Sheffield by the Glen.' Peter looked over at her.

'Go ahead,' replied Ruth, making a second notation.

'The equipment to be inspected is microscopes.'

'Very well.' Ruth made a third mark on the left of the page, went back to her previous notes, and then darted her eyes to the bottom right. 'Are you ready?'

'Yes.'

Ruth Wells Jensen, paleontologist, proceeded to recite a series of numbers. Her husband started at the top of the body of the cablegram and began circling words with his pencil. Several times he asked his wife to repeat a number. As she did so, he counted from the previous circle and circled another word.

Three minutes later, they had finished the exercise. Peter Jensen swallowed some tea and reread the cablegram to himself. His wife spread jam on two scones and covered the teapot with the cozy.

'Warfield is flying over next week. He agrees. McAuliff has been reached.'

Part Three

The North Coast

Hammond's words kept coming back to McAuliff: *You'll find it quite acceptable to operate on different levels. Actually, it evolves rather naturally, even instinctively. You'll discover that you tend to separate your concentrations.*

The British Intelligence agent had been right. The survey was in its ninth day, and Alex found that for hours at a time he had no other thoughts but the immediate work at hand.

The equipment had been trucked from Boscobel Airfield straight through to Puerto Seco, on Discovery Bay. Alex, Sam Tucker, and Alison Booth flew into Ocho Rios ahead of the others and allowed themselves three days of luxury at the Sans Souci while McAuliff ostensibly hired a crew – two of the five of which had been agreed upon in an isolated farmhouse high in the hills of the Blue Mountains. Alex found – as he'd expected – that Sam and Alison got along extremely well. Neither was difficult to like; each possessed an easy humor, both were professionals. And there was no reason to conceal from Sam the fact that they were lovers. As Tucker phrased it: 'I'd be shocked if you weren't, Alexander.'

Sam's approval was important to McAuliff. For at no time was Alison to be left alone when he was away. Under no circumstances. Ever.

Sam Tucker was the ideal protective escort. Far superior to himself, Alex realized. Tuck was the most resourceful man he had ever known, and just about the hardest. He had within him an aggressiveness that when called upon was savage. He was not a man to have as an enemy. In his care, Alison was as safe as a human being could be.

The fourth day had been the first day of the survey work. The team was housed halfway between Puerto Seco and Rio Bueno Harbour, in a pleasant beach motel called Bengal Court. Work began shortly after six in the morning. The initial objective of the survey was to plot the coastline definitively. Alex and Sam Tucker operated the equipment. Azimuths were shot along the shoreline, recorded by transit cameras. The angular-degree demarcations were correlated with the coastal charts provided by the Jamaican Institute. By and large, these charts were sectional and imperfect, acceptable for the details of road maps and small-craft navigation, but inadequate for geophysical purposes. To set up accurate perimeters, McAuliff employed sonic geodometers which bounced sound waves back and forth between instruments, giving what amounted to perfect bearings. Each contour, each elevation was recorded on both sonic graphs and transit cameras.

These chores were dull, laborious, and sweat-provoking under the hot sun. The single relief was the constant presence of Alison, as much as she herself objected to it. Alex was adamant, however. He instructed Barak Moore's two men to stay within a hundred feet of her at all times, and then commanded Alison not to stroll out of his sight.

It was an impossible demand, and McAuliff realized he could not prolong it more than a few days. Alison had work to do; minor over the coastal area, a great deal once they started inland. But all beginnings were awkward under pressure; he could not separate this particular concentration that easily, nor did he wish to.

Very rapidly your own personal antennae will be activated automatically. Their function will be second nature, as it were. You will fall into a rhythm, actually. It is the connecting link between your divided objectives. You will recognize it and build a degree of confidence in the process.

Hammond.

But not during the first few days; there was no confidence to speak of. He did grant, however, that the fear was lessening . . . partially, imperceptibly. He thought this was due to the constant physical activity and the fact that he *could* require such men as Sam and Barak Moore's 'special forces' to take up posts around Alison. And at any given moment he could turn his head and there she was – on the beach, in a small boat – chipping rocks, instructing one of the crew in the manipulation of a drill bore.

But, again, were not all these his antennae? And was not the lessening of · fear the beginnings of confidence? *R. C. Hammond. Supercilious son of a bitch. Manipulator. Speaker of truths.*

But not the whole truth.

The areas bordering Braco Beach were hazardous. Sheets of coral overlay extended hundreds of yards out into the surf. McAuliff and Sam Tucker crawled over the razor-sharp miniature hills of ocean polyps and set up their geodometers and cameras. Both men incurred scores of minor cuts, sore muscles, and sorer backs.

That was the third day, marked by the special relief of Alison's somehow commandeering a fisherman's flat-bottomed boat and, with her two 'escorts', bringing a picnic lunch of cold chicken out to the reef. It was a comfortable hour on the most uncomfortable picnic grounds imaginable.

The Jamaican revolutionary, Floyd, who had guided the boat into its precarious coral mooring succinctly observed that the beach was flatter and far less wet.

'But then they'd have to crawl all the way out here again,' Alison had replied, holding onto her wide-brimmed cloth sun hat.

'Mon, you have a good woman!' This observation came from Floyd's companion, the huge, quiet Jamaican named Lawrence.

The five of them perched – there was no other description – on the highest ridges of the coral jetty, the spray cascading up from the base of the reef, creating faint rainbow prisms of color in its mist. Far out on the water two freighters were passing each other, one heading for the open sea, the second aiming for the bauxite docks east of Runaway Bay. A luxurious cabin cruiser rigged for deep-sea fishing sliced through the swells several hundred yards in front of them, the passengers pointing in astonishment at the strange sight of five humans picnicking on a reef.

McAuliff watched the others respond to the cruiser's surprised riders. Sam Tucker stood up, gestured at the coral, and yelled, 'Diamonds!'

Floyd and Lawrence, their black, muscular bodies bared to the waist, roared at Sam's antics. Lawrence pried loose a coral stone and held it up, then chucked it to Tucker, who caught it and shouted again, 'Twenty carats!'

Alison, her blue jeans and light field blouse drenched with the spray, joined in the foolish game. She elaborately accepted the coral stone, presented by Sam, and held it on top of her outstretched hand as though it were a jeweled ring of great value. A short burst of breeze whipped across the reef; Alison dropped the stone in an effort to hold her hat, whose brim had caught the wind. She was not successful; the hat glided off and disappeared over a small mound of coral. Before Alex could rise and go after it, Lawrence was on his feet, dashing surefootedly over the rocks and down toward the water. Within seconds he had the hat, now soaked, and effortlessly leaped back up from the water's edge and handed it to Alison.

The incident had taken less than ten seconds.

'You keep the hat on the head, Mis Aleesawn. Them sun very hot; roast skin like cooked chicken, mon.'

'Thank you, Lawrence,' said Alison gratefully, securing the wet hat over her head. 'You run across this reef as though it were a golf green!'

'Lawrence is a fine caddy, Mis Alison,' said Floyd smiling, still sitting. 'At the Negril Golf Club he is a favorite, is that not so, Lawrence?'

Lawrence grinned and glanced at McAuliff knowingly. 'Eh, mon. At Negril they alla time ask for me. I cheat good, mon. Alla time I move them golf balls out of bad places to the smooth grass. I think everybody know. Alla time ask for Lawrence.'

Sam Tucker chuckled as he sat down again. 'Alla time big goddamn tips, I'd say.'

'Plenty good tips, mon,' agreed Lawrence.

'And probably something more,' added McAuliff, looking at Floyd and remembering the exclusive reputation of the Negril Golf Club. 'Alla time plenty of information.'

'Yes, mon.' Floyd smiled conspiratorially. 'It is as they say: the rich Westmorelanders talk a great deal during their games of golf.'

Alex fell silent. It seemed strange, the whole scene. Here they were, the five of them, eating cold chicken on a coral reef three hundred yards from shore, playing children's games with passing cabin cruisers and joking casually about the surreptitious gathering of information on a golf course.

Two black revolutionaries – recruits from a band of hill country guerillas.

A late-middle-aged 'soldier of fortune'. (Sam Tucker would object to the cliché, but if it was ever applicable, he was the applicant.) A strikingly handsome ... lovely English divorcée whose background just happened to include undercover work for an international police organization. And one forty-four-year-old ex-infantry man who six weeks ago flew to London thinking he was going to negotiate a geological survey contract.

The five of them. Each knowing that he was not what he appeared to be; each doing what he was doing ... she was doing ... because there were no alternatives. Not really.

It wasn't strange; it was insane. And it struck McAuliff once again that he was the least qualified among these people, under these circumstances. Yet because of the circumstances – having nothing to do with qualifications – he was their leader.

Insanity.

By the seventh day, working long hours with few breaks, Alex and Sam had charted the coastline as far as Burwood, five miles from the mouth of the Martha Brae, their western perimeter. The Jensens and James Ferguson kept a leisurely parallel pace, setting up tables with microscopes, burners, vials, scales, and chemicals as they went about their work. None found anything exceptional, nor did they expect to in the coastal regions. The areas had been studied fairly extensively for industrial and resort purposes; there was nothing of consequence not previously recorded. And since Ferguson's botanical analyses were closely allied with Sam Tucker's soil evaluations, Ferguson volunteered to make the soil tests, freeing Tucker to finish the topographics with Alex.

These were the geophysical concerns. There was something else, and none could explain it. It was first reported by the Jensens.

A sound. Only a sound. A low wail or cry that seemed to follow them throughout an entire afternoon.

When they first heard it, it came from the underbrush beyond the dunes. They thought that perhaps it was an animal in pain. Or a small child in some horrible anguish, an agony that went beyond a child's tears. In a very real sense, it was terrifying.

So the Jensens raced beyond the dunes into the underbrush, thrashing at the tangled foliage to find the source of the dreadful, frightening cry.

They had found nothing.

The animal, or the child, or whatever it was, had fled.

Shortly thereafter – late in the same afternoon – James Ferguson came running down to the beach, his face an expression of bewildered panic. He had been tracing a giant mollusk fern to its root source; the trek had taken him up into a rocky precipice above the shore. He had been in the center of the overhanging vines and macca-fats when a vibration – at first a vibration – caused his whole body to tremble. There followed a wild, piercing screech, both high-pitched and full, that pained his ears beyond – he said – endurance.

He had gripped the vines to keep from plummeting off the precipice.

Terrified, he had scrambled down hysterically to firmer ground and raced back to the others.

James had not been more than a few hundred yards away.

Yet none but he had heard the terrible thing.

Whitehall had another version of the madness. The black scholar had been walking along the shoreline, half sand, half forest, of Bengal Bay. It was an aimless morning constitutional; he had no destination other than the point, perhaps.

About a mile east of the motel's beach, he rested briefly on a large rock overlooking the water. He heard a noise from behind, and so he turned, expecting to see a bird or a mongoose fluttering or scampering in the woods.

There was nothing.

He turned back to the lapping water beneath him, when suddenly there was an explosion of sound – sustained, hollowlike, a dissonant cacophony of wind. And then it stopped.

Whitehall had gripped the rock and stared into the forest. At nothing, aware only that he was afflicted with a terrible pain in his temples.

But Charles was a scholar, and a scholar was a sceptic. He had concluded that, somewhere in the forest, an enormous unseen tree had collapsed from the natural weight of ages. In its death fall, the tons of ripping, scraping wood against wood within the huge trunk had caused the phenomenon.

And none was convinced.

As Whitehall told his story, McAuliff watched him. He did not think Charles believed it himself. Things not explicable had occurred, and they were all – if nothing else – scientists of the physical. The explainable. Perhaps they all took comfort in Whitehall's theory of sonics. Alexander thought so; they could not dwell on it. There was work to do.

Divided objectives.

Alison thought she had found something, and with Floyd's and Lawrence's help she made a series of deep bores arcing the beaches and coral jetties. Her samplings showed that there were strata of soft lignite interspersed throughout the limestone beds on the ocean floor. Geologically it was easily explained: hundreds of thousands of years ago, volcanic disturbances swallowed whole land masses of wood and pulp. Regardless of explanations, however, if there were plans to sink pilings for piers or even extended docks, the construction firms were going to have to add to their base supports.

Alison's concentrations were a relief to McAuliff. She was absorbed, and so complained less about his restrictions, and, more important, he was able to observe Floyd and Lawrence as they went about the business of watching over her. The two guerillas were extremely thorough. And gracefully subtle. Whenever Alison wandered along the beach or up into the shore grass, one or both had her flanked or preceded or followed. They were like stalking panthers prepared to spring, yet they did not in their tracking call attention to themselves. They seemed to become natural appendages, always carrying something – binoculars, sampling boxes, clipboards, whatever was handy – to divert any zeroing in on their real function.

And during the nights, McAuliff found a protective bonus he had neither asked for nor expected: Floyd and Lawrence alternated patrols around the lawns and in the corridors of the Bengal Court motel. Alex discovered this on the night of the eighth day, when he got up at four in the morning to get himself a plastic bucket of ice from the machine down the hall. He wanted ice water.

As he turned the corner into the outside alcove where the machine was situated, he was suddenly aware of a figure behind the latticework that fronted the lawn. The figure had moved quickly; there had been no sound of footsteps.

McAuliff rapidly scooped the cubes into the small bucket, closed the metal door, and walked back around the corner into the hallway. The instant he was out of sight, he silently placed the ice at his feet and pressed his back against the wall's edge.

There was movement.

McAuliff whipped around the corner, with every intention of hurling himself at whoever came into view. His fists were clenched, his spring accurate; he lunged into the figure of Lawrence. It was too late to regain his footing.

'Eh, *mon*!' cried the Jamaican softly as he recoiled and fell back under Alex's weight. Both men rolled out of the alcove onto the lawn.

'Christ!' whispered McAuliff, next to Lawrence on the ground. 'What the hell are you doing here?'

Lawrence smiled in the darkness; he shook his hand, which had been pinned by Alex under his back. 'You're a big fella, mon! You pretty quick, too.'

'I was pretty damn excited. What *are* you doing out here?'

Lawrence explained briefly, apologetically. He and Floyd had made an arrangement with the night watchman, an old fisherman who prowled around at night with a shotgun neither guerilla believed he knew how to use. Barak Moore had ordered them to stand evening patrols; they would have done so whether commanded to or not, said Lawrence.

'When do you sleep?'

'Sleep *good*, mon,' replied Lawrence. 'We take turns alla time.'

Alex returned to his room. Alison sat up in bed when he closed the door. 'Is everything all right?' she asked apprehensively.

'Better than I expected. We've got our own miniature army. We're fine.'

On the afternoon of the ninth day, McAuliff and Tucker reached the Martha Brae River. The geodometer charts and transit photographs were sealed hermetically and stored in the cool vaults of the equipment truck. Peter Jensen gave his summary of the coastal ore and mineral deposits; his wife, Ruth, had found traces of plant fossils embedded in the coral, but her findings were of little value, and James Ferguson, covering double duty in soil and flora, presented his unstartling analyses. Only Alison's discovery of the lignite strata was unexpected.

All reports were to be driven into Ocho Rios for duplication. McAuliff said he would do this himself; it had been a difficult nine days, and the tenth was a day off. Those who wanted to go into Ochee could come with him; the others could go to Montego or laze around the Bengal Court beach, as they preferred. The survey would resume on the morning of the eleventh day.

They made their respective plans on the riverbank, with the inevitable picnic lunches put up by the motel. Only Charles Whitehall, who had done little but lie around the beach, knew precisely what he wanted to do, and he could not state it publicly. He spoke to Alex alone.

'I really *must* see Piersall's papers. Quite honestly, McAuliff, it's been driving me crazy.'

'We wait for Moore. We agreed to that.'

'When? For heaven's sake, when will he show up? It will be ten days tomorrow; he said ten days.'

'There were no guarantees. I'm as anxious as you. There's an oilcloth packet buried somewhere on his property, remember?'

'I haven't forgotten for an instant.'

Separation of concentrations; divided objectives.

Hammond.

Charles Whitehall was as concerned academically as he was conspiratorially. Perhaps more so, thought Alex. The black scholar's curiosity was rooted in a lifetime of research.

The Jensens remained at Bengal Court. Ferguson requested an advance from McAuliff and hired a taxi to drive him into Montego Bay. McAuliff, Sam Tucker, and Alison Booth drove the truck to Ocho Rios. Charles Whitehall followed in an old station wagon with Floyd and Lawrence; the guerillas insisted that the arrangements be thus.

Barak Moore lay in the tall grass, binoculars to his eyes. It was sundown; rays of orange and yellow lights filtered through the green trees above him and bounced off the white stone of Walter Piersall's house, four hundred yards away. Through the grass he saw the figures of the Trelawny Parish police circling the house, checking the windows and the doors; they would leave at least one man on watch. As usual.

The police had finished the day's investigation, the longest investigation, thought Barak, in the history of the parish. They had been at it nearly two weeks. Teams of civilians had come up from Kingston: men in pressed clothes, which meant they were more than police.

They would find nothing, of that Barak Moore was certain.

If Walter Piersall had accurately described his caches.

And Barak could not wait any longer. It would be a simple matter to retrieve the oilcloth packet – he was within a hundred and fifty yards of it at the moment – but it was not that simple. He needed Charles Whitehall's total cooperation – more than Whitehall realized – and that meant he had to get inside Piersall's house and bring out the rest of Piersall's legacy. The anthropologist's papers.

The papers. They were cemented in the wall of an old, unused cistern in Piersall's basement.

Walter Piersall had carefully removed several cistern blocks, dug recesses in the earth beyond, and replaced the stones. It was in one of these recesses that he had buried his studies of the Halidon.

Charles Whitehall would not help unless he saw those papers. Barak needed Charley-mon's help.

The Trelawny police got into their vehicles; a single uniformed guard waved as the patrol cars started down the road.

He, Barak, the people's revolutionary, had to work with Whitehall, the political criminal. Their own war – perhaps a civil war – would come later, as it had in so many developing lands.

First, there was the white man. And his money and his companies and his unending thirst for the sweat of the black man. That was first, very much first, mon!

Barak's thoughts had caused him to stare blindly into the binoculars. The guard was nowhere in sight now. Moore scanned the area, refocusing the Zeiss Ikon lenses as he covered the sides and the sloping back lawn of Piersall's house. It was a comfortable white man's home, thought Barak.

It was on top of a hill, the entrance road a long climb from George's Valley to the west and the Martha Brae to the east. Mango trees, palms, hibiscus, and orchids lined the entrance and surrounded the one-and-a-half-storied white stone structure. The house was long, most of the wide spacious rooms on the first floor. There was black iron grillwork everywhere, across the windows and over the door entrances. The only glass was in the second-floor bedrooms; all the windows had teak shutters.

The rear of High Hill, as the house was called, was the most striking. To the east of the old pasture of high grass, where Barak lay, the gently sloping back lawn had been carved out of the forests and the fields, seeded with a Caribbean fescue that was as smooth as a golf course; the rocks, painted a shiny white, gave the appearance of white-caps in a green sea.

In the center of the area was a medium-sized pool, installed by Piersall, with blue and white tiles that reflected the sun as sharply as the blue-green water in it. Around the pool and spreading out over the grass were tables and chairs – white wrought iron – delicate in appearance, sturdy in design.

The guard came into view again, and Moore caught his breath, as much in astonishment as in anger. The guard was playing with a dog, a vicious-looking Doberman. There had been no dogs before. It was a bad thing, thought Barak . . . yet, perhaps, not so bad. The presence of the dog probably meant that this policeman would stay alone at his post longer than the normal time span. It was a police custom to leave dogs with men for two reasons: because the district they patrolled was dangerous, or because the men would remain for a relatively long time at their watches. Dogs served several purposes: they were alarms, they protected, and they helped pass the hours.

The guard threw a stick; the Doberman raced beyond the pool, nearly crashing into a wrought-iron table, and snatched it up in his mouth. Before the dog could bring it back the policeman threw another stick, bewildering the Doberman, who dropped the first retrieval and went after the second.

He is a stupid man, thought Barak, watching the laughing guard. He did not know animals, and a man who did not know animals was a man who could be trapped.

He would be trapped tonight.

18

It was a clear night. The Jamaican moon – three-quarters of it – shone brightly between the high banks of the river. They had poled a stolen bamboo raft down the rushing waters of the Martha Brae until they had reached the point of shortest distance to the house in Carrick Foyle. They manoeuvred the raft into a pitch-black recess and pulled it out of the water, hiding it under cascading umbrellas of full-leaved mangroves and maiden palms.

They were the raiding party: Barak, Alex, Floyd, and Whitehall. Sam Tucker and Lawrence had stayed at Bengal Court to protect Alison.

They crept up the slope through the dense, ensnaring foliage. The slope was steep, the traveling slow and painfully difficult. The distance to the High Hill property was no more than a mile – perhaps a mile and a quarter – but it took the four of them nearly an hour to reach it. Charles Whitehall thought the route was foolish. If there was one guard and one dog, why not drive to the road below the winding, half-mile entrance and simply walk up to the outer gates?

Barak's reasoning held more sophistication than Whitehall would have conceded to the Trelawny police. Moore thought it possible that the parish authorities had set up electronic tripwires along the entrance drive. Barak knew that such instruments had been in use in Montego Bay, Kingston, and Port Antonio hotels for months. They could not take the chance of setting one off.

Breathing heavily, they stood at the southern border of Piersall's sloping lawn and looked up at the house called High Hill. The moon's illumination on the white stone made the house stand out like an alabaster monument, still, peaceful, graceful, and solid. Light spilled out of the teak shutters in two areas of the house: the downstairs back room opening onto the lawn and the center bedroom on the second floor. All else was in darkness.

Except the underwater spotlights in the pool. A slight breeze caused ripples on the water; the bluish light danced from underneath.

'We must draw him out,' said Barak. 'Him and the dog, mon.'

'Why? What's the point?' asked McAuliff, the sweat from the climb rolling down into his eyes. 'He's one, we're four.'

'Moore is right,' answered Charles Whitehall. 'If there are electronic devices outside, then certainly he has the equivalent within.'

'He would have a police radio, at any rate, mon,' interjected Floyd. 'I know those doors; by the time we broke one down, he would have time – easy to reach others.'

'It's a half-hour from Falmouth; the police are in Falmouth,' pressed Alex. 'We'd be in and out by then.'

'Not so, mon,' argued Barak. 'It will take us a while to select and pry loose the cistern stones. We'll dig up the oilcloth packet first. Come!'

Barak Moore led them around the edge of wooded property, to the opposite side, into the old grazing field. He shielded the glass of his flashlight with his fingers and raced to a cluster of breadfruit trees at the northern end of the rock-strewn pasture. He crouched at the trunk of the farthest tree; the others did the same. Barak spoke – whispered.

'Talk quietly. These hill winds carry voices. The packet is buried in the earth forty-four paces to the right of the fourth large rock on a northwest diagonal from this tree.'

'He was a man who knew Jamaica,' said Whitehall softly.

'How do you mean?' McAuliff saw the grim smile on the scholar's face in the moonlight.

'The Arawak symbols for a warrior's death march were in units of four, always to the right of the setting sun.'

'That's not very comforting,' said Alex.

'Like your American Indians,' replied Whitehall, 'the Arawaks were not comforted by the white man.'

'Neither were the Africans, Charley-mon.' Barak locked eyes with Whitehall in the moonlight. 'Sometimes I think you forget that.' He addressed McAuliff and Floyd. 'Follow me. In a line.'

They ran in crouched positions through the tall grass behind the black revolutionary, each man slapping a large prominent rock as he came upon it. One, two, three, four.

At the fourth rock, roughly a hundred and fifty yards from the base of the breadfruit tree, they knelt around the stone. Barak cupped his flashlight and shone it on the top. There was a chiseled marking, barely visible. Whitehall bent over it.

'Your Dr Piersall had a progressive imagination; progressive in the historical sense. He's jumped from Arawak to Coromantee. See?' Whitehall traced his index finger over the marking under the beam of the flashlight and continued softly. 'This twisted crescent is an Ashanti moon the Coromantees used to leave a trail for members of the tribe perhaps two or three days behind in a hunt. The chips on the convex side of the crescent determine the direction: one – to the left; two – to the right. Their replacement on the rim shows the angle. Here: two chips, dead center; therefore, directly to the right of the stone facing the base of the crescent.' Whitehall gestured with his right hand northeast.

'As Piersall instructed.' Barak nodded his head: he did not bother to conceal his pique at Charley-mon's explanation. Yet there was respect in that pique, thought McAuliff, as he watched Moore begin pacing off the forty-four steps.

Piersall had disguised the spot chosen for burial. There was a thicket of mollusk ferns spreading out in a free-form spray within the paced-off area of the grass. They had been rerooted expertly; it was illogical to assume any sort of digging had taken place there in years.

Floyd took a knapsack shovel from his belt, unfolded the stem, and began removing the earth. Charles Whitehall bent down on his knees and joined the revolutionary, clawing at the dirt with his bare hands.

The rectangular box was deep in the ground. Had not the instructions been so precise, the digging might have stopped before reaching it. The depth was over three feet. Whitehall suspected it was exactly four feet when deposited. The Arawak unit of four.

The instant Floyd's small shovel struck the metal casing, Whitehall lashed his right hand down, snatched the box out of the earth, and fingered the edges, trying to pry it apart. It was not possible, and Whitehall realized it within seconds. He had used this type of receptacle perhaps a thousand times: It was a hermetically sealed archive case whose soft, rubberized edges created a vacuum within. It had two locks, one at each end, with separate keys; once the keys were inserted and turned, air was allowed in, and after a period of minutes the box could be forced open. It was the sort of repository used in the most heavily endowed libraries to house old manuscripts, manuscripts that were studied by scholars no more than once every five years or so and thus preserved with great care. The name 'archive case' was well suited for documents in archives for a millennium.

'Give me the keys!' whispered Charles urgently to Barak.

'I have no keys, mon. Piersall said nothing about keys.'

'*Damn!*'

'Keep quiet!' ordered McAuliff.

'Push that dirt back,' said Moore to Floyd. 'So it is not obvious, mon. Push back the ferns.'

Floyd did as he was told; McAuliff helped him. Whitehall stared at the rectangular box in his hands; he was furious.

'He was paranoid!' whispered the scholar, turning to Barak. 'You said it was a packet. An oilcloth packet! Not this. This will take a blowtorch to open!'

'Charley's got a point,' said Alex, shoveling in dirt with his hands, realizing that he had just called Whitehall 'Charley'. 'Why did he go to this trouble? Why didn't he just put the box with the rest of the papers in the cistern?'

'You ask questions I cannot answer, mon. He was very concerned, that's all I can tell you.'

The dirt was back in the hole. Floyd smoothed out the surface and pushed the roots of the mollusk ferns into the soft earth. 'That will do, I think, mon,' he said, folding the stem of the shovel and replacing it in his belt.

'How are we going to get inside?' asked McAuliff. 'Or get the guard outside?'

'I have thought of this for several hours,' replied Barak. 'Wild pigs, I think.'

'Very *good*, mon!' interrupted Floyd.

'In the pool?' added Whitehall knowingly.

'Yes.'

'What the hell are you talking about?' Alex watched the faces of the three black men in the moonlight.

Barak answered. 'In the Cock Pit there are many wild pigs. They are vicious and troublesome. We are perhaps ten miles from the Cock Pit's borders. It is not unusual for pigs to stray this far. Floyd and I will imitate the sounds. You and Charley-mon throw rocks into the pool.'

'What about the dog?' asked Whitehall. 'You'd better shoot it.'

'No shooting, mon! Gunfire would be heard for miles. I will take care of the dog.' Moore withdrew a small anesthetizing dart gun from his pocket. 'Our arsenal contains many of these. Come.'

Five minutes later McAuliff thought he was part of some demonic children's charade. Barak and Floyd had crept to the edge of the tall grass bordering the elegant lawn. On the assumption that the Doberman would head directly to the first human smell, Alex and Whitehall were in parallel positions ten feet to the right of the revolutionaries, a pile of stones between them. They were to throw the rocks as accurately as possible into the lighted pool sixty feet away at the first sounds emanating from Moore and his comrade.

It began.

The shrieks intruded on the stillness of the night with terrible authenticity. They were the bellows of panicked beasts, shrill and somehow horrible.

'*Eeewahhee ... gnnrahha, nggrahhaaa ... eeaww, eeaww ... eeeowahhee ...*'

McAuliff and Whitehall lobbed rocks into the pool; the splashes were interspersed with the monstrous shrieks. A weird cacophony filled the air.

The shutters from the first floor were thrown open. The guard could be seen behind the grillwork, a rifle in his hand.

Suddenly a stone hit Alex's cheek. The blow was gentle, not stunning. He whipped his head toward the direction of the throw. Floyd was waving his arm in the tall grass, commanding McAuliff to stop hurling the rocks. Alex grabbed Whitehall's hand. They stopped.

The shrieks then became louder, accompanied by blunt thuds of pounding earth. Alex could see Barak and Floyd in the moonlight. They were slapping the ground like crazed animals; the horrible noises coming from their shaking heads reached a crescendo.

Wild pigs fighting in the high grass.

The door of Piersall's house crashed open. The guard, rifle in hand, released the dog at his side. The animal lurched out onto the lawn and raced toward the hysterical sounds and all-too-human odors.

McAuliff knelt, hypnotized by what followed in the Jamaican moonlight. Barak and Floyd scrambled back into the field without raising their bodies above the grass and without diminishing the pitch of their animal screams. The Doberman streaked across the lawn and sprang headlong over the border of the field and into the tall grass.

The continuing shrieks and guttural roars were joined by the savage barking of the vicious dog. And, amid the terrible sounds, Alex could distinguish a series of spits; the dart gun was being fired repeatedly.

A yelping howl suddenly drowned out the man-made bellowing; the guard ran to the edge of the lawn, his rifle raised to fire. And before McAuliff could absorb or understand the action, Charles Whitehall grabbed a handful of rocks and threw them toward the lighted pool. And then a second handful hard upon the first.

The guard spun around to the water; Whitehall slammed Alex out of the way, raced along the edge of the grass, and suddenly leaped out on the lawn at the patrolman.

McAuliff watched, stunned.

Whitehall, the elegant academic – the delicately boned Charley-mon – lashed his arm out into the base of the guard's neck, crashed his foot savagely into the man's midsection, and seized a wrist, twisting it violently so that the rifle flew out of the guard's hands; the man jerked off his feet, spun into the air, and whipped to the ground. As the guard vibrated off the grass, Whitehall took swift aim and crashed his heel into the man's skull below his forehead.

The body contorted, then lay still.

The shrieking stopped; all was silent.

It was over.

Barak and Floyd raced out from the high grass onto the lawn. Barak spoke. 'Thank you, Charley-mon. Indiscriminate gunfire might have found us.'

'It was necessary,' replied Whitehall simply. 'I must see those papers.'

'Then let us go,' said Barak Moore. 'Floyd, take this real pig inside; tie him up somewhere.'

'Don't waste time,' countered Whitehall, starting for the house, the receptacle under his arm. 'Just throw him into the grass. He's dead.'

Inside, Floyd led them to the cellar stairs and down into Piersall's basement. The cistern was in the west section, about six feet deep and five wide. The walls were dry; cobwebs laced the sides and the top. Barak brushed aside the filmy obstructions and lowered himself into the pit.

'How do you know which are the blocks?' asked Whitehall urgently, the black rectangular box clasped in his hand.

'There is a way; the Doctor explained,' replied Moore, taking out a small box of safety matches. He struck one and stared at the north center line, revolving slowly clockwise, holding the lighted match against the cracks in the blocks on the lower half of the pit.

'Ground phosphorus,' stated Whitehall quietly. 'Packed into the concrete edges.'

'Yes, mon. Not much; enough to give a little flame, or a sputter, perhaps.'

'You're wasting time!' Whitehall spat out the words. 'Swing to your *left*, toward the northwest point! Not to your right.'

The three men looked abruptly at the scholar. '*What*, Charley-mon?' Barak was bewildered.

'Do as I say! ... Please.'

'The Arawak symbols?' asked McAuliff. 'The odyssey to death, or whatever you called it? To the right of the setting sun?'

'I'm glad you find it amusing.'

'I don't, Charley. Not one goddamn bit,' answered Alex softly.

'Ayee ...' Barak whistled softly as tiny spits of flame burst out of the cistern's cracks. 'Charley, you got brains, mon! Here they are. Floyd, mon, give me the tools.'

Floyd reached into his field jacket and produced a five-inch stone chisel and an all-metal folding hammer. He handed them down to his superior. 'You want help?' he asked.

'There is not room for two,' replied Barak as he started hammering along the cracks.

Three minutes later Moore had managed to dislodge the first block from its surrounding adhesive; he tugged at it, pulling it slowly out of the cistern wall. Whitehall held the flashlight now, his eyes intent on Moore's manipulations. The block came loose; Floyd reached down and took it from Barak's hands.

'What's behind?' Whitehall pierced the beam of light into the gaping hole.

'Space, mon. Red dirt and space,' said Moore. 'And I think the top of another box. A larger box.'

'For God's sake, *hurry!*'

'Okay, Charley-mon. There is no dinner engagement at the Mo'Bay Hilton, mon.' Barak chuckled. 'Nothing will be rewritten by a hidden mongoose.'

'Relax.' McAuliff did not look at Whitehall when he spoke. He did not want to. 'We have all night, don't we? You killed a man out there. He was the only one who could have interfered. And you decided he had to die for that.'

Whitehall turned his head and stared at McAuliff. 'I killed him because it was necessary.' Whitehall transferred his attention back to Barak Moore. The second block came loose with far less effort than the first. Barak reached into the space and rocked the stone until the cracks widened and it slid out. Floyd took the block and placed it carefully to one side.

Whitehall crouched opposite the hole, shining the flashlight into it. 'It's an archive case. Let me have it.' He handed Floyd the flashlight and reached across the pit as Barak pulled the receptacle out of the dirt and gave it to him. 'Extraordinary!' said Charley, fingering the oblong box, his knee pressed against the top of the first receptacle on the floor beside him. Whitehall was not going to let either out of his possession.

'The case, you mean, mon?' asked Moore.

'Yes.' Whitehall turned the box over, then held it up as Floyd shone the beam of light on it. 'I don't think any of you understand. Without the keys or proper equipment, these bloody things take hours to open. Watertight, airtight, vacuumed, and crushproof. Even a starbit drill could not penetrate the metal ... Here! See.' The scholar pointed to some lettering on the bottom surface. 'Hitchcock Vault Company, Indianapolis. The finest in the world. Museums, libraries ... government archives everywhere use Hitch-cock. Simply extraordinary.'

When the sound came, it had the impact of an earth-shattering explosion. Although the noise was distant – that of the whining low gear of an automobile racing up the long entrance drive from the road below.

And then another.

The four men looked back and forth at one another. They were stunned. Outside there was an intrusion that was not to be. *Could* not be.

'Oh my *God, Jesus, mon!*' Barak jumped out of the pit.

'Take these tools, you damn fool!' cried Whitehall. 'Your fingerprints!'

Floyd, rather than Barak, leaped into the cistern, grabbed the hammer and chisel, and put them into the pockets of his field jacket. 'There is only the staircase, mon! No other way!'

Barak ran to the stairs. McAuliff reached down for the first receptacle at Whitehall's side; simultaneously, Whitehall's hand was on it.

'You can't carry both, Charley,' said Alex in answer to Whitehall's manic stare. 'This one's mine!' He grabbed the box, jerked it out from under Whitehall's grip, and followed Moore to the stairs. The automobiles, in grinding counterpoint, were getting nearer.

The four men leaped up the stairs in single file and raced through the short corridor into the darkened, rugless living room. The beams of headlights could be seen shining through the slits in the teak shutters. The first car had reached the compact parking area; the sounds of doors opening could be heard. The second vehicle roared in only seconds behind. In the corner of the room could be seen, in the strips of light, the cause for the intrusion: an open-line portable radio. Barak ran to it and with a single blow of his fist into the metal, smashed the front and then tore out the back antennae.

Men outside began shouting. Predominately one name:

'*Raymond!*'

'Raymond!'

'Raymond! Where are you at, mon!'

Floyd assumed the lead and raced to the rear center door. 'This way! Quick, mon!' he whispered to the others. He yanked the door open and held it as they all gathered. McAuliff could see in the reflection of the pool's light that Floyd held a pistol in his free hand. Floyd spoke to Barak. 'I will deflect them, mon. To the west. I know the property good, mon!'

'Be careful! You two,' said Barak to Whitehall and McAuliff. 'Go straight into the woods; we'll meet at the raft. One half-hour from now. No more.

Whoever is there, leave. Pole down, mon. The Martha Brae is no good without a raft, mon. *Go!* He shoved Alex through the door.

Outside, McAuliff started across the strangely peaceful lawn, with the blue-green light of the pool illuminating from behind. Men had raced up from the entrance drive to the sides of the house. Alex wondered if they could see him; he was running as fast as he could toward the seemingly impenetrable wall of forest beyond the sloping lawn. He gripped the oblong receptacle under his right arm.

He got his answer instantly.

The insanity had started.

Gunshots!

Bullets cracked above him; abrupt detonations spaced erratically behind him.

Men were firing pistols indiscriminately.

Oh, Jesus; he was back there again!

Long-forgotten instructions returned once more. Diagonals; make diagonals. *Short, quick spurts; but not too short. Just enough to give the enemy a half-second to assume zero aim.*

He had given those instructions. To scores of men in the Che San hills.

The shouting became an overlapping chorus of hysteria; and then a single scream pierced the symphony.

McAuliff hurled himself into the air, into the sudden growth of dense foliage that bordered the lawn. He fell into a thicket and rolled to his left.

On the ground, out of sight lines, roll! Roll for all you're worth into a second position!

Basics.

Fundamentals.

He was positive he would see men coming after him down the hill.

There weren't.

Instead, what he saw hypnotized him, as he had been hypnotized watching the two black revolutionaries in the high grass pretending to be wild pigs.

Up by the house – to the west of it, actually – Floyd was reeling around and around, the light of the pool catching the dull green of his field jacket. He was allowing himself to be an open target, firing a pistol, pinning the police to the sides of the house. He ran out of ammunition, reached into his pocket, withdrew another gun, and started firing again – now racing to the edge of the pool, in full sacrificial view.

He had been hit. Repeatedly. Blood was spreading throughout the cloth of the field jacket and all over his trousers. The man had at least a half-dozen bullets in him, ebbing away his life, leaving him only moments to live.

McAuliff!' The whispered shout was from his right. Barak Moore, his grotesque shaved head glistening with sweat in the filtered moonlight, threw himself down beside Alex. 'We get out of here, mon! Come!' He tugged at McAuliff's drenched shirt.

'For God's sake! Can't you see what's happening up there? That man's dying!'

Barak glanced up through the tangled overgrowth. He spoke calmly. 'We are committed till death. In its way, it is a luxury. Floyd knows that.'

'For *what*, for Christ's sake? For goddamn stinking *what*? You're goddamn madmen!'

'Let us *go*!' commanded Moore. 'They will follow us in seconds. Floyd is giving us this chance, you white shit, mon!'

Alex grabbed Barak's hand, which was still gripping his shirt, and threw it off. 'That's it, isn't it? I'm a white shit. And Floyd has to die because you think so. And that guard had to die because Whitehall thinks so! . . . You're sick.'

Barak Moore paused. 'You are what you are, mon. And you will not take this island. Many, many will die, but this island will not be yours . . . You will be dead, too, if you do not run with me.' Moore suddenly stood up and ran into the forest darkness.

McAuliff looked after him, holding the black oblong box to his chest. Then he rose from the ground and followed the black revolutionary.

They waited at the water's edge, the raft bobbing up and down in the onrushing current. They were waist-deep in the river, Barak checking his wristwatch, Alex shifting his feet in the soft mud to hold the bamboo sides of the raft more firmly.

'We cannot wait much longer, mon,' said Barak. 'I can hear them in the hills. They come closer!'

McAuliff could not hear anything but the sounds of the rushing river and the slapping of water against the raft. And Barak. 'We can't leave him here!'

'No choice. You want your head blown off, mon?'

'No. And it *won't* be. We stole papers from a dead man. At his instructions. That's no call for being shot at. Enough's enough, goddammit!'

Barak laughed. 'You have a short memory, mon! Up in the tall grass there is a dead policeman. Without doubt, Floyd took at least one other life with him; Floyd was an expert shot. Your head will be blown off; the Falmouth police will not hesitate.'

Barak Moore was right. *Where the hell was Whitehall?*

'Was he shot? Do you know if he was wounded?'

'I think not, mon. I cannot be sure . . . Charley-mon did not do as I told him. He ran southwest into the field.'

A single shaft of light was seen a hundred yards upstream, streaking down through the overgrown banks.

'Look!' cried Alex. Moore turned.

There was a second, then a third beam. Three dancing columns of light, wavering toward the river below.

'No time now, mon! Get in and pole fast!'

The two of them shoved the raft toward the center current and jumped onto the bamboo-sided surface.

'I get in front, mon!' yelled Moore, scrambling over the platformed, high-backed seat used by tourists viewing the beauty of the Martha Brae. 'You stay in the rear, mon! Use the pole and when I tell you, stop and put your legs over the backside!'

McAuliff focused his eyes in the moonlight, trying to distinguish which was the loose pole among the strapped cylinders of bamboo. It was wedged between the low railing and the deck; he picked it up and plunged it into the mud below.

The raft entered the rapids and began careening downstream. Moore stood up in the bow and used his pole as a deflector, warding the racing bamboo float off the treacherous series of flesh-cutting rocks that broke the surface of the water. They were approaching a bend in the river. Barak shouted.

'Sit on the backside, mon! Put your feet into the water. *Quick, mon!*'

Alex did as he was ordered; he soon understood. The drag created by his weight and his feet gave Moore the slightly slower speed he needed to navigate the raft through a miniature archipelago of hazardous rocks. The bamboo sides crashed back and forth, into and over the mounds of jagged stones. McAuliff thought the raft would list right out of the water.

It was the sound of the harsh scrapings and his concentration on the rapids that caused Alex to delay his realization of the gunshots. And then that realization was complete with the stinging, searing pain in his left arm. A bullet had grazed his flesh; the blood trickled down his sleeve in the moonlight.

There was a staccato burst of gunfire.

'You get down, mon!' yelled Barak. 'Get flat! They cannot follow us; we get around the bend, there is a grotto. Many caves. They lead up to the Brae Road, mon ... *Ayeee!*'

Moore buckled; he let go of the pole, grabbed his stomach, and fell onto the bamboo deck. Alex reached down for the oblong archive case, crammed it into his belt, and crawled as fast as he could to the front of the raft. Barak Moore was writhing; he was alive.

'How bad are you hurt?'

'Pretty bad, mon! ... Stay *down*! If we get stuck, jump out and push us off ... around bend, mon.'

Barak was unconscious. The bamboo raft plunged over a shallow, graveled surface and then into the final curve of the bend, where the water was deep, the current powerful and faster than before. The sounds of gunfire stopped; they were out of sight of the Trelawny police.

McAuliff raised his shoulders; the archive case was cutting into his skin beneath his belt. His left arm stung with pain. The river now became a huge flat pool, the waters rushing under the surface. There were stone cliffs diagonally across, rising sharply out of the riverbank.

Suddenly Alex saw the beam of the lone flashlight, and the terrible pain of fear pierced his stomach. The enemy was not behind – he was waiting.

Involuntarily, he reached into his pocket for his gun. The Smith & Wesson given him by Westmore Tallon. He raised it as the raft steered itself toward the stone cliffs and the flashlight.

He lowered himself over the unconscious body of Barak Moore and waited, his arm outstretched, the pistol aimed at the body beyond the flashlight.

He was within forty yards of the silent figure. He was about to squeeze the trigger and take a life.

'*Barak, mon!*' came the words.

The man on the riverbank was Lawrence.

Charles Whitehall waited in the high brass by the cluster of breadfruit trees. The archive case was securely under his arm; he knelt immobile in the moonlight and watched Piersall's house and grounds two hundred yards away. The body of the dead guard had not been found. Floyd's corpse had been carried into the house for the light necessary for a complete search of the dead body.

One man remained behind. The others had all raced into the eastern forests and down to the Martha Brae in pursuit of Moore and McAuliff.

That was precisely what Charles Whitehall thought would happen. And why he had not done as Barak Moore commanded.

There was a better way. If one acted alone.

The single Trelawny policeman was fat. He waddled back and forth by the wooded border of the lawn; he was pacing nervously, as if afraid to be alone. He carried a rifle in his hands, jerking it toward every sound he heard or thought he heard.

Suddenly there was gunfire far below in the distance, down at the river. It was full, rapid. Either much ammunition was being wasted, or Moore and McAuliff were having a bad time of it.

But it was his moment to move. The patrolman was gunning the edge of the forest, peering down. The gunfire was both his protection and the source of his fear. He cradled his rifle and nervously lighted a cigarette.

Charles got up and, clutching the archive case, raced through the tall grass behind the west flank of the field. He then turned right and ran toward Piersall's house, through the diminishing woods to the border of the entrance drive.

The two patrol cars stood peacefully in the moonlight, in front of the wide stone steps to High Hill. Whitehall emerged from the woods and crossed to the first vehicle. One door was open – the driver's door. The dim interior shone over the black leather.

The keys were in the ignition. He removed them and then reached under the dashboard radio and ripped every wire out of the panel. He closed the door silently, ran to the second car, and saw that its keys were also in place. He walked rapidly back to the first car and as quietly as possible unlatched the hood. He yanked off the distributor cap and tugged at the rubber lid until it sprang loose from the wires.

He returned to the second vehicle, got in, and placed the archive case beside him. He pressed the accelerator several times. He checked the gearshift mechanism and was satisfied.

He turned the key in the ignition. The motor started instantly.

Charles Whitehall backed the patrol car out of the parking area, swung the wheel, and sped off down the drive.

19

The doctor closed the patio door and walked out onto Bengal Court's terrace, which connected Alison's and McAuliff's rooms. Barak Moore was in Alison's bed. She had insisted; no comments were offered, the decision was not debated.

Alex's upper-left arm was bandaged; the wound was surface, painful, and not serious. He sat with Alison on the waist-high terrace sea wall. He did not elaborate on the night raid; there would be time later. Sam Tucker and Lawrence had taken positions at each end of the patio in order to keep any wanderers from coming into the small area.

The doctor from Falmouth, whom Lawrence had contacted at midnight, approached McAuliff. 'I have done what I can. I wish I felt more confident.'

'Shouldn't he be in a hospital?' Alison's words were as much a rebuke as a question.

'He should be,' agreed the doctor wearily. 'I discussed it with him; we concluded it was not feasible. There is only a government clinic in Falmouth. I think this is cleaner.'

'Barak is wanted,' explained Alex quietly. 'He'd be put in prison before they got the bullet out.'

'I sincerely doubt they would take the trouble to remove the bullet, Mr McAuliff.'

'What do you think?' asked Alex, lighting a cigarette.

'He will have a chance if he remains absolutely still. But only a chance. I have cauterized the abdominal wall; it could easily rerupture. I have replaced blood ... yes, my office has a discreet file of certain individuals' blood classifications. He is extremely weak. If he survives two or three days, there is hope.'

'But you don't think he will,' stated McAuliff.

'No. There was too much internal bleeding. My ... portable operating kit is not that good. Oh, my man is cleaning up. He will take out the sheets, clothing, anything that has been soiled. Unfortunately, the odor of ether and disinfectant will remain. Keep the outside doors open when you can. Lawrence will make sure no one enters.'

Alex slid off the wall and leaned against it. 'Doctor? I gather you're part of Barak's organization, if that's the word.'

542

'It is too precise at this juncture.'

'But you know what's going on.'

'Not specifically. Nor do I wish to. My function is to be available for medical purposes. The less involvement otherwise, the better for everyone.'

'You can get word to people, though, can't you?'

The doctor smiled. 'By "people" I assume you mean Barak's followers.'

'Yes.'

'There are telephone numbers ... public telephones, and specific hours. The answer is yes.'

'We're going to need at least one other man. Floyd was killed.'

Alison Booth gasped. Her eyes riveted on Alex; her hand reached out for his arm. He covered it gently. 'Oh my God,' she whispered.

The doctor looked at Alison but did not comment on her reaction. He turned back to McAuliff. 'Barak told me. There may be a problem; we do not know yet. The survey is being watched. Floyd was part of it, and the police will find out. You will be questioned, of course. Naturally, you know absolutely nothing; wear long sleeves for a while – a few days, until the wound can be covered with a large plaster. To replace Floyd now with one of our men could be a self-induced trap.'

Reluctantly, Alex nodded. 'I see,' he said softly. 'But I need another man. Lawrence can't do triple duty.'

'May I make a suggestion?' asked the doctor with a thin smile and a knowing look in his eyes.

'What's that?'

'Use British Intelligence. You really should not ignore them.'

'Get some sleep, Sam. Lawrence, you do the same,' said Alex to the two men on the terrace. The doctor had left; his assistant remained with Barak Moore. Alison had gone into McAuliff's room and shut the door. 'Nothing will happen tonight, except possibly the police ... to ask me questions about a crewman I haven't seen since early afternoon.'

'You know what to say, mon?' Lawrence asked the question with authority, as if he would provide the answer.

'The doctor explained; Barak told him.'

'You must be angry, mon! Floyd alla time a no-good thief from Ochee. Now you know: supplies stolen. You drum-drum angry, mon!'

'It doesn't seem fair, does it?' said Alex sadly.

'Do as he says, lad,' countered Sam Tucker. 'He knows what he's talking about ... I'll nap out here. Hate the goddamn bed, anyway.'

'It isn't necessary, Sam.'

'Has it occurred to you, boy, that the police may just come here without announcing themselves? I'd hate like hell for them to get the rooms mixed up.'

'Oh, Lord ...' McAuliff spoke with weariness. It was the exhaustion of inadequacy, the pressure of continually being made aware of it. 'I didn't think of that.'

'Neither did the goddamn doctor,' replied Sam. 'Lawrence and I have, which is why we'll stand turns.'

'Then I'll join you.'

'You do enough tonight, mon,' said Lawrence firmly. 'You have been hurt. Maybe policemen do not come so quick. Floyd carry no papers. Early morning Sam Tucker and me take Barak away.'

'The doctor said he was to stay where he is.'

'The doctor is a kling-kling, mon! Two, three hours Barak will sleep. If he is not dead, we take him to Braco Beach. The ocean is still before sunrise; a flat-bottom is very gentle, mon. We take him away.'

'He makes sense again, Alex.' Tucker gave his approval without regret. 'Our medical friend notwithstanding, it's a question of alternatives. And we both know most wounded men can travel gentle if you give 'em a couple of hours.'

'What'll we do if the police come tonight? And search?'

Lawrence answered, again with authority. 'I tell Tuck, mon. The person in that room has Indie Fever. The bad smell helps us. Falmouth police plenty scared of Indie Fever.'

'So is everybody else,' added Sam, chuckling.

'You're inventive,' said McAuliff. And he meant it. 'Indie Fever' was the polite term for a particularly nasty offshoot of elephantiasis, infrequent but nevertheless very much a reality, usually found in the hill country. It could swell a man's testicles many times their size and render him impotent as well as a figure of grotesque ridicule.

'You go get sleep now, McAuliff, mon . . . please.'

'Yes. Yes, I will. See you in a few hours.' Alex looked at Lawrence for a moment before turning to go inside. It was amazing. Floyd was dead, Barak barely alive, and the grinning, previously carefree youngster who had seemed so naïve and playful in comparison to his obvious superiors was no longer the innocent. He had, in a matter of hours, become the leader of his faction, lord of his pack. A hard authority had been swiftly developed, although he still felt the need to qualify that authority.

Get sleep now . . . please.

In a day or two the 'please' would be omitted. The command would be all. So forever the office made the man.

Sam Tucker smiled at McAuliff in the bright Jamaican moonlight. He seemed to be reading Alex's thoughts. Or was Sam remembering McAuliff's first independent survey? Tucker had been there. It had been in the Aleutians, in springtime, and a man had died because Alex had not been firm enough in his disciplining the team regarding the probing of ice fissures. Alexander Tarquin McAuliff had matured quickly that springtime in the Aleutians.

'See you later, Sam.'

Inside the room, Alison lay in bed, the table lamp on. By her side was the archive case he had carried out of Carrick Foyle. She was outwardly calm, but there was no mistaking the intensity beneath the surface. McAuliff removed his shirt, threw it on a chair, and crossed to the dial on the wall that regulated the overhead fan. He turned it up; the four blades suspended from the ceiling accelerated, the whirr matching the sound of distant surf outside. He walked to the bureau, where the bucket of ice had melted halfway. Cubes were bunched together in the water, enough for drinks.

'Would you like a Scotch?' he asked without looking at her.

'No thank you,' she replied in her soft British accent. Soft, but laced – as all British speech was laced – with that core of understated, superior rationality.

'I would.'

'I should think so.'

He poured the whisky into a hotel glass, threw in two ice cubes, and turned around. 'To answer you before you ask, I had no idea tonight would turn out the way it did.'

'Would you have gone had you known?'

'Of course not . . . But it's over. We have what we need now.'

'This?' Alison touched the archive case.

'Yes.'

'From what you've told me . . . on the word of a dying primitive. Told to him by a dead fanatic.'

'I think those descriptions are a little harsh.' McAuliff went to the chair by the bed and sat down facing her. 'But I won't defend either one yet. I'll wait. I'll find out what's in here, do what they say I should do, and see what happens.'

'You sound positively confident, and I can't imagine why. You've been shot at. A bullet came within five inches of killing you. Now you sit here calmly and tell me you'll simply bide your time and see what happens? Alex, for God's sake, what are you *doing*?'

McAuliff smiled and swallowed a good deal of whisky. 'What I never thought was possible,' he said slowly, abruptly serious. 'I mean that . . . And I've just seen a boy grow up into a man. In one hour. The act cost a terrible price, but it happened . . . and I'm not sure I can understand it, but I saw it. That transformation had something to do with belief. We haven't got it. We act out of fear or greed or both . . . all of us. He doesn't. He does what he does, becomes what he becomes, because he believes . . . And, strangely enough, so does Charley Whitehall.'

'What in heaven's name are you talking about?'

McAuliff lowered his glass and looked at her. 'I have an idea we're about to turn this war over to the people who should be fighting it.'

Charles Whitehall exhaled slowly, extinguished the acetylene flame, and removed his goggles. He put the torch down on the long narrow table and took off the asbestos gloves. He noted with satisfaction that his every movement was controlled; he was like a confident surgeon, no motion wasted, his mind ahead of his every muscle.

He rose from the stool and stretched. He turned to see that the door of the small room was still bolted. A foolish thing to do, he thought; he had bolted the door. He was alone.

He had driven over back roads nearly forty miles away from Carrick Foyle to the border of St Anne's. He had left the police car in a field and walked the last mile into the town.

Ten years ago St Anne's was a meeting place for those of the Movement between Falmouth and Ocho Rios. The 'nigger rich', they had called themselves, with good-sized fields in Drax Hall, Chalky Hill, and Davis Town. Men of property and certain wealth, which they had forced from the earth and were not about to turn over to the Commonwealth sycophants in Kingston. Whitehall remembered names, as he remembered most things – a necessary discipline – and within fifteen minutes after he reached St Anne's, he was picked up by a man in a new Pontiac, who cried at seeing him.

When his needs were made known, he was driven to the house of another man in Drax Hall, whose hobby was machinery. The introductions were brief; this second man embraced him, held on to him for such a length of time – silently – that Charles found it necessary to disengage him.

He was taken to a toolshed at the side of the house, where everything he had requested was laid out on the long narrow table that butted the wall, a sink at midpoint. Besides the overhead light, there was a goosenecked lamp, whose bright illumination could be directed at a small area. Charles was amused to see that along with these requirements was a bowl of fresh fruit and a huge pewter tankard filled with ice.

A messiah had returned.

And now the archive case was open. He stared down at the severed end, the metal edges still glowing with dying orange, then yellow – lingering – soon to be black again. Inside he could see the brown folds of a document roll – the usual encasement for folded papers, each sheet against the imperceptibly moist surface of the enveloping shield.

In the earth a living vault. Precise for a thousand years.

Walter Piersall had buried a rock for many ages in the event his own overlooked it. He was a professional.

As a physician might with a difficult birth, Charles reached in and pulled the priceless child from its womb. He unraveled the document and began reading.

Acquaba.

The tribe of Acquaba.

Walter Piersall had gone back into the Jamaican archives and found the brief allusion in the records pertaining to the Maroon Wars.

On January 2, 1739, a descendant of the Coromanteen tribal chieftains, one Acquaba, led his followers into the mountains. The tribe of Acquaba would not be a party to the Cudjoe treaty with the British, insofar as said treaty called upon the Africans to recapture slaves for the white garrisons...

There was the name of an obscure army officer who had supplied the information to His Majesty's Recorder in Spanish Town, the colony's capital.

Middlejohn, Robt. Maj. W.I. Reg. 641.

What made the name of 'Middlejohn, Robt.' significant was Piersall's discovery of the following.

His Majesty's Recorder. Spanish Town. February 9, 1739. *[Docm'ts. recalled. Middlejohn. W.I. Reg. 641.]*

And . . .

His Majesty's Recorder. Spanish Town. April 20, 1739. *[Docm'ts recalled. R. M. W.I. Reg. 641.]*

Robert Middlejohn. Major. West Indian Regiment 641, in the Year of Our Lord 1739, had been significant to someone.

Who?

Why?

It took Walter Piersall weeks at the Institute to find the next clue. A second name.

But not in the eighteenth century; instead, 144 years later, in the year 1883. *Fowler, Jeremy. Clerk. Foreign Service.*

One Jeremy Fowler had removed several documents from the archives in the new capital of Kingston on the *instructions of Her Majesty's Foreign Office, June 7, 1883. Victoria Regina.*

The colonial documents in question were labeled simply 'Middlejohn papers'. 1739.

Walter Piersall speculated. Was it possible that the Middlejohn papers continued to speak of the Tribe of Acquaba, as the first document had done? Was the retention of that first document in the archives an oversight? An omission committed by one Jeremy Fowler on June 7, 1883?

Piersall had flown to London and used his academic credentials to gain access to the Foreign Office's West Indian records. Since he was dealing in matters of research over a hundred years old, F.O. had no objections. The archivists were most helpful.

And there were no transferred documents from Kingston in the year 1883.

Jeremy Fowler, clerk of the Foreign Service, had stolen the Middlejohn papers!

If there was a related answer, Walter Piersall now had two specifics to go on: the name Fowler and the year 1883 in the colony of Jamaica.

Since he was in London, he traced the descendants of Jeremy Fowler. It was not a difficult task.

The Fowlers – sons and uncles – were proprietors of their own brokerage house on the London Exchange. The patriarch was Gordon Fowler Esquire, great-great-grandson of Jeremy Fowler, clerk, Foreign Service, colony of Jamaica.

Walter Piersall interviewed old Fowler on the premise that he was researching the last two decades of Victoria's rule in Jamaica; the Fowler name was prominent. Flattered, the old gentleman gave him access to all papers, albums, and documents relative to Jeremy Fowler.

These materials told a not unfamiliar story of the times, a young man of 'middle breeding' entering the Colonial Service, spending a number of years in a distant outpost, only to return to England far richer than when he left.

Sufficiently rich to be able to buy heavily into the Exchange during the last decade of the nineteenth century. A propitious time; the source of the current Fowler wealth.

One part of the answer.

Jeremy Fowler had made his connection in the Colonial Service.

Walter Piersall had returned to Jamaica to look for the second part.

He studied, day by day, week by week, the recorded history of Jamaica for the year 1883. It was laborious.

And then he found it. May 25, 1883.

A disappearance that was not given much attention insofar as small groups of Englishmen – hunting parties – were constantly getting lost in the Blue Mountains and tropic jungles, usually to be found by scouting parties of blacks led by other Englishmen.

As this lone man had been found.

Her Majesty's Recorder, Jeremy Fowler.

Not a clerk, but the official Crown Recorder.

Which was why his absence justified the space in the papers. The Crown Recorder was not insignificant. Not landed gentry, of course, but a person of substance.

The ancient newspaper accounts were short, imprecise, and strange.

A Mr Fowler had last been observed in his government office on the evening of May 25, a Saturday. He did not return on Monday and was not seen for the rest of the work week. Nor had his quarters been slept in.

Six days later, Mr Fowler turned up in the garrison of Fleetcourse, south of the impenetrable Cock Pit, escorted by several Maroon 'Negroes'. He had gone on horseback alone . . . for a Sunday ride. His horse had bolted him; he had gotten lost and wandered for days until found by the Maroons.

It was illogical. In those years, Walter Piersall knew, men did not ride alone into such territories. And if one did, a man who was sufficiently intelligent to be Her Majesty's Recorder would certainly know enough to take a left angle from the sun and reach the south coast in a matter of hours, at best a day.

And one week later Jeremy Fowler stole the Middlejohn papers from the archives. The documents concerning a sect led by a Coromanteen chieftain named Acquaba . . . that had disappeared into the mountains 144 years before.

And six months later he left the Foreign – Colonial – Service and returned to England a very, very wealthy man.

He had discovered the Tribe of Acquaba.

It was the only logical answer. And if that were so, there was a second, logical speculation: Was the Tribe of Acquaba . . . the Halidon?

Piersall was convinced it was. He needed only current proof.

Proof that there was substance to the whispers of the incredibly wealthy sect high in the Cock Pit mountains. An isolated community that sent its members out into the world, into Kingston, to exert influence.

Piersall tested five men in the Kingston government, all in positions of trust, all with obscure backgrounds. Did any of them belong to the Halidon?

He went to each, telling each that he alone was the recipient of his startling information: *the Tribe of Acquaba.*

The Halidon.

Three of the five were fascinated but bewildered. They did not understand.

Two of the five disappeared.

Disappeared in the sense of being removed from Kingston. Piersall was told one man had retired suddenly to an island in the Martinique chain. The other was transferred out of Jamaica to a remote post.

Piersall had his current proof.

The Halidon was the Tribe of the Acquaba.

It existed.

If he needed further confirmation, final proof, the growing harassment against him was it. The harassment now included the selected rifling and theft of his files and untraceable university inquiries into his current academic studies. Someone beyond the Kingston government was concentrating on him. The acts were not those of concerned bureaucrats.

The Tribe of Acquaba ... Halidon.

What was left was to reach the leaders. A staggeringly difficult thing to do. For throughout the Cock Pit there were scores of insulated sects who kept to themselves; most of them poverty-stricken, scraping an existence off the land. The Halidon would not proclaim its self-sufficiency; which one was it?

The anthropologist returned once again to the volumes of African minutiae, specifically seventeenth- and eighteenth-century Coromanteen. The key had to be there.

Piersall had found the key; he had not footnoted its source.

Each tribe, each offshoot of a tribe, had a *single sound applicable to it only. A whistle, a slap, a word. This symbol was known only within the highest tribal councils, understood by only a few, who communicated it to their out-tribal counterparts.*

The symbol, the sound, the word ... was 'Halidon'.

Its meaning.

It took him nearly a month of sleepless days and nights, using logarithmic charts of phonetics, hieroglyphs, and African symbols of daily survival.

When he was finished, he was satisfied. He had broken the ancient code.

It was too dangerous to include it in this summary. For in the event of his death – or murder – this summary might fall into the wrong hands. Therefore, there was a second archive case containing the secret.

The second without the first was meaningless.

Instructions were left with one man. To be acted upon in the event he was no longer capable of doing so himself.

Charles Whitehall turned over the last page. His face and neck were drenched with sweat. Yet it was cool in the shack. Two partially opened windows in the south wall let in the breezes from the hills of Drax Hall, but they could not put out the nervous fires of his anxiety.

Truths had been learned. A greater, overwhelming truth was yet to be revealed.

That it would be now, he was certain.

The scholar and the patriot were one again.

The Praetorian of Jamaica would enlist the Halidon.

20

James Ferguson, at the fashionable bar in Montego Bay, was exhilarated. It was the feeling he had when momentous things happened in the lens of a microscope and he knew he was the first observer – or, at least, the first witness who recognized a causal effect for what it was.

Like the baracoa fiber.

He was capable of great imagination when studying the shapes and densities of microscopic particles. A giant manipulating a hundred million infinitesimal subjects. It was a form of control.

He had control now. Over a man who did not know what it was like to have to protest too loudly over the inconsequential because no one paid attention; to be forever down to his last few quid in the bank because none paid him the value of his work.

All that was changing. He could think about a great many things that were preposterous fantasies only yesterday: his own laboratories with the most expensive equipment – electronic, computerized, data-banked; throwing away the little budget pads that told him whom he had last borrowed from.

A Maserati. He would buy a Maserati. Arthur Craft had one, why shouldn't he?

Arthur Craft was paying for it.

Ferguson looked at his watch – his too inexpensive Timex – and signaled the bartender to total his bill.

When the bartender did not come over in thirty seconds, Ferguson reached for the tab in front of him and turned it over. It was simple enough to add: a dollar and fifty cents, twice.

James Ferguson then did what he had never done in his life. He took out a five-dollar bill, crumpled it up in his hand, got off the bar stool, and threw the wadded bill toward the cash register several yards in front of him. The bill bounced off the bottles on the lighted shelf and arced to the floor.

He started for the entrance.

There was *machismo* in his gesture; that was the word, that was the feeling.

In twenty minutes, he would meet the emissary from Craft the Younger. Down off Harbour Street, near Parish Wharf, on Pier Six. The man would be obsequious – he had no choice – and give him an envelope containing three thousand dollars.

Three thousand dollars.

In a single envelope; not saved in bits and pieces over months of budgeting, nor with the tentacles of Inland Revenue or debtors past, reaching out to cut it in half. It was his to do with as he pleased. To squander, to throw away on silly things, to pay a girl to get undressed and undress him and do things to him that were fantasies . . . only yesterday.

He had borrowed – taken a salary advance, actually – from McAuliff. Two hundred dollars. There was no reason to repay it. Not now. He would simply tell McAuliff . . . Alex; from now on it would be Alex, or perhaps Lex – very informal, very sure . . . to deduct the silly money from his paycheck. All at once, if he felt like it. It was inconsequential; it didn't really matter.

And it certainly didn't, thought Ferguson.

Every month Arthur Craft would give him an envelope. The agreed-upon amount was three thousand dollars in each envelope, but that was subject to change. Related to cost of living, as it were. Increased as his appetites and comforts increased. Just the beginning.

Ferguson crossed St James Square and proceeded toward the waterfront. It was a warm night, with no breeze, and humid. Fat clouds, flying low and threatening rain, blocked the moon; the antiquated streetlamps threw a subdued light in counterpoint to the gaudy neons of white and orange that announced the diversions of Montego Bay night life.

Ferguson reached Harbour Street and turned left. He stopped under a streetlamp and checked his watch again. It was ten minutes past midnight; Craft had specified twelve fifteen. In five minutes, he would have three thousand dollars.

Pier Six was directly ahead on his right, across the street. There was no ship in the dock, no activity within the huge loading area beyond the high linked fence; only a large naked bulb inside a wire casing that lit up the sign:

PIER SIX

MONTEGO LINES

He was to stand under the lamp, in front of the sign, and wait for a man to drive up in a Triumph sportscar. The man would ask him for identification. Ferguson would show him his passport and the man would give him the envelope.

So simple. The entire transaction would take less than thirty seconds. And change his life.

Craft had been stunned; speechless, actually, until he had found his voice and screamed a torrent of abuse . . . until, again, he realized the futility of his position. Craft the Younger had gone too far. He had broken laws and would be an object of scorn and embarrassment. James Ferguson could tell a story of airport meetings and luggage and telephone calls and industrial espionage . . . and promises.

Such promises.

But his silence could be purchased. Craft could buy his confidence for a first payment of three thousand dollars. If Craft did not care to do so, Ferguson was sure the Kingston authorities would display avid interest in the details of his story.

No, he had not spoken to anyone yet. But things had been written down. (Lies Craft could not trace, of course.) That did not mean he was incapable of finding the spoken words; such capability was very much within his province . . . as the first payment was within Craft's province. One canceled the other: which would it be?

And so it was.

Ferguson crossed Harbour Street and approached the wire-encased light and the sign. A block and a half away, crowds of tourists swelled into the street, a one-way flow toward the huge passenger terminal and the gangplanks of a cruise ship. Taxis emerged out of side streets and alleys from the center of Montego Bay, blowing their horns anxiously, haltingly making their way to the dock. Three bass-toned whistles filled the air, vibrating the night, signifying that the ship was giving a warning: all passengers were to be on board.

He heard the Triumph before he saw it. There was the gunning of an engine from the darkness of a narrow side street diagonally across from Pier Six. The shiny, red, low-slung sportscar sped out of the dark recess and coasted to a stop in front of Ferguson. The driver was another Craft employee, one he recognized from a year ago. He did not recall the man's name; only that he was a quick, physical person, given to arrogance. He would not be arrogant now.

He wasn't. He smiled in the open car and gestured Ferguson to come over. 'Hello, *Fergy*! It's been a long time.'

Ferguson hated the nickname 'Fergy'; it had dogged him for most of his life. Just when he had come to think it was part of a schoolboy past, someone – always someone unpleasant, he reflected – used it. He felt like correcting the man, reminding him of his messenger status, but he did not. He simply ignored the greeting.

'Since you recognize me, I assume there's no need to show you my identification,' said James, approaching the Triumph.

'Christ, no! How've you been?'

'Well, thank you. Do you have the envelope? I'm in a hurry.'

'Sure. Sure, I do, Fergy . . . Hey, you're a pistol, buddy! Our friend is pissing rocks! He's half out of his skull, you know what I mean?'

'I know what you mean. He should be. The envelope, please.'

'Sure.' The driver reached into his jacket and withdrew an envelope. He then leaned over and handed it to Ferguson. 'You're supposed to count it. If it's all there, just give me back the envelope . . . make any kind of mark on it you like. Oh, here's a pen.' The man opened the glove compartment and took out a ballpoint pen and held it up for Ferguson.

'That's not necessary. He wouldn't try to cheat me.'

'Hey, come on, Fergy! It's my ass that'll be in a sling! Count it, mark it; what's the difference?'

Ferguson opened the bulky envelope. The denominations were all fives, tens, and twenties. He had not asked for small denominations; it was convenient, though, he had to admit that. Less suspicious than hundreds or fifties.

He started counting the bills.

Twice Craft's man interrupted him with insignificant questions, causing James to lose his count. He had to start over again both times.

When he had finished, the driver suddenly handed him a wrapped package. 'Oh, because our friend wants to show there's no bad feeling – he's a sport, you know what I mean? – he sent you one of those new Yashica thirty-five millimeters. He remembered you're crazy about photography.'

Ferguson saw the Yashica label on top of the package. A seven-hundred-dollar instrument! One of the very best! Craft the Younger was indeed a frightened man. 'Thank . . . Arthur for me. But tell him this isn't deductible from any future payments.'

'Oh, I'll tell him . . . Now, I'm going to tell you something, Fergy baby. You're on fuckin' *Candid Camera.*' The driver spoke quietly.

'What are you talking about?'

'Right behind you, Fergy baby.'

Ferguson whipped around toward the high linked fence and the deserted area beyond. There were two men in the shadows of a doorway. They came out slowly, perhaps thirty yards away from him. And one of the men carried a camcorder. 'What have you done?'

'Just a little insurance, Fergy baby. Our friend is contract-conscious, you know what I mean? Infrared tape, babe. I think you know what that is. And you just gave a terrific performance counting out money and taking Christ knows what from a guy who hasn't been seen in public north of Caracas for over six months. You see, our friend flew me out of Rio just to get my picture taken . . . with you.'

'You can't do this! Nobody would believe this!'

'Why not, babe? You're a hungry little prick, you know what I mean? Hungry little pricks like you get hung easy. Now, you listen to me, asshole. You and Arthur, you're one on one. Only his one is a little heavier. That tape would raise a lot of questions you couldn't find any answers for. I'm a very unpopular man, Fergy. You'd get thrown off the island . . . but probably you'd get thrown into the can first. You wouldn't last fifteen minutes with those social rejects, you know what I mean? They'd peel your white skin, babe, layer by layer . . . Now, you be a good boy, Fergy. Arthur says for you to keep the three thousand. You'll probably earn it.' The man held up the empty envelope. 'Two set of prints on this. Yours and mine. Ciao, baby. I've got to get out of here and back to nonextradition country.'

The driver gunned the engine twice and slapped the gearshift effortlessly. He swung the Triumph expertly in a semicircle and roared off into the darkness of Harbour Street.

Julian Warfield was in Kingston now. He had flown in three days ago and used all of Dunstone's resources to uncover the strange activities of Alexander McAuliff. Peter Jensen had followed instructions to the letter; he had kept McAuliff under the closest scrutiny, paying desk clerks and doormen and taxi drivers to keep him informed of the American's every move.

And always he and his wife were out of sight, in no way associated with that scrutiny.

It was the least he could do for Julian Warfield. He would do anything Julian asked, anything Dunstone Limited, demanded. He would deliver nothing but his best to the man and the organization that had taken him and his wife out of the valley of despair and given them a world with which they could cope and in which they could function.

Work they loved, money and security beyond the reach of most academic couples. Enough to forget.

Julian had found them years ago, beaten, finished, destroyed by events . . . impoverished, with nowhere and no one to turn to. He and Ruth had been caught; it was a time of madness, MI5's Fourth Man and two Soviet moles in the Foreign Office, convictions born of misplaced zeal. He and his wife had supplemented their academic income by working for the government on covert geological operations – oil, gold, minerals of value. And they had willingly turned over everything in the classified files to a contact at the Soviet embassy.

Another blow for equality and justice. And they were caught.

But Julian Warfield came to see them.

Julian Warfield offered them their lives again . . . in exchange for certain assignments he might find for them. Inside the government and out; on the temporary staffs of companies . . . within England and without; always in the highest professional capacities, pursuing their professional labours.

All charges were dropped by the Crown. Terrible mistakes had been made against the most respected members of the academic community. Scotland Yard had apologized. Actually *apologized*.

Peter and Ruth never refused Julian; their loyalty was unquestioned. Which was why Peter was now on his stomach in the cold, damp sand while the light of a Caribbean dawn broke over the eastern horizon. He was behind a mound of coral rock with a perfect view of McAuliff's oceanside terrace. Julian's last instructions had been specific.

Find out who comes to see him. Who's important to him. Get identities, if you can. But for God's sake, stay in the background. We'll need you both in the interior.

Julian had agreed that McAuliff's disappearances – into Kingston, into taxis, into an unknown car at the gates of Courtleigh Manor – all meant that he had interests in Jamaica other than Dunstone Limited.

It had to be assumed that he had broken the primary article of faith. Secrecy.

If so, McAuliff could be transferred . . . forgotten without difficulty. But before that happened, it was essential to discover the identity of Dunstone's island enemy. Or enemies.

In a very real sense, the survey itself was secondary to that objective. Definitely secondary. If it came down to it, the survey could be sacrificed if, by that sacrifice, identities were revealed.

And Peter Jensen knew he was nearer those identities now . . . in this early dawn on the beach of Bengal Court. It had begun three hours ago.

Peter and Ruth had retired a little past midnight. Their room was in the east wing of the motel, along with Ferguson's and Charles Whitehall's. McAuliff, Alison, and Sam Tucker were in the west wing, the division signifying only old friends, new lovers, and late drinkers.

They heard it around one o'clock: an automobile swerving into the front drive, its wheels screeching, then silent, as if the driver had heard the noise and suddenly become alarmed by it.

It had been strange. Bengal Court was no kind of nightclub, no 'drum-drum' watering hole that catered to the swinging and/or younger tourist crowds. It was quiet, with very little to recommend it to the image of fast drivers. As a matter of fact, Peter Jensen could not remember having heard *any* automobiles drive into Bengal Court after nine o'clock in the evening since they had been there.

He had risen from the bed and walked out on the terrace, and had seen nothing. He had walked around the east end of the motel to the edge of the front parking lot, where he did see something; something extremely alarming, barely visible.

In the far section of the lot, in shadows, a large black man – he believed he was black – was lifting the unconscious figure of another man out of the rear seat of an automobile. Then, farther beyond, a white man ran across the lawn from around the corner of the west wing. It was Sam Tucker. He approached the black man carrying the unconscious form, gave instructions – pointing to the direction from which he had come – and continued to the automobile, silently closing the rear door.

Sam Tucker was supposed to be in Ocho Rios with McAuliff. It seemed unlikely that he would have returned to Bengal Court alone.

And as Jensen pondered this, there was the outline of another figure on the west lawn. It was Alison Booth. She gestured to the black man; she was obviously excited, trying to remain in control of herself. She led the large black man into the darkness around the far corner.

Peter Jensen suddenly had a sinking feeling. Was the unconscious figure Alexander McAuliff? Then he rethought the immediate visual picture. He could not be sure – he could barely see, and everything was happening so rapidly – but as the black man passed under the spill of a parking light, the bobbing head of his charge extended beyond his arms. Peter had been struck by the oddness of it. The head appeared to be completely bald . . . as if shaved.

Sam Tucker looked inside the automobile, seemed satisfied, then raced back across the west lawn after the others.

Peter remained crouched in his concealed position after the figure had disappeared. It was extraordinary. Tucker and Alison Booth were not in Ocho Rios; a man had been hurt, apparently quite seriously, and instead of taking him directly inside the motel's front entrance, they furtively carried him in, smuggled him in. And it might be conceivable that Sam Tucker would come back to Bengal Court without McAuliff; it was inconceivable that Alison Booth would do so.

What were they doing? What in heaven's name had happened . . . was happening?

The simplest way to find out, thought Peter, was to get dressed, return to the tiny bar, and, for reasons he had not yet created, call McAuliff for drink.

He would do this alone. Ruth would remain in their room. But first Peter would walk down to the beach, to the water's edge, where he would have a full view of the motel and the oceanside terraces.

Once in the miniature lounge, Peter invented his reason to phone McAuliff. It was simple to the point of absurdity. He had been unable to sleep, taken a stroll on the beach, seen a light behind the drawn curtains in Alexander's room, and gathered he had returned from Ocho Rios. Would he and Alison be his guests for a nightcap?

Jensen went to the house phone at the end of the bar. When McAuliff answered, his voice was laced with the frustration of a man forced to be civil in the most undesirable of circumstances. And McAuliff's lie was apparent.

'Oh, Jesus, Peter, thanks, but we're *beat*. We just got settled at the Sans Souci when Latham called from the Ministry. Some damned bureaucratic problem with our interior permits; we had to drive all the way back for some kind of goddamned . . . inspection first thing in the morning . . . inoculation records, medical stuff. Crew, mainly.'

'Terribly inconsiderate, old boy. Nasty bastards, I'd say.'

'They are . . . We'll take a raincheck, though. Perhaps tomorrow.'

Peter had wanted to keep McAuliff on the phone a bit longer. The man was breathing audibly; each additional moment meant the possibility of Jensen's learning something. 'Ruth and I thought we'd hire a car and go to Dunn's Falls around noon tomorrow. Surely you'll be finished by then. Care to come along?'

'Frankly, Peter,' said McAuliff haltingly, 'we were hoping to get back to Ochee, if we could.'

'Then that would rule out Dunn's Falls, of course. You've seen it, though, haven't you? Is it all they say?'

'Yes . . . yes, it certainly is. Enjoy yourselves—'

'You *will* be back tomorrow night, then?' interjected Jensen.

'Sure . . . Why?'

'Our raincheck, old boy.'

'Yes,' said McAuliff slowly, carefully. 'We'll be back tomorrow night. Of course we'll be back tomorrow night . . . Good night, Peter.'

'Good night, chap. Sleep well.' Jensen hung up the house phone. He carried his drink slowly back to a table in the corner, nodding pleasantly to the other guests, giving the impression that he was waiting for someone, probably his wife. He had no wish to join anyone; he had to think out his moves.

Which was why he was now lying in the sand behind a small mound of surfaced coral on the beach, watching Lawrence and Sam Tucker talking.

He had been there for nearly three hours. He had seen things he knew he was not supposed to see: two men arriving – one obviously a doctor with the inevitable bag, the other some sort of assistant carrying a large trunklike case and odd-shaped paraphernalia.

There had been quiet conferences between McAuliff, Alison, and the doctor, later joined by Sam Tucker and the black crewman, Lawrence.

Finally, all left the terrace but Tucker and the crewman. They stayed outside.

On guard.

Guarding not only Alexander and the girl, but also whoever was in that adjoining room. The injured man with the oddly shaped head who had been carried from the automobile. Who was he?

The two men had stayed at their posts for three hours now. No one had come or gone. But Peter knew he could not leave the beach. Not yet.

Suddenly, Jensen saw the black crewman, Lawrence, walk down the terrace steps and start across the dunes toward the beach. Simultaneously, Tucker made his way over the grass to the corner of the building. He stood immobile on the lawn; he was waiting for someone. Or watching.

Lawrence reached the surf, and Jensen lay transfixed as the huge black man did a strange thing. He looked at his watch and then proceeded to light two matches, one after the other, holding each aloft in the breezeless dawn air for several seconds and throwing each into the lapping water.

Moments later, the action was explained. Lawrence cupped his hand over his eyes to block the blinding, head-on light of the sun as it broke the space above the horizon, and Peter followed his line of sight.

Across the calm ocean surface in the massive land shadows by the point, there were two corresponding flickers of light. A small boat had rounded the waters of the cove's entrance, its gray-black hull slowly emerging in the early sunlight.

Its destination was that section of the beach where Lawrence stood.

Several minutes later, Lawrence struck another match and held it up until there was an acknowledgment from the approaching craft, at which instant both were extinguished and the black crewman started running back over the sand toward Bengal Court.

On the lawn, by the corner of the building, Sam Tucker turned and saw the racing Lawrence. He walked to the stairs in the sea wall and waited for him. The black man reached the steps; he and Tucker spoke briefly, and together they approached the terrace doors of the adjoining room – Alison Booth's room. Tucker opened them, and the two men went inside, leaving the double doors ajar.

Peter kept shifting his eyes from the motel to the beach. There was no visible activity from the terrace; the small boat plodded its way over the remarkably still waters toward the beach, now only three or four hundred yards from the shore. It was a long, flat-bottomed fishing boat, propelled by a muffled engine. Sitting in the stern was a black man in what appeared to be ragged clothes and a wide straw sun hat. Hook poles shot up from the small deck, nets were draped over the sides of the hull; the effect was that of a perfectly normal Jamaican fisherman out for the dawn catch.

When the boat came within several hundred feet of the shore, the skipper lit a match, then extinguished it quickly. Jensen looked up at the terrace. In seconds, the figure of Sam Tucker emerged from the darkness beyond the open doors. He held one end of a stretcher on which a man lay wrapped in blankets; Lawrence followed, holding the other end.

Gently, but swiftly, the two men ran – glided – the stretcher across the terrace, down the sea-wall steps, over the sand, and toward the beach. The timing was precise, not a moment wasted. It seemed to Jensen that the instant the boat hit shallow water, Tucker and Lawrence waded into the calm surf with the stretcher and placed it carefully over the sides onto the deck. The nets were swung over on top of the blanketed man and the fishing boat was immediately pushed back into the water by Sam Tucker as Lawrence slid onto the bow slat. Seconds later, Lawrence had removed his shirt and from some recess in the boat lifted out a torn, disheveled straw hat, clamped it on his head, and yanked a hook pole from its clasp. The transformation was complete. Lawrence the conspirator was now a lethargic native fisherman.

The small flat-bottomed craft turned, rippling the glasslike surface of the water, and headed out. The motor chugged a bit louder than before; the skipper wanted to get away from the beach with his concealed cargo.

Sam Tucker waved; Lawrence nodded and dipped the hook pole. Tucker came out of the miniature surf and walked swiftly back toward Bengal Court.

Peter Jensen watched as the fishing boat veered in open water toward the point. Several times Lawrence leaned forward and down, fingering nets but obviously checking the condition of the man on the stretcher. Intermittently, he seemed to be issuing quiet commands to the man at the engine tiller. The sun had now cleared the edge of the Jamaican horizon. It would be a hot day.

Up at the terrace Peter saw that the double doors of Alison Booth's room remained open. With the additional light, he could also see that there was new activity inside. Sam Tucker came out twice, carrying tan plastic bags, which he left on the patio. Then a second man – the doctor's assistant, Peter realized – emerged, holding a large cylinder by its neck and a huge black suitcase in his other hand. He placed them on the stone, bent down below them on the sea wall, and stood up moments later with two elongated cans – aerosol cans, thought Jensen – and handed one to Tucker as he came through the door. The two men talked briefly and then went back inside the room.

No more than three minutes had elapsed when Tucker and the doctor's aide were seen again, this time somewhat comically as they backed into the door frame simultaneously. Each held his arm outstretched; in each hand was an aerosol can, clouds of mist spewing from both.

Tucker and the black aide had systematically sprayed the interior of the room.

Once finished, they crossed to the plastic bags, the case, and the large cylinder. They picked up the objects, spoke briefly again, and started for the lawn.

Out on the water, the fishing boat was halfway to the point of the cove. But something had happened. It had stopped; it bobbed gently on the calm surface, no longer traveling forward. Peter could see the now tiny figure of Lawrence standing up in the bow, then crouching, then standing up again. The skipper was gesturing, his movements excited.

The boat pushed forward once more, only to turn slowly and change direction. It did not continue on its course – if the point was, indeed, its course. Instead, it headed for the open sea.

Jensen lay on the moist sand for the next fifteen minutes, watching the small craft progressively become a black dot within a gray-black ocean splashed with orange sunlight. He could not read the thoughts of the two Jamaicans; he could not see the things that were happening on that boat so illogically far out on the water. But his knowledge of tides and currents, his observations during the last three hours, led his conclusions to one end.

The man on the stretcher had died. His corpse would soon be stripped of identification, weighted down with net lead, and thrown into the water, eventually to be carried by floor currents far away from the island of Jamaica. Perhaps to be washed ashore weeks or months from now on some Cayman reef or, more fortuitously, torn apart and devoured by the predators of the deep.

Peter knew it was time to call Warfield, meet with Julian Warfield.

Immediately.

McAuliff rolled over on his side, the sharp pain in his shoulder suddenly surging through his chest. He sat up quickly, momentarily bewildered. He focused his thoughts. It was morning; the night before had been a series of terrifying confusions. The pieces would have to be put back together, plans made.

He looked down at Alison, beside him. She was breathing deeply, steadily, in complete sleep. If the evening had been a nightmare for him, it had been no less a torment for her. Perhaps worse. At least he had been in motion, constant, unceasing movement. She had been waiting, thinking; he had had no time for thoughts. It was worse to wait. In some ways.

Slowly, as silently as he could, he swung his legs over the side of the bed and stood up. His whole body was stiff; his joints pained him, especially his kneecaps.

It was understandable. The muscles he had used last night were dormant strings of an unused instrument, called into play by a panicked conductor. The allusion was proper, thought Alex – about his thoughts. He nearly smiled as he conjured up the phrase: so out of tune. Everything was out of tune.

But the notes *were* forming recognizable chords ... somewhere. In the distance. There was a melody of sorts that could be vaguely distinguished.

Yet not *distinguished*. Hardly noble. Not yet.

An odor assaulted his nostrils. It was not the illusion of spice and vanilla, but nevertheless sweet. If there was an association, it was south Oriental ... Java, the Sunda Trench, pungent, a bit sickening. He crossed quietly to the terrace door, about to open it, when he realized he was naked. He walked silently to a chair by the curtained window, where he had thrown a pair of swimming trunks several days ago. He removed them from the wooden rim and put them on.

'I hope they're not wet,' said Alison from the bed. 'The maid service here is a touch lacking, and I didn't hang them up.'

'Go back to sleep,' Alex replied. 'You were asleep a moment ago. Very much asleep.'

'I'm very much awake now. Good heavens, it's a quarter past eight.'

'And?'

'Nothing, really ... I just didn't think we'd sleep this long.'

'It's not long. We didn't get to bed until after three. Considering everything that happened, noon would have been too early.'

'How's your arm? The shoulder?'

'A little sore ... like most of me. Not crippling.'

'What is that terrible smell?' Alison sat up; the sheet fell away, revealing a curiously prim nightgown, opaque cotton with buttons. She saw Alex's gaze, the beginning of a smile on his lips. She glanced down and laughed. 'My granny nightshirt. I put it on after you fell asleep. It was chilly, and you hadn't the slightest interest in anything but philosophical discourse.'

He walked to the edge of the bed and sat down beside her. 'I was long-winded, wasn't I?'

'I couldn't shut you up; there was simply no way. You drank a great deal of Scotch – how's your head, incidentally?'

'Fine. As though I'd had Ovaltine.'

'... straight alcohol wouldn't have stayed with you either. I've seen that kind of reaction before, too ... Sorry. I forgot you object to my British pronouncements.'

'I made a few myself last night. I withdraw my objections.'

'Do you still believe them? Your pronouncements? As they say ... in the cold logic of the morning?'

'I think I do; the thrust of my argument being that no one fights better for his own turf than he who lives on it, depends on it ... Yes, I believe it. I'd feel more confident if Barak hadn't been hurt.'

'Strange name, Barak.'

'Strange man. And very strong. He's needed, Alison. Boys can become men quickly, but they're still not seasoned. His ken is needed.'

'By whom?'

McAuliff looked at her, at the lovely way her eyebrows rose quizzically above her clear, light blue eyes. 'By his own side,' he answered simply.

'Which is not Charles Whitehall's side.' There was no question implied.

'No. They're very different. And I think it's necessary ... at this point, under these circumstances ... that Barak's faction be as viable as Charley-mon's.'

'That concern strikes me as dangerously close to interference, darling.'

'I know. It's just that everything seems so complicated to me. But it doesn't to Whitehall. And it doesn't to Barak Moore. They see a simple division muddled up by second and third parties ... Don't you see? They're not distracted. They first go after one objective, then another, and another, knowing ultimately they'll have to deal with each other. Neither one loses sight of that. Each stores his apples as he goes along.'

'What?' Alison leaned back on the pillow, watching McAuliff as he stared blankly at the wall. 'I don't follow that.'

'I'm not sure I can explain it. A wolf pack surrounds its victims, who huddle into the center. The dogs set up an erratic rhythm of attack, taking turns lunging in and out around the circle until the quarry's confused to the point of exhaustion. Then the wolves close in.' Alex stopped; he was uncertain.

'I gather Charles and this Barak are the victims,' said Alison, trying to help him.

'Jamaica's the victim, and they're Jamaica. The wolves – the enemies – are Dunstone and all it represents: Warfield and his crowd of ... global manipulators – the Chatelleraults of this world; British Intelligence, with its elitists, like Tallon and *his* crowd of opportunists; the Crafts of this island ... internal bleeders, you could call them. Finally, maybe even this Halidon, because you can't control what you can't find; and even if you find it, it may not be controllable ... There are a lot of wolves.'

'There's a lot of confusion,' added Alison.

McAuliff turned and looked at her. 'For *us*. Not for *them*. That's what's remarkable. The victims have worked out a strategy: Take each wolf as it lunges. Destroy it.'

'What's that got to do with apples?'

'I jumped out of the circle and went into a straight line.'

'Aren't we abstract,' stated Alison Booth.

'It's valid. As any army – and don't kid yourself, Charles Whitehall and Barak Moore have their armies – as any army moves forward, it maintains its lines of supply. In this case, support. Remember. When all the wolves have been killed, they face each other. Whitehall and Moore are both piling up apples ... support.' McAuliff stopped again and got up from the bed. He walked toward the window to the right of the terrace doors, pulled the curtain, and looked out at the beach. 'Does any of this make sense to you?' he asked softly.

'It's very political, I think, and I'm not much at that sort of thing. But you're describing a rather familiar pattern. I'd say—'

'You bet your *life* I am,' interrupted Alex, speaking slowly and turning from the windows. 'Historical precedents unlimited . . . and *I'm* no goddamn historian. Hell, where do you want to start? Caesar's Gaul? Rome's Ferrara? China in the thirties? The Koreas, the Vietnams, the Cambodias? Half a dozen African countries? The words are there, over and over again. Exploitation from the outside, inside revolt – insurgence and counterinsurgence. Chaos, bloodbath, expulsion. Ultimately reconstruction in so-called compromise. That's the pattern. That's what Barak and Charley expect to play out. And each knows that while he's joining the other to kill a wolf, he's got to entrench himself further in the turf at the same time. Because when the compromise comes . . . as it must . . . he wants it more *his* way than less.'

'What you're saying – getting away from circles and straight lines – is that you don't approve of Barak's "army" being weakened. Is that it?'

'Not *now*. Not at this moment.'

'Then you *are* interfering. You're an outsider taking an inside position. It's not your . . . turf, my darling.'

'But I brought Charley here. I gave him his respectability, his cover. Charley's a son-of-a-bitch.'

'Is Barak Moore a saint?'

'Not for a second. He's a son-of-a-bitch, too. And it's important that he is.' McAuliff returned to the window. The morning sun was striking the panes of glass, causing tiny nodules of condensation. It was going to be a hot day.

'What are you going to do?' Alison sat forward, prepared to get up as she looked over at Alex.

'Do?' he asked quietly, his eyes concentrating on something outside the window. 'What I was sent here to do; what I'm being paid two million dollars to do. Complete the survey or find this Halidon. Whichever comes first. Then get us out of here . . . on our terms.'

'That sounds reasonable,' said Alison, rising from the bed. 'What is that sickening odor?'

'Oh, I forgot to tell you. They were going to spray down your room, get rid of the medicine smells.' McAuliff stepped closer to the window and shaded his eyes from the rays of the morning sun.

'The ether or disinfectant or whatever it was was far more palatable. My bathing suit's in there. May I get it?'

'What?' Alex was not listening, his attention on the object of his gaze outside.

'My bathing suit, darling. It's in my room.'

McAuliff turned from the window, oblivious to her words. 'Wait here. I'll be right back.' He walked rapidly to the terrace door, opened it, and ran out.

Alison looked after him, bewildered. She crossed to the window to see what Alex had seen. It took several seconds to understand; she was helped by watching McAuliff run across the sand toward the water. In the distance, down at the beach, was the lone figure of a large black man staring out at the ocean. It was Lawrence.

Alex approached the tall Jamaican, wondering if he should call out.

Instinctively, he did not. Instead, he cleared his throat when he was within ten yards; cleared it loud enough to be heard over the sound of the lapping small waves.

Lawrence turned around. Tears were in his eyes, but he did not blink or change the muscles of his face. He was a child-man accepting the agonies of a very personal torment.

'What happened?' asked McAuliff softly, walking up to the shirtless boy-giant.

'I should have listened to you, mon. Not to him. He was wrong, mon.'

'Tell me what happened,' repeated Alex.

'Barak is dead. I did what he ordered me to do and he is dead. I listened to him and he is dead, mon.'

'He knew the risk; he had to take it. I think he was probably right.'

'No. He was wrong because he is dead. That makes him wrong, mon.'

'Floyd's gone ... Barak. Who is there now?'

Lawrence's eyes bored into McAuliff's; they were red from silent weeping, and beyond the pride and summoned strength, there was the anguish of a child. And the pleading of a boy. 'You and me, mon. There is no one else ... You will help me, mon?'

Alex returned the rebel's stare; he did not speak.

Welcome to the seat of revolution, McAuliff thought to himself.

21

The Trelawny police made Floyd's identification at 7:02 in the morning. The delay was caused by the lack of any print facilities in Falmouth and the further lack of cooperation on the part of several dozen residents who were systematically routed from their beds during the night to identify the corpse. The captain was convinced that any number of them recognized the bullet-pierced body, but it was not until two minutes past seven when one old man – a gardener from Carrick Foyle – had reacted sufficiently to the face of the bloody mess on the table for the captain to decide to apply sterner methods. He held a lighted cigarette millimeters in front of the old man's left eye, which he stretched open with his free hand. He told the trembling gardener that he would burn the gelatin of his eyeball unless he told the truth.

The ancient gardener screamed and told the truth. The man who was the corpse on the table had worked for Walter Piersall. His name was Floyd Cotter.

The captain then telephoned several parish precincts for further information on one Cotter, Floyd. There was nothing; they had never heard of him. But the captain had persisted; Kingston's interest in Dr Walter Piersall, before and after his death, was all-inclusive. Even to the point of around-the-clock patrols at the house on the hill in Carrick Foyle. The captain did not know why; it was not his province to question, much less analyse, Kingston's commands. That they were was enough. Whatever the motives that resulted in the harassment of the white scholar before his death, and the continued concern about his residence after, was Kingston's bailiwick, not his. He simply followed orders. He followed them well, even enthusiastically. That was why he was the prefect captain of the parish police in Falmouth.

And that was why he kept making telephone calls about one Floyd Cotter, deceased, whose corpse lay on the table and whose blood would not stop oozing out of the punctures on his face and in his chest and stomach and legs; blood that dried on the pages of *The Gleamer*, hastily scattered about the floor.

At five minutes to eight, as the captain was about to lift the receiver off its base and call the precinct in Sherwood Content, the telephone rang. It was his counterpart in Puerto Seco, near Discovery Bay, whom he had contacted twenty minutes ago. The man said that after their conversation, he had talked with his deputies on the early shift. One of the men reported that there was a Floyd with a survey team, headed by an American named McAuliff, who had begun work about ten days ago on the shoreline. The survey had hired a carrier crew out of Ocho Rios. The Government Employment Office had been involved.

The captain then woke up the director of the G.E.O. in Ochee. The man was thoroughly awake by the time he got on the line, because he had no telephone and consequently had had to leave his house and walk to a Johnny Canoe store where he – and most of the neighborhood – took calls. The employment chief recalled that among the crewmen hired by the American named McAuliff, there had been a Floyd, but he did not remember the last name. This Floyd had simply shown up with other applicants who had heard of the available work from the Ochee grapevine. He had not been listed in the employment files; neither had one or two others eventually hired.

The captain listened to the director, thanked him, and said nothing to contradict or enlighten him. But after hanging up the phone, he put in a call to Gordon House in Kingston. To the inspector who headed the search teams that had meticulously gone over Piersall's house in Carrick Foyle.

The inspector's conclusion was the same as the captain's: The deceased Floyd Cotter – former employee of Walter Piersall – had returned with friends to loot the house and been interrupted.

Was anything missing?

Digging in the cellar? In an old cistern out of use for years?

The inspector would fly back to Falmouth by noon. In the meantime, the captain might discreetly interrogate Mr McAuliff. If nothing else, ascertain his whereabouts.

At twenty minutes past nine, the captain and his first deputy drove through the gates of Bengal Court.

Alexander was convincingly agitated. He was appalled – and naturally sorry – that Floyd Cotter had lost his life, but goddammit, the episode answered several questions. Some very expensive equipment was missing from the supply truck, equipment that could bring high prices in a thieves' market. This Floyd Cotter obviously had been the perpetrator; he was a thief, had been a thief.

Did the captain want a list of the missing items? There was a geodometer, a water scope, half a dozen jeweled compasses, three Polaroid filter screens, five brand-new medicine kits in Royal Society cases, a Rolleiflex camera, and a number of other things of lesser value – but not inexpensive. The captain's deputy wrote as rapidly as he could on a notepad as Alex rattled off the 'missing' items. Twice he asked for spellings; once the point of his pencil broke. It was a harried few minutes.

After the interview was over, the captain and his deputy shook hands with the American geologist and thanked him for his cooperation. McAuliff watched them get into the police car and waved a friendly goodbye as the vehicle sped out of the parking lot through the gates.

A quarter of a mile down the road, the captain braked the patrol car to a stop. He spoke quietly to his deputy.

'Go back through the woods to the beach, mon. Find out who he is with, who comes to see him.'

The deputy removed his visor cap and the creased khaki shirt of his uniform with the yellow insignias of his rank, and reached into the back for a green T-shirt. He slipped it over his head and got out of the car. He stood on the tarred pavement, unbuckled his belt, and slid his holster off the leather strip. He handed it through the window to the captain.

The captain reached down below the dashboard and pulled out a rumpled black baseball cap that was discolored with age and human sweat. He gave it to his deputy and laughed.

'We all look alike, mon. Aren't you the fella who alla time sell *cocoruru*?'

'Alla time John Crow, mon. Mongoose him not.'

The deputy grinned and started toward the woods beyond the bank of the pavement, where there was a rusty, torn wire fence. It was the demarcation of the Bengal Court property.

The patrol car roared off down the road. The prefect captain of the Falmouth police was in a hurry. He had to drive to Halfmoon Bay and meet a seaplane that was flying in from Kingston.

Charles Whitehall stood in the tall grass on a ridge overlooking the road from Priory-on-the-Sea. Under his arm was the black archive case, clamped shut and held together with three-inch strips of adhesive. It was shortly after twelve noon, and McAuliff would be driving up the road soon.

Alone.

Charles had insisted on it. That is, he had insisted before he had heard McAuliff's words – spoken curtly, defensively – that Barak Moore was dead.

Bramwell Moore, schoolboy chum from so many years ago in Savanna-la-Mar, dead from Jamaican bullets.

Jamaican bullets.

Jamaican *police* bullets. That was better. In adding the establishmentarian, there was a touch of compassionate logic – a contradiction in terms, thought Whitehall; logic was neither good nor evil, merely logic. Still, words defined logic and words could be interpreted – thus the mendacity of all official statistics: self-serving logic.

His mind was wandering and he was annoyed with himself. Barak had known, as he knew, that they were not playing chicken-in-de-kitchen any longer. There was no bandanna-headed mother wielding a straw broom, chasing child and fowl out into the yard, laughing and scolding simultaneously. This was a different sort of insurgence. Bandanna-headed mothers were replaced by visor-capped men of the state; straw brooms became high-powered rifles. The chickens were ideas . . . far more deadly to the uniformed servants of the state than the loose feathers were to the bandanna-headed servants of the family.

Barak dead.

It seemed incredible. Yet not without its positive effect. Barak had not understood the problems of their island; therefore, he had not understood the proper solutions. Barak's solutions were decades away.

First there had to be strength. The many led by a very strong, militant few. Perhaps one.

In the downhill distance there was a billow of dust; a station wagon was traveling much too fast over the old dirt road.

McAuliff was anxious too.

Charles stared back across the field to the entrance drive of the house. He had requested that his Drax Hall host be absent between the hours of twelve and three. No explanations were given, and no questions asked.

A messiah had returned. That was enough.

'Here it is,' said McAuliff, standing in front of Whitehall in the cool toolshed, holding the smaller archive case in his left hand. 'But before you start fiddling around, I want a couple of things clear.'

Charles Whitehall stared at the American. 'Conditions are superfluous. We both know what must be done.'

'What's not superfluous,' countered Alex, 'is that you understand there'll be no . . . unilateral decisions. This isn't your private war, *Charley-mon.*'

'Are you trying to sound like Barak?'

'Let's say I'm looking after his interests. And mine.'

'Yours I can comprehend. Why his? They're not compatible, you know.'

'They're not even connected.'

'So why concern yourself?' Whitehall shifted his eyes to the archive case. He realized that his breathing had become audible; his anxiety was showing, and again he was annoyed with himself. 'Let me have that, please.'

'You asked me a question. I'm going to answer it first,' replied McAuliff. 'I don't trust you, Charley. You'll use anyone. Anything. Your kind always does. You make pacts and agreements with anything that moves, and you do it very well. You're so flexible you meet yourself around corners. But all the time it's Sturm und Drang, and I'm not much for that.'

'Oh, I see. You subscribe to Barak's canefield paratroopers. The chaos of the Fidelisti, where the corporals spit and chew cigars and rape the generals' daughters so society is balanced. Three-year plans and five-year plans and crude uneducated bullies managing the affairs of state. Into disaster, I might add. Don't be a fool, McAuliff. You're better than that.'

'Cut it out, Charley. You're not on a podium addressing your chiefs of staff,' said Alex wearily. 'I don't believe in that oversimplification any more than I believe in your two-plus-two solutions. Pull in your hardware. I'm still the head of this survey. I can fire you in a minute. Very publicly. Now, that might not get you off the island, but your situation won't be the same.'

'What guarantee do I have that you won't force me out?'

'Not much of one. You'll just have to take my word that I want those bastards off my back as badly as you do. For entirely different reasons.'

'Somehow I think you're lying.'

'I wouldn't gamble on that.'

Whitehall searched McAuliff's eyes. 'I won't. I said this conversation was superfluous, and it is. Your conditions are accepted because of what must be done ... Now, may I have that case, please?'

Sam Tucker sat on the terrace, alternately reading the newspaper and glancing over the sea wall to the beach, where Alison and James Ferguson were in deck chairs near the water. Every now and then, when the dazzling Caribbean sun had heated their skin temperatures sufficiently, Alison and the young botanist waded into the water. They did not splash or jump or dive; they simply fell onto the calm surface, as though exhausted. It seemed to be an exercise of weariness for both of them.

There was no joy *sur la plage*, thought Sam, who nevertheless picked up a pair of binoculars whenever Alison began paddling about and scanned the immediate vicinity around which she swam. He focused on any swimmer who came near her; there were not many, and all were recognizable as guests of Bengal Court.

None was a threat, and that's what Sam Tucker was looking for.

Ferguson had returned from Montego Bay a little before noon, just after Alex had driven off to Drax Hall. He had wandered onto the connecting terraces, startling Sam and the temporarily disoriented Lawrence, who had been sitting on the sea wall talking quietly about the dead Barak Moore. They had been stunned because Ferguson had been expansive about his day-off plans in Mo'Bay.

Ferguson arrived looking haggard, a nervous wreck. The assumption was that he had overindulged and was hung to his fuzzy-cheeked gills; the jokes were along this line, and he accepted them with a singular lack of humor. But Sam Tucker did not subscribe to the explanation. James Ferguson was not ravaged by the whisky input of the night before; he was a frightened young man who had not slept. His fear, thought Sam, was not anything he cared to discuss; indeed, he would not even talk about his night in Montego, brushing it off as a dull, unrewarding interlude. He appeared only to want company, as if there was immediate security in the familiar. He seemed to cling to the presence of Alison Booth, offering to fetch and carry ... A schoolboy's crush or a gay's devotion? Neither fit, for he was neither.

He was afraid.

Very inconsistent behavior, concluded Sam Tucker.

Tucker suddenly heard the quiet, rapid footsteps behind him and turned. Lawrence, fully clothed now, came across the terrace from the west lawn. The black revolutionary walked over to Sam and knelt – not in fealty, but in a conscious attempt to conceal his large frame behind the sea wall. He spoke urgently.

'I don't like what I see and hear, mon.'

'What's the matter?'

'John Crow hide wid' block chicken!'

'We're being watched?' Tucker put down the newspaper and sat forward.

'Yes, mon. Three, four hours now.'

'Who?'

'A digger been walking on the sand since morning. Him keep circling the west-cove beach too long for tourist leave-behinds. I watch him good. His trouser pants rolled up, look too new, mon. I go behind in the woods and find his shoes. Then I know the trouser pants, mon. Him policeman.'

Sam's gnarled features creased in thought. 'Alex spoke with the Falmouth police around nine-thirty. In the lobby. He said there were two: a chief and an Indian.'

'What, mon?'

'Nothing ... That's what you saw. What did you hear?'

'Not all I saw.' Lawrence looked over the sea wall, east toward the center beach. Satisfied, he returned his attention to Sam. 'I follow the digger to the kitchen alley, where he waits for a man to come outside to speak with him. It is the clerk from the lobby desk. Him shake his head many times. The policeman angry, mon.'

'But what did you *hear*, boy?'

'A porter fella was plenty near, cleaning snapper in his buckets. When the digger-policeman left I ask him hard, mon. He tells me this digger kep' asking where the American fella went, who had telephoned him.'

'And the clerk didn't know.'

'That's right, mon. The policeman was angry.'

'Where is he now?'

'Him wait down at the east shore.' Lawrence pointed over the sea wall, across the dunes to a point on the other side of the central beach. 'See? In front of the sunfish boats, mon.'

Tucker picked up the binoculars and focused on the figure near the shallow-bottomed sailboats by the water. The man and boats were about four hundred yards away. The man was in a torn green T-shirt and rumpled baseball cap; the trousers were a contradiction. They were rolled up to the knees, like most scavengers of the beach wore them, but Lawrence was right, they were creased, too clean. The man was chatting with a *cocoruru* peddler, a thin, very dark Jamaican who rolled a wheelbarrow filled with coconuts up and down the beach, selling them to the bathers, cracking them open with a murderous-looking machete. From time to time the man glanced over toward the west-wing terraces, directly into the binoculars, thought Sam. Tucker knew the man did not realize he was being observed; if he did, the reaction would appear on his face. The only reaction was one of irritation, nothing else.

'We'd better supply him with the proper information, son,' said Sam, putting down the binoculars.

'What, mon?'

'Give him something to soothe that anger ... so he won't think about it too much.'

Lawrence grinned. 'We make up a story, eh, mon?

'McAuliff went shopping Ochee, maybe? Ochee is six, seven miles from Drax Hall, mon. Same road.'

'Why didn't Mrs Booth – Alison go with him?'

'Him buy the lady a present. Why not, mon?'

Sam looked at Lawrence, then down at the beach, where Alison was standing up, prepared to go back into the water. 'It's possible, boy. We should make it a little festive, though.' Tucker got out of the chair and walked to the sea wall. 'I think Alison should have a birthday.'

The telephone rang in McAuliff's room. The doors were closed against the heat, and the harsh bell echoed from beyond the slatted panels. Tucker and Lawrence looked at each other, each knowing the other's thoughts. Although McAuliff had not elaborated on his late-morning departure from Bengal Court, neither had he concealed it. Actually, he had asked the desk for a road map, explaining only that he was going for a drive. Therefore, the front desk knew that he was not in his room.

Tucker crossed rapidly to the double doors, opened them, and went inside to the telephone.

'Mr McAuliff?' The soft, precise Jamaican voice was that of the switchboard operator.

'No, Mr McAuliff is out. May I give him a message?'

'Please, sir, I have a call from Kingston. From a Mr Latham. Will you hold the line, please?'

'Certainly. Tell Mr Latham you've got Sam Tucker on the phone. He may want to speak with me.'

Sam held the telephone under his wrinkled chin as he struck a match to a thin cigar. He had barely drawn the first smoke when he heard the double click of the connecting line. The voice was now Latham's. Latham, the proper bureaucrat from the Ministry, who was also committed to the cause of Barak Moore. As Latham spoke, Tucker made the decision not to tell him of Barak's death.

'Mr Tucker?'

'Yes, Mr Latham. Alex drove into Ocho Rios.'

'Very well. You can handle this, I'm sure. We were able to comply with McAuliff's request. He's got his interior runners several days early. They're in Duanvale and will be driving on Route Eleven into Queenhythe later this afternoon.'

'Queenhythe's near here, isn't it?'

'Three or four miles from your motel, that's all. They'll telephone when they get in.'

'What are their names?'

'They're brothers. Marcus and Justice Hedrik. They're Maroons, of course. Two of the best runners in Jamaica; they know the Cock Pit extremely well, and they're trustworthy.'

'That's good to hear. Alexander will be delighted.'

Latham paused but obviously was not finished. 'Mr Tucker?'

'Yes, Mr Latham?'

'McAuliff's altered the survey's schedule, it would appear. I'm not sure we understand ...'

'Nothing to understand, Mr Latham. Alex decided to work from a geographical midpoint. Less room for error that way; like bisecting a triangle from semicircular coordinates. I agree with him.' Tucker inhaled on his thin cigar while Latham's silence conveyed his bewilderment. 'Also,' continued Sam, 'it gives everyone a lot more to do.'

'I see ... The reasons, then, are quite compatible with ... let us say, professional techniques?'

'Very professional, Mr Latham.' Tucker realized that Latham would not speak freely on the telephone. Or felt he could not. 'Beyond criticism, if you're worried about the Ministry's concerns. Actually, Alexander could be saving you considerable sums of money. You'll get a lot more data much quicker.'

Latham paused again, as though to telegraph the importance of the following statement. 'Naturally, we're always interested in conserving funds ... and I assume you all agree with the decision to go in so quickly. Into the Cock Pit, that is.'

Sam knew that Latham's statement could be translated into the question: *Does Barak Moore agree?*

'We *all* agree, Mr Latham. We're all professionals.'

'Yes ... well, that's splendid. One last item, Mr Tucker.'

'Yes, Mr Latham?'

'We want Mr McAuliff to use all the resources provided him. He's not to stint in an effort to save money; the survey's too important for that.'

Tucker again translated Latham's code easily: *Alex was to maintain contact with British Intelligence liaisons. If he avoided them, suspicions would be aroused.*

'I'll tell him that, Mr Latham, but I'm sure he's aware of it. These past two weeks have been very routine, very dull – simple coastline geodometrics. Not much call for equipment. Or resources.'

'As long as he knows our feelings,' said Latham rapidly, now anxious to terminate the conversation. 'Goodbye, Mr Tucker.'

'Goodbye, Mr Latham.' Sam held his finger down on the telephone button for several moments, then released it and waited for the switchboard. When the operator came on the line, Tucker asked for the front desk.

'Bengal Court, good afternoon.'

'This is Mr Tucker, west wing six, Royal Society survey.'

'Yes, Mr Tucker?'

'Mr McAuliff asked me to make arrangements for tonight. He didn't have time this morning; besides, it was awkward; Mrs Booth was with him.' Sam paused, letting his words register.

The clerk automatically responded. 'Yes, Mr Tucker. What can we do for you?'

'It's Mrs Booth's birthday. Do you think the kitchen could whip up a little cake? Nothing elaborate, you understand.'

'Of course! We'd be *delighted*, sir.' The clerk was effusive. 'Our pleasure, Mr Tucker.'

'Fine. That's very kind of you. Just put it on Mr McAuliff's bill—'

'There'll be no charge,' interjected the clerk, fluidly subservient.

'Very kind indeed. We'll be dining around eight thirty, I guess. Our usual table.'

'We'll take care of everything.'

'That is, it'll be eight thirty,' continued Sam, 'if Mr McAuliff finds his way back in time ...' Tucker paused again, listening for the clerk's appropriate response.

'Oh? Is there a problem, Mr Tucker?'

'Well, the damn fool drove south of Ocho Rios, around Fern Gully, I think, to locate some stalactite sculpture. He told me there were natives who did that sort of thing down there.'

'That's true, Mr Tucker. There are a number of stalactite craftsmen in the Gully. However, there are government restrictions—'

'Oh Lord, son!' interrupted Sam defensively. 'He's just going to find Mrs Booth a little present, that's all.'

The clerk laughed, softly and obsequiously. 'Please don't mistake me, Mr Tucker. Government interference is often most unwarranted. I only meant that I hope Mr McAuliff is successful. When he asked for the petrol map, he should have mentioned where he was going. I might have helped him.'

'Well ...' drawled Sam conspiratorially, 'he was probably embarrassed, if you know what I mean. I wouldn't mention it; he'd be mad as hell at me.'

'Of course.'

'And thanks for the cake tonight. That's really very nice of you, son.'

'Not at all, sir.'

The goodbyes were rapid, more so on the clerk's part. Sam replaced the telephone and walked back out onto the terrace. Lawrence turned from peering over the wall and sat on the flagstone deck, his back against the sea wall, his body hidden from the beach.

'Mrs Booth and Jimbo-mon are out of water,' said the black revolutionary. 'They are in chairs again.'

'Latham called. The runners will be here this afternoon ... And I talked with the front desk. Let's see if our information gets transmitted properly.' Tucker lowered himself on the chair slowly and reached for the binoculars on the table. He picked up the newspaper and held it next to the binoculars as he focused on the swimming-pool patio fronting the central beach of Bengal Court.

Within ten seconds he saw the figure of a man dressed in a coat and tie come out of the rear entrance of the pool, past a group of wooden, padded sun chairs, nodding to guests, chatting with several. He reached the stone steps leading to the sand and stood there several moments, surveying the beach. Then he started down the steps and across the white, soft sand. He walked diagonally to the right, to the row of sunfish sailboats.

Sam watched as the clerk approached the digger-policeman in the sloppy baseball cap and the *cocoruru* peddler. The *cocoruru* man saw him coming, picked up the handles of his wheelbarrow, and rolled it on the hard sand near the water to get away. The digger-policeman stayed where he was and acknowledged the clerk.

The magnified features in the glass conveyed all that was necessary to Sam Tucker. The policeman's features contorted with irritation. The man was apparently lamenting his waste of time and effort, commodities not easily expended on such a hot day.

The clerk turned and started back across the sand toward the patio. The digger-policeman began walking west, near the water's edge. His gait was swifter now; gone was the stooped posture indigenous to a scavenger of the beach.

He wasn't much of an undercover man, thought Sam Tucker as he watched the man's progress toward the woods of Bengal Court's west property. On his way to his shoes and the egress to the shore road, he never once looked down at the sand for tourist leave-behinds.

McAuliff stood looking over Charles Whitehall's left shoulder as the black scholar ridged the flame of the acetylene torch across the seamed edge of the archive case. The hot point of flame bordered no more than an eighth of an inch behind the seam, at the end of the case.

The top edge of the archive case cracked. Charles extinguished the flame quickly and thrust the end of the case under the faucet in the sink. The thin stream of water sizzled into vapor as it touched the hot steel. Whitehall removed his tinted goggles, picked up a miniature hammer, and tapped the steaming end.

It fell off, cracking and sizzling, into the metal sink. Within the case could be seen the oilcloth of a packet. His hands trembling slightly, Charles Whitehall pulled it out. He got off the stool, carrying the rolled-up oilcloth to a deserted area of the bench, and untied the nylon laces. He unwound the packet until it was flat, unzipped the inner lining, and withdrew two sheets of single-spaced typing. As he reached for the bench lamp, he looked at McAuliff.

Alex was fascinated by what he saw. Whitehall's eyes shone with a strange intensity. It was a fever. A messianic fever. A kind of victory rooted in the absolute.

A fanatic's victory, thought McAuliff.

Without speaking, Whitehall began to read. As he finished the first page, he slid it across the bench to Alex.

The word 'Halidon' was in reality three words – or sounds – from the African Ashanti, so corrupted by later phonetics as to be hardly traceable. (Here Piersall included hieroglyphs that were meaningless to Alex.) The root word, again a hieroglyph, was in the sound *leedaw*, translated to convey the picture of a hollowed-out piece of wood that could be held in the hand. The *leedaw* was a primitive instrument of sound, a means of communication over distances in the jungles and hills. The pitch of its wail was controlled by the breath of the blower and the placement of his hand over slits carved through the surface – the basic principle of the woodwind.

The historical parallel had been obvious to Walter Piersall. Whereas the Maroon tribes, living in settlements, used an *abeng* – a type of bugle made from the horns of cattle – to signal their warriors or spread the alarm of an approaching white enemy, the followers of Acquaba were nomadic and could not rely on animal products with any certainty. They returned to the African custom of utilizing the most prolific material of their surroundings: wood.

Once having established the root symbol as the primitive horn, it remained for Piersall to specify the modification of the accompanying sounds. He went back to the Ashanti-Coromanteen studies to extract compatible noun roots. He found the final syllable, or sound, first. It was in the hieroglyph depicting a deep river current, or undertow, that periled man or animal in the water. Its sonic equivalent was a bass-toned wail or cry. The phonetic spelling was *nwa*.

The pieces of the primitive puzzle were nearly joined.

The initial sound was the symbol *hayee*, the Coromanteen word meaning the council of their tribal gods.

Hayee-leedaw-nwa.

The low cry of a jungle horn signifying a peril, a supplication to the council of the gods.

Acquaba's code. The hidden key that would admit an outsider into the primitive tribal sect.

Primitive and not primitive at all.

Halidon. Hollydawn. A wailing instrument whose cry was carried by the wind to the gods.

This, then, was Dr Walter Piersall's last gift to his island sanctuary. The means to reach, enlist, and release a powerful force for the good of Jamaica. To convince 'it' to accept its responsibility.

There remained only to determine which of the isolated communities in the Cock Pit mountains was the Halidon. Which would respond to the code of the Acquaba?

Finally, the basic scepticism of the scholar inserted itself into Piersall's document. He did not question the existence of the Halidon; what he did speculate on was its rumored wealth and commitment. Were these more myth than current fact? Had the myth grown out of proportion to the conceivably diminished resources?

The answer was in the Cock Pit.

McAuliff finished the second page and looked over at Charles Whitehall. The black fascist had walked from the workbench to the small window overlooking the Drax Hall fields. Without turning, he spoke quietly, as though he knew Alex was staring at him, expecting him to speak.

'Now we know what must be done. But we must proceed cautiously, sure of every step. A wrong move on our part and the cry of the Halidon will vanish with the wind.'

22

The Caravel prop plane descended on its western approach to the small Boscobel airfield in Oracabessa. The motors revved in short bursts to counteract the harsh wind and rain of the sudden downpour, forcing the aircraft to enter the strip cleanly. It taxied to the far end, turned awkwardly, and rolled back toward the small, one-lever concrete passenger terminal.

Two Jamaican porters ran through the low gates to the aircraft, both holding umbrellas. Together they pushed the metal step unit to the side of the plane, under the door; the man on the left then knocked rapidly on the fuselage.

The door was slapped open by a large white man who immediately stepped out, waving aside the offer of the two umbrellas. He jumped from the top level to the ground and looked around in the rain.

His right hand was in his jacket pocket.

He turned up to the aircraft door and nodded. A second large white man disembarked and ran across the muddy space toward the concrete terminal. His right hand, too, was in his pocket. He entered the building, glanced around, and proceeded out of the exit to the parking area.

Sixty seconds later the gate by the luggage depot was swung open by the second man and a Mercedes 660 limousine drove through toward the Caravel, its wheels spinning frequently in the drenched earth.

The two Jamaicans remained by the step unit, their umbrellas waiting.

The Mercedes pulled alongside the plane, and the tiny, ancient figure of Julian Warfield was helped down the steps, his head and body shielded by the black aides. The second white man held the door of the Mercedes; his large companion was in front of the automobile, scanning the distance and the few passengers who had come out of the terminal.

When Warfield was enclosed in the back seat, the Jamaican driver stepped out and the second white man got behind the wheel. He honked the horn once; his companion turned and raced around to the left front door and climbed in.

The Mercedes's deep-throated engine roared as the limousine backed up beyond the tail assembly of the Caravel, then belched forward and sped through the gate.

With Julian Warfield in the back seat were Peter Jensen and his wife, Ruth.

'We'll drive to Peale Court, it's not far from here,' said the small, gaunt financier, his eyes alive and controlled. 'How long do you have? With reasonable caution.'

'We rented a car for a trip to Dunn's Falls,' replied Peter. 'We left it in the lot and met the Mercedes outside. Several hours, at least.'

'Did you make it clear you were going to the Falls?'

'Yes, I invited McAuliff.'

Warfield smiled. 'Nicely done, Peter.'

The car raced over the Oracabessa road for several miles and turned into a gravel drive flanked by two while stone posts. On both were identical plaques reading PEALE COURT. They were polished to a high gloss, a rich mixture of gold and black.

At the end of the drive was a long parking area in front of a longer, one-story white stucco house with expensive wood in the doors, and many windows. It was perched on top of a steep incline above the beach.

Warfield and the Jensens were admitted by a passive, elderly black woman in a white uniform, and Julian led the way to a veranda overlooking the waters of Golden Head Bay.

The three of them settled in chairs, and Warfield politely asked the Jamaican servant to bring refreshments. Perhaps a light rum punch.

The rain was letting up; streaks of yellow and orange could be seen beyond the gray sheets in the sky.

'I've always been fond of Peale Court,' said Warfield. 'It's so peaceful.'

'The view is breathtaking,' added Ruth. 'Do you own it, Julian?'

'No, my dear. But I don't believe it would be difficult to acquire. Look around, if you like. Perhaps you and Peter might be interested.'

Ruth smiled and, as if one cue, rose from her chair. 'I think I shall.'

She walked back through the veranda doors into the larger living room with the light brown marble floor. Peter watched her, then looked over at Julian. 'Are things that serious?'

'I don't want her upset,' replied Warfield.

'Which, of course, gives me my answer.'

'Possibly. Not necessarily. We've come upon disturbing news. MI5, and over here its brother, MI6.'

Peter reacted as though he'd been jolted unnecessarily. 'I thought we had that area covered. Completely. It was passive.'

'On the island, perhaps. Sufficient for our purposes. Not in London. Obviously.' Warfield paused and took a deep breath, pursing his narrow, wrinkled lips. 'Naturally, we'll take steps immediately to intercede, but it may have gone too far. Ultimately, we can control the Service . . . if we must, right out of the Foreign Office. What bothers me now is the current activity.'

Peter Jensen looked out over the veranda railing. The afternoon sun was breaking through the clouds. The rain had stopped.

'Then we have two adversaries. This Halidon – whatever in blazes it is. And British Intelligence.'

'Precisely. What is of paramount importance, however, is to keep the two separate. Do you see?'

Jensen returned his gaze to the old man. 'Of course. Assuming they haven't already joined forces.'

'They have not.'

'You're sure of that, Julian?'

'Yes. Don't forget, we first learned of this Halidon through MI5 personnel – specialist level. Dunstone's payrolls are diverse. If contact had been made, we'd know it.'

Again Jensen looked out at the waters of the bay, his expression pensive and questioning. 'Why? *Why?* The man was offered two million dollars . . . There is nothing, *nothing* in his dossier that would give an inkling of this. McAuliff is suspicious of *all* governmental interferences . . . quite rabid on the subject, actually. It was one of the reasons I proposed him.'

'Yes,' said Warfield noncommittally. 'McAuliff was your idea, Peter . . . Don't mistake me, I am not holding you responsible, I concurred with your choice . . . Describe what happened last night. This morning.'

Jensen did so, ending with the description of the fishing boat veering off into open water and the removal of the medical equipment from the motel room. 'If it was an MI6 operation, it was crude, Julian. Intelligence has too many facilities available to be reduced to motels and fishing boats. If we only knew what happened.'

'We do. At least, I think we do,' replied Warfield. 'Late last night the house of a dead white man, an anthropologist named Piersall, was broken into, ten, twelve miles from the coast. There was a skirmish. Two men were killed that we know of; others could have been wounded. They officially called it a robbery, which, of course, it wasn't really. Not in the sense of larceny.'

'I know the name Piersall—'

'You should. He was the university radical who filed that insane letter of intent with the Department of Territories.'

'Of course! He was going to purchase half of the Cock Pit! That was months ago. He was a lunatic.' Jensen lighted his pipe; he gripped the bowl as he did so, he did not merely hold it. 'So there is a third intruder,' he said, his words drifting off quietly, nervously.

'Or one of the first two, Peter.'

'How? What do you mean?'

'You ruled out MI6. It could be the Halidon.'

Jensen stared at Warfield. 'If so, it would mean McAuliff is working with both camps. And if Intelligence has not made contact, it's because McAuliff has not permitted it.'

'A very complicated young man.' The old financier placed his glass down carefully on a tiled table next to his chair. He turned slightly to look through the veranda doors; the voice of Ruth Jensen could be heard chatting with the Jamaican maid inside the house. Warfield looked back at Peter. He pointed his thin, bony finger to a brown leather case on a white wicker table across the porch. 'That is for you, Peter. Please get it.'

Jensen rose from his chair, walked to the table, and stood by the case. It was smaller than the attaché variety. And thicker. Its two hasps were secure by combination locks. 'What are the numbers?'

'The left lock is three zeros. The right, three fives. You may alter the combinations as you wish.' Peter bent down and began manipulating the tiny vertical dials. Warfield continued. 'Tomorrow you will start into the interior. Learn everything you can. Find out who comes to see him, for certainly he will have visitors. And the minute you establish the fact that he is in actual contact, and with whom, send out Ruth on some medical pretext with the information ... Then, Peter, you must kill him. McAuliff is a keystone. His death will panic both camps, and we shall know all we need to know.'

Jensen lifted the top of the leather case. Inside, recessed in the green felt, was a brand-new Luger pistol. Its steel glistened, except for a dull space below the trigger housing where the serial number had been removed. Below the weapon was a five-inch cylinder, one end grooved.

A silencer.

'You've never asked this of me, Julian. Never ... You mustn't.'

Jensen turned and stared at Warfield.

'I am not asking, Peter. I am demanding. Dunstone Limited, has given you everything. And now it needs you in a way it has not needed you before. You must, you see.'

Part Four

The Cock Pit

23

They began at the midpoint of the western perimeter, two and a half miles south of Weston Favel, on the edge of the Cock Pit range. They made base camp on the bank of a narrow offshoot of the Martha Brae. All but the runners, Marcus and Justice Hedrik, were stunned by the seemingly impenetrable walls of jungle that surrounded them.

Strange, contradictory forests that were filled with the west verdance of tropic growth and the cold massiveness of sky-reaching black and green associated with northern climates. Dense macca-fat palms stood next to silk-cotton, or ceiba, trees that soared out of sight, their tops obscured by the midgrowth. Mountain cabbage and bull thatch, orchid and moss, fungi and eucalyptus battled for their individual rights to coexist in the Oz-like jungle primeval.

The ground was covered with ensnaring spreads of fern and pteridophyte, soft, wet and treacherous. Pools of swamp-like mud were hidden in the thick, crowded sprays of underbrush. Sudden hills rose out of nowhere, remembrances of Oligocene upheavals, never to be settled back into the cradle of the earth.

The sounds of the screeching bat and parrot and tanager intruded on the forest's undertones; jungle rats and the mongoose could be heard intermittently in their unseen games of death. Every now and then there was the scream of a wild pig, pursuing or in panic.

And far in the distance, in the clearing of the riverbank, were the mountains, preceded by sudden stretches of untamed grassland. Strangely gray with streaks of deep green and blue and yellow – rain and hot sunlight in an unceasing interchange.

All this fifteen minutes by air from the gaudy strips of Montego.

Unbelievable.

McAuliff had made contact with the north-coast contacts of British Intelligence. There were five, and he had reached each one.

They had given him another reason to consign R. C. Hammond to the despised realm of the manipulator. For the Intelligence people were of small comfort. They stated perfunctorily their relief at his reporting, accepted his explanations of routine geographic chores that kept him occupied, and assured him – with more sound than conviction – that they were at his beck and call.

One man, the MI6 contact from Port Maria, drove down the coast to Bengal Court to meet with Alex. He was a portly black merchant who limited his identification to the single name of Garvey. He insisted on a late-night rendezvous in the tiny bar of the motel, where he was known as a liquor distributor.

It did not take McAuliff long to realize that Garvey, ostensibly there to assure him of total cooperation and safety, was actually interrogating him for a report that would be sent back to London. Garvey had the stench and look of a practised informer about him. The stench was actual: the man suffered from body odor, which could not be concealed by liberal applications of bay rum. The look was in his eyes – ferretlike, and a touch bloodshot. Garvey was a man who sought out opportunities and enjoyed the fruits thereof.

His questions were precise, McAuliff's answers apparently not satisfactory. And all questions led to the one question, the only one that mattered: Any progress concerning the Halidon?

Anything?

Unknown observers, strangers in the distance ... a signal, a sign – no matter how remote or subtle?

Anything?

'Absolutely nothing' was a hard reply for Garvey to accept.

What about the men in the green Chevrolet who had followed him in Kingston? Tallon had traced them to the anthropologist Walter Piersall. Piersall had been a white agitator ... common knowledge. Piersall had telephoned McAuliff ... the Courtleigh switchboard cooperated with MI6. What did Piersall want?

Alex claimed he did not – could not – know, as Piersall had never reached him. An agitator, white *or* black, was an unpredictable bearer of unpredictable news. Predictably, this agitator had had an accident. It might be presumed – from what little McAuliff had been told by Tallon and others – that Piersall had been closing in on Dunstone Limited; without a name, of course. If so, he, McAuliff, was a logical person to reach. But this was conjecture; there was no way to confirm it as fact.

What had happened to the late-arriving Samuel Tucker? Where had he been?

Drinking and whoring in Montego Bay. Alex was sorry he had caused so much trouble about Sam; he should have known better. Sam Tucker was an incorrigible wanderer, albeit the best soil analyst in the business.

The perspiring Garvey was bewildered, frustrated by his confusion. There was too much activity for McAuliff to remain so insulated.

Alex reminded the liaison in short, coarse words that there was far too much survey activity – logistical, employment, above all government paperwork – for him not to be insulated. What the hell did Garvey think he had been doing?

The interview lasted until one thirty in the morning. Before leaving the

MI6 contact reached into his filthy briefcase and withdrew a metallic object the size of a pen-and-pencil case, with its approximate thickness. It was a miniaturized radio-signal transmitter, set to a specific frequency. There were three thick, tiny glass lights across the top of the small panel. The first, explained Garvey, was a white light that indicated sufficient power for sending when turned on – not unlike the illuminated filigree of a strobe light. The second, a red light, informed the operator that his signal was being transmitted. The third, a green light, confirmed the reception of the signal by a corresponding device within a radius of twenty-five miles. There would be two simple codes, one for normal conditions, one for emergency. Code One was to be transmitted twice daily, once every twelve hours. Code Two, when aid was needed.

The receiving set, said Garvey, was capable of defining the signal within a diameter of one thousand yards by means of an attached radarscope with terrain coordinates. Nothing was left to chance. Unbelievable.

The incredible assumption, therefore, was that the Intelligence men would never be more than twenty-five miles away, and Hammond's 'guaranteed' safety factor was the even more ridiculous assumption that the jungle distance could be traversed and the exact location pinpointed within a time period that precluded danger.

R. C. Hammond was a winner, thought McAuliff.

'Is this everything?' McAuliff asked the sweating Garvey. 'This goddamn metal box is our protection?'

'There are additional precautions,' Garvey replied enigmatically. 'I told you, nothing is left to chance—'

'What the hell does that mean?'

'It means you are protected. I am not authorized to speak further. As a matter of fact, mon, I do not *know* anything further. I am, like you, merely an employee. I do what I am told to do, say what I am told to say ... And now I have said enough. I have an uncomfortable drive back to Port Maria.'

The man named Garvey rose from the table, picked up his tattered briefcase, and waddled toward the door of the dimly lit room. Before leaving, however, he could not help himself. He stopped at the bar, where one of the motel's managers was standing, and solicited an order of liquor.

McAuliff shook his thoughts loose as he heard the voices of Ruth and Peter Jensen behind him. He was sitting on a dried mudflat above the riverbank; the Jensens were talking as they walked across the clearing from their bivouac tent. It amazed Alex – *they* amazed him. They walked so casually, so normally, over the chopped Cock Pit ground cover; one might think they had entered Regent's Park for a stroll.

'Majestic place in its way, rather,' said Peter, removing the ever-present pipe from between his teeth.

'It is the odd combination of color and substance, don't you think, Alex?' Ruth had her arm linked through her husband's. A noonday walk down the Strand. 'One is so very sensuous, the other so massive and intricate.'

'You make the terms sound contradictory, darling. They're not, you know.' Peter chuckled as his wife feigned minor exasperation.

'He has an incorrigibly pornographic mind, Alex. Pay no attention. Still, he's right. It is majestic. And positively *dense*. Where's Alison?'

'With Ferguson and Sam. They're testing the water.'

'Jimbo-mon's going to use up all of his film, I dare say,' muttered Peter as he helped his wife to sit down next to McAuliff. 'That new camera he brought back from Montego has consumed him.'

'Frightfully expensive, I should think.' Ruth smoothed the unsmoothable cloth of her bivouac slacks, like a woman not used to being without a skirt. Or a woman who was nervous. 'For a boy who's always saying he's bone-stony, quite an extravagance.'

'He didn't buy it; he borrowed it,' said Alex. 'From a friend he knew last year in Port Antonio.'

'That's right, I forgot.' Peter relit his pipe as he spoke. 'You were all here last year, weren't you?'

'Not all, Peter. Just Sam and me; we worked for Kaiser. And Ferguson. He was with the Craft Foundation. No one else.'

'Well, Charles is Jamaican,' intruded Ruth nervously. 'Surely he flies back and forth. Heaven knows, he must be rich enough.'

'That's a rather brass speculation, luv.'

'Oh come off it, Peter. Alex knows what I mean.'

McAuliff laughed. 'I don't think he worries about money. He's yet to submit his bills for the survey outfits. I have an idea they're the most expensive in Harrod's Safari Shop.'

'Perhaps he's embarrassed,' said Peter, smiling. 'He looks as though he had jumped right off the cinema screen. The black hunter; very impressive image, if somewhat contrived.'

'Now you're the one who's talking brass, luv. Charles *is* impressive.' Ruth turned to Alex. 'My overage Lochinvar is green with envy.'

'That camera's damn well new ... not the sort of thing one lends, I shouldn't think.' Peter looked at McAuliff as he spoke the non sequitur.

'Depends on the friend, I guess,' replied Alex, aware that Peter was implying something beyond his words. 'Ferguson can be a likable guy.'

'*Very*,' added Ruth. 'And so helpless, somehow. Except when he's over his equipment. Then he's positively a whiz.'

'Which is all I really care about.' McAuliff addressed this judgment to Peter. 'But then, you're all whizzes, cameras and fancy clothes and aromatic pipes notwithstanding.' Alex laughed.

'Got me there, chap.' Peter removed his pipe and shook his head. 'Dreadful habit.'

'Not at all,' said McAuliff. 'I like the smell, I really do. I'd smoke one myself but my tongue burns. Then stings.'

'There are preventive measures, but it's a dull subject ... What's fascinating is this jungle laboratory we're in. Have you decided on crew assignments?'

'Vaguely,' answered Alex. 'Doesn't make an awful lot of difference. Who do you want?'

'One of those brothers for me,' said Ruth. 'They seem to know exactly where they are. I'd be lost in half a mo'! . . . Of course, that's selfish; my work is least important.'

'We still don't want to lose you, do we, Peter?' McAuliff leaned forward.

'Not as long as she behaves.'

'Take your pick,' said Alex. 'Marcus or Justice?'

'What marvelously dotty names!' cried Ruth. 'I choose Justice.' She looked at her husband. 'Always justice.'

'Yes, of course, my dear.'

'All right,' agreed McAuliff. 'Then Marcus'll be with me. One of them has to. And Alison asked for Lawrence, if you don't mind, Peter.'

'Not at all, chap. Sorry his friend . . . what was his name? Floyd? Yes, Floyd. Sorry he jumped ship, as it were. Did you ever find out what happened to him?'

'No,' replied Alex. 'He just disappeared. Unreliable guy. Something of a thief, too, according to Lawrence.'

'Pity . . . He seemed rather intelligent.'

'*That's* condescending, darling. Worse than brass.' Ruth Jensen picked up a tiny stone and chucked it into the narrow river offshoot.

'Then just pick out a stout fellow who'll promise to lead me back to camp for meals and sleep.'

'Fine. I'll do that. We'll work four-hour field sessions, staying in touch by radio. I don't want anyone going beyond a sonic mile from camp for the first few days.'

'*Beyond!*' Ruth looked at McAuliff, her voice having risen an octave. '*Dear* Alex, if I stumble more than twenty feet into that maze of overgrowth, commit me!'

'Rubbish,' countered her husband, 'when you start cracking rocks, you lose time *and* distance . . . Speaking of which, Alex, old boy, I presume there'll be a fairly steady flow of visitors. To observe our progress; that sort of thing.'

'Why?' McAuliff was now aware that both husband and wife were sending out abstract, perhaps unconscious, signals. Peter less than Ruth. He was subtler, surer of himself than she was. But not completely sure. 'We'll bring out field reports every ten days or so. Rotate days off that way. That'll be good enough.'

'Well, we're not exactly at the end of nowhere; although I grant you, it looks like it. I should think the moneymen would want to check up on what they're paying for.'

Peter Jensen had just made a mistake, and McAuliff was suddenly alarmed. 'What moneymen?'

Ruth Jensen had picked up another stone, about to throw it into the brackish river. Arm poised, she froze for a second before hurling it. The moment was not lost on any of them. Peter tried to minimize it.

'Oh ... some Royal Society titans or perhaps a few of these buggers from the Ministry. I know the R.S. boys, and God knows the Jamaicans have been less than cordial. I just thought ... Oh, well, perhaps I'm off-center.'

'Perhaps,' said Alex quietly, 'you're ahead of me. On-site inspectors aren't unusual. I was thinking about the convenience. Or lack of it. It took us nearly a day to get here. Of course, we had the truck and the equipment ... Still it seems like a lot of trouble.'

'Not really.' Peter Jensen tapped his pipe on his boots. 'I've been checking the maps, looking about from the river clearing. The grasslands are nearer than we think. Less than a couple of miles, I'd say. Light planes or helicopters could easily land.'

'That's a good point. I hadn't thought of it.' McAuliff leaned forward once again to engage Peter, but Peter did not look at him now. 'I mean if we needed ... equipment or supplies, we could get them much quicker than I'd anticipated. Thanks, Peter.'

'Oh, don't *thank* him.' Ruth spoke with a nervous giggle. 'Don't *cater* to him.' She looked briefly at her husband; McAuliff wished he could have seen her eyes. 'Peter just wants to convince himself he's a hop-skip from a pub.'

'Rubbish. Just idle conversation, old girl ...'

'I think he's bored with us, Ruth,' said Alex, laughing softly, almost intimately. 'I think he wants to see new faces.'

'As long as it's not new bodies, my dear, the tolerance is possible,' retorted Ruth Jensen with throated caricature.

The three of them laughed out loud.

McAuliff knew the humor was forced. Mistakes had been made, and the Jensens were afraid.

Peter *was* looking for new faces ... or a new face. A face he believed Alex expected.

Who was it?

Was it possible ... remotely possible that the Jensens were not what they seemed?

There was the sound of whistling from a path in the north bush. Charles Whitehall emerged into the clearing, his safari uniform pressed and clean, in counterpoint to the rumpled clothes of Marcus Hedrik, the older brother of the two Cock Pit runners. Marcus remained a respectful distance behind Whitehall, his passive black face inscrutable.

McAuliff rose from the ground and spoke to the Jensens. 'It's Charley. There's a hill community several miles west of the river; he was going to try to hire a couple of hands.'

Ruth and Peter took their cue, because they very much wanted to. 'Well, we've still got some equipment sorting to do,' said the husband, rising quickly.

'Indeed we do! Help me up, luv.'

The Jensens waved to Charles Whitehall and rapidly started for their tent.

McAuliff met Whitehall at the midpoint of the clearing. The black scholar dismissed Marcus Hedrik, instructing him to issue preparation orders to the rest of the crew about the evening patrols. Alex was fascinated to watch and listen to Charley-mon speaking to the runner. He fell easily into the hill country patois – damn near indecipherable to McAuliff – and used his hands and eyes in gestures and looks that were absolutely compatible with the obtuse speech.

'You do that very well,' said Alex as the runner trudged out of hearing.

'I should. It's what you hired me for. I am the best there is.'

'That's one of the things I like about you, Charley. You take compliments so gracefully.'

'You did not hire me for my graces. They are a bonus you don't deserve.' Whitehall allowed himself a slight smile. 'You enjoy calling me "Charley", McAuliff?' he added.

'Do you object?'

'Not really. Because I understand. It is a defense mechanism; you Americans are rife with them. "Charley" is an idiomatic leveler, peculiarly indigenous to the sixties and seventies. The Vietcong became "Charley", so too the Cambodians and the Laotians; even your man on the American street. It makes you feel superior. Strange that the name should be Charley, is it not?'

'It happens to be *your* name.'

'Yes, of course, but I think that is almost beside the point.' The black scholar looked away briefly, then back at Alex. 'The name Charles is Germanic in origin, actually. Its root meaning is "full grown" or possibly – here scholars differ – "great size". Is it not interesting that you Americans take just such a name and reverse its connotation?'

McAuliff exhaled audibly and spoke wearily. 'I accept the lesson for the day and all its subtle anticolonialism. I gather you'd prefer I call you Charles, or Whitehall, or perhaps "Great Black Leader".'

'Not for a moment. Charley is perfectly fine. Even amusing. And, after all, it is better than Rufus.'

'Then what the hell is this all about?'

Whitehall smiled – again, only slightly – and lowered his voice. 'Until ten seconds ago, Marcus Hedrik's brother has been standing behind the lean-to on our left. He was trying to listen to us. He is gone now.'

Alex whipped his head around. Beyond the large tarpaulin lean-to, erected to cover some camp furniture against a forest shower, Justice Hedrik could be seen walking slowly toward two other crewmen across the clearing. Justice was younger than his brother Marcus, perhaps in his late twenties, and stockily muscular.

'Are you sure? I mean, that he was listening to us?'

'He was carving a piece of ceiba wood. There is too much to do to waste time carving artifacts. He was listening. Until I looked over at him.'

'I'll remember that.'

'Yes. Do. But do not give it undue emphasis. Runners are splendid fellows when they are taking in tourist groups; the tips are generous. I suspect neither brother is too pleased to be with us. Our trip is professional – worse, academically professional. There is not much in it for them. So there will be some hostility.'

McAuliff started to speak, then hesitated. He was bewildered. 'I . . . I may have missed something. What's that got to do with his listening?'

Whitehall blinked slowly, as if patiently explaining to an inept pupil – which, obviously, he felt was the case. 'In the primitive intelligence, hostility is usually preceded by an overt, blunt curiosity.'

'Thank you, Dr Strangelove.' Alex did not hide his irritation. 'Let's get off this. What happened over in the hill community?'

'I sent a messenger to the Maroon Town. I asked for a very private meeting with the Colonel of the Maroons. He will listen; he will accept.'

'I wasn't aware a meeting was that tough to get. If I remember what Barak said, and I do, we just offer money.'

'We do not want a tourist audience, McAuliff. No tribal artifacts or Afro-Carib beads bought for an extra two-dollah-Jamaican. Our business is more serious than tourist trade. I want to prepare the colonel psychologically; make him think.'

Alex paused; Whitehall was probably right. If what Barak Moore had said had validity. If the Colonel of the Maroons was the sole contact with the Halidon, the decision to make that contact would not be lightly arrived at; a degree of psychological preparation would be preferable to none at all. But not so much as to make him run, avoid the decision.

'How do you think you accomplished that?' asked McAuliff.

'I hired the leader of the community to act as courier. I gave him a hundred dollars, which is like offering either of us roughly a quarter of a million. The message requests a meeting in four days, four hours after the sun descends over the mountains—'

'The Arawak symbols?' interrupted Alex.

'Precisely. Completed by specifying that the meeting should take place to the right of the Coromanteen crescent, which I would presume to be the colonel's residence. The colonel was to send back the exact location with our courier . . . Remember, the Colonel of the Maroon Tribes is an ancestral position; he is a descendant and, like all princes of the realm, schooled in its traditions. We shall know soon enough if he perceives us to be quite out of the ordinary.'

'How?'

'If the location he chooses is in some unit of four. Obviously.'

'Obviously . . . So for the next few days we wait.'

'Not just wait, McAuliff. We will be watched, observed very closely. We must take extreme care that we do not appear as a threat. We must go about our business quite professionally.'

'I'm glad to hear that. We're being paid to make a geological survey.'

24

With the first penetration into the Cock Pit, the work of the survey consumed each member of the team. Whatever their private fears or foreign objectives, they were professionals, and the incredible laboratory that was the Cock Pit demanded their professional attentions.

Portable tables, elaborately cased microscopes, geoscopes, platinum drills, sediment prisms, and depository vials were transported by scientist and carrier alike into the barely penetrable jungles and into the grasslands. The four-hour field sessions were more honored in the breach; none cared to interrupt his experiments or analyses for such inconveniences as meals or routine communications. The disciplines of basic precautions were swiftly consigned to aggravating nuisances. It took less than a full working day for the novelty of the ever-humming, ever-irritating walkie-talkies to wear off. McAuliff found it necessary to remind Peter Jensen and James Ferguson angrily that it was mandatory to leave the radio receiving switches on, regardless of the intermittent chatter between stations.

The first evenings lent credence to the wisdom of Charles Whitehall's purchases at Harrod's Safari Shop. The team sat around the fires in canvas chairs, as though recuperating from the day's hunt. But instead of talk of cat, horn, spore, and bird, other words flew around, spoken with no less enthusiasm. *Zinc, manganese, and bauxite; ochers, gypsum, and phosphate . . . Cretaceous, Eocene, shale, and igneous; wynne grass, tamarind, bloodwood; guano, gros-michel, and woman's tongue . . . arid and acid and peripatus; water runoffs, gas pockets, and layers of vesicular lava – honeycombs of limestone.*

The overriding generalization was shared by everyone: the Cock Pit was an extraordinarily fruitful landmass with abundant reserves of rich soil, available water, and unbelievable deposits of gases and ores.

All this was accepted as fact before morning of the third day. McAuliff listened as Peter Jensen summed it up with frightening clarity.

'It's inconceivable that no one's gone in and developed. I daresay Brasilia couldn't hold a candle! Three-quarters of the life force is right here, waiting to be used!'

The reference to the city carved out of the Brazilian jungles made Alex swallow and stare at the enthusiastic, middle-aged, pipe-smoking minerals expert.

We're going to build a city ... Julian Warfield's words.

Unbelievable. And viable.

It did not take great imagination to understand Dunstone Limited, now. The project was sound, taking only gigantic sums of capital to set it in motion; sums available to Dunstone. And once set in motion, the entire island could be tied to the incredible development. Armies of workers, communities, *one source*.

Ultimately, the government.

Kingston could not, *would* not turn it off. Once in motion – *one source* – the benefits would be overwhelming and undeniable. The enormity of the cash flow alone could subvert the parliament. Slices of the gigantic pie.

Economically and psychologically, Kingston would become dependent on Dunstone Limited.

So complicated, yet so basically, ingeniously simple.

Once they have Kingston, they have the laws of the land in their vaults. To shape as they will. Dunstone will own a nation ... R. C. Hammond's words.

It was nearly midnight; the carriers were banking the fires under the scrutiny of the two runners, Marcus and Justice Hedrik. The black revolutionary, Lawrence, was playing his role as one of the crew, subservient and pleasant, but forever scanning the forests beyond, never allowing himself to be too far away from Alison Booth.

The Jensens and Ferguson had gone to their tents. McAuliff, Sam Tucker, and Alison sat around a small bivouac table, the light of the dying fires flickering across their faces as they talked quietly.

'Jensen's right, Alexander,' said Tucker, lighting a thin cigar. 'Those behind this know exactly what they're doing. I'm no expert, but one strike, one hint of a mother lode, and you couldn't stop the speculation money.'

'It's a company named Dunstone.'

'What is?'

'Those behind ... the company's called Dunstone; the man's name is Warfield. Julian Warfield. Alison knows.'

Sam held the cigar between his fingers and looked at McAuliff. 'They hired you.' Tucker's statement was spoken slowly, a touch gruffly.

'He did,' replied Alex. 'Warfield did.'

'Then this Royal Society grant ... the Ministry, and the Institute, *are* covers.'

'Yes.'

'And you knew it from the beginning.'

'So does British Intelligence. I wasn't just acting as an informer, Sam. They trained me ... as best they could over a couple of weeks.'

'Was there any particular reason why you kept it a secret, Alexander?' Tucker's voice – especially as capped with McAuliff's name – was not comforting. 'I think you should have told me. Especially after that meeting in the hills. We've been together a long time, boy ... No, I don't think you acted properly.'

'He was generously proper, Sam,' said Alison, with a combination of precision and warmth. 'For your benefit. I speak from experience. The less you're aware of, the better your prospects. Take my word for it.'

'Why should I?' asked Tucker.

'Because I've been there. And because I was there, I'm here now.'

'She tied in against Chatellerault. That's what I couldn't tell you. She worked for Interpol. A data bank picked out her name; it was made to look so completely logical. She wanted to get out of England—'

'*Had* to get out, my darling ... Do you see, Sam? The computer was Interpol's; all the intelligence services are first cousins, and don't let anyone tell you otherwise. MI5 ran a cross-reference, and here I am. Valuable bait, another complication ... Don't be anxious to learn too much. Alex was right.'

The ensuing silence was artificial. Tucker inhaled on his thin cigar, the unasked questions more pronounced by their absence. Alison whisked strands of hair, let down for the evening, off her forehead. McAuliff poured himself a small quantity of Scotch. Finally Sam Tucker spoke.

'It's fortunate I trust you, Alexander.'

'I know that. I counted on it.'

'But *why*?' continued Sam quietly. 'Why in hell did you *do* it? You're not that hungry. Why did you work for *them*?'

'For whom? Or which? Dunstone or British Intelligence?'

Tucker paused, staring at Alex before he replied. '*Jesus*, I don't know. Both, I guess, boy.'

'I accepted the first before the second showed up. It was a good contract, the best I'd ever been offered. Before I realized it, I was locked in. I was convinced I couldn't get out ... by both sides. At one point, it was as simple as staying alive. Then there were guarantees and promises ... and more guarantees and more promises.' McAuliff stared across the clearing; it was strange. Lawrence was crouched over the embers of a fire, looking at them. 'Before you know it, you're in some kind of crazy cell block, hurtling around the confining space, bouncing off the walls ... that's not a very sane picture.'

'Move and countermove, Sam,' interrupted Alison. 'They're experts.'

'Who? Which?' Tucker leaned forward in his chair, holding Alison with his old eyes.

'Both,' answered the girl firmly. 'I saw what Chatellerault did to my husband. I know what Interpol did to me.'

The silence returned once more, less strained than before. And once again, Sam Tucker broke it softly.

'You've got to define your enemies, Alexander. I get the feeling you haven't done that ... present company expected as allies, I sincerely hope.'

'I've defined them as best I can. I'm not sure those definitions will hold. It's complicated, at least for me.'

'Then simplify, boy. When you're finished, who wants you hanged the quickest?'

McAuliff looked at Alison. 'Again, both. Dunstone literally; MI5 and

MI6 figuratively. One dead, the other dependent – subject to recall. A name in a data bank. That's very real.'

'I agree,' said Tucker, relighting his thin cigar. 'Now, let's reverse the process. Who can *you* hang the quickest? The surest?'

Alex laughed quietly, joined by Alison. The girl spoke. 'My Lord, you *do* think alike.'

'That doesn't answer the question. Who the quickest?'

'Dunstone, I imagine. At the moment, it's more vulnerable. Warfield made a mistake; he thinks I'm *really* hungry. He thinks he bought me because he made me a part of them. They fall, I fall . . . I'd have to say Dunstone.'

'All right,' replied Sam, assuming the mantle of a soft-spoken attorney. 'Enemy number one defined as Dunstone. You can extricate yourself by simple blackmail: third-person knowledge, documents tucked away in lawyers' offices. Agreed?'

'Yes.'

'That leaves enemy number two: Her Majesty's Intelligence boys. Let's define them. What's their hook into you?'

'Protection. It's supposed to be protection.'

'Not noticeably successful, would you say, son?'

'Not noticeably successful,' said Alex in agreement. 'But we're not finished yet.'

'We'll get to that; don't rush. What's your hook into them?'

McAuliff paused in thought. 'Their methods . . . and their contacts, I think. Exposing their covert operations.'

'Really the same as with Dunstone, isn't it?' Tucker was zeroing in on his target.

'Again, yes.'

'Let's go back a second. What does Dunstone offer?'

'Money. A great deal of money. They need this survey.'

'Are you prepared to lose it?'

'Hell, yes! But I may not have to—'

'That's immaterial. I assume that's part of the "guarantees and promises".'

'That's right.'

'But it's not a factor. You haven't stolen from the thieves. In any way can they get you indicted as one of them?'

'Christ, no! They may think so, but they're wrong.'

'Then there are your answers. Your definitions. Eliminate the hooks and the offers. Theirs. The money and the protection. Lose one – the money; make the other unnecessary – the protection. You're dealing from strength, with your own hooks. *You* make whatever offers you wish.'

'You jumped, Sam,' said McAuliff slowly. 'Or you forgot. We're not finished; we may need the protection. If we take it, we can't deny it. We'd be a joke. The Iran-Contra syndrome. Worms crawling over each other.'

Sam Tucker put down his thin cigar in the ashtray on the table and reached for the bottle of Scotch. He was about to speak, but was interrupted by the sight of Charles Whitehall walking out of a jungle path into the clearing. Whitehall looked around, then crossed rapidly to Lawrence, who was still over the coals of the banked fire, the orange glow coloring his skin a bronzed black. The two men spoke. Lawrence stood up, nodded once, and started toward the jungle path. Whitehall watched him briefly, then turned and looked over at McAuliff, Sam, and Alison.

With urgency, he began walking across the clearing to them.

'There's your protection, Alexander,' said Sam quietly as Whitehall approached. 'The two of them. They may despise each other, but they've got a common hate that works out fine for you. For all of us, goddammit . . . Bless their beautiful hides.'

'The courier has returned.' Charles Whitehall adjusted the light of the Coleman lantern in his tent. McAuliff stood inside the canvas flap of the doorway – Whitehall had insisted that Alex come with him; he did not wish to speak in front of Alison and Sam Tucker.

'You could have told the others.'

'That will be a . . . multilateral decision. Personally, I would not subscribe to it.'

'Why not?'

'We must be extremely careful. The less that is known by them, the better.'

McAuliff pulled out a pack of cigarettes and walked to the single nylon-strapped chair in the center of the tent. He sat down, knowing that Charley-mon would not; the man was too agitated, trying almost comically to remain calm. 'That's funny. Alison used the same words a little while ago. For different reasons . . . What's the message from Maroon Town?'

'Affirmative! The colonel will meet with us. What's more important – *so* much more important – is that his reply was in units of four!'

Whitehall approached the chair, his eyes filled with that messianic anxiety Alex had seen in Drax Hall. 'He made a counterproposal for our meeting. Unless he hears otherwise, he will assume it is acceptable. He asks for eight days. And rather than four hours after sundown, he requests the same four hours after two in the morning. *Two* in the *morning*! Diagrammatically to the *right* of the setting sun. Don't you see? He *understands*, McAuliff. He understands! Piersall's first step is confirmed!'

'I thought it would be,' replied Alex lamely, not quite sure how to handle Whitehall's agitation.

'It doesn't matter to you, does it?' The Jamaican stared at McAuliff incredulously. 'A scholar made an extraordinary discovery. He'd followed elusive threads in the archives going back over two hundred years. His work proved out; it could have enormous academic impact. The story of Jamaica might well have to be rewritten . . . Can't you *see*?'

'I can see you're excited, and I can understand that. You should be. But right now, I'm concerned with a less erudite problem. I don't like the delay.'

Whitehall silently exploded in exasperation. He looked up at the canvas ceiling, inhaled deeply, and quickly regained his composure. The judgment he conveyed was obvious: the blunt mind in front of him was incapable of being reached. He spoke with condescending resignation. 'It's good. It indicates progress.'

'Why?'

'I did not tell you, but I included a message with our request for a meeting. It was admittedly a risk but I felt – unilaterally – that it was worth taking. It could expedite our objective with greater speed. I told the courier to say the request came from . . . new believers of Acquaba.'

McAuliff tensed; he was suddenly angry with Whitehall, but had the presence to minimize his anger. The horrible memory of the fate of the first Dunstone survey came to mind. 'For such a brilliant guy, I think that was pretty stupid, Charley-*mon*.'

'Not stupid. A calculated risk. If the Halidon decides to make contact on the strength of Piersall's code, it will arrive at that decision only after it learns more about us. It will send out for information; it will see that I am part of the unit. The elders of the Halidon will know of my credentials, my scholarship, my contributions to the Jamaican story. These will be in our favor.'

Alex leaped out of the chair and spoke quietly, viciously. 'You egomaniacal son-of-a-bitch! Has it occurred to you that your . . . *other* credentials may *not* be favorable? You could be the one piece of rotten meat!'

'*Impossible!*'

'You arrogant prick! I won't have the lives of this team jeopardized by your inflated opinion of yourself! I want protection, and I'm going to get it!'

There was a rustling outside the tent. Both men whipped around toward the canvas flap of the entrance. The canvas parted, and the black revolutionary, Lawrence, walked in slowly, his hands in front of him, bound by rope. Behind Lawrence was another man. In the shadowed darkness it appeared to be the runner Marcus Hedrik. In his hand was a gun. It was jabbed into the flash of his prisoner.

The captor spoke quietly. 'Do not go for your weapons. Don't make noise. Just stay exactly where you are.'

'Who are you?' asked McAuliff, amazed that Hedrik's voice had lost the hesitant, dull tones he had heard for the better part of a week. 'You're not Marcus!'

'For the moment, that is not important.'

'*Garvey!*' whispered Alex. 'Garvey said it! He said there were others . . . he didn't know who. You're with British Intelligence!'

'No,' replied the large man softly, even politely. 'Two of your carriers were English agents. They're dead. And the obese Garvey had an accident on the road to Port Maria. He is dead also.'

'Then—'

'It is not you who will ask the questions, Mr McAuliff. It is I. You will tell me . . . you new believers . . . what you know of Acquaba.'

25

They talked for several hours, and McAuliff knew that for the time being he had saved their lives. At one point Sam Tucker interrupted, only to receive and acknowledge the plea in Alexander's eyes: Sam *had* to leave them alone. Tucker left, making it clear that he would be with Alison. He expected Alex to speak with them before retiring. Sam did not notice the ropes on Lawrence's hands in the shadowed corner, and McAuliff was grateful that he did not.

Marcus Hedrik was *not* the runner's name. Marcus and Justice Hedrik had been replaced: where they were was of no consequence, insisted this unnamed member of the Halidon. What was of paramount consequence was the whereabouts of the Piersall documents.

Always leave something to trade off . . . in the last extremity. The words of R. C. Hammond.

The documents.

McAuliff's ploy.

The Halidonite probed with infinite care every aspect of Piersall's conclusions as related by Charles Whitehall. The black scholar traced the history of the Acquaba sect, but he would not reveal the *nagarro*, the meaning of the Halidon. The 'runner' neither agreed nor disagreed; he was simply an interrogator. He was also a perceptive and cautious man.

Once satisfied that Charles Whitehall would tell him no more, he ordered him to remain inside his tent with Lawrence. They were not to leave; they would be shot if they tried. His fellow 'runner' would stay on guard.

The Halidonite recognized the intransigence of McAuliff's position. Alex would tell him nothing. Faced with that, he ordered Alex under gunpoint to walk out of the campsite. As they proceeded up a path toward the grasslands, McAuliff began to understand the thoroughness of the Halidon – that small part of it to which he was exposed.

Twice along the alley of dense foliage, the man with the weapon commanded him to stop. There followed a brief series of guttural parrot calls, responded to in kind. Alex heard the softly spoken words of the man with the gun.

'The bivouac is surrounded, Mr McAuliff. I'm quite sure Whitehall and

Tucker, as well as your couriers, know that now. The birds we imitate do not sing at night.'

'Where are we going?'

'To meet with someone. My superior, in fact. Continue, please.'

They climbed for another twenty minutes; a long jungle hill suddenly became an open grassland, a field that seemed extracted from some other terrain, imposed on a foreign land surrounded by wet forests and steep mountains.

The moonlight was unimpeded by clouds; the field was washed with dull yellow. And in the center of the wild grass stood two men. As they approached, McAuliff saw that one of the men was perhaps ten feet behind the first, his back to them. The first man faced them.

The Halidonite facing them was dressed in what appeared to be ragged clothes, but with a loose field jacket and boots. The combined effect was a strange, unkempt paramilitary appearance. Around his waist was a pistol belt and holster. The man ten feet away and staring off in the opposite direction was in a caftan held together in the middle by a single thick rope.

Priestlike. Immobile.

'Sit on the ground, Dr McAuliff,' instructed the strangely ragged paramilitary man; in clipped tones used to command.

Alex did so. The use of the title 'Doctor' told him the unfamiliarity was more his than theirs.

The subordinate who had marched him up from the camp approached the priest figure. The two men fell into quiet conversation, walking slowly into the grass while talking. The two figures receded over a hundred yards into the dull yellow field.

They stopped.

'Turn around, Dr McAuliff.' The order was abrupt; the black man above him had his hand on his holster. Alex pivoted in his sitting position and faced the descending forest from which he and the runner had emerged.

The waiting was long and tense. Yet McAuliff understood that his strongest weapon – perhaps his only viable strength – was calm determination. He was determined; he was not calm.

He was frightened in the same way he had experienced fear before. In the Vietnam jungles; alone, no matter the number of troops. Waiting to witness his own single annihilation.

Pockets of fear.

'It is an extraordinary story, is it not, Dr McAuliff?'

That voice. My God! He knew that voice.

He pressed his arms against the ground and started to whip his head and body around.

His temple crashed into the hard steel of a pistol; the agonizing pain shot through his face and chest. There was a series of bright flashes in front of his eyes as the pain reached a sensory crescendo. It subsided to a numbing ache, and he could feel a trickle of blood on his neck.

'You will remain the way you are while we talk,' said the familiar voice.

Where had he heard it before?

'I know you.'

'You don't *know* me, Dr McAuliff.'

'I've heard your voice ... somewhere.'

'Then you have remarkable recall. So much has happened ... I shall not waste words. Where are Piersall's documents? I am sure it is unnecessary to tell you that your life and the lives of those you brought to Jamaica depend on our having them.'

'How do you know they'd do you any good? What if I told you I had copies made?'

'I would say you were lying. We know the placement of every Xerox machine, every photostat copier, every store, hotel, and individual that does much work along the coast. Including Bueno, the Bays, and Ocho Rios. You have had no copies made.'

'You're not very bright, Mr Halidon ... It is Mr Halidon, isn't it?' There was no response, so Alex continued. 'We photographed them.'

'Then the films are not developed. And the only member of your team possessing a camera is the boy, Ferguson. He is hardly a confidant. ... But this is immaterial, Dr McAuliff. When we say documents, we assume any and all reproductions thereof. Should any surface ... *ever* ... there will be, to put it bluntly, a massacre of innocents. Your survey team, their families, children ... all those held dear by everyone. A cruel and unnecessary prospect.'

... to the last extremity. R. C. Hammond.

'It would be the Halidon's last action, wouldn't it?' McAuliff spoke slowly but sharply, stunned by his own calm. 'A kind of final ... *beau geste* before extinction. If you want it that way, I don't give a damn.'

'*Stop it, McAuliff!*' The voice suddenly screamed, a piercing shriek over the blades of wild grass, its echo muted by the surrounding jungles.

Those words ... they were the words he had heard before!

Stop it. Stop it ... stop it ...

Where? For God's sake, where had he heard them?

His mind raced; images were blurred with blinding colored lights, but he could not focus.

A man. A black man – tall and lithe and muscular ... a man following orders. A man commanding but not with his own commands. The voice that had just roared was the same voice from the past ... *following orders.* In panic ... as before.

Something ...

'You said we would talk. Threats are one-sided conversations; you take turns, you don't talk. I'm not on anybody's side. I want your ... superiors to know that.' Alex held his breath during the silence that followed.

The quiet reply came with measure authority ... and a small but recognizable trace of fear. 'There *are* no superiors as far as you are concerned. My temper is short. These have been difficult days. You should realize that you are very close to losing your life.'

The man with the pistol had moved slightly; Alex could see him now out of the corner of his eye. And what he saw convinced him he was on the track of an immediate truth. The man's head had snapped up at the priest figure; the man with the weapon dangling was questioning the priest figure's words.

'If you kill me . . . or any member of the team, the Halidon will be exposed in a matter of hours.'

Again silence. Again the measured authority; again the now unmistakable undertone of fear. 'And how is this remarkable exposure going to take place, Dr McAuliff?'

Alex drew a deep breath silently. His right hand was clasping his left wrist; he pressed his fingers into his own flesh as he replied.

'In my equipment there is a radio signaling device. It is standard and operates on a frequency that rides above interference. It's functional within a radius of twenty-five miles. Every twelve hours I send out one of two codes; a light on the miniature panel confirms reception and pinpoints location-identification. The first code says everything's normal, no problems. The second says something else. It instructs the man on the receiving end to implement two specific orders: fly the documents out and send help in. The absence of transmissions is the equivalent of the second code, only more so. It alerts all the factions in Kingston, including British Intelligence. They'll be forced in; they'll start with our last location and fan out. The Cock Pit will be swarming with planes and troops . . . I'd better transmit the code, Mr Halidon. And even when I do, you won't know which one I'm sending, will you?' McAuliff stopped for precisely three seconds. And then he said quietly, 'Checkmate, Mr Bones.'

A macaw's screech could be heard in the distance. From somewhere in the wet forests a pride of wild pigs was disturbed. The warm breeze bent the reeds of the tall grass ever so slightly; cicadas were everywhere. All these were absorbed by Alex's senses. And he understood, too, the audible, trembling intake of breath from the darkness behind him. He could feel the mounting, uncontrollable pitch of anger.

'No, mon!' The man with the pistol cried out, lunging forward.

Simultaneously, McAuliff felt the rush of air and heard the rustle of cloth that precedes the instant of impact from behind. Too late to turn; defence only in crouching, hugging the earth.

One man tried to stop the priest figure as he lunged forward; the weight of two furious bodies descended on Alex's shoulders and back. Arms were thrashing, fingers spastically clutched; hard steel and soft cloth and warm flesh enveloped him. He reached above and grasped the first objects his hands touched, yanked with all his strength, and rolled forward.

The priest figure somersaulted over his back; Alex crashed his shoulders downward, rising on one knee for greater weight, and threw himself on the coarse cloth of the caftan. As he pinned the priest, he felt himself instantly pulled backward, with such force that the small of his back arched in pain.

The two Halidonites locked his arms, stretching his chest to the breaking point; the man with the pistol held the barrel to his temple, digging it into his skin.

'That will be *enough*, mon.'

Below him on the ground, the yellow moonlight illuminating a face creased with fury, was the priest figure.

McAuliff instantly understood the bewildering, unfocused images of blinding, colored lights his mind had associated with the panicked words *stop it, stop it.*

He had last seen this 'priest' of the Halidon in London's Soho. During the psychedelic madness that was The Owl of Saint George. The man lying on the ground in a caftan had been dressed in a dark suit then, gyrating on the crowded dance floor. He had screamed at McAuliff, *Stop . . . stop it!* He had delivered a crushing fist into Alex's midsection; he had disappeared into the crowds, only to show up an hour later in a government car on the street by a public telephone.

This 'priest' of the Halidon was an agent of British Intelligence.

'You said your name was Tallon.' McAuliff strained his speech through the pain, the words interrupted by his lack of breath. 'In the car that night you said your name was Tallon. And . . . when I called you on it, you said you were . . . testing me.'

The priest figure rolled over and slowly began to rise. He nodded to the two Halidonites to relax their grips and addressed them. 'I would not have killed him. You know that.'

'You were angry, mon,' said the man who had taken Alex out of the camp.

'Forgive us,' added the man who had cried out and lunged at the priest figure. 'It was necessary.'

The 'priest' smoothed his cassock and tugged at the thick rope around his waist. He looked down at McAuliff. 'Your recollection is sharp, doctor. I sincerely hope your ability to think is equally acute.'

'Does that mean we talk?'

'We talk.'

'My arms hurt like hell. Will you tell your sergeants to let go of me?'

The 'priest' nodded once again, and flicked his wrist in accord. Alex's arms were released; he shook them.

'My sergeants, as you call them, are more temperate men than I. You should be grateful to them.'

The man with the pistol belt demurred, his voice respectful. 'Not so, mon. When did you last sleep?'

'That does not matter. I should have more control . . . My friend refers to a hectic several weeks, McAuliff. Not only did I have to get myself out of England, avoiding Her Majesty's Service, but also a colleague who had disappeared in a Bentley around a Soho corner. A West Indian in London has a thousand hiding places.'

Alex remembered vividly. 'That Bentley tried to run me down. The driver wanted to kill me. Only someone else was killed . . . because of a neon light.'

The priest figure stared at McAuliff. He, too, seemed to recall the evening vividly. 'It was a tragedy born of the instant. We thought a trap had been set, the spring caught at the last moment.'

'Three lives were lost that night. Two with cyanide—'

'We are committed,' interrupted the Halidonite, who looked at his two companions and spoke gently. 'Leave us alone, please.'

In warning, both men removed the weapons from their belts as they pulled Alex to his feet. As ordered, they retreated into the field. McAuliff watched them. A ragged-clothed twosome with the unlikely jackets and pistol belts. 'They not only do as you say, they protect you from yourself.'

The priest figure also looked at his retreating subordinates. 'When we are in our formative years, we are all given batteries of tests. Each is assigned areas of instruction and future responsibility from the results. I often think grave errors are made.' The man tugged at his caftan and turned to McAuliff. 'We must deal now with each other, must we not? As I am sure you have surmised, I was an impermanent member of MI5.'

'An "infiltrator" is the word that comes to mind.'

'A very successful one, doctor. Hammond himself twice recommended me for citations. I was one of the best West Indian specialists. I was reluctant to leave. You – and those manoeuvring you – created the necessity.'

'How?'

'Your survey suddenly contained too many dangerous components. We could live with several, but when we found out that your closest associate on the geological team – Mr Tucker – was apparently a friend of Walter Piersall, we knew we had to keep you under a microscope . . . Obviously, we were too late.'

'What were the other components?'

The priest figure hesitated. He touched his forehead, where a grass burn had developed from his fall to the ground. 'Do you have a cigarette? This very comfortable sheet has one disadvantage: there are no pockets.'

'Why do you wear it?'

'It is a symbol of authority, nothing more.'

McAuliff reached into his pocket, withdrew a pack of cigarettes, and shook one up for the Halidonite. As he lighted it for him, he saw that the black hollows in the very black skin beneath the eyes were stretched in exhaustion. 'What were the dangerous components?'

'Oh, come, doctor, you know them as well as I do.'

'Maybe I don't; enlighten me. Or is that too dangerous, too?'

'Not now. Not at this point. The *reality* is the danger. Piersall's documents are the reality. The . . . components are inconsequential.'

'Then tell me.'

The priest figure inhaled on his cigarette and blew the smoke into the soft breeze of the dull yellow light. 'The woman you know about. There are many who fear her on the Continent. Among those, one of the Dunstone hierarchy . . . the Marquis de Chatellerault. Where she is, so is an arm of the Intelligence service. The boy, Ferguson, is deep with the Craft interests; actually, they fear him. Or did. And rightly so. He never understood the calamitous economic potential of his fiber work.'

'I think he did,' interrupted Alex. 'And he does. He expects to make money out of Craft.'

The Halidonite laughed quietly. 'They will never let him. But he is a component. Where does Craft stand? Is he part of Dunstone? Nothing happens in Jamaica that the soiled hand of Craft has not touched . . . Samuel Tucker I have told you about: his association with the suddenly vital Walter Piersall. Whose summons did he answer? Is he on the island because of his old friend McAuliff? Or his new friend, Piersall? Or is it coincidence?'

'It's coincidence,' said Alex. 'You'd have to know Sam to understand that.'

'But we do not, you see. We only understand that among the first telephone calls he made was one to a man who was disturbing us profoundly. Who was walking around Kingston with the secrets of two hundred years in his brain . . . and somewhere on paper.' The priest figure looked at McAuliff – stared at him, really. His eyes in the moonlight conveyed a supplication for Alex to understand. He looked away and continued. 'Then there is Charles Whitehall. A very . . . *very* dangerous and unpredictable component. You must know his background; Hammond certainly did. Whitehall feels his time on the island has come. His is the hot mysticism of the fanatic. The black Caesar come to ride up Victoria Park on nigger-Pompey's horse. He has followers throughout Jamaica. If there is anyone who might expose Dunstone – wittingly or otherwise – it could well be Whitehall and his fascists.'

'Hammond didn't know that,' protested McAuliff. 'He made it clear that you . . . the Halidon . . . were the only ones who could stop Dunstone.'

'Hammond is a professional. He creates internal chaos, knowing that his breakthrough can come at any instant during the panic. Would it surprise you to know that Hammond is in Kingston now?'

Alex thought for a moment. 'No . . . but I'm surprised he hasn't let me know it.'

'There is a reason. He doesn't want you to fall back on him. He flew in when word was received that Chatellerault was in Savanna-la-Mar . . . You knew *that*, didn't you?'

'*He* knows it because I told Westmore Tallon.'

'And then there are the Jensens. That charming, devoted couple. So normal, so lovable, really . . . who send back word to Julian Warfield of every move you make, of every person you make contact with; who bribe Jamaicans to spy on you . . . The Jensens made a huge mistake once, years ago. Dunstone Limited, stepped in and recruited them. In exchange for obliterating that mistake.'

McAuliff looked up at the clear night sky. A single elongated cloud was drifting from a distant mountain toward the yellow moon. He wondered if the condensation would disappear before it reached the shining satellite, or blur it from beneath . . . envelop it from the ground.

As he was so enveloped.

'So there are the components,' said Alex aimlessly. 'The Halidon knows a lot more than anyone else, it seems. And I'm not sure what that means.'

'It means, doctor, that we are the silent caretakers of our land.'

'I don't recall any election. Who gave you the job?'

'To quote an American writer: "It comes with the territory." It is our heritage. We do not swim in the political rivers, however. We leave those to the legitimate competitors. We *do* try our best to keep the pollution to a minimum.' The priest figure finished his cigarette and crushed the burning end under his sandaled foot.

'You're killers,' said McAuliff simply. 'I know that. I think that's the worst kind of human pollution.'

'Are you referring to Dunstone's previous survey?'

'I am.'

'You don't know the circumstances. And I'm not the one to define them. I am here only to persuade you to give me Piersall's documents.'

'I won't do that.'

'*Why?*' The Halidonite's voice rose in anger, as before. His black eyes above the black hollows pierced into McAuliff's.

'*Mon?*' came the shouted query from the field. The priest figure waved his arm in dismissal.

'This is not your business, McAuliff. Understand that and get out. Give me the documents and take your survey off the island before it is too late.'

'If it was that simple, I would. I don't *want* your fight, goddammit. It has no appeal for me ... On the other hand, I don't relish being chased all over the globe by Julian Warfield's guns. Can't *you* understand *that?*'

The priest figure stood immobile. His eyes softened; his lips parted in concentration as he stared at Alexander. He spoke slowly; he was barely audible. 'I warned them that it might come to this. Give me the *nagarro*, doctor. What is the meaning of the Halidon?'

McAuliff told him.

26

They returned to the river campsite, McAuliff and the runner who had assumed the name and function of Marcus Hedrik. There was no pretense now. As they neared the bivouac area, black men in rags could be seen in the bush, the early dawn light shafting through the dense foliage, intermittently reflecting off the barrels of their weapons.

The survey camp was surrounded, the inhabitants prisoners of the Halidon.

A hundred yards from the clearing, the runner – now preceding Alex on the narrow jungle path, pistol secure in his field-jacket belt – stopped and summoned a Halidon patrol. He did so by snapping his fingers repeatedly until a large black man emerged from between the trees.

The two men spoke briefly, quietly, and when they were finished the patrol returned to his post in the tropic forest. The runner turned to McAuliff.

'Everything is peaceful. There was a skirmish with Charles Whitehall, but it was anticipated. He severely wounded the guard, but others were nearby. He is bound and back in his tent.'

'What about Mrs Booth?'

'The woman? She is with Samuel Tucker. She was asleep a half-hour ago . . . That Tucker, he will not sleep. He sits in the chair in front of his tent, a rifle in his hands. The others are quiet. They will be rising soon.'

'Tell me,' said Alex while the runner still faced him, 'what happened to all that Arawak language? The Maroon colonel, the units of four, the eight days?'

'You forgot, doctor. I led the Whitehall-mon to his courier. The Colonel of the Maroons never got the message. The reply you received came from us.' The runner smiled. Then he turned, gesturing for Alex to follow him into the clearing.

Under the eyes of the runner, McAuliff waited for the white light of the miniature panel to reach full illumination. When it did, he pressed the signal-transmitter button, holding his left hand over his fingers as he did so. He knew the concealment was unnecessary; he would not radio for aid. He would not jam the frequency with cries of emergency. It had been made clear that at the first sight of hostile forces, each member of the survey would be shot through the head, Alison Booth and Sam Tucker the first to be executed.

The remainder of the understanding was equally clear. Sam Tucker would continue to send the signals every twelve hours. Alexander would return with the runner into the grassland. From there, with the 'priest' he would be taken to the hidden community of the Halidon. Until he returned, the team was a collective hostage.

Alison, Sam, Charles Whitehall, and Lawrence would be told the truth. The others would not. The Jensens, James Ferguson, and the crew would be given another explanation, a bureaucratic one readily acceptable to professional surveyors: During the night a radio message from Kingston had been relayed by Falmouth; the Ministry of the Interior required McAuliff's presence in Ocho Rios; there were difficulties with the Institute. It was the sort of complication to which survey directors were subjected. Fieldwork was constantly interrupted by administrative foul-ups.

When the priest figure suggested the time of absence be no less than three full days, Alex demanded to know the reason for so long a period.

'I can't answer that, McAuliff.'

'Then why should I agree to it?'

'It is only time. Then, too, are we not at checkmate . . . Mr Bones? We fear exposure perhaps more than you fear for your lives.'

'I won't concede that.'

'You do not know us. Give yourself the margin to learn. You will not be disappointed.'

'You were told to say three days, then?'

'I was.'

'Which presumes that whoever told you to say it expected you to bring me to them.'

'It was a distinct probability.'

Alexander agreed to three full days.

Lawrence, was rubbing a penicillin salve over Charles Whitehall's bare back. The rope burns were deep; whoever had lashed Charley-mon had done so in fever-pitch anger. The ropes on both men had been removed after McAuliff's talk with them. Alexander had made it clear he would brook no further interference. Their causes were expendable.

'Your arrogance is beyond understanding, McAuliff!' said Charles Whitehall, suppressing a grimace as Lawrence touched a sensitive burn.

'I accept the rebuke. You're very qualified in that department.'

'You are not *equipped* to deal with these people. I have spent my life, my *entire life*, stripping away the layers of Jamaican – Caribbean – history!'

'Not your entire life, Charley,' replied Alex, calmly but incisively. 'I told you last night. There's the little matter of your extrascholastic activity. "The black Caesar riding up Victoria Park on nigger-Pompey's horse."'

'*What?*'

'They're not my words, Charley.'

Lawrence suddenly pressed his fist into a raw lash mark on Whitehall's shoulder. The scholar arched back his neck in pain. The revolutionary's other hand was close to his throat. Neither man moved; Lawrence spoke. 'You don't ride no nigger horse, mon. You den walk like everybody else.'

Charles Whitehall stared over his shoulder at the blur of the brutal, massive hand poised for assault. 'You play the fool, you know. Do you think any political entity with a power structure based on wealth will tolerate *you*? Not for a minute, you egalitarian jackal. You will be crushed.'

'You do not seek to crush us, mon?'

'I seek only what is best for Jamaica. Everyone's energies will be used to that end.'

'You're a regular Pollyanna,' broke in Alex, walking toward the two men.

Lawrence looked up at McAuliff, his expression equal parts of suspicion and dependence. He removed his hand and reached for the tube of penicillin salve. 'Put on your shirt, mon. Your skin is covered,' he said, twisting the small cap onto the medicine tube.

'I'm leaving in a few minutes,' said McAuliff, standing in front of Whitehall. 'Sam will be in charge; you're to do as he says. Insofar as possible, the work is to continue normally. The Halidon will stay out of sight . . . at least as far as the Jensens and Ferguson are concerned.'

'How can that be?' asked Lawrence.

'It won't be difficult,' answered Alex. 'Peter is drilling for gas-pocket sediment a mile and a half southwest. Ruth is due east in a quarry; the runner we know as Justice will be with her. Ferguson is across the river working some fern groves. All are separated, each will be watched.'

'And me?' Whitehall buttoned his expensive cotton safari shirt as though dressing for a concert at Covent Garden. 'What do you propose for me?'

'You're confined to the clearing, Charley-mon. For your own sake, don't try to leave it. I can't be responsible if you do.'

'You think you have any say about anything now, McAuliff?'

'Yes, I do. They're as much afraid of me as I am of them. Just don't try to upset the balance, either of you. I buried a man on an Alaskan job a number of years ago. Sam will tell you, I know the standard prayers.'

Alison stood on the riverbank, looking down at the water. The heat of the early sun was awakening the late sleepers of the forest. The sounds were those of combative foraging; flyer against flyer, crawler fighting crawler. The green vines dangling from the tall macca-fat palms glistened with the moisture rising from below; fern and moss and matted cabbage growth bordered the slowly flowing currents of the Martha Brae offshoot. The water was morning-clear, bluish-green.

'I went to your tent,' said McAuliff, walking up to her. 'Sam said you were out here.'

She turned and smiled. 'I wasn't really disobeying, my darling. I'm not running anywhere.'

'Nowhere to go. You'll be all right . . . The runner's waiting for me.'

Alison took two steps and stood in front of him. She spoke quietly, barely above a whisper. 'I want to tell you something, Alexander T. McAuliff. And I refuse to be dramatic or tearful or anything remotely theatrical because those are crutches and both of us can walk without them. Six weeks ago I was running. Quite desperately, trying my goddamnedest to convince myself that by running I was escaping – which I knew underneath was absurd. In Kingston I told you how absurd it was. They can find you. Anywhere. The computers, the data banks, the horrid, complicated tracers they have in their cellars and in their hidden rooms are too real now. Too thorough. And there is no life underground, in remote places, always wondering. I don't expect you to understand this, and, in a way, it's why what you're doing is right . . . "Do unto others *before* they do unto you." That's what you said. I believe that's a terrible way to think. And I also believe it's the only way we're going to have a life of our own.'

McAuliff touched her face with his fingers. Her eyes were bluer than he had ever seen them. 'That sounds dangerously like a proposal.'

'My wants are simple, my expressions uncomplicated. And, as you said once, I'm a damned fine professional.'

'"McAuliff and Booth. Surveyors. Offices: London and New York." That'd look good on the letterhead.'

'You wouldn't consider "Booth and McAuliff"? I mean, alphabetically—'

'No, I wouldn't,' he interrupted gently as he put his arms around her.

'Do people always say silly things when they're afraid?' she asked, her face buried in his chest.

'I think so,' he replied.

Peter Jensen reached down into the full pack and felt his way among the soft articles of clothing. The canvas was stuffed. Jensen winced as he slid the object of his search up the sides of the cloth.

It was the Luger. It was wrapped in plastic, the silencer detached, tied to the barrel in plastic also.

His wife stood by the entrance flap of their tent, the slit folded back just sufficiently for her to look outside. Peter unwrapped both sections of the weapon and put the silencer in the pocket of his field jacket. He pressed the release, slid out the magazine, and reached into his other pocket for a box of cartridges. Methodically he inserted the magazine until the spring was taut, the top bullet ready for chamber insertion. He slid the magazine back into the handle slot and cracked it into position.

Ruth heard the metallic click and turned around. 'Do you have to do this?'

'Yes. Julian was very clear. McAuliff was my selection, his concurrence a result of that choice. McAuliff's made contact. With whom? With what? I must find out.' Peter pulled open his jacket and shoved the Luger down between a triangle of leather straps sewn into the lining. He buttoned the field jacket and stood up straight. 'Any bulges, old girl? Does it show?'

'No.'

'Good. Hardly the fit of Whitehall's uniform, but I dare say a bit more comfortable.'

'You will be careful? It's so dreadful out there.'

'All that camping you dragged me on had a purpose. I see that now, my dear.' Peter smiled and returned to his pack, pushing down the contents, pulling the straps into buckling position. He inserted the prongs, tugged once more, and slapped the bulging outsides. He lifted the canvas sack by the shoulder harness and let it fall to the dirt. 'There! I'm set for a fortnight if need be.'

'How will I know?'

'When I don't come back with my carrier. If I pull it off right, he might even be too petrified to return himself.' Peter saw the tremble on his wife's lips, the terrible fear in her eyes. He motioned for her to come to him, which she did. Rushing into his arms.

'Oh, God, *Peter—*'

'Please, Ruth. *Shhh.* You mustn't,' he said, stroking her hair. 'Julian has been everything to us. We both know that. And Julian thinks we'd be very happy at Peale Court. Dunstone will need many people in Jamaica, he said. Why not us?'

When the unknown carrier came into camp, James Ferguson could see that the runner he knew as Marcus Hedrik was as angry as he was curious. They were all curious. McAuliff had left early that morning for the coast; it seemed strange that the carrier had not met him on the river. The carrier insisted he had seen no one but wandering hill people, some fishing, some hunting – no white man.

The carrier had been sent by the Government Employment Office, a branch in Falmouth that knew the survey was looking for additional hands. The carrier was familiar with the river offshoot, having grown up in Weston Favel, and was anxious for work. Naturally, he had the proper papers, signed by some obscure functionary at G.E.O., Falmouth.

At two thirty in the afternoon, James Ferguson, having rested after lunch, sat on the edge of his cot, prepared to gather up his equipment and head back into the field. There was a rustling outside his tent. He looked up, and the new carrier suddenly slapped open the flap and walked in. He was carrying a plastic tray.

'I say—'

'I pick up dishes, mon,' said the carrier rapidly. 'Alla time be very neat.'

'I have no dishes here. There's a glass or two need washing . . .'

The carrier lowered his voice. 'I got message for Fergomon. I give it to you. You read it quick.' The runner reached into his pocket and withdrew a sealed envelope. He handed it to Ferguson.

James ripped the back and pulled out a single page of stationery. It was the stationery of the Craft Foundation, and Ferguson's eyes were immediately pulled to the signature. It was known throughout Jamaica – the scrawl of

Arthur Craft Senior, the semiretired but all-powerful head of the Craft enterprises.

My dear James Ferguson:

Apologies from a distance are always most awkward and often the most sincere. Such is the present case.

My son has behaved badly, for which he, too, offers his regrets. He sends them from the South of France where he will be residing for an indeterminate – but long – period of time.

To the point: your contributions in our laboratories on the baracoa experiments were immense. They led the way to what we believe can be a major breakthrough that can have a widespread industrial impact. We believe this breakthrough can be accelerated by your immediate return to us. Your future is assured, young man, in the way all genius should be rewarded. You will be a very wealthy man.

However, time is of the essence. Therefore I recommend that you leave the survey forthwith – the messenger will explain the somewhat odd fashion of departure but you may be assured that I have apprised Kingston of my wishes and they are in full agreement. (The baracoa is for all Jamaica.) We're also in mutual agreement that it is unnecessary to involve the survey director, Dr McAuliff, as his immediate interests are rightfully in conflict with ours. A substitute botanist will join the survey within a matter of days.

I look forward to renewing our acquaintance.
Very truly yours,
Arthur Craft Senior

James Ferguson held his breath in astonishment as he reread the letter.
He had done it.
He had really done it.
Everything.
He looked up at the carrier, who smiled and spoke softly.
'We leave late afternoon, mon. Before dark. Come back early from your work. I will meet you on the riverbank and we will go.'

27

The priest figure identified himself by the single name of Malcolm. They traveled south on hidden routes that alternated between steep rocky climbs, winding grottoes, and dense jungle. The Halidonite in the ragged clothes and the field jacket led the way, effortlessly finding concealed paths in the forests and covered openings that led through long dark tunnels of ancient stone – the dank smell of deep grotto waters ever present, the bright reflection of stalactites, suspended in alabaster isolation, caught in the beams of flashlights.

It seemed to McAuliff that at times they were descending into the cellars of the earth, only to emerge from the darkness of a grotto onto higher ground. A geological phenomenon, tunneled caves that inexorably progressed upward, evidence of oceanic-terrestrial upheavals that bespoke an epoch of incredible geophysical combustion. The cores of mountains rising out of the faults and trenches, doing infinite battle to reach the heat of the sun.

Twice they passed hill communities by circling above them on ridges at the edge of the forest. Malcolm both times identified the sects, telling of their particular beliefs and the religious justification for their withdrawal from the outside world. He explained that there were approximately twenty-three Cock Pit communities dedicated to isolation. The figure had to be approximate, for there was ever present the rebellion of youth who found in their intermittent journeys to the marketplace temptations outweighing the threats of Obeah. Strangely enough, as one community, or two or three, disintegrated, there were always others that sprang up to take their places . . . and often their small villages.

'The "opiate of the people" is often an escape from simple hardship and the agonizing pointlessness of the coastal towns.'

'Then eliminate the pointlessness.' Alex remembered the sights of Old Kingston, the corrugated tin shacks across from the abandoned, filthy barges peopled by outcasts; the emaciated dogs, the bone-thin cats, the eyes of numbed futility on the young-old women. The man with no teeth praying for the price of a pint of wine, defecating in the shadows of dark alleys.

And three blocks above, the shining, immaculate banks with their shining, tinted windows. Shining, immaculate, and obscene in their choice of location.

'Yes, you are right,' replied Malcolm the Halidonite. 'It is the pointlessness that erodes the people most rapidly. It is so easy to say "give meaning". And so difficult to know how. So many complications.'

They continued their journey for eight hours, resting after difficult sections of jungle and steep clifflike inclines and endless caves. McAuliff judged that they had gone no further than seventeen, perhaps eighteen miles into the Cock Pit country, each mile more treacherous and enervating than the last.

Shortly after five in the afternoon, while high in the Flagstaff range, they came to the end of a mountain pass. Suddenly in front of them was a plateau of grassland about a half mile long and no more than five hundred yards wide. The plateau fronted the banks of a mountain cliff, at three-quarters altitude. Malcolm led them to the right, to the western edge. The slope of the plateau descended into thick jungle, as dense and forbidding as any McAuliff had ever seen.

'That is called the Maze of Acquaba,' said Malcolm, seeing the look of astonishment on Alex's face. 'We have borrowed a custom from ancient Sparta. Each male child, on his eleventh birthday, is taken into the core and must remain for a period of four days and nights.'

'Units of four . . .' McAuliff spoke as much to himself as to Malcolm as he stared down at the unbelievably cruel density of jungle beneath. 'The odyssey of death.'

'We're neither that Spartan nor Arawak,' said Malcolm, laughing softly. 'The children do not realize it, but there are others with them . . . Come.'

The two Halidonites turned and started toward the opposite ledge of the plateau. Alex took a last look at the Maze of Acquaba and joined them.

At the eastern edge, the contradictory effect was immediate.

Below was a valley no more than a half a mile in length, perhaps a mile wide, in the center of which was a quiet lake. The valley itself was enclosed by hills that were the first inclines of the mountains beyond. On the north side were mountain streams converging into a high waterfall that cascaded down into a relatively wide, defined avenue of water.

On the far side of the lake were fields – pastures, for there were cattle grazing lazily. Cows, goats, a few burros, and several horses. This area had been cleared and seeded – generations ago, thought Alex.

On the near side of the lake, below them, were thatched huts, protected by tall ceiba trees. At first glance, there seemed to be seventy or eighty such dwellings. They were barely visible because of the trees and arcing vines and dense tropical foliage that filled whatever spaces might have been empty with the bright colors of the Caribbean. A community roofed by nature, thought Alex.

Then he pictured the sight from the air. Not as he was seeing it, on a vertical-diagonal, but from above, from a plane. The village – and it was a village – would look like any number of isolated hill communities with thatched roofs and nearby grazing fields. But the difference was in the surrounding mountains. The plateau was an indentation formed at high altitude. This section of the Flagstaff range was filled with harsh updrafts and uncontrollable wind variants; jets would remain at a twelve-thousand-foot minimum, light aircraft would avoid direct overhead. The first would have no place to land, the second would undoubtedly crash if it attempted to do so.

The community was protected by natural phenomena above it and by a tortuous passage on the ground that could never be defined on a map.

'Not very prepossessing, is it?' Malcolm stood next to McAuliff. A stream of children were running down a bordered path toward the lake, their shouts carried on the wind. Natives could be seen walking around the huts; larger groups strolled by the avenue of water that flowed from the waterfall.

'It's all . . . very neat.' It was the only word McAuliff could think of at the moment.

'Yes,' replied the Halidonite. 'It's orderly. Come, let's go down. There is a man waiting for you.'

The runner-guide led them down the rocky slope. Five minutes later the three of them were on the western level of the thatched community. From above Alex had not fully realized the height of the trees that were on all sides of the primitive dwellings. Thick vines sloped and twisted, immense ferns sprayed out of the ground and from within dark recesses of the underbrush.

Had the view from the plateau above been fifty feet high, thought McAuliff, none of what he had seen would have been visible.

Roofed by nature.

The guide started across a path that seemed to intersect a cluster of huts within the junglelike area.

The inhabitants were dressed, like most Jamaican hill people, in a variety of soft, loose clothing, but there was something different that McAuliff could not at first discern. There was a profusion of rolled-up khaki trousers and dark-colored skirts and white cotton shirts and printed blouses – all normal, all seen throughout the island. Seen really in all outback areas – Africa, Australia, New Zealand – where the natives had taken what they could – stolen what they could – of the white invaders' protective comforts. Nothing unusual . . . but something was very different, and Alex was damned if he could pinpoint that difference.

And then he did so. At the same instant that he realized there was something else he had been observing. Books.

A few – three of four or five, perhaps – of the dozens of natives within this jungle community were carrying books. Carrying *books* under their arms and in their hands.

And the clothing was *clean*. It was as simple as that. There were stains of wetness, of sweat, obviously, and the dirt of fieldwork and the mud of the lake, but there was a cleanliness, a neatness, that was *not* usual in the hill or outback communities. Africa, Australia, New Guinea, or Jacksonville, Florida.

It was a normal sight to see clothing worn by natives in varying stages of disrepair – torn, ripped, even shredded. But the garments worn by these hill people were whole, untorn, unripped.

Not castoffs, not ill-fitting stolen property.

The Tribe of Acquaba was deep within a jungle primeval but it was not – like so many of the isolated hill people – a worn-out race of poverty-stricken primitives scratching a bare subsistence from the land.

Along the paths and around the dwellings Alex could see strong black bodies and clear black eyes, the elements of balanced diets and sharp intelligence.

'We shall go directly to Daniel,' said Malcolm to the guide. 'You are relieved now. And thank you.'

The guide turned right, down a dirt path that seemed to be tunneled under a dense web of thick jungle vines. He was removing his pistol belt, unbuttoning his field jacket. The commando was home, reflected McAuliff. He could take off his costume – so purposely ragged.

Malcolm gestured, interrupting Alex's thought. The path on which they had been walking under an umbrella of macca-fats and ceibas veered left into a clearing of matted spider grass. This open area extended beyond the conduit of rushing water that shot out from the base of the high waterfall streaming down the mountain. On the other side of the wide, banked gully the ground sloped toward a barricade of rock; beyond were the grazing fields that swung right, bordering the eastern shore of the lake.

In the huge pasture, men could be seen walking with staffs toward the clusters of livestock. It was late afternoon, the heat of the sun was lessening. It was time to shelter the cattle for the night, thought McAuliff.

He had been absently following Malcolm, more concerned with observing everything he could of the strange, isolated village, when he realized where the Halidonite was leading them.

Toward the base of the mountain and the waterfall.

They reached the edge of the lake-feeding channel and turned left. Alex saw that the conduit of water was deeper than it appeared from a distance. The banks were about eight feet in height; the definition he had seen from the plateau was a result of carefully placed rocks, embedded in the earth of the embankments. This natural phenomenon had been controlled by man, like the seeded fields, generations ago.

There were three crossings of wooden planks with waist-high railings, each buttressed into the sides of the embankments, where there were stone steps . . . placed many decades ago. The miniature bridges were spaced about fifty yards apart.

Then McAuliff saw it; barely saw it, as it was concealed behind a profusion of tall trees, immense giant fern, and hundreds of flowering vines at the base of the mountain.

It was a wooden structure. A large cabinlike dwelling whose base straddled the channel, the water rushing out from under the huge pilings that supported the hidden edifice. On each side of the pilings were steps – again in stone, again placed generations ago – that led up to a wide catwalk fronting the building. In the center of the planked catwalk was a door. It was closed.

From any distance – certainly from the air – the building was completely concealed.

Its length was perhaps thirty feet, its width impossible to determine, as it seemed to disappear into the jungle and the crashing waterfall.

As they approached the stone steps, McAuliff saw something else, which so startled him that he had to stop and stare.

On the west side of the building, emerging from within and scaling upward into the tangling mass of foliage, were thick black cables.

Malcolm turned and smiled at Alex's astonishment. 'Our contact with the outside, McAuliff. Radio signals that are piped into telephone trunk lines throughout the island. Not unlike cellular phones, but generally much clearer than the usual telephone service. All untraceable, of course. Now let us see Daniel.'

'Who is Daniel?'

'He is our Minister of Council. He is an elective office. Except that his term is not guided by the calendar.'

'Who elects him?'

The Halidonite's smile faded somewhat. 'The council.'

'Who elects *it*?'

'The tribe.'

'Sounds like regular politics.'

'Not exactly,' said Malcolm enigmatically. 'Come. Daniel's waiting.'

The Halidonite opened the door, and McAuliff walked into a large high-ceilinged room with windows all around the upper wall. The sounds of the waterfall could be heard; these were mingled with the myriad noises of the jungle outside.

There were wooden chairs – chairs fashioned by hand, not machinery. In the center of the back wall, in front of a second, very large, thick door was a table, at which sat a black girl in her late twenties. On her 'desk' were papers, and at her left was a word processor on a white computer table. The incongruity of such equipment in such a place caused Alex to stare.

And then he swallowed as he saw a telephone – a sophisticated, push-button console – on a stand to the girl's right.

'This is Jeanine, Dr McAuliff. She works for Daniel.'

The girl stood, her smile brief and tenuous. She acknowledged Alex with a hesitant nod; her eyes were concerned as she spoke to Malcolm. 'Was the trip all right?'

'Since I brought back our guest, I cannot say it was wildly successful.'

'Yes,' replied Jeanine, her expression of concern now turned to fear. 'Daniel wants to see you right away. This way ... Dr McAuliff.'

The girl crossed to the door and rapped twice. Without waiting for a reply, she twisted the knob and opened it. Malcolm came alongside Alex and gestured him inside. McAuliff walked hesitantly through the door frame and into the office of the Halidon's Minister of Council.

The room was large, with a single, enormous leaded-glass window taking up most of the rear wall. The view was both strange and awesome. Twenty feet beyond the glass was the midsection of the waterfall; it took up the entire area; there was nothing but endless tons of crashing water, its sound muted but discernible. In front of the window was a long, thick hatch table, its dark wood glistening. Behind it stood the man named Daniel, Minister of Council.

He was a Jamaican with sharp Afro-European features, slightly more than medium height and quite slender. His shoulders were broad, however; his body tapered like that of a long-distance runner. He was in his early forties, perhaps. It was difficult to tell: his face had lean youth, but his eyes were not young.

He smiled – briefly, cordially, but not enthusiastically – at McAuliff and came around the table, his hand extended.

As he did so, Alex saw that Daniel wore white casual slacks and a dark blue shirt open at the neck. Around his throat was a white silk kerchief, held together by a gold ring. It was a kind of uniform, thought Alex. As Malcolm's robes were a uniform.

'Welcome, doctor. I will not ask you about your trip. I have made it too many times myself. It's a bitch.'

Daniel shook McAuliff's hand. 'It's a bitch,' said Alex warily.

The minister abruptly turned to Malcolm. 'What's the report? I can't think of any reason to give it privately. Or is there?'

'No ... Piersall's documents are valid. They're sealed, and McAuliff has them ready to fly out from a location within a twenty-five-mile radius of the Martha Brae base camp. Even he doesn't know where. We have three days, Daniel.'

The minister started at the priest figure. Then he walked slowly back to his chair behind the hatch table without speaking. He stood immobile, his hands on the surface of the wood, and looked up at Alex.

'So by the brilliant persistence of an expatriate island fanatic we face ... castration. Exposure renders us impotent, you know, Dr McAuliff. We will be plundered. Stripped of our possessions. And the responsibility is yours ... *you*. A geologist in the employ of Dunstone Limited. And a most unlikely recruit in the service of British Intelligence.' Daniel looked over at Malcolm. 'Leave us alone, please. And be ready to start out for Montego.'

'When?'

'That will depend on our visitor. He will be accompanying you.'

'I *will*?'

'Yes, Dr McAuliff. If you are alive.'

28

'There is but a single threat one human being can make against another that must be listened to. That threat is obviously the taking of life.' Daniel had walked to the enormous window framing the cascading, unending columns of water. 'In the absence of overriding ideological issues, usually associated with religion or national causes, I think you will agree.'

'And because I'm not motivated religiously or nationally, you expect the threat to succeed.' McAuliff remained standing in front of the long, glistening hatch table. He had not been offered a chair.

'Yes,' replied the Halidon's Minister of Council, turning from the window. 'I am sure it has been said to you before that Jamaica's concerns are not your concerns.'

'It's ... "not my war" is the way it was phrased.'

'Who said that to you? Charles Whitehall or Barak Moore?'

'Barak Moore is dead,' said Alex.

The minister was obviously surprised. His reaction, however, was a brief moment of thoughtful silence. Then he spoke quietly. 'I am sorry. His was a necessary check to Whitehall's thrust. His faction has no one else, really. Someone will have to be brought up to take his place ...' Daniel walked to the table, reached down for a pencil, and wrote a note on a small pad. He tore off the page and put it to the side.

McAuliff saw without difficulty the words the minister had written. They were: 'Replace Barak Moore.' In this day of astonishments, the implication of the message was not inconsiderable.

'Just like that?' asked Alex, nodding his head in the direction of the page of notepaper.

'It will not be simple, if that is what you mean,' replied Daniel. 'Sit down, Dr McAuliff. I think it is time you understood. Before we go further ...'

Alexander Tarquin McAuliff, geologist, with a company on 38th Street in New York City, United States of America, sat down in a native-made chair in an office room high in the inaccessible mountains of the Flagstaff range, deep within the core of the impenetrable Cock Pit country on the island of Jamaica, and listened to a man called Daniel, Minister of Council for a covert sect with the name Halidon.

He could not think any longer. He could only listen.

Daniel covered the initial groundwork rapidly. He asked Alex if he had read Walter Piersall's papers. McAuliff nodded.

The minister then proceeded to confirm the accuracy of Piersall's studies by tracing the Tribe of Acquaba from its beginnings in the Maroon wars in the early eighteenth century.

'Acquaba was something of a mystic, but essentially a simple man. A Christ figure without the charity or extremes of mercy associated with the Jesus beliefs. After all, his forebears were born to the violence of the Coromanteen jungles. But his ethics were sound.'

'What is the source of your wealth?' asked Alex, his faculties returning. 'If there *is* wealth. And a source.'

'Gold,' replied Daniel simply.

'Where?'

'In the ground. On our lands.'

'There is no gold in Jamaica.'

'You are a geologist. You know better than that. There are traces of crystalline deposit in scores of minerals throughout the island—'

'Infinitesimal,' broke in McAuliff. 'Minute, and so impacted with worthless ores as to make any attempt at separation prohibitive. More expensive than the product.'

'But ... gold, nevertheless.'

'Worthless.'

Daniel smiled. 'How do you think the crystalline traces became impacted? I might even ask you – theoretically, if you like – how the island of Jamaica came to be.'

'As any isolated landmass in the oceans. Geologic upheavals—' Alex stopped. The theory was beyond imagination, made awesome because of its simplicity. A section of a vein of gold, millions upon millions of years ago, exploding out of the layers of earth beneath the sea, impacting deposits through the mass that was disgorged out of the waters. 'My God ... there's a vein ...'

'There is no point in pursuing this,' said Daniel. 'For centuries the colonial law of Jamaica spelled out an absolute: all precious metals discovered on the island were the possession of the Crown. It was the primary reason no one searched.'

'*Fowler*,' said McAuliff softly. 'Jeremy Fowler ...'

'I beg your pardon?'

'The Crown Recorder in Kingston. More than a hundred years ago ...'

Daniel paused. 'Yes. In 1883, to be exact. So that was Piersall's fragment.' The minister of the Halidon wrote on another page of notepaper. 'It will be removed.'

'This Fowler,' said Alex softly. 'Did he know?'

Daniel looked up from the paper, tearing it off the pad as he did so. 'No. He believed he was carrying out the wishes of a dissident faction of Maroons conspiring with a group of north-coast landowners. The object was to destroy the records of a tribal treaty so thousands of acres could be cleared for plantations. It was what he was told and what he was paid for.'

'The family in England still believes it.'

'Why not? It was' – the minister smiled – '*Colonial Service.* Shall we return to more currently applicable questions? You see, Dr McAuliff, we want you to understand. *Thoroughly.*'

'Go ahead.'

According to Daniel, the Halidon had no ambitions for political power. It never had such ambitions; it remained outside the body politic, accepting the historical view that order emerges out of the chaos of different, even conflicting ideologies. Ideas were greater monuments than cathedrals, and a people must have free access to them. That was the lesson of Acquaba. Freedom of mobility, freedom of thought ... freedom to do battle, if need be. The religion of the Halidon was essentially humanist, its jungle gods symbols of continuously struggling forces battling for the mortals' freedom. Freedom to survive in the world in the manner agreed upon within the tribe, without imposing that manner on the other tribes.

'Not a bad premise, is it?' asked Daniel confidently, again rapidly.

'No,' answered McAuliff. 'And not particularly original, either.'

'I disagree,' said the minister. 'The thoughts may have a hundred precedents, but the practice is almost unheard of ... Tribes, as they develop self-sufficiency, tend to graduate to the point where they are anxious to impose themselves on as many other tribes as possible. From the pharaohs to Caesar; from the Empire – several empires, Holy Roman, British, et cetera – to Adolf Hitler; from Stalin to your own conglomeratized government of self-righteous proselytizers. Beware the pious believers, McAuliff. They were all pious in their fashions. Too many are still.'

'But you're not.' Alex looked over at the enormous leaded glass and the rushing, plummeting water beyond. 'You just decide who is ... and act accordingly. Free to "do battle", as you call it.'

'You think that is a contradiction of purpose?'

'You're damned right I do. When "doing battle" includes killing people ... because they don't conform to your idea of what's acceptable.'

'Whom have we killed?'

Alex shifted his gaze from the waterfall to Daniel. 'I can start with last night. Two carriers on the survey who were probably picking up a few dollars from British Intelligence; for what? Keeping their eyes open? Reporting what we had for dinner? Who came to see us? Your runner, the one I called Marcus, said they were agents; he killed them. And a fat pig named Garvey, who was a pretty low-level, uniformed liaison and, I grant you, smelled bad. But I think a fatal accident on the road to Port Maria was a bit drastic.' McAuliff paused for a moment and leaned forward in the chair. 'You massacred an entire survey team – every member – and for all you know, they were hired by Dunstone the same way I was: just looking for work. Now, maybe you can justify all those killings, but neither you nor anyone else can justify the death of Walter Piersall ... Yes, Mr High and Mighty Minister, I think you're pretty violently pious yourself.'

Daniel had sat down in the chair behind the hatch table during Alex's angry narrative. He now pushed his foot against the floor, sending the chair gently to his right, toward the huge window. 'Over a hundred years ago, this office was the entire building. One of my early predecessors had it placed here. He insisted that the minister's room – "chamber", it was called then – overlook this section of our waterfall. He claimed the constant movement and the muffled sound forced a man to concentrate, blocked out small considerations ... That long-forgotten rebel proved right. I never cease to wonder at the different bursts of shapes and patterns. And while wondering, the mind really concentrates.'

'Is that your way of telling me those who were killed were ... small considerations?'

Daniel pushed the chair back in place and faced McAuliff. 'No, doctor. I was trying to think of a way to convince you. I shall tell you the truth, but I am not sure you will believe it. Our runners, our guides – our infiltrators, if you will – are trained to use *effect* wherever possible. Fear, McAuliff, is an extraordinary weapon. A nonviolent weapon; not that we are necessarily nonviolent ... Your carriers are not dead. They were taken prisoner, blindfolded, led to the outskirts of Weston Favel, and released. They were not hurt, but they were frightened severely. They will not work for MI5 or MI6 again. Garvey *is* dead, but we did not kill him. Your Mr Garvey sold anything he could get his hands on, including women, especially young girls. He was shot on the road to Port Maria by a distraught father, the motive obvious. We simply took the credit ... You say we massacred the Dunstone survey. Reverse that, doctor. Three of the four white men tried to massacre our scouting party. They killed six of our young men after asking them into the camp for conference.'

'One of those ... white men was a British agent.'

'So Malcolm tells us.'

'I don't believe a trained Intelligence man would kill indiscriminately.'

'Malcolm agrees with you. But the facts are there. An Intelligence agent is a man first. In the sudden pitch of battle, a man takes sides. This man, whichever one he was, chose his side ... He did not have to choose the way he did.'

'The fourth man? He was different, then?'

'Yes.' Daniel's eyes were suddenly reflective. 'He was a good man. A Hollander. When he realized what the others were doing, he objected violently. He ran out to warn the rest of our party. His own men shot him.'

For several moments, neither men spoke. Finally McAuliff asked, 'What about Walter Piersall? Can you find a story for that?'

'No,' said Daniel. 'We do not know what happened. Or who killed him. We have ideas, but nothing more. Walter Piersall was the last man on earth we wanted dead. Especially under the circumstances. And if you do not understand that, then you're stupid.'

McAuliff got out of the chair and walked aimlessly to the huge window. He could feel Daniel's eyes on him. He forced himself to watch the crashing streams of water in front of him. 'Why did you bring me here? Why have you told me so much? About you ... and everything else.'

'We had no choice. Unless you lied or unless Malcolm was deceived, neither of which I believe ... And we understand your position as well as your background. When Malcolm flew out of England, he brought with him MI5's complete dossier on you. We are willing to make you an offer.'

Alex turned and looked down at the minister. 'I'm sure it's one I can't refuse.'

'Not readily. Your life. And, not incidentally, the lives of your fellow surveyors.'

'Piersall's documents?'

'Somewhat more extensive, but those, too, of course,' answered Daniel.

'Go on.' McAuliff remained by the window. The muted sound of the waterfall was his connection to the outside somehow. It was comforting.

'We know what the British want: the list of names that comprise the Dunstone hierarchy. The international financiers that fully expect to turn this island into an economic sanctuary, another Switzerland. Not long ago, a matter of weeks, they gathered here on this island from all over the world. In Port Antonio. A few used their real names, most did not. The timing is propitious. The Swiss banking institutions are breaking down their traditional codes of account-secrecy one after another. They are under extraordinary pressures, of course ... We have the Dunstone list. We will make an exchange.'

'It for our lives? And the documents ...'

Daniel laughed, neither cruelly nor kindly. It was a genuine expression of humor. 'Doctor, I am afraid it is you who are obsessed with small considerations. It is true we place great value on Piersall's documents, but the British do not. We must think as our adversaries think. The British want the Dunstone list above all things. And above all things, we want British Intelligence, and everything it represents, out of Jamaica. That is the exchange we offer.'

McAuliff stood motionless by the window. 'I don't understand you.'

The minister leaned forward. 'We demand an end to English influence ... as we demand an end to the influence of all other nations – *tribes*, if you wish, doctor – over this island. In short words, Jamaica is to be left to the Jamaicans.'

'Dunstone wouldn't leave it to you,' said Alex, groping. 'I'd say its influence was a hell of a lot more dangerous than anyone else's.'

'Dunstone is *our* fight; we have our own plans. Dunstone was organized by financial geniuses. But once confined in our territory, our alternatives are multiple. Among other devices, expropriation ... But these alternatives take time, and we both know the British do not have the time. England cannot afford the loss of Dunstone Limited.'

McAuliff's mind raced back to the room in the Savoy Hotel ... and R. C.

Hammond's quiet admission that *economics were a factor. A rather significant one.*

Hammond the manipulator.

Alex walked back to the armchair and sat down. He realized Daniel was allowing him the time to think, to absorb the possibilities of the new information. There were so many questions; most, he knew, could not be answered, but several touched him. He had to try.

'A few days ago,' he began awkwardly, 'when Barak Moore died, I found myself concerned that Charles Whitehall had no one to oppose him. So did you. I saw what you wrote down—'

'What is your question?' asked Daniel civilly.

'I was right, wasn't I? They're the two extremes. They have followers. They're not just hollow fanatics.'

'Whitehall and Moore?'

'Yes.'

'Hardly. They're the charismatic leaders. Moore *was*, Whitehall *is*. In all emerging nations there are generally three factions: right, left, and the comfortable middle – the entrenched holdovers who have learned the daily functions. The middle is eminently corruptible, for it continues the same dull, bureaucratic chores with sudden new authority. It is the first to be replaced. The healthiest way is by an infusion of the maturest elements from both extremes. Peaceful balance.'

'And that's what you're waiting for? Like a referee? An umpire?'

'Yes. That's very good, doctor. There's merit in the struggle, you know; neither side is devoid of positive factors ... Unfortunately, Dunstone makes our task more difficult. We must observe the combatants carefully.'

The minister's eyes had strayed again; and, again, there was the brief nearly imperceptible reflection. 'Why?' asked Alex.

Daniel seemed at first reluctant to answer. And then he sighed audibly. 'Very well ... Barak Moore's reaction to Dunstone would be violent. A bloodbath ... chaos. Whitehall's would be equally dangerous. He would seek temporary collusion, the power base being completely financial. He could be used as many of the German industrialists honestly believed they were using Hitler. Only the association feeds on absolute power ... absolutely.'

McAuliff leaned back in the chair. He was beginning to understand. 'So if Dunstone's out, you're back to the – what was it – the healthy struggle?'

'Yes,' said Daniel quietly.

'Then you and the British want the same thing. How can you make conditions?'

'Because our solutions are different. We have the time and the confidence of final control. The English ... and the French and the Americans and the Germans ... do not have either. The economic disasters they would suffer could well be to our advantage. And that is all I will say on the subject. We have the Dunstone list. You will make the offer to the British.'

'I go to with Malcolm to Montego—'

'You will be escorted, and guarded,' interrupted Daniel harshly. 'The members of your geological survey are hostages. Each will be summarily executed should there be the slightest deviation from our instructions.'

'Suppose British Intelligence doesn't believe you? What the hell am I supposed to do then?'

Daniel stood up. 'They will believe you, McAuliff. For your trip to Montego Bay is merely part of the news that will soon be worldwide. There will be profound shock in several national capitals. And you will tell British Intelligence that this is our proof. It is only the tip of the Dunstone iceberg. Oh, they will believe you, McAuliff. Precisely at noon, London time. Tomorrow.'

'That's all you'll tell me?'

'No. One more thing. When the acts take place, the panicked giant – Dunstone – will send out its killers. Among others, you will be a target.'

McAuliff found himself standing up in anger. 'Thank you for the warning,' he said.

'You are welcome,' replied Daniel. 'Now, if you will come with me.'

Outside the office, Malcolm, the priest figure, was talking quietly with Jeanine. At the sight of Daniel, both fell silent. Jeanine blocked Daniel's path and spoke.

'There is news from the Martha Brae.'

Alex looked at the minister and then back at the girl. 'Martha Brae' had to mean the survey's campsite. He started to speak, but was cut off by Daniel.

'Whatever it is, tell us both.'

'It concerns two men. The young man, Ferguson, and the ore specialist, Peter Jensen.'

Alex breathed again.

'What happened?' asked Daniel. 'The young man first.'

'A runner came into camp bringing him a letter from Arthur Craft Senior. In it Craft made promises, instructing Ferguson to leave the survey, come up to Port Antonio, to the Foundation. Our scouts followed and intercepted them several miles down the river. They are being held there, south of Weston Favel.'

'Craft found out about his son,' said Alex. 'He's trying to buy off Ferguson.'

'The purchase might well be to Jamaica's advantage, and Ferguson is not a hostage high on your scale of values.'

'I brought him to the island. He is valuable to me,' answered Alex coldly.

'We shall see.' Daniel turned to the girl. 'Tell the scouts to stay where they are. Hold Ferguson and the runner; instructions will follow. What about the Jensen man?'

'He is all right. The scouts are tracking him.'

'He left camp?'

'He's pretending to be lost, our men think. Early this morning, soon after Dr McAuliff left, he had his carrier stretch what is called an . . . azimuth line. He had the man walk quite a distance while he reeled out the nylon string. The signals were by tugs, apparently—'

'And Jensen cut the line and tied his end to a sapling,' interrupted Alex in a rapid monotone. 'With a loop around a nearby limb.'

'How do you know this?' Daniel seemed fascinated.

'It's a very old, unfunny trick in the field. A distasteful joke. It's played on green recruits.'

Daniel turned again to the girl. 'So his carrier could not find him. Where is Jensen now?'

'He tried to pick up Malcolm's trail,' replied the secretary. 'The scouts say he came very close. He gave up and circled back to the west hill. From there he can watch the entire campsite. All means of entrance.'

'He will wait the full three days, starving and trapped by cats, if he thinks it will help him. He does not dare go back to Warfield without something.' Daniel looked at Alex. 'Did you know you were *his* choice to direct the survey?'

'*I* was *his* . . .' McAuliff did not finish the statement. There was no point, he thought.

'Tell our people to stay with him,' ordered the minister. 'Get close, but don't take him . . . unless he uses a radio that could reach the coast. If he does, kill him.'

'What the hell are you saying?' demanded McAuliff angrily. 'Goddammit, you have no right!'

'We have every right, doctor. You adventurers come to this land. Soil it with your *filth*. Don't speak to me of *rights*, McAuliff!' And then as suddenly as he had raised his voice, he lowered it. He spoke to the girl. 'Convene the Council.'

29

Daniel led McAuliff down the steps into the matted grass on the left bank of the miniature channel of rushing water. Neither man spoke. Alex looked at his watch; it was nearly eight o'clock. The rays of the twilight of sun shot up from behind the western mountains in spectral shafts of orange; the intercepting hills were silhouetted in brownish black, emphasizing their incredible height, their fortress-immensity. The lake was a huge sheet of very dark glass, polished beyond the ability of man, reflecting the massive shadows of the mountains and the streaks of the orange sun.

They walked down the slope of the clearing to the stone fence bordering the grazing fields. At the far left was a gate; Daniel approached it, unlatched the large single bolt, and swung it open. He gestured McAuliff to go through.

'I apologize for my outburst,' said the minister as they walked into the field. 'It was misdirected. You are a victim, not an aggressor. We realize that.'

'And what are you? Are you a victim? Or an aggressor?'

'I am the Minister of Council. And *we* are neither. I explained that.'

'You explained a lot of things, but I still don't know anything about you,' said McAuliff, his eyes on a lone animal approaching them in the darkening field. It was a young horse, and it whinnied and pranced hesitantly as it drew near.

'This colt is forever breaking out,' laughed Daniel as he patted the neck of the nervous animal. 'He will be difficult to train, this one. *Hyee! Hyee!*' cried the Halidonite as he slapped the colt's flank, sending it kicking and prancing and snorting toward the center of the field.

'Maybe that's what I mean,' said Alex. 'How do you train . . . people? Keep them from breaking out?'

Daniel stopped and looked at McAuliff. They were alone in the large pasture, awash with the vivid colors of the dying Jamaican sun. The light silhouetted the minister and caused McAuliff to shield his face. He could not see Daniel's eyes, but he could feel them.

'We are an uncomplicated people in many ways,' said the Halidonite. 'What technology we require is brought in, along with our medical supplies, basic farm machinery, and the like. Always by our own members, using untraceable mountain routes. Other than these, we are self-sufficient on our lands. Our training – as you call it – is a result of understanding the immense riches we possess. Our isolation is hardly absolute. As you will see.'

From childhood, Daniel explained, the Halidonite was told he was privileged and must justify his birthright by his life's actions. The ethic of contribution we imbued in him early in his education; the need to use his potential to the fullest. The outside world was shown in all its detail – its simplicities, its complications; its peace and its violence; its good and its evil. Nothing was concealed; exaggeration was not left to young imaginations. Realistic temptation was balanced – perhaps a bit strongly, admitted Daniel – with realistic punishment.

As near to his or her twelfth birthday as possible, the Halidonite was tested extensively by teachers, the elders of the Council, and finally by the minister himself. On the basis of these examinations, individuals were selected for training for the outside world. There followed three years of preparation, concentrating on specific skills or professions.

When he or she reached sixteen, the Halidonite was taken from the community and brought to a family residence on the outside, where the father and mother were members of the tribe. Except for infrequent returns to the community and reunions with his own parents, the outside family would be the Haldonite's guardians for a number of years to come.

'Don't you have defections?' asked Alex.

'Rarely,' replied Daniel. 'The screening process is most thorough.'

'What happens if it isn't thorough enough? If there are—'

'That is an answer I will not give you,' interrupted the minister. 'Except to say the Maze of Acquaba is a threat no prison can compete with. It keeps offenders – within and without – to a minimum. Defections are extremely rare.'

From the tone of Daniel's voice, Alex had no desire to pursue the subject. 'They're brought back?'

Daniel nodded.

The population of the Halidon was voluntarily controlled. Daniel claimed that for every couple that wanted more children, there invariably was a couple that wanted fewer or none. And, to McAuliff's astonishment, the minister added: 'Marriages take place between ourselves and those of the outside. It is, of course, unavoidable and, by necessity, desirable. But it is a complicated procedure taking place over many months and with stringent regulations.'

'A reverse screening process?'

'The harshest imaginable. Controlled by the guardians.'

'What happens if the marriage doesn't ...'

'That answer, too, is not in bounds, doctor.'

'I have an idea the penalties are stiff,' said Alex softly.

'You may have all the ideas you like,' said Daniel, starting up again across the field. 'But what is of the greatest importance is that you understand that we have scores ... hundreds of guardians – halfway houses – throughout the countries of the world. In every profession, in all governments, in dozens of universities and institutions everywhere. You will never know who is a member of the Halidon. And that is our threat, our ultimate protection.'

'You're saying that if I reveal what I know, you'll have me killed?'

'You and every member of your family. Wife, children, parents ... in the absence of the formal structure, lovers, closest associates, every person who was or is an influence on your life. Your identity, even your memory, will be erased.'

'You can't know every person I talk to, every telephone call I make. Where I am every minute. *No* one can! I could mount an army; I could find you!'

'But you will not,' said Daniel quietly, in counterpoint to McAuliff's outburst. 'For the same reason others have not ... Come. We are here.'

They were standing now on the edge of the field. Beyond was the tentacled foliage of the Cock Pit forest, in shadowed blackness.

Suddenly, startlingly, the air was filled with a penetrating sound of terrible resonance. It was a wailing, inhuman lament. The tone was low, breathless, enveloping everything and echoing everywhere. It was the sound of a giant woodwind, rising slowly, receding into a simple obscure theme and swelling again to the plaintive cry of a higher melody.

It grew louder and louder, the echoes now picking up the bass tones and hurling them through the jungles, crashing them off the sides of the surrounding mountains until the earth seemed to vibrate.

And then it stopped, and McAuliff stood transfixed as he saw in the distance the outlines of figures walking slowly, purposefully, in the measured cadence, across the fields in the chiaroscuro shadows of the early darkness. A few carried torches, the flames low.

At first there were only four or five, coming from the direction of the gate. Then there were some from the south bank of the black, shining lake; others from the north, emerging out of the darkness. Flat-bottomed boats could be seen crossing the surface of the water, each with a single torch.

Within minutes there were ten, then twenty, thirty ... until McAuliff stopped counting. From everywhere. Dozens of slowly moving bodies swaying gently as they walked across the darkened fields.

They were converging toward the spot where Alex stood with Daniel.

The inhuman wailing began again. Louder – if possible – than before, and McAuliff found himself bringing his hands up to his ears; the vibrations in his head and throughout his body were causing pain – actual *pain*.

Daniel touched him on the shoulder; Alex whipped around as if he had been struck violently. For an instant he thought he had been, so severe were the agonizing sensations brought on by the deafening sound of the horrible lament.

'Come,' said Daniel gently. 'The *hollydawn* can injure you.'

McAuliff heard him accurately; he knew that. Daniel had pronounced the word: not 'halidon' but 'hollydawn'. As though the echoing, deafening sound had caused him to revert to a more primitive tongue.

Daniel walked rapidly ahead of Alex into what McAuliff thought was a wall of underbrush. Then the Halidonite suddenly began to descend into what appeared to be a trench dug out of the jungle. Alex ran to catch up, and nearly plummeted down a long, steep corridor of steps carved out of rock.

The strange staircase widened, flaring out more on both sides the deeper it went, until McAuliff could see that they had descended into a primitive amphitheater, the walls rising thirty or forty feet to the surface of the earth.

What was the staircase became an aisle, the curving rock on both sides forming rows of descending seats.

And suddenly the deafening, agonizing sound from above was no more. It had stopped. Everything was silent.

The amphitheater, carved out of some kind of quarry, blocked out all other sound.

McAuliff stood where he was and looked down at the single source of light: a low flame that illuminated the wall of rock at the center rear of the amphitheater. In that wall was embedded a slab of dull yellow metal. And on the slab of metal was a withered corpse. In front of the corpse was a latticework of thin reeds made of the same yellow substance.

McAuliff needed to go no closer to realize what the substance was: gold.

And the withered, ancient body – once huge – was that of the mystic descendant of the Coromanteen chieftains.

Acquaba.

The preserved remains of the progenitor ... spanning the centuries. The true cross of the Tribe of Acquaba. For the believers to see. And sense.

'Down here.' Daniel's words were whispered, but Alex heard them clearly. 'You will sit with me. Please, hurry.'

McAuliff walked down the remaining staircase to the floor of the quarry shell and over to the Halidonite on the right side of the primitive stage. Jutting out from the wall were two stone blocks; Daniel pointed to one: the seat nearest the corpse of Acquaba, less than eight feet away.

McAuliff lowered himself on to the hard stone, his eyes drawn to the open catafalque of solid and webbed gold. The leathered corpse was dressed in robes of reddish black; the feet and hands were bare ... and huge, as the head was huge. Allowing for the contraction of two centuries, the man must have been enormous – nearer seven feet than six.

The single torch below the coffin of gold shot flickering shadows against the wall; the thin reeds crisscrossing the front of the carved-out casket picked up the light in dozens of tiny reflections. The longer one stared, thought Alex, the easier it would be to convince oneself this was the shell of a god lying in state. A god who had walked the earth and worked the earth – two hundred years could not erase the signs on the enormous hands and feet. But this god, this man did not toil as other men ...

He heard the sounds of muted steps and looked up into the small amphitheater. Through the entrance, hidden in darkness, and down the staircase they came, a procession of men and women separating and spreading throughout the later stone aisles, taking their seats.

In silence.

Those with torches stood equidistant from each other on graduating levels against opposite walls.

All eyes were on the withered body beyond the latticework of gold. Their concentration was absolute; it was as if they drew sustenance from it.

In silence.

Suddenly, without warning, the sound of the *hollydawn* shattered the stillness with the impact of an explosion. The thunderous, wailing lament seemed to burst from the bowels of rock-covered earth, crashing upward against the stone, thrusting out of the huge pit that was the grave of Acquaba.

McAuliff felt the breath leaving his lungs, the blood rushing to his head. He buried his face between his knees, his hands clamped over his ears, his whole body shaking.

The cry reached a crescendo, a terrible screaming rush of air that swelled to a pitch of frenzy. *No human ears could stand it!* thought Alex as he trembled . . . as he had never before trembled in his life.

And then it was over and the silence returned.

McAuliff slowly sat up, lowering his hands, gripping the stone beneath him in an effort to control the violent spasms he felt shooting through his flesh. His eyes were blurred from the blood which had raced to his temples; they cleared slowly, in stages, and he looked out at the rows of Halidonites, at these chosen members of the Tribe of Acquaba.

They were – each one all – still staring, eyes fixed on the ancient, withered body behind the golden reeds.

Alex knew they had remained exactly as they were throughout the shattering madness that had nearly driven him out of his mind.

He turned to Daniel; involuntarily he gasped. The Minister of Council, too, was transfixed, his black eyes wide, his jaw set, his face immobile. But he was different from all the others; there were tears streaming down Daniel's cheeks.

'You're mad . . . all of you,' said Alex quietly. 'You're insane.'

Daniel did not respond. Daniel could not hear him. He was in a hypnotic state.

They all were. Everyone in that carved-out shell beneath the earth. Nearly a hundred men and women inextricably held by some force beyond his comprehension.

Autosuggestion. Self-somnipathy. Group hypnosis. Whatever the catalyst, each individual in that primitive amphitheater was mesmerized beyond reach. On another plane . . . time and space unfamiliar.

Alexander felt himself an intruder; he was observing a ritual too private for his eyes.

Yet he had not asked to be here. He had been forced in – ripped out of place – and made to bear witness.

Still, the witnessing filled him with sorrow. And he could not understand. So he looked over at the body that was once the giant, Acquaba.

He stared at the shriveled flesh of the once-black face. At the closed eyes, so peaceful in death. At the huge hands folded so strongly across the reddish-black robe.

Then back at the face ... the eyes ... the eyes ...

Oh my God! Oh, Christ!

The shadows were playing tricks ... terrible, horrible tricks.

The body of Acquaba moved.

The eyes opened; the fingers of the immense hands spread, the wrists turned, the arms raised ... inches above the ancient cloth.

In supplication.

And then there was nothing.

Only a shriveled corpse behind a latticework of gold.

McAuliff pressed himself back against the wall of stone, trying desperately to find his sanity. He closed his eyes and breathed deeply, gripping the rock beneath him. It could *not* have *happened!* It was some sort of mass hallucination by way of theatrical trickery accompanied by group expectation and that damned unearthly ear-shattering sound! Yet he had *seen* it! And it was horrifyingly effective. He did not know how long it was – a minute, an hour, a decade of terror – until he heard Daniel's words.

'You *saw* it.' A statement made gently. 'Do not be afraid. We shall never speak of it again. There is no harm. Only good.'

'I ... I ...' Alexander could not talk. The perspiration rolled down his face. And the carved-out council ground was cool.

Daniel stood up and walked to the center of the platform of rock. Instead of addressing the Tribe of Acquaba, he turned to McAuliff. His words were whispered, but, as before, they were clear and precise, echoing off the walls.

'The lessons of Acquaba touch all men, as the lessons of all prophets touch all men. But few listen. Still, the work must go on. For those who can do it. It is really as simple as that. Acquaba was granted the gift of great riches ... beyond the imaginations of those who will never listen; who will only steal and corrupt. So we go out into the world without the world's knowledge. And we do what we can. It must ever be so, for if the world knew, the world would impose itself and the Halidon, the Tribe of Acquaba, and the lessons of Acquaba would be destroyed ... We are not fools, Dr McAuliff. We know with whom we speak, with whom we share our secrets. And our love. But do not mistake us. We can kill; we will kill to protect the vaults of Acquaba. In that we are dangerous. In that we are absolute. We will destroy ourselves and the vaults if the world outside interferes with us.

'I, as Minister of Council, ask you to rise, Dr McAuliff. And turn yourself away from the Tribe of Acquaba, from this Council of the Halidon, and face the wall. What you will hear, staring only at stone, are voices, revealing locations and figures. As I mentioned, we are not fools. We understand the specifics of the marketplace. But you will not see faces, you will never know the identities of those who speak. Only know that they go forth bearing the wealth of Acquaba.

'We dispense vast sums throughout the world, concentrating as best we can on the areas of widespread human suffering. Pockets of famine, displacement, futility. Untold thousands are helped daily by the Halidon. Daily. In practical ways.

'Please rise and face the wall, Dr McAuliff.'

Alexander got up from the block of stone and turned. For a brief instant his eyes fell on the corpse of Acquaba. He looked away and stared at the towering sheet of rock.

Daniel continued. 'Our contributions are made without thought of political gain or influence. They are made because we have the concealed wealth and the commitment to make them. The lessons of Acquaba.

'But the world is not ready to accept our ways, Acquaba's ways. The global mendacity would destroy us, cause us to destroy ourselves, perhaps. And that we cannot permit.

'So understand this, Dr McAuliff. Beyond the certainty of your own death, should you reveal what you know of the Tribe of Acquaba, there is another certainty of far greater significance than your life: the work of the Halidon will cease. That is our ultimate threat.'

One by one, the voices recited their terse statements:

Afro axis. Ghana. Fourteen thousand bushels of grain. Conduit: Smythe Brothers, Capetown. Barclay's Bank.'

'Sierra Leone. Three tons of medical supplies. Conduit: Baldazi Pharmaceuticals, Algiers. Bank of Constantine.'

'Indo-China axis. Vietnam, Mekong, Quan Tho provinces. Radiology and laboratory personnel and supplies. Conduit: Swiss Red Cross. Bank of America.'

'Southwest Hemisphere axis. Brazil. Rio de Janeiro. Typhoid serum. Conduit: Surgical Salizar. Banco Terceiro, Rio.'

'Northwest Hemisphere axis. West Virginia. Appalachia. Twenty-four tons food supplies. Conduit: Atlantic Warehousing. Chase Manhattan. New York.'

'India axis. Dacca. Refugee camps. Inoculation serums, medicals. Conduit: International Displacement Organization. World Bank. Burma . . .'

The voices of men and women droned on, the phrases clipped, yet somehow gentle. It took nearly an hour, and McAuliff began to recognize that many spoke twice, but always with different information. Nothing was repeated.

Finally there was silence.

A long period of silence. And then Alexander felt a hand on his shoulder. He turned, and Daniel's eyes bore in on him.

'Do you understand?'

'Yes, I understand,' McAuliff said.

They walked across the field toward the lake. The sounds of the forest mingled with the hum of the mountains and the crashing of the waterfall nearly a mile to the north.

They stood on the embankment, and Alex bent down, picked up a small stone, and threw it into the black, shining lake that reflected the light of the moon. He looked at Daniel.

'In a way, you're as dangerous as the rest of them. One man ... with so much ... operating beyond reach. No checks, no balances. It would be so simple for good to become evil, evil good. Malcolm said your ... term isn't guided by a calendar.'

'It is not. I am elected for life. Only I can terminate my office.'

'And pick your successor?'

'I have influence. The Council, of course, has the final disposition.'

'Then I think you're more dangerous.'

'I do not deny it.'

30

The trip to Montego was far easier than the circuitous march from the Martha Brae. To begin with, most of the journey was by vehicle.

Malcolm, his robes replaced by Savile Row clothing, led Alexander around the lake to the southeast, where they were met by a runner who took them to the base of a mountain cliff, hidden by jungle. A steel lift, whose thick chains were concealed by mountain rocks, carried them up the enormous precipice to a second runner, who placed them in a small tram, which was transported by cable on a path below the skyline of the forest.

At the end of the cable ride, a third runner took them through a series of deep caves, identified by Malcolm as the Quick Step Grotto. He told Alex that the Quick Step was named for seventeenth-century buccaneers who raced from Bluefield's Bay overland to bury treasure at the bottom of the deep pools within the caves. The other derivation – the one many believed to be more appropriate – was that if a traveler did not watch his feet, he could easily slip and plummet into a crevice. Injury was certain, death not impossible.

McAuliff stayed close to the runner, his flashlight beamed at the rocky darkness in front of him.

Out of the caves, they proceeded through a short stretch of jungle to the first definable road they had seen. The runner activated a portable radio; ten minutes later a Land Rover came out of the pitch-black hollows from the west and the runner bid them goodbye.

The rugged vehicle traveled over a crisscross pattern of back country roads, the driver keeping his engine as quiet as possible, coasting on descending hills, shutting off his headlights whenever they approached a populated area. The drive lasted a half-hour. They passed through the Maroon village of Accompong and swung south several miles to a flat stretch of grassland.

In the darkness, on the field's edge, a small airplane was rolled out from under a camouflage of fern and acacia. It was a two-seater Comanche; they climbed in, and Malcolm took the controls.

'This is the only difficult leg of the trip,' he said as they taxied for takeoff. 'We must fly close to the ground to avoid interior radar. Unfortunately, so do the ganja aircraft, the drug smugglers. But we will worry less about the authorities than we will about collision.'

Without incident, but not without sighting several ganja planes, they landed on the grounds of an outlying farm, southwest of Unity Hall. From there it was a fifteen-minute ride into Montego Bay.

'It would arouse suspicions for us to stay in the exclusively black section of the town. You, for your skin, me for my speech and my clothes. And tomorrow we must have mobility in the white areas.'

They drove to the Cornwall Beach Hotel and registered ten minutes apart. Reservations had been made for adjoining but not connecting rooms.

It was two o'clock in the morning, and McAuliff fell into bed exhausted. He had not slept in forty-eight hours. And yet, for a very long time, sleep did not come.

He thought about so many things. The brilliant, lonely, awkward James Ferguson and his sudden departure to the Craft Foundation. Defection, really. Without explanation. Alex hoped Craft was Jimbo-mon's solution. For he would never be trusted again.

And of the sweetly charming Jensens . . . up to their so-respectable chins in the manipulations of Dunstone Limited.

Of the 'charismatic leader' Charles Whitehall, waiting to ride 'nigger-Pompey's horse' through Victoria Park. Whitehall was no match for the Halidon. The Tribe of Acquaba would not tolerate him.

Nor did the lessons of Acquaba include the violence of Lawrence, the boy-man giant . . . successor to Barak Moore. Lawrence's 'revolution' would not come to pass. Not the way he conceived it.

Alex wondered about Sam Tucker. Tuck, the gnarled rocklike force of stability. Would Sam find what he was looking for in Jamaica? For surely he was looking.

But most of all McAuliff thought about Alison. Of her lovely half laugh and her clear blue eyes and the calm acceptance that was her understanding. How very much he loved her.

He wondered, as his consciousness drifted into the gray, blank void that was sleep, if they would have a life together.

After the madness.

If he was alive.

If they were alive.

He had left a wake-up call for six forty-five. Quarter to twelve, London time. Noon. For the Halidon.

The coffee arrived in seven minutes. Eight minutes to twelve. The telephone rang three minutes later. Five minutes to noon, London time. It was Malcolm, and he was not in his hotel room. He was at the Associated Press Bureau, Montego Bay office, on St James Street. He wanted to make sure that Alex was up and had his radio on. Perhaps his television set as well.

McAuliff had both instruments on.

Malcolm the Halidonite would call him later.

At three minutes to seven – twelve, London time – there was a rapid knocking on his hotel door. Alexander was startled. Malcolm had said nothing about visitors; no one knew he was in Montego Bay. He approached the door.

'Yes?'

The words from the other side of the wood were spoken hesitantly, in a deep, familiar voice.

'Is that you ... McAuliff?'

And instantly Alexander understood. The symmetry, the timing was extraordinary; only extraordinary minds could conceive and execute such a symbolic coup.

He opened the door.

R. C. Hammond, British Intelligence, stood in the corridor, his slender frame rigid, his face an expression of suppressed shock.

'Good God. It is you. I didn't believe him. Your signals from the river ... There was nothing irregular, nothing at all!'

'That,' said Alex, 'is about as disastrous a judgment as I've ever heard.'

'They dragged me out of my rooms in Kingston before daylight. Drove me up into the hills—'

'And flew you to Montego,' completed McAuliff, looking at his watch. 'Come in, Hammond. We've got a minute and fifteen seconds to go.'

'For what?'

'We'll both find out.'

The lilting, high-pitched Caribbean voice on the radio proclaimed over the music the hour of seven in the 'sunlight paradise of Montego Bay'. The picture on the television set was a sudden fade-in shot of a long expanse of white beach ... a photograph. The announcer, in overly anglicized tones, was extolling the virtues of 'our island life' and welcoming 'alla visitors from the cold climate', pointing out immediately that there was a blizzard in New York.

Twelve o'clock London time.

Nothing unusual.

Nothing.

Hammond stood by the window, looking out at the blue-green waters of the bay. He was silent; his anger was the fury of a man who had lost control because he did not know the moves his opponents were making. And, more important, why they were making them.

The manipulator manipulated.

McAuliff sat on the bed, his eyes on the television set, now a travelogue fraught with lies about the 'beautiful city of Kingston'. Simultaneously, the radio on the bedside table blared its combination of cacophonic music and frantic commercials for everything from Coppertone to Hertz. Intermittently, there was the syrupy female Voice-of-the-Ministry-of-Health, telling the women of the island that 'you do not have to get pregnant', followed by the repetition of the weather ... the forecasts never 'partly cloudy', always 'partly sunny.'

Nothing unusual.

Nothing.

It was eleven minutes past twelve London time.

Still nothing.

And then it happened.

'We interrupt this broadcast ...'

And, like an insignificant wave born of the ocean depths – unnoticed at first, but gradually swelling, suddenly bursting out of the waters and cresting in controlled fury – the pattern of terror was clear.

The first announcement was merely the prelude – a single flute outlining the significant notes of a theme shortly to be developed.

Explosion and death in Port Antonio.

The east wing of the estate of Arthur Craft had been blown up by explosives, the resulting conflagration gutting most of the house. Among the dead was feared to be the patriarch of the Foundation.

There were rumors of rifle fire preceding the series of explosions. Port Antonio was in panic.

Rifle fire. Explosives.

Rare, yes. But not unheard of on this island of scattered violence. Of contained anger.

The next 'interruption' followed in less than ten minutes. It was – appropriately, thought McAuliff – a news report out of London. This intrusion warranted a line of moving print across the television screen: KILLINGS IN LONDON FULL REPORT ON NEW HOUR. The radio allowed a long musical commercial to run its abrasive course before the voice returned, now authoritatively bewildered.

The details were still sketchy, but not the conclusions. Four high-ranking figures in government and industry had been slain. A director of Lloyds, an accounts official of the Inland Revenue, and two members of the House of Commons, both chairing trade committees of consequence.

The methods: two now familiar, two new – dramatically oriented.

A high-powered rifle fired from a window into a canopied entrance in Belgrave Square. A dynamited automobile, blown up in the Westminster parking area. Then the new: poison – temporarily identified as strychnine – administered in a Beefeater martini, causing death in two minutes; a horrible, contorted, violent death ... the blade of a knife thrust into moving flesh on a crowded corner of the Strand.

Killings accomplished; no killers apprehended.

R. C. Hammond stood by the hotel window, listening to the excited tones of the Jamaican announcer. When Hammond spoke, his shock was clear.

'My *God* ... Every one of those men at one time or another was under the glass—'

'The what?'

'Suspected of high crimes. Malfeasance, extortion, fraud ... Nothing was ever proved out.'

'Something's been proved out now.'

Paris was next. Reuters sent out the first dispatches, picked up by all the wire services within minutes. Again, the number was four. Four Frenchmen – actually, three French men and one woman. But still four.

Again, they were prominent figures in industry and government: And the M.Os were identical: rifle, explosives, strychnine, knife.

The Frenchwoman was a proprietor of a Paris fashion house. A ruthless sadist long considered an associate of the Corsicans. She was shot from a distance as she emerged from a doorway on the St-Germain-des-Prés. Of the three men, one was a member of the president's all-important Elysée Financial; his Citroën exploded when he turned his ignition on in the Rue du Bac. The two other Frenchmen were powerful executives in shipping companies – Marseilles-based, under the Paraguayan flag ... owned by the Marquis de Chatellerault. The first spastically lurched and died over a café table in the Montmartre – strychnine in his late-morning espresso. The second had his chest torn open by a butcher's knife on the crowded sidewalk outside the Georges V Hotel.

Minutes after Paris came Berlin.

On the Kurfurstendam Strasse, the *Unter Schriftführer* of the Bundestag's *AuBenpolitik* was shot from the roof of a nearby building as he was on his way to a luncheon appointment. A *Direktor* of Mercedes-Benz stopped for a traffic light on the Autobahn, where two grenades were thrown into the front seat of his car, demolishing automobile and driver in seconds. A known narcotics dealer was given poison in his glass of heavy lager at the bar of the Grand Hotel, and an appointee of the *Einkunfte Finanzamt* was stabbed expertly – death instantaneous – through the heart in the crowded lobby of the government building.

Rome followed. A financial strategist for the Vatican, a despised cardinal devoted to the church militants' continuous extortion of the uninformed poor, was dropped by an assassin firing a rifle from behind a Bernini in St Peter's Square. A *funzionario* of Milan's Mondadori drove into a cul-de-sac on the Via Condotti, where his automobile exploded. A lethal dose of strychnine was administered with cappuccino to a *direttore* of Customs at Rome's Fiumicino Airport. A knife was plunged into the ribs of a powerful broker of the *Borsa Valori* as he walked down the Spanish Steps into the Via Due Marcelli.

London, Paris, Berlin, Rome.

And always the figure was four ... and the methods identical: rifle, explosives, strychnine, knife. Four diverse, ingenious modi operandi. Each strikingly news-conscious, oriented for shock. All killings the work of expert professionals; no killers caught at the scenes of violence.

The radio and the television stations no longer made attempts to continue regular programming. As the names came, so too did progressively illuminating biographies. And another pattern emerged, lending credence of Hammond's summary of the four slain Englishmen: the victims were not ordinary men of stature in industry and government. There was a common stain running through the many that aroused suspicions about the rest. They were individuals not alien to official scrutinies. As the first hints began to surface, curious newsmen dug swiftly and furiously, dredging up scores of rumors, and more than rumor – facts: indictments (generally reduced to the inconsequential), accusations from injured competitors, superiors, and subordinates (removed, recanted . . . unsubstantiated), litigations (settled out of court or dropped for lack of evidence).

It was an elegant cross-section of the suspected. Tarnished, soiled, an aura of corruption.

All this before the hands on McAuliff's watch read nine o'clock. Two hours past twelve, London time. Two o'clock in the afternoon in Mayfair.

Commuter time in Washington and New York.

There was no disguising the apprehension felt as the sun made its way from the east over the Atlantic. Speculation was rampant, growing in hysteria: a conspiracy of international proportions was suggested, a cabal of self-righteous fanatics violently implementing its vengeances throughout the world.

Would it touch the shores of the United States?

But, of course, it had.

Two hours ago.

The awkward giant was just beginning to stir, to recognize the signs of the spreading plague.

The first news reached Jamaica out of Miami. Radio Montego picked up the overlapping broadcasts, sifting, sorting . . . finally relaying by tape the words of the various newscasters as they rushed to verbalize the events spewing out of the wire service teletypes.

Washington. Early morning. The Undersecretary of the Budget – a patently political appointment resulting from openly questioned campaign contributions – was shot while jogging on a back-country road. The body was discovered by a motorist at eight twenty; the time of death estimated to be within the past two hours.

Noon. London time.

New York. At approximately seven o'clock in the morning, when one Gianni Dellacroce – reputed Mafia figure – stepped into his Lincoln Continental in the attached garage of his Scarsdale home, there was an explosion that ripped the entire enclosure out of its foundation, instantly killing Dellacroce and causing considerable damage to the rest of the house. Dellacroce was rumored to be . . .

Noon. London time.

Phoenix, Arizona. At approximately five fifteen in the morning, one Harrison Renfield, international financier and real-estate magnate with extensive Caribbean holdings, collapsed in his private quarters at the Thunderbird Club after a late party with associates. He had ordered a predawn breakfast; poison was suspected, as a Thunderbird waiter was found unconscious down the hall from Renfield's suite. An autopsy was ordered . . .

Five o'clock, Mountain time.

Twelve, noon. London.

Los Angeles, California. At precisely four A.M. the junior senator from Nevada – recently implicated (but not indicted) in a Las Vegas tax fraud – stepped off a launch onto a pier in Marina del Ray. The launch was filled with guests returning from the yacht of a motion-picture producer. Somewhere between the launch and the base of the pier, the junior senator from Nevada had his stomach ripped open with a blade so long and a cut so deep that the cartilage of his backbone protruded through spinal lacerations. He fell among the revelers, carried along by the boisterous crowd until the eruptions of the warm fluid that covered so many was recognized for the blood that it was. Panic resulted, the terror alcoholic but profound. Four in the morning. Pacific time.

Twelve noon. London.

McAuliff looked over at the silent, stunned Hammond.

'The last death reported was four in the morning ... twelve o'clock in London. In each country four died, with four corresponding – identical – methods of killing ... The Arawak units of four – the death odyssey ... that's what they call it.'

'What are you talking about?'

'Deal with the Halidon, Hammond. You have no choice; this is their proof. They said it was only the tip.'

'The tip?'

'The tip of the Dunstone iceberg.'

'Impossible demands!' roared R. C. Hammond, the capillaries in his face swollen, forming splotches of red anger over his skin. 'We will *not* be dictated to by goddamn *niggers!*'

'Then you won't get the list.'

'We'll *force* it out of them. This is no time for treaties with *savages!*'

Alexander thought of Daniel, of Malcolm, of the incredible lakeside community, of the grave of Acquaba, the vaults of Acquaba. Things he could not, would not, talk about. He did not have to, he considered. 'You think what's happened the work of savages? Not the killings, I won't defend that. But the methods, the victims ... Don't kid yourself.'

'I don't give a *damn* for your opinions.' Hammond walked rapidly to the telephone on the bedside table. Alex remained in a chair by the television set. It was the sixth time Hammond had tried to place his call. The Britisher had only one telephone number he could use in Kingston; embassy telephones were off-limits for clandestine operations. Each time he had managed to get a line through to Kingston – not the easiest feat in Montego – the number was busy.

'*Damn! Goddammit!*' exploded the agent.

'Call the embassy before you have a coronary,' said McAuliff. 'Deal with them.'

'Don't be an ass,' replied Hammond. 'They don't know who I am. We don't use embassy personnel.'

'Talk to the ambassador.'

'What in God's name for? What am I supposed to say? "Pardon me, Mr Ambassador, but my name's so-and-so. I happen to be ..." The bloody explanation – if he'd listen to it without cutting me off – would take the better part of an hour. And then the damn fool would start sending cables to Downing Street!' Hammond marched back to the window.

'What are you going to do?'

'They've isolated me, you understand that, don't you?' Hammond remained at the window, his back to McAuliff.

'I think so.'

'The purpose is to cut me off, force me to absorb the full impact of the ... past three hours ...' The Britisher's voice trailed off in thought.

McAuliff wondered. 'That presupposes they know the Kingston telephone, that they shorted it out somehow.'

'I don't think so,' said Hammond, his eyes still focused on the waters of the bay. 'By now Kingston knows I've been taken. Our men are no doubt activating every contact on the island, trying to get a bearing on my whereabouts. The telephone would be in constant use.'

'You're not a prisoner; the door's not locked.' Alex suddenly wondered if he was correct. He got out of the chair, crossed to the door, and opened it.

Down the corridor were two Jamaicans by the bank of the elevators. They looked at McAuliff, and although he did not know them, he recognized the piercing, controlled calm of their expressions. He had seen such eyes, such expressions high in the Flagstaff Mountains. They were members of the Halidon.

Alex closed the door and turned to Hammond, but before he could say anything, the Britisher spoke, his back still to Alex.

'Does that answer you?' he asked quietly.

'There are two men in the corridor,' said McAuliff pointlessly. 'You knew that.'

'I didn't know it, I merely assumed it. There are fundamental rules.'

'And you still think they're savages?'

'Everything's relative.' Hammond turned from the window and faced Alex. 'You're the conduit now. I'm sure they've told you that.'

'If "conduit" means I take back your answer, then yes.'

'Merely the answer? They've asked for no substantive guarantees?' The Englishman seemed bewildered.

'I think that comes in Phase Two. This is a step contract, I gather. I don't think they'll take the word of Her Majesty's obedient servant. He uses the term "nigger" too easily.'

'You're an ass,' said Hammond.

'You're an autocratic cipher,' replied McAuliff, with equal disdain. 'They've got you, agent-mon. They've also got the Dunstone list. You play in *their* sandbox ... with their "fundamental rules".'

Hammond hesitated, repressing his irritation. 'Perhaps not. There's an avenue we haven't explored. They'll take you back ... I should like to be taken with you.'

'They won't accept that.'

'They may not have a choice—'

'Get one thing straight,' interrupted Alex. 'There's a survey team in the Cock Pit – white *and* black – and *no one's* going to jeopardize a single life.'

'You forget,' said Hammond softly – aloofly. 'We know the location within a thousand yards.'

'You're no match for those guarding it. Don't think you are. One misstep, one deviation, and there are mass executions.'

'Yes,' said the Britisher. 'I believe just such a massacre took place previously. The executioners being those whose methods and selections you admire so.'

'The circumstances were different. You don't know the truth—'

'Oh, come off it, McAuliff! I shall do my best to protect the lives of your team, but I'm forced to be honest with you. They are no more the first priority for me than they are for the Halidon! There are more important considerations.' The Englishman stopped briefly, for emphasis. 'And I can assure you, our resources are considerably more than those of a sect of fanatic . . . coloreds. I'd advise you not to change your allegiances at this late hour.'

The announcer on the television screen had been droning, reading from pages of script handed to him by others in the studio. Alex couldn't be sure – he had not been listening – but he thought he had heard the name, spoken differently . . . as if associated with new or different information. He looked down at the set, holding up his hand for Hammond to be quiet.

He *had* heard the name.

And as the first announcement three hours ago had been the prelude – a single instrument marking a thematic commencement – McAuliff recognized this as the coda. The terror had been orchestrated to a conclusion.

The announcer looked earnestly into the camera, then back to the papers in his hand.

'To repeat the bulletin. Savanna-la-Mar. Shooting broke out at the private Negril airfield. A band of identified men ambushed a party of Europeans as they were boarding a small plane for Weston Favel.

'The French industrialist Henri Salanne, the Marquis de Chatellerault, was killed along with three men said to be in his employ. No motive is known. The marquis was the house guest of the Wakefield family. The pilot, a Wakefield employee, reported that his final instructions from the marquis were to fly south of Weston Favel at low altitude toward the interior grasslands. The parish police are questioning . . .'

Alex walked over to the set and switched it off. He turned to Hammond; there was very little to say, and he wondered if the Intelligence man would understand.

'That was a priority you forgot about, wasn't it, Hammond? Alison Booth. Your filthy link to Chatellerault. The expendable Mrs Booth, the bait from Interpol . . . Well, you're *here*, agent-mon, and Chatellerault is dead. You're in a hotel room in Montego Bay. Not in the Cock Pit. Don't talk to me about resources, you son-of-a-bitch. You've only got one. And it's me.'

The telephone rang. McAuliff reached it first.

'Yes?'

'Don't interrupt me; there is no time,' came the agitated words from Malcolm. 'Do as I say. I have been spotted. MI6 . . . a Jamaican. One I knew in London. We realized they would fan out; we did not think they would reach Montego so quickly—'

'Stop running,' broke in Alex, looking at Hammond. 'MI6 will cooperate. They have no choice—'

'You damn fool, I said *listen*! There are two men in the corridor. Go out and tell them I called. Say the word "Ashanti". Have you got that, mon? *"Ashantee."'*

Alex had not heard the anglicized Malcolm use 'mon' before. Malcolm was in a state of panic. 'I've got it.'

'Tell them I said to get out! *Now!* The hotels will be watched. You will all have to move fast—'

'Goddammit!' interrupted Alex again. 'Now you listen to me. Hammond's right here and—'

'*McAuliff.*' The sound of Malcolm's voice was low, cutting, demanding attention. 'British Intelligence, Caribbean Operations, has a total of fifteen West Indian specialists. That is the budget. Of those fifteen, seven have been bought by Dunstone Limited.'

The silence was immediate, the implication clear. 'Where are you?'

'In a pay phone outside McNab's. It is a crowded street; I will do my best to melt.'

'Be careful in crowded streets. I've been listening to the news.'

'Listen well, my friend. That is what this is all about.'

'You said they spotted you. Are they there now?'

'It is difficult to tell. We are dealing with Dunstone now. Even we do not know everyone on its payroll. But they will not want to kill me. Any more than I want to be taken alive . . . Good luck, McAuliff. We are doing the right thing.'

With these words, Malcolm hung up the telephone. Alexander instantly recalled a dark field at night on the outskirts of London, near the banks of the River Thames. And the sight of two dead West Indians in a government automobile.

Any more than I want to be taken alive . . .

Cyanide.

We are doing the right thing . . .

Death.

Unbelievable. Yet very, very real.

McAuliff gently replaced the telephone in its cradle. As he did, he had the fleeting thought that his gesture was funereal.

This was no time to think of funerals.

'Who was that?' asked Hammond.

'A fanatic who, in my opinion, is worth a dozen men like you. You see, he doesn't lie.'

'I've had enough of your sanctimonious claptrap, McAuliff!' The Englishman spat out his words in indignation. 'Your fanatic doesn't pay two million dollars, either. Nor, I suspect, does he jeopardize his own interests for your well-being, as *we* have done constantly. Furthermore—'

'He just did,' interrupted Alex as he crossed the room. 'And if I'm a target, so are you.'

McAuliff reached the door, opened it swiftly, and ran out into the corridor toward the bank of elevators. He stopped.

There was no one there.

31

It was a race in blinding sunlight, somehow macabre because of the eye-jolting reflections from the glass and chrome and brightly colored metals on the Montego streets. And the profusion of people. Crowded, jostling, black and white; thin men and fat women – the former with the goddamned cameras, the latter in foolish-looking rhinestone sunglasses. Why did he notice these things? Why did they irritate him? There were fat men, too. Always with angry faces; silently, stoically reacting to the vacuous-looking thin women at their sides.

And the hostile black eyes staring out from wave after wave of black skin. Thin, black faces – somehow always thin – on top of bony, black bodies – angular, beaten, slow.

These then were the blurred, repeating images imprinted on the racing pages of his mind.

Everything . . . everyone was instantly categorized in the frantic, immediate search for an enemy.

The enemy was surely there.

It had been there . . . minutes ago.

McAuliff had rushed back into the room. There was no time to explain to the furious Hammond; it was only necessary to make the angry Britisher obey. Alex did so by asking him if he had a gun, then pulling out his own, furnished him by Malcolm on the night before.

The sight of McAuliff's weapon caused the agent to accept the moment. He removed a small, inconspicuous Rycee automatic from a belt holster under his jacket.

Alexander had grabbed the seersucker coat – this too furnished by Malcolm on the previous night – and thrown it over his arm, concealing his revolver.

Together the two men had slipped out of the room and run down the corridor to the staircase beyond the bank of elevators. On the concrete landing they had found the first of the Halidonites.

He was dead. A thin line of blood formed a perfect circle around his neck below the swollen skin of his face and the extended tongue of blank, dead, bulging eyes. He had been garroted swiftly, professionally.

Hammond had bent down; Alexander was too repelled by the sight to get closer. The Englishman had summarized.

Professionally.

'They know we're on this floor. They don't know which rooms. The other poor bastard's probably with them.'

'That's impossible. There wasn't time. *Nobody* knew where we were.'

Hammond had stared at the lifeless black man, and when he spoke, McAuliff recognized the profound shock of the Intelligence's man's anger.

'Oh, *God*, I've been *blind*!'

In that instant, Alexander, too, understood.

British Intelligence, Caribbean Operations, has a total of fifteen West Indian specialists. That's the budget. Of those fifteen, seven have been bought by Dunstone Limited.

The words of Malcolm the Halidonite.

And Hammond the manipulator had just figured it out.

The two men raced down the staircase. When they reached the lobby floor, the Englishman stopped and did a strange thing. He removed his belt, slipping the holster off and placing it in his pocket. He then wound the belt in a tight circle, bent down, and placed it in a corner. He stood up, looked around, and crossed to a cigarette-butt receptacle and moved it in front of the belt.

'It's a signaling device, isn't it?' McAuliff had said.

'Yes. Long-range. External scanner reception; works on vertical arcs. No damn good inside a structure. Too much interference . . . thank heaven.'

'You wanted to be *taken*?'

'No, not actually. It was always a possibility, I knew that . . . Any ideas, chap? At the moment, it's your show.'

'One, and I don't know how good it is. An airfield; it's a farm, I guess. West, on the highway. Near a place called Drax Hall . . . Let's go.' Alex reached for the knob on the door to the lobby.

'Not that way,' said Hammond. 'They'll be watching the lobby. The street, too, I expect. Downstairs. Delivery entrance . . . maintenance, that sort of thing. There's bound to be one in the cellar.'

'*Wait* a minute.' McAuliff had grabbed the Englishman's arm, physically forcing him to respond. 'Let's you and I get something clear. Right now. You've been *had*. *Taken*. Your own people sold you out. So there won't be any stopping for phone calls, for signaling anyone on the street. We run but we don't stop. For anything. You do and you're on your own. I disappear and I don't think you can handle that.'

'Who in hell do you think I'm going to get in touch with? The Prime Minister?'

'I don't know. I just know that I don't trust you. I don't trust liars. Or manipulators. And you're both, Hammond.'

'We all do what we can,' replied the agent coldly, his eyes unwavering. 'You've learned quickly, Alexander. You're an apt pupil.'

'Reluctantly. I don't think much of the school.'

And the race in the blinding sunlight had begun.

They ran up the curving driveway of the basement garage, directly into a tan Mercedes sedan that was not parked at that particular entrance by coincidence. Hammond and Alexander saw the startled look on the face of the white driver; then the man reached over across the seat for a transistor radio.

In the next few seconds Alex witnessed an act of violence he would never forget as long as he lived. An act performed with cold precision.

R. C. Hammond reached into both of his pockets and took out the Rycee automatic in his right hand, a steel cylinder in his left. He slapped the cylinder onto the barrel of the weapon, snapped in a clip, and walked directly to the door of the tan Mercedes-Benz. He opened it, held his hand low, and fired two shots into the driver, killing him instantly.

The shots were spits. The driver fell onto the dashboard; Hammond reached down and picked up the radio with his left hand.

The sun was bright; the strolling crowds kept moving. If anyone knew an execution had taken place, none showed it.

The British agent closed the door almost casually.

'*My God ...*' It was as far as Alex got.

'It was the last thing he expected,' said Hammond rapidly. 'Let's find a taxi.'

The statement was easier made than carried out. Cabs did not cruise in Montego Bay. The drivers homed like giant pigeons back to appointed street corners, where they lined up in European fashion, as much to discuss the progress of the day with their peers as to find additional fares. It was a maddening practice; during these moments it was a frightening one for the two fugitives. Neither knew where the cab locations were, except the obvious – the hotel entrance – and that was out.

They rounded the corner of the building, emerging on a free-port strip. The sidewalks were steaming hot; the crowds of gaudy, perspiring shoppers were pushing, hauling, tugging, pressing faces against the window fronts, foreheads and fingers smudging the glass, envying the unenviable ... the shiny. Cars were immobilized in the narrow street, the honking of horns, interspersed with oaths and threats as Jamaican tried to out-chauffeur Jamaican for the extra tip ... and his manhood.

Alexander saw him first, under a green-and-white sign that read MIRANDA HILL with an arrow pointing south. He was a heavyset, dark-haired white man in a brown gabardine suit, the jacket buttoned, the cloth stretched across muscular shoulders. The man's eyes were scanning the streams of human traffic, his head darting about like that of a huge pink ferret. And clasped in his left hand, buried in the flesh of his immense left hand, was a walkie-talkie identical to the one Hammond had taken out of the Mercedes.

Alex knew it would be only seconds before the man spotted them. He grabbed Hammond's arm and wished to God both of them were shorter than they were.

'At the corner! Under the sign ... Miranda Hill. The brown suit.'

'Yes. I see.' They were by a low-hanging awning of a free-port liquor store. Hammond swung into the entrance, begging his pardon through the swarm of tourists, their Barbados shirts and Virgin Island palm hats proof of yet another cruise ship. McAuliff followed involuntarily; the Britisher had locked Alex's arm in a viselike grip, propelling the American in a semicircle, forcing him into the crowded doorway.

The agent positioned the two of them inside the store, at the far corner of the display window. The line of sight was direct; the man under the green-and-white sign could be seen clearly, his eyes still searching the crowds. 'It's the same radio,' said Alex.

'If we're lucky he'll use it. I'm sure they've set up relays. I know that's him. He's Unio Corso.'

'That's like a Mafia, isn't it?'

'Not unlike. And far more efficient. He's a Corsican gun. Very high-priced. Warfield would pay it.' Hammond clipped his phrases in a quiet monotone; he was considering strategies. 'He may be our way out.'

'You'll have to be clearer than that,' said Alex.

'Yes, of course.' The Englishman was very imperiously polite. And maddening. 'By now they've circled the area, I should think. Covering all streets. Within minutes they'll know we've left the hotel. The signal won't fool them for long.' Hammond lifted the transistor radio as unobtrusively as possible to the side of his head and snapped the circular switch. There was a brief burst of static; the agent reduced the volume. Several nearby tourists looked curiously; Alexander smiled foolish at them. Outside on the corner, underneath the sign, the Corsican suddenly brought his radio to his ear. Hammond looked at McAuliff. 'They've just reached your room.'

'How do you know?'

'They report a cigarette still burning in the ashtray. Nasty habit. Radio on ... I should have thought of that.' The Englishman pursed his lips abruptly; his eyes indicated recognition. 'An outside vehicle is circling. The ... W.I.S. claims the signal is still inside.'

'W.I.S.?'

Hammond replied painfully. 'West Indian Specialist. One of my men.'

'Past tense,' corrected Alex.

'They can't raise the Mercedes,' said Hammond quickly. 'That's it.' He swiftly shut off the radio, jammed it into his pocket, and looked outside. The Corsican could be seen listening intently to his instrument. Hammond spoke again. 'We'll have to be very quick. Listen and commit. When our Italian finishes his report, he'll put the radio to his side. At that instant we'll break through at him. Get your hands on that radio. Hold it no matter *what*.'

'Just like that?' asked McAuliff apprehensively. 'Suppose he pulls a gun?'

'I'll be beside you. He won't have time.'

And the Corsican did not.

As Hammond predicted, the man under the sign spoke into the radio. The agent and Alex were beneath the low awning on the street, concealed by the crowds. The second the Corsican's arm began to descend from the side of his head, Hammond jabbed McAuliff's ribs. The two men broke through the flow of people toward the professional killer.

Alexander reached him first; the man started. His right hand went for his belt, his left automatically raised the radio. McAuliff grabbed the Corsican's wrist and threw his shoulder into the man's chest, slamming him against the pole supporting the sign.

Then the Coriscan's whole face contorted spastically; a barking, horrible sound emerged from his twisted mouth. And McAuliff felt a burst of warm blood exploding below.

He looked down. Hammond's hand held a long switchblade. The agent had ripped the Corsican's stomach open from pelvis to rib cage, severing the belt, cutting the cloth of the brown gabardine suit.

'Get the radio!' commanded the agent. 'Run south on the east side of the street. I'll meet you at the next corner. *Quickly* now!'

Alex's shock was so profound that he obeyed without thought. He grabbed the radio from the dead hand and plunged into the crowds crossing the intersection. Only when he was halfway across did he realize what Hammond was doing: he was holding up the dead Coriscan against the pole. He was giving *him* time to get away!

Suddenly he heard the first screams behind him. Then a mounting crescendo of screams and shrieks and bellowing roars of horror. And within the pandemonium, there was the piercing shrill of a whistle . . . then more whistles, then the thunder of bodies running in the steaming-hot street.

McAuliff raced . . . *was* he running south? *Was* he on the east side? He could not think. He could only feel the panic. And the blood. The blood! The goddamn blood was all over him! People had to see that!

He passed an outdoor restaurant, a sidewalk café. The diners were all rising from their seats, looking north toward the panicked crowds and the screams and the whistles . . . and now the sirens. There was an empty table by a row of planter boxes. On the table was the traditional red-checked tablecloth beneath a sugar bowl and shakers of salt and pepper.

He reached over the flowers and yanked the cloth, sending the condiments crashing to the cement deck, one or all smashing to pieces; he did not, could not, tell. His only thought was to cover the goddamn blood, now saturated through his shirt and trousers.

The corner was thirty feet away. What the hell was he supposed to do? Suppose Hammond had not gotten away? Was he supposed to stand there with the goddamn tablecloth over his front looking like an imbecile while the streets were in chaos?

'*Quickly now!*' came the words.

McAuliff turned, grateful beyond his imagination. Hammond was directly behind him, and Alex could not but help notice his hands. They were deep red and shining; the explosion of Corsican blood had left its mark.

The intersecting street was wider; the sign read QUEEN'S DRIVE. It curved upward toward the west, and Alex thought he recognized the section. On the diagonal corner an automobile pulled to a stop; the driver peered out the window, looking north at the racing people and the sounds of a riot.

Alex had to raise his voice to be heard. 'Over there!' he said to Hammond. 'That car!'

The Englishman nodded in agreement.

They dashed across the street. McAuliff by now had his wallet out of his pocket, removing bills. He approached the driver – a middle-aged black Jamaican – and spoke rapidly.

'We need a ride. I'll pay you whatever you want!'

But the Jamaican just stared at Alexander, his eyes betraying his sudden fear. And then McAuliff saw: The tablecloth was under his arm – how did it get under his arm? – and the huge stain of dark red blood was everywhere.

The driver reached for the gearshift; Alex thrust his right hand through the window and grabbed the man's shoulder, pulling his arm away from the dashboard. He threw his wallet to Hammond, unlatched the door, and yanked the man out of the seat. The Jamaican yelled and screamed for help. McAuliff took the bills in his hand and dropped them on the curb as he pummeled the driver across the sidewalk.

A dozen pedestrians looked on, and most ran, preferring noninvolvement; others watched, fascinated by what they saw. Two white teenagers ran toward the money and bent down to pick it up.

McAuliff did not know why, but that bothered him. He took the necessary three steps and lashed his foot out, smashing one of the young men in the side of the head.

'Get the hell out of here!' he roared as the teenager fell back, blood matted instantly along his blond hairline.

'*McAuliff!*' yelled Hammond, racing around the car toward the opposite front door. 'Get in and drive, for God's sake!'

As Alex climbed into the seat, he saw what he knew instantly was the worst sight he could see at that moment. A block away, from out of the milling crowds on the street, a tan Mercedes-Benz had suddenly accelerated, its powerful, deep-throated engine signifying its anticipated burst of speed.

McAuliff pulled the gearshift into drive and pressed the pedal to the floor. The car responded, and Alex was grateful for the surge of the racing wheels. He steered into the middle of Queen's Drive, on what had to be Miranda Hill, and immediately passed two cars . . . dangerously close, nearly colliding.

'The Mercedes was coming down the street,' he said to Hammond. 'I don't know if they spotted us.'

The Britisher whipped around in the seat, simultaneously withdrawing the Rycee automatic and the transistorized radio from both pockets. He snapped on the radio; the static was interspersed with agitated voices issuing commands and answering excitedly phrased questions.

The language, however, was not English.

Hammond supplied the reason. 'Dunstone has half the Unio Corso in Jamaica.'

'Can you understand?'

'Sufficiently . . . They're at the corner of Queen's Drive and Essex. In the Miranda Hill district. They've ascertained that the secondary commotion was us.'

'Translated: they've spotted us.'

'Can this car get a full throttle?'

'It's not bad; no match for a Mercedes, though.'

Hammond kept the radio at full volume, his eyes still on the rear window. There was a burst of chatter from the tiny speaker, and at the same instant McAuliff saw a speeding black Pontiac come over the incline in front of him, on the right, its brakes screeching, the driver spinning the wheel. 'Jesus!' he yelled.

'It's theirs!' cried Hammond. 'Their west patrol just reported seeing us. Turn! The first chance you get.'

Alex sped to the top of the hill. 'What's he doing?' He yelled again, his concentration on the road in front, on whatever automobile might lie over the crest.

'He's turning . . . side-slipped halfway down. He's righting it now.'

At the top of the incline, McAuliff spun the wheel to the right, pressed the accelerator to the floor, and raced past three automobiles on the steep descent, forcing a single approaching car to crowd the curb. 'There's some kind of park about a half a mile down.' He couldn't be sure of the distance; the blinding sun was careening off a thousand metal objects . . . or so it seemed. But he couldn't think of that; he could only squint. His mind was furiously abstracting flashes of recent memory. Flashes of another park . . . in Kingston; St George's. And another driver . . . a versatile Jamaican named Rodney.

'So?' Hammond was bracing himself now, his right hand, pistol firmly gripped against the dashboard, the radio, at full volume, against the seat.

'There's not much traffic. Not too many people either . . .' Alex swerved the car once again to pass another automobile. He looked in the rear-view mirror. The black Pontiac was at the top of the hill behind them; there were now four cars between them.

'The Mercedes is heading west on Gloucester,' said Hammond, breaking in on Alex's thoughts. 'They said Gloucester . . . Another car is to proceed along . . . Sewell . . .' Hammond translated as rapidly as the voices spoke, overlapping each other.

'Sewell's on the other side of the district,' said McAuliff, as much to himself as to the agent. 'Gloucester's the shore road.'

'They've alerted two vehicles. One at North and Fort Streets, the other at Union.'

'That's Montego proper. The business area. They're trying to cut us off at all points. For Christ's sake, there *is* nothing else left!'

'What are you talking about?' Hammond had to shout; the screaming tires, the wind, the roaring engine did not permit less.

Explanations took time, if only seconds – there were no seconds left. There would be no explanations, only commands . . . as there had been commands years ago. Issued in the frozen hills with no more confidence than McAuliff felt now.

'Get in the back seat,' he ordered, firmly but not tensely. 'Smash the rear window; get yourself a clear area. When I swing into the park, he'll follow. As soon as I'm inside, I'm going to swerve right and stop. *Hard!* Start firing the second you see the Pontiac behind us. Do you have extra clips?'

'Yes.'

'Put in a full one. You've used two shells. Forget that goddamn silencer, it'll throw you off. Try to get clean shots. Through the front and side windows. Stay away from the gas tank and the tires.'

The stone gates to the park were less than a hundred yards away, seconds away. Hammond stared at Alex – for but an instant – and began climbing over the seat to the rear of the automobile.

'You think we can switch cars—'

Perhaps it was a question; McAuliff did not care. He interrupted. 'I don't know. I just know we can't use this one any longer and we have to get to the other side of Montego.'

'They'll surely spot their own vehicle.'

'They won't be looking for it. Not for the next ten minutes . . . if you can aim straight.'

The gates were on the left now. Alex whipped the steering wheel around; the car skidded violently as Hammond began smashing the glass in the rear window. The automobile behind swerved to the right to avoid a collision, its horn blaring, the driver screaming. McAuliff sped through the gate, now holding down the bar of his horn as a warning.

Inside the gates he slammed on the brakes, spun the wheel to the right, pressed the accelerator, and jumped the curb of the drive over onto the grass. He crashed his foot once again onto the brake pedal; the car jolted to a stop on the soft turf. In the distance strollers in the park turned; a couple picnicking stood up.

Alex was not concerned. In seconds the firing would start; the pedestrians would run for cover, out of the danger zone. Away from the fire base.

Danger zone. Fire base. Cover. Terms from centuries ago.

So then it followed that the strollers were not pedestrians. Not pedestrians at all.

They were *civilians*.

It *was* war.

Whether the civilians knew it or not.

There was the sudden, ear-shattering screech of tires.

Hammond fired through the smashed rear window. The Pontiac swerved off the drive, hurtled over the opposite curb, careened off a cluster of tropic shrubbery, and slammed into a mound of loose earth dug for one of a thousand unending park projects. The engine continued at high speed, but the gears had locked, the wheels still, the horn blasting in counterpoint to the whining roar of the motor.

Screams could be heard in the distance.

From the civilians.

McAuliff and Hammond jumped out of the car and raced over grass and concrete onto grass again. Both had their weapons drawn; it was not necessary. R. C. Hammond had performed immaculately. He had fired with devastating control through the open side window of the Pontiac. The automobile was untouched but the driver was dead, sprawled over the wheel. Dead weight against the horn.

The two fugitives divided at the car, each to a door of the front seat, Alexander on the driver's side. Together they shoved the lifeless body away from the wheel; the blaring horn ceased, the engine continued to roar. McAuliff reached in and turned the ignition key.

The silence was incredible.

Yet, still, there were the screams from the distance, from the grass.

The civilians.

They yanked at the dead man and threw the body over the plastic seat onto the floor behind. Hammond picked up the transistor radio. It was in the 'on' position. He turned it off. Alexander got behind the wheel and feverishly tugged at the gearshift.

It did not move, and the muscles in McAuliff's stomach tensed; he felt his hands trembling.

From out of a boyhood past, long, long, forgotten, came the recall. There was an old car in an old garage; the gears were always sticking.

Start the motor for only an instant.

Off-on. Off-on.

Until the gear teeth unlocked.

He did so. How many times, he would never remember. He would only remember the cold, calm eyes of R. C. Hammond watching him.

The Pontiac lurched. First into the mound of earth; then, as Alex jammed the stick into *R*, backward – wheels spinning furiously – over the grass.

They were mobile.

McAuliff whipped the steering wheel into a full circle, pointing the car toward the cement drive. He pressed the accelerator, and the Pontiac gathered speed on the soft grass in preparation for its jarring leap over the curb.

Four seconds later they sped through the stone gates.

And Alexander turned right. East. Back toward Miranda Hill.

He knew Hammond was stunned; that did not matter. There was still no time for explanations, and the Englishman seemed to understand. He said nothing.

Several minutes later, at the first intersecting road, McAuliff jumped the light and swung left. North. The sign read CORNICHE ANNEX.

Hammond spoke.

'You're heading toward the shore road?'

'So you're behind the Dunstone car ... the Mercedes.'

'Yes.'

'And may I presume that since the last word' – here Hammond held up the walkie-talkie – 'any of them received was from that park, there's a more direct way back to it? A faster way?'

'Yes. Two. Queen's Drive and Corniche Road. They branch off from Gloucester.'

'Which, of course, would be the routes they would take.'

'They'd better.'

'And naturally, they would search the park.'

'I hope so.'

R. C. Hammond pressed back into the seat. It was a gesture of temporary relaxation. Not without a certain trace of admiration.

'You're a *very* apt student, Mr McAuliff.'

'To repeat myself, it's a rotten school,' said Alexander.

They waited in the darkness, in the overgrowth at the edge of the field. The crickets hammered out the passing seconds. They had left the Pontiac miles away on a deserted back road in Catherine Mount and walked to the farm on the outskirts of Drax Hall, where they found a stream and cleaned themselves up, washing the blood off their skin and soaking their clothes. They had waited until nightfall before making the last few miles of the trip. Cautiously, shelter to shelter; when on the road, as far out of sight as possible. Finally using the tracks of the Jamaica Railway as their guideline.

There had been a road map in the glove compartment of the automobile, and they studied it. It was maddening. Most of the streets west of Montego proper were unmarked, lines without names, and always there were the alleys without lines. They passed through a number of ghetto settlements, aware that the inhabitants had to be sizing them up – two white men without conceivable business in the area. There was profit in an assault on such men.

Hammond had insisted that they both carry their jackets, their weapons very much in evidence in their belts.

Subalterns crossing through hostile colonial territory, letting the wog natives know they carried the magic firesticks that spat death.

Ludicrous.

But there was no assault.

They crossed the Montego River at Westgate; a half-mile away were the railroad tracks. They ran into an itinerant tramp enclave – a hobo camp, Jamaica-style – and Hammond did the talking.

The Englishman said they were insurance inspectors for the company; they had no objections to the filthy campsite so long as there was no interference with the line. But should there be interference, the penalties would be stiff indeed.

Ludicrous.

Yet no one bothered them, although the surrounding black eyes were filled with hatred.

There was a freight pick-up at Drax Hall. A single platform with two wire-encased light bulbs illuminating the barren site. Inside the weather-beaten rain shelter was an old man drunk on cheap rum. Painstakingly they elicited enough information from him for McAuliff to get his bearings. Vague, to be sure, but enough to determine the related distances from the highway, which veered inland at Parish Wharf, to the farm district in the southwest section.

By nine thirty they had reached the field.

Now, Alex looked at his watch. It was ten thirty.

He was not sure he had made the right decision. He was only sure that he could not think of any other. He had recalled the lone farmhouse on the property, remembered seeing a light on inside. There was no light now. It was deserted.

There was nothing else to do but wait.

An hour passed, and the only sounds were those of the Jamaican night: the predators foraging, victims taken, unending struggles – immaterial to all but the combatants.

It was nearly the end of the second hour when they heard it.

Another sound.

An automobile. Driving slowly, its low-geared, muted engine signaling its apprehension. An intruder very much aware of its transgression.

Minutes later, in the dim light of a moon sheeted with clouds, they watched a long figure run across the field, first to the north end, where a single torch was ignited, then to the south – perhaps four hundred yards – where the action was repeated. Then the figure dashed once more to the opposite end.

Another sound. Another intruder. Also muted – this from the darkness of the sky.

An airplane, its engine idling, was descending rapidly.

It touched ground, and simultaneously the torch at the north end was extinguished. Seconds later the aircraft came to a stop by the flame at the south end. A man jumped out of the small cabin; the fire was put out instantly.

'Let's go!' said McAuliff to the British agent. Together the two men started across the field.

They were no more than fifty yards into the grass when it happened.

The impact was so startling, the shock so complete, that Alex screamed involuntarily and threw himself to the ground, his pistol raised, ready to fire.

Hammond remained standing.

For two immensely powerful searchlights had caught them in the blinding convergence of the cross-beams.

'Put down your weapon, McAuliff,' came the words from beyond the blinding glare.

And Daniel, Minister of Council for the Tribe of Acquaba, walked through the light.

32

'When you came into the area you tripped the photo-electric alarms. Nothing mysterious.'

They were in the automobile, Daniel in front with the driver, Hammond and Alexander in the back seat. They had driven away from the field, out of Drax Hall, along the coast into Lucea Harbour. They parked on a deserted section of a dirt road overlooking the water. The road was one of those native offshoots on the coastal highway unspoiled by trespassing tourists. The moon was brighter by the ocean's edge, reflected off the rippling surface, washing soft yellow light over their faces.

As they were driving, McAuliff had a chance to study the car they were in. From the outside it looked like an ordinary, not-very-distinguished automobile of indeterminate make and vintage – like hundreds of island vehicles, made from parts cannibalized from other cars. Yet inside the fundamental difference was obvious: it was a precision-tooled mobile fortress and communications center. The windows were of thick, bullet-proof glass; rubber slots were evident in the rear and side sections – slots that were for the high-blasting, short-barreled shotguns clamped below the back of the front seat. Under the dashboard was a long panel with dials and switches; a telephone was locked into a recess between two microphones. The engine, from the sound of it, was one of the most powerful Alex had ever heard.

The Halidon went first class in the outside world.

Daniel was in the process of dismissing McAuliff's astonishment at the events of the past two hours. It seemed important to the minister that he convey the reality of the situation. The crisis was sufficiently desperate for Daniel to leave the community; to risk his life to be in command.

It was as though he wanted very much for R. C. Hammond to realize he was about to deal with an extremely sensible and hard-nosed adversary.

'We had to make sure you were alone ... the two of you, of course. That you were not somehow followed. There were tense moments this afternoon. You handled yourselves expertly, apparently. We could not help you. Congratulations.'

'What happened to Malcolm?' asked Alex.

Daniel paused, then spoke quietly, sadly. 'We do not know yet. We are looking ... He is safe – or dead. There is no middle ground.' Daniel looked at Hammond. 'Malcolm is the man you know as Joseph Myers, Commander Hammond.'

McAuliff shifted his gaze to the agent. So Hammond the manipulator was a commander. Commander Hammond, liar, manipulator . . . and risker-of-life to save another's.

Hammond reacted to Daniel's words by closing his eyes for precisely two seconds. The information was a professional burden he did not care for; the manipulator was outflanked again.

'Do I have a single black man working for me? For the Service?'

The minister smiled gently. 'By our count, seven. Three, however, are quite ineffectual.'

'Thank you for enlightening me. I'm sure you can furnish me with identities . . . They all look so much alike you see.'

Daniel accepted the clichéd insult calmly, his smile disappearing, his eyes cold in the yellow moonlight. 'Yes. I understand the problem. There appears to be so little to distinguish us . . . from such a viewpoint. Fortunately, there are other standards. You will not be needing the identities.'

Hammond returned Daniel's look without intimidation. 'McAuliff conveyed your demands. I say to you what I said to him. They're impossible, of course—'

'Please, Commander Hammond,' said Daniel rapidly, interrupting, 'there are so many complications, let us not compound them with lies. From the beginning your instructions were clear. Would you prefer we deal with the Americans? Or the French? The Germans, perhaps?'

The silence was abrupt. There was a cruelty to it, a blunt execution of pain. Alexander watched as the two enemies exchanged stares. He saw the gradual, painful cognizance in Hammond's eyes.

'Then you know,' said the Englishman softly.

'We know,' replied Daniel simply.

Hammond remained silent and looked out the window.

The Minister of the Halidon turned to McAuliff. 'The global mendacity, doctor. Commander Hammond is the finest Intelligence officer in the British service. The unit he directs is a coordinated effort between the aforementioned governments. It is, however, coordinated in name only. For MI5 – as the prime investigatory agency – does nothing to apprise its fellow signatories of its progress.'

'There are good and sufficient reasons for our actions,' said Hammond, still looking out the window.

'Reduced to one, is that not right, Commander? . . . Security. You cannot trust your allies.'

'Our counterparts are leak-prone. Experience has confirmed this.' The agent did not take his eyes off the water.

'So you mislead them,' said Daniel. 'You give false information, tell them you are concentrating in the Mediterranean, then South America – Argentina, Nicaragua. Even nearby Haiti . . . but never Jamaica.' The minister paused for emphasis. 'No, never Jamaica.'

'Standard procedure,' answered Hammond, allowing Daniel a brief, wary look.

'Then it will not surprise you to learn that this mistrust is shared by your foreign confederates. They have sent out teams, their best men. They are presently tracking down every scrap of information MI6 has made available. They are working furiously.'

Hammond snapped his head back to Daniel. 'That is contrary to our agreement,' he said in an angry monotone.

The minister did not smile. 'I do not think you are in a position to be sanctimonious, Commander.' Daniel shifted his eyes again to Alexander. 'You see, McAuliff, since Dunstone Limited, was a London-based conglomerate, it was agreed to give the first-level assignment to British Intelligence. It was understandable; MI5 and 6 are the finest in the West; the Commander is their finest. On the theory that the fewer clandestine services operating, the less likely were breaches of security, the British agreed to function alone and keep everyone current. Instead, they continuously furnished erroneous data.' Daniel now permitted himself a minor smile. 'In a sense, they were justified. The Americans, the French, and the Germans were *all* breaking the agreement, none had any intention of keeping it. Each was going after Dunstone, while claiming to leave the field to the English ... Dunstone *has* to be dismantled. Taken apart economic brick by economic brick. The world markets can accept no less. But there are so many bricks. Each government believes that if only it can get there first – get the Dunstone list before the others – well, arrangements can be made, assets transferred.'

Hammond could not remain silent. 'I submit – whoever you are – that we are the logical ... executors.'

'The term "logic" being interchangeable with "deserving". I will say this for your cause. God, Queen, and Empire have paid heavily in recent decades. Somewhat out of proportion to their relative sins, but that is not our concern, Commander. As I said, your instructions were clear at the outset: Get the Dunstone list at all costs. The cost is now clear. We will give you the list. You will get out of Jamaica. That is the price.'

Again, the silence; once more, the exchange of analysing stares. A cloud passed over the Montego moon, causing a dark shadow to fall over the faces. Hammond spoke.

'How can be we be sure of its authenticity?'

'Can you doubt us after the events of the day? Remember, it is in our mutual interest that Dunstone be eliminated.'

'What guarantees do you expect from us?'

Daniel laughed. A laugh formed in humor. 'We do not need *guarantees*, Commander. We will *know*. Can you not understand that? Our island is not a continent; we know every liaison, conduit, and contact with whom you function.' The smile from the laugh formed in humor disappeared. 'These operations will stop. Make whatever settlements you must, but then no more. Give – really give – Jamaica to its rightful owners. Struggles, chaos, and all.'

'And' – the Englishman spoke softly – 'if these decisions are outside my control—'

'Make no mistake, Commander Hammond!' Daniel's voice rose, cutting off the agent. 'The executions that took place today began at noon London time. And each day, the chimes in Parliament's clocktower ring out another noon. When you hear them, remember. What we were capable of today, we are capable of tomorrow. And we will add the truth of our motives. England will be a pariah in the community of nations. You cannot afford that.'

'Your threat is ludicrous!' countered Hammond, with equal fever. 'As you said, this island is not a continent. We'd go in and destroy you.'

Daniel nodded and replied quietly. 'Quite possible. And you should know that we are prepared for that eventuality. We *have* been for over two hundred years. Remarkable, isn't it? ... By all you believe holy, pay the price, Hammond; take the list and salvage what you can from Dunstone. You *do* deserve that. Not that you'll salvage much; the vultures will fly in from their various geographies and dive for the carrion. We offer you time, perhaps only a few days. Make the best of it!'

A red light on the panel beneath the dashboard lit up, throwing a glow over the front seat. There were the sharp, staccato repeats of a high-pitched buzzer. The driver reached for the telephone and pulled it to his ear, held it there for several seconds, and then handed the instrument to Daniel.

The Minister of the Halidon listened. Alexander saw his face in the rearview mirror. Daniel could not conceal his alarm.

And then his anger.

'Do what you can but risk *no lives*. Our men are to pull out. *No one* is to leave the community. That is final. *Irreversible!*' He replaced the telephone in its upright recess firmly and turned his eyes on the Englishman as he spoke sarcastically. 'British *expertise*, Commander. John Bull *know-how*. The West Indian specialists, MI6, Caribbean, have just received their orders from Dunstone. They are to go into the Cock Pit and intercept the survey. They are to make sure it does not come out.'

'Oh, my God!' McAuliff pitched forward on the seat. 'Can they reach them?'

'Ask the eminent authority,' said Daniel bitingly, his eyes wide on Hammond. 'They are his men.'

The agent was rigid, as though he had stopped breathing. Yet it was obvious his mind was operating swiftly, silently. 'They are in contact with the radio receivers ... the signals transmitted from the campsite. The location can be pinpointed—'

'Within a thousand yards,' cut in Alexander, completing Hammond's statement.

'Yes.'

'You've got to stop them!'

'I'm not sure there's a way—'

'*Find* one. For Christ's sake, Hammond, they're going to be killed!'

McAuliff grabbed Hammond by the lapels of his jacket, yanking him forward viciously. 'You *move*, mister. Or I'll kill you!'

'Take your hands—'

Before the agent could finish the obvious, Alexander whipped his right hand across Hammond's face, breaking the skin on the Englishman's lips. 'There isn't anything more, *Commander*! I want those guarantees! *Now!*'

The agent spoke through rivulets of blood. 'I'll do my best. All I've ever given you was . . . our best efforts.'

'You son-of-a-bitch!' McAuliff brought his hand back once again. The driver and Daniel grabbed his arm.

'McAuliff! You'll accomplish *nothing*!' roared the minister.

'You tell *him* to start accomplishing!' Then Alexander stopped and turned to Daniel, releasing the Englishman. 'You've got people there.' And then McAuliff remembered the terrible words Daniel had spoken into the telephone: *Risk no lives. Our men . . . pull back. No one is to leave the community.* 'You've got to get on that phone. Take back what you said. *Protect them!*'

The minister spoke quietly. 'You must try to understand. There were traditions, revelations . . . a way of life extending over two hundred years. We cannot jeopardize these things.'

Alexander stared at the black man. 'You'd watch them *die*? My God, you *can't*!'

'I am afraid we could. And would. And we would then be faced with the taking of your life. It would be taken as swiftly . . .' Daniel turned up the collar of his shirt, revealing a tiny bulge in the cloth. *Tablets, sewn into the fabric.* '. . . as I would bite into these, should I ever find myself in a position where it was necessary. I would not think twice about it.'

'For God's sake, that's *you*! They're not you; they're no part of you. They don't *know* you. Why should they pay with their lives?'

Hammond's voice was startling in its quiet incisiveness. 'Priorities, McAuliff. I told you. For them . . . for us.'

'The accidents of war, doctor. Combat's slaughter of innocents, perhaps.' Daniel spoke simply, denying the implication of his words. 'Things written and unwritten—'

'*Bullshit!*' screamed McAuliff. The driver removed a pistol from his belt; his action was obvious. Alexander looked rapidly back and forth between the Minister of the Halidon and the British Intelligence officer. 'Listen to me. You said on that phone for them to do what they can. You. Hammond. You offered your . . . goddamned "best efforts". All right. Give *me* a chance!'

'How?' asked Daniel. 'There can be no Jamaican police, no Kingston troops.'

The words came back to Alexander. Words spoken by Sam Tucker in the glow of the campsite fire. A quiet statement made as Sam watched the figure of Charles Whitehall and the black giant, Lawrence, talking in the compound. *They're our protection. They may hate each other . . .*

They're our protection.

McAuliff whirled on Hammond. 'How many defectors have you got here?'

'I brought six specialists from London—'

'All but one has sold out to Dunstone,' interrupted Daniel.

'That's five. How many others could they pick up?' McAuliff addressed the Halidonite.

'On such short notice, perhaps three or four; probably mercenaries. That is only a guess . . . They would be more concerned with speed than numbers. One automatic rifle in the hands of a single soldier—'

'When did they get the Dunstone orders?' asked Alex swiftly, breaking off Daniel's unnecessary observations.

'Within the hour is our estimate. Certainly no more than an hour.'

'Could they get a plane?'

'Yes. Ganja aircraft are always for hire. It would take a little time; ganja pilots are a suspicious breed, but it could be done.'

Alex turned to Hammond. The agent was wiping his lips with his fingers . . . his goddamn fingers, as if dusting the pastry crumbs off his mouth during tea at the Savoy! 'Can you raise the people monitoring the signals from the campsite? With that radio?' McAuliff pointed to the panel under the dashboard.

'I have the frequency—'

'Does that mean *yes*?'

'Yes.'

'What is the point?' asked Daniel.

'To see if his goddamn specialists have reached them. To get the position—'

'You want our plane?' interrupted the Minister of the Halidon, knowing the answer to his question.

'*Yes!*'

Daniel signaled to the driver to start the car. 'You don't need the position. There is only one place to land: the grassland two miles southwest of the campsite. We have the coordinates.'

The automobile lurched out of the parking area, careened off the primitive border, and sped into the darkness toward the highway.

Hammond gave the frequency-band decimals to Daniel; the minister transmitted them, handing the microphone to the British agent.

There was no pick-up.

No answer over the airways.

'It will take time to get the plane.' Daniel spoke quietly as the car roared over the wide roadway.

Alex suddenly put his hand on the minister's shoulder. 'Your runner, the one who used the name Marcus. Tell him to get word to Sam Tucker.'

'I have instructed our men to pull out,' answered Daniel icily. 'Please remember what I told you.'

'For Christ's sake, send him back. Give them a chance!'

'Don't you mean give *her* a chance?'

McAuliff wanted – as he had never wanted anything before – to kill the man. 'You had to say it, didn't you?'

'Yes,' replied Daniel, turning in his seat to look Alexander in the eye. 'Because it is related to the condition on which you have use of the plane. If you fail, if the woman is killed, your life is taken also. You will be executed. Quite simply, with her death you could never be trusted.'

Alexander acknowledged the penetrating stare of Daniel the Halidonite. 'Quite simply,' he said, 'my answer is easy. I'll give the firing order myself.'

R. C. Hammond leaned forward. His speech was measured, precise as ever. 'I am going in with you, McAuliff.'

Both Daniel and Alex looked at the Englishman. Hammond, in a few words, had quietly moved into a strange defenceless position. It astonished both men.

'Thank you.' It was all McAuliff could say, but he meant it profoundly.

'I'm afraid that is not possible, Commander,' said Daniel. 'You and I . . . we have matters between us. If McAuliff goes, he goes alone.'

'You're a barbarian.' Hammond spoke sharply.

'I am the Halidon. And we *do* have priorities. Both of us.'

33

McAuliff nosed the small plane above cloud cover. He loosened the field jacket provided him by the driver of the car. It was warm in the tiny cabin. The Halidon aircraft was different from the plane he and Malcolm had flown from the field west of Accompong. It was similar to the two-seater Comanche in size and appearance, but its weight and manoeuvrability were heavier and greater.

McAuliff was not a good pilot. Flying was a skill he had half mastered through necessity, not from any devotion. Ten years ago, when he had made the decision to go field-commercial, he had felt the ability to fly would come in handy, and so he had taken the prescribed lessons that eventually led to a very limited licence.

It had proved worthwhile. On dozens of trips over most continents. In small, limited aircraft.

He hoped to Christ it would prove worthwhile now. If it did not, nothing mattered anymore.

On the seat beside him was a small blackboard, a slate common to grammar school, bordered by wood. On it was chalked his primitive flight plan in white lettering that stood out in the dim light of the instrument panel.

Desired air speed, compass points, altitude requirements, and sightings that, with luck and decent moonlight, he could distinguish.

From the strip outside Drax Hall he was to reach a height of one thousand feet, circling the field until he had done so. Leaving the strip perimeter, he was to head southeast at 115 degrees, air speed 90. In a few minutes he would be over Mount Carey – two brush fires would be burning in a field; he would spot them.

He did.

From Mount Carey, maintaining air speed and dropping to 700 feet, he was to swing east-northeast at 84 degrees and proceed to Kempshot Hill. An automobile with a spotlight would be on a road below; the spotlight would flicker its beam into the sky.

He saw it and followed the next line on the chalkboard. His course change was minor – 8 degrees to 92 on the compass, maintaining air speed and

662

altitude. Three minutes and thirty seconds later, he was over Amity Hall. Again brush fires, again a fresh instruction; this, too, was minimal.

East at 87 degrees into Weston Favel.

Drop altitude to 500 feet, maintain air speed, look for two automobiles facing each other with blinking headlights at the south section of the town. Correct course to exactly 90 degrees and reduce air speed to 75.

The instant he reached Martha Brae River, he was to alter course 35 degrees southeast, to precisely 122 on the compass.

At this point he was on his own. There would be no more signals from the ground, and, of course, no radio contact whatsoever.

The coordination of air speed, direction, and timing was all he had ... everything he had. Altitude was by pilotage – as low as possible, cognizant of the gradual ascent of the jungle hills. He might spot campfires, but he was not to assume any to be necessarily those of the survey. There were roving hill people, often on all-night hunts. He was to proceed on course for exactly four minutes and fifteen seconds.

If he had followed everything precisely and if there were no variants of magnitude such as sudden wind currents or rainfall, he would be in the vicinity of the grasslands. Again, if the night was clear and if the light of the moon was sufficient, he would see them.

And – most important – if he spotted other aircraft, he was to dip his right wing twice. This would indicate to any other plane that he was a ganja runner. It was the current courtesy-of-recognition among such gentlemen of the air.

The hills rose suddenly, far more rapidly than McAuliff had expected. He pulled back the half wheel and felt the updrafts carry him into a one-o'clock soar. He reduced the throttle and countered the high bank with pressure on the left pedal; the turbulence continued, the winds grew.

Then he realized the cause of the sudden shifts and cross-currents. He had entered a corridor of harsh jungle showers. Rain splattered against the glass and pelted the fuselage; wipers were inadequate. In front of him was a mass of streaked, opaque gray. He slammed down the left window panel, pulled out the throttle, went into a swift ten-o'clock bank, and peered down. His altimeter inched toward 650; the ground below was dense and black ... nothing but jungle forest, no breaks in the darkness. He retraced the leg from the Martha Brae in his mind. Furiously, insecurely. His speed had been maintained, so too his compass. But there had been slippage; not much but recognizable. He was not that good a pilot – only twice before had he flown at night; his lapsed licence forbade it – and slippage, or drift, was an instrument or pilotage problem corrected by dials, sightings, or radio.

But the slight drift had been there. And it had come from aft starboard. Jesus, he was better in a sailboat! He leveled the aircraft and gently banked to the right, back into the path of the rain squall. The windshield was useless now; he reached across the seat and pulled down the right window panel. The burst of noise from the cross-drafted openings crashed abruptly through the small cabin. The wind roared at high velocity; the rain swept in streaking sheets, covering the seats and the floor and the instrument panel. The blackboard was soaked, its surface glistening, the chalk marks seemingly magnified by the rushing water sloshing within the borders.

And then he saw it ... them. The plateau of grassland. Through the starboard – goddammit, *right* window. A stretch of less-black in the middle of the total blackness. A dull gray relief in the center of the dark wood.

He had overshot the fields to the left, no more than a mile, perhaps two.

But he had reached them. Nothing else mattered at the moment. He descended rapidly, entering a left bank above the trees – the top of a figure eight for landing. He made a 280-degree approach and pushed the half wheel forward for touch down.

He was at the fifty-foot reading when behind him, in the west, was a flash of heat lightning. He was grateful for it; it was an additional, brief illumination in the night darkness. He trusted the instruments and could distinguish the approaching grass in the beam of the forelamps, but the dull, quick fullness of dim light gave him extra confidence.

And it gave him the visibility to detect the outlines of another plane. It was on the ground, stationary, parked on the north border of the field.

In the area of the slope that led to the campsite two miles away.

Oh, God! He had not made it at all. He was too late!

He touched earth, revved the engine, and taxied toward the immobile aircraft, removing his pistol from his belt as he manipulated the controls.

A man waved in the beam of the front lights. No weapon was drawn; there was no attempt to run or seek concealment. Alex was bewildered. It did not make sense; the Dunstone men were killers, he knew that. The man in the beam of light, however, gave no indication of hostility. Instead, he did a peculiar thing. He stretched out his arms at his sides, lowering the right and raising the left simultaneously. He repeated the gesture several times as McAuliff's aircraft approached.

Alex remembered the instructions at the field at Drax Hall. If you sight other planes, dip your right wing. *Lower* your right wing ... arm.

The man in the beam of light was a ganja pilot!

McAuliff pulled to a stop and switched off the ignition, his hand gripped firmly around the handle of his weapon, his finger poised in the trigger frame.

The man came up behind the wind and shouted through the rain to Alex in the open window. He was a white man, his face framed in the canvas of a poncho hood. His speech was American ... Deep South. Delta origins.

'Gawd*damn*! This is one busy fuckin' place! Good to see your white skin, man! I'll fly 'em an' I'll fuck 'em, but I don't *lak* 'em!' The pilot's voice was high-pitched and strident, easily carried over the sound of the rain. He was medium height, and, if his face was any indication, he was slender but flabby; a thin man unable to cope with the middle years. He was past forty.

'When did you get in?' asked Alex loudly, trying not to show his anxiety.

'Flew in these six blacks 'bout ten minutes ago. Mebbe a little more, not much. You with 'em, I sup'ose? You runnin' things?'

'Yes.'

'They don't get so *uppity* when there's trouble, huh? Nothin' but trouble in these mountain fields. They sure need whitey, then, you betcha balls!'

McAuliff put his pistol back in his belt beneath the panel. He had to move fast now. He had to get past the ganja pilot. 'They said there was trouble?' Alex asked the question casually as he opened the cabin door, stepped on the wing into the rain, and jumped to the wet ground.

'Gawd*damn*! The way they tell it, they got stole blind by a bunch of fuckin' bucks out there. Resold a bundle after takin' their cash. Let me tell you, those niggers are loaded with hardware!'

'That's a mistake,' said McAuliff with conviction. 'Jesus ... goddamn *idiots!*'

'They're lookin' for black blood, man! Those brothers gonna lay out a lotta other brothers! *Eeeaww!*'

'They do and New Orleans will go up in smoke! ... Christ!' Alexander knew the Louisiana city was the major port of entry for narcotics throughout the Southern and Southwestern states. This particular ganja pilot would know that. 'Did they head down the slope?' McAuliff purposely gestured a hundred yards to the right, away from the vicinity of the path he remembered.

'Damned if they was too fuckin' sure, man! They got one a them Geigers like an air-radar hone, but not so good. They took off more like down there.' The pilot pointed to the left of the hidden jungle path.

Alex calculated rapidly. The scanner used by the Dunstone men was definitive only in terms of a thousand-yard radius. The signals would register, but there were no hot or cold levels that would be more specific. It was the weakness of miniaturized long-distance radio arcs, operating on vertical principals.

One thousand yards was three thousand feet – over a half a mile within the dense, almost impenetrable jungle of the Cock Pit. If the Dunstone team had a ten-minute advantage, it was not necessarily fatal. They did not know the path – he didn't *know* it either, but he had traveled it. Twice. Their advantage had to be reduced. And if their angle of entry was indirect – according to the ganja pilot, it was – and presuming they kept to a relatively straight line, anticipating a sweep ... the advantage conceivably might be removed.

If ... if he could find the path and keep to it.

He pulled up the lapels of his field jacket to ward off the rain and turned toward the cabin door above the wind of the plane. He opened it, raised himself with one knee to the right of the strut, and reached into the small luggage compartment behind the seat. He pulled out a short-barreled, high-powered automatic rifle – one of the two that had been strapped below the front seat of the Halidon car. The clip was inserted, the safety on. In his pockets were four additional clips; each clip held twenty cartridges.

One hundred shells.

His arsenal.

'I've got to reach them,' he yelled through the downpour at the ganja pilot. 'I sure as hell don't want to answer to New Orleans!'

'Them New Orleens boys is a tense bunch. I don't fly for 'em if I got other work. They don' lak nobody!'

Without replying, McAuliff raced toward the edge of the grassland slope. The path was to the right of a huge cluster of nettled fern – he remembered that; his face had been scratched because his hand had not been quick enough when he had entered the area with the Halidon runner.

Goddammit! Where was it?

He began feeling the soaked foliage, gripping every leaf, every branch, hoping to find his hand scratched, scraped by nettles. He had to find it; he had to start his entry at precisely the right point. The wrong spot would be fatal. Dunstone's advantage would be too great; he could not overcome it.

'What are you lookin' for?'

'*What?*' Alex whipped around into a harsh glare of light. His concentration was such that he found himself unlatching the safety on the rifle. He had been about to fire in shock.

The ganja pilot had walked over. 'Gawddamn. Ain't you got a flashlight, man? You expect to find your way in that mess without no flashlight?'

Jesus! He had left the flashlight in the Halidon plane. Daniel had said something about being careful ... with the flashlight. So he had left it behind! 'I forgot. There's one in the plane.'

'I hope to fuck there is,' said the pilot.

'You take mine. Let me use yours, okay?'

'You promise to shoot me a couple a bucks, you got it man.' The pilot handed him the light. 'This rain's too fuckin' wet, I'm going back inside. Good huntin', hear!'

McAuliff watched the pilot run toward his aircraft and then quickly turned back to the jungle's edge. He was no more than five feet from the cluster of fern; he could see the matted grass at the entry point of the concealed path.

He plunged in.

He ran as fast as he could, his feet ensnared by the underbrush, his face and body whipped by the unseen tentacles of overgrowth. The path twisted – right, left, right, right, *right, Jesus! circles* – and then became straight again for a short stretch at the bottom of the slope.

But it was still true. He was still on it. That was all that mattered.

Then he veered off. The path wasn't there. It was gone!

There was an ear-shattering screech in the darkness, magnified by the jungle downpour. In the beam of his flashlight, deep within a palm-covered hole below him, was a wild pig suckling its blind young. The hairy, monstrous face snarled and screeched once more and started to rise, shaking its squealing offspring from its teats. McAuliff ran to his left, into the wall of the jungle. He stumbled on a rock. Two, three rocks. He fell to the wet earth, the flashlight rolling on the ground. The ground was flat, unobstructed.

He had found the path again!

He got to his feet, grabbed the light, shifted the rifle under his arm, and raced down the relatively clear jungle corridor.

Clear for no more than a hundred yards, where it was intersected by a stream, bordered by soft, foot-sucking mud. He remembered the stream. The runner who had used the name Marcus had turned left. Was it left? Or was it the from the opposite direction? . . . No, it *was* left. There had been palm trunks and rocks showing through the surface of the water, crossing the narrow stream. He ran to the left, his flashlight aimed at the midpoint of the water.

There were the logs! The rocks. A hastily constructed bridge to avoid the ankle-swallowing mud.

And on the right palm trunk were two snakes in lateral slow motion, curving their way toward him. Even the Jamaican mongoose did not have the stomach for Jamaica's Cock Pit.

Alexander knew these snakes. He had seen them in Brazil. Anaconda strain. Blind, swift-striking, vicious. Not fatal, but capable of causing paralysis – for days. If flesh came within several feet of the flat heads, the strikes were inevitable.

He turned back to the overgrowth, the beam of light crisscrossing the immediate area. There was a dangling branch of a ceiba tree about six feet long. He ran to it, bending it back and forth until it broke off. He returned to the logs. The snakes had stopped, alarmed. Their oily, ugly bodies were entwined, the flat heads poised near each other, the blind, pinlike eyes staring fanatically in the direction of the scent. At him.

Alex shoved the ceiba limb out on the log with his left hand, the rifle and flashlight gripped awkwardly in his right.

Both snakes lunged simultaneously, leaping off the surface of the log, whipping their bodies violently around the branch, their heads zeroing toward McAuliff's hand, soaring through the soft leaves.

Alex threw – dropped? he would never know – the limb into the water. The snakes thrashed; the branch reeled in furious circles and sank beneath the surface.

McAuliff ran across the logs and picked up the path.

He had gone perhaps three-quarters of a mile, certainly no more than that. The time elapsed was twelve minutes by his watch. As he remembered it, the path veered sharply to the right through a particularly dense section of fern and maidenhead to where there was a small clearing recently used by a band of hill-country hunters. Marcus – the man who used the name of Marcus – had remarked on it.

From the clearing it was less than a mile to the banks of the Martha Brae and the campsite. The Dunstone advantage had to be diminishing.

It *had* to be.

He reached the nearly impossible stretch of overgrowth, his flashlight close to the earth, inspecting the ground for signs of passage. If he stepped away from the path now – if he moved into the underbrush that had not seen human movement – it would take him hours to find it again. Probably not until daylight – or when the rains stopped.

It was painfully slow, agonizingly concentrated. Bent weeds, small broken branches, swollen borders of wet ground where once there had been the weight of recent human feet; these were signs, his codes. He could not allow the tolerance of a single error.

'Hey, mon!' came the muted words.

McAuliff threw himself to the ground and held his breath. Behind him, to his left, he could see the beam of another flashlight. Instantly he snapped off his own.

'Hey, mon, where are you? Contact, please. You went off your pattern. Or I did.'

Contact, please ... Off your pattern. The terms of an agent, not the language of a carrier. The man was MI6.

Past tense. *Was.*

Now Dunstone Limited.

The Dunstone team had separated, each man assigned an area ... a pattern. That could only mean they were in radio contact.

Six men in radio contact.

Oh, *Jesus!*

The beam of light came nearer, dancing, flickering through the impossible foliage.

'Here, mon!' whispered Alex gutturally, hoping against reasonable hope that the rain and the whisper would not raise an alarm in the Dunstone ear.

'Put on your light, please, mon.'

'Trying to, mon.' No more, thought McAuliff. Nothing.

The dancing beam reflected off a thousand shining, tiny mirrors in the darkness, splintering the light into hypnotically flickering shafts.

Closer.

Alex rolled silently off the path into the mass of wet earth and soft growth, the rifle under him cutting into his thighs.

The beam of light was nearly above him, its shaft almost clear of interference. In the spill he could see the upper body of the man. Across his chest were two wide straps: one was connected to an encased radio, the other to the stock of a rifle, its thick barrel silhouetted over his shoulder. The flashlight was in the left hand; in the right was a large, ominous-looking pistol.

The MI6 defector was a cautious agent. His instincts had been aroused.

McAuliff knew he had to get the pistol; he could not allow the man to fire. He did not know how near the others were, how close the other patterns.

Now!

He lashed his right hand up, directly onto the barrel of the pistol, jamming his thumb into the curvature of the trigger housing, smashing his shoulder into the man's head, crashing his left knee up under the man's leg into his testicles. With the impact, the man buckled and expunged a tortured gasp; his hand went momentarily limp, and Alex ripped the pistol from it, propelling the weapon into the darkness.

From his crouched agony the Jamaican looked up, his left hand still holding the flashlight, its beam directed nowhere at the earth, his face contorted ... about to take the necessary breath to scream.

McAuliff found himself thrusting his fingers into the man's mouth, tearing downward with all his strength. The man lurched forward, bringing the hard metal of the flashlight crashing into Alex's head, breaking the skin. Still McAuliff ripped at his mouth, feeling the teeth puncturing his flesh, sensing the screams.

They fell, twisting in midair, into the overgrowth. The Jamaican kept smashing the flashlight into McAuliff's temple; Alex kept tearing grotesquely, viciously, at the mouth that could sound the alarm he could not allow.

They rolled over into a patch of sheer jungle mud. McAuliff felt a rock, he tore his left hand loose, ripped the rock up from the ground, and brought it crashing into the black mouth, over his own fingers. The man's teeth shattered; he choked on his own saliva. Alex whipped out his bleeding hand and instantly grabbed the matted hair, twisting the entire head into the soft slime of the mud. There were the muffled sounds of expulsion beneath the surface. A series of miniature filmy domes burst silently out of the soggy earth in the spill of the fallen flashlight.

And then there was nothing.

The man was dead.

And no alarms had been sent.

Alexander reached over, picked up the light, and looked at the fingers of his right hand. The skin was slashed, there were teeth marks, but the cuts were not deep; he could move his hand freely, and that was all he cared about.

His left temple was bleeding, and the pain terrible, but not immobilizing. Both would stop ... sufficiently.

He looked over at the dead Jamaican and he felt like being sick. There was no time. He crawled back to the path and started once again the painstaking task of following it. And he tried to focus his eyes into the jungle. Twice, in the not-too-distant denseness, he saw sharp beams of flashlights.

The Dunstone team was continuing its sweep. It was zeroing in.

There was not an instant to waste in thought.

Eight minutes later he reached the clearing. He felt the accelerated pounding in his chest; there was less than a mile to go. The easiest leg of the terrible journey. He looked at his watch. It was exactly four minutes after twelve midnight.

Twelve was also the house of noon.

Four was the ritual Arawak unit.

The odyssey of death.

No time for thought.

He found the path at the opposite side of the small clearing and began to run, gathering speed as he raced toward the banks of the Martha Brae. There was no air left in his lungs now, not breath as he knew it; only the steady explosion of exhaustion from his throat, blood and perspiration falling from his head, rivering down his neck onto his shoulders and chest.

There was the river. He had reached the river!

It was only then that he realized the pounding rain had stopped; the jungle storm was over. He swung the flashlight to his left; there were the rocks of the path bordering the final few hundred yards into the campsite.

He had heard no rifle fire. There had been no shots. There were five experienced killers in the darkness behind him, and the terrible night was not over ... but he had a chance.

That's all he had asked for, all that was between him and his command to a firing squad ending his life.

Willingly, if he failed. Willingly to end it without Alison.

He ran the last fifty yards as fast as his exhausted muscles could tolerate. He held the flashlight directly in front of him; the first object caught by its beam was the lean-to at the mouth of the campsite area. He raced into the clearing.

There were no fires, no signs of life. Only the dripping of a thousand reminders of the jungle storm, the tents silent monuments of recent living.

He stopped breathing. Cold terror gripped him. The silence was an overpowering portent of horror.

'Alison. *Alison!*' he screamed and raced blindly toward the tent. '*Sam! Sam!*'

When the words came out of the darkness, he knew what it was to be taken from death and be given life again.

'*Alexander* ... You damn near got killed, boy,' said Sam Tucker from the black recesses of the jungle's edge.

34

Sam Tucker and the runner called Marcus walked out of the bush. McAuliff stared at the Halidonite, bewildered. The runner saw his expression and spoke.

'There is no time for lengthy explanations. I have exercised an option, that is all.' The runner pointed to the lapel of his jacket. Alex needed no clarification. Sewn into the cloth were the tablets he had seen in the wash of yellow moonlight on the back road above Lucea Harbour.

I would not think twice about it, Daniel had said.

'Where is Alison?'

'With Lawrence and Whitehall. They're farther down the river,' answered Sam.

'What about the Jensens?'

Tucker paused. 'I don't know, Alexander.'

'*What?*'

'They disappeared. That's all I can tell you. Yesterday Peter was lost; his carrier returned to camp, he couldn't find him. Ruth bore up well, poor girl ... a lot of guts in her. We sent out a search. Nothing. And then this morning, I can't tell you why – I don't know – I went to the Jensen tent. Ruth was gone. She hasn't been seen since.'

McAuliff wondered. Had Peter Jensen seen something? Sensed something? And fled with his wife? Escaped past the tribe of Acquaba?

Questions for another time.

'The carriers?' asked Alex warily, afraid to hear the answer.

'Check with our friend here,' replied Tucker, nodding to the Halidonite.

'They have been sent north, escorted north on the river,' said the man with the usurped name of Marcus. 'Jamaicans will not die tonight unless they know why they are dying. Not in this fight.'

'And you? Why you? Is this your fight?'

'I know the men who come for you. I have the option to fight.'

'The limited freedoms of Acquaba?' asked Alex softly.

Marcus shrugged; his eyes betrayed nothing. 'An individual's freedom of choice, doctor.'

There was a barely perceptible cry of a bird, or the muted screech of a bat, from the dense, tropic jungle. Then there followed another. And another.

McAuliff would not have noticed ... there were so many sounds, so continuously. A never-ending nocturnal sympathy; pleasant to hear, not pleasant to think about.

But he was compelled to notice now.

Marcus snapped his head up, reacting to the sound. He swiftly reached over and grabbed Alexander's flashlight and ripped it out of his hand while shouldering Tucker away.

'*Get down!*' he cried, as he pushed McAuliff violently, reeling him backward, away from the spot where he was standing.

Seven rifle shots came out of the darkness, some thumping into trees, others cracking into the jungle distance, two exploding into the dirt of the clearing.

Alex rolled on the ground, pulling his rifle into position, and aimed in the direction of the firing. He kept his finger on the trigger; a shattering fusillade of twenty bullets sprayed the area. It was over in seconds. The stillness returned.

He felt a hand grabbing his leg. It was Marcus.

'Pull back. Down to the river, mon,' he whispered harshly.

McAuliff scrambled backward in the darkness. More shots were fired from the bush; the bullets screamed above him to the right.

Suddenly there was a burst of rifle fire from only feet away. Marcus had leaped up to the left and delivered a cross-section barrage that drew the opposing fire away. Alex knew Marcus's action was his cover. He lurched to the right, to the edge of the clearings. He heard Sam Tucker's voice.

'*McAuliff!* Over *here!*'

As he raced into the brush, he saw Sam's outline on the ground. Tucker was crouched on one knee, his rifle raised. '*Where?* For Christ's sake, where's Alison? The others?'

'Go down to the river, boy! South, about three hundred yards. Tell the others. We'll hold here.'

'No, Sam! come with me ... *Show* me.'

'I'll be there, son ...' Another volley of shots spat out of the jungle. Marcus answered from the opposite side of the clearing. Tucker continued speaking as he grabbed the cloth in Alex's field jacket and propelled him beyond. 'That black son-of-a-bitch is willing to get his tar ass shot off for us! Maybe he's given me a little time I don't deserve. He's my countryman, boy. My new *landsmann, Jesus!* I knew I liked this fucking island. Now get the hell down there and watch out for the girl. We'll join you, don't you worry about that. The *girl,* Alexander!'

'There are five men out there, Sam. I killed one of them a mile back. They must have seen my flashlight when I was running. I'm sorry ...' With these words McAuliff plunged into the soaking-wet forest and slashed his way to the riverbank. He tumbled down the short slope, there life clattering against the metal buttons of his jacket, and fell into the water.

South. *Left.*

Three hundreds yards. Nine hundred feet ... a continent.

He stayed close to the riverbank, where he could make the best time. As he slopped through the mud and the growth and over fallen rocks, he realized his magazine was empty. Without stopping he reached into his pocket and pulled out a fresh clip, snapping the old one out of its slot and slamming the new one in. He cracked back the insertion bar; the cartridge entered the chamber.

Gunfire broke his nonthoughts. Behind him men were trying to kill other men.

There was a bend in the narrow river. He had traveled over a hundred yards; nearer two, he thought.

My new landsmann ... Christ! Sam Tucker, itinerant wanderer of the globe, schooler of primitives, lover of all lands – in search of one to call his own, at this late stage of his life. And he had found it in a violent moment of time in the cruelest wilds of Jamaica's Cock Pit. In a moment of sacrifice.

Suddenly, in an instant of terror, from out of the darkness above, a huge black form descended. A giant arm fell viselike around his neck; clawing fingers tore at his face; his kidneys were being hammered by a vicious, powerful fist. He slammed the rifle butt into the body behind him, sank his teeth into the flesh below his mouth, and lunged forward into the water.

'Mon! Jesus, mon!'

The voice of Lawrence cried as he pummeled McAuliff's shoulder. Stunned, each man released the other; each held up his hands, Alex's awkwardly thrusting out the rifle, Lawrence's holding a long knife.

'My God!' said McAuliff. 'I could have *shot* you!'

There was another fusillade of gunfire to the north.

'I might have put the blade in ... not the handle,' said the black giant, waist-deep in water. 'We wanted a hostage.'

Both men recognized there was no time for explanations. 'Where *are* you? Where's Alison and Whitehall?'

'Downstream, mon. Not far.'

'Is she all right?'

'She is frightened ... But she is a brave woman. For a white English lady. You see, mon?'

'I saw, mon,' replied Alexander. 'Let's go.'

Lawrence preceded him, jumping out of the water about thirty yards beyond the point of the near-fatal encounter. McAuliff saw that the revolutionary had tied a cloth around his forearm; Alex spat the blood out of his mouth as he noticed it, and rubbed the area of his kidneys in abstract justification.

The Jamaican pointed up the slope with his left hand and put his right hand to his mouth at the same time. A whistled treble emerged from his lips. A bird, a bat, an owl ... it made no difference. There was a corresponding sound from the top of the riverbank, beyond in the jungle.

'Go up, mon, I will wait here,' said Lawrence.

McAuliff would never know whether it was the panic of the moment or whether his words spoke the truth as he saw it, but he grabbed the black revolutionary by the shoulder and pushed him forward. 'There won't be any more orders given. You don't know what's back there. I do! Get your ass up there!'

An extended barrage of rifle fire came from the river.

Lawrence blinked. He blinked in the new moonlight that flooded the riverbank of this offshoot of the Martha Brae.

'Okay, mon! Don't *push*.'

They crawled to the top of the slope and started into the overgrowth.

The figure came rushing out of the tangled darkness, a darker racing object out of a void of black. It was Alison. Lawrence reached back to McAuliff and took the flashlight out of Alex's hand. A gesture of infinite understanding.

She ran into his arms. The world . . . the universe stopped its insanity for an instant, and there was stillness. And peace and comfort. But for only an instant.

There was not time for thought. Or reflection.

Or words.

Neither spoke.

They held each other, and then looked at each other in the dim spill of the new moonlight in the isolated space that was their own on the banks of the Martha Brae.

In a terrible, violent moment of time. And sacrifice.

Charles Whitehall intruded, as Charley-mon was wont to do. He approached, his safari outfit still creased, his face an immobile mask, his eyes penetrating.

'Lawrence and I agreed he would stay down at the river. Why have you changed that?'

'You blow my mind, Charley . . .'

'You *bore* me, McAuliff!' replied Whitehall. 'There was gunfire up there!'

'I was in the middle of it, you black son-of-a-bitch!' *Jesus, why did he have to say that?* 'And you're going to learn what the problem is. Do you understand that?'

Whitehall smiled. 'Do tell . . . *whitey*.'

Alison slapped her hands off McAuliff and looked at both men. '*Stop it!*'

'I'm sorry,' said Alex quickly.

'I'm *not*,' replied Whitehall. 'This is his moment of truth. Can't you see that, *Miss* Alison?'

Lawrence's great hands interfered. They touched both men, and his voice was that of a thundering child-man. 'Neither no more, mon! McAuliff, mon, you say what you know! *Now!*'

Alexander did. He spoke of the grasslands, the plane – a plane, not the Halidon's – the redneck ganja pilot who had brought six men into the Cock Pit to massacre the survey, the race to the campsite, the violent encounter in the jungle that ended in death in a small patch of jungle mud. Finally, those minutes ago when the runner called Marcus saved their lives by hearing a cry in the tropic bush.

'Five men, mon,' said Lawrence, interrupted by a new burst of gunfire, closer now but still in the near-distance to the north. He turned to Charles Whitehall. 'How many do you want, *fascisti?*'

'Give me a figure, *agricula.*'

'Goddammit!' yelled McAuliff. 'Cut it out. Your games don't count anymore.'

'You do not understand,' said Whitehall. 'It is the only thing that does count. We are prepared. We are the viable contestants. Is this not what the fictions create? One on one, the victor sets the course?'

The charismatic leaders are not the foot soldiers . . . They change or are replaced . . . the words of Daniel, Minister of the Tribe of Acquaba.

'You're both insane,' said Alex, more rationally than he thought was conceivable. 'You make me sick, and goddamn you—'

'Alexander! *Alexander!*' The cry came from the riverbank less than twenty yards away. Sam Tucker was yelling.

McAuliff began running to the edge of the jungle. Lawrence raced ahead, his huge body crashing through the foliage, his hands pulverizing into sudden diagonals everything in their path.

The black giant jumped to the water's edge; Alex started down the short slope and stopped.

Sam Tucker was cradling the body of Marcus the runner in his arms. The head protruding out of the water was a mass of blood, sections of the skull were shot off.

Still, Sam Tucker would not let go.

'One of them circled and caught us at the bank. Caught me at the bank . . . Marcus jumped out between us and took the fire. He killed the son-of-a-bitch; he kept walking right up to him. Into the gun.'

Tucker lowered the body into the mud of the riverbank.

McAuliff thought. Four men remained, four killers left of the Dunstone team.

They were five. But Alison could not be counted now.

They were four, too.

Killers.

Four. The Arawak four.

The death odyssey.

Alex felt the woman's hands on his shoulders, her face pressed against his back in the moonlight.

The grasslands.

Escape was in the grasslands and the two aircraft that could fly them out of the Cock Pit.

Yet Marcus had implied that there was no other discernible route but the narrow, twisting jungle path – a danger in itself.

The path was picked east of the river at the far right end of the campsite clearing. It would be watched; the MI6 defectors were experienced agents. *Egress* was a priority; the single avenue of escape would have automatic rifles trained on it.

Further, the Dunstone killers knew their prey was downstream. They would probe, perhaps, but they would not leave the hidden path unguarded.

But they had to separate. They could not gamble on the unknown, on the possibility that the survey team might slip through, try to penetrate the net.

It was this assumption that led McAuliff and Sam Tucker to accept the strategy. A variation on the deadly game proposed by Lawrence and Charles Whitehall. Alexander would stay with Alison. The others would go out. Separately. And find the enemy.

Quite simply, kill or be killed.

Lawrence lowered his immense body into the dark waters. He hugged the bank and pulled his way slowly upstream, his pistol just above the surface, his long knife out of its leather scabbard, in his belt – easily, quickly retrievable.

The moon was brighter now. The rain clouds were gone; the towering jungle overgrowth obstructed but did not blot out the moonlight. The river currents were steady; incessant, tiny whirlpools spun around scores of fallen branches and protruding rocks, the latter's tips glistening with buffeted moss and matted green algae.

Lawrence stopped; he dropped farther into the water, holding his breath, his eyes just above the surface. Diagonally across the narrow river offshoot a man was doing exactly what he was doing, but without the awareness Lawrence now possessed.

Waist-deep in water, the man held a lethal-looking rifle in front of and above him. He took long strides, keeping his balance by grabbing the overhanging foliage on the riverbank, his eyes straight ahead.

In seconds, the man would be directly opposite him.

Lawrence placed his pistol on a bed of fern spray. He reached below and pulled the long knife from his belt.

He sank beneath the surface and began swimming underwater.

Sam Tucker crawled over the ridge above the riverbank and rolled toward the base of the ceiba trunk. The weight of his body pulled down a loose vine; it fell like a coiled snake across his chest, startling him.

He was north of the campsite now, having made a wide half-circle west, on the left side of the river. His reasoning was simple, he hoped not too simple. The Dunstone patrol would be concentrating downstream; the path was east of the clearing. They would guard it, expecting any who searched for it to approach from below, not above the known point of entry.

Tucker shouldered his way up the ceiba trunk into a sitting position. He loosened the strap of his rifle, lifted the weapon, and lowered it over his head diagonally across his back. He pulled the strap taut. Rifle fire was out of the question, to be used only in the last extremity, for its use meant – more than likely – one's own execution.

That was not out of the question, thought Sam, but it surely would take considerable persuasion.

He rolled back to a prone position and continued his reptilelike journey through the tangled labyrinth of jungle underbrush.

He heard the man before he saw him. The sound was peculiarly human, a casual sound that told Sam Tucker his enemy was casual, not primed for alarm. A man who somehow felt his post was removed from immediate assault, the patrol farthest away from the area of contention.

The man had sniffed twice. A clogged nostrils, or nostrils, caused a temporary blockage and a passage for air was casually demanded. Casually obtained.

It was enough.

Sam focused in the direction of the sound. His eyes of fifty-odd years were strained, tired from lack of sleep and from peering for nights on end into the tropic darkness. But they would serve him, he knew that.

The man was crouched by a giant fern, his rifle between his legs, stock butted against the ground. Beyond, Tucker could see in the moonlight the outlines of the lean-to at the far left of the clearing. Anyone crossing the campsite was in the man's direct line of fire.

The fern ruled out a knife. A blade that did not enter precisely at the required location could cause a victim to lunge, to shout. The fern concealed the man's back too well. It was possible, but awkward.

There was a better way. Sam recalled the vine that had dropped from the trunk of the ceiba tree.

He reached into his pocket and withdrew a coil of ordinary azimuth line. Thin steel wire encased in nylon, so handy for so many things . . .

He crept silently toward the giant spray of tiny leaves.

His enemy sniffed again.

Sam rose, half-inch by half-inch, behind the fern. In front of him now, unobstructed, was the silhouette of the man's neck and head.

Sam Tucker slowly separated his gnarled, powerful hands. They were connected by the thin steel wire encased in nylon.

Charles Whitehall was furious. He had wanted to use the river; it was the swiftest route, far more direct than the torturously slow untangling that was demanded in the bush. But it was agreed that since Lawrence had been on guard at the river, he knew it better. So the river was his.

Whitehall looked at the dial of his watch; there were still twelve minutes to go before the first signal. If there was one.

Simple signals.

Silence meant precisely that. Nothing.

The short, simulated, guttural cry of a wild pig meant success. One kill. If two, two kills.

Simple.

If he had been given the river, Charles was convinced, he would have delivered the first cry. At least one.

Instead, his was the southwest sweep, the least likely of the three routings to make contact. It was a terrible waste. An old man, authoritative, inventive, but terribly tired, and a plodding, unskilled hill boy, not without potential, perhaps, but still a misguided, awkward giant.

A terrible waste! Infuriating.

Yet not as infuriating as the sharp, hard steel that suddenly made contact with the base of his skull. And the words that followed, whispered in a harsh command:

'Open your mouth and I blow your head off, mon!'

He had been taken! His anger had caused his concentration to wander. *Stupid.*

But his captor had not fired. His taker did not want the alarm of a rifle shot any more than he did. The man kept thrusting the barrel painfully into Charles's head, veering him to the right, away from the supposed line of Whitehall's march. The man obviously wanted to interrogate, discover the whereabouts of the others.

Stupid.

The *release-seizure* was a simple manoeuvre requiring only a hard surface to the rear of the victim for execution.

And it was, indeed, execution.

It was necessary for the victim to rebound following impact, not be absorbed in space or elastically swallowed by walled softness. The impact was the most important; otherwise the trigger of the rifle might be pulled. There was an instant of calculated risk – nothing was perfect – but the reverse jamming of the weapon into the victim allowed for that split-second diagonal slash that invariably ripped the weapon out of the hands of the hunter.

Optimally, the slash coincided with the impact.

It was all set forth clearly in the Oriental training manuals.

In front of them, to the left, Whitehall could distinguish the sudden rise of a hill in the jungle darkness. One of those abrupt protrusions out of the earth that was so common to the Cock Pit. At the base of the hill was a large boulder reflecting the wash of moonlight strained through trees.

It would be sufficient ... actually, more than sufficient; very practical indeed.

He stumbled, just slightly, as if his foot had been ensnared by an open root. He felt the prod of the rifle barrel. It was the moment.

He slammed his head back into the steel and whipped to his right, clasping the barrel with his hands and jamming it forward. As the victim crashed into the boulder, he swung the weapon violently away, ripping it out of the man's grasp.

As the man blinked in the moonlight, Charles Whitehall rigidly extended three fingers on each hand and completed the assault with enormous speed and control. The hands were trajectories – one toward the right eye, the other into the soft flesh below the throat.

McAuliff had given Alison his pistol. He had been startled to see her check the clip with such expertise, releasing it from its chamber, pressing the spring, and reinserting it with a heel-of-the-palm impact that would have done justice to Bonnie of Clyde notoriety. She had smiled at him and mentioned the fact that the weapon had been in the water.

There were eight minutes to go. Two units of four; the thought was not comforting.

He wondered if there would be any short cries in the night. Or whether a measured silence would signify an extension of the nightmare.

Was any of them good enough? Quick enough? Sufficiently alert?

'Alex!' Alison grabbed his arm, whispering softly but with sharp intensity. She pulled him down and pointed into the forest, to the west.

A beam of light flickered on and off.

Twice.

Someone had been startled in the overgrowth; something perhaps. There was a slapping flutter and short, repeated screeches that stopped as rapidly as they had started.

The light went on once again, for no more than a second, and then there was darkness.

The invader was perhaps thirty yards away. It was difficult to estimate in the dense surroundings. But it was an opportunity. And if Alexander Tarquin McAuliff had learned anything during the past weeks of agonizing insanity, it was to accept opportunities with the minimum of analysis.

He pulled Alison to him and whispered instructions into her ear. He released her and felt about the ground for what he knew was there. Fifteen seconds later he silently clawed his way up the trunk of a ceiba tree, rifle across his back, his hands noiselessly testing the low branches, discomforted by the weight of the object held in place inside his field jacket by the belt.

In position, he scratched twice on the bark of the tree.

Beneath him Alison whistled – a very human whistle, the abrupt notes of a signaling warble. She then snapped on her flashlight for precisely one second, shut it off, and dashed away from her position.

In less than a minute the figure was below him – crouched, rifle extended, prepared to kill.

McAuliff dropped from the limb of the ceiba tree, the sharp point of the heavy rock on a true, swift course toward the top of the invader's skull.

The minute hand on his watch reached twelve; the second hand was on one. It was time.

The first cry came from the river. An expert cry, the sound of a wild pig.

The second came from the southwest, quite far in the distance, equally expert, echoing through the jungle.

The third came from the north, a bit too guttural, not expert at all, but sufficient unto the instant. The message was clear.

McAuliff looked at Alison, her bright, stunningly blue eyes bluer still in the Caribbean moonlight.

He lifted his rifle in the air and shattered the stillness of the night with a burst of gunfire. Perhaps the ganja pilot in the grasslands would laugh softly in satisfaction. Perhaps, with luck, one of the stray bullets might find its way to his head.

It did not matter.

It mattered only that they had made it. They were good enough, after all.

He held Alison in his arms and screamed joyfully into the darkness above. It did not sound much like a wild pig, but that did not matter either.

35

They sat at the table on the huge free-form pool deck overlooking the beds of coral and the blue waters beyond. The conflict between wave and rock resulted in cascading arcs of white spray surging upward and forward, blanketing the jagged crevices.

They had flown from the grasslands directly to Port Antonio. They had done so because Sam Tucker had raised Robert Hanley on the airplane's radio, and Hanley had delivered his instructions in commands that denied argument. They had landed at the small Sam Jones Airfield at two thirty-five in the morning. A limousine sent from the Trident Villas awaited them.

So, too, did Robert Hanley. And the moment Sam Tucker alighted from the plane, Hanley shook his hand and proceeded to crash his fist into Tucker's face. He followed this action by reaching down and picking Sam up off the ground, greeting him a bit more cordially but explaining in measured anger that the past several weeks had caused him unnecessary anxiety, obviously Sam Tucker's responsibility.

The two very young old reprobates then drank the night through at the bar of the Trident Villas. The young manager, Timothy Durell, surrendered at five ten in the morning, dismissed the bartender, and turned the keys over to Hanley and Sam. Durell was not aware that in a very real sense, the last strategies of Dunstone Limited had been created at Trident that week when strangers had converged from all over the world. Strangers, and not strangers at all ... only disturbing memories now.

Charles Whitehall left with Lawrence, the revolutionary. Both black men said their goodbyes at the airfield; each had places to go to, things to do, men to see. There would be no questions, for there would be no answers. That was understood.

They would separate quickly.

But they had communicated; perhaps that was all that could be expected.

Alison and McAuliff had been taken to the farthest villa on the shoreline. She had bandaged his hand and washed the cuts on his face and made him soak for nearly an hour in a good British tub of hot water.

They were in Villa 20.

They had slept in each other's arms until noon.

It was now a little past one o'clock. They were alone at the table, a note having been left for Alexander from Sam Tucker. Sam and Robert Hanley were flying to Montego Bay to see an attorney. They were going into partnership.

God help the island, thought McAuliff.

At two thirty Alison touched his arm and nodded toward the alabaster portico across the lawn. Down the marble steps came two men, one black, one white, dressed in proper business suits.

R. C. Hammond and Daniel, Minister of Council for the Tribe of Acquaba, high in the Flagstaff range.

'We'll be quick,' said Hammond, taking the chair indicated by Alexander. 'Mrs Booth, I am Commander Hammond.'

'I was sure you were,' said Alison, her voice warm, her smile cold.

'May I present . . . an associate? Mr Daniel, Jamaican Affairs. I believe you two have met, McAuliff.'

'Yes.'

Daniel nodded pleasantly and sat down. He looked at Alex and spoke sincerely. 'There is much to be thankful for. I am very relieved.'

'What about Malcolm?'

The sadness flickered briefly across Daniel's eyes. 'I am sorry.'

'So am I,' said McAuliff. 'He saved our lives.'

'That was his job,' replied the Minister of the Halidon.

'May I assume,' interrupted Hammond gently, 'that Mrs Booth has been apprised . . . up to a point?'

'You certainly may assume that, Commander.' Alison gave that answer herself.

'Very well.' The British agent reached into his pocket, withdrew the yellow paper of a cablegram, and handed it to Alexander. It was a deposit confirmation from Barclay's Bank, London. The sum of $2,000,000 had been deposited to the account of A. T. McAuliff, Chase Manhattan, New York, Further, a letter of credit had been forwarded to said A. T. McAuliff that could be drawn against for all taxes upon receipt of the proper filing papers approved by the United States Treasury Department, Bureau of Internal Revenue.

Alex read the cable twice and wondered at his own indifference. He gave it to Alison. She started to read it but did not finish; instead, she lifted McAuliff's cup and saucer and placed it underneath.

She said nothing.

'Our account is settled, McAuliff.'

'Not quite, Hammond . . . In simple words, I never want to hear from you again. We never want to hear from you. Because if we do, the longest deposition on record will be made public—'

'My *dear* man,' broke in the Englishman wearily, 'let me save you the time. Gratitude and marked respect would obligate me socially any time you're in London. And, I should add, I think you're basically a quite decent chap. But I can assure you that *professionally* we shall remain at the farthest distance. Her

Majesty's Service has no desire to involve itself with international irregularities. I might as well be damned blunt about it.'

'And Mrs Booth?'

'The same, obviously.' Here Hammond looked directly, even painfully, at Alison. 'Added to which it is our belief that she has gone through a great deal. Most splendidly and with our deepest appreciation. The terrible past is behind you, my dear. Public commendation is uncalled for, we realize. But the highest citation will be entered into your file. Which shall be closed. Permanently.'

'I want to believe that,' said Alison.

'You may, Mrs Booth.'

'What about Dunstone?' asked McAuliff. 'What's going to happen? When?'

'It has already begun,' replied Hammond. 'The list was cabled in the early hours of the morning.'

'Several hours ago,' said Daniel quietly. 'Around noon, London time.'

'In all the financial centers, the work is proceeding,' continued Hammond. 'All the governments are cooperating ... it is to everyone's benefit.'

McAuliff looked up at Daniel. 'What does that do for global mendacity?'

Daniel smiled. 'Perhaps a minor lesson has been learned. We shall know in a few years, will we not?'

'And Piersall? Who killed him?'

Hammond replied. 'Real-estate interests along the North Coast, which stood to gain by the Dunstone purchase. His work was important, not those who caused his death. They were tragically insignificant.'

'And so it is over,' said Daniel, pushing back his chair. 'The Westmore Tallons will go back to selling fish, the disciples of Barak Moore will take up the struggle against Charles Whitehall, and the disorderly process of advancement continues. Shall we go, Commander Hammond?'

'By all means, Mr Daniel.' Hammond rose from the chair, as did the Minister of Council for the Tribe of Acquaba.

'What happened to the Jensens?' Alexander looked at Daniel, for it was the Halidonite who could answer him.

'We allowed him to escape. To leave the Cock Pit. We knew Julian Warfield was on the island, but we did not know where. We only knew that Peter Jensen would lead us to him. He did so. In Oracabessa. Julian Warfield's life was ended on the balcony of a villa named Peale Court.'

'What will happen to them? The Jensens.' McAuliff shifted his eyes to Hammond.

The commander glanced briefly at Daniel. 'There is an understanding. A man and a woman answering the description of the Jensens boarded a Mediterranean flight this morning at Palisados. We think he is retired. We shall leave him alone. You see, he shot Julian Warfield ... because Warfield had ordered him to kill someone else. And he could not do that.'

'It is time, Commander,' said Daniel.

'Yes, of course. There's a fine woman in London I've rather neglected. She liked you very much that night in Soho, McAuliff. She said you were attentive.'

'Give her my best.'

'I shall.' The Englishman looked up at the clear sky and the hot sun. 'Retirement in the Mediterranean. Interesting.' R. C. Hammond allowed himself a brief smile, and replaced the chair quite properly under the table.

They walked on the green lawn in front of the cottage that was called a villa and looked out at the sea. A white sheet of ocean spray burst up from the coral rock and appeared suspended, the pitch-blue waters of the Caribbean serving as a backdrop, not a source. The spray cascaded forward and downward and then receded back over the crevices that formed the coral overlay. It became ocean again, at one with its source; another form of beauty.

Alison took McAuliff's hand.

They were free.

The Rhinemann
Exchange

For Norma and Ed Marcum –
for so many things, my thanks

Preface

'David?'

The girl came into the room and stood silently for a moment, watching the tall army officer as he stared out the hotel window. The March rain fell through a March chill, creating pockets of wind and mist over the Washington skyline.

Spaulding turned, aware of her presence, not of her voice. 'I'm sorry. Did you say something?' He saw that she held his raincoat. He saw, too, the concern in her eyes – and the fear she tried to conceal.

'It's over,' she said softly.

'It's over,' he replied. 'Or will be in an hour from now.'

'Will they all be there?' she asked as she approached him, holding the coat in front of her as though it were a shield.

'Yes. They have no choice . . . I have no choice.' Spaulding's left shoulder was encased in bandages under his tunic, the arm in a wide, black sling. 'Help me on with that, will you? The rain's not going to let up.'

Jean Cameron unfolded the coat reluctantly and opened it.

She stopped, her eyes fixed on the collar of his army shirt. Then on the lapels of his uniform.

All the insignia had been removed.

There were only slight discolorations in the cloth where the emblems had been.

There was no rank, no identifying brass or silver. Not even the gold initials of the country he served.

Had served.

He saw that she had seen.

'It's the way I began,' he said quietly. 'No name, no rank, no history. Only a number. Followed by a letter. I want them to remember that.'

The girl stood motionless, gripping the coat. 'They'll kill you, David.' Her words were barely audible.

'That's the one thing they won't do,' he said calmly. 'There'll be no assassins, no accidents, no sudden orders flying me out to Burma or Dar es Salaam. That's finished . . . They can't know what I've done.'

687

He smiled gently and touched her face. Her lovely face. She breathed deeply and imposed a control on herself he knew she did not feel. She slipped the raincoat carefully over his left shoulder as he reached around for the right sleeve. She pressed her face briefly against his back; he could feel the slight trembling as she spoke.

'I won't be afraid. I promised you that.'

He walked out the glass entrance of the Shoreham Hotel and shook his head at the doorman under the canopy. He did not want a taxi; he wanted to walk. To let the dying fires of rage finally subside and burn themselves out. A long walk.

It would be the last hour of his life that he would wear the uniform.

The uniform now with no insignia, no identification.

He would walk through the second set of doors at the War Department and give his name to the military police.

David Spaulding.

That's all he would say. It would be enough; no one would stop him, none would interfere.

Orders would be left by unnamed commanders – divisional recognition only – that would allow him to proceed down the gray corridors to an unmarked room.

Those orders would be at that security desk because another order had been given. An order no one could trace. No one comprehended . . .

They claimed. In outrage.

But none with an outrage matching his.

They knew that, too, the unknown commanders.

Names meaning nothing to him only months ago would be in the unmarked room. Names that now were symbols of an abyss of deceit that so revolted him, he honestly believed he had lost his mind.

Howard Oliver.

Jonathan Craft.

Walter Kendall.

The names were innocuous-sounding in themselves. They could belong to untold hundreds of thousands. There was something so . . . American about them.

Yet these names, these men, had brought him to the brink of insanity.

They would be there in the unmarked room, and he would remind them of those who were absent.

Erich Rhinemann. Buenos Aires.

Alan Swanson. Washington.

Franz Altmüller. Berlin.

Other symbols. Other threads . . .

The abyss of deceit into which he had been plunged by . . . enemies.

How in God's name had it *happened*?

How *could* it have happened?

But it did happen. And he had written down the facts as he knew them.

Written them down and placed . . . the document in an archive case inside a deposit box within a bank vault in Colorado.

Untraceable. Locked in the earth for a millennium . . . for it was better that way.

Unless the men in the unmarked room forced him to do otherwise.

If they did . . . if they forced him . . . the sanities of millions would be tested. The revulsion would not acknowledge national boundaries or the cause of any global tribe.

The leaders would become pariahs.

As he was a pariah now.

A number followed by a letter.

He reached the steps of the War Department; the tan stone pillars did not signify strength to him now. Only the appearance of light-brown paste.

No longer substance.

He walked through the sets of double doors up to the security desk, manned by a middle-aged lieutenant colonel flanked by two sergeants.

'Spaulding, David,' he said quietly.

'Your ID . . .' the lieutenant colonel looked at the shoulders of the raincoat, then at the collar, 'Spaulding . . .'

'My name is David Spaulding. My source is Fairfax,' repeated David softly. 'Check your papers, soldier.'

The lieutenant colonel's head snapped up in anger, gradually replaced by bewilderment as he looked at Spaulding. For David had not spoken harshly, or even impolitely. Just factually.

The sergeant to the left of the lieutenant colonel shoved a page of paper in front of the officer without interrupting. The lieutenant colonel looked at it.

He glanced back up at David – briefly – and waved him through.

As he walked down the gray corridor, his raincoat over his arm, Spaulding could feel the eyes on him, scanning the uniform devoid of rank or identification. Several salutes were rendered hesitantly.

None was acknowledged.

Men turned; others stared from doorways.

This was the . . . officer, their looks were telling him. They'd heard the rumors, spoken in whispers, in hushed voices in out-of-the-way corners. This was the man.

An order had been given . . .

The *man*.

Prologue

1

The two army officers, their uniforms creased into steel, their hats removed, watched the group of informally dressed men and women through the glass partition. The room in which the officers sat was dark.

A red light flashed; the sounds of an organ thundered out of the two webbed boxes at each corner of the glass-fronted, light-less cubicle. There followed the distant howling of dogs – large, rapacious dogs – and then a voice – deep, clear, forbidding – spoke over the interweaving sounds of the organ and the animals.

Wherever madness exists, wherever the cries of the helpless can be heard, there you will find the tall figure of Jonathan Tyne – waiting, watching in shadows, prepared to do battle with the forces of hell. The seen and the unseen...

Suddenly there was a piercing, mind-splitting scream. 'Eeaagh!' Inside the lighted, inner room an obese woman winked at the short man in thick glasses who had been reading from a typed script and walked away from the microphone, chewing her gum rapidly.

The deep voice continued. *Tonight we find Jonathan Tyne coming to the aid of the terror-stricken Lady Ashcroft, whose husband disappeared into the misty Scottish moors at precisely midnight three weeks ago. And each night at precisely midnight, the howls of unknown dogs bay across the darkened fields. They seem to be challenging the very man who now walks stealthily into the enveloping mist. Jonathan Tyne. The seeker of evil; the nemesis of Lucifer. The champion of the helpless victims of darkness...*

The organ music swelled once more to a crescendo; the sound of the baying dogs grew more vicious.

The older officer, a colonel, glanced at his companion, a first lieutenant. The younger man, his eyes betraying his concern, was staring at the group of nonchalant actors inside the lighted studio.

The colonel winced.

'Interesting, isn't it?' he said.

'What?' ... Oh, yes, sir. Yes, sir; very interesting. Which one is he?'

'The tall fellow over in the corner. The one reading a newspaper.'

'Does he play Tyne?'

'Who? Oh no, lieutenant. He has a small role, I think. In a Spanish dialect.'

'A small role . . . in a Spanish dialect.' The lieutenant repeated the colonel's words, his voice hesitant, his look bewildered. 'Forgive me, sir, I'm confused. I'm not sure what we're doing here; what *he*'s doing here. I thought he was a construction engineer.'

'He is.'

The organ music subsided to pianissimo; the sound of the howling dogs faded away. Now another voice – this one lighter, friendlier, with no undercurrent of impending drama – came out of the two webbed boxes.

Pilgrim. The soap with the scent of flowers in May; the Mayflower soap. Pilgrim brings you once again . . . 'The Adventures of Jonathan Tyne'.

The thick corked door of the dark cubicle opened and a balding man, erect, dressed in a conservative business suit, entered. He carried a manila envelope in his left hand; he reached over and extended his right hand to the colonel. He spoke quietly, but not in a whisper. 'Hello, Ed. Nice to see you again. I don't have to tell you your call was a surprise.'

'I guess it was. How are you, Jack? . . . Lieutenant, meet Mr John Ryan; formerly Major John N. M. I. Ryan of Six Corps.'

The officer rose to his feet.

'Sit down, lieutenant,' said Ryan, shaking the young man's hand.

'Nice to meet you, sir. Thank you, sir.'

Ryan edged his way around the rows of black leather armchairs and sat down next to the colonel in front of the glass partition. The organ music once more swelled, matching the reintroduced sounds of the howling dogs. Several actors and actresses crowded around two microphones, all watching a man behind a panel in another glass booth – this one lighted – on the other side of the studio.

'How's Jane?' asked Ryan. 'And the children?'

'She hates Washington; so does the boy. They'd rather be back in Oahu. Cynthia loves it, though. She's eighteen, now; all those DC dances.'

A hand signal was given by the man in the lighted booth across the way. The actors began their dialogue.

Ryan continued. 'How about you? "Washington" looks good on the roster sheet.'

'I suppose it does, but nobody knows I'm there. That won't help me.'

'Oh?'

'G-2.'

'Yes, I gathered that.'

'You look as though you're thriving, Jack.'

Ryan smiled a little awkwardly. 'No sweat. Ten other guys in the agency could do what I'm doing . . . better. But they don't have the Point on their résumés. I'm an agency symbol, strong-integrity version. The clients sort of fall in for muster.'

The colonel laughed. 'Horseshit. You were always good with the beady-bags. Even the high brass used to turn the congressmen over to you.'

'You flatter me. At least I *think* you're flattering me.'

'Eeaagh!' The obese actress, still chewing her gum, had screeched into the second microphone. She backed away, goosing a thin, effeminate-looking actor who was about to speak.

'There's a lot of screaming, isn't there.' The colonel wasn't really asking a question.

'And dogs barking and off-key organ music and a hell of a lot of groaning and heavy breathing. "Tyne's" the most popular program we have.'

'I admit I've listened to it. The whole family has; since we've been back.'

'You wouldn't believe it if I told you who writes most of the scripts.'

'What do you mean?'

'A Pulitzer poet. Under another name, of course.'

'That seems strange.'

'Not at all. Survival. We pay. Poetry doesn't.'

'Is that why *he*'s on?' The colonel gestured with a nod of his head toward the tall, dark-haired man who had put down the newspaper but still remained in the corner of the studio, away from the other actors, leaning against the white corked wall.

'Beats the hell out of me. I mean, I didn't know who he was – that is, I knew who he *was*, but I didn't know anything about him – until you called.' Ryan handed the colonel the manila envelope. 'Here's a list of the shows and the agencies he's worked for. I called around; implied that we were considering him for a running lead. The Hammerts use him a lot ...'

'The who?'

'They're packagers. They've got about fifteen programs; daytime, serials and evening shows. They say he's reliable; no sauce problems. He's used exclusively for dialects, it seems. And language fluency when it's called for.'

'German and Spanish.' It was a statement.

'That's right ...'

'Only it's not Spanish, it's Portuguese.'

'Who can tell the difference? You know who his parents are.'

Another statement, only agreement anticipated.

'Richard and Margo Spaulding. Concert pianists, very big in England and the Continent. Current status: semiretirement in Costa del Santiago, Portugal.'

'They're American, though, aren't they?'

'Very. Made sure their son was born here. Sent him to American settlement schools wherever they lived. Shipped him back here for his final two years in prep school and college.'

'How come Portugal, then?'

'Who knows? They had their first successes in Europe and decided to stay there. A fact I *think* we're going to be grateful for. They only return here for tours; which aren't very frequent anymore ... Did you know that he's a construction engineer?'

'No, I didn't. That's interesting.'

'Interesting? Just "interesting"?'

Ryan smiled; there was a trace of sadness in his eyes. 'Well, during the last six years or so there hasn't been a lot of building, has there? I mean, there's no great call for engineers . . . outside of the CCC and the NRA.' He lifted his right hand and waved it laterally in front of him, encompassing the group of men and women inside the studio. 'Do you know what's in there? A trial lawyer whose clients – when he can get a few – can't pay him; a Rolls-Royce executive who's been laid off since thirty-eight; and a former state senator whose campaign a few years ago not only cost him his job but also a lot of potential employers. They think he's a Red. Don't fool yourself, Ed. You've got it good. The Depression isn't over by a long shot. These people are the lucky ones. They found avocations they've turned into careers . . . As long as they last.'

'If I do *my* job, *his* career won't last any longer than a month from now.'

'I figured it was something like that. The storm's building, isn't it? We'll be in it pretty soon. And I'll be back, too . . . Where do you want to use him?'

'Lisbon.'

David Spaulding pushed himself away from the white studio wall. He held up the pages of his script as he approached the microphone, preparing for his cue.

Pace watched him through the glass partition, wondering how Spaulding's voice would sound. He noticed that as Spaulding came closer to the group of actors clustered around the microphone, there was a conscious – or it seemed conscious – parting of bodies, as if the new participant was in some way a stranger. Perhaps it was only normal courtesy, allowing the new performer a chance to position himself, but the colonel didn't think so. There were no smiles, no looks, no indications of familiarity as there seemed to be among the others.

No one winked. Even the obese woman who screamed and chewed gum and goosed her fellow actors just stood and watched Spaulding, her gum immobile in her mouth.

And then it happened; a curious moment.

Spaulding grinned, and the others, even the thin, effeminate man who was in the middle of a monologue, responded with bright smiles and nods. The obese woman winked.

A curious moment, thought Colonel Pace.

Spaulding's voice – mid-deep, incisive, heavily accented – came through the webbed boxes. His role was that of a mad doctor and bordered on the comic. It *would* have been comic, thought Pace, except for the authority Spaulding gave the writer's words. Pace didn't know anything about acting, but he knew when a man was being convincing. Spaulding was convincing.

That would be necessary in Lisbon.

In a few minutes Spaulding's role was obviously over. The obese woman screamed again; Spaulding retreated to the corner and quietly, making sure the pages did not rustle, picked up his folded newspaper. He leaned against the wall and withdrew a pencil from his pocket. He appeared to be doing *The New York Times* crossword puzzle.

Pace couldn't take his eyes off Spaulding. It was important for him to observe closely any subject with whom he had to make contact whenever possible. Observe the small things: the way a man walked; the way he held his head; the steadiness or lack of it in his eyes. The clothes, the watch, the cuff links; whether the shoes were shined, if the heels were worn down; the quality – or lack of quality – in a man's posture.

Pace tried to match the human being leaning against the wall, writing on the newspaper, with the dossier in his Washington office.

His name first surfaced from the files of the Army Corps of Engineers. David Spaulding had inquired about the possibilities of a commission – not volunteered: what would his opportunities be? were there any challenging construction projects? what about the length-service commitments? The sort of questions thousands of men – skilled men – were asking, knowing that the Selective Service Act would become law within a week or two. If enlistment meant a shorter commitment and/or the continued practice of their professional skills, then better an enlistment than be drafted with the mobs.

Spaulding had filled out all the appropriate forms and had been told the army would contact him. That had been six weeks ago and no one had done so. Not that the Corps wasn't interested; it was. The word from the Roosevelt men was that the draft law would be passed by Congress any day now, and the projected expansion of the army camps was so enormous, so incredibly massive, that an engineer – especially a *construction* engineer of Spaulding's qualifications – was target material.

But those high up in the Corps of Engineers were aware of the search being conducted by the Intelligence Division of the Joint Chiefs of Staff and the War Department.

Quietly, slowly. No mistakes could be made.

So they passed along David Spaulding's forms to G-2 and were told in turn to stay away from him.

The man ID was seeking had to have three basic qualifications. Once these were established, the rest of the portrait could be microscopically scrutinized to see if the whole being possessed the other desirable requirements. The three basics were difficult enough in themselves: the first was fluency in the Portuguese language; the second, an equal mastery of German; the third, sufficient professional experience in structural engineering to enable swift and accurate understanding of blueprints, photographs – even verbal descriptions – of the widest variety of industrial designs. From bridges and factories to warehousing and railroad complexes.

The man in Lisbon would need each of these basic requirements. He would employ them throughout the war that was to be; the war that the United States inevitably would have to fight.

The man in Lisbon would be responsible for developing an Intelligence network primarily concerned with the destruction of the enemy's installations deep within its own territories.

Certain men – and women – traveled back and forth through hostile territories, basing their undefined activities in neutral countries. These were the people the man in Lisbon would use ... before others used them.

These plus those he would train for infiltration. Espionage units. Teams of bi- and trilingual agents he would send up through France into the borders of Germany. To bring back their observations; eventually to inflict destruction themselves.

The English agreed that such an American was needed in Lisbon. British Intelligence admitted its Portuguese weakness; they had simply been around too long, too obviously. And there were current, very serious lapses of security in London. MI5 had been infiltrated.

Lisbon would become an American project.

If such an American could be found.

David Spaulding's preapplication forms listed the primary requisites. He spoke three languages, had spoken them since he was a child. His parents, the renowned Richard and Margo Spaulding, maintained three residences: a small, elegant Belgravia flat in London; a winter retreat in Germany's Baden-Baden; and a sprawling oceanside house in the artists' colony of Costa del Santiago in Portugal. Spaulding had grown up in these environs. When he was sixteen, his father – over the objections of his mother – insisted that he complete his secondary education in the United States and enter an American university.

Andover in Massachusetts; Dartmouth in New Hampshire; finally Carnegie Institute in Pennsylvania.

Of course, the Intelligence Division hadn't discovered *all* of the above information from Spaulding's application forms. These supplementary facts – and a great deal more – were revealed by a man named Aaron Mandel in New York.

Pace, his eyes still riveted on the tall, lean man who had put down his newspaper and was now watching the actors around the microphones with detached amusement, recalled his single meeting with Mandel. Again, he matched Mandel's information with the man he saw before him.

Mandel had been listed on the application under 'References.' *Power-of-attorney, parents' concert manager.* An address was given: a suite of rooms in the Chrysler Building. Mandel was a very successful artists' representative, a Russian Jew who rivaled Sol Hurok for clients, though not as prone to attract attention or as desirous of it.

'David has been as a son to me,' Mandel told Pace. 'But I must presume you know that.'

'Why must you? I know only what I've read on his application forms. And some scattered information; academic records, employment references.'

'Let's say I've been expecting you. Or someone like you.'

'I beg your pardon?'

'Oh, come. David spent a great many years in Germany; you might say he almost grew up there.'

'His application ... as a matter of fact his passport information, also includes family residences in London and a place called Costa del Santiago in Portugal.'

'I said almost. He converses easily in the German language.'

'Also Portuguese, I understand.'

'Equally so. And its sister tongue, Spanish ... I wasn't aware that a man's enlistment in the army engineers called for a full colonel's interest. And passport research.' Mandel, the flesh creased around his eyes, smiled.

'I wasn't prepared for you.' The colonel's reply had been stated simply. 'Most people take this sort of thing as routine. Or they convince themselves it's routine ... with a little help.'

'Most people did not live as Jews in tsarist Kiev ... What do you want from me?'

'To begin with, did you tell Spaulding you expected us? Or someone ...'

'Of course not,' Mandel interrupted gently. 'I told you, he is as a son to me. I wouldn't care to give him such ideas.'

'I'm relieved. Nothing may come of it anyway.'

'However, you hope it will.'

'Frankly, yes. But there are questions we need answered. His background isn't just unusual, it seems filled with contradictions. To begin with, you don't expect the son of well-known musicians ... I mean ...'

'Concert artists.' Mandel had supplied the term Pace sought.

'Yes, concert artists. You don't expect the children of such people to become engineers. Or accountants, if you know what I mean. And then – and I'm sure you'll understand this – it seems highly illogical that once that fact is accepted, the son *is* an engineer, we find that the major portion of his income is currently earned as a ... as a radio performer. The pattern indicates a degree of instability. Perhaps more than a degree.'

'You suffer from the American mania for consistency. I don't say this unkindly. I would be less than adequate as a neurosurgeon; you may play the piano quite well, but I doubt that I'd represent you at Covent Garden ... The questions you raise are easily answered. And, perhaps, the word *stability* can be found at the core ... Have you any idea, any *conception*, of what the world of the concert stage is like? *Madness* ... David lived in this world for nearly twenty years; I suspect ... no, I don't suspect, I know ... he found it quite distasteful ... And so often people overlook certain fundamental characteristics of musicianship. Characteristics easily inherited. A great musician is often, in his own way, an exceptional mathematician. Take Bach. A genius at mathematics ...'

According to Aaron Mandel, David Spaulding found his future profession while in his second year in college. The solidity, the permanence of structural creation combined with the precision of engineering detail were at once his answer to and escape from the mercurial world of the 'concert stage'. But there were other inherited characteristics equally at work inside him.

Spaulding had an ego, a sense of independence. He needed approval, wanted recognition. And such rewards were not easily come by for a junior engineer, just out of graduate school, in a large New York firm during the late thirties. There simply wasn't that much to do; or the capital to do it with.

'He left the New York firm,' Mandel continued, 'to accept a number of individual construction projects where he believed the money would grow faster, the jobs be his own. He had no ties; he could travel. Several in the Midwest, one ... no, two, in Central America; four in Canada, I think. He got the first few right out of the newspapers; they led to the others. He returned to New York about eighteen months ago. The money didn't really grow, as I told him it wouldn't. The projects were not his own; provincial ... local interference.'

'And somehow this led to the radio work?'

Mandel had laughed and leaned back in his chair. 'As you may know, Colonel Pace, I've diversified. The concert stage and a European war – soon to reach these shores, as we all realize – do not go well together. These last few years my clients have gone into other performing areas, including the highly paid radio field. David quickly saw opportunities for himself and I agreed. He's done extremely well, you know.'

'But he's not a trained professional.'

'No, he's not. He has something else, however ... Think. Most children of well-known performers, or leading politicians, or the immensely rich, for that matter, have it. It's a public confidence, an assurance, if you will; no matter their private insecurities. After all, they've generally been on display since the time they could walk and talk. David certainly has it. And he has a good ear; as do both of his parents, obviously. An aural memory for musical or linguistic rhythms ... He doesn't act, he *reads*. Almost exclusively in the dialects or the foreign languages he knows fluently ...'

David Spaulding's excursion into the 'highly paid radio field' was solely motivated by money; he was used to living well. At a time when owners of engineering companies found it difficult to guarantee themselves a hundred dollars a week, Spaulding was earning three or four hundred from his 'radio work' alone.

'As you may have surmised,' said Mandel, 'David's immediate objective is to bank sufficient monies to start his own company. Immediate, that is, unless otherwise shaped by world or national conditions. He's not blind; anyone who can read a newspaper sees that we are being drawn into the war.'

'Do you think we should be?'

'I'm a Jew. As far as I'm concerned, we're late.'

'This Spaulding. You've described what seems to me a very resourceful man.'

'I've described only what you could have found out from any number of sources. And *you* have described the conclusion you have drawn from that surface information. It's not the whole picture.' At this point, Pace recalled, Mandel had gotten out of his chair, avoiding any eye contact, and walked about his office. He was searching for negatives; he was trying to find the words that would disqualify 'his son' from the government's interests. And Pace had been aware of it. 'What certainly must have struck you – from what I've told you – is David's preoccupation with himself, with his comforts, if you wish. Now, in a business sense this might be applauded; therefore, I disabused you of your concerns for stability. However, I would not be candid if I didn't tell you that David is abnormally headstrong. He operates – I think – quite poorly under authority. In a word, he's a selfish man, not given to discipline. It pains me to say this; I love him dearly . . .'

And the more Mandel had talked, the more indelibly did Pace imprint the word *affirmative* on Spaulding's file. Not that he believed for a minute the extremes of behavior Mandel suddenly ascribed to David Spaulding – no man could function as 'stably' as Spaulding had if it were true. But if it were only half true, it was no detriment; it was an asset.

The last of the requirements.

For if there were any soldier in the United States Army – in or out of uniform – who would be called upon to operate solely on his own, without the comfort of the chain of command, without the knowledge that difficult decisions could be made by his superiors, it was the Intelligence officer in Portugal.

The man in Lisbon.

October 8, 1939 – Fairfax, Virginia

There were no names.

Only numbers and letters.

Numbers followed by letters.

Two-Six-B. Three-Five-Y. Five-One-C.

There were no personal histories, no individual backgrounds . . . no references to wives, children, fathers, mothers . . . no countries; cities, hometowns, schools, universities; there were only bodies and minds and separate, specific, reacting intelligences.

The location was deep in the Virginia hunt country, 220 acres of fields and hills and mountain streams. There were sections of dense forest bordering stretches of flat grasslands. Swamps – dangerous with body-sucking earth and hostile inhabitants, reptile and insect – were but feet from sudden masses of Virginia boulders fronting abrupt inclines.

The area had been selected with care, with precision. It was bordered by a fifteen-foot-high hurricane fence through which a paralysing – not lethal – electrical current flowed continuously; and every twelve feet there was a forbidding sign that warned observers that this particular section of the land . . . forest, swamp, grassland and hill . . . was the exclusive property of the United States Government. Trespassers were duly informed that entry was not only prohibited, it was exceedingly dangerous. Titles and sections of the specific laws pertaining to the exclusivity were spelled out along with the voltage in the fence.

The terrain was as diverse as could be found within a reasonable distance from Washington. In one way or another – one place or another – it conformed remarkably to the topography of the locations projected for those training inside the enormous compound.

The numbers followed by the letters.

No names.

There was a single gate at the center of the north perimeter, reached by a back-country road. Over the gate, between the opposing guard houses, was a metal sign. In block letters it read: FIELD DIVISION HEADQUARTERS – FAIRFAX.

No other description was given, no purpose identified.

On the front of each guard house were identical signs, duplicates of the warnings placed every twelve feet in the fence, proclaiming the exclusivity, the laws and the voltage.

No room for error.

David Spaulding was assigned an identity – his Fairfax identity. He was Two-Five-L.

No name. Only a number followed by a letter.

Two-Five-L.

Translation: his training was to be completed by the fifth day of the second month. His destination: Lisbon.

It was incredible. In the space of four months a new way of life – of *living* – was to be absorbed with such totality that it strained acceptance.

'You probably won't make it,' said Colonel Edmund Pace.

'I'm not sure I want to,' had been Spaulding's reply.

But part of the training was motivation. Deep, solid, ingrained beyond doubt ... but not beyond the psychological reality as perceived by the candidate.

With Two-Five-L, the United States Government did not wave flags and roar espousals of patriotic causes. Such methods would not be meaningful; the candidate had spent his formative years outside the country in a sophisticated, international environment. He spoke the language of the enemy-to-be; he knew them as people – taxi drivers, grocers, bankers, lawyers – and the vast majority of those he knew were not the Germans fictionalized by the propaganda machines. Instead – and this was Fairfax's legitimate hook – they were goddamned fools being led by psychopathic criminals. The leaders were, indeed, fanatics, and the overwhelming evidence clearly established their crimes beyond doubt. Those crimes included wanton, indiscriminate murder, torture and genocide.

Beyond doubt.

Criminals.

Psychopaths.

Too, there was Adolf Hitler.

Adolf Hitler killed Jews. By the thousands – soon to be millions if his *final solution* was read accurately.

Aaron Mandel was a Jew. His other 'father' was a Jew; the 'father' he loved more than the parent. And the goddamned fools tolerated an exclamation point after the word *Juden!*

David Spaulding could bring himself to hate the goddamned fools – the taxi drivers, the grocers, the bankers, the lawyers – without much compunction under the circumstances.

Beyond this very rational approach, Fairfax utilized a secondary psychological 'weapon' that was standard in the compound; for some more than others, but it was never absent.

The trainees at Fairfax had a common gift – or flaw – depending on one's approach. None was accepted without it.

A highly developed sense of competition; a thrust to win.

There was no question about it; arrogance was not a despised commodity at Fairfax.

With David Spaulding's psychological profile – a dossier increasingly accepted by the Intelligence Division – the Fairfax commanders recognized that the candidate-in-training for Lisbon had a soft core which the field might harden – undoubtedly *would* harden if he lived that long – but whatever advances could be made in the compound, so much the better. Especially for the subject.

Spaulding was confident, independent, extremely versatile in his surroundings ... all to the very good; but Two-Five-L had a weakness. There was within his psyche a slowness to take immediate advantage, a hesitancy to spring to the kill when the odds were his. Both verbally and physically.

Colonel Edmund Pace saw this inadequacy by the third week of training. Two-Five-L's abstract code of fairness would never do in Lisbon. And Colonel Pace knew the answer.

The mental adjustment would be made through the physical processes.

'Seizures, Holds and Releases' was the insipid title of the course. It disguised the most arduous physical training at Fairfax: hand-to-hand combat. Knife, chain, wire, needle, rope, fingers, knees, elbows ... never a gun.

Reaction, reaction, reaction.

Except when one initiated the assault.

Two-Five-L had progressed nicely. He was a large man but possessed the quick coordination usually associated with a more compact person. Therefore his progress had to be stymied; the man himself humiliated. He would learn the practical advantages of the odds.

From smaller, more arrogant men.

Colonel Edmund Pace 'borrowed' from the British commando units the best they had in uniform. They were flown over by the Bomber Ferry Command; three bewildered 'specialists' who were subtly introduced to the Fairfax compound and given their instructions.

'Kick the shit out of Two-Five-L.'

They did. For many weeks of sessions.

And then they could not do so with impunity any longer.

David Spaulding would not accept the humiliation; he was becoming as good as the 'specialists'.

The man for Lisbon was progressing.

Colonel Edmund Pace received the reports in his War Department office. Everything was on schedule.

The weeks became months. Every known portable offensive and defensive weapon, every sabotage device, every conceivable method of ingress and egress – apparent and covert – was exhaustively studied by the Fairfax trainees. Codes and variations became fluent languages; instant fabrications second nature. And Two-Five-L continued to advance. Whenever there appeared a slackening, harsher instructions were given to the 'specialists' in 'Seizures, Holds and Releases.' The psychological key was in the observable, physical humiliation.

Until it was no longer viable. The commandos were bested.

Everything on schedule.

'You may make it after all,' said the colonel.

'I'm not sure what I've made,' replied David in his first lieutenant's uniform, over a drink in the Mayflower Cocktail Lounge. And then he laughed quietly. 'I suppose if they gave degrees in Advanced Criminal Activities, I'd probably qualify.'

Two-Five-L's training would be completed in ten days. His twenty-four-hour pass was an irregularity, but Pace had demanded it. He had to talk with Spaulding.

'Does it bother you?' asked Pace.

Spaulding looked across the small table at the colonel. 'If I had time to think about it, I'm sure it would. Doesn't it bother you?'

'No ... Because I understand the reasons.'

'Okay. Then so do I.'

'They'll become clearer in the field.'

'Sure,' agreed David tersely.

Pace watched Spaulding closely. As was to be expected, the young man had changed. Gone was the slightly soft, slightly pampered grace of inflection and gesture. These had been replaced by a tautness, a conciseness of movement and speech. The transformation was not complete, but it was well in progress.

The patina of the professional was beginning to show through. Lisbon would harden it further.

'Are you impressed by the fact that Fairfax skips you a rank? It took me eighteen months to get that silver bar.'

'Again, time. I haven't had time to react. I haven't worn a uniform before today; I think it's uncomfortable.' Spaulding flicked his hand over his tunic.

'Good. Don't get used to it.'

'That's a strange thing to say ...'

'How do you feel?' said Pace, interrupting.

David looked at the colonel. For a moment or two, the grace, the softness

– even the wry humor – returned. 'I'm not sure ... As though I'd been manufactured on a very fast assembly line. A sort of high-speed treadmill, if you know what I mean.'

'In some ways that's an accurate description. Except that you brought a lot to the factory.'

Spaulding revolved his glass slowly. He stared at the floating cubes, then up at Pace. 'I wish I could accept that as a compliment,' he said softly. 'I don't think I can. I know the people I've been training with. They're quite a collection.'

'They're highly motivated.'

'The Europeans are as crazy as those they want to fight. They've got their reasons; I can't question them ...'

'Well,' interrupted the colonel, 'we don't have that many Americans. Not yet.'

'Those you do are two steps from a penitentiary.'

'They're not army.'

'I didn't know that,' said Spaulding quickly, adding the obvious with a smile. 'Naturally.'

Pace was annoyed with himself. The indiscretion was minor but still an indiscretion. 'It's not important. In ten days you'll be finished in Virginia. The uniform comes off then. To tell you the truth, it was a mistake to issue you one in the first place. We're still new at this kind of thing; rules of requisition and supply are hard to change.' Pace drank and avoided Spaulding's eyes.

'I thought I was supposed to be a military attaché at the embassy. One of several.'

'For the record, yes. They'll build a file on you. But there's a difference; it's part of the cover. You're not partial to uniforms. We don't think you should wear one. Ever.' Pace put down his glass and looked at David. 'You hustled yourself a very safe, very comfortable job because of the languages, your residences and your family connections. In a nutshell, you ran as fast as you could when you thought there was a chance your pretty neck might be in the real army.'

Spaulding thought for a moment. 'That sounds logical. Why does it bother you?'

'Because only one man at the embassy will know the truth. He'll identify himself ... After a while others may suspect – after a long while. But they won't know. Not the ambassador, not the staff ... What I'm trying to tell you is, you won't be very popular.'

David laughed quietly. 'I trust you'll rotate me before I'm lynched.'

Pace's reply was swift and quiet, almost curt. 'Others will be rotated. Not you.'

Spaulding was silent as he responded to the colonel's look. 'I don't understand.'

'I'm not sure I can be clear about it.' Pace put down his drink on the small cocktail table. 'You'll have to start slowly, with extreme caution. British MI5 has given us a few names – not many but something to start with. You'll have to build up your own network, however. People who will maintain contact only with you, no one else. This will entail a great deal of traveling. We think you'll gravitate to the north country, across the borders into Spain. Basque country ... by and large anti-Falangist. We think those areas south of the Pyrenees will become the data and escape routes ... We're not kidding ourselves: the Maginot won't hold. France will fall ...'

'*Jesus*,' interrupted David softly. 'You've done a lot of projecting.'

'That's almost *all* we do. It's the reason for Fairfax.'

Spaulding leaned back in the chair, once more revolving his glass. 'I understand about the network; in one form or another it's what the compound's training all of us for. This is the first I've heard about the north of Spain, the Basque areas. I know that country.'

'We could be wrong. It's only a theory. You might find the water routes ... Mediterranean, Málaga, or Biscay, or the Portuguese coast ... more feasible. That's for you to decide. And develop.'

'All right. I understand ... What's that got to do with rotation?'

Pace smiled. 'You haven't reached your post. Are you angling for a leave already?'

'You brought it up. Sort of abruptly, I think.'

'Yes, I did.' The colonel shifted his position in the small chair. Spaulding was very quick; he locked in on words and used brief time spans to maximize their effectiveness. He would be good in interrogations. Quick, harsh inquiries. In the field. 'We've decided that you're to remain in Portugal for the duration. Whatever normal and "abnormal" leaves you take should be spent in the south. There's a string of colonies along the coast ...'

'Costa del Santiago among them,' interjected Spaulding under his breath. 'Retreats for the international rich.'

'That's right. Develop covers down there. Be seen with your parents. Become a fixture.' Pace smiled again; the smile was hesitant. 'I could think of worse duty.'

'You don't know those colonies ... If I read you – as we say in Fairfax – Candidate Two-Five-L had better take a good, hard look at the streets of Washington and New York because he's not going to see them again for a very long time.'

'We can't risk bringing you back once you've developed a network, assuming you *do* develop one. If, for whatever reason, you flew out of Lisbon to Allied territory, there'd be an enemy scramble to microscopically trace every movement you made for months. It would jeopardize everything. *You're* safest – *our interests* are safest – if you remain permanent. The British taught us this. Some of their operatives have been local fixtures for years.'

'That's not very comforting.'

'You're not in MI5. Your tour is for the duration. The war won't last forever.'

It was Spaulding's turn to smile; the smile of a man caught in a matrix he had not defined. 'There's something insane about that statement ... "The war won't last forever." ...'

'Why?'

'We're not in it yet.'

'You are,' Pace said.

2

September 8, 1943 – Peenemünde, Germany

The man in the pinstriped suit, styled by tailors in Alte Strasse, stared in disbelief at the three men across the table. He would have objected strenuously had the three laboratory experts not worn the square, red, metal insignias on the lapels of their starched white laboratory jackets, badges that said these three scientists were permitted to walk through passageways forbidden to all but the elite of Peenemünde. He, too, had such a badge attached to his pinstriped lapel; it was a temporary clearance he was not sure he wanted.

Certainly he did not want it now.

'I can't accept your evaluation,' he said quietly. 'It's preposterous.'

'Come with us,' replied the scientist in the center, nodding to his companion on the right.

'There's no point procrastinating,' added the third man.

The four men got out of their chairs and approached the steel door that was the single entrance to the room. Each man in succession unclipped his red badge and pressed it against a gray plate in the wall. At the instant of contact, a small white bulb was lighted, remained so for two seconds and then went off; a photograph had been taken. The last man – one of the Peenemünde personnel – then opened the door and each went into the hallway.

Had only three men gone out, or five, or any number not corresponding to the photographs, alarms would have been triggered.

They walked in silence down the long, starched-white corridor, the Berliner in front with the scientist who sat between the other two at the table, and was obviously the spokesman; his companions were behind.

They reached a bank of elevators and once more went through the ritual of the red tags, the gray plate and the tiny white light that went on for precisely two seconds. Below the plate a number was also lighted.

Six.

From elevator number six there was the sound of a single muted bell as the thick steel panel slid open. One by one each man walked inside.

The elevator descended eight stories, four below the surface of the earth, to the deepest levels of Peenemünde. As the four men emerged into yet another white corridor, they were met by a tall man in tight-fitting green coveralls, an outsized holster in his wide brown belt. The holster held a Lüger *Sternlicht,* a specially designed arm pistol with a telescopic sight. As the man's visor cap indicated, such weapons were made for the Gestapo.

The Gestapo officer obviously recognized the three scientists. He smiled perfunctorily and turned his attention to the man in the pinstriped suit. He held out his hand, motioning the Berliner to remove the red badge.

The Berliner did so. The Gestapo man took it, walked over to a telephone on the corridor wall and pushed a combination of buttons. He spoke the Berliner's name and waited, perhaps ten seconds.

He replaced the phone and crossed back to the man in the pinstriped suit. Gone was the arrogance he had displayed moments ago.

'I apologize for the delay, Herr Strasser. I should have realized . . .' He gave the Berliner his badge.

'No need for apologies, Herr Oberleutnant. They would be necessary only if you overlooked your duties.'

'*Danke,*' said the Gestapo man, gesturing the four men beyond his point of security.

They proceeded towards a set of double doors; clicks could be heard as locks were released. Small white bulbs were lighted above the mouldings; again photographs were taken of those going through the double doors.

They turned right into a bisecting corridor – this one not white, but instead, brownish black; so dark that Strasser's eyes took several seconds to adjust from the pristine brightness of the main halls to the sudden night quality of the passageway. Tiny ceiling lights gave what illumination there was.

'You've not been here before,' said the scientist-spokesman to the Berliner. 'This hallway was designed by an optics engineer. It supposedly prepares the eyes for the high-intensity microscope lights. Most of us think it was a waste.'

There was a steel door at the end of the long, dark tunnel. Strasser reached for his red metal insignia automatically; the scientist shook his head and spoke with a slight wave of his hand.

'Insufficient light for photographs. The guard inside has been alerted.'

The door opened and the four men entered a large laboratory. Along the right wall was a row of stools, each in front of a powerful microscope, all the microscopes equidistant from one another on top of a built-in workbench. Behind each microscope was a high-intensity light, projected and shaded on a goose-necked stem coming out of the immaculate white surface. The left wall was a variation of the right. There were no stools, however, and fewer microscopes. The work shelf was higher: it was obviously used for conferences, where many pairs of eyes peered through the same sets of lenses; stools would only interfere, men stood as they conferred over magnified particles.

At the far end of the room was another door, not an entrance. A vault. A seven-foot-high, four-foot-wide, heavy steel vault. It was black; the two levers and the combination wheel were in glistening silver.

The spokesman-scientist approached it.

'We have fifteen minutes before the timer seals the panel and the drawers. I've requested closure for a week. I'll need your counterauthorization, of course.'

'And you're sure I'll give it, aren't you?'

'I am.' The scientist spun the wheel right and left for the desired locations. 'The numbers change automatically every twenty-four hours,' he said as he held the wheel steady at its final mark and reached for the silver levers. He pulled the top one down to the accompaniment of a barely audible whirring sound, and seconds later, pulled the lower one up.

The whirring stopped, metallic clicks could be heard and the scientist pulled open the thick steel door. He turned to Strasser. 'These are the tools for Peenemünde. See for yourself.'

Strasser approached the vault. Inside were five rows of removable glass trays, top to bottom; each row had a total of one hundred trays, five hundred in all.

The trays that were empty were marked with a white strip across the facing glass, the word *Auffüllen* printed clearly.

The trays that were full were so designated by strips of black across their fronts.

There were four and a half rows of white trays. Empty.

Strasser looked closely, pulled open several trays, shut them and stared at the Peenemünde scientist.

'This is the sole repository?' he asked quietly.

'It is. We have six thousand casings completed; God knows how many will go in experimentation. Estimate for yourself how much further we can proceed.'

Strasser held the scientist's eyes with his own. 'Do you realize what you're saying?'

'I do. We'll deliver only a fraction of the required schedules. Nowhere near enough. Peenemünde is a disaster.'

September 9, 1943 – The North Sea

The fleet of B-17 bombers had aborted the primary target of Essen due to cloud cover. The squadron commander, over the objections of his fellow pilots, ordered the secondary mission into operation: the shipyards north of Bremerhaven. No one liked the Bremerhaven run; Messerschmitt and Stuka interceptor wings were devastating. They were called the Luftwaffe suicide squads, maniacal young Nazis who might as easily collide with enemy aircraft as fire at them. Not necessarily due to outrageous bravery; often it was merely inexperience or worse: poor training.

Bremerhaven-north was a terrible secondary. When it was a primary objective, the Eighth Air Force fighter escorts took the sting out of the run; they were not there when Bremerhaven was a secondary.

The squadron commander, however, was a hardnose. Worse, he was West Point: the secondary would not only be hit, it would be hit at an altitude that guaranteed maximum accuracy. He did not tolerate the very vocal criticism of his second-in-command aboard the flanking aircraft, who made it clear that such an altitude was barely logical *with* fighter escorts; *without* them, considering the heavy ack-ack fire, it was ridiculous. The squadron commander had replied with a terse recital of the new navigational headings and termination of radio contact.

Once they were into the Bremerhaven corridors, the German interceptors came from all points; the antiaircraft guns were murderous. And the squadron commander took his lead plane directly down into maximum-accuracy altitude and was blown out of the sky.

The second-in-command valued life and the price of aircraft more than his West Point superior. He ordered the squadron to scramble altitudes, telling his bombardiers to unload on anything below but for-God's-sake-release-the-goddamn-weight so all planes could reach their maximum heights and reduce antiaircraft and interceptor fire.

In several instances it was too late. One bomber caught fire and went into a spin; only three chutes emerged from it. Two aircraft were riddled so badly both planes began immediate descents. Pilots and crew bailed out. Most of them.

The remainder kept climbing; the Messerschmitts climbed with them. They went higher and still higher, past the safe altitude range. Oxygen masks were ordered; not all functioned.

But in four minutes, what was left of the squadron was in the middle of the clear midnight sky, made stunningly clearer by the substratosphere absence of air particles. The stars were extraordinary in their flickering brightness, the moon more a bombers' moon than ever before.

Escape was in these regions.

'Chart man!' said the exhausted, relieved second-in-command into his radio, 'give us headings! Back to Lakenheath, if you'd be so kind.'

The reply on the radio soured the moment of relief. It came from an aerial gunner aft of navigation. 'He's dead, colonel. Nelson's dead.'

There was no time in the air for comment, 'Take it, aircraft three. It's your chart,' said the colonel in aircraft two.

The headings were given. The formation grouped and, as it descended into safe altitude with cloud cover above, sped toward the North Sea.

The minutes reached five, then seven, then twelve. Finally twenty. There was relatively little cloud cover below; the coast of England should have come into sighting range at least two minutes ago. A number of pilots were concerned. Several said so.

'Did you give accurate headings, aircraft three?' asked the now squadron commander.

'Affirmative, colonel,' was the radioed answer.

'Any of you chart men disagree?'

A variety of negatives was heard from the remaining aircraft.

'No sweat on the headings, colonel,' came the voice of the captain of aircraft five. 'I fault your execution, though.'

'What the hell are you talking about?'

'You pointed two-three-niner by my reading. I figured my equipment was shot up . . .'

Suddenly there were interruptions from every pilot in the decimated squadron.

'I read one-seven . . .'

'My heading was a goddamned two-niner-two. We took a direct hit on . . .'

'*Jesus!* I had sixer-four . . .'

'Most of our middle took a load. I discounted my readings totally!'

And then there was silence. All understood.

Or understood what they could not comprehend.

'Stay off all frequencies,' said the squadron commander, 'I'll try to reach base.'

The cloud cover above broke; not for long, but long enough. The voice over the radio was the captain of aircraft three.

'A quick judgment, colonel, says we're heading due northwest.'

Silence again.

After a few moments, the commander spoke. 'I'll reach somebody. Do all your gauges read as mine? Fuel for roughly ten to fifteen minutes?'

'It's been a long haul, colonel,' said aircraft seven. 'No more than that, it's for sure.'

'I figured we'd be circling, if we had to, five minutes ago,' said aircraft eight.

'We're not,' said aircraft four.

The colonel in aircraft two raised Lakenheath on an emergency frequency.

'As near as we can determine,' came the strained, agitated, yet controlled English voice, 'and by that I mean open lines throughout the coastal defence areas – water and land – you're approaching the Dunbar sector. That's the Scottish border, colonel. What in blazes are you doing there?'

'For Christ's sake, I don't *know!* Are there any fields?'

'Not for *your* aircraft. Certainly not a formation; perhaps, one or two . . .'

'I don't want to hear that, you son-of-a-bitch! Give me emergency instructions!'

'We're really quite unprepared . . .'

'Do you *read me*?! I have what's left of a very chopped-up squadron! We have less than six minutes' fuel! Now you *give*!'

The silence lasted precisely four seconds. Lakenheath conferred swiftly. With finality.

'We believe you'll sight the coast, probably Scotland. Put your aircraft down at sea . . . We'll do our best, lads.'

'We're eleven *bombers*, Lakenheath! We're not a bunch of ducks!'

'There isn't time, squadron Leader ... The logistics are insurmountable. After all, we didn't guide you there. Put down at sea. We'll do our best ... Godspeed.'

Part One

1

September 10, 1943 – Berlin, Germany

Reichsminister of Armaments Albert Speer raced up the steps of the Air Ministry on the Tiergarten. He did not feel the harsh, diagonal sheets of rain that plummeted down from the gray sky; he did not notice that his raincoat – unbuttoned – had fallen away, exposing his tunic and shirt to the inundation of the September storm. The pitch of his fury swept everything but the immediate crisis out of his mind.

Insanity! Sheer, unmitigated, unforgivable insanity!

The industrial reserves of all Germany were about exhausted; but he could handle that immense problem. Handle it by properly utilizing the manufacturing potential of the occupied countries; reverse the unmanageable practices of importing the labour forces. Labour forces? Slaves!

Productivity disastrous; sabotage continuous, unending.

What did they expect?

It was a time for sacrifice! Hitler could not continue to be all things to all people! He could not provide outsized Duesenbergs and grand operas and populated restaurants; he had to provide, instead, tanks, munitions, ships, aircraft! *These* were the priorities!

But the Führer could never erase the memory of the 1918 revolution.

How totally inconsistent! The sole man whose will was shaping history, who was close to the preposterous dream of a thousand-year Reich, was petrified of a long-ago memory of unruly mobs, of unsatisfied masses.

Speer wondered if future historians would record the fact. If they would comprehend just how weak Hitler really was when it came to his own countrymen. How he buckled in fear when consumer production fell below anticipated schedules.

Insanity!

But still *he*, the Reichsminister of Armaments, could control this calamitous inconsistency as long as he was convinced it was just a question of time. A few months; perhaps six at the outside.

For there was Peenemünde.

The rockets.

Everything reduced itself to Peenemünde!

713

Peenemünde was irresistible. Peenemünde would cause the collapse of London and Washington. Both governments would see the futility of continuing the exercise of wholesale annihilation.

Reasonable men could then sit down and create reasonable treaties.

Even if it meant the silencing of *unreasonable* men. Silencing Hitler.

Speer knew there were others who thought that way, too. The Führer was manifestly beginning to show unhealthy signs of pressure – fatigue. He now surrounded himself with mediocrity – an ill-disguised desire to remain in the comfortable company of his intellectual equals. But it went too far when the Reich itself was affected. A wine merchant, the foreign minister! A third-rate party propagandizer, the minister of eastern affairs! An erstwhile fighter pilot, the overseer of the *entire economy*!

Even himself. Even the quiet, shy architect; now the minister of armaments.

All that would change with Peenemünde.

Even himself. *Thank God!*

But first there *had* to be Peenemünde. There could be no *question* of its operational success. For without Peenemünde, the war was lost.

And now they were telling him there *was* a question. A flaw that might well be the precursor of Germany's defeat.

A vacuous-looking corporal opened the door of the cabinet room. Speer walked in and saw that the long conference table was about two-thirds filled, the chairs in cliquish separation, as if the groups were suspect of one another. As, indeed, they were in these times of progressively sharpened rivalries within the Reich.

He walked to the head of the table, where – to his right – sat the only man in the room he could trust. Franz Altmüller.

Altmüller was a forty-two-year-old cynic. Tall, blond, aristocratic; the vision of the Third Reich Aryan who did not, for a minute, subscribe to the racial nonsense proclaimed by the Third Reich. He did, however, subscribe to the theory of acquiring whatever benefits came his way by pretending to agree with anyone who might do him some good.

In public.

In private, among his *very* close associates, he told the truth.

When that truth might also benefit him.

Speer was not only Altmüller's associate, he was his friend. Their families had been more than neighbours; the two fathers had often gone into joint merchandising ventures; the mothers had been school chums.

Altmüller had taken after his father. He was an extremely capable businessman; his expertise was in production administration.

'Good morning,' said Altmüller, flicking an imaginary thread off his tunic lapel. He wore his party uniform far more often than was necessary, preferring to err on the side of the archangel.

'That seems unlikely,' replied Speer, sitting down rapidly. The groups – and they were groups – around the table kept talking among themselves but the voices were perceptibly quieter. Eyes kept darting over in Speer's direction, then swiftly away; everyone was prepared for immediate silence yet none wished to appear apprehensive, guilty.

Silence would come when either Altmüller or Speer himself rose from his chair to address the gathering. That would be the signal. Not before. To render attention before that movement might give the appearance of fear. Fear was equivalent to an admission of error. No one at the conference table could afford that.

Altmüller opened a brown manila folder and placed it in front of Speer. It was a list of those summoned to the meeting. There were essentially three distinct factions with subdivisions within each, and each with its spokesman. Speer read the names and unobtrusively – he thought – looked up to ascertain the presence and the location of the three leaders.

At the far end of the table, resplendent in his general's uniform, his tunic a field of decorations going back thirty years, sat Ernst Leeb, Chief of the Army Ordnance Office. He was of medium height but excessively muscular, a condition he maintained well into his sixties. He smoked his cigarette through an ivory holder which he used to cut off his various subordinates' conversations at will. In some ways Leeb was a caricature, yet still a powerful one. Hitler liked him, as much for his imperious military bearing as for his abilities.

At the midpoint of the table, on the left, sat Albert Vögler, the sharp, aggressive general manager of Reich's Industry. Vögler was a stout man, the image of a burgomaster; the soft flesh of his face constantly creased into a questioning scowl. He laughed a great deal, but his laughter was hard; a device, not an enjoyment. He was well suited to his position. Vögler liked nothing better than hammering out negotiations between industrial adversaries. He was a superb mediator because all parties were usually frightened of him.

Across from Vögler and slightly to the right, toward Altmüller and Speer, was Wilhelm Zangen, the Reich official of the German Industrial Association. Zangen was thin-lipped, painfully slender, humorless; a fleshed-out skeleton happiest over his charts and graphs. A precise man who was given to perspiring at the edge of his receding hairline and below the nostrils and on his chin when nervous. He was perspiring now, and continuously brought his handkerchief up to blot the embarrassing moisture. Somewhat in contradiction to his appearance, however, Zangen was a persuasive debater. For he never argued without the facts.

They were all persuasive, thought Speer. And if it were not for his anger, he knew such men could – probably would – intimidate him. Albert Speer was honest in self-assessment; he realized that he had no substantial sense of authority. He found it difficult to express his thoughts forthrightly among such potentially hostile men. But now the potentially hostile men were in a defensive position. He could not allow his anger to cause them to panic, to seek only absolution for themselves.

They needed a remedy. Germany needed a remedy.

Peenemünde had to be saved.

'How would you suggest we begin?' Speer asked Altmüller, shading his voice so no one else at the table could hear him.

'I don't think it makes a particle of difference. It will take an hour of very loud, very boring, very obtuse explanations before we reach anything concrete.'

'I'm not interested in explanations . . .'

'Excuses, then.'

'Least of all, excuses. I want a solution.'

'If it's to be found at this table – which, frankly, I doubt – you'll have to sit through the excess verbiage. Perhaps something will come of it. Again, I doubt it.'

'Would you care to explain that?'

Altmüller looked directly into Speer's eyes. 'Ultimately, I'm not sure there is a solution. But if there is, I don't think it's at this table . . . Perhaps I'm wrong. Why don't we listen first?'

'All right. Would you please open with the summary you prepared? I'm afraid I'd lose my temper midway through.'

'May I suggest,' Altmüller whispered, 'that it will be necessary for you to lose your temper at some point during this meeting. I don't see how you can avoid it.'

'I understand.'

Altmüller pushed back his chair and stood up. Grouping by grouping the voices trailed off around the table.

'Gentlemen. This emergency session was called for reasons of which we assume you are aware. At least you should be aware of them. Apparently it is only the Reichsminister of Armaments and his staff who were not informed; a fact which the Reichsminister and his staff find appalling . . . In short words, the Peenemünde operation faces a crisis of unparalleled severity. In spite of the millions poured into this most vital weaponry development, in spite of the assurances consistently offered by your respective departments, we now learn that production may be brought to a complete halt within a matter of weeks. Several months prior to the *agreed-upon* date for the first operational rockets. That date has never been questioned. It has been the keystone for whole military strategies; entire armies have been manoeuvred to coordinate with it. Germany's victory is predicated on it . . . But now Peenemünde is threatened; Germany is threatened . . . If the projections the Reichsminister's staff have compiled – *unearthed* and compiled – are valid, the Peenemünde complex will exhaust its supply of industrial diamonds in less than ninety days. Without industrial diamonds the precision tooling in Peenemünde cannot continue.'

The babble of voices – excited, guttural, vying for attention – erupted the second Altmüller sat down. General Leeb's cigarette holder slashed the air in front of him as though it were a saber; Albert Vögler scowled and wrinkled his flesh-puffed eyes, placed his bulky hands on the table and spoke harshly in a loud monotone; Wilhelm Zangen's handkerchief was working furiously around his face and his neck, his high-pitched voice in conflict with the more masculine tones around him.

Franz Altmüller leaned toward Speer. 'You've seen cages of angry ocelots in the zoo? The zookeeper can't let them hurl themselves into the bars. I suggest you lose your benign temper far earlier than we discussed. Perhaps now.'

'This is not the way.'

'Don't let them think you are cowed . . .'

'Nor that I am cowering.' Speer interrupted his friend, the slightest trace of a smile on his lips. He stood up. 'Gentlemen.'

The voices trailed off.

'Herr Altmüller speaks harshly; he does so, I'm sure, because I spoke harshly with him. That was this morning, very early this morning. There is greater perspective now; it is no time for recriminations. This is not to lessen the critical aspects of the situation, for they are great. But anger will solve nothing. And we need solutions ... Therefore, I propose to seek your assistance – the assistance of the finest industrial and military minds in the Reich. First, of course, we need to know the specifics. I shall start with Herr Vögler. As manager of Reich's Industry, would you give us your estimate?'

Vögler was upset; he didn't wish to be the first called. 'I'm not sure I can be of much enlightenment, Herr Reichsminister. I, too, am subject to the reports given me. They have been optimistic; until the other week there was no suggestion of difficulty.'

'How do you mean, optimistic?' asked Speer.

'The quantities of bortz and carbonado diamonds were said to be sufficient. Beyond this there are the continuing experiments with lithicum, carbon and paraffin. Our intelligence tells us that the Englishman Storey at the British Museum reverified the Hannay-Moissan theories. Diamonds *were* produced in this fashion.'

'Who verified the Englishman?' Franz Altmüller did not speak kindly. 'Had it occurred to you that such data was meant to be passed?'

'Such verification is a matter for Intelligence. I am not with Intelligence, Herr Altmüller.'

'Go on,' said Speer quickly. 'What else?'

'There is an Anglo-American experiment under the supervision of the Bridgemann team. They are subjecting graphite to pressures in excess of six million pounds per square inch. So far there is no word of success.'

'Is there word of failure?' Altmüller raised his aristocratic eyebrows, his tone polite.

'I remind you again, I am not with Intelligence. I have received no word whatsoever.'

'Food for thought, isn't it,' said Altmüller, without asking a question.

'Nevertheless,' interrupted Speer before Vögler could respond, 'you had reason to assume that the quantities of bortz and carbonado were sufficient. Is that not so?'

'Sufficient. Or at least obtainable, Herr Reichsminister.'

'How so obtainable?'

'I believe General Leeb might be more knowledgeable on that subject.'

Leeb nearly dropped his ivory cigarette holder. Altmüller noted his surprise and cut in swiftly. 'Why would the army ordnance officer have that information, Herr Vögler? I ask merely for my own curiosity.'

'The reports, once more. It is my understanding that the Ordnance Office is responsible for evaluating the industrial, agricultural and mineral potentials of occupied territories. Or those territories so projected.'

Ernst Leeb was not entirely unprepared. He *was* unprepared for Vögler's insinuations, not for the subject. He turned to an aide, who shuffled papers top to bottom as Speer inquired.

'The Ordnance Office is under enormous pressure these days; as is your department, of course, Herr Vögler. I wonder if General Leeb has had the time . . .'

'We *made* the time,' said Leeb, his sharp military bearing pitted in counterpoint to Vögler's burgomaster gruffness. 'When we received word – from Herr Vögler's subordinates – that a crisis was imminent – not upon us, but imminent – we immediately researched the possibilities for extrication.'

Franz Altmüller brought his hand to his mouth to cover an involuntary smile. He looked at Speer, who was too annoyed to find any humor in the situation.

'I'm relieved the Ordnance Office is so confident, general,' said Speer. The Reichsminister of Armaments had *little* confidence in the military and had difficulty disguising it. 'Please, your extrication?'

'I said *possibilities*, Herr Speer. To arrive at practical solutions *will* take more time than we've been given.'

'Very well. Your possibilities?'

'There is an immediate remedy with historical precedent.' Leeb paused to remove his cigarette, crushing it out, aware that everyone around the table watched him intently. 'I have taken the liberty of recommending preliminary studies to the General Staff. It involves an expeditionary force of less than four battalions . . . Africa. The diamond mines east of Tanganyika.'

'*What?*' Altmüller leaned forward; he obviously could not help himself. 'You're not serious.'

'Please!' Speer would not allow his friend to interrupt. If Leeb had even conceived of such drastic action, it might have merit. No military man, knowing the thin line of combat strength – chewed up on the Eastern Front, under murderous assault by the Allies in Italy – could suggest such an absurdity unless he had a realistic hope of success. 'Go ahead, general.'

'The Williamson Mines at Mwadui. Between the districts of Tanganyika and Zanzibar in the central sector. The mines at Mwadui produce over a million carats of the carbonado diamond annually. Intelligence – the intelligence that is forwarded regularly to me at my insistence – informs us that there are supplies going back several months. Our agents in Dar es Salaam are convinced such an incursion would be successful.'

Franz Altmüller passed a sheet of paper to Speer. On it he had scribbled: 'He's lost his senses!'

'What is the historical precedent to which you refer?' asked Speer, holding his hand over Altmüller's paper.

'All of the districts east of Dar es Salaam rightfully belong to the Third Reich, German West Africa. They were taken from the fatherland after the Great War. The Führer himself made that clear four years ago.'

There was silence around the table. An embarrassed silence. The eyes of even his aides avoided the old soldier. Finally Speer spoke quietly.

'That is justification, not precedent, general. The world cares little for our justifications, and although I question the logistics of moving battalions halfway around the globe, you may have raised a valid point. Where else nearer . . . in *East* Africa, perhaps, can the bortz or the carbonado be found?'

Leeb looked to his aides; Wilhelm Zangen lifted his handkerchief to his nostrils and bowed his thin head in the direction of the general. He spoke as if exhaling, his high voice irritating.

'I'll answer you, Herr Reichsminister. And then, I believe, you will see how fruitless this discussion is . . . Sixty per cent of the world's crushing-bortz diamonds are in the Belgian Congo. The two principal deposits are in the Kasai and the Bakwanga fields, between the Kanshi and the Bushimaie rivers. The district's governor-general is Pierre Ryckmans; he is devoted to the Belgian government in exile in London. I can assure Leeb that the Congo's allegiances to Belgium are far greater than ours ever were in Dar es Salaam.'

Leeb lit a cigarette angrily. Speer leaned back in his chair and addressed Zangen.

'All right. Sixty per cent crushing-bortz; what of carbonado and the rest?'

'French Equatorial: totally allied to de Gaulle's Free French. Gold Coast and Sierra Leone: the tightest of British controls. Angola: Portuguese domination and their neutrality's inviolate; we know that beyond doubt. French West Africa: not only under Free French mandate but with Allied forces manning the outposts . . . Here, there was only one possibility and we lost it a year and a half ago. Vichy abandoned the Ivory Coast . . . There is no access in Africa, Reichsminister. None of a military nature.'

'I see.' Speer doodled on top of the paper Altmüller had passed to him. 'You are recommending a nonmilitary solution?'

'There is no other. The question is what.'

Speer turned to Franz Altmüller. His tall, blond associate was staring at them all. Their faces were blank. Baffled.

2

September 11, 1943 – Washington, DC

Brigadier General Alan Swanson got out of the taxi and looked up at the huge oak door of the Georgetown residence. The ride over the cobblestone streets had seemed like a continuous roll of hammering drums.

Prelude to execution.

Up those steps, inside that door, somewhere within that five-story brownstone-and-brick aristocratic home, was a large room. And inside that room thousands of executions would be pronounced, unrelated to any around the table within that room.

Prelude to annihilation.

If the schedules were kept. And it was inconceivable that they would be altered.

Wholesale murder.

In line with his orders he glanced up and down the street to make sure he hadn't been followed. Asinine! CIC had all of them under constant surveillance. Which of the pedestrians or slowly moving automobiles had him in their sights? It didn't matter; the choice of the meeting place was asinine, too. Did they really believe they could keep the crisis a secret? Did they think that holding conferences in secluded Georgetown houses would help?

Asses!

He was oblivious to the rain; it came down steadily, in straight lines. An autumn rainstorm in Washington. His raincoat was open, the jacket of his uniform damp and wrinkled. He didn't give a damn about such things; he couldn't think about them.

The only thing he could think about was packaged in a metal casing no more than seven inches wide, five high, and perhaps a foot long. It was designed for those dimensions; it had the appearance of sophisticated technology; it was tooled to operate on the fundamental properties of inertia and precision.

And it wasn't functional; it didn't work.

It failed test after test.

Ten thousand high-altitude B-17 bomber aircraft were emerging from production lines across the country. Without high-altitude, radio-beam gyroscopes to guide them, they might as well stay on the ground!

And without those aircraft, Operation Overlord was in serious jeopardy. The invasion of Europe would extract a price so great as to be obscene.

Yet to send the aircraft up on massive, round-the-clock, night and day bombing strikes throughout Germany without the cover of higher altitudes was to consign the majority to destruction, their crews to death. Examples were constant reminders ... whenever the big planes soared too high. The labels of pilot error, enemy fire and instrument fatigue were not so. It was the higher altitudes ... Only twenty-four hours ago a squadron of bombers on the Bremerhaven run had scrambled out of the strike, exacting the maximum from their aircraft and regrouped far above oxygen levels. From what could be determined, the guidance systems went crazy; the squadron ended up in the Dunbar sector near the Scottish border. All but one plane crashed into the sea. Three survivors were picked up by coastal patrols. Three out of God knows how many that had made it out of Bremerhaven. The one aircraft that attempted a ground landing had blown up on the outskirts of a town ... No survivors.

Germany was in the curve of inevitable defeat, but it would not die easily. It was ready for counterstrike. The Russian lesson had been learned; Hitler's generals were prepared. They realized that ultimately their only hope for any surrender other than *unconditional* lay in their ability to make the cost of an Allied victory so high it would stagger imagination and sicken the conscience of humanity.

Accommodation would then be reached.

And *that* was unacceptable to the Allies. *Unconditional surrender* was now a tripartite policy; the absolute had been so inculcated that it dared not be tampered with. The fever of total victory had swept the lands; the leaders had shaped that, too. And at this pitch of frenzy, the leaders stared into blank walls seeing nothing others could see and said heroically that losses would be tolerated.

Swanson walked up the steps of the Georgetown house. As if on cue, the door opened, a major saluted and Swanson was admitted quickly. Inside the hallway were four noncommissioned officers in paratroop leggings standing at ready-at-ease; Swanson recognized the shoulder patches of the Ranger battalions. The War Department had set the scene effectively.

A sergeant ushered Swanson into a small, brass-grilled elevator. Two stories up the elevator stopped and Swanson stepped out into the corridor. He recognized the face of the colonel who stood by a closed door at the end of the short hallway. He could not recall his name, however. The man worked in Clandestine Operations and was never much in evidence. The colonel stepped forward, saluting.

'General Swanson? Colonel Pace.'

Swanson nodded his salute, offering his hand instead. 'Oh, yes. Ed Pace, right?'

'Yes, sir.'

'So they pulled you out of the cellars. I didn't know this was your territory.'

'It's not, sir. Just that I've had occasion to meet the men you're seeing. Security clearances.'

'And with you here they know we're serious.' Swanson smiled.

'I'm sure we are, but I don't know what we're serious about.'

'You're lucky. Who's inside?'

'Howard Oliver from Meridian. Jonathan Craft from Packard. And the lab man, Spinelli, from ATCO.'

'They'll make my day; I can't wait. Who's presiding? Christ, there should be *one* person on our side.'

'Vandamm.'

Swanson's lips formed a quiet whistle; the colonel nodded in agreement. Frederic Vandamm was undersecretary of state and rumored to be Cordell Hull's closest associate. If one wanted to reach Roosevelt, the best way was through Hull; if that avenue was closed, one pursued Vandamm.

'That's impressive artillery,' Swanson said.

'When they saw him, I think he scared the hell out of Craft and Oliver. Spinelli's in a perpetual daze. He'd figure Patton for a doorman.'

'I don't know Spinelli, except by rep. He's supposed to be the best gyro man in the labs . . . Oliver and Craft I know *too* well. I wish to hell you boys had never cleared them for road maps.'

'Not much you can do when they own the roads, sir.' The colonel shrugged. It was obvious he agreed with Swanson's estimate.

'I'll give you a clue, Pace. Craft's a social-register flunky. Oliver's the bad meat.'

'He's got a lot of it on him,' replied the colonel, laughing softly.

Swanson took off his raincoat. 'If you hear gunfire, colonel, it's only me fooling around. Walk the other way.'

'I accept that as an order, general. I'm deaf,' answered Pace as he reached for the handle and opened the door swiftly for his superior.

Swanson walked rapidly into the room. It was a library with the furniture pushed back against the walls and a conference table placed in the center. At the head of the table sat the white-haired, aristocratic Frederic Vandamm. On his left was the obese, balding Howard Oliver, a sheaf of notes in front of him. Opposite Oliver were Craft and a short, dark, bespectacled man Swanson assumed was Gian Spinelli.

The empty chair at the end of the table, facing Vandamm, was obviously for him. It was good positioning on Vandamm's part.

'I'm sorry to be late, Mr Undersecretary. A staff car would have prevented it. A taxi wasn't the easiest thing to find . . . Gentlemen?'

The trio of corporate men nodded; Craft and Oliver each uttered a muted 'General.' Spinelli just stared from behind the thick lenses of his glasses.

'I apologize, General Swanson,' said Vandamm in the precise, Anglicized speech that bespoke a background of wealth. 'For obvious reasons we did not want this conference to take place in a government office, nor, if known, did we wish any significance attached to the meeting itself. These gentlemen represent War Department gossip, I don't have to tell you that. The absence of urgency was desirable. Staff cars speeding through Washington – don't ask me why, but they never seem to slow down – have a tendency to arouse concern. Do you see?'

Swanson returned the old gentleman's veiled look. Vandamm was a smart one, he thought. It was an impetuous gamble referring to the taxi, but Vandamm had understood. He'd picked it up and used it well, even impartially.

The three corporate men were on notice. At this conference, they were the enemy.

'I've been discreet, Mr Undersecretary.'

'I'm sure you have. Shall we get down to points? Mr Oliver has asked that he be permitted to open with a general statement of Meridian Aircraft's position.'

Swanson watched the heavy-jowled Oliver sort out his notes. He disliked Oliver intensely; there was a fundamental gluttony about him. He was a manipulator; there were so many of them these days. They were everywhere in Washington, piling up huge sums of money from the war; proclaiming the power of the deal, the price of the deal, the price of the power – which they held.

Oliver's rough voice shot out from his thick lips. 'Thank you. It's our feeling at Meridian that the ... *assumed* gravity of the present situation has obscured the real advancements that *have* been made. The aircraft in question has proved beyond doubt its superior capabilities. The new, improved Fortress is ready for operational combat; it's merely a question of desired altitudes.'

Oliver abruptly stopped and put his obese hands in front of him, over his papers. He had finished his statement; Craft nodded in agreement. Both men looked noncommittally at Vandamm. Gian Spinelli simply stared at Oliver, his brown eyes magnified by his glasses.

Alan Swanson was astounded. Not necessarily by the brevity of the statement but by the ingenuousness of the lie.

'If that's a position statement, I find it wholly unacceptable. The aircraft in question has *not* proved its capabilities until it's operational at the altitudes specified in the government contracts.'

'It's operational,' replied Oliver curtly.

'Operational. Not functional, Mr Oliver. It is not functional until it can be guided from point A to point B at the altitudes called for in the specifications.'

'*Specified* as "intended maximum", General Swanson,' shot back Oliver, smiling an obsequious smile that conveyed anything but courtesy.

'What the hell does that mean?' Swanson looked at Undersecretary Vandamm.

'Mr Oliver is concerned with a contractual interpretation.'

'I'm *not*.'

'I *have* to be,' replied Oliver. 'The War Department has refused payment to Meridian Aircraft Corporation. We have a contract . . .'

'Take the goddamned contract up with someone else!'

'Anger won't solve anything.' Vandamm spoke harshly.

'I'm sorry, Mr Undersecretary, but I'm not here to discuss *contractual interpretations.*'

'I'm afraid you'll have to, General Swanson.' Vandamm now spoke calmly. 'The Disbursement Office has withheld payment to Meridian on *your* negative authorization. You haven't cleared it.'

'Why should I? The aircraft can't do the job we expected.'

'It *can* do the job you contracted for,' said Oliver, moving his thick neck from Vandamm to the brigadier general. 'Rest assured, general, our best efforts are being poured into the *intended* maximum guidance system. We're expending all our resources. We'll reach a breakthrough, we're convinced of that. But until we do, we expect the contracts to be honored. We've met the guarantees.'

'Are you suggesting that we take the aircraft *as is*?'

'It's the finest bomber in the air.' Jonathan Craft spoke. His soft, high voice was a weak exclamation that floated to a stop. He pressed his delicate fingers together in what he believed was emphasis.

Swanson disregarded Craft and stared at the small face and magnified eyes of the ATCO scientist, Gian Spinelli. 'What about the *gyros*? Can you give me an answer, Mr Spinelli?'

Howard Oliver intruded bluntly. 'Use the existing systems. Get the aircraft into combat.'

'*No!*' Swanson could not help himself. His was the roar of disgust, let Undersecretary Vandamm say what he liked. 'Our strategies call for round-the-clock strikes into the deepest regions of Germany. From all points – known and unknown. Fields in England, Italy, Greece . . . yes, even unlisted bases in Turkey and Yugoslavia; carriers in the Mediterranean and, goddamn it, the Black Sea! Thousands and thousands of planes crowding the air corridors for space. We need that extra altitude! We need the guidance systems to operate at those altitudes! Anything less is unthinkable! . . . I'm sorry, Mr Vandamm. I believe I'm justifiably upset.'

'I understand,' said the white-haired undersecretary of state. 'That's why we're here this afternoon. To look for solutions . . . as well as money.' The old gentleman shifted his gaze to Craft. 'Can you add to Mr Oliver's remarks, from Packard's vantage point?'

Craft disengaged his lean, manicured fingers and took a deep breath through his nostrils as if he were about to deliver essential wisdom. The executive font of knowledge, thought Alan Swanson, jockeying for a chairman's approval.

'Of course, Mr Undersecretary. As the major subcontractor for Meridian, we've been as disturbed as the general over the lack of guidance results. We've spared nothing to accommodate. Mr Spinelli's presence is proof of that. After all, we're the ones who brought in ATCO . . .' here Craft smiled heroically, a touch sadly. 'As we all know, ATCO is the finest – and most costly. We've spared *nothing.*'

'You brought in ATCO,' said Swanson wearily, 'because your own laboratories couldn't do the job. You submitted cost overruns to Meridian which were passed on to us. I don't see that you spared a hell of a lot.'

'Good Lord, general!' exclaimed Craft with very little conviction. 'The *time*, the *negotiations* . . . time is money, sir; make no mistake about *that*, I could show you . . .'

'The general asked *me* a question. I should like to answer him.'

The words, spoken with a trace of dialect, came from the tiny scientist, who was either dismissing Craft's nonsense, or oblivious to it, or, somehow, both.

'I'd be grateful, Mr Spinelli.'

'Our progress has been consistent, steady if you like. Not rapid. The problems are great. We believe the distortion of the radio beams beyond certain altitudes varies with temperatures and land-mass curvatures. The solutions lie in alternating compensations. Our experiments continuously narrow that field . . . Our rate of progress would be more rapid were it not for constant interferences.'

Gian Spinelli stopped and shifted his grotesquely magnified eyes to Howard Oliver, whose thick neck and jowled face were suddenly flushed with anger.

'You've had no interference from *us*!'

'And certainly not from Packard!' chimed in Craft. 'We've stayed in almost daily contact. Our concerns have never flagged!'

Spinelli turned to Craft. 'Your concerns . . . as those of Meridian . . . have been exclusively budgetary, as far as I can see.'

'That's preposterous! Whatever financial inquiries were made, were made at the request of the . . . contractor's audit division . . .'

'And totally necessary!' Oliver could not conceal his fury at the small Italian. 'You *laboratory* . . . people don't reconcile! You're *children*!'

For the next thirty seconds the three agitated men babbled excitedly in counterpoint. Swanson looked over at Vandamm. Their eyes met in understanding.

Oliver was the first to recognize the trap. He held up his hand . . . a corporate command, thought Swanson.

'Mr Undersecretary.' Oliver spoke, stifling the pitch of his anger. 'Don't let our squabbling convey the wrong impression. We turn out the products.'

'You're not turning out this one,' said Swanson. 'I recall vividly the projections in your bids for the contract. You had everything *turned out then.*'

When Oliver looked at him, Alan Swanson instinctively felt he should reach for a weapon to protect himself. The Meridian executive was close to exploding.

'We relied on subordinates' evaluations,' said Oliver slowly, with hostility. 'I think the military has had its share of staff errors.'

'Subordinates don't plan major strategies.'

Vandamm raised his voice. 'Mr Oliver. Suppose General Swanson were convinced it served no purpose withholding funds. What kind of time limits could you *now* guarantee?'

Oliver looked at Spinelli. 'What would you estimate?' he asked coldly.

Spinelli's large eyes swept the ceiling. 'In candor, I cannot give you an answer. We *could* solve it next week. Or next year.'

Swanson quickly reached into his tunic pocket and withdrew a folded page of paper. He spread it out in front of him and spoke swiftly. 'According to this memorandum . . . our last communication from ATCO . . . once the guidance system *is* perfected, you state you need six weeks of inflight experimentation. The Montana Proving Grounds.'

'That's correct, general. I dictated that myself,' said Spinelli.

'Six weeks from next week. Or next year. And assuming the Montana experiments are positive, another month to equip the fleets.'

'Yes.'

Swanson looked over at Vandamm, 'In light of this, Mr Undersecretary, there's no other course but to alter immediate priorities. Or at least the projections. We can't meet the logistics.'

'Unacceptable, General Swanson. We have to meet them.'

Swanson stared at the old man. Each knew precisely what the other referred to.

Overlord, the invasion of Europe.

'We must postpone, sir.'

'Impossible. That's the word, general.'

Swanson looked at the three men around the table.

The enemy.

'We'll be in touch, gentlemen,' he said.

3

September 12, 1943 – The Basque Hills, Spain

David Spaulding waited in the shadows of the thick, gnarled tree on the rocky slope above the ravine. It was Basque country and the air was damp and cold. The late afternoon sun washed over the hills; his back was to it. He had years ago – it seemed a millennium but it wasn't – learned the advantage of catching the reflections of the sun off the steel of small weapons. His own rifle was dulled with burnt, crushed cork.

Four.

Strange, but the number *four* kept coming to mind as he scanned the distance.

Four.

Four years and four days ago exactly. And this afternoon's contact was scheduled for precisely four o'clock in the afternoon.

Four years and four days ago he had first seen the creased brown uniforms behind the thick glass partition in the radio studio in New York. Four years and four days ago since he had walked toward that glass wall to pick up his raincoat off the back of a chair and realized that the eyes of the older officer were looking at him. Steadily. Coldly. The younger man avoided him, as if guilty of intrusion, but not his superior, not the lieutenant colonel.

The lieutenant colonel had been studying him.

That was the beginning.

He wondered now – as he watched the ravine for signs of movement – when it would end. Would he be alive to see it end?

He intended to be.

He had called it a treadmill once. Over a drink at the Mayflower in Washington. Fairfax had *been* a treadmill; still, he had not known at the time how completely accurate that word would continue to be; a racing treadmill that never stopped.

It slowed down occasionally. The physical and mental pressures demanded deceleration at certain recognizable times – recognizable to him. Times when he realized he was getting careless . . . or too sure of himself. Or too absolute with regard to decisions that took human life.

Or might take his.

They were often too easily arrived at. And sometimes that frightened him. Profoundly.

During such times he would take himself away. He would travel south along the Portuguese coast where the enclaves of the temporarily inconvenienced rich denied the existence of war. Or he would stay in Costa del Santiago – with his perplexed parents. Or he would remain within the confines of the embassy in Lisbon and engross himself in the meaningless chores of neutral diplomacy. A minor military attaché who did not wear a uniform. It was not expected in the streets; it was inside the 'territory'. He did not wear one, however; no one cared. He was not liked very much. He socialized too frequently, had too many prewar friends. By and large, he was ignored ... with a certain disdain.

At such times he rested. Forced his mind to go blank; to recharge itself.

Four years and four days ago such thoughts would have been inconceivable.

Now they consumed him. When he had the time for such thoughts.

Which he did not have now.

There was still no movement in the ravine. Something was wrong. He checked his watch; the team from San Sebastián was too far behind schedule. It was an abnormal delay. Only six hours ago the French underground had radioed that everything was secure; there were no complications, the team had started out.

The runners from San Sebastián were bringing out photographs of the German airfield installations north of Mont-de-Marsan. The strategists in London had been screaming for them for months. Those photographs had cost the lives of four ... again, that goddamned number ... four underground agents.

If anything, the team should have been early; the runners should have been waiting for the man from Lisbon.

Then he saw it in the distance; perhaps a half a mile away, it was difficult to tell. Over the ravine, beyond the opposite slope, from one of the miniature hills. A flashing.

An intermittent but rhythmic flashing. The measured spacing was a mark of intent, not accident.

They were being signaled. *He* was being signaled by someone who knew his methods of operation well; perhaps someone he had trained. It was a warning.

Spaulding slung the rifle over his shoulder and pulled the strap taut, then tighter still so that it became a fixed but flexible appendage to his upper body. He felt the hasp of his belt holster; it was in place, the weapon secure. He pushed himself away from the trunk of the old tree and, in a crouching position, scrambled up the remainder of the rock-hewn slope.

On the ridge he ran to his left, into the tall grass toward the remains of a dying pear orchard. Two men in mud-caked clothes, rifles at their sides, were sitting on the ground playing trick knife, passing the time in silence. They snapped their heads up, their hands reaching for their guns.

Spaulding gestured to them to remain on the ground. He approached and spoke quietly in Spanish.

'Do either of you know who's on the team coming in?'

'Bergeron, I think,' said the man on the right. 'And probably Chivier. That old man has a way with patrols; forty years he's peddled across the border.'

'Then it's Bergeron,' said Spaulding.

'What is?' asked the second man.

'We're being signaled. They're late and someone is using what's left of the sun to get our attention.'

'Perhaps to tell you they're on their way.' The first man put the knife back in his scabbard as he spoke.

'Possible but not likely. We wouldn't go anywhere. Not for a couple of hours yet.' Spaulding raised himself partially off the ground and looked eastward. 'Come on! We'll head down past the rim of the orchard. We can get a cross view there.'

The three men in single file, separated but within hearing of each other, raced across the field below the high ground for nearly four hundred yards. Spaulding positioned himself behind a low rock that jutted over the edge of the ravine. He waited for the other two. The waters below were about a hundred feet straight down, he judged. The team from San Sebastián would cross them approximately two hundred yards west, through the shallow, narrow passage they always used.

The two other men arrived within seconds of each other.

'The old tree where you stood was the mark, wasn't it?' asked the first man.

'Yes,' answered Spaulding, removing his binoculars from a case opposite his belt holster. They were powerful, with Zeiss Ikon lenses, the best Germany produced. Taken from a dead German at the Tejo River.

'Then why come down here? If there's a problem, your line of vision was best where you were. It's more direct.'

'If there's a problem, they'll know that. They'll flank to their left. East. To the west the ravine heads *away* from the mark. Maybe it's nothing. Perhaps you were right; they just want us to know they're coming.'

A little more than two hundred yards away, just west of the shallow passage, two men came into view. The Spaniard who knelt on Spaulding's left touched the American's shoulder.

'It's Bergeron and Chivier,' he said quietly.

Spaulding held up his hand for silence and scanned the area with the binoculars. Abruptly he fixed them in one position. With his left hand he directed the attention of his subordinates to the spot.

Below them, perhaps fifty yards, four soldiers in Wehrmacht uniforms were struggling with the foliage, approaching the waters of the ravine.

Spaulding moved his binoculars back to the two Frenchmen, now crossing the water. He held the glasses steady against the rock until he could see in the woods behind the two men what he knew was there.

A fifth German, an officer, was half concealed in the tangled mass of weeds and low branches. He held a rifle on the two Frenchmen crossing the ravine.

Spaulding passed the binoculars quickly to the first Spaniard. He whispered, 'Behind Chivier.'

The man looked, then gave the glasses to his countryman.

Each knew what had to be done; even the methods were clear. It was merely a question of timing, precision. From a scabbard behind his right hip, Spaulding withdrew a short carbine bayonet, shortened further by grinding. His two associates did the same. Each peered over the rock at the Wehrmacht men below.

The four Germans, faced with waters waist-high and a current – though not excessively strong, nevertheless considerable – strapped their rifles across their shoulders laterally and separated in a downstream column. The lead man started across, testing the depths as he did so.

Spaulding and the two Spaniards came from behind the rock swiftly and slid down the incline, concealed by the foliage, their sounds muffled by the rushing water. In less than half a minute they were within thirty feet of the Wehrmacht men, hidden by fallen tree limbs and overgrowth. David entered the water, hugging the embankment. He was relieved to see that the fourth man – now only fifteen feet in front of him – was having the most difficulty keeping his balance on the slippery rocks. The other three, spaced about ten yards apart, were concentrating on the Frenchmen upstream. Concentrating intently.

The Nazi saw him; the fear, the bewilderment was in the German's eyes. The split second he took to assimilate the shock was the time David needed. Covered by the sounds of the water, Spaulding leaped on the man, his knife penetrating the Wehrmacht throat, the head pushed violently under the surface, the blood mingling with the rushing stream.

There was no time, no second to waste. David released the lifeless form and saw that the two Spaniards were parallel with him on the embankment. The first man, crouched and hidden, gestured toward the lead soldier; the second nodded his head toward the next man. And David knew that the third Wehrmacht soldier was his.

It took no more than the time necessary for Bergeron and Chivier to reach the south bank. The three soldiers were dispatched, their blood-soaked bodies floating downstream, careening off rocks, filling the waters with streaks of magenta.

Spaulding signaled the Spaniards to cross the water to the north embankment. The first man pulled himself up beside David, his right hand bloodied from a deep cut across his palm.

'Are you all right?' whispered Spaulding.

'The blade slipped. I lost my knife.' The man swore.

'Get out of the area,' said David. 'Get the wound dressed at the Valdero farm.'

'I can put on a tight bandage. I'll be fine.'

The second Spaniard joined them. He winced at the sight of his countryman's hand, an action Spaulding thought inconsistent for a guerilla who had just minutes ago plunged a blade into the neck of a man, slicing most of his head off.

'That looks bad,' he said.

'You can't function,' added Spaulding, 'and we don't have time to argue.'

'I can . . .'

'You *can't*.' David spoke peremptorily, 'Go back to Valdero's. I'll see you in a week or two. Get going and stay out of sight!'

'Very well.' The Spaniard was upset but it was apparent that he would not, could not, disobey the American's commands. He started to crawl into the woods to the east.

Spaulding called quietly, just above the rush of the water. 'Thank you. Fine work today.'

The Spaniard grinned and raced into the forest, holding his wrist.

Just as swiftly, David touched the arm of the second man, beckoning him to follow. They sidestepped their way along the bank upstream. Spaulding stopped by a fallen tree whose trunk dipped down into the ravine waters. He turned and crouched, ordering the Spaniard to do the same. He spoke words quietly.

'I want him alive. I want to question him.'

'I'll get him.'

'No, I will. I just don't want you to fire. There could be a back-up patrol.' Spaulding realized as he whispered that the man couldn't help but smile. He knew why: his Spanish had the soft lilt of Castilian, a foreigner's Castilian at that. It was out of place in Basque country.

As he was out of place, really.

'As you wish, good friend,' said the man. 'Shall I cross farther back and reach Bergeron? He's probably sick to his stomach by now.'

'No, not yet. Wait'll we're secure over here. He and the old man will just keep walking.' David raised his head over the fallen tree trunk and estimated distances. The German officer was about sixty yards away, hidden in the woods. 'I'll head in there, get behind him. I'll see if I can spot any signs of another patrol. If I do, I'll come back and we'll get out. If not, I'll try to grab him . . . If anything goes wrong, if he hears me, he'll probably head for the water. Take him.'

The Spaniard nodded. Spaulding checked the tautness of his rifle strap, giving it a last-second hitch. He gave his subordinate a tentative smile and saw that the man's hands – huge, calloused – were spread on the ground like claws. If the Wehrmacht officer headed this way, he'd never get by those hands, thought David.

He crept swiftly, silently into the woods, his arms and feet working like a primitive hunter's, warding off branches, sidestepping rocks and tangled foliage.

In less than three minutes he had gone thirty yards behind the German on the Nazi's left flank. He stood immobile and withdrew his binoculars. He scanned the forest and the trail. There were no other patrols. He doubled back cautiously, blending every movement of his body with his surroundings.

When he was within ten feet of the German, who was kneeling on the ground, David silently unlatched his holster and withdrew his pistol. He spoke sharply, though not impolitely, in German.

'Stay where you are or I'll blow your head off.'

The Nazi whipped around and awkwardly fumbled for his weapon. Spaulding took several rapid steps and kicked it out of his hands. The man started to rise, and David brought his heavy leather boot up into the side of the German's head. The officer's visor hat fell to the ground; blood poured out of the man's temple, spreading throughout the hairline, streaking down across his face. He was unconscious.

Spaulding reached down and tore at the Nazi's tunic. Strapped across the Oberleutnant's chest was a traveling pouch. David pulled the steel zipper laterally over the waterproofed canvas and found what he was sure he would find.

The photographs of the hidden Luftwaffe installations north of Mont-de-Marsan. Along with the photographs were amateurish drawings that were, in essence, basic blueprints. At least, schematics. Taken from Bergeron, who had then led the German into the trap.

If he could make sense out of them – along with the photographs – he would alert London that sabotage units could inflict the necessary destruction, immobilizing the Luftwaffe complex. He would send in the units himself.

The Allied air strategists were manic when it came to bombing runs. The planes dove from the skies, reducing to rubble and crater everything that was – and was not – a target, taking as much innocent life as enemy. If Spaulding could prevent air strikes north of Mont-de-Marsan, it might somehow . . . abstractly make up for the decision he now had to face.

There were no prisoners of war in the Galician hills, no internment centers in the Basque country.

The Wehrmacht lieutenant, who was so ineffectual in his role of the hunter . . . who might have had a life in some peaceful German town in a peaceful world . . . had to die. And he, the man from Lisbon, would be the executioner. He would revive the young officer, interrogate him at the point of a knife to learn how deeply the Nazis had penetrated the underground in San Sebastián. Then kill him.

For the Wehrmacht officer had seen the man from Lisbon; he could identify that man as David Spaulding.

The fact that the execution would be mercifully quick – unlike a death in partisan hands – was of small comfort to David. He knew that at the instant he pulled the trigger, the world would spin insanely for a moment or two. He would be sick to his stomach and want to vomit, his whole being in a state of revulsion.

But he would not show these things. He would say nothing, indicate nothing . . . silence. And so the legend would continue to grow. For that was part of the treadmill.

The man in Lisbon was a killer.

4

September 20, 1943 – Mannheim, Germany

Wilhelm Zangen brought the handkerchief to his chin, and then to the skin beneath his nostrils, and finally to the border of his receding hairline. The sweat was profuse; a rash had formed in the cleft below his lips, aggravated by the daily necessity to shave and the continuous pressure.

His whole face was stinging, his embarrassment compounded by Franz Altmüller's final words:

'Really, Wilhelm, you should see a doctor. It's most unattractive.'

With that objective solicitousness, Altmüller had gotten up from the table and walked out the door. Slowly, deliberately, his briefcase – the briefcase containing the reports – held down at arm's length as though it had been some diseased appendage.

They had been alone. Altmüller had dismissed the group of scientists without acknowledging any progress whatsoever. He had not even allowed him, the Reich official of German Industry, to thank them for their contributions. Altmüller knew that these were the finest scientific minds in Germany, but he had no understanding of how to handle them. They were sensitive, they were volatile in their own quiet way; they needed praise constantly. He had no patience for tact.

And there *had* been progress.

The Krupp laboratories were convinced that the answer lay in the graphite experiments. Essen had worked around the clock for nearly a month, its managers undergoing one sleepless night after another. They had actually *produced carbon particles* in sealed iron tubes and were convinced these carbons held all the properties required for precision tooling. It was merely a question of time; time to create larger particles, sufficient for tolerance placement within existing machinery.

Franz Altmüller had listened to the Krupp team without the slightest indication of enthusiasm, although enthusiasm certainly had been called for under the circumstances. Instead, when the Krupp spokesman had finished his summary, Altmüller had asked one question. Asked it with the most bored expression imaginable!

'Have these ... particles been subjected to the pressures of operational tooling?'

Of course they hadn't! How could they have been? They *had* been subjected to artificial, substitute pressures; it was all that was possible at the moment.

That answer had been unacceptable; Altmüller dismissed the most scientifically creative minds in the Reich without a single sentence of appreciation, only ill-disguised hostility.

'Gentlemen, you've brought me words. We don't need words, we need diamonds. We need them, we *must have* them within weeks. Two months at the outside. I suggest you return to your laboratories and consider our problem once again. Good day, gentlemen.'

Altmüller was impossible!

After the scientists had left, Altmüller had become even more abrasive.

'Wilhelm,' he had said with a voice bordering on contempt, 'was *this* the nonmilitary solution of which you spoke to the minister of armaments?'

Why hadn't he used Speer's name? Was it necessary to threaten with the use of titles?

'Of course. Certainly more realistic than that insane march into the Congo. The mines at the Bushimaie River! Madness!'

'The comparison is odious. I overestimated you; I gave you more credit than you deserve. You understand, of course, that you failed.' It was not a question.

'I disagree. The results aren't in yet. You can't make such a judgment.'

'I can and I have!' Altmüller had slammed the flat of his hand against the tabletop; a crack of soft flesh against hard wood. An intolerable insult. 'We have no time! We can't waste weeks while your laboratory misfits play with their bunsen burners, creating little stones that could fall apart at the first contact with steel! We need the *product!*'

'You'll have it!' The surface of Zangen's chin became an oily mixture of sweat and stubble. 'The finest minds in all Germany are . . .'

'Are *experimenting.*' Altmüller had interrupted quietly, with scornful emphasis. 'Get us the *product.* That's my order to you. Our powerful companies have long histories that go back many years. Certainly one of them can find an old friend.'

Wilhelm Zangen had blotted his chin; the rash was agonizing. 'We've covered those areas. Impossible.'

'Cover them again.' Altmüller had pointed an elegant finger at Zangen's handkerchief. 'Really, Wilhelm, you should see a doctor. It's most unattractive.'

September 24, 1943 – New York City

Jonathan Craft walked up Park Avenue and checked his wristwatch under the spill of a streetlamp. His long, thin fingers trembled; the last vestige of too many martinis, which he had stopped drinking twenty-four hours ago in

Ann Arbor. Unfortunately, he had been drunk for the three previous days. He had not been to the office. The office reminded him of General Alan Swanson; he could not bear that memory. Now he had to.

It was a quarter to nine; another fifteen minutes and he would walk into 800 Park Avenue, smile at the doorman and go to the elevator. He did not want to be early, dared not be late. He had been inside the apartment house exactly seven times, and each occasion had been traumatic for him. Always for the same reason: he was the bearer of bad news.

But they needed him. He was the impeccable man. His family was old, fine money; he had been to the right schools, the best cotillions. He had access into areas – social and institutional – the *merchants* would never possess. No matter he was stuck in Ann Arbor; it was a temporary situation, a wartime inconvenience. A sacrifice.

He would be back in New York on the Exchange as soon as the damn thing was over.

He had to keep these thoughts in mind tonight because in a few minutes he would have to repeat the words Swanson had screamed at him in his Packard office. He had written a confidential report of the conversation ... the *unbelievable* conversation ... and sent it to Howard Oliver at Meridian.

If you've done what I think you've done, it falls under the heading of treasonable acts! And we're at war!

Swanson.

Madness.

He wondered how many would be there, in the apartment. It was always better if there were quite a few, say a dozen. Then they argued among themselves; he was almost forgotten. Except for his information.

He walked around the block, breathing deeply, calming himself ... killing ten minutes.

Treasonable acts!

And we're at war!

His watch read five minutes to nine. He entered the building, smiled at the doorman, gave the floor to the elevator operator and, when the brass grill opened, he walked into the private foyer of the penthouse.

A butler took his overcoat and ushered him across the hall, through the door and down three steps into the huge sunken living room.

There were only two men in the room. Craft felt an immediate sharp pain in his stomach. It was an instinctive reaction partly brought on by the fact that there were only two people for this extremely vital conference, but mainly caused by the sight of Walter Kendall.

Kendall was a man in shadows, a manipulator of figures who was kept out of sight. He was fiftyish, medium-sized, with thinning, unwashed hair, a rasping voice and an undistinguished – shoddy – appearance. His eyes darted continuously, almost never returning another man's look. It was said his mind concentrated incessantly on schemes and counterschemes; his whole purpose in life was apparently to outmanoeuvre other human beings – friend or enemy, it made no difference to Kendall, for he did not categorize people with such labels.

All were vague opponents.

But Walter Kendall was brilliant at what he did. As long as he could be kept in the background, his manipulations served his clients. And made him a great deal of money – which he hoarded, attested to by ill-fitting suits that bagged at the knees and sagged below the buttocks. But he was always kept out of sight; his presence signified crisis.

Jonathan Craft despised Kendall because he was frightened by him.

The second man was to be expected under the circumstances. He was Howard Oliver, Meridian Aircraft's obese debater of War Department contracts.

'You're on time,' said Walter Kendall curtly, sitting down in an armchair, reaching for papers in an open, filthy briefcase at his feet.

'Hello, Jon.' Oliver approached and offered a short, neutral handshake.

'Where are the others?' asked Craft.

'No one wanted to be here,' answered Kendall with a furtive glance at Oliver. 'Howard has to be, and I'm paid to be. You had one hell of a meeting with this Swanson.'

'You've read my report?'

'He's read it,' said Oliver, crossing to a copper-topped wheelcart in the corner on which there were bottles and glasses. 'He's got questions.'

'I made everything perfectly clear . . .'

'Those aren't the questions,' interrupted Kendall while squeezing the tip of a cigarette before inserting it into his mouth. As he struck a match, Craft walked to a large velvet chair across from the accountant and sat down. Oliver had poured himself a whisky and remained standing.

'If you want a drink, Jon, it's over there,' said Oliver.

At the mention of alcohol, Kendall glanced up at him from his papers with ferret-like eyes. 'No, thank you,' Craft replied. 'I'd like to get this over with as soon as possible.'

'Suit yourself,' Oliver looked at the accountant. 'Ask your questions.'

Kendall, sucking on his cigarette, spoke as the smoke curled around his nostrils. 'This Spinelli over at ATCO. Have you talked to him since you saw Swanson?'

'No. There was nothing to say; nothing *I could say* . . . without instructions. As you know, I spoke with Howard on the phone. He told me to wait; write a report and do nothing.'

'Craft's the funnel to ATCO,' said Oliver. 'I didn't want him running scared, trying to smooth things over. It'd look like we were hiding something.'

'We are,' Kendall removed his cigarette, the ash falling on his trousers. He continued while slowly shuffling the papers on his lap. 'Let's go over Spinelli's complaints. As Swanson brought them up.'

The accountant touched briefly, concisely on each point raised. They

covered Spinelli's statements regarding delayed deliveries, personnel transfers, blueprint holdups, a dozen other minor grievances. Craft replied with
equal brevity, answering when he could, stating ignorance when he could
not. There was no reason to hide anything.

He had been carrying out instructions, not issuing them.

'Can Spinelli substantiate these charges? And don't kid yourselves, these
are charges, not complaints.'

'What *charges*?' Oliver spat out the words. 'That guinea bastard's fucked up
everything! Who's he to make charges?'

'Get off it,' said Kendall in his rasping voice. 'Don't play games. Save them
for a congressional committee, unless I can figure something.'

At Kendall's words the sharp pain returned to Craft's stomach. The
prospects of disgrace – even remotely associated – could ruin his life. The life
he expected to lead back in New York. The financial boors, the *merchants*,
could never understand. 'That's going a little far . . .'

Kendall looked over at Craft. 'Maybe you didn't *hear* Swanson. It's not
going far enough. You got the Fortress contracts because your *projections* said
you could do the job.'

'Just a minute!' yelled Oliver. 'We . . .'

'*Screw* the legal crap!' countered Kendall, shouting over Oliver's interruption. 'My firm . . . *me, I* . . . squared those projections. I know what they say,
what they implied. You left the other companies at the gate. They wouldn't
say what you said. Not Douglas, not Boeing, not Lockheed. You were hungry
and you got the meat and now you're not delivering . . . So what else is new?
Let's go back: can Spinelli substantiate?'

'*Shit*,' exploded Oliver, heading for the bar.

'How do you mean . . . substantiate?' asked Jonathan Craft, his stomach in
agony.

'Are there any memorandums floating around,' Kendall tapped the pages
in his hand, 'that bear on any of this?'

'Well . . .' Craft hesitated; he couldn't stand the pain in his stomach.
'When personnel transfers were expedited, they were put into interoffice . . .'

'The answer's yes,' interrupted Oliver in disgust, pouring himself a drink.

'What about financial cutbacks?'

Oliver once again replied. 'We obscured those. Spinelli's requisitions just
got lost in the paper shuffle.'

'Didn't he scream? Didn't *he* shoot off memos?'

'That's Craft's department,' answered Oliver, drinking most of his whisky
in one swallow. 'Spinelli was his little guinea boy.'

'Well?' Kendall looked at Craft.

'Well . . . he sent numerous communications.' Craft leaned forward in the
chair, as much to relieve the pain as to appear confidential. 'I removed
everything from the files,' he said softly.

'*Christ*,' exploded Kendall quietly. 'I don't give a *shit* what *you* removed.
He's got copies. Dates.'

'Well, I couldn't say . . .'

'He didn't type the goddamned things *himself*, did he? You didn't take away the fucking secretaries, *too,* did you?'

'There's no call to be offensive . . .'

'*Offensive!* You're a funny man! Maybe they've got fancy stripes for you in Leavenworth.' The accountant snorted and turned his attention to Howard Oliver. 'Swanson's got a case; he'll hang you. Nobody has to be a lawyer to see that. You held back. *You figured to use the existing guidance systems.*'

'Only because the new gyroscopes couldn't be developed! Because that guinea bastard fell so far behind he couldn't catch up!'

'Also it saved you a couple of hundred million . . . You should have primed the pumps, not cut off the water. You're big ducks in a short gallery; a blind man could knock you off.'

Oliver put his glass down and spoke slowly. 'We don't pay you for that kind of judgment, Walter. You'd better have something else.'

Kendall crushed out his mutilated cigarette, his dirty fingernails covered with ash. 'I do,' he said. 'You need company; you're in the middle of a very emotional issue. It'll cost you but you don't have a choice. You've got to make deals, ring in everybody. Get hold of Sperry Rand, GM, Chrysler, Lockheed, Douglas, Rolls-Royce, if you have to . . . every son-of-a-bitch with an engineering laboratory. A patriotic crash program. Cross-reference your data, open up everything you've got.'

'They'll steal us blind!' roared Oliver. 'Millions!'

'Cost you more if you don't . . . I'll prepare supplementary financial stats. I'll pack the sheets with so much ice, it'll take ten years to thaw. That'll cost you, too.' Kendall smirked, baring soiled teeth.

Howard Oliver stared at the unkempt accountant. 'It's crazy,' he said quietly. 'We'll be giving away fortunes for something that can't be bought because it doesn't exist.'

'But you said it *did* exist. You told Swanson it existed – at least a hell of a lot more confidently than anybody else. You sold your great industrial know-how, and when you couldn't deliver, you covered up. Swanson's right. You're a menace to the war effort. Maybe you *should* be shot.

Jonathan Craft watched the filthy, grinning bookkeeper with bad teeth and wanted to vomit. But he was their only hope.

5

September 25, 1943 – Stuttgart, Germany

Wilhelm Zangen stood by the window overlooking Stuttgart's Reichssieg Platz, holding a handkerchief against his inflamed, perspiring chin. This outlying section of the city had been spared the bombing; it was residential, even peaceful. The Neckar River could be seen in the distance, its waters rolling calmly, oblivious to the destruction that had been wrought on the other side of the city.

Zangen realized he was expected to speak, to answer von Schnitzler, who spoke for all of IG Farben. The two other men were as anxious to hear his words as was von Schnitzler. There was no point in procrastinating. He had to carry out Altmüller's orders.

'The Krupp laboratories have failed. No matter what Essen says, there is no time for experimentation. The Ministry of Armaments has made that clear; Altmüller is resolute. He speaks for Speer.' Zangen turned and looked at the three men. 'He holds you responsible.'

'How can that be?' asked von Schnitzler, his guttural lisp pronounced, his voice angry. 'How can we be responsible for something we know nothing about? It's illogical. Ridiculous!'

'Would you wish me to convey that judgment to the ministry?'

'I'll convey it myself, thank you,' replied von Schnitzler. 'Farben is not involved.'

'We are all involved,' said Zangen quietly.

'How can *our* company be?' asked Heinrich Krepps, Direktor of Schreibwaren, the largest printing complex in Germany. 'Our work with Peenemünde has been practically nothing; and what there was, obscured to the point of foolishness. Secrecy is one thing; lying to ourselves, something else again. Do not include us, Herr Zangen.'

'You *are* included.'

'I reject your conclusion. I've studied our communications with Peenemünde.'

'Perhaps you were not cleared for all the facts.'

'Asinine!'

'Quite possibly. Nevertheless...'

'Such a condition would hardly apply to *me*, Herr Reich official,' said Johann Dietricht, the middle-aged effeminate son of the Dietricht Chemikalien empire. Dietricht's family had contributed heavily to Hitler's National Socialist coffers; when the father and uncle had died, Johann Dietricht was allowed to continue the management – more in name than in fact. 'Nothing occurs at Dietricht of which I am unaware. We've had nothing to do with Peenemünde!'

Johann Dietricht smiled, his fat lips curling, his blinking eyes betraying an excess of alcohol, his partially plucked eyebrows his sexual proclivity – excess, again. Zangen couldn't stand Dietricht; the man – although no man – was a disgrace, his life-style an insult to German industry. Again, felt Zangen, there was no point in procrastinating. The information would come as no surprise to von Schnitzler and Krepps.

'There are many aspects of the Dietricht Chemikalien of which you know *nothing.* Your own laboratories have worked consistently with Peenemünde in the field of chemical detonation.'

Dietricht blanched; Krepps interrupted.

'What is your purpose, Herr Reich official? You call us here only to insult us? You tell us, directors, that we are not the masters of our own companies? I don't know Herr Dietricht so well, but I can assure you that von Schnitzler and myself are not puppets.'

Von Schnitzler had been watching Zangen closely, observing the Reich official's use of his handkerchief. Zangen kept blotting his chin nervously. 'I presume you have specific information – such as you've just delivered to Herr Dietricht – that will confirm your statements.'

'I have.'

'Then you're saying that isolated operations – within our own factories – were withheld from us.'

'I am.'

'Then how can we be held responsible? These are insane accusations.'

'They are made for practical reasons.'

'Now you're talking in circles!' shouted Dietricht, barely recovered from Zangen's insult.

'I must agree,' said Krepps, as if agreement with the obvious homosexual was distasteful, yet mandatory.

'Come, gentlemen. Must I draw pictures? These are *your companies.* Farben has supplied eighty-three per cent of all chemicals for the rockets; Schreibwaren has processed every blueprint; Dietricht, the majority of detonating compounds for the casing explosives. We're in a crisis. If we don't overcome that crisis, no protestations of ignorance will serve you. I might go so far as to say that there are those in the ministry and elsewhere who will deny that anything was withheld. You simply buried your collective heads. I'm not even sure myself that such a judgment is in error.'

'Lies!' screamed Dietricht.

'Absurd!' added Krepps.

'But obscenely practical,' concluded von Schnitzler slowly, staring at

Zangen. 'So this is what you're telling us, isn't it? What Altmüller tells us. We either employ our resources to find a solution – to come to the aid of our industrial *Schwachling* – or we face equilateral disposition in the eyes of the ministry.'

'And in the eyes of the Führer; the judgment of the Reich itself.'

'But *how*?' asked the frightened Johann Dietrich.

Zangen remembered Altmüller's words precisely. 'Your companies have long histories that go back many years. Corporate and individual. From the Baltic to the Mediterranean, from New York to Rio de Janeiro, from Saudi Arabia to Johannesburg.'

'And from Shanghai down through Malaysia to the ports in Australia and the Tasman Sea,' said von Schnitzler quietly.

'They don't concern us.'

'I thought not.'

'Are you suggesting, Herr Reich official, that the solution for Peenemünde lies in our past associations?' Von Schnitzler leaned forward in his chair, his hands and eyes on the table.

'It's a crisis. No avenues can be overlooked. Communications can be expedited.'

'No doubt. What makes you think they'd be exchanged?' continued the head of IG Farben.

'Profits,' replied Zangen.

'Difficult to spend facing a firing squad.' Von Schnitzler shifted his large bulk and looked up at the window, his expression pensive.

'You assume the commission of specific transactions. I refer more to acts of *omission*.'

'Clarify that, please.' Krepps's eyes remained on the tabletop.

'There are perhaps twenty-five acceptable sources for the bortz and carbonado diamonds – acceptable in the sense that sufficient quantities can be obtained in a single purchase. Africa and South America; one or two locations in Central America. These mines are run by companies under fiat security conditions: British, American, Free French, Belgian ... you know them. Shipments are controlled, destinations cleared ... We are suggesting that shipments can be sidetracked, destinations altered in neutral territories. By the expedient of omitting normal security precautions. Acts of incompetence, if you will; human error, not betrayal.'

'Extraordinarily profitable mistakes,' summed up von Schnitzler.

'Precisely,' said Wilhelm Zangen.

'Where do you find such men?' asked Johann Dietrich in his high-pitched voice.

'Everywhere,' replied Heinrich Krepps.

Zangen blotted his chin with his handkerchief.

6

November 29, 1943 – Basque Country, Spain

Spaulding raced across the foot of the hill until he saw the converging limbs of the two trees. They were the mark. He turned right and started up the steep incline, counting off an approximate 125 yards; the second mark. He turned left and walked slowly around to the west slope, his body low, his eyes darting constantly in all directions; he gripped his pistol firmly.

On the west slope he looked for a single rock – one among so many on the rock-strewn Galician hill – that had been chipped on its downward side. Chipped carefully with three indentations. It was the third and final mark.

He found it, spotting first the bent reeds of the stiff hill grass. He knelt down and looked at his watch: two forty-five.

He was fifteen minutes early, as he had planned to be. In fifteen minutes he would walk down the west slope, directly in front of the chipped rock. There he would find a pile of branches. Underneath the branches would be a short-walled cave; in that cave – if all went as planned – would be three men. One was a member of an infiltration team. The other two were *Wissenschaftler* – German scientists who had been attached to the Kindorf laboratories in the Ruhr Valley. Their defections – escape – had been an objective of long planning.

The obstacles were always the same.

Gestapo.

The Gestapo had broken an underground agent and was on to the *Wissenschaftler*. But, typical of the SS elite, it kept its knowledge to itself, looking for bigger game than two disaffected laboratory men. Gestapo *Agenten* had given the scientists wide latitude; surveillance dismissed, laboratory patrols relaxed to the point of inefficiency, routine interrogation disregarded.

Contradictions.

The Gestapo was neither inefficient nor careless. The SS was setting a trap.

Spaulding's instructions to the underground had been terse, simple: let the trap be sprung. With no quarry in its net.

Word was leaked that the scientists, granted a weekend leave to Stuttgart, were in reality heading due north through underground routing to

743

Bremerhaven. There contact was being made with a high-ranking defecting German naval officer who had commandeered a small craft and would make a dramatic run to the Allies. It was common knowledge that the German navy was rife with unrest. It was a recruiting ground for the anti-Hitler factions springing up throughout the Reich.

The *word* would give everyone something to think about, reasoned Spaulding. And the Gestapo would be following two men it assumed were the *Wissenschaftler* from Kindorf, when actually they were two middle-aged Wehrmacht security patrols sent on a false surveillance.

Games and countergames.

So much, so alien. The expanded interests of the man in Lisbon.

This afternoon was a concession. Demanded by the German underground. He was to make the final contact alone. The underground claimed the man in Lisbon had created too many complications; there was too much room for error and counter-infiltration. There wasn't, thought David, but if a solo run would calm the nervous stomachs of the anti-Reichists, it was little enough to grant them.

He had his own Valdero team a half-mile away in the upper hills. Two shots and they would come to his help on the fastest horses Castilian money could buy.

It was time. He could start toward the cave for the final contact.

He slid down the hard surface, his heels digging into the earth and rocks of the steep incline until he was above the pile of branches and limbs that signified the hideout's opening. He picked up a handful of loose dirt and threw it down into the broken foliage.

The response was as instructed: a momentary thrashing of a stick against the piled branches. The fluttering of bird's wings, driven from the bush.

Spaulding quickly sidestepped his way to the base of the enclosure and stood by the camouflage.

'*Alles in Ordnung. Kommen Sie,*' he said quietly but firmly. 'There isn't much traveling time left.'

'*Halt!*' was the unexpected shout from the cave.

David spun around, pressed his back into the hill and raised his Colt. The voice from inside spoke again. In English.

'Are you . . . Lisbon?'

'For God's sake, yes! Don't *do* that! You'll get your head shot off!' *Christ*, thought Spaulding, the infiltration team must have used a child, or an imbecile, or both as its runner. 'Come on out.'

'I am with apologies, Lisbon,' said the voice, as the branches were separated and the pile dislodged. 'We've had a bad time of it.'

The runner emerged. He was obviously not anyone David had trained. He was short, very muscular, no more than twenty-five or twenty-six; nervous fear was in his eyes.

'In the future,' said Spaulding, 'don't acknowledge signals, then question the signaler at the last moment. Unless you intend to kill him. *Es ist Schwarztuch-chiffre.*'

'*Was ist das?* Black . . .'

'Black drape, friend. Before our time. It means . . . confirm and terminate. Never mind, just don't do it again. Where are the others?'

'Inside. They are all right; very tired and very afraid, but not injured.' The runner turned and pulled off more branches. 'Come out. It's the man from Lisbon.'

The two frightened, middle-aged scientists crawled out of the cave cautiously, blinking at the hot, harsh sun. They looked gratefully at David; the taller one spoke in halting English.

'This is a . . . minute we have waited for. Our very much thanks.'

Spaulding smiled. 'Well, we're not out of the woods, yet. *Frei.* Both terms apply. You're brave men. We'll do all we can for you.'

'There was . . . *nichts* . . . remaining,' said the shorter laboratory man. 'My friend's socialist . . . *Politik* . . . was unpopular. My late wife was . . . *eine Jüdin.*'

'No children?'

'*Nein,*' answered the man. '*Gott sel dank.*'

'I have one son,' said the taller scientist coldly. '*Er ist . . . Gestapo.*'

There was no more to be said, thought Spaulding. He turned to the runner, who was scanning the hill and the forests below. 'I'll take over now. Get back to Base Four as soon as you can. We've got a large contingent coming in from Koblenz in a few days. We'll need everyone. Get some rest.'

The runner hesitated; David had seen his expression before . . . so often. The man was now going to travel alone. No company, pleasant or unpleasant. Just alone.

'That is not my understanding, Lisbon. I am to stay with you . . .'

'Why?' interrupted Spaulding.

'My instructions . . .'

'From whom?'

'From those in San Sebastián. Herr Bergeron and his men. Weren't you informed?'

David looked at the runner. The man's fear was making him a poor liar, thought Spaulding. Or he was something else. Something completely unexpected because it was not logical; it was not, at this point, even remotely to be considered. Unless . . .

David gave the runner's frayed young nerves the benefit of the doubt. A benefit, not an exoneration. That would come later.

'No, I wasn't told,' he said. 'Come on. We'll head to Beta camp. We'll stay there until morning.' Spaulding gestured and they started across the foot of the slope.

'I haven't worked this far south,' said the runner, positioning himself behind David. 'Don't you travel at night, Lisbon?'

'Sometimes,' answered Spaulding, looking back at the scientists, who were walking side by side. 'Not if we can help it. The Basque shoot indiscriminately at night. They have too many dogs off their leashes at night.'

'I see.'

'Let's walk single file. Flank our guests,' said David to the runner.

The four traveled several miles east. Spaulding kept up a rapid pace; the middle-aged scientists did not complain but they obviously found the going difficult. A number of times David told the others to remain where they were while he entered the woods at various sections of the forest and returned minutes later. Each time he did so, the older men rested, grateful for the pauses. The runner did not. He appeared frightened – as if the American might not come back. Spaulding did not encourage conversation, but after one such disappearance, the young German could not restrain himself.

'What are you *doing*?' he asked.

David looked at the *Widerstandskämpfer* and smiled. 'Picking up messages.'

'Messages?'

'These are drops. Along our route. We establish marks for leaving off information we don't want sent by radio. Too dangerous if intercepted.'

They continued along a narrow path at the edge of the woods until there was a break in the Basque forest. It was a grazing field, a lower plateau centered beneath the surrounding hills. The *Wissenschaftler* were perspiring heavily, their breaths short, their legs aching.

'We'll rest here for a while,' said Spaulding, to the obvious relief of the older men. 'It's time I made contact anyway.'

'*Was ist los?*' asked the young runner. 'Contact?'

'Zeroing our position,' replied David, taking out a small metal mirror from his field jacket. 'The scouts can relax if they know where we are . . . If you're going to work the north country – what you call south – you'd better remember all this.'

'I shall, I shall.'

David caught the reflection of the sun on the mirror and beamed it up to a northern hill. He made a series of motions with his wrist, and the metal plate moved back and forth in rhythmic precision.

Seconds later there was a reply from halfway up the highest hill in the north. Flashes of light shafted out of an infinitesimal spot in the brackish green distance. Spaulding turned to the others.

'We're not going to Beta,' he said. 'Falangist patrols are in the area. We'll stay here until we're given clearance. You can relax.'

The heavyset Basque put down the knapsack mirror. His companion still focused his binoculars on the field several miles below, where the American and his three charges were now seated on the ground.

'He says they are being followed. We are to take up counter-positions and stay out of sight,' said the man with the metal mirror. 'We go down for the scientists tomorrow night. He will signal us.'

'What's *he* going to do?'

'I don't know. He says to get word to Lisbon. He's going to stay in the hills.'

'He's a cold one,' the Basque said.

December 2, 1943 – Washington, DC

Alan Swanson sat in the back of the army car trying his best to remain calm. He looked out the window; the late morning traffic was slight. The immense Washington labour force was at its appointed destinations; machines were humming, telephones ringing, men were shouting and whispering and, in too many places, having the first drink of the day. The exhilaration that was apparent during the first hours of the working day faded as noon approached. By eleven thirty a great many people thought the war was dull and were bored by their mechanical chores, the unending duplicates, triplicates and quadruplicates. They could not understand the necessity of painstaking logistics, of disseminating information to innumerable chains of command.

They could not understand because they could not be given whole pictures, only fragments, repetitious statistics. Of course they were bored.

They were weary. As he had been weary fourteen hours ago in Pasadena, California.

Everything had failed.

Meridian Aircraft had initiated – was *forced* to initiate – a crash program, but the finest scientific minds in the country could not eliminate the errors inside the small box that was the guidance system. The tiny, whirling spheroid discs would not spin true at maximum altitudes. They were erratic; absolute one second, deviant the next.

The most infinitesimal deviation could result in the midair collision of giant aircraft. And with the numbers projected for the saturation bombing prior to Overlord – scheduled to commence in less than four months – collisions *would* occur.

But this morning everything was different.

Could be different, if there was substance to what he had been told. He hadn't been able to sleep on the plane, hardly been able to eat. Upon landing at Andrews, he had hurried to his Washington apartment, showered, shaved, changed uniforms and called his wife in Scarsdale, where she was staying with a sister. He didn't remember the conversation between them; the usual endearments were absent, the questions perfunctory. He had no time for her.

The army car entered the Virginia highway and accelerated. They were going to Fairfax; they'd be there in twenty minutes or so. In less than a half hour he would find out if the impossible was, conversely, entirely possible. The news had come as a last-minute stay of execution; the cavalry in the distant hills – the sounds of muted bugles signaling reprieve.

Muted, indeed, thought Swanson as the army car veered off the highway onto a back Virginia road. In Fairfax, covering some two hundred acres in the middle of the hunt country, was a fenced-off area housing Quonset huts beside huge radar screens and radio signal towers that sprang from the ground like giant steel malformities. It was the Field Division Headquarters of Clandestine Operations; next to the underground rooms at the White

House, the most sensitive processing location of the Allied Intelligence services.

Late yesterday afternoon, FDHQ-Fairfax had received confirmation of an Intelligence probe long since abandoned as negative. It came out of Johannesburg, South Africa. It had not been proved out, but there was sufficient evidence to believe that it could be.

High-altitude directional gyroscopes had been perfected. Their designs could be had.

December 2, 1943 – Berlin, Germany

Altmüller sped out of Berlin on the Spandau highway toward Falkensee in the open Duesenberg. It was early in the morning and the air was cold and that was good.

He was so exhilarated that he forgave the theatrically secretive ploys of the *Nachrichtendienst*, code name for a select unit of the espionage service known to only a few of the upper-echelon ministers, not to many of the High Command itself. A Gehlen specialty.

For this reason it never held conferences within Berlin proper; always outside the city, always in some remote, secluded area or town and even then in private surroundings, away from the potentially curious.

The location this morning was Falkensee, twenty-odd miles northwest of Berlin. The meeting was to take place in a guest house on the estate belonging to Gregor Strasser.

Altmüller would have flown to Stalingrad itself if what he'd been led to believe was true.

The *Nachrichtendienst* had found the solution for Peenemünde!

The solution *was true*; it was up to others to expedite it.

The solution that had eluded teams of 'negotiators' sent to all parts of the world to explore – unearth – prewar 'relationships'. Capetown, Dar es Salaam, Johannesburg, Buenos Aires . . .

Failure.

No company, no individual would touch German negotiations. Germany was in the beginning of a death struggle. It would go down to defeat.

That was the opinion in Zürich. And what Zürich held to be true, international business did not debate.

But the *Nachrichtendienst* had found another truth.

So he was told.

The Duesenberg's powerful engine hummed; the car reached high speed; the passing autumn foliage blurred.

The stone gates of Strasser's estate came into view on the left, Wehrmacht eagles in bronze above each post. He swung into the long, winding drive and stopped at the gate guarded by two soldiers and snarling shepherd dogs. Altmüller thrust his papers at the first guard, who obviously expected him.

'Good morning, Herr Unterstaatssekretär. Please follow the drive to the right beyond the main house.'

'Have the others arrived?'

'They are waiting, sir.'

Altmüller manoeuvred the car past the main house, reached the sloping drive and slowed down. Beyond the wooded bend was the guest cottage; it looked more like a hunting lodge than a residence. Heavy dark-brown beams everywhere; a part of the forest.

In the graveled area were four limousines. He parked and got out, pulling his tunic down, checking his lapels for lint. He stood erect and started toward the path to the door.

No names were ever used during a *Nachrichtendienst* conference; if identities were known – and certainly they had to be – they were never referred to in a meeting. One simply addressed his peer by looking at him, the group by gesture.

There was no long conference table as Altmüller had expected; no formal seating arrangement by some hidden protocol. Instead, a half-dozen informally dressed men in their fifties and sixties were standing around the small room with the high Bavarian ceiling, chatting calmly, drinking coffee. Altmüller was welcomed as 'Herr Unterstaatssekretär' and told that the morning's conference would be short. It would begin with the arrival of the final expected member.

Altmüller accepted a cup of coffee and tried to fall into the casual atmosphere. He was unable to do so; he wanted to roar his disapproval and demand immediate and serious talk. Couldn't they *understand*?

But this was the *Nachrichtendienst*. One didn't yell; one didn't demand.

Finally, after what seemed an eternity to his churning stomach, Altmüller heard an automobile outside the lodge. A few moments later the door opened; he nearly dropped his cup of coffee. The man who entered was known to him from the few times he had accompanied Speer to Berchtesgaden. He was the Führer's valet, but he had no subservient look of a valet now.

Without announcement, the men fell silent. Several sat in armchairs, others leaned against walls or stayed by the coffee table. An elderly man in a heavy tweed jacket stood in front of the fireplace and spoke. He looked at Franz, who remained by himself behind a leather couch.

'There is no reason for lengthy discussions. We believe we have the information you seek. I say "believe", for we gather information, we do not act upon it. The ministry may not care to act.'

'That would seem inconceivable to me,' said Altmüller.

'Very well. Several questions then. So there is no conflict, no misrepresentation.' The old man paused and lit a thick meerschaum pipe. 'You have exhausted all normal intelligence channels? Through Zürich and Lisbon?'

'We have. And in numerous other locations – occupied, enemy and neutral.'

'I was referring to the acknowledged conduits, Swiss, Scandinavian and Portuguese, primarily.'

'We made no concentrated efforts in the Scandinavian countries. Herr Zangen did not think . . .'

'No names, please. Except in the area of Intelligence confrontation or public knowledge. Use governmental descriptions, if you like. Not individuals.'

'The Reichsamt of Industry – which has continuous dealings in the Baltic areas – was convinced there was nothing to be gained there. I assume the reasons were geographical. There are no diamonds in the Baltic.'

'Or they've been burnt too often,' said a nondescript middle-aged man below Altmüller on the leather sofa. 'If you want London and Washington to know what you're doing before you do it, deal with the Scandinavians.'

'An accurate analysis,' concurred another member of the *Nachrichtendienst*, this one standing by the coffee table, cap in hand. 'I returned from Stockholm last week. We can't trust even those who publicly endorse us.'

'Those least of all,' said the old man in front of the fireplace, smiling and returning his eyes to Franz. 'We gather you've made substantial offers? In Swiss currency, of course.'

'Substantial is a modest term for the figures we've spoken of,' replied Altmüller. 'I'll be frank. No one will touch us. Those who could, subscribe to Zürich's judgment that we shall be defeated. They fear retribution; they even speak of postwar bank deposit reclamations.'

'If such whispers reach the High Command there'll be a panic.' The statement was made humorously by the Führer's valet, sitting in an armchair. The spokesman by the fireplace continued.

'So you must eliminate money as an incentive . . . even extraordinary sums of money.'

'The negotiating teams were not successful. You know that.' Altmüller had to suppress his irritation. Why didn't they get to the *point*?

'And there are no ideologically motivated defectors on the horizon. Certainly none who have access to industrial diamonds.'

'Obviously, *mein Herr*.'

'So you must look for another motive. Another incentive.'

'I fail to see the point of this. I was told . . .'

'You will,' interrupted the old man, tapping his pipe on the mantel. 'You see, we've uncovered a panic as great as yours . . . The enemy's panic. We've found the most logical motive for all concerned. Each side possesses: the other's solution.'

Franz Altmüller was suddenly afraid. He could not be sure he fully understood the spokesman's implications. 'What are you saying?'

'Peenemünde has perfected a high-altitude, directional guidance system, is this correct?'

'Certainly. Indigenous to the basic operation of the rockets.'

'But there'll be no rockets – or at best, a pitiful few – without shipments of industrial diamonds.'

'Obviously.'

'There are business interests in the United States who face insurmounta-ble...' the old man paused for precisely one second and continued, '*insurmountable* problems that can only be resolved by the acquisition of functional high-altitude gyroscopes.'

'Are you suggesting...'

'The *Nachrichtendienst* does not suggest, Herr Unterstaatssekretär. We say what is.' The spokesman removed the meerschaum from his lips. 'When the occasion warrants, we transmit concrete information to diverse recipients. Again, only what is. We did so in Johannesburg. When the man IG Farben sent in to purchase diamonds from the Koening mines met with failure, we stepped in and confirmed a long-standing Intelligence probe we knew would be carried back to Washington. Our agents in California had apprised us of the crisis in the aircraft industry. We believe the timing was propitious.'

'I'm not sure I understand...'

'Unless we're mistaken, an attempt will be made to re-establish contact with one of the Farben men. We assume contingencies were made for such possibilities.'

'Of course. Geneva. The acknowledged conduits.'

'Then our business with you is concluded, sir. May we wish you a pleasant drive back to Berlin.'

December 2, 1943 – Fairfax, Virginia

The interior of the Quonset belied its stark outside. To begin with, it was five times larger than the usual Quonset structure, and its metal casing was insulated with a sound-absorbing material that swept seamless down from the high ceiling. The appearance was not so much that of an airplane hangar – as it should have been – as of a huge, windowless shell with substantial walls. All around the immense room were banks of complicated high-frequency radio panels; opposite each panel were glass-enclosed casings with dozens of detailed maps, changeable by the push of a button. Suspended above the maps were delicate, thin steel arms – markers, not unlike polygraph needles – that were manipulated by the radio operators, observed by men holding clipboards. The entire staff was military, army, none below the rank of first lieutenant.

Three-quarters into the building was a floor-to-ceiling wall that obviously was not the end of the structure. There was a single door, centered and closed. The door was made of heavy steel.

Swanson had never been inside this particular building. He had driven down to Field Division, Fairfax, many times – to get briefed on highly classified Intelligence findings, to observe the training of particular insurgence or espionage teams – but for all his brigadier's rank and regardless of the secrets he carried around in his head, he had not been cleared for this particular building. Those who were, remained within the two-hundred-acre compound for weeks, months at a time; leaves were rare and taken only in emergency and with escort.

It was fascinating, thought Swanson, who honestly believed he had lost all sense of awe. No elevators, no back staircases, no windows; he could see a washroom door in the left wall and without going inside, knew it was machine ventilated. And there was only a single entrance. Once inside there was no place for a person to conceal himself for any length of time, or to exit without being checked out and scrutinized. Personal items were left at the entrance; no briefcases, envelopes, papers or materials were removed from the building without signed authorization by Colonel Edmund Pace and with the colonel personally at the side of the individual in question.

If there was ever total security, it was here.

Swanson approached the steel door; his lieutenant escort pushed a button. A small red light flashed above a wall intercom, and the lieutenant spoke.

'General Swanson, colonel.'

'Thank you, lieutenant,' were the words that came from the webbed circle below the light. There was a click in the door's lock and the lieutenant reached for the knob.

Inside, Pace's office looked like any other Intelligence headquarters – huge maps on the walls, sharp lighting on the maps, lights and maps changeable by pushbuttons on the desk. Teletype machines were equidistant from one another below printed signs designating theaters of operation – all the usual furnishings. Except the furniture itself. It was simple to the point of primitiveness. No easy chairs, no sofas, nothing comfortable. Just plain metal straight-backed chairs, a desk that was more a table than a desk, and a rugless hardwood floor. It was a room for concentrated activity; a man did not relax in such a room.

Edmund Pace, Commander of Field Division, Fairfax, got up from his chair, came around his table and saluted Alan Swanson.

There was one other man in the room, a civilian, Frederic Vandamm, Undersecretary of State.

'General. Good to see you again. The last time was at Mr Vandamm's house, if I remember.'

'Yes, it was. How are things here?'

'A little isolated.'

'I'm sure.' Swanson turned to Vandamm. 'Mr Undersecretary? I got back here as soon as I could. I don't have to tell you how anxious I am. It's been a difficult month.'

'I'm aware of that,' said the aristocratic Vandamm, smiling a cautious smile, shaking Swanson's hand perfunctorily. 'We'll get right to it. Colonel Pace, will you brief the general as we discussed?'

'Yes, sir. And then I'll leave.' Pace spoke noncommittally; it was the military's way of telegraphing a message to a fellow officer: *be careful.*

Pace crossed to a wall map, present with markings. It was an enlarged, detailed section of Johannesburg, South Africa. Frederic Vandamm sat in a chair in front of the desk; Swanson followed Pace and stood beside him.

'You never know when a probe will get picked up. Or where.' Pace took a wooden pointer from a table and indicated a blue marker on the map. 'Or even if the location is important. In this case it *may* be. A week ago a member of the Johannesburg legislature, an attorney and a former director of Koening Mines Ltd, was contacted by what he believed were two men from the Zürich Staats-Bank. They wanted him to middle-man a negotiation with Koening: simple transaction of Swiss francs for diamonds – on a large scale, with the anticipation that the diamond standard would remain more constant than the gold fluctuations.' Pace turned to Swanson. 'So far, so good. With lend-lease, and monetary systems going up in smoke everywhere, there's a lot of speculation in the diamond market. Postwar killings could be made. When he accepted the contact, you can imagine his shock when he arrived for the meeting and found that one of the "Swiss" was an old friend – a very old and good friend – from the prewar days. A German he'd gone to school with – the Afrikaner's mother was Austrian, father, a Boer. The two men had kept in close touch until thirty-nine. The German worked for IG Farben.'

'What was the point of the meeting?' Swanson was impatient.

'I'll get to that. This background's important.'

'Okay. Go on.'

'There was no diamond market speculation involved, no transaction with any Zürich bank. It was a simple purchase. The Farben man wanted to buy large shipments of bortz and carbonado . . .'

'Industrial diamonds?' interrupted Swanson.

Pace nodded. 'He offered a fortune to his old friend if he could pull it off. The Afrikaner refused; but his long-standing friendship with the German kept him from reporting the incident. Until three days ago.' Pace put down the pointer and started for his desk. Swanson understood that the colonel had additional information, written information, that he had to refer to; the general crossed to the chair beside Vandamm and sat down.

'Three days ago,' continued Pace, standing behind the desk, 'the Afrikaner was contacted again. This time there was no attempt to conceal identities. The caller said he was German and had information the Allies wanted; had wanted for a long time.'

'The probe?' asked Swanson, whose impatience was carried by his tone of voice.

'Not exactly the probe we expected . . . The German said he would come to the Afrikaner's office, but he protected himself. He told the lawyer that if any attempt was made to hold him, his old friend at IG Farben would be executed back in Germany.' Pace picked up a sheet of paper from his desk. He spoke as he leaned across and handed it to Swanson. 'This is the information, the report flown in by courier.'

Swanson read the typewritten words below the Military Intelligence letterhead; above the large, stamped *Top Secret. Eyes Only. Fairfax 4–0.*

Nov. 28, 1943. Johannesburg: Confirmed by *Nachrichtendienst*. Substratospheric directional gyroscopes perfected. All tests positive. Peenemünde. Subsequent contact: Geneva. Johannesburg contingent.

Swanson let the information sink in; he read the statement over several times. He asked a question of Edmund Pace with a single word: 'Geneva?'

'The conduit. Neutral channel. Unofficial, of course.'

'What is this ... Nachrichtendienst?'

'Intelligence unit. Small, specialized; so rarefied it's above even the most classified crowds. Sometimes we wonder if it takes sides. It often appears more interested in observing than participating; more concerned with after the war than now. We suspect that it's a Gehlen operation. But it's never been wrong. Never misleading.'

'I see.' Swanson held out the paper for Pace.

The colonel did not take it. Instead, he walked around the desk toward the steel door. 'I'll leave you gentlemen. When you're finished, please signify by pushing the white button on my desk.' He opened the door and left quickly. The heavy steel frame closed into an airtight position; a subsequent click could be heard in the lock housing.

Frederic Vandamm looked at Swanson. 'There is your solution, general. Your gyroscope. In Peenemünde. All you have to do is send a man to Geneva. Someone wants to sell it.'

Alan Swanson stared at the paper in his hand.

7

December 4, 1943 – Berlin, Germany

Altmüller stared at the paper in his hand. It was after midnight, the city in darkness. Berlin had withstood another night of murderous bombardment; it was over now. There would be no further raids until late morning, that was the usual pattern. Still, the black curtains were pulled tight against the windows. As they were everywhere in the ministry.

Speed was everything now. Yet in the swiftness of the planning, mandatory precautions could not be overlooked. The meeting in Geneva with the conduit was only the first step, the prelude, but it had to be handled delicately. Not so much *what* was said but *who* said it. The *what* could be transmitted by anyone with the proper credentials or acknowledged authority. But in the event of Germany's collapse, that *someone* could not represent the Third Reich. Speer had been adamant.

And Altmüller understood: if the war was lost, the label of traitor could not be traced to the Reichsministry. Or to those leaders Germany would need in defeat. In 1918 after Versailles, there had been mass internal recrimina-tions. Polarization ran deep, unchecked, and the nation's paranoia over betrayal from within laid the groundwork for the fanaticism of the twenties. Germany had not been able to accept defeat, could not tolerate the destruction of its identity by traitors.

Excuses, of course.

But the prospects of repetition, no matter how remote, were to be avoided at all costs. Speer was himself fanatic on the subject. The Geneva representative was to be a figure isolated from the High Command. Someone from the ranks of German industry, in no way associated with the rulers of the Third Reich. Someone expendable.

Altmüller tried to point out the inconsistency of Speer's manipulation: high-altitude gyroscopic designs would hardly be given to an expendable mediocrity from German business. Peenemünde was buried – literally buried in the earth; its military security measures absolute.

But Speer would not listen, and Altmüller suddenly grasped the Reichsminister's logic. He was shifting the problem precisely where it belonged: to those whose lies and concealments had brought Peenemünde to the brink of disaster. And as with so much in the wartime Reich – the labour forces, the death camps, the massacres – Albert Speer conveniently looked away. He wanted positive results, but he would not dirty his tunic.

In this particular case, mused Altmüller, Speer was right. If there were to be risks of great disgrace, let German industry take them. Let the German businessman assume complete responsibility.

Geneva was vital only in the sense that it served as an introduction. Cautious words would be spoken that could – or could not – lead to the second stage of the incredible negotiation.

Stage two was geographical: the location of the exchange, should it actually take place.

For the past week, day and night, Altmüller had done little else but concentrate on this. He approached the problem from the enemy's viewpoint as well as his own. His worktable was covered with maps, his desk filled with scores of reports detailing the current political climates of every neutral territory on earth.

For the location had to be neutral; there had to be sufficient safeguards each side could investigate and respect. And perhaps most important of all, it had to be thousands of miles away ... from either enemy's corridors of power.

Distance.

Remote.

Yet possessing means of instant communication.

South America.

Buenos Aires.

An inspired choice, thought Franz Altmüller. The Americans might actually consider it advantageous to them. It was unlikely that they would reject it. Buenos Aires had much each enemy considered its own; both had enormous influence, yet neither controlled with any real authority.

The third stage, as he conceived of it, was concerned with the human factor, defined by the word *Schiedsrichter.*

Referee.

A man who was capable of overseeing the exchange, powerful enough within the neutral territory to engineer the logistics. Someone who had the appearance of impartiality ... above all, acceptable to the Americans.

Buenos Aires had such a man.

One of Hitler's gargantuan errors.

His name was Erich Rhinemann. A Jew, forced into exile, disgraced by Goebbels's insane propaganda machine, his lands and companies expropriated by the Reich.

Those lands and companies he had not converted before the misplaced thunderbolts struck. A minor percentage of his holdings, sufficient for the manic screams of the anti-Semitic press, but hardly a dent in his immense wealth.

Erich Rhinemann lived in exiled splendor in Buenos Aires, his fortunes secure in Swiss banks, his interests expanding throughout South America,

And what few people knew was that Erich Rhinemann was a more dedicated fascist than Hitler's core. He was a supremacist in all things financial and military, an elitist with regard to the human condition. He was an empire builder who remained strangely – stoically – silent.

He had reason to be.

He would be returned to Germany regardless of the outcome of the war. He knew it.

If the Third Reich was victorious, Hitler's asinine edict would be revoked – as, indeed, might be the Führer's powers should he continue to disintegrate. If Germany went down to defeat – as Zürich projected – Rhinemann's expertise and Swiss accounts would be needed to rebuild the nation.

But these things were in the future. It was the present that mattered, and presently Erich Rhinemann was a Jew, forced into exile by his own countrymen, Washington's enemy.

He would be acceptable to the Americans.

And he would look after the Reich's interests in Buenos Aires.

Stages two and three, then, felt Altmüller, had the ring of clarity. But they were meaningless without an accord in Geneva. The prelude had to be successfully played by the minor instruments.

What was needed was a man for Geneva. An individual no one could link to the leaders of the Reich, but still one who had a certain recognition in the market place.

Altmüller continued to stare at the pages under the desk lamp. His eyes were weary, as he was weary, but he knew he could not leave his office or sleep until he had made the decision.

His decision; it was his alone. To be approved by Speer in the morning with only a glance. A name. Not discussed; someone instantly acceptable.

He would never know whether it was the letters in Johannesburg or the subconscious process of elimination, but his eyes riveted on one name, and he circled it. He recognized immediately that it was, again, an inspired choice.

Johann Dietricht, the bilious heir of Dietricht Fabriken; the unattractive homosexual given to alcoholic excess and sudden panic. A completely expendable member of the industrial community; even the most cynical would be reluctant to consider him a liaison to the High Command.

An expendable mediocrity.

A messenger.

December 5, 1943 – Washington, DC

The bass-toned chimes of the clock on the mantel marked the hour somberly. It was six in the morning and Alan Swanson stared out the window at the dark buildings that were Washington. His apartment was on the twelfth floor, affording a pretty fair view of the capital's skyline, especially from the living room, where he now stood in his bathrobe, no slippers on his feet.

He had been looking at Washington's skyline most of the night ... most of the hours of the night for the past three days. God knew what sleep he managed was fitful, subject to sudden torments and awakenings; and always there was the damp pillow that absorbed the constant perspiration that seeped from the pores in the back of his neck.

If his wife were with him, she would insist that he turn himself in to Walter Reed for a check-up. She would force the issue with constant repetition until he was nagged into submission. But she was *not* with him; he had been adamant. She was to remain with her sister in Scarsdale. The nature of his current activities was such that his hours were indeterminate. Translation: the army man had no time for his army wife. The army wife understood: there was a severe crisis and her husband could not cope with even her minor demands and the crisis, too. He did not like her to observe him in these situations; he knew she knew that. She would stay in Scarsdale.

Oh, Christ! It was beyond belief!

None said the words; perhaps no one allowed himself to think them.

That was it, of course. The few – and there were *very few* – who had access to the data turned their eyes and their minds away from the ultimate judgment. They cut off the transaction at midpoint, refusing to acknowledge the final half of the bargain. That half was for others to contend with. Not them.

As the wily old aristocrat Frederic Vandamm had done.

There's your solution, general. Your guidance system. In Peenemünde ... Someone wants to sell it.

That's all.

Buy it.

None wanted to know the price. The price was insignificant ... let others concern themselves with details. Under no circumstances – *no circumstances* – were insignificant details to be brought up for discussion! They were merely to be expedited.

Translation: the chain of command depended upon the execution of general orders. It did not – repeat, *not* – require undue elaboration, clarification or justification. Specifics were an anathema; they consumed time. And by all that was military holy writ, the highest echelons *had* no time. Goddamn it, man, there was a *war on*! We must tend to the great military issues of state!

The garbage will be sorted out by lesser men ... whose hands may on occasion reek with the stench of their lesser duties, but that's what the chain of command is all about.

Buy it!

We have no time. Our eyes are turned. Our minds are occupied elsewhere.

Carry out the order on your own initiative as a good soldier should who understands the chain of command. No one will be inquisitive; it is the result that matters. We all know that; the chain of command, old boy.

Insanity.

By the *strangest coincidence* an Intelligence probe is returned by a man in Johannesburg through which the purchase of industrial diamonds was sought. A purchase for which a fortune in Swiss currency was tendered by Germany's IG Farben, the armaments giant of the Third Reich.

Peenemünde had the guidance system; it could be had. For a price.

It did not take a major intellect to arrive at that price.

Industrial diamonds.

Insanity.

For reasons beyond inquiry, Germany desperately needed the diamonds. For reasons all too clear, the Allies desperately needed the high-altitude guidance system.

An exchange between enemies at the height of the bitterest war in the history of mankind.

Insanity. Beyond comprehension.

And so General Alan Swanson removed it from his immediate . . . totality.

The single deep chime of the clock intruded, signifying the quarter hour. Here and there throughout the maze of dark concrete outside, lights were being turned on in a scattering of tiny windows. A grayish purple slowly began to impose itself on the black sky; vague outlines of cloud wisps could be discerned above.

In the higher altitudes.

Swanson walked away from the window to the couch facing the fireplace and sat down. It had been twelve hours ago . . . eleven hours and forty-five minutes, to be precise . . . when he had taken the first step of *removal.*

He had placed . . . delegated the insanity where it belonged. To the men who had created the crisis; whose lies and manipulations had brought Overlord to the precipice of obscenity.

He had ordered Howard Oliver and Jonathan Craft to be in his apartment at six o'clock. Twelve hours and fifteen minutes ago. He had telephoned them on the previous day, making it clear that he would tolerate no excuses. If transportation were a problem, he would resolve it, but they were to be in Washington, in his apartment, by six o'clock.

Exposure was a viable alternative.

They had arrived at precisely six, as the somber chimes of the mantel clock were ringing. At that moment Swanson knew he was dealing from absolute strength. Men like Oliver and Craft – especially Oliver – did not adhere to such punctuality unless they were afraid. It certainly was not courtesy.

The transference had been made with utter simplicity.

There was a telephone number in Geneva, Switzerland. There was a man at that number who would respond to a given code phrase and bring together two disparate parties, act as an interpreter, if necessary. It was understood that the second party – for purposes of definition – had access to a perfected high-altitude guidance system. The first party, in turn, should have knowledge of . . . perhaps access to . . . shipments of industrial diamonds. The Koening mines of Johannesburg might be a place to start.

That was all the information they had.

It was recommended that Mr Oliver and Mr Craft act on this information immediately.

If they failed to do so, extremely serious charges involving individual and corporate deceit relative to armaments contracts would be leveled by the War Department.

There had been a long period of silence. The implications of his statement – with all its ramifications – were accepted gradually by both men.

Alan Swanson then added the subtle confirmation of their worst projections: whoever was chosen to go to Geneva, it could *not* be anyone known to him. Or to any War Department liaison with *any* of their companies. That was paramount.

The Geneva meeting was exploratory. Whoever went to Switzerland should be knowledgeable and, if possible, capable of spotting deception. Obviously a man who practised deception.

That shouldn't be difficult for them; not in the circles they traveled. Surely they knew such a man.

They did. An accountant named Walter Kendall.

Swanson looked up at the clock on the mantel. It was twenty minutes past six.

Why did the time go so slowly? On the other hand, why didn't it stop? Why didn't everything stop but the sunlight? Why did there have to be the nights to go through?

In another hour he would go to his office and quietly make arrangements for one Walter Kendall to be flown on neutral routes to Geneva, Switzerland. He would bury the orders in a blue pouch along with scores of other transport directives and clearances. There would be no signature on the orders, only the official stamp of Field Division, Fairfax; standard procedure with conduits.

Oh, Christ! thought Swanson. If there could be control . . . *without participation.*

But he knew that was not possible. Sooner or later he would have to face the reality of what he had done.

8

December 6, 1943 – Basque Country, Spain

He had been in the north country for eight days. He had not expected it to be this long, but Spaulding knew it was necessary ... an unexpected dividend. What had begun as a routine escape involving two defecting scientists from the Ruhr Valley had turned into something else.

The scientists were throwaway bait. Gestapo bait. The runner who had made their escape possible out of the Ruhr was not a member of the German underground. He was Gestapo.

It had taken Spaulding three days to be absolutely sure. The Gestapo man was one of the best he had ever encountered, but his mistakes fell into a pattern: he was *not* an experienced runner. When David *was* sure, he knew exactly what had to be done.

For five days he led his 'underground' companion through the hills and mountain passes to the east as far as Sierra de Guara, nearly a hundred miles from the clandestine escape routes. He entered remote villages and held 'conferences' with men he knew were Falangists – but who did *not* know him – and then told the Gestapo man they were partisans. He traveled over primitive roads and down the Guayardo River and explained that these routes were the avenues of escape ... Contrary to what the Germans believed, the routes were to the *east*, into the *Mediterranean, not* the Atlantic. This confusion was the prime reason for the success of the Pyrenees network. On two occasions he sent the Nazi into towns for supplies – both times he followed and observed the Gestapo man entering buildings that had thick telephone wires sagging into the roofs.

The information was being transmitted back to Germany. That was reason enough for the investment of five additional days. The German interceptors would be tied up for months concentrating on the eastern 'routes'; the network to the west would be relatively unencumbered.

But now the game was coming to an end. It was just as well, thought David; he had work to do in Ortegal, on the Biscay coast.

The small campfire was reduced to embers, the night air cold. Spaulding looked at his watch. It was two in the morning. He had ordered the 'runner' to stay on guard quite far from the campsite ... out of the glow of the fire. In darkness. He had given the Gestapo man enough time and isolation to make his move, but the German had *not* made his move; he had remained at his post.

So be it, thought David. Perhaps the man wasn't as expert as he thought he was. Or perhaps the information his own men in the hills had given him was not accurate. There was no squad of German soldiers – suspected Alpine troops – heading down from the mountain borders to take out the Gestapo agent.

And him.

He approached the rock on which the German sat. 'Get some rest. I'll take over.'

'*Danke*,' said the man, getting to his feet. 'First, nature calls; I must relieve my bowels. I'll take a spade into the field.'

'Use the woods. Animals graze here. The winds carry.'

'Of course. You're thorough.'

'I try to be,' said David.

The German crossed back toward the fire, to his pack. He removed a camp shovel and started for the woods bordering the field. Spaulding watched him, now aware that his first impression was the correct one. The Gestapo agent *was* expert. The Nazi had not forgotten that six days ago the two Ruhr scientists had disappeared during the night – at a moment of the night when he had dozed. David had seen the fury in the German's eyes and knew the Nazi was now remembering the incident.

If Spaulding assessed the current situation accurately, the Gestapo man would wait at least an hour into his watch, to be sure he, David, was not making contact with unseen partisans in the darkness. Only then would the German give the signal that would bring the Alpine troops out of the forest. With rifles leveled.

But the Gestapo man had made a mistake. He had accepted too readily – without comment – Spaulding's statement about the field and the wind and the suggestion that he relieve himself in the woods.

They had reached the field during late daylight; it was barren, the grass was sour, the slope rocky. Nothing would graze here, not even goats.

And there was no wind at all. The night air was cold, but dead.

An experienced runner would have objected, no doubt humorously, and say he'd be damned if he'd take a crap in the pitch-black woods. But the Gestapo agent could not resist the gratuitous opportunity to make his own contact.

If there *was* such a contact to be made, thought Spaulding. He would know in a few minutes.

David waited thirty seconds after the man had disappeared into the forest. Then he swiftly, silently threw himself to the ground and began rolling his body over and over again, away from the rock, at a sharp angle from the point where the runner had entered the forest.

When he had progressed thirty-five to forty feet into the grass, he stood up, crouching, and raced to the border of the woods, judging himself to be about sixty yards away from the German.

He entered the dense foliage and noiselessly closed the distance between them. He could not see the man but he knew he would soon find him.

Then he saw it. The German's signal. A match was struck, cupped, and extinguished swiftly.

Another. This one allowed to burn for several seconds, then snuffed out with a short spit of breath.

From deep in the woods came two separate, brief replies. Two matches struck. In opposite directions.

David estimated the distance to be, perhaps, a hundred feet. The German, unfamiliar with the Basque forest, stayed close to the edge of the field. The men he had signaled were approaching. Spaulding – making no sound that disturbed the hum of the woods – crawled closer.

He heard the voices whispering. Only isolated words were distinguishable. But they were enough.

He made his way rapidly back through the overgrowth to his original point of entry. He raced to his sentry post, the rock. He removed a small flashlight from his field jacket, clamped separated fingers over the glass and aimed it southwest. He pressed the switch five times in rapid succession. He then replaced the instrument in his pocket and waited.

It wouldn't be long now.

It wasn't.

The German came out of the woods carrying the shovel, smoking a cigarette. The night was black, the moon breaking only intermittently through the thick cover of clouds; the darkness was nearly total. David got up from the rock and signaled the German with a short whistle. He approached him.

'What is it, Lisbon?'

Spaulding spoke quietly. Two words.

'Heil Hitler.'

And plunged his short bayonet into the Nazi's stomach, ripping it downward, killing the man instantly.

The body fell to the ground, the face contorted; the only sound was a swallow of air, the start of a scream, blocked by rigid fingers thrust into the dead man's mouth, yanked downward, as the knife had been, shorting out the passage of breath.

David raced across the grass to the edge of the woods, to the left of his previous entry. Nearer, but not much, to the point where the Nazi had spoken in whispers to his two confederates. He dove into a cluster of winter fern as the moon suddenly broke through the clouds. He remained immobile for several seconds, listening for sounds of alarm.

There were none. The moon was hidden again, the darkness returned. The corpse in the field had not been spotted in the brief illumination. And that fact revealed to David a very important bit of knowledge.

Whatever Alpine troops were in the woods, they were not on the *edge* of the woods. Or if they were, they were not concentrating on the field.

They were waiting. Concentrating in other directions.

Or just waiting.

He rose to his knees and scrambled rapidly west through the dense underbrush, flexing his body and limbs to every bend in the foliage, making sounds compatible to the forest's tones. He reached the point where the three men had conferred but minutes ago, feeling no presence, seeing nothing.

He took out a box of waterproof matches from his pocket and removed two. He struck the first one, and the instant it flared, he blew it out. He then struck the second match and allowed it to burn for a moment or two before he extinguished it.

About forty feet into the woods there was a responding flash of a match. Directly north.

Almost simultaneously came a second response. This one to the west, perhaps fifty or sixty feet away.

No more.

But enough.

Spaulding quickly crawled into the forest at an angle. Northeast. He went no more than fifteen feet and crouched against the trunk of an ant-ridden ceiba tree.

He waited. And while he waited, he removed a thin, short, flexible coil of wire from his field jacket pocket. At each end of the wire was a wooden handle, notched for the human hand.

The German soldier made too much noise for an Alpiner, thought David. He was actually hurrying, anxious to accommodate the unexpected command for rendezvous. That told Spaulding something else: the Gestapo agent he had killed was a demanding man. That meant the remaining troops would stay in position, awaiting orders. There would be a minimum of individual initiative.

There was no time to think of them now. The German soldier was passing the ceiba tree.

David sprang up silently, the coil held high with both hands. The loop fell over the soldier's helmet, the reverse pull so swift and brutally sudden that the wire sliced into the flesh of the neck with complete finality.

There was no sound but the expunging of air again.

David Spaulding had heard that sound so often it no longer mesmerized him. As it once had done.

Silence.

And then the unmistakable breaking of branches; footsteps crushing the ground cover of an unfamiliar path. Rushing, impatient, as the dead man at his feet had been impatient.

Spaulding put the bloody coil of wire back into his pocket and removed the shortened carbine bayonet from the scabbard on his belt. He knew there was no reason to hurry; the third man would be waiting. Confused, frightened perhaps ... but probably not, if he was an Alpiner. The Alpine troops were rougher than the Gestapo. The rumors were that the Alpiners were chosen primarily for streaks of sadism. Robots who could live in mountain passes and nurture their hostilities in freezing isolation until the order for attack were given.

There was no question about it, thought David. There was a certain pleasure in killing Alpiners.

The treadmill.

He edged his way forward, his knife leveled.

'*Wer? ... Wer ist dort?*' The figure in darkness whispered in agitation.

'*Hier, mein Soldat,*' replied David. His carbine bayonet slashed into the German's chest.

The partisans came down from the hills. There were five men, four Basque and one Catalonian. The leader was a Basque, heavyset and blunt.

'You gave us a wild trip, Lisbon. There were times we thought you were *loco.* Mother of God! We've traveled a hundred miles.'

'The Germans will travel many times that, I assure you. What's north?'

'A string of Alpiners. Perhaps twenty. Every six kilometers, right to the border. Shall we let them sit in their wastes?'

'No,' said Spaulding thoughtfully. 'Kill them ... All but the last three; harass them back. They'll confirm what we want the Gestapo to believe.'

'I don't understand.'

'You don't have to.' David walked to the dying fire and kicked at the coals. He had to get to Ortegal. It was all he could think about.

Suddenly he realized that the heavyset Basque had followed him. The man stood across the diminished campfire; he wanted to say something. He looked hard at David and spoke over the glow.

'We thought you should know now. We learned how the pigs made the contact. Eight days ago.'

'What are you talking about?' Spaulding was irritated. Chains of command in the north country were at best a calculated risk. He would get the written reports; he did not want conversation. He wanted to sleep, wake up, and get to Ortegal. But the Basque seemed hurt; there was no point in that. 'Go on, *amigo.*'

'We did not tell you before. We thought your anger would cause you to act rashly.'

'How so? Why?'

'It was Bergeron.'

'I don't believe that ...'

'It is so. They took him in San Sebastiàn. He did not break easily, but they broke him. Ten days of torture ... wires in the genitals, among other devices, including hypodermics of the drug. We are told he died spitting at them.'

David looked at the man. He found himself accepting the information without feeling. *Without feeling.* And that lack of feeling warned him ... to be on guard. He had trained the man named Bergeron, lived in the hills with him, talked for hours on end about things only isolation produces between men. Bergeron had fought with him, sacrificed for him. Bergeron was the closest friend he had in the north country.

Two years ago such news would have sent him into furious anger. He would have pounded the earth and called for a strike somewhere across the borders, demanding that retribution be made.

A year ago he would have walked away from the bearer of such news and demanded a few minutes to be by himself. A brief silence to consider ... by himself ... the whole of the man who had given his life, and the memories that man conjured up.

Yet now he felt nothing.

Nothing at all.

And it was a terrible feeling to feel nothing at all.

'Don't make that mistake again,' he said to the Basque. 'Tell me next time. I don't act rashly.'

9

December 13, 1943 – Berlin, Germany

Johann Dietricht shifted his immense soft bulk in the leather chair in front of Altmüller's desk. It was ten thirty at night and he had not had dinner; there had been no time. The Messerschmitt flight from Geneva had been cramped, petrifying; and all things considered, Dietricht was in a state of aggravated exhaustion. A fact he conveyed a number of times to the Unterstaatssekretär.

'We appreciate everything you've been through, Herr Dietricht. And the extraordinary service you've rendered to your country.' Altmüller spoke solicitously. 'This will take only a few minutes longer, and then I'll have you driven anywhere you like.'

'A decent restaurant, if you can find one open at this hour,' said Dietricht petulantly.

'We apologize for rushing you away. Perhaps a pleasant evening; a really good meal. Schnapps, good company. Heaven knows you deserve it ... There's an inn several miles outside the city. Its patronage is restricted; mostly young flight lieutenants, graduates in training. The kitchen is really excellent.'

There was no need for Johann Dietricht to return Altmüller's smiling look; he accepted certain things as indigenous to his life-style. He had been catered to for years. He was a very important man, and other men were invariably trying to please him. As Herr Altmüller was trying to please him now.

'That might be most relaxing. It's been a dreadful day. Days, really.'

'Of course, if you've some other ...'

'No, no. I'll accept your recommendation ... Let's get on with it, shall we?'

'Very well. Going back over several points so there's no room for error ... The American was not upset with regard to Buenos Aires?'

'He jumped at it. Revolting man; couldn't look you in the eye, but he meant what he said. Simply revolting, though. His clothes, even his fingernails. Dirty fellow!'

'Yes, of course. But you couldn't have misinterpreted?'

'My English is fluent. I understand even the nuances. He was very pleased. I gathered that it served a dual purpose; far removed – thousands of miles away – and in a city nominally controlled by American interests.'

'Yes, we anticipated that reaction. Did he have the authority to confirm it?'

'Indeed, yes. There was no question. For all his uncouth manner, he's obviously highly placed, very decisive. Unquestionably devious, but most anxious to make the exchange.'

'Did you discuss – even peripherally – either's motives?'

'My word, it was unavoidable! This Kendall was most direct. It was a financial matter, pure and simple. There were no other considerations. And I believe him totally; he talks only figures. He reduces everything to numbers. I doubt he has capacities for anything else. I'm extremely perceptive.'

'We counted on that. And Rhinemann? He, too, was acceptable?'

'Immaterial. I pointed out the calculated risk we were taking in an effort to allay suspicions; that Rhinemann was in forced exile. This Kendall was impressed only by Rhinemann's wealth.'

'And the time element; we must be thoroughly accurate. Let's go over the projected dates. It would be disastrous if I made any mistake. As I understand you, the American had graduated estimates of carbonado and bortz shipping requirements . . .'

'Yes, yes,' broke in Dietrich, as if enlightening a child. 'After all, he had no idea of our needs. I settled on the maximum, of course; there was not that much difference in terms of time. They must divert shipments from points of origin; too great a risk in commandeering existing supplies.'

'I'm not sure I understand that. It could be a ploy.'

'They're trapped in their own security measures. As of a month ago, every repository of industrial diamonds has excessive controls, dozens of signatures for every kiloweight. To extract our requirements would be massive, lead to exposure.'

'The inconvenience of the democratic operation. The underlings are given responsibility. And once given, difficult to divest. Incredible.'

'As this Kendall phrased it, there would be too many questions, far too many people would be involved. It would be very sensitive. Their security is filled with Turks.'

'We have to accept the condition,' said Altmüller with resignation – his own, not for the benefit of Dietrich. 'And the anticipated time for these shipment diversions is four to six weeks. It can't be done in less?'

'Certainly. If we are willing to process the ore ourselves.'

'Impossible. We could end up with tons of worthless dirt. We must have the finished products, of course.'

'Naturally. I made that clear.'

'It strikes me as an unnecessary delay. I have to look for inconsistencies, Herr Dietrich. And you said this Kendall was devious.'

'But anxious. I said he was anxious, too. He drew an analogy that lends weight to his statements. He said that their problem was no less than that of a man entering the national vaults in the state of Kentucky and walking out with crates of gold bullion . . . Are we concluded?'

'Just about. The conduit in Geneva will be given the name of the man in Buenos Aires? The man with whom we make contact?'

'Yes. In three or four days. Kendall believed it might be a scientist named Spinelli. An expert in gyroscopics.'

'That title could be questioned, I should think. He's Italian?'

'A citizen, however.'

'I see. That's to be expected. The designs will be subject to scrutiny, of course. What remains now are the checks and counterchecks each of us employ up to the moment of the exchange. A ritual dance.'

'*Ach!* That's for your people. I'm out of it. I have made the initial and, I believe, the most important contribution.'

'There's no question about it. And, I assume, you have abided by the Führer's trust in you, conveyed through this office. You have spoken to no one of the Geneva trip?'

'No one. The Führer's trust is not misplaced. He knows that. As my father and his brother, my uncle, the Dietricht loyalty and obedience are unswerving.'

'He's mentioned that often. We are finished, *mein Herr*.'

'Good! It's been absolutely nerve-wracking! . . . I'll accept your recommendation of the restaurant. If you'll make arrangements, I'll telephone for my car.'

'As you wish, but I can easily have my personal driver take you there. As I said, it's somewhat restricted; my chauffeur is a young man who knows his way around.' Altmüller glanced at Dietricht. Their eyes met for the briefest instant. 'The Führer would be upset if he thought I inconvenienced you.'

'Oh, very well. I suppose it *would* be easier. And we don't want the Führer upset.' Dietricht struggled out of the chair as Altmüller rose and walked around the desk.

'Thank you, Herr Dietricht,' said the Unterstaatssekretär, extending his hand. 'When the time comes we will make known your extraordinary contribution. You are a hero of the Reich, *mein Herr*. It is a privilege to know you. The adjutant outside will take you down to the car. The chauffeur is waiting.'

'Such a relief! Good evening, Herr Altmüller.' Johann Dietricht waddled toward the door as Franz reached over and pushed a button on his desk.

In the morning Dietricht would be dead, the circumstances so embarrassing no one would care to elaborate on them except in whispers.

Dietricht, the misfit, would be eliminated.

And all traces of the Geneva manipulation to the leaders of the Reich canceled with him. Buenos Aires was now in the hands of Erich Rhinemann and his former brothers in German industry.

Except for him – for Franz Altmüller.

The true manipulator.

December 15, 1943 – Washington, DC

Swanson disliked the methods he was forced to employ. They were the beginnings, he felt, of an unending string of deceits. And he was not a deceitful man. Perhaps better than most at spotting deceitful men, but that was due to continuous exposure, not intrinsic characteristics.

The methods were distasteful: observing men who did not know they were being watched and listened to; who spoke without the inhibitions they certainly would have experienced had they any idea there were eyes and ears and wire recorders eavesdropping. It all belonged to that other world, Edmund Pace's world.

It had been easy enough to manipulate. Army Intelligence had interrogation rooms all over Washington. In the most unlikely places. Pace had given him a list of locations; he'd chosen one at the Sheraton Hotel. Fourth floor, Suite 4-M; two rooms in evidence and a third room that was not. This unseen room was behind the wall with openings of unidirectional glass in the two rooms of the suite. These observation holes were fronted by impressionist paintings hung permanently in the bedroom and the sitting room. Wire recorders with plug-in jacks were on shelves beneath the openings within the unseen room. Speakers amplified the conversation with minor distortion. The only visual obstructions were the light pastel colors of the paintings.

Not obstructions at all, really.

Neither had it been difficult to manoeuvre the three men to this room at the Sheraton. Swanson had telephoned Packard's Jonathan Craft and informed him that Walter Kendall was due in on an early afternoon flight from Geneva. The authoritative general also told the frightened civilian that it was possible the military might want to be in telephone communication. Therefore he suggested that Craft reserve a room at a busy, commercial hotel in the center of town. He recommended the Sheraton.

Craft was solicitous; he was running for his life. If the War Department suggested the Sheraton, then the Sheraton it would be. He had booked it without bothering to tell Meridian Aircraft's Howard Oliver.

The front desk took care of the rest.

When Walter Kendall had arrived an hour ago, Swanson was struck by the accountant's disheveled appearance. It was innate untidiness, not the result of traveling. A slovenliness that extended to his gestures, to his constantly darting eyes. He was an outsized rodent in the body of a medium-sized man. It seemed incongruous that men like Oliver and Craft – especially Craft – would associate with a Walter Kendall. Which only pointed up Kendall's value, he supposed. Kendall owned a New York auditing firm. He was a financial analyst, hired by companies to manipulate projections and statistics.

The accountant had not shaken hands with either man. He had gone straight to an easy chair opposite the sofa, sat down, and opened his briefcase. He had begun his report succinctly.

'The son of a bitch was a homo, I swear to Christ!'

As the hour wore on, Kendall described in minute detail everything that had taken place in Geneva. The quantities of bortz and carbonado agreed upon; the quality certifications; Buenos Aires; Gian Spinelli, the gyroscopic designs – *their* certifications and delivery; and the liaison, Erich Rhinemann, exiled Jew. Kendall was an authoritative rodent who was not awkward in the tunnels of negotiated filth. He was, in fact, very much at home.

'How can we be sure they'll bargain in good faith?' asked Craft.

'Good *faith*?' Kendall smirked and winced and grinned at the Packard executive. 'You're too goddamned much. Good *faith*!'

'They might not give us the proper designs,' continued Craft. 'They could pass off substitutes, worthless substitutes!'

'He's got a point,' said the jowled Oliver, his lips taut.

'And we could package crates of cut glass. You think that hasn't crossed their minds? ... But they won't and we won't. For the same shit-eating reason. Our respective necks are on chopping blocks. We've got a common enemy and it's not each other.'

Oliver, sitting across from Kendall, stared at the accountant. 'Hitler's generals there; the War Department here.'

'That's right. We're both lines of supply. For God, country and a dollar or two. And we're both in a lousy position. We don't tell the goddamned generals how to fight a war, and they don't tell us how to keep up production. If they screw up strategy or lose a battle, no screams come from us. But if we're caught short, if we don't deliver, those fuckers go after our necks. It's goddamned unfair. This homo Dietricht, he sees it like I do. We have to protect ourselves.'

Craft rose from the couch; it was a nervous action, a gesture of doubt. He spoke softly, hesitantly. 'This isn't exactly protecting ourselves in any normal fashion. We're dealing with the enemy.'

'Which enemy?' Kendall shuffled papers on his lap; he did not look up at Craft. 'But right, again. It's better than "normal". No matter who wins, we've each got a little something going when it's over. We agreed on that, too.'

There was silence for several moments. Oliver leaned forward in his chair, his eyes still riveted on Kendall. 'That's a dividend, Walter. There could be a lot of common sense in that.'

'A lot,' replied the accountant, allowing a short glance at Oliver. 'We're kicking the crap out of their cities, bombing factories right off the map; railroads, highways – they're going up in smoke. It'll get worse. There's going to be a lot of money made putting it all back together. Reconstruction money.'

'Suppose Germany wins?' asked Craft, by the window.

'Goddamned unlikely,' answered Kendall. 'It's just a question of how much damage is done to both sides, and we've got the hardware. The more damage, the more it'll cost to repair. That includes England. If you boys are smart, you'll be prepared to convert and pick up some of the postwar change.'

'The diamonds ...' Craft turned from the window. 'What are they for?'

'What difference does it make?' Kendall separated a page on his lap and wrote on it. 'They ran out; their asses are in a sling. Same as yours with the guidance system ... By the way, Howard, did you have a preliminary talk with the mines?'

Oliver was deep in thought. He blinked and raised his eyes. 'Yes. Koening. New York offices.'

'How did you put it?'

'That it was top secret, War Department approval. The authorization would come from Swanson's office but even *he* wasn't cleared.'

'They bought that?' The accountant was still writing.

'I said the money would be up front. They stand to make a few million. We met at the Bankers' Club.'

'They bought it.' A statement.

'Walter ...' continued Oliver, 'you said Spinelli before. I don't like it. He's a bad choice.'

Kendall stopped writing and looked up at the Meridian man. 'I didn't figure to tell him anything. Just that we were buying; he was to clear everything before we paid, make sure the designs were authentic.'

'No good. He wouldn't be taken off the project. Not now; too many questions. Find somebody else.'

'I see what you mean.' Kendall put down the pencil. He picked his nose; it was a gesture of thought. 'Wait a minute ... There *is* someone. Right in Pasadena. He's a weird son of a bitch, but he could be perfect.' Kendall laughed while breathing through his mouth. 'He doesn't even talk; I mean he *can't* talk.'

'Is he any good?' asked Oliver.

'He's got problems but he may be better than Spinelli,' replied Kendall, writing on a separate piece of paper. 'I'll take care of it ... It'll cost you.'

Oliver shrugged. 'Include it in the overruns, you prick. What's next?'

'A contact in Buenos Aires. Someone who can deal with Rhinemann, work out the details of the transfer.'

'Who?' asked Craft apprehensively, both hands clasped in front of him.

The accountant grinned, baring his discolored teeth. 'You volunteering? You look like a priest.'

'Good Lord, no! I was simply ...'

'How much, Kendall?' interrupted Oliver.

'More than you want to pay but I don't think you've got a choice. I'll pass on what I can to Uncle Sam; I'll save you what I can.'

'You do that.'

'There's a lot of military down in Buenos Aires. Swanson will have to run some interference.'

'He won't touch it,' said Oliver quickly. 'He was specific. He doesn't want to hear or see your name again.'

'I don't give a shit if he does. But this Rhinemann's going to want certain guarantees. I can tell you that right now.'

'Swanson will be upset.' Craft's voice was high and intense. 'We don't *want* him upset.'

'Upset, shit! He wants to keep that pretty uniform nice and clean . . . Tell you what, don't push him now. Give me some time; I've got a lot of things to figure out. Maybe I'll come up with a way to keep his uniform clean after all. Maybe I'll send him a bill.'

He wants to keep that pretty uniform nice and clean . . .

So devoutly to be wished, Mr Kendall, thought Swanson as he approached the bank of elevators.

But not possible now. The uniform had to get dirty. The emergence of a man named Erich Rhinemann made that necessary.

Rhinemann was one of Hitler's fiascos. Berlin knew it; London and Washington knew it. Rhinemann was a man totally committed to power: financial, political, military. For him all authority must emanate from a single source and he would ultimately settle for nothing less than being at the core of that source.

The fact that he was a Jew was incidental. An inconvenience to end with the end of the war.

When the war was over, Erich Rhinemann would be called back. What might be left of German industry would demand it; the world's financial leaders would demand it.

Rhinemann would re-enter the international market place with more power than ever before.

Without the Buenos Aires manipulation.

With it his leverage would be extraordinary.

His knowledge, his participation in the exchange would provide him with an unparalleled weapon to be used against all sides, all governments.

Especially Washington.

Erich Rhinemann would have to be eliminated.

After the exchange.

And if only for this reason, Washington had to have another man in Buenos Aires.

10

It was unusual for the ranking officer of Fairfax to leave the compound for any reason, but Colonel Edmund Pace was so ordered.

Pace stood in front of General Swanson's desk and began to understand. Swanson's instructions were brief, but covered more territory than their brevity implied. Intelligence files would have to be culled from dozens of double-locked cabinets, a number examined minutely.

Swanson knew that at first Pace disapproved. The Fairfax commander could not conceal his astonishment – at first. The agent in question had to be fluent in both German and Spanish. He had to have a working knowledge – not expert but certainly more than conversational – of aircraft engineering, including metallurgical dynamics and navigational systems. He had to be a man capable of sustaining a cover perhaps on the embassy level. That meant an individual possessing the necessary graces to function easily in monied circles, in the diplomatic arena.

At this juncture Pace had balked. His knowledge of the Johannesburg probe and the Geneva conduit caused him to object. He interrupted Swanson, only to be told to hold his remarks until his superior had finished.

The last qualification of the man for Buenos Aires – and the general conceded its inconsistency when included with the previous technical qualifications – was that the agent be experienced in 'swift dispatch.'

The man was to be no stranger to killing. Not combat fire with its adversaries separated, pitched into frenzy by the sights and sounds of battle. But a man who could kill in silence, facing his target. Alone.

This last qualification mollified Pace. His expression conveyed the fact that whatever his superiors were involved in, it was not wholly what he suspected it to be – might be. The War Department did not request such a man if it intended to keep surface agreements.

The ranking officer of Fairfax made no comment. It was understood that he, alone, would make the file search. He asked for a code, a name to which he could refer in any communications.

774

Swanson had leaned forward in his chair and stared at the map on his desk. The map that had been there for over three hours.

'Call it "Tortugas",' he said.

December 18, 1943 – Berlin, Germany

Altmüller stared at the unbroken seal on the wide, brown manila envelope. He moved it under his desk lamp and took a magnifying glass from his top drawer. He examined the seal under the magnification; he was satisfied. It had not been tampered with.

The embassy courier had flown in from Buenos Aires – by way of Senegal and Lisbon – and delivered the envelope in person, as instructed. Since the courier was based permanently in Argentina, Altmüller did not want him carrying back gossip, so he indulged the man in innocuous conversation, referring to the communication several times in an offhand, derogatory manner. He implied it was a nuisance – a memorandum concerned with embassy finances and really belonged at the Finanzministerium, but what could he do? The ambassador was reputed to be an old friend of Speer's.

Now that the courier was gone and the door shut, Altmüller riveted his attention on the envelope. It was from Erich Rhinemann.

He sliced open the top edge. The letter was written by hand, in Rhinemann's barely decipherable script.

My Dear Altmüller:

To serve the Reich is a privilege I undertake with enthusiasm. I am, of course, grateful for your assurances that my efforts will be made known to my many old friends. I assumed you would do no less under the circumstances.

You will be pleased to know that in the coastal waters from Punta Delgada north to the Caribbean, my ships are honored under the neutrality of the Paraguayan flag. This convenience may be of service to you. Further, I have a number of vessels, notably small and medium-sized craft converted with high-performance engines. They are capable of traveling swiftly through the coastal waters, and there are refueling depots, thus enabling considerable distances to be traversed rapidly. Certainly no comparison to the airplane, but then the trips are made in utter secrecy, away from the prying eyes that surround all airfields these days. Even we neutrals must constantly outflank the blockades.

This information should answer the curiously obscure questions you raised.

I beg you to be more precise in future communications. Regardless, you may be assured of my commitment to the Reich.

Along these lines, associates in Bern inform me that your Führer is showing marked signs of fatigue. It was to be expected, was it not?

Remember, my dear Franz, the concept is always a greater monument than the man. In the current situation, the concept came *before* the man. *It* is the monument.

I await word from you.

Erich Rhinemann

How delicately unsubtle was Rhinemann! ... *commitment to the Reich* ... *associates in Bern* ... *marked signs of fatigue* ... *to be expected* ...

... *a greater monument than the man* ...

Rhinemann spelled out his abilities, his financial power, his 'legitimate' concerns and his unequivocal commitment to Germany. By including, *juxtaposing* these factors, he elevated himself above even the Führer. And by so doing, condemned Hitler – for the greater glory of the Reich. No doubt Rhinemann had photostats made of his letter: Rhinemann would start a very complete file of the Buenos Aires operation. And one day he would use it to manoeuvre himself to the top of postwar Germany. Perhaps of all Europe. For he would have the weapon to guarantee his acceptance.

In victory *or* defeat. Unswerving devotion or, conversely, blackmail of such proportions the Allies would tremble at the thought of it.

So be it, thought Altmüller. He had no brief with Rhinemann. Rhinemann was an expert at whatever he entered into. He was methodical to the point of excess; conservative in progress – only in the sense of mastering all details before going forward. Above everything, he was boldly imaginative.

Altmüller's eyes fell on Rhinemann's words:

I beg you to be more precise in future communications.

Franz smiled. Rhinemann was right. He *had* been obscure. But for a sound reason: he wasn't sure where he was going; where he was being led, perhaps. He only knew that the crates of carbonado diamonds had to be thoroughly examined, and that would take time. More time than Rhinemann realized if the information he had received from Peenemünde was accurate. According to Peenemünde, it would be a simple matter for the Americans to pack thousands of low-quality bortz that; to the inexperienced eye, would be undetectable. Stones that would crack at the first touch to steel.

If the operation was in the hands of the British, that would be the expected manoeuvre.

And even the Americans had decent Intelligence manipulators. *If* the Intelligence services were intrinsic to the exchange. Yet Altmüller doubted their active involvement. The Americans were governmentally hypocritical. They would make demands of their industrialists and expect those demands to be met. However, they would close their eyes to the methods; the unsophisticated Puritan streak was given extraordinary lip service in Washington.

Such children. Yet angry, frustrated children were dangerous.

The crates would have to be examined minutely.

In Buenos Aires.

And once accepted, no risks could be taken that the crates would be blown out of the sky or the water. So it seemed logical to ask Rhinemann what avenues of escape were available. For somewhere, somehow, the crates would have to make rendezvous with the most logical method of transportation back to Germany.

Submarine.

Rhinemann would understand; he might even applaud the precision of future communications.

Altmüller got up from his desk and stretched. He walked absently around his office, trying to rid his back of the cramps resulting from sitting too long. He approached the leather armchair in which Johann Dietricht had sat several days ago.

Dietricht was dead. The expendable, misfit messenger had been found in a blood-soaked bed, the stories of the evening's debauchery so demeaning that it was decided to bury them and the body without delay.

Altmüller wondered if the Americans had the stomach for such decisions. He doubted it.

December 19, 1943 – Fairfax, Virginia

Swanson stood silently in front of the heavy steel door inside the Quonset structure. The security lieutenant was on the wall intercom for only the length of time it took for him to give the general's name. The lieutenant nodded, replaced the phone, saluted the general for a second time. The heavy steel door clicked and Swanson knew he could enter.

The Fairfax commander was alone, as Swanson had ordered. He was standing to the right of his table-desk, a file folder in his hand. He saluted his superior.

'Good morning, general.'

'Morning. You worked fast; I appreciate it.'

'It may not be everything you want but it's the best we can come up with ... Sit down, sir. I'll describe the qualifications. If they meet with your approval, the file's yours. If not, it'll go back into the vaults.'

Swanson walked to one of the straight-backed chairs in front of the colonel's desk and sat down. He did so with a touch of annoyance. Ed Pace, as so many of his subordinates in Clandestine Operations, functioned as though he were responsible to no one but God; and even He had to be cleared by Fairfax. It struck Swanson that it would be much simpler if Pace simply gave him the file and let him read it for himself.

On the other hand, Fairfax's indoctrination had at its core the possibility – however remote – that any pair of eyes might be captured by the enemy. A man could be in Washington one week, Anzio or the Solomons the next. There was logic in Pace's methods; a geographical network of underground agents could be exposed with a single break in the security chain.

Still, it was annoying as hell. Pace seemed to enjoy his role; he was humorless, thought Swanson.

'The subject under consideration is a proven field man. He's acted as independently as anyone in one of our touchiest locations. Languages: acceptable fluency. Deportment and cover: extremely flexible. He moves about the civilian spectrum facilely, from embassy teacups to bricklayers' saloons – he's very mobile and convincing.'

'You're coming up with a positive print, colonel.'

'If I am, I'm sorry. He's valuable where he is. But you haven't heard the rest. You may change your mind.'

'Go on.'

'On the negative side, he's not army. I don't mean he's a civilian – he holds the rank of captain, as a matter of fact, but I don't think he's ever used it. What I'm saying is that he's never operated within a chain of command. He set up the network; he *is* the command. He has been for nearly four years now.'

'Why is that negative?'

'There's no way to tell how he reacts to discipline. Taking orders.'

'There won't be much latitude for deviation. It's cut and dried.'

'That *is* important!' Swanson spoke harshly; Pace was wasting his time. The man in Buenos Aires had to understand what the hell was going on; perhaps more than understand.

'He's in a related field, sir. One that our people say primes him for crash instructions.'

'What is it?'

'He's a construction engineer. With considerable experience in mechanical, electrical and metal design. His background includes full responsibility for whole structures – from foundations through the finished productions. He's a blueprint expert.'

Swanson paused, then nodded noncommittally. 'All right. Go on.'

'The most difficult part of your request was to find someone – someone with these technical qualifications – who had practical experience in "dispatch". You even conceded that.'

'I know.' Swanson felt it was the time to show a little more humanity. Pace looked exhausted; the search had not been easy. 'I handed you a tough one. Does your nonmilitary, mobile engineer have any "dispatches" of record?'

'We try to avoid records, because . . .'

'You know what I mean.'

'Yes. He's stationed where it's unavoidable, I'm sorry to say. Except for the men in Burma and India, he's had more occasions to use last-extremity solutions than anyone in the field. To our knowledge, he's never hesitated to implement them.'

Swanson started to speak, then hesitated. He creased his brow above his questioning eyes. 'You can't help but wonder about such men, can you?'

'They're trained. Like anyone else they do a job . . . for a purpose. He's not a killer by nature. Very few of our really good men are.'

'I've never understood your work, Ed. Isn't that strange?'

'Not at all. I couldn't possibly function in your end of the War

Department. Those charts and graphs and civilian double-talkers confuse me
... How does the subject sound to you?'

'You have no alternates?'

'Several. But with each there's the same negative. Those that have the
languages *and* the aeronautical training have no experience in "dispatch". No
records of ... extreme prejudice. I worked on the assumption that it was as
important as the other factors.'

'Your assumption was correct ... Tell me, do you know him?'

'Very well. I recruited him, I observed every phase of his training. I've seen
him in the field. He's a pro.'

'I want one.'

'Then maybe he's your man. But before I say it, I'd like to ask you a
question. I have to ask it, actually; I'll be asked the same question myself.'

'I hope I can give an answer.'

'It's within bounds. It's not specific.'

'What is it?'

Pace came to the edge of the desk toward Swanson. He leaned his back
against it and folded his arms. It was another army signal: *I'm your
subordinate but this puts us on equal footing right now – at this moment.*

'I said the subject was valuable where he is. That's not strong enough. He's
*in*valuable, essential. By removing him from his station we jeopardize a very
sensitive operation. We can handle it, but the risks are considerable. What I
have to know is, does the assignment justify his transfer?'

'Let me put it this way, colonel,' said Swanson, the tone of his voice gentle
but strong. 'The assignment has no priority equal, with the possible
exception of the Manhattan Project. You've heard of the Manhattan Project,
I assume.'

'I have.' Pace got off his desk. 'And the War Department – through your
office – will confirm this priority?'

'It will.'

'Then here he is, general.' Pace handed Swanson the file folder. 'He's one
of the best we've got. He's our man in Lisbon ... Spaulding. Captain David
Spaulding.'

11

December 26, 1943 – Ribadavia, Spain

David sped south on the motorcycle along the dirt road paralleling the Minho River. It was the fastest route to the border, just below Ribadavia. Once across he would swing west to an airfield outside Valença. The flight to Lisbon would take another two hours, if the weather held and if an aircraft was available. Valença didn't expect him for another two days; its planes might all be in use.

His anxiety matched the intensity of the spinning, careening wheels beneath him. It was all so extraordinary; it made no *sense* to him. There was *no one* in *Lisbon* who could issue such orders as he had received from Ortegal!

What had *happened?*

He felt suddenly as though a vitally important part of his existence was being threatened. And then he wondered at his own reaction. He had no love for his temporary world; he took no pleasure in the countless manipulations and countermanipulations. In fact, he despised most of his day-to-day activities, was sick of the constant fear, the unending high-risk factors to be evaluated with every decision.

Yet he recognized what bothered him so: he had grown in his work. He had arrived in Lisbon centuries ago, beginning a new life, and he had mastered it. Somehow it signified all the buildings he wanted to build, all the blueprints he wanted to turn into mortar and steel. There was precision and finality in his work; the results were there every day. Often many times every day. Like the hundreds of details in construction specifications, the information came to him and he put it all together and emerged with reality.

And it was this reality that others depended upon.

Now someone wanted him out of Lisbon! Out of Portugal and Spain! Was it as simple as that? Had his reports angered one general too many? Had a strategy session been nullified because he sent back the truth of a supposedly successful operation? Were the London and Washington brass finally annoyed to the point of removing a critical thorn? It was possible; he had been told often enough that the men in the underground rooms in London's Tower Road had exploded more than once over his assessments. He knew that Washington's Office of Strategic Services felt he was encroaching on their territory; even G-2, ostensibly his own agency, criticized his involvement with the escape teams.

But beyond the complaints there was one evaluation that overrode them all: he was good. He had welded together the best network in Europe.

Which was why David was confused. And not a little disturbed, for a reason he tried not to admit: he needed praise.

There were no buildings of consequence, no extraordinary blueprints turned into more extraordinary edifices. Perhaps there never would be. He would be a middle-aged engineer when it was over. A middle-aged engineer who had not practised his profession in years, not even in the vast army of the United States, whose Corps of Engineers was the largest construction crew in history.

He tried not to think about it.

He crossed the border at Mendoso, where the guards knew him as a rich, irresponsible ex-patriot avoiding the risks of war. They accepted his gratuities and waved him over.

The flight from Valença to the tiny airfield outside Lisbon was hampered by heavy rains. It was necessary to put down twice – at Agueda and Pombal – before the final leg. He was met by an embassy vehicle; the driver, a cryptographer named Marshall, was the only man in the embassy who knew his real function.

'Rotten weather, isn't it?' said the code man, settling behind the wheel as David threw his pack in the back seat. 'I don't envy you up in a crate like that. Not in this rain.'

'Those grass pilots fly so low you could jump down. I worry more about the trees.'

'I'd just worry.' Marshall started up and drove toward the broken-down pasture gate that served as the field's entrance. On the road he switched on his high beams; it was not yet six o'clock, but the sky was dark, headlights necessary. 'I thought you might flatter me and ask why an expert of my standing was acting as chauffeur. I've been here since four. Go on, ask me. It was a hell of a long wait.'

Spaulding grinned. 'Jesus, Marsh, I just figured you were trying to get in my good graces. So I'd take you north on the next trip. Or have I been made a brigadier?'

'You've been made something, David.' Marshall spoke seriously. 'I took the DC message myself. It was that high up in the codes: eyes-only, senior cryp.'

'I'm flattered,' said Spaulding softly, relieved that he could talk to someone about the preposterous news of his transfer. 'What the hell is it all about?'

'I have no idea what they want you for, of course, but I can spell out one conclusion: they want you yesterday. They've covered all avenues of delay. The orders were to compile a list of your contacts with complete histories of each: motives, dates, repeats, currency, routings, codes ... everything.

Nothing left out. Subsequent order: alert the whole network that you're out of strategy.'

'Out of . . .' David trailed off the words in disbelief. *Out of strategy* was a phrase used as often for defectors as it was for transfers. Its connotation was final, complete breakoff. 'That's insane! This is *my network!*'

'Not anymore. They flew a man in from London this morning. I think he's Cuban; rich, too. Studied architecture in Berlin before the war. He's been holed up in an office studying your files. He's your replacement . . . I wanted you to know.'

David stared at the windshield, streaked with the harsh Lisbon rain. They were on the hard-surfaced road that led through the Alfama district, with its winding, hilly streets below the cathedral towers of the Moorish St George and the Gothic Sé. The American embassy was in the Baixa, past the Terreiro do Paço. Another twenty minutes.

So it was really over, thought Spaulding. They were sending him out. A Cuban architect was now the man in Lisbon. The feeling of being dispossessed took hold of him again. So much was being taken away and under such extraordinary conditions. *Out of strategy . . .*

'Who signed the orders?'

'That's part of the craziness. The use of high codes presumes supreme authority; no one else has access. But no one signed them, either. No name other than yours was in the cable.'

'What am I supposed to do?'

'You get on a plane tomorrow. The flight time will be posted by tonight. The bird makes one stop. At Lajes Field on Terceira, the Azores. You pick up your orders there.'

12

December 26, 1943 – Washington, DC

Swanson reached for the tiny lever on his desk intercom and spoke: 'Send Mr Kendall in.' He stood up, remaining where he was, waiting for the door to open. He would not walk around his desk to greet the man; he would not offer his hand in even a symbol of welcome. He recalled that Walter Kendall had avoided shaking hands with Craft and Oliver at the Sheraton. The handshake would not be missed; his avoidance of it, however, might be noted.

Kendall entered; the door closed. Swanson saw that the accountant's appearance had changed little since the afternoon conference he had observed from the unseen room two days ago. Kendall wore the same suit, conceivably the same soiled shirt. God knew about his underwear; it wasn't a pleasant thought to dwell on. There was the slightest curl on Kendall's upper lip. It did not convey anger or even disdain. It was merely the way the man breathed: mouth and nostrils simultaneously. As an animal might breathe.

'Come in, Mr Kendall. Sit down.'

Kendall did so without comment. His eyes locked briefly with Swanson's but only briefly.

'You're listed on my appointment calendar as being called in to clarify a specific overrun on a Meridian contract,' said the general, sitting down promptly. 'Not to justify, simply enumerate. As the . . . outside auditing firm you can do that.'

'But that's not why I'm here, is it?' Kendall reached into his pocket for a crumpled pack of cigarettes. He squeezed the end before lighting one. Swanson noted that the accountant's fingernails were unkempt, ragged, soiled at the tips. The brigadier began to see – but would not ponder it – that there was a sickness about Walter Kendall, the surface appearance merely one manifestation.

'No, that's not why you're here,' he answered curtly. 'I want to set up ground rules so neither of us misunderstands . . . So *you* don't misunderstand, primarily.'

'Ground rules mean a game. What's the game we're playing, general?'

'Perhaps . . . "Clean Uniforms" might be a good name for it. Or how to run some "Interference in Buenos Aires". That might strike you as more inclusive.'

Kendall, who had been gazing at his cigarette, abruptly shifted his eyes to the general. 'So Oliver and Craft couldn't wait. They had to bring their teacher his big fat apple. I didn't think you wanted it.'

'Neither Craft nor Howard Oliver have been in touch with this office – or with me – in over a week. Since you left for Geneva.'

Kendall paused before speaking. 'Then your uniform's pretty goddamned dirty now . . . The Sheraton. I thought that was a little unritzy for Craft; he's the Waldorf type . . . So you had the place *wired*. You trapped those fuckers.' Kendall's voice was hoarse, not angry, not loud. 'Well, you just remember how I got to where I was going. How I got to Geneva. You got that on the wire, too.'

'We accommodated a request of the War Production Board; relative to a business negotiation with a firm in Geneva. It's done frequently. However, we often follow up if there's reason to think *anything prejudicial* . . .'

'Horseshit!'

Swanson exhaled an audible breath. That reaction is pointless. I don't want to argue with you. The *point* had been *made*. I have an . . . edited spool of wire that could send you straight to the hangman or the electric chair. Oliver, too . . . Craft might get off with a life sentence. You ridiculed his doubts; you didn't let him talk . . . The point, however, *has been made*.'

Kendall leaned forward and crushed out his cigarette in an ashtray on Swanson's desk. His sudden fear made him look at the general; he was searching. 'But you're more interested in Buenos Aires than the electric chair. That's right, isn't it?'

'I'm forced to be. As distasteful as it may be to me. As loathsome . . .'

'Cut out the horseshit,' Kendall interrupted sharply; he was no amateur in such discussions. He knew when to assert himself and his contributions. 'As you said, the point's been made. I think you're in the barnyard with the rest of us pigs . . . So don't play Jesus. Your halo smells.'

'Fair enough. But don't you forget, I've got a dozen different pigsties to run to. A great big War Department that could get me to Burma or Sicily in forty-eight hours. You don't. You're right out there . . . in the barnyard. For everyone to see. And I've got a spool of wire that would make you *special*. *That's* the understanding I want you to have clear in your mind. I hope it is.'

Kendall squeezed the tip of a second cigarette and lit the opposite end. The smoke drifted over his nostrils; he was about to speak, then stopped, staring at the general, his look a mixture of fear and hostility.

Swanson found himself consciously avoiding Kendall's eyes. To acknowledge the man at that moment was to acknowledge the pact. And then he realized what would make the pact bearable. It was the answer, *his* answer; at least a surface one. He was amazed it had not occurred to him before this moment.

Walter Kendall would have to be eliminated.

As Erich Rhinemann would be eliminated.

When Buenos Aires was in reach of completion, Kendall's death was mandatory.

And then all specific traces to the government of the United States would be covered.

He wondered briefly if the men in Berlin had the foresight for such abrupt decisions. He doubted it.

He looked up at the filthy – sick – accountant and returned his stare in full measure. General Alan Swanson was no longer afraid. Or consumed with guilt.

He was a soldier.

'Shall we continue, Mr Kendall?'

The accountant's projections for Buenos Aires were well thought out. Swanson found himself fascinated by Walter Kendall's sense of manoeuvre and countermeasure. The man thought like a sewer rat: instinctively, probing sources of smell and light; his strength in his suspicions, in his constantly varying estimates of his adversaries. He was indeed an animal: predator and evader.

The Germans' prime concerns could be reduced to three: the quality of the bortz and carbonado diamonds; the quantity of the shipment; and finally the methods of safe transport to Germany. Unless these factors could be guaranteed, there would be no delivery of the gyroscopic designs – the guidance system.

Kendall assumed that the shipment of diamonds would be inspected by a team of experts – not one man or even two.

A team, then, three to five men, would be employed; the length of time required might extend to the better part of a week depending upon the sophistication of the instruments used. This information he had learned from Koening in New York. During this period simultaneous arrangements would be agreed to that allowed an aerophysicist to evaluate the gyroscopic designs brought from Peenemünde. If the Nazis were as cautious as Kendall assumed they would be, the designs would be delivered in stages, timed to the schedule the inspection team considered adequate for its examination of the diamonds. The gyroscope scientist would no doubt be fed step-blueprints in isolation, with no chance of photostats or duplication until the diamond team had completed its work.

Once both sides were satisfied with the deliveries, Kendall anticipated that an ultimate threat would be imposed that guaranteed safe transport to the respective destinations. And it was logical that this 'weapon' be identical for each party; threat of exposure. Betrayal of cause and country.

Penalties: death.

The same 'weapon' the general held on him, on Walter Kendall.

What else was new?

Did Kendall think it was possible to get the designs and subsequently sabotage or reclaim the diamond shipment?

No. Not as long as it remained a civilian exchange. The threat of exposure was too complete; there was too much proof of contact. Neither crisis could be denied and names were known. The taint of collaboration could ruin men and corporations. 'Authenticated' rumors could be circulated easily.

And if the military moved in, the civilians would move out instantly – the responsibility of delivery no longer theirs.

Swanson should know this; it was precisely the situation he had engineered.

Swanson knew it.

Where would the diamonds be inspected? Where was the most advantageous location?

Kendall's reply was succinct: any location that seemed advantageous to one side would be rejected by the other. He thought the Germans foresaw this accurately and for that reason suggested Buenos Aires. It was on the spool of wire. Didn't Swanson listen?

Powerful men in Argentina were unquestionably, if quietly, pro-Axis, but the government's dependency on Allied economics took precedence. The neutrality essentially was controlled by the economic factors. Each side, therefore, had something: the Germans would find a sympathetic environment, but the Americans were capable of exerting a strong enough influence to counteract that sympathy – without eliminating it.

Kendall respected the men in Berlin who centered in on Buenos Aires. They understood the necessity of balancing the psychological elements, the need to give up, yet still retain spheres of influence. They were good.

Each side would be extremely cautious; the environment demanded it. Timing would be everything.

Swanson knew how the designs would be gotten out: a string of pursuit aircraft flying up the coastal bases under diplomatic cover. This cover would extend to the military. Only *he* would be aware of the operation; no one else in the services or, for that matter, in the government would be apprised. He would make the arrangements and give them to Kendall at the proper time.

'What transport would the Germans arrive at?' asked the general.

'They've got a bigger problem. They recognize it so they'll probably make some kind of airtight demands. They could ask for a hostage, but I don't think so.'

'Why not?'

'Who've we got – that's involved – that's not expendable? Christ! If it was me, you'd be the first to say, "Shoot the son of a bitch!" ' Kendall again locked his eyes briefly with Swanson's. 'Of course, you wouldn't know what particular safeguards *I* took; a lot of uniforms would be dirty as hell.'

Swanson recognized Kendall's threat for what it was. He also knew he could handle it. It would take some thought, but such consideration could come later. It would be no insurmountable hurdle to prepare for Kendall's dispatch. The isolation would come first; then an elaborate dossier . . .

'Let's concentrate on how they expect to ship out the bortz and carbonado. There's no point in going after each other,' said Swanson.

'We're beyond that, then?'

'I think we are.'

'Good. Just don't forget it,' said Kendall.

'The diamonds will be brought to Buenos Aires. Have those arrangements been made?'

'They're being made. Delivery date in three, three-and-a-half weeks. Unless there's a fuck-up in the South Atlantic. We don't expect any.'

'The inspection team does its work in Buenos Aires. We send the physicist . . . who will it be? Spinelli?'

'No. For both our sakes we ruled him out. But you know that . . .'

'Yes. Who, then?'

'Man named Lyons. Eugene Lyons. I'll get you a file on him. You'll sweat bullets when you read it, but if there's anyone better than Spinelli, it's him. We wouldn't take any chances. He's in New York now.'

Swanson made a note. 'What about the German transport? Any ideas?'

'A couple. Neutral cargo plane north to Recife in Brazil, across east to Palmas or someplace in Guinea on the African coast. Then straight up to Lisbon and out. That's the fastest routing. But they may not want to chance the air corridors.'

'You sound military.'

'When I do a job, it's thorough.'

'What else?'

'I think they'll probably settle for a submarine. Maybe two, for diversion purposes. It's slower but the safest.'

'Subs can't enter Argentine ports. Our southern patrols would blow them out of the water. If they put in, they're impounded. We're not going to change those rules.'

'You may have to.'

'Impossible. There has to be another way.'

'You may have to find it. Don't forget those clean uniforms.'

Swanson looked away. 'What about Rhinemann?'

'What about him? He's on his way back. With his kind of money, even Hitler can't freeze him out.'

'I don't trust him.'

'You'd be a goddamned fool if you did. But the worst he can do is hold out for market concessions – or money – from both sides. So what? He'll deliver. Why wouldn't he?'

'I'm sure he'll deliver; that's the one thing I'm positive about . . . Which brings me to the main point of this meeting. I want a man in Buenos Aires. At the embassy.'

Kendall absorbed Swanson's statement before replying. He reached for the ashtray and put it on the arm of his chair. 'One of your men or one of ours? We need someone; we figured you'd have us supply him.'

'You figured wrong. I've picked him.'

'That could be dangerous. I tell you this with no charge . . . since I already said it.'

'If we move in, the civilian contingent moves out?' A question.

'It makes sense . . .'

'Only if the man I send *knows* about the diamonds. You're to make sure he doesn't.' A statement. 'Make *very* sure, Kendall. Your life depends on it.'

The accountant watched Swanson closely. 'What's the point?'

'There are six thousand miles between Buenos Aires and the Meridian Aircraft plants. I want that trip made without any mishaps. I want those designs brought back by a professional.'

'You're taking a chance on dirtying up the uniforms, aren't you, general?'

'No. The man will be told that Rhinemann made a deal for the designs out of Peenemünde. We'll say Rhinemann brought in the German underground. For escape routings.'

'Full of holes! Since when does the underground work for a price? Why would they go three thousand miles out of their way? Or work with Rhinemann?'

'Because they need him and he needs them. Rhinemann was exiled as a Jew; it was a mistake. He rivaled Krupp. There are many in German industry still loyal to him; and he maintains offices in Bern . . . Our crisis in gyroscopics is no secret, we know that. Rhinemann would use that knowledge; make deals in Bern.'

'Why even bring in the underground?'

'I have my own reasons. They're not your concern.' Swanson spoke curtly, clipping his words. It crossed his mind – fleetingly – that he was getting overtired again. He had to watch that; his strength was hollow when he was tired. And now he had to be convincing. He had to make Kendall obey without question. The important thing was to get Spaulding within reach of Erich Rhinemann. Rhinemann was the target.

The brigadier watched the filthy man in front of him. It sickened him to think that such a human slug was so necessary to the moment. Or was it, he wondered, that he was reduced to using such a man? Using him and then ordering his execution. It made their worlds closer.

'All right, Mr Kendall, I'll spell it out . . . The man I've picked for Buenos Aires is one of the best Intelligence agents we've got. He'll bring those designs back. But I don't want to take the slightest chance that he could learn of the diamond transfer. Rhinemann operating alone is suspect; the inclusion of the German underground puts it above suspicion.'

Swanson had done his homework; everyone spoke of the French and Balkan undergrounds, but the *German* underground had worked harder and more effectively, with greater sacrifice, than all the others combined. The former man in Lisbon would know that. It would make the Buenos Aires assignment palatable and legitimate.

'Wait a minute . . . Jesus Christ! *Wait* a minute.' Kendall's disagreeable expression abruptly changed. It was as if suddenly – with reluctant enthusiasm – he had found merit in something Swanson said. 'That could be a good device.'

'What do you mean, *device*?'

'Just that. You say you're going to use it for this agent. The underground's above suspicion and all that shit . . . Okay, let's go further. You just spelled out the guarantee we have to give.'

'What guarantee?'

'That the shipment of Koening diamonds can get *out* of Buenos Aires. It's going to be *the* ball-breaker . . . Let me ask you a couple of questions. And give me straight answers.'

The *sewer rat*, thought Swanson, looking at the excited, disheveled figure-man. 'Go ahead.'

'This underground. They've gotten a lot of people out of Germany, very important people. I mean everybody knows that.'

'They've – it's – been very effective.'

'Does it have any hooks into the German *navy*?'

'I imagine so. Allied Central Intelligence would know specifically . . .'

'But you don't want to go to them. Or do you?'

'Out of the question.'

'But is it possible?'

'What?'

'The German *navy*, goddamn it! The submarine fleet!' Kendall was leaning forward, his eyes now boring into Swanson's.

'I would think so. I'm not . . . not primarily an Intelligence man. The German underground has an extensive network. I assume it has contacts in the naval command.'

'Then it *is* possible.'

'Yes, *anything's* possible.' Swanson lowered his voice, turning away from his own words. 'This is possible.'

Kendall leaned back in the chair and crushed out his cigarette. He grinned his unattractive grin and wagged his forefinger at Swanson. 'Then there's your story. Clean as a goddamned whistle and way above any goddamned suspicion . . . While we're buying those designs, it just so happens that a German submarine is floating around, ready to surface and bring out one – even two, if you like – very important defectors. Courtesy of the underground. What better reason for a submarine to surface in hostile waters? Protected from patrols . . . Only nobody gets off. Instead, some fresh cargo gets put on board.'

Swanson tried to assimilate Kendall's rapidly delivered manoeuvres. 'There'd be complications . . .'

'Wrong! It's *isolated. One* has nothing to do with the *other*! It's just talk, anyway.'

Brigadier General Alan Swanson knew when he had met a man more capable in the field than himself. 'It's possible. Radio blackout; Allied Central instructions.'

Kendall rose from his chair; he spoke softly. 'Details. I'll work them out . . . And you'll pay me. Christ, will you pay.'

13

December 27, 1943 – The Azores

The island of Terceira in the Azores, 837 miles due west of Lisbon, was a familiar stop to the trans-Atlantic pilots flying the southern route to the United States mainland. As they descended there was always the comfortable feeling that they would encounter minor traffic to be serviced by efficient ground crews who allowed them to be rapidly airborne again. Lajes Field was good duty; those assigned there recognized that and performed well.

Which was why the major in command of the B-17 cargo and personnel carrier which had a Captain David Spaulding as its single passenger couldn't understand the delay. It had begun at descent altitude, fourteen thousand feet. The Lajes tower had interrupted its approach instructions and ordered the pilot to enter a holding pattern. The major had objected; there was no necessity from his point of view. The field was clear. The Lajes tower radioman agreed with the major but said he was only repeating telephone instructions from American headquarters in Ponta Delgada on the adjacent island of São Miguel. Az-Am-HQ gave the orders; apparently it was expecting someone to meet the plane and that someone hadn't arrived. The tower would keep the major posted and, incidentally, was the major carrying some kind of priority cargo? Just curiosity.

Certainly not. There was *no* cargo; only a military attaché named Spaulding from the Lisbon embassy. One of those goddamned diplomatic teaparty boys. The trip was a routine return flight to Norfolk, and why the hell couldn't he land?

The tower would keep the major posted.

The B-17 landed at 1300 hours precisely, its holding pattern lasting twenty-seven minutes.

David got up from the removable seat, held to the deck by clamps, and stretched. The pilot, an aggressive major who looked roughly thirteen years old to Spaulding, emerged from the enclosed cockpit and told him a jeep was outside – or would be outside shortly – to drive the captain off the base.

'I'd like to maintain a decent schedule,' said the young pilot, addressing his outranked elder humorlessly. 'I realize you diplomatic people have a lot of friends in these social posts, but we've got a long lap to fly. Bear it in mind, please.'

'I'll try to keep the polo match down to three chukka,' replied David wearily.

'Yeah, you do that.' The major turned and walked to the rear of the cabin, where an air force sergeant had sprung open the cargo hatch used for the aircraft's exit. Spaulding followed, wondering who would meet him outside.

'My name's Ballantyne, captain,' said the middle-aged civilian behind the wheel of the jeep, extending his hand to Spaulding. 'I'm with Azores-American. Hop in; we'll only be a few minutes. We're driving to the provost's house, a few hundred yards beyond the fence.'

David noticed that the guards at the gate did not bother to stop Ballantyne, they just waved him through. The civilian turned right on the road paralleling the field and accelerated. In less time than it took to adequately light a cigarette, the jeep entered the driveway of a one-story Spanish hacienda and proceeded past the house to what could only be described as an out-of-place gazebo.

'Here we are. Come on, captain,' said Ballantyne getting out, indicating the screen door of the screened enclosure. 'My associate, Paul Hollander, is waiting for us.'

Hollander was another middle-aged civilian. He was nearly bald and wore steel-rimmed spectacles that gave him an appearance beyond his years. As with Ballantyne, there was a look of intelligence about him. Both small and capital *I*. Hollander smiled genuinely.

'This is a distinct pleasure, Spaulding. As so many others, I've admired the work of the man in Lisbon.'

Capital *I*, thought David.

'Thank you. I'd like to know why I'm not him any longer.'

'I can't answer that. Neither can Ballantyne, I'm afraid.'

'Perhaps they thought you deserved a rest,' offered Ballantyne. 'Good Lord, you've been there – how long is it now? Three years with no break.'

'Nearer four,' answered David. 'And there were plenty of "breaks". The Costa Brava beats the hell out of Palm Beach. I was told that you – I assume it's you – have my orders . . . I don't mean to seem impatient but there's a nasty teenager with a major's rank flying the plane. *He's* impatient.'

'Tell him to go to blazes,' laughed the man named Hollander. 'We *do* have your orders and also a little surprise for you: you're a lieutenant colonel. Tell the major to get his uniform pressed.'

'Seems I jumped one.'

'Not really. You got your majority last year. Apparently you don't have much use for titles in Lisbon.'

'Or military associations,' interjected Ballantyne.

'Neither, actually,' said David. 'At least I wasn't broken. I had premonitions of walking guard duty around latrines.'

'Hardly.' Hollander sat down in one of the four deck chairs, gesturing David to do the same. It was his way of indicating that their meeting might not be as short as Spaulding had thought. 'If it was a time for parades or revelations, I'm sure you'd be honored in the front ranks.'

'Thanks,' said David, sitting down. 'That removes a very real concern. What's this all about?'

'Again, we don't have answers, only *ex cathedra* instructions. We're to ask you several questions – only one of which could preclude our delivering your orders. Let's get that over with first; I'm sure you'd like to know at least where you're going.' Hollander smiled his genuine smile again.

'I would. Go on.'

'Since you were relieved of your duties in Lisbon, have you made contact – intentional or otherwise – with *anyone* outside the embassy? I mean by this, even the most innocuous goodbye? Or a settling of a bill – a restaurant, a store; or a chance run-in with an acquaintance at the airport, or on the way to the airport?'

'No. And I had my luggage sent in diplomatic cartons; no suitcases, no traveling gear.'

'You're thorough,' said Ballantyne, still standing.

'I've had reason to be. Naturally, I had engagements for the week after I returned from the north country . . .'

'From *where*?' asked Hollander.

'Basque and Navarre. Contact points below the border. I always scheduled engagements right after; it kept a continuity. Not many, just enough to keep in sight. Part of the cover. I had two this week; lunch and cocktails.'

'What about them?' Ballantyne sat down next to David.

'I instructed Marshall – he's the cryp who took my orders – to call each just before I was supposed to show up. Say I'd be delayed. That was all.'

'Not that you wouldn't *be* there?' Hollander seemed fascinated.

'No. Just delayed. It fit the cover.'

'I'll take your word for it,' laughed Hollander. 'You answered affirmatively and then some. How does New York strike you?'

'As it always has: pleasantly for limited periods.'

'I don't know for how long but that's your assignment. And out of uniform, colonel.'

'I lived in New York. I know a lot of people there.'

'Your new cover is simplicity itself. You've been discharged most honorably after service in Italy. Medical reasons, minor wounds.' Hollander took out an envelope from the inside pocket of his jacket and handed it across to David. 'It's all here. Terribly simple, papers . . . everything.'

'Okay,' said David, accepting the envelope. 'I'm a ruptured duck in New York. So far, very nice. You couldn't make it the real thing, could you?'

'The papers are simple, I didn't say authentic. Sorry.'

'So am I. What happens then?'

'Someone's very solicitous of you. You have an excellent job; good pay, too. With Meridian Aircraft.'

'Meridian?'

'Blueprint Division.'

'I thought Meridian was in the Midwest. Illinois or Michigan.'

'It has a New York office. Or it does now.'

'Aircraft blueprints, I assume.'

'I should think so.'

'Is it counterespionage?'

'We don't know,' answered Ballantyne. 'We weren't given any data except the names of the two men you'll report to.'

'They're in the envelope?'

'No,' said Hollander. 'They're verbal and to be committed. Nothing written until you're on the premises.'

'Oh, Christ, this all sounds like Ed Pace. He loves this kind of nonsense.'

'Sorry, again. It's above Pace.'

'What? . . . I didn't think anything was, except maybe Holy Communion . . . Then how do *you* report? And to whom?'

'Priority courier straight through to an address in Washington. No department listing, but transmission *and* priority cleared through Field Division, Fairfax.'

Spaulding emitted a soft, nearly inaudible whistle. 'What are the two names?'

'The first is Lyons. Eugene Lyons. He's an aerophysicist. We're to tell you that he's a bit strange, but a goddamned genius.'

'In other words, reject the man; accept the genius.'

'Something like that. I suppose you're used to it,' said Ballantyne.

'Yes,' answered Spaulding. 'And the other?'

'A man named Kendall.' Hollander crossed his legs. 'Nothing on him; he's just a name. Walter Kendall. Have no idea what he does.'

David pulled the strap across his waist in the removable seat. The B-17's engines were revving at high speed, sending vibrations through the huge fuselage. He looked about in a way he hadn't looked at an airplane before, trying to reduce the spans and the plating to some kind of imaginary blueprint. If Hollander's description of his assignment was accurate – and why shouldn't it be? – he'd be studying aircraft blueprints within a few days.

What struck him as strange were the methods of precaution. In a word, they were unreasonable; they went beyond even abnormal concerns for security. It would have been a simple matter for him to report to Washington, be reassigned, and be given an in-depth briefing. Instead, apparently there would be *no* briefing.

Why not?

Was he to accept open-ended orders from two men he'd never met before? Without the sanction of recognition – even introduction – from any military authority? What the hell was Ed Pace doing?

Sorry . . . It's above Pace.

Those were the words Hollander had used.

. . . cleared through Field Division, Fairfax.

Hollander again.

Except for the White House itself, David realized that Fairfax was about as high up as one could go. But Fairfax was still *military*. And he wasn't being instructed by Fairfax, simply 'cleared'.

Hollander's remaining 'questions' had not been questions at all, really. They had been introduced with interrogatory words: *do you, have you, can you*. But not questions; merely further instructions.

'Do you have friends in any of the aircraft companies? On the executive level?'

He didn't know, for God's sake. He'd been out of the country so damned long he wasn't sure he had any friends, period.

Regardless, Hollander had said, he was to avoid any such 'friends' – should they exist. Report their names to Walter Kendall, if he ran across them.

'Have you any women in New York who are in the public eye?'

What kind of question was *that*? Silliest goddamned thing he'd ever heard of! What the hell did Hollander mean?

The balding, bespectacled Az-Am agent had clarified succintly. It was listed in David's file that he had supplemented his civilian income as a radio performer. That meant he knew actresses.

And actors, Spaulding suggested. And so what?

Friendships with well-known actresses could lead to newspaper photographs, Hollander rejoined. Or speculations in columns; his name in print. That, too, was to be avoided.

David recalled that he did know – knew – several girls who'd done well in pictures since he'd left. He'd had a short-lived affair with an actress who was currently a major star for Warner Brothers. Reluctantly he agreed with Hollander; the agent was right. Such contacts would be avoided.

'Can you absorb quickly, commit to memory, blueprint specifications unrelated to industrial design?'

Given a breakdown key of correlative symbols and material factors, the answer was probably yes.

Then he was to prepare himself – however it was done – for aircraft design.

That, thought Spaulding, was obvious.

That, Hollander had said, was all he could tell him.

The B-17 taxied to the west extreme of the Lajes runway and turned for takeoff. The disagreeable major had made it a point to be standing by the cargo hatch looking at his wristwatch when Spaulding returned. David had climbed out of the jeep, shaken hands with Ballantyne and held up three fingers to the major.

'The timer lost count during the last chukka,' he said to the pilot. 'You know how it is with these striped-pants boys.'

The major had not been amused.

The aircraft gathered speed, the ground beneath hammered against the landing gear with increasing ferocity. In seconds the plane would be airborne. David bent over to pick up an Azores newspaper that Hollander had given him and which he'd placed at his feet when strapping himself in.

Suddenly it happened. An explosion of such force that the removable seat flew out of its clamps and jettisoned into the right wall of the plane, carrying David, bent over, with it. And he'd never know but often speculate on whether that Azores newspaper had saved his life.

Smoke was everywhere; the aircraft careened off the ground and spun laterally. The sound of twisting metal filled the cabin with a continuous, unending scream; steel ribs whipped downward from the top and sides of the fuselage – snapping, contorted, sprung from their mountings.

A second explosion blew out the front cabin; sprays of blood and pieces of flesh spat against the crumbling, spinning walls. A section of human scalp with traces of burnt hairline under the bright, viscous red fluid slapped into Spaulding's forearm. Through the smoke David could see the bright sunlight streaming through the front section of the careening plane.

The aircraft had been severed!

David knew instantly that he had only one chance of survival. The fuel tanks were filled to capacity for the long Atlantic flight; they'd go up in seconds. He reached for the buckle at his waist and ripped at it with all his strength. It was locked; the hurling fall had caused the strap to bunch and crowd the housing with cloth. He tugged and twisted, the snap sprung and he was free.

The plane – what was left of it – began a series of thundering convulsions signifying the final struggle to come to a halt on the rushing, hilly ground beyond the runway. David crashed backward, crawling as best he could toward the rear. Once he was forced to stop and hug the deck, his face covered by his arms, a jagged piece of metal piercing the back of his right shoulder.

The cargo hatch was blown open; the air force sergeant lay half out of the steel frame, dead, his chest ripped open from throat to rib cage.

David judged the distance to the ground as best his panic would allow and hurled himself out of the plane, coiling as he did so for the impact of the fall and the necessary roll away from the onrushing tail assembly.

The earth was hard and filled with rocks, but he was *free*. He kept rolling, rolling, crawling, digging, gripping his bloodied hands into the dry, hard soil until the breath in his lungs was exhausted.

He lay on the ground and heard the screaming sirens far in the distance.

And then the explosion that filled the air and shook the earth.

Priority high-frequency radio messages were sent back and forth between the operations room of Lajes Airfield and Field Division, Fairfax.

David Spaulding was to be airlifted out of Terceira on the next flight to Newfoundland, leaving in less than an hour. At Newfoundland he would be met by a pursuit fighter plane at the air force base and flown directly to Mitchell Field, New York. In light of the fact that Lieutenant Colonel Spaulding had suffered no major physical disability, there would be no change in the orders delivered to him.

The cause of the B-17 explosions and resultant killings was, without question, sabotage. Timed out of Lisbon or set during the refueling process at Lajes. An intensive investigation was implemented immediately.

Hollander and Ballantyne had been with David when he was examined and treated by the British army doctor. Bandages around the sutures in his right shoulder, the cuts on his hands and forearms cleaned, Spaulding pronounced himself shaken but operable. The doctor left after administering an intravenous sedative that would make it possible for David to rest thoroughly on the final leg of his trip to New York.

'I'm sure it will be quite acceptable for you to take a leave for a week or so,' said Hollander. 'My God, you're lucky to be among us!'

'*Alive* is the word,' added Ballantyne.

'Am I a mark?' asked Spaulding. 'Was it connected with me?'

'Fairfax doesn't think so,' answered the balding Hollander. 'They think it's coincidental sabotage.'

Spaulding watched the Az-Am agent as he spoke. It seemed to David that Hollander hesitated, as if concealing something.

'Narrow coincidence, isn't it? I *was* the only passenger.'

'If the enemy can eliminate a large aircraft and a pilot in the bargain, well, I imagine he considers that progress. And Lisbon security *is* rotten.'

'Not where I've been. Not generally.'

'Well, perhaps here at Terceira, then ... I'm only telling you what Fairfax thinks.'

There was a knock on the dispensary door and Ballantyne opened it. A first lieutenant stood erect and spoke gently, addressing David, obviously aware that Spaulding had come very close to death.

'It's preparation time, sir. We should be airborne in twenty minutes. Can I help you with anything?'

'I haven't *got* anything, lieutenant. Whatever I had is in that mass of burnt rubble in the south forty.'

'Yes, of course. I'm sorry.'

'Don't be. Better it than me ... I'll be right with you.' David turned to Ballantyne and Hollander, shaking their hands.

As he said his last goodbye to Hollander, he saw it in the agent's eyes.

Hollander *was* hiding something.

The British naval commander opened the screen door of the gazebo and walked in. Paul Hollander rose from the deck chair.

'Did you bring it?' he asked the officer.

'Yes.' The commander placed his attaché case on the single wrought-iron table and snapped up the hasps. He took out an envelope and handed it to the American. 'The photo lab did a rather fine job. Well lighted, front and rear views. Almost as good as having the real item.'

Hollander unwound the string on the envelope's flap and removed a photograph. It was an enlargement of a small medallion, a star with six points.

It was the Star of David.

In the center of the face was the scrolled flow of a Hebrew inscription. On the back was the bas-relief of a knife with a streak of lightning intersecting the blade.

'The Hebrew spells out the name of a prophet named Haggai; he's the symbol of an organization of Jewish fanatics operating out of Palestine. They call themselves the Haganah. Their business, they claim, is vengeance – two thousand years' worth. We anticipate quite a bit of trouble from them in the years to come; they've made that clear, I'm afraid.'

'But you say it was welded to the bottom main strut of the rear cabin.'

'In such a way as to escape damage from all but a direct explosion. Your aircraft was blown up by the Haganah.'

Hollander sat down staring at the photograph. He looked up at the British commander. 'Why? For God's sake, *why?*'

'I can't answer that.'

'Neither can Fairfax. I don't think they even want to acknowledge it. They want it buried.'

14

December 27, 1943 – Washington, DC

When the words came over his intercom in the soft, compensating voice of the WAC lieutenant who was his secretary, Swanson knew it was no routine communication.

'Fairfax on line one, sir. It's Colonel Pace. He says to interrupt you.'

Since delivering David Spaulding's file, the Fairfax commander had been reluctant to call personally. He hadn't spoken of his reluctance, he simply relegated messages to subordinates. And since they all concerned the progress of getting Spaulding out of Portugal, Pace's point was clear: he would expedite but not personally acknowledge his participation.

Edmund Pace was still not satisfied with the murky 'highest priority' explanations regarding his man in Lisbon. He would follow orders once-removed.

'General, there's a radio emergency from Lajes Field in Terceira,' said Pace urgently.

'What the hell does that mean? *Where?*'

'Azores. The B-17 carrier with Spaulding on it was sabotaged. Blown up on takeoff.'

'Jesus!'

'May I suggest you come out here, sir?'

'Is Spaulding dead?'

'Preliminary reports indicate negative, but I don't want to guarantee anything. Everything's unclear. I wanted to wait till I had further confirmations but I can't now. An unexpected development. Please, come out, general.'

'On my way. Get the information on Spaulding!'

Swanson gathered the papers on his desk – the information from Kendall – that had to be clipped together, sealed in a thin metal box and locked in a file cabinet with two combinations and a key.

If there was ever a reason for total security, it was symbolized by those papers.

He spun the two combination wheels, turned the key and then thought for a second that he might reverse the process and take the papers with him ...

No, that was unsound. They were safer in the cabinet. A file cabinet riveted to the floor was better than a cloth pocket on a man who walked in the street and drove in automobiles. A file cabinet could not have accidents; was not subject to the frailties of a tired, fifty-three-year-old brigadier.

He saluted the guard on duty at the entrance and walked rapidly down the steps to the curb. His driver was waiting, alerted by the WAC secretary, whose efficiency overcame her continuous attempts to be more than an efficient secretary to him. He knew that one day when the pressures became too much, he'd ask her in, lock the door and hump the ass off her on the brown leather couch.

Why was he thinking about his secretary? He didn't give a goddamn about the WAC lieutenant who sat so protectively outside his office door.

He sat back in the seat and removed his hat. He knew why he thought about his secretary: it gave him momentary relief. It postponed thoughts about the complications that may or may not have exploded on a runway in the Azores.

Oh *Christ*! The thought of rebuilding what he'd managed to put together was abhorrent to him. To go back, to reconstruct, to research for the right man was impossible. It was difficult enough for him to go over the details as they now stood.

The details supplied by the sewer rat.

Kendall.

An enigma. An unattractive puzzle even G-2 couldn't piece together. Swanson had run a routine check on him, based on the fact that the accountant was privy to Meridian's aircraft contracts; the Intelligence boys and Hoover's tight-lipped maniacs had returned virtually nothing but names and dates. They'd been instructed *not* to interview Meridian personnel or anyone connected with ATCO or Packard; orders that apparently made their task close to impossible.

Kendall was forty-six, severely asthmatic and a CPA. He was unmarried, had few if any friends and lived two blocks from his firm, which he solely owned, in mid-Manhattan.

The personal evaluations were fairly uniform: Kendall was a disagreeable, antisocial individualist who happened to be a brilliant statistician.

The dossier might have told a desolate story – paternal abandonment, lack of privilege, the usual – but it didn't. There was no indication of poverty, no record of deprivation or hardship anywhere near that suffered by millions, especially during the Depression years.

No records of depth on anything, for that matter.

An enigma.

But there was nothing enigmatic about Walter Kendall's 'details' for Buenos Aires. They were clarity itself. Kendall's sense of manipulation had been triggered; the challenge stimulated his already primed instincts for manoeuvring. It was as if he had found the ultimate 'deal' – and indeed, thought Swanson, he had.

The operation was divided into three isolated exercises: the arrival and inspection of the diamond shipment; the simultaneous analysis of the gyroscopic blueprints, as they, too, arrived; and the submarine transfer. The crates of bortz and carbonado from the Koening mines would be secretly cordoned off in a warehouse in the Dársena Norte district of the Puerto Nuevo. The Germans assigned to the warehouse would report only to Erich Rhinemann.

The aerophysicist, Eugene Lyons, would be billeted in a guarded apartment in the San Telmo district, an area roughly equivalent to New York's Gramercy Park – rich, secluded, ideal for surveillance. As the step-blueprints were delivered, he would report to Spaulding.

Spaulding would precede Lyons to Buenos Aires and be attached to the embassy on whatever pretext Swanson thought feasible. His assignment – as *Spaulding* thought it to be – was to coordinate the purchase of the gyroscopic designs, and if their authenticity was confirmed, authorize payment. This authorization would be made by a code radioed to Washington that supposedly cleared a transfer of funds to Rhinemann in Switzerland.

Spaulding would then stand by at a mutually agreed-upon airfield, prepared to be flown out of Argentina. He would be given airborne clearance when Rhinemann received word that 'payment' had been made.

In reality, the code sent by Spaulding was to be a signal for the German submarine to surface at a prearranged destination at sea and make rendezvous with a small craft carrying the shipment of diamonds. Ocean and air patrols would be kept out of the area; if the order was questioned – and it was unlikely – the cover story of the underground defectors would be employed.

When the transfer at sea was made, the submarine would radio confirmation – Rhinemann's 'payment'. It would dive and start its journey back to Germany. Spaulding would then be cleared for takeoff to the United States.

These safeguards were the best either side could expect. Kendall was convinced he could sell the operation to Erich Rhinemann. He and Rhinemann possessed a certain objectivity lacking in the others.

Swanson did not dispute the similarity; it was another viable reason for Kendall's death.

The accountant would fly to Buenos Aires in a week and make the final arrangements with the German expatriot. Rhinemann would be made to understand that Spaulding was acting as an experienced courier, a custodian for the eccentric Eugene Lyons – a position Kendall admitted was desirable. But Spaulding was nothing else. He was not part of the diamond transfer; he knew nothing of the submarine. He would provide the codes necessary for the transfer, but he'd never know it. There was no way he could learn of it.

Airtight, ironclad: acceptable.

Swanson had read and reread Kendall's 'details'; he could not fault them. The ferret-like accountant had reduced an enormously complicated negotiation to a series of simple procedures and separate motives. In a way Kendall had created an extraordinary deception. Each step had a checkpoint, each move a countermove.

And Swanson would add the last deceit: David Spaulding would kill Erich Rhinemann.

Origin of command: instructions from Allied Central Intelligence. By the nature of Rhinemann's involvement, he was too great a liability to the German underground. The former man in Lisbon could employ whatever methods he thought best. Hire the killers, do it himself; whatever the situation called for. Just make sure it was done.

Spaulding would understand. The shadow world of agents and double agents had been his life for the past several years. David Spaulding – if his dossier was to be believed – would accept the order for what it was: a reasonable, professional solution.

If Spaulding was alive.

Oh, Christ! What had *happened*? Where was it? Lapess, Lajes. Some goddamned airfield in the Azores! Sabotage. Blown up on takeoff!

What the hell did it *mean*?

The driver swung off the highway onto the back Virginia road. They were fifteen minutes from the Fairfax compound; Swanson found himself sucking his lower lip between his teeth. He had actually bitten into the soft tissue; he could taste a trickle of blood.

'We have further information,' said Colonel Edmund Pace, standing in front of a photograph map frame. The map was the island of Terceira in the Azores. 'Spaulding's all right. Shaken up, of course. Minor sutures, bruises; nothing broken, though. I tell you he pulled off a miracle. Pilot, copilot, a crewman: all dead. Only survivors were Spaulding and a rear aerial gunner who probably won't make it.'

'Is he mobile? Spaulding?'

'Yes. Hollander and Ballantyne are with him now. I assumed you wanted him out . . .'

'Jesus, *yes*,' interrupted Swanson.

'I got him on a Newfoundland transfer. Unless you want to switch orders, a coastal patrol flight will pick him up there and bring him south. Mitchell Field.'

'When will he get in?'

'Late tonight, weather permitting. Otherwise, early morning. Shall I have him flown down here?'

Swanson hesitated. 'No . . . Have a doctor at Mitchell give him a thorough going-over. But keep him in New York. If he needs a few days' rest, put him up at a hotel. Otherwise, everything remains.'

'Well . . .' Pace seemed slightly annoyed with his superior. 'Someone's going to have to see him.'

'Why?'

'His papers. Everything we prepared went up with the plane. They're a packet of ashes.'

'Oh. Yes, of course. I didn't think about that.' Swanson walked away from Pace to the chair in front of the stark, plain desk. He sat down.

The colonel watched the brigadier. He was obviously concerned with Swanson's lack of focus, his inadequate concentration. 'We can prepare new ones easily enough, that's no problem.'

'Good. Do that, will you? Then have someone meet him at Mitchell and give them to him.'

'Okay ... But it's possible you may want to change your mind.' Pace crossed to his desk chair but remained standing.

'Why? About what?'

'Whatever it is ... The plane was sabotaged, I told you that. If you recall, I asked you to come out here because of an unexpected development.'

Swanson stared up at his subordinate. 'I've had a difficult week. And I've told *you* the gravity of this project. Now, don't play Fairfax games with me. I make no claims of expertise in your field. I asked only for assistance; ordered it, if you like. Say what you mean without the preamble, please.'

'I've tried to give you that assistance.' Pace's tone was rigidly polite. 'It's not easy, sir. And I've just bought you twelve hours to consider alternatives. That plane was blown up by the Haganah.'

'The *what?*'

Pace explained the Jewish organization operating out of Palestine. He watched Swanson closely as he did so.

'That's insane! It doesn't make sense! How do you *know?*'

'The first thing an inspection team does at the site of sabotage is to water down, pick over debris, look for evidence that might melt from the heat, or burn, if explosives are used. It's a preliminary check and it's done fast ... A Haganah medallion was found riveted to the tail assembly. They wanted full credit.'

'Good God! What did you say to the Azores people?'

'I bought you a day, general. I instructed Hollander to minimize any connection, keep it away from Spaulding. Frankly, to imply coincidence if the subject got out of hand. The Haganah is independent, fanatic. Most Zionist organizations won't touch it. They call it a group of savages.'

'How could it get out of hand?' Swanson was disturbed on another level.

'I'm sure you're aware that the Azores are under British control. An old Portuguese treaty gives them the right to military installations.'

'I know that,' said Swanson testily.

'The British found the medallion.'

'What will they do?'

'Think about it. Eventually make a report to Allied Central.'

'But you know about it *now.*'

'Hollander's a good man. He does favors; gets favors in return.'

Swanson got out of the chair and walked aimlessly around it. 'What do you think, Ed? Was it meant for Spaulding?' he looked at the colonel.

The expression on Pace's face let Swanson know that Pace was beginning to understand his anxiety. Not so much about the project – that was out of bounds and he accepted it – but that a fellow officer was forced to deal in an area he was out-of-sync with; territory he was not trained to cross. At such times a decent army man had sympathy.

'All I can give you are conjectures, very loose, not even good guesses . . . It could be Spaulding. And even if it was, it doesn't necessarily mean it's connected with *your* project.'

'What?'

'I don't know what Spaulding's field activities have been. Not specifically. And the Haganah is filled with psychopaths – deadly variety. They're about as rational as Julius Streicher's units. Spaulding may have had to kill a Portuguese or Spanish Jew. Or use one in a "cover trap". In a Catholic country that's all a Haganah cell would need . . . Or it could be someone else on the plane. An officer or crewman with an anti-Zionist relative, especially a *Jewish* anti-Zionist relative. I'd have to run a check . . . Unless you'd read the book, you couldn't possibly understand those kikes.'

Swanson remained silent for several moments. When he spoke he did so acknowledging Pace's attitude. 'Thank you . . . But it probably isn't any of those things, is it? I mean, Spanish Jews or "cover traps" or some pilot's uncle . . . it's Spaulding.'

'You don't *know* that. Speculate, sure; don't assume.'

'I can't understand *how*.' Swanson sat down again, thinking aloud, really. 'All things considered . . .' His thoughts drifted off into silence.

'May I make a suggestion?' Pace went to his chair. It was no time to talk down to a bewildered superior.

'By all means,' said Swanson, looking over at the colonel, his eyes conveying gratitude to this hard-nosed, confident Intelligence man.

'I'm not cleared for your project, let's face it, I don't want to be. It's a DW exercise, and that's where it belongs. I said a few minutes ago that you should consider alternatives . . . maybe you should. But *only* if you see a direct connection. I watched you and you didn't.'

'Because there isn't any.'

'You're not involved – and even I don't see how, considering what I *do* know from the probe and Johannesburg – with the concentration camps? Auschwitz? Belsen?'

'Not even remotely.'

Pace leaned forward, his elbows on the desk. 'Those are Haganah concerns. Along with the "Spanish Jews" and "cover traps". . . . Don't make any new decisions now, general. You'd be making them too fast, without supportive cause.'

'Sup*port* . . .' Swanson looked incredulous. 'A plane was blown up. Men were killed!'

'And a medallion could be planted on a tail assembly by anyone. It's quite possible you're being tested.'

'By *whom*?'

'I couldn't answer that. Warn Spaulding; it'll strike him as funny, he was *on* that aircraft. But let my man at Mitchell Field tell him there could be a recurrence; to be careful ... He's been there, general. He'll handle himself properly ... And in the meantime, may I also suggest you look for a replacement.'

'A replacement?'

'For Spaulding. If there *is* a recurrence, it could be successful. He'd be taken out.'

'You mean he'd be killed.'

'Yes.'

'What kind of world do you people live in?' asked Swanson softly.

'It's complicated,' said Pace.

15

December 29, 1943 – New York City

Spaulding watched the traffic below from the hotel window overlooking Fifth Avenue and Central Park. The Montgomery was one of those small, elegant hotels his parents had used while in New York, and there was a pleasant sense of nostalgia in his being there again. The old desk clerk had actually wept discreet tears while registering him. Spaulding had forgotten – fortunately he remembered before his signature was dry – that the old man years ago had taken him for walks in the park. Over a quarter of a century ago!

Walks in the park. Governesses. Chauffeurs standing in foyers, prepared to whisk his parents away to a train, a concert, a rehearsal. Music critics. Record company executives. Endless dinner parties where he'd make his usual 'appearance' before bed time and be prompted by his father to tell some guest at what age Mozart composed the Fortieth; dates and facts he was forced to memorize and which he gave not one goddamn about. Arguments. Hysterics over an inadequate conductor or a bad performance or a worse review.

Madness.

And always the figure of Aaron Mandel, soothing, placating – so often fatherly to his overbearing father while his mother faded, waiting in a secondary status that belied her natural strength.

And the quiet times. The Sundays – except for concert Sundays – when his parents would suddenly remember his existence and try to make up in one day the attention they thought they had allocated improperly to governesses, chauffeurs and nice, polite hotel managements. At these times, the quiet times, he had felt his father's honest yet artificial attempts; had wanted to tell him it was all right, he wasn't deprived. They didn't have to spend autumn days wandering around zoos and museums; the zoos and museums were much better in Europe, anyway. It wasn't necessary that he be taken to Coney Island or the beaches of New Jersey in summer. What were they, compared to the Lido or Costa del Santiago? But whenever they were in America, there was this parental compulsion to fit into a mold labeled 'An American Father and Mother'.

Sad, funny, inconsistent, impossible, really.

And for some buried reason, he had never come back to this small, elegant hotel during the later years. There was rarely a need, of course, but he could have made the effort; the management was genuinely fond of the Spaulding family. Now it seemed right, somehow. After the years away he wanted a secure base in a strange land, secure at least in memories.

Spaulding walked away from the window to the bed where the bellboy had placed his new suitcase with the new civilian clothes he had purchased at Rogers Peet. Everything, including the suitcase. Pace had had the foresight to send money with the major who had brought him duplicates of the papers destroyed in Terceira. He had to sign for the money, not for the papers; that amused him.

The major who met him at Mitchell Field – on the field – had escorted him to the base infirmary, where a bored army doctor pronounced him fit but 'run down'; had professionally criticized the sutures implanted by the British doctor in the Azores but saw no reason to change them; and suggested that David take two APCs every four hours and rest.

Caveat patient.

The courier-major had played a tune on the Fairfax piano and told him Field Division was still analysing the Lajes sabotage; it could have been aimed at him for misdeeds out of Lisbon. He should be careful and report any unusual incidents directly to Colonel Pace at Fairfax. Further, Spaulding was to commit the name of Brigadier General Alan Swanson, DW. Swanson was his source control and would make contact in a matter of days, ten at the outside.

Why call Pace then? Regarding any 'incidents'. Why not get in touch directly with this Swanson? Since he was the SC.

Pace's instructions, replied the major – until the brigadier took over; just simpler that way.

Or further concealment, thought David, remembering the clouded eyes of Paul Hollander, the Az-Am agent in Terceira.

Something was happening. The source control transfer was being handled in a very unorthodox manner. From the unsigned, high-priority codes received in Lisbon to the extraordinary command: out of strategy. From the mid-ocean delivery of papers from Az-Am agents who said they had to question him first, to the strange orders that had him reporting to two civilians in New York without prior briefing.

It was all like a hesitation waltz. It was either very professional or terribly amateur; really, he suspected, a combination of both. It would be interesting to meet this General Swanson. He had never heard of him.

He lay down on the hotel bed. He would rest for an hour and then shower and shave and see New York at night for the first time in over three years. See what the war had done to a Manhattan evening; it had done little or nothing to the daylight hours, from what he'd seen – only the posters. It would be good to have a woman tonight. But if it happened, he'd want it to be comfortable, without struggle or urgency. A happy coincidence would be just right; a likable, really likable interlude. On the other hand, he wasn't about to browse through a telephone directory to create one. Three years and nine months had passed since he last picked up a telephone in New York City. During that time he had learned to be wary of the changes taking place over a matter of days, to say nothing of three years and nine months.

And he recalled pleasantly how the Stateside transfers to the embassy in Lisbon often spoke of the easy accessibility of the women back home. Especially in Washington and New York, where the numbers and the absence of permanency worked in favor of one-night stands. Then he remembered, with a touch of amused resignation, that these same reports usually spoke of the irresistible magnetism of an officer's uniform, especially captain and over.

He had worn a uniform exactly three times in the past four years: at the Mayflower Hotel lounge with Ed Pace, the day he arrived in Portugal and the day he left Portugal.

He didn't even own one now.

His telephone rang and it startled him. Only Fairfax and, he assumed, this brigadier, Swanson, knew where he was. He had called the Montgomery from the Mitchell Field infirmary and secured the reservation; the major had said to take seventy-two hours. He needed the rest; no one would bother him. Now someone was bothering him.

'Hello?'

'*David!*' It was a girl's voice; low, cultivated at the Plaza. 'David *Spaulding!*'

'Who is this?' He wondered for a second if his just-released fantasies were playing tricks on reality.

'*Leslie*, darling! Leslie *Jenner*! My God, it must be nearly *five years!*'

Spaulding's mind raced. Leslie Jenner was part of the New York scene but not the radio world; she was the up-from-college crowd. Meetings under the clock at the Biltmore; late nights at LaRue; the cotillions – which he'd been invited to, not so much from social bloodlines as for the fact that he was the son of the concert Spauldings. Leslie was Miss Porter's, Finch and the Junior League.

Only her name had been changed to something else. She had married a boy from Yale. He didn't remember the name.

'Leslie, this is ... well, Jesus, a surprise. How did you know I was here?' Spaulding wasn't engaging in idle small talk.

'*Nothing* happens in New York that I don't know about! I have eyes and ears everywhere, darling! A veritable spy network!'

David Spaulding could feel the blood draining from his face; he didn't like the girl's joke. 'I'm serious, Leslie ... Only because I haven't called anyone. Not even Aaron. How did you find out?'

'If you must know, Cindy Bonner – she was Cindy Tottle, married Paul Bonner – Cindy was exchanging some dreary Christmas gifts for Paul at Rogers Peet and she *swore* she saw you trying on a suit. Well, you know Cindy! Just too shy for words...'

David *didn't* know Cindy. He couldn't even recall the name, much less a face. Leslie Jenner went on as he thought about that.

'. . . and so she ran to the nearest phone and called me. After all, darling, we *were* a major item!'

If a 'major item' described a couple of summer months of weekending at East Hampton and bedding the daughter of the house, then David had to agree. But he didn't subscribe to the definition; it had been damned transient, discreet and before the girl's very social marriage.

'I'd just as soon you kept that information from your husband . . .'

'Oh, *God*, you poor lamb! It's *Jenner*, darling, not Hawkwood! Didn't even keep the *name*. Damned if I would.'

That was it, thought David. She'd married a man named Hawkwood: Roger or Ralph; something like that. A football player, or was it tennis?

'I'm sorry. I didn't know . . .'

'Richard and I called it quits simply *centuries* ago. It was a *disaster*. The son-of-a-bitch couldn't even keep his hands off my best friends! He's in London now; air corps, but very hush-hush, I think. I'm sure the English girls are getting their fill of him . . . and I do mean fill! I *know*!'

There was a slight stirring in David's groin. Leslie Jenner was proffering an invitation.

'Well, they're allies,' said Spaulding humorously. 'But you didn't tell me, how did you find me here?'

'It took exactly four telephone calls, my lamb. I tried the usual: Commodore, Biltmore and the Waldorf; and then I remembered that your dad and mum always stopped off at the Montgomery. Very Old World, darling . . . I thought, with reservations simply *hell*, you might have thought of it.'

'You'd make a good detective, Leslie.'

'Only when the object of my detecting is worthwhile, lamb . . . We *did* have fun.'

'Yes, we did,' said Spaulding, his thoughts on an entirely different subject. 'And we can't let your memory prowess go to waste. Dinner?'

'If you hadn't asked, I would have *screamed*.'

'Shall I pick you up at your apartment? What's the address?'

Leslie hesitated a fraction of a moment. 'Let's meet at a restaurant. We'd never get out of here.'

An invitation, indeed.

David named a small Fifty-first Street café he remembered. It was on Park. 'At seven thirty? Eight?'

'Seven thirty's lovely, but not *there*, darling. It closed simply years ago. Why not the Gallery? It's on Forty-sixth. I'll make reservations; they know me.'

'Fine.'

'You poor lamb, you've been away so *long*. You don't know *anything*. I'll take you in tow.'

'I'd like that. Seven thirty, then.'

'Can't wait. And I promise not to cry.'

Spaulding replaced the telephone; he was bewildered – on several levels.

To begin with, a girl didn't call a former lover after nearly four war years without asking – especially in these times – where he'd been, how he was; at least the length of his stay in town. It wasn't natural, it denied curiosity in these curiosity-prone days.

Another reason was profoundly disturbing.

The last time his parents had been at the Montgomery was in 1934. And he had not returned since then. He'd met the girl in 1936; in October of 1936 in New Haven at the Yale Bowl. He remembered distinctly.

Leslie Jenner couldn't possibly know about the Montgomery Hotel. Not as it was related to his parents.

She was lying.

16

December 29, 1943 – New York City

The Gallery was exactly as David thought it would be: a lot of deep-red velvet with a generous sprinkling of palms in varying shapes and sizes, reflecting the soft-yellow pools of light from dozens of wall sconces far enough above the tables to make the menus unreadable. The clientele was equally predictable: young, rich, deliberately casual; a profusion of wrinkled eyebrows and crooked smiles and very bright teeth. The voices rose and subsided, words running together, the diction glossy.

Leslie Jenner was there when he arrived. She ran into his arms in front of the cloak room; she held him fiercely, in silence, for several minutes – or it seemed like minutes to Spaulding; at any rate, too long a time. When she tilted her head back, the tears had formed rivulets on her cheeks. The tears were genuine, but there was something – was it the tautness of her full mouth? the eyes themselves? – something artificial about the girl. Or was it him? The years away from places like the Gallery and girls like Leslie Jenner.

In all other respects she was as he remembered her. Perhaps older, certainly more sensual – the unmistakable look of experience. Her dark blonde hair was more a light brown now, her wide brown eyes had added subtlety to her innate provocativeness, her face was a touch lined but still sculptured, aristocratic. And he could feel her body against his; the memories were sharpened by it. Lithe, strong, full-breasted; a body that centered on sex. Shaped by it and for it.

'God, God, God! Oh, *David*!' She pressed her lips against his ear.

They went to their table; she held his hand firmly, releasing it only to light a cigarette, taking it back again. They talked rapidly. He wasn't sure she listened, but she nodded incessantly and wouldn't take her eyes off him. He repeated the simple outlines of his cover: Italy, minor wounds; they were letting him out to go back into an essential industry where he'd do more good than carrying a rifle. He wasn't sure how long he'd be in New York. (He was honest about that, he thought to himself. He had no idea how long he'd be in town; he wished he did know.) He was glad to see her again.

The dinner was a prelude to bed. They both knew it; neither bothered to conceal the excitement of reviving the most pleasant of experiences: young sex that was taken in shadows, beyond the reprimands of elders. Enjoyed more because it was prohibited, dangerous.

'Your apartment?' he asked.

'No, lamb. I share it with my aunt, Mum's younger sister. It's very chic these days to share an apartment; very patriotic.'

The reasoning escaped David. 'Then my place,' he said firmly.

'David?' Leslie squeezed his hand and paused before speaking. 'Those old family retainers who run the Montgomery, they know so many in our crowd. For instance, the Allcotts have a suite there, so do the Dewhursts . . . I have a key to Peggy Webster's place in the Village. Remember Peggy? You were at their wedding. Jack Webster? You know Jack. He's in the navy; she went out to see him in San Diego. Let's go to Peggy's place.'

Spaulding watched the girl closely. He hadn't forgotten her odd behavior on the telephone, her lie about the old hotel and his parents. Yet it was possible that his imagination was overworking – the years in Lisbon made one cautious. There could be explanations, memory lapses on his part; but now he was as curious as he was stimulated.

He was very curious. Very stimulated.

'Peggy's place,' he said.

If there was anything beyond the sexual objective, it escaped him.

Their coats off, Leslie made drinks in the kitchen while David bunched newspapers beneath the fireplace grill and watched the kindling catch.

Leslie stood in the kitchen doorway looking down at him separating the logs, creating an airflow. She held their drinks and smiled. 'In two days it's New Year's Eve. We'll jump and call this ours. Our New Year's. The start of many, I hope.'

'Of many,' he replied, standing up and going to her. He took both glasses, not the one extended. 'I'll put them over here.' He carried them to the coffee table in front of the small couch that faced the fireplace. He turned rapidly, politely to watch her eyes. She wasn't looking at the glasses. Or his placement of them.

Instead, she approached the fire and removed her blouse. She dropped it on the floor and turned around, her large breasts accentuated by a tight, transparent brassiere that had webbed stitching at the tips.

'Take off your shirt, David.'

He did so and came to her. She winced at his bandages and gently touched them with her fingers. She pressed herself against him, her pelvis firm against his thighs, moving laterally, expertly. He reached around her back and undid the hasps of the brassiere; she hunched slightly as he pulled it away; then she turned, arching her breasts upward into his flesh. He cupped her left breast with his right hand; she reached down, stepping partially away, and undid his trousers.

'The drinks can wait, David. It's New Year's Eve. Ours, anyway.'

Still holding her breast, he put his lips to her eyes, her ears. She felt him and moaned.

'Here, David,' she said 'Right here on the floor.' She sank to her knees, her skirt pulled up to her thighs, the tops of her stockings visible.

He lay down beside her and they kissed.

'I remember,' he whispered with a gentle laugh. 'The first time; the cottage by the boathouse. The floor. I remember.'

'I wondered if you would. I've never forgotten.'

It was only one forty-five in the morning when he took her home. They had made love twice, drunk a great deal of Jack and Peggy Webster's good whisky and spoken of the 'old days' mostly. Leslie had no inhibitions regarding her marriage. Richard Hawkwood, ex-husband, was simply not a man who could sustain a permanent relationship. He was a sexual glutton as long as the sex was spread around; not much otherwise. He was also a failure – as much as his family would allow – in the business world. Hawkwood was a man brought up to enjoy fifty thousand a year with the ability to make, perhaps, six.

The war was created, she felt, for men like Richard. They would excel in it, as her ex-husband had done. He should 'go down in flames' somewhere, exiting brilliantly rather than returning to the frustrations of civilian inadequacy. Spaulding thought that was harsh; she claimed she was being considerate. And they laughed and made love:

Throughout the evening David kept alert, waiting for her to say something, reveal something, ask something unusual. Anything to clarify – if nothing else – the reasons behind her earlier lies about finding him. There was nothing.

He asked her again, claiming incredulity that she would remember his parents and the Montgomery. She stuck to her infallible memory, adding only that 'love makes any search more thorough'.

She was lying again; he knew that. What they had was not love.

She left him in the taxi; she didn't want him to come up. Her aunt would be asleep; it was better this way.

They'd meet again tomorrow. At the Websters'. Ten o'clock in the evening; she had a dinner date she'd get rid of early. And she'd break her engagement for the real New Year's Eve. They'd have the whole day to themselves.

As the doorman let her in and the taxi started up toward Fifth Avenue, he thought for the first time that Fairfax had him beginning his assignment at Meridian Aircraft the day after tomorrow. New Year's Eve. He expected it would be a half-day.

It was strange. New Year's Eve. Christmas.

He hadn't even thought about Christmas. He'd remembered to send his parents' gifts to Santiago, but he'd done that before his trip to the north country. To Basque and Navarre.

Christmas had no meaning. The Santa Clauses ringing their clinking bells on the New York streets, the decorations in the store windows – none had meaning for him.

He was sad about that. He had always enjoyed the holidays.

David paid the driver, said hello to the Montgomery night clerk and took the elevator to his floor. He got off and approached his door. Automatically, because his eyes were tired, he flipped his finger above the Do Not Disturb sign beneath the lock.

Then he felt the wood and looked down, punching his cigarette lighter for better vision.

The field thread was gone.

Second nature and the instructions from Fairfax to stay alert had caused him to 'thread' his hotel room. Strands of invisible tan and black silk placed in a half-dozen locations, that if missing or broken meant a trespasser.

He carried no weapon and he could not know if anyone was still inside.

He returned to the elevator and pushed the button. He asked the operator if he had a passkey; his door wouldn't open. The man did not; he was taken to the lobby.

The night clerk obliged, ordering the elevator operator to remain at the desk while he went to the aid of Mr Spaulding and his difficult lock.

As the two men walked out of the elevator and down the corridor, Spaulding heard the distinct sound of a latch being turned, snapped shut quietly but unmistakably. He rapidly turned his head in both directions, up and down corridor, trying to locate the origin of the sound.

Nothing but closed hotel doors.

The desk clerk had no trouble opening the door. He had more difficulty understanding Mr Spaulding's arm around his shoulder ushering him into the single room with him.

David looked around quickly. The bathroom and closet doors were open as he had left them. There were no other places of concealment. He released the desk clerk and tipped him with a five-dollar bill.

'Thank you very much. I'm embarrassed; I'm afraid I had too much to drink.'

'Not at all, sir. *Thank* you, sir.' The man left, pulling the door shut behind him.

David rapidly began his thread check. In the closet: his jacket breast pocket, leafed out, centered.

No thread.

The bureau: the first and third drawers, inserted.

Both threads out of place. The first inside on top of a handkerchief; the second, wedged between shirts.

The bed: laterally placed along the spread in line with the pattern.

Nowhere. Nothing.

He went to his suitcase, which lay on a luggage rack by the window. He knelt down and inspected the right lock; the thread had been clamped inside the metal hasp up under the tiny hinge. If the suitcase was opened, it had to break.

It was broken, only one half remaining.

The inside of the suitcase housed a single strand at the rear, crossing the elastic flap three fingers from the left side.

It was gone.

David stood up. He crossed to the bedside table and reached underneath for the telephone directory. There was no point in delay; what advantage he had was in surprise. His room had been searched professionally; he was not expected to know.

He would get Leslie Jenner's number, return to her apartment house and find a telephone booth near the entrance – with luck, in sight of it. He would then call her, tell her some wildly incredible story about anything and ask to see her. No mention of the search, nothing of his borne-out suspicions. Throw her off completely and listen acutely to her reaction. If she agreed to see him, all well and good. If she didn't, he'd keep her apartment under surveillance throughout the night, if necessary.

Leslie Jenner had a story to tell and he'd find out what it was. The man in Lisbon had not spent three years in the north provinces without gaining expertise.

There was no Jenner at the address of the apartment building.

There were six Jenners listed in Manhattan.

One by one he gave the hotel switchboard the numbers, and one by one – in varying stages of sleep and anger – the replies were the same.

No Leslie Jenner. None known.

Spaulding hung up. He'd been sitting on the bed; he got up and walked around the room.

He would go to the apartment building and ask the doorman. It was possible the apartment was in the aunt's name but it wasn't plausible. Leslie Jenner would put her name and number in the Yellow Pages, if she could; for her the telephone was an instrument of existence, not convenience. And if he went to the apartment and started asking questions, he would be announcing unreasonable concern. He wasn't prepared to do that.

Who was the girl at Rogers Peet? The one exchanging Christmas gifts. Cynthia? Cindy? . . . Cindy. Cindy Tuttle . . . Tottle. But not Tottle . . . Bonner. Married to Paul Bonner, exchanging 'dreary gifts for Paul'.

He crossed to the bed and picked up the telephone directory.

Paul Bonner was listed: 480 Park Avenue. The address was appropriate. He gave the number to the switchboard.

The voice of a girl more asleep than awake answered.

'Yes? . . . Hello?'

'Mrs Bonner?'

'Yes. What is it? This is Mrs Bonner.'

'I'm David Spaulding. You saw me this afternoon at Rogers Peet; you were exchanging gifts for your husband and I was buying a suit . . . Forgive me for disturbing you but it's important. I had dinner with Leslie . . . Leslie Jenner; you called her. I just left her at her apartment; we were to meet tomorrow and now I find that I may not be able to. It's foolish but I forgot to get her telephone number, and I can't find it in the book. I wondered . . .'

'Mr Spaulding.' The girl interrupted him, her tone sharp, no longer blurred with sleep. 'If this is a joke, I think it's in bad taste. I *do* remember your name . . . I did *not* see you this afternoon and I wasn't exchanging . . . I wasn't in Rogers Peet. My husband was killed four months ago. In Sicily . . . I haven't spoken to Leslie Jenner . . . Hawkwood, I think now . . . in over a year. She moved to California, Pasadena, I believe . . . We haven't been in touch. Nor is it likely we would be.'

David heard the abrupt click of the broken connection.

17

December 31, 1943 – New York City

It was the morning of New Year's Eve.

His first day of 'employment' for Meridian Aircraft, Blueprint Division.

He had stayed most of the previous day in his hotel room, going out briefly for lunch and magazines, dinner through room service, and finally a pointless taxi to Greenwich Village, where he knew he would not find Leslie Jenner at ten o'clock.

He had remained confined for two reasons. The first was a confirmation of the Mitchell Field doctor's diagnosis: he was exhausted. The second reason was equally important. Fairfax was running checks on Leslie Jenner Hawkwood, Cindy Tottle Bonner, and a naval officer named Jack or John Webster, whose wife was conveniently in California. David wanted this data before progressing further, and Ed Pace had promised to be as thorough as forty-eight hours allowed.

Spaulding had been struck by Cindy Bonner's words concerning Leslie Jenner.

She moved to California. Pasadena, I believe . . .

And a routine phone call to the Greenwich Village apartment's superintendent had confirmed that, indeed, the Websters *did* live there; the husband was in the navy, the wife was visiting him someplace in California. The superintendent was holding the mail.

Someplace in California.

She moved to California . . .

Was there a connection? Or simple coincidence?

Spaulding looked at his watch. It was eight o'clock. The morning of New Year's Eve. Tomorrow would be 1944.

This morning, however, he was to report to one Walter Kendall and one Eugene Lyons at Meridian's temporary offices on Thirty-eighth Street.

Why would one of the largest aircraft companies in the United States have 'temporary' offices?

The telephone rang. David reached for it.

'Spaulding?'

'Hello, Ed.'

816

'I got what I could. It doesn't make a hell of a lot of sense. To begin with, there's no record of a divorce between the Hawkwoods. And he *is* in England. Eighth Air Force, but nothing classified. He's a pilot, Tenth Bomber Command down in Surrey.'

'What about her living in California?'

'Eighteen months ago she left New York and moved in with an aunt in Pasadena. Very rich aunt, married to a man named Goldsmith; he's a banker – Social Register, polo set. From what we've learned – and it's sketchy – she just likes California.'

'Okay. What about this Webster?'

'Checks out. He's a gunner officer on the *Saratoga*. It pulled into San Diego for combat repairs. It's scheduled for sea duty in two weeks, and the date holds. Until then there are a lot of forty-eights, seventy-twos; no extended leaves, though. The wife Margaret joined her lieutenant a couple of days ago. She's at the Greenbrier Hotel.'

'Anything on the Bonners?'

'Only what you know, except that he was a bona fide hero. Posthumous Silver Star, Infantry. Killed on a scout patrol covering an ambush evacuation. Sicily invasion.'

'And that's it?'

'That's it. Obviously they all know each other, but I can't find anything to relate to your DW assignment.'

'But you're not the control, Ed. You said you didn't know what the assignment was.'

'True. But from the fragments I *do* know about, I can't find anything.'

'My room was searched. I'm not mistaken about that.'

'Maybe theft. Rich soldier in a rich hotel, home from an extended tour. Could be someone figured you were carrying a lot of back pay, discharge money.'

'I doubt that. It was too pro.'

'A lot of pros work those hotels. They wait for guys to start off on an alcoholic evening and . . .'

Spaulding interrupted. 'I want to follow up something.'

'What?'

'The Bonner girl said "it wasn't likely" she'd be in touch with Leslie Jenner, and she wasn't kidding. That's an odd thing to say, isn't it? I'd like to know why she said it.'

'Go ahead. It was your hotel room, not mine . . . You know what I think? And I've thought about it; I've had to.'

'What?'

'That New York crowd plays a fast game of musical beds. Now, you didn't elaborate, but isn't it logical the lady was in New York for a few days, perhaps saw you herself, or knew someone who had, and figured, why not? I mean, what the hell, she's headed back to California; probably never see you again . . .'

'No, it's not logical. She was too complicated; she didn't have to be. She was keeping me away from the hotel.'

'Well, you were there . . .'

'I certainly was. You know, it's funny. According to your major at Mitchell Field, you think the Azores thing was directed at me . . .'

'I said *might* be,' interjected Pace.

'And I don't. Yet here I am, convinced the other night was, and *you* don't. Maybe we're both getting tired.'

'Maybe I'm also concerned for your source control. This Swanson, he's very nervous; this isn't his ball park. I don't think he can take many more complications.'

'Then let's not give him any. Not now. I'll know if I should.'

Spaulding watched the disheveled accountant as he outlined the Buenos Aires operation. He had never met anyone quite like Walter Kendall. The man was positively unclean. His body odor was only partially disguised by liberal doses of bay rum. His shirt collar was dirty, his suit unpressed, and David was fascinated to watch the man breathe simultaneously through his mouth and nostrils. The agent in Terceira had said Eugene Lyons was 'odd'; if this Kendall was 'normal', he couldn't wait to meet the scientist.

The Buenos Aires operation seemed simple enough, far less complicated than most of the Lisbon work. So simple, in fact, that it angered him to think he had been removed from Lisbon for it. Had anyone bothered to fill him in a few weeks ago, he could have saved Washington a lot of planning, and probably money. He had been dealing with the German underground since that organization had consolidated its diverse factions and become an effective force. If this Erich Rhinemann was capable of buying the designs, removing them from the Peenemünde complex, he – the man in Lisbon – could have gotten them out of the country. Probably with more security than trying to slip them out of North Sea or Channel ports. Those ports were clamped tight, obsessively patrolled. Had they not been, much of his own work would have been unnecessary. The only really remarkable aspect of the operation was that Rhinemann *could* get blueprints – on *anything* – related to Peenemünde. That *was* extraordinary. Peenemünde was a concrete and steel vault buried in the earth. With the most complex system of safeguards and back-ups ever devised. It would be easier to get a man out – for any number of invented reasons – than to remove a single page of paper.

Further, Peenemünde kept its laboratories separate, vital stages coordinated by only a handful of elite scientific personnel under Gestapo check. In Buenos Aires terms, this meant that Erich Rhinemann was able to (1) reach and buy diverse laboratory heads in a systematic order; (2) circumvent or buy (impossible) the Gestapo; or (3) enlist the cooperation of those handful of scientists who crossed laboratory lines.

David's experience led him to disqualify the last two possibilities; there was too much room for betrayal. Rhinemann must have concentrated on the laboratory heads; that was dangerous enough but more feasible.

As Kendall talked, David decided to keep his conclusions to himself. He would ask several questions, one or two of which he really wanted answered, but he would not form a partnership with Walter Kendall at this time. It was an easy decision to make. Kendall was one of the least likable men he'd ever met.

'Is there any particular reason why the designs have to be delivered in stages?' Spaulding asked.

'They may not be. But Rhinemann's smuggling them out section by section. Everybody's got a schedule; he says it's safer that way. From his projections, we figure a period of a week.'

'All right, that makes sense ... And this Lyons fellow can authenticate them?'

'There's no one better. I'll get to him in a few minutes; there are a couple of things you'll have to know. Once in Argentina, he's your property.'

'That sounds ominous.'

'You can handle him. You'll have help ... The point is, as soon as he's cleared those blueprints, you send the codes and Rhinemann gets paid. Not before.'

'I don't understand. Why so complicated? If they check out, why not pay him off in Buenos Aires?'

'He doesn't want that money in an Argentine bank.'

'It must be a bundle.'

'It is.'

'From what little I know of this Rhinemann, isn't it unusual for him to be working with the German underground?'

'He's a Jew.'

'Don't tell any graduates of Auschwitz. They won't believe you.'

'War makes necessary relationships. Look at us. We're working with the Reds. Same thing: common goals, forget the disagreements.'

'In this case, that's a little cold-blooded.'

'Their problem, not ours.'

'I won't pursue it ... One obvious question. Since I'm on my way to Buenos Aires, the embassy, why this stop in New York? Wouldn't it have been easier to just rotate from Lisbon to Argentina?'

'A last-minute decision, I'm afraid. Awkward, huh?'

'Not too smooth. Am I on a transfer list?'

'A what?'

'Foreign Service transfer sheet. State Department. Military attaché.'

'I don't know. Why?'

'I'd like to find out if it's common knowledge that I left Lisbon. Or could be common knowledge. I didn't think it was supposed to be.'

'Then it wasn't. *Why?*'

'So I know how to behave, that's all.'

'We thought you should spend a few days getting familiar with everything. Meet Lyons, me; go over the schedule. What we're after, that sort of thing.'

'Very considerate.' David saw the questioning look on Kendall's face. 'No,

I mean that. So often we get thrown field problems knowing too little background. I've done it to men myself . . . Then this discharge, the combat in Italy, they're the cover for my Lisbon activities? For New York only.'

'Yeah, I guess that's right.' Kendall, who'd been sitting on the edge of his desk, got up and walked around to his chair.

'How far am I to carry it?'

'Carry what?' Kendall avoided looking at David, who was leaning forward on an office couch.

'The cover. The papers mention Fifth Army – that's Clark; Thirty-Fourth Division, One Hundred and Twelfth Battalion, et cetera. Should I bone up? I don't know much about the Italian Theater. Apparently I got hit beyond Salerno; are there circumstances?'

'That's army stuff. As far as I'm concerned you'll be here five, six days, then Swanson will see you and send you down to Buenos Aires.'

'All right, I'll wait for General Swanson.' David realized there was no point in pursuing G-2 rituals with Kendall . . . Part professional, part amateur. The hesitation waltz.

'Until you leave you'll spend whatever time you think is necessary with Lyons. In his office.'

'Fine. I'd like to meet him.' David stood up.

'Sit down, he's not here today. Nobody's here today but the receptionist. Till one o'clock. It's New Year's Eve.' Kendall slumped into his chair and took out a cigarette, which he squeezed. 'I've got to tell you about Lyons.'

'All right.' David returned to the couch.

'He's a drunk. He spent four years in jail, in a penitentiary. He can hardly talk because his throat got burned out with raw alcohol . . . He's also the smartest son-of-a-bitch in aerophysics.'

Spaulding stared at Kendall without replying for several moments. When he did speak, he made no attempt to conceal his shock. 'That's kind of a contradictory recommendation, isn't it?'

'I said he's smart.'

'So are half the lunatics in Bellevue. Can he *function*? Since he's going to be my "property" – as you put it – I'd like to know what the hell you've given me. And *why*, not incidentally.'

'He's the best.'

'That doesn't answer my question. Questions.'

'You're a soldier. You take orders.'

'I give them, too. Don't start that way.'

'All right . . . Okay. You're entitled, I guess.'

'I'd say so.'

'Eugene Lyons wrote the book on physical aerodynamics; he was the youngest full professor at the Massachusetts Institute of Technology. Maybe he was too young; he went downhill fast. Bum marriage, a lot of drinking, a lot of debts; the debts did it, they usually do. That and too many brains no one wants to pay for.'

'Did what?'

'He went out of his skull, a week's bender. When he woke up in a South Side Boston hotel room, the girl he was with was dead. He'd beaten her to death . . . She was a whore so nobody cared too much; still, he did it. They called it unpremeditated murder and MIT got him a good lawyer. He served four years, got out and nobody would hire him, wouldn't touch him . . . That was 1936. He gave up; joined the skid row bums. I mean he really joined them.' Kendall paused and grinned.

David was disturbed by the accountant's smile; there was nothing funny in the story. 'Obviously he didn't stay there.' It was all he could think to say.

'Did for damn near three years. Got his throat burned out right down on Houston Street.'

'That's very sad.'

'Best thing that happened to him. In the hospital ward they took his history and a doctor got interested. He was shipped off to the goddamned CCC, was reasonably rehabilitated, and what with the war coming he got into defence work.'

'Then he's all right now.' Spaulding made the statement positively. Again, it was all he could think to say.

'You don't clean out a man like that overnight. Or in a couple of years . . . He has lapses, falls into the booze barrel now and then. Since working on classified stuff he's cooped up with his own personal wardens. For instance, here in New York he's got a room at St Luke's Hospital. He's taken back and forth just like your socialite drunks . . . In California, Lockheed's got him in a garden apartment with male nurses round the clock, when he's away from the plants. Actually, he's got it pretty good.'

'He must be valuable. That's a lot of trouble . . .'

'I told you,' interrupted Kendall. 'He's *the best*. He's just got to be watched.'

'What happens when he's on his own? I mean, I've known alcoholics; they can slip away, often ingeniously.'

'That's no problem. He'll get liquor – when he wants it; he'll be ingenious about that. But he doesn't go outside by himself. He won't go where there are any people, if you know what I mean.'

'I'm not sure I do.'

'He doesn't talk. The best he can manage is a hoarse whisper; remember, his throat was boiled out. He stays away from people . . . Which is fine. When he's not drinking – which is most of the time – he's reading and working. He'll spend days in a laboratory stone sober and never go outside. It's just fine.'

'How does he communicate? In the lab? In a meeting?'

'Pad and pencil, a few whispers, his hands. Mostly a pad and pencil. It's just numbers, equations, diagrams. That's his language.'

'His entire language?'

'That's right . . . If you're thinking about holding a conversation with him, forget it. He hasn't had a conversation with anyone in ten years.'

18

Spaulding hurried down Madison Avenue to the northeast corner of B. Altman's. There was a light snow falling; taxis rushed past the few pedestrians signaling in the middle of the block. The better fares were at the department store's entrance, carrying last-minute purchases for New Year's Eve. People who shopped at Altman's on the afternoon of New Year's Eve were prime passengers. Why waste gas on less?

David found himself walking faster than he had reason to; he wasn't going anywhere, to any specific place that required his presence at a specific time; he was getting away from Walter Kendall as fast as he could.

Kendall had finished his briefing on Eugene Lyons with the statement that 'two hulks' would accompany the scientist to Buenos Aires. There'd be no liquor for the hermit-mute with his throat burned out; the male nurses carried 'horse pills' at all times. Eugene Lyons, with no drink available, would spend hours over the work problems. Why not? He didn't do anything *else*. No conversations, David mused.

David turned down Kendall's offer of lunch on the pretext of looking up family friends. After all, it had been over three years . . . He'd be in the office on January 2.

The truth was that Spaulding just wanted to get away from the man. And there was another reason: Leslie Jenner Hawkwood.

He didn't know where he'd begin, but he had to begin quickly. He had roughly a week to learn the story behind that incredible evening two nights ago. The beginning would include a widow named Bonner, that much he knew.

Perhaps Aaron Mandel could help him.

He took a dollar bill from his pocket and approached the doorman in front of Altman's. A taxi was found in less than a minute.

The ride uptown was made to the accompanying loquaciousness of the driver, who seemed to have an opinion on most any subject. David found the man annoying; he wanted to think and it was difficult. Then suddenly he was grateful to him.

'I was gonna catch the New Year's Eve crowds, like up at the Plaza, you

822

know what I mean? There's big tips over at those war relief things. But the wife said no. She said come home, drink a little wine, pray to God our boy gets through the year. Now, I gotta. I mean if anything happened, I'd figure it was the tips I made New Year's Eve. Superstitions! What the hell, the kid's a typist in Fort Dix.'

David had forgotten the obvious. No, not forgotten; he just hadn't considered the possibilities because they did not relate to him. Or he to them. He was in New York. On New Year's Eve. And that meant parties, dances, charity balls and an infinite variety of war-created celebrations in a dozen ballrooms and scores of townhouses.

Mrs Paul Bonner would be at one of those places, at one of those parties. It had been four months since her husband had been killed. It was sufficient mourning under the circumstances, for the times. Friends – other women like Leslie Jenner, but of course not Leslie Jenner – would make that clear to her. It was the way social Manhattan behaved. And quite reasonable, all things considered.

It shouldn't be too difficult to find out where she was going. And if he found her, he'd find others ... it was a place to start.

He tipped the driver and walked rapidly into the Montgomery lobby.

'Oh, Mr Spaulding!' The old desk clerk's voice echoed in the marble enclosure. 'There's a message for you.'

He crossed to the counter. 'Thank you.' He unfolded the paper; Mr Fairfax had telephoned. Would he return the call as soon as possible?

Ed Pace wanted to reach him.

The thread was intact under the door lock. He entered his room and went directly to the telephone.

'We got something in on the Hawkwood girl,' Pace said. 'Thought you'd want to know.'

'What is it?' Why, oh *why*, did Pace *always* start conversations like that? Did he expect him to say, no, I don't want to know anything, and hang up?

'It fits in, I'm afraid, with my opinion of the other night. Your antenna's been working overtime.'

'For Christ's sake, Ed, I'll pin a medal on you whenever you like. What *is* it?'

'She plays around. She's got a wide sex life in the Los Angeles area. Discreet but busy. A high-class whore, if I don't offend you.'

'You don't offend me. What's the source?'

'Several brother officers to begin with; navy and air force. Then some of the movie people, actors and a couple of studio executives. And the social-industrial crowd: Lockheed, Sperry Rand. She's not the most welcome guest at the Santa Monica Yacht Club.'

'Is there a G-2 pattern?'

'First thing we looked for. Negative. No classified personnel in her bed. Just rank: military and civilian. And she *is* in New York. Careful inquiry says she went back to visit her parents for Christmas.'

'There are no Jenners listed in the phone book who've ever heard of her.'

'In Bernardsville, New Jersey?'

'No,' said David wearily. 'Manhattan. You *did* say New York.'

'Try Bernardsville. If you want to find her. But don't hand in any expense vouchers; you're not on a courier run in the north country.'

'No. Bernardsville is hunt country.'

'What?'

'Very social territory. Stables and stirrup cups ... Thanks, Ed. You just saved me a lot of work.'

'Think nothing of it. All you've had is the conduit center of Allied Intelligence solving the problems of your sex life. We try to please our employees.'

'I promise to re-enlist when it's all over. Thanks again.'

'Dave?'

'Yes?'

'I'm not cleared for the Swanson job, so no specifics, but how does it strike you?'

'I'll be damned if I know why you're *not* cleared. It's a simple purchase being handled by some oddballs – at least one ... no, two that I know about. The one I've met is a winner. It seems to me they've complicated the deal, but that's because they're new at it ... We could have done it better.'

'Have you met Swanson?'

'Not yet. After the holidays, I'm told. What the hell, we wouldn't want to interfere with the brigadier's Christmas vacation. School doesn't start until the first week in January.'

Pace laughed on the other end of the line. 'Happy New Year, Dave.'

'The same, Ed. And thanks.'

Spaulding replaced the receiver. He looked at his watch, it was one fifteen. He could requisition an army vehicle somewhere, he supposed, or borrow a car from Aaron Mandel. Bernardsville was about an hour outside New York, west of the Oranges, if he remembered correctly. It might be best to take Leslie Jenner by surprise, giving her no chance to run. On the other hand, on the premise he had considered before Pace's call, Leslie was probably in New York, preparing for the New Year's Eve she'd promised him. Somewhere, someplace. In an apartment or a brownstone or a hotel room like his own.

Spaulding wondered for a moment whether Pace had a point. Was he trying to find Leslie for reasons quite apart from his suspicions? The lies, the search ... It was possible. Why not? But a two- to three-hour drive to west Jersey and back would bring him no closer to either objective, investigatory or Freudian. If she wasn't there.

He asked the Montgomery switchboard to get him the number of the Jenner residence in Bernardsville, New Jersey. Not to place the call, just get the telephone number. And the address. Then he called Aaron Mandel.

He had postponed it for as long as he could; Aaron would be filled with tears and questions and offers of anything under the Manhattan sun and moon. Ed Pace told him he had interviewed the old concert manager four years ago before approaching David for Lisbon; that would mean he could reasonably avoid any lengthy discussions about his work.

And Aaron might be able to help him, should he need the old man's particular kind of assistance. Mandel's New York contacts were damn near inexhaustible. David would know more after he reached Bernardsville; and it would be less awkward to have made his duty call to Aaron before asking favors.

At first Spaulding thought the old man would have a coronary over the telephone. Aaron's voice choked, conveying his shock, his concern . . . and his love. The questions came faster than David could answer them; his mother, his father, his own well-being.

Mandel did not ask him about his work, but neither would he be satisfied that David was as healthy as he claimed. Aaron insisted on a meeting, if not this evening then certainly tomorrow.

David agreed. In the morning, late morning. They would have a drink together, perhaps a light lunch; welcome the New Year together.

'God be praised. You are well. You'll come around tomorrow?'

'I promise,' David said.

'And you've never broken a promise to me.'

'I won't. Tomorrow. And Aaron . . .'

'Yes?'

'It's possible I may need to find someone tonight. I'm not sure where to look but probably among the Social Register crowd. How are your Park Avenue connections?'

The old man chuckled in the quiet, good-humored, slightly arrogant way David remembered so well. 'I'm the only Jew with a Torah stand in St John the Divine. Everybody wants an artist – for nothing, of course. Red Cross, green cross; debutantes for war bandages, dances for fancy-sounding French medal winners. You name it, Mandel's on the hook for it. I got three coloraturas, two pianists and five Broadway baritones making appearances for "our boys" tonight. All on the Upper East Side.'

'I may call you in a little while. Will you still be at the office?'

'Where else? For soldiers and concert managers, when are the holidays?'

'You haven't changed.'

'The main thing is that you're well . . .'

No sooner had David hung up the phone than it rang.

'I have the telephone number and the address of your party in Bernardsville, Mr Spaulding.'

'May I have them, please?'

The operator gave him the information and he wrote it down on the ever-present stationery next to the phone.

'Shall I put the call through, sir?'

David hesitated, then said, 'Yes, please. I'll stay on the line. Ask for a Mrs Hawkwood, please.'

'Mrs Hawkwood. Very well, sir. But I can call you back when I have the party.'

'I'd rather stay on an open circuit . . .' David caught himself, but not in time. The blunder was minor but confirmed by the operator. She replied in a knowing voice.

'Of course, Mr Spaulding. I assume if someone other than Mrs Hawkwood answers, you'll wish to terminate the call?'

'I'll let you know.'

The operator, now part of some sexual conspiracy, acted her role with firm efficiency. She dialed the outside operator and in moments a phone could be heard ringing in Bernardsville, New Jersey. A woman answered; it was not Leslie.

'Mrs Hawkwood, please.'

'Mrs . . .' The voice on the Bernardsville line seemed hesitant.

'Mrs Hawkwood, please. Long distance calling,' said the Montgomery operator, as if she were from the telephone company, expediting a person-to-person call.

'Mrs Hawkwood isn't here, operator.'

'Can you tell me what time she's expected, please?'

'What time? Good heavens, she's not expected. At least, I didn't think she was . . .'

Not fazed, the Montgomery employee continued, interrupting politely. 'Do you have a number where Mrs Hawkwood can be reached, please?'

'Well . . .' The voice in Bernardsville was now bewildered. 'I suppose in California . . .'

David knew it was time to intercede. 'I'll speak to the party on the line, operator.'

'Very well, sir.' There was a *ther-ump* sound indicating the switchboard's disengagement from the circuit.

'Mrs Jenner?'

'Yes, this is Mrs Jenner,' answered Bernardsville, obviously relieved with the more familiar name.

'My name is David Spaulding, I'm a friend of Leslie's and . . .' *Jesus!* He'd forgotten the husband's first name. '. . . Captain Hawkwood's. I was given this number . . .'

'Well, *David Spaulding!* How are you, dear? This is Madge Jenner, you silly boy! Good heavens, it must be eight, ten years ago. How's your father and mother? I hear they're living in London. So very brave!'

Christ! thought Spaulding, it never occurred to him that Leslie's mother would remember two East Hampton months almost a decade ago. 'Oh, Mrs Jenner . . . They're fine. I'm sorry to disturb you . . .'

'You could never disturb us, you dear boy. We're just a couple of old stablehands out here. James has doubled our colors; no one wants to keep horses anymore . . . You thought Leslie was here?'

'Yes, that's what I was told.'

'I'm sorry to say she's not. To be quite frank, we rarely hear from her. She moved to California, you know.'

'Yes, with her aunt.'

'Only half-aunt, dear. My stepsister; we've not gotten along too well, I'm afraid. She married a Jew. He calls himself Goldsmith – hardly a disguise for Goldberg or Goldstein, is it? We're convinced he's in the black market and all that profiteering, if you know what I mean.'

'Oh? Yes, I see . . . Then Leslie didn't come East to visit you for Christmas?'

'Good heavens, no! She barely managed to send us a card . . .'

He was tempted to call Ed Pace in Fairfax; inform the Intelligence head that California G-2 had come up with a Bernardsville zero. But there was no point. Leslie Jenner Hawkwood was in New York.

He had to find out why.

He called Mandel back and gave him two names: Leslie's and Cindy Tottle Bonner, widow of Paul Bonner, hero. Without saying so, David indicated that his curiosity might well be more professional than personal. Mandel did not question; he went to work.

Spaulding realized that he could easily phone Cindy Bonner, apologize and ask to see her. But he couldn't risk her turning him down; which she probably would do in light of the crude telephone call he had placed two nights ago. There simply wasn't the time. He'd have to see her, trust the personal contact.

And even then she might not be able to tell him anything. Yet there were certain instincts one developed and came to recognize. Inverted, convoluted, irrational . . . Atavistic.

Twenty minutes passed; it was a quarter to three. His telephone rang.

'David?'

'Aaron.'

'This Hawkwood lady, there's absolutely nothing. Everyone says she moved to California and nobody's heard a word . . . Mrs Paul Bonner: there's a private party tonight, on Sixty-second Street, name of Warfield. Number 212.'

'Thanks. I'll wait outside and crash it with my best manners.'

'No need for that. You have an invitation. Personal from the lady of the house. Her name's Andrea and she's delighted to entertain the soldier son of the famous you-know-who. She also wants a soprano in February, but that's my problem.'

19

The dinner clientele from the Gallery could have moved intact to the Warfield brownstone on Sixty-second Street. David mixed easily. The little gold emblem in his lapel served its purpose; he was accepted more readily, he was also more available. The drinks and buffet were generous, the small Negro jazz combo better than good.

And he found Cindy Bonner in a corner, waiting for her escort—an army lieutenant — to come back from the bar. She was petite, with reddish hair and very light, almost pale skin. Her posture was *Vogue*, her body slender, supporting very expensive, very subdued clothes. There was a pensive look about her; not sad, however. Not the vision of a hero's widow, not heroic at all.

A rich little girl.

'I have a sincere apology to make,' he told her. 'I hope you'll accept it.'

'I can't imagine what for. I don't think we've met.' She smiled but not completely, as if his presence triggered a memory she could not define. Spaulding saw the look and understood. It was his voice. The voice that once had made him a good deal of money.

'My name is Spaulding. David . . .'

'You telephoned the other night,' interrupted the girl, her eyes angry. 'The Christmas gifts for Paul. Leslie . . .'

'That's why I'm apologizing. It was all a terrible misunderstanding. Please forgive me. It's not the sort of joke I'd enter into willingly; I was as angry as you were.' He spoke calmly, holding her eyes with his own. It was sufficient; she blinked, trying to understand, her anger fading. She looked briefly at the tiny brass eagle in his lapel, the small insignia that could mean just about anything.

'I think I believe you.'

'You should. It was sick; I'm not sick.'

The army lieutenant returned carrying two glasses. He was drunk and hostile. Cindy made a short introduction; the lieutenant barely acknowledged the civilian in front of him. He wanted to dance; Cindy did not. The situation — abruptly created — was about to deteriorate.

David spoke with a trace of melancholy. 'I served with Mrs Bonner's husband. I'd like to speak with her for just a few minutes. I'll have to leave shortly, my wife's waiting for me uptown.'

The combination of facts – reassurances – bewildered the drunken lieutenant as well as mollified him. His gallantry was called; he bowed tipsily and walked back toward the bar.

'Nicely done,' Cindy said. 'If there *is* a Mrs Spaulding uptown, it wouldn't surprise me. You said you were out with Leslie; that's par for her course.'

David looked at the girl. *Trust the developed instincts*, he thought to himself. 'There is no Mrs Spaulding. But there was a Mrs Hawkwood the other night. I gather you're not very fond of her.'

'She and my husband were what is politely referred to as "an item", A long-standing one. There are some people who say I forced her to move to California.'

'Then I'll ask the obvious question. Under the circumstances, I wonder why she used your name? And then disappeared. She'd know I'd try to reach you.'

'I think you used the term *sick*. She's sick.'

'Or else she was trying to tell me something.'

David left the Warfields' shortly before the New Year arrived. He reached the corner of Lexington Avenue and turned south. There was nothing to do but walk, think, try to piece together what he had learned; find a pattern that made sense.

He couldn't. Cindy Bonner was a bitter widow; her husband's death on the battlefield robbed her of any chance to strike back at Leslie. She wanted, according to her, simply to forget. But the hurt had been major. Leslie and Paul Bonner had been more than an 'item'. They had reached – again, according to Cindy – the stage where the Bonners had mutually sued for divorce. A confrontation between the two women, however, did not confirm Paul Bonner's story; Leslie Jenner Hawkwood had no *intention* of divorcing *her* husband.

It was all a messy, disagreeable Social Register foul-up; Ed Pace's 'musical beds'.

Why, then, would Leslie use Cindy's name? It was not only provocative and tasteless, it was senseless.

Midnight arrived as he crossed Fifty-second Street. A few horns blared from passing automobiles. In the distance could be heard tower bells and whistles; from inside bars came the shrill bleats of noisemakers and a cacophony of shouting. Three sailors, their uniforms filthy, were singing loudly off-key to the amusement of pedestrians.

He walked west toward the string of cafés between Madison and Fifth. He considered stopping in at Shor's or 21 . . . in ten minutes or so. Enough time for the celebrations to have somewhat subsided.

'Happy New Year, Colonel Spaulding.'

The voice was sharp and came from a darkened doorway.

'What?' David stopped and looked into the shadows. A tall man in a light-gray overcoat, his face obscured by the brim of his hat, stood immobile. 'What did you say?'

'I wished you a Happy New Year,' said the man. 'Needless to say, I've been following you. I overtook you several minutes ago.'

The voice was lined with an accent, but David couldn't place it. The English was British-tutored, the origin somewhere in Middle Europe. Perhaps the Balkans.

'I find that a very unusual statement and ... needless to say ... quite disturbing.' Spaulding held his place; he had no weapon and wondered if the man recessed in the doorway was, conversely, armed. He couldn't tell. 'What do you want?'

'To welcome you home, to begin with. You've been away a long time.'

'Thank you ... Now, if you don't mind ...'

'I mind! Don't move, colonel! Just stand there as if you were talking with an old friend. Don't back away; I'm holding a .45 leveled at your chest.'

Several passers-by walked around David on the curb side. A couple came out of an apartment entrance ten yards to the right of the shadowed doorway; they were in a hurry and crossed rapidly between Spaulding and the tall man with the unseen gun. David was first tempted to use them, but two considerations prevented him. The first was the grave danger to the couple, the second, the fact that the man with the gun had something to say. If he'd wanted to kill him, he would have done so by now.

'I won't move ... What is it?'

'Take two steps forward. Just *two*. No more.'

David did so. He could see the face better now, but not clearly. It was a thin face, gaunt and lined. The eyes were deep-set with hollows underneath. Tired eyes. The dull finish of the pistol's barrel was the clearest object David could distinguish. The man kept shifting his eyes to his left, behind Spaulding. He was looking for someone. Waiting.

'All right. Two steps. Now no one can walk between us ... Are you expecting someone?'

'I'd heard that the main agent in Lisbon was very controlled. You bear that out. Yes, I'm waiting; I'll be picked up shortly.'

'Am I to go with you?'

'It won't be necessary. I'm delivering a message, that is all ... The incident at Lajes. It is to be regretted, the work of zealots. Nevertheless, accept it as a warning. We can't always control deep angers; surely you must know that. Fairfax should know it. Fairfax *will* know it before this first day of the New Year is over. Perhaps by now ... There is my car. Move to my right, your *left*.' David did so as the man edged toward the sidewalk, hiding the pistol under the cloth of his coat. 'Heed us, colonel. There are to be no negotiations with Franz Altmüller. They are finished!'

'Wait a minute! I don't know what you're talking about. I don't *know* any Altmüller!'

'*Finished!* Heed the lesson of Fairfax!'

A dark-brown sedan with bright headlights pulled up to the curb. It stopped, the rear door was thrown open, and the tall man raced across the sidewalk between the pedestrians and climbed in. The car sped away.

David rushed to the curb. The least he could do was get the vehicle's licence number.

There was none. The rear licence plate was missing.

Instead, above the trunk in the oblong rear window, a face looked back at him. His shock caused him to lose his breath. For the briefest of moments he wondered if his eyes, his senses were playing tricks on him, transporting his imagination back to Lisbon.

He started after the car, running in the street, dodging automobiles and the goddamned New Year's Eve revelers.

The brown sedan turned north on Madison Avenue and sped off. He stood in the street, breathless.

The face in the rear window was that of a man he had worked with in the most classified operations out of Portugal and Spain.

Marshall. Lisbon's master cryptographer.

The taxi driver accepted David's challenge to get him to the Montgomery in five minutes or less. It took seven, but considering the traffic on Fifth Avenue, Spaulding gave him five dollars and raced into the lobby.

There were no messages.

He hadn't bothered to thread his door lock; a conscious oversight, he considered. In addition to the maid service, if he could have offered an open invitation to those who had searched his room two nights ago, he would have done so. A recurrence might cause carelessness, some clues to identities.

He threw off his coat and went to his dresser, where he kept a bottle of Scotch. Two clean glasses stood on a silver tray next to the liquor. He'd take the necessary seconds to pour himself a drink before calling Fairfax.

'A very Happy New Year,' he said slowly as he lifted the glass to his lips.

He crossed to the bed, picked up the telephone and gave the Virginia number to the switchboard. The circuits to the Washington area were crowded; it would take several minutes to get through.

What in God's name did the man mean? *Heed the lesson of Fairfax.* What the hell was he talking about? Who was Altmüller? . . . What was the first name? . . . Franz. Franz Altmüller.

Who was he?

So the Lajes Field 'incident' *was* aimed at him. For Christ's sake, what *for*?

And *Marshall.* It *was* Marshall in that rear window! He *hadn't* been mistaken!

'Field Division Headquarters' were the monotoned words from the State of Virginia, County of Fairfax.

'Colonel Edmund Pace, please.'

There was a slight pause at the other end of the line. David's ears picked up a tiny rush of air he knew very well.

It was a telephone intercept, usually attached to a wire recorder.

'Who's calling Colonel Pace?'

It was David's turn to hesitate. He did so thinking that perhaps he'd missed the interceptor sound before. It was entirely possible, and Fairfax was, after all ... well, Fairfax.

'Spaulding. Lieutenant Colonel David Spaulding.'

'Can I give the colonel a message, sir? He's in conference.'

'No, you may not. You may and can give me the colonel.'

'I'm sorry, sir.' Fairfax's hesitation was now awkward. 'Let me have a telephone number ...'

'Look, soldier, my name is Spaulding. My clearance is four-zero and this is a four-zero priority call. If those numbers don't mean anything to you, ask the son-of-a-bitch on your intercept. Now, it's an emergency. Put me through to Colonel Pace!'

There was a loud double click on the line. A deep, hard voice came over the wire.

'And this is Colonel Barden, Colonel Spaulding. I'm also four-zero and any four-zeros will be cleared with this son-of-a-bitch. Now, I'm in no mood for any rank horseshit. What do you want?'

'I like your directness, colonel,' said David, smiling in spite of his urgency. 'Put me through to Ed. It's really priority. It concerns Fairfax.'

'I can't put you through, colonel. We don't have any circuits, and I'm not trying to be funny. Ed Pace is dead. He was shot through the head an hour ago. Some goddamned son-of-a-bitch killed him right here in the compound.'

20

January 1, 1944 – Fairfax, Virginia

It was four thirty in the morning when the army car carrying Spaulding reached the Fairfax gate.

The guards had been alerted; Spaulding, in civilian clothes, possessing no papers of authorization, was matched against his file photograph and waved through. David had been tempted to ask to see the photograph; to the best of his knowledge, it was four years old. Once inside, the automobile swung left and headed to the south area of the huge compound. About a half-mile down the gravel road, past rows of metal Quonset huts, the car pulled up in front of a barracks structure. It was the Fairfax Administration Building.

Two corporals flanked the door. The sergeant driver climbed out of the car and signaled the noncoms to let Spaulding through; he was already in front of them.

David was shown to an office on the second floor. Inside were two men: Colonel Ira Barden and a doctor named McCleod, a captain. Barden was a thick, short man with the build of a football tackle and close-cropped black hair. McCleod was stooped, slender, bespectacled – the essence of the thoughtful academician.

Barden wasted the minimum time with introductions. Completed, he went immediately to the questions at hand.

'We've doubled patrols everywhere, put men with K-9s all along the fences. I'd like to think no one could get out. What bothers us is whether someone got out beforehand.'

'How did it happen?'

'Pace had a few people over for New Year's. Twelve, to be exact. Four were from his own Quonset, three from Records, the rest from Administration. Very subdued ... what the hell, this is Fairfax. As near as we can determine, he went out his back door at about twenty minutes past midnight. Carrying out garbage, we think; maybe just to get some air. He didn't come back ... A guard down the road came to the door, saying he'd heard a shot. No one else had. At least, not inside.'

'That's unusual. These quarters are hardly soundproof.'

'Someone had turned up the phonograph.'

'I thought it was a subdued party.'

Barden looked hard at Spaulding. His glare was not anger, it was his way of telegraphing his deep concern. 'That record player was turned up for no more than thirty seconds. The rifle used – and ballistics confirms this – was a training weapon, .22 caliber.'

'A sharp crack, no louder,' said David.

'Exactly. The phonograph was a signal.'

'Inside. At the party,' added Spaulding.

'Yes . . . McCleod here is the base psychiatrist. We've been going over everyone who was inside . . .'

'Psychiatrist?' David was confused. It was a security problem, not medical.

'Ed was a hardnose, you know that as well as I do. He trained you . . . I looked you up, Lisbon. It's one angle. We're covering the others.'

'Look,' interrupted the doctor, 'you two want to talk, and I've got files to go over. I'll call you in the morning; later this morning, Ira. Nice to meet you, Spaulding. Wish it wasn't this way.'

'Agreed,' said Spaulding, shaking the man's hand.

The psychiatrist gathered up the twelve file folders on the colonel's desk and left.

The door closed. Barden indicated a chair to Spaulding. David sat down, rubbing his eyes. 'One hell of a New Year's, isn't it?' said Barden.

'I've seen better,' Spaulding replied.

'Do you want to go over what happened to you?'

'I don't think there's any point. I was stopped; I told you what was said. Ed Pace was obviously the "Fairfax lesson". It's tied to a brigadier named Swanson at DW.'

'I'm afraid it isn't.'

'It has to be.'

'Negative. Pace wasn't involved with the DW thing. His only tie was recruiting you; a simple transfer.'

David remembered Ed Pace's words: *I'm not cleared . . . how does it strike you? Have you met Swanson?* He looked at Barden. 'Then someone thinks he was. Same motive. Related to the sabotage at Lajes. In the Azores.'

'How?'

'The son-of-a-bitch said so on Fifty-second Street! Five *hours* ago . . . Look, Pace is dead; that gives you certain latitude under the circumstances. I want to check Ed's four-zero files. Everything connected to my transfer.'

'I've already done that. After your call there was no point in waiting for an inspector general. Ed was about my closest friend . . .'

'And?'

'There are no files. Nothing.'

'There *has* to be! There's got to be a record for Lisbon. For *me.*'

'There is. It states simple transfer to DW. No names. Just a word. A single word: "Tortugas".'

'What about the papers you prepared? The discharge, the medical record;

Fifth Army, One Hundred and Twelfth Battalion? Italy? ... Those papers aren't manufactured without a Fairfax file!'

'This is the first I've heard of them. There's nothing about them in Ed's vaults.'

'A major – Winston, I think his name is – met me at Mitchell Field. I flew in from Newfoundland on a coastal patrol. He brought me the papers.'

'He brought you a sealed envelope and gave you verbal instructions. That's all he knows.'

'*Jesus!* What the hell happened to the so-called Fairfax efficiency?'

'You tell me. And while you're at it, who murdered Ed Pace?'

David looked over at Barden. The word *murder* hadn't occurred to him. One didn't commit *murder;* one killed, yes, that was part of it. But murder? Yet it *was* murder.

'I can't tell you that. But I can tell you where to start asking questions.'

'Please do.'

'Raise Lisbon. Find out what happened to a cryptographer named Marshall.'

January 1, 1944 – Washington, DC

The news of Pace's murder reached Alan Swanson indirectly; the effect was numbing.

He had been in Arlington, at a small New Year's Eve dinner party given by the ranking general of Ordnance when the telephone call came. It was an emergency communication for another guest, a lieutenant general on the staff of the Joint Chiefs. Swanson had been near the library door when the man emerged; the staffer had been white, his voice incredulous.

'My God!' he had said to no one in particular. 'Someone shot Pace over at Fairfax. He's dead!'

Those few in that small gathering in Arlington comprised the highest echelons of the military; there was no need for concealing the news; they would all, sooner or later, be told.

Swanson's hysterical first thoughts were of Buenos Aires. Was there *any possible connection?*

He listened as the brigadiers and the two- and three-stars joined in controlled but excited speculations. He heard the words ... *infiltrators, hired assassins, double agents.* He was stunned by the wild theories ... advanced rationally ... that one of Pace's undercover agents had to be behind the murder. Somewhere a defector had been paid to make his way back to Fairfax; somewhere there was a weak link in a chain of Intelligence that had been bought.

Pace was not just a crack Intelligence man, he was one of the best in Allied Central. So much so that he twice had requested that his brigadier star be officially recorded but not issued, thus protecting his low profile.

But the profile was not low enough. An extraordinary man like Pace would

have an extraordinary price on his head. From Shanghai to Bern; with
Fairfax's rigid security the killing had to have been planned for months.
Conceived as a long-range project, to be executed internally. There was no
other way it could have been accomplished. And there were currently over
five hundred personnel in the compound, including a rotating force of
espionage units-in-training – nationals from many countries. No security
system could be that absolute under the circumstances. All that was needed
was one man to slip through.

*Planned for months . . . a defector who had made his way back to Fairfax . . .
a double agent . . . a weak Intelligence link paid a fortune. Berne to Shanghai.*

A long-range project!

These were the specific words and terms and judgments that Swanson
heard clearly because he wanted to hear them.

They removed the motive from Buenos Aires. Pace's death had nothing to
do with Buenos Aires because the time element prohibited it.

The Rhinemann exchange had been conceived barely three weeks ago; it
was inconceivable that Pace's murder was related. For it to be so would mean
that he, himself, had broken the silence.

No one else on earth knew of Pace's contribution. And even Pace had
known precious little.

Only fragments.

And all the background papers concerning the man in Lisbon had been
removed from Pace's vault. Only the War Department transfer remained.

A fragment.

Then Alan Swanson thought of something and he marveled at his own
cold sense of the devious. In a way, it was chilling that it could escape the
recesses of his mind. With Edmund Pace's death, not even Fairfax could
piece together the events leading up to Buenos Aires. The government of the
United States was removed one step further.

As if abstractly seeking support, he ventured aloud to the small group of
his peers that he recently had been in communication with Fairfax, with Pace
as a matter of fact, over a minor matter of clearance. It was insignificant
really, but he hoped to Christ . . .

He found his support instantly. The lieutenant general from staff, two
brigs and a three-star all volunteered that they, too, had used Pace.

Frequently, Obviously more than he did.

'You could save a lot of time dealing directly with Ed,' said the staffer. 'He
cut tape and shot you off a clearance right away.'

One step further removed.

Once back in his Washington apartment, Swanson experienced the doubts
again. Doubts and opportunities alike. Pace's murder was potentially a
problem because of the shock waves it would produce. There would be a
major investigation, all avenues explored. On the other hand, the concentration would be on Fairfax. It would consume Allied Central Intelligence. At
least for a while. He had to move now. Walter Kendall had to get to Buenos
Aires and conclude the arrangements with Rhinemann.

The guidance designs from Peenemünde. Only the designs were important.

But first tonight, this morning. David Spaulding. It was time to give the former man in Lisbon his assignment.

Swanson picked up the telephone. His hand shook.

The guilt was becoming unbearable.

January 1, 1944 – Fairfax, Virginia

'Marshall was killed several miles from a place called Valdero's. In the Basque province. It was an ambush.'

'That's horseshit! Marshall never went into the north country! He wasn't trained, he wouldn't know what to do!' David was out of the chair, confronting Barden.

'Rules change. You're not the man in Lisbon now ... He went, he was killed.'

'Source?'

'The ambassador himself.'

'*His* source?'

'Your normal channels, I assume. He said it was confirmed. Identification was brought back.'

'Meaningless!'

'What do you want? A body?'

'This may surprise you, Barden, but a hand or a finger isn't out of the question. *That's* identification ... Any photographs? Close shots, wounds, the eyes? Even those can be doctored.'

'He didn't indicate any. What the hell's eating you? This is *confirmed.*'

'Really?' David stared at Barden.

'For Christ's sake, Spaulding! What the hell is ... "Tortugas"? If it killed Ed Pace, I want to know! And I'm going to goddamned well find out! I don't give a shit about Lisbon cryps!'

The telephone rang on Barden's desk; the colonel looked briefly at it, then pulled his eyes back to Spaulding.

'Answer it,' said David. 'One of those calls is going to be Casualty. Pace has a family ... Had.'

'Don't complicate my life any more than you have.' Barden crossed to his desk. 'Ed was due for an escort leave this Friday. I'm putting off calling – till morning ... Yes?' The colonel listened to the phone for several seconds, then looked at Spaulding. 'It's the trip-line operator in New York; the one we've got covering you. This General Swanson's been trying to reach you. He's got him holding now. Do you want him to put the old man through?'

David remembered Pace's appraisal of the nervous brigadier. 'Do you have to tell him I'm here?'

'Hell, no.'

'Then put him through.'

Barden walked from behind the desk as Spaulding took the phone and repeated the phrase 'Yes, sir' a number of times. Finally he replaced the instrument. 'Swanson wants me in his office this morning.'

'I want to know why the hell they ripped you out of Lisbon,' Barden said.

David sat down in the chair without at first answering. When he spoke he tried not to sound military or officious. 'I'm not sure it has anything to do with . . . anything. I don't want to duck; on the other hand, in a way I have to. But I want to keep a couple of options open. Call it instinct, I don't know . . . There's a man named Altmüller. Franz Altmüller . . . Who he is, where he is – I have no idea. German, Swiss, I don't know . . . Find out what you can on a four-zero basis. Call me at the Hotel Montgomery in New York. I'll be there for at least the rest of the week. Then I go to Buenos Aires.'

'I will if you flex the clearances . . . tell me what the hell is going on.'

'You won't like it. Because if I do, and if it is connected, it'll mean Fairfax has open code lines in Berlin.'

January 1, 1944 – New York City

The commercial passenger plane began its descent toward La Guardia Airport. David looked at his watch. It was a little past noon. It had all happened in twelve hours: Cindy Bonner, the stranger on Fifty-second Street, Marshall, Pace's murder, Barden, the news from Valdero's . . . and finally the awkward conference with the amateur source control, Brigadier General Alan Swanson, DW.

Twelve hours.

He hadn't slept in nearly forty-eight. He needed sleep to find some kind of perspective, to piece together the elusive pattern. Not the one that was clear.

Erich Rhinemann was to be killed.

Of *course* he had to be killed. The only surprise for David was the bumbling manner in which the brigadier had given the order. It didn't require elaboration or apology. And it – at *last* – explained his transfer from Lisbon. It filled in the gaping hole of why. He was no gyroscope specialist; it hadn't made sense. But now it did. He was a good selection; Pace had made a thoroughly professional choice. It was a job for which he was suited – in addition to being a bilingual liaison between the mute gyroscopic scientist, Eugene Lyons, and Rhinemann's blueprint man.

That picture was clear; he was relieved to see it come into focus.

What bothered him was the unfocused picture.

The embassy's Marshall, the cryp who five days ago picked him up at a rain-soaked airfield outside of Lisbon. The man he *had* seen looking at him through the automobile window on Fifty-second Street; the man supposedly killed in an ambush in the north country, into which he never had ventured. Or would venture.

Leslie Jenner Hawkwood. The resourceful ex-lover who had lied and kept him away from his hotel room, who foolishly used the ploy of Cindy Bonner and the exchange of gifts for a dead husband she had stolen. Leslie was not an idiot. She *was* telling him something.

But what?

And Pace. Poor, humorless Ed Pace cut down within the most security-conscious enclosure in the United States.

The *lesson of Fairfax*, predicted with incredible accuracy – nearly to the moment – by a tall, sad-eyed man in shadows on Fifty-second Street.

That . . . *they* were the figures in the unfocused picture.

David had been harsh with the brigadier. He had demanded – professionally, of course – to know the exact date the decision had been reached to eliminate Erich Rhinemann. Who had arrived at it? How was the order transmitted? Did the general know a cryptographer named Marshall? Had Pace ever mentioned him? Had *anyone* ever mentioned him? And a man named Altmüller. Franz Altmüller. Did that name mean anything?

The answers were no help. And God knew Swanson wasn't lying. He wasn't pro enough to get away with it.

The names Marshall and Altmüller were unknown to him. The decision to execute Rhinemann was made within hours. There was absolutely no way Ed Pace could have known; he was not consulted, nor was anyone at Fairfax. It was a decision emanating from the cellars of the White House; no one at Fairfax or Lisbon could have been involved. For David that absence of involvement was the important factor. It meant simply that the whole unfocused picture had nothing to do with Erich Rhinemann. And thus, as far as could be determined, was unrelated to Buenos Aires. David made the quick decision not to confide in the nervous brigadier. Pace had been right: the man couldn't take any more complications. He'd use Fairfax, source control be damned.

The plane landed; Spaulding walked into the passenger terminal and looked for the signs that read Taxis. He went through the double doors to the platform and heard the porters shouting the various destinations of the unfilled cabs. It was funny, but the shared taxis were the only things that caused him to think La Guardia Airport knew there was a war going on somewhere.

Simultaneously he recognized the foolishness of his thoughts. And the pretentiousness of them.

A soldier with no legs was being helped into a cab. Porters and civilians were touched, helpful.

The soldier was drunk. What was left of him, unstable.

Spaulding shared a taxi with three other men, and they talked of little but the latest reports out of Italy. David decided to forget his cover in case the inevitable questions came up. He wasn't about to discuss any mythical combat in Salerno. But the questions did not arise. And then he saw why.

The man next to him was blind; the man shifted his weight and the afternoon sun caused a reflection in his lapel. It was a tiny metal replica of a ribbon: South Pacific.

David considered again that he was terribly tired. He was about the most unobservant agent ever to have been given an operation, he thought.

He got out of the cab on Fifth Avenue, three blocks north of the Montgomery. He had overpaid his share; he hoped the other two men would apply it to the blind veteran whose clothes were one hell of a long way from Leslie Jenner's Rogers Peet.

Leslie Jenner ... Hawkwood.

A cryptographer named Marshall.

The unfocused picture.

He had to put it all out of his mind. He had to sleep, forget; let everything settle before he thought again. Tomorrow morning he would meet Eugene Lyons and begin ... again. He had to be ready for the man who'd burned his throat out with raw alcohol and had not had a conversation in ten years.

The elevator stopped at the sixth floor. His was the seventh. He was about to tell the elevator operator when he realized the doors were not opening.

Instead, the operator turned in place. In his hand he gripped a short-barreled Smith & Wesson revolver. He reached behind him to the lever control and pushed it to the left, the enclosed box jerked and edged itself up between floors.

'The lobby lights go out this way, Colonel Spaulding. We may hear buzzers, but there's a second elevator used in emergencies. We won't be disturbed.'

The accent was the same, thought David. British overlay. Middle Europe. 'I'm glad of that. I mean, Jesus, it's been so long.'

'I don't find you amusing.'

'Nor I, you ... obviously.'

'You've been to Fairfax, Virginia. Did you have a pleasant journey?'

'You've got an extraordinary pipeline.' Spaulding wasn't only buying time with conversation. He and Ira Barden had taken the required precautions. Even if the Montgomery switchboard reported everything he said, there was no evidence that he had flown to Virginia. The arrangements were made from telephone booths, the flight from Mitchell to Andrews under an assumed name on a crew sheet. Even the Manhattan number he had left with the Montgomery desk had a New York address under constant surveillance. And *in* the Fairfax compound, only the security gate had his name; he had been seen by only four, perhaps five men.

'We have reliable sources of information ... Now you have learned firsthand the lesson of Fairfax, no?'

'I've learned that a good man was murdered. I imagine his wife and children have been told by now.'

'There is no murder in war, colonel. A misapplication of the word. And don't speak to us ...'

A buzzer interrupted the man. It was short, a polite ring.

'Who is "us"?' asked David.

'You'll know in time, if you cooperate. If you don't cooperate, it will make no difference; you'll be killed ... We don't make idle threats. Witness Fairfax.'

The buzzer sounded again. This time prolonged, not quite polite.

'How am I supposed to cooperate? What about?'

'We must know the precise location of Tortugas.'

Spaulding's mind raced back to five o'clock that morning. In Fairfax. Ira Barden had said that the name 'Tortugas' was the single word opposite his transfer specification. No other data, nothing but the word 'Tortugas'. And it had been buried in Pace's 'vaults'. Cabinets kept behind steel doors, accessible only to the highest-echelon Intelligence personnel.

'Tortugas is part of an island complex off the coast of Florida. It's usually referred to as the Dry Tortugas. It's on any map.'

The buzzer again. Now repeated; in short, angry spurts.

'Don't be foolish, colonel.'

'I'm not being anything. I don't know what you're talking about.'

The man stared at Spaulding. David saw that he was unsure, controlling his anger. The elevator buzzer was incessant now; voices could be heard from above and below.

'I'd prefer not to have to kill you but I will. *Where is Tortugas?*'

Suddenly a loud male voice, no more than ten feet from the enclosure, on the sixth floor, shouted.

'*It's up here! It's stuck!* Are you all *right* up there?'

The man blinked, the shouting had unnerved him. It was the instant David was waiting for. He lashed his right hand out in a diagonal thrust and gripped the man's forearm, hammering it against the metal door. He slammed his body into the man's chest and brought his knee up in a single, crushing assault against the groin. The man screamed in agony; Spaulding grabbed the arched throat with his left hand and tore at the veins around the larynx. He hammered the man twice more in the groin, until the pain was so excruciating that no more screams could emerge, only low, wailing moans of anguish. The body went limp, the revolver fell to the floor, and the man slid downward against the wall.

Spaulding kicked the weapon away and gripped the man's neck with both hands, shaking the head back and forth to keep him conscious.

'Now, you tell *me*, you son-of-a-bitch! What is "Tortugas"?'

The shouting outside the elevator was now deafening. There was a cacophony of hysteria brought on by the screams of the battered operator. There were cries for the hotel management. For the police.

The man looked up at David, tears of terrible pain streaming from his eyes. 'Why not kill me, pig,' he said between agonizing chokes of breath. '... You've tried before.'

David was bewildered. He'd never *seen* the man. The north country? Basque? Navarre?

There was no time to think.

'What is "*Tortugas*"?'

'Altmüller, pig. The pig Altmüller ...' The man fell into unconsciousness.

There was the name again.

Altmüller.

Spaulding rose from the unconscious body and grabbed the control lever of the elevator. He swung it to the far left, accelerating the speed as fast as possible. There were ten floors in the Montgomery; the panel lights indicated that the first-, third-, and sixth-floor buttons had been activated. If he could reach the tenth before the hysterical voices followed him up the stairs, it was possible that he could get out of the elevator, race down the corridor to one of the corners, then double back into the crowd which surely would gather around the open elevator doors.

Around the unconscious man on the floor.

It *had* to be possible! This was no time for him to be involved with the New York police.

The man was carried away on a stretcher; the questions were brief.

No, he didn't know the elevator operator. The man had dropped him off at his floor ten or twelve minutes ago. He'd been in his room and came out when he'd heard all the shouting.

The same as everyone else.

What was New York coming to?

David reached his room on seven, closed the door and stared at the bed. Christ, he was exhausted! But his mind refused to stop racing.

He would postpone everything until he had rested, except for two items. He had to consider those now. They could not wait for sleep because a telephone might ring, or someone might come to his hotel room. And he had to make his decisions in advance. Be prepared.

The first item was that Fairfax no longer could be used as a source. It was riddled, infiltrated. He had to function without Fairfax, which, in a way, was akin to telling a cripple he had to walk without braces.

On the other hand, he was no cripple.

The second item was a man named Altmüller. He had to find a man named Franz Altmüller; find out who he was, what he meant to the unfocused picture.

David lay down on the bed; he didn't have the energy to remove his clothes, even his shoes. He brought his arm up to shade his eyes from the afternoon sun streaming in the hotel windows. The afternoon sun of the first day of the new year, 1944.

Suddenly, he opened his eyes in the black void of tweed cloth. There was a third item. Inextricably bound to the man named Altmüller.

What the hell did 'Tortugas' mean?

21

Eugene Lyons sat at a drafting board in the bare office. He was in shirtsleeves. There were blueprints strewn about on tables. The bright morning sun bouncing off the white walls gave the room the antiseptic appearance of a large hospital cubicle.

And Eugene Lyons's face and body did nothing to discourage such thoughts.

David had followed Kendall through the door, apprehensive at the forthcoming introduction. He would have preferred not knowing anything about Lyons.

The scientist turned on the stool. He was among the thinnest men Spaulding had ever seen. The bones were surrounded by flesh, not protected by it. Light blue veins were in evidence throughout the hands, arms, neck and temples. The skin wasn't old, it was worn out. The eyes were deep-set but in no way dull or flat; they were alert and, in their own way, penetrating. His straight gray hair was thinned out before its time; he could have been any age within a twenty-year span.

There was, however, one quality about the man that seemed specific: disinterest. He acknowledged the intrusion, obviously knew who David was, but made no move to interrupt his concentration.

Kendall forced the break. 'Eugene, this is Spaulding. You show him where to start.'

And with those words Kendall turned on his heel and went out the door, closing it behind him.

David stood across the room from Lyons. He took the necessary steps and extended his hand. He knew exactly what he was going to say.

'It's an honor to meet you, Dr Lyons. I'm no expert in your field, but I've heard about your work at MIT. I'm lucky to have you spread the wealth, even if it's only for a short time.'

There was a slight, momentary flicker of interest in the eyes. David had gambled on a simple greeting that told the emaciated scientist several things, among which was the fact that David was aware of Lyons's tragedy in Boston – thus, undoubtedly, the rest of his story – and was not inhibited by it.

843

Lyons's grip was limp; the disinterest quickly returned. Disinterest, not necessarily rudeness. On the borderline.

'I know we haven't much time and I'm a neophyte in gyroscopics,' said Spaulding, releasing the hand, backing off to the side of the drafting board. 'But I'm told I don't have to recognize much more than pretty basic stuff; be able to verbalize in German the terms and formulas you write out for me.'

David emphasized – with the barest rise in his voice – the words *verbalize . . . you write out for me.* He watched Lyons to see if there was any reaction to his open acknowledgment of the scientist's vocal problem. He thought he detected a small hint of relief.

Lyons looked up at him. The thin lips flattened slightly against the teeth; there was a short extension at the corners of the mouth and the scientist nodded. There was even an infinitesimal glint of appreciation in the deep-set eyes. He got up from his stool and crossed to the nearest table where several books lay on blueprints. He picked up the top volume and handed it to Spaulding. The title on the cover was *Diagrammatics: Inertia and Precession.*

David knew it would be all right.

It was past six o'clock.

Kendall had gone; the receptionist had bolted at the stroke of five, asking David to close the doors if he was the last person to leave. If not, tell one of the others.

The 'others' were Eugene Lyons and his two male nurses.

Spaulding met them – the male nurses – briefly in the reception room. Their names were Hal and Johnny. Both were large men; the talkative one was Hal, the leader was Johnny, an ex-marine.

'The old guy is on his real good behavior,' said Hal. 'Nothing to worry about.'

'It's time to get him back to St Luke's,' said Johnny. 'They get pissed off if he's too late for the night meal.'

Together the men went into Lyons's office and brought him out. They were polite with the cadaverous physicist, but firm. Eugene Lyons looked indifferently at Spaulding, shrugged and walked silently out the door with his two keepers.

David waited until he heard the sound of the elevator in the hallway. Then he put down the *Diagrammatics* volume the physicist had given him on the receptionist's desk and crossed to Walter Kendall's office.

The door was locked, which struck him as strange. Kendall was on his way to Buenos Aires, he might not be back for several weeks. Spaulding withdrew a small object from his pocket and knelt down. At first glance, the instrument in David's hand appeared to be an expensive silver pocket knife, the sort so often found at the end of an expensive key chain, especially in very expensive men's clubs. It wasn't. It was a locksmith's pick designed to give that appearance. It had been made in London's Silver Vaults, a gift from an MI5 counterpart in Lisbon.

David spun out a tiny cylinder with a flat tip and inserted it into the lock housing. In less than thirty seconds the appropriate clicks were heard and Spaulding opened the door. He walked in, leaving it ajar.

Kendall's office had no file cabinets, no closets, no bookshelves; no recesses whatsoever other than the desk drawers. David turned on the fluorescent reading lamp at the far edge of the blotter and opened the top center drawer.

He had to stifle a genuine laugh. Surrounded by an odd assortment of paper clips, toothpicks, loose Lifesavers, and note paper were two pornographic magazines. Although marked with dirty fingerprints, both were fairly new.

Merry Christmas, Walter Kendall, thought David a little sadly.

The side drawers were empty, at least there was nothing of interest. In the bottom drawer lay crumpled yellow pages of note paper, meaningless doodles drawn with a hard pencil, piercing the pages.

He was about to get up and leave when he decided to look once more at the incoherent patterns on the crumpled paper. There was nothing else; Kendall had locked his office door out of reflex, not necessity. And again by reflex, perhaps, he had put the yellow pages – not in a wastebasket, which had only the contents of emptied ashtrays – but in a drawer. Out of sight.

David knew he was reaching. There was no choice; he wasn't sure what he was looking for, if anything.

He spread two of the pages on top of the blotter, pressing the surfaces flat. Nothing.

Well, something. Outlines of women's breasts and genitalia. Assorted circles and arrows, diagrams: a psychoanalyst's paradise.

He removed another single page and pressed it out. More circles, arrows, breasts. Then to one side, childlike outlines of clouds – billowy, shaded; diagonal marks that could be rain or multiple sheets of thin lightning.

Nothing.

Another page.

It caught David's eye. On the bottom of the soiled yellow page, barely distinguishable between crisscross penciling, was the outline of a large swastika. He looked at it closely. The swastika had circles at the right-hand points of the insignia, circles that spun off as if the artist were duplicating the ovals of a Palmer writing exercise. And flowing out of these ovals were unmistakable initials. *J.D..* Then *Joh D., J Diet . . .* The letters appeared at the end of each oval line. And beyond the final letters in each area were elaborately drawn *? ? ?*

? ? ?

David folded the paper carefully and put it in his jacket pocket.

There were two remaining pages, so he took them out simultaneously. The page to the left had only one large, indecipherable scribble – once more circular, now angry – and meaningless. But on the second paper, again toward the bottom of the page, was a series of scroll-like markings that could be interpreted as *J*s and *D*s, similar in flow to the letters after the swastika points on the second page. And opposite the final *D* was a strange horizontal obelisk, its taper on the right. There were lines on the side as though they were edges ... A bullet, perhaps, with bore markings. Underneath, on the next line of the paper to the left, were the same oval motions that brought to mind the Palmer exercise. Only they were firmer here, pressed harder into the yellow paper.

Suddenly David realized what he was staring at.

Walter Kendall had subconsciously outlined an obscene caricature of an erect penis and testicles.

Happy New Year, Mr Kendall, thought Spaulding.

He put the page carefully into his pocket with its partner, returned the others and shut the drawer. He switched off the lamp, walked to the open door, turning to see if he had left everything as it was, and crossed into the reception room. He pulled Kendall's door shut and considered briefly whether to lock the tumblers in place.

It would be pointless to waste the time. The lock was old, simple; janitorial personnel in just about any building in New York would have a key, and it was more difficult inserting tumblers than releasing them. To hell with it.

A half-hour later it occurred to him – in an instant of reflection – that this decision probably saved his life. The sixty, or ninety, or one-hundred-odd seconds he eliminated from his departure placed him in the position of an observer, not a target.

He put on the Rogers Peet overcoat, turned off the lights, and walked into the corridor to the bank of elevators. It was nearly seven, the day after New Year's, and the building was practically deserted. A single elevator was working. It had passed his floor, ascending to the upper stories, where it seemed to linger. He was about to use the stairs – the offices were on the third floor, it might be quicker – when he heard rapid, multiple footsteps coming up the staircase. The sound was incongruous. Moments ago the elevator had been in the lobby; why would two – more than two? – people be racing up the stairs at seven at night? There could be a dozen reasonable explanations, but his instincts made him consider *un*reasonable ones.

Silently, he ran to the opposite end of the short floor, where an intersecting corridor led to additional offices on the south side of the building. He rounded the corner and pressed himself against the wall. Since the assault in the Montgomery elevator, he carried a weapon – a small Beretta revolver – strapped to his chest, under his clothes. He flipped open his overcoat and undid the buttons of his jacket and shirt. Access to the pistol would be swift and efficient, should it be necessary.

It probably wouldn't be, he thought, as he heard the footsteps disappear.

Then he realized that they had not disappeared, they had faded, slowed down to a walk – a quiet, cautious walk. And then he heard the voices: whisper-like, indistinguishable. They came from around the edge of the wall, in the vicinity of the unmarked Meridian office, no more than thirty feet away.

He inched the flat of his face to the sharp, concrete corner and simultaneously reached his right hand under his shirt to the handle of the Beretta.

There were two men with their backs to him, facing the darkened glass of the unmarked office door. The shorter of the two put his face against the pane, hands to both temples to shut out the light from the corridor. He pulled back and looked at his partner, shaking his head negatively.

The taller man turned slightly, enough for Spaulding to recognize him.

It was the stranger in the recessed, darkened doorway on Fifty-second Street. The tall, sad-eyed man who spoke gently, in bastardized British-out-of-the-Balkans, and held him under the barrel of a thick, powerful weapon.

The man reached into his left overcoat pocket and gave a key to his friend. With his right hand he removed a pistol from his belt. It was a heavy-duty .45, army issue. At close range, David knew it would blow a person into the air and off the earth. The man nodded and spoke softly but clearly.

'He has to be. He didn't leave. I want him.'

With these words the shorter man inserted the key and shoved at the door. It swung back slowly. Together, both men walked in.

At that precise moment the elevator grill could be heard opening, its metal frames ringing throughout the corridor. David could see the two men in the darkened reception room freeze, turn toward the open door and quickly shut it.

'*Chee-ryst Almighty!*' was the irate shout from the angry elevator operator as the grill rang shut with a clamor.

David knew it was the instant to move. Within seconds one or both men inside the deserted Meridian offices would realize that the elevator had stopped on the third floor because someone had pushed the button. Someone not in evidence, someone they had not met on the stairs. Someone still on the floor.

He spun around the edge of the wall and raced down the corridor toward the staircase. He didn't look back; he didn't bother to muffle his steps – it would have reduced his speed. His only concern was to get down those steps and out of the building. He leaped down the right-angled staircase to the in-between landing and whipped around the corner.

And then he stopped.

Below him, leaning against the railing, was the third man. He *knew* he'd heard more than two sets of feet racing up the staircase minutes ago. The man was startled, his eyes widened in shocked recognition and his right hand jerked backwards toward his coat pocket. Spaulding didn't have to be told what he was reaching for.

David sprang off the landing straight down at the man, making contact in midair, his hands clawing for the man's throat and right arm. He gripped the skin on the neck below the left ear and tore at it, slamming the man's head into the concrete wall as he did so. David's heavier body crushed into the would-be sentry's chest; he twisted the right arm nearly out of its shoulder socket.

The man screamed and collapsed; the scalp was lacerated, blood flowing out of the section of his skull that had crashed into the wall.

David could hear the sounds of a door being thrown open and men running. Above him, of course, one floor above him.

He freed his entangled legs from the unconscious body and raced down the remaining flight of stairs to the lobby. The elevator had, moments ago, let out its cargo of passengers; the last few were going out the front entrance. If any had heard the prolonged scream from the battered man sixty feet away up the staircase, none acknowledged it.

David rushed into the stragglers, elbowing his way through the wide double doors and onto the sidewalk. He turned east and ran as fast as he could.

He had walked over forty city blocks – some two miles in Basque country, but here infinitely less pleasant.

He had come to several decisions. The problem was how to implement them.

He could not stay in New York; not without facing risks, palpably unacceptable. And he had to get to Buenos Aires at once, before any of those hunting him in New York knew he was gone.

For they were hunting him now; that much was clear.

It would be suicide to return to the Montgomery. Or, for that matter, to the unmarked Meridian offices in the morning. He could handle both with telephone calls. He would tell the hotel that he had been suddenly transferred to Pennsylvania; could the Montgomery management pack and hold his things? He'd call later about his bill . . .

Kendall was on his way to Argentina. It wouldn't make any difference what the Meridian office was told.

Suddenly, he thought of Eugene Lyons.

He was a little sad about Lyons. Not the man (of course the man, he reconsidered quickly, but not the man's affliction, in this instance), but the fact that he would have little chance to develop any sense of rapport before Buenos Aires. Lyons might take his sudden absence as one more rejection in a long series. And the scientist might really need his help in Buenos Aires, at least in the area of German translation. David decided that he had to have the books Lyons selected for him; he had to have as solid a grasp of Lyons's language as was possible.

And then David realized where his thoughts were leading him.

For the next few hours the safest places in New York were the Meridian offices and St Luke's Hospital.

After his visits to both locations he'd get out to Mitchell Field and telephone Brigadier General Swanson.

The answer to the violent enigma of the past seven days – from the Azores to a staircase on Thirty-eighth Street and everything in between – was in Buenos Aires.

Swanson did not know it and could not help; Fairfax was infiltrated and could not be told. And *that* told *him* something.

He was on his own. A man had two choices in such a dilemma: take himself out of strategy, or dig for identities and blow the covers off.

The first choice would be denied him. The brigadier, Swanson, was paranoid on the subject of the gyroscopic designs. And Rhinemann. There'd be no out of strategy.

That left the second: the identity of those behind the enigma.

A feeling swept over him, one he had not experienced in several years: the fear of sudden inadequacy. He was confronted with an extraordinary problem for which there was no pat – or complicated – solution in the north country. No unraveling that came with moves or countermoves whose strategies he had mastered in Basque and Navarre.

He was suddenly in another war. One he was not familiar with; one that raised doubts about himself.

He saw an unoccupied taxi, its roof light dimly lit, as if embarrassed to announce its emptiness. He looked up at the street sign; he was on Sheridan Square – it accounted for the muted sounds of jazz that floated up from cellars and surged down crowded side streets. The Village was warming up for another evening.

He raised his hand for the taxi; the driver did not see him. He started running as the cab proceeded up the street to the corner traffic light. Suddenly he realized that someone else on the other side of the square was rushing toward the empty taxi; the man was closer to it than Spaulding, his right hand was gesturing.

It was now terribly important to David that he reach the car first. He gathered speed and ran into the street, dodging pedestrians, momentarily blocked by two automobiles that were bumper to bumper. He spread his hands from hood to trunk and jumped over into the middle of the street and continued racing toward his objective.

Objective.

He reached the taxi no more than half a second after the other man.

Goddamn it! It was the obstruction of the two automobiles!

Obstruction.

He slammed his hand on the door panel, preventing the other man from pulling it open. The man looked up at Spaulding's face, at Spaulding's eyes.

'Christ, fella. I'll wait for another one,' the man said quickly.

David was embarrassed. What the hell was he *doing*?

The doubts? The goddamned doubts.

'No, really, I'm terribly sorry.' He mumbled the words, smiling apologetically. 'You take it. I'm in no hurry ... Sorry again.'

He turned and walked rapidly across the street into the crowds of Sheridan Square.

He could have had the taxi. That was the important thing.

Jesus! The treadmill never let up.

Part Two

22

1944 – Buenos Aires, Argentina

The Pan American Clipper left Tampa at eight in the morning, with scheduled coastline stops at Caracas, São Luis, Salvador, and Rio de Janeiro before the final twelve hundred miles to Buenos Aires. David was listed on the passenger invoice as Mr Donald Scanlan of Cincinnati, Ohio; occupation: mining surveyor. It was a temporary cover for the journey only. 'Donald Scanlan' would disappear after the Clipper landed at the aeroparque in Buenos Aires. The initials were the same as his own for the simple reason that it was so easy to forget a monogrammed gift or the first letter of a hastily written signature. Especially if one was preoccupied or tired ... or afraid.

Swanson had been close to panic when David reached him from the Mitchell Field Operations Room in New York. As a source control, Swanson was about as decisive as a bewildered bird dog. Any deviation from Kendall's schedule – Kendall's instructions, really – was abhorrent to him. And Kendall wasn't even *leaving* for Buenos Aires until the following morning.

David had not wasted complicated explanations on the general. As far as he was concerned, three attempts had been made on his life – at least, they could be so interpreted – and if the general wanted his 'services' in Buenos Aires, he'd better get down there while he was still in one piece and functioning.

Were the attempts – the attacks – related to Buenos Aires? Swanson had asked the question as though he were afraid to name the Argentine city.

David was honest: there was no way to tell. The answer was in Buenos Aires. It was reasonable to consider the possibility, but not to assume it.

'That's what Pace said,' had been Swanson's reply. 'Consider, don't assume.'

'Ed was generally right about such things.'

'He said when you operated in Lisbon, you were often involved in messy situations in the field.'

'True. I doubt that Ed knew the particulars, though. But he was right in what he was trying to tell you. There are a lot of people in Portugal and Spain who'd rather see me dead than alive. Or at least they think they would. They could never be sure. Standard procedure, general.'

There had been a prolonged pause on the Washington line. Finally, Swanson had said the words. 'You realize, Spaulding, that we may have to replace you.'

'Of course. You can do so right now, if you like.' David had been sincere. He wanted very much to return to Lisbon. To go into the north country. To Valdero's. To find out about a cryp named Marshall.

'No . . . No, everything's too far along. The designs. They're the important thing. Nothing else matters.'

The remainder of the conversation concerned the details of transportation, American and Argentine currency, replenishing of a basic wardrobe, and luggage. Logistics which were not in the general's frame of reference and for which David took responsibility. The final command – request – was delivered, not by the general, but by Spaulding.

Fairfax was not to be informed of his whereabouts. Nor was anyone else for that matter, except the embassy in Buenos Aires; but make every effort to keep the information from Fairfax.

Why? Did Spaulding think . . .

'There's a leak in Fairfax, general. You might pass that on to the White House cellars.'

'That's impossible!'

'Tell that to Ed Pace's widow.'

David looked out the Clipper window. The pilot, moments ago, had informed the passengers that they were passing over the huge coastal lake of Mirim in Uruguay. Soon they'd be over Montevideo, forty minutes from Buenos Aires.

Buenos Aires. The unfocused picture, the blurred figures of Leslie Jenner Hawkwood, the cryptographer Marshall, a man named Franz Altmüller; strange but committed men on Fifty-second and Thirty-eighth streets – in a darkened doorway, in a building after office hours, on a staircase. A man in an elevator who was so unafraid to die. An enemy who displayed enormous courage . . . or misguided zealousness. A maniac.

The answer to the enigma was in Buenos Aires, less than an hour away. The city was an hour away, the answer much longer. But no more than three weeks if his instincts were right. By the time the gyroscopic designs were delivered.

He would begin slowly, as he always did with a new field problem. Trying first to melt into the surroundings, absorb his cover; be comfortable, facile in his relationships. It shouldn't be difficult. His cover was merely an extension of Lisbon's: the wealthy trilingual attaché whose background, parents, and prewar associations in the fashionable centers of Europe made him a desirable social buffer for any ambassador's dinner table. He was an attractive addition to the delicate world of a neutral capital; and if there were those who thought someone, somewhere, had used money and influence to secure him such combat-exempt employment, so be it. It was denied emphatically, but not vehemently; there was a difference.

The 'extension' for Buenos Aires was direct and afforded him top-secret classification. He was acting as a liaison between New York–London banking circles and the German ex-patriot Erich Rhinemann. Washington approved, of course; postwar financing in areas of reconstruction and industrial rebuilding were going to be international problems. Rhinemann could not be overlooked, not in the civilized marble halls of Bern and Geneva.

David's thoughts returned to the book on his lap. It was the second of six volumes Eugene Lyons had chosen for him.

'Donald Scanlan' went through the aeroparque customs without difficulty. Even the embassy liaison, who checked in all Americans, seemed unaware of his identity.

His single suitcase in hand, David walked to the taxi station and stood on the cement platform looking at the drivers standing beside their vehicles. He wasn't prepared to assume the name of Spaulding or to be taken directly to the embassy just yet. He wanted to assure himself that 'Donald Scanlan' was accepted for what he was – a mining surveyor, nothing more, that there was no unusual interest in such a man. For if there were, it would point to David Spaulding, Military Intelligence, Fairfax and Lisbon graduate.

He selected an obese, pleasant-looking driver in the fourth cab from the front of the line. There were protests from those in front, but David pretended not to understand. 'Donald Scanlan' might know a smattering of Spanish, but certainly not the epithets employed by the disgruntled drivers cheated out of a fare.

Once inside he settled back and gave instructions to the unctuous driver. He told the man he had nearly an hour to waste before he was to be met – the meeting place not mentioned – and asked if the driver would give him a short tour of the city. The tour would serve two purposes: he could position himself so that he could constantly check for surveillance, and he would learn the main points of the city.

The driver, impressed by David's educated, grammatical Spanish, assumed the role of tour director and drove out of the airport's winding lanes to the exit of the huge Parque 3 de Febrero in which the field was centered.

Thirty minutes later David had filled a dozen pages with notes. The city was like a European insert on the southern continent. It was a strange mixture of Paris, Rome and middle Spain. The streets were not city streets, they were boulevards: wide, lined with color. Fountains and statuary everywhere. The Avenida 9 de Julio might have been a larger Via Veneto or Saint-Germain-des-Prés. The sidewalk cafes, profuse with brightly decorated awnings and greenery from hundreds of planter boxes, were doing a brisk summer afternoon business. The fact that it *was* summer in Argentina was emphasized for David by the perspiration on his neck and shirt front. The driver admitted that the day was inordinately warm, in the high seventies.

David asked to be driven – among other places – to a district called San Telmo. The cab owner nodded appreciatively, as if he had accurately assessed the rich American. Soon Spaulding understood. San Telmo was as Kendall had noted: elegant, secluded, beautifully kept old houses and apartment buildings with wrought-iron balustrades and brilliantly blossoming flowers lining the spotless streets.

Lyons would be comfortable.

From San Telmo the driver doubled back into the inner city and began the tour from the banks of the Rio de la Plata.

The Plaza de Mayo, the Cabildo, the Casa Rosada, Calle Rivadavia. The names filled David's notebook; these were the streets, the squares, the locations he would absorb quickly.

La Boca. The waterfront, south of the city; this, the driver said, was no place for the tourist.

The Calle Florida. Here was the finest shopping area in all South America. The driver could take his American to several store owners personally known to him and extraordinary purchases could be made.

Sorry, there was no time. But David wrote in his notebook that traffic was banned at the borders of the Calle Florida.

The driver then sped out on the Avenida Santa Fé toward the Palermo. No sight in Buenos Aires was as beautiful as the Palermo.

What interested David more than the beauty was the huge park – or series of individual parks; the quiet, immense, artificial lake. The acres of botanical gardens; the enormous zoo complex with rows of cages and buildings.

Beauty, yes. Secure areas of contact, more so. The Palermo might come in handy.

An hour had passed; there were no automobiles following the taxi. 'Donald Scanlan' had not been under surveillance; David Spaulding could emerge.

Quietly.

He instructed the driver to leave him off at the cabstand outside the entrance to the Palermo zoo. He was to meet his party there. The driver looked crestfallen. Was there no hotel? No place of residence?

Spaulding did not reply, he simply asked the fare and quickly held out the amount. No more questions were in order.

David spent an additional fifteen minutes inside the zoo, actually enjoying it. He bought an ice from a vendor, wandered past the cages of marmosets and orangutans – finding extraordinary resemblances to friends and enemies – and when he felt comfortable (as only a field man can feel comfortable), walked out to the cabstand.

He waited another five minutes while mothers and governesses and children entered the available taxis. It was his turn.

'The American embassy, *por favor.*'

Ambassador Henderson Granville allowed the new attaché a half-hour. There would be other days when they could sit and chat at length, but Sundays were hectic. The rest of Buenos Aires might be at church or at play; the diplomatic corps was at work. He had two garden parties still to attend – telephone calls would be made detailing the departures and arrivals of the German and the Japanese guests; *his* arrivals and departures would be timed accordingly. And after the second garden-bore there was dinner at the

Brazilian embassy, Neither German nor Japanese interference was anticipated. Brazil was close to an open break.

'The Italians, you realize,' said Granville, smiling at David, 'don't count
any longer. Never did really; not down here. They spend most of their time
cornering us in restaurants, or calling from public phones, explaining how
Mussolini ruined the country.'

'Not too different from Lisbon.'

'I'm afraid they're the only pleasant similarity . . . I won't bore you with a
tedious account of the upheavals we've experienced here, but a quick sketch
– and emphasis – will help you adjust. You've read up, I assume.'

'I haven't had much time. I left Lisbon only a week ago. I know that the
Castillo government was overthrown.'

'Last June. Inevitable . . . Ramón Castillo was as inept a president as
Argentina ever had, and it's had its share of buffoons. The economy was
disastrous: agriculture and industry came virtually to a halt; his cabinet never
made provisions to fill the beef market void created by the British struggle,
even though the lot of them figured John Bull was finished. He deserved to
be thrown out . . . Unfortunately, what came in the front door – marched in
phalanx up the Rivadavia, to be more precise – hardly makes our lives easier.'

'That's the military council, isn't it? The junta?'

Granville gestured with his delicate hands, the chiseled features of his
aging, aristocratic face formed a sardonic grimace. 'The Grupo de Oficiales
Unidos! As unpleasant a band of goose-stepping opportunists as you will
meet . . . I daresay, anywhere. You know, of course, the entire army was
trained by the Wehrmacht officer corps. Add to that jovial premise the hot
Latin temperament, economic chaos, a neutrality that's enforced but not
believed in, and what have you got? A suspension of the political apparatus;
no checks and balances. A police state rife with corruption.'

'What maintains the neutrality?'

'The infighting, primarily. The GOU – that's what we call it – has more
factions than the '29 Reichstag. They're all jockeying for the power spots.
And naturally, the cold fear of an American fleet and air force right up the
street, so to speak . . . The GOU has been reappraising its judgments during
the past five months. The colonels are beginning to wonder about their
mentors' thousand-year crusade; extremely impressed by our supply and
production lines.'

'They should be. We've . . .'

'And there's another aspect,' interrupted Granville thoughtfully. 'There's a
small, very wealthy community of Jews here. Your Erich Rhinemann, for
example. The GOU isn't prepared to openly advocate the solutions of Julius
Streicher . . . It's already used Jewish money to keep alive lines of credit pretty
well chewed up by Castillo. The colonels are afraid of financial manipulations, most military people are. But there's a great deal of money to be made
in this war. The colonels intend to make it . . . Do I sketch a recognizable
picture?'

'A complicated one.'

'I daresay . . . We have a maxim here that serves quite well. Today's friend will probably be on the Axis payroll tomorrow; conversely, yesterday's Berlin courier might be for sale next week. Keep your options open and your opinions private. And publicly . . . allow for a touch more flexibility than might be approved of at another post. It's tolerated.'

'And expected?' asked David.

'Both.'

David lit a cigarette. He wanted to shift the conversation; old Granville was one of those ambassadors, professorial by nature, who would go on analysing the subtleties of his station all day if someone listened. Such men were usually the best diplomats but not always the most desirable liaisons in times of active practicality. Henderson Granville was a good man, though his concerns shone in his eyes, and they were fair concerns.

'I imagine Washington has outlined my purpose here.'

'Yes. I wish I could say I approved. Not of you; you've got your instructions. And I suppose international finance will continue long after Herr Hitler has shrieked his last scream . . . Perhaps I'm no better than the GOU. Money matters can be most distasteful.'

'These in particular, I gather.'

'Again, yes. Erich Rhinemann is a sworn companion of the wind. A powerful companion, make no mistake, but totally without conscience; a hurricane's morality. Unquestionably the least honorable man I've ever met. I think it's criminal that his resources make him acceptable to London and New York.'

'Perhaps necessary is a more appropriate term.'

'I'm sure that's the rationalization, at any rate.'

'It's mine.'

'Of course. Forgive an old man's obsolete limits of necessity. But we have no quarrel. You have an assignment. What can I do for you? I understand it's very little.'

'Very little indeed, sir. Just have me listed on the embassy index; any kind of office space will do as long as it has a door and a telephone. And I'd like to meet your cryp. I'll have codes to send.'

'My word, that sounds ominous,' said Granville, smiling without humor.

'Routine, sir. Washington relay; simple Yeses and Nos.'

'Very well. Our head cryptographer is named Ballard. Nice fellow; speaks seven or eight languages and is an absolute whiz at parlor games. You'll meet him directly. What else?'

'I'd like an apartment . . .'

'Yes, we know,' interrupted Granville gently, snatching a brief look at the wall clock. 'Mrs Cameron has scouted one she thinks you'll approve of . . . Of course, Washington gave us no indication of your length of stay. So Mrs Cameron took it for three months.'

'That's far too long. I'll straighten it out . . . I think that's almost all, Mr Ambassador. I know you're in a hurry.'

'I'm afraid I am.'

David got out of his chair, as did Granville. 'Oh, one thing, sir. Would this Ballard have an embassy index? I'd like to learn the names here.'

'There aren't that many,' said Granville, leveling his gaze at David, a subtle note of disapproval in his voice. 'Eight or ten would be those you'd normally come in contact with. And I can assure you we have our own security measures.'

David accepted the rebuke. 'That wasn't my point, sir. I really *do* like to familiarize myself with the names.'

'Yes, of course.' Granville came around the desk and walked Spaulding to the door. 'Chat with my secretary for a few minutes. I'll get hold of Ballard; he'll show you around.'

'Thank you, sir.' Spaulding extended his hand to Granville, and as he did so he realized for the first time how tall the man was.

'You know,' said the ambassador, releasing David's hand, 'there was a question I wanted to ask you, but the answer will have to wait for another time. I'm late already.'

'What was that?'

'I've been wondering why the boys on Wall Street and the Strand sent *you.* I can't imagine there being a dearth of experienced bankers in New York or London, can you?'

'There probably isn't. But then I'm only a liaison carrying messages; information best kept private, I gather. I *have* had experience in those areas ... in a neutral country.'

Granville smiled once more and once more there was no humor conveyed. 'Yes, of course. I was sure there was a reason.'

23

Ballard shared two traits common to most cryptographers, thought David. He was a casual cynic and a fount of information. Qualities, Spaulding believed, developed over years of deciphering other men's secrets only to find the great majority unimportant. He was also cursed with the first name of Robert, by itself acceptable but when followed by Ballard, invariably reduced to Bobby. Bobby Ballard. It had the ring of a 1920s socialite or the name in a cereal box cartoon.

He was neither. He was a linguist with a mathematical mind and a shock of red hair on top of a medium-sized, muscular body; a pleasant man.

'That's our home,' Ballard was saying. 'You've seen the working sections; big, rambling, baroque and goddamned hot this time of year. I hope you're smart and have your own apartment.'

'Don't you? Do you live *here*?'

'It's easier. My dials are very inconsiderate, they hum at all hours. Better than scrambling down from Chacarita or Telmo. And it's not bad; we stay out of each other's way pretty much.'

'Oh? A lot of you here?'

'No. They alternate. Six, usually. In the two wings, east and south. Granville has the north apartments. Besides him, Jean Cameron and I are the only permanents. You'll meet Jean tomorrow, unless we run into her on the way out with the old man. She generally goes with him to the diplobores.'

'The what?'

'Diplobores. The old man's word ... contraction. I'm surprised he didn't use it with you. He's proud of it. Diplobore is an embassy duty bash.' They were in a large empty reception room; Ballard was opening a pair of French doors leading out onto a short balcony. In the distance could be seen the waters of the Rio de la Plata and the estuary basin of the Puerto Nuevo, Buenos Aires's main port. 'Nice view, isn't it?'

'Certainly is.' David joined the cryptographer on the balcony. 'Does this Jean Cameron and the ambassador ... I mean, are they ...?'

'Jean and the old *man*?' Ballard laughed loud and good-naturedly. 'Christ, no! ... Come to think of it, I don't know why it strikes me so funny. I suppose there're a lot of people who think that. And *that's* funny.'

'Why?'

'Sad-funny, I guess I should say,' continued Ballard without interruption. 'The old man and the Cameron family go back to the original Maryland money. Eastern Shore yacht clubs, blazer jackets, tennis in the morning – you know: diplomat territory. Jean's family was part of it, too. She married this Cameron; knew him since they could play doctor together in their Abercrombie pup tents. A rich-people romance, childhood sweethearts. They got married; the war came; he chucked his law books for a TBF – aircraft carrier pilot. He was killed in the Leyte Gulf. That was last year. She went a little crazy; maybe more than a little.'

'So the ... Granville brought her down here?'

'That's right.'

'Nice therapy, if you can afford it.'

'She'd probably agree with that.' Ballard walked back into the reception room; Spaulding followed. 'But most people will tell you she pays her dues for the treatment. She works damned hard and knows what she's doing. Has rotten hours, too; what with the diplobores.'

'Where's *Mrs* Granville?'

'No idea. She divorced the old man ten, fifteen years ago.'

'I still say it's nice work if you can get it.' David was thinking, in an offhand way, of several hundred thousand other women whose husbands had been killed, living with reminders every day. He dismissed his thoughts; they weren't his concerns.

'Well, she's qualified.'

'What?' David was looking at a rococo-styled corner pillar in the wall, not really listening.

'Jean spent four years – off and on – down here as a kid. Her father was in Foreign Service; probably would have been an ambassador by now if he'd stuck with it ... Come on, I'll show you the office Granville assigned you. Maintenance should have it tidied up by now,' Ballard smiled.

'You've been employing a diversion,' laughed David, following the cryp out the door into another hallway.

'I had to. You've got a room in the back. So far back it's been used for storage, I think.'

'Obviously I made points with Granville.'

'You sure did. He can't figure you out ... Me? I don't try.' Ballard turned left into still another intersecting hallway. 'This is the south wing. Offices on the first and second floors; not many, three on each. Apartments on the third and fourth. The roof is great for sunbathing, if you like that sort of thing.'

'Depends on the company, I suppose.'

The two men approached a wide staircase, preparing to veer to the left beyond it, when a feminine voice called down from the second landing.

'Bobby, is that you?'

'It's Jean,' said Ballard. 'Yes,' he called out. 'I'm with Spaulding. Come on down and meet the new recruit with enough influence to get his own apartment right off.'

'Wait'll he sees the apartment!'

Jean Cameron came into sight from around the corner landing. She was a moderately tall woman, slender and dressed in a floor-length cocktail gown at once vivid with color yet simple in design. Her light-brown hair was shoulder length, full and casual. Her face was a combination of striking features blended into a soft whole; wide, alive blue eyes; a thin, sharply etched nose; lips medium full and set as if in a half-smile. Her very clear skin was bronzed by the Argentine sun.

David saw that Ballard was watching him, anticipating his reaction to the girl's loveliness. Ballard's expression was humorously sardonic, and Spaulding read the message: Ballard had been to the font and found it empty – for those seeking other than a few drops of cool water. Ballard was now a friend to the lady; he knew better than to try being anything else.

Jean Cameron seemed embarrassed by her introduction on the staircase. She descended rapidly, her lips parted into one of the most genuine smiles David had seen in years. Genuine and totally devoid of innuendo.

'Welcome,' she said, extending her hand. 'Thank heavens I have a chance to apologize before you walk into that place. You may change your mind and move right back here.'

'It's that bad?' David saw that Jean wasn't quite as young at close range as she seemed on the staircase. She was past thirty; comfortably past. And she seemed aware of his inspection, the approbation – or lack of it – unimportant to her.

'Oh, it's all right for a limited stay. You can't get anything else on that basis, not if you're American. But it's small.'

Her handshake was firm, almost masculine, thought Spaulding. 'I appreciate your taking the trouble. I'm sorry to have caused it.'

'No one else here could have gotten you anything but a hotel,' said Ballard, touching the girl's shoulder; was the contact protective? wondered David. 'The *porteños* trust Mother Cameron. Not the rest of us.'

'*Porteños*,' said Jean in response to Spaulding's questioning expression, 'are the people who live in BA . . .'

'And BA – don't tell me – stands for Montevideo,' replied David.

'Aw, they sent us a *bright* one,' said Ballard.

'You'll get used to it,' continued Jean. 'Everyone in the American and English settlements calls it BA. Montevideo, of course,' she added, smiling. 'I think we see it so often on reports, we just do it automatically.'

'Wrong,' interjected Ballard. 'The vowel juxtaposition in "Buenos Aires" is uncomfortable for British speech.'

'That's something else you'll learn during your stay, Mr Spaulding,' said Jean Cameron, looking affectionately at Ballard. 'Be careful offering opinions around Bobby. He has a penchant for disagreeing.'

'Never so,' answered the cryp. 'I simply care enough for my fellow prisoners to want to enlighten them. Prepare them for the outside when they get paroled.'

'Well, I've got a temporary pass right now, and if I don't get over to the ambassador's office, he'll start on that damned address system . . . Welcome again, Mr Spaulding.'

'Please. The name's David.'

'Mine's Jean. Bye,' said the girl, dashing down the hallway, calling back to Ballard. 'Bobby? You've got the address and the key? For . . . David's place?'

'Yep. Go get irresponsibly drunk, I'll handle everything.'

Jean Cameron disappeared through a door in the right wall.

'She's very attractive,' said Spaulding, 'and you two are good friends. I should apologize for . . .'

'No, you shouldn't,' interrupted Ballard. 'Nothing to apologize for. You formed a quick judgment on isolated facts. I'd've done the same, thought the same. Not that you've changed your mind; no reason to, really.'

'She's right. You disagree . . . before you know what you're disagreeing to; and then you debate your disagreement. And if you go on, you'll probably challenge your last position.'

'You know what? I can follow that. Isn't it frightening?'

'You guys are a separate breed,' said David, chuckling, following Ballard beyond the stairs into a smaller corridor.

'Let's take a quick look at your Siberian cubicle and then head over to your other cell. It's on Córdoba; we're on Corrientes. It's about ten minutes from here.'

David thanked Bobby Ballard once again and shut the apartment door. He had pleaded exhaustion from the trip, preceded by too much welcome home in New York – and God knew that was the truth – and would Ballard take a raincheck for dinner?

Alone now, he inspected the apartment; it wasn't intolerable at all. It was small: a bedroom, a sitting room-kitchen, and a bath. But there was a dividend Jean Cameron hadn't mentioned. The rooms were on the first floor, and at the rear was a tiny brick-leveled patio surrounded by a tall concrete wall, profuse with hanging vines and drooping flowers from immense pots on the ledge. In the center of the enclosure was a gnarled fruit-bearing tree he could not identify; around the trunk were three rope-webbed chairs that had seen better days but looked extremely comfortable. As far as he was concerned, the dividend made the dwelling.

Ballard had pointed out that his section of the Avenida Córdoba was just over the borderline from the commercial area, the 'downtown' complex of Buenos Aires. Quasi-residential, yet near enough to stores and restaurants to be easy for a newcomer.

David picked up the telephone; the dial tone was delayed but eventually there. He replaced it and walked across the small room to the refrigerator, an American Sears Roebuck. He opened it and smiled. The Cameron girl had provided – or had somebody provide – several basic items: milk, butter, bread, eggs, coffee. Then happily he spotted two bottles of wine: an Orfila *tinto* and a Colón *blanco*. He closed the refrigerator and went back into the bedroom.

He unpacked his single suitcase, unwrapping a bottle of Scotch, and remembered that he'd have to buy additional clothes in the morning. Ballard had offered to go with him to a men's shop in the Calle Florida – if his goddamned dials weren't 'humming.' He placed the books Eugene Lyons had given him on the bedside table. He had gone through two of them; he was beginning to gain confidence in the aerophysicists' language. He would need comparable studies in German to be really secure. He would cruise around the bookshops in the German settlement tomorrow; he wasn't looking for definitive texts, just enough to understand the terms. It was really a minor part of his assignment, he understood that.

Suddenly, David remembered Walter Kendall. Kendall was either in Buenos Aires by now or would be arriving within hours. The accountant had left the United States at approximately the same time he had, but Kendall's flight from New York was more direct, with far fewer stopovers.

He wondered whether it would be feasible to go out to the aeroparque and trace Kendall. If he hadn't arrived, he could wait for him; if he had, it would be simple enough to check the hotels – according to Ballard there were only three or four good ones.

On the other hand, any additional time – more than absolutely essential – spent with the manipulating accountant was not a pleasant prospect. Kendall would be upset at finding him in Buenos Aires before he'd given the order to Swanson. Kendall, no doubt, would demand explanations beyond those David wished to give; probably send angry cables to an already strung-out brigadier general.

There were no benefits in hunting down Walter Kendall until Kendall expected to find him. Only liabilities.

He had other things to do: the unfocused picture. He could begin that search far better alone.

David walked back into the living room-kitchen carrying the Scotch and took out a tray of ice from the refrigerator. He made himself a drink and looked over at the double doors leading to his miniature patio. He would spend a few quiet twilight moments in the January summertime breeze of Buenos Aires.

The sun was fighting its final descent beyond the city; the last orange rays were filtering through the thick foliage of the unidentified fruit tree. Underneath, David stretched his legs and leaned back in the rope-webbed chair. He realized that if he kept his eyes closed for any length of time, they would not reopen for a number of hours. He had to watch that; long experience in the field had taught him to eat something before sleeping.

Eating had long since lost its pleasure for him – it was merely a necessity directly related to his energy level. He wondered if the pleasure would ever come back; whether so much he had put aside would return. Lisbon had probably the best accommodations – food, shelter, comfort – of all the major cities, excepting New York, on both continents. And now he was on a third continent, in a city that boasted undiluted luxury.

But for him it was the field – as much as was the north country in Spain.

As much as Basque and Navarre, and the freezing nights in the Galician hills or the sweat-prone silences in ravines, waiting for patrols – waiting to kill.

So much. So alien.

He brought his head forward, took a long drink from the glass and let his neck arch back into the frame of the chair. A small bird was chattering away in the midsection of the tree, annoyed at his intrusion. It reminded David of how he would listen for such birds in the north country. They telegraphed the approach of men unseen, often falling into different rhythms that he began to identify – or thought he identified – with the numbers of the unseen, approaching patrols.

Then David realized that the small chattering bird was not concerned with him. It hopped upward, still screeching its harsh little screech, only faster now, more strident.

There was someone else.

Through half-closed eyes, David focused above, beyond the foliage. He did so without moving any part of his body or head, as if the last moments were approaching before sleep took over.

The apartment house had four stories and a roof that appeared to have a gentle slope covered in a terra-cotta tile of sorts – brownish pink in color. The windows of the rooms above him were mostly open to the breezes off the Rio de la Plata. He could hear snatches of subdued conversation, nothing threatening, no loud vibrations. It was the Buenos Aires siesta hour, according to Ballard; quite different from Rome's afternoon or the Paris lunch. Dinner in BA was very late, by the rest of the world's schedule. Ten, ten thirty, even midnight was not out of the question.

The screeching bird was not bothered by the inhabitants of the Córdoba apartment house; yet still he kept up his strident alarms.

And then David saw why.

On the roof, obscured but not hidden by the branches of the fruit tree, were the outlines of two men.

They were crouched, staring downward; staring, he was sure, at him.

Spaulding judged the position of the main intersecting tree limb and rolled his head slightly, as if the long-awaited sleep were upon him, his neck resting in exhaustion on his right shoulder, the drink barely held by a relaxed hand, millimeters from the brick pavement.

It helped; he could see better, not well. Enough, however, to make out the sharp, straight silhouette of a rifle barrel, the orange sun careening off its black steel. It was stationary, in an arrest position under the arm of the man on the right. No movement was made to raise it, to aim it; it remained immobile, cradled.

Somehow, it was more ominous that way, thought Spaulding. As though in the arms of a killer guard who was sure his prisoner could not possibly vault the stockade; there was plenty of time to shoulder and fire.

David carried through his charade. He raised his hand slightly and let his drink fall. The sound of the minor crash 'awakened' him; he shook the pretended sleep from his head and rubbed his eyes with his fingers. As he did so, he manoeuvred his face casually upward. The figures on the roof had stepped back on the terra-cotta tiles. There would be no shots. Not directed at him.

He picked up a few pieces of the glass, rose from the chair and walked into the apartment as a tired man does when annoyed with his own carelessness. Slowly, with barely controlled irritation.

Once he crossed the saddle of the door, beneath the sightline of the roof, he threw the glass fragments into a wastebasket and walked rapidly into the bedroom. He opened the top drawer of the bureau, separated some handkerchiefs and withdrew his revolver.

He clamped it inside his belt and picked up his jacket from the chair in which he'd thrown it earlier. He put it on, satisfied that it concealed the weapon.

He crossed out into the living room, to the apartment door, and opened it silently.

The staircase was against the left wall and David swore to himself, cursing the architect of this particular Avenida Córdoba building – or the profuseness of lumber in Argentina. The stairs were made of wood, the brightly polished wax not concealing the obvious fact that they were ancient and probably squeaked like hell.

He closed his apartment door and approached the staircase, putting his feet on the first step.

It creaked the solid creak of antique shops.

He had four flights to go; the first three were unimportant. He took the steps two at a time, discovering that if he hugged the wall, the noise of his ascent was minimized.

Sixty seconds later he faced a closed door marked with a sign – in goddamned curlicued Castilian lettering:

El Techo.

The roof.

The door, as the stairs, was old. Decades of seasonal heat and humidity had caused the wood to swell about the hinges; the borders were forced into the frame.

It, too, would scream his arrival if he opened it slowly.

There was no other way: he slipped the weapon out of his belt and took one step back on the tiny platform. He judged the frame – the concrete walls – surrounding the old wooden door and with an adequate intake of breath, he pulled at the handle, yanked the door open and jumped diagonally into the right wall, slamming his back against the concrete.

The two men whirled around, stunned. They were thirty feet from David at the edge of the sloping roof. The man with the rifle hesitated, then raised the weapon into waist-firing position. Spaulding had his pistol aimed directly into the man's chest. However, the man with the gun did not have the look of one about to fire at a target; the hesitation was deliberate, not the result of panic or indecision.

The second man shouted in Spanish; David recognized the accent as southern Spain, not Argentine. *'Por favor, señor!'*

Spaulding replied in English to establish their understanding, or lack of it. 'Lower that rifle. *Now!'*

The first man did so, holding it by the stock. 'You are in error,' he said in halting English: 'There have been ... how do you say, *ladrones* ... thieves in the neighbourhood.'

David walked over the metal transom onto the roof, holding his pistol on the two men. 'You're not very convincing. *Se dan corte, amigos.* You're not from Buenos Aires.'

'There are a great many people in this neighborhood who are as we: displaced, *señor.* This is a community of ... not the native born,' said the second man.

'You're telling me you weren't up here for my benefit? You weren't watching me?'

'It was coincidental, I assure you,' said the man with the rifle.

'Es la verdad,' added the other. 'Two *habitaciones* have been broken into during the past week. The police do not help; we are ... *extranjeros*, foreigners to them. We protect ourselves.'

Spaulding watched the men closely. There was no waver in either man's expression, no hint of lies. No essential fear.

'I'm with the American embassy,' said David curtly. There was no reaction from either *extranjero.* 'I must ask you for identification.'

'Qué cosa?' The man with the gun.

'Papers. Your names ... *Certificados.'*

'Por cierto, en seguida.' The second man reached back into his trousers pocket; Spaulding raised the pistol slightly, in warning.

The man hesitated, now showing his fear. 'Only a *registro, señor.* We all must carry them ... Please. In my *cartera.'*

David held out his left hand as the second man gave him a cheap leather wallet. He flipped it open with minor feelings of regret. There was a kind of helplessness about the two *extranjeros*; he'd seen the look thousands of times. Franco's Falangistas were experts at provoking it.

He looked quickly down at the cellophane window of the billfold; it was cracked with age.

Suddenly, the barrel of the rifle came crashing across his right wrist; the pain was excruciating. Then his hand was being twisted expertly inward and down; he had no choice but to release the weapon and try to kick it away on the sloping roof. To hold it would mean breaking his wrist.

He did so as his left arm was being hammerlocked – again expertly – up over his neck. He lashed his foot out at the unarmed *extranjero,* who had hold of his hand. He caught him in the stomach and as the man bent forward, David crossed his weight and kicked again, sending the man tumbling down on the tiled incline.

David fell in the thrust direction of the hammerlock – downward, to his rear – and as the first man countered the position, Spaulding brought his right elbow back up, crushing into the man's groin. The arm was released as the *extranjero* tried to regain his balance.

He wasn't quick enough; Spaulding whipped to his left and brought his knee up into the man's throat. The rifle clattered on the tiles and rolled downward on the slope. The man sank, blood dribbling from his mouth where his teeth had punctured the skin.

Spaulding heard the sound behind him and turned.

He was too late. The second *extranjero* was over him, and David could hear the whistling of his own pistol piercing the air above him, crashing down into his skull.

All was black. Void.

'They described the right attitude but the wrong section of town,' said Ballard, sitting across the room from David, who held an ice pack to his head. 'The *extranjeros* are concentrated in the west areas of the La Boca district. They've got a hell of a crime rate over there; the *polica* prefer strolling the parks rather than those streets. And the Grupo – the GOU – has no love for *extranjeros*.'

'You're no help,' said Spaulding, shifting the ice pack around in circles on the back of his head.

'Well, they weren't out to kill you. They could have thrown you off or just left you on the edge; five to one you'd've rolled over and down four flights.'

'I knew they weren't intent on killing me . . .'

'How?'

'They could have done that easily before. I think they were waiting for me to go out. I'd unpacked; they'd have the apartment to themselves.'

'What for?'

'To search my things. They *have* done that before.'

'Who?'

'Damned if I know.'

'Now who's no help?'

'Sorry . . . Tell me, Bobby, who exactly knew I was flying in? How was it handled?'

'First question: three people. I did, of course; I'm on the dials. Granville, obviously. And Jean Cameron; the old man asked her to follow up on an apartment . . . but you know that. Question two: very confidentially. Remember, your orders came through at night. From Washington. Jean was playing chess with Granville in his quarters when I brought him the eggs . . .'

'The what?' interrupted David.

'The scrambler; it's marked. Washington had your sheet radioed in on a scrambler code. That means only myself or my head man can handle it, deliver it to the ambassador.'

'Okay. Then what?'

'Nothing. I mean nothing you don't know about.'

'Tell me anyway.'

Ballard exhaled a long, condescending breath. 'Well, the three of us were alone; what the hell, I'd read the scramble and the instructions were clear about the apartment. So Granville figured – apparently – that Jean was the logical one to scout one up. He told her you were coming in; to do what she could on such short notice.' Ballard looked about the room and over at the patio doors. 'She didn't do badly, either.'

'Then that's it; they've got a network fanned out over the city; nothing unusual. They keep tabs on unoccupied places: apartments, rooming houses; hotels are the easiest.'

'I'm not sure I follow you,' said Ballard, trying to.

'We can all be smart as whips, Bobby, but we can't change a couple of basics: we have to have a place to sleep and take a bath.'

'Oh, I follow *that*, but you can't apply it here. Starting tomorrow you're no secret; until then you are. DC said you were coming down on your own; we had no idea precisely when or how . . . Jean didn't get this apartment for *you*. Not in *your name*.'

'Oh?' David was far more concerned than his expression indicated. The two *extranjeros* had to have been on the roof before he arrived. Or, at least, within minutes after he did so. 'How did she lease it then? Whose name did she use? I didn't want a cover; we didn't ask for one.'

'Jesus, I thought *I* talked fast. Sunday is *Sunday*, Monday is *Monday*. Sunday we don't know you; Monday we do. That's what Washington spelled out. They wanted no advance notice of your arrival and, incidentally, if *you* decided to stay out of sight, we were to adhere to your wishes. I'm sure Granville will ask you what you want to do in the morning . . . How did Jean lease the place? Knowing her, she probably implied the ambassador had a girl on the side, or something. The *porteños* are very *simpático* with that sort of thing; the Paris of South America and all that . . . One thing I *do* know, she wouldn't have used your name. Or any obvious cover. She'd use her own first.'

'Oh, boy,' said Spaulding wearily, removing the ice pack and feeling the back of his head. He looked at his fingers. Smudges of blood were apparent.

'I hope you're not going to play hero with that gash. You should see a doctor.'

'No hero.' David smiled. 'I've got to have some sutures removed, anyway. Might as well be tonight, if you can arrange it.'

'I can arrange it. Where did you get the stitches?'

'I had an accident in the Azores.'

'Christ, you travel, don't you?'

'So does something ahead of me.'

24

'Mrs Cameron is here at my request, Spaulding. Come in. I've talked with Ballard and the doctor. Stitches taken out and new ones put in; you must feel like a pincushion.'

Granville was behind his baroque desk, reclining comfortably in his highbacked chair. Jean Cameron sat on the couch against the left wall; one of the chairs in front of the desk was obviously meant for David. He decided to wait until Granville said so before sitting down. He remained standing; he wasn't sure he liked the ambassador. The office assigned to him was, indeed, far back and used for storage.

'Nothing serious, sir. If it was, I'd say so.' Spaulding nodded to Jean and saw her concern. Or, at least, that's what he thought he read in her eyes.

'You'd be foolish not to. The doctor says the blow to the head fortunately fell between concussion areas. Otherwise, you'd be in rather bad shape.'

'It was delivered by an experienced man.'

'Yes, I see . . . Our doctor didn't think much of the sutures he removed.'

'That seems to be a general medical opinion. They served their purpose; the shoulder's fine. He strapped it.'

'Yes . . . Sit down, sit down.'

David sat down. 'Thank you, sir.'

'I gather the two men who attacked you last evening were *provincianos.* Not *porteños.*'

Spaulding gave a short, defeated smile and turned to Jean Cameron. 'I got to *porteños*; I guess *provincianos* means what it says. The country folk? Outside the cities.'

'Yes,' said the girl softly. '*The* city. BA.'

'Two entirely different cultures,' continued Granville. 'The *provincianos* are hostile and with much legitimacy. They're really quite exploited; the resentments are flaring up. The GOU has done nothing to ease matters, it only conscripts them in the lowest ranks.'

'The *provincianos* are native to Argentina, though, aren't they?'

'Certainly. From their point of view, much more so than Buenos Airens, *porteños.* Less Italian and German blood, to say nothing of Portuguese, Balkan and Jewish. There were waves of immigrations, you see . . .'

'Then, Mr Ambassador,' interrupted David, hoping to stem another post analysis by the pedagogical diplomat, 'these were not *provincianos*. They called themselves *extranjeros*. Displaced persons, I gathered.'

'*Extranjero* is a rather sarcastic term. Inverse morbidity. As though employed by a reservation Indian in our Washington. A foreigner in his own native land, you see what I mean?'

'These men were not from Argentina,' said David quietly, dismissing Granville's question. 'Their speech pattern was considerably alien.'

'Oh? Are you an expert?'

'Yes, I am. In these matters.'

'I see.' Granville leaned forward. 'Do you ascribe the attack to embassy concerns? Allied concerns?'

'I'm not sure. It's my opinion I was the target. I'd like to know how they knew I was here.'

Jean Cameron spoke from the couch. 'I've gone over everything I said, David.' She stopped and paused briefly, aware that the ambassador had shot her a look at her use of Spaulding's first name. 'Your place was the fourth apartment I checked into. I started at ten in the morning and got there around two o'clock. And leased it immediately. I'm sorry to say it was the patio that convinced me.'

David smiled at her.

'Anyway, I went to a real estate office at Viamonte. Geraldo Baldez is the owner; we all know him. He's partisan; has no use for Germans. I made it clear that I wanted to rent the apartment for one of our people who was living here and who, frankly, found the embassy restrictions too limiting. He laughed and said he was sure it was Bobby. I didn't disagree.'

'But it was a short lease,' said David.

'I used it as an excuse in case you didn't like the apartment. It's a standard three-month clause.'

'Why wouldn't Bobby – or anyone else – get his own place?'

'Any number of reasons. Also standard . . . here.' Jean smiled, a touch embarrassed, thought David. 'I know the city better than most; I lived here for several years. Also there's a little matter of expense allowance; I'm a pretty good bargainer. And men like Bobby have urgent work to do. My hours are more flexible; I have the time.'

'Mrs Cameron is too modest, Spaulding. She's an enormous asset to our small community.'

'I'm sure she is, sir . . . Then you don't think anyone had reason to suspect you were finding a place for an incoming attaché.'

'Absolutely not. It was all done in such a . . . lighthearted way, if you know what I mean.'

'What about the owner of the building?' David asked.

'I never saw him. Most apartments are owned by wealthy people who live in the Telmo or Palermo districts. Everything's done through rental agencies.'

David turned to Granville. 'Have there been any calls for me? Messages?'

'No. Not that I'm aware of, and I'm sure I would be. You would have been contacted, of course.'

'A man named Kendall . . .'

'Kendall?' interrupted the ambassador. 'I know that name . . . Kendall. Yes, Kendall.' Granville riffled through some papers on his desk. 'Here. A Walter Kendall came in last night. Ten-thirty flight. He's staying at the Alvear; that's near the Palermo Park. Fine old hotel.' Granville suddenly looked over at Spaulding. 'He's listed on the sheet as an industrial economist. Now that's a rather all-inclusive description, isn't it? Would he be the banker I referred to yesterday?'

'He'll make certain arrangements relative to my instructions.' David did not conceal his reluctance to go into the matter of Walter Kendall. On the other hand, he instinctively found himself offering a token clarification to Jean Cameron. 'My primary job here is to act as liaison between financial people in New York and London and banking interests here in Buenos . . . BA.' David smiled; he hoped as genuinely as Jean smiled. 'I think it's a little silly. I don't know a debit from an asset. But Washington okayed me. The ambassador is worried that I'm too inexperienced.'

Spaulding quickly shifted his gaze to Granville, reminding the old man that 'banking interests' was the limit of identities. The name of Erich Rhinemann was out of bounds.

'Yes, I admit, I was . . . But that's neither here nor there. What do you wish to do about last night? I think we should lodge a formal complaint with the police. Not that it will do a damn bit of good.'

David fell silent for a few moments, trying to consider the pros and cons of Granville's suggestion. 'Would we get press coverage?'

'Very little, I'd think,' answered Jean.

'Embassy attachés usually have money,' said Granville. 'They've been robbed. It will be called an attempted robbery. Probably was.'

'But the Grupo doesn't like that kind of news. It doesn't fit in with the colonels' view of things, and they control the press.' Jean was thinking out loud, looking at David. 'They'll play it down.'

'And if we don't complain – assuming it was not robbery – we're admitting we think it was something else. Which I'm not prepared to do,' said Spaulding.

'Then by all means, a formal complaint will be registered this morning. Will you dictate a report of the incident and sign it, please?' Obviously, Granville wished to terminate the meeting. 'And to be frank with you, Spaulding, unless I'm considerably in the dark, I believe it *was* an attempt to rob a newly arrived rich American. I'm told the airport taxi drivers have formed a veritable thieves' carnival. *Extranjeros* would be perfectly logical participants.'

David stood up; he was pleased to see that Jean did the same. 'I'll accept that, Mr Ambassador. The years in Lisbon have made me overly . . . concerned. I'll adjust.'

'I daresay. Do write up the report.'

'Yes, sir.'

'I'll get him a stenographer,' said Jean. 'Bilingual.'

'Not necessary. I'll dictate it in Spanish.'

'I forgot.' Jean smiled. 'Bobby said they'd sent us a bright one.'

David supposed it began with that first lunch. Later she told him it was before, but he didn't believe her. She claimed it was when he said that BA stood for Montevideo; that was silly, it didn't make sense.

What made sense – and they both recognized it without any attempt to verbalize it – was the total relaxation each felt in the other's company. It was as simple as that. It was a splendid comfort; the silences never awkward, the laughter easy and based in communicated humor, not forced response.

It was remarkable. Made more so, David believed, because neither expected it, neither sought it. Both had good and sufficient reasons to avoid any relationships other than surface or slightly below. He was an impermanent man, hoping only to survive and start somewhere again with a clear head and suppressed memories. That was important to him. And he knew she still mourned a man so deeply she couldn't possibly – without intolerable guilt – push that man's face and body and mind behind her.

She told him partially why herself. Her husband had not been the image of the dashing carrier pilot so often depicted by navy public relations. He'd had an extraordinary fear – not for himself – but of taking lives. Were it not for the abuse he knew would have been directed at his Maryland wife and Maryland family, Cameron would have sought conscientious objector status. Then, too, perhaps he hadn't the courage of his own convictions.

Why a pilot?

Cameron had been flying since he was in his teens. It seemed natural and he believed his civilian training might lead to a Stateside instructor's berth. He rejected military law; too many of his fellow attorneys had gone after it and found themselves in the infantry and on the decks of battleships. The military had enough lawyers; they wanted pilots.

David thought he understood why Jean told him so much about her dead husband. There were two reasons. The first was that by doing so openly, she was adjusting to what she felt was happening between them; atoning, perhaps. The second was less clear but in no way less important. Jean Cameron hated the war; hated it for what it had taken away from her. She wanted him to know that.

Because – David realized – her instincts told her he was very much involved. And she would have no part of that involvement; she owed that much to Cameron's memory.

They'd gone to lunch at a restaurant overlooking the waters of the Riachúelo Basin near the piers of Dársena Sud. She had suggested it – the restaurant and the lunch. She saw that he was still exhausted; what sleep he'd managed had been interrupted constantly with pain. She insisted that he needed a long, relaxing lunch, then home to bed and a day's recuperation.

She hadn't meant to go with him.

He hadn't meant for her to.

'Ballard's a nice guy,' said Spaulding, pouring a clear white Colón.

'Bobby's a dear,' she agreed. 'He's a kind person.'

'He's very fond of you.'

'And I of him . . . What you're speculating on is perfectly natural, and I'm sorry to spoil the wilder melody. Is melody right? Granville told me who your parents were. I'm impressed.'

'I've refused to read music since the age of eight. But "melody's" fine. I just wondered.'

'Bobby gave me a thoroughly professional try, with enormous charm and good humor. A better girl would have responded. He had every right to be angry . . . I wanted his company but gave very little in return for it.'

'He accepted your terms,' said David affirmatively.

'I said he was kind.'

'There must be ten other fellows here . . .'

'Plus the marine guard,' interjected Jean, feigning a lovely, unmilitary salute. 'Don't forget them.'

'A hundred and ten, then. You're Deanna Durbin.'

'Hardly. The marines rotate off the FMF base south of La Boca; the staff – those without wives and kinder – are plagued with the embassy syndrome.'

'What's that?'

'State Department-itis . . . The quivers. You seem to be singularly lacking in them.'

'I don't know whether I am or not. I don't know what they are.'

'Which tells me something about you, doesn't it?'

'What does it tell you?'

'You're not a State Department climber. The "itis" syndrome is treading lightly and making damned sure everybody above you – especially the ambassador – is happy with your *sincerest efforts*.' Jean grimaced like a boxer puppy, her delicate chin forward, her eyebrows down – mocking the words. Spaulding broke out laughing; the girl had captured the embassy look and voice with devastating accuracy.

'Christ, I'm going to put you on the radio.' He laughed again. 'You've described the syndrome. I see it, Lord! I see it!'

'But you're not infected by it.' Jean stopped her mimicry and looked into his eyes. 'I watched you with Granville; you were just barely polite. You weren't looking for a fitness report, were you?'

He returned her gaze. 'No, I wasn't . . . To answer the question that's rattling around that lovely head of yours so loud it vibrates – I'm not a Foreign Service career officer. I'm strictly wartime. I *do* work out of embassies on a variety of related assignments for a couple of related reasons. I speak four languages and because of those parents that impressed you so, I have what is euphemistically described as access to important people in government, commerce, those areas. Since I'm not a complete idiot, I often circulate confidential information among corporations in various countries. The marketplace doesn't stop humming for such inconveniences as war . . .

That's my contribution. I'm not very proud of it, but it's what they handed me.'

She smiled her genuine smile and reached for his hand. '*I* think you do whatever you do very intelligently and well. There aren't many people who can say that. And God knows you can't choose.'

' "What did you do in the war, daddy?" ... "Well, son," ' David tried his own caricature. ' "I went from place to place telling friends of the Chase Bank to sell high and buy low and clear a decent profit margin." ' He kept her hand in his.

'And got attacked on Argentine rooftops and ... and what were those stitches in your shoulder?'

'The cargo plane I was on in the Azores made a rotten landing. I think the pilot and his whole crew were plastered.'

'There. See? You live as dangerously as any man at the front ... If I meet that boy you're talking to, I'll tell him that.'

Their eyes were locked; Jean withdrew her hand, embarrassed. But for Spaulding the important thing was that she believed him. She accepted his cover extension without question. It occurred to him that he was at once greatly relieved and yet, in a way, quite sorry. He found no professional pride in lying to her successfully.

'So now you know how I've avoided the State Department syndrome. I'm still not sure why it's relevant. What the hell, with a hundred and ten men and marines ...'

'The marines don't count. They have sundry interests down here in La Boca.'

'Then the staff – those without the "Wives and kinder" – they can't all be quivering.'

'But they do and I've been grateful. They'd like to get to the Court of St James's someday.'

'Now you're playing mental gymnastics. I'm not following you.'

'No, I'm not. I wanted to see if Bobby had told you. He hasn't. I said he was kind ... He was giving me the chance to tell you myself.'

'Tell me what?'

'My husband was Henderson Granville's stepson. They were very close.'

They left the restaurant shortly past four and walked around the docks of the Dársena Sud waterfront, breathing in the salt air. It seemed to David that Jean was enjoying herself in a way she hadn't in too long a time. That it was part of the instant comfort between them, he realized, but it went further. As if some splendid relief had swept over her.

Her loveliness had been evident from those first moments on the staircase, but as he thought back on that brief introduction, he knew what the difference was. Jean Cameron had been outgoing, good-natured ... welcoming charm itself. But there'd been something else: a detachment born of self-control. Total control. A patina of authority that had nothing to do with her status at the embassy or whatever other benefits derived from her marriage to the ambassador's stepson. It was related solely to her own decisions, her own outlook.

He had seen that detached authority throughout the morning – when she introduced him to various embassy employees; when she gave directions to her secretary; when she answered her telephone and rendered quick instructions.

Even in the byplay with Bobby Bollard she glided firmly, with the assurance of knowing her own pattern. Ballard could shout humorously that she could 'get irresponsibly drunk' because by no stretch of the imagination would she allow herself to do that.

Jean kept a tight rein on herself.

The rein was loosening now.

Yesterday he had looked at her closely, finding the years; and she was completely unconcerned, without vanity. Now, walking along the docks, holding his arm, she was pleasantly aware of the looks she received from the scores of waterfront *Bocamos*. Spaulding knew she hoped he was aware of those looks.

'Look, David,' she said excitedly. 'Those boats are going to crash head on.'

Several hundred yards out in the bay, two trawlers were on a collision course, both steam whistles filling the air with aggressive warnings, both crews shouting at each other from port and starboard railings.

'The one on the right will veer.'

It did. At the last moment, amid dozens of guttural oaths and gestures.

'How did you know?' she said.

'Simple right of way; the owner would get clobbered with damages. There'll be a brawl on one of these piers pretty soon, though.'

'Let's not wait for it. You've had enough of that.'

They walked out of the dock area into the narrow La Boca streets, teeming with small fish markets, profuse with fat merchants in bloodied aprons and shouting customers. The afternoon catch was in, the day's labour on the water over. The rest was selling and drinking and retelling the misadventures of the past twelve hours.

They reached a miniature square called – for no apparent reason – Plaza Ocho Calle; there was no street number eight, no plaza to speak of. A taxi hesitantly came to a stop at the corner, let out its fare and started up again, blocked by pedestrians unconcerned with such vehicles. David looked at Jean and she nodded, smiling. He shouted at the driver.

Inside the taxi he gave his address. It didn't occur to him to do otherwise.

They rode in silence for several minutes, their shoulders touching, her hand underneath his arm.

'What are you thinking of?' David asked, seeing the distant but happy expression on her face.

'Oh, the way I pictured you when Henderson read the scramble the other night ... Yes, I call him Henderson; I always have.'

'I can't imagine anyone, even the president, calling him Henderson.'

'You don't know him. Underneath that Racquet Club jacket is lovable Henderson.'

'How did you picture me?'

'Very differently.'

'From what?'

'You ... I thought you'd be terribly short, to begin with. An attaché named David Spaulding who's some kind of financial whiz and is going to have conferences with the banks and the colonels about money things is short, at least fifty years old and has *very* little hair. He also wears spectacles – not glasses – and has a thin nose. Probably has an allergy as well – he sneezes a lot and blows his nose all the time. And he speaks in short, clipped sentences; very precise and quite disagreeable.'

'He chases secretaries, too; don't leave that out.'

'My David Spaulding doesn't chase secretaries. He reads dirty books.'

David felt a twinge. Throw in an unkempt appearance, a soiled handkerchief and replace the spectacles with glasses – worn occasionally – and Jean was describing Walter Kendall.

'Your Spaulding's an unpleasant fellow.'

'Not the new one,' she said, tightening her grip on his arm.

The taxi drew up to the curb in front of the entrance on Córdoba. Jean Cameron hesitated, staring momentarily at the apartment house door. David spoke softly, without emphasis.

'Shall I take you to the embassy?'

She turned to him. 'No.'

He paid the driver and they went inside.

The field thread was invisibly protruding from the knob; he felt it.

He inserted the key in the lock and instinctively, gently shouldered her aside as he pushed the door open. The apartment was as he had left it that morning; he knew she felt his relief. He held the door for her. Jean entered and looked around.

'It really *isn't* so bad, is it?' she said.

'Humble but home.' He left the door open and with a smile, a gesture – without words – he asked her to stay where she was. He walked rapidly into the bedroom, returned and went through the double doors onto his miniature, high-walled patio. He looked up, scanning the windows and the roof carefully. He smiled again at her from under the branches of the fruit tree. She understood, closed the door and came out to him.

'You did that very professionally, Mr Spaulding.'

'In the best traditions of extreme cowardice, Mrs Cameron.'

He realized his mistake the minute he'd made it. It was not the moment to use the married title. And yet, in some oblique way she seemed grateful that he had. She moved again and stood directly in front of him.

'Mrs Cameron thanks you.'

He reached out and held her by the waist. Her arms slowly, haltingly, went up to his shoulders; her hands cupped his face and she stared into his eyes.

He did not move. The decision, the first step, had to be hers; he understood that.

She brought her lips to his. The touch was soft and lovely and meant for earthbound angels. And then she trembled with an almost uncontrollable sense of urgency. Her lips parted and she pressed her body with extraordinary strength into his, her arms clutched about his neck.

She pulled her lips away from his and buried her face into his chest, holding him with fierce possession.

'Don't say anything,' she whispered. 'Don't say anything at all . . . *Just take me.*'

He picked her up silently and carried her into the bedroom. She kept her face pressed into his chest, as if she were afraid to see light or even him. He lowered her gently onto the bed and closed the door.

In a few moments they were naked and he pulled the blankets over them. It was a moist and beautiful darkness. A splendid comfort.

'I want to say something,' she said, tracing her finger over his lips, her face above his, her breasts innocently on his chest. And smiling her genuine smile.

'I know. You want the other Spaulding. The thin one with spectacles.' He kissed her fingers.

'He disappeared in an explosion of sorts.'

'You're positively descriptive, young lady.'

'And not so young . . . That's what I want to talk about.'

'A pension. You're angling for Social Security. I'll see what I can do.'

'Be serious, silly boy.'

'And not so silly . . .'

'There's no commitment, David,' she said, interrupting him. 'I want you to know that . . . I don't know how else to say it. Everything happened so fast.'

'Everything happened very naturally. Explanations aren't required.'

'Well, I think some are. I didn't expect to be here.'

'I didn't expect that you would be. I suppose I hoped, I'll admit that . . . I didn't plan; neither of us did.'

'I don't know; I think I did. I think I saw you yesterday and somewhere in the back of my mind I made a decision. Does that sound brazen of me?'

'If you did, the decision was long overdue.'

'Yes, I imagine it was.' She lay back, pulling the sheet over her. 'I've been very selfish. Spoiled and selfish and behaving really quite badly.'

'Because you haven't slept around?' It was his turn to roll over and touch her face. He kissed both her eyes, now open; the deep speckles of blue made bluer, deeper, by the late afternoon sun streaming through the blinds. She smiled; her perfect white teeth glistening with the moisture of her mouth, her lips curved in that genuine curve of humor.

'That's funny. I must be unpatriotic. I've withheld my charms only to deliver them to a noncombatant.'

'The Visigoths wouldn't have approved. The warriors came first, I'm told.'

'Let's not tell them.' She reached up for his face. 'Oh, David, David, *David.*'

25

'I hope I didn't wake you. I wouldn't have troubled you but I thought you'd want me to.'

Ambassador Granville's voice over the telephone was more solicitous than David expected it to be. He looked at his watch as he replied. It was three minutes of ten in the morning.

'Oh? . . . No, sir. I was just getting up. Sorry I overslept.'

There was a note on the telephone table. It was from Jean.

'Your friend was in contact with us.'

'Friend?' David unfolded the note. *My Darling – You fell into such a beautiful sleep it would have broken my heart to disturb you. Called a taxi. See you in the morning. At the Bastille. Your ex-regimented phoenix.* David smiled, remembering her smile.

'. . . the details, I'm sure, aren't warranted.' Granville had said something and he hadn't been listening.

'I'm sorry, Mr Ambassador. This must be a poor connection; your voice fades in and out.' All telephones beyond the Atlantic, north, middle and south, were temperamental instruments. An unassailable fact.

'Or something else, I'm afraid,' said Granville with irritation, obviously referring to the possibility of a telephone tap. 'When you get in, please come to see me.'

'Yes, sir. I'll be there directly.'

He picked up Jean's note and read it again.

She had said last night that he was complicating her life. But there were no commitments; she'd said that, too.

What the hell was a commitment? He didn't want to speculate. He didn't want to think about the awful discovery – the instant, splendid comfort they both recognized. It wasn't the time for it . . .

Yet to deny it would be to reject an extraordinary reality. He was trained to deal with reality.

He didn't want to think about it.

His 'friend' had been in contact with the embassy.

Walter Kendall.

That was another reality. It couldn't wait.

He crushed out his cigarette angrily, watching his fingers stab the butt into the metal ashtray.

Why was he angry?

He didn't care to speculate on that, either. He had a job to do. He hoped he had the commitment for it.

'Jean said you barely made it through dinner. You needed a good night's sleep; I must say you look better.' The ambassador had come from around his desk to greet him as he entered the large, ornate office. David was a little bewildered. The old diplomat was actually being solicitous, displaying a concern that belied his unconcealed disapproval of two days ago. Or was it his use of the name Jean instead of the forbidding Mrs Cameron.

'She was very kind. I couldn't have found a decent restaurant without her.'

'I daresay ... I won't detain you, you'd better get cracking with this Kendall.'

'You said he's been in contact ...'

'Starting last night; early this morning to be accurate. He's at the Alvear and apparently quite agitated, according to the switchboard. At two thirty this morning he was shouting, demanding to know where you were. Naturally, we don't give out that information.'

'I'm grateful. As you said, I needed the sleep; Kendall would have prevented it. Do you have his telephone number? Or shall I get it from the book?'

'No, right here.' Granville walked to his desk and picked up a sheet of notepaper. David followed and took it from the ambassador's outstretched hand.

'Thank you, sir. I'll get on it.' He turned and started for the door, Granville's voice stopping him.

'Spaulding?'

'Yes, sir?'

'I'm sure Mrs Cameron would like to see you. Assess your recovery, I daresay. Her office is in the south wing. First door from the entrance, on the right. Do you know where that is?'

'I'll find it, sir.'

'I'm sure you will. See you later in the day.'

David went out the heavy baroque door, closing it behind him. Was it his imagination or was Granville reluctantly giving an approval to his and Jean's sudden ... alliance? The words were approving, the tone of voice reluctant.

He walked down the connecting corridor toward the south wing and reached her door. Her name was stamped on a brass plate to the left of the doorframe. He had not noticed it yesterday.

Mrs Andrew Cameron.

So his name had been Andrew. Spaulding hadn't asked his first name; she hadn't volunteered it.

As he looked at the brass plate he found himself experiencing a very strange reaction. He resented Andrew Cameron; resented his life, his death.

The door was open and he entered. Jean's secretary was obviously an Argentine. A *porteña*. The black Spanish hair was pulled back into a bun, her features Latin.

'Mrs Cameron, please. David Spaulding.'

'Please go in. She's expecting you.' David approached the door and turned the knob.

She was taken by surprise, he thought. She was at the window looking out at the south lawn, a page of paper in her hand, glasses pushed above her forehead, resting on top of her light-brown hair.

Startled, she removed her glasses from their perch and stood immobile. Slowly, as if studying him first, she smiled.

He found himself afraid. More than afraid, for a moment. And then she spoke and the sudden anguish left him, replaced by a deeply felt relief.

'I woke up this morning and reached for you. You weren't there and I thought I might cry.'

He walked rapidly to her and they held each other. Neither spoke. The silence, the embrace, the splendid comfort returning.

'Granville acted like a procurer a little while ago,' he said finally, holding her by the shoulders, looking at her blue speckled eyes that held such intelligent humor.

'I told you he was lovable. You wouldn't believe me.'

'You didn't *tell* me we had dinner, though. Or that I could barely get through it.'

'I was hoping you'd slip; give him more to think about.'

'I don't understand him. Or you, maybe.'

'Henderson has a problem ... Me. He's not sure how to handle it – me. He's overprotective because I've led him to believe I wanted that protection. I did; it was easier. But a man who's had three wives and at least twice that many mistresses over the years is no Victorian ... And he knows you're not going to be here long. As he would put it: do I sketch a reasonable picture?'

'I daresay,' answered David in Granville's anglicized manner.

'That's unkind.' Jean laughed. 'He probably doesn't approve of you, which makes his unspoken acceptance very difficult for him.'

David released her. 'I know damned well he doesn't approve ... Look, I have to make some calls; go out and meet someone ...'

'Just someone?'

'A ravishing beauty who'll introduce me to lots of other ravishing beauties. And between the two of us, I can't stand him. But I have to see him ... Will you have dinner with me?'

'Yes, I'll have dinner with you. I'd planned to. You didn't have a choice.'

'You're right; you're brazen.'

'I made that clear. You broke down the regimens; I'm flying up out of my own personal ash heap ... The air feels good.'

'It was going to happen ... I was here.' He wasn't sure why he said it but he had to.

*

Walter Kendall paced the hotel room as though it were a cage. Spaulding sat on the couch watching him, trying to decide which animal Kendall reminded him of; there were several that came to mind, none pets.

'You listen to *me*,' Kendall said. 'This is no military operation. You *take* orders, you don't give them.'

'I'm sorry; I think you're misreading me.' David was tempted to answer Kendall's anger in kind, but he decided not to.

'I misread, bullshit! You told Swanson you were in some trouble in New York. That's *your* problem, not *ours*.'

'You can't be sure of that.'

'Oh yes I can! You tried to sell that to Swanson and he bought it. You could have involved *us*!'

'Now just a minute.' Spaulding felt he could object legitimately – within the boundaries he had mentally staked off for Kendall. 'I told Swanson that in my opinion the "trouble" in New York might have been related to Buenos Aires. I didn't say it *was*, I said it might have been.'

'That's not possible!'

'How the hell can you be so sure?'

'Because I am.' Kendall was not only agitated, thought David, he was impatient. 'This is a business proposition. The deal's been made. There's no one trying to stop it. Stop *us*.'

'Hostilities don't cease because a deal's been made. If the German command got wind of it they'd blow up Buenos Aires to stop it.'

'Yeah ... well, that's not possible.'

'You *know* that?'

'We know it ... So don't go confusing that stupid bastard, Swanson. I'll level with you. This is strictly a money-line negotiation. We could have completed it without any help from Washington, but they insisted – Swanson insisted – that they have a man here. Okay, you're him. You can be helpful; you can get the papers out and you speak the languages. But that's *all* you've got to do. Don't call attention to yourself. We don't want anyone upset.'

Grudgingly, David began to understand the subtle clarity of Brigadier General Swanson's manipulation. Swanson had manoeuvred him into a clean position. The killing of Erich Rhinemann – whether he did it himself or whether he bought the assassin – would be totally unexpected. Swanson wasn't by any means the 'stupid bastard' Kendall thought he was. Or that David had considered.

Swanson was nervous. A neophyte. But he was pretty damned good.

'All right. My apologies,' said Spaulding, indicating a sincerity he didn't feel. 'Perhaps the New York thing was exaggerated. I made enemies in Portugal, I can't deny that ... I got out under cover, you know.'

'What?'

'There's no way the people in New York could know I left the city.'

'You're sure?'

'As sure as you are that no one's trying to stop your negotiations.'

'Yeah ... Okay. Well, everything's set. I got a schedule.'

'You've seen Rhinemann?'

'Yesterday. All day.'

'What about Lyons?' asked David.

'Swanson's packing him off at the end of the week. With his nursemaids. Rhinemann figures the designs will be arriving Sunday or Monday.'

'In steps or all together?'

'Probably two sets of prints. He's not sure. It doesn't make any difference; they'll be here in full by Tuesday. He guaranteed.'

'Then we've moved up. You estimated three weeks.' David felt a pain in his stomach. He knew it wasn't related to Walter Kendall or Eugene Lyons or designs for high-altitude gyroscopes: It was Jean Cameron and the simple fact that he'd have only one week with her.

It disturbed him greatly and he speculated – briefly – on the meaning of this disturbance.

And then he knew he could not allow himself the indulgence; the two entities had to remain separate, the worlds separate.

'Rhinemann's got good control,' said Kendall, more than a hint of respect showing in his voice. 'I'm impressed with his methods. Very precise.'

'If you think that, you don't need me.' David was buying a few seconds to steer their conversation to another area. His statement was rhetorical.

'We don't, that's what I said. But there's a lot of money involved and since the War Department – one way or another – is picking up a large share of the tab, Swanson wants his accounts covered. I don't sweat him on that. It's business.'

Spaulding recognized his moment. 'Then let's get to the codes. I haven't wasted the three days down here. I've struck up a friendship of sorts with the embassy cryp.'

'The what?'

'The head cryptographer. He'll send out the codes to Washington; the payment authorization.'

'Oh ... Yeah, that.' Kendall was squeezing a cigarette, prepared to insert it in his mouth. He was only half concerned with codes and cryptographers, thought David. They were the wrap-up, the necessary details relegated to others. Or was it an act? wondered Spaulding.

He'd know in a moment or two.

'As you pointed out, it's a great deal of money. So we've decided to use a scrambler with code switches every twelve hours. We'll prepare the cryp schedule tonight and send it out by patrol courier to Washington tomorrow. The master plate will allow for fifteen hours ... Naturally, the prime word will be "Tortugas".'

Spaulding watched the disheveled accountant.

There was no reaction whatsoever.

'Okay ... Yeah, Okay.' Kendall sat down in an easy chair. His mind seemed somewhere else.

'That meets with your approval, doesn't it?'

'Sure. Why not? Play any games you like. All I give a shit about is that Geneva radios the confirmation and you fly out of here.'

'Yes, but I thought the reference had to include the . . . code factor.'

'What the hell are you talking about?'

' "Tortugas." Hasn't it got to be "Tortugas"?'

'Why? What's "Tortugas"?'

The man wasn't acting. David was sure of that. 'Perhaps I misunderstood. I thought "Tortugas" was part of the authorization code.'

'Christ! You and Swanson! All of you. Military geniuses! *Jesus!* If it doesn't sound like Dan Dunn, Secret Agent, it's not the real McCoy, huh? . . . Look. When Lyons tells you everything's in order, just say so. Then drive out to the airport . . . it's a small field called Mendarro . . . and Rhinemann's men will tell you when you can leave. Okay? You got that?'

'Yes, I've got it,' said Spaulding. But he wasn't sure.

Outside, David walked aimlessly down the Buenos Aires streets. He reached the huge park of the Plaza San Martin, with its fountains, its rows of white gravel paths, its calm disorder.

He sat down on a slatted bench and tried to define the elusive pieces of the increasingly complex puzzle.

Walter Kendall hadn't lied, 'Tortugas' meant nothing to him.

Yet a man in an elevator in New York City had risked his life to learn about 'Tortugas'.

Ira Barden in Fairfax had told him there was only a single word opposite his name in the DW transfer in Ed Pace's vaults: 'Tortugas.'

There was an obvious answer, perhaps. Ed Pace's death prohibited any real knowledge, but the probability was genuine.

Berlin had gotten word of the Peenemünde negotiation – too late to prevent the theft of the designs – and was now committed to stopping the sale. Not only stopping it, but if possible tracing the involvement of everyone concerned. Trapping the entire Rhinemann network.

If this was the explanation – and what other plausible one existed? – Pace's code name, 'Tortugas', had been leaked to Berlin by Fairfax infiltration. That there was a serious breach of security at Fairfax was clear; Pace's murder was proof.

His own role could be easily assessed by Berlin, thought David. The man in Lisbon suddenly transferred to Buenos Aires. The expert whose skill was proven in hundreds of espionage transactions, whose own network was the most ruthlessly efficient in southern Europe, did not walk out of his own creation unless his expertise was considered vital someplace else. He'd long ago accepted the fact that Berlin more than suspected him. In a way it was his protection; he'd by no means won every roll of the dice. If the enemy killed him, someone else would take his place. The enemy would have to start all over again. He was a known commodity . . . accept an existing devil.

Spaulding considered carefully, minutely, what he might do were he the enemy. What steps would he take at this specific juncture?

Barring panic or error, the enemy would not kill him. Not now. Because he could *not* by himself inhibit the delivery of the designs. He could, however, lead his counterparts to the moment and place of delivery.

What is the location of Tortugas?!

The desperate ... hysterical man in the Montgomery elevator had screamed the question, preferring to die rather than reveal those whose orders he followed. The Nazis reveled in such fanaticism. And so did others, for other reasons.

He – Spaulding – would therefore be placed under *äusserste Überwachung* – foolproof surveillance, three- to four-man teams, twenty-four hours a day. That would account for the recruitment of the extraterritorial personnel on the Berlin payroll. Agents who operated outside the borders of Germany, *had* operated – for profit – for years. The languages and dialects would vary; deep-cover operatives who could move with impunity in neutral capitals because they had no Gestapo or Gehlen or *Nachrichtendienst* histories.

The Balkans and the Middle East countries had such personnel for hire. They were expensive; they were among the best. Their only morality was to the pound sterling and the American dollar.

Along with this round-the-clock surveillance, Berlin would take extraordinary measures to prevent him from developing his own network in Buenos Aires. That would mean infiltrating the American embassy. Berlin would not overlook that possibility. A great deal of money would be offered.

Who at the embassy could be bought?

To attempt corrupting an individual too highly placed could backfire; give him, Spaulding, dangerous information ... Someone not too far up on the roster; someone who could gain access to doors and locks and desk-drawer vaults. And codes ... A middle-level attaché. A man who'd probably never make it to the Court of St James's anyway; who'd settle for another kind of security. Negotiable at a very high price.

Someone at the embassy would be Spaulding's enemy.

Finally, Berlin would order him killed. Along with numerous others, of course. Killed at the moment of delivery; killed after the *äusserste Überwachung* had extracted everything it could.

David got up from the slatted green bench and stretched, observing the beauty that was the Plaza San Martin park. He wandered beyond the path onto the grass, to the edge of a pond whose dark waters reflected the surrounding trees like a black mirror. Two white swans paddled by in alabaster obliviousness. A little girl was kneeling by a rock on the tiny embankment, separating the petals from a yellow flower.

He was satisfied that he had adequately analysed the immediate options of his counterparts. Options and probable courses of action. His gut feeling was positive – not in the sense of being enthusiastic, merely not negative.

He had now to evolve his own counterstrategy. He had to bring into play the lessons he had learned over the years in Lisbon. But there was so little time allowed him. And because of this fact, he understood that a misstep could be fatal here.

Nonchalantly – but with no feelings of nonchalance – he looked around at the scores of strollers on the paths, on the grass; the rowers and the passengers in the small boats on the small dark lake. Which of them were the enemy?

Who were the ones watching him, trying to think what he was thinking?

He would have to find them – one or two of them anyway – before the next few days were over.

That was the genesis of his counterstrategy.

Isolate and break.

David lit a cigarette and walked over the miniature bridge. He was primed. The hunter and the hunted were now one. There was the slightest straining throughout his entire body; the hands, the arms, the legs: there was a muscular tension, an awareness. He recognized it. He was back in the north country.

And he was good in that jungle. He was the best there was. It was here that he built his architectural monuments, his massive structures of concrete and steel. In his mind.

It was all he had sometimes.

26

He looked at his watch. It was five thirty; Jean had said she'd be at his apartment around six. He had walked for nearly two hours and now found himself at the corner of Viamonte, several blocks from his apartment. He crossed the street and walked to a newsstand under a storefront awning, where he bought a paper.

He glanced at the front pages, amused to see that the war news – what there was of it – was relegated to the bottom, surrounded by accounts of 'the Grupo de Oficiales' latest benefits to Argentina. He noted that the name of a particular colonel, one Juan Perón, was mentioned in three separate subheadlines.

He folded the paper under his arm and, because he realized he had been absently musing, looked once again at his watch.

It was not a deliberate move on David's part. That is to say, he did not calculate the abruptness of his turn; he simply turned because the angle of the sun caused a reflection on his wristwatch and he unconsciously shifted his body to the right, his left hand extended, covered by his own shadow.

But his attention was instantly diverted from his watch. Out of the corner of his eye he could discern a sudden, sharp break in the sidewalk's human traffic. Thirty feet away across the street two men had swiftly turned around, colliding with oncoming pedestrians, apologizing, stepping into the flow on the curbside.

The man on the left had not been quick enough; or he was too careless – too inexperienced, perhaps – to angle his shoulders, or hunch them imperceptibly so as to melt into the crowd.

He stood out and David recognized him.

He was one of the men from the roof of the Córdoba apartment. His companion David couldn't be sure of, but he *was* sure of that man. There was even the hint of a limp in his gait; David remembered the battering he'd given him.

He was being followed, then, and that was good.

His point of departure wasn't as remote as he'd thought.

He walked another ten yards, into a fairly large group approaching the corner of Córdoba. He sidestepped his way between arms and legs and packages, and entered a small jewelry store whose wares were gaudy, inexpensive. Inside, several office girls were trying to select a gift for a departing secretary. Spaulding smiled at the annoyed proprietor, indicating that he could wait, he was in no hurry. The proprietor made a gesture of helplessness.

Spaulding stood by the front window, his body concealed from outside by the frame of the door.

Before a minute was up he saw the two men again. They were still across the street; David had to follow their progress through the intermittent gaps in the crowd. The two men were talking heatedly, the second man annoyed with his limping companion. Both were trying to glance above the heads of the surrounding bodies, raising themselves up on their toes, looking foolish, amateur.

David figured they would turn right at the corner and walk east on Córdoba, toward his apartment. They did so and, as the owner of the jewelry store protested, Spaulding walked swiftly out into the crowds and ran across the Avenida Callao, dodging cars and angry drivers. He had to reach the other side, staying out of the sightlines of the two men. He could not use the crosswalks or the curbs. It would be too easy, too logical, for the men to look backward as men did when trying to spot someone they had lost in surveillance.

David knew his objective now. He had to separate the men and take the one with a limp. Take him and force answers.

If they had any experience, he considered, they would reach his apartment and divide, one man cautiously going inside to listen through the door, ascertaining the subject's presence, the other remaining outside, far enough from the entrance to be unobserved. And common sense would dictate that the man unknown to David would be the one to enter the apartment.

Spaulding removed his jacket and held up the newspaper – not full but folded; not obviously but casually, as if he were uncertain of the meaning of some awkwardly phrased headline – and walked with the crowds to the north side of Córdoba. He turned right and maintained a steady, unbroken pace east, remaining as far left on the sidewalk as possible.

His apartment was less than a block and a half away now. He could see the two men; intermittently they *did* look back, but on their own side of the street.

Amateurs. If he taught surveillance, they'd fail his course.

The men drew nearer to the apartment, their concentration on the entrance. David knew it was his moment to move. The only moment of risk, really; the few split seconds when one or the other might turn and see him across the street, only yards away. But it was a necessary gamble. He had to get beyond the apartment entrance. That was the essence of his trap.

Several lengths ahead was a middle-aged *porteña* housewife carrying groceries, hurrying, obviously anxious to get home. Spaulding came alongside and without breaking stride, keeping in step with her, he started asking directions in his best, most elegant Castilian, stating among other points that he knew this was the right street and he was late. His head was tilted from the curb.

If anyone watched them, the housewife and the shirtsleeved man with a jacket under one arm and a newspaper under the other looked like two friends hastening to a mutual destination.

Twenty yards beyond the entrance on the other side, Spaulding left the smiling *porteña* and ducked into a canopied doorway. He pressed himself into the wall and looked back across the street. The two men stood by the curb and, as he expected, they separated. The unknown man went into his apartment house; the man with the limp looked up and down the sidewalk, checked oncoming vehicles, and started across Córdoba to the north side. David's side.

Spaulding knew it would be a matter of seconds before the limping figure passed him. Logic, again; common sense. The man would continue east – he would not reverse direction – over traversed ground. He would station himself at a vantage point from which he could observe those approaching the apartment from the west. David's approach.

The man did not see him until David touched him, grabbed his left arm around the elbow, forced the arm into a horizontal position, and clamped the man's hand downward so that the slightest force on David's part caused an excruciating pain in the man's bent wrist.

'Just keep walking or I'll snap your hand off,' said David in English, pushing the man to the right of the sidewalk to avoid the few pedestrians walking west on Córdoba.

The man's face grimaced in pain; David's accelerated walk caused him to partially stumble – his limp emphasized – and brought further agony to the wrist.

'You're breaking my arm. You're *breaking* it!' said the anguished man, hurrying his steps to relieve the pressure.

'Keep up with me or I will,' David spoke calmly, even politely. They reached the corner of the Avenida Paraná and Spaulding swung left, propelling the man with him. There was a wide, recessed doorway of an old office building – the type that had few offices remaining within it. David spun the man around, keeping the arm locked, and slammed him into the wooden wall at the point farthest inside. He released the arm; the man grabbed for his strained wrist. Spaulding took the moment to flip open the man's jacket, forcing the arms downward, and removed a revolver strapped in a large holster above the man's left hip.

It was a Luger. Issued less than a year ago.

David clamped it inside his belt and pushed a lateral forearm against the man's throat, crashing his head into the wood as he searched the pockets of the jacket. Inside he found a large rectangular European billfold. He slapped it open, removed his forearm from the man's throat, and shoved his left shoulder into the man's chest, pinning him unmercifully against the wall. With both hands, David removed identification papers.

A German driver's licence; an Autobahn vehicle pass; rationing cards countersigned by Oberführers, allowing the owner to utilize them through-out the Reich – a privilege granted to upper-level government personnel and above.

And then he found it.

An identity pass with a photograph affixed; for the ministries of Information, Armaments, Air and Supply.

Gestapo.

'You're about the most inept recruit Himmler's turned out,' said David, meaning the judgment profoundly, putting the billfold in his back pocket. 'You must have relatives ... *Was ist "Tortugas"?'* Spaulding whispered harshly, suddenly. He removed his shoulder from the man's chest and thrust two extended knuckles into the Nazi's breastbone with such impact that the German coughed, the sharp blow nearly paralysing him. *'Wer ist Altmüller? Was wissen Sie über Marshall?'* David repeatedly hammered the man's ribs with his knuckles, sending shock waves of pain throughout the Gestapo agent's rib cage. *'Sprechen Sie! Sofort!'*

'Nein! Ich weiss nichts!' the man answered between gasps. *'Nein!'*

Spaulding heard it again. The dialect. Nowhere near *Berliner;* not even a mountainized *Bavarian.* Something else.

What was it?

'Noch 'mal! Again! Sprechen Sie!'

And then the man did something quite out of the ordinary. In his pain, his fear, he stopped speaking German. He spoke in English. 'I have not the information you want! I follow orders ... That is all!'

David shifted his stand to the left, covering the Nazi from the intermittent looks they both received from the passers-by on the sidewalk. The doorway was deep, however, in shadows; no one stopped. The two men could have been acquaintances, one or both perhaps a little drunk.

Spaulding clenched his right fist, his left elbow against the wall, his left hand poised to clamp over the German's mouth. He leaned against the slatted wood and brought his fist crashing into the man's stomach with such force that the agent lurched forward, held only by David's hand, now gripping him by the hairline.

'I can keep this up until I rupture everything inside you. And when I'm finished I'll throw you in a taxi and drop you off at the German embassy with a note attached. You'll get it from both sides then, won't you? ... Now, tell me what I want to know!' David brought his two bent knuckles up into the man's throat, jabbing twice.

'Stop ... *Mein Gott!* Stop!'

'Why don't you yell? You can scream your head off, you know ... Of course, then I'll have to put you to sleep and let your own people find you. Without your credentials, naturally ... Go on! Yell!' David knuckled the man once more in the throat. 'Now, you start telling me. What's "Tortugas"? Who's Altmüller? How did you get a cryp named Marshall?'

'I swear to God! I know nothing!'

David punched him again. The man collapsed; Spaulding pulled him up against the wall, leaning against him, hiding him, really. The Gestapo agent opened his lids, his eyes swimming uncontrollably.

'You've got five seconds. Then I'll rip your throat out.'

'No! ... Please! Altmüller ... Armaments ... Peenemünde ...'

'What about Peenemünde?'

'The tooling ... "Tortugas".'

'What does that *mean*?!' David showed the man his two bent fingers. The recollection of pain terrified the German. 'What is "Tortugas"?'

Suddenly the German's eyes flickered, trying to focus. Spaulding saw that the man was looking above his shoulder. It wasn't a ruse, the Nazi was too far gone for strategies.

And then David felt the presence behind him. It was an unmistakable feeling that had been developed over recent years; it was never false.

He turned.

Coming into the dark shadows from the harsh Argentine sunlight was the second part of the surveillance team, the man who'd entered his apartment building. He was Spaulding's size, a large man and heavily muscular.

The light and the onrushing figure caused David to wince. He released the German, prepared to throw himself onto the opposite wall.

He couldn't!

The Gestapo agent – in a last surge of strength – held onto his arms!

Held his arms, threw his hands around David's chest and hung his full weight on him!

Spaulding lashed out with his foot at the man attacking, swung his elbows back, slamming the German back into the wood.

It was too late and David knew it.

He saw the huge hand – the long fingers spread – rushing into his face. It was as if a ghoulish film was being played before his eyes in slow motion. He felt the fingers clamp into his skin and realized that his head was being shoved with great strength into the wall.

The sensations of diving, crashing, spinning accompanied the shock of pain above his neck.

He shook his head; the first thing that struck him was the stench. It was all around him, sickening.

He was lying in the recessed doorway, curled up against the wall in a fetal position. He was wet, drenched around his face and shirt and in the crotch area of his trousers.

It was cheap whisky. Very cheap and very profuse.

His shirt had been ripped, collar to waist; one shoe was off, the sock removed. His belt was undone, his fly partially unzipped.

He was the perfect picture of a derelict.

He rose to a sitting position and remedied as best he could his appearance. He looked at his watch.

Or where his watch had been; it was gone.

His wallet, too. And money. And whatever else had been in his pockets.

He stood up. The sun was down, early night had begun; there were not so many people on the Avenida Paraná now.

He wondered what time it was. It couldn't be much more than an hour later, he supposed.

He wondered if Jean were still waiting for him.

She removed his clothes, pressed the back of his head with ice and insisted that he take a long, hot shower.

When he emerged from the bathroom, she fixed him a drink, then sat down next to him on the small couch.

'Henderson will insist on your moving into the embassy; you know that, don't you?'

'I can't.'

'Well, you can't go on being beaten up every day. And don't tell me they were *thieves*. You wouldn't swallow that when Henderson and Bobby *both* tried to tell you that about the men on the roof!'

'This was different. For God's *sake*, Jean, I was robbed of everything on me!' David spoke sternly. It was important to him that she believe him now. And it was entirely possible that he'd find it necessary to avoid her from now on. That might be important, too. And terribly painful.

'People don't rob people and then douse them with whisky!'

'They do if they want to create sufficient time to get out of the area. It's not a new tactic. By the time a mark gets finished explaining to the police that he's a sober citizen, the hustlers are twenty miles away.'

'I don't believe you, I don't even think you expect me to.' She sat up and looked at him.

'I do expect you to because it's the truth. A man doesn't throw away his wallet, his money, his watch . . . in order to impress a girl with the validity of a lie. Come *on*, Jean! I'm very thirsty and my head still hurts.'

She shrugged, obviously realizing it was futile to argue.

'You're just about out of Scotch, I'm afraid. I'll go buy a bottle for you. There's a liquor store on the corner of Talcahuano. It's not far . . .'

'No,' he said interrupting, recalling the man with huge hands who'd entered his building. 'I will. Lend me some money.'

'We'll both go,' she responded.

'Please? . . . Would you mind waiting? I may get a phone call; I'd like the person to know I'll be right back.'

'Who?'

'A man named Kendall.'

Out on the street, he asked the first man he saw where the nearest pay phone could be found. It was several blocks away, on Rodriguez Peña, in a newspaper store.

David ran as fast as he could.

The hotel page found Kendall in the dining room. When he got on the phone he spoke while chewing. Spaulding pictured the man, the doodled obscenities, the animal-like breathing. He controlled himself. Walter Kendall was sick.

'Lyons is coming in in three days,' Kendall told him. 'With his nurses. I got him a place in this San Telmo district. A quiet apartment, quiet street. I wired Swanson the address. He'll give it to the keepers and they'll get him set up. They'll be in touch with you.'

'I thought *I* was to get him settled.'

'I figured you'd complicate things,' interrupted Kendall. 'No piss lost. They'll call you. Or I will. I'll be here for a while.'

'I'm glad ... Because so's the Gestapo.'

'*What?*'

'I said so's the Gestapo. You figured a little inaccurately, Kendall. Someone *is* trying to stop you. It doesn't surprise me.'

'You're out of your fucking mind!'

'I'm not.'

'What happened?'

So David told him, and for the first time in his brief association with the accountant, he detected fear.

'There was a break in Rhinemann's network. It doesn't mean the designs won't get here. It does mean we have obstacles – if Rhinemann's as good as you say. As I read it, Berlin found out the designs were stolen. They know they're filtering down or across or however Rhinemann's routing them out of Europe. The High Command got wind of the transactions. The Reichsführers aren't going to broadcast, they're going to try and intercept. With as little noise as possible. But you can bet your ass there's been a slew of executions in Peenemünde.'

'It's crazy ...' Kendall could hardly be heard. And then he mumbled something; David could not understand the words.

'What did you say?'

'The address in this Telmo. For Lyons. It's three rooms. Back entrance.' Kendall still kept his voice low, almost indistinct.

The man was close to panic, thought Spaulding. 'I can barely hear you, Kendall ... Now, calm down! I think it's time I introduced myself to Rhinemann, don't you?'

'The Telmo address. It's Fifteen Terraza Verde ... it's quiet.'

'Who's the contact for Rhinemann?'

'The what?'

'Rhinemann's contact.'

'I don't know ...'

'For Christ's sake, Kendall, you held a five-hour conference with him!'

'I'll be in touch ...'

David heard the click. He was stunned. Kendall had hung up on him. He considered calling again but in Kendall's state of anxiety it might only make matters worse.

Goddamned amateurs! What the hell did they expect? Albert Speer himself to get in touch with Washington and lend the army air corps a few designs because he heard they had problems?

Jesus!

David walked angrily out of the telephone booth and the store and into the street.

Where the goddamned hell was he? Oh, yes, the Scotch. The store was back at Talcahuano, Jean said. Four blocks west. He looked at his watch and, of course, there was no watch.

Goddamn.

'I'm sorry I took so long. I got confused. I walked the wrong way for a couple of blocks.' David put the package of Scotch and soda water on the sink. Jean was sitting on the sofa; disturbed about something, he thought. 'Did I get the call?'

'Not the one you expected,' said Jean softly. 'Someone else. He said he'd phone you tomorrow.'

'Oh? Did he leave a name?'

'Yes, he did.' When she answered, David heard the questioning fear in her voice. 'It was Heinrich Stoltz.'

'Stoltz? Don't know him.'

'You should. He's an undersecretary at the German embassy . . . David, what are you doing?'

27

'Sorry, *señor*. Mister Kendall checked out last night. At ten thirty, according to the card.'

'Did he leave any other address or telephone number here in Buenos Aires?'

'No, *señor*. I believe he was going back to the United States. There was a Pan American flight at midnight.'

'Thank you.' David put down the telephone and reached for his cigarettes. It was incredible! Kendall had shot out at the first moment of difficulty. Why?

The telephone rang, startling David.

'Hello?'

'Herr Spaulding?'

'Yes.'

'Heinrich Stoltz. I called last night but you were out.'

'Yes, I know ... I understand you're with the German embassy. I hope I don't have to tell you that I find your contacting me unorthodox. And not a little distasteful.'

'Oh, come, Herr Spaulding. The man from *Lisbon*? *He* finds unorthodoxy?' Stoltz laughed quietly but not insultingly.

'I am an embassy attaché specializing in economics. Nothing more. If you know anything about me, surely you know that ... Now, I'm late ...'

'Please,' interrupted Stoltz. 'I call from a public telephone. Surely *that* tells *you* something.'

It did, of course.

'I don't talk on telephones.'

'Yours is clean, I checked thoroughly.'

'If you want to meet, give me a time and an address ... Somewhere in the downtown area. With people around; no outside locations.'

'There's a restaurant, Casa Langosta del Mar, several blocks north of the Parque Lezama. It's out of the way, not outside. There are back rooms. Curtains, no doors; no means of isolation. Only seclusion.'

'Time?'

'Half past twelve.'

'Do you smoke?' asked David sharply.

'Yes.'

'Carry a pack of American cigarettes from the moment you get out of the car. In your left hand; the foil off one end of the top, two cigarettes removed.'

'It's quite unnecessary. I know who you are. I'll recognize you.'

'That's not my concern. I don't know you.' David hung up the phone abruptly. As in all such rendezvous, he would arrive at the location early, through a delivery entrance if possible, and position himself as best he could to observe his contact's arrival. The cigarettes were nothing more than a psychological device: the contact was thrown off balance with the realization that he was an identified mark. A target. A marked contact was reluctant to bring trouble. And if trouble was his intent, he wouldn't show up.

Jean Cameron walked down the corridor toward the metal staircase that led to the cellars.

To the 'Caves'.

The 'Caves' – a name given without affection by Foreign Service officers the world over – were those underground rooms housing file cabinets containing dossiers on just about everybody who had the slightest contact with an embassy, known and unknown, friend and adversary. They included exhaustive checks and counterchecks on all embassy personnel; service background, State Department evaluations, progress reports. Nothing was left out if it was obtainable.

Two signatures were required to gain entrance into the 'Caves'. The ambassador's and that of the senior attaché seeking information.

It was a regulation that was occasionally bypassed in the interests of haste and emergency. The marine officer of the guard generally could be convinced that an established attaché *had* to have immediate background material; the marine would list both the names of the embassy man and his subject on the check sheet, then stand in attendance while the file was removed. If there were repercussions, they were the attaché's responsibility.

There never were. Violations of this sort guaranteed a post in Uganda. The check sheet was sealed daily and sent only to the ambassador.

Jean rarely took advantage of her relationship to Henderson Granville in embassy matters. In truth, the occasion rarely arose, and when it did, the matter was always insignificant.

It was not insignificant now. And she intended to use fully her status as *family*, as well as a respected member of the staff. Granville had left for lunch; he would not return for several hours. She had made up her mind to tell the marine guard that her 'father-in-law, the ambassador' had asked her to make a discreet inquiry regarding a new transfer.

Spaulding, David.

If Henderson wished to call her down for it, she would tell him the truth. She found herself very, *very* involved with the enigmatic Mr Spaulding, and if Henderson did not realize it, he was a damn fool.

The marine officer of the guard was a young lieutenant from the FMF base south of La Boca. The personnel from FMF were sped in civilian clothes through the city to their posts at the embassy; the treaty that permitted the small, limited base did not condone uniformed men outside either territory. These restrictions tended to make the young officers sensitive to the functionary, faceless roles they were forced to play. So it was understandable that when the ambassador's daughter-in-law called him by name and spoke confidentially of a discreet matter, the marine complied without question.

Jean stared at David's file. It was frightening. It was not like any file she had ever seen. There was no dossier, no State Department records, no reports, no evaluations, no listing of post assignments.

There was only a single page.

It gave his description by sex, height, weight, coloring and visible markings.

Beneath this cursory data, separated by a three-line space, was the following:

War Dept. Transfer. Clandestine Operations. Finance. Tortugas.

And nothing more.

'Finding what you need, Mrs Cameron?' asked the marine lieutenant by the steel-grilled gate.

'Yes . . . Thank you.' Jean slipped David's thin folder back into place in the cabinet, smiled at the marine, and left.

She reached the staircase and walked slowly up the steps. She accepted the fact that David was involved with an undercover assignment – accepted it while hating it; loathing the secrecy, the obvious danger. But in a conscious way she had prepared herself, expecting the worst and finding it. She was not at all sure she could handle the knowledge, but she was willing to try. If she could not handle it she'd take what moments of selfish pleasure she could and kiss David Spaulding goodbye. She had made up her mind to that . . . unconsciously, really. She could not allow herself more pain.

And there was something else. It was only a dim shadow in a half-lit room but it kept falling across her eyes. It was the word.

'Tortugas.'

She had seen it before. Recently. Only days ago.

It had caught her attention because she'd thought of the Dry Tortugas . . . and the few times she and Andrew had sailed there from the Keys.

Where was it? Yes . . . Yes, she remembered.

It had been in a very mechanical paragraph within the context of an area surveillance report on Henderson Granville's desk. She had read it rather absently one morning . . . only a few days ago. But she hadn't read it closely. Area surveillance reports were comprised of short, choppy informational sentences devoid of rhythm and color. Written by unimaginative men concerned only with what they could describe briefly, with data.

It had been down at La Boca.

Something about the captain of a trawler . . . and cargo. Cargo that had a lading destination of Tortugas. A violation of coastal limits; said destination rescinded, called an obvious error by the trawler's captain.

Yet the lading papers had said Tortugas.

And David Spaulding's classified operation – *clandestine* operation – was coded 'Tortugas'.

And Heinrich Stoltz of the German embassy had called David.

And Jean Cameron was suddenly afraid.

Spaulding was convinced that Stoltz was alone. He signaled the German to follow him to the back of the restaurant, to the curtained cubicle David had arranged for with the waiter a half-hour ago.

Stoltz entered carrying the pack of cigarettes in his left hand. Spaulding circled the round table and sat facing the curtain.

'Have a seat,' said David indicating the chair opposite him. Stoltz smiled, realizing that his back would be to the entrance.

'The man from Lisbon is a cautious man.' The German pulled out the chair and sat down, placing the cigarettes on the table. 'I can assure you I'm not armed.'

'Good. I am.'

'You are *too* cautious. The colonels look askance at belligerents carrying weapons in their neutral city. Your embassy should have told you.'

'I understand they also arrest Americans quicker than they do you fellows.'

Stoltz shrugged. 'Why not? After all, we trained them. You only buy their beef.'

'There'll be no lunch, incidentally. I paid the waiter for the table.'

'I'm sorry. The langosta . . . the lobster here is excellent. Perhaps a drink?'

'No drinks. Just talk.'

Stoltz spoke, his voice flat. 'I bring a welcome to Buenos Aires. From Erich Rhinemann.'

David stared at the man. 'You?'

'Yes. I'm your contact.'

'That's interesting.'

'That's the way of Erich Rhinemann. He pays for allegiances.'

'I'll want proof.'

'By all means. From Rhinemann himself . . . Acceptable?'

Spaulding nodded. 'When? Where?'

'That's what I'm here to discuss. Rhinemann is as cautious as the man from Lisbon.'

'I was attached to the diplomatic corps in Portugal. Don't try to make anything more of it than that.'

'Unfortunately, I have to speak the truth. Herr Rhinemann is most upset that the men in Washington saw fit to send you as the liaison. Your presence in Buenos Aires could attract attention.'

David reached for the cigarettes Stoltz had placed on the table. He lit one . . . The German was right, of course; Rhinemann was right. The one liability in his having been chosen was the enemy's probable knowledge of his Lisbon operations. Ed Pace, he was sure, had considered that aspect, discarding it in favor of the overriding assets. Regardless, it was not a subject to discuss with Heinrich Stoltz. The German attaché was still an unproven factor.

'I have no idea what you're referring to. I'm in Buenos Aires to transmit preliminary recommendations from New York and London banking circles relative to postwar reconstruction negotiations. You see, we *do* believe we'll win. Rhinemann can't be overlooked in such projected discussions.'

'The man from Lisbon is most professional.'

'I wish you'd stop repeating that nonsense . . .'

'And convincing,' interrupted Stoltz. 'The cover is one of your better ones. It has more stature than a cowardly American socialite . . . Even Herr Kendall agrees with that.'

David paused before replying. Stoltz was circling in, about to deliver his proof. 'Describe Kendall,' he said quietly.

'In short words?'

'It doesn't matter.'

Stoltz laughed under his breath. 'I'd prefer as few as possible. He's a most unattractive biped. He must be an extraordinary man with figures; there's no other earthly reason to stay in the same room with him.'

'Have you stayed in the same room with him?'

'For hours, unfortunately. With Rhinemann . . . Now. May we talk?'

'Go ahead.'

'Your man Lyons will be here the day after tomorrow. We can accomplish everything very quickly. The designs will be delivered in one package, not two as Kendall believes.'

'Does he believe that?'

'It's what he was told.'

'Why?'

'Because until late last evening Herr Rhinemann thought it was so. I myself did not know of the change until this morning.'

'Then why did you call me last night?'

'Instructions from Walter Kendall.'

'Please explain that.'

'Is it necessary? One has nothing to do with the other. Herr Kendall telephoned *me*. Apparently he had just spoken with you. He said he was called back to Washington suddenly; that I was to contact you immediately so there's no break in communications. He was most adamant.'

'Did Kendall say why he was returning to the States?'

'No. And I saw no reason to inquire. His work here is finished. He's of no concern to us. You are the man with the codes, not him.'

David crushed out his cigarette, staring at the tablecloth. 'What's your rank at the embassy?'

Stoltz smiled. 'Third . . . fourth in command would be a modest appraisal. My loyalty, however, is to the Rhinemann interests. Surely that's apparent.'

'I'll know when I talk to Rhinemann, won't I?' David looked up at the German. 'Why are the Gestapo here in Buenos Aires?'

'They're not ... Well, there's one man; no more than a clerk really. As all Gestapo he thinks of himself as the personal spokesman for the Reich and overburdens the couriers – who, incidentally, cooperate with us. He is, as you *Amerikaner* say, a jackass. There is no one else.'

'Are you sure?'

'Of course. I would be the first to know; before the ambassador, I assure you. This game is quite unnecessary, Herr Spaulding.'

'You'd better set up that meeting with Rhinemann ... *that's* necessary.'

'Yes. Certainly ... Which brings us back to Herr Rhinemann's concerns. Why is the man from Lisbon in Buenos Aires?'

'I'm afraid he has to be. You said it. I'm cautious. I'm experienced. And I have the codes.'

'But why *you*? To remove you from Lisbon is costly. I speak both as an enemy and as an objective neutral, allied with Rhinemann. Is there some side issue of which we're not aware?'

'If there is, I'm not aware of it, either,' answered Spaulding, neutralizing Stoltz's inquisitorial look with one of his own. 'Since we're talking plain, I want to get those designs okayed, send the codes for your goddamned money and get the hell out of here. Since a large share of that financing will come from the government, Washington obviously thinks I'm the best man to see we're not cheated.'

Both men remained silent for several moments. Stoltz spoke.

'I believe you. You Americans always worry about being cheated, don't you?'

'Let's talk about Rhinemann. I want the meeting immediately. I won't be satisfied that Kendall's arrangements are solid until I hear it from him. And I won't organize a code schedule with Washington until I'm satisfied.'

'There's no schedule?'

'There won't be any until I see Rhinemann.'

Stoltz breathed deeply. 'You are what they say, a thorough man. You'll see Rhinemann ... It will have to be after dark, two transfers of vehicles, his residence. He can't take the chance of anyone seeing you together ... Do these precautions disturb you?'

'Not a bit. Without the codes there's no money transferred in Switzerland. I think Herr Rhinemann will be most hospitable.'

'Yes, I'm sure ... Very well. Our business is concluded. You'll be contacted this evening. Will you be at home?'

'If not, I'll leave word at the embassy switchboard.'

'*Dann auf Wiedersehen, mein Herr.*' Stoltz got out of the chair and gave a diplomatic nod of his head. '*Heute Abend.*'

'*Heute Abend,*' replied Spaulding as the German parted the curtain and walked out of the cubicle. David saw that Stoltz had left his cigarettes on the table; a minor gift or a minor insult. He removed one and found himself squeezing the tip as he remembered Kendall doing – incessantly, with every cigarette the accountant prepared to smoke. David broke the paper around the tobacco and dropped it in the ashtray. Anything reminding him of

Kendall was distasteful now. He couldn't think about Kendall and his sudden, fear-induced departure.

He had something else to think about.

Heinrich Stoltz, 'third, fourth in command' at the German embassy, was not so highly placed as he believed. The Nazi had not been lying – he *did not* know the Gestapo was in Buenos Aires. And if he didn't know, that meant someone wasn't telling him.

It was ironic, thought David, that he and Erich Rhinemann would be working together after all. Before he killed Rhinemann, of course.

Heinrich Stoltz sat down at his desk and picked up the telephone. He spoke in his impeccable academic German.

'Get me Herr Rhinemann in Luján.'

He replaced the phone, leaned back in his chair and smiled. Several moments later his buzzer hummed.

'Herr Rhinemann? ... Heinrich Stoltz ... Yes, yes, everything went smoothly. Kendall spoke the truth. This Spaulding knows nothing about Koening or the diamonds; his only concerns are the designs. His only threat – that of withholding funds. He plays unimpressive games but we need the codes. The American fleet patrols could be ordered to seal off the harbour; the trawler will have to get out ... Can you imagine? All this Spaulding is interested in is not being cheated!'

28

At first he thought he was mistaken ... No, that wasn't quite right, he considered; that wasn't his first thought. He didn't have a first *thought*, he had only a *reaction*.

He was stunned.

Leslie Hawkwood!

He saw her from his taxi window talking with a man at the south end of the fountain in the Plaza de Mayo. The cab was slowly making its way through the traffic around the huge square; he ordered the driver to pull over and stop.

David paid the driver and got out. He was now directly opposite Leslie and the man; he could see the blurred figures through the spray of the fountain.

The man handed Leslie an envelope and bowed a European bow. He turned and went to the curb, his hand held up for a taxi. One stopped and the man got in; the cab entered the flow of traffic and Leslie went to the crosswalk, waiting for the pedestrian signal.

David made his way cautiously around the fountain and dashed to the curb just as the crosswalk light flashed.

He dodged the anxious vehicles, arousing horns and angry shouts, angling his path to the left in case she turned around at the commotion. She was at least fifty yards ahead of him; she couldn't spot him, he was sure of that.

On the boulevard, Leslie headed west toward Avenida 9 de Julio. David closed the gap between them but kept himself obscured by the crowds. She stopped briefly at several store windows, twice obviously trying to make up her mind whether to enter or not.

So like Leslie; she had always hated to give up the acquisition of something new.

She kept walking, however. Once she looked at her wristwatch; she turned north on Julio and checked the numbers of two store-front addresses, apparently to determine the directional sequence.

Leslie Hawkwood had never been to Buenos Aires.

She continued north at a leisurely pace, taking in the extraordinary color and size of the boulevard. She reached the corner of Corrientes, in the middle of the theater district, and wandered past the billboards, looking at the photographs of the performers.

Spaulding realized that the American embassy was less than two blocks away – between the Avenidas Supacha and Esmeralda. There was no point in wasting time.

She saw him before he spoke. Her eyes widened, her jaw fell, her whole body trembled visibly. The blood drained from her suntanned face.

'You have two alternatives, Leslie,' said Spaulding as he came within a foot of her, looking down at her terrified face. 'The embassy is right up there; it's United States territory. You'll be arrested as a citizen interfering with national security, if not espionage. Or you can come with me ... And answer questions. Which will it be?'

The taxi took them to the airport, where Spaulding rented a car with the papers identifying him as 'Donald Scanlan, mining surveyor'. They were the sort of identifications he carried when making contact with such men as Heinrich Stoltz.

He had held Leslie by the arm with sufficient pressure to warn her not to attempt running; she was his prisoner and he was deadly serious about the fact. She said nothing at all during the ride to the airport, she simply stared out the window, avoiding his eyes.

Her only words at the rental counter were, 'Where are we going?'

His reply was succinct: 'Out of Buenos Aires.'

He followed the river road north toward the outskirts, into the hills above the city. A few miles into the Sante Fé province, the Rio Luján curved westward, and he descended the steep inclines onto the highway paralleling the water's edge. It was the territory of the Argentine rich. Yachts were moored or cruising slowly; sailboats of all classes were lazily catching the upriver winds, tacking harmoniously among the tiny green islands which sprung out of the water like lush gardens. Private roads veered off the highway – now subtly curving west, away from the water. Enormous villas dotted the banks; nothing was without visual effect.

He saw a road to his left that was the start of a hill. He swung up into it, and after a mile there was a break in the bordering forest and a sign in front of a flat, graveled area.

Vigia Tigre.

A lookout. A courtesy for tourists.

He drove the car to the front of the parking ground and pulled to a stop, next to the railing. It was a weekday; there were no other automobiles.

Leslie had said nothing throughout the hour's ride. She had smoked cigarettes, her hands trembling, her eyes refusing to make contact with his. And through experience, David knew the benefits of silence under such conditions.

The girl was close to breaking.

'All right. Now come the questions.' Spaulding turned in the seat and faced her. 'And please believe me, I won't hesitate to run you into military arrest if you refuse.'

She swung her head around and stared at him angrily – yet still in fear. 'Why didn't you do that an hour ago?'

'Two reasons,' he answered simply. 'Once the embassy is involved, I'd be locked into a chain of command; the decisions wouldn't be mine. I'm too curious to lose that control . . . And second, old friend, I think you're in way the hell over your head. What is it, Leslie? What *are* you into?'

She put a cigarette to her lips and inhaled as though her life depended on the smoke. She closed her eyes briefly and spoke barely above a whisper. 'I can't tell you. Don't force me to.'

He sighed. 'I don't think you understand. I'm an Intelligence officer assigned to Clandestine Operations – I'm not telling you anything you don't know. You made it possible for my hotel room to be searched; you lied; you went into hiding; for all I know, you were responsible for several assaults which nearly cost me my life. Now, you turn up in Buenos Aires, four thousand miles away from that Park Avenue apartment. You followed me four thousand miles! . . . *Why?*'

'I can't *tell* you! I haven't been *told* what I can tell you!'

'You haven't been . . . *Christ!* With what I can piece together – and testify to – you could spend twenty years in prison!'

'I'd like to get out of the car. May I?' she said softly, snuffing out her cigarette in the ashtray.

'Sure. Go ahead.' David opened his door and rapidly came around the automobile. Leslie walked to the railing, the waters of the Rio Luján far below in the distance.

'It's very beautiful here, isn't it?'

'Yes . . . Did you try to have me killed?'

'Oh, *God*!' She whirled on him, spitting out the words. 'I tried to save your *life*! I'm here because I don't *want* you killed!'

It took David a few moments to recover from the girl's statement. Her hair had fallen carelessly around her face, her eyes blinking back tears, her lips trembling.

'I think you'd better explain that,' he said in a quiet monotone.

She turned away from him and looked down at the river, the villas, the boats. 'It's like the Riviera, isn't it?'

'*Stop it, Leslie!*'

'Why? It's part of it.' She put her hands on the railing. 'It used to be all there was. Nothing else mattered. *Where* next; *who* next? *What* a lovely party! . . . You were part of it.'

'Not really. You're wrong if you thought that. Just as you're wrong now . . . I won't be put off.'

'I'm not putting you off.' She gripped the railing harder; it was a physical gesture telegraphing her indecision with her words. 'I'm trying to tell you something.'

'That you followed me because you wanted to save my *life?*' He asked the question with incredulity. 'You were filled with dramatics in New York, too, if I recall. You waited, how long was it? Five, six, eight years to get me on the boathouse floor again. You're a bitch.'

'And *you're insignificant*!' She flung the words at him in heat. And then she subsided, controlling herself. 'I don't mean you . . . *you*. Just compared to everything else. We're all insignificant in that sense.'

'So the lady has a cause.'

Leslie stared at him and spoke softly. 'One she believes in very deeply.'

'Then you should have no reservations explaining it to me.'

'I *will*. I promise you. But I can't *now* . . . Trust me!'

'Certainly,' said David casually. And then he suddenly whipped out his hand, grabbing her purse, which hung from her shoulder by a leather strap. She started to resist; he looked at her.

She stopped and breathed deeply.

He opened the purse and took out the envelope she had been given at the fountain in the Plaza de Mayo. As he did so, his eyes caught sight of a bulge at the bottom of the bag, covered by a silk scarf. He held the envelope between his fingers and reached down. He separated the scarf from the object and pulled out a small Remington revolver. Without saying anything, he checked the chamber and the safety and put the weapon in his jacket pocket.

'I've learned to use it,' said Leslie tentatively.

'Good for you,' replied Spaulding, opening the envelope.

'At least you'll see how efficient we are,' she said turning, looking down at the river.

There was no letterhead, no origin of writer or organization.

The heading on the top of the paper read:

Spaulding. David. Lt. Col. Military Intelligence. US Army. Classification 4-0. Fairfax.

Beneath were five complicated paragraphs detailing every move he had made since he was picked up on Saturday afternoon entering the embassy. David was pleased to see that 'Donald Scanlan' was not mentioned; he'd gotten through the airport and customs undetected.

Everything else was listed: his apartment, his telephone, his office at the embassy, the incident on the Córdoba roof, the lunch with Jean Cameron at La Boca, the meeting with Kendall at the hotel, the assault on the Avenida Paraná, his telephone call in the store on Rodriguez Peña.

Everything.

Even the 'lunch' with Heinrich Stoltz at the Langosta del Mar, on the border of Lezuma. The meeting with Stoltz was estimated to last 'a minimum of one hour'.

It was the explanation for her leisurely pace on the Avenida de Mayo. But David had cut the meeting short; there'd been no lunch. He wondered if he had been picked up after he'd left the restaurant. He had not been concerned. His thoughts had been on Heinrich Stoltz and the presence of a Gestapo Stoltz knew nothing about.

'Your people are *very* thorough. Now, who are they?'

'Men . . . and women who have a calling. A purpose. A *great* calling.'

'That's not what I asked you . . .'

There was the sound of an automobile coming up the hill below the parking area. Spaulding reached inside his jacket for his pistol. The car came into view and proceeded upward, past them. The people in the car were laughing. David turned his attention back to Leslie.

'I asked you to trust me,' said the girl. 'I was on my way to an address on that street, the boulevard called Julio. I was to be there at one thirty. They'll wonder where I am.'

'You're not going to answer me, are you?'

'I'll answer you in one way. I'm here to convince you to get out of Buenos Aires.'

'Why?'

'Whatever it is you're doing – and I don't *know* what it is, they haven't told me – it can't happen. We can't let it happen. It's wrong.'

'Since you don't know what it is, how can you say it's wrong?'

'Because I've been told. That's enough!'

'*Ein Volk, ein Reich, ein Führer*,' said David quietly. 'Get in the car!'

'No. You've got to listen to me! Get out of Buenos Aires! Tell your generals it can't be done!'

'Get in the car!'

There was the sound of another automobile, this time coming from the opposite direction, from above. David put his hand once more under his jacket, but then removed it casually. It was the same vehicle with the laughing tourists that had passed by moments ago. They were still laughing, still gesturing; probably drunk with luncheon wine.

'You can't take me to the embassy! You *can't!*'

'If you don't get in the car, you'll just wake up there! Go *on*.'

There was the screeching of tires on the gravel. The descending automobile had turned abruptly – at the last second – and swung sharply into the parking area and come to a stop.

David looked up and swore to himself, his hand immobile inside his jacket.

Two high-powered rifles protruded from the open windows of the car. They were aimed at him.

The heads of the three men inside were covered with silk stockings, the faces flattened, grotesque beyond the translucent masks. The rifles were held by one man next to the driver and by another in the back.

The man in the rear opened the door, his rifle held steady. He gave his command in a calm voice in English.

'Get in the car, Mrs Hawkwood ... And you, colonel. Remove your weapon by the handle – with two fingers.'

David did so.

'Walk to the railing,' commanded the man in the back seat, 'and drop it over the side, into the woods.'

David complied. The man got out of the car to let Leslie climb in. He then returned to his seat and closed the door.

There was the gunning of the powerful engine and the sound once more of spinning tires over the loose gravel. The car lurched forward out of the parking area and sped off down the hill.

David stood by the railing. He would go over it and find his pistol. There was no point in trying to follow the automobile with Leslie Hawkwood and three men in stocking masks. His rented car was no match for a Duesenberg.

29

The restaurant had been selected by Jean. It was out of the way in the north section of the city, beyond Palermo Park, a place for assignation. Telephone jacks were in the wall by the booths; waiters could be seen bringing phones to and from the secluded tables.

He was mildly surprised that Jean would know such a restaurant. Or would choose it for them.

'Where did you go this afternoon?' she asked, seeing him looking out over the dim room from their booth.

'A couple of conferences. Very dull. Bankers have a penchant for prolonging any meeting way beyond its finish. The Strand or Wall Street, makes no difference.' He smiled at her.

'Yes . . . Well, perhaps, they're always looking for ways to extract every last dollar.'

'No "perhaps". That's it . . . This is quite a place, by the way. Reminds me of Lisbon.'

'Rome,' she said. 'It's more like Rome. Way out. Via Appia. Did you know that the Italians comprise over thirty per cent of the population in Buenos Aires?'

'I knew it was considerable.'

'The Italian hand . . . That's supposed to mean evil.'

'Or clever. Not necessarily evil. The "fine Italian hand" is usually envied.'

'Bobby brought me here one night . . . I think he brings lots of girls here.'

'It's . . . discreet.'

'I think he was worried that Henderson might find out he had dishonorable designs. And so he brought me here.'

'Which confirms his designs.'

'Yes . . . It's for lovers. But we weren't.'

'I'm glad you chose it for us. It gives me a nice feeling of security.'

'Oh, no! Don't look for that. No one's in the market for that this year. No . . . Security's out of the question. And commitments. Those, too. No commitments for sale.' She took a cigarette from his open pack; he lit it for her. Over the flame he saw her eyes staring at him. Caught, she glanced downward, at nothing.

'What's the matter?'

'Nothing . . . Nothing at all.' She smiled, but only the outlines were there; not the ingenuousness, not the humor. 'Did you talk to that man Stoltz?'

'Good Lord, is that what's bothering you? . . . I'm sorry, I suppose I should have said something. Stoltz was selling fleet information; I'm in no position to buy. I told him to get in touch with Naval Intelligence. I made a report to the base commander at FMF this morning. If they want to use him, they will.'

'Strange he should call you.'

'That's what I thought. Apparently German surveillance picked me up the other day and the financial data was on their sheet. That was enough for Stoltz.'

'He's a defector?'

'Or selling bad stuff. It's FMF's problem, not mine.'

'You're very glib.' She drank her coffee unsteadily.

'What's that supposed to mean?'

'Nothing . . . Just that you're quick. Quick and facile. You must be very good at your work.'

'And you're in a godawful mood. Does an excess of gin bring it on?'

'Oh, you think I'm drunk?'

'You're not sober. Not that it matters.' He grinned. 'You're hardly an alcoholic.'

'Thanks for the vote of confidence. But don't speculate. That implies some kind of permanence. We must avoid that, mustn't we?'

'Must we? It seems to be a point with you tonight. It wasn't a problem I was considering.'

'You just brushed it aside, I assume. I'm sure you have other, more pressing matters.' In replacing her cup, Jean spilled coffee on the tablecloth. She was obviously annoyed with herself. 'I'm doing it badly,' she said after a moment of silence.

'You're doing it badly,' he agreed.

'I'm frightened.'

'Of what?'

'You're not here in Buenos Aires to talk to bankers, are you? It's much more than that. You won't tell me, I know. And in a few weeks, you'll be gone . . . if you're alive.'

'You're letting your imagination take over.' He took her hand; she crushed out her cigarette and put her other hand over his. She gripped him tightly.

'All right. Let's say you're right.' She spoke quietly now; he had to strain to hear her. 'I'm making everything up. I'm crazy and I drank too much. Indulge me. Play the game for a minute.'

'If you want me to . . . Okay.'

'It's hypothetical. My David isn't a State Department syndromer, you see. He's an agent. We've had a few here; I've met them. The colonels call them *provocarios* . . . So, my David is an agent and being an agent is called . . . high-risk something-or-other because the rules are different. That is, the rules don't have any meaning ... There aren't any rules for these people ... like my hypothetical David. Do you follow?'

'I follow,' he replied simply. 'I'm not sure what the object is or how a person scores.'

'We'll get to that.' She drank the last of her coffee, holding the cup firmly – too firmly; her fingers shook. 'The point is, such a man as my ... mythical David could be killed or crippled or have his face shot off. That's a horrible thought, isn't it?'

'Yes. I imagine that possibility has occurred to several hundred thousand men by now. It's horrible.'

'But they're different. They have armies and uniforms and certain rules. Even in airplanes ... their chances are better. And I say this with a certain expertise.'

He looked at her intently. 'Stop.'

'Oh, not yet. Now, I'm going to tell you how you can score a goal. Why does my hypothetical David do what he does? ... No, don't answer yet.' She stopped and smiled weakly. 'But you weren't about to answer, were you? It doesn't matter; there's a second part to the question. You get extra points for considering it.'

'What's the second part?' He thought that Jean was recapitulating an argument she had memorized. Her next words proved it.

'You see, I've thought about it over and over again ... for this make-believe game ... this make-believe agent. He's in a very unique position; he works alone ... or at least with very, *very* few people. He's in a strange country and he's alone ... Do you understand the second part now?'

David watched her. She had made some abstract connection in her mind without verbalizing it. 'No, I don't.'

'If David is working alone and in a strange country and has to send codes to Washington ... Henderson told me that ... that means the people he's working for have to believe what he tells them. He can tell them anything he wants to ... So now we come back to the question. Knowing all this, why does the mythical David do what he does? He can't really believe that he'll influence the outcome of the whole war. He's only one among millions and millions.'

'And ... if I'm following you ... this make-believe man can send word to his superiors that he's having difficulties ...'

'He has to stay on in Buenos Aires. For a long time,' she interrupted, holding his hand fiercely.

'And if they say no, he can always hide out in the pampas.'

'Don't make fun of me!' she said intensely.

'I'm not. I won't pretend that I can give you logical answers, but I don't think the man you're talking about has such a clear field. Tight reins are kept on such men, I believe. Other men could be sent into the area ... would be sent, I'm sure. Your strategy is only a short-term gain; the penalties are long and damned stiff.'

She withdrew her hands slowly, looking away from him. 'It's a gamble that might be worth it, though. I love you very much. I don't want you hurt and I know there are people trying to hurt you.' She stopped and turned her eyes back to him. 'They're trying to kill you, aren't they? . . . One among so many millions . . . and I keep saying to myself, "Not him. Oh, God, not him." Don't you see? . . . Do we need them? Are those people – whoever they are – so important? To us? Haven't you done enough?'

He returned her stare and found himself understanding the profundity of her question. It wasn't a pleasant realization . . . He *had* done enough. His whole life had been turned around until the alien was an everyday occurrence.

For what?

The amateurs? Alan Swanson? Walter Kendall?

A dead Ed Pace. A corrupt Fairfax.

One among so many millions.

'Señor Spaulding?' The words shocked him momentarily because they were so completely unexpected. A tuxedoed maître d' was standing by the edge of the booth, his voice low.

'Yes?'

'There's a telephone call for you.'

David looked at the discreet man. 'Can't you bring the telephone to the table?'

'Our sincere apologies. The instrument plug at this booth is not functioning.'

A lie, of course, Spaulding knew.

'Very well.' David got out of the booth. He turned to Jean. 'I'll be right back. Have some more coffee.'

'Suppose I wanted a drink?'

'Order it.' He started to walk away.

'David?' She called out enough to be heard; not loudly.

'Yes?' He turned back; she was staring at him again.

' "Tortugas" isn't worth it,' she said quietly.

It was as if he'd been hit a furious blow in the stomach. Acid formed in his throat, his breath stopped, his eyes pained him as he looked down at her.

'I'll be right back.'

'Heinrich Stoltz here,' the voice said.

'I've been expecting your call. I assume the switchboard gave you the number.'

'It was not necessary to telephone. The arrangements have been made. In twenty minutes a green Packard automobile will be outside the restaurant. A man will have his left arm out the window, holding an open pack of German cigarettes this time. I thought you would appreciate the symbolic repetition.'

'I'm touched. But you may have to alter the time and the car.'

'There can be no changes. Herr Rhinemann is adamant.'

'So am I. Something's come up.'

'Sorry. Twenty minutes. A green Packard automobile.'

The connection was severed.

Well, that was Stoltz's problem, thought David. There was only one thought in mind. To get back to Jean.

He made his way out of the dimly lit corner and sidled awkwardly past the bar patrons whose stools were blocking the aisle. He was in a hurry; the human and inanimate obstructions were frustrating, annoying. He reached the arch into the dining area and walked rapidly through the tables to the rear booth.

Jean Cameron was gone. There was a note on the table.

It was on the back of a cocktail napkin, the words written in the heavy wax of an eyebrow pencil. Written hastily, almost illegibly:

David. I'm sure you have things to do –
places to go – and I'm a bore tonight

Nothing else. As if she'd just stopped.

He crumpled the napkin in his pocket and raced back across the dining room to the front entrance. The maître d' stood by the door.

'*Señor?* Is there a problem?'

'The lady at the booth. Where did she go?!'

'Mrs Cameron?'

Christ! thought David, looking at the calm *porteño*. What was happening? The reservation was in *his* name. Jean had indicated that she'd been to the restaurant only once before.

'Yes! Mrs Cameron! Goddamn you, where is she?!'

'She left a few minutes ago. She took the first taxi at the curb.'

'You *listen* to me . . .'

'*Señor,*' interrupted the obsequious Argentine, 'there is a gentleman waiting for you outside. He will take care of your bill. He has an account with us.'

Spaulding looked out the large windowpanes in the heavy front door. Through the glass he could see a man standing on the sidewalk. He was dressed in a white Palm Beach suit.

David pushed the door open and approached him.

'You want to see me?'

'I'm merely waiting for you, Herr Spaulding. To escort you. The car should be here in fifteen minutes.'

30

The green Packard sedan came to a stop across the street, directly in front of the restaurant. The driver's arm appeared through the open window, an indistinguishable pack of cigarettes in his hand. The man in the white Palm Beach suit gestured politely for Spaulding to accompany him.

As he drew nearer, David could see that the driver was a large man in a black-knit, short-sleeved shirt that both revealed and accentuated his muscular arms. There was a stubble of beard, thick eyebrows; he looked like a mean-tempered longshoreman, the rough image intended, Spaulding was sure. The man walking beside him opened the car door and David climbed in.

No one spoke. The car headed south back toward the center of Buenos Aires; then northeast into the aeroparque district. David was mildly surprised to realize that the driver had entered the wide highway paralleling the river. The same road he had taken that afternoon with Leslie Hawkwood. He wondered whether the route was chosen deliberately, if they expected him to make some remark about the coincidence.

He sat back, giving no indication that he recognized anything.

The Packard accelerated on the wide river road which now swung to the left, following the water into the hills of the northwest. The car did not, however, go up any of the offshoot roads as David had done hours ago. Instead the driver maintained a steady, high speed. A reflecting highway sign was caught momentarily in the glare of the headlights: *Tigre 12 kil.*

The traffic was mild; cars rushed past intermittently from the opposite direction; several were overtaken by the Packard. The driver checked his rear- and side-view mirrors constantly.

In the middle of a long bend in the road, the Packard slowed down. The driver nodded his head to the man in the white Palm Beach suit beside David.

'We will exchange cars now, Herr Spaulding,' said the man, reaching into his jacket, withdrawing a gun.

Ahead of them was a single building, an outskirts restaurant or an inn with a circular drive that curved in front of an entrance and veered off into a large parking area on the side. Spotlights lit the entrance and the lawn in front.

The driver swung in; the man beside Spaulding tapped him.

'Get out here, please. Go directly inside.'

David opened the door. He was surprised to see a uniformed doorman remain by the entrance, making no move toward the Packard. Instead, he crossed rapidly in front of the entrance and started walking on the graveled drive in the direction of the side parking lot. Spaulding opened the front door and stepped into the carpeted foyer of the restaurant; the man in the white suit was at his heels, his gun now in his pocket.

Instead of proceeding toward the entrance of the dining area, the man held David by the arm – politely – and knocked on what appeared to be the door of a small office in the foyer. The door opened and the two of them walked inside.

It was a tiny office but that fact made no impression on Spaulding. What fascinated him were the two men inside. One was dressed in a white Palm Beach suit; the other – and David instantly, involuntarily, had to smile – was in the identical clothes he himself was wearing. A light-blue, striped cord jacket and dark trousers. The second man was his own height, the same general build, the same general coloring.

David had no time to observe further. The light in the small office – a desk lamp – was snapped off by the newly appeared white suit. The German who had accompanied Spaulding walked to the single window that looked out on the circular drive. He spoke softly.

'Schnell. Beeilen Sie sich ... Danke.'

The two men quickly walked to the door and let themselves out. The German by the window was silhouetted in the filtered light of the front entrance. He beckoned David.

'Kommen Sie her.'

He went to the window and stood beside the man. Outside, their two counterparts were on the driveway, talking and gesturing as if in an argument – a mild disagreement, not violent. Both smoked cigarettes, their faces more often covered by their hands than not. Their backs were to the highway beyond.

Then an automobile came from the right, from the direction of the parking lot, and the two men got inside. The car moved slowly to the left, to the entrance of the highway. It paused for several seconds, waiting for an opportune moment in the thinned-out night traffic. Suddenly it lurched forward, crossed to the right of the highway and sped off south, toward the city.

David wasn't sure why the elaborate ploy was considered necessary, he was about to ask the man beside him. Before he spoke, however, he noticed the smile on the man's face, inches from his in the window. Spaulding looked out.

About fifty yards away, off the side of the river road, headlights were snapped on. A vehicle, facing north, made a fast U-turn on the wide highway and headed south in a sudden burst of speed.

The German grinned. 'Amerikanische ... Kinder.'

David stepped back. The man crossed to the desk and turned on the lamp.

'That was an interesting exercise,' said Spaulding.

The man looked up. 'Simply a – what are your words, *eine Vorsichtsmass-nahme – a . . .*'

'A precaution,' said David.

'*Ja.* That's right, you speak German . . . Come. Herr Rhinemann must not be kept waiting longer than the . . . *precautions* require.'

Even in daylight, Spaulding realized, the dirt road would be difficult to find. As it was, with no street lamps and only the misty illumination of the moon, it seemed as though the Packard had swung off the hard pavement into a black wall of towering overgrowth. Instead, there was the unmistakable sound of dirt beneath the wheels as the car plunged forward, the driver secure in his knowledge of the numerous turns and straightaways. A half-mile into the forest the dirt road suddenly widened and the surface became smooth and hard again.

There was an enormous parking area. Four stone gateposts – wide, medieval in appearance – were spaced equidistant from one another at the far end of the blacktopped field. Above each stone post was a massive floodlamp, the spills intersecting, throwing light over the entire area and into the woods beyond. Between the huge posts was a thick-grilled iron fence, in the center of which was a webbed steel gate, obviously operated electrically.

Men dressed in dark shirts and trousers – quasi-military in cut – stood around, several with dogs on leashes.

Dobermans. Massive, straining at their leather straps, barking viciously.

Commands could be heard from the handlers and the dogs subsided.

The man in the white Palm Beach suit opened the door and got out. He walked to the main gatepost, where a guard appeared at the fence from inside the compound. The two men talked briefly; David could see that beyond the guard stood a dark concrete or stucco enclosure, perhaps twenty feet in length, in which there were small windows with light showing through.

The guard returned to the miniature house; the man in the white suit came back to the Packard.

'We will wait a few minutes,' he said, climbing into the rear seat.

'I thought we were in a hurry.'

'To be here; to let Herr Rhinemann know we have arrived. Not necessarily to be admitted.'

'Accommodating fellow,' said David.

'Herr Rhinemann can be what he likes.'

Ten minutes later the steel-webbed gate swung slowly open and the driver started the engine. The Packard cruised by the gatehouse and the guards; the Dobermans began their rapacious barking once again, only to be silenced by their masters. The road wound uphill, ending in another huge parking area in front of an enormous white mansion with wide marble steps leading to the largest pair of oak doors David had ever seen. Here, too, floodlights covered the whole area. Unlike the outside premises, there was a fountain in the middle of the courtyard, the reflection of the lights bouncing off the spray of the water.

It was as if some extravagant plantation house from the antebellum South had been dismantled stone by stone, board by board, marble block by marble block, and rebuilt deep within an Argentine forest.

An extraordinary sight, and not a little frightening in its massive architectural concept. The construction engineer in David was provoked and stunned at the same time. The materials-logistics must have been staggering; the methods of leveling and transport incredible.

The cost unbelievable.

The German got out of the car and walked around to David's door. He opened it.

'We'll leave you now. It's been a pleasant trip. Go to the door; you'll be admitted. *Auf Wiedersehen.*'

David got out and stood on the hard surface before the marble steps. The green Packard started off down the winding descent.

Spaulding stood alone for nearly a minute. If he was being watched – and the thought crossed his mind – the observer might think he was an astonished caller overwhelmed by the magnificence in front of him. That judgment would have been partially accurate; his remaining concentration, however, was on the mansion's more mundane specifics: the windows, the roof, the grounds on both visible sides.

Ingress and egress were matters to be considered constantly; the unexpected was never to be projected as too unlikely.

He walked up the steps and approached the immense, thick wooden doors. There was no knocker, no bell; he hadn't thought there would be.

He turned and looked down at the floodlit area. Not a person in sight; neither guards nor servants. No one.

Quiet. Even the sounds of the forest seemed subdued. Only the splash of the fountain interrupted the stillness.

Which meant, of course, that there were eyes unseen and whispers unheard, directing their attention on him.

The door opened. Heinrich Stolz stood in the frame.

'Welcome to Habichtsnest, Herr Spaulding. The Hawk's Lair; appropriately – if theatrically – named, is it not?'

David stepped inside. The foyer, as might be expected, was enormous; a marble staircase rose beyond a chandelier of several thousand crystal cones. The walls were covered with gold cloth; Renaissance paintings were hung beneath silver portrait lamps.

'It's not like any bird's nest I've ever seen.'

'True. However, Habichtsnest, I think, loses something in your translation. Come with me, please. Herr Rhinemann is outside on the river balcony. It's a pleasant evening.'

They walked underneath the grotesque yet beautiful chandelier, past the marble staircase to an archway at the end of the great hall. It led out to an enormous terrace that stretched the length of the building. There were white wrought-iron tables topped with spotless glass, chairs of varying sizes with brightly colored cushions. A series of large double doors could be seen on both sides of the arch; they presumably led to diverse sections of the huge house.

Bordering the terrace was a stone balustrade, waist-high, with statuary and plants on the railing. Beyond the balcony, in the distance, were the waters of the Río Luján. At the left end of the terrace was a small platform, blocked by a gate. Enormously thick wires could be seen above. It was a dock for a cable car, the wires evidently extending down to the river.

David absorbed the splendor, expecting his first view of Rhinemann. There was no one; he walked to the railing and saw that beneath the balcony was another terrace perhaps twenty feet below. A large swimming pool – complete with racing lines in the tile – was illuminated by floodlights under the blue green water. Additional metal tables with sun umbrellas and deck chairs were dotted about the pool and the terrace. And surrounding it all was a manicured lawn that in the various reflections of light looked like the thickest, fullest putting green David had ever seen. Somewhat incongruously, there were the silhouettes of poles and wickets; a croquet course had been imposed on the smooth surface.

'I hope you'll come out one day and enjoy our simple pleasures, Colonel Spaulding.'

David was startled by the strange, quiet voice. He turned. The figure of a man stood in shadows alongside the arch of the great hall.

Erich Rhinemann had been watching him, of course.

Rhinemann emerged from the darkened area. He was a moderately tall man with graying straight hair combed rigidly back – partless. He was somewhat stocky for his size – 'powerful' would be the descriptive word, but his stomach girth might deny the term. His hands were large, beefy, yet somehow delicate, dwarfing the wineglass held between his fingers.

He came into a sufficient spill of light for David to see his face clearly. Spaulding wasn't sure why, but the face startled him. It was a broad face; a wide forehead above a wide expanse of lip beneath a rather wide, flat nose. He was deeply tanned, his eyebrows nearly white from the sun. And then David realized why he was startled.

Erich Rhinemann was an aging man. The deeply tanned skin was a cover for the myriad lines the years had given him; his eyes were narrow, surrounded by swollen folds of age; the faultlessly tailored sports jacket and trousers were cut for a much, much younger man.

Rhinemann was fighting a battle his wealth could not win for him.

'*Habichtsnest ist prächtig. Unglaublich,*' said David politely but without commensurate enthusiasm.

'You are kind,' replied Rhinemann, extending his hand. 'And also courteous; but there is no reason not to speak English . . . Come, sit down. May I offer you a drink?' The financier led the way to the nearest table.

'Thank you, no,' said David, sitting across from Rhinemann. 'I have urgent business in Buenos Aires. A fact I tried to make clear to Stolz before he hung up.'

Rhinemann looked over at an unperturbed Stolz, who was leaning against the stone balustrade. 'Was that necessary? Herr Spaulding is not to be so treated.'

'I'm afraid it *was* necessary, *mein Herr*. For our American friend's own benefit. It was reported to us that he was followed; we were prepared for such an occurrence.'

'If I was followed, you were doing the following.'

'*After* the fact, colonel; I don't deny it. Before, we had no *reason*.'

Rhinemann's narrow eyes pivoted to Spaulding. 'This is disturbing. Who would have you followed?'

'May we talk privately?' David said, glancing at Heinrich Stoltz.

The financier smiled. 'There's nothing in our arrangements that excludes the *Botschaftssekretär*. He is among my most valued associates in South America. Nothing should be withheld.'

'I submit that you won't know unless we speak alone.'

'Our American colonel is perhaps embarrassed,' interrupted Stoltz, his voice laced with invective. 'The man from Lisbon is not considered competent by his own government. He's placed under American surveillance.'

David lit a cigarette; he did not reply to the German attaché. Rhinemann spoke, gesturing with his large, delicate hands.

'If this is so, there is no cause for exclusion. And obviously, there can be no other explanation.'

'We're buying,' said David with quiet emphasis. 'You're selling . . . Stolen property.'

Stoltz was about to speak but Rhinemann held up his hand.

'What you are implying is not possible. Our arrangements were made in complete secrecy; they have been totally successful. And Herr Stoltz is a confidant of the High Command. More so than the ambassador.'

'I don't like repeating myself.' David spoke angrily. 'Especially when I'm paying.'

'Leave us, Heinrich,' said Rhinemann, his eyes on Spaulding.

Stoltz bowed stiffly and walked rapidly, furiously, through the arch into the great hall.

'Thank you.' David shifted his position in the chair and looked up at several small balconies on the second and third stories of the house. He wondered how many men were near the windows; watching, prepared to jump if he made a false move.

'We're alone as requested,' said the German ex-patriot, hardly concealing his irritation. 'What is it?'

'Stoltz is marked,' said Spaulding. He paused to see what kind of reaction the financier would register at such news. As he might have expected, there was none. David continued, thinking perhaps that Rhinemann did not entirely understand. 'He's not being given straight information at the embassy. He may do better at ours.'

'Preposterous.' Rhinemann remained immobile, his narrow eyelids half squinting, staring at David. 'On what do you base such an opinion?'

'The Gestapo. Stoltz claims there's no active Gestapo in Buenos Aires. He's wrong. It's here. It's active. It's determined to stop you. Stop us.'

Erich Rhinemann's composure cracked – if only infinitesimally. There was the slightest, tiny vibration within the rolls of flesh beneath his eyes, and his stare – if possible, thought David – was harder than before.

'Please clarify.'

'I want questions answered first.'

'*You want questions . . .*?' Rhinemann's voice rose, his hand gripped the table; the veins were pronounced at his graying temples. He paused and continued as before. 'Forgive me. I'm not used to conditions.'

'I'm sure you're not. On the other hand, I'm not used to dealing with a contact like Stoltz who's blind to his own vulnerability. That kind of person annoys me . . . and worries me.'

'These questions. What are they?'

'I assume the designs have been gotten out?'

'They have.'

'En route?'

'They arrive tonight.'

'You're early. Our man won't be here until the day after tomorrow.'

'Now it is you who have been given erroneous information, Herr Colonel. The American scientist, Lyons, will be here tomorrow.'

David was silent for several moments. He'd used such a ploy on too many others in the past to show surprise.

'He's expected in San Telmo the day *after* tomorrow,' David said. 'The change is insignificant but that's what Kendall told me.'

'Before he boarded the Pan American Clipper. We spoke subsequently.'

'Apparently he spoke to a lot of people. Is there a point to the change?'

'Schedules may be slowed or accelerated as the necessities dictate . . .'

'Or altered to throw someone off balance,' interrupted David.

'Such is not the case here. There would be no reason. As you phrased it – most succinctly – we're selling, you're buying.'

'And, of course, there's no reason why the Gestapo's in Buenos Aires . . .'

'May we *return* to that subject, please?' interjected Rhinemann.

'In a moment,' answered Spaulding, aware that the German's temper was again stretched. 'I need eighteen hours to get my codes to Washington. They have to go by courier, under chemical seal.'

'Stoltz told me. You were foolish. The codes should have been sent.'

'*Eine Vorsichtsmassnahme, mein Herr,*' said David. 'Put plainly, I don't know who's been bought at our embassy but I'm damned sure someone has. Codes have ways of getting sold. The authentic ones will be radioed only when Lyons verifies the designs.'

'Then you must move quickly. You fly out your codes in the morning; I will bring the first set of prints to San Telmo tomorrow night ... *Eine Vorsichtsmassnahme.* You get the remaining set when you have assured us Washington is prepared to make payment in Switzerland ... as a result of receiving your established code. You won't leave Argentina until I have word from Bern. There is a small airfield called Mendarro. Near here. My men control it. Your plane will be there.'

'Agreed.' David crushed out his cigarette. 'Tomorrow evening, the first set of prints. The remaining within twenty-four hours ... Now we have a schedule. That's all I was interested in.'

'*Gut!* And now we will return to this Gestapo business.' Rhinemann leaned forward in his chair, the veins in his temples once more causing blue rivulets in his sun-drenched skin. 'You said you would clarify!'

Spaulding did.

When he was finished, Erich Rhinemann was breathing deeply, steadily. Within the rolls of flesh, his narrow eyes were furious but controlled.

'Thank you. I'm sure there is an explanation. We'll proceed on schedule ... Now, it has been a long and complicated evening. You will be driven back to Córdoba. Good night.'

'*Altmüller!*' Rhinemann roared. 'An *idiot!* A *fool!*'

'I don't understand,' Stoltz said.

'Altmüller ...' Rhinemann's voice subsided but the violence remained. He turned to the balcony, addressing the vast darkness and the river below. 'In his insane attempts to *disassociate* the High Command from Buenos Aires ... to *absolve* his precious ministry, he's *caught* by his own *Gestapo!*'

'There is *no Gestapo* in Buenos Aires, Herr Rhinemann,' said Stoltz firmly. 'The man from Lisbon lies.'

Rhinemann turned and looked at the diplomat. His speech was ice. 'I know when a man is lying, Herr Stoltz. This Lisbon told the truth; he'd have no reason to do otherwise ... So if Altmüller was *not* caught, he's betrayed me. He's sent in the Gestapo, he has no intention of going through with the exchange. He'll take the diamonds and destroy the designs. The Jew-haters have led me into a trap.'

'I, myself, am the sole coordinator with Franz Altmüller.' Stoltz spoke in his most persuasive tones, nurtured for decades in the Foreign Corps. 'You, Herr Rhinemann, arranged for that. You have no cause to question me. The men at the warehouse in Ocho Calle have nearly finished. The Koening diamonds will be authenticated within a day or two; the courier will deliver the designs before the night is over. Everything is as we planned. The exchange will be made.'

Rhinemann turned away again. He put his thick yet delicate hands on the railing and looked into the distance. 'There is one way to be sure,' he said quietly. 'Radio Berlin. I want Altmüller in Buenos Aires. There will be no exchange otherwise.'

31

The German in the white Palm Beach suit had changed into the paramilitary dress worn by the Rhinemann guards. The driver was not the same one as before. He was Argentine.

The automobile was different, too. It was a Bentley six-seater complete with mahogany dashboard, gray felt upholstery, and window curtains. It was a vehicle suited to the upper-level British diplomatic service, but not so high as to be ambassadorial; just eminently respectable. Another Rhinemann touch, David assumed.

The driver swung the car out onto the dark river highway from the darker confines of the hidden dirt road. He pressed the accelerator to the floor and the Bentley surged. The German beside Spaulding offered him a cigarette; David declined with a shake of his head.

'You say you wish to be driven to the American embassy, *señor*?' said the driver, turning his head slightly, not taking his eyes off the onrushing road. 'I'm afraid I cannot do so. *Señor* Rhinemann's orders were to bring you to the apartment house on Córdoba. Forgive me.'

'We may not deviate from instructions,' added the German.

'Hope you never do. We win the wars that way.'

'The insult is misdirected. I'm completely indifferent.'

'I forgot. Habichtsnest is neutral.' David ended the conversation by shifting in the seat, crossing his legs and staring in silence out the window. His only thought was to get to the embassy and to Jean. She had used the word 'Tortugas'.

Again the elusive 'Tortugas'!

How could she know? Was it conceivable she was part of it?

'*Tortugas*' *isn't worth it*. Jean had said those words. She had pleaded.

Leslie Hawkwood had pleaded, too. Leslie had traveled four thousand miles to plead in defiance. Fanatically so.

Get out of Buenos Aires, David!

Was there a connection?

Oh, Christ! he thought. *Was there really a connection?*

'*Señors!*'

The driver spoke harshly, jolting David's thoughts. The German instantly –

instinctively – whipped around in his seat and looked out the rear window. His question was two words.

'How long?'

'Too long for doubt. Have you watched?'

'No.'

'I passed three automobiles. Without pattern. Then I slowed down, into the far right lane. He's with us. Moving up.'

'We're in the Hill Two district, yes?' asked the German.

'*Si* ... He's coming up rapidly. It's a powerful car; he'll take us on the highway.'

'Head up into the Colinas Rojas! Take the next road on the right! Any one!' commanded Rhinemann's lieutenant, taking his pistol from inside his jacket as he spoke.

The Bentley skidded into a sudden turn, swerving diagonally to the right, throwing David and the German into the left section of the back seat. The Argentine gunned the engine, starting up a hill, slamming the gears into first position, reaching maximum speed in seconds. There was a slight leveling off, a connecting, flatter surface before a second hill, and the driver used it to race the motor in a higher gear for speed. The car pitched forward in a burst of acceleration, as if it were a huge bullet.

The second hill was steeper but the initial speed helped. They raced upward; the driver knew his machine, thought David.

'There are the lights!' yelled the German. 'They follow!'

'There are flat stretches ... I think,' said the driver, concentrating on the road. 'Beyond this section of hills. There are many side roads; we'll try to hide in one. Perhaps they'll pass.'

'No.' The German was still peering out the rear window. He checked the magazine of his pistol by touch; satisfied, he locked it in place. He then turned from the window and reached under the seat. The Bentley was pitching and vibrating on the uphill, back-country road, and the German swore as he worked his hand furiously behind his legs.

Spaulding could hear the snap of metal latches. The German slipped the pistol into his belt and reached down with his free hand. He pulled up a thick-barreled automatic rifle that David recognized as the newest, most powerful front-line weapon the Third Reich had developed. The curved magazine, rapidly inserted by the German, held over forty rounds of .30 caliber ammunition.

Rhinemann's lieutenant spoke. 'Reach your flat stretches. Let them close in.'

David belted up; he held onto the leather strap across the rear of the front seat and braced his left hand against the window frame. He spoke to the German harshly.

'Don't use that! You don't know who they are.'

The man with the gun glanced briefly at Spaulding, dismissing him with a look. 'I know my responsibilities.' He reached over to the right of the rear window where there was a small metal ring imbedded in the felt. He inserted his forefinger, pulled it up, and yanked it toward him, revealing an open-air slot about ten inches wide, perhaps four inches high.

David looked at the left of the window. There was another ring, another opening.

Rhinemann's car was prepared for emergencies. Clean shots could be fired at any automobile pursuing it; the sightlines were clear and there was a minimum of awkwardness at high speeds over difficult terrain.

'Suppose it's American surveillance covering *me*?' David shouted as the German knelt on the seat, about to insert the rifle into the opening.

'It's not.'

'You don't *know* that!'

'*Señors!*' shouted the driver. 'We go down the hill; it's very long, a wide bend. I remember it! Below there are high-grass fields. Flat ... Roads. Hold *on*!'

The Bentley suddenly dipped as if it had sped off the edge of a precipice. There was an immediate, sustained thrust of speed so abrupt that the German with the rifle was thrown back, his body suspended for a fraction of a second in midair. He crashed into the front seat support, his weapon held up to break the fall.

David did not – could not – hesitate. He grabbed the rifle, gripping his fingers around the trigger housing, twisting the stock inward and jerking it out of the German's hands. Rhinemann's lieutenant was stunned by Spaulding's action. He reached into his belt for his pistol.

The Bentley was now crashing down the steep incline at an extraordinary speed. The wide bend referred to by the Argentine was reached; the car entered a long, careening pattern that seemed to be sustaining an engineering improbability: propelled by the wheels of a single side, the other off the surface of the ground.

David and the German braced themselves with their backs against opposite sides, their legs taut, their feet dug into the felt carpet.

'Give me that *rifle*!' The German held his pistol on David's chest. David had the rifle stock under his arm, his finger on the trigger, the barrel of the monster weapon leveled at the German's stomach.

'You fire, I fire,' he shouted back. 'I might come out of it. You won't. You'll be all over the car!'

Spaulding saw that the driver had panicked. The action in the back seat, coupled with the problems of the hill, the speed and the curves created a crisis he was not capable of handling.

'*Señors! Madre de Jesús!* ... You'll *kill* us!'

The Bentley briefly struck the rocky shoulder of the road; the jolt was staggering. The driver swung back toward the center line. The German spoke.

'You behave stupidly. Those men are after you, not us!'

'I can't be sure of that. I don't kill people on speculation.'

'You'll kill us, then? For what purpose?'

'I don't want anyone killed ... Now, put down that gun! We both know the odds.'

The German hesitated.

There was another jolt; the Bentley had struck a large rock or a fallen limb. It was enough to convince Rhinemann's lieutenant. He placed the pistol on the seat.

The two adversaries braced themselves; David's eyes on the German's hand, the German's on the rifle.

'*Madre de Dios!*' The Argentine's shout conveyed relief, not further panic. Gradually the Bentley was slowing down.

David glanced through the windshield. They were coming out of the hill's curve; in the distance were flat blankets of fields, miniature pampas reflecting the dull moonlight. He reached over and took the German's pistol from the seat. It was an unexpected move; Rhinemann's lieutenant was annoyed with himself.

'Get your breath,' said Spaulding to the driver. 'Have a cigarette. And get me back to town.'

'Colonel!' barked the German. 'You may hold the weapons, but there's a car back there! If you won't follow my advice, at least let us get off the road!'

'I haven't the time to waste. I didn't tell him to slow down, just to relax.'

The driver entered a level stretch of road and reaccelerated the Bentley. While doing so he took David's advice and lit a cigarette. The car was steady again.

'Sit back,' ordered Spaulding, placing himself diagonally in the right corner, one knee on the floor – the rifle held casually, not carelessly.

The Argentine spoke in a frightened monotone. 'There are the headlights again. They approach faster than I can drive this car ... What would you have me do?'

David considered the options. 'Give them a chance to respond ... Is there enough moon to see the road? With your lights off?'

'For a while. Not long. I can't remember ...'

'Flick them on and off! Twice ... Now!'

The driver did as he was instructed. The effect was strange: the sudden darkness, the abrupt illumination – while the Bentley whipped past the tall grass on both sides of the road.

David watched the pursuing vehicle's lights through the rear window. There was no response to the signals. He wondered whether they'd been clear, whether they conveyed his message of accommodation.

'Flick them again,' he commanded the driver. 'Hold a couple of beats ... seconds. Now!'

The clicks were heard from the dashboard; the lights remained off for three, four seconds. The clicks again; the darkness again.

And then it happened.

There was a burst of gunfire from the automobile in pursuit. The glass of the rear window was shattered; flying, imbedding itself into skin and upholstery. David could feel blood trickling down his cheek; the German screamed in pain, grasping his bleeding left hand.

The Bentley swerved; the driver swung the steering wheel back and forth, zigzagging the car in the road's path.

'There is your *reply!*' roared Rhinemann's lieutenant, his hand bloodied, his eyes a mixture of fury and panic.

Quickly, David handed the rifle to the German. 'Use it!'

The German slipped the barrel into the opening; Spaulding sprung up into the seat and reached for the metal ring on the left side of the window, pulled it back and brought the pistol up.

There was another burst from the car behind. It was the volley of a submachine gun, scattershot, heavy caliber; spraying the rear of the Bentley. Bulges appeared throughout the felt top and sides, several bullets shattered the front windshield.

The German began firing the automatic; David aimed as best he could – the swerving, twisting Bentley kept pushing the pursuing car out of sightlines. Still he pulled the trigger, hoping only to spray the oncoming tires.

The roars from the German's weapon were thunderous; repeated crescendos of deafening *booms*, the shock waves of each discharge filling the small, elegant enclosure.

David could see the explosion the instant it happened. The hood of the onrushing automobile was suddenly a mass of smoke and steam.

But still the machine-gun volleys came *out* of the enveloping vapor.

'*Eeaagh!*' the driver screamed. David looked and saw blood flowing out of the man's head; the neck was half shot off. The Argentine's hands sprung back from the wheel.

Spaulding leaped forward, trying to reach the wheel, but he couldn't. The Bentley careened off the road, side-slipping into the tall grass.

The German took his automatic weapon from the opening. He smashed the side window with the barrel of the rifle and slammed in a second magazine as the Bentley came to a sharp, jolting stop in the grass.

The pursuing car – a cloud of smoke and spits of fire – was parallel now on the road. It braked twice, lurched once and locked into position, immobile.

Shots poured from the silhouetted vehicle. The German kicked the Bentley's door open and jumped out into the tall grass. David crouched against the left door, fingers searching for the handle, pushing his weight into the panel so that upon touch, the door would fly open and he could thrust himself into cover.

Suddenly the air was filled with the overpowering thunder of the automatic rifle held steady in a full-firing discharge.

Screams pierced the night; David sprung the door open, and as he leaped out he could see Rhinemann's lieutenant rising in the grass. *Rising* and *walking* through the shots, his finger depressing the automatic's trigger, his whole body shaking, staggering under the impact of the bullets entering his flesh.

He fell.

As he did so a second explosion came from the car on the road.

The gas tank burst from under the trunk, sending fire and metal into the air.

David sprang around the tail of the Bentley, his pistol steady.

The firing stopped. The roar of the flames, the hissing of steam was all there was.

He looked past the Bentley's trunk to the carnage on the road.

Then he recognized the automobile. It was the Duesenberg that had come for Leslie Hawkwood that afternoon.

Two dead bodies could be seen in the rear, rapidly being enveloped by fire. The driver was arched over the seat, his arms limp, his neck immobile, his eyes wide in death.

There was a fourth man, splayed out on the ground by the open right door.

The hand moved! Then the head!

He was alive!

Spaulding raced to the flaming Duesenberg and pulled the half-conscious man away from the wreckage.

He had seen too many men die to mistake the rapid ebbing of life. There was no point in trying to stem death; only to use it.

David crouched by the man. 'Who are you? Why did you want to kill me?'

The man's eyes – swimming in their sockets – focused on David. A single headlight flickered from the smoke of the exploded Duesenberg; it was dying, too.

'Who *are* you? Tell me who you are!'

The man would not – or could not – speak. Instead, his lips moved, but not a whisper.

Spaulding bent down further.

The man died trying to spit in David's face. The phlegm and blood intermingled down the man's chin as his head went limp.

In the light of the spreading flames, Spaulding pulled the man's jacket open.

No identification.

Nor in the trousers.

He ripped at the lining in the coat, tore the shirt to the waist.

Then he stopped. Stunned, curious.

There were marks on the dead man's stomach. Wounds but not from bullets. David had seen those marks before.

He could not help himself. He lifted the man by the neck and yanked the coat off the left shoulder, tearing the shirt at the seams to expose the arm.

They were there. Deep in the skin. Never to be erased.

The tattooed numbers of a death camp.

Ein Volk, ein Reich, ein Führer.

The dead man was a Jew.

32

It was nearly five o'clock when Spaulding reached his apartment on Córdoba. He had taken the time to remove what obvious identification he could from the dead Argentine driver and Rhinemann's lieutenant. He found tools in the trunk and unfastened the Bentley's licence plates; moved the dials of the dashboard clock forward, then smashed it. If nothing else, these details might slow police procedures – at least a few hours – giving him valuable time before facing Rhinemann.

Rhinemann would demand that confrontation.

And there was too much to learn, to piece together.

He had walked for nearly an hour back over the two hills – the Colinas Rojas – to the river highway. He had removed the fragments of window glass from his face, grateful they were few, the cuts minor. He had carried the awesome automatic rifle far from the scene of death, removed the chamber loading clip and smashed the trigger housing until the weapon was inoperable. Then he threw it into the woods.

A milk truck from the Tigre district picked him up; he told the driver an outrageous story of alcohol and sex – he'd been expertly rolled and had no one to blame but himself.

The driver admired the foreigner's spirit, his acceptance of risk and loss. The ride was made in laughter.

He knew it was pointless, even frivolous, to attempt sleep. There was too much to do. Instead he showered and made a large pot of coffee.

It was time. Daylight came up from the Atlantic. His head was clear; it was time to call Jean.

He told the astonished marine night operator on the embassy switchboard that Mrs Cameron expected the call; actually he was late, he'd overslept. Mrs Cameron had made plans for deep-sea fishing; they were due at La Boca at six.

'Hello? . . . Hello.' Jean's voice was at first dazed, then surprised.

'It's David. I haven't time to apologize. I've got to see you right away.'

'David? Oh, God! . . .'

'I'll meet you in your office in twenty minutes.'

'*Please . . .*'

'There's no *time*! Twenty minutes. Please, be there ... I need you, Jean. *I need you!*'

The OD lieutenant at the embassy gate was cooperative, if disagreeable. He consented to let the inside switchboard ring Mrs Cameron's office; if she came out and personally vouched for him, the marine would let him pass.

Jean emerged on the front steps. She was vulnerable, lovely. She walked around the driveway path to the gatehouse and saw him. The instant she did so, she stifled a gasp.

He understood.

The styptic pencil could not eradicate the cuts from the half-dozen splinters of glass he had removed from his cheeks and forehead. Partially conceal, perhaps; nothing much more than that.

They did not speak as they walked down the corridor. Instead, she held his arm with such force that he shifted to her other side. She had been tugging at the shoulder not yet healed from the Azores crash.

Inside her office she closed the door and rushed into his arms. She was trembling.

'David, I'm *sorry, sorry, sorry*. I was dreadful. I behaved so badly.'

He took her shoulders, holding her back very gently. 'You were coping with a problem.'

'It seems to me I *can't* cope anymore. And I always thought I was so good at it ... What happened to your face?' She traced her fingers over his cheek. 'It's swollen here.'

' "Tortugas." ' He looked into her eyes. ' "Tortugas" happened.'

'Oh, God.' She whispered the words and buried her head in his chest. 'I'm too disjointed; I can't say what I want to say. Don't. Please, don't ... let anything more happen.'

'Then you'll have to help me.'

She pulled back. '*Me*? How can I?'

'Answer my questions ... I'll know if you're lying.'

'*Lying*? ... Don't joke. *I* haven't lied to *you*.'

He believed her ... which didn't make his purpose any easier. Or clearer. 'Where did you learn the name "Tortugas"?'

She removed her arms from around his neck; he released her. She took several steps away from him but she was not retreating.

'I'm not proud of what I did; I've never done it before.' She turned and faced him.

'I went down to the "Caves" ... without authorization ... and read your file. I'm sure it's the briefest dossier in the history of the diplomatic corps.'

'What did it say?'

She told him.

'So you see, my mythical David of last evening had a distinct basis in reality.'

Spaulding walked to the window overlooking the west lawn of the embassy. The early sun was up, the grass flickered with dew; it brought to mind the manicured lawn seen in the night floodlights below Rhinemann's terrace. And that memory reminded him of the codes. He turned. 'I have to talk to Ballard.'

'Is that all you're going to say?'

'The not-so-mythical David has work to do. That doesn't change.'

'I can't change it, you mean.'

He walked back to her. 'No, you can't . . . I wish to God you could; I wish *I* could. I can't convince myself – to paraphrase a certain girl – that what I'm doing will make that much difference . . . but I react out of habit, I guess. Maybe ego; maybe it's as simple as that.'

'I said you were good, didn't I?'

'Yes. And I am . . . Do you know *what* I am?'

'An intelligence officer. An agent. A man who works with other men; in whispers and at night and with a great deal of money and lies. That's the way I think, you see.'

'Not that. That's new . . . What I *really* am . . . I'm a construction engineer. I build buildings and bridges and dams and highways. I once built an extension for a zoo in Mexico; the best open-air enclosure for primates you ever saw. Unfortunately, we spent so much money the Zoological Society couldn't afford monkeys, but the space is there.'

She laughed softly. 'You're funny.'

'I liked working on the bridges best. To cross a natural obstacle without marring it, without destroying its own purpose . . .'

'I never thought of engineers as romantics.'

'*Construction* engineers are. At least, the best ones . . . But that's all long ago. When this mess is over I'll go back, of course, but I'm not a fool. I know the disadvantages I'll be faced with . . . It's not the same as a lawyer putting down his books only to pick them up again; the law doesn't change that much. Or a stockbroker; the market solutions *can't* change.'

'I'm not sure what you're driving at . . .'

'Technology. It's the only real, civilized benefit war produces. In construction it's been revolutionary. In three years whole new techniques have been developed . . . I've been out of it. My postwar references won't be the best.'

'Good Lord, you're sorry for yourself.'

'Christ, *yes*! In one way . . . More to the point, I'm angry. Nobody held a gun to my head; I walked into this . . . this job for all the wrong reasons and without any foresight . . . That's why I have to be good at it.'

'What about us? Are we an "us"?'

'I love you,' he said simply. 'I know that.'

'After only a week? That's what I keep asking myself. We're not children.'

'We're not children,' he replied. 'Children don't have access to State Department dossiers.' He smiled, then grew serious. 'I need your help.'

She glanced at him sharply. 'What is it?'

'What do you know about Erich Rhinemann?'

'He's a despicable man.'

'He's a Jew.'

'Then he's a despicable Jew. Race and religion notwithstanding, immaterial.'

'Why is he despicable?'

'Because he uses people. Indiscriminately. Maliciously. He uses his money to corrupt whatever and whomever he can. He buys influence from the junta; that gets him land, government concessions, shipping rights. He forced a number of mining companies out of the Patagonia Basin; he took over a dozen or so oil fields at Comodoro Rivadavia . . .'

'What are his politics?'

Jean thought for a second; she leaned back in the chair, looking for an instant at the window, then over to Spaulding. 'Himself,' she answered.

'I've heard he's openly pro-Axis.'

'Only because he believed England would fall and terms would be made. He still owns a power base in Germany, I'm told.'

'But he's a Jew.'

'Temporary handicap. I don't think he's an elder at the synagogue. The Jewish community in Buenos Aires has no use for him.'

David stood up. 'Maybe that's it.'

'What?'

'Rhinemann turned his back on the tribe, openly supports the creators of Auschwitz. Maybe they want him killed. Take out his guards first, then go after him.'

'If by "they" you mean the Jews here, I'd have to say no. The Argentine *judios* tread lightly. The colonels' legions are awfully close to a goose step; Rhinemann has influence. Of course, nothing stops a fanatic or two . . .'

'No . . . They may be fanatics, but not one or two. They're organized; they've got backing – considerable amounts, I think.'

'And they're after Rhinemann? The Jewish community would panic. Frankly, we'd be the first they'd come to.'

David stopped his pacing. The words came back to him again; *there'll be no negotiations with Altmüller*. A darkened doorway on New York's Fifty-second Street.

'Have you ever heard the name Altmüller?'

'No. There's a plain Müller at the German embassy, I think, but that's like Smith or Jones. No Altmüller.'

'What about Hawkwood? A woman named Leslie Jenner Hawkwood?'

'No, again. But if these people are Intelligence-oriented, there'd be no reason for me to.'

'They're Intelligence but I didn't think they were undercover. At least not this Altmüller.'

'What does that mean?'

'His name has been used in a context that assumes recognition. But I can't find him.'

'Do you want to check the "Caves"?' she asked.

'Yes. I'll do it directly with Granville. When do they open?'

'Eight thirty. Henderson's in his office by a quarter to nine.' She saw David hold up his wrist, forgetting he had no watch. She looked at her office clock. 'A little over two hours. Remind me to buy you a watch.'

'Thanks ... Ballard. I have to see him. How is he in the early morning? At this hour?'

'I trust that question's rhetorical ... He's used to being roused up for code problems. Shall I call him?'

'Please. Can you make coffee here?'

'There's a hotplate out there.' Jean indicated the door to the anteroom. 'Behind my secretary's chair. Sink's in the closet ... Never mind. I'll do it. Let me get Bobby first.'

'I make a fine pot of coffee. You call, I'll cook. You look like such an executive, I'd hate to interfere.'

He was emptying the grounds from the pot when he heard it. It was a footstep. A single footstep outside in the corridor. A footstep that should have been muffled but wasn't. A second step would ordinarily follow but didn't.

Spaulding put the pot on the desk, reached down and removed both his shoes without a sound. He crossed to the closed door and stood by the frame.

There it was again. Steps. Quiet; unnatural.

David opened his jacket, checking his weapon, and put his left hand on the knob. He turned it silently, then quickly opened the door and stepped out.

Fifteen feet away a man walking down the corridor spun around at the noise. The look on his face was one Spaulding had seen many times.

Fright.

'Oh, hello there, you must be the new man. We haven't met ... The name's Ellis. Bill Ellis ... I have a beastly conference at seven.' The attaché was not convincing.

'Several of us were going fishing but the weather reports are uncertain. Care to come with us?'

'I'd love to except I have this damned ungodly hour meeting.'

'Yes. That's what you said. How about coffee?'

'Thanks, old man. I really should bone up on some paperwork.'

'Okay. Sorry.'

'Yes, so am I ... Well, see you later.' The man named Ellis smiled awkwardly, gestured a wave more awkwardly – which David returned – and continued on his way.

Spaulding went back into Jean's office and closed the door. She was standing by the secretary's desk.

'Who in heaven's name were you talking to at this hour?'

'He said his name was Ellis. He said he had a meeting with someone at seven o'clock ... He doesn't.'

'What?'

'He was lying. What's Ellis's department?'

'Import–export clearances.'

'That's handy . . . What about Ballard?'

'He's on his way. He says you're a mean man . . . What's "handy" about Ellis?'

Spaulding went to the coffee pot on the desk, picked it up and started for the closet. Jean interrupted his movement, taking the pot from him. 'What's Ellis's rating?' he asked.

'Excellent. Strictly the syndrome; he wants the Court of St James's. You haven't answered me. What's "handy"?'

'He's been bought. He's a funnel. It could be serious or just penny-ante waterfront stuff.'

'Oh?' Jean, perplexed, opened the closet door where there was a washbasin. Suddenly, she stopped. She turned to Spaulding. 'David. What does "Tortugas" mean?'

'Oh, Christ, stop kidding.'

'Which means you can't tell me.'

'Which means I don't *know*. I wish to heaven I *did*.'

'It's a code word, isn't it? That's what it says in your file.'

'It's a code I've never been told about and I'm the one responsible!'

'Here, fill this; rinse it out first.' Jean handed him the coffee pot and walked rapidly into her office, to the desk. David followed and stood in the doorway.

'What are you doing?'

'Attachés, even undersecretaries, if they have very early appointments, list them with the gate.'

'Ellis?'

Jean nodded and spoke into the telephone; her conversation was brief. She replaced the instrument and looked over at Spaulding. 'The first gate pass is listed for nine. Ellis has no meeting at seven.'

'I'm not surprised. Why are you?'

'I wanted to make sure . . . You said you didn't know what "Tortugas" meant. I might be able to tell you.'

David, stunned, took several steps into the office. '*What?*'

'There was a surveillance report from La Boca – that's Ellis's district. His department must have cleared it up, given it a clean bill. It was dropped.'

'What was dropped? What are you talking about?'

'A trawler in La Boca. It had cargo with a destination lading that violated coastal patrols . . . they called it an error. The destination was Tortugas.'

The outer office door suddenly opened and Bobby Ballard walked in.

'*Jesus!*' he said. 'The Munchkins go to work early in this wonderful world of Oz!'

33

The code schedules with Ballard took less than a half-hour. David was amazed at the cryptographer's facile imagination. He developed – on the spot – a geometrical progression of numbers and corresponding letters that would take the best cryps Spaulding knew a week to break.

At maximum, all David needed was ninety-six hours.

Bobby placed Washington's copy in an official courier's envelope, sealed it chemically, placed it in a triple-locked pouch and called the FMF base for an officer – captain's rank or above – to get to the embassy within the hour. The codes would be on a coastal pursuit aircraft by nine; at Andrews Field by late afternoon; delivered to General Alan Swanson's office in the War Department by armored courier van shortly thereafter.

The confirmation message was simple; Spaulding had given Ballard two words; *Cable Tortugas.*

When the code was received in Washington, Swanson would know that Eugene Lyons had authenticated the guidance designs. He could then radio the bank in Switzerland and payment would be made to Rhinemann's accounts. By using the name 'Tortugas', David hoped that someone, somewhere, would understand his state of mind. His anger at being left with the full responsibility without all of the facts.

Spaulding was beginning to think that Erich Rhinemann was demanding more than he was entitled to. A possibility that would do him little good.

Rhinemann was to be killed.

And the outlines of a plan were coming into focus that would bring about that necessary death. The act itself might be the simplest part of his assignment.

There was no point in *not* telling Jean and Bobby Ballard about the guidance designs. Kendall had flown out of Buenos Aires – without explanation; David knew he might need assistance at a moment when there was no time to brief those helping him. His cover was superfluous now. He described minutely Rhinemann's schedule, the function of Eugene Lyons and Heinrich Stoltz's surfacing as a contact.

Ballard was astonished at Stoltz's inclusion. '*Stoltz!* That's a little bit of lightning . . . I mean, he's a *believer.* Not the Hitler fire 'n' brimstone – he dismisses that, I'm told. But *Germany.* The Versailles motive, the reparations

– bled giant, export or die – the whole thing. I figured him for the real Junker item . . .'

David did not pay much attention.

The logistics of the morning were clear in Spaulding's mind and at eight forty-five he began.

His meeting with Henderson Granville was short and cordial. The ambassador was content not to know David's true purpose in Buenos Aires, as long as there was no diplomatic conflict. Spaulding assured him that to the best of his knowledge there was none; certainly less of a possibility if the ambassador remained outside the hard core of the assignment. Granville agreed. On the basis of David's direct request, he had the 'Caves' checked for files on Franz Altmüller and Leslie Jenner Hawkwood.

Nothing.

Spaulding went from Granville's office back to Jean's. She had received the incoming passengers manifest from Aeroparque. Eugene Lyons was listed on clipper flight 101, arriving at two in the afternoon. His profession was given as 'physicist'; the reason for entry, 'industrial conferences'.

David was annoyed with Walter Kendall. Or, he thought, should his annoyance be with the bewildered amateur, Brigadier General Alan Swanson? The least they could have done was term Lyons a 'scientist'; 'physicist' was stupid. A physicist in Buenos Aires was an open invitation to surveillance – even *Allied* surveillance.

He walked back to his own isolated, tiny office. To think.

He decided to meet Lyons himself. Walter Kendall had told him that Lyons's male nurses would settle the mute, sad man in San Telmo. Recalling the two men in question, David had premonitions of disaster. It wasn't beyond Johnny and Hal – those were the names, weren't they? – to deliver Lyons to the steps of the German embassy, thinking it was another hospital.

He would meet Pan Am Clipper 101. And proceed to take the three men on a complicated route to San Telmo.

Once he'd settled Lyons, David estimated that he would have about two, possibly three, hours before Rhinemann – or Stoltz – would make contact. Unless Rhinemann was hunting him now, in panic over the killings in the Colinas Rojas. If so, Spaulding had 'built his shelter'. His irrefutable alibi . . . He hadn't been there. He'd been dropped off at Córdoba by two in the morning.

Who could dispute him?

So, he would have two or three hours in midafternoon.

La Boca.

Discreetly, Jean had checked naval surveillance at FMF. The discretion came with her utterly routine, bored telephone call to the chief of operations. She had a 'loose end' to tie up, for a 'dead file'; there was no significance, only a bureaucratic matter – someone was always looking for a good rating on the basis of closing out. Would the lieutenant mind filling in? . . . The trawler erroneously listed for Tortugas was moored by a warehouse complex in Ocho Calle. The error was checked and confirmed by the embassy attaché, Mr William Ellis, Import–Export Clearance Division.

Ocho Calle.

David would spend an hour or so looking around. It could be a waste of time. What connection would a fishing trawler have with his assignment? There was none that he could see. But there was the name 'Tortugas'; there *was* an attaché named Ellis who crept silently outside closed doors and lied about nonexistent conferences in the early morning.

Ocho Calle was worth looking into.

Afterward, he would stay by his telephone at Córdoba.

'Are you going to take me to lunch?' asked Jean, walking into his office. 'Don't look at your watch; you haven't got one.'

Spaulding's hand was in midair, his wrist turned. 'I didn't realize it was so late.'

'It's not. It's only eleven, but you haven't eaten – probably didn't sleep, either – and you said you were going to the airport shortly after one.'

'I was right; you're a corporate executive. Your sense of organization is frightening.'

'Nowhere near yours. We'll stop at a jewelry store first. I've already called. You have a present.'

'I like presents. Let's go.' Spaulding got out of his chair as the telephone rang. He looked down at it. 'Do you know that's the first time that thing has made a sound?'

'It's probably for me. I told my secretary I was here ... I don't think I really *had* to tell her.'

'Hello?' said David into the phone.

'Spaulding?'

David recognized the polished German of Heinrich. Stolz. His tension carried over the wire. 'Isn't it a little foolish to call me here?'

'I have no choice. Our mutual friend is in a state of extreme anxiety. Everything is jeopardized.'

'What are you talking about?'

'This is no time for foolishness! The situation is grave.'

'It's no time for games, either. What the hell are you talking about?'

'Last night! This morning. What happened?'

'What happened where?'

'*Stop it!* You *were there!*'

'Where?'

Stoltz paused; David could hear his breath. The German was in panic, desperately trying to control himself. 'The men were killed. We must know what happened!'

'Killed? ... You're crazy. How?'

'*I warn you ...*'

'Now *you* cut it out! I'm *buying*. And don't forget it ... I don't want to be mixed up in any organization problems. Those men dropped me off around one thirty. Incidentally, they met your other boys, the ones covering my apartment. And also incidentally, I don't like this round-the-clock surveillance!'

Stoltz was blanked – as David expected he would be. 'The others? . . . What others?'

'Get off it! You know perfectly well.' Spaulding let the inference hang.

'This is all most disturbing . . .' Stoltz tried to compose himself.

'I'm sorry,' said David noncommittally.

Exasperated, Stoltz interrupted. 'I'll call you back.'

'Not here. I'll be out most of the afternoon . . . As a matter of fact,' added Spaulding quickly, pleasantly, 'I'll be in one of those sailboats our mutual friend looks down upon so majestically. I'm joining some diplomatic friends almost as rich as he is. Call me after five at Córdoba.'

David hung up instantly, hearing the beginning of Stoltz's protest. Jean was watching him, fascinated.

'You did that very well,' she said.

'I've had more practice than him.'

'Stoltz?'

'Yes. Let's go into your office.'

'I thought we were going to lunch.'

'We are. Couple of things first . . . There's a rear exit, isn't there?'

'Several. Back gate.'

'I want to use an embassy vehicle. Any trouble?'

'No, of course not.'

'Your secretary. Could you spare her for a long lunch?'

'You're sweet. I had the insane idea you were taking *me*.'

'I am. Could she put her hair up and wear a floppy hat?'

'Any woman can.'

'Good. Get that yellow coat you wore last night. And point out any man around here relatively my size. One that your secretary might enjoy that long lunch with. Preferably wearing dark trousers. He'll have my jacket.'

'What *are* you *doing*?'

'Our friends are good at playing jokes on other people. Let's see how they take it when one's played on them.'

Spaulding watched from the third-floor window, concealed by the full-length drapes. He held the binoculars to his eyes. Below, on the front steps, Jean's secretary – in a wide-brimmed hat and Jean's yellow coat – walked rapidly down to the curb of the driveway. Following her was one of Ballard's assistants, a tall man in dark trousers and David's jacket. Both wore sunglasses. Ballard's man paused momentarily on the top step, looking at an unfolded road map. His face was covered by the awkward mass of paper. He descended the stairs and together he and the girl climbed into the embassy limousine – an upper-level vehicle with curtains.

Spaulding scanned the Avenida Corrientes in front of the gates. As the limousine was passed through, a Mercedes coupe parked on the south side of the street pulled away from the curb and followed it. And then a second automobile on the north side made a cautious U-turn and took up its position several vehicles behind the Mercedes.

Satisfied, David put down the binoculars and went out of the room. In the corridor he turned left and walked swiftly past doors and around staircases toward the rear of the building, until he came to a room that corresponded to his observation post in front. Bobby Ballard sat in an armchair by the window; he turned around at the sound of David's footsteps, binoculars in his hands.

'Anything?' Spaulding asked.

'Two,' answered the cryp. 'Parked facing opposite directions. They just drove away.'

'Same up front. They're in radio contact.'

'Thorough, aren't they?'

'Not as much as they think,' Spaulding said.

Ballard's sports coat was loose around the midsection and short in the sleeves, but it showed off David's new wristwatch. Jean was pleased about that. It was a very fine chronometer.

The restaurant was small, a virtual hole-in-the-wall on a side street near San Martin. The front door was open; a short awning protected the few outside tables from the sun. Their table, however, was inside. Spaulding sat facing the entrance, able to see clearly the passers-by on the sidewalk.

But he was not watching them now. He was looking at Jean. And what he saw in her face caused him to say the words without thinking.

'It's going to be over soon. I'm getting out.'

She took his hand, searching his eyes. She did not reply for several moments. It was as if she wanted his words suspended, isolated, thought about. 'That's a remarkable thing to say. I'm not sure what it means.'

'It means I want to spend years and years with you. The rest of my life . . . I don't know any other way to put it.'

Jean closed her eyes briefly, for the duration of a single breath of silence. 'I think you've put it . . . very beautifully.'

How could he tell her? How could he explain? He had to try. It was so damned important. 'Less than a month ago,' he began softly, 'something happened in a field. At night, in Spain. By a campfire . . . *To me.* The circumstances aren't important, but what happened to me was . . . the most frightening thing I could imagine. And it had nothing to do with the calculated risks in my work; nothing to do with being afraid – and I was always afraid, you can bet your life on that . . . But I suddenly found I had no *feeling.* No feeling at all. I was given a report that should have shaken me up – made me weep, or made me angry, *goddamned angry.* But I didn't feel anything. I was numb. I accepted the news and criticized the man for withholding it. I told him not to make that mistake again . . . That I did not act rashly under any conditions . . . You see, he *rightfully* thought that I would.' David stopped and put his hand over Jean's. 'What I'm trying to tell you is that you've given me back something I thought I'd lost. I don't ever want to take the chance of losing it again.'

'You'll make me cry,' she said quietly, her eyes moist, her lips trembling to a smile. 'Don't you know girls cry when things like that are said to them? . . . I'll have to teach you so much . . . Oh, Lord,' she whispered. 'Please, *please* . . . years.'

David leaned over the small table; their lips touched and as they held lightly together, he removed his hand from hers and gently ran his fingers over the side of her face.

The tears were there.

He felt them, too. They would not come for him, but he *felt* them.

'I'm going back with you, of course,' she said.

Her words brought back the reality . . . the other reality, the lesser one. 'Not *with* me. But soon. I'm going to need a couple of weeks to settle things . . . And you'll have to transfer your work down here.'

She looked at him questioningly but did not ask a question. 'There are . . . special arrangements for you to take back the blueprints or designs or whatever they are.'

'Yes.'

'When?'

'If everything goes as we expect, in a day or two. At the most, three.'

'Then why do you need a couple of weeks?'

He hesitated before answering. And then he realized he wanted to tell her the truth. It was part of the beginning for him. The truth. 'There's a breach of security in a place called Fairfax . . .'

'Fairfax,' she interrupted. 'That was in your file.'

'It's an intelligence center in Virginia. Very classified. A man was killed there. He was a friend of mine. I purposely withheld information that might stop the leaks and, more important, find out who killed him.'

'For heaven's sake, why?'

'In a way, I was forced to. The men in Fairfax weren't cleared for the information I had; the one man who was, is ineffectual . . . especially in something like this. He's not Intelligence-oriented; he's a requisition general. He buys things.'

'Like gyroscopic designs?'

'Yes. When I get back I'll force him to clear the data.' David paused and then spoke as much to himself as to Jean. 'Actually, I don't give a damn whether he does or not. I've got a long accumulated leave coming to me. I'll use a week or two of it in Fairfax. There's a German agent walking around in that compound with a four-zero rating. He killed a very good man.'

'That frightens me.'

'It shouldn't.' David smiled, answering her with the truth. 'I have no intention of risking those years we talked about. If I have to, I'll operate from a maximum security cell . . . Don't worry.'

She nodded. 'I won't. I believe you . . . I'll join you in, say, three weeks. I owe that to Henderson; there *will* be a lot of adjustments for him. Also, I'll have something done about Ellis.'

'Don't touch him. We don't *know* anything yet. If we find out he's on an outside payroll he can be valuable right where he is. Reverse conduits are jewels. When we uncover one we make sure he's the healthiest man – or woman – around.'

'What kind of a world do you live in?' Jean asked the question with concern, not humor.

'One that you'll help me leave ... After Fairfax, I'm finished.'

Eugene Lyons edged into the back seat of the taxi between Spaulding and the male nurse named Hal. The other attendant, Johnny, sat in front with the driver. David gave his instructions in Spanish; the driver started out on the long, smooth roadway of the aeroparque.

David looked at Lyons; it wasn't easy to do so. The proximity of the sad, emaciated face emphasized the realization that what he saw was self-inflicted. Lyons's eyes were not responding; he was exhausted from the flight, suspicious of the new surroundings, annoyed by David's aggressive efficiency at hurrying them all out of the terminal.

'It's good to see you again,' David told him.

Lyons blinked; Spaulding wasn't sure whether it was a greeting or not.

'We didn't expect you,' said Johnny from the front seat. 'We expected to get the professor set ourselves.'

'We've got it all written down,' added Hal, leaning forward on Lyons's right, taking number of index cards out of his pocket. 'Look. The address. Your telephone number. And the embassy's. And a wallet full of Argentine money.'

Hal pronounced Argentine, 'Argentyne'. David wondered how he could be given a course in hypodermic injection; who would read the labels? On the other hand, his partner Johnny – less talkative, more knowing somehow – was obviously the leader of the two.

'Well, these things are usually fouled up. Communications break down all the time ... Did you have a good flight down, doctor?'

'It wasn't bad,' answered Hal. 'But bumpy as a son-of-a-bitch over Cuba.'

'Those were probably heavy air masses coming up from the island,' said David, watching Lyons out of the corner of his eye. The physicist responded now; a slight glance at Spaulding. And there was humor in the look.

'Yeah,' replied Hal knowingly, 'that's what the stewardess said.'

Lyons smiled a thin smile.

David was about to capitalize on the small breakthrough when he saw a disturbing sight in the driver's rear-view mirror – instinctively he'd been glancing at the glass.

It was the narrow grill of an automobile he'd previously spotted, though with no alarm. He had seen it twice: on the long curb in the taxi lineup and again on the turnout of the front park. Now it was there again, and David slowly shifted his position and looked out the taxi's rear window. Lyons seemed to sense that Spaulding was concerned; he moved to accommodate him.

The car was a 1937 La Salle, black, with rusted chrome on the grillwork and around the headlights. It remained fifty to sixty yards behind, but the driver – a blond-haired man – refused to let other vehicles come between them. He would accelerate each time his position was threatened. The blond-haired man, it appeared, was either inexperienced or careless. If he *was* following them.

David spoke to the taxi driver in urgent but quiet Spanish. He offered the man five dollars over the meter if he would reverse his direction and head away from San Telmo for the next several minutes. The *porteño* was less of an amateur than the driver of the La Salle; he understood immediately, with one look in his mirror. He nodded silently to Spaulding, made a sudden, awkwardly dangerous U-turn, and sped west. He kept the taxi on a fast zigzag course, weaving in and around the traffic, then turned abruptly to his right and accelerated the car south along the ocean drive. The sight of the water reminded David of Ocho Calle.

He wanted very much to deposit Eugene Lyons in San Telmo and get back to Ocho Calle.

The La Salle was no longer a problem.

'Christ!' said Hal. 'What the hell was that?' And then he answered his own question. 'We were being followed, right?'

'We weren't sure,' said David.

Lyons was watching him, his look inexpressive. Johnny spoke from the front seat.

'Does that mean we can expect problems? You had this guy tooling pretty hard. Mr Kendall didn't mention anything about trouble ... Just our job.' Johnny did not turn around as he spoke.

'Would it bother you if there were?'

Johnny turned to face Spaulding; he was a very serious fellow, thought David. 'It depends,' said the male nurse. 'Our job is to watch out for the professor. Take care of him. If any trouble interfered with that, I don't think I'd like it.'

'I see. What would you do?'

'Get him the hell out of here,' answered Johnny simply.

'Dr Lyons has a job to do in Buenos Aires. Kendall must have told you that.'

Johnny's eyes leveled with Spaulding's. 'I'll tell you straight, mister. That dirty pig can go screw. I never took so much shit from anyone in my life.'

'Why don't you quit?'

'We don't work for Kendall,' said Johnny, as if the thought was repulsive. 'We're paid by the Research Center of Meridian Aircraft. That son-of-a-bitch isn't even from Meridian. He's a lousy bookkeeper.'

'You understand, Mr Spaulding,' said Hal, retreating from his partner's aggressiveness. 'We have to do what's best for the professor. That's what the Research Center hires us for.'

'I understand. I'm in constant touch with Meridian Research. The last thing anyone would wish is to harm Dr Lyons. I can assure you of that.' David lied convincingly. He couldn't give assurance because he himself was far from sure. His only course with Johnny and Hal was to turn this newfound liability into an asset. The key would be Meridian's Research Center and his fictional relationship to it; and a common repugnance for Kendall.

The taxi slowed down, turning a corner into a quiet San Telmo street. The driver pulled up to a narrow, three-storied, white stucco house with a sloping, rust-tiled roof. It was 15 Terraza Verde. The first floor was leased to Eugene Lyons and his 'assistants'.

'Here we are.' said Spaulding, opening the door.

Lyons climbed out after David. He stood on the sidewalk and looked up at the quaint, colorful little house on the peaceful street. The trees by the curb were sculptured. Everything had a scrubbed look; there was an Old World serenity about the area. David had the feeling that Lyons had suddenly found something he'd been looking for.

And then he thought he saw what it was. Eugene Lyons was looking up at a lovely resting place. A final resting place. A grave.

34

There wasn't the time David thought there would be. He had told Stoltz to call him after five at Córdoba; it was nearly four now.

The first boats were coming into the piers, whistles blowing, men throwing and catching heavy ropes, nets everywhere, hanging out for the late drying rays of the sun.

Ocho Calle was in the Dársena Norte, east of the Retiro freight yards in a relatively secluded section of La Boca. Railroad tracks, long out of use, were implanted in the streets along the row of warehouses. Ocho Calle was not a prime storage or loading area. Its access to the sea channels wasn't as cumbersome as the inner units of the La Plata, but the facilities were outmoded. It was as if the management couldn't decide whether to sell its fair waterfront real estate or put it into good operating order. The indecision resulted in virtual abandonment.

Spaulding was in shirtsleeves; he had left Ballard's tan jacket at Terraza Verde. Over his shoulder was a large used net he had bought at an outdoor stall. The damn thing was rancid from rotting hemp and dead fish but it served its purpose. He could cover his face at will and move easily, comfortably among his surroundings – at one with them. David thought that should he ever – God forbid! – instruct recruits at Fairfax, he'd stress the factor of comfort. Psychological comfort. One could feel it immediately; just as swiftly as one felt the discomfort of artificiality.

He followed the sidewalk until it was no more. The final block of Ocho Calle was lined on the far side by a few old buildings and fenced-off abandoned lots once used for outside storage, now overgrown with tall weeds. On the water side were two huge warehouses connected to each other by a framed open area. The midships of a trawler could be seen moored between the two buildings. The next pier was across a stretch of water at least a quarter of a mile away. The Ocho Calle warehouses were secluded indeed.

David stopped. The block was like a miniature peninsula; there were few people on it. No side streets, no buildings beyond the row of houses on his left, only what appeared to be other lots behind the houses and further pilings that were sunk into the earth, holding back the water of a small channel.

The last stretch of Ocho Calle *was* a peninsula. The warehouses were not only secluded, they were isolated.

David swung the net off his right shoulder and hoisted it over his left. Two seamen walked out of a building; on the second floor a woman opened a window and shouted down, berating her husband about the projected hour of his return. An old man with dark Indian features sat in a wooden chair on a small, dilapidated stoop in front of a filthy bait store. Inside, through the glass stained with salt and dirt, other old men could be seen drinking from wine bottles. In the last house, a lone whore leaned out a first-floor window, saw David and opened her blouse, displaying a large, sagging breast. She squeezed it several times and pointed the nipple at Spaulding.

Ocho Calle was the end of a particular section of the earth.

He walked up to the old Indian, greeted him casually, and went into the bait store. The stench was overpowering, a combination of urine and rot. There were three men inside, more drunk than sober, nearer seventy than sixty.

The man behind the planked boards which served as a counter seemed startled to see a customer, not really sure what to do. Spaulding took a bill from his pocket – to the astonishment of all three surrounding him – and spoke in Spanish.

'Do you have squid?'

'No ... No, no squid. Very little supplies today,' answered the owner, his eyes on the bill.

'What have you got?'

'Worms. Dog meat, some cat. Cat is very good.'

'Give me a small container.'

The man stumbled backward, picked up pieces of intestine and wrapped them in a dirty newspaper. He put it on the plank next to the money. 'I have no change, *señor? ...*'

'That's all right,' replied Spaulding. 'The money's for you. And keep the bait.'

The man grinned, bewildered. '*Señor? ...*'

'You keep the money. Understand? ... Tell me. Who works over there?' David pointed at the barely translucent front window. 'In those big dock houses?'

'Hardly anybody ... A few men come and go ... now and then. A fishing boat ... now and then.'

'Have you been inside?'

'Oh, yes. Three, four years ago, I work inside. Big business, three, four ... five years ago. We all work.' The other two old men nodded, chattering old men's chatter.

'Not now?'

'No, no ... All closed down. Finished. Nobody goes inside now. The owner is a very bad man. Watchmen break heads.'

'Watchmen?'

'Oh, yes. With guns. Many guns. Very bad.'

'Do automobiles come here?'

'Oh, yes. Now and then ... One or two ... They don't give us work.'

'Thank you. You keep the money. Thank you, again.' David crossed to the filthy store-front window, rubbed a small section of the glass and looked out at the block-long stretch of warehouse. It appeared deserted except for the men on the pier. And then he looked closer at those men.

At first he wasn't sure; the glass – though rubbed – still had layers of film on the outside pane; it wasn't clear and the men were moving about, in and out of the small transparent area.

Then he was sure. And suddenly very angry.

The men in the distance on the pier were wearing the same paramilitary clothes the guards at Rhinemann's gate had worn.

They were Rhinemann's men.

The telephone rang at precisely five thirty. The caller was not Stoltz, and because it wasn't, David refused to accept the instructions given him. He hung up and waited less than two minutes for the phone to ring again.

'You are most obstinate,' said Erich Rhinemann. 'It is we who should be cautious, not you.'

'That's a pointless statement. I have no intention of following the directions of someone I don't know. I don't expect airtight controls but that's too loose.'

Rhinemann paused. Then he spoke harshly. 'What happened last night?'

'I told Stoltz exactly what happened to *me*. I don't know anything else.'

'I don't believe you.' Rhinemann's voice was tense, sharp, his anger very close to the surface.

'I'm sorry,' said David. 'But that doesn't really concern me.'

'Neither of those men could have left Córdoba! Impossible!'

'They left; take my word for it ... Look, I told Stoltz I don't want to get mixed up in your problems...'

'How do you know you're not ... mixed up?'

It was, of course, the logical question and Spaulding realized that. 'Because I'm here in my apartment, talking to you. According to Stoltz, the others are dead; that's a condition I intend to avoid. I'm merely purchasing some papers from you. Let's concentrate on that.'

'We'll talk further on this subject,' said Rhinemann.

'Not now. We have business to transact.'

Again the German Jew paused. 'Do as the man told you. Go to the Casa Rosada on the Plaza de Mayo. South gate. If you take a taxi, get off at the Julio and walk.'

'Your men will pick me up when I leave the apartment, I assume.'

'Discreetly. To see if you're followed.'

'Then I'll walk from here. It'll be easier.'

'Very intelligent. A car will be waiting for you at the Rosada. The same automobile that brought you here last evening.'

'Will you be there?' asked David.

'Of course not. But we'll meet shortly.'

'I take the designs straight to Telmo?'

'If everything is clear, you may.'

'I'll leave in five minutes. Will your men be ready?'

'They are ready now,' answered Rhinemann. He hung up.

David strapped the Beretta to his chest and put on his jacket.

He went into the bathroom, grabbed a towel from the rack and rubbed his shoes, removing the Aeroparque and La Boca dirt from the leather. He combed his hair and patted talcum powder over the scratches on his face.

He couldn't help but notice the dark crescents under his eyes. He needed sleep badly, but there was no time. For his own sake – survival, really – he knew he had to take the time.

He wondered when it would be.

He returned to the telephone. He had two calls to make before he left.

The first was to Jean. To ask her to stay in the embassy; he might have reason to call her. At any rate, he would talk to her when he returned. He said he would be with Eugene Lyons at Terraza Verde. And that he loved her.

The second call was to Henderson Granville.

'I told you I wouldn't involve the embassy or yourself in my work here, sir. If that's changed it's only because a man on your staff closed a naval surveillance file improperly. I'm afraid it directly affects me.'

'How do you mean "improperly"? That's a serious implication. If not a chargeable offense.'

'Yes, sir. And for that reason it's imperative we raise no alarm, keep everything very quiet. It's an Intelligence matter.'

'Who is this man?' asked Granville icily.

'An attaché named Ellis. William Ellis – please don't take *any* action, sir.' Spaulding spoke rapidly, emphatically. 'He may have been duped; he may *not* have been. Either way we can't have him alerted.'

'Very well. I follow you . . . Then why have you told me . . . if you want no action taken?'

'Not against Ellis, sir. We *do* need a clarification on the surveillance.' David described the warehouses on Ocho Calle and the trawler moored between the two buildings.

Granville interrupted quietly. 'I remember the report. Naval surveillance. It was a lading destination . . . let me think.'

'Tortugas,' supplied Spaulding.

'Yes, that was it. Coastal violations. An error, of course. No fishing boat would attempt such a trip. The actual destination was *Torugos*, a small port in northern Uruguay, I think.'

David thought for a second. Jean hadn't mentioned the switch – or similarity of names. 'That may be, sir, but it would be advantageous to know the cargo.'

'It was listed. Farm machinery, I believe.'

'We don't think so,' said Spaulding.

'Well, we have no right to inspect cargo . . .'

'Mr Ambassador?' David cut off the old gentleman. 'Is there anyone in the junta we can trust, *completely* trust?'

Granville's reply was hesitant, cautious; Spaulding understood. 'One. Two, perhaps.'

'I won't ask you their names, sir. I *will* ask you to request their help. With priority security measures. Those warehouses are guarded ... by Erich Rhinemann's men.'

'*Rhinemann?*' The ambassador's distaste carried over the telephone. That was an asset, thought David.

'We have reason to believe he's aborting a negotiation or tying contraband into it. Smuggling, sir. We have to know what that cargo is.' It was all David could think to say. A generalization without actual foundation. But if men were willing to kill and be killed for 'Tortugas', perhaps that was foundation enough. If Fairfax could list the name on his transfer orders without telling him – that was *more* than enough.

'I'll do what I can, Spaulding. I can't promise anything, of course.'

'Yes, sir. I realize. And thank you.'

The Avenida de Mayo was jammed with traffic, the Plaza worse. At the end of the square the pinkish stone of Casa Rosada reflected the orange flood of the setting sun. Befitting a capital controlled by soldiers, thought David.

He crossed the Plaza, stopping at the fountain, recalling yesterday and Leslie Jenner Hawkwood. Where was she now? In Buenos Aires; but where? And more important, why?

The answer might lie in the name 'Tortugas' and a trawler in Ocho Calle.

He circled the fountain twice, then reversed his steps once, testing himself, testing Erich Rhinemann. Where were the men watching him? Or were they women?

Were they in cars or taxis or small trucks? Circling as he was circling?

He spotted one. It wasn't hard to do. The man had seated himself on the edge of the fountain's pool, the tail of his jacket in the water. He'd sat down too quickly, trying to be inconspicuous.

David started across the pedestrian walk – the same pedestrian walk he'd used following Leslie Hawkwood – and at the first traffic island waited for a change of light. Instead of crossing, however, he walked back to the fountain. He stepped up his pace and sat down at the pool's edge and watched the crosswalk.

The man with the wet jacket emerged with the next contingent of pedestrians and looked anxiously around. Finally he saw Spaulding.

David waved.

The man turned and raced back across the street,

Spaulding ran after him, just making the light. The man did not look back; he seemed hell-bent to reach a contact, thought David; to have someone take over, perhaps. The man turned left at the Casa Rosada and Spaulding followed, keeping himself out of sight.

The man reached a corner and to David's surprise he slowed down, then stopped and entered a telephone booth.

It was a curiously amateurish thing to do, mused Spaulding. And it told him something about Erich Rhinemann's personnel: they weren't as good as they thought they were.

There was a long blasting of a horn that seemed louder than the normally jarring sounds of the Mayo's traffic. The single horn triggered other horns and in a few seconds a cacophony of strident honking filled the streets. David looked over. It was nothing; an irritated motorist had momentarily reached the end of his patience. Everything returned to normal chaos with the starting up of the automobiles at the crosswalk.

And then there was a scream. A woman's scream. And another; and still another.

A crowd gathered around the telephone booth.

David pushed his way through, yanking arms, pulling shoulders, shoving. He reached the edge of the booth and looked inside.

The man with the wet jacket was slumped awkwardly to the floor of the tiny glass enclosure, his legs buckled under him, his arms stretched above, one hand still gripping the telephone receiver so that the wire was taut. His head was sprung back from his neck. Blood was streaming down the back of his skull. Spaulding looked up at the walls of the booth. On the street side were three distinct holes surrounded by cracked glass.

He heard the piercing sounds of police whistles and pushed his way back through the crowd. He reached the iron fence that surrounded the Casa Rosada, turned right and started rapidly around the building to the south side.

To the south gate.

The Packard was parked in front of the entrance, its motor running. A man about his size approached him as David started for the automobile.

'Colonel Spaulding?'

'Yes?'

'If you'll hurry, please?' The man opened the back door and David climbed in quickly.

Heinrich Stoltz greeted him. 'You've had a long walk. Sit. The ride will be relaxing.'

'Not now.' David pointed to the panels below the front dashboard. 'Can you reach Rhinemann on that thing? Right away?'

'We're in constant contact. Why?'

'Get him. Your man was just killed.'

'Our man?'

'The one following me. He was shot in a telephone booth.'

'He wasn't our man, colonel. And *we* shot him,' said Stoltz calmly.

'*What?*'

'The man was known to us. He was a hired killer out of Rio de Janeiro. You were his target.'

Stoltz's explanation was succinct. They'd picked up the killer within moments after David left his apartment house. He was a Corsican, deported out of Marseilles before the war; a gun for the Unio Corso who had murdered one prefect too many under orders from the *contrabandistes* of southern France.

'We couldn't take a chance with the American who possesses the codes. A silencer in heavy traffic you'll agree is adequate.'

'I don't think he was trying to kill me,' said Spaulding. 'I think you moved too soon.'

'Then he was waiting for you to meet with *us*. Forgive me, but we couldn't permit that. You agree?'

'No. I could have taken him.' David sat back and brought his hand to his forehead, tired and annoyed. 'I was *going* to take him. Now we both lose.'

Stoltz looked at David. He spoke cautiously; a question. 'The same? You wonder also.'

'Don't you? ... You still think the Gestapo's not in Buenos Aires?'

'*Impossible!*' Stoltz whispered the words intensely through his teeth.

'That's what our mutual friend said about your men last night ... I don't know a goddamned thing about that, but I understand they're dead. So what's impossible?'

'The Gestapo *can't* be involved. We've learned that at the highest levels.'

'Rhinemann's Jewish, isn't he?' David watched Stoltz as he asked the unexpected question.

The German turned and looked at Spaulding. There was a hint of embarrassment in his expression. 'He practises no religion; his mother was Jewish ... Frankly, it's not pertinent. The racial theories of Rosenberg and Hitler are not shared unequivocally; far too much emphasis has been placed upon them ... It is – was – primarily an economic question. Distribution of banking controls, decentralization of financial hierarchies ... An unpleasant topic.'

David was about to reply to the diplomat's evasions when he stopped himself ... Why did Stoltz find it necessary even to attempt a rationalization? To offer a weak explanation he himself knew was devoid of logic?

Heinrich Stoltz's loyalty was supposedly to Rhinemann, not the Third Reich.

Spaulding looked away and said nothing. He was, frankly, confused, but it was no time to betray that confusion. Stoltz continued.

'It's a curious question. Why did you bring it up?'

'A rumor ... I heard it at the embassy.' And that was the truth, thought David. 'I gathered that the Jewish community in Buenos Aires was hostile to Rhinemann.'

'Mere speculation. The Jews here are like Jews elsewhere. They keep to themselves, have little to do with those outside. Perhaps the ghetto is less definable, but it's there. They have no argument with Rhinemann; there's no contact, really.'

'Cross off one speculation,' said Spaulding.

'There's another,' said Stoltz. 'Your own countrymen.'

David turned slowly back to the German. 'This is a good game. How did you arrive at that?'

'The purchase of the designs is being made by one aircraft corporation. There are five, six major companies in competition for your unending government contracts. Whoever possesses the gyroscope designs will have a powerful – I might even say irresistible – lever. All other guidance systems will be obsolete.'

'Are you serious?'

'Most assuredly. We have discussed the situation at length ... in depth. We are nearly convinced that this is the logical answer.' Stoltz looked away from David and stared to the front. 'There's no other. Those trying to stop us are American.'

35

The green Packard made crisscross patterns over the Buenos Aires streets. The route was programmed aimlessness, and Spaulding recognized it for what it was: an extremely thorough surveillance check. Intermittently, the driver would pick up the microphone from beneath the dashboard and recite a prearranged series of numbers. The crackling response over the single speaker would repeat the numbers and the Packard would make yet another – seemingly aimless – turn.

Several times David spotted the corresponding vehicles making the visual checks. Rhinemann had a minimum of five automobiles involved. After three-quarters of an hour, it was certain beyond doubt that the trip to San Telmo was clean.

The driver spoke to Stoltz.

'We are clear. The others will take up their positions.'

'Proceed,' said Stoltz.

They swung northwest; the Packard accelerated toward San Telmo. David knew that at least three other cars were behind them; perhaps two in front. Rhinemann had set up his own transport column, and that meant the gyroscopic designs were in one of the automobiles.

'Have you got the merchandise?' he asked Stoltz.

'Part of it,' replied the attaché, leaning forward, pressing a section of the felt backing in front of him. A latch sprung; Stoltz reached down and pulled out a tray from beneath the seat. Inside the concealed drawer was a thin metal box not unlike the containers used in libraries to protect rare manuscripts from possible loss by fire. The German picked it up, held it in his lap and pushed the drawer back with his foot. 'We'll be there in a few minutes,' he said.

The Packard pulled up to the curb in front of the white stucco house in San Telmo. Spaulding reached for the door handle but Stoltz touched his arm and shook his head. David withdrew his hand; he understood.

About fifty yards ahead, one of the checkpoint automobiles had parked and two men got out. One carried a thin metal container, the other an oblong leather case – a radio. They walked back toward the Packard.

David didn't have to look out the rear window to know what was happening behind him, but to confirm his thoughts he did so. Another automobile had parked. Two additional men were coming up the sidewalk; one, of course, carrying a container, the second, a leather-encased radio.

The four men met by the door of the Packard. Stoltz nodded to Spaulding; he got out of the car and walked around the vehicle, joining Rhinemann's contingent. He was about to start up the short path to the front entrance when Stoltz spoke through the automobile window.

'Please wait. Our men are not yet in position. They'll tell us.'

Static could be heard over the radio beneath the Packard's dashboard. There followed a recitation of numbers; the driver picked up his microphone and repeated them.

Heinrich Stoltz nodded and got out of the car. David started toward the door.

Inside, two of Rhinemann's men remained in the hallway; two walked through the apartment to the kitchen and a rear door that opened onto a small, terraced backyard. Stoltz accompanied David into the living room where Eugene Lyons was seated at a large dining table. The table was cleared except for two notepads with a half dozen pencils.

The male nurses, Johnny and Hal, accepted Spaulding's terse commands. They stood at opposite ends of the room in front of a couch, in shirtsleeves, their pistols strapped in shoulder holsters emphasized by the white cloth of their shirts.

Stoltz had relieved one man of his metal case and told David to take the other. Together, Stoltz and Spaulding placed the three containers on the large table, and Stoltz unlocked them. Lyons made no effort to greet his visitors – his intruders – and only the most perfunctory salutation came from Stoltz. It was apparent that Kendall had described the scientist's afflictions; the German diplomat conducted himself accordingly.

Stoltz spoke from across the table to the seated Lyons. 'From your left, the designs are in order of sequence. We have prepared bilingual keys attached to each of the schematics, and wherever processes are described, they have been translated verbatim, utilizing English counterpart formulae or internationally recognized symbols, and often both ... Not far from here, and easily contacted by our automobile radio, is an aeronautical physicist from Peenemünde. He is available for consultation at your request ... Finally, you understand that no photographs may be taken.'

Eugene Lyons picked up a pencil and wrote on a pad. He tore off the page and handed it to Spaulding. It read:

How long do I have? Are these complete?

David handed the note to Stoltz, who replied.

'As long as you need, *Herr Doktor* ... There is one last container. It will be brought to you later.'

'Within twenty-four hours,' interrupted Spaulding. 'I insist on that.'

'When we receive confirmation that the codes have arrived in Washington.'

'That message is undoubtedly at the embassy now.' David looked at his watch. 'I'm sure it is.'

'If you say it, I believe it,' said Stoltz. 'It would be pointless to lie. You won't leave Argentina until *we* have received word from . . . Switzerland.'

Spaulding couldn't define why but there was something questioning about the German's statement; a questioning that didn't belong with such a pronouncement. David began to think that Stoltz was far more nervous than he wanted anyone to realize. 'I'll confirm the codes when we leave . . . By the way, I also insist the designs remain here. Just as Doctor Lyons has checked them.'

'We anticipated your . . . request. You Americans are so mistrustful. Two of our men will also remain. Others will be outside.'

'That's a waste of manpower. What good is three-fourths of the merchandise?'

'Three-fourths better than you have,' answered the German.

The next two and a half hours were marked by the scratches of Lyons's pencil; the incessant static of the radios from the hallway and the kitchen, over which came the incessant, irritating recitation of numbers; the pacing of Heinrich Stoltz – his eyes constantly riveting on the pages of notes taken by an exhausted Lyons, making sure the scientist did not try to pocket or hide them; the yawns of the male nurse, Hal; the silent, hostile stares of his partner, Johnny.

At ten thirty-five, Lyons rose from the chair. He placed the pile of notes to his left and wrote on a pad, tearing off the page and handing it to Spaulding.

So far – authentic. I have no questions.

David handed the note to an anxious Stoltz.

'Good,' said the German. 'Now, colonel, please explain to the doctor's companions that it will be necessary for us to relieve them of their weapons. They will be returned, of course.'

David spoke to Johnny. 'It's all right. Put them on the table.'

'It's all right by who-says?' said Johnny, leaning against the wall, making no move to comply.

'I do,' answered Spaulding. 'Nothing will happen.'

'These fuckers are Nazis! You want to put us in blindfolds, too?'

'They're German. Not Nazis.'

'Horseshit!' Johnny pushed himself off the wall and stood erect. 'I don't like the way they talk.'

'Listen to me.' David approached him. 'A great many people have risked their lives to bring this thing off. For different reasons. You may not like them any more than I do, but we can't louse it up now. Please, do as I ask you.'

Johnny stared angrily at Spaulding. 'I hope to Christ you know what you're doing . . .' He and his partner put down their guns.

'Thank you, gentlemen,' said Stoltz, walking into the hallway. He spoke quietly in German to the two guards. The man with the radio walked rapidly through the sitting room into the kitchen; the other picked up the two weapons, placing one in his belt, the second in his jacket pocket. He then returned to the hallway without speaking.

Spaulding went to the table, joined by Stoltz. Lyons had replaced the designs in the manila envelopes; there were three. 'I'd hate to think of the money our mutual friend is getting for these,' said David.

'You wouldn't pay it if they weren't worth it.'

'I suppose not ... No reason not to put them in one case. Along with the notes.' Spaulding looked over at Lyons, who stood immobile at the end of the table. 'Is that all right, doctor?'

Lyons nodded, his sad eyes half closed, his pallor accentuated.

'As you wish,' said Stoltz. Picking up the envelopes and the notes, he put them in the first container, locked it, closed the other two and placed them on top of the first, as if he were performing a religious exercise in front of an altar.

Spaulding took several steps toward the two men by the window. 'You've had a rough day. Doctor Lyons, too. Turn in and let your guests walk guard duty; I think they're on overtime.'

Hal grinned. Johnny did not.

'Good evening, doctor. It's been a privilege meeting such a distinguished man of science.' Across the room, Stoltz spoke in diplomatic tones, bowing a slight diplomatic bow.

The guard with the radio emerged from the kitchen and nodded to the German attaché. They left the room together. Spaulding smiled at Lyons; the scientist turned without acknowledging and walked into his bedroom to the right of the kitchen door.

Outside on the sidewalk, Stoltz held the car door for David. 'A very strange man, your Doctor Lyons,' he said as Spaulding got into the Packard.

'He may be, but he's one of the best in his field ... Ask your driver to stop at a pay phone. I'll check the embassy's radio room. You'll get your confirmation.'

'Excellent idea ... Then, perhaps, you'll join me for dinner?'

David looked at the attaché who sat so confidently, so half-mockingly, beside him. Stoltz's nervousness had disappeared. 'No, Herr Botschaftssekre-tär. I have another engagement.'

'With the lovely Mrs Cameron, no doubt. I defer.'

Spaulding did not reply. Instead, he looked out the window in silence.

The Terraza Verde was peaceful. The streetlamps cast a soft glow on the quiet, darkened sidewalks; the sculptured trees in front of the picturesque Mediterranean houses were silhouetted against pastel-colored brick and stone. In windows beyond flower boxes, the yellow lamps of living rooms and bedrooms shone invitingly. A man in a business suit, a newspaper under his arm, walked up the steps to a door, taking a key from his pocket; a young couple were laughing quietly, leaning against a low wrought-iron fence. A little girl with a light brown cocker spaniel on a leash was skipping along the sidewalk, the dog jumping happily out of step.

Terraza Verde was a lovely place to live.

And David thought briefly of another block he'd seen that day. With old men who smelled of rot and urine; with a toothless whore who leaned on a filthy sill. With cat intestines and dirt-filmed windows. And with two huge warehouses that provided no work, and a trawler at anchor, recently destined for Tortugas.

The Packard turned the corner into another street. There were a few more lights, less sculptured trees, but the street was very much like Terraza Verde. It reminded David of those offshoot streets in Lisbon that approached the rich *caminos*; dotted with expensive shops, convenient for wealthy inhabitants a few hundred yards away.

There were shops here, too; with windows subtly lit, wares tastefully displayed.

Another block; the Packard slowed down at the intersecting street and then started across. More shops, less trees, more dogs – these often walked by maids. A group of teenagers were crowded around an Italian sportscar.

And then David saw the overcoat. It was just an overcoat at first; a light-gray overcoat in a doorway.

A gray overcoat. A recessed doorway.

The man was tall and thin. A tall, thin man in a light-gray overcoat. In a doorway!

My God! thought David. *The man on Fifty-second Street!*

The man was turned sideways, looking down into a dimly lit store window. Spaulding could not see them but he could picture the dark, hollow eyes; could hear the bastardized English out of somewhere in the Balkans; sense the desperation in the man's eyes:

There are to be no negotiations with Franz Altmüller . . . Heed the lesson of Fairfax!

He had to get out of the Packard. Quickly!

He had to go back to Terraza Verde. Without Stoltz. He *had* to!

There's a café in the next block,' said Spaulding, pointing to an orange canopy with lights underneath, stretching across the sidewalk. 'Stop there. I'll call the embassy.'

'You seem anxious, colonel. It can wait. I believe you.'

Spaulding turned to the German. 'You want me to spell it out? Okay, I'll do that . . . I don't like you, Stoltz. And I don't like Rhinemann; I don't like men who yell and bark orders and have me followed . . . I'm buying from you, but I don't have to associate with you. I don't have to have dinner or ride in your automobile once our business for the day is over. Do I make myself clear?'

'You're clear. Though somewhat uncivilized. And ungrateful, if you don't mind my saying so. We saved your life earlier this evening.'

'That's your opinion. Not mine. Just let me off, I'll telephone and come out with your confirmation . . . As you said, there's no point in my lying. You go on your way, I'll grab a taxi.'

Stoltz instructed the driver to pull up at the orange canopy. 'Do as you please. And should your plans include Doctor Lyons, be advised we have men stationed about the area. Their orders are harsh. Those designs will stay where they are.'

'I'm not paying for three-quarters of the merchandise regardless of what there is back home. And I have no intention of walking into that phalanx of robots.'

The Packard drew up to the canopy. Spaulding opened the door quickly, slamming it angrily behind him. He walked swiftly into the lighted entrance and asked for the telephone.

'The ambassador has been trying to reach you for the past half-hour or so,' said the night operator. 'He says it's urgent. I'm to give you a telephone number.' The operator drawled out the digits.

'Thank you,' David said. 'Now connect me with Mr Ballard in Communications, please.'

'O'Leary's Saloon,' came the uninterested voice of Bobby Ballard over the wire.

'You're a funny man. I'll laugh next Tuesday.'

'The "switch" said it was you. You know Granville's trying to find you.'

'I heard. Where's Jean?'

'In her room; pining away just like you ordered.'

'Did you get word from DC?'

'All wrapped. Came in a couple of hours ago; your codes are cleared. How's the erector set?'

'The instructions – three-quarters of them – are in the box. But there are too many playmates.'

'Terraza Verde?'

'Around there.'

'Shall I send out a few FMF playground attendants?'

'I think I'd feel better,' said Spaulding. 'Tell them to cruise. Nothing else. I'll spot them and yell if I need them.'

'It'll take a half-hour from the base.'

'Thanks. No parades, please, Bobby.'

'They'll be so quiet no one'll know but us Munchkins. Take care of yourself.'

Spaulding held down the receiver with his finger, tempted to lift it, insert another coin and call Granville . . . There wasn't time. He left the booth and walked out the restaurant door to the Packard. Stoltz was at the window; David saw that a trace of his previous nervousness had returned.

'You've got your confirmation. Deliver the rest of the goods and enjoy your money . . . I don't know where you come from, Stoltz, but I'll find out and have it bombed off the map. I'll tell the Eighth Air Force to name the raid after you.'

Stoltz seemed relieved at David's surliness – as David thought he might be. 'The man from Lisbon is complicated. I suppose that's proper for a complicated assignment . . . We'll call you by noon.' Stoltz turned to the driver. '*Los, abfahren, machen Sie schnell!*'

The green Packard roared off down the street. Spaulding waited under the canopy to see if it made any turns; should it do so, he would return to the cafe and wait.

It did not; it maintained a straight course. David watched until the taillights were infinitesimal red dots. Then he turned and walked as fast as he could without calling attention to himself toward Terraza Verde.

He reached the short block in which he'd seen the man in the light-gray overcoat and stopped. His concerns made him want to rush on; his instincts forced him to wait, to look, to move cautiously.

The man was not on the block now; he was nowhere to be seen. David reversed his direction and walked to the end of the sidewalk. He turned left and raced down the street to the next corner, turning left again, now slowing down, walking casually. He wished to God he knew the area better, knew the buildings behind Lyons's white stucco house. Others did; others were positioned in dark recesses he knew nothing about.

Rhinemann's guards. The man in the light-gray overcoat; how many more were with *him*?

He approached the intersection of Terraza Verde and crossed the road diagonally, away from the white stucco house. He stayed out of the spill of the lamps as best he could and continued down the pavement to the street behind the row of houses on Terraza Verde. It was, of course, a block lined with other houses; quaint, picturesque, quiet. Spaulding looked up at the vertical sign: *Terraza Amarilla*.

San Telmo fed upon itself.

He remained at the far end of the corner under a sculptured tree and looked toward the section of the adjacent street where he judged the rear of Lyons's house to be. He could barely make out the sloping tiled roof, but enough to pinpoint the building behind it – about 150 yards away.

He also saw Rhinemann's automobile, one of those he'd spotted during the long, security-conscious drive from the Casa Rosada. It was parked opposite a light-bricked Italian townhouse with large gates on both sides. David assumed those gates opened to stone paths leading to a wall or a fence separating Lyons's back terrace from the rear entrance of the townhouse. It had to be something like that; Rhinemann's guards were posted so that anyone emerging from those gates was equally in their sightlines.

And then Spaulding remembered the crackling static of the radios from the hallway and the kitchen and the incessant repetition of the German numbers. Those who carried the radios had weapons. He reached beneath his jacket to his holster and took out the Beretta. He knew the clip was filled; he unlatched the safety, shoved the weapon into his belt and started across the street toward the automobile.

Before he reached the opposite corner, he heard a car drive up behind him. He had no time to run, no moment to make a decision – good or bad. His hand went to his belt; he tried to assume a posture of indifference.

He heard the voice and was stunned.

'Get in, you goddamned *fool*!'

Leslie Hawkwood was behind the wheel of a small Renault coupe. She had reached over and unlatched the door. David caught it, his attention split between his shock and his concern that Rhinemann's guard – or guards – a hundred yards away might hear the noise. There were fewer than a dozen pedestrians within the two-block area. Rhinemann's men *had* to have been alerted.

He jumped into the Renault and with his left hand he grabbed Leslie's right leg above the knee, his grip a restraining vise, pressing on the nerve lines. He spoke softly but with unmistakable intensity.

'You back this car up as quietly as you can, and turn left down that street.'

'Let *go*! Let . . .'

'Do as I say or I'll break your kneecap off!'

The Renault was short; there was no need to use the reverse gear. Leslie spun the wheel and the car veered into a sharp turn.

'Slowly!' commanded Spaulding, his eyes on Rhinemann's car. He could see a head turn – two heads. And then they were out of sight.

David took his hand off the girl's leg; she pulled it up and doubled her shoulders down in agony. Spaulding grabbed the wheel and forced the gears into neutral. The car came to a stop halfway down the block, at the curb.

'You bastard! You broke my leg!' Leslie's eyes were filled with tears of pain, not sorrow. She was close to fury but she did not shout. And that told David something about Leslie he had not known before.

'I'll break more than a leg if you don't start telling me what you're doing here! How many others are there? I saw one; how many more?'

She snapped her head up, her long hair whipping back, her eyes defiant. 'Did you think we couldn't find him?'

'Who?'

'Your *scientist*. This Lyons! We found him!'

'Leslie, for Christ's sake, what are you *doing*?'

'Stopping you!'

'*Me?*'

'You. Altmüller, Rhinemann. Koening! Those pigs in Washington . . . Peenemünde! It's all over. They won't trust you anymore. "Tortugas" is finished!'

The faceless name – Altmüller again. Tortugas . . . Koening? Words, names . . . meaning and no meaning. The tunnels had no light.

There was no *time*!

Spaulding reached over and pulled the girl toward him. He clutched the hair above her forehead, yanking it taut, and with his other hand he circled his fingers high up under her throat, just below the jawbone. He applied pressure in swift, harsh spurts, each worse than the last.

So much, so alien.

'You want to play this game, you play it out! Now tell me! What's *happening*? *Now*?'

She tried to squirm, lashing out her arms, kicking at him; but each time she moved he ripped his fingers into her throat. Her eyes widened until the sockets were round. He spoke again.

'Say it, Leslie! I'll have to kill you if you don't. I don't have a choice! Not now . . . For Christ's sake, don't *force* me!'

She slumped; her body went limp but not unconscious. Her head moved up and down; she sobbed deep-throated moans. He released her and gently held her face. She opened her eyes.

'Don't touch me! Oh, *God*, don't touch me!' She could barely whisper, much less scream. 'Inside ... We're going inside. Kill the scientists; kill Rhinemann's men ...'

Before she finished, Spaulding clenched his fist and hammered a short, hard blow into the side of her chin. She slumped, unconscious.

He'd heard enough. There *was* no time.

He stretched her out in the small front seat, removing the ignition keys as he did so. He looked for her purse; she had none. He opened the door, closed it firmly and looked up and down the street. There were two couples halfway down the block; a car was parking at the corner; a window was opened on the second floor of a building across the way, music coming from within.

Except for these – nothing. San Telmo was at peace.

Spaulding ran to within yards of Terraza Amarilla. He stopped and edged his way along an iron fence that bordered the corner, swearing at the spill of the streetlamp. He looked through the black grillwork at Rhinemann's car less than a hundred yards away. He tried to focus on the front seat, on the two heads he'd seen moving minutes ago. There was no movement now, no glow of cigarettes, no shifting of shoulders.

Nothing.

Yet there was a break in the silhouette of the left window frame; an obstruction that filled the lower section of the glass.

David rounded the sharp angle of the iron fence and walked slowly toward the automobile, his hand clamped on the Beretta, his finger steady over the trigger. *Seventy yards, sixty, forty-five.*

The obstruction did not move.

Thirty-five, thirty ... he pulled the pistol from his belt, prepared to fire. Nothing.

He saw it clearly now. The obstruction was a head, sprung back into the glass – not resting, but wrenched, twisted from the neck; immobile.

Dead.

He raced across the street to the rear of the car and crouched, his Beretta level with his shoulders. There was no noise, no rustling from within.

The block was deserted now. The only sounds were the muffled, blurred hums from a hundred lighted windows. A latch could be heard far down the street; a small dog barked; the wail of an infant was discernible in the distance.

David rose and looked through the automobile's rear window.

He saw the figure of a second man sprawled over the felt top of the front seat. The light of the streetlamps illuminated the upper part of the man's back and shoulders. The whole area was a mass of blood and slashed cloth.

Spaulding slipped around the side of the car to the front right door. The window was open, the sight within sickening. The man behind the wheel had been shot through the side of his head, his companion knifed repeatedly.

The oblong, leather-cased radio was smashed, lying on the floor beneath the dashboard.

It had to have happened within the past five or six minutes, thought David. Leslie Hawkwood had rushed down the street in the Renault to intercept him – at the precise moment men with silenced pistols and long-bladed knives were heading for Rhinemann's guards.

The killings complete, the men with knives and pistols must have raced across the street into the gates towards Lyons's house. Raced without thought of cover or camouflage, knowing the radios were in constant contact with those inside 15 Terraza Verde.

Spaulding opened the car door, rolled up the window, and pulled the lifeless form off the top of the seat. He closed the door; the bodies were visible, but less so than before. It was no moment for alarms in the street if they could be avoided.

He looked over at the gates across the way on each side of the townhouse. The left one was slightly ajar.

He ran over to it and eased himself through the opening, touching nothing, his gun thrust laterally at his side, aiming forward. Beyond the gate was a cement passageway that stretched the length of the building to some sort of miniature patio bordered by a high brick wall.

He walked silently, rapidly to the end of the open alley; the patio was a combination of slate paths, plots of grass and small flower gardens. Alabaster statuary shone in the moonlight; vines crawled up the brick wall.

He judged the height of the wall: seven feet, perhaps, seven and a half. Thickness: eight, ten inches – standard. Construction: new, within several years, strong. It was the construction with which he was most concerned. In 1942 he took a nine-foot wall in San Sebastián that collapsed under him. A month later it was amusing; at the time it nearly killed him.

He replaced the Beretta in his shoulder holster, locking the safety, shoving in the weapon securely. He bent down and rubbed his hands in the dry dirt at the edge of the cement, absorbing whatever sweat was on them. He stood up and raced towards the brick wall.

Spaulding leaped. Once on top of the wall, he held – silent, prone; his hands gripping the sides, his body motionless – a part of the stone. He remained immobile, his face towards Lyons's terrace, and waited several seconds. The back door to Lyons's flat was closed – no lights were on in the kitchen; the shades were drawn over the windows throughout the floor. No sounds from within.

He slid down from the wall, removed his gun and ran to the side of the kitchen door, pressing his back against the white stucco. To his astonishment he saw that the door was *not* closed; and then he saw why. At the base, barely visible in the darkness of the room beyond, was a section of a hand. It had gripped the bottom of the doorframe and been smashed into the saddle; the fingers were the fingers of a dead man.

Spaulding reached over and pressed the door. An inch. Two inches. Wood against dead weight; his elbow ached from the pressure.

Three, four, five inches. A foot.

Indistinguishable voices could be heard now; faint, male, excited.

He stepped swiftly in front of the door and pushed violently – as quietly as possible – against the fallen body that acted as a huge, soft, dead weight against the frame. He stepped over the corpse of Rhinemann's guard, noting that the oblong radio had been torn from its leather case, smashed on the floor. He closed the door silently.

The voices came from the sitting room. He edged his way against the wall, the Beretta poised, unlatched, ready to fire.

An open pantry against the opposite side of the room caught his eye. The single window, made of mass-produced stained glass, was high in the west wall, creating eerie shafts of colored light from the moon. Below, on the floor, was Rhinemann's second guard. The method of death he could not tell; the body was arched backward – probably a bullet from a small-caliber pistol had killed him. A pistol with a silencer attached. It would be very quiet. David felt the perspiration rolling down his forehead and over his neck.

How many were there? They'd immobilized a garrison.

He had no commitment matching those odds.

Yet he had a strange commitment to Lyons. He had commitment enough for him at the moment. He dared not think beyond that instant.

And he was good; he could – should – never forget that. He was the best there was.

If it was important to anyone.

So much, so alien.

He pressed his cheek against the molding of the arch and what he saw sickened him. The revulsion, perhaps, was increased by the surroundings: a well-appointed flat with chairs and couches and tables meant for civilized people involved with civilized pursuits.

Not death.

The two male nurses – the hostile Johnny, the affable, dense Hal – were sprawled across the floor, their arms linked, their heads inches from each other. Their combined blood had formed a pool on the parquet surface. Johnny's eyes were wide, angry – dead; Hal's face composed, questioning, at rest.

Behind them were Rhinemann's two other guards, their bodies on the couch like slaughtered cattle.

I hope you know what you're doing!

Johnny's words vibrated painfully – in screams – in David's brain.

There were three other men in the room – standing, alive, in the same grotesque stocking masks that had been worn by those in the Duesenberg who had cut short the few moments he'd had alone with Leslie Hawkwood high in the hills of Luján.

The Duesenberg that had exploded in fire in the hills of Colinas Rojas.

The men were standing – none held weapons – over the spent figure of Eugene Lyons – seated gracefully, without fear, at the table. The look in the scientist's eyes told the truth, as Spaulding saw it: he welcomed death.

'You see what's around you!' The man in the light-gray overcoat spoke to him. 'We will not hesitate further! You're dead! ... Give us the designs!'

Jesus Christ! thought David. Lyons had hidden the plans!

'There's no point in carrying on, please believe me,' continued the man in the overcoat, the man with the hollow crescents under his eyes Spaulding remembered so well. 'You may be spared, but only if you tell us! *Now!*'

Lyons did not move; he looked up at the man in the overcoat without shifting his head, his eyes calm. They touched David's.

'Write it!' said the man in the light-gray overcoat.

It was the moment to move.

David spun around the molding, his pistol leveled.

'Don't reach for guns! *You!*' he yelled at the man nearest him. 'Turn around!'

In shock, without thinking, the man obeyed. Spaulding took two steps forward and brought the barrel of the Beretta crashing down into the man's skull. He collapsed instantly.

David shouted at the man next to the interrogator in the gray overcoat. 'Pick up that chair! *Now!*' He gestured with his pistol to a straight-backed chair several feet from the table. '*Now*, I said!'

The man reached over and did as he was told; he was immobilized. Spaulding continued. 'You drop it and I'll kill you ... Doctor Lyons. Take their weapons. You'll find pistols and knives. Quickly, please.'

It all happened so fast. David knew his only hope of avoiding gunfire was in the swiftness of the action, the rapid immobilization of one or two men, an instant reversal of the odds.

Lyons got out of the chair and went first to the man in the light-gray overcoat. It was apparent that the scientist had observed where the man had put his pistol. He took it out of the overcoat pocket. He went to the man holding the chair and removed an identical gun, then searched the man and took a large knife from his jacket and a second, short revolver from a shoulder holster. He placed the weapons on the far side of the table and walked to the unconscious third man. He rolled him over and removed two guns and a switchblade knife.

'Take off your coats. *Now!*' Spaulding commanded both men. He took the chair from the one next to him and pushed him toward his companion. The men began removing their coats when Spaulding suddenly spoke, before either had completed their actions. 'Stop right there! Hold it! ... Doctor, please bring over two chairs and place them behind them.'

Lyons did so.

'Sit down,' said Spaulding to his captives.

They sat, coats half off their shoulders. David approached them and yanked the garments further – down to the elbows.

The two men in the grotesque stocking masks were seated now, their arms locked by their own clothes.

Standing in front of them, Spaulding reached down and ripped the silk masks off their faces. He moved back and leaned against the dining table, his pistol in his hand.

'All right,' he said. 'I estimate we've got about fifteen minutes before all hell breaks loose around here ... I have a few questions. You're going to give me the answers.'

36

Spaulding listened in disbelief. The enormity of the charge was so far-reaching it was – in a very real sense – beyond his comprehension.

The man with the hollow eyes was Asher Feld, commander of the Provisional Wing of the Haganah operating within the United States. He did the talking.

'The operation . . . the exchange of the guidance designs for the industrial diamonds . . . was first given the name "Tortugas" by the Americans – one American, to be exact. He had decided that the transfer should be made in the Dry Tortugas, but it was patently rejected by Berlin. It was, however, kept as a code name by this man. The misleading association dovetailed with his own panic at being involved. It came – for him and for Fairfax – to mean the activities of the man from Lisbon.

'When the War Department clearances were issued to the Koening company's New York offices – an Allied requisite – this man coded the clearance as "Tortugas". If anyone checked, "Tortugas" was a Fairfax operation. It would not be questioned.

'The concept of the negotiation was first created by the *Nachrichtendienst*. I'm sure you've heard of the *Nachrichtendienst*, colonel . . .'

David did not reply, He could not speak. Feld continued.

'We of the Haganah learned of it in Geneva. We had word of an unusual meeting between an American named Kendall – a financial analyst for a major aircraft company – and a very despised German businessman, a homosexual, who was sent to Switzerland by a leading administrator in the Ministry of Armaments, Unterstaatssekretär Franz Altmüller . . . The Haganah is everywhere, colonel, including the outer offices of the ministry and in the Luftwaffe . . .'

David continued to stare at the Jew, so matter of fact in his extraordinary . . . unbelieveable . . . narrative.

'I think you'll agree that such a meeting was unusual. It was not difficult to manoeuvre these two messengers into a situation that gave us a wire recording. It was in an out-of-the-way restaurant and they were amateurs.

'We then knew the basics. The materials and the general location. But not the specific point of transfer. And that was the all-important factor. Buenos

Aires is enormous, its harbour more so – stretching for miles. Where in this vast area of land and mountains and water was the transfer to take place?'

'Then, of course, came word from Fairfax. The man in Lisbon was being recalled. A most unusual action. But then how well thought out. The finest network specialist in Europe, fluent German and Spanish, an expert in blueprint designs. How logical. Don't you agree!'

David started to speak, but stopped. Things were being said that triggered flashes of lightning in his mind. And unbelievable cracks of thunder ... as unbelievable as the words he was hearing. He could only nod his head. Numbly.

Feld watched him closely. Then spoke.

'In New York I explained to you, albeit briefly, the sabotage at the airfield in Terceira. Zealots. The fact that the man in Lisbon could turn and be a part of the exchange was too much for the hot-tempered Spanish Jews. No one was more relieved than we of the Provisional Wing when you escaped. We assumed your stopover in New York was for the purposes of refining the logistics in Buenos Aires. We proceeded on that assumption.

'Then quite abruptly there was no more time. Reports out of Johannesburg – unforgivably delayed – said that the diamonds had arrived in Buenos Aires. We took the necessary violent measures, including an attempt to kill you. Prevented, I presume, by Rhinemann's men.' Asher Feld stopped. Then added wearily, 'The rest you know.'

No! The rest he did not know! Nor any other part!

Insanity!

Madness!

Everything was nothing! Nothing was everything!

The years! The lives! ... The terrible nightmares of fear ... the killing! Oh, my God, the killing!

For what?! ... Oh, my God! For what?!

'You're *lying!*' David crashed his hand down on the table. The steel of the pistol cracked against the wood with such force the vibration filled the room. 'You're *lying!*' he cried; he did not shout. 'I'm in Buenos Aires to buy gyroscopic designs! To have them authenticated! Confirmed by code so that son of a bitch gets paid in Switzerland! That's *all. Nothing else! Nothing else at all! Not this!*'

'Yes ...' Asher Feld spoke softly. 'It is this.'

David whirled around at nothing. He stretched his neck: the crashing thunder in his head would not stop, the blinding flashes of light in front of his eyes were causing a terrible pain. He saw the bodies on the floor, the blood ... the corpses on the sofa, the blood.

Tableau of death.

Death.

His whole shadow world had been ripped out of orbit. A thousand gambles ... pains, manipulations, death. And more death ... all faded into a meaningless void. The betrayal – if it was a betrayal – was so immense ... hundreds of thousands had been sacrificed for absolutely nothing.

He had to stop. He had to think. To concentrate.

He looked at the painfully gaunt Eugene Lyons, his face a sheet of white.

The man's dying, thought Spaulding.

Death.

He had to concentrate.

Oh, Christ! He had to *think.* Start *somewhere. Think.*

Concentrate.

Or he would go out of his mind.

He turned to Feld. The Jew's eyes were compassionate. They might have been something else, but they were not. They were compassionate.

And yet, they were the eyes of a man who killed in calm deliberation.

As he, the man in Lisbon, had killed.

Execution.

For what?

There were questions. *Concentrate on the questions. Listen.* Find error. *Find error* – if error was needed in this world it was *now*!

'I don't believe you,' said David, trying as he had never tried in his life to be convincing.

'I think you do,' replied Feld quietly. 'The girl, Leslie Hawkwood, told us you didn't know. A judgment we found difficult to accept . . . I accept it now.'

David had to think for a moment. He did not, at first, recognize the name. *Leslie Hawkwood.* And then, of course, he did instantly. Painfully. 'How is she involved with you?' he asked numbly.

'Herold Goldsmith is her uncle. By marriage, of course, she's not Jewish.'

'Goldsmith? The name . . . doesn't mean anything to me.' . . . *Concentrate!* He had to concentrate and speak rationally.

'It does to thousands of Jews. He's the man behind the Baruch and Lehman negotiations. He's done more to get our people out of the camps than any man in America . . . He refused to have anything to do with us until the civilized, compassionate men in Washington, London and the Vatican turned their backs on him. Then he came to us . . . in fury. He created a hurricane, his niece was swept up in it. She's overly dramatic, perhaps, but committed, effective. She moves in circles barred to the Jew.'

'*Why?*' . . . *Listen! For God's sake, listen. Be rational. Concentrate!*

Asher Feld paused for a moment, his dark, hollow eyes clouded with quiet hatred. 'She met dozens . . . hundreds, perhaps, of those Herold Goldsmith got out. She saw the photographs, heard the stories. It was enough. She was ready.'

The calm was beginning to return to David. Leslie was the springboard he needed to come back from the madness. There were questions . . .

'I can't reject the premise that Rhinemann bought the designs . . .'

'Oh, come!' interrupted Feld. 'You were the man in Lisbon. How often did your own agents – your best men – find Peenemünde invulnerable? Has not the German underground itself given up penetration?'

'No one ever gives up. On either side. The German underground is *part* of this!' *That was the error*, thought David.

'If that were so,' said Feld, gesturing his head toward the dead Germans on the couch, 'then those men were members of the underground. You know the Haganah, Lisbon. We don't kill such men.'

Spaulding stared at the quiet-spoken Jew and knew he told the truth.

'The other evening,' said Spaulding quickly, 'on Paraná. I was followed, beaten up . . . but I saw the IDs. They were Gestapo!'

'They were Haganah,' replied Feld. 'The Gestapo is our best cover. If they had been Gestapo that would presume knowledge of your function . . . Would they have let you live?'

Spaulding started to object. The Gestapo would not risk killing in a neutral country; not with identification on their persons. Then he realized the absurdity of his logic. Buenos Aires was not Lisbon. Of course, they would kill him. And then he recalled the words of Heinrich Stoltz.

We've checked at the highest levels . . . not the Gestapo . . . impossible . . .

And the strangely inappropriate apologia: *the racial theories of Rosenberg and Hitler are not shared . . . primarily an economic . . .*

A defence of the indefensible offered by a man whose loyalty was purportedly *not* to the Third Reich but to *Erich Rhinemann*. A Jew.

Finally, Bobby Ballard:

. . . he's a believer . . . the real Junker item . . .

'Oh, my God,' said David under his breath.

'You have the advantage, colonel. What is your choice? We're prepared to die; I say this in no sense heroically, merely as a fact.'

Spaulding stood motionless. He spoke softly, incredulously. 'Do you understand the implications? . . .'

'We've understood them,' interrupted Feld, 'since that day in Geneva your Walter Kendall met with Johann Dietrich.'

David reacted as though slapped, 'Johann . . . *Dietrich*?'

'The expendable heir of Dietrich Fabriken.'

'J.D.,' whispered Spaulding, remembering the crumpled yellow pages in Walter Kendall's New York office. The breasts, the testicles, the swastikas . . . the obscene, nervous scribblings of an obscene, nervous man. 'Johann Dietrich . . . *J.D.*'

'Altmüller had him killed. In a way that precluded any . . .'

'*Why?*' asked David.

'To remove any connection with the Ministry of Armaments, is our thought; any association with the High Command. Dietrich initiated the negotiations to the point where they could be shifted to Buenos Aires. To Rhinemann. With Dietrich's death the High Command was one more step removed.'

The items raced through David's mind: Kendall had fled Buenos Aires in panic; something had gone wrong. The accountant would not allow himself to be trapped, to be killed. And he, David, was to kill – or have killed – Erich Rhinemann. Second to the designs, Rhinemann's death was termed paramount. And with his death, Washington, too, was 'one more step removed' from the exchange.

Yet there was Edmund Pace.

Edmund *Pace*.

Never.

'A man was killed,' said David, 'A Colonel Pace ...'

'In Fairfax,' completed Asher Feld. 'A necessary death. He was being used as you are being used. We deal in pragmatics ... Without knowing the consequences – or refusing to admit them to himself – Colonel Pace was engineering "Tortugas".'

'You could have *told* him. Not killed him! You could have stopped it! You *bastards!*'

Asher Feld sighed. 'I'm afraid you don't understand the hysteria among your industrialists. Or those of the Reich. He would have been eliminated ... By removing him ourselves, we neutralized Fairfax. And all its considerable facilities.'

There was no point in dwelling on the *necessity* of Pace's death, thought David. Feld, the pragmatist, was right: Fairfax had been removed from 'Tortugas'.

'Then Fairfax doesn't know.'

'Our man does. But not enough.'

'Who is he? Who's your man in Fairfax?'

Feld gestured to his silent companion. 'He doesn't know and I won't tell you. You may kill me but I won't tell you.'

Spaulding knew the dark-eyed Jew spoke the truth. 'If Pace was used ... and me. Who's using us?'

'I can't answer that.'

'You know this much. You must have ... thoughts. Tell me.'

'Whoever gives you orders, I imagine.'

'One man ...'

'We know. He's not very good, is he? There are others.'

'*Who?* Where does it *stop*? State? The War Department? *The White House? Where*, for Christ's sake!?'

'Such territories have no meaning in these transactions. They vanish.'

'*Men don't!* Men don't vanish!'

'Then look for those who dealt with Koening. In South Africa. Kendall's men. They created "Tortugas".' Asher Feld's voice grew stronger. 'That's your affair, Colonel Spaulding. We only wish to stop it. We'll gladly *die* to stop it.'

David looked at the thin-faced, sad-faced man. 'It means that much? With what you know, what you believe? Is either side worth it?'

'One must have priorities. Even in lessening descent. If Peenemünde is saved ... put back on schedule ... the Reich has a bargaining power that is unacceptable to us. Look to Dachau; look to Auschwitz, to Belsen. Unacceptable.'

David walked around the table and stood in front of the Jews. He put his Beretta in his shoulder holster and looked at Asher Feld.

'If you've lied to me, I'll kill you. And then I'll go back to Lisbon, into the north country, and wipe out every Haganah fanatic in the hills. Those I don't kill, I'll expose ... Put on your coats and get out of here. Take a room at the Alvear under the name of ... Pace. *E. Pace.* I'll be in touch.'

'Our weapons?' asked Feld, pulling his light-gray overcoat over his shoulders.

'I'll keep them. I'm sure you can afford others ... And don't wait for us outside. There's an FMF vehicle cruising for me.'

'What about "Tortugas"?' Asher Feld was pleading.

'I said I'll be in touch!' shouted Spaulding. 'Now, get out of here! ... Pick up the Hawkwood girl; she's around the corner in the Renault. Here are the keys.' David reached in his pocket and threw the keys to Asher Feld's companion, who caught them effortlessly. 'Send her back to California. Tonight, if you can. No later than tomorrow morning. Is that clear?'

'Yes ... You *will* be in touch?'

'Get out of here,' said Spaulding in exhaustion.

The two Haganah agents rose from their chairs, the younger going to the unconscious third man and lifting him off the floor, onto his shoulders. Asher Feld stood in the front hallway and turned, his gaze resting momentarily on the dead bodies, then over to Spaulding.

'You and I. We must deal in priorities ... The man from Lisbon is an extraordinary man.' He turned to the door and held it open as his companion carried out the third man. He went outside, closing the door behind him.

David turned to Lyons. 'Get the designs.'

37

When the assault on 15 Terraza Verde had begun, Eugene Lyons had done a
remarkable thing. It was so simple it had a certain cleanliness to it, thought
Spaulding. He had taken the metal container with the designs, opened his
bedroom window and dropped the case five feet below into the row of tiger
lilies that grew along the side of the house. The window shut, he had then
run into his bathroom and locked the door.

All things considered – the shock, the panic, his own acknowledged
incapacities – he had taken the least expected action: he had kept his head.
He had removed the container, not tried to conceal it; he had transferred it
to an *accessible* place, and that was not to be anticipated by the fanatic men
who dealt in complicated tactics and convoluted deceits.

David followed Lyons out of the house through the kitchen door and
around to the side. He took the container from the physicist's trembling
hands and helped the near-helpless man over the small fence separating the
adjacent property. Together they ran behind the next two houses and
cautiously edged their way toward the street. Spaulding kept his left hand
extended, gripping Lyons's shoulder, holding him against the wall, prepared
to throw him to the ground at the first hint of hostilities.

Yet David was not really expecting hostilities; he was convinced the
Haganah had eliminated whatever Rhinemann guards were posted in front,
for the obvious reason that Asher Feld had left by the front door. What he
did think was possible was a last-extremity attempt by Asher Feld to get the
designs. Or the sudden emergence of a Rhinemann vehicle from some near
location – a vehicle whose occupants were unable to raise a radio signal from
15 Terraza Verde.

Each possible; neither really expected.

It was too late and too soon.

What David profoundly hoped he would find, however, was a blue-green
sedan cruising slowly around the streets. A car with small orange insignias on
the bumpers that designated the vehicle as US property. Ballard's 'playground attendants'; the men from the FMF base.

It wasn't cruising. It was stationary, on the far side of the street, its parking
lights on. Three men inside were smoking cigarettes, the glows illuminating
the interior. He turned to Lyons.

'Let's go. Walk slowly, casually. The car's over there.'

The driver and the man next to him got out of the automobile the moment Spaulding and Lyons reached the curb. They stood awkwardly by the hood, dressed in civilian clothes. David crossed the street, addressing them.

'Get in that goddamned car and get us out of here! And while you're at it, why don't you paint bull's-eyes all over the vehicle? You wouldn't be any more of a target than you are now!'

'Take it easy, buddy,' replied the driver. 'We just got here.' He opened the rear door as Spaulding helped Lyons inside.

'You were supposed to be cruising, not parked like watch-dogs!' David climbed in beside Lyons; the man at the far window squeezed over. The driver got behind the wheel, closed his door and started the engine. The third man remained outside. 'Get him in here!' barked Spaulding.

'He'll remain where he is, colonel,' said the man in the back seat next to Lyons. 'He stays here.'

'Who the hell are you?'

'Colonel Daniel Meehan, Fleet Marine Force, Naval Intelligence. And we want to know what the fuck's going on.'

The car started up.

'You have no control over this exercise,' said David slowly, deliberately. 'And I don't have time for bruised egos. Get us to the embassy, please.'

'Screw egos! We'd like a little simple clarification! You know what the hell is going on down in our section of town? This side trip to Telmo's just a minor inconvenience! I wouldn't be here except your goddamned name was mentioned by that smart-ass cryp! ... *Jesus!*'

Spaulding leaned forward on the seat, staring at Meehan. 'You'd better tell me what's going on in your section of town. And why my name gets you to Telmo.'

The marine returned the look, glancing once – with obvious distaste – at the ashen Lyons. 'Why not? Your friend cleared?'

'He is now. No one more so.'

'We have three cruisers patrolling the Buenos Aires coastal zone plus a destroyer and a carrier somewhere's out there ... Five hours ago we get a blue alert: prepare for a radio-radar blackout, all sea and aircraft to hold to, no movement. Forty-five minutes later there's a scrambler from Fairfax, source four-zero. Intercept one Colonel David Spaulding, also four-zero. He's to make contact pronto.'

'With Fairfax?'

'*Only* with Fairfax ... So we send a man to your address on Córdoba. He doesn't find you but he *does* find a weird son-of-a-bitch tearing up your place. He tries to take him and gets laid out ... He gets back to us a couple of hours later with creases in his head and guess who calls? Right on an open-line telephone!'

'Ballard,' answered David quietly. 'The embassy cryp.'

'The smart-ass! He makes jokes and tells us to play games out at Telmo!

Wait for you to decide to show.' The marine colonel shook his head in disgust.

'You said the blue alert was preparation for radar silence ... and radio.'

'And all ships and planes immobilized,' interrupted Meehan. 'What the hell's coming *in* here? The whole goddamned General *Staff*? *Roosevelt*? *Churchill*? *Rin-tin-tin*? And what are *we*? The *enemy*!'

'It's not what's coming in, colonel,' said David softly. 'It's what's going out ... What's the time of activation?'

'It's damn loose. Anytime during the next forty-eight hours. How's that for a tight schedule?'

'Who's my contact in Virginia?'

'Oh ... Here.' Meehan shifted in his seat, proffering a sealed yellow envelope that was the mark of a scrambled message. David reached across Lyons and took it.

There was the crackling static of a radio from the front seat followed by the single word 'Redbird!' out of the speaker. The driver quickly picked up the dashboard microphone.

'Redbird acknowledge,' said the marine.

The static continued but the words were clear. 'The Spaulding intercept. Pick him up and bring him in. Four-zero orders from Fairfax. No contact with the embassy.'

'You heard the man,' laughed Meehan. 'No embassy tonight, colonel.'

David was stunned. He started to object – angrily, furiously; then he stopped ... Fairfax. No Nazi, but Haganah. Asher Feld had said it. The Provisional Wing dealt in practicalities. And the most practical objective during the next forty-eight hours was to immobilize the man with the codes. Washington would not activate a radio-radar blackout without them; and an enemy submarine surfacing to rendezvous with a trawler would be picked up on the screens and blown out of the water. The Koening diamonds – the Peenemünde tools – would be sent to the bottom of the South Atlantic.

Christ! The *irony*, thought David. Fairfax – *someone* at Fairfax – was doing precisely what *should* be done, motivated by concerns Washington – and the aircraft companies – refused to acknowledge! It – they – had other concerns: three-quarters of them were at Spaulding's feet. High-altitude gyroscopic designs.

David pressed his arm into Lyons's shoulder. The emaciated scientist continued to stare straight ahead but responded to Spaulding's touch with a hesitant nudge of his left elbow.

David shook his head and sighed audibly. He held up the yellow envelope and shrugged, placing it into his jacket pocket

When his hand emerged it held a gun.

'I'm afraid I can't accept those orders, Colonel Meehan.' Spaulding pointed the automatic at the marine's head; Lyons leaned back into the seat.

'What the hell are you doing?!' Meehan jerked forward; David clicked the firing pin of the weapon into hair-release.

'Tell your man to drive where I say. I don't want to kill you, colonel, but I will. It's a matter of priorities.'

'You're a goddamned double agent! That's what Fairfax was onto!'

David sighed. 'I wish it were that simple.'

Lyons's hands trembled as he tightened the knots around Meehan's wrists. The driver was a mile down the dirt road, bound securely, lying in the border of the tall grass. The area was rarely traveled at night. They were in the hills of Colinas Rojas.

Lyons stepped back and nodded to Spaulding.

'Get in the car.'

Lyons nodded again and started toward the automobile. Meehan rolled over and looked up at David.

'You're dead, Spaulding. You got a firing squad on your duty sheet. You're stupid, too. Your Nazi friends are going to lose this war!'

'They'd better,' answered David. 'As to executions, there may be a number of them. Right in Washington. That's what this is all about, colonel ... Someone'll find you both tomorrow. If you like, you can start inching your way west. Your driver's a mile or so down the road ... I'm sorry.'

Spaulding gave Meehan a half-felt shrug of apology and ran to the FMF automobile. Lyons sat in the front seat and when the door light spilled over his face, David saw his eyes. Was it possible that in that look there was an attempt to communicate a sense of gratitude? Or approval? There wasn't time to speculate, so David smiled gently and spoke quietly.

'This has been terrible for you, I know ... But I can't think what else to do. I don't know. If you like, I'll get you back to the embassy. You'll be safe there.'

David started the car and drove up a steep incline – one of many – in the Colinas Rojas. He would double back on a parallel road and reach the highway within ten or fifteen minutes; he would take Lyons to an outskirts taxi and give the driver instructions to deliver the physicist to the American embassy. It wasn't really what he wanted to do; but what else was there?

Then the words came from beside him. *Words!* Whispered, muffled, barely audible but clear! From the recesses of a tortured throat.

'I ... stay with ... you. Together ...'

Spaulding had to grip the wheel harshly for fear of losing control. The shock of the pained speech – and it *was* a speech for Eugene Lyons – had nearly caused him to drop his hands. He turned and looked at the scientist. In the flashing shadows he saw Lyons return his stare; the lips were set firmly, the eyes steady. Lyons knew exactly what he was doing; what they both were doing – *had* to do.

'All right,' said David, trying to remain calm and precise. 'I read you clearly. God knows I need all the help I can get. We both do. It strikes me we've got two powerful enemies. Berlin *and* Washington.'

'I don't want any interruptions, Stoltz!' David yelled into the mouthpiece of the telephone in the small booth near Ocho Calle. Lyons was now behind the wheel of the FMF car ten yards away on the street. The motor was running. The scientist hadn't driven in twelve years but with half-words and gestures he convinced Spaulding he would be capable in an emergency.

'You can't behave this way!' was the panicked reply.

'I'm Pavlov, you're the dog! Now shut up and listen! There's a mess in Terraza Verde, if you don't know it by now. Your men are dead; so are mine. I've got the designs *and* Lyons . . . Your nonexistent Gestapo are carrying out a number of executions!'

'*Impossible!*' screamed Stoltz.

'Tell that to the corpses, you incompetent son-of-a-bitch! While you clean up that mess! . . . I want the rest of those designs, Stoltz. Wait for my call!' David slammed down the receiver and bolted out of the booth to the car. It was time for the radio. After that the envelope from Fairfax. Then Ballard at the embassy. One step at a time.

Spaulding opened the door and slid into the seat beside Lyons. The physicist pointed to the dashboard.

'Again . . .' was the single, painful word.

'Good,' said Spaulding. 'They're anxious. They'll listen hard.' David snapped the panel switch and lifted the microphone out of its cradle. He pressed his fingers against the tiny wire speaker with such pressure that the mesh was bent; he covered the instrument with his hand and held it against his jacket as he spoke, moving it in circles so as to further distort the sound.

'Redbird to base . . . Redbird to base.'

The static began, the voice angry. 'Christ, Redbird! We've been trying to raise you for damn near two hours! That Ballard keeps calling! Where the hell are you?!'

'Redbird . . . Didn't you get our last transmission?'

'*Transmission?* Shit, man! I can hardly hear this one. Hold on; let me get the CO.'

'Forget it! No sweat. You're fading here again. We're on Spaulding. We're following him; he's in a vehicle . . . twenty-seven, *twenty-eight miles north . . .*' David abruptly stopped talking.

'Redbird! Redbird! . . . Christ, this frequency's puke! . . . Twenty-eight miles north *where?* . . . I'm not reading you, Redbird! Redbird, acknowledge!'

'. . . bird, acknowledge,' said David directly into the microphone. 'This radio needs maintenance, pal. Repeat. No problems. Will *return to base in approximately . . .*'

Spaulding reached down and snapped the switch into the 'off' position.

He got out of the car and went back to the telephone booth.

One step at a time. No blurring, no overlapping – each action defined, handled with precision.

Now it was the scramble from Fairfax. The deciphered code that would tell him the name of the man who was having him intercepted; the source four-zero, whose priority rating allowed him to send such commands from the transmission core of the intelligence compound.

The agent who walked with impunity in the highest classified alleyways and killed a man named Ed Pace on New Year's Eve.

The Haganah infiltration.

He had been tempted to rip open the yellow envelope the moment the FMF officer had given it to him in San Telmo, but he had resisted the almost irresistible temptation. He knew that he would be stunned no matter who it was – whether known to him or not; and no *matter* who it was he would have a name to fit the revenge he planned for the killer of his friend.

Such thoughts were obstructions. Nothing could hinder their swift but cautious ride to Ocho Calle; nothing could interfere with his thought-out contact with Heinrich Stoltz.

He withdrew the yellow envelope and slid his finger across the flap.

At first, the name meant nothing.

Lieutenant Colonel Ira Barden.

Nothing.

Then he remembered.

New Year's Eve!

Oh, *Christ*, did he remember! The rough-talking hardnose who was second in command at Fairfax. Ed Pace's 'best friend' who had mourned his 'best friend's' death with army anger; who secretly had arranged for David to be flown to the Virginia base and participate in the wake-investigation; who had used the tragic killing to enter his 'best friend's' dossier vaults . . . only to find nothing.

The man who insisted a Lisbon cryptographer named Marshall had been killed in the Basque country; who said he would run a check on Franz Altmüller.

Which, of course, he never did.

The man who tried to convince David that it would be in everyone's interest if Spaulding would flex the clearance regulations and explain his War Department assignment.

Which David nearly did. And now wished he had.

Oh, God! Why hadn't Barden *trusted* him? On the other hand, he could not. For to do so would have raised specific, unwanted speculations on Pace's murder.

Ira Barden was no fool. A fanatic, perhaps, but not foolish. He knew the man from Lisbon would kill him if Pace's death was laid at his feet.

Heed the lesson of Fairfax . . .

Jesus! thought David. We fight each other, kill each other . . . we don't know our enemies any longer.

For *what*?

There was now a second reason to call Ballard. A name was not enough; he needed more than just a name. He would confront Asher Feld.

He picked up the telephone's receiver off the hook, held his coin and dialed.

Ballard got on the line, no humor in evidence.

'*Look*, David.' Ballard had not used his first name in conversation before.

Ballard was suppressing a lot of anger. 'I won't pretend to understand how you people turn your dials, but if you're going to use *my* set, keep me informed!'

'A number of people were killed; I wasn't one of them. That was fortunate but the circumstances prohibited my contacting you. Does that answer your complaint?'

Ballard was silent for several seconds. The silence was not just his reaction to the news, thought David. There was someone with Bobby. When the cryp spoke, he was no longer angry; he was hesitant, afraid.

'You're all right?'

'Yes. Lyons is with me.'

'The FMF were too late . . .' Ballard seemed to regret his statement. 'I keep phoning, they keep avoiding. I think their car's lost.'

'Not really. I've got it . . .'

'Oh, Christ!'

'They left one man at Telmo – for observation. There were two others. They're not hurt; they've disqualified.'

'What the hell does *that* mean?'

'I haven't got time to explain . . . There's an intercept order out for me. From Fairfax. The embassy's not supposed to know. It's a setup; I can't let them take me. Not for a while . . .'

'Hey, we don't mess with Fairfax,' said Ballard firmly.

'You can this time. I told Jean. There's a security breach in Fairfax. I'm not it, believe that . . . I've *got* to have time. Maybe as much as forty-eight hours. I need questions answered. Lyons can help. For God's sake, trust me!'

'I can trust you but I'm no big deal here . . . Wait a minute. Jean's with me . . .'

'I thought so,' interrupted Spaulding. It had been David's intention to ask Ballard for the help he needed. He suddenly realized that Jean could be far more helpful.

'Talk to her before she scratches the skin off my hand.'

'Before you get off, Bobby . . . Could you run a priority check on someone in Washington? In Fairfax, to be exact?'

'I'd have to have a reason. The subject – an Intelligence subject, *especially* Fairfax – would probably find out.'

'I don't give a damn if he does. Say I demanded it. My rating's four-zero; G-2 has that in the records. I'll take the responsibility.'

'Who is it?'

'A lieutenant colonel named Ira Barden. Got it?'

'Yes. Ira Barden. Fairfax.'

'Right. Now let me talk to . . .'

Jean's words spilled over one another, a mixture of fury and love, desperation and relief.

'Jean,' he said when she had finished a half-dozen questions he couldn't possibly answer, 'the other night you made a suggestion I refused to take seriously. I'm taking it seriously now. That mythical David of yours needs a place to hide out. It can't be the pampas, but any place nearer will do . . . Can you help me? Help us? For *God's sake!*'

38

He would call Jean later, before daybreak. He and Lyons had to move in darkness, wherever they were going. Wherever Jean could find them sanctuary.

There would be no codes sent to Washington, no clearance given for the obscene exchange, no radio or radar blackouts that would immobilize the fleet. David understood that; it was the simplest, surest way to abort 'Tortugas'.

But it was not enough.

There were the men behind 'Tortugas'. They had to be yanked up from the dark recesses of their filth and exposed to the sunlight. If there was any meaning left, if the years of pain and fear and death made any sense at all, they had to be given to the world in all their obscenity.

The world deserved that. Hundreds of thousands – on both sides – who would carry the scars of war throughout their lives, deserved it.

They had to understand the meaning of *For what*.

David accepted his role; he would face the men of 'Tortugas'. But he could not face them with the testimony of a fanatical Jew. The words of Asher Feld, leader of the Haganah's Provisional Wing, were no testimony at all. Fanatics were madmen; the world had seen enough of both, for both were one. And they were dismissed. Or killed. Or both.

David knew he had no choice.

When he faced the men of 'Tortugas'. it would not be with the words of Asher Feld. Or with deceptive codes and manipulations that were subject to a hundred interpretations.

Deceits. Cover-ups. Removals.

He would face them with what he saw. What he knew, because he had borne witness. He would present them with the irrefutable. And then he would destroy them.

To do this – all this – he had to get aboard the trawler in Ocho Calle. The trawler that would be blown out of the water should it attempt to run the harbour and rendezvous with a German submarine.

That it ultimately would attempt such a run was inevitable. The fanatic mind would demand it. Then there would be no evidence of things seen. Sworn to.

He had to get aboard that trawler now.

He gave his final instructions to Lyons and slid into the warm, oily waters of the Rio de la Plata. Lyons would remain in the car – drive it, if necessary – and, if David did not return, allow ninety minutes to elapse before going to the FMF base and telling the commanding officer that David was being held prisoner aboard the trawler. An American agent held prisoner.

There was logic in the strategy. FMF had priority orders to bring in David; orders from Fairfax, it would be three thirty in the morning. Fairfax called for swift, bold action. Especially at three thirty in the morning in a neutral harbor.

It was the bridge David tried always to create for himself in times of high-risk infiltration. It was the trade-off; his life for a lesser loss. The lessons of the north country.

He did not want it to happen that way. There were too many ways to immobilize him; too many panicked men in Washington and Berlin to let him survive, perhaps. At best there would be compromise. At worst ... The collapse of 'Tortugas' was not enough, the indictment was everything.

His pistol was tight against his head, tied with a strip of his shirt, the cloth running through his teeth. He breaststroked toward the hull of the ship, keeping his head out of the water, the firing-pin mechanism of his weapon as dry as possible. The price was mouthfuls of filthy, gasoline-polluted water, made further sickening by the touch of a large conger eel attracted, then repelled, by the moving white flesh.

He reached the hull. Waves slapped gently, unceasingly, against the hard expanse of darkness. He made his way to the stern of the ship, straining his eyes and his ears for evidence of life.

Nothing but the incessant lapping of water.

There was light from the deck but no movement, no shadows, no voices. Just the flat, colorless spill of naked bulbs strung on black wires, swaying in slow motion to the sluggish rhythm of the hull. On the port side of the ship – the dockside – were two lines looped over the aft and midships pilings. Rat disks were placed every ten feet or so; the thick manila hemps were black with grease and oil slick. As he approached, David could see a single guard sitting in a chair by the huge loading doors, which were shut. The chair was tilted back against the warehouse wall; two wire-mesh lamps covered by metal shades were on both sides of the wide doorframe. Spaulding treaded backward to get a clearer view. The guard was dressed in the paramilitary clothes of Habichtsnest. He was reading a book; for some reason that fact struck David as odd.

Suddenly, there were footsteps at the west section of the warehouse dock. They were slow, steady; there was no attempt to muffle the noise.

The guard looked up from his book. Between the pilings David could see a second figure come into view. It was another guard wearing the Rhinemann uniform. He was carrying a leather case, the same radio case carried by the men – dead men – at 15 Terraza Verde.

The guard in the chair smiled and spoke to the standing sentry. The language was German.

'I'll trade places, if you wish,' said the man in the chair. 'Get off your feet for a while.'

'No, thanks,' replied the man with the radio. 'I'd rather walk. Passes the time quicker.'

'Anything new from Luján?'

'No change. Still a great deal of excitement. I can hear snatches of yelling now and then. Everybody's giving orders.'

'I wonder what happened in Telmo.'

'Bad trouble is all I know. They've blocked us off; they've sent men to the foot of Ocho Calle.'

'You heard that?'

'No. I spoke with Geraldo. He and Luis are here. In front of the warehouse; in the street.'

'I hope they don't wake up the whores.'

The man with the radio laughed. 'Even Geraldo can do better than those dogs.'

'Don't bet good money on that,' replied the guard in the chair.

The guard on foot laughed again and proceeded east on his solitary patrol around the building. The man in the chair returned to his book.

David sidestroked his way back toward the hull of the trawler.

His arms were getting tired; the foul-smelling-waters of the harbour assaulted his nostrils. And now he had something else to consider: Eugene Lyons.

Lyons was a quarter of a mile away, diagonally across the water, four curving blocks from the foot of Ocho Calle. If Rhinemann's patrols began cruising the area, they would find the FMF vehicle with Lyons in it. It was a bridge he hadn't considered. He should have considered it.

But he couldn't think about that now.

He reached the starboard midships and held onto the waterline ledge, giving the muscles of his arms and shoulders a chance to throb in relief. The trawler was in the medium-craft classification, no more than seventy or eighty feet in length, perhaps a thirty-foot midship beam. By normal standards, and from what David could see as he approached the boat in darkness, the mid and aft cabins below the wheel shack were about fifteen and twenty feet long, respectively, with entrances at both ends and two portholes per cabin on the port and starboard sides. If the Koening diamonds *were* on board, it seemed logical that they'd be in the aft cabin, farthest away from the crew's normal activity. Too, aft cabins had more room and fewer distractions. And if Asher Feld was right, if two or three Peenemünde scientists were microscopically examining the Koening products, they would be under a pressured schedule and require isolation.

David found his breath coming easier. He'd know soon enough whether and where the diamonds were or were not. In moments.

He untied the cloth around his head, treading water as he did so, holding the pistol firmly. The shirt piece drifted away; he held onto the line ledge and looked above. The gunwale was six to seven feet out of the water; he would need both his hands to claw his way up the tiny ridges of the hull.

He spat out what harbour residue was in his mouth and clamped the barrel of the gun between his teeth. The only clothing he wore was his trousers; he plunged his hands beneath the water, rubbing them against the cloth in an effort to remove what estuary slick he could.

He gripped the line ledge once again and with his right hand extended, kicked his body out of the water and reached for the next tiny ridge along the hull. His fingers grasped the half-inch sprit; he pulled himself up, slapping his left hand next to his right, pushing his chest into the rough wood for leverage. His bare feet were near the water's surface, the gunwale no more than three feet above him now.

Slowly he raised his knees until the toes of both feet rested on the waterline ledge. He paused for breath, knowing that his fingers would not last long on the tiny ridge. He tensed the muscles of his stomach and pressed his aching toes against the ledge, pushing himself up as high as possible, whipping out his hands; knowing, again, that if he missed the gunwale he would plunge back into the water. The splash would raise alarms.

The left hand caught; the right slipped off. But it was enough.

He raised himself to the railing, his chest scraping against the rough, weathered hull until spots of blood emerged on his skin. He looped his left arm over the side and removed the pistol from his mouth. He was – as he hoped he would be – at the midpoint between the fore and aft cabins, the expanse of wall concealing him from the guards on the loading dock.

He silently rolled over the gunwale onto the narrow deck and took the necessary crouching steps to the cabin wall. He pressed his back into the wooden slats and slowly stood up. He inched his way toward the first aft porthole; the light from within was partially blocked by a primitive curtain of sorts, pulled back as if parted for the night air. The second porthole farther down had no such obstruction, but it was only feet from the edge of the wall; there was the possibility that a sentry – unseen from the water – might be on stern watch there. He would see whatever there was to see in the first window.

His wet cheek against the rotted rubber surrounding the porthole, he looked inside. The 'curtain' was a heavy sheet of black tarpaulin folded back at an angle. Beyond, the light was as he had pictured it; a single bulb suspended from the ceiling by a thick wire – a wire that ran out a port window to a pier outlet. Ship generators were not abused while at dock. There was an oddshaped, flat piece of metal hanging on the side of the bulb, and at first David was not sure why it was there. And then he understood; the sheet of metal deflected the light of the bulb from the rear of the cabin, where he could make out – beyond the fold of the tarp – two bunk beds. Men were sleeping; the light remained on but they were in relative shadow.

On the far side of the cabin, butted against the wall, was a long table that had the incongruous appearance of a hospital laboratory workbench. It was covered by a taut, white, spotless oilcloth and on the cloth, equidistant from one another, were four powerful microscopes. Beside each instrument was a high-intensity lamp – all the wires leading to a twelve-volt utility battery under the table. On the floor in front of the microscopes were four high-backed stools – four white, spotless stools standing at clinical attention.

That was the effect, thought David. Clinical. This isolated section of the trawler was in counterpoint to the rest of the filthy ship; it was a small, clinical island surrounded by rotted sea waste and rat disks.

And then he saw them. In the corner.

Five steel crates, each with metal strips joined at the top edges and held in place with heavy vault locks. On the front of each crate was the clearly stenciled name: KOENING MINES LTD.

He'd seen it now. The undeniable, the irrefutable.

Tortugas.

The obscene exchange funneled through Erich Rhinemann.

And he was so close, so near possession. The final indictment.

Within his fear – and he *was* afraid – furious anger and deep temptation converged. They were sufficient to suspend his anxiety, to force him to concentrate only on the objective. To believe – knowing the belief was false – in some mystical invulnerability, granted for only a few precious minutes.

That was enough.

He ducked under the first porthole and approached the second. He stood up and looked in; the door of the cabin was in his direct line of sight. It was a new door, not part of the trawler. It was steel and in the center was a bolt at least an inch thick, jammed into a bracket in the frame.

The Peenemünde scientists were not only clinically isolated, they were in a self-imposed prison.

That bolt, David realized, was his personal Alpine pass – to be crossed without rig.

He crouched and passed under the porthole to the edge of the cabin wall. He remained on his knees and, millimeter by millimeter, the side of his face against the wood, looked around the corner.

The guard was there, of course, standing his harbour watch in the tradition of such sentry duty: on deck, the inner line of defence; bored, irritated with his boredom, relaxed in his inactivity yet annoyed by its pointlessness.

But he was not in the paramilitary clothes of Habichtsnest. He was in a loose-fitting suit that did little to conceal a powerful – military – body. His hair was cut short, Wehrmacht style.

He was leaning against a large fishing-net winch, smoking a thin cigar, blowing the smoke aimlessly into the night air. At his side was an automatic rifle, .30 caliber, the shoulder strap unbuckled, curled on the deck. The rifle had not been touched for quite some time, the strap had a film of moisture on the surface of the leather.

The strap . . . David took the belt from his trousers. He stood up, inched back towards the porthole, reached underneath the railing and removed one of two gunwale spikes which were clamped against the inner hull for the fish nets. He tapped the railing softly twice; then twice again. He heard the shuffling of the guard's feet. No forward movement, just a change of position.

He tapped again. Twice. Then twice more. The quietly precise tapping – intentional, spaced evenly – was enough to arouse curiosity, insufficient to cause alarm.

He heard the guard's footsteps now. Still relaxed, the forward motion easy, not concerned with danger, only curious. A piece of harbour driftwood, perhaps, slapping against the hull, caught in the push-pull of the current.

The guard rounded the corner; Spaulding's belt whipped around his neck, instantly lashed taut, choking off the cry.

David twisted the leather as the guard sank to his knees, the face darkening perceptibly in the dim spill of light from the porthole, the lips pursed in strangled anguish.

David did not allow his victim to lose consciousness; he had the Alpine pass to cross. Instead, he wedged his pistol into his trousers, reached down to the scabbard on the guard's waist, and took out the carbine bayonet – a favorite knife of combat men, rarely used on the front of any rifle. He held the blade under the guard's eyes and whispered.

'*Español* or *Deutsch*?'

The man stared up in terror. Spaulding twisted the leather tighter; the guard choked a cough and struggled to raise two fingers. David whispered again, the blade pushing against the skin under the right eyeball.

'*Deutsch?*'

The man nodded.

Of course he was German, thought Spaulding. And Nazi. The clothes, the hair. Peenemünde *was* the Third Reich. Its scientists would be guarded by their own. He twisted the blade of the carbine bayonet so that a tiny laceration appeared under the eye. The guard's mouth opened in fright.

'You do exactly what I tell you,' whispered David in German into the guard's ear, 'or I'll carve out your sight. Understand?'

The man, nearly limp, nodded.

'Get up and call through the porthole. You have an urgent message from ... Altmüller, Franz Altmüller! They must open the door and sign for it ... Do it! Now! And remember, this knife is inches from your eyes.'

The guard, in shock, got up. Spaulding pushed the man's face to the open porthole, loosened the belt only slightly, and shifted his position to the side of the man and the window, his left hand holding the leather, his right the knife.

'*Now!*' whispered David, flicking the blade in half-circles.

At first the guard's voice was strained, artificial. Spaulding moved in closer; the guard knew he had only seconds to live if he did not perform.

He performed.

There was stirring in the bunk beds within the cabin. Grumbling complaints to begin with, ceasing abruptly at the mention of Altmüller's name.

A small, middle-aged man got out of the left lower bunk and walked sleepily to the steel door. He was in undershorts, nothing else. David propelled the guard around the corner of the wall and reached the door at the sound of the sliding bolt.

He slammed the guard against the steel panel with the twisted belt; the door flung open, David grabbed the knob, preventing it from crashing into the bulkhead. He dropped the knife, yanked out his pistol, and crashed the barrel into the skull of the small scientist.

'*Schweigen!*' he whispered hoarsely. '*Wenn Ihnen Ihr Leben Lieb ist!*'

The three men in the bunks – older men, one old man – stumbled out of their beds, trembling and speechless. The guard, choking still, began to focus around him and started to rise. Spaulding took two steps and slashed the pistol diagonally across the man's temple, splaying him out on the deck.

The old man, less afraid than his two companions, stared at David. For reasons Spaulding could not explain to himself, he felt ashamed. Violence was out of place in this antiseptic cabin.

'I have no quarrel with you,' he whispered harshly in German. 'You follow orders. But don't mistake me, I'll kill you if you make a sound!' He pointed to some papers next to a microscope; they were filled with numbers and columns. 'You!' He gestured his pistol at the old man. 'Give me those! Quickly!'

The old man trudged haltingly across the cabin to the clinical-work area. He lifted the papers off the table and handed them to Spaulding, who stuffed them into his wet trousers pocket.

'Thanks . . . Now!' He pointed his weapon at the other two. 'Open one of those crates! Do it now!'

'No! . . . No! For God's sake!' said the taller of the middle-aged scientists, his voice low, filled with fear.

David grabbed the old man standing next to him, He clamped his arm around the loose flesh of the old neck and brought his pistol up to the head. He thumbed back the firing pin and spoke calmly. 'You will open a crate or I will kill this man. When he's dead, I'll turn my pistol on you. Believe me, I have no alternative.'

The shorter man whipped his head around, pleading silently with the taller one. The old man in David's grasp was the leader; Spaulding knew that. An old . . . *alter-Anführer;* always take the German leader.

The taller Peenemünde scientist walked – every step in fear – to the far corner of the clinical workbench, where there was a neat row of keys on the wall. He removed one and hesitantly went to the first steel crate. He bent down and inserted the key in the vault lock holding the metal strip around the edge; the strip snapped apart in the center.

'Open the lid!' commanded Spaulding, his anxiety causing his whisper to become louder; too loud, he realized.

The cover of the steel crate was heavy; the German had to lift it with both hands, the wrinkles around his eyes and mouth betraying the effort required.

Once at a ninety-degree angle, chains on both sides became taut; there was a click of a latch and the cover was locked in place.

Inside were dozens of identically matched compartments in what appeared to be sliding trays – something akin to a large complicated fishing-tackle box. Then David understood: the front of the steel case was on hinges; it too could be opened – or lowered, to be exact – allowing the trays to slide out.

In each compartment were two small heavy, paper envelopes, apparently lined with layers of soft tissue. There were dozens of envelopes on the top tray alone.

David released the old man, propelling him back toward the bunk beds. He waved his pistol at the tall German who had opened the crate, ordering him to join the other two. He reached down into the steel crate, picked out a small envelope and brought it to his mouth, tearing the edge with his teeth. He shook it toward the ground; tiny translucent nuggets spattered over the cabin deck.

The Koening diamonds.

He watched the German scientists as he crumpled the envelope. They were staring at the stones on the floor.

Why not? thought David. In that cabin was the solution for Peenemünde. In those crates were the tools to rain death on untold thousands . . . as the gyroscopic designs for which they were traded would make possible further death, further massacre.

He was about to throw away the envelope in disgust and fill his pockets with others when his eyes caught sight of some lettering. He unwrinkled the envelope, his pistol steady on the Germans, and looked down. The single word:

echt

True. Genuine. This envelope, this tray, this steel case had passed inspection.

He reached down and grabbed as many envelopes as his left hand could hold and stuffed them into his trousers pocket.

It was all he needed for the indictment.

It was everything. It was the meaning.

There was one thing more he could do. Of a more immediately practical nature. He crossed to the workbench and went down the line of four microscopes, crashing the barrel of his pistol up into each lens and down into the eyepieces. He looked for a laboratory case, the type which carried optical equipment. There had to be one!

It was on the floor beneath the long table. He kicked it out with his bare foot and reached down to open the hasp.

More slots and trays, only these filled with lenses and small black tubes in which to place them.

He bent down and overturned the case; dozens of circular lenses fell out onto the deck. As fast as he could he grabbed the nearest white stool and brought it down sideways into the piles of glass.

The destruction wasn't total, but the damage was enough, perhaps, for forty-eight hours.

He started to get up, his weapon still on the scientists, his ears and eyes alert.

He heard it! He sensed it! And simultaneously he understood that if he did not spin out of the way he would be dead!

He threw himself on the floor to the right, the hand above and behind him came down, the carbine bayonet slicing the air, aimed for the spot where his neck had been less than a second ago.

He had left the goddamned bayonet on the floor! He had discarded the goddamned *bayonet*! The guard had revived and *taken* the goddamned *bayonet*!

The Nazi's single cry emerged before Spaulding leaped on his kneeling form, smashing his skull into the wood floor with such force that blood spewed out in tiny bursts throughout the head.

But the lone cry was enough.

'Is something wrong?' came a voice from outside, twenty yards away on the loading dock. 'Heinrich! Did you call?'

There was no second, no instant, to throw away on hesitation.

David ran to the steel door, pulled it open and raced around the corner of the wall to the concealed section of the gunwale. As he did so, a guard – the sentry on the bow of the trawler – came into view. His rifle was waist-high and he fired.

Spaulding fired back. But not before he realized he was hit. The Nazi's bullet had creased the side of his waist; he could feel the blood oozing down into his trousers.

He threw himself over the railing into the water; screams and shouts started from inside the cabin and farther away on the pier.

He thrashed against the dirty Rio slime and tried to keep his head. Where was he? What direction? Where? For Christ's sake, *where?*

The shouts were louder now; searchlights were turned on all over the trawler, crisscrossing the harbor waters. He could hear men screaming into radios as only panicked men can scream. Accusing, helpless.

Suddenly, David realized there were no boats! No boats were coming out of the pier with the searchlights and high-powered rifles that would be his undoing!

No boats!

And he nearly laughed. The operation at Ocho Calle was so totally secretive they had allowed no small craft to put into the deserted area!

He held his side, going under water as often as he could, as fast as he could.

The trawler and the screaming Rhinemann-Altmüller guards were receding in the harbour mist. Spaulding kept bobbing his head up, hoping to God he was going in the right direction.

He was getting terribly tired, but he would not allow himself to grow weak. He *could not* allow that! Not now!

He had the 'Tortugas' indictment!

He saw the pilings not far away. Perhaps two, three hundred yards. They *were* the right pilings, the right piers! They . . . it, *had* to be!

He felt the waters around him stir and then he saw the snake-like forms of the conger eels as they lashed blindly against his body. The blood from his wound was attracting them! A horrible mass of slashing giant worms were converging!

He thrashed and kicked and fought down a scream. He pulled at the waters in front of him, his hands in constant contact with the oily snakes of the harbour. His eyes were filled with flashing dots and streaks of yellow and white; his throat was dry in the water, his forehead pounded.

When it seemed at last the scream would come, *had* to come, he felt the hand in his hand. He felt his shoulders being lifted, heard the guttural cries of his own terrified voice – deep, frightened beyond his own endurance. He could look down and see, as his feet kept slipping off the ladder, the circles of swarming eels below.

Eugene Lyons carried him – *carried* him! – to the FMF automobile. He was aware – yet not aware – of the fact that Lyons pushed him gently into the back seat.

And then Lyons climbed in after him, and David understood – yet did not understand – that Lyons was slapping him. Hard. Harder.

Deliberately. Without rhythm but with a great deal of strength.

The slapping would not stop! He couldn't make it stop! He couldn't stop the half-destroyed, throatless Lyons from slapping him.

He could only cry. Weep as a child might weep.

And then suddenly he *could* make him stop. He took his hands from his face and grabbed Lyons's wrists, prepared, if need be, to break them.

He blinked and stared at the physicist.

Lyons smiled in the shadows. He spoke in his tortured whisper.

'I'm sorry . . . You were . . . in temporary . . . shock. My friend.'

39

An elaborate naval first-aid kit was stored in the trunk of the FMF vehicle. Lyons filled David's wound with sulfa powder, laid on folded strips of gauze and pinched the skin together with three-inch adhesive. Since the wound was a gash, not a puncture, the bleeding stopped; it would hold until they reached a doctor. Even should the wait be a day or a day and a half, there would be no serious damage.

Lyons drove.

David watched the emaciated man behind the wheel. He was unsure but willing; that was the only way to describe him. Every now and then his foot pressed too hard on the accelerator, and the short bursts of speed frightened him – then annoyed him. Still, after a few minutes, he seemed to take a careful delight in manipulating the car around corners.

David knew he had to accomplish three things: reach Henderson Granville, talk to Jean and drive to that sanctuary he hoped to Christ Jean had found for them. If a doctor could be brought to him, fine. If not, he would sleep; he was beyond the point of functioning clearly without rest.

How often in the north country had he sought out isolated caves in the hills? How many times had he piled branches and limbs in front of small openings so his body and mind could restore the balance of objectivity that might save his life? He had to find such a resting place now.

And tomorrow he would make the final arrangements with Erich Rhinemann.

The final pages of the indictment.

'We have to find a telephone,' said David. Lyons nodded as he drove.

David directed the physicist back into the center of Buenos Aires. By his guess they still had time before the FMF base sent out a search. The orange insignias on the bumpers would tend to dissuade the BA police from becoming too curious; the Americans were children of the night.

He remembered the telephone booth on the north side of the Casa Rosada. The telephone booth in which a hired gun from the Unio Corso – sent down from Rio de Janeiro – had taken his last breath.

They reached the Plaza de Mayo in fifteen minutes, taking a circular route, making sure they were not followed. The Plaza was not deserted. It was, as the prewar travel posters proclaimed, a Western Hemisphere Paris. Like

Paris, there were dozens of early stragglers, dressed mainly in expensive clothes. Taxis stopped and started; prostitutes made their last attempts to find profitable beds; the streetlights illuminated the huge fountains; lovers dabbled their hands in the pools.

The Plaza de Mayo at three thirty in the morning was not a barren, dead place to be. And David was grateful for that.

Lyons pulled the car up to the telephone booth and Spaulding got out.

'Whatever it is, you've hit the rawest nerve in Buenos Aires.' Granville's voice was hard and precise. 'I must demand that you return to the embassy. For your own protection as well as the good of our diplomatic relations.'

'You'll have to be clearer than that, I'm afraid,' replied David.

Granville was.

The 'one or two' contacts the ambassador felt he could reach in the Grupo were reduced, of course, to one. That man made inquiries as to the trawler in Ocho Calle and subsequently was taken from his home under guard. That was the information Granville gathered from a hysterical wife.

An hour later the ambassador received word from a GOU liaison that his 'friend' had been killed in an automobile accident. The GOU wanted him to have the news. It was most unfortunate.

When Granville tried reaching the wife, an operator cut in explaining that the telephone was disconnected.

'You've involved us, Spaulding! We can't function with Intelligence dead weight around our necks. The situation in Buenos Aires is extremely delicate.'

'You *are* involved, sir. A couple of thousand miles away people are shooting at each other.'

'Shit!' It was just about the most unexpected expletive David thought he could hear from Granville. 'Learn your lines of demarcation! We all have jobs to do within the ... artificial, if you like, parameters that are set for us! I repeat, sir. Return to the embassy and I'll expedite your immediate return to the United States. Or if you refuse, take yourself to FMF. *That's* beyond my jurisdiction; you will be no part of the embassy!'

My God! thought David. *Artificial parameters. Jurisdictions. Diplomatic niceties.* When men were dying, armies destroyed, cities obliterated! And men in high-ceilinged rooms played games with words and attitudes!

'I can't go to FMF. But I can give you something to think about. Within forty-eight hours all American ships and aircraft in the coastal zones are entering a radio and radar blackout! Everything grounded, immobilized. That's straight military holy writ. And I think you'd better find out why! Because I think I know, and if I'm right, your *diplomatic wreck* is filthier than anything you can imagine! Try a man named Swanson at the War Department. Brigadier Alan Swanson! And tell him I've found "Tortugas"!'

David slammed down the receiver with such force that chips of Bakelite fell off the side of the telephone. He wanted to run. Open the door of the suffocating booth and race away.

But where to? There was nowhere.

He took several deep breaths and once more dialed the embassy.

Jean's voice was soft, filled with anxiety. But she had found a place!

He and Lyons were to drive due west on Rivadavia to the farthest outskirts of Buenos Aires. At the end of Rivadavia was a road bearing right – it could be spotted by a large statue of the Madonna at its beginning. The road led to the flat grass country, *provinciales* country. Thirty-six miles beyond the Madonna was another road – on the left – this marked by telephone junction wires converging into a transformer box on top of a double-strapped telephone pole. The road led to a ranch belonging to one Alfonzo Quesarro. Señor Quesarro would not be there ... under the circumstances. Neither would his wife. But a skeleton staff would be on; the remaining staff quarters would be available for Mrs Cameron's unknown friends.

Jean would obey his orders: she would not leave the embassy.

And she loved him. Terribly.

Dawn came up over the grass country. The breezes were warm; David had to remind himself that it was January. The Argentine summer. A member of the skeleton staff of Estancia Quesarro met them several miles down the road past the telephone junction wires, on the property border, and escorted them to the *ranchera* – a cluster of small one-story cottages – near but not adjacent to the main buildings. They were led to an adobe hut farthest from the other houses; it was on the edge of a fenced grazing area, fields extending as far as the eye could see. The house was the residence of the *caporal* – the ranch foreman.

David understood as he looked up at the roof, at the single telephone line. Ranch foremen had to be able to use a telephone.

Their escort opened the door and stood in the frame, anxious to leave. He touched David's arm and spoke in a Spanish tempered with pampas Indian.

'The telephones out here are with operators. The service is poor; not like the city. I am to tell you this, señor.'

But that information was not what the gaucho was telling him. He was telling him to be careful.

'I'll remember,' said Spaulding. 'Thank you.'

The man left quickly and David closed the door. Lyons was standing across the room, in the center of a small monastery arch that led to some sort of sunlit enclosure. The metal case containing the gyroscopic designs was in his right hand; with his left he beckoned David.

Beyond the arch was a cubicle; in the center, underneath an oblong window overlooking the fields, there was a bed.

Spaulding undid the top of his trousers and peeled them off.

He fell with his full weight into the hard mattress and slept.

40

It seemed only seconds ago that he had walked through the small arch into the sunlit cubicle.

He felt the prodding fingers around his wound; he winced as a cold-hot liquid was applied about his waist and the adhesive ripped off.

He opened his eyes fiercely and saw the figure of a man bent over the bed. Lyons was standing beside him. At the edge of the hard mattress was the universal shape of a medical bag. The man bending over him was a doctor. He spoke in unusually clear English.

'You've slept nearly eight hours. That is the best prescription one could give you ... I'm going to suture this in three places; that should do it. There will be a degree of discomfort, but with the tape, you'll be quite mobile.'

'What time is it?' asked David.

Lyons looked at his watch. He whispered, and the words were clear. 'Two ... o'clock.'

'Thank you for coming out here,' said Spaulding, shifting his weight for the doctor's instruments.

'Wait until I'm back at my office in Palermo.' The doctor laughed softly, sardonically. 'I'm sure I'm on one of their lists.' He inserted a suture, reassuring David with a tight smile. 'I left word I was on a maternity call at an outback ranch ... There.' He tied off the stitch and patted Spaulding's bare skin. 'Two more and we're finished.'

'Do you think you'll be questioned?'

'No. Not actually. The junta closes its eyes quite often. There's not an abundance of doctors here ... And amusingly enough, interrogators invariably seek free medical advice. I think it goes with their mentalities.'

'And I think you're covering. I think it *was* dangerous.'

The doctor held his hands in place as he looked at David. 'Jean Cameron is a very special person. If the history of wartime Buenos Aires is written, she'll be prominently mentioned.' He returned to the sutures without elaboration. David had the feeling that the doctor did not wish to talk further. He was in a hurry.

Twenty minutes later Spaulding was on his feet, the doctor at the door of the adobe hut. David shook the medical man's hand. 'I'm afraid I can't pay you,' he said.

'You already have, colonel. I'm a Jew.'

Spaulding did not release the doctor's hand. Instead, he held it firmly – not in salutation. 'Please explain.'

'There's nothing to explain. The Jewish community is filled with rumors of an American officer who pits himself against the pig . . . Rhinemann the pig.'

'That's all?'

'It's enough.' The doctor removed his hand from Spaulding's and walked out. David closed the door.

Rhinemann the pig. It was time for Rhinemann.

The teutonic, guttural voice screamed into the telephone. David could picture the blue-black veins protruding on the surface of the bloated, suntanned skin. He could see the narrow eyes bulging with fury.

'*It was you! It was you!*' The accusation was repeated over and over again, as if the repetition might provoke a denial.

'It was me,' said David without emphasis.

'You are *dead*! You are a *dead man*!'

David spoke quietly, slowly. With precision. 'If I'm dead, no codes are sent to Washington; no radar or radio blackout. The screens will pick up that trawler and the instant a submarine surfaces anywhere near it, it'll be blown out of the water.'

Rhinemann was silent. Spaulding heard the German Jew's rhythmic breathing but said nothing. He let Rhinemann's thoughts dwell upon the implication. Finally Rhinemann spoke. With equal precision.

'Then you have something to say to me. Or you would not have telephoned.'

'That's right,' agreed David. 'I have something to say. I assume you're taking a broker's fee. I can't believe you arranged this exchange for nothing.'

Rhinemann paused again. He replied cautiously, his breathing heavy, carried over the wire. 'No . . . It is a transaction. Accommodations must be paid for.'

'But that payment comes later, doesn't it?' David kept his words calm, dispassionate. 'You're in no hurry; you've got everyone where you want them . . . There won't be any messages radioed out of Switzerland that accounts have been settled. The only message you'll get – or *won't* get – is from a submarine telling you the Koening diamonds have been transferred from the trawler. That's when I fly out of here with the designs. That's the signal.' Spaulding laughed a brief, cold, quiet laugh. 'It's very pro, Rhinemann. I congratulate you.'

The financier's voice was suddenly low, circumspect. 'What's your point?'

'It's also very pro . . . I'm the only one who can bring about that message from the U-boat. No one else. I have the codes that turn the lights off; that make the radar screens go dark . . . But I expect to get paid for it.'

'I see . . .' Rhinemann hesitated, his breathing still audible. 'It is a presumptuous demand. Your superiors expect the gyroscopic designs. Should you impede their delivery, your punishment, no doubt, will be execution. Not formally arrived at, of course, but the result will be the same. Surely you know that.'

David laughed again, and again the laugh was brief – but now good-natured. 'You're way off. *Way off*. There may be executions, but not mine. Until last night I only knew half the story. Now I know it *all* . . . No, not *my* execution. On the other hand, you *do* have a problem. I know *that*; four years in Lisbon teaches a man some things.'

'What is my problem?'

'If the Koening merchandise in Ocho Calle is not delivered, Altmüller will send an undercover battalion into Buenos Aires. You won't survive it.'

The silence again. And in that silence was Rhinemann's acknowledgement that David was right.

'Then we are allies,' said Rhinemann. 'In one night you've gone far. You took a dangerous risk and leaped many plateaus. I admire such aggressive ambitions. I'm sure arrangements can be made.'

'I was sure you'd be sure.'

'Shall we discuss figures?'

Again David laughed softly. 'Payment from you is like . . . before last night. Only half the story. Make your half generous. In Switzerland. The second half will be paid in the States. A lifetime of *very* generous retainers.' David suddenly spoke tersely. 'I want names.'

'I don't understand . . .'

'*Think* about it. The men *behind* this operation. The Americans. Those are the names I want. Not an accountant, not a confused brigadier. The others . . . Without those names there's no deal. No codes.'

'The man from Lisbon is remarkably without conscience,' said Rhinemann with a touch of respect. 'You are . . . as you Americans say . . . quite a rotten fellow.'

'I've watched the masters in action. I thought about it . . . Why not?'

Rhinemann obviously had not listened to David's reply. His tone was abruptly suspicious. 'If this . . . gain of personal wealth is the conclusion you arrived at, why did you do what you did last night? I must tell you that the damage is not irreparable, but why *did* you?'

'For the simplest of reasons. I hadn't thought about it last night. I hadn't arrived at this conclusion . . . last night.' God knew, that was the truth, thought David.

'Yes. I think I understand,' said the financier. 'A very human reaction . . .'

'I want the rest of these designs,' broke in Spaulding. 'And you want the codes sent out. To stay on schedule, we have thirty-six hours, give or take two or three. I'll call you at six o'clock. Be ready to move.'

David hung up. He took a deep breath and realized he was perspiring . . . and the small concrete house was cool. The breezes from the fields were coming through the windows, billowing the curtains. He looked at Lyons, who sat watching him in a straight-backed wicker chair.

'How'd I do?' he asked.

The physicist swallowed and spoke, and it occurred to Spaulding that either he was getting used to Lyons's strained voice or Lyons's speech was improving.

'Very ... convincing. Except for the ... sweat on your face and the expression ... in your eyes.' Lyons smiled; then followed it instantly with a question he took seriously. 'Is there a chance ... for the remaining blueprints?'

David held a match to a cigarette. He inhaled the smoke, looked up at the gently swaying curtains of an open window, then turned to the physicist. 'I think we'd better understand one another, doctor. I don't give a goddamn about those designs. Perhaps I should, but I don't. And if the way to get our hands on them is to risk that trawler reaching a U-boat, it's out of the question. As far as I'm concerned we're bringing out three-quarters more than what we've got. And that's too goddamn much ... There's only one thing I want: the names ... I've got the evidence; now I want the names.'

'You want revenge,' said Lyons softly.

'*Yes! ... Jesus! Yes, I do!*' David crushed out his barely touched cigarette, crossed to the open window and looked out at the fields. 'I'm sorry, I don't mean to yell at you. Or maybe I should. You heard Feld; you saw what I brought back from Ocho Calle. You know the whole putrid ... obscene thing.'

'I know ... the men who fly those planes ... are not responsible ... I know I believe that ... Germany must lose this war.'

'For Christ's *sake*!' roared David, whirling from the window. 'You've *seen*! You've *got* to *understand*!'

'Are you saying ... there's no difference? I don't believe that ... I don't think you believe it.'

'I don't know *what* I believe! ... No. I *do* know. I know what I object to; because it leaves no *room* for belief ... And I know I want those names.'

'You should have them ... Your questions are great ... moral ones. I think they will pain you ... for years.' Lyons was finding it difficult to sustain his words now. 'I submit only ... no matter what has happened ... that Asher Feld was right. This war must *not* be settled ... it must be won.'

Lyons stopped talking and rubbed his throat. David walked to a table where Lyons kept a pitcher of water and poured a glass. He carried it over to the spent physicist and handed it to him. It occurred to David, as he acknowledged the gesture of thanks, that it was strange ... Of all men, the emaciated recluse in front of him would profit least from the outcome of the war. Or the shortening of it. Yet Eugene Lyons had been touched by the commitment of Asher Feld. Perhaps, in his pain, Lyons understood the simpler issues that his own anger had distorted.

Asher Feld. The Alvear Hotel.

'Listen to me,' said Spaulding. 'If there's a chance ... and there may be, we'll try for the blueprints. There's a trade-off possible; a dangerous one ... not for us, but for your friend, Asher Feld. We'll see. No promises. The names come first ... It's a parallel route; until I get the names, Rhinemann has to believe I want the designs as much as he wants the diamonds . . . We'll see.'

The weak, erratic bell of the country telephone spun out its feeble ring. Spaulding picked it up.

'It's Ballard,' said the voice anxiously.

'Yes, Bobby?'

'I hope to Christ you're clean, because there's a lot of flak to the contrary. I'm going on the assumption that a reasonable guy doesn't court-martial himself into a long prison term for a few dollars.'

'A reasonable assumption. What is it? Did you get the information?'

'First things first. And the first thing is that the Fleet Marine Force wants you dead or alive; the condition is immaterial, and I think they'd prefer you dead.'

'They found Meehan and the driver . . .'

'You bet your ass they did! After they got rolled and stripped to their skivvies by some wandering *vagos*. They're mad as hell! They threw out the bullshit about not alerting the embassy that Fairfax wants you picked up. Fairfax's incidental; *they* want you. Assault, theft, et cetera.'

'All right. That's to be expected.'

'Expected? Oh, you're a pistol! I don't suppose I have to tell you about Granville. You got him burning up my dials! Washington's preparing a top-level scramble, so I'm chained to my desk till it comes in.'

'Then he doesn't know. They're covering,' said Spaulding, annoyed.

'The hell he doesn't! The hell they *are*! This radio silence; you walked into a High Command *defection*! An Allied Central project straight from the War Department.'

'I'll bet it's from the War Department. I can tell you which office.'

'It's true . . . There's a U-boat bringing in a couple of very important Berliners. You're out of order; it's not your action. Granville will tell you that.'

'Horseshit!' yelled David. 'Pure horseshit! *Transparent* horseshit! Ask any network agent in Europe. You couldn't get a *Breifmarke* out of *any* German port! No one knows that better than me!'

'Interesting, ontologically speaking. Transparency isn't a quality one associates . . .'

'No jokes! My humor's strained!' And then suddenly David realized he had no cause to yell at the cryp. Ballard's frame of reference was essentially the same as it had been eighteen hours ago – with complications, perhaps, but not of death and survival. Ballard did not know about the carnage at San Telmo or the tools for Peenemünde in Ocho Calle; and a Haganah that reached into the most secret recesses of Military Intelligence. Nor would he be told just now. 'I'm sorry. I've got a lot on my mind.'

'Sure, sure.' Ballard replied as if he were used to other people's tempers. Another trait common to most cryptographers, David reflected. 'Jean said you were hurt; fell and cut yourself pretty badly. Did somebody push?'

'It's all right. The doctor was here . . . Did you get the information? On Ira Barden.'

'Yeah . . . I used straight G-2 in Washington. A dossier Teletype request over your name. This Barden's going to know about it.'

'That's Okay. What's it say?'

'The whole damn *thing*?'

'Whatever seems . . . unusual. Fairfax qualifications, probably.'

'They don't use the name Fairfax. Just high-priority classification . . . He's in the Reserves, not regular army. Family company's in importing. Spent a number of years in Europe and the Middle East; speaks five languages . . .'

'And one of them's Hebrew,' interrupted David quietly.

'That's right. How did . . . ? Never mind. He spent two years at the American University in Beirut while his father represented the firm in the Mediterranean areas. The company was very big in Middle East textiles. Barden transferred to Harvard, then transferred again to a small college called Brandeis . . . I don't know it. He majored in Near East studies, it says here. When he graduated he went into the family business until the war . . . I guess it was the languages.'

'Thanks,' said David. 'Burn the Teletype, Bobby.'

'With pleasure . . . When are you coming in? You better get here before the FMF finds you. Jean can probably convince old Henderson to cool things off.'

'Pretty soon. How's Jean?'

'Huh? Fine . . . Scared; nervous, I guess. You'll see. She's a strong girl, though.'

'Tell her not to worry.'

'Tell her yourself.'

'She's there with you?'

'No . . .' Ballard drew out the word, telegraphing a note of concern that had been absent. 'No, she's not with me. She's on her way to see you . . .'

'*What?*'

'The nurse. The doctor's nurse. She called about an hour ago. She said you wanted to see Jean.' Ballard's voice suddenly became hard and loud. '*What the hell's going on, Spaulding?*'

41

'Surely the man from Lisbon expected countermeasures. I'm amazed he was so derelict.' Heinrich Stoltz conveyed his arrogance over the telephone. 'Mrs Cameron was a flank you took for granted, yes? A summons from a loved one is difficult to resist, is it not?'

'Where is she?'

'She is on her way to Luján. She will be a guest at Habichtsnest. An honored guest, I can assure you. Herr Rhinemann will be immensely pleased; I was about to telephone him. I wanted to wait until the interception was made.'

'You're out of line!' David said, trying to keep his voice calm. 'You're asking for reprisals in every neutral area. Diplomatic hostages in a neutral . . .'

'A guest,' interrupted the German with relish. 'Hardly a prize; a *step*-daughter-in-law; the husband *deceased*. With no official status. So complicated, these American social rituals.'

'You know what I mean! You don't need diagrams!'

'I said she was a *guest*! Of an eminent financier you yourself were sent to contact . . . concerning international economic matters, I believe. A Jew expelled from his own country, that country your enemy. I see no cause for immediate alarm . . . Although, perhaps, you should.'

There was no reason to procrastinate. Jean was no part of the bargain, no part of the indictment. To hell with the indictment! To hell with a meaningless commitment! There *was* no meaning!

Only Jean.

'Call the moves,' said David.

'I was sure you'd cooperate. What difference does it make to you? Or to me, really . . . You and I, we take orders. Leave the philosophy to men of great affairs. We survive.'

'That doesn't sound like a true believer. I was told you were a believer.' David spoke aimlessly; he needed time, only seconds. To think.

'Strangely enough, I am. In a world that passed, I'm afraid. Only partially in the one that's coming . . . The remaining designs are at Habichtsnest. You and your aerophysicist will go there at once. I wish to conclude our negotiations this evening.'

'Wait a minute!' David's mind raced over conjectures – his counterpart's options. 'That's not the cleanest nest I've been in; the inhabitants leave something to be desired.'

'So do the guests . . .'

'Two conditions. One: I see Mrs Cameron the minute I get there. Two: I don't send the codes – if they're to be sent – until she's back at the embassy. With Lyons.'

'We'll discuss these points later. There is one prior condition, however.' Stoltz paused. 'Should you not be at Habichsnest this afternoon, you will *never* see Mrs Cameron. As you last saw her . . . Habichtsnest has so many diversions; the guests enjoy them so. Unfortunately, there have been some frightful accidents in the past. On the river, in the pool . . . on horseback . . .'

The foreman gave them a road map and filled the FMF automobile's gas tank with fuel from the ranch pump. Spaulding removed the orange medallions from the bumpers and blurred the numbers of the licence plates by chipping away at the paint until the 1s looked like 7s, and 3s like 8s. Then he smashed the ornament off the tip of the hood, slapped black paint over the grill and removed all four hubcaps. Finally, he took a sledgehammer and, to the amazement of the silent gaucho, he crashed it into the side door panels, trunk and roof of the car.

When he had finished, the automobile from Fleet Marine Force looked like any number of back-country wrecks.

They drove out the road to the primitive highway by the telephone junction box and turned east toward Buenos Aires. Spaulding pressed the accelerator; the vibrations caused the loose metal to rattle throughout the car. Lyons held the unfolded map on his knees; if it was correct, they could reach the Luján district without traveling the major highways, reducing the chances of discovery by the FMF patrols that were surely out by now.

The goddamned irony of it! thought David. Safety . . . safety for Jean, for him, too, really . . . lay in contact with the same enemy he had fought so viciously for over three years. An enemy made an ally by incredible events . . . treasons taking place in Washington and Berlin.

What had Stoltz said? *Leave the philosophy to men of great affairs.*

Meaning and no meaning at all.

David nearly missed the half-concealed entrance to Habichtsnest. He was approaching it from the opposite direction on the lonely stretch of road he had traveled only once, and at night. What caused him to slow down and look to his left, spotting the break in the woods, were sets of black tire marks on the light surface of the entrance. They had not been there long enough to be erased by the hot sun or succeeding traffic. And Spaulding recalled the words of the guard on the pier in Ocho Calle.

. . . There is a lot of shouting.

David could visualize Rhinemann screaming his orders, causing a column of racing Bentleys and Packards to come screeching out of the hidden road from Habichtsnest on its way to a quiet street in San Telmo.

And no doubt later – in the predawn hours – other automobiles, more sweating, frightened henchmen – racing to the small isolated peninsula that was Ocho Calle.

With a certain professional pride, Spaulding reflected that he had interdicted well.

Both enemies. All enemies.

A vague plan was coming into focus, but only the outlines. So much depended on what faced them at Habichtsnest.

And the soft-spoken words of hatred uttered by Asher Feld.

The guards in their paramilitary uniforms leveled their rifles at the approaching automobile. Others held dogs that were straining at leashes, teeth bared, barking viciously. The man behind the electric gate shouted orders to those in front; four guards ran to the car and yanked the smashed panels open. Spaulding and Lyons got out; they were pushed against the FMF vehicle and searched.

David kept turning his head, looking at the extended fence beyond both sides of the gate. He estimated the height and the tensile strength of the links, the points of electrical contact between the thick-poled sections. The angles of direction.

It was part of his plan.

Jean ran to him from across the terraced balcony. He held her, silently, for several moments. It was a brief span of sanity and he was grateful for it.

Rhinemann stood at the railing twenty feet away, Stoltz at his side. Rhinemann's narrow eyes stared at David from out of the folds of suntanned flesh. The look was one of despised respect, and David knew it.

There was a third man. A tall, blond-haired man in a white Palm Beach suit seated at a glass-topped table. Spaulding did not know him.

'David, *David*. What have I *done*?' Jean would not let him go; he stroked her soft brown hair, replying quietly.

'Saved my life among other things . . .'

'The Third Reich has extraordinarily thorough surveillance, Mrs Cameron,' interrupted Stoltz, smiling. 'We keep watch on all Jews. Especially professional men. We knew you were friendly with the doctor in Palermo; and that the colonel was wounded. It was all quite simple.'

'Does your surveillance of Jews include the man beside you?' asked Spaulding in a monotone.

Stoltz paled slightly, his glance shifting unobtrusively from Rhinemann to the blond-haired man in the chair. 'Herr Rhinemann understands my meaning. I speak pragmatically; of the necessary observation of hostile elements.'

'Yes, I remember,' said David, releasing Jean, putting his arm around her shoulders. 'You were very clear yesterday about the regrettable necessity of certain practicalities. I'm sorry you missed the lecture, Rhinemann. It concerned the concentration of Jewish money ... We're here. Let's get on with it.'

Rhinemann stepped away from the railing. 'We shall. But first, so the ... circle is complete, I wish to present to you an acquaintance who has flown in from Berlin. By way of neutral passage, of course. I want you to have the opportunity of knowing you deal *directly* with *him*. The exchange is more *genuine* this way.'

Spaulding looked over at the blond-haired man in the white Palm Beach suit. Their eyes locked.

'Franz Altmüller, Ministry of Armaments. Berlin,' said David.

'Colonel David Spaulding. Fairfax. Late of Portugal. The man in Lisbon,' said Altmüller.

'You are jackals,' added Rhinemann, 'who fight as traitors fight and dishonor your houses. I say this to you both. For both to hear ... Now, as you say, colonel, we shall get on with it.'

Stoltz took Lyons below to the manicured lawn by the pool. There, at a large, round table, a Rhinemann guard stood with a metal attaché case in his hand. Lyons sat down, his back to the balcony; the guard lifted the case onto the table.

'Open it,' commanded Erich Rhinemann from above.

The guard did so; Lyons took out the plans and spread them on the table.

Altmüller spoke. 'Remain with him, Stoltz.'

Stoltz looked up, bewildered. However, he did not speak. He walked to the edge of the pool and sat in a deck chair, his eyes fixed on Lyons.

Altmüller turned to Jean. 'May I have a word with the colonel, please?'

Jean looked at Spaulding. She took her hand from his and walked to the far end of the balcony. Rhinemann remained in the center, staring down at Lyons.

'For both our sakes,' said Altmüller, 'I think you should tell me what happened in San Telmo.'

David watched the German closely. Altmüller was not lying; he was not trying to trap him. *He did not know about the Haganah. About Asher Feld.* It was Spaulding's only chance.

'Gestapo,' said David, giving the lie the simplicity of conviction.

'*Impossible!*' Altmüller spat out the word. 'You *know* that's impossible! *I* am here!'

'I've dealt with the Gestapo – in various forms – for nearly four years. I know the enemy ... Grant me that much credit.'

'You're wrong! There's *no possible way*!'

'You've spent too much time in the ministry, not enough in the field. Do you want a professional analysis?'

'What is it?'

David leaned against the railing. 'You've been had.'

'*What?*'

'Just as I've been had. By those who employ our considerable talents. In Berlin and Washington. There's a remarkable coincidence, too . . . They both have the same initials . . . A.S.'

Altmüller stared at Spaulding, his blue eyes penetrating, his mouth parted slightly – in disbelief. He spoke the name under his breath.

'*Albert Speer . . .*'

'*Alan Swanson,*' countered David softly.

'It can't *be*,' said Altmüller with less conviction than he wished to muster. 'He doesn't know . . .'

'Don't go into the field without some advanced training. You won't last . . . Why do you think I offered to make a deal with Rhinemann?'

Altmüller was listening but not listening. He took his eyes from Spaulding, seemingly consumed with the pieces of an incredible puzzle. 'If what you say is true – and by no means do I agree – the codes would not be sent, the transfer aborted. There would be no radio silence; your fleet cruising, radar and aircraft in operation. Everything lost!'

David folded his arms in front of him. It was the moment when the lie would either be bought or rejected out of hand. He knew it; he felt as he had felt scores of times in the north country when *the lie* was the keystone. 'Your side plays rougher than mine. It goes with the New Order. My people won't kill me; they just want to make sure I don't know anything. All they care about are those designs . . . With you it's different. Your people keep their options open.'

David stopped and smiled at Rhinemann, who had turned from his sentry position by the balcony and was looking at them. Altmüller kept his eyes on Spaulding . . . the inexperienced 'runner' being taught, thought David.

'And in your judgment, what are these options?'

'A couple I can think of,' replied Spaulding. 'Immobilize me, force in another code man at the last minute, substitute faulty blueprints; or get the diamonds out from Ocho Calle some other way than by water – difficult with those crates, but not impossible.'

'Then why should I not let these options be exercised? You tempt me.'

Spaulding had been glancing up, at nothing. Suddenly he turned and looked at Altmüller. 'Don't *ever* go into the field; you won't last a day. Stay at your ministry.'

'What does that mean?'

'Any alternate strategy used, you're dead. You're a liability now. You "dealt" with the enemy. Speer knows it, the Gestapo knows it. Your only chance is to *use* what you know. Just like me. You for your life; me for a great deal of money. Christ knows the aircraft companies will make a pile; I deserve some of it.'

Altmüller took two steps to the railing and stood alongside David, looking down at the distant river below. 'It's all so pointless.'

'Not when you think about it,' said Spaulding. 'Something for nothing never is in this business.'

David, staring straight ahead, could feel Altmüller's eyes abruptly on him. He could sense the new thought coming into focus in Altmüller's mind.

'Your generosity may be your undoing, colonel ... We can still have something for nothing. And I, a hero's medal from the Reich. We have you. Mrs Cameron. The physicist's expendable, I'm sure ... You *will* send the codes. You were willing to negotiate for money. Surely you'll negotiate for your lives.'

Like Altmüller, David stared straight ahead when he replied. His arms still folded, he was irritatingly relaxed, as he knew he had to be. 'Those negotiations have been concluded. If Lyons approves the blueprints, I'll send the codes when he and Mrs Cameron are back at the embassy. Not before.'

'You'll send them when I *order* you to.' Altmüller was finding it difficult to keep his voice low. Rhinemann looked over again but made no move to interfere. Spaulding understood. Rhinemann was toying with his jackals.

'Sorry to disappoint you,' said David.

'Then extremely unpleasant things will happen. To Mrs Cameron first.'

'Give it up.' David sighed. 'Play by the original rules. You haven't a chance.'

'You talk confidently for a man alone.'

Spaulding pushed himself off the railing and turned, facing the German. He spoke barely above a whisper. 'You really are a goddamned fool. You wouldn't last an hour in Lisbon ... Do you think I drove in here without any back-ups? Do you think Rhinemann *expected* me to? ... We men in the field are very cautious, very cowardly; we're not heroic at all. We don't blow up buildings if there's a chance we'll still be inside. We won't destroy an enemy bridge unless there's another way back to our side.'

'You *are* alone. There are no bridges left for you!'

David looked at Altmüller as if appraising a bad cut of meat, then glanced at his watch. 'Your Stolz was a fool. If I don't make a call within fifteen minutes, there'll be a lot of busy telephones resulting in God knows how many very official automobiles driving out to Luján. I'm a military attaché stationed at the American embassy. I accompanied the ambassador's daughter to Luján. That's enough.'

'That's preposterous! This is a neutral city. Rhinemann would ...'

'*Rhinemann* would open the gates and throw the jackals out,' interrupted Spaulding quietly and very calmly. 'We're liabilities both of us. "Tortugas" could blow up in his postwar face. He's not going to allow that. Whatever he thinks of the systems, yours *or* mine, it doesn't matter. Only one thing matters to him: the cause of Erich Rhinemann ... I thought you knew that. You picked him.'

Altmüller was breathing steadily, a bit too deeply, thought David. He was imposing a control on himself and he was only barely succeeding.

'You ... have made arrangements to send the codes? From here?'

The lie was bought. The keystone was now in place.

'The rules are back in force. Radio and radar silence. No air strikes on surfacing submarines. No interception of trawlers ... under Paraguayan flags entering the coastal zones. We both win ... Which do you want, jackal?'

Altmüller turned back to the railing and placed his hands on the marble top. His fingers were rigid against the stone. The tailored folds of his white Palm Beach suit were starchly immobile. He looked down at the river and spoke.

'The rules of "Tortugas" are reinstated.'

'I have a telephone call to make.' said David.

'I expected you would,' replied Rhinemann, looking contemptuously at Franz Altmüller. 'I have no stomach for an embassy kidnapping. It serves no one.'

'Don't be too harsh,' said Spaulding agreeably. 'It got me here in record time.'

'Make your call.' Rhinemann pointed to a telephone on a table next to the archway. 'Your conversation will be amplified, of course.'

'Of course,' answered David, walking to the phone.

'Radio room ...' came the words from the unseen speakers.

'This is Lieutenant Colonel Spaulding, military attaché,' said David, interrupting Ballard's words.

There was the slightest pause before Ballard replied.

'Yes, sir, Colonel Spaulding?'

'I issued a directive of inquiry prior to my conference this afternoon. You may void it now.'

'Yes, sir ... Very good, sir.'

'May I speak with the head cryptographer, please? A Mr Ballard, I believe.'

'I'm ... Ballard, sir.'

'Sorry,' said David curtly, 'I didn't recognize you, Ballard. Be ready to send out the sealed code schedules I prepared for you. The green envelope; open it and familiarize yourself with the progressions. When I give you the word, I want it transmitted immediately. On a black-drape priority.'

'What ... sir?'

'My authorization is black drape, Ballard. It's in the lex, so clear all scrambler channels. You'll get no flak with that priority. I'll call you back.'

'Yes, sir ...'

David hung up, hoping to Christ that Ballard was as good at his job as David thought he was. Or as good at parlor games as Henderson Granville thought he was.

'You're very efficient,' said Rhinemann.

'I try to be,' said David.

Ballard stared at the telephone. What was Spaulding trying to tell him? Obviously that Jean was all right; that he and Lyons were all right, too. At least for the time being.

Be ready to send out the sealed code schedules I prepared ...

David had not prepared any codes. *He* had. Spaulding had memorized the progressions, that was true, but only as a contingency.

What goddamned *green envelope?*

There was no envelope, red, blue or green!

What the hell was that nonsense ... *black-drape priority?*

What was a black drape? It didn't make sense!

But it *was* a key.

It's in the lex ...

Lex ... Lexicon. The Lexicon of Cryptography!

Black drape ... He recalled something ... something very obscure, way in the past. *Black drape* was a very old term, long obsolete. But it *meant* something.

Ballard got out of his swivel chair and went to the bookshelf on the other side of the small radio room. He had not looked at *The Lexicon of Cryptography* in years. It was a useless, and, academic tome ... Obsolete.

It was on the top shelf with the other useless reference books and, like the others, had gathered dust.

He found the term on page 71. It was a single paragraph sandwiched between equally meaningless paragraphs. But it had meaning now.

'The Black Drape, otherwise known as *Schwarzes Tuch*, for it was first employed by the German Imperial Army in 1916, is an entrapment device. It is hazardous for it cannot be repeated in a sector twice. It is a signal to proceed with a code, activating a given set of arrangements with intent to terminate, canceling said arrangements. The termination factor is expressed in minutes, specifically numbered. As a practice, it was abandoned in 1917 for it nullified ...'

Proceed ... with intent to terminate.

Ballard closed the book and returned to his chair in front of the dials.

Lyons kept turning the pages of the designs back and forth as if double-checking his calculations. Rhinemann called down twice from the balcony, inquiring if there were problems. Twice Lyons turned in his chair and shook his head. Stoltz remained in the deck chair by the pool, smoking cigarettes. Altmüller talked briefly with Rhinemann, the conversation obviously unsatisfactory to both. Altmüller returned to the chair by the glass-topped table and leafed through a Buenos Aires newspaper.

David and Jean remained at the far end of the terrace, talking quietly. Every once in a while Spaulding let his voice carry across; if Altmüller listened, he heard references to New York, to architectural firms, to vague postwar plans. Lovers' plans.

But these references were non sequiturs.

'At the Alvear Hotel,' said David softly, holding Jean's hand, 'there's a man registered under the name of E. Pace. *E. Pace.* His real name is Asher Feld. Identify yourself as the contact from me ... and a Fairfax agent named Barden. Ira Barden. Nothing else. Tell him I'm calling his ... priorities. In

precisely two hours from . . . the minute you telephone from the embassy . . .
I *mean* the minute, Jean, he'll understand . . .'

Only once did Jean Cameron gasp, an intake of breath that caused David
to glare at her and press her hand. She covered her shock with artificial
laughter.

Altmüller looked up from the newspaper. Contempt was in his eyes;
beyond the contempt, and also obvious, was his anger.

Lyons got up from the chair and stretched his emaciated frame. He had spent
three hours and ten minutes at the table; he turned and looked up at the
balcony. At Spaulding.

He nodded.

'Good,' said Rhinemann, crossing to Franz Altmüller. 'We'll proceed. It
will be dark soon; we'll conclude everything by early morning. No more
delay! Stoltz! *Kommen Sie her! Bringen Sie die Aktenmappe!*'

Stoltz went to the table and began replacing the pages in the attaché case.

David took Jean's arm and guided her towards Rhinemann and Altmüller.
The Nazi spoke.

'The plans comprise four hundred and sixty-odd pages of causal data and
progressive equations. No man can retain such information; the absence of
any part renders the designs useless. As soon as you contact the
cryptographer and relay the codes, Mrs Cameron and the physicist are free to
leave.'

'I'm sorry,' said Spaulding. 'My agreement was to send the codes when
they were back at the embassy. That's the way it has to be.'

'*Surely,*' interjected Rhinemann angrily, 'you don't think I would
permit . . .'

'No, I don't,' broke in David. 'But I'm not sure what you can control
outside the gates of Habichtsnest. This way, I know you'll try harder.'

42

It was an hour and thirty-one minutes before the telephone rang. Nine fifteen, exactly. The sun had descended behind the Luján hills; the lights along the distant riverbank flickered in the enveloping darkness.

Rhinemann picked up the receiver, listened and nodded to David.

Spaulding got out of his chair and crossed to the financier, taking the receiver. Rhinemann flicked a switch on the wall. The speakers were activated.

'We're here, David.' Jean's words were amplified on the terrace.

'Fine,' answered Spaulding. 'No problems then?'

'Not really. After five miles or so I thought Doctor Lyons was going to be sick. They drove so fast . . .'

After . . . five . . .

Asher . . . Feld . . .

Jean had done it!

'But he's all right now?'

'He's resting. It'll take some time before he feels himself . . .'

Time.

Jean had given Asher Feld the precise *time.*

'All right . . .'

'*Genug! Genug!*' said Altmüller, standing by the balcony. 'That's enough. You have your proof; they are there. The codes!'

David looked over at the Nazi. It was an unhurried look, not at all accommodating.

'Jean?'

'Yes?'

'You're in the radio room?'

'Yes.'

'Let me speak to that Ballard fellow.'

'Here he is.'

Ballard's voice was impersonal, efficient. 'Colonel Spaulding?'

'Ballard, have you cleared all scrambler channels?'

'Yes, sir. Along with your priority. The drape's confirmed, sir.'

'Very good. Stand by for my call. It shouldn't be more than a few minutes.' David quickly hung up the phone.

'What are you doing?!' yelled Altmüller furiously. 'The *codes*! *Send them!*'

'He's *betraying* us!' screamed Stoltz, jumping up from his chair.

'I think you should explain yourself.' Rhinemann spoke softly, his voice conveying the punishment he intended to inflict.

'Just last-minute details,' said Spaulding, lighting a cigarette. 'Only a few minutes ... Shall we talk alone, Rhinemann?'

'That is unnecessary. What is it?' asked the financier. 'Your method of departure? It's arranged. You'll be driven to the Mendarro field with the designs. It's less than ten minutes from here. You won't be airborne, however, until we have confirmation of the Koening transfer.'

'How long will that be?'

'What difference does it make?'

'Once the blackout starts I have no protection, *that's* the difference.'

'*Ach!*' Rhinemann was impatient. 'For four hours you'll have the best protection in the world. I have no stomach for offending the men in Washington!'

'You see?' said David to Franz Altmüller. 'I told you we were liabilities.' He turned back to Rhinemann. 'All right. I accept that. You've got too much to lose. Detail number one, crossed off. Now detail number two. My payment from you.'

Rhinemann squinted his eyes. 'You *are* a man of details ... The sum of five hundred thousand American dollars will be transferred to the Banque Louis Quatorze in Zürich. It's a non-negotiable figure and a generous one.'

'Extremely. More than I would have asked for ... What's my guarantee?'

'Come, colonel. We're not *salesmen*. You know where I live; your abilities are proven. I don't wish the specter of the man from Lisbon on my personal horizon.'

'You flatter me.'

'The money will be deposited, the proper papers held in Zürich for you. At the bank; normal procedures.'

David crushed out his cigarette. 'All right, Zürich ... Now the last detail. Those generous payments I'm going to receive right at home ... The names, please. Write them on a piece of paper.'

'Are you so sure I possess these names?'

'It's the only thing I'm really sure of. It's the one opportunity you wouldn't miss.'

Rhinemann took a small black leather notebook from his jacket pocket and wrote hastily on a page. He tore it out and handed it to Spaulding.

David read the names:

Kendall, Walter
Swanson, A. US Army
Oliver, H. Meridian Aircraft
Craft, J. Packard

'Thank you,' said Spaulding. He put the page in his pocket and reached for the telephone. 'Get me the American embassy, please.'

Ballard read the sequence of the code progressions David had recited to him. They were not perfect but they were not far off, either; Spaulding had confused a vowel equation, but the message was clear.

And David's emphasis on the 'frequency megacycle of 120 for all subsequent scrambles' was meaningless gibberish. But it, too, was very clear.

120 minutes.

Black Drape.

The original code allowed for thirteen characters:

CABLE TORTUGAS

The code Spaulding had recited, however, had fifteen characters.
Ballard stared at the words.

DESTROY TORTUGAS

In two hours.

David had a final 'detail' which none could fault professionally, but all found objectionable. Since there were four hours – more or less – before he'd be driven to the Mendarro airfield, and there were any number of reasons during this period why he might be out of sight of the designs – or Rhinemann might be out of sight of the designs – he insisted that they be placed in a single locked metal case and chained to any permanent structure, the chain held by a new padlock, the keys given to him. Further, he would also hold the keys to the case and thread the hasps. If the designs were tampered with, he'd know it.

'Your precautions are now obsessive,' said Rhinemann disagreeably. 'I should ignore you. The codes have been sent.'

'Then humor me. I'm a Fairfax four-zero. We might work again.'

Rhinemann smiled. 'That is always the way, is it not? So be it.'

Rhinemann sent for a chain and a padlock, which he took a minor delight in showing to David in its original box. The ritual was over in several minutes, the metal case chained to the banister of the stairway in the great hall. The four men settled in the huge living room, to the right of the hall, an enormous archway affording a view of the staircase ... and the metal briefcase.

The financier became genial host. He offered brandies; only Spaulding accepted at first, then Heinrich Stoltz followed. Altmüller would not drink.

A guard, his paramilitary uniform pressed into starched creases, came through the archway.

'Our operators confirm radio silence, sir. Throughout the entire coastal zone.'

'Thank you,' said Rhinemann. 'Stand by on all frequencies.'

The guard nodded. He turned and left the room as quickly as he had entered.

'Your men are efficient,' observed David.

'They're paid to be,' answered Rhinemann, looking at his watch. 'Now, we wait. Everything progresses and we have merely to wait. I'll order a buffet. Canapés are hardly filling ... and we have the time.'

'You're hospitable,' said Spaulding, carrying his brandy to a chair next to Altmüller.

'And generous. Don't forget that.'

'It would be hard to ... I was wondering, however, if I might impose further?' David placed his brandy glass on the side table and gestured at his rumpled, ill-fitting clothes. 'These were borrowed from a ranch hand. God knows when they were last washed. Or me ... I'd appreciate a shower, a shave; perhaps a pair of trousers and a shirt, or a sweater ...'

'I'm sure your army personnel can accommodate you,' said Altmüller, watching David suspiciously.

'For Christ's sake, Altmüller, I'm not *going* anywhere! Except to a shower. The designs are over there!' Spaulding pointed angrily through the archway to the metal case chained to the banister of the stairway. 'If you think I'm leaving without *that*, you're retarded.'

The insult infuriated the Nazi; he gripped the arms of his chair controlling himself. Rhinemann laughed and spoke to Altmüller.

'The colonel has had a tiresome few days. His request is minor; and I can assure you he is going nowhere but to the Mendarro airfield ... I wish he were. He'd save me a half-million dollars.'

David responded to Rhinemann's laugh with one of his own. 'A man with that kind of money in Zürich should at least *feel* clean.' He rose from the chair. 'And you're right about the last few days. I'm bushed. And sore all over. If the bed is soft I'll grab a nap.' He looked over at Altmüller. 'With a battalion of armed guards at the door if it'll ease the little boy's concerns.'

Altmüller shot up, his voice harsh and loud. '*Enough!*'

'Oh sit down,' said David. 'You look foolish.'

Rhinemann's guard brought him a pair of trousers, a lightweight turtleneck sweater and a tan suede jacket, David saw that each was expensive and he knew each would fit. Shaving equipment was in the bathroom; if there was anything else he needed, all he had to do was open the door and ask. The man would be outside in the hall. Actually, there would be two men.

David understood.

He told the guard – a *porteño* – that he would sleep for an hour, then shower and shave for his journey. Would the guard be so considerate as to make sure he was awake by eleven o'clock?

The guard would do so.

It was five minutes past ten on David's watch. Jean had phoned at precisely nine fifteen. Asher Feld had exactly two hours from nine fifteen.

David had one hour and five minutes.

Eleven fifteen.

If Asher Feld really believed in his priorities.

The room was large, had a high ceiling and two double-casement windows three stories above the ground, and was in the east wing of the house. That was all Spaulding could tell – or wanted to study – while the lights were on.

He turned them off and went back to the windows. He opened the left casement quietly, peering out from behind the drapes.

The roof was slate; that wasn't good. It had a wide gutter; that was better. The gutter led to a drainpipe about twenty feet away. That was satisfactory.

Directly beneath, on the second floor, were four small balconies that probably led to four bedrooms. The farthest balcony was no more than five feet from the drainpipe. Possibly relevant; probably not.

Below, the lawn like all the grounds at Habichtsnest: manicured, greenish black in the moonlight, full; with white wrought-iron outdoor furniture dotted about, and flagstone walks bordered by rows of flowers. Curving away from the area beneath his windows was a wide, raked path that disappeared into the darkness and the trees. He remembered seeing that path from the far right end of the terrace overlooking the pool; he remembered the intermittent, unraked hoofprints. The path was for horses; it had to lead to stables somewhere beyond the trees.

That *was* relevant; relevancy, at this point, being relative.

And then Spaulding saw the cupped glow of a cigarette behind a latticed arbour thirty-odd feet from the perimeter of the wrought-iron furniture. Rhinemann may have expressed confidence that he, David, would be on his way to Mendarro in a couple of hours, but that confidence was backed up by men on watch.

No surprise; the surprise would have been the absence of such patrols. It was one of the reasons he counted on Asher Feld's priorities.

He let the drapes fall back into place, stepped away from the window and went to the canopied bed. He pulled down the blankets and stripped to his shorts – coarse underdrawers he had found in the adobe hut to replace his own bloodstained ones. He lay down and closed his eyes with no intention of sleeping. Instead, he pictured the high, electrified fence down at the gate of Habichtsnest. As he had seen it while Rhinemann's guards searched him against the battered FMF automobile.

To the right of the huge gate. To the east.

The floodlights had thrown sufficient illumination for him to see the slightly angling curvature of the fence line as it receded into the woods. Not much but definite.

North by northeast.

He visualized once again the balcony above the pool. Beyond the railing at the far right end of the terrace where he had talked quietly with Jean. He concentrated on the area below – in front, to the right.

North by northeast.

He saw it clearly. The grounds to the right of the croquet course and the tables sloped gently downhill until they were met by the tall trees of the surrounding woods. It was into these woods that the bridle path below him now entered. And as the ground descended – ultimately a mile down to the riverbanks – he remembered the breaks in the patterns of the far-off treetops. Again to the right.

Fields.

If there were horses – and there *were* horses – and stables – and there *had* to be stables – then there were fields. For the animals to graze and race off the frustrations of the wooded, confining bridle paths.

The spaces between the descending trees were carved-out pasture lands, there was no other explanation.

North by northeast.

He shifted his thoughts to the highway two miles south of the marble steps of Habichtsnest, the highway that cut through the outskirts of Luján toward Buenos Aires. He remembered: the road, although high above the river at the Habichtsnest intersection, curved to the *left* and went *downhill* into the Tigre district. He tried to recall precisely the first minutes of the nightmare ride in the Bentley that ended in smoke and fire and death in the Colinas Rojas. The car had swung out of the hidden entrance and for several miles sped east *and* down *and* slightly north. It finally paralleled the shoreline of the river.

North by northeast.

And then he pictured the river below the terraced balcony, dotted with white sails and cabin cruisers. It flowed diagonally away . . . to the right.

North by northeast.

That was his escape.

Down the bridle path into the protective cover of the dark woods and northeast toward the breaks in the trees – the fields. Across the fields, always heading to the right – east, and downhill, north. Back into the sloping forest, following the line of the river, until he found the electrified fence bordering the enormous compound that was Habichtsnest.

Beyond that fence was the highway to Buenos Aires. And the embassy. And Jean.

David let his body go limp, let the ache of his wound run around in circles on his torn skin. He breathed steadily, deeply. He had to remain calm; that was the hardest part.

He looked at his watch – his gift from Jean. It was nearly eleven o'clock. He got out of the bed and put on the trousers and the sweater. He slipped into his shoes and pulled the laces as tight as he could, until the leather pinched his feet, then reached for the pillow and wrapped the soiled shirt from the outback ranch around it. He replaced the pillow at the top of the bed and pulled the blanket partially over it. He lifted the sheets, bunched them, inserted the ranch hand's trousers and let the blankets fall back in place.

He stood up. In the darkness, and with what light would come from the hallway, the bed looked sufficiently full at least for his immediate purpose.

He crossed to the door and pressed his back into the wall beside it.

His watch read one minute to eleven.

The tapping was loud; the guard was not subtle.

The door opened.

'*Señor? . . . Señor?*'

The door opened further.

'*Señor*, it's time. It's eleven o'clock.'

The guard stood in the frame, looking at the bed. '*Él duerme,*' he said casually over his shoulder.

'Señor *Spaulding*!' The guard walked into the darkened room.

The instant the man cleared the door panel, David took a single step and with both hands clasped the guard's neck from behind. He crushed his fingers into the throat and yanked the man diagonally into him.

No cry emerged; the guard's windpipe was choked of all air supply. He went down, limp.

Spaulding closed the door slowly and snapped on the wall switch.

'*Thanks very much,*' he said loudly. 'Give me a hand, will you please? My stomach hurts like *hell . . .*'

It was no secret at Habichtsnest that the American had been wounded.

David bent over the collapsed guard. He massaged his throat, pinched his nostrils, put his lips to the man's mouth and blew air into the damaged windpipe.

The guard responded; conscious but not conscious. In semi-shock.

Spaulding removed the man's Luger from his belt holster and a large hunting knife from a scabbard beside it. He put the blade underneath the man's jaw and drew blood with the sharp point. He whispered. In Spanish.

'Understand me! I want you to laugh! You start laughing *now*! If you don't, this goes home. Right up through your neck! . . . Now. *Laugh!*'

The guard's crazed eyes carried his total lack of comprehension. He seemed to know only that he was dealing with a maniac. A madman who would kill him.

Feebly at first, then with growing volume and panic, the man laughed.

Spaulding laughed with him.

The laughter grew; David kept staring at the guard, gesturing for louder, more enthusiastic merriment. The man – perplexed beyond reason and totally frightened – roared hysterically.

Spaulding heard the click of the doorknob two feet from his ear. He crashed the barrel of the Luger into the guard's head and stood up as the second man entered.

'*Qué pasa, Antonio? Te re—*'

The Luger's handle smashed into the Argentine's skull with such force that the guard's expulsion of breath was as loud as his voice as he fell.

David looked at his watch. It was eight minutes past eleven. Seven minutes to go.

If the man named Asher Feld believed the words he spoke with such commitment.

Spaulding removed the second guard's weapons, putting the additional

Luger into his belt. He searched both men's pockets, removing whatever paper currency he could find. And a few coins.

He had no money whatsoever. He might well need money.

He ran into the bathroom and turned on the shower to the hottest position on the dial. He returned to the hallway door and locked it. Then he turned off all lights and went to the left casement window, closing his eyes to adjust to the darkness outside. He opened them and blinked several times, trying to blur out the white spots of anxiety.

It was nine minutes past eleven.

He rubbed his perspiring hands over the expensive turtleneck sweater; he took deep breaths and waited.

The waiting was nearly unendurable.

Because he could not know.

And then he heard it! And he knew.

Two thunderous explosions! So loud, so stunning, so totally without warning that he found himself trembling, his breathing stopped.

There followed bursts of machine-gun fire that ripped through the silent night.

Below him on the ground, men were screaming at one another, racing toward the sounds that were filling the perimeter of the compound with growing ferocity.

David watched the hysteria below. There were five guards beneath his window, all running now out of their concealed stations. He could see the spill of additional floodlights being turned on to his right, in the elegant front courtyard of Habichtsnest. He could hear the roar of powerful automobile engines and the increasing frequency of panicked commands.

He eased himself out of the casement window, holding onto the sill until his feet touched the gutter.

Both Lugers were in his belt, the knife between his teeth. He could not chance a blade next to his body; he could always spit it out if necessary. He sidestepped his way along the slate roof. The drainpipe was only feet away.

The explosions and the gunfire from the gate increased. David marveled – not only at Asher Feld's commitment, but at his logistics. The Haganah leader must have brought a small, well-supplied army into Habichtsnest.

He lowered his body cautiously against the slate roof; he reached out, gripped the gutter on the far side of the drainpipe with his right hand and slowly, carefully crouched sideways, inched his feet into a support position. He pushed against the outside rim of the gutter, testing its strength, and in a quick-springing short jump, he leaped over the side, holding the rim with both hands, his feet against the wall, straddling the drainpipe.

He began his descent, hand-below-hand on the pipe.

Amid the sounds of the gunfire, he suddenly heard loud crashing above him. There were shouts in both German and Spanish and the unmistakable smashing of wood.

The room he had just left had been broken into.

The extreme north second-floor balcony was parallel with him now. He reached out with his left hand, gripped the edge, whipped his right hand across for support and swung underneath, his body dangling thirty feet above the ground but out of sight.

Men were at the casement windows above. They forced the lead frames open without regard to the handles; the glass smashed; metal screeched against metal.

There was another thunderous explosion from the battleground a quarter of a mile away in the black-topped field cut out of the forest. A far-off weapon caused a detonation in the front courtyard; the spill of floodlight suddenly disappeared. Asher Feld was moving up. The crossfire would be murderous. Suicidal.

The shouts above Spaulding receded from the window, and he kicked his feet out twice to get sufficient swing to lash his hands once more across and around the drainpipe.

He did so, the blade between his teeth making his jaws ache.

He slid to the ground, scraping his hands against the weathered metal, insensitive to the cuts on his palms and fingers.

He removed the knife from his mouth, a Luger from his belt and raced along the edge of the raked bridle path toward the darkness of the trees. He ran into the pitch-black, tree-lined corridor, skirting the trunks, prepared to plunge between them at the first sound of nearby shots.

They came, four in succession, the bullets thumping with terrible finality into the surrounding tall shafts of wood.

He whipped around a thick trunk and looked toward the house. The man firing was alone, standing by the drainpipe. Then a second guard joined him, racing from the area of the croquet course, a giant Doberman straining at its leash in his hand. The men shouted at one another, each trying to assert command, the dog barking savagely.

As they stood yelling, two bursts of machine-gun fire came from within the front courtyard; two more floodlights exploded.

David saw the men freeze, their concentration shifted to the front. The guard with the dog yanked at the straps, forcing the animal back into the side of the house. The second man crouched, then rose and started sidestepping his way rapidly along the building toward the courtyard, ordering his associate to follow.

And then David saw him. Above. To the right. Through foliage. On the terrace overlooking the lawn and the pool.

Erich Rhinemann had burst through the doors, screaming commands in fury, but not in panic. He was marshaling his forces, implementing his defences . . . somehow in the pitch of the assault, he was the messianic Caesar ordering his battalions to attack, attack, *attack*. Three men came into view behind him; he roared at them and two of the three raced back into Habichtsnest. The third man argued; Rhinemann shot him without the slightest hesitation. The body collapsed out of David's sight. Then Rhinemann ran to the wall, partially obscured by the railing, but not entirely. He seemed to be yelling into the wall.

Screeching *into the wall.*

Through the bursts of gunfire, David heard the muted, steady whirring and he realized what Rhinemann was doing.

The cable car from the riverbank was being sent up for him.

While the battle was engaged, this Caesar would escape the fire.

Rhinemann the pig. The ultimate manipulator. Corruptor of all things, honoring nothing.

We may work again ...

That is always the way, is it not?

David sprang out of his recessed sanctuary and ran back on the path to the point where the gardens and woods joined the lawn below the balcony. He raced to a white metal table with the wrought-iron legs – the same table at which Lyons had sat, his frail body bent over the blueprints. Rhinemann was nowhere in sight.

He *had to be there*!

It was suddenly ... inordinately clear to Spaulding that the one meaningful aspect of his having been ripped out of Lisbon and transported half a world away – through the fire and the pain – was the man above him now, concealed on the balcony.

'*Rhinemann! ... Rhinemann! I'm here!*'

The immense figure of the financier came rushing to the railing. In his hand was a Sternlicht automatic. Powerful, murderous.

'*You. You are a dead man!*' He began firing; David threw himself to the ground behind the table, overturning it, erecting a shield. Bullets thumped into the earth and ricocheted off the metal. Rhinemann continued screaming. 'Your tricks are *suicide*, Lisbon! My men come from everywhere! *Hundreds!* In minutes! ... Come, Lisbon! Show yourself. You merely move up your death! You think I would have let *you live*? *Never!* Show yourself! You're *dead!*'

David understood. The manipulator would not offend the men in Washington, but neither would he allow the man from Lisbon to remain on his *personal horizon*. The designs would have gone to Mendarro. Not the man from Lisbon.

He would have been killed on his way to Mendarro.

It was *so* clear.

David raised his Luger, he would have only an instant. A diversion, then an instant.

It would be enough ...

The lessons of the north country.

He reached down and clawed at the ground, gathering chunks of earth and lawn with his left hand. When he had a large fistful, he lobbed it into the air, to the *left* of the rim of metal. Black dirt and blades of grass floated up, magnified in the dim spills of light and the furious activity growing nearer.

There was a steady burst of fire from the Sternlicht. Spaulding sprang to the *right* of the table and squeezed the trigger of the Luger five times in rapid succession.

Erich Rhinemann's face exploded in blood. The Sternlicht fell as his hands sprang up in the spasm of death. The immense body snapped backward, then forward; then lurched over the railing.

Rhinemann plummeted down from the balcony.

David heard the screams of the guards above and raced back to the darkness of the bridle path. He ran with all his strength down the twisting black corridor, his shoes sinking intermittently into the soft, raked edges.

The path abruptly curved. To the *left*.

Goddamn it!

And then he heard the whinnies of frightened horses. His nostrils picked up their smells and to his right he saw the one-story structure that housed the series of stalls that was the stables. He could hear the bewildered shouts of a groom somewhere within trying to calm his charges.

For a split second, David toyed with an idea, then rejected it. A horse would be swift, but possibly unmanageable.

He ran to the far end of the stables, turned the corner and stopped for breath, for a moment of orientation. He thought he knew where he was; he tried to picture an aerial view of the compound.

The fields! The fields had to be nearby.

He ran to the opposite end of the one-story structure and saw the pastures beyond. As he had visualized, the ground sloped gently downward – north – but not so much as to make grazing or running difficult. In the distance past the fields, he could see the wooded hills rise in the moonlight. To the right – east.

Between the slope of the fields and the rise of the hills was the line he had to follow. It was the most direct, concealed route to the electrified fence.

North by northeast.

He sped to the high post-and-rail fence that bordered the pasture, slipped through and began racing across the field. The volleys and salvos of gunfire continued behind him – in the distance now, but seemingly no less brutal. He reached a ridge in the field that gave him a line of sight to the river a half-mile below. It, too, was bordered by a high post-and-rail, used to protect the animals from plummeting down the steeper inclines. He could see lights being turned on along the river; the incessant crescendos of death were being carried by the summer winds to the elegant communities below.

He spun in shock. A bullet whined above him. It had been *aimed* at him! He had been spotted!

He threw himself into the pasture grass and scrambled away. There was a slight incline and he let himself roll down it, over and over again until his body hit the hard wood of a post. He had reached the opposite border of the field; beyond, the woods continued.

He heard the fierce howling of the dogs, and knew it was directed at him.

On his knees, he could see the outlines of a huge animal streaking toward him across the grass. His Luger was poised, level, but he understood that by firing it, he would betray his position. He shifted the weapon to his left hand and pulled the hunting knife out of his belt.

The black monstrosity leaped through the air, honed by the scent into his target of human flesh. Spaulding lashed out his left hand with the Luger, feeling the impact of the hard, muscular fur of the Doberman on his upper body, watching the ugly head whip sideways, the bared teeth tearing at the loose sweater and into his arm.

He swung his right hand upward, the knife gripped with all the strength he had, into the soft stomach of the animal. Warm blood erupted from the dog's lacerated belly; the swallowed sound of a savage roar burst from the animal's throat as it died.

David grabbed his arm. The Doberman's teeth had ripped into his skin below the shoulder. And the wrenching, rolling, twisting movements of his body had broken at least one of the stitches in his stomach wound.

He held onto the rail of the pasture fence and crawled east.

North by northeast! Not *east*, goddamn it!

In his momentary shock, he suddenly realized there was a perceptible reduction of the distant gunfire. How many minutes had it *not* been there? The explosions seemed to continue but the small-arms fire was subsiding. Considerably.

There were shouts now; from across the field by the stables. He looked between and over the grass. Men were running with flashlights, the beams darting about in shafting diagonals. David could hear shouted commands.

What he saw made him stop all movement and stare incredulously. The flashlights of the men across the wide pasture were focused on a figure coming out of the stable – on horseback! The spill of a dozen beams picked up the glaring reflection of a white Palm Beach suit.

Franz Altmüller!

Altmüller had chosen the madness he, David, had rejected.

But, of course, their roles were different.

Spaulding knew he was the quarry now. Altmüller, the hunter.

There would be others following, but Altmüller would not, *could* not wait. He kicked at the animal's flanks and burst through the opened gate.

Spaulding understood again. Franz Altmüller was a dead man if David lived. His only means of survival in Berlin was to produce the corpse of the man from Lisbon. The Fairfax agent who had crippled 'Tortugas'; the body of the man the patrols and the scientists in Ocho Calle could identify. The man the 'Gestapo' had unearthed and provoked.

So much, so alien.

Horse and rider came racing across the field. David stayed prone and felt the hard earth to the east. He could not stand; Altmüller held a powerful, wide-beamed flashlight. If he rolled under the railing, the tall weeds and taller grass beyond might conceal him but just as easily might bend, breaking the pattern.

If ... might.

He knew he was rationalizing. The tall grass would be best; out of sight. But also out of strategy. And he knew why that bothered him.

He wanted to be the hunter. Not the quarry.

He wanted Altmüller dead.

Franz Altmüller was not an enemy one left alive. Altmüller was every bit as lethal in a tranquil monastery during a time of peace as he was on a battlefield in war. He was the absolute enemy; it was in his eyes. Not related to the cause of Germany, but from deep within the man's arrogance: Altmüller had watched his masterful creation collapse, had seen 'Tortugas' destroyed. By another man who had told him he was inferior.

That, Altmüller could not tolerate.

He would be scorned in the aftermath.

Unacceptable!

Altmüller would lie in wait. In Buenos Aires, in New York, in London; no matter where. And his first target would be Jean. In a rifle sight, or a knife in a crowd, or a concealed pistol at night. Altmüller would make him pay. It was in his eyes.

Spaulding hugged the earth as the galloping horse reached the midpoint of the field, plunging forward, directed by the search-light beam from the patrols back at the stables a quarter of a mile away. They were directed at the area where the Doberman was last seen.

Altmüller reined in the animal, slowing it, not stopping it. He scanned the ground in front with his beam, approaching cautiously, a gun in his hand, holding the straps but prepared to fire.

Without warning, there was a sudden, deafening explosion from the stables. The beams of light that had come from the opposite side of the field were no more; men who had started out across the pasture after Altmüller stopped and turned back to the panic that was growing furiously at the bordering fence. Fires had broken out.

Altmüller continued; if he was aware of the alarms behind him he did not show it. He kicked his horse and urged it forward.

The horse halted, snorted; it pranced its front legs awkwardly and backstepped in spite of Altmüller's commands. The Nazi was in frenzy; he screamed at the animal, but the shouts were in vain. The horse had come upon the dead Doberman; the scent of the fresh blood repelled it.

Altmüller saw the dog in the grass. He swung the light first to the left, then to the right, the beam piercing the space above David's head. Altmüller made his decision instinctively – or so it seemed to Spaulding. He whipped the reins of the horse to his right, toward David. He walked the horse; he did not run it.

Then David saw why. Altmüller was following the stains of the Doberman's blood in the grass.

David crawled as fast as he could in front of the spill of Altmüller's slow-moving beam. Once in relative darkness, he turned abruptly to his right and ran close to the ground back toward the *center* of the field. He waited until horse and rider were between him and the bordering post-and-rail, then inched his way toward the Nazi. He was tempted to take a clean shot with the Luger, but he knew that had to be the last extremity. He had several miles to go over unfamiliar terrain, with a dark forest that others knew better. The loud report of heavy-caliber pistol shot would force men out of the pandemonium a quarter of a mile away.

Nevertheless, it might be necessary.

He was within ten feet now, the Luger in his left hand, his right free ... A little closer, just a bit closer. Altmüller's flashlight slowed to a near stop. He had approached the point where he, David, had lain in the grass immobile.

Then Spaulding felt the slight breeze from behind and knew – in a terrible instant of recognition – that it was the moment to move.

The horse's head yanked up, the wide eyes bulged. The scent of David's blood-drenched clothing had reached its nostrils.

Spaulding sprang out of the grass, his right hand aimed at Altmüller's wrist. He clasped his fingers over the barrel of the gun – it was a Colt! A US Army issue Colt .45! – and forced his thumb into the trigger housing. Altmüller whipped around in shock, stunned by the totally unexpected attack. He pulled his arms back and lashed out with his feet. The horse reared high on its hind legs; Spaulding held on, forcing Altmüller's hand down, *down*. He yanked with every ounce of strength he had and literally ripped Altmüller off the horse into the grass. He slammed the Nazi's wrist into the ground again and again, until flesh hit rock and the Colt sprang loose. As it did so, he crashed his Luger into Altmüller's face.

The German fought back. He clawed at Spaulding's eyes with his free left hand, kicked furiously with his knees and feet at David's testicles and legs and rocked violently, his shoulders and head pinned by Spaulding's body. He screamed.

'*You!* You and ... *Rhinemann! Betrayal!*'

The Nazi saw the blood beneath David's shoulder and tore at the wound, ripping the already torn flesh until Spaulding thought he could not endure the pain.

Altmüller heaved his shoulder up into David's stomach, and yanked at David's bleeding arm, sending him sprawling off to the side. The Nazi leaped up on his feet, then threw himself back down on the grass where the Colt .45 had been pried loose. He worked his hands furiously over the ground.

He found the weapon.

Spaulding pulled the hunting knife from the back of his belt and sprang across the short distance that separated him from Altmüller. The Colt's barrel was coming into level position, the small black opening in front of his eyes.

As the blade entered the flesh, the ear-shattering fire of the heavy revolver exploded at the side of David's face, burning his skin, but missing its mark.

Spaulding tore the knife downward into Altmüller's chest and left it there.

The absolute enemy was dead.

David knew there was no instant to lose, or he was lost. There would be other men, other horses ... many dogs.

He raced to the bordering pasture fence, over it and into the darkness of the woods. He ran blindly, trying desperately to swing partially to his left. North.

North by northeast.

Escape!

He fell over rocks and fallen branches, then at last penetrated deepening foliage, lashing his arms for a path, any kind of path. His left shoulder was numb, both a danger and a blessing.

There was no gunfire in the distance now; only darkness and the hum of the night forest and the wild, rhythmic pounding of his chest. The fighting by the stables had stopped. Rhinemann's men were free to come after him now.

He had lost blood; how much and how severely he could not tell. Except that his eyes were growing tired, as his body was tired. The branches became heavy, coarse tentacles; the inclines, steep mountains. The slopes were enormous ravines that had to be crossed without ropes. His legs buckled and he had to force them taut again.

The fence! There was the fence!

At the bottom of a small hill, between the trees.

He began running, stumbling, clawing at the ground, pushing forward to the base of the hill.

He was there. *It* was there.

The fence.

Yet he could not touch it. But, perhaps . . .

He picked up a dry stick from the ground and lobbed it into the wire. Sparks and crackling static. To touch the fence meant death.

He looked up at the trees. The sweat from his scalp and forehead stung his eyes, blurring his already blurred vision. There had to be a tree.

A tree. The *right* tree.

He couldn't be sure. The darkness played tricks on the leaves, the limbs. There were shadows in the moonlight where substance should be.

There were no limbs! No limbs hanging over the fence whose touch meant oblivion. Rhinemann had severed – on both sides – whatever growths approached the high, linked steel wires!

He ran as best he could to his left – north. The river was perhaps a mile away. Perhaps.

Perhaps the water.

But the river, if he could reach it down the steep inclines barred to horses, would slow him up, would rob him of the time he needed desperately. And Rhinemann would have patrols on the riverbanks.

Then he saw it.

Perhaps.

A sheared limb several feet above the taut wires, coming to within a few feet of the fence! It was thick, widening into suddenly greater thickness as it joined the trunk. A labourer had taken the means of least resistance and had angled his chain saw just before the final thickness. He would not be criticized; the limb was too high, too far away, for all practical purposes.

But Spaulding knew it was his last chance. The only one left. And that fact was made indelibly clear to him with the distant sounds of men and dogs. They were coming after him now.

He removed one of the Lugers from his belt and threw it over the fence. One bulging impediment in his belt was enough.

He jumped twice before gripping a gnarled stub; his left arm aching, no longer numb, no longer a blessing. He scraped his legs up the wide trunk until his right hand grasped a higher branch. He struggled against the sharp bolts of pain in his shoulder and stomach and pulled himself up.

The sawed-off limb was just above.

He dug the sides of his shoes into the bark, jabbing them repeatedly to make tiny ridges. He strained his neck, pushing his chin into the calloused wood, and whipped both arms over his head, forcing his left elbow over the limb, pulling maniacally with his right hand. He hugged the amputated limb, peddling his feet against the tree until the momentum allowed him the force to throw his right leg over it. He pressed his arms downward and thrust himself into a sitting position, his back against the trunk.

He had managed it. Part of it.

He took several deep breaths and tried to focus his sweat-filled, stinging eyes. He looked down at the electrified barbed wire on top of the fence. It was less than four feet below him but nearly three feet in front. From the crest of the ground, about eight. If he was going to clear the wire, he had to twist and jack his body into a lateral vault. And should he be able to do that, he was not at all sure his body could take the punishment of the fall.

But he could hear the dogs and the men clearly now. They had entered the woods beyond the fields. He turned his head and saw dim shafts of light piercing the dense foliage.

The other punishment was death.

There was no point in thinking further. Thoughts were out of place now. Only motion counted.

He reached above with both hands, refusing to acknowledge the silent screams from his shoulder, grabbed at the thin branches, pulled up his legs until his feet touched the top of the thick limb and lunged, hurling himself straight out, above the taut wires until he could see their blurred image. At that split-instant, he twisted his body violently to the right and down, jackknifing his legs under him.

It was a strange, fleeting sensation: disparate feelings of final desperation and, in a very real sense, clinical objectivity. He had done all he could do. There wasn't any more.

He hit the earth, absorbing the shock with his right shoulder, rolling forward, his knees tucked under him – rolling, rolling, not permitting the roll to stop; distributing the impact throughout his body.

He was propelled over a tangle of sharp roots and collided with the base of a tree. He grabbed his stomach; the surge of pain told him the wound was open now. He would have to hold it, clutch it . . . blot it. The cloth of the turtleneck sweater was drenched with sweat and blood – his own and the Doberman's – and torn in shreds from the scores of falls and stumbles.

But he had made it.

Or nearly.

He was out of the compound. He was free from Habichtsnest.

He looked around and saw the second Luger on the ground in the moonlight ... The one in his belt would be enough. If it wasn't, a second wouldn't help him; he let it stay there.

The highway was no more than half a mile away now. He crawled into the underbrush to catch his spent breath, to temporarily restore what little strength he had left. He would need it for the remainder of his journey.

The dogs were louder now; the shouts of the patrols could be heard no more than several hundred yards away. And suddenly the panic returned. What in God's name had he been *thinking* of?! What was he *doing*?!

What *was* he doing?

He was lying in the underbrush assuming – *assuming* he was *free*!

But *was* he?

There were men with guns and savage – viciously savage – animals within the sound of his voice and the sight of his running body.

Then suddenly he heard the words, the commands, shouted – screamed in anticipation. In rage.

'Freilassen! Die Hunde freilassen!'

The dogs were being released! The handlers thought their quarry was cornered! The dogs were unleashed to tear the quarry apart!

He saw the beams of light come over the small hill before he saw the animals. Then the dogs were silhouetted as they streaked over the ridge and down the incline. Five, eight, a dozen racing, monstrous forms stampeding toward the hated object of their nostrils; growing nearer, panicked into wanting, needing the wild conclusion of teeth into flesh.

David was mesmerized – and sickened – by the terrible sight that followed.

The whole area lit up like a flashing diadem; crackling, hissing sounds of electricity filled the air. Dog after dog crashed into the high wire fence. Short fur caught fire; horrible, prolonged, screeching yelps of animal deaths shattered the night.

In alarm or terror or both, shots were fired from the ridge. Men ran in all directions – some to the dogs and the fence, some to the flanks, most away in retreat.

David crawled out of the brush and started running into the forest.

He *was* free!

The prison that was Habichtsnest confined his pursuers ... but *he* was free!

He held his stomach and ran into the darkness.

The highway was bordered by sand and loose gravel. He stumbled out of the woods and fell on the sharp, tiny stones. His vision blurred; nothing stayed level; his throat was dry, his mouth rancid with the vomit of fear. He realized that he could not get up. He could not stand.

He saw an automobile far in the distance, to his right. West. It was traveling at high speed; the headlights kept flashing. Off ... on, off ... on. On, on, on ... off, off, off, interspersed.